Oscar Fay Adams

A dictionary of American authors

Oscar Fay Adams

A dictionary of American authors

ISBN/EAN: 9783337280192

Printed in Europe, USA, Canada, Australia, Japan

Cover: Foto ©Andreas Hilbeck / pixelio.de

More available books at **www.hansebooks.com**

A DICTIONARY OF AMERICAN AUTHORS

BY

OSCAR FAY ADAMS

AUTHOR OF "THE STORY OF JANE AUSTEN'S LIFE," "POST-LAUREATE IDYLS," ETC.; EDITOR OF "THROUGH THE YEAR WITH THE POETS," ETC.

BOSTON AND NEW YORK
HOUGHTON, MIFFLIN AND COMPANY
The Riverside Press, Cambridge
1898

To

My Mother

NOTE TO SECOND EDITION.

As there seems to have been a misunderstanding in some quarters regarding the employment of brackets in authors' names in this volume, it may be well to explain here that in names of men the portions within brackets have been dropped from the owner's signature; in names of women the bracketed portions indicate the maiden name, and, in case of a second marriage, the first married name. In this second edition the writer has corrected such errors and misprints as he or others have discovered, has inserted the dates of many deaths which have occurred since the printing of the first edition, and has extended the addenda by more than two hundred names. That his work is still imperfect he is fully aware, but he trusts that credit will be given him for having put forth all reasonable effort to make it of service to those who have occasion to consult its pages.

JANUARY 1, 1898.

PREFACE.

The present volume is an outgrowth of the writer's "Handbook of American Authors," first published in 1884, several features which the judgment of the public approved in the earlier work having been retained in this. Without pretending to contain an exhaustive list of American writers, it may nevertheless lay claim to be fairly inclusive, as the more than six thousand names herein mentioned will serve to show. A few names that might naturally be looked for here have been omitted at the request of their owners; while some others have not been included, for the reason that diligent search failed to discover any trustworthy data concerning them. Here and there, too, the reader may chance upon unfilled dates of birth, or initials unexpanded. Yet in the majority of such cases application by letter made directly to the owners of the names aforesaid, or to relatives and immediate friends of such persons, has failed to elicit any response. All reasonable effort has been made to obtain trustworthy information upon such points, but failure to obtain replies to letters of inquiry must account for the greater number of such omissions; and here it may not be out of place to mention that information of more general character obtained from private sources has now and then been received too late to be of service, owing to the fact that the work was already electrotyped before it came to hand.

In a comprehensive work like this, including so large a number of names and so many thousand dates, errors must of necessity occur, and the author cannot hope to escape adverse criticism in this respect. While absolute accuracy would have been impossible to attain, he has nevertheless taken no little pains to approach this ideal; and to this end, besides resorting to the ordinary means of information, he has consulted hundreds of catalogues of libraries, colleges, and publishers, as well as denominational year-books, and in numberless instances has availed himself of trustworthy information received directly from private sources. It thus happens that in certain cases dates given in this volume differ from those in other works of reference, and where this occurs the reason for the adoption of a different date herein is supported by excellent authority.

It has been thought advisable to retain the "u" in the spelling of such words as "colour," "favour," and the like, the exceptions to this occurring in titles where the spelling of the original has been followed. In connection with this it may not be amiss to note that the original spelling of titles has been very commonly though not invariably retained. To have done this in every instance, however, would have entailed more labour than it was desirable to incur.

For several reasons the author has thought best in his classification of certain authors to discriminate between poets and verse-writers. To apply the name of poet to each and every writer of verse would have been manifestly unjust. The poets of a generation are not numerous, but the verse-writers are very many. If the term "poet" be loosely applied it loses its signification, while to deny that name to many a writer of excellent verse is to do him no injustice, but rather a service, as it is no disparagement to a private soldier not to be addressed as colonel.

To the many persons who have so cordially responded to his letters of inquiry, and whom he may not thank by name, the writer desires in this place to express his acknowledgments. To Mr. Arthur Mason Knapp, the superintendent of the Bates Hall department of the Boston Public Library, he has been indebted for very much in the way of help and suggestion from the time the work was begun, and to other officials of that department he is under obligations likewise. He also gratefully acknowledges much timely assistance received from the publishing firms of Lee & Shepard, T. Y. Crowell & Co., and Lamson, Wolffe & Co. In the reading of the proofs many valuable suggestions have been received from the proof-readers at the Riverside Press; but his especial thanks are due his friend, Mr. Francis H. Allen, of Boston, whose watchful, critical supervision has been exercised upon every page of proof from first to last. The debt of gratitude which the writer owes him for this service may not be lightly estimated. Without his help, the book would have fallen far short of whatever measure of excellence it may now be judged to attain.

THE HERMITAGE,
BOSTON, MASSACHUSETTS,
JUNE 17, 1897.

PUBLISHERS NAMED IN THIS VOLUME.

Am.	American Book Co	New York.
Ap.	D. Appleton & Co	New York.
Ar.	Arena Publishing Co.	Boston.
A. U. A.	American Unitarian Association.	Boston.
Ba	Baker & Taylor Co.	New York.
Bai.	Henry Carey Baird & Co.	Philadelphia.
Ban.	Banner of Light Publishing Co.	Boston.
Bap	American Baptist Publication Society.	Philadelphia.
Bar.	A. S. Barnes & Co.	New York.
Bo.	Bowen-Merrill Co.	Indianapolis.
Bur.	Burrows Brothers Co.	Cleveland.
Cas.	Cassell Publishing Co.	New York.
Cent.	Century Co.	New York.
Clke.	Robert Clarke Co.	Cincinnati.
Co.	Henry T. Coates & Co.	Philadelphia.
Cop.	Copeland & Day	Boston.
C. P. S.	Congregational S. S. & Publishing Society.	Boston.
Cr.	Thomas Y. Crowell & Co.	New York and Boston.
Dil.	G. W. Dillingham Co.	New York.
Dit.	Oliver Ditson Co.	Boston.
Do.	Dodd, Mead & Co.	New York.
Dut.	E. P. Dutton & Co.	New York.
El.	George H. Ellis.	Boston.
Est.	Estes & Lauriat.	Boston.
Fl.	Flood & Vincent	Meadville, Pa.
Fo.	Fords, Howard & Hulbert.	New York.
Fu.	Funk & Wagnalls Co.	New York.
Gi.	Ginn & Co.	Boston.
Har.	Harper & Bros.	New York.
He.	D. C. Heath & Co.	Boston.
Hi.	J. A. Hill & Co.	New York.
Ho.	Henry Holt & Co.	New York.
Hou.	Houghton, Mifflin & Co.	Boston.
Int.	International Book Co.	Chicago.
J. H. U.	Johns Hopkins University	Baltimore.
Ju.	Orange Judd Co.	New York.
Ke.	Charles H. Kerr & Co.	Chicago.
Kt.	Joseph Knight Co.*	Boston.
Lai.	Laird & Lee.	Chicago.
Lam.	Lamson, Wolffe & Co.	Boston.
Le.	Lee & Shepard.	Boston.
Lgs.	Longmans, Green & Co.	London and New York.
Lip.	J. B. Lippincott Co.	Philadelphia.
Lit.	Little, Brown & Co.	Boston.
Ll.	Lovell, Coryell & Co.	New York.
Lo.	Lothrop Publishing Co.	Boston.

* Since the above was in type the firm name has become L. C. Page & Co.

Lov..........A. Lovell & Co.........................New York and Chicago.
Mac..........Macmillan & Co.........................New York and London.
Mer..........Merriam Co.........................New York.
Meth..........Methodist Book Concern.........................New York.
Mg..........A. C. McClurg & Co.........................Chicago.
Mor..........John P. Morton & Co.........................Louisville.
My..........David McKay.........................Philadelphia.
Ne..........F. Tennyson Neely.........................New York.
Pr..........Preston & Rounds.........................Providence.
Put..........G. P. Putnam's Sons.........................New York.
Ra..........Rand, McNally & Co.........................Chicago and New York.
Ran..........A. D. F. Randolph & Co.........................New York.
Rev..........Fleming H. Revell Co.........................Chicago.
Ric..........George H. Richmond & Co.........................New York.
Rob..........Roberts Brothers.........................Boston.
S..........Herbert S. Stone & Co.........................Chicago.
Sc..........Scott, Foresman & Co.........................Chicago.
Scr..........Charles Scribner's Sons.........................New York.
Se..........N. J. Stone & Co.........................San Francisco.
Sh..........Sheldon & Co.........................New York.
Sil..........Silver, Burdett & Co.........................Boston.
St..........Stone & Kimball.........................New York.
Sto..........Frederick A. Stokes Co.........................New York.
Vn..........D. Van Nostrand Co.........................New York.
Wat..........John D. Wattles & Co.........................Philadelphia.
We..........W. A. Wilde & Co.........................Boston.
Wh..........Thomas Whittaker.........................New York.
Wil..........John Wiley & Sons.........................New York.
Wn..........Bradlee Whidden.........................Boston.
Wy..........Way & Williams.........................Chicago.

PLACE OF BIRTH OF AUTHORS.

The place of birth of the larger number of the authors mentioned in this volume is indicated by an abbreviation placed before the date of birth, which the following list will serve to explain: —

A.	Austria.
Al.	Alabama.
A. M.	Asia Minor.
Ar.	Argentina.
Ark.	Arkansas.
B.	Brazil.
Ba.	Bermuda.
B. G.	British Guiana.
Bh.	Burmah.
Bm.	Belgium.
Bo.	Bohemia.
Bv.	Bavaria.
C.	Cuba.
Cal.	California.
Ch.	China.
Ct.	Connecticut.
Cy.	Ceylon.
Del.	Delaware.
D. C.	District of Columbia.
Dk.	Denmark.
E.	England.
E. I.	East Indies.
F.	France.
Fl.	Florida.
G.	Germany.
Ga.	Georgia.
Gr.	Greece.
H.	Holland.
H. I.	Hawaiian Islands.
Hy.	Hungary.
I.	Ireland.
Ia.	Iowa.
Il.	Illinois.
Ind.	Indiana.
Ion.	Ionian Islands.
Iy.	Italy.
J.	Jamaica.
Ky.	Kentucky.
La.	Louisiana.
L. I.	Long Island.
Ma.	Moravia.
Mch.	Michigan.
Md.	Maryland.
Me.	Maine.
Mg.	Mecklenburg.
Mi.	Mississippi.
Min.	Minnesota.
Mo.	Missouri.
Ms.	Massachusetts.
N.	Norway.
N. B.	New Brunswick.
N. C.	North Carolina.
N. H.	New Hampshire.
N. J.	New Jersey.
N. M.	New Mexico.
N. S.	Nova Scotia.
N. Y.	New York.
O.	Ohio.
Ont.	Ontario.
Or.	Oregon.
P.	Prussia.
Pa.	Pennsylvania.
P. E. I.	Prince Edward Island.
Per.	Persia.
Ph.	Philippine Islands.
Pl.	Portugal.
Po.	Poland.
Q.	Quebec.
R.	Russia.
R. I.	Rhode Island.
S.	Scotland.
Sa.	Syria.
S. C.	South Carolina.
Sd.	Switzerland.
Sg.	Schleswig.
S. I.	Staten Island.
Sil.	Silesia.
Sl.	Senegal.
Sn.	Sweden.
Sp.	Spain.
Sxy.	Saxony.
Sy.	Sicily.
Tn.	Tennessee.
Ts.	Texas.
Ty.	Turkey.
Va.	Virginia.
Vt.	Vermont.
W.	Wales.
Wa.	Westphalia.
Wg.	Wurtemburg.
Wis.	Wisconsin.
W. I.	West Indies.
W. Va.	West Virginia.

A DICTIONARY OF AMERICAN AUTHORS.*

Abbe, Cleveland. *N. Y.*, 1838——. A meteorologist of distinction who in 1871 became professor of meteorology in the national weather bureau and has since continued in that position. The more important of his many publications include Solar Spots and Terrestrial Temperature; A Plea for Terrestrial Physics; Atmospheric Radiation; Treatise on Meteorological Apparatus; Preparatory Studies for Deductive Methods in Meteorology.

Abbe, Frederick Randolph. *Ct.*, 1827–1889. A Congregational clergyman in Massachusetts. The Temple Rebuilt, a Poem of Christian Faith.

Abbey, Henry. *N. Y.*, 1842——. A resident of Kingston, New York, who has published several collections of pleasant unpretentious verse. Ballads of Good Deeds; The City of Success; May Dreams; Ralph and Other Poems; Stories in Verse.

Abbey, Richard. *N. Y.*, 1805——. A prominent clergyman of the Southern Methodist Church, among whose many theological and controversial writings are, End of the Apostolical Succession; Creed of All Men; Diuturnity; Ecce Ecclesia, a reply to Ecce Homo; The City of God and the Church Makers.

Abbot, Abiel. *N. H.*, 1765–1859. A Congregational clergyman of Connecticut and Massachusetts. History of Andover; Genealogy of the Abbot Family.

Abbot, Abiel. *Ms.*, 1770–1828. A Congregational clergyman of Beverly, Massachusetts. Letters from Cuba. His Sermons with Memoir were published in 1831.

Abbot, Ezra. *Me.*, 1819–1884. A Unitarian biblical scholar of much prominence, who was for many years a professor in the Divinity School of Harvard University, and widely known for the extent of his bibliographical acquirements. Literature of the Doctrine of a Future Life; Authenticity of the Fourth Gospel; The Fourth Gospel and Other Critical Essays. With H. B. Hackett, *infra*, he prepared the American edition of Smith's Bible Dictionary. *See Memorial of, 1884. El.*

Abbot, Francis Ellingwood. *Ms.*, 1836——. A religious and philosophical thinker of advanced views, for some years editor of The Index, whose home is at Cambridge. Scientific Theism; The Way out of Agnosticism. *Lit.*

Abbot, Gorham Dummer. *Me.*, 1807–1874. A Congregational clergyman, long an educator of New York city. He was a brother of Jacob Abbott, *infra*, but returned to an older spelling of his surname. Prayer-Book for the Young; Pleasure and Profit; The Family at Home.

Abbot, Henry Larcom. *Ms.*, 1831——. A general in the United States army, of prominence as an engineer. Besides several series of Professional Papers, his writings include Lectures on the Defence of the Sea Coast of the United States; Physics and Hydraulics of the Mississippi River. *Vn.*

Abbot, Willis John. *Ct.*, 1863——. Grandson of J. S. C. Abbott, *infra*, but using an older spelling of the surname. A journalist of New York city. Blue Jackets of 1776; Blue Jackets of 1812; Blue Jackets of '61, three volumes of history for young people; Battle Fields of '61; Battle Fields and Camp Fires; Battle Fields and Victory; Life of Carter Harrison. *Do.*

Abbott, Arthur Vaughan. *N. Y.*, 1854——. Son of B. V. Abbott, *infra.*

 * See Addenda, p. 441.

A civil, electrical, and mechanical engineer of Chicago. Electrical Transmission of Energy; The Evolution of a Switchboard; History and Use of Testing Machines; Treatise on Fuel. *Vn.*

Abbott, Austin. *Ms.*, 1831–1896. Son of Jacob Abbott, *infra.* A lawyer of New York city who was dean of the Law School of New York University at the time of his death. Besides preparing several works with his brother Benjamin, *infra*, he published Legal Remembrancer, Principles and Forms of Practice in Civil Actions in Courts of Record; The Law of Evidence; Select Cases on Code Pleading; Digest of New York Statutes.

Abbott, Benjamin Vaughan. *Ms.*, 1830–1890. Son of Jacob Abbott, *infra.* A lawyer of New York city. Law Dictionary; Travelling Law School and Famous Trials; First Lessons in Government and Law; Patent Laws of All Nations; Year-Book of Jurisprudence for 1880; Judge and Jury. *Har. Lit. Lo.*

Abbott, Charles Conrad. *N. J.*, 1843——. A naturalist and physician of Trenton, New Jersey, whose writings show a very close and sympathetic observation of nature. The Stone Age in New Jersey; Primitive Industry; A Naturalist's Rambles about Home; Cyclopædia of Natural History; Upland and Meadow; Wasteland Wanderings; The Birds About Us; Days Out of Doors; Outings at Odd Times; Recent Rambles; Travels in a Treetop; Notes of the Night; A Colonial Wooing, a novel; Bird-Land Echoes. *Ap. Cent. Har. Lip.*

Abbott, Charles Edward. *Me.*, 1811–1880. Brother of Jacob Abbott, *infra.* An educator in Connecticut. Down the Hill; Village Boys.

Abbott, Edward. *Me.*, 1841——. Son of Jacob Abbott, *infra.* An Episcopal clergyman of Cambridge, but prior to 1878 a Congregational minister and editor of The Congregationalist. He is now [1897] the editor of The Literary World. Dialogues of Christ; The Long Look series of juvenile tales; A Trip Eastward; Revolutionary Times; Paragraph History of the United States; Paragraph History of the American Revolution. *Rob.*

Abbott, Jacob. *Me.*, 1803–1879. An educator of New England, who was a voluminous and popular writer for young people. Among his numerous writings the best known are The Franconia Stories; Marco Paul's Adventures; The Rollo Books; Histories of Celebrated Sovereigns; Harper's Story Books. *See Bibliography of Maine. Cr. Har.*

Abbott, John Stevens Cabot. *Me.*, 1805–1877. Brother of Jacob Abbott, *supra.* An historical writer, whose partisan spirit seriously impairs the value of his very readable works. He was for some years a Congregational minister, but after 1844 devoted himself to literature and educational work. Among his works are comprised The Mother at Home; Practical Christianity; Romance of Spanish History; American Pioneers and Patriots; History of Napoleon; Napoleon at St. Helena; History of the French Revolution; History of the Civil War in America; Lives of the Presidents; History of Maine from its Discovery by Northmen; Christopher Carson; History of Napoleon III.; History of Frederick the Great; History of Christianity. *See Bibliography of Maine. Do. Har.*

Abbott, Lyman. *Ms.*, 1835——. Son of Jacob Abbott, *supra.* A Congregational minister of broad views, who as editor of The Outlook and successor to H. W. Beecher as pastor of Plymouth Church, Brooklyn, has exercised a wide influence. Christianity and Social Problems; Jesus of Nazareth; Old Testament Shadows of New Testament Truths; Illustrated Commentary on the New Testament; A Layman's Story; How to Study the Bible; Life of Christ; In Aid of Faith; The Evolution of Christianity; A Study in Human Nature; Dictionary of Religious Knowledge (with T. J. Conant, *infra*). *Bar. Do. Dut. Fo. Har. Hou. Meth. Put.*

Abeel, David. *N. J.*, 1804–1846. A Reformed Dutch missionary in China. Journal of a Residence in China; A Missionary Convention at Jerusalem; The Claims of the World to the Gospel. *See Memoirs by G. R. Williamson, 1849.*

Abert [ā'bert], **Silvanus Thayer.** *Pa.*, 1828——. A civil engineer in the United States service. Notes Historical and Statistical upon the Projected Route for an Interoceanic Canal between the Atlantic and Pacific.

Adams, Mrs. Abigail [Smith]. *Ms.*, 1744–1818. Wife of President John Adams, *infra*. Known to literature by her entertaining Letters edited by her grandson.

Adams, Brooks. *Ms.*, 1848——. Son of Charles Francis Adams, *infra*. A lawyer of Boston. The Gold Standard; The Emancipation of Massachusetts, a careful study of the evolution of religious freedom; The Law of Civilization and Decay, an Essay in History. *See The Forum, January, 1897. Hou. Mac.*

Adams, Charles. *N. H.*, 1808–1890. A Methodist clergyman who wrote extensively, and among whose works are Evangelism in the Middle of the 19th Century; Women of the Bible; The Poet Preacher, a Memorial of Charles Wesley; The Earth and its Wonders; Life of Cromwell; Life Sketches of Macaulay. *Meth.*

Adams, Charles Baker. *Ms.*, 1814–1853. A naturalist, who published Contributions to Conchology; Monographs of Several Species of Shells.

Adams, Charles Coffin. 182—1888. An Episcopal clergyman. Creation, a Recent Work of God; Life of Christ; Anthrosophy; The Bible, a Scientific Revelation.

Adams, Charles Follen. *Ms.*, 1842——. A humourous verse-writer of Boston, principally known as the author of Leedle Yawcob Strauss. Leedle Yawcob Strauss, and Other Poems; Dialect Ballads. *Har. Le.*

Adams, Charles Francis. *Ms.*, 1807–1886. Son of President John Quincy Adams, *infra*. An eminent diplomatist, who was Minister to England during the period of the Civil War. He edited The Life and Works of John Adams; Letters of Mrs. Abigail Adams; Life and Works of John Q. Adams; Familiar Letters of John and Abigail Adams, with Memoir of Mrs. Adams. *See Life by his son, C. F. Adams, infra. Hou.*

Adams, Charles Francis, Jr. *Ms.*, 1835——. Son of C. F. Adams, *supra*. An officer in the Union army during the Civil War, and subsequently an expert in railway science and president of the Union Pacific Railway. Since resigning that office he has devoted his attention to historical writing, his estimates of men and motives often differing materially from those of other writers in the same field. Notes on Railway Accidents; Chapters of Erie; Railroads; A College Fetich; Massachusetts, its Historians and its History; Three Episodes of Massachusetts History; Richard Henry Dana [*infra*], a Biography; Life of Charles Francis Adams. *Hou. Le. Put.*

Adams, Charles Kendall. *Vt.*, 1835——. The president of Wisconsin University and formerly of Cornell University. Manual of Historical Literature; Democracy and Monarchy in France; Christopher Columbus. *Har.*

Adams, Francis Colburn. *Circa* 1850. A writer of Charleston, South Carolina, who wrote under various pseudonyms. Manuel Pereira, or the Sovereign Rule of South Carolina; Uncle Tom at Home; Our World, or the Democrats' Rule; Justice in the Byways; Life and Adventures of Major Potter; An Outcast, a novel; The Story of a Trooper; Siege of Washington, for Little People; The Von Toodleburgs, or the Memoirs of a Very Distinguished Family.

Adams, George Burton. *Vt.*, 1851——. An historical writer, professor of history at Yale University. Civilization during the Middle Ages; The Growth of the French Nation. *Fl. Scr.*

Adams, Hannah. *Ms.*, 1755–1832. An industrious and painstaking writer on religious and historical subjects, whose chief claim to distinction at present is that she was the first woman in America who made literature a profession. A View of Religious Opinions; History of New England; History of the Jews; Evidences of Christianity. *See Memoir by herself, with additions by another hand, 1832.*

Adams, Henry. *Ms.*, 1838——. Son of Charles Francis Adams, *supra*. An historian and political biographer, living in Washington. Life of John Randolph; Life of Albert Gallatin; History of the United States, 1801–17; Historical Essays; Essays in Anglo-Saxon Law. *Hou. Lip. Scr.*

Adams, Henry Carter. *Ia.*, 1852–——. A political economist of note. Public Debts: an Essay in the Science of Finance; Taxation in the United States, 1789–1816. *Ap.*

Adams, Herbert Baxter. *Ms.*, 1850–——. A professor of history at Johns Hopkins University, and the secretary of the American Historical Association from its beginning. The Germanic Origin of New England Towns; Saxon Tithingmen in America; Norman Constables in America; Village Communities of Cape Ann and Salem; Thomas Jefferson and the University of Virginia; Methods of Historical Study; History of the United States Constitution. He has edited the Life and Writings of Jared Sparks, *infra. Hou.*

Adams, Jasper. *Ms.*, 1793–1841. An Episcopal clergyman, once noted as an educator at West Point, Charleston, and elsewhere, who published The Elements of Moral Philosophy.

Adams, John. *N. S.*, 1704–1740. A clergyman of Newport and Philadelphia, much esteemed in his day as a poet. Poems on Several Occasions, a volume of his verses posthumously collected and printed, shows, however, no very especial marks of poetic talent.

Adams, John. *Ms.*, 1735–1826. The second President of the United States, and a political writer of great ability and force. A Dissertation on Canon and Feudal Law, a work relating to the constitutional rights of New England; Thoughts on Government; Novanglus: a History of the Dispute with America from 1754 to 1774; Defence of the American Constitution; Discourses on Davila: a Series of Papers on Political History. *See complete Works in 10 volumes, 1850–56. See, also, Lives by J. Q. and C. F. Adams, 1871; John Adams, by Morse, 1885; Histories of the United States, by Bancroft, McMaster, Henry Adams, and Schouler; Parker's Historic Americans; Appleton's American Biography.*

Adams, John Coleman. *Ms.*, 1849–——. Son of J. G. Adams, *infra.* A Universalist clergyman and editor of New York city. Christian Types of Heroism; The Fatherhood of God; The Leisure of God and Other Studies in Spiritual Evolution.

Adams, John Greenleaf. *N. H.*, 1810–1887. A Universalist clergyman, among whose writings the chief are The Universalist Church, its Faith and its Works; Universalism of the Lord's Prayer; Talks About the Bible to Young Folks; Fifty Notable Years, or Views of the Ministry of Universalism.

Adams, John Quincy. *Ms.*, 1767–1848. Son of President John Adams, *supra.* The sixth President of the United States, and a statesman whose writings, though mainly political in their character, include several purely literary works. Lectures on Rhetoric and Oratory; The Bible and its Teachings; Poems of Religion and Society; Letters on Freemasonry; Lives of Celebrated Statesmen, and many State Papers. *See Complete Works, edited by C. F. Adams, with Life; also Diary of; Lives by Seward, Quincy, Morse; Histories of the United States by Bancroft, McMaster, Schouler. Lip.*

Adams, John Turrell. *B. G.*, 1805–1882. A lawyer of Norwich, Connecticut. The Knight of the Golden Melice, an historical tale; The Lost Hunter.

Adams, Julius Walker. *Ms.*, 1812–——. An engineer of distinction, who has been employed in many important engineering works. Sewers and Drains for Populous Districts.

Adams, Myron. *N. Y.*, 1841–1895. A Congregational clergyman of Rochester, New York, from 1876 until his death. The Creation of the Bible; The Continuous Creation, an Application of the Evolutionary Philosophy to the Christian Religion. *Hou.*

Adams, Nehemiah. *Ms.*, 1806–1878. A once noted Congregational clergyman of Boston, whose most famous work, A South Side View of Slavery, provoked much hostile criticism. Among other works by him are Walks to Emmaus; Scriptural Argument for Endless Punishment; Remarks on Unitarian Belief; Life of John Eliot; Agnes and the Little Key; Evenings with the Doctrines.

Adams, Robert Chamblet. *Ms.*, 1839——. Son of Nehemiah Adams, *supra.* History of England in Rhyme; History of the United States in Rhyme; On Board the Rocket; Aids to Endeavour, Evolution, a Summary of Evidence; Travels in Faith from Tradition to Reason; Pioneer Pith. *Lo.*

Adams, Samuel. *Ms.*, 1722–1803. Cousin of President John Adams, *supra.* A statesman and orator who fills a large place in the annals of the American Revolution. *See Lives by Wells, Hosmer, 1885; Harper's Magazine, vol. 53.*

Adams, William. *Ct.*, 1807–1880. A Presbyterian clergyman of prominence in New York city, 1835–80. The Three Gardens: Eden, Gethsemane, Paradise; Conversations of Jesus Christ with Representative Men; In the World, not of the World; Thanksgiving, Memories of the Day and Helps to the Habit.

Adams, William. *I.*, 1813–1897. An Episcopal clergyman who was one of the founders of Nashotah Theological Seminary, Wisconsin, and professor of systematic divinity there from 1841. Mercy to Babes; Elements of Christian Science; New Treatise of Baptismal Regeneration.

Adams, William Taylor, "Oliver Optic." *Ms.*, 1822–1897. A prolific and popular writer of books for boys, who was for many years a teacher in the Boston public schools. Among his writings are Army and Navy Series; Young America Abroad Series; Lake Shore Series; Starry Flag Series. *Le.*

Ade, George. *Il.*, 1866——. A Chicago journalist. Artie: a Story of the Streets and Town. *S.*

Adeler, Max. *See Clark, C. H.*

Adler, Felix. *G.*, 1851——. An ethical reformer of New York city. Creed and Deed; The Moral Instruction of Children. *Ap. Put.*

Adler, Georg. *G.*, 1821–1868. A philologist of New York city who was the author of a valuable German and English Dictionary and other educational works. *Ap.*

Agassiz [ag'a-see or ä-gäs-se'], **Alexander.** *Sd.*, 1835——. Son of L. Agassiz, *infra.* Marine zoölogist. Born in Neuchatel, he came to America with his father, and has distinguished himself in lines of special scientific research. Exploration of Lake Titicaca; List of the Echinoderms; Three Cruises of the Blake: a Contribution to American Thalassography. *Hou.*

Agassiz, Mrs. Elizabeth [Cary]. *Ms.*, 1822——. Wife of L. Agassiz, *infra.* Life of Louis Agassiz; Seaside Studies in Natural History (with A. Agassiz, *supra*).

Agassiz, Jean Louis Rodolphe. *Sd.*, 1807–1873. A naturalist of eminence. Founder of the Museum of Natural History at Cambridge. Recherches sur les Poissons Fossiles; Lake Superior, Natural History of Fresh-Water Fishes of Central Europe; Etudes sur les Glaciers; Système Glacière; Methods of Study in Natural History; Geological Sketches; Structure of Animal Life; Journey in Brazil. *See Whipple's Character and Characteristic Men; Louis Agassiz and Evolution, Popular Science Monthly, vol. 32; Lives by Mrs. E. Agassiz, Holder, 1892, Jules Marcou, 1896; Lowell's ode, Agassiz.*

Agnew, David Hayes. *Pa.*, 1810–1892. A physician who was for a long time professor of surgery in the University of Pennsylvania. His writings were the outcome of wide experience. Handbook of Practical Anatomy; Principles and Practice of Surgery: a treatise on Surgical Diseases and Injuries. *See Life of, by J. H. Adams, 1892. Lip.*

Aikman, William. *I.*, 1824——. A Presbyterian clergyman. The Moral Power of the Sea; Life at Home, or the Family and its Members; The Altar in the Home; A Bachelor's Talks about Married Life.

Aimwell, Walter. *See Simonds.*

Ainslie, Hew. *S.*, 1792–1878. A Scottish poet who emigrated to America in 1822 and lived mainly in Kentucky. Pilgrimage to the Land of Burns, a prose work with lyrics interspersed; Scottish Songs, Ballads, and Poems.

Akers, Elizabeth. *See Allen, Mrs.*

Albee, John. *Ms.*, 1833——. Formerly a clergyman; now living at Chocorua, New Hampshire. Literary Art;

St. Aspenquid: an Indian Idyl; Prose Idyls. *Hou. Put.*

Alcott [awl'kot], **Amos Bronson.** *Ct.*, 1799–1888. A philosopher of a singularly unpractical type, whose personality was of greater interest than his writings. Conversations with Children on the Gospels; Table Talk, Emerson; Essays; Tablets, Concord Days, Sonnets, and Canzonets; New Connecticut: a poem. *See Miss E. P. Peabody's Records of a School; Life, by F. B. Sanborn and W. T. Harris, 1893. Rob.*

Alcott, Louisa May. *Pa.*, 1832–1888. Daughter of A. B. Alcott, *supra.* A writer whose books for young people have been widely popular. They cannot, however, claim consideration as examples of literary art. Among them are Little Women; Little Men; An Old-Fashioned Girl; Eight Cousins; Under the Lilacs. Moods; Hospital Sketches; A Modern Mephistopheles, are works for older readers. The thoughtful poem, Thoreau's Flute, is her finest effort. *See Life, Letters, and Journals, edited by Mrs. Cheney; Recollections of, by Mrs. M. S. Porter, 1893. Rob.*

Alcott, William Alexander. *Ct.*, 1798–1859. Cousin of A. B. Alcott, *supra.* An energetic, earnest writer upon diet reform. The House I Live in; Vegetable Diet; Library of Health.

Alden [awl'den], **Henry Mills.** *Vt.*, 1836——. A thoughtful and suggestive writer on religious themes who has been editor of Harper's Magazine from 1869. God in his World; A Study of Death. *Har.*

Alden, Mrs. Isabella [Macdonald]. "Pansy." *N. Y.*, 1841——. A very prolific writer of religious tales for young people, the literary worth of which is inconsiderable. Four Girls at Chautauqua; Chautauqua Girls at Home, are among the earlier ones. *Lo.*

Alden, Joseph. *N. Y.*, 1807–1885. An industrious contributor to educational and Sunday-school literature. He was for many years president of the Normal School at Albany. Example of Washington; Citizen's Manual; Christian Ethics; The Science of Government; Studies in Bryant; Elements of Intellectual Philosophy. *Ap. Le. Meth.*

Alden, William Livingston. *Ms.*, 1837——. Son of J. Alden, *supra.* A humourous writer who has for some time resided in London. A New Robinson Crusoe; Domestic Explosions; Shooting Stars; Moral Pirates; Cruise of the Canoe Club; Life of Christopher Columbus. *Har. Ho. Put.*

Aldrich [awl'dritch], **Annie Reeve.** *N. Y.*, 1866–1892. A New York city writer of notably erotic verse and fiction. The Rose of Flame and Other Poems of Love; Songs about Life, Love, and Death; The Feet of Love: a novel. *Put.*

Aldrich, James. *N. Y.*, 1810–1856. A littérateur of New York, who established The Literary Gazette in 1840, in which a number of his verses appeared. His Poems were privately printed by his daughter in 1884.

Aldrich, Thomas Bailey. *N. H.*, 1837——. A poet and novelist whose work in both verse and prose is distinguished for grace of expression and delicacy of execution. Verse: The Bells; Ballad of Baby Bell; Pampinea; Flower and Thorn; Cloth of Gold; Friar Jerome's Beautiful Book; XXXVI Lyrics and XII Sonnets; The Sisters' Tragedy; Wyndham Towers; Unguarded Gates; Mercedes and Later Lyrics; Judith and Holofernes. Prose: Prudence Palfrey; The Queen of Sheba; The Stillwater Tragedy; Marjorie Daw and Other Stories; Two Bites at a Cherry, with Other Tales; The Story of a Bad Boy; An Old Town by the Sea: a description of Portsmouth, the author's birthplace; From Ponkapog to Pesth: Travel Sketches. *See Stedman's Poets of America; Vedder's American Writers. Hou.*

Alexander, Archibald. *Va.*, 1772–1851. A Presbyterian clergyman who was professor at Princeton Theological Seminary 1812–51. Evidences of Christianity; The Canon of Scripture; Moral Science; Bible Dictionary, are some of his many works. *See Life, by J. W. Alexander; Sprague's Annals of the American Pulpit. Scr.*

Alexander, Caleb. *N. Y.*, 1755–1828. A clergyman, much of whose life was spent in teaching at Onondaga, New

York. He published Latin and English grammars; Essay on the Deity of Christ; The Columbian Dictionary; Grammar Elements: a literal prose version of Virgil.

Alexander, James Waddel. *Va.*, 1804–1859. Son of A. Alexander, *supra.* A Presbyterian clergyman of New York city. Plain Words to a Young Communicant; Sacramental Discourses; Thoughts on Preaching; Life of Archibald Alexander; Consolation; The American Mechanic and Workingman, are among his writings. *Ran. Scr.*

Alexander, John Henry. *Md.*, 1812–1867. A once noted Maryland scientist. History of the Metallurgy of Iron; Universal Dictionary of Weights and Measures, Ancient and Modern; International Tonnage; Treatise of Mathematical Instruments; Introits; Catena Dominica: a collection of religious poems.

Alexander, Joseph Addison. *Pa.*, 1809–1860. Son of A. Alexander, *supra.* A Presbyterian clergyman, professor at Princeton College, and Theological Seminary, 1820–60. He was the author of Commentaries on the Psalms, Isaiah, Acts, Matthew, and Mark; and many theological reviews, often as sarcastic as they were forcible. *See Life, by H. C. Alexander; Hart's American Literature. Scr.*

Alexander, Samuel Davies. *N. J.*, 1819–1894. Son of A. Alexander, *supra.* A Presbyterian clergyman of New York city from 1855. Princeton College in the 18th Century. *Scr.*

Alexander, Stephen. *N. Y.*, 1806–1883. An astronomer who was a professor at Princeton College, 1834–78. Physical Phenomena of Solar Eclipses; Certain Harmonies of the Solar System.

Alger [ăl′jẽr], **Horatio, Jr.** *Ms.*, 1832——. The author of a long series of popular juvenile tales, among which the Ragged Dick stories are best known. *Co.*

Alger, William Rounseville. *Ms.*, 1822——. A Unitarian clergyman and lecturer of Boston. Symbolic History of the Cross; The School of Life; History of the Doctrine of a Future Life; The Solitudes of Nature and Man; The Friendships of Women; Poetry of the Orient; Life of Edwin Forrest. *A. U. A. Lip. Rob.*

Alice, Aunt. *See Graves, Mrs.*

Alice, Cousin. *See Haven, Mrs.*

Allan, William. *Va.*, 1837–1889. A lieutenant-colonel in the Confederate army during the Civil War. Battle-fields of Virginia; Jackson's Valley Campaign; Army of Northern Virginia. *Hou. Lip.*

Allen, Alexander Viets Griswold. *Ms.*, 1841——. An Episcopal clergyman, prominent among leaders of modern religious thought, and a professor in the Episcopal Theological School at Cambridge. The Continuity of Christian Thought: a Study of Modern Theology in the Light of its History; Life of Jonathan Edwards; The Greek Theology and the Renaissance of the 19th Century; Religious Progress. *Hou.*

Allen, Mrs. Elizabeth Ann [Chase] [Akers], "Florence Percy." *Me.* 1832——. A writer of verse, whose song, "Rock Me to Sleep, Mother," is her most famous though not her best poem. The Triangular Society; Queen Catharine's Rose; Forest Buds; Poems by Florence Percy; The Silver Bridge; The High Top Sweeting. *Hou. Scr.*

Allen, Frederick De Forest. *O.*, 1844–1897. A professor of classical philology at Harvard University from 1880. Remnants of Early Latin; Greek Versification in Inscriptions.

Allen, Fred Hovey. *N. H.*, 1845——. A clergyman, author of the text in a number of popular art works, such as Great Cathedrals of the World; Modern German Masters; The Bowdoin Collection; The Doré Album; The Gerome Album; Discovery and Conquest of Peru; Discovery and Conquest of Mexico. *Meth.*

Allen, Harrison. *Pa.*, 1841–1897. A surgeon of Philadelphia, professor in the University of Pennsylvania from 1865. Outlines of Comparative Anatomy; System of Human Anatomy. *Lip.*

Allen, Ira. *Ct.*, 1751–1814. An officer in the American army during the Revolutionary War, who was afterwards instrumental in settling the disputes between Vermont and its neighbours. Natural and Political History of Vermont.

Allen, James Lane. *Ky.*, 1849——. At one time a teacher, now devoted to literature. A writer of short stories, notable for literary excellence. Flute and Violin; The Blue Grass Region and Other Sketches of Kentucky; John Gray: a Novel; The Kentucky Cardinal; Aftermath; A Summer in Arcady; The Choir Invisible. *See Atlantic Monthly, January, 1897. Har. Lip. Mac.*

Allen, Jerome. *Vt.*, 1830–1894. An educator of New York, dean of the School of Pedagogy. Handbook of Experimental Chemistry; Methods for Teachers in Grammar; Mind Studies for Young Teachers; Temperament in Education.

Allen, Joel Asaph. *Ms.*, 1838——. A naturalist who since 1885 has been curator of ornithology and mammalogy in the American Museum of Natural History in New York city. History of North American Pinnipeds; Monographs of North American Rodentia (with E. Coues, *infra*).

Allen, Joseph Henry. *Ms.*, 1820——. A Unitarian clergyman of Cambridge, who is also noted as the author of a number of valuable and popular classical text-books. Ten Discourses on Orthodoxy; Hebrew Men and Times; Christian History in Three Great Periods; Fragments of Christian History; Historical Sketch of the Unitarian Movement since the Reformation; Our Liberal Movement in Theology; Outline of Christian History, A. D. 50–1880; are some of his religious works. *El. Gi. Rob.*

Allen's Wife, Josiah. *See Holley.*

Allen, Lewis Fally. *N. Y.*, 1799–18—. A once prominent cattle broker. Rural Architecture; The American Herd Book; American Cattle.

Allen, Nathan. *Ms.*, 1813–1889. A physician of Lowell. The Law of Human Increase; The Opium Trade; Physical Development.

Allen, Paul. *R. I.*, 1775–1826. A journalist of Philadelphia. Poems: Noah, a poem in five cantos; Life of Alexander I.; Lewis and Clark's Novels. The Life of Washington, which bears his name, was written by John Neal, *infra*, and others.

Allen, Richard Lamb. *Ms.*, 1803–1869. Brother of L. F. Allen, *supra*, with whom, in 1842, he founded the American Agriculturalist. Domestic Animals; Diseases of Domestic Animals; New American Farm Book (with *L. F. Allen*). *See Last Letters of, with Memoir.*

Allen, Stephen Merrill. *N. H.*, 1819–1894. A banker and merchant of Boston. Fibrilia and Fibrous Manufactures, Ancient and Modern; Theories of Light; Religion and Science.

Allen, Timothy Field. *Vt.*, 1837——. A physician of New York city, dean of the Homœopathic Medical College since 1882. Characcæ Americanæ; General Symptom-Register of Homœopathic Materia Medica. He has edited Encyclopædia of Pure Materia Medica.

Allen, William. *Ms.*, 1784–1868. The author of an American Biographical and Historical Dictionary, the first edition of which appeared in 1809, the earliest work of the kind in the United States. From 1820 to 1829 he was president of Bowdoin College. Lectures to Young Men; Junius Unmasked; Wunissoo: a poem, with notes.

Allen, William Francis. *Ms.*, 1830–1889. Brother of J. H. Allen, *supra*. A professor in the University of Wisconsin. He published Outline Studies in the History of Ireland; Monographs and Essays; and edited a collection of Slave Songs.

Allen, Willis Boyd. *Me.*, 1855——. A Boston littérateur whose writings are popular with juvenile readers. Among them are The Red Mountain of Alaska; Pine Cones; Silver Rags; Kelp; The Mammoth Hunters. He has published In the Morning, a collection of verse. *Est. Lo. Ran.*

Allen, Zachariah. *R. I.*, 1795–1882. A noted inventor and manufacturer of Providence. Practical Tourist; Practical Mechanics; Philosophy of the Mechanics of Nature; Solar Light and Heat. *See Memorial by A. Perry, 1883. Ap.*

Allerton, Mrs. Ellen [Palmer]. *N.*

Y., 1835——. A Kansas writer living at Padonia in that State. Poems of the Prairies.

Allibone, Samuel Austin. *Pa.*, 1816–1889. A Philadelphia author widely known by his Critical Dictionary of English Literature and British and American Authors, a work of immense labour and research. It is of great value as a work of reference, but is not an infallible guide, and is more or less marred by trivial comment and moralizing. *See Pennsylvania Magazine, vol. 15, 1891. Lip.*

Allmond, Marcus Blakey. *Va.*, 1851——. An educator of Louisville who has published Estelle, an Idyl of Old Virginia, a volume of verse; Agricola, an Eastern Idyl; Outlines of Latin Syntax.

Allston [awl'ston], **Robert Francis Withers.** *S. C.*, 1801–1864. A South Carolina statesman well known at one time as an agricultural reformer. Memoir on Rice; Essay on Sea Coast Crops; Report on Public Schools.

Allston, Washington. *S. C.*, 1779–1843. A once famous artist of Cambridge who was also known as a poet and romancer. Sylphs of the Seasons and Other Poems; The Romance of Monaldi; Lectures on Art. *See Tuckerman's Book of the Artists; Life and Letters, edited by J. Flagg, 1892.*

Alsop [awl'sop], **Richard.** *Ct.*, 1761–1815. A once noted political satirist, chief of the "Hartford Wits," who wrote The Echo, a series of metrical parodies upon current publications, orations, state papers, and the like. Other works by Alsop are The Charms of Fancy; A Monody on the Death of Washington; The Enchanted Lake of the Fairy Morgana.

Alvord [awl'vord], **Benjamin.** *Vt.*, 1813–1884. A United States officer who served in the Mexican and Civil wars. Tangencies of Circles and Spheres; Interpretation of Imaginary Roots in Questions of Maxima and Minima.

Ames, Charles Gordon. *Ms.*, 1828——. A Unitarian clergyman who became pastor of the Church of the Disciples in Boston on the death of J. F. Clarke, *infra.* George Eliot's Two Marriages; As Natural as Life: Studies of the Inner Kingdom.

Ames, Mrs. Eleanor Maria [**Easterbrook**], "Eleanor Kirk." 1830——. A littérateur of Brooklyn. Up Broadway and Its Sequel; Information for Authors; Perpetual Youth.

Ames, Fisher. *Ms.*, 1758–1808. Son of N. Ames, *infra.* A statesman whose speeches are marked examples of condensed effective statement as well as of felicitous expression. Laocoon and Other Essays. *See Works of, with Memoir, 1854; Magoon's Orators of the American Revolution.*

Ames, Lucia True. *N. H.*, 1856——. A Boston writer who has published Great Thoughts for Little Thinkers; Memoirs of a Millionaire, a novel. *Hou. Put.*

Ames, Mary Clemmer. *See Hudson, Mrs.*

Ames, Nathaniel. *Ms.*, 1708–1764. A physician of Dedham, Massachusetts, who published, 1725–64, an Astronomical Diary and Almanac which contained much shrewd humour and original philosophy and was widely popular. *See Tyler's American Literatures; Essays, Humour and Poems of Nathaniel Ames, father and son, edited by S. Briggs, 1891.*

Ammen, Daniel. *O.*, 1820——. A rear-admiral of the United States navy, the designer of the Ammen life raft. The Atlantic Coast; Country Homes and their Improvement; The Old Navy and the New. *Lip. Scr.*

Amory, Thomas Coffin. *Ms.*, 1812–1889. A lawyer of Boston. Life of James Sullivan, Governor of Massachusetts; Military Services of Major-General John Sullivan; Life of Sir Isaac Coffin.

Anagnos, Mrs. Julia Romana [**Howe**]. 1844–1886. Daughter of Dr. S. G. and Julia Ward Howe, *infra*, and wife of M. Anagnos, the Superintendent of the Perkins Institute for the Blind in Boston. Stray Chords, a volume of verse; Philosophiæ Questor.

Anderson, Alexander. *N. Y.*, 1775–1870. The first wood-engraver in the United States. He was the author of an illustrated General History of Quadrupeds.

Anderson, John Jacob. *N. Y.*, 1821——. An educator of New York city who prepared a number of historical text books, among which are A History of France; Common School History of the United States. *My.*

Anderson, Mary. *See Navarro.*

Anderson, Rasmus Björn. *Wis.*, 1846——. A Norse scholar of Norwegian descent who has translated Björnson's novels and written much in relation to Norse mythology. America not Discovered by Columbus; Norse Mythology; Viking Tales of the North; The Younger Edda; The Elder Edda. *Sc.*

Anderson, Rufus. *Me.*, 1796–1880. A clergyman, who was secretary of the American Board of Foreign Missions, 1824–74. Foreign Missions, their Relations and Claims; History of the American Board's Missions in the Sandwich Islands, Turkey and India, Peloponnesus and Greek Islands. *C. P. S.*

Andrew, James Osgood. *Ga.*, 1794–1871. A bishop of the Methodist Church South. Family Government; Miscellanies.

Andrews, Christopher Columbus. *N. H.*, 1829——. A brevet major-general in the United States army, who was minister to Sweden 1869–77, and consul-general to Brazil 1882–85. Minnesota and Dakota (1857); Practical Treatise on the Revenue Laws of the United States; Hints to Company Officers on their Military Duties; History of the Campaign of Mobile; Digests of the Opinions of the Attorneys-General of the United States; Brazil, its Condition and Prospects (1887). third enlarged edition (1895). *Ap.*

Andrews, Elisha Benjamin. *N. H.*, 1844——. A prominent educator, president of Brown University. Institutes of General History; Institutes of Economics; Brief Institutes of our Economical History; An Honest Dollar; Eternal Words and Other Sermons; History of the United States; Wealth and Moral Law; History of the Last Quarter Century in the United States, 1870–95. *Gi. Scr. Sil.*

Andrews, Eliza Frances. *Ga.*, 1850——. An educator of Macon, Georgia, whose writing is mainly in the line of fiction. A Mere Adventurer; A Family Secret; How he was Tempted; Prince Hal.

Andrews, Ethan Allen. *Ct.*, 1787–1858. An educator who was at one time professor of ancient languages in the University of North Carolina. Beside a Latin-English Dictionary, he published a valuable series of classical text-books. *Hou.*

Andrews, Israel Ward. *Ct.*, 1815–1888. President of Marietta College. His only published work of importance is a Manual of the Constitution of the United States. *Va.*

Andrews, Jane. *Ms.*, 1833–1887. A writer of Newburyport whose books for children have long been deservedly popular. Seven Little Sisters who Live on the Round Ball that Floats in the Air; The Seven Little Sisters Prove their Sisterhood; The Stories Mother Nature Told; Ten Boys who Lived on the Road from Long Ago to Now; Only a Year and what it Brought. *Gi.*

Andrews, Samuel James. *Ct.*, 1817——. Brother of I. W. Andrews, *supra.* An Irvingite clergyman of Hartford, Connecticut. The Life of Our Lord upon Earth; God's Revelations of Himself to Men. *Scr.*

Andrews, Sidney. 1837–1880. A Boston journalist. The Art of Flying; The South since the War.

Andrews, Stephen Pearl. *Ms.*, 1812–1886. An eccentric writer of New York city, the originator of phonographic reporting and at one period prominent as an abolitionist. Among his many and varied works are Basic Outline of Universalogy, in which he advocated the adoption of a universal language called Alwato; Discourses in Chinese; Comparison of Common Law with Roman, French, or Spanish Law on Entails and Other Limited Property; Love, Marriage and Divorce.

Angell, Henry Clay. *R. I.*, 1829——. A professor of ophthalmology in Boston University. Diseases of the Eye; How to Take Care of our Eyes; Records of W. M. Hunt. *Rob.*

Angell, James Burrill. *R. I.*, 1829——. President of Michigan University since 1871. Manual of French Literature; Progress in International Law.

Angell, Joseph Kinnicut. *R. I.*, 1794–1857. A legal writer of Rhode Island, among whose works are Treatise on the Common Law of Watercourses; The Law of Tide Waters; The Limitation of Actions. *Lit.*

Anspach, Frederick Rinehart. *Pa.*, 1815–1867. A Lutheran clergyman of Hagerstown, Maryland. Sons of the Sires; Sepulchres of Our Departed; The Two Pilgrims.

Anthon, Charles. *N. Y.*, 1797–1867. A noted classical scholar, for many years professor of ancient languages at Columbia College. He was the author of some fifty classical text-books, including a Classical Dictionary. *Har.*

Anthon, John. *Mch.*, 1784–1863. Brother of Charles Anthon, *supra.* A jurist of New York city. Essay on the Study of Law; Analysis of Blackstone; Nisi Prius Cases; American Precedents.

Appleton, Jesse. *N. H.*, 1772–1819. A Congregational clergyman, president of Bowdoin College, 1807–19. Addresses; Lectures. His works, with Memoir by A. S. Packard, *infra*, appeared in 1837.

Appleton, John. 1804–1891. A former chief justice of Maine eminent as a legal reformer. The Rules of Evidence Stated and Discussed.

Appleton, John Howard. *Me.*, 1844——. A professor of chemistry at Brown University since 1868. The Young Chemist; Qualitative Analysis; Quantitative Analysis; Chemistry of Non Metals. *Sil.*

Appleton, Thomas Gold. *Ms.*, 1812–1884. An artist and littérateur of Boston. A Sheaf of Papers; A Nile Journal; Windfalls; Syrian Sunshine; Chequer-Work; Faded Leaves, a volume of verse. *See Life and Letters, edited by Susan Hale, 1885. Rob.*

Apthorp, William Foster. *Ms.*, 1848——. A musical newspaper critic of Boston. Musicians and Music Lovers and Other Essays. He has translated Zola's Jacques Damour. *Cop. Scr.*

Archibald, Andrew Webster. *N. Y.*, 1851——. A Congregational clergyman of prominence in Iowa. The Bible Verified.

Archibald, Mrs. George. *See Palmer, Mrs. Anna.*

Arey, Mrs. Harriet Ellen [Grannis]. *Vt.*, 1819——. An educator whose home is in Cleveland. Household Songs and Other Poems; Home and School Training. *Lip.*

Arkwright, Peleg. *See Proudfit, D.*

Armitage, Thomas. *E.*, 1819–1896. A prominent Baptist clergyman of New York city. Jesus, his Self Introspection; Lectures on Preaching; History of the Baptists.

Armstrong, George Dodd. *N. J.*, 1813——. A Presbyterian clergyman of Norfolk, Virginia. The Summer of the Pestilence; The Doctrine of Baptisms; The Christian Doctrine of Slavery; Theology of Christian Experience; The Sacraments of the New Testament; The Books of Nature and Revelation, a criticism of the theory of evolution. *Fu.*

Armstrong, John. *Pa.*, 1758–1843. An officer of note in the American army at the time of the Revolution. He was the author of the first of the famous Newburg Letters, and in later life published Notes on the War of 1812; Treatise on Gardening; Treatise on Agriculture; Memoirs of Generals Montgomery and Wayne.

Arnold, Albert Nicholas. *R. I.*, 1814–1883. A Baptist clergyman who held professorships in several Baptist seminaries successively. Pre-requisites to Communion; Evils of Infant Baptism; One Woman's Mission.

Arnold, George. *N. Y.*, 1834–1865. A journalist and poet of New York city, whose verse is musical without being especially strong. Drift and Other Poems; Poems Grave and Gay. *See Biographical Sketch by W. Winter, infra. Hou.*

Arnold, Isaac Newton. *N. Y.*, 1815–1884. A prominent Chicago lawyer and politician, member of Congress, 1861–65. Life of Abraham Lincoln; Life of Benedict Arnold; Recollections of the Early Chicago and Illinois Bar. *Mg.*

Arnold, Lauren Briggs. *N. Y.*, 1814–1888. An agriculturist of western New York who lectured frequently upon dairy husbandry and was the author of American Dairying.

Arnold, Samuel Greene. *R. I.*, 1821–1880. A lawyer who was several times lieutenant-governor of Rhode Island. History of the State of Rhode Island and Providence Plantations; Life of Patrick Henry. *Pr.*

Arp, Bill. *See Smith, C. H.*

Arr, E. H. *See Rollins, Mrs. Ellen.*

Arria. *See Pugh, Mrs.*

Arrington, Alfred W. *N. C.*, 1810–1867. A prominent lawyer in the Southwest, and, later, in Chicago. The Rangers and Regulators of the Tanaha; Sketches of the Southwest; Poems (with Memoir), 1869.

Arthur, Timothy Shay. *N.Y.*, 1809–1885. A prolific writer of moral tales, with much more excellence of intention than literary merit to recommend them, but which have enjoyed a very extensive popularity. Ten Nights in a Bar-Room; Six Nights with the Washingtonians; Tales of Married Life, are some of the best known. His life was nearly all spent in Philadelphia. *Co. Lip. Pet.*

Ashhurst, John. *Pa.*, 1839——. A distinguished surgeon of Philadelphia. Injuries of the Spine; Principles and Practice of Surgery. He has edited the International Encyclopædia of Surgery. *Lip.*

Astor, William Waldorf. *N. Y.*, 1848——. A noted millionaire of New York city, minister to Italy, 1882–85, and more recently the proprietor of the Pall Mall Gazette and Pall Mall Magazine in London. Valentino, an Historical Romance of the 16th Century in Italy; Sforza, a Story of Milan. *Scr.*

Atkinson, Edward. *Ms.*, 1827——. A Boston reformer active in matters of diet and political economy. The Distribution of Products; Labor and Capital; Industrial Progress of the Nation; The Science of Nutrition; Margin of Profits; Taxation and Work. *Put.*

Atkinson, John. *N. J.*, 1835–1897. A clergyman of prominence in the Methodist church. The Living Way; Memorials of Methodism in New Jersey; The Garden of Sorrows; The Class Leader; Centennial History of American Methodism. *Meth.*

Atkinson, William Parsons. *Ms.*, 1820–1890. Brother of E. Atkinson, *supra*. A professor of history at the Massachusetts Institute of Technology. The Right Use of Books; History and the Study of History; Classical and Scientific Studies. *Rob.*

Atwater, Horace Cowles. *N. Y.*, 1819–1879. A clergyman of the Methodist Church South, who published Incidents of a Southern Tour (1857).

Atwater, Lyman Hotchkiss. *Ct.*, 1813–1883. A professor of philosophy at Princeton College and long a noted contributor to the Princeton Review. He published a Manual of Elementary Logic. *Lip.*

Atwater, Wilbur Olin. *N.Y.*, 1844——. A professor of chemistry at Wesleyan University since 1873. He has written extensively upon agricultural chemistry, and published Co-operative Experimenting as a Means of Studying the Effect of Fertilizers; Results of Field Experiments with Various Fertilizers.

Atwood, Anthony. *N. J.*, 1801–1888. A Methodist clergyman, whose only published work is The Abiding Comforter.

Atwood, Isaac Morgan. *N. Y.*, 1838——. A Universalist clergyman, president of the Theological Seminary at St. Lawrence University. Have we Outgrown Christianity; Glance at the Religious Progress of the United States; Latest Word of Universalism; Walks about Zion; Manual of Revelation.

Audubon, John James. *La.*, 1780–1851. An ornithologist of eminence, whose entire life was devoted to the pursuit of his favorite study. Birds of America; Quadrupeds of North America; Ornithological Biography. *See Audubon, the Naturalist, by Mrs. St. John; Journal of Life and Labours of Audubon.*

Auringer, Obadiah Cyrus. *N. Y.*, 1849——. A Presbyterian clergyman of New York state, whose writings in verse include Scythe and Sword; The Heart of the Golden Roan; The Episode of Jane McCrea; The Book of the Hills. *Lo.*

Austen, Peter Townsend. *N. Y.*, 1852——. A professor of chemistry at Rutgers College since 1877, who has contributed much to scientific journals, and published Chemical Lecture Notes; Organic Chemistry, from the German of Pinner. *Wil.*

Austin, Arthur Williams. *Ms.*, 1807–1884. A lawyer of Boston. The Woman and the Queen, and Other Specimens of Verse, (1875).

Austin, Benjamin. *Ms.*, 1752–1820. A Boston merchant, active as a political writer and an especially violent champion of democracy. Constitutional Republicanism is a collection of some of his contributions to the newspapers of his day.

Austin, Coe Finch. *N. Y.*, 1831–1880. A botanist of Closter, New York, who published Musci Appalachani, a description of American mosses.

Austin, George Lowell. *Ms.*, 1849–1893. A Boston physician whose miscellaneous writings include Perils of American Women, a Doctor's Talk with Maiden, Wife, and Mother; Water-Analysis, a Handbook for Water-Drinkers; Under the Tide; Life of Franz Schubert; Popular History of Massachusetts; Life and Deeds of General Grant; Longfellow; Life of Wendell Phillips. *Le.*

Austin, Henry. *Ms.*, 1856——. A lawyer of Boston, who has written The Law Concerning Farms; American Farm and Game Laws; American Fish and Game Laws; Liquor Law in New England.

Austin, Henry Willard. *Ms.*, 1858——. A journalist and littérateur of Boston. Vagabond Verses.

Austin, James Trecothick. *Ms.*, 1784–1870. A once prominent lawyer of Boston, who published a Life of Elbridge Gerry.

Austin, Mrs. Jane [Goodwin]. *Ms.*, 1831–1894. A talented writer of historical fiction, much of whose life was spent in Boston. She was a careful student of colonial history, and will be long remembered for her series of romances relating to the Plymouth Pilgrims and their descendants. These include A Nameless Nobleman; Standish of Standish; Betty Alden: the First-Born Daughter of the Pilgrims; Dr. Le Baron and his Daughters; David Alden's Daughter and Other Stories of Colonial Times. Other novels by her are Cipher; The Shadow of Moloch Mountain; Mrs. Beauchamp Brown; The Desmond Hundred; Dora Darling; Outpost. Nantucket Scraps is a volume of travel sketches; Moonfolk, a fairy tale. *Hou. Le. Put. Rob.*

Austin, Samuel. *Ct.*, 1760–1830. A Congregational clergyman of Worcester, Massachusetts, 1790–1815, and afterwards president of the University of Vermont. Views of the Church; Theological Essays; Letters on Baptism.

Austin, William. *Ms.*, 1778–1841. A Boston lawyer whose best claim to remembrance is that he was author of the famous sketch Peter Rugg: the Missing Man, which appeared in the New England Galaxy in 1824. It is a very remarkable imaginative study that in some respects anticipates the later work of Hawthorne. Other works of his are Letters from London (1804); The Human Character of Jesus Christ. *See Literary Papers of, with Biographical Sketch, 1890. Lit.*

Avery, Benjamin Parke. *N. Y.*, 1829–1875. A Californian journalist who was appointed minister to China in 1874. Californian Pictures in Prose and Verse.

Ayres, Alfred. *See Osmun.*

Ayres, Anne. *E.*, 1816–1896. The first member of an American sisterhood in the Protestant Episcopal Church, becoming a sister of the Holy Communion in 1845. Evangelical Sisterhoods; Life of W. H. Muhlenberg, *infra.*

Azarias, Brother. *See Mullany.*

B

Bache [baych], Alexander Dallas. *Pa.*, 1806–1867. A scientist who was superintendent of the United States Court Survey, 1843–67. His annual reports to Congress are works of great value. *See Commemorative Address by B. A. Gould, infra, 1868.*

Bache, Franklin. *Pa.*, 1792–1864. Cousin of A. D. Bache, *supra*, and like him a great-grandson of Benjamin

Franklin, *infra.* A Philadelphia physician, professor of chemistry in Jefferson Medical College, 1841–64. A System of Chemistry for Students in Medicine; The Dispensatory of the United States (with *G. B. Wood*). *See Memoir, by G. B. Wood, infra.*

Bacheller, Irving. *N. Y.*, 1859——. A journalist and littérateur of New York city. The Master of Silence, a romance; The Still House of O'Darrow, a novel. *Cas.*

Bachman [bäk′man], **John.** *N. Y.*, 1790–1874. A naturalist of Charleston, where he was pastor of a Lutheran church, 1815–74. He assisted Audubon, preparing the greater part of the text of The Quadrupeds of North America, and wrote several religious and scientific works. Two Letters on Heredity; Defence of Luther and the Reformation. *See American Lutheran Biographies.*

Backus, Isaac. *Ct.*, 1724–1806. A Baptist clergyman of Rhode Island. A History of New England, with Particular Reference to the Baptists. *See Sprague's Annals of the American Pulpit.*

Bacon, Delia Salter. *O.*, 1811–1859. The earliest exponent of the Baconian theory of the authorship of Shakespeare. Philosophy of the Plays of Shakespeare Unfolded; Tales of the Puritans; The Bride of Fort Edward: a Drama. *See Hawthorne's Recollections of a Gifted Woman; Mrs. Farrar's Recollections of Seventy Years; Life, by Theodore Bacon; Saturday Review, vol. 67.*

Bacon, Edwin Munroe. *R. I.*, 1844——. A journalist of Boston. Dictionary of Boston; Boston of To-Day. *Hou.*

Bacon, Henry. *Ms.*, 1839——. An artist who has lived principally in Paris. A Parisian Year; Parisian Art and Artists. *Hou. Rob.*

Bacon, Leonard. *Mch.*, 1802–1881. Brother of D. S. Bacon, *supra.* The pastor of a Congregational church in New Haven, Connecticut, 1825–81, and a prominent figure in the denomination to which he belonged. Historical Discourses; Slavery Discussed in Occasional Essays; Genesis of the New England Churches; Christian Self-Culture. *See Century Magazine, vol. 3. Har.*

Bacon, Leonard Woolsey. *Ct.*, 1830——. Son of L. Bacon, *supra.* A Congregational clergyman. A Life Worth Living; Church Papers; Sermons; The Simplicity that is in Christ. *Fu.*

Bacon, Thomas Scott. *N. Y.*, 1825——. An Episcopal controversialist of Maryland. Both Sides of the Controversy between the Roman and Reformed Churches; The Reign of God and the Reign of Law; The Beginnings of Religion; Primitive Man in Christian Thought; It is Written; The Primitive and Catholic Doctrine as to Holy Scripture.

Badeau, Adam. *N. Y.*, 1831–1895. A general in the United States army. The Vagabond; Military History of General Grant; Conspiracy: a Cuban Romance; Aristocracy in England; Grant in Peace: a Personal Memoir. *Ap. Har.*

Bagg, Lyman Hotchkiss. "Karl Kron." *Ms.*, 1846——. Four Years at Yale; Ten Thousand Miles on a Bicycle.

Bailey, Jacob Montgomery. *N. Y.*, 1841–1894. Widely known at one time as "The Danbury News Man." A journalist of Danbury, Connecticut, who was among the earliest to exploit a kind of native humour chiefly concerned with local allusion and application. He has had many imitators whose methods have been much less legitimate than his. Life in Danbury; England from a Back Window; The Danbury Boom; Mr. Phillis' Goneness; They All Do It. *Le.*

Bailey, Liberty Hyde. *Mich.*, 1858——. A prominent horticulturist. American Grape Training; Cross-breeding and Hybridization; Field Notes on Apple Culture; Annals of Horticulture; The Horticulturist Rule-Book; The Nursery-Book: a Complete Guide to the Multiplication and Pollination of Plants; Talks Afield about Plants; Plant Breeding. *Hou. Mac.*

Bailey, Loring Woart. *N. Y.*, 1839——. A professor of natural history in the University of New Brunswick.

Mines and Minerals of New Brunswick; Geology of Southern New Brunswick; Elementary Natural History.

Bailey, William Whitman. *N. Y.*, 1843——. Brother of L. W. Bailey, *supra.* A professor of botany at Brown University. New England Wild Flowers and Their Seasons; Among Rhode Island Wild Flowers; Botanical Collector's Hand-Book. *Pr.*

Baird, Charles Washington. *N. J.*, 1828–1887. Son of R. Baird, *supra.* A Presbyterian minister of Rye, New York. Eutaxia, or the Presbyterian Liturgies; Book of Public Prayer; History of Rye; History of the Huguenot Emigration to America. *Do.*

Baird, Henry Carey. *Pa.*, 1825——. Nephew of Henry Carey, *infra*, and a political economist holding similar views. Rights of American Producers and Wrongs of British Free Trade Revenue Reformers; Protection of Home Labour and Home Production necessary to the Protection of the American Farmer; Miscellaneous Papers on Economic Questions. *Bai.*

Baird, Henry Martyn. *Pa.*, 1832——. Son of R. Baird, *infra.* Professor of Greek at the University of New York from 1859. An historian who is conscientious but not absolutely impartial. Life of Robert Baird; Modern Greece; Narrative of a Residence and Travels; History of the Rise of the Huguenots of France; The Huguenots and Henry of Navarre; The Huguenots and the Revocation of the Edict of Nantes. *Har. Ran. Scr.*

Baird, Robert. *Pa.*, 1798–1863. A Presbyterian clergyman, active in the cause of temperance and in promoting the extension of Protestantism in Europe. History of the Temperance Societies; View of Religion in America; History of the Waldenses, Albigenses, and Vaudois; Protestantism in Italy. *See Life, by H. M. Baird. Har.*

Baird, Samuel John. *O.*, 1817——. A Presbyterian clergyman whose writings are chiefly concerned with the polity and history of the Presbyterian church. The Church of Christ: its Constitution and Order; History of the Early Polity of the Presbyterian Church in the Training of Ministers; The Socinian Apostasy of the English Presbyterian Church; History of the New School.

Baird, Spencer Fullerton. *Pa.*, 1823–1887. A naturalist of prominence, who was from 1878 the secretary of the Smithsonian Institution. The translator and editor of the Iconographic Encyclopedia, co-author with J. Cassin of Birds of North America and Mammals of North America; editor Annual Record of Science and Industry from 1872–78. A History of North American Birds, written in collaboration with T. M. Brewer and R. Ridgway, is one of his most valuable works. *See Popular Science Monthly, vol. 33. Har. Lip. Lit.*

Baker, Abijah Richardson. *Ms.*, 1805–1876. A Congregational clergyman of Lynn, Massachusetts. School History of the United States; The Catechism Tested by the Bible; Topics in Christ's Sermon on the Mount.

Baker, George Augustus. *N. Y.*, 1849——. A lawyer of New York. Point Lace and Diamonds, a collection of sparkling society verse; The Bad Habits of Good Society; Mrs. Hephaestus and Other Short Stories; West Point: a Comedy. *Sto.*

Baker, George Melville. *Me.*, 1832–1890. The author and compiler of Amateur Dramas, the Social Stage, and works of like character. *Le.*

Baker, George Pierce. *R. I.*, 1866——. An instructor at Harvard University. Plot Book of Elizabethan Plays; Principles of Argumentation. *Gi. Ho.*

Baker, Mrs. Harriette Newell [Woods]. "Madeline Leslie." *Ms.*, 1815–1893. Wife of A. R. Baker, *supra*, and daughter of Leonard Woods, *infra.* Beside two novels, — Cora and the Doctor, The Courtesies of Wedded Life, — her writings include nearly two hundred moral and religious tales, among which Tim the Scissors Grinder is the best known.

Baker, Mrs. Julie Keim [Wetherill]. *Mi.*, 1858——. A journalist of New Orleans. Wings: a Novel.

Baker, William Mumford. *D. C.*, 1825–1883. A popular novelist who was a Presbyterian clergyman in the Southwest until 1870, and afterwards the pastor of a church in Boston. He was a vigourous writer of considerable originality, whose earlier works possess historic interest as pictures of a now past stage of civilization in the Southern States. Inside: a Chronicle of Secession; The Virginians in Texas; Oak Mot; The New Timothy; Mose Evans; His Majesty Myself; Blessed St. Certainty; Thirlmore; Carter Quarterman; A Year Worth Living; Colonel Dunwoddie: Millionaire; The Making of a Man; The Ten Theophanies: the Manifestations of Christ before his Birth in Bethlehem; John Westacott, a juvenile tale. *Har. Le. Ran. Rob.*

Balch, William Stevens. *Vt.*, 1806–1887. A Universalist clergyman, long resident at Elgin, Illinois, and author of Lectures on Language; Grammar of the English Language; Ireland as I Saw It; A Peculiar People.

Baldwin, James Mark. *S. C.*, 1861–——. A professor of psychology at Princeton University since 1893. Psychology; Elements of Psychology; Mental Development in the Child and Man; a translation of Ribot's "German Psychology of To-Day." *Ho. Mac.*

Baldwin, John Denison. *Ct.*, 1809–1883. A journalist of Worcester, Massachusetts. Raymond Hill, a Poem; Pre-Historic Nations; Ancient America. *Har.*

Baldwin, Joseph G. *Va.*, 1811–1864. A once popular humourous writer who was a jurist of prominence in Alabama and afterwards of California, of which State he became chief justice. Flush Times in Alabama and Mississippi; Party Leaders, able papers on Southern statesmen.

Baldwin, Mrs. Lydia Wood. *Ms.*, 1836——. Rubina; A Yankee School-Teacher in Virginia. *Fu.*

Balestier, Charles Wolcott. 1861–1891. An American writer who established himself as a publisher in London, and whose sister was married to Rudyard Kipling the novelist. A Fair Device; Life of Blaine; A Victorious Defeat; Benefits Forgot; The Naulahka (with Rudyard Kipling); A Common Story. *See Century Magazine, April, 1892. Ap. Har.*

Ballou, Adin. *R. I.*, 1803–1890. A Universalist clergyman of Milford, Massachusetts. Christian Non-Resistance Defended; Treatise on Spirit Manifestations; Primitive Christianity and its Corruptions; History of the Town of Milford. *See New England Magazine, April, 1891.*

Ballou, Hosea. *N. H.*, 1771–1852. A Universalist theologian of note in New England, and one of the founders of American Universalism. With his son he established the Universalist Quarterly. Treatise on Atonement; Notes on the Parables; An Examination of the Doctrine of Future Retribution. *See Lives, by M. M. Ballou; Whittemore, 1854; Safford, 1889. See Universalist Review, vol. 41.*

Ballou, Hosea. *Vt.*, 1796–1861. Nephew of H. Ballou, *supra*. A Universalist clergyman who was the first president of Tufts College, 1854–61. Ancient History of Universalism.

Ballou, Maturin Murray. *Ms.*, 1820–1895. Son of H. Ballou, 2nd. The founder and editor of several periodicals in Boston which bore his name, and, in his later years, a traveler to all parts of the world. History of Cuba; Life of Hosea Ballou; Due West, or Round the World in Ten Months; Due South, or Cuba Past and Present; Due North: Glimpses of Scandinavia and Russia; Under the Southern Cross: Travels in Australia, Tasmania, New Zealand, etc.; Alaska: The New Eldorado; Aztec Land; The Story of Malta; The Pearl of India, a description of Ceylon; Equatorial America, a description of visits to the Lesser Antilles and to South American capitals; Footprints of Travel. *Gi. Hou.*

Ballou, Moses. *Ms.*, 1811–1879. A nephew of H. Ballou, 1st, and, like him, a Universalist clergyman. The Divine Character Vindicated.

Bancroft, Aaron. *Ms.*, 1755–1839. A Unitarian clergyman of Worcester, Massachusetts, 1785–1839, who was prominent in the earlier days of the Unitarian movement as a writer in its behalf. Sermons on the Doctrines of the Gospel; A Life of Washington. *Co.*

Bancroft, Edward. *Ms.*, 1744–1821.

A physician who resided chiefly in London, where he was supposed to have been a spy of the English Government during the American Revolution. Natural History of Guiana; Researches concerning the Philosophy of Permanent Colors; Charles Wentworth: a Novel; and several political works.

ancroft, George. *Ms.*, 1800–1891. Son of A. Bancroft, *supra*. An eminent historian who was United States minister to England, 1846–49, and to Prussia and Germany, 1867–74. He was inclined to view history from the philosophic standpoint, and his political experiences gave him insight into motives. In his estimates of men he made smaller allowance for the relative values of the testimony of different periods than is now customary among historians. He paid much attention to style, but sometimes erred in regard to over-ornament. His manner, however, where not laboured, is attractive and often dramatic. The first volume of The History of the United States appeared in 1834, the second in 1837, the third in 1840, and the succeeding ones 1852–74. A revised edition was issued in 1876, while volumes 11 and 12 of the first edition were published in 1882 as The History of the Formation of the Constitution of the United States. The latest revised edition was printed 1884–85. Minor works include Martin Van Buren to the End of his Public Career; Literary and Historical Miscellanies; Memorial Address on Abraham Lincoln; A Plea for the Constitution of the United States wounded in the House of its Guardians. *See Annual Cyclopedia, 1891; Century Magazine, vol. 11; Jameson's Historical Writing in America, pp. 100–110. Ap. Har.*

ancroft, Hubert Howe. *O.*, 1832–——. An historical writer whose works, exceedingly comprehensive in their scope, were prepared with the assistance of a number of collaborateurs. The Native Races of the Pacific States, 5 volumes; History of the Pacific States of North America, including Central America, Mexico, California, Oregon, British Columbia, 39 volumes; The Early American Chroniclers; Popular History of the Mexican People; Literary Industries. *See Jameson's Historical Writing in America, pp. 152–156. Ap. Har.*

Bandelier, Adolph Francis Alphonse. *Sd.*, 1830——. An archæologist of Swiss birth, whose life has been chiefly spent in the United States. The Art of War and Mode of Warfare; Tenure of Land and Inheritances of the Ancient Mexicans; Historical Introduction to Studies among the Sedentary Indians of New Mexico; Archæological Tour in Mexico in 1881; The Delight Makers, a novel of Pueblo Indian Life. *Ap. Do.*

Bangs, John Kendrick. *N.Y.*, 1862–——. A humourous writer of Yonkers, New York, and one of the founders of "Life." Three Weeks in Politics; Coffee and Repartee; The Idiot; The Water Ghost; Mr. Bonaparte of Corsica; A House Boat on the Styx; The Bicyclers and Other Farces; Toppleton's Client; A Rebellious Heroine. *Har.*

Bangs, Nathan. *Ct.*, 1778–1862. An active Methodist theologian and controversialist, very prominent in the literary history of his church and a most prolific writer. Among his works are comprised History of the Methodist Episcopal Church to 1840; Errors of Hopkinsianism; Life of Arminius; Letters to a Young Preacher; Letters on Sanctification; Methodist Episcopacy. *See Life and Times of, by Abel Stevens. Meth.*

Banks, Louis Albert. *Or.*, 1855–——. A prominent Methodist clergyman. The Saloon Keeper's Ledger, a series of Temperance Discourses; The Fisherman and his Friends; Common Folks' Religion; Revival Quiver, a Record of Revival Campaigns; The People's Christ; White Slaves, or the Oppression of the Worthy Poor; The Honeycombs of Life; Christ and His Friends. *Fu. Le. Meth.*

Banister, John. *E.*, 16—1692. A Virginia botanist who assisted the English naturalist, John Ray. Observations on the Natural Productions of Jamaica; Insects of Virginia; Curiosities of Virginia; The Unseen Lupus; The Pistolochia, or Serpentaria Virginiana. The genus Banisteria was named in his honour.

Banneker, Benjamin. *Md.*, 1731–

1806. An astronomer and mathematician of African descent, who assisted in the original survey of the District of Columbia and published an astronomical almanac 1792–1806. *See Lives, by Latrobe, 1845; Norris, 1854; Atlantic Monthly, January, 1863; Catholic World, vol. 38.*

Banvard, John. 1814–1891. An artist and poet whose famous panorama of the Mississippi covered 3 miles of canvas. He wrote much indifferent verse, and published books of a miscellaneous nature. Amasis, The Last of the Pharaohs, afterwards dramatized by him; Carrinia: a Drama; Description of the Mississippi River; Pilgrimage to the Holy Land; The Private Life of a King; A Tradition of the Temple: a Poem.

Banvard, Joseph. *N. Y.*, 1810–1887. Brother of J. Banvard, *supra*. A Baptist clergyman of Massachusetts who beside contributing somewhat largely to Sunday-school literature wrote much in other directions. Romance of American History; Plymouth and the Pilgrims; Novelties of the New World, or Adventures and Discoveries of the First Explorers; Tragic Scenes in the History of Maryland; The American Statesman: a Memoir of Webster; Southern Explorers; Soldiers and Patriots of the Revolution; Priscilla: an Historical Tale. *Lo. Mer.*

Baraga, Friedric. *A.*, 1797–1868. A Roman Catholic missionary who came to America in 1830 from Austria, and became bishop of Sault St. Marie in 1852. He devoted himself to mission work among the Chippewa or Ojibway Indians, and beside writing several books in their tongue prepared a Grammar and Dictionary of the Otchipewe Language.

Barbe, Waitman. *W. Va.*, 1864——. A resident of Parkersburg, West Virginia. Ashes and Incense, a volume of notable verse; In the Virginias, a collection of short stories. *Lip.*

Barber, John Warner. *Ct.*, 1798–1885. An industrious annalist whose compilations though of slight literary merit are valuable as historical material not so readily accessible elsewhere. Historical Collections of Massachusetts, Connecticut, New York, New Jersey, Virginia, and Ohio, the four last being prepared with the assistance of Henry Howe, *infra*; History of New Haven; Elements of General History; Historical Scenes in the United States.

Barbour, John Humphrey. *Ct.*, 1854——. An Episcopal clergyman, professor of New Testament interpretation at the Berkeley Divinity School at Middletown, Connecticut. Beginnings of the Historic Episcopate.

Barbour, Oliver Lorenzo. *N. Y.*, 1811–1889. An eminent lawyer of New York State. Equity Digest; Criminal Law; The Law of Set-Off; Practice of the Court of Chancery; Summary of the Law of Parties to Actions at Law, and many legal reports.

Barclay, James Turner. *Va.*, 1807–1874. A leading clergyman of the Campbellite faith, for many years a missionary at Jerusalem. He is best known as the author of The City of the Great King, a description of Jerusalem.

Barker, Fordyce. *N. H.*, 1818–1891. A New York physician of prominence and a professor in the Bellevue Hospital from 1860. On Sea-Sickness; On Puerperal Diseases. *Ap.*

Barker, George Frederic. *Ms.*, 1835——. A professor of physics in the University of Pennsylvania since 1873. Correlation of Vital and Physical Forces; Text Book of Elementary Chemistry.

Barker, James Nelson. *Pa.*, 1784–1858. A Philadelphia poet and playwright who was comptroller of the United States Treasury 1838–50. His dramas include Marmion; The Indian Princess; Superstition; Smiles and Tears.

Barlow, Joel. *Ct.*, 1754–1812. A prominent literary figure in the early days of the republic. His verse for the most part is stilted and declamatory. The Columbiad, his most ambitious poem, is now unread, but Hasty Pudding, a poetical reminiscence of New England among Italian scenes, still affords pleasant reading, and is genuinely humourous. The Vision of Columbus, The Conspiracy of Kings, are his only other works of any note. *See Life by Todd, 1886; Tyler's Three Men of*

Letters, 1895; Atlantic Monthly, vol. 58.

Barnard, Charles. *Ms.*, 1838——. A journalist whose work is very miscellaneous in character and of momentary value only. The Tone Masters; The Soprano; My Ten Rod Farm; Farming by Inches; A Simple Flower Garden; The Strawberry Garden; Legilda Romanoff; Knights of To-Day; Co-operation as a Business; A Dead Town, a Romance of the Old Country; Talks about the Weather; Talks about the Soil. *Put. Scr.*

Barnard, Frederick Augustus Porter. *Ms.*, 1809–1889. An educational writer who was president of Columbia College, 1864–89. History of the United States Coast Survey; Imaginary Metrological System of the Great Pyramid; The Undulatory Theory of Light; Letters on College Government. *See Memoirs of, by John Fulton, 1896. Wil.*

Barnard, Henry. *Ct.*, 1811——. A noted advocate of educational reforms. National Education in Europe; School Architecture; Hints and Methods for Teachers; Pestalozzi and Pestalozzianism; History of Education in Connecticut; Educational Biography; German Educational Reformers. *See New England Magazine, vol. 4.*

Barnard, John. *Ms.*, 1681–1770. A Congregational minister of Boston who was among the earliest New England dissenters from Calvinism. A robust and logical thinker. Version of the Psalms; Sermons; The Strange Adventures of Philip Ashton. *See Tyler's American Literature.*

Barnard, John Gross. *Ms.*, 1815–1882. Brother of F. Barnard, *supra.* A major-general of the United States Army. Survey of the Isthmus of Tehuantepec; Phenomena of the Gyroscope; Dangers and Defences of New York; Sea Coast Defence; The Peninsular Campaign and its Antecedents; Problems of Rotary Motion.

Barnes, Albert. *N. Y.*, 1798–1870. A leader of New School Presbyterian thought and an able scriptural commentator. He was a clergyman of Philadelphia, and was at one time tried for heresy. Notes on the New Testament; Scriptural Views of Slavery; The Atonement; Life at Three Score; Prayers for Family Worship; Evidences of Christianity in the Nineteenth Century. *See Theological Works of, 1875. Har.*

Barnes, James. *Md.*, 1865——. For King or Country, a Story of the Revolution; Admiral Farragut; Naval Actions of the War of 1812; A Princetonian. *Ap. Har. Put.*

Barnes, Mrs. Mary Downing [Sheldon]. *N. Y.*, 1850——. An educator who has published Studies in General History; Teachers' Manual.

Barnum, Mrs. Frances Courtenay [Baylor]. *Ark.*, 1848——. A novelist now living in Savannah. On Both Sides, an international novel; Behind the Blue Ridge; Juan and Juanita, a juvenile tale; Claudia Hyde. *Hou. Lip.*

Barnum, Phineas Taylor. *Ct.*, 1810–1891. A showman of world-wide fame. Humbugs of the World; Struggles and Triumphs, or Forty Years' Recollections; Lion Jack, or How Menageries are Made; Autobiography. *See Saturday Review, vol. 71.*

Barr, Mrs. Amelia Edith [Huddleston.] *E.*, 1831——. A novelist of English birth who was educated in Glasgow and came to America in 1854. Her literary career did not begin, however, until 1871. Her books exhibit many excellencies of construction and characterization, are wholesome in tone, and have been deservedly popular. Among the best of them may be named Jan Vedder's Wife; Paul and Christina; A Daughter of Fife; A Border Shepherdess; The Bow of Orange Ribbon, a tale of colonial life in New York; Between Two Loves; Friend Olivia; Bernicia, a story in which Whitefield, the famous preacher, is a prominent figure. Other works by Mrs. Barr include: Scottish Sketches; Flower of Gala Water; Romance and Reality; Young People of Shakespeare's Time; Cluny McPherson; The Hallam Succession; The Lost Silver of Briffault; The Last of the McAlisters; Scottish Sketches; The Squire of Sandal Side; Master of his Fate; Christopher; Remember the Alamo, a story of Texas; She Loved a Sailor; A Rose of a Hundred Leaves;

Michael and Theodora; A Sister to Esau; Feet of Clay; The Household of McNeil; The Preacher's Daughter; Love for an Hour is Love Forever; A Singer from the Sea; The Lone House. *See Andover Review, vol. 11. Ap. Do. Har.*

Barrett, Benjamin Fisk. *Me.*, 1808–1892. A Swedenborgian clergyman of Philadelphia who wrote extensively in behalf of his faith. Among his many books are A Life of Swedenborg; The New View of Hell; Swedenborg and Channing; Heaven Revealed: a Popular Presentation of Swedenborg's Disclosures about Heaven.

Barrett, Walter. *See Scoville.*

Barron, Elwyn Alfred. *Tn.*, 1855——. A Chicago journalist on the editorial staff of The Inter-Ocean from 1879, who has written The Viking, a blank-verse drama; A Moral Crime, and other plays.

Barrow, Mrs. Frances Elizabeth [Mease]. "Aunt Fanny." *S. C.*, 1822–1894. A writer of juvenile tales which have been widely circulated. Among them are The Night Cap Series; The Pop Gun Series; The Six Mitten Books. *Est.*

Barrows, John Henry. *Mich.*, 1847——. A Presbyterian clergyman of Chicago. The Gospels are True History; I believe in God the Father Almighty; Henry Ward Beecher, the Pulpit Jupiter; Life of Henry Ward Beecher. *Fu. Lo.*

Barrows, Mrs. Katherine Isabel Hayes [Chapin]. *Vt.*, 1846——. Wife of S. J. Barrows, *infra*, and with him author of The Shaybacks in Camp, a volume of leisurely travel notes. *Hou.*

Barrows, Samuel June. *N. Y.*, 1845——. A Unitarian clergyman of Boston, editor of The Christian Register since 1881. A Baptist Meeting House, a narrative of a transition from the Baptist to the Unitarian faith; The Doom of the Majority of Mankind. *A. U. A.*

Barrows, William. *Ms.*, 1815–1891. A Congregational clergyman of Massachusetts. The Church and the Children; The Indian's Side of the Indian Question; Oregon, the Struggle for Possession; The United States of Yesterday and To-morrow; Twelve Nights in the Hunter's Camp. *Hou. Le. Lo. Rob.*

Barry, John Daniel. *Ms.*, 1866——. A littérateur of New York city. A Daughter of Thespis; The Intriguers, a novel; Mademoiselle Blanche; The Princess Margarethe, a fairy tale. *Ap. St.*

Barry, John Stetson. *Ms.*, 1819–1872. A Universalist clergyman. The Stetson Genealogy; History of Massachusetts.

Barry, Patrick. *I.*, 1816–1890. A prominent horticulturist of Rochester, N.Y. Treatise on the Fruit Garden. *Ju.*

Barry, William. *Ms.*, 1805–1885. Brother of J. S. Barry, *supra*. A Congregational clergyman of Chicago. Rights and Duties of Neighboring Churches; Thoughts on Christian Doctrine; History of Framingham; Antiquities of Wisconsin.

Bartholow, Roberts. *Md.*, 1831——. A physician and medical professor of Philadelphia. Materia Medica and Therapeutics; Practice of Medicine; Medical Electricity; The Antagonism between Medicines and between Remedies and Diseases. *Ap. Lip.*

Bartlett, Elisha. *R. I.*, 1804–1855. A Rhode Island physician. The Fevers of the United States; Simple Settings in Verse for Portraits and Pictures in Mr. Dickens's Gallery.

Bartlett, John. *Ms.*, 1820——. Formerly a Boston publisher, well known as the editor of Familiar Quotations, which reached a ninth edition in 1891; The Shakespeare Phrase-Book; A Complete Concordance to Shakespeare. *Lit. Mac.*

Bartlett, John Russell. *R. I.*, 1805–1886. At one time Secretary of State in Rhode Island. Records of the Colony of Rhode Island; Memoir of Rhode Island Officers in the War of the Rebellion; Primeval Man; Genealogy of the Russell Family; Dictionary of Americanisms; Progress of Ethnology. He edited the Letters of Roger Williams. *Lit.*

Bartlett, Joseph. *Ms.*, 1762–1827. A satirical poet whose New Vicar of Bray once attracted considerable attention.

Bartlett, Samuel Colcord. *N. H.*, 1817——. President of Dartmouth College 1877–92. Life and Death Eternal, a Refutation of the Doctrine of Annihilation; Future Punishment; From Egypt to Palestine: observations of a Journey; Sources of History in the Pentateuch. *See The Forum, vol. 2. Har.*

Bartlett, William Holms Chambers. *Pa.*, 1804–1893. A prominent scientist, who was from 1834–71 an instructor at West Point. Treatise on Optics; Analytical Mechanics; Spherical Astronomy.

Bartol, Cyrus Augustus. *Me.*, 1813——. A Unitarian clergyman of Boston, prominent as a leader of radical religious thought. Pictures of Europe; Christian Spirit and Life; Radical Problems; The Rising Faith; Principles and Portraits; Church and Congregation; Christian Body and Form. *A. U. A. Rob.*

Barton, Benjamin Smith. *Pa.*, 1766–1815. A once noted physician of Philadelphia. Observations on Some Parts of Natural History; New Views on the Origin of the Tribes of North America; Elements of Botany.

Barton, William Paul Crillon. *Pa.*, 1786–1856. Nephew of B. S. Barton, *supra*. He organized the United States Naval Bureau of Medicine and Surgery, and was known both as botanist and surgeon. Vegetable Materia Medica of the United States; Flora of North America; Medical Botany; Compendium Floræ Philadelphiæ.

Bartram, John. *Pa.*, 1699–1777. "The Father of American Botany." A shrewd, careful observer whom Linnæus termed "the greatest natural botanist in the world." Observations on the Inhabitants. Climate, etc., as made by Mr. John Bartram in his Travels from Pennsylvania to Onondaga, etc. A similar record of travels in eastern Florida appeared in 1766. *See Memorials of, by Darlington, 1849.*

Bartram, William. *Pa.*, 1739–1823. Son of J. Bartram, *supra*. A botanist and traveller of Pennsylvania. Travel Through North and South Carolina, Georgia, etc.; Observations on the Creek and Cherokee Indians.

Bascom, Henry Bidleman. *N. Y.*, 1796–1850. A bishop of the Methodist church. Sermons from the Pulpit; Mental and Moral Science; Methodism and Slavery. *See Life by Heuhle, 1854; Methodist Quarterly, vol. 45.*

Bascom, John. *N. Y.*, 1827——. A philosophical writer, from 1874–87, president of Wisconsin University, subsequently professor of political science at Williams College. Elements of Psychology; Æsthetics; Political Economy for Colleges; Science, Philosophy, and Religion; Natural Theology; The Science of Mind; The Words of Christ; Philosophy of English Literature; Comparative Psychology; Problems in Philosophy; Sociology, Social Theory; Ethics; The New Theology; Historical Interpretation of Philosophy; A Philosophy of Religion. *Cr. Put.*

Bassett, James. *Ont.*, 1834——. A Presbyterian missionary in Persia. Hymns in Persian; Among the Turcomans; Persia, the Land of the Imams: a Narrative of Travel; Grammatical Note on the Simnuni Dialects of the Persian. *Scr.*

Batchelor, George. *Ct.*, 1836——. A Unitarian clergyman. Social Equilibrium and Other Problems, Ethical and Religious. *El.*

Bates, Arlo. *Me.*, 1850——. Professor of English Literature in Massachusetts Institute of Technology, and novelist. Talks on Writing English; The Pagans; Patty's Perversities; A Wheel of Fire; In the Bundle of Time; A Lad's Love; The Philistines; A Book o' Nine Tales. His verse includes Berries of the Brier; Sonnets in Shadow; A Poet and his Self; Told in the Gate; The Torch-Bearers. *Ho. Hou. Rob. Scr.*

Bates, Charlotte Fiske. *See Rogé.*

Bates, Mrs. Clara [Doty]. *Mch.*, 1838–1895. A writer of juvenile tales. Classics of Babyland Versified; Child Lore; On the Way to Wonderland; Heart's Content. *Lo.*

Bates, Mrs. Harriet Leonora [Vose]. "Eleanor Putnam." *It.*, 1856–1886. Wife of A. Bates, *supra*. A Woodland Wooing; Old Salem; Prince Vance (with A. Bates).

Bates, Katherine Lee. *Ms.*, 1859——. A professor of literature at Wellesley College. The English Religious Drama; Hermit Island: a Story for Girls. *Lo. Mac.*

Bates, Mrs. Margaret Holmes [Ernsperger]. *O.*, 1844——. A fiction-writer of Indianapolis. Manitou; The Chamber Over the Gate.

Bates, Samuel Penniman. *Ms.*, 1827——. A Pennsylvania educator of note. Mental and Moral Culture; Liberal Education; History of Pennsylvania Volunteers; History of the Colleges of Pennsylvania.

Batterson, Hermon Griswold. *Ct.*, 1827——. An Episcopal clergyman of Philadelphia. The Missionary Tune Book; The Churchman's Hymn Book; Christmas Carols and Other Verses; The Pathway of Faith; A Sketch Book of the American Episcopate. *Lip.*

Baxley, Isaac Rieman. *Md.*, 1850——. A California versifier whose thought as a whole gains nothing by being expressed in verse. The Temple of Alanthur; The Prophet and Other Poems; Songs of the Spirit; The Bank of Mist.

Baxter, James Phinney. *Me.*, 1831——. An historical writer of Portland, Maine. George Cleves of Casco Bay, 1630–67; Sir Ferdinando Gorges and his Province of Maine; Idyls of the Year, a collection of verse.

Baxter, Lydia. *N. Y.*, 1809–1814. Gems by the Wayside, a collection of poems. The hymn, The Gates Ajar, is by her.

Baxter, Sylvester. *Ms.*, 1850——. A journalist of Boston, prominent in exploiting the Metropolitan Park system. The Cruise of a Land Yacht, a Boy's Book of Mexican Travel. *Lit.*

Baxter, William. *E.*, 1820——. A clergyman of Cincinnati, whose War Lyrics as originally published in Harper's Weekly were once widely popular. The Loyal West in the Times of the Rebellion; Pea Ridge and Prairie Grove, or Scenes and Incidents of the War in Arkansas. *Meth.*

Bayley, James Roosevelt. *N. Y.*, 1814–1877. A clergyman who entered the Roman Catholic Church from the Episcopal and became archbishop of Baltimore. History of the Catholic Church of New York; Memoirs of Bruté, First Bishop of Vincennes; Pastorals for the People.

Baylies, Francis. *Ms.*, 1783–1852. An eminent lawyer of Taunton, Massachusetts. Historical Memoir of the Colony of New Plymouth.

Baylor, Frances Courtenay. *See Barnum, Mrs.*

Beach, David Nelson. *N. J.*, 1848——. A prominent Congregational clergyman of Cambridge, and, since 1895, of Minneapolis. The Newer Religious Thinking; How we Rose; Plain Words on Our Lord's Work; The Intent of Jesus. *Lit. Rob.*

Beal, William James. *Mch.*, 1833——. A botanical professor in the Michigan Agricultural College from 1870. The New Botany; The Grasses of North America.

Beale, Mrs. Maria [Taylor]. *Va.*, 1849——. A novelist of Arden, North Carolina. Jack O'Doon.. *Ho.*

Beard, George Miller. *Ct.*, 1839–1883. A New York physician. American Nervous Diseases: Causes and Consequences; The Scientific Basis of Delusions; Clinical Researches in Electro-Surgery; Medical Uses of Electricity; Physiology of Mind-Reading; Stimulants and Narcotics; Psychology of the Salem Witchcraft and its Practical Application in Our Own Time. Some works of lesser note. *Har. Wo.*

Beardsley, Eben Edwards. *Ct.*, 1808–1891. An Episcopal clergyman of New Haven. History of the Episcopal Church in Connecticut; Lives of Samuel Johnson, the First President of King's College, New York, William Samuel Johnson, President of Columbia College, and Samuel Seabury, Bishop of Connecticut. *Hou.*

Beasley, Frederick. *N. C.*, 1777–1845. An Episcopal clergyman who was provost of the University of Pennsylvania. An Examination of the Oxford Divinity; Search of Truth in the Science of the Human Mind; Reply to Dr. Channing.

Beck, Theodric Romeyn. *N. Y.*, 1791–1855. A medical writer of Albany. Elements of Medical Jurisprudence (with J. B. Beck).

Becker, George Ferdinand. *N.Y.*, 1847——. A geologist in the United States service. Geology of the Comstock Lode; Atomic Weight Determinations; Geometrical Value of Volcanic Cones; A New Law of Thermo-Chemistry; Geology of the Quicksilver Deposits of the Pacific Slope. Several lesser works.

Beckett, Sylvester Breakmore. *Me.*, 1812–1882. An author and publisher of Portland, Maine. Hester, the Bride of the Islands, a Poem; Guide Book of the Atlantic and St. Lawrence.

Bedell [bē-dĕll′], **Gregory Thurston.** *N. Y.*, 1817–1892. The third Protestant Episcopal bishop of Ohio, and a valued writer of the evangelical school. The Divinity of Christ; The Profit of Godliness; Pastoral Theology; Principles of Pastorship; The Age of Indifference; Episcopacy; Fact and Law. A few minor works.

Bedell, Gregory Townsend. *N.Y.*, 1793–1834. Father of G. T. Bedell, *supra*. An Episcopal clergyman of Philadelphia, once famous as a preacher. Renunciation; Ezekiel's Vision; Sermons were his chief works. *See Life by Tyng, 1836.*

Beecher, Catherine Esther. *L. I.*, 1800–1878. Daughter of L. Beecher, *infra*. A New England educator of much celebrity at one time, who wrote with the ardour of sincerest conviction. Domestic Economy; Physiology and Calisthenics; Letters to the People; Religious Training of Children; Domestic Service, True Remedy for the Wrongs of Woman. *See Mrs. Hale's Woman's Record. Har.*

Beecher, Charles. *Ct.*, 1815——. Son of L. Beecher, *infra*. A Congregational clergyman. Patmos; Pen Pictures of the Bible; The Eden Tableau; Redeemer and Redeemed. He edited his father's Life and Correspondence. *Har. Le.*

Beecher, Edward. *L. I.*, 1803–1895. Son of L. Beecher, *infra*. A Congregational clergyman of Illinois, and later of Brooklyn, whose attainments must be considered as the most solid of those of any of the famous children of Lyman Beecher. In his Conflict of Ages (1853) was struck the earliest note of the liberal theology now dominant in the Congregational churches. The more important of his other works include Papal Conspiracy Exposed; Baptism; History of Opinions on the Scriptural Doctrine of Future Retribution. *Ap.*

Beecher, Mrs. Eunice White [Bullard]. *Ms.*, 1812–1897. Wife of H. W. Beecher, *infra*. From Dawn to Daylight: a Simple Story; Motherly Talks with Young Housekeepers; All around the House, or How to Make Homes Happy; Letters from Florida; Mr. Beecher as I Knew Him. *Ap.*

Beecher, Henry Ward. *Ct.*, 1813–1887. Son of Lyman Beecher, *infra*. A Congregational clergyman widely famous as the pastor of Plymouth Church, Brooklyn, 1847–87. He was an earnest, large-hearted man, though not a deep thinker, and his cheerful influence upon middle-class American thought was very extensive. His literary work can hardly be said to possess enduring excellence, and much of it is already forgotten, graphic and picturesque as it often is. Eyes and Ears; Life Thoughts; Star Papers; Yale Lectures on Preaching; Lectures to Young Men; Speeches on the American Rebellion; Doctrinal Beliefs and Unbeliefs; Life of Jesus the Christ. His only novel, Norwood, is a collection of successful character studies rather than a finished story. *See Parton's Famous Americans; Lives by Lyman Abbott, 1883; J. Howard, 1887; Barrows, 1893; Henry Ward Beecher: a Study, 1891; Mr. Beecher as I Knew Him, by his wife; North American Review, vol. 144. Ap. Fo. Har.*

Beecher, Lyman. *Ct.*, 1775–1863. A Congregational clergyman of wide fame. While in Boston he was a zealous opponent of Unitarianism, and as president of Lane Theological Seminary at Cincinnati was noted as an outspoken enemy of slavery. He was a bold thinker, much in advance of his contemporaries. Sermons on Temperance; Views in Theology; Scepticism; Political Atheism. *See Life and Correspondence, edited by Charles Beecher, 1864. Har.*

Beecher, Thomas Kinnicut. *Ct.*, 1824——. Son of L. Beecher, *supra*. A Congregational clergyman of Elmira, N. Y. Our Seven Churches.

Beecher, Willis Judson. *O.*, 1838——. A professor of Hebrew in the Auburn Theological Seminary. Farmer Tompkins and his Bible; Drill Lessons in Hebrew; Testimony of the Historical Books.

Beers, Mrs. Ethelinda [Eliot]. "Ethel Lynn." *N. J.*, 1827–1879. General Frankie, a juvenile tale; All Quiet Along the Potomac and Other Poems. *Co.*

Beers, Henry Augustin. *N. Y.*, 1847——. A professor of English literature at Yale University. The Ways of Yale; A Suburban Pastoral and Other Stories; From Chaucer to Tennyson; Life of N. P. Willis, *infra;* Outline Sketch of English Literature; Initial Studies in American Letters. Verse: Odds and Ends; The Thankless Muse. *Fl. Ho. Hou. Meth.*

Belcher, Joseph. *E.*, 1794–1859. A Baptist clergyman of Philadelphia, who came thither from England in 1844. His complete works number over 200 volumes. Among them are The Baptist Pulpit of the United States; The Clergy of America; History of Religious Denominations in the United States; Hymns and their Authors.

Belknap [bĕl'năp], **Jeremy.** *Ms.*, 1744–1798. A Congregational clergyman of Boston, whose History of New Hampshire ranks as the best among local State histories, and is accurate as it is entertaining. His other works include American Biographies; The Foresters: an American Tale. *See Atlantic Monthly, vol. 67.*

Bell, Charles Henry. *N. H.*, 1823–1893. A New Hampshire lawyer and Congressman, governor of his State, 1881–83. The Bench and Bar of New Hampshire. *Hou.*

Bell, John. *I.*, 1796–1872. A physician and medical lecturer, among whose writings are Health and Beauty; Regimen and Longevity.

Bell, Lilian. *Ky.*, 1867——. A Chicago novelist. The Love Affairs of An Old Maid; A Little Sister to the Wilderness. *Har. St.*

Bell, Zura. *See Williamson, Julia.*

Bellamy, Charles Joseph. *Ms.*, 1852——. A journalist of Springfield, Massachusetts. The Breton Mills: a Novel; Everybody's Lawyer; The Way Out: Suggestions for Social Reform. *Put.*

Bellamy, Edward. *Ms.*, 1850——. Brother of C. J. Bellamy, *supra.* A socialist reformer whose Utopian theories embodied in the tale Looking Backward, 2000–1887, have been very widely read, and have resulted in the formation of several societies and communities that endeavour to put some of them in practice. His other works include Six to One: a Nantucket Idyl; Dr. Heidenhoff's Process, a novel; Miss Ludington's Sister: a Romance of Immortality. *See North American Review, vol. 160; The Forum, vol. 8; New Englander, vol. 52. Ap. Hou.*

Bellamy, Mrs. Elizabeth Whitfield [Croom]. "Kamba Thorpe." *Fl.*, 1838——. A novelist of Mobile. Four Oaks; Little Joanna; Penny Lancaster Farmer; Old Man Gilbert; The Luck of the Pendennings. *Ap.*

Bellamy, Joseph. *Ct.*, 1719–1790. A Congregational minister of the Edwards school, settled at Bethlehem, Connecticut, for a half century. He founded a divinity school in his parish, and trained many men there who were afterwards famous among New England ministers. True Religion Delineated; The Law our Schoolmaster; The Half-Way Covenant; The Nature and Glory of the Gospel, are a few of his publications. *See Bibliotheca Sacra, vol. 43; Sprague's Annals of the American Pulpit.*

Bellamy, William. *Ms.*, 1840——. A Boston writer who has published, in verse, A Century of Charades; A Second Century of Charades. *Hou.*

Bellows, Henry Whitney. *N. H.*, 1814–1882. A Unitarian clergyman of prominence in New York city, well known at one time as the president of the United States Sanitary Commission. Restatements of Christian Doctrine; Sermons; Relation of Public Amusements to Public Morality; The Old World in its New Face. *See Unitarian Review, vol. 67. A. U. A. Har.*

Belrose, Louis. *Pa.*, 1845–189–. A writer whose only published work of note is Thorns and Flowers, a volume of verse.

Bemis, Edward Webster. *Ms.*, 1860——. A professor of economics in the University of Chicago. History of Co-operation in the United States; Municipal Ownership of Gas in the United States.

Bender, Prosper. *Q.*, 1844——. A Canadian physician, a littérateur, who since 1883 has practiced his profession in Boston. Old and New Canada; Literary Sheaves, or La Littérature au Canada-Français.

Benedict, David. *Ct.*, 1779–1874. A Baptist clergyman of Pawtucket. History of the Baptists; History of All Religions; Fifty Years Among the Baptists; Compendium of Ecclesiastical History; History of the Donatists, comprise his principal works.

Benedict, Erastus Cornelius. *Ct.*, 1800–1880. A jurist of New York city. The American Admiralty: its Jurisdiction and Practice.

Benedict, Frank Lee. *N.Y.*, 1834——. A novelist of New York city. Miss Van Kortland; My Daughter Elinor; The Price She Paid; John Worthington's Name; Miss Dorothy's Charge; St. Simon's Niece; 'Twixt Hammer and Anvil; Her Friend Laurence; A Late Remorse; Madame; The Shadow-Worshipper and Other Poems. *Har. Lip.*

Benezet, Anthony. *F.*, 1713–1784. A Quaker philanthropist of Philadelphia, whose tracts on slavery first aroused the attention of Clarkson and Wilberforce to the subject. *See Memoir by R. Vaux, 1817.*

Benjamin, Judah Philip. *W. I.*, 1811–1884. A prominent New Orleans lawyer who became attorney-general of the Confederacy during the Civil War. At its close he went to England, and speedily became eminent in his profession there. His Treatise on the Law of Sale of Personal Property is the standard work on the subject. *See The Athenæum, vol. 88.*

Benjamin, Park. *B. G.*, 1809–1864. A poet and journalist of New York city, whose verse, mainly lyrical in character, has not been collected. The Old Sexton is the best remembered example.

Benjamin, Park, Jr. *N. Y.*, 1849——. Son of P. Benjamin, *supra*. A New York lawyer whose specialty is patent law. Shakings: Etchings for the Naval Academy; Wrinkles and Receipts: Suggestions for the Mechanic, Engineer, etc.; The Age of Electricity; The Intellectual Rise in Electricity: a History. *Ap. Scr. Wil.*

Benjamin, Samuel Green Wheeler. *Gr.*, 1837——. A contributor to the field of general literature; at one period minister to Persia. Art in America; Contemporary Art in Europe; The Atlantic Islands; Troy: its Legend, Literature, and Topography; A Group of Etchers; Persia and the Persians; The Story of Persia; The Cruise of the Alice May in the Gulf of St. Lawrence; Sea Spray, or Facts and Fancies of a Yachtsman. *Ap. Har. Hou. Lo. Scr.*

Bennett, Charles Wesley. *N. Y.*, 1828–1891. A Methodist clergyman prominent in educational matters. National Education in Italy, France, Germany, England, and Wales, Popularly Considered; Christian Art and Archæology of the First Six Centuries. *Meth.*

Bennett, De Robique Mortimer. *N. Y.*, 1818–1882. A noted freethinker who was several times arrested and imprisoned on account of his extreme views. The World's Reformers; Champions of the Church; From Behind the Bars; An Infidel Abroad; A Truth Seeker Around the World.

Bennett, Edmund Hatch. *Vt.*, 1824–1898. A New England jurist, dean of the Boston University Law School. English Law and Equity Reports; Fire Insurance Cases; Leading Cases in Criminal Law. He has also edited many legal works of importance. *Hou.*

Bennett, Emerson. *Ms.*, 1822——. A Philadelphia writer of sensational romances quite worthless as literature, but which have been very popular. Prairie Flower, Leni Leoti, are perhaps the most noted of his fifty or more novels.

Bensel, James Berry. *N. Y.*, 1856–1886. A verse-writer whose lines are often musical and pathetic, though sometimes lacking in finish. In the King's Garden, and Other Poems; King Cophetua's Wife, a novel. *Lo.*

Benson, Carl. *See Bristed.*

Benson, Egbert. *N. Y.*, 1746–1833. A jurist and politician. Vindication of the Captors of Major André; Memoir on Dutch Names of Places.

Benson, Eugene. *N. Y.*, 1840——. An American artist long resident in Italy. Gaspara Stampa, a biography; Art and Nature in Italy. *Rob.*

Benton, Joel. *N. Y.*, 1832——. A verse-writer and critic. Under the Apple Boughs, a collection of verse; Emerson as a Poet. *Ho.*

Benton, Thomas Hart. *N. C.*, 1782–1858. An eminent statesman who represented Missouri in the United States Senate for 30 years. His political writing is notable for its simple, direct style and absence of invective. Speeches; Thirty Years' View; History of the Workings of Congress, 1820–50; Abridgment of the Debates of Congress, 1789–1856. *See Life by T. Roosevelt. Ap.*

Berard, Augusta Blanche. *N. Y.*, 1824——. An educational writer of West Point. School History of the United States; School History of England; Manual of Spanish Art and Literature; Reminiscences of West Point in the Olden Time.

Berg, Joseph Frederick. *W. I.*, 1812–1871. A Dutch Reformed clergyman of Philadelphia and a once noted controversialist. Lectures on Romanism; Rome's Policy towards the Bible are among his writings.

Berg, Louis De Coppet. 1856——. An architect and civil engineer of New York city, who has published a valuable work on Safe Building.

Bergh, Henry. *N. Y.*, 1823–1888. A New York philanthropist who founded the American Society for the Prevention of Cruelty to Animals. The Streets of New York, a volume of sketches; Love's Alternative, a drama; Married Off, a poem.

Bernheim, Gotthardt Dellman. 1827——. A Lutheran clergyman at Phillipsburg, New Jersey, from 1883. The Success of God's Work; Localities of the Reformation; History of the German Settlements in North and South Carolina.

Berrian, William. 1787–1862. An Episcopal clergyman who was rector of Trinity Church, New York city, 1830–62. Travels in France and Italy; Devotions for the Sick Room; On Communion; Enter thy Closet; The Sailors' Manual; Recollections of Departed Friends; Family and Private Prayers; Historical Sketch of Trinity Church.

Bessey, Charles Edwin. *O.*, 1845——. A botanical professor in the University of Nebraska. Geography of Iowa; Botany for High Schools and Colleges; The Essentials of Botany. *Ho.*

Bethune [beh-thoon'], **George Washington.** *N. Y.*, 1805–1862. A Dutch Reformed clergyman of Brooklyn of considerable note as a preacher. Orations and Discourses; Fruits of the Spirit; History of a Penitent; Lays of Love and Faith, a volume of verse, are some of his works. He was an ardent fisherman, and edited Walton's Complete Angler. *See Memoir by Van Nest.*

Betts, Craven Langstroth. *N. B.*, 1853——. Songs from Béranger; The Perfume Holder: A Persian Love Poem; co-author with A. W. H. Eaton (*infra*) of Tales of a Garrison Town. *Sto.*

Beverley, Robert. *Va.*, 1675–1716. A writer whose one work, a History of the Present State of Virginia, 1705, is full of life and vigour. In it occurs the phrase "the almighty power of gold," which anticipates Irving's "almighty dollar." *See Tyler's American Literature; Jameson's Historical Writing in America, pp. 62–67.*

Bianciardi, Mrs. Elizabeth Dickinson [Rice]. *Ms.*, *c.* 1833–1885. At Home in Italy. *Hou.*

Bickmore, Albert Smith. *Me.*, 1839——. An ethnologist, since 1885 the curator of the American Museum of Natural History in New York city. Travels in the East Indian Archipelago; The Ainos or Hairy Men of Jesso, Saghalien, etc.; Sketch of a Journey from Canton to Hankow.

Biddle, Anthony Joseph Drexel. *Pa.*, 1874——. A journalist and publisher of Philadelphia. A Dual Role, and Other Stories; An Allegory and Three Essays; The Madeira Islands; The Froggy Fairy Book.

Biddle, Charles John. *Pa.*, 1819–1873. Son of N. Biddle, *infra*. An officer in the United States Army, and afterwards a journalist in Philadelphia, who is best known by his careful monograph, The Case of Major André.

Biddle, Nicholas. *Pa.*, 1786–1844. A financier of Philadelphia famous in political history as the president of the United States Bank. A Commercial Digest; History of the Expedition under Lewis and Clark to the Missouri River. *See Memoir, by Conrad.*

Biddle, Richard. *Pa.*, 1796–1847. Brother of N. Biddle, *supra*. A lawyer of Philadelphia. Memoir of Sebastian Cabot, with a Review of the History of Maritime Discovery.

Bigelow, Mrs. Edith Evelyn [Jaffray]. *N.Y.*, 1861——. Wife of P. Bigelow, *infra*. Diplomatic Disenchantments, a novel. *Har.*

Bigelow, Erastus Brigham. *Ms.*, 1814–1879. A noted New England inventor of carpet looms. The Tariff Question considered in regard to the Policy of England and the Interest of the United States; The Tariff Policy of England and United States Contrasted.

Bigelow, Jacob. *Ms.*, 1787–1879. A famous physician of Boston who established Mount Auburn cemetery. History of Mount Auburn; A Brief Exposition of Rational Medicine; Modern Inquiries, classical, professional, and miscellaneous; Remarks on Classical and Utilitarian Studies; American Medical Botany; Nature in Disease. *See Memoir, by Ellis.*

Bigelow, John. *N. Y.*, 1817——. A prominent New York journalist, at one time United States Minister to France. Life of Benjamin Franklin; Life of William Cullen Bryant; Life of Samuel Tilden; Jamaica in 1850; Les États Unis d'Amériqne en 1863; Some Recollections of Antoine Pierre Berryer; France and Hereditary Monarchy; Wit and Wisdom of the Haytiens; Molinos the Quietist; France and the Confederate Navy: an International Episode; The Mystery of Sleep. He has edited complete editions of the works of Franklin and Tilden. *Har. Hou. Lip. Scr.*

Bigelow, John, Jr. *N. Y.*, 1854——. Son of John Bigelow, *supra*. A United States cavalry officer. The Principles of Strategy, illustrated chiefly from American Campaigns. *Lip.*

Bigelow, Melville Madison. *Mch.*, 1846——. A lawyer and law lecturer of Boston. The Law of Bills; English Procedure in the Norman Period; The Law of Fraud; Elements of Equity; Elements of the Law of Torts; Placita Anglo-Normannica: Law Cases from William I. to Richard I.; Law of Wills, Notes, and Cheques; The Law of Fraud on its Civil Side; The Law of Estoppel and its Application to Practice; Leading Cases in the Law of Torts, comprise his principal works. He has also edited the 8th edition of Story's Conflict of Laws, and published a volume of original verse, Rhymes of a Barrister. *Hou. Lit.*

Bigelow, Poultney. *N. Y.*, 1855——. Son of John Bigelow, *supra*. The German Emperor and his Eastern Neighbors; The Borderland of Czar and Kaiser; History of the German Struggle for Liberty; White Man's Africa. *Har.*

Biglow, William. *Ms.*, 1773–1844. An educator of Boston. History of Natick; History of Sherburne; The Youth's Library; Introduction to the Making of Latin.

Billings, John Shaw. *Ind.*, 1838——. Formerly surgeon U. S. A. Upon the consolidation of the New York city libraries, he was made chief librarian. His chief work is a voluminous Index Catalogue of the Library of the Surgeon-General's office. Others are Hygienics of the United States Army Barracks; Mortality and Vital Statistics of the United States Army.

Billings, Josh. *See Shaw, Henry.*

Binney, Amos. *Ms.*, 1803–1847. A once prominent physician and naturalist of Boston. Terrestrial Air-Breathing Mollusks of the United States.

Binney, Horace. *Pa.*, 1780–1875. A noted jurist of Philadelphia. Reports of Cases in the Supreme Court of Pennsylvania, 1799–1814; Leaders of the Old Bar of Philadelphia; Inquiry into the Formation of Washington's Farewell Address.

Binney, William Greene. *Ms.*, 1833——. Son of A. Binney, *supra.* A well-known conchologist of Burlington, New Jersey. Besides completing his father's work on mollusks he has written Bibliography of North American Conchology; Land and Fresh Water Shells of North America; Catalogues of the Terrestrial Air-Breathing Mollusks of North America.

Bird, Frederick Mayer. *Pa.*, 1838——. Son of R. M. Bird, *infra.* An Episcopal clergyman widely known as an hymnologist. He has edited The Lutheran Ministerium Hymns (with Smucker); Songs of the Spirit (with Bishop Odenheimer); published Charles Wesley seen in his Finer and Less Familiar Pieces; and contributed extensively to the critical literature of his subject.

Bird, Robert Montgomery. *Del.*, 1803–1854. A romantic novelist of Philadelphia whose Nick of the Woods was his most popular work. His two Mexican stories, Calavar: a Knight of the Conquest; The Infidel, or the Fall of Mexico, were commended by the historian Prescott. His other works include Peter Pilgrim, a collection of Tales and Sketches, notable as containing almost the earliest description of the Mammoth Cave; Sheppard Lee; The Hawks of Hawk Hollow; Adventures of Robin Day; and three successful dramas, The Broker of Bogota; Oraoosa; The Gladiator.

Birney, James Gillespie. *Ky.*, 1792–1857. A statesman famous for his opposition to slavery. Ten Letters on Slavery and Colonization; Addresses and Speeches; American Churches the Bulwarks of American Slavery, are among his writings. *See Nation, vol. 50; Birney and his Times, by W. Birney.*

Bishop, Joel Prentiss. *N. Y.*, 1814——. An eminent jurist of Boston. Commentaries on Criminal Law; Marriage and Divorce; The Law of Married Women; Thoughts for the Times; First Book of The Law; Directions and Forms; Criminal Procedure; Statutory Crimes; Prosecution and Defence; The Written Laws, are among the more important works of his. *Lit.*

Bishop, Nathaniel Holmes. *Ms.*, 1837——. A writer of entertaining travels. A Thousand Miles' Walk across South America; The Voyage of the Paper Canoe; Four Months in a Sneak Box. *Le.*

Bishop, Robert Hamilton. *S.*, 1777–1855. A Presbyterian clergyman of Ohio, president of Miami University, 1824–41. Sermons; Elements of Logic; Philosophy of the Bible; Science of Government; Western Peacemaker; Memoirs of David Rice.

Bishop, William Henry. *Ct.*, 1847——. A novelist and professor in Yale University. Fish and Men in the Maine Islands; A Househunter in Europe; Writing to Rosina: a novelette; A Pound of Cure: a Story of Monte Carlo; Detmold; The House of a Merchant Prince; The Golden Justice; Choy Susan and Other Stories; The Brown Stone Boy and Other Queer People; Old Mexico and her Lost Provinces, a volume of travel; The Garden of Eden. *Cas. Cent. Har. Ho. Hou. Ke. Scr.*

Bisland, Elizabeth. *See Wetmore, Mrs.*

Bissell, Edwin Cone. *N. Y.*, 1832——. A Congregational clergyman of Chicago. Analysis of the Codes; The Historic Origin of the Bible; The Pentateuch: its Origin and Structure; Biblical Antiquities; Practical Introductory Hebrew Grammar; Genesis Printed in Colours, showing original sources of compilation. *Fu. Ran. Scr.*

Bixby, James Thompson. *N. Y.*, 1843——. A Unitarian clergyman of Yonkers, New York. Similarities of Physical and Religious Knowledge, reprinted with the title Religion and Science as Allies; The Crisis in Morals. *Ap. Rob.*

Bixby, John Munson. "E. Grayson." *Ct.*, 1800–1876. A lawyer of New York city, whose two novels were issued under a pseudonym. Standish the Puritan; Overing, or the Heir of Wycherly.

Black, Alexander. *N. Y.*, 1859——. A Brooklyn journalist, literary editor of the Brooklyn Times. The Story of Ohio; Photography Indoors and Out; Miss Jerry, a Picture Play. *Hou. Lo. Scr.*

Black, James. *Pa.*, 1823–1894. A noted Pennsylvania advocate of temperance who was the presidential nominee of the prohibitionists in 1872. Is Prohibition a Necessity; History of the Prohibition Party; The Prohibition Party.

Black, James Rush. *S.*, 1827——. An Ohio physician, since 1876 a professor of hygiene in the medical college of Columbus. Ten Laws of Health, a valuable work on hygiene; Guide to Protection against Epidemic Disease.

Black, Warren Columbus. *Mi.*, 1843——. A Methodist clergyman of Mississippi. Temperance and Teetotalism; Christian Womanhood.

Black, William Henry. *Ind.*, 1854——. A Presbyterian clergyman of St. Louis. God our Father; Womanhood; Sermons for the Sunday School.

Blackburn, William Maxwell. *Ind.*, 1828——. A Presbyterian clergyman, since 1886 president of Pierre University, South Dakota. Among his many works, chiefly on religion and biography, are History of the Christian Church; Geneva's Shield; Exiles of Madeira; Judas the Maccabee; The Rebel Prince; College Days of Calvin; Young Calvin in Paris; St. Patrick and the Early Irish Church; Admiral Coligny and the Rise of the Huguenots; The Theban Legion; and the Uncle Alick series of juvenile tales. *Meth.*

Blackwell, Mrs. Antoinette Louisa [Brown]. *N. Y.*, 1825——. A Unitarian minister prominent in the woman suffrage movement. Studies in General Science; The Market Woman; The Island Neighbours: a novel of American life; The Sexes Throughout Nature; The Physical Basis of Immortality; The Philosophy of Individuality. *Har.*

Blackwell, Elizabeth. *E.*, 1821——. A physician of New York city who, with her sister Emily, organized the woman's medical college of the New York Infirmary. Laws of Life, or the Physical Education of Girls; Counsel to Parents in the Moral Education of their Children; Pioneer Work in opening the Medical Profession to Women. *Lgs.*

Blaikie, William. *N. Y.*, 1843——. A lawyer and athlete of New York city. How to Get Strong; Sound Bodies for our Boys and Girls. *Har.*

Blaine, James Gillespie. *Pa.*, 1830–1893. A very prominent Republican leader who was an unsuccessful candidate for the presidency in 1884. Twenty Years of Congress, an able and reasonably impartial work; Eulogy on James Abram Garfield. *See Appleton's American Biography, vol. 1, and Annual Cyclopedia, 1893; Lives, by Cressey, 1884; Balestier, 1884; Ramsdell; Dodge, 1895; Mr. Blaine and his Foreign Policy, 1884; North American Review, vol. 147.*

Blair, Andrew Alexander. *Ky.*, 1846——. A chemist of Philadelphia. The Chemical Analysis of Iron; Methods in Analysis of Iron, Steel, Copper, and Alloys of Copper, Zinc, and Tin. *Lip.*

Blair, Mrs. Eliza [Nelson]. *N. H.*, 185 ——. A writer of Manchester, New Hampshire. Her novel, 'Lisbeth Wilson, gives an excellent picture of New Hampshire rural life a half century ago. *Le.*

Blair, James. *S.*, 1656–1743. An Episcopal clergyman of Virginia who founded William and Mary College, and was its president for 50 years. The State of His Majesty's Colony in Virginia; Our Saviour's Divine Sermon on the Mount, a series of 117 sermons written in a simple, unornamental style; moderate in tone and very much to the point. *See Tyler's American Literature.*

Blake, Mrs. Euphemia [Vale]. *E.*, 1824——. Daughter of G. Vale, *infra.* Teeth, Ether, and Chloroform; History of Newburyport; Arctic Experiences, a history of the Polaris Expedition.

Blake, James Vila. *N. Y.*, 1842——. A Unitarian clergyman of Chicago. Poems; Essays; A Grateful Spirit; Anchor of the Soul; St. Solifer; Legends from Story Land. *Ke.*

Blake, John Lauris. *N. H.*, 1788–1857. An Episcopal clergyman of Boston long prominent as an educator. Text Book of Geography and Chronology; Family Encyclopædia of Agriculture and Domestic Economy; Farmer's Every-Day Book; Modern Farmer; Letters on Confirmation; General Biographical Dictionary; Book of Nature Laid Open; Wonders of the Earth; Wonders of Art.

Blake, Mrs. Lillie [Devereux] [Umstead]. *N. C.*, 1835——. A prominent advocate of woman suffrage. Fettered for Life; Southwold; Rockford; Woman's Place To-Day; The Hypocrite, or Sketches of American Society.

Blake, Mrs. Mary Elizabeth [McGrath]. *I.*, 1840——. A Boston writer of prose and verse. Poems; Youth in Twelve Centuries; Verses by the Way. Her prose includes On the Wing, sketches of American travel; A Summer Holiday: travel experiences in Europe; Mexico: Picturesque, Political, Progressive (with Mrs. Sullivan, *infra*). *Hou. Le.*

Blake, William Phipps. *N. Y.*, 1826——. A mineralogist of prominence. Silver Ores and Silver Mines; California Minerals; Production of the Precious Metals; Iron and Steel; Ceramic Art and Glass; History of Hamden, Ct.; Life of Captain Jonathan Mix.

Blauvelt, Augustus. *N. Y.*, 1832——. A Dutch Reformed clergyman of New Jersey, deposed from the ministry on account of his liberal doctrinal views embodied in papers in the Century Magazine. The Kingdom of Satan; The Present Religious Crisis.

Blavatsky, Helene Petrovna [Hahn-Hahn]. *R.*, 1831–1891. A writer of Russian birth but naturalized in the United States, who visited India, and, embracing Buddhism, founded the Theosophical Society of New York. Isis Unveiled; The Secret Doctrine; Voices of Silence; Key to Theosophy. *See Memoirs of, by Sinnett, 1886; Review of Reviews, vol. 3.*

Bledsoe, Albert Taylor. *Ky.*, 1808–1877. A Southern clergyman who left the Episcopal for the Methodist church, and wrote extensively on metaphysics and mathematics. Liberty and Slavery; Examination of Edwards on the Will; Philosophy of Mathematics; Is Davis a Traitor? or was Secession a Constitutional Right previous to the War of 1861?; Theodicy. *Lip. Meth.*

Bliss, Daniel. *Vt.*,, 1826——. A Congregational missionary, president of the Protestant college at Beyrout since 1864. Mental Philosophy; Natural Philosophy (in Arabic).

Bliss, Porter Cornelius. *N. Y.*, 1838–1885. A journalist and diplomat of some repute as a philologist. The Ethnography of Gran Chaco, a district of Argentina; Historia Secreta de la mision, del ciudadano noto Americano, Charles A. Washburn, cerca de gobierno de la república del Paraguay; The Conquest of Turkey 1877–78 (with L. Blodgett, *infra*).

Bliss, William Dwight Porter. *Iy.*, 1856——. An Episcopal clergyman of Boston, prominent as a leader among Christian Socialists. A Handbook of Socialism; The Social Faith of the Catholic Church; What is Christian Socialism? He has edited The Encyclopædia of Socialism. *Fu. Scr.*

Bliss, William Root. *Ct.*, 1825——. A business man of New York city. Side Glimpses from the Colonial Meeting-House; The Old Colony Town and other Sketches; Colonial Times on Buzzard's Bay; Quaint Nantucket; Paradise in the Pacific. *Hou.*

Blodget, Lorin. *N. Y.*, 1823——. An eminent statistician of Philadelphia who has published over 150 volumes, mainly reports upon finance, revenue, and industrial progress. The Climatology of the United States; Commercial and Financial Resources of the United States. *Lip.*

Bloede, Gertrude. "Stuart Sterne." *Sxy.*, 1845——. A poet and novelist of Brooklyn who has usually written under a pseudonym. Angelo; Giorgio and Other Poems; Beyond the Shadow; Pièro da Castiglione, a tale in verse of the time of Savonarola; The Story of Two Lives: a novel. *Hou.*

Bloomfield-Moore, Mrs. Clara Sophia [Jessup]. *Pa.*, 1824——. A Philadelphia writer who has lived much abroad, and chiefly in England. Miscellaneous Poems; On Dangerous Ground, a romance of American Society; Sensible Etiquette; Gondaline's Lesson and Other Poems; Slander and Gossip; The Warden's Tale and Other Poems. *Co.*

Blot, Pierre. *F.*, 1818–1874. A once noted cooking instructor of New York city. What to Eat and How to Cook It; Lectures on Cookery; Handbook of Practical Cookery. *Ap.*

Blunt, Edmond March. *N. H.*, 1770–1802. A bookseller of Newburyport whose chief work, The American Coast Pilot (1796), is still in use.

Blunt, George William. *Ms.*, 1802–1878. Son of E. M. Blunt, *supra*. Hydrographer. Atlantic Memoir; Sheet Anchor; Harbour Laws of New York; Plan to Avoid the Centre of Violent Gales.

Blunt, Joseph. *Ms.*, 1792–1860. Son of E. M. Blunt, *supra*. A lawyer who was one of the founders of the Republican party. Historical Sketch of the Formation of the American Confederacy; Speeches, Reviews, and Reports; Merchants' and Shipmasters' Assistant.

Boardman, George Dana. *Bh.*, 1828——. A prominent Baptist clergyman of Philadelphia. Coronation of Love; Studies in the Creative Week; Epiphanies of the Risen Lord; Studies in the Mountain Instruction; University Lectures on the Ten Commandments; The Divine Man. *Ap. Bap.*

Boardman, Henry Augustus. *N. Y.*, 1808–1880. A once noted Presbyterian divine of Philadelphia. The Bible in the Family; The Bible in the Counting-House; The Christian Ministry not a Priesthood; Earthly Suffering and Heavenly Glory; A Handful of Corn, are among his writings. *Lip. Ran.*

Bogart, William Henry. *N. Y.*, 1810–1888. A writer of New York state. Life of Daniel Boone; Who Goes There? or Men and Events. *Le.*

Bok, Edward William. *H.*, 1863——. Editor of the Ladies' Home Journal. The Young Man in Business; Successward, a Young Man's Book for Young Men. *Rev.*

Boker, George Henry. *Pa.*, 1823–1890. A poet and diplomat of Philadelphia, United States Minister to Turkey and Russia successively. His verse is of uneven excellence, but at its best is notably good, as, for example, the familiar Dirge for a Soldier. Of his four tragedies, Calaynos; Anne Boleyn; Lenor de Guzman; Francesca da Rimini, the first and last are the finest, the last having been revived with success in very recent years. His volumes of verse include The Lesson of Life; Poems of War; The Book of the Dead; Königsmark; Street Lyrics; Our Heroic Themes. Plays of lesser rank are The Widow's Marriage; The Betrothal. *See Atlantic Monthly, vol. 65; Lippincott's Magazine, vol. 45. Lip.*

Bollan, William. *E.*, 17—–1776. An English lawyer who settled in Boston in 1740, and was subsequently colonial agent in London for Massachusetts. He was active in its behalf and wrote many political tracts for that end, among which The Mutual Interests of Great Britain and the American Colonies Considered, is a favourable example.

Boller, Alfred Pancoast. *Pa.*, 1840——. An engineer of note whose specialty is bridge construction. Practical Treatise on the Construction of Iron Highway Bridges; Report on Thames River Bridge. *Wil.*

Bolles, Albert Sidney. *Ct.*, 1845——. A political economist of prominence, professor in the University of Pennsylvania. Chapters in Political Economy; The Conflict between Labour and Capital; Industrial History of the United States; Financial History of the United States, 1774–1860; Elements of Commercial Law. *Ap.*

Bolles, Frank. *Ms.*, 1856–1894. A writer of nature studies of the school of Jefferies and Thoreau, though with important differences from either. From Blomidon to Smoky; At the North of Bearcamp Water; Land of the Lingering Snow; Chocorua's Tenants, a volume of verse. *Hou.*

Bolster, William Wheeler. *Me.*, 1823——. A lawyer of Auburn, Maine. Digest of the Law of Tax Titles; The Authority and Duty of Town Officers.

Bolton, Charles Knowles. *O.*, 1867——. Son of S. K. Bolton, *infra*; librarian of Brookline, Massachusetts. The Boltons of Old and New England; Gossiping Guide to Harvard; Saskia the Wife of Rembrandt; Notes on Special Collections in American Libraries (with W. C. Lane). Verse: Poems: from Heart and Nature; The Wooing of Martha Pitkin; the Love Story of Ursula Wolcott. *Cop. Lam.*

Bolton, Henry Carrington. *N. Y.*, 1843——. Scientist and professor of chemistry at Trinity College. Application of Organic Acids to the Examination of Minerals; Literature of Uranium; Literature of Manganese; Student's Guide in Quantitative Analysis; Counting-out Rhymes of Children; their Antiquity, Origin, and Wide Distribution. *Wil.*

Bolton, Mrs. Sarah [Knowles]. *Ct.*, 1841——. A miscellaneous writer of Cleveland whose successive collections of biographical sketches have been extremely popular. Famous Givers and Their Gifts; How Success is Won; Poor Boys who Became Famous; Girls who Became Famous; Famous American Authors; Famous American Statesmen; Successful Women; Social Studies in England; Famous Types of Womanhood; Famous Voyages and Explorers; Famous Leaders among Men; The Inevitable, a collection of pleasing, unpretentious verse. *Cr. Lo.*

Bolton, Mrs. Sarah Tittle [Barritt]. *Ky.*, 1820–1893. A writer whose name is kept in mind by her oft quoted poem, Paddle Your Own Canoe. The Songs of a Life Time; Life and Poems of, 1880.

Bomberger, John Henry Augustus. *Pa.*, 1817–1890. A German Reformed theologian, president of Ursinus College, 1870–90. Infant Salvation and Baptism; Revised Liturgy; Reformed not Ritualistic.

Bond, George Phillips. *Ms.*, 1825–1865. An astronomer of note, professor in Harvard University. On the Construction of the Rings of Saturn; The Method of Least Squares; Mathematical Memoirs upon Mechanical Quadrations.

Boner, John Henry. *N. C.*, 1845——. A poet and littérateur of New York city. Whispering Pines: poems.

Bonner, Sherwood. *See MacDowell.*

Bonney, Charles Carroll. *N. Y.*, 1831——. A lawyer of Chicago. Rules of Law for Carriage and Delivery of Persons and Property by Railway; Summary of the Law of Marine, Fire, and Life Insurance; Our Remedy in the Laws.

Booth, Henry Matthias. *N. Y.*, 1843——. A Presbyterian clergyman of New Jersey. The Heavenly Vision and other Sermons; Sunrise, Noonday, and Sunset of the Day of Grace; First Communion. *Ran.*

Booth, Mary Louise. *L. I.*, 1831–1889. Editor of Harper's Bazar from its establishment in 1867 to 1889. She made over 30 valuable translations from the French. A History of the City of New York was her only piece of original writing.

Bostwick, Mrs. Helen Louise [Barron]. *N.*, *H.*, 1826——. A verse-writer of Bucyrus, Ohio. Buds, Blossoms and Berries.

Botta, Mrs. Anne Charlotte [Lynch]. *Vt.*, 1820–1891. Wife of V. Botta, *infra.* A well-known New York writer whose weekly receptions were for many years the nearest approach in New York city to a *salon.* Handbook of Universal Literature; Leaves from the Diary of a Recluse; Poems. *Hou.*

Botta, Vincenzo. *Iy.*, 1818–1894. An Italian educator who came to the United States in 1853, and was for a long period a professor of Italian Literature in the University of New York. The System of Education in Piedmont: Life of Cavour; Historical Account of Modern Philosophy in Italy; Dante as Philosopher, Patriot, and Poet. *Scr.*

Botts, John Minor. *Va.*, 1802–1869. A Virginia lawyer eminent for his devotion to the Union during the Civil War. Letters on the Nebraska Question; The Great Rebellion: its Secret History, Rise, Progress, and Disastrous Failure. *Har.*

Boudinot [boo'de-not], **Elias.** *Pa.*, 1740–1821. A philanthropist of Burlington, New Jersey, and the first president of the American Bible Society. The Second Advent of the Messiah; The Age of Revelation, a reply to Paine; The Star in the West, an attempt to identify the American Indians with the Ten Lost Tribes of Israel. *See Life, edited by J. J. Boudinot, 1896.*

Boughton, Willis. *N. Y.*, 1854——. An educator, professor of English literature in Ohio University from 1892. A History of Ancient Peoples; Mythology in Art. *Put.*

Bourke, John Gregory. *Pa.*, 1846–1896. A United States army officer. The Snake Dance of the Moquis of Arizona, a valuable contribution to ethnology; An Apache Campaign in the Sierra Madre; On the Border with Crook. *Scr.*

Bouton, John Bell. *N. H.*, 1830–——. Son of N. Bouton, *infra.* A New York littérateur. Loved and Lost: essays; Round the Block, a novel; Treasury of Travel and Adventure; Memoir of General Bell; Roundabout to Moscow, an Epicurean Journey; Uncle Sam's Church. *Ap. Lam.*

Bouton, Nathaniel. *Ct.*, 1797–1878. State historian of New Hampshire. He is best known for his edition of ten volumes of Provincial Records and for a History of Concord, New Hampshire.

Boutwell, George Sewall. *Ms.*, 1818——. A Massachusetts statesman; Governor of the State, 1852–53; Secretary of the Treasury, 1869–73. Thoughts on Educational Topics; Manual of the Direct and Excise Tax System of the United States; The Tax-Payer's Manual; Speeches and Papers relating to the Rebellion; Why I am a Republican: a History of the Republican Party; The Lawyer, the Statesman, the Soldier; The Constitution of the United States at the end of the First Century. *Ap. He.*

Bouvé, Edward Tracy. 18——. A Boston writer of fiction. Centuries Apart. *Lit.*

Bouvet, Marguerite. *La.*, 1865——. A writer of children's books of notable excellence. Sweet William; Prince Tip-Top; Little Marjorie's Love Story; My Lady; A Child of Tuscany; Pierrette. *Mg.*

Bouvier [boo-veer'], **Hannah.** Daughter of J. Bouvier, *infra. See Peterson, Mrs.*

Bouvier, John. *Iy.*, 1787–1851. A jurist of Philadelphia. Law Dictionary; Institutes of American Law. *Lip.*

Bovee, Christian Nestell. *N. Y.*, 1820——. An epigrammatic writer, some of whose sayings have been much quoted. Thoughts, Feelings, and Fancies; Intuitions and Summaries of Thought.

Bowditch, Henry Ingersoll. *Ms.*, 1808–1892. Son of N. Bowditch, *infra.* An eminent physician of Boston. Life of Nathaniel Bowditch for the Young; The Young Stethoscopist; Public Hygiene in America.

Bowditch, Nathaniel. *Ms.*, 1773–1838. A famous mathematician of Salem, Massachusetts, whose translation of La Place's Mécanique Céleste, with extensive commentary, was his greatest work. The New American Navigator was his only original work of note. *See Memoir, by H. I. Bowditch.*

Bowen, Eli. *Pa.*, 1824–188–. A once popular Pennsylvania author. Coal Regions of Pennsylvania; Pictorial Sketch Book of Pennsylvania; Rambles in the Path of the Iron Horse; The Creation of the Earth; United States Post-Office System; Coal and Coal Oil.

Bowen, Francis. *Ms.*, 1811–1890. A professor of philosophy at Harvard University for many years, and eminent both as philosopher and political economist. He opposed the systems of Kant, Fichte, Cousin, Comte, and Mill, and was answered by the latter in a third edition of his Logic. Critical Essays in Speculative Philosophy; Modern Philosophy from Descartes to Schopenhauer and Hartmann; Treatise on Logic; American Political Economy; Principles of Political Economy; A Layman's Study of the English Bible considered in its Literary and Secular Aspects; Gleanings from a Literary Life. *Scr.*

Bowen, John Eliot. *N. Y.*, 1858–1890. A New York journalist. The Conflict of East and West in Egypt; Songs of Toil, a translation from Carmen Sylva.

Bowen, Mrs. Sue [Petigru] [King]. *S. C.*, 1824–1875. A novelist of Charleston, South Carolina. Sylvia's World; Gerald Gray's Wife; Lily; Busy Moments of an Idle Woman, a collection of stories.

Bowker, Richard Rogers. *Ms.*, 1848——. The editor for some years of the Publishers' Weekly. Work and Wealth: a Summary of Economics; A Primer for Political Education; Economics for the People; The Library List; Electoral Reform. *Har.*

Bowles, Samuel. *Ms.*, 1826–1878. Journalist of Springfield, Massachusetts, editor of the Springfield Republican. Across the Continent; Our New West. *See Life of, by Merriam, 1885.*

Bowne, Borden Parker. *N. J.*, 1847–——. A philosophical writer and professor of philosophy in Boston University. The Philosophy of Herbert Spencer; Studies in Theism; Metaphysics: a Study of First Principles; Introduction to Psychological Theory; Philosophy of Theism; Principles of Ethics. *Har. Meth.*

Boyd, James Robert. *N. Y.*, 1804–1890. A Presbyterian clergyman, formerly professor of moral philosophy at Hamilton College. Elements of Rhetoric and Literary Criticism; Moral Philosophy; The Westminster Shorter Catechism, with Analysis; Elements of Logic; Last Days of a Christian Philosopher; Memoir of Doddridge, are some among his rather numerous publications. *Har.*

Boyesen, Hjalmar Hjorth. *N.*, 1848–1895. A writer of Norwegian birth, long resident in New York, and a professor in Columbia College at the time of his death. His novels and sketches are pleasantly written, but as essays in fiction are not much above average merit. Gunnar; A Norseman's Pilgrimage; Tales from Two Hemispheres; Falconberg; A Daughter of the Philistines; Queen Titania; Ilka on the Hill Top and Other Stories; Goethe and Schiller, their Lives and Works; Literary and Social Silhouettes; The Story of Norway, an historical work; Social Strugglers; Essays on Scandinavian Literature; Essays on German Literature; Idylls of Norway and Other Poems; the Norseland series of books for boys, including: Norseland Tales; Boyhood in Norway; The Modern Vikings; Against Heavy Odds; The Golden Calf. *Fl. Har. Mac. Scr.*

Boynton, Edward Carlisle. *Vt.*, 1825——. A United States army officer. History of West Point.

Bozman, John Leeds. *Md.*, 1757–1823. A once noted Maryland lawyer. Historical Sketch of the Prime Causes of the Revolutionary War; History of Maryland. *See Memoir by S. A. Harrison, 1888.*

Brace, Charles Loring. *Ct.*, 1826–1890. Son of J. P. Brace, *infra.* A noted clergyman and philanthropist of New York city who founded the Children's Aid Society, and gave much of his time to philanthropic work. Norsefolk; Home Life in Germany; The Races of the Old World; Gesta Christi; The Dangerous Classes of New York. *See Life, chiefly told in his own Letters. Scr.*

Brace, John Peirce. *Ct.*, 1793–1872. A once prominent educator of Litchfield, Connecticut. Lectures to Young Converts; Tales of the Devil; The Fawn of the Pale Faces: a Novel.

Brackenridge, Henry Marie. *Pa.*, 1786–1871. Son of H. H. Brackenridge, *infra.* A noted Florida jurist. History of the Late War between the United States and Great Britain (1816); Voyage to South America; Views of Louisiana; Recollections of Persons and Places in the West; Essay on Trusts and Trustees; History of the Western Insurrection.

Brackenridge, Hugh Henry. *S.*, 1748–1816. A Pennsylvania lawyer and humourist whose writing enjoyed great popularity in the early years of the 19th century. His principal work was Modern Chivalry, or the Adventures of Captain Farrago and Teague O'Regan, his Servant, a rough, sharp piece of humourous fiction, partaking, to some extent, of the nature of an autobiography. *See edition of 1848, with illustrations by Darley; Hart's American Literature.*

Brackett, Albert Gallatin. *N. Y.*, 1829–1896. A United States cavalry officer. General Lane's Brigade in Central Mexico; History of the United States Cavalry, 1854. *Har.*

Brackett, Anna Callender. *Ms.*, 1836——. An educational writer. The Education of American Girls; Woman and the Higher Education; The Technique of Rest. *Har.*

Brackett, Edward Augustus. *Me.*, 1819——. A sculptor of Boston. Twilight Hours, a volume of verse.

Bradford, Alden. *Ms.*, 1765–1843. Secretary of State for Massachusetts, 1812–24. Eulogy on Washington; History of Massachusetts, 1764–1820; Life of Jonathan Mayhew; History of the Federal Government; Biographical Notices of Distinguished Men of Massachusetts; New England Chronology, 1497–1843.

Bradford, Alexander Warfield. *N. Y.*, 1815–1867. A New York jurist of prominence. He edited American Antiquities, and prepared many volumes of legal reports, among which the six commonly called Bradford's Reports have become standard authority.

Bradford, Amory Howe. *Ms.*, 1846——. A Congregational clergyman of Montclair, New Jersey. The Pilgrim in Old England; Old Wine: New Bottles; Spirit and Life, Thought for To-Day; Heredity and Christian Problems. *Fo. Mac.*

Bradford, William. • *E.*, 1590–1657. Governor of the Plymouth Colony, 1621–57. He left in manuscript a History of Plymouth Plantation, the leisurely composition of 20 years, which was drawn from by Morton, Prince, and Hutchinson as a basis for their respective histories, and after being lost for nearly a century was found in the library of the Bishop of London in 1855, and published soon after. He was the earliest American historian, and his work exhibits judicial impartiality, broad conceptions, and a direct, vigourous style. *See Tyler's American Literature; Young's Chronicles of the Pilgrims; Mrs. Austin's Betty Alden and Standish of Standish. Hou.*

Bradlee, Caleb Davis. *Ms.*, 1831–1897. A Unitarian clergyman. Sermons for the Church; Sermons for All Sects; Life of Starr King. *El.*

Bradley, Mrs. Mary Emily [Neeley]. *Md.*, 1835——. A writer of tales for girls. Among her 20 or more volumes of this class are Douglass Farm; Story of a Summer; Brave Girls; Grace's Visit. Hidden Sweetness is a volume of verse. *Le. Lo.*

Bradley, Warren Ives. "Glance Gaylord." *Ct.*, 1847–1868. A talented writer of tales for boys. Among his twelve volumes, all written before he was twenty-one, Culm Rock is as well known as any.

Bradstreet, Mrs. Anne [Dudley]. *E.*, 1612–1672. The first American woman of letters, and called by her contemporaries "The Tenth Muse." Her prose work includes a brief autobiographic sketch, Religious Experiences; Meditations Divine and Moral, a series of shrewd, strong aphorisms. In her lifetime she was known only as a poet, and her verse, the bulk of which is considerable, comprises elegies, epitaphs; The Four Monarchies, a rhymed chronicle of ancient history; The Four Elements; The Four Humours of Man; The Four Ages of Man; The Four Seasons of the Year; Dialogue between Old England and New; Contemplations. She followed artificial models, and her lines reflect the grotesque conceits of the time, but here and there are gleams of real poetic vigour, while in the poem Contemplations, the least laboured of them all, she exhibits true poetic inspiration. *See Works of, edited by John Harvard Ellis, with sketch of the author, 1867; Tyler's American Literature; Life, by Helen Campbell; New England Magazine, 1887.*

Brainard, John Gardiner Calkins. *Ct.*, 1796–1828. A Hartford journalist whose Poems were published first in 1825, and reissued as Literary Remains in 1832 in an enlarged edition, with Memoir by his friend Whittier. His verse was temporarily popular, but his chief claim to present remembrance is the fine poem beginning, "I saw two clouds at morning."

Brainerd, David. *Ct.*, 1718–1747. A famous missionary among the Indians of New England. Selections from his journals have been printed, entitled Miriabilia Dei apud Indicos; Divine Grace Displayed. *See Life, by Jonathan Edwards, 1749, enlarged, 1822; Sparks's American Biography.*

Branch, Mrs. Mary Lydia [Bolles]. *Ct.*, 1840——. A New York writer, best known by her poem, The Petrified Fern. The Kanter Girls is a story for young people. *Scr.*

Brannan, William Penn. "Vandyke Brown." *O.*, 1825–1866. A portrait painter of Cincinnati. Vagaries of Vandyke Brown; The Harp of a Thousand Strings, or Laughter for a Life Time.

Brattle, Thomas. *Ms.*, 1657–1713. A once famous Boston merchant. Eclipse of the Sun and Moon observed in New England; Lunar Eclipse in New England, 1707.

Brazza, Cora [Slocomb], Countess di. *La.*, 1862——. A writer of New York city. An American Idyl; A Literary Farce; Guide to the Old and New Lace in Italy. *Ar.*

Breckinridge, Robert Jefferson. *Ky.*, 1800–1871. A once noted Presbyterian clergyman of Lexington, Kentucky. Popery; Internal Evidence of Christianity; Memoranda of Foreign Travel; Travels in France, Germany, etc. His chief work was a system of theology, The Knowledge of God, Objectively and Subjectively Considered. He was a writer of very positive views, and one of the leaders in the division of the Presbyterian church into Old and New School in 1837.

Breed, David Riddle. *Pa.*, 1848——. A Presbyterian minister of Chicago since 1885. More Light; Abraham, the Typical Life of Faith; History of the Preparation of the World for Christ; Heresy and Heresy. *Rev.*

Breed, William Pratt. *N. Y.*, 1816——. A Presbyterian clergyman of Philadelphia. His works are mainly religious juveniles, and among them are Jenny Geddes; Home Songs for Home Birds; Grapes from the Great Vine; A Board and Abroad. *Fu.*

Breidenbaugh, Edward Swoyer. *Pa.*, 1849——. A professor of chemistry at Pennsylvania College. Notes on Inorganic Chemistry; Mineralogy of the Farm, are among his purely technical papers and monographs.

Breitman, Hans. *See Leland.*

Brewer, Thomas Mayo. *Ms.*, 1821–1880. A Massachusetts ornithologist who was the principal author of the History of North American Birds prepared with Ridgway and S. F. Baird, *supra.* Oölogy of North America is also by him.

Brewer, William Henry. *N. Y.*, 1828——. A professor of agriculture in the Sheffield Scientific School at New Haven since 1864. Botany of California.

Brewerton, George Douglas. *C.*, 1820——. A United States army officer. The War in Kansas, a Rough Trip to the Border; Fitzpoodle at Newport; Ida Lewis, the Heroine of Lime Rock; The Automaton Company; The Automaton Battery.

Bridge, James Howard. "Harold Brydges." *E.*, 1858——. A Fortnight in Heaven: an Unconventional Romance; Uncle Sam at Home.

Bridges, Madeline. *See De Vere.*

Bridges, Robert. "Droch." *Pa.*, 1858——. A littérateur of New York city; literary critic of Life from 1883, and assistant editor of Scribner's Magazine since 1887. Overheard in Arcady, dialogues about contemporary writers; Suppressed Chapters and Other Bookishness. *Scr.*

Briggs, Charles Augustus. 1841——. A Presbyterian clergyman prominent among the leaders of newer religious thought and a professor at Union Theological Seminary, New York, since 1875. In 1892 he was tried for heresy and acquitted. Biblical Study; American Presbyterianism; Messianic Prophecy, notable for its display of the true historical spirit; The Authority of Holy Scripture; The Messiah of the Apostles; The Messiah of the Gospels; The Higher Criticism of the Hexateuch; The Bible, the Church, and the Reason; Whither? a Theological Question for the Times. *See New Englander, vol. 55; Andover Review, vol. 16; Catholic World, vol. 53. Scr.*

Briggs, Charles Frederick. *Ms.*, 1804–1877. A journalist and editor of New York city, the valued friend of many of the prominent literary Americans of his time. Adventures of Harry Franco, a Tale of the Great Panic; The Haunted Merchant; The Trippings of Tom Pepper; Working a Passage, or Life on a Liner. *See Lowell's Fable for Critics.*

Brigham, Amariah. *Ms.*, 1798–1849. A physician of Hartford, and subsequently superintendent of the lunatic asylum at Utica, New York. The Anatomy, Physiology, and Pathology of the Brain.

Brigham, William Tufts. *Ms.*, 1841——. A lawyer and naturalist now at Honolulu in charge of the government museum. Volcanic Manifestations in New England; Guatemala: the Land of the Quetzal, a volume of travels. *Scr.*

Brightly, Francis Frederick. *Pa.*, 1845——. Son of F. C. Brightly, *infra.* Digest of the Laws of Philadelphia, 1701–1887.

Brightly, Frederick Charles. *E.*, 1812–1888. An eminent Philadelphia jurist. Treatise on Law of Costs; Nisi Prius Reports; Equitable Jurisdiction of the Laws of Pennsylvania; Digest of the Laws of the United States, 1789–1869; Digest of the Decisions of the Federal Courts; Bankrupt Law of the United States; Leading Cases in the Law of Elections, include the larger number of his legal writings.

Brinton, Daniel Garrison. *Pa.*, 1837——. An archæological writer and publisher, as well as physician, of Philadelphia, whose researches in aboriginal history and literature have been very extensive. A professor of archæology in the University of Pennsylvania since 1880. The Myths of the New World; The Religions Sentiment; American Hero-Myths; Aboriginal American Authors; The Floridian Peninsula; Races and Peoples; Essays of an Americanist; The Lenape and their Legends. He has edited The Maya Chronicles; The Comedy-Ballet of Güegüence; Aboriginal American Anthology. *See Popular Science Monthly, vol. 38. Co. Gi. Ho.*

Brisbin, James Sanks. *Pa.*, 1837–1892. A United States cavalry officer. Campaign Lives of Grant and Colfax; The Beef Bonanza; Trees and Tree Planting. *Har. Lip.*

Bristed, Charles Astor. "Carl Benson." *N. Y.*, 1820–1874. Son of J. Bristed, *infra.* A magazinist of New York city. Five Years in an English University; The Upper Ten Thousand; Pieces of a Broken-down Critic; The Interference Theory of Government; Anacreontics.

Bristed, John. *E.*, 1778–1855. An Episcopal clergyman of Rhode Island. His principal works, none of which rise much above the level of dullness, are Critical and Philosophical Essays; Resources of the United States, 1818; Anglo-American Churches; Edward and Anna: a Novel; A Pedestrian Tour through the Highlands of Scotland.

Bristol, Mrs. Augusta [Cooper]. *N. H.*, 1835——. An educator of Vineland, New Jersey. Poems; The Relation of the Maternal Function to the Woman's Intellect; The Philosophy of Art; Science and its Relations to Character; The Present Phase of Woman's Advancement; The Web of Life, a collection of verse.

Britton, Nathaniel Lord. *S. I.*, 1859——. A botanical professor in the School of Mines at Columbia College. Catalogue of the Flora of Staten Island; The Geology of Staten Island; Catalogue of the Flora of New Jersey; An Illustrated Flora of the Northern United States, Canada, and the British Possessions, from Newfoundland to the Parallel of the Southern Boundary of Virginia, and from the Atlantic Ocean to the 102d Meridian (with A. Brown). *Scr.*

Britts, Mrs. Mattie [Dyer]. *N. Y.*, 1842——. Daughter of S. Dyer, *infra.* The author of many juvenile tales, among which are Edward Lee; Nobody's Boy.

Broaddus, Andrew. *Va.*, 1770–1848. A Baptist clergyman once noted as a pulpit orator. History of the Bible; Form of Church Discipline; Letters and Sermons.

Broadus, John Albert. *Va.*, 1827–1895. A Baptist clergyman, the president of the Southern Baptist Theological Seminary. Preparation and Delivery of Sermons; Lectures on Preaching; Sermons and Addresses; Jesus of Nazareth. *Bap.*

Brockett, Linus Pierpont. *Ct.*, 1820–1893. A prolific writer of Hartford, among whose many productions are History of Education; Our Great Captains; The Year of Battles: a History of the Franco-German War of 1870; Epidemics and Contagious Diseases; The Silk Industry in America; Our Western Empire, an account of the resources of the United States west of the Mississippi; The Great Metropolis.

Brodhead, Mrs. Eva Wilder [McGlasson]. 18— ——. A popnlar novelist. One of the Visconti; Diana's Livery; An Earthly Paragon; Ministers of Grace; Bound In Shallows. *Har. Scr.*

Brodhead, John Romeyn. *Pa.*, 1814–1873. A painstaking, accurate writer, whose work, if somewhat lacking in picturesqueness, is of lasting value. History of the State of New York; The Government of Sir Edmund Andros over New England. *Har.*

Brooks, Arthur. *Ms.*, 1845–1895. Brother of Phillips Brooks, *infra.* An Episcopal clergyman of New York city. A volume of his Sermons was reprinted in London with the title, Christ for To-Day. *Wh.*

Brooks, Charles. *Ms.*, 1795–1872. A once prominent Massachusetts educator. History of Medford; The Christian in his Closet; Daily Monitor; Family Prayer-Book; Elements of Ornithology; Introduction to Ornithology, and ten volumes of biography.

Brooks, Charles Timothy. *Ms.*, 1813–1883. A Unitarian clergyman of Newport, Rhode Island, 1837–73, whose English versions of Schiller, Richter, Goethe, and Schefer take high rank. His other work includes Songs of Field and Flood; The Simplicity of Christ; William Ellery Channing: a Centennial Memory; Poems Original and Translated. *See Memoir by Wendte. Rob.*

Brooks, Edward. *N. Y.*, 1831——. The principal of the Millersville Normal School, Pennsylvania, 1866–86, and since then superintendent of the Philadelphia public schools. His writings are mainly, though not entirely, mathematical, and among them are The Normal Written Arithmetic; Philosophy of Arithmetic; Mental Science and Methods of Culture; The Story of the Iliad; The Story of the Odyssey.

Brooks, Elbridge Gerry. *N. H.*, 1816–1878. A Universalist clergyman of Philadelphia. Universalism a Practical Power; Our New Departure; Universalism in Life and Doctrine. *See Life by E. S. Brooks.*

Brooks, Elbridge Streeter. *Ms.*, 1846——. A Boston writer for young people. Life Work of Elbridge Gerry Brooks; In No Man's Land; Historic Boys; In Leisler's Times; Chivalric Days; Storied Holidays; Historic Girls; Story of the American Indian; The Story of New York; Story of the American Sailor; Story of the United States; The True Story of Columbus; Heroic Happenings; A Son of Issachar; The True Story of George Washington; The Century Book for Young Americans; A Boy of the First Empire; Great Men's Sons; The Story of Miriam of Magdala; The True Story of Abraham Lincoln; The Story of the American Soldier; The Century Book of Famous Americans; Under the Tamaracks; The Long Walls (with J. Alden). *Cent. Lo. Put.*

Brooks, Mrs. Maria [Gowen]. *Ms.*, 1795–1845. Called by Southey "Maria del Occidente." A poet whose fate it has been to be utterly neglected after being once extravagantly praised. Zophiel, or The Bride of Seven, her chief work, is a poem whose incidents are taken from the story of Sara in the apocryphal book of Tobit. It is a work of considerable power but extravagant sentiment. Idomen, or the Vale of Yumuri, is to some extent autobiographic. *See Griswold's Female Poets; Harper's Magazine, January and May, 1879; Mrs. Hale's Woman's Record.*

Brooks, Nathan Covington. *Md.*, 1819——. A prominent educator of Baltimore, who besides publishing an excellent series of classical text-books, chief among which are editions of Ovid's Metamorphoses and Virgil's Æneid, is the author of A Complete History of the Mexican War.

Brooks, Noah. *Me.*, 1830——. A New York writer of popular books for boys. The Boy Emigrants; The Fairport Nine; Our Baseball Club; Abraham Lincoln; The Boy Settlers; American Statesmen; Tales of the Maine Coast; Abraham Lincoln and the Downfall of American Slavery; How the Republic is Governed; Short Studies in American Party Politics; Washington in Lincoln's Time, a volume of gossipy recollections; The Mediterranean Trip. *Cent. Scr.*

Brooks, Phillips. *Ms.*, 1835–1893. The sixth Protestant Episcopal bishop of Massachusetts. He was rector of Holy Trinity Church at Philadelphia, 1862–69, and of Trinity Church, Boston, from 1869 until his consecration as bishop in 1891. He was a leader of Broad Church opinion, but had no hostility towards forms of thought opposed to his. For many years before his death he had been accounted the foremost preacher in America. The Influence of Jesus; Lectures on Preaching; The Candle of the Lord and Other Sermons; The Light of the World and Other Sermons; Sermons in English Churches; Twenty Sermons; Sermons for the Principal Festivals and Fasts; Tolerance; A Century of Church Growth in Boston; Essays and Addresses; Letters of Travel; The Oldest School in America. O Little Town of Bethlehem is a popular poem by him. *See Phillips Brooks in Boston; Five Years' Editorial Estimates; Phillips Brooks, by Dunbar; Annual Cyclopedia, 1893; Andover Review, vol. 15; Phillips Brooks in Massachusetts, by J. H. Ward, infra. Dut. Mer.*

Brooks, William Keith. *O.*, 1848——. A professor of morphology at Johns Hopkins University. Hand-book of Invertebrate Zoölogy; Development of the American Oyster; Conifer, a Study in Morphology; Development of Lingula; The Law of Heredity. *Wn.*

Bross, William. *N. J.*, 1813-1890. A Chicago journalist. History of Chicago (1866); Tom Quick, a romance of Indian warfare; Chicago and her Future Growth.

Brotherton, Mrs. Alice [Williams]. *Ind.*, 18——. A magazinist of Cincinnati, whose work is mainly in verse. Beyond the Veil; The Sailing of King Olaf; What the Wind told the Tree-Tops, prose and verse for children.

Brougham [broo'am or broo'm], **John.** *I.*, 1814-1880. A once noted dramatist who was the author of over a hundred comedies and farces, many of which, like Vanity Fair and The Irish Emigrant, have been very successful. *See Life, by William Winter.*

Brown, Abram English. *Ms.*, 1849——. A resident of Bedford, Massachusetts. Beneath Old Roof Trees, a volume of local history; Beside Old Hearthstones; History of Bedford; Bedford Old Families; Glimpses of New England Life; Flag of the Minute Men. *Le.*

Brown, Alexander. *Va.*, 1843——. A writer of Nelson County, Virginia, who has published The Cabells and their Kin, a genealogy; The Genesis of the United States. *Hou.*

Brown, Alice. *N. H.*, 185——. A Boston writer on the staff of the Youth's Companion. Fools of Nature, a novel; Meadow Grass, a collection of New England stories; By Oak and Thorn, a volume of English travel; Robert Louis Stevenson: a Study (with L. Guiney, *infra*); Life of Mercy Otis Warren. *Cop. Hou. Scr.*

Brown, Anna Robeson. *Pa.*, 1873——. Daughter of H. A. Brown, *infra*, and great niece of C. B. Brown, *infra*. A novelist who has published Sir Mark; The Black Lamb. *Ap.*

Brown, Charles Brockden. *Pa.*, 1771-1810. A novelist of Philadelphia, and the first of native authors who adopted literature as a profession. In his novels probability plays a very small part, the local colour is faint, though the scenes are American, and all are overshadowed by an overpowering element of mystery. In spite of extravagances and faults, his work possesses undeniable power of a very high order, and does not deserve the neglect into which it has fallen. Wieland; Ormond, or the Secret Witness; Arthur Mervyn, in some respects the most powerful of his works; Edgar Huntley, or the Memories of a Sleep Walker; Clara Howard, reprinted in England as Philip Stanley; Jane Talbot. *See Lives by Dunlap, 1815, Prescott, 1831; Atlantic Monthly, vol. 61; Nichol's American Literature. My.*

Brown, Charles Rufus. *N. H.*, 1849——. A professor of Old Testament interpretation at Union Theological Seminary since 1883. An Aramaic Method: Text and Grammar. *Scr.*

Brown, David Paul. *Pa.*, 1795-1872. A Philadelphia lawyer who was the author of two unsuccessful tragedies, Sestorius; The Trial; a melodrama and a comedy, equally unsuccessful, and The Forum, or Forty Years' Practice at the Philadelphia Bar. His Forensic Speeches were edited by his son in 1873.

Brown, Emma Elizabeth. *N. H.*, 1847——. A writer of popular biographies living at Newton, Massachusetts. Her works include lives of

Washington; Grant; Garfield; Wendell Holmes; Russell Lowell; From Night to Light, a story of Bible times; The Child Toilers of Boston Streets; An Hundred Years Ago, a story in verse. *Lo. Me.*

Brown, Francis. *N. H.*, 1849——. A professor of Hebrew and cognate languages at Union Theological Seminary since 1890. Assyriology: its Use and Abuse; The Teachings of the Apostles (with R. D. Hitchcock). *Scr.*

Brown, Goold. *R. I.*, 1791–1857. An educator of New York city and a once famous grammarian. Grammar of English Grammars; Institutes of English Grammar; First Lines of English Grammar.

Brown, Helen Dawes. *Ms.*, 18——. A lecturer on English literature in New York city. The Petrie Estate, a novel; Two College Girls; Little Miss Phœbe Gay. *Hou.*

Brown, Henry Armitt. 1846–1878. A lawyer and orator of Philadelphia, whose Four Historical Orations have been much admired. *See Memoir, by Hoppin; Atlantic Monthly, August, 1880.*

Brown, Henry Billings. *Ms.*, 1836——. A justice of the United States Supreme Court since 1890. Admiralty Reports for Western, Lake, and River Districts.

Brown, James Allen. *Pa.*, 1821–1883. A Lutheran clergyman and educator, professor in Gettysburg Seminary, 1864–77. The New Theology.

Brown, John Walker. *N. Y.*, 1814–1849. An Episcopal clergyman who won some fleeting notice as a poet. Christmas Bells, a Tale of Holy Tide, and Other Poems.

Brown, Mrs. Phoebe [Hinsdale]. *N. Y.*, 1783–1861. A hymn-writer remembered for her popular religious lyric, "I love to steal awhile away."

Brown, Samuel Gilman. *Me.*, 1813–1885. A Congregational clergyman who was president of Hamilton College, 1867–81. Biography of Self-Taught Men; Life of Rufus Choate. *Lit.*

Brown, Theron. *Ct.*, 1832——. A Baptist clergyman of Boston, who has written several books for young people, among which are The Blount Family; Walter Neil's Example; Life Songs, a collection of verse. *Le. Lo.*

Brown, Thomas Edwin. *D. C.*, 1841——. A Baptist clergyman of Rochester, New York. Studies in Modern Socialism and Labor Problems.

Brown, Thurlow Weed. ——1866. A Wisconsin journalist prominent as a temperance advocate. Why I am a Temperance Man; Minnie Hermon, the Landlord's Daughter; Temperance Tales.

Browne, Charles Farrar, "Artemus Ward." *Me.*, 1834–1867. A very genuine though grotesque humourist, whose satire is invariably good-natured and whose humour is based on shrewd sense. While a printer in the office of The Plaindealer, in Cleveland, he began publishing his series of letters from "Artemus Ward, Showman.". Later he became known as a popular humourous lecturer, and was lecturing in England with success at the time of his death. Artemus Ward: his Book; Artemus Ward Among the Mormons; Artemus Ward in London; Artemus Ward: His Travels; Artemus Ward's Lecture at Egyptian Hall. *See Haweis's American Humourists.*

Browne, Francis Fisher. *Vt.*, 1843——. A literary critic of Chicago and editor of The Dial since 1880. Every-day Life of Abraham Lincoln; Volunteer Grain, a collection of poems. *Wy.*

Browne, Irving. *N. Y.*, 1835——. A lawyer of Albany. Humourous Phases of the Law; Short Studies of Great Lawyers; Judicial Interpretation of Common Words and Phrases; Law and Lawyers in Literature; Iconoclasm and Whitewash; The Character of the Nurse's Deceased Husband in Romeo and Juliet; Our Best Society, a comedy; The Elements of Criminal Law. *See The Green Bag, vol. 1.*

Browne, John Ross. *I.*, 1817–1875. A writer of amusing travels, illustrated by original drawings, which enjoyed a transient but profitable popularity. An American Family in Germany; Yusef, a Crusade in the East; Land of Thor, a volume of Icelandic experiences; Etchings of a Whaling Voyage;

Crusoe's Island; Adventures in the Apache Country. *Ap. Har.*

Browne, Junius Henri. *N. Y.*, 1833——. A journalist of New York city. Four Years in Secessia; The Great Metropolis, a Memoir of New York; Lights and Sensations in Europe. *See Lippincott's Magazine, vol. 40.*

Browne, William Hand. *Md.*, 1828——. An historical writer of Baltimore who, besides assisting Scharf and other writers, has also written Maryland, the History of a Palatinate; George Calvert and Cecilius Calvert, barons Baltimore. *Do. Hou.*

Browne, William Hardcastle. *Pa.*, 1840——. A lawyer of Philadelphia. Digest of the Law of Divorce and Alimony in the United States; Famous Women of History; Bible Heroes.

Brownell, Henry Howard. *R. I.*, 1820–1872. Nephew of T. C. Brownell, *infra.* A writer who served in the Civil War as ensign under Farragut, and was present in the two engagements described in his famous battle poems, The Bay Fight, The River Fight, which rank among the finest verses of their kind. Poems; People's Book of Ancient and Modern History; Discoverers of North and South America; Lyrics of a Day; War Lyrics.

Brownell, Thomas Church. *Ms.*, 1779–1865. The third Protestant-Episcopal bishop of Connecticut. Family Prayer-Book; Commentary on the Prayer-Book; Youthful Christian's Guide; Consolation for the Afflicted; Christian's Walk and Consolation; Religion of Heart and Life, comprise the greater number of his works.

Brownell, William Crary. *N. Y.*, 1851——. A New York journalist and critic. Newport; French Art; Classic and Contemporary Painting and Sculpture; French Traits: an essay in Comparative Criticism. *See The Bookman, December, 1896. Scr.*

Brownell, William Craig. *S.*, 1784–1860. A Reformed Dutch clergyman of New York city, and a very active controversialist, whose batteries were chiefly directed at the Quakers and Roman Catholics. Inquiry into the Principles of the Quakers; The Roman Catholic Controversy; Treatise on Popery; Lights and Shadows of Scottish Life; Christian Youths' Book; Christian Father at Home; Deity of Christ; History of the Western Apostolic Church; The Converted Murderer; The Whigs of Scotland, a romance.

Brownlow, William Gannaway. *Va.*, 1805–1877. A Methodist preacher and journalist of Knoxville, Tennessee, conspicuous for his fidelity to the Union during the Civil War. At its close he served two terms as governor of his state. The Iron Wheel Examined and its False Spokes Extracted, a reply to attacks upon Methodism; Ought American Slavery to be Perpetuated; Sketches of the Rise, Progress, and Decline of Secession.

Brownson, Orestes Augustus. *Vt.*, 1803–1876. A prominent philosophical thinker who in early life was successively a Presbyterian, a Universalist clergyman, a Socialist leader associated with Robert Owen, and a Unitarian clergyman, as well as an able political speaker at all times. In 1844 he became a Roman Catholic, and in Brownson's Review, from that date until 1864, he ably defended the Roman Catholic faith from the standpoint of a liberal. His philosophy is more or less influenced by the thought of Cousin. New Views of Christianity, Society, and the Church; Charles Elwood, or the Infidel Converted (1840), a more or less autobiographic novel; Leaves from my Experience; Essays and Reviews; The Spirit-Rapper, an autobiography; The American Republic, a work on political ethics; Conversations on Liberalism. *See Complete Works, in 20 volumes, 1882–87, published in Detroit by his son Henry F. Brownson; Catholic World, volumes 45 and 46; Atlantic Monthly, June, 1896.*

Bruce, Wallace. *N. Y.*, 1844——. A poet and lecturer of Poughkeepsie. From the Hudson to the Yosemite; The Land of Burns; The Connecticut Daylight; in verse, The Hudson; Yosemite; Old Homestead Poems; Wayside Poems; In Clover and Heather; Here 's a Hand. *Har.*

Brush, Mrs. Constance [Chaplin]. *Me.*, 1842–1892. Daughter of J. Chaplin, *infra.* An artist in water-colours whose home was in Brooklyn. Her most important book, The Colonel's Opera Cloak, a novel, was first published anonymously. Her only other works are the two stories, Inside our Gate; One Summer's Lessons in Perspective. *Rob.*

Bryan, Mrs. Mary [Edwards]. *Fl.* 1846——. A journalist of New York city who has written the novels Manch; Wild Work, a story of the reconstruction period in Louisiana; The Bayou Bride; Kildee.

Bryant, John Howard. *Ms.*, 1807——. Brother of W. C. Bryant, *infra*. A poet and farmer of Princeton, Illinois. Poems; Poems written from Youth to Old Age, 1824–84.

√ **Bryant, William Cullen.** *Ms.*, 1794–1878. A poet and journalist of New York city. In early life he began the practice of law, but soon abandoned it for journalism and, removing to New York in 1825, became in 1828 the editor of the Evening Post, with which he remained associated until his death. His earliest poem, The Embargo, a political satire, was published when its author was but thirteen, but the first collection of his poems was not made until 1821, the famous Thanatopsis being one of the eight which the volume comprised. The quantity of Bryant's verse is small, the quality high, but not uniformly so. Its tone is usually calmly philosophic, and it rarely makes any very effective appeal to the sympathies, its coldness arising partly from lack of humour, partly from natural reserve. The Embargo; The Spanish Revolution; The Ages; The Fountain of Youth, and Other Poems; The White-Footed Deer; The Flood of Years; Thirty Poems; translations of the Iliad and Odyssey, both in unrhymed heroic pentameter; Letters of a Traveller, a prose work; Orations and Addresses. *See Commemorative Address by G. W. Curtis; Lives by J. Bigelow, Parke Godwin, A. J. Symington; Stedman's Poets of America; Appleton's American Biography; Wilson's Bryant and his Friends, 1886; Gosse's Questions at Issue; Magazine of American History, vol. 23; Atlantic Monthly, March, 1897. Ap. Cr. Hou.*

Bryant, William McKendree. *Ind.*, 1843——. A prominent educator of St. Louis. Philosophy of Landscape Painting; The World Energy and its Self-Conservation; Syllabus of Psychology; Ethics and the New Education; Text Book of Psychology, are some of his writings. *Sc.*

Bryce, Lloyd. *L. I.*, 1852——. A novelist of New York city, editor of the North American Review, 1889–96. Paradise; A Dream of Conquest; The Romance of An Alter Ego; Friends in Exile.

Brydges, Harold. *See Bridge, J. H.*

Buchanan, James. *Pa.*, 1791–1868. The fifteenth president of the United States. Mr. Buchanan's Administration (1866) is his own defence of his policy as President. *See Life of, by G. T. Curtis, infra.*

Buchanan, Joseph. *Va.*, 1785–1829. A once noted mechanical inventor of Kentucky who published The Philosophy of Human Nature.

Buchanan, Joseph Rodes. *Ky.*, 1814——. Son of J. Buchanan, *supra*. A Boston physician who claimed to have invented the sciences of sarcognomy and psychometry. He published Buchanan's Journal of Medicine, 1849–56, and wrote Outlines of Lectures on the Neurological System of Anthropology; Eclectric Practice of Medicine and Surgery; The New Education; Therapeutic Sarcognomy; Manual of Psychometry. *See One of a Thousand.*

Buck, Dudley. *Ct.*, 1839——. A composer and organist of Brooklyn. Dictionary of Musical Terms; The Influence of the Organ in History.

Buck, Gurdon. *N. Y.*, 1807–1877. An eminent surgeon of New York city. He wrote much for medical journals and a treatise on Contributions to Reparative Surgery.

Buckingham, Joseph Tinker. *Ct.*, 1779–1861. A Boston journalist of note who published, 1831–34, The New England Magazine, in which Dr. Holmes began his famous "Autocrat," and The Boston Courier, 1828–48. Specimens of Newspaper Literature; Personal Memoirs and Recollections of Editorial Life.

Buckley, James Monroe. *N. J.*, 1836——. A Methodist clergyman, editor since 1881 of the New York Christian Advocate. Two Weeks in the Yosemite Valley; Supposed Miracles; Christians and the Theatre; Oats or Wild Oats; The Land of the Czar and the Nihilist; Faith-Healing, Christian Science, and Kindred Phenomena; Travels in Three Continents, Europe, Africa, Asia. *Cent. Har. Lo. Meth.*

Buckminster, Joseph Stevens. *N. H.*, 1784–1812. A talented Unitarian clergyman of Boston, the first appointed lecturer on biblical criticism at Harvard University. Sermons, with Memoir by S. C. Thacher, 1814.

Buel, Jesse. *Ct.*, 1778–1839. A noted agriculturist of Albany who effected many reforms in farming. He established the Albany Argus, The Cultivator, and published The Farmer's Instructor, in ten volumes; and also The Farmer's Companion, or Essays in Husbandry. *Har.*

Buel, Samuel. *N. Y.*, 1815–1892. An Episcopal clergyman of High Church proclivities, who was professor of divinity at the General Theological Seminary of New York from 1871. The Apostolic System Defended; Eucharistic Presence, Sacrifice, and Adoration; A Treatise on Dogmatic Theology. *Wh.*

Buell, Richard Hooker. *Md.*, 1842–——. A United States civil engineer. The Cadet Engineer; Safety Valves; The Compound Steam-Engine and its Steam-Generating Plant.

Bulfinch, Ellen Susan. *Ms.*, 1844–——. An artist of Cambridge. Life and Letters of Charles Bulfinch, Architect. *Hou.*

Bulfinch, Stephen Greenleaf. *Ms.*, 1809–1870. A Unitarian clergyman of Boston, and son of Charles Bulfinch, the noted architect. Poems, Lays of the Gospel, Communion Thoughts; Contemplations of the Saviour; The Holy Land and its Inhabitants; The Harp and the Cross; Honour, or The Slave Dealer's Daughter; Manual of the Evidences of Christianity; Studies in the Evidences of Christianity. *A. U. A. Le.*

Bulfinch, Thomas. *Ms.*, 1796–1867. Brother of S. G. Bulfinch, *supra.* A Boston banker whose leisure was devoted to literary pursuits. Hebrew Lyrical History; The Age of Fable; The Age of Chivalry; Boy Inventors; Legends of Charlemagne; Poetry of the Age of Fable; Oregon and Eldorado, or Romance of the Rivers. *Le.*

Bulkley, Peter. *E.*, 1583–1659. A Congregational clergyman of Concord, Massachusetts. His one work, The Gospel Covenant, or The Covenant of Grace Opened, is a ponderous series of sermons notable for its intellectual vigour. *See Tyler's History of American Literature.*

Bullard, Asa. *Ms.*, 1804–1888. Brother-in-law of H. W. Beecher, *supra.* A Congregational clergyman of Massachusetts, long prominent in Sunday-school work. His principal writings are Sunnybank Stories; Shady Dell Stories; Fifty Years with the Sabbath School; Incidents in a Busy Life, an autobiography. *Le. Lo.*

Bullions, Peter. *S.*, 1791–1864. A United Presbyterian clergyman of Troy, New York, well known as a classical scholar. Among his text-books for schools are Principles of English Grammar; Principles of Greek Grammar; Latin and English Dictionary.

Bullock, Alexander Hamilton. *Ms.*, 1816–1882. A prominent Massachusetts politician, at one period governor of the State. Intellectual Leaderships; Address on Several Occasions, with Memoir by G. F. Hoar. *Lit.*

Bump, Orlando Franklin. *N. Y.*, 1841–1881. A Baltimore lawyer, author of The Law and Practice of Bankruptcy; Federal Procedure.

Bumstead, Freeman Josiah. *Ms.*, 1826–1879. A physician of New York city. Pathology and Treatment of Venereal Diseases, and translations from the French of Ricord and Cullerier.

Bunce, Oliver Bell. *N. Y.*, 1828–1890. A New York littérateur, editor of Appleton's Journal for the period of its existence, and well known as the author of Don't (1883), a small volume of social negations which was widely circulated. He wrote also Bachelor Bluff, his Opinions, a volume of essays; My House; Marco Bozzaris, a drama; Love in '76, a comedy; Romance of the Revolution; four stories, including Life Before Him; Bensly; A Bachelor's Story; The Adventures of Timias

Terrystone; Happinolande and Other Legends, a collection of sketches. *Ap. Co. Scr.*

Bundy, Jonas Mills. *N. H.*, 1835–1891. A New York journalist, prominent as editor of the Mail and Express from 1868. State Rights; Are we a Nation?; Life of Garfield (1880). *Bar.*

Bungay, George Washington. *E.*, 1818–1892. A New York journalist well known as a temperance lecturer. He wrote many poems, among which The Creeds of the Bells has long been popular. His other writings include The Abraham Lincoln Songster; The Poets of Queen Elizabeth's Time; Offhand Takings; Crayon Sketches; Pen Portraits of Illustrious Abstainers.

Bunner, Henry Cuyler. *N. Y.*, 1855–1896. A New York journalist, the editor of Puck, and well known as a writer of graceful, delicate verse and very readable fiction. Jersey Street and Jersey Lane; Love in Old Cloathes; Zadoc Pine and Other Stories; The Story of a New York House; The Midge; In Partnership (with J. B. Matthews, *infra*); Short Sixes, a collection of humourous tales; The Woman of Honour. His verse includes Airs from Arcady and Elsewhere; Rowen: "second crop" Songs. *Hou. Scr.*

Burdett, Charles. *N. Y.*, 1815–18—. A journalist and novelist of New York whose writings were transiently popular. Life of Kit Carson; The Second Marriage; The Beautiful Spy; Margaret Moncrieffe; Emma, or The Lost Found; Marion Desmond; The Gambler; The Adopted Child; Trials and Triumphs; Never too Late; Chances and Changes. *Har.*

Burdette, Robert Jones. *Pa.*, 1844–——. A newspaper humourist who was for some years editor of The Hawkeye, of Burlington, Iowa. Hawkeyes; Rise and Fall of the Mustache; Innach Garden and Other Comic Sketches; Life of William Penn. *Ho.*

Burgess, Edward. *Ms.*, 1848–1891. A noted naval architect of Boston. English and American Yachts. *See New England Magazine, vol. 5.*

Burgess, George. *R. I.*, 1809–1866. The first Protestant Episcopal bishop of Maine. Pages from the Ecclesiastical History of New England; The Christian Life; The Book of Psalms in English Verse; The Last Enemy Conquering and Conquered; Strife of Brothers, a poem, comprise the most of his writings. *See Memoir, by A. Burgess; Bibliography of Maine. Ran.*

Burgess, John William. *Tn.*, 1844–——. The dean of the school of physical science in Columbia College. The American University: When Shall it Be, Where Shall it Be, and What Shall it Be?; Political Science and Comparative Constitutional Law; The Middle Period. *Gi.*

Burk, John Daly. *I.*, 17—1808. An Irish author who came to America in 1796, and for the last years of his life was a lawyer in Virginia. History of the Late War in Ireland; History of Virginia; Bunker Hill, a once popular tragedy; Bethlem Gaber, an historical drama.

Burleigh, George Shepard. *Ct.*, 1821——. A writer of Little Compton, Rhode Island. Anti-Slavery Hymns; The Maniac and Other Poems; Signal Fires, or The Trail of the Pathfinder.

Burleigh, William Henry. *Ct.*, 1812–1871. Brother of G. S. Burleigh, *supra*. An anti-slavery journalist of Hartford and elsewhere who won some notice as a poet. *See Poems of, with biographical sketch by Celia Burleigh. Hou.*

Burnap, George Washington. *N. H.*, 1802–1859. A Unitarian clergyman of Baltimore, prominent as a controversialist. Popular Objections to Unitarian Christianity Considered; What is a Unitarian; Lectures to Young Men; Lectures on the History of Christianity; Christianity, its Essence and Evidence, are his more important works.

Burney, Stanford Guthrie. *Tn.*, 1814——. A Cumberland Presbyterian divine, professor of systematic theology at Cumberland University. Treatise on Elocution; Baptismal Regeneration; Atonement and Law Reviewed; Chart of Duty; Soteriology; Studies in Moral Science; Studies in Psychology; Studies in Theology.

Burnett, Mrs. Frances Eliza [Hodgson]. *E.*, 1849——. A popular writer of fiction, whose first successful book was That Lass o' Lowrie's, a powerful tale of Lancashire life. Her other works, of varying degrees of excellence, include Earlier Stories, first and second series; Haworth; A Fair Barbarian; Through One Administration; Louisiana; Esmeralda; Vagabondia, Surly Tim, and Other Stories; The Pretty Sister of José; A Lady of Quality. As a writer for young people her success has been very marked; and besides Little Lord Fauntleroy, the most popular of all her books, her juvenile writings comprise Sara Crewe; Piccino and Other Child Stories; Little Saint Elizabeth; Two Little Pilgrims' Progress; Giovanni and the Other; The One I Knew the Best of All, an autobiographic tale. *See Vedder's American Writers. Scr.*

Burnett, James G. *N. Y.*, 1868–1893. A verse-writer who published Love and Laughter, a collection of verse. *Put.*

Burnett, Peter Hardeman. *Tn.*, 1807–1895. A California lawyer who was the first governor of that state. The Path which led a Protestant Lawyer to the Catholic Church; The American Theory of Government; Recollections and Opinions of an Old Pioneer; Reasons why *we* should believe in God. *Ap.*

Burnett, Waldo Irving. *Ms.*, 1828–1854. A naturalist of Boston. The Cell, its Physiology, Pathology, and Philosophy.

Burnham, Mrs. Clara Louise [Root]. *Ms.*, 1854——. A popular novelist of Chicago. "No Gentlemen"; A Sane Lunatic; Dearly Bought; Next Door; Young Maids and Old; The Mistress of Beech Knoll; Miss Bagg's Secretary, a West Point romance; Dr. Latimer, a story of Casco Bay; Sweet Clover; The Wise Woman. *Hou.*

Burr, Aaron. *Ct.*, 1716–1757. A Presbyterian clergyman who was president of Princeton College. He married a daughter of Jonathan Edwards, *infra*, and his son was the noted politician of the same name. His Latin Grammar was long in use at Princeton as "the Newark Grammar." His only other work was The Supreme Divinity of our Lord Jesus Christ.

Burr, Enoch Fitch. *Ct.*, 1818——. A Congregational clergyman of Lyme, Connecticut, since 1850. Pater Mundi; Ad Fidem; Doctrine of Evolution; Ecce Cœlum; Sunday Afternoons for Little People; About Spiritualism; Toward the Strait Gate; Ecce Terra; Work in the Vineyard; From Dark to Day; Facts in Aid of Faith; Celestial Empires; Universal Beliefs; Long Ago as Interpreted by the 19th Century; Tempted to Unbelief; Dio the Athenian; The Voyage, and Other Poems; Aleph, the Chaldean.

Burr, George Lincoln. *N.Y.*, 1857——. A professor of history at Cornell University from 1892. The Literature of Witchcraft; The Fate of Dietrick Flade; Charlemagne.

Burr, William Hubert. *Ct.*, 1851——. A civil engineer of prominence, professor of engineering at Columbia College from 1893. Stresses in Bridge and Roof Trusses; The Theory of the Masonry Arch; Elasticity and Resistance of the Materials of Engineering. *Wil.*

Burrage, Henry Sweetser. *Ms.*, 1837——. The editor of Zion's Advocate, Portland, Maine. Brown University in the Civil War; The Act of Baptism in the History of the Christian Church; History of the Anabaptists in Switzerland; History of Baptists in New England; History of the 36th Massachusetts Regiment; Baptist Hymn Writers and their Hymns. *Bap.*

Burrill, Alexander Mansfield. *N. Y.*, 1807–1869. A noted New York jurist. Practice of the Supreme Court of New York; Law Dictionary and Glossary; Law and Practice of Voluntary Assignments; Circumstantial Evidence.

Burritt, Elihu. *Ct.*, 1811–1879. A famous linguist who was called "The Learned Blacksmith," from the fact that much of his education was obtained while working at the forge in Worcester, Massachusetts. He was a noted peace reformer, and was for some years consul at Birmingham. Few of his writings have the literary quality to any extent, and they form rather dry reading. Sparks from the Anvil; A Voice from the Forge; Peace Papers for the People; Olive Leaves; Thoughts of Things at Home and Abroad; Handbook of the Nations; A Walk from John O' Groat's to Land's End; The Mission of Great Sufferings; Walks in the Black Country; Lectures and Speeches; Ten-Minute Talks; Chips from Many Blocks; Prayers and Devotional Meditations. *See Memorial, by C. Northend, 1879; Leisure Hour, vol. 28. Ran.*

Burroughs, John. *N. Y.*, 1837——. A noted essayist of Esopus, New York, whose keen, sympathetic studies of nature have been very popular both in America and England. Wake-Robin; Winter Sunshine; Birds and Poets; Locusts and Wild Honey; Pepacton; Fresh Fields; Signs and Seasons; Indoor Studies; Riverby; Whitman: a Study. *See Gentleman's Magazine, vol. 42; Lippincott's Magazine, vol. 39. Hou.*

Burrowes, George. *N. Y.*, 1811——. A Presbyterian clergyman of San Francisco, professor of Hebrew in the Presbyterian seminary there. Commentary on the Song of Solomon; Octorara, a Poem and Occasional Pieces; Advanced Growth in Grace.

Burt, Nathaniel Clark. *N. J.*, 1825–1874. A Presbyterian clergyman of Ohio. Hours among the Gospels; The Far East; The Land and its Story, the Sacred Geography of Palestine. *Ap.*

Burton, Asa. *Ct.*, 1752–1836. A Congregational clergyman, pastor at Thetford, Vermont, for more than fifty years. Essays on Some of the First Principles of Metaphysics, Ethics, and Theology. *See Memoir by T. Adams.*

Burton, Ernest De Witt. *O.*, 1856——. A professor of sacred literature in the University of Chicago. Records and Letters of the Apostolic Age; Syntax of Moods and Tenses in New Testament Greek; A Harmony of the Four Gospels (with W. A. Stevens). *Scr. Sil.*

Burton, Richard [Eugene]. *Ct.*, 1859——. A littérateur and journalist of Hartford, Connecticut. Dogs and Dog Literature; Dumb in June, and Other Poems; Memorial Day and Other Poems; Men of Progress (edited). *Cop.*

Burton, Warren. *N. H.*, 1800–1866. An educational writer of Boston. Cheering Views of Man and Providence; My Religious Experience at my Native Home; The Divine Agency in the Material Universe; Uncle Sam's Recommendations of Phrenology; The District School as it Was; Helps to Education; Culture of the Observing Faculties in the Family and School; Scenery Showing.

Burton, William Evans. *E.*, 1804–1860. A popular comedian of New York city. The Actor's Alloquy; Waggeries and Vagaries; Cyclopædia of Wit and Humor. *Ap.*

Bush, George. *Vt.*, 1796–1859. A Swedenborgian clergyman who was long a professor of Hebrew in the University of New York. Beside Commentaries on Genesis, Exodus, Leviticus, Numbers, Joshua, Judges, the Psalms, his writings include Life of Mohammed; New Church Miscellanies; Priesthood and Clergy unknown to Christianity; Mesmer and Swedenborg; Treatise on the Millennium; The Resurrection of Christ. *Har.*

Bushnell, Charles Ira. *N. Y.*, 1826–1883. An antiquarian writer of New York city, among whose works are Crumbs for Antiquarians; Adventures of Sir Christopher Hawkins (edited).

Bushnell, Horace. *Ct.*, 1802–1876. A Congregational clergyman of Hartford, who was one of the foremost thinkers in his denomination. He was a fearless reasoner, and his literary style exhibits both clearness and beauty. Christian Nurture; God in Christ; Christ in Theology; The Vicarious Sacrifice; Politics the Law of God; Nature and the Supernatural; Moral Uses of Dark Things, his ablest work; Sermons for the New Life; Sermons on Living Subjects; Forgiveness and Law; The Age of Homespun; Woman Suffrage; Moral Tendencies and Results of Human History; Building Eras in Religion; The Character of Jesus; Work and Play; Christ and His Salvation. *See Life and Letters, edited by his daughter, Mrs. Cheney; Atlantic Monthly, January, 1881.*

Bushnell, William H. *N. Y.*, 1823——. A littérateur of Washington. Biographical Sketches of the Early Settlers of Chicago; The Hermit of the

Colorado Hills, a Story of the Texan Pampas; Ah Meek the Beaver, or The Copper Hunters of Lake Superior.

Butler, Clement Moore. *N. Y.*, 1810–1890. An Episcopal clergyman of the evangelical type, professor of ecclesiastical history in the Episcopal Divinity School at Philadelphia, 1864–1884. Book of Common Prayer Interpreted by its History; Old Truths and New Errors; The Flock Fed; St. Paul in Rome; Inner Rome; Manual of Ecclesiastical History from the 1st to the 18th Century; The Reformation in Sweden, are his most important works. *Ran.*

Butler, Frederick. *Circa* 1766–1843. A writer of Hartford. History of the United States to 1820; The Farmer's Manual; Memorial of Lafayette and his Tour in the United States.

Butler, James Glentworth. *N. Y.*, 1821——. A Presbyterian clergyman of New York. The Bible Work, an extended scriptural commentary; The Fourfold Gospel. *Fu.*

Butler, John Jay. *Me.*, 1814–1891. A Free Baptist clergyman of Michigan, professor of sacred literature in Hillsdale College from 1873. Natural and Revealed Theology; Commentary on the Gospels, are his principal works.

Butler, Nicholas Murray. *N. J.*, 1862——. An educator of New York city, professor of philosophy in Columbia College. Horace Mann and American Systems of Education.

Butler, Noble. *Pa.*, 1810–1882. A classical professor in the University of Louisville, who published A Practical and Critical English Grammar and other valuable text-books.

Butler, Thomas Belden. *Ct.*, 1806–1873. A Connecticut jurist whose Philosophy of the Weather, 1856, appeared later in enlarged form as a Concise Analytical and Logical Development of the Atmospheric System.

Butler, William. *I.*, 1818——. A Methodist missionary. The Land of the Veda; From Boston to Bareilly and Back; Mexico in Transition from the Power of Political Romanism to Civil and Religious Liberty.

Butler, William Allen. *N. Y.*, 1825——. A lawyer of New York city well known as a writer of poetical satires, among which Nothing to Wear has long been famous. Others are, Two Millions; General Average, a satire upon mercantile life; Barnum's Parnassus. His prose writings include, Martin Van Buren, a Biography; Mrs. Limber's Raffle, an able attack on the morality of church fairs; Domesticus, a Story; Oberammergau. *Ap. Har. Scr.*

Butterfield, Consul Willshire. *N. Y.*, 1824——. A Wisconsin educator. Historical Account of the Expedition against Sandusky, 1782; System of Punctuation for Schools; History of the Discovery of the Northwest by John Nicollet, 1634, comprise his chief works. *Clke.*

Butterfield, Daniel. *N. Y.*, 1831——. A major-general in the United States army. Camp and Outpost Duty. *Har.*

Butterworth, Hezekiah. *R. I.*, 1837——. A Boston writer, for many years editor of The Youth's Companion. Besides publishing several volumes of Zig-Zag Journeys, Great Composers, The Knight of Liberty, In the Boyhood of Lincoln, The Patriot Schoolmaster, and other popular juvenile books, he is the author of two collections of musical verse, Songs of History; Poems for Christmas, Easter, and New Year's. *Ap. Cr. Est. Lo. Mer.*

Butts, Mrs. Mary Frances [Barber]. *R. I.*, 1836——. A writer of popular juvenile works. Three Girls; Lottie; Nellie's New Home; Lizzie and her Friends; The Frolic Series, are some of them.

Byerly, William Ellwood. *Pa.*, 1849——. A professor of mathematics at Harvard University. Elements of Differential Calculus; Elements of Integral Calculus. *Gi.*

Byers, Samuel Hawkins Marshall. *Ms.*, 1838——. A United States consul at Zurich, subsequently a consul-general to Italy and now a resident of Des Moines. Switzerland; Switzerland and the Swiss: Historical and Descriptive; Florence; History of Switzerland; What I Saw in Dixie; Military History of Iowa; The Happy Isles, and Other Poems.

Byfield, Nathaniel. *E.*, 1653–1733. A jurist of note in Massachusetts in the colonial period. Account of the Late War in England, 1689.

Byford, William Heath. *O.*, 1817–1890. A physician of prominence in Chicago. Practice of Medicine and Surgery Applied to Diseases and Accidents Peculiar to Women; Theory and Practice of Obstetrics; Philosophy of Domestic Life, are his more important works.

Byington, Ezra Hoyt. *Vt.*, 1828——. A Congregational clergyman of Newton, Massachusetts, who beside a number of historical monographs has written The Puritan in England and New England. *Rob.*

Byles, Mather. *Ms.*, 1706–1788. A Congregational clergyman of Boston famous both as preacher and wit. After 43 years' ministry in the Hollis Street Church, his Tory sympathies obliged him to give up his charge in 1776. *See Sprague's Annals of the American Pulpit; Tyler's American Literature; Unitarian Review, vol. 27; Atlantic Monthly, vol. 59.*

Bynner, Edwin Lassetter. *N. Y.*, 1842–1893. A popular historical novelist of Boston. His best work is included in the three historical tales, Agnes Surriage; The Begum's Daughter; Zachary Phips. Of lesser importance are Nimport; Tritons; Damen's Ghost; Penelope's Suitors; An Uncloseted Skeleton (with L. P. Hale, *infra*); The Chase of the Meteor, a book for boys. *Hou.*

Byrd, William. *Va.*, 1674–1744. A colonial Virginian and man of letters, whose Journals, first published in 1841, are known as The Westover Manuscripts, from Westover, the family mansion of Byrd. A fuller collection, styled The Byrd Manuscripts, was printed in 1866, edited by T. Wynne. They are well worth reading for their wit, keen observations, and vigourous style. They comprise The Story of the Dividing Line, an account of the expedition to fix the boundary between Virginia and North Carolina; A Progress to the Mines; A Journey to the Land of Eden. *See Hart's American Literature; Tyler's American Literature; Century Magazine, vol. 20.*

Byrn, Marcus Lafayette. 18——. A physician. Complete Practical Brewer; Rattlehead's Travels, or the Recollections of a Backwoodsman; Complete Practical Distiller; Repository of Wit and Humour; Book of Nature, an expositor of the Science of Life and Sexual Physiology; Family Physician.

C

Cabell, James Lawrence. *Va.*, 1813–1889. An eminent Virginia physician. The Testimony of Modern Science to the Unity of Mankind.

Cabell, Mrs. Julia [Mayo]. *Va.*, 18—185–. An Odd Volume of Facts and Fiction in Prose and Verse; Sketches and Recollections of Lynchburg.

Cable, George Washington. *La.*, 1844——. A writer of fiction who has reproduced with much success the life and dialect among the creoles of Louisiana. He served in the Confederate army during the Civil War, and is now a resident of Northampton, Massachusetts. Old Creole Days; The Grandissimes; Madame Delphine; Dr. Sevier; John March, Southerner; Bonaventure; Strange True Stories of Louisiana; The Creoles of Louisiana; The Silent South; The Busy Man's Bible; The Negro Question. *See Vedder's American Writers. Fl. Scr.*

Cabot, James Elliot. *Ms.*, 1821——. A Boston writer whose principal work is A Memoir of Ralph Waldo Emerson. *Hou.*

Cahan, Abraham. *R.*, 1860——. A New York city journalist, editor of Zukunft. Yekl, a Tale of the New York Ghetto; Raphael Narizokh (in Yiddish). *Ap.*

Cain, William. *N. C.*, 1847——. A professor of civil engineering in the University of North Carolina. Theory of Voussoir; Solid and Braced Arches; Maximum Stress in Framed Bridges; Solid and Braced Elastic Bridges; Symbolic Algebra; Practical Designing of Retaining Walls.

Caines, George. 1771–1825. A reporter of the New York Supreme Court. Lex Mercatoria Americana; Cases in the Court of Errors; Forms of New York Supreme Court; Summary of Practice in New York Supreme Court; Cases in the Court for Trial of Impeachments; New York Supreme Court Reports.

Caldwell, Charles. *N. C.*, 1772–1853. A Kentucky physician, who beside publishing some 200 technical monographs and pamphlets, wrote The Life and Campaigns of General Greene, and translated Blumenbach's Elements of Physiology. *See Autobiography, 1855; Life, by Caruthers, infra; Sketches of Contemporaries, by S. D. Gross, infra.*

Caldwell, George Chapman. *Ms.*, 1834——. A professor of agricultural chemistry at Cornell University. Agricultural Qualitative and Quantitative Analysis; Manual of Introductory Chemical Practice (with A. Breneman); Manual of Qualitative Chemical Analysis (with S. M. Babcock).

Caldwell, Joseph. *N. J.*, 1773–1835. A once noted educator who was president of the University of North Carolina. A Compendious System of Elementary Geometry; Letters of Carleton.

Caldwell, Linus Boues. *N. Y.*, 1834——. A Methodist clergyman and educator, of Tennessee. Wines of Palestine, or The Bible Defended; Beyond the Grave.

Caldwell, Merritt. *Me.*, 1806–1848. A professor of metaphysics at Dickinson College. The Doctrine of the English Verb; Manual of Elocution; Philosophy of Christian Perfection; Christianity Tested by Eminent Men. *See Memoir by S. M. Vail. Meth.*

Caldwell, Samuel Lunt. *Ms.*, 1820–1889. A Baptist clergyman whose later life was passed in Providence. Cities of Our Faith and Other Addresses and Discourses. *Hou.*

Caldwell, William Warren. *Ms.*, 1823——. A resident of Newburyport who has published Poems, Original and Translated, and has translated many lyrics from the German.

Calef, Robert. *Ms.*, *c.* 1648–1719. A Boston merchant who published in 1700 More Wonders of the Invisible World, a satirical reply to Cotton Mather's Wonders of the Invisible World. Its line of argument was in direct opposition to the witchcraft persecutions, and the book was publicly burnt by Increase Mather in the grounds of Harvard College. *See Tyler's American Literature.*

Calhoun [kăl-hoon′], **John Caldwell.** *S. C.*, 1782–1850. A South Carolina statesman who was secretary of state under Monroe, and again under Tyler, vice-president under John Quincy Adams, and United States senator from 1845 till his death. He was one of the ablest of political leaders, a great orator, and a political thinker of the first rank. His literary style is both vigourous and concise, and displays at times a remarkable intensity of expression. A Disquisition on Government; The Constitution and Government of the United States. *See Works in 6 volumes; Parton's Famous Americans; Lives by Jenkins; Von Holst. Ap.*

Calkins, Norman Allison. *N. Y.*, 1822–1895. The first assistant superintendent of primary schools in New York city for thirty-three years. Primary Object Lessons; How to Teach; Manual of Object Teaching; Aids for Object Teaching; Trades and Occupations; Natural History Series for Children.

Callender, James Thomas. *E.*, 17—1803. A writer who was exiled from England on account of his pamphlet, The Political Progress of Great Britain. He was at first the friend and soon the violent political opponent of Thomas Jefferson. Sketches of the History of America; The Prospect before Us.

Callender, John. *Ms.*, 1706–1748. A Baptist clergyman of Newport, Rhode Island, whose Historical Discourse, 1739, is a careful monograph of Rhode Island history for the first century of the colony's existence. *See edition of 1838, with notes and memoir.*

Calthrop, Samuel Robert. *E.*, 1829——. A Unitarian clergyman of Syracuse. Essay on Religion and Science; The Rights of the Body.

Calvert, George Henry. *Md.*, 1803–1889. A littérateur of Newport, Rhode Island, who published a great number of volumes of verse that never was mistaken for poetry by any reader, and almost as many prose works. Among his writings are Goethe: his Life and Works; Dante and his Latest Translators; St. Beuve, the Critic; Count Julian, a tragedy; Three Score, and Other Poems; a translation of Schiller's Don Carlos.

Cameron, Henry Clay. *W. Va.*, 1827——. A professor at Princeton College since 1877. Princeton Roll of Honour; History of American Whig Society.

Camp, Walter. *Ct.*, 1859——. A writer of prominence on athletic matters. Book of College Sports; American Football; Football Facts and Figures; Football (with L. F. Deland). *Har. Hou.*

Campbell, Alexander. *I.*, 1788–1866. A Baptist clergyman of West Virginia, who was the founder of the sect of Campbellites, or Disciples of Christ. He established Bethany College in 1841, and was its first president. His writings, mainly controversial, are nearly sixty in number, among them being Christian Baptism; Infidelity Refuted by Infidels; Essay on Life and Death; Popular Lectures and Addresses; Christianity as it Was; Familiar Lectures on the Pentateuch; Six Letters to a Sceptic. *See Hart's American Literature; Memoir by Richardson, 1868.*

Campbell, Alexander Augustus. *Va.*, 1789–1846. A Presbyterian clergyman and physician, once prominent in Tennessee, whose only book was a work on Scripture Baptism.

Campbell, Alexander James. 18——. Son of A. Campbell, *supra.* The Power of Christ to Save to the Uttermost; American Practical Cyclopædia; A True Friend, reflections on Life, Character, and Conduct.

Campbell, Bartley. *Pa.*, 1843–1888. A journalist of Pittsburg, who turned his attention to the stage and became a popular playwright. My Partner; The Galley Slave; Matrimony; Siberia; The Big Bonanza; The White Slave; and Peril, comprising his most successful plays.

Campbell, Charles. *Va.*, 1807–1876. An educator of Petersburg, Virginia, whose father, John Wilson Campbell, a bookseller there for many years, wrote a History of Virginia to 1781. The writings of Charles Campbell include History of the Colony of Virginia; Genealogy of the Spotswood Family; The Bland Papers; Memoir of John Daly Burk, *supra. Lip.*

Campbell, Douglas. *N. Y.*, 1840–1893. Son of W. W. Campbell, *infra.* A lawyer of New York city, whose notable historical work, The Puritan in Holland, England, and America, has attracted much attention. *Har.*

Campbell, Douglas Houghton. *Mch.*, 1859——. A professor of botany in Stanford University. Elements of Structural and Systematic Botany; Structure and Development of the Mosses and Ferns. *Mac.*

Campbell, Mrs. Helen [Stuart]. 1839——. A writer who is deeply concerned in philanthropic and social reforms, and whose work covers a wide range of topics. In Foreign Kitchens; The Easiest Way in Housekeeping, are books for the housekeeper. Prisoners of Poverty; Prisoners of Poverty Abroad; Some Passages in the Life of Dr. Martha Scarborough; Women Wage-Earners; Problem of the Poor; Darkness and Daylight in New York, relate to the social problems of the time. Six Sinners; His Grandmothers; Roger Berkeley's Probation; Miss Melinda's Opportunity; Mrs. Herndon's Income; The What-to-Do-Club; Under Green Apple-Boughs; Unto the Third and Fourth Generation; Patty Pearson's Boy, are fictions. Other works are Girls' Handbook of Work and Play; A Sylvan City, a description of Philadelphia; The Ainslee Stories, for juvenile readers; Anne Bradstreet and her Time, *supra. Fo. Hou. Lo. Rob.*

Campbell, James Valentine. *N. Y.*, 1823–1890. A Michigan jurist. Outlines of the Political History of Michigan.

Campbell, John Lyle. *Va.*, 1818–1886. A professor of chemistry at Washington and Lee College, 1851–86. Manual of Scientific and Practical Agriculture; Idaho, Six Months in the New Gold Diggings; Guide to the Agricultural and Mineral West; Geology and Mineral Resources of the James River Valley, Virginia.

Campbell, John Poage. *Va.*, 1767–1814. A once popular clergyman on the Ohio border. The Passenger; Strictures on Stone's Letters on the Atonement; Vindex; Letters to the Rev. Mr. Craighead; The Pelagian Defeated; An Answer to Jones.

Campbell, William Henry. *Md.*, 1808–1890. A Dutch Reformed clergyman, president of Rutgers College, 1863–82. Subjects and Modes of Baptism; Influence of Christianity in Civil and Religious Liberty; System of Catechetical Instruction.

Campbell, William W. *N. Y.*, 1806–1881. A jurist of New York city. Annals of Tryon County, reissued as Border Warfare; Memoirs of Mrs. Grant, Missionary to Persia; Life and Writings of De Witt Clinton; Sketches of Robin Hood and Captain Kidd.

Canfield, Henry Judson. *Ct.*, 1789–1856. An agriculturist who published a serviceable Treatise on the Breed, Management, Structure, and Diseases of Sheep.

Cannon, Charles James. *N. Y.*, 1810–1860. A New York littérateur who besides compiling a series of readers published, among other works, Poems, Dramatic and Miscellaneous; Pencillings from the Web of Life, and a number of dramas now forgotten.

Cannon, James Spencer. *W. I.*, 1776–1852. A Dutch Reformed clergyman of New Jersey, professor of metaphysics at Rutgers College, 1826–56. Lectures on Chronology; Lectures on Pastoral Theology.

Capen, Nahum. *Ms.*, 1804–1886. A Boston publisher who was postmaster 1857–61, and introduced the custom of street letter-box collections. The Republic of the United States; Reminiscences of Spurzheim and Combe; History of Democracy, or Political Progress Historically Illustrated.

Capers, William. *S. C.*, 1790–1855. A Methodist bishop once prominent in the South. Cathechisms for Negro Missions; Short Sermons and True Tales for Children. *See Life, by Wightman, 1859.*

Carey, Henry Charles. *Pa.*, 1793–1879. Son of M. Carey, *infra*. One of the foremost of American political economists, who advocated protection as a preliminary step toward ultimate free trade. He opposed such theorists as Malthus and Ricardo, holding that human progress depends upon success in subjugating nature; that land values depend upon labour; and that the social well-being is directly dependent upon existing conditions. Principles of Political Economy; The Credit System; The Principles of Social Science; Lectures on the Currency; Letters on Political Economy; Letters on International Copyright; Financial Crises; The Unity of Law, comprise his chief works. *See Allibone's Dictionary; Memoir by Elder; Gross's Sketches of Contemporaries. Bai. Lip.*

Carey, Matthew. *I.*, 1760–1839. An Irishman who came to America in 1785, entered into politics, and established himself in Philadelphia as a bookseller. His writings include The Olive Branch, or Faults on Both Sides, Federal and Democratic (1814), which soon entered a tenth edition; Vindiciæ Hibernicæ; Thoughts on Penitentiaries and Prison Discipline; Essays on Political Economy; The Yellow Fever of 1793.

Carleton, Henry Guy. *N. M.*, 1856–——. A journalist of New York city who is best known as a writer of plays, among which are Memnon; The Pembertons; Victor Durand.

Carleton, Osgood. 1742–1816. A Massachusetts mathematician. American Navigator; South American Pilot; Practice of Arithmetic.

Carleton, William. *Mch.*, 1845——. A writer of homely verse which appeals with great force to imperfectly educated tastes, and has been very popular, but which is without literary merit. Farm Ballads; Farm Festivals; Farm Legends; City Legends; City Ballads; City Festivals; Rhymes of onr Planet; Young Folks' Centennial Rhymes; The Old Infant, and Similar Stories. *Har.*

Carman [William], Bliss. *N. B.*, 1861——. A poet of Canadian birth, whose literary work has been done mainly in New York and Boston. Low Tide on Grand Pré; A Seamark; Behind the Arras; Songs from Vagabondia (with R. Hovey, *infra*); More Songs from Vagabondia (with R. Hovey); Ballads of Lost Haven, a Book of the Sea. *Cop. Lam.*

Carnegie, Andrew. *S.*, 1835——. A noted steel-manufacturer of Pittsburg who came to America in 1845. He has made many important gifts to his native Scotland and to Pittsburg, and as a writer is distinguished for the rather exuberant Americanism of his work. An American Four-in-Hand in Europe; Round the World; Triumphant Democracy, or Fifty Years' March of the Republic. *Scr.*

Carnochan, John Murray. *Ga.*, 1817-1887. A New York surgeon of distinction. Treatise on Congenital Dislocations; Contributions to Operative Surgery. *Har.*

Carpenter, Edmund Janes. *Ms.*, 1845——. A journalist of Boston. A Woman of Shawmut, a Romance of Colonial Times; History of Roger Williams. *Lit.*

Carpenter, Esther Bernon. *R. I.*, 1848-1893. A writer of southern Rhode Island, whose South Country Neighbours is a series of sympathetic studies in fiction of Rhode Island types of character. *Rob.*

Carpenter, Francis Bicknell. *N. Y.*, 1830——. A portrait painter of New York city, who painted The Emancipation Proclamation in the Capitol at Washington. Six Months in the White House with Abraham Lincoln.

Carpenter, Henry Bernard. *I.*, 1840-1890. A Unitarian clergyman of Boston, brother of W. Boyd Carpenter, the Anglican bishop of Ripon. He wrote principally in verse, his only published books including The Oatmeal Crusaders; Liber Amoris, a Metrical Romaunt of the Middle Ages; A Poet's Last Songs. The last-named volume was issued after his death, with memorial sketch by J. J. Roche, *infra. Hou.*

Carpenter, Stephen Cutter. *E.*, c. 17—1820. An English journalist who came to America in 1803 and settled in Charleston. Memoir of Thomas Jefferson, containing a Concise History of the United States (1809); An Overland Journey to India, published under the pseudonym "Donald Campbell."

Carpenter, Stephen Haskins. *N. J.*, 1831-1878. A Wisconsin educator, professor of literature at the University of Wisconsin. Evidences of Christianity; English of the 14th Century; Introduction to the Study of Anglo-Saxon; Elements of English Analysis. *Gi.*

Carr, Lucien. *Mo.*, 1829——. An archæologist of Cambridge, assistant curator of the Peabody Museum, 1876-1894. The Mounds of the Mississippi Valley Historically Considered; Missouri, a brief history of the State; Prehistoric Remains of Kentucky (with N. S. Shaler, *infra*). *Clke. Hou.*

Carrier, Augustus Stiles. *N. Y.*, 1857. A Presbyterian clergyman of Chicago, professor of Hebrew in McCormick Theological Seminary from 1892. The Hebrew Verb, a Series of Tabular Studies.

Carrington, Henry Beebe. *Ct.*, 1824——. A general in the United States army living in Boston. His principal writings include Crisis Thoughts; Battles of the American Revolution; Apsaraka, or Indian Operations on the Plains; Hints to Soldiers Taking the Field; The Washington Obelisk and its Voices. *See One of a Thousand. Bar. Le. Lip.*

Carrol, John. *Md.*, 1735-1817. The first Roman Catholic archbishop of Baltimore. His writings are mainly of a controversial cast. Concise View of the Principal Points of Controversy between the Protestant and Catholic Churches; Discourse on General Washington.

Carroll, Anna Ella. *Md.*, 1815-1894. A political writer who was the real author of the Federal campaign of 1862 in Tennessee. The Great American Battle, or The Contest between Christianity and Political Romanism; The Star of the West, or National Men and National Measures; The Union of the States; The War Powers of the General Government; The Relation of the National Government to the Revolted Citizens Defined. *See S. E. Blackwell's A Military Genius.*

Carroll, Henry King. *N. J.*, 1847——. A Methodist clergyman and religious statistician. The World of Missions; The Catholic Dogma of

Church Authority; The Religious Forces of the United States.

Carryl, Charles Edward. *N. Y.*, 1841——. A broker of New York city, the author of the popular juvenile tales, Davy and the Goblin; The Admiral's Caravan. *Cent. Hou.*

Carson, Joseph. 1808–1876. A medical professor at the University of Pennsylvania from 1850. Illustrations of Medical Botany; Lectures on Materia Medica and Pharmacy.

Carter, Franklin. *Ct.*, 1837——. President of Williams College. Life of Mark Hopkins, *infra*, and a scholarly translation of Goethe's Iphigenie auf Tauris. *Hou.*

Carter, James Gordon. *Ms.*, 1795–1849. A once prominent educator of Massachusetts. Essays on Popular Education; Geography of New Hampshire; Geography of Massachusetts; Letters to William Prescott on the Free Schools of New England.

Carter, Nathaniel Franklin. *N. H.*, 1830——. A Congregational clergyman in New Hampshire. The Ride for Life, and Other Poems; History of Pembroke, New Hampshire.

Carter, Nathaniel Hazeltine. *N. H.*, 1787–1830. A New York journalist who published Letters from Europe (1827), and wrote many poems of reflection.

Carter, Peter. *S.*, 1825——. A prominent New York publisher. Crumbs from the Land of Cakes, a volume of travels in Scotland; Scotia's Bards; and three juvenile tales, including Bertie Lee; Donald Fraser; Effie's Home.

Carter, Robert. *N. Y.*, 1819–1879. A New York writer who was one of the editors of Appleton's American Cyclopædia, to which he contributed many articles. A Summer Cruise on the Coast of New England was his only book of importance.

Carter, Russel Kelso. *Md.*, 1849——. A mathematician of Chester, Pennsylvania, prominent in the "Holiness" movement in the Methodist church and as a Faith healer. The Atonement for Sin and Sickness; Miracles of Healing.

Cartwright, Peter. *Va.*, 1785–1872. A once famous Methodist preacher of Illinois. Controversy with the Devil; Autobiography of a Backwoods Preacher; Fifty Years a Presiding Elder.

Caruthers, William Alexander. *Va.*, 1800–1850. A physician of Savannah who wrote a number of romances now quite forgotten. The Kentuckian in New York; The Cavaliers of Virginia; Knights of the Horse Shoe; Life of Charles Caldwell, *supra*.

Cary, Alice. *O.*, 1820–1871. An Ohio writer who came with her sister Phœbe to New York city in 1852, and as poet and novelist became prominent in literary circles there. The weekly receptions of the sisters were attended by artists and writers for many years. Her books of verse include Lyra, and Other Poems; A Lover's Diary; Ballads, Lyrics, and Hymns; Early and Late Poems (with Phœbe Cary, *infra*). Her other works are Clovernook, a book of the type of Miss Mitford's Our Village; Pictures of Country Life; the novels, Hagar; The Bishop's Son; Married, not Mated. Snowberries, a juvenile; From Year to Year, a Token of Remembrance (with P. Cary). *See Memorials of Alice and Phœbe Cary, by Mrs. [Clemmer] Hudson. Hou. Lip.*

Cary, Edward. *N. Y.*, 1840——. A journalist of New York city on the editorial staff of The Times. Life of George William Curtis, *infra*. *Hou.*

Cary, George Lovell. *Ms.*, 1830——. A professor of New Testament literature at Meadville Theological Seminary since 1862. Introduction to the Greek of the New Testament.

Cary, Phœbe. *O.*, 1824–1871. Sister of A. Cary, *supra*. Poems and Parodies; Poems of Faith, Hope, and Love. She will be longest remembered by the well-known hymn, Nearer Home. *Hou. Lip.*

Casey, Silas. *R. I.*, 1807–1882. A general in the United States army who published Infantry Tactics; Infantry Tactics for Colored Troops.

Cass, Lewis. *N. H.*, 1782–1866. A statesman of Michigan who was the Democratic candidate for president in 1845. Inquiries Concerning the History, Traditions, and Languages of the Indians in the United States; France, its King, Court, and Government, 1840. *See Lives by Schoolcraft, 1848; W. L. G. Smith, 1856; McLaughlin, 1891.*

Cassin, John. *Pa.*, 1813–1869. A naturalist of Philadelphia whose American Ornithology is a continuation of Audubon's work on that subject. Other works of his are Ornithology of the Japan Expedition; Mammalogy and Ornithology of the Wilkes Exploring Expedition; Illustrations of the Birds of California, Texas, etc.; A General Synopsis of North American Ornithology. *Lip.*

Castlemon, Harry. *See Fosdick.*

Caswall, Henry. *E.*, 1810–1870. An Episcopal clergyman of English birth, but ordained in the United States, where the most of his life was spent. He lived for a time in England, however, and was a prebend of Salisbury. An Epitome of the History of the American Episcopal Church (1836); Didascalus, or The Teacher; Mormonism and its Author; The Jerusalem Chamber, or Convocation and its Possibilities; The Californian Crusoe, a Tale of Mormonism; Scotland and the Scottish Church; The Western World Revisited; The Martyr of the Pongas; The American Church and the American Union, include the majority of his writings.

Caswell, Alexis. *Ms.*, 1799–1877. A Baptist clergyman and educator; for 35 years a professor at Brown University, and its president, 1868-72. Lectures on Astronomy; Meteorological Observations.

Cathcart, William. *I.*, 1826——. A Baptist clergyman of Philadelphia. The Baptists and the American Revolution; The Papal System; The Baptism of the Ages and the Nations; The Baptist Encyclopædia.

Catherwood, Mrs. Mary [Hartwell]. *O.*, 1847——. A writer of Hoopeston, Illinois, whose historical romances dealing with the early days of Canada and the Northwest are as notable for their careful attention to historical details as for their graphic and picturesque style. A Woman in Armour; The Lady of Fort St. John; The Romance of Dollard; Story of Tonty; Old Kaskaskia; The Chase of St. Castin, and Other Tales; The Spirit of an Illinois Town; The White Islander, a story of Mackinac; Craque o' Doom. Her books for young people include Old Caravan Days; The Dogberry Bunch; Rocky Fork; The Secrets of Roseladies. *Cent. Hou. Lip. Lo. Mg.*

Catlin, George. *Pa.*, 1796–1872. An artist who spent many years among the Indians. Notes of Eight Years in Europe; Illustrations of the Manners, Customs, and Condition of the North American Indians; Notes for the Emigrant to America; Life among the Indians, a Book for Youth; The Breath of Life, or Mal-Respiration and its Effects; O-Kee-Pa, a Religious Ceremony, and other Customs of the Mandans; Last Rambles Among the Indians of the Rocky Mountains; The Lifted and Subsided Rocks of America. *See Tuckerman's Book of the Artists.*

Catlin, George Lynde. *S. I.*, 1840–1896. A journalist and diplomat, consul at Limoges, Stuttgart, and Zurich. Bilbigheim, a story; The Presidential Campaign of 1896, written in 1888; Titbits for Travellers; The Postilion of Nagold and Other Poems. *Fu.*

Caton, John Dean. *N. Y.*, 1812–1895. A jurist of Chicago. A Summer in Norway; The Last of the Illinois and a Sketch of the Pottawatomies; The Antelope and the Deer of America; Miscellanies, Speeches, and Essays.

Caulkins, Frances Mainwaring. *Ct.*, 1796–1869. A local historian of Connecticut. A History of Norwich; A History of New London.

Cawein, Madison Julius. *Ky.*, 1865——. A poet of Louisville, Kentucky, whose verse is very musical, and shows much individuality. Days and Dreams; Moods and Memories; Intimations of the Beautiful; Blooms of the Berry; The Triumph of Music; Accolon of Gaul; Lyrics and Idyls; Poems of Nature and Love; Red Leaves and Roses; The Garden of Dreams; Undertones. *Cop. Mor. Put.*

Cesnola [ches-no'la], **Luigi Palma di.** *It.*, 1832——. An archæologist who served in the Union army during the War and became a colonel, but has for

Castle, Edgerton.

a number of years filled the position of director of the Metropolitan Museum of New York city. Cyprus, its Ancient Cities, Tombs, and Temples; The Metropolitan Museum of Art. *Ap. Har.*

Chadbourne, Paul Ansel. *Me.*, 1823–1883. A Congregational clergyman who was president of Williams College, 1872–81. Relations of Natural History to Intellect, Taste, Wealth, and Religion; Natural Theology; Instinct in Animals and Men; Strength of Men and Stability of Nations; The Hope of the Righteous; The Public Services of the State of New York [with W. B. Moore]. *Bar. Put.*

Chadwick, Henry. *N. H.*, 1824——. An authority on games and sports. Base Ball Players' Book of Reference; Base Ball, How to Learn, Play, and Teach It; Base Ball Manual; Sports and Pastimes of American Boys.

Chadwick, John White. *Ms.*, 1840——. A Unitarian clergyman of Brooklyn, prominent among the more radical thinkers of his denomination. The Man Jesus; The Faith of Reason; The Bible of To-Day; Old and New Unitarian Belief; The Power of an Endless Life; The Revelation of God, and Other Sermons; Thomas Paine: the Method and Value of his Religious Teachings; George William Curtis: an Address; A Book of Poems; In Nazareth Town, and Other Poems. *Har. Put. Rob.*

Chaffin, William Ladd. 18——. A Unitarian clergyman of Easton, Massachusetts, whose History of Easton is of notable excellence.

Chaillé, Stanford Emerson. *Mi.*, 1830——. A prominent physician of New Orleans. Yellow Fever in Havana and Cuba; Laws of Population and Voters; Living, Dying, Registering, and Voting Population of Louisiana; Intimidation of Voters in Louisiana; Origin and Progress of Medical Jurisprudence, 1776–1876.

Chalkley, Thomas. *E.*, 1675–1741. A Quaker itinerant preacher born in London, who spent his life preaching throughout New England and the Southern colonies. His writings, consisting of religious tracts and a Journal of his experiences, published as Life, Labours, and Travels, are noted for their quaint simplicity. His Journal has been very popular among the Friends, and has been several times reprinted. *See Dictionary of National Biography, vol. 9.*

Chalmers, Lionel. *S.*, c. 1715–1777. A once noted physician of Charleston. Treatise on the Weather and Diseases of South Carolina; Essay on Fevers.

Chamberlain, Jacob. *Ct.*, 1835——. A Reformed Dutch missionary to India. The Bible Tested is his most important work.

Chamberlain, Nathan Henry. *Ms.*, 1830——. An Episcopal clergyman of Massachusetts, whose principal writings include The Autobiography of a New England Farm House; Samuel Sewell and the World he Lived In; The Sphinx in Aubrey Parish.

Chamberlayne, Israel. *N.Y.*, 1795–1875. A Methodist clergyman. The Past and the Future; The Australian Captive; Saving Faith: its Rationale; The Great Specific against Despair of Pardon. *Meth.*

Chamberlin, Joseph Edgar. *Vt.*, 1851——. A Boston journalist on the staffs of The Transcript and the Youth's Companion. The Listener in the Town; The Listener in the Country. *Cop.*

Chamberlin, Thomas Chrowder. *Il.*, 1843——. A prominent geologist of Wisconsin. Outline of a Course of Oral Instruction; Geology of Wisconsin.

Chambers, Charles Julius. *O.*, 1850——. A journalist long connected with the New York Herald. A Mad World and its Inhabitants, a description of lunatic asylums founded on the author's personal experience in one in disguise; On a Margin, a Story of These Times; Lovers Four and Maidens Five, a Story. *Ap. Fu.*

Chambers, Robert William. *L. I.*, 1865——. A novelist and artist of New York city. In the Quarter; The King in Yellow; The Red Republic; The Maker of Moons; The Mystery of Choice; A King and a Few Dukes; With the Band, a book of ballads. *Ne. Put. St.*

Chambers, Talbot Wilson. *Pa.*, 1819–1896. A noted Reformed Dutch clergyman of New York city. The Noon Prayer Meeting in Fulton Street;

Memoir of Theodore Frelinghuysen; The Psalter a Witness to the Divine Origin of the Bible; Companion to the Revised Version of the Old Testament. *Fu.*

Champlin, James Tifft. *Ct.*, 1811-1882. A Baptist clergyman of Portland, Maine, president of Colby University, 1857-73. First Principles of Ethics; Lessons on Political Economy; Text-Book of Intellectual Philosophy; Scripture Reading Lessons; The Constitution of the United States, with Brief Comments; and a series of classical text-books. *See Bibliography of Maine.*

Champlin, John Denison. *Ct.*, 1834——. A littérateur of New York city. Young Folks' Cyclopædia of Common Things; Young Folks' Cyclopædia of Persons and Places; Young Folks' History of the War for the Union; Young Folks' Catechism of Common Things; Young Folks' Cyclopædia of Games and Sports; Young Folks' Astronomy; Chronicle of the Coach: Charing Cross to Ilfracombe. With W. F. Apthorp, *supra*, he has edited a Cyclopædia of Music and Musicians, and with C. C. Perkins, *infra*, a Cyclopædia of Painters and Paintings. *Ho. Scr.*

Champney, Mrs. Elizabeth [Williams]. *O.*, 1850——. A popular New York writer for young people, and wife of the artist, J. Wells Champney, who has illustrated many of her books. The Three Vassar Girls Series; The Witch Winnie Books; The Bubbling Teapot; Howling Wolf and his Trick-Pony; All Around a Palette; Children's Art Sketches; In the Sky Garden; Fables in Astronomy, and other juveniles; and the novels, Bourbon Lilies; Sebia's Tangled Web; Rosemary and Rue. *Do. Est. Lo. Ran.*

Chancellor, Charles Williams. *Va.*, 1833——. An eminent physician of Baltimore. Prisons, Reformatories, and Charitable Institutions of Maryland; Mineral Waters and Seaside Resorts; Contagious and Infectious Diseases; Drainage of the Marsh Lands of Maryland; Heredity; The Sewerage of Cities.

Chandler, Bessie. *See Parker, Mrs.*

Chandler, Elizabeth Margaret. *Del.*, 1807-1835. A verse-writer whose themes were mainly those relating to the subject of anti-slavery, in which she was greatly interested. *See Poetical Works and Essays, with Memoir by Benjamin Lundy.*

Chandler, Peleg Whitman. *Me.*, 1816-1889. A prominent lawyer of Boston. The Bankrupt Law of the United States; American Criminal Trials; Memoir of Governor Andrew; Observations on the Authenticity of the Gospels. *Rob.*

Chaney, George Leonard. *Ms.*, 1836——. A Unitarian clergyman, pastor of the Hollis Street Church in Boston, 1862-79, and subsequently pastor in Atlanta, Georgia, where he edited the Southern Unitarian, 1893-96. F. Grant & Co., a story for boys; Tom, a Home Story; Aloha, travels in the Sandwich Islands; Every Day Life and Every Day Morals; Belief. *Rob.*

Chaney, Lucien West. *N. Y.*, 1857——. A naturalist, professor of biology in Carleton College, Minnesota, since 1882, and author of Guides for the Laboratory.

Chanler, Mrs. Amélie Rives. *See Troubetzkoy.*

Channing, Edward. *Ms.*, 1856——. Son of W. E. Channing, 2d. A professor of history at Harvard University since 1883. Guide to the Study of American History (with A. B. Hart, *infra*); Town and County Government of the English Colonies of North America; Narragansett Planters; The United States of America, 1765-1865. *Gi. Mac.*

Channing, Edward Tyrrel. *R. I.*, 1790-1856. Brother of W. E. Channing, *infra.* A professor of rhetoric and oratory at Harvard University. Life of William Ellery; Lectures on Rhetoric and Oratory (with Memoir by R. H. Dana, Jr.).

Channing, Walter. *R. I.*, 1786-1876. Brother of W. E. Channing, *infra.* A physician of prominence in Boston for many years, and medical professor in Harvard University. The Prevention of Pauperism; Etherization in Childbirth; Professional Reminiscences of Foreign Travel; New and Old; Miscellaneous Poems; A Physician's Vacation, or A Summer in Europe; Reformation of Medical Science.

Channing, William Ellery. *R. I.*, 1780–1842. A Unitarian theologian of eminence, who became pastor of the Federal Street Church in Boston in 1803. He was the foremost theologian in America in his time, and his influence is still great. He wrote upon philanthropic and social as well as religious and ethical questions, and was a noted opponent of slavery. His writings have been translated into French, Italian, German, Icelandic, Russian, and Hungarian. Evidences of Revealed Religion; Self-Culture; Essay on Milton; The Duty of the Free States, are among his most notable works. *See Sprague's Annals of the American Pulpit; Lives by W. H. Channing, infra; C. T. Brooks, supra; Reminiscences by Miss Peabody; Correspondence of Channing and Lucy Aikin; New England Magazine, December, 1896. A. U. A.*

Channing, William Ellery. *Ms.*, 1818——. Son of W. Channing, *supra.* A poet and essayist of Concord, Massachusetts, who married a sister of Margaret Fuller, *infra.* His verse is thoroughly original in tone and more or less willful in form. His work in verse includes The Youth of the Painter, a series of psychological essays; Poems 1843–47; The Woodman; The Wanderer; Near Home; Eliot; John Brown. Thoreau, the Poet Naturalist; Conversations in Rome between an Artist, a Catholic, and a Critic, are prose volumes.

Channing, William Francis. *Ms.*, 1820——. Son of W. E. Channing, 1st. A physician, scientist, and inventor. Davis's Manual of Magnetism; Medical Application of Electricity; The American Fire Alarm Telegraph.

Channing, William Henry. *Ms.*, 1810–1884. Nephew of W. E. Channing. A Unitarian clergyman who settled in England, and succeeded James Martineau as pastor of the Unitarian Chapel in Hope Street, Liverpool. The Christian Church and Social Reform; Memoirs of Wm. E. Channing; Memoirs of James H. Perkins; Memoirs of Margaret Fuller (with R. W. Emerson and J. F. Clarke). *A. U. A.*

Chapin, Aaron Lucius. *Ct.*, 1817–1892. A Congregational clergyman of Wisconsin, who was president of Beloit College, 1849–86. First Principles of Political Economy.

Chapin, Alonzo Bowen. *Ct.*, 1808–1858. An Episcopal clergyman of Hartford. Classical Spelling-Book; Organization and Order of the Primitive Church; Views of Gospel Truth; Glastenbury for 200 Years (1853); Puritanism not Protestantism.

Chapin, Edwin Hubbell. *N. Y.*, 1814–1881. A Universalist clergyman of New York city, long the foremost preacher in his denomination. The Crown of Thorns; Humanity in the City; Christianity the Perfection of True Manliness; Moral Aspects of City Life; Discourses on the Lord's Prayer; Hours of Communion; Token for the Sorrowing; Characters in the Gospels. *See Life, by Sumner Ellis.*

Chapin, James Henry. *Ind.*, 1832–1892. A Universalist clergyman and educator, professor of geology in St. Lawrence University, 1871–92. Sketches of the Huguenots; The Creation and Early Development of Mankind; From Japan to Granada, a Tour Around the World. *See Life of, by G. S. Weaver. Put.*

Chaplin, Mrs. Ada C. *Ms.*, 1842–1883. A Massachusetts writer of religious juveniles, some of which are Christ's Cadets; Charity Hurlburt; Our Gold Mine, the Story of American Baptist Missions in India.

Chaplin, Heman White. *R. I.*, 1847——. Son of J. Chaplin, 2d. A lawyer of Boston, whose Five Hundred Dollars, and Other Stories of New England Life, are exceptionally faithful and delicate studies of character, and rank among the foremost of American short stories. *Lit.*

Chaplin, Mrs. Jane [Dunbar]. *S.*, 1819–1884. Wife of J. Chaplin, 2d, *infra*, and daughter of Duncan Dunbar. Among her various writings, mainly religious juveniles, are The Transplanted Shamrock; Black and White; The Convent and the Manse.

Chaplin, Jeremiah. *Ms.*, 1776–1841. A Baptist clergyman and educator, the first president of Colby University, 1822–33. The Evening of Life.

Chaplin, Jeremiah. *Ms.*, 1813–1886. Son of J. Chaplin, *supra.* A Baptist clergyman of Newton, Massachusetts, who after leaving the ministry devoted himself to literary pursuits in Boston. The Memorial Hour; The Hand of Jesus; Riches of Bunyan; Life of Henry Dunster, First President of Harvard College; Chips from the White House; Life of Benjamin Franklin; Life of Galen; Life of Duncan Dunbar; Life of Charles Sumner (with Jane Chaplin). *Lo.*

Chapman, Alvan Wentworth. *Ms.*, 1809——. A botanist for whom the genus Chapmannia was named. Flora of the Southern United States.

Chapman, George Thomas. *E.*, 1786–1872. An Episcopal clergyman. Sketches of Alumni of Dartmouth College from 1771–1868.

Chapman, Henry Cadwalader. *Pa.*, 1845——. Grandson of N. Chapman, *infra.* A physician of Philadelphia. Evolution of Life; History of the Discovery of the Circulation of the Blood.

Chapman, Nathaniel. *Va.*, 1780–1853. A Philadelphia physician and professor of medicine in the University of Pennsylvania, 1814–50. Materia Medica and Therapeutics, long a valued text-book; Select Speeches (edited); Lectures on Eruptive Fevers, Hemorrhages and Dropsies; Lectures on Thoracic Viscera. *See Gross's Sketches of Contemporaries.*

Charles, Mrs. Emily [Thornton]. *Ind.*, 1845——. A Washington journalist who has published two volumes of verse, Hawthorn Blossoms; Lyrical Poems. *Lip.*

Chase, George. *Me.*, 1849——. A professor of criminal law at Columbia College. The American Students' Blackstone.

Chase, George Wingate. *Ms.*, 1826–1867. A native and resident of Haverhill, Massachusetts. History of Haverhill, 1640-1860; The Freemason's Monitor; Masonic Dictionary and Manual of Masonic Law; Tactics for Knights Templars and Appendant Authors.

Chase, Irah. *Vt.*, 1793–1864. A Baptist clergyman of prominence who founded the theological seminary at Newton Centre, Massachusetts, and was professor there, 1825–45. Life of Bunyan; Design of Baptism; The Jewish Tabernacle; Infant Baptism an Invention of Men; The Constitutions of the Holy Apostles, are his principal works.

Chase, Lucien B. *Vt.*, 1817–1864. A member of Congress from Tennessee, who wrote the History of Polk's Administration.

Chase, Philander. *N. H.*, 1775–1852. The first Protestant Episcopal bishop of Ohio, and, later, of Illinois. He founded Kenyon College at Gambier, Ohio. A Plea for the West; Defence of Kenyon College; Reminiscences.

Chase, Pliny Earle. *Ms.*, 1820–1886. An educator and scientist of Philadelphia. Numerical Relations of Gravity and Magnetism; Elements of Meteorology; Elements of Arithmetic; Common School Arithmetic.

Chase, Thomas. *Ms.*, 1827-1892. Brother of P. E. Chase, *supra.* An educator of Pennsylvania, and president of Haverford College. He was co-editor with George Stuart of a series of classical text-books, and also published Hellas, her Monuments and Scenery, descriptive of his travels in Greece.

Chatard, Francis Silas. *Md.*, 1835——. The Roman Catholic bishop of Vincennes, Indiana. Christian Truths.

Chatfield-Taylor, Hobart Chatfield. *Il.*, 1865——. A novelist of Chicago. With Edge Tools; An American Peeress; Two Women and a Fool; The Land of the Castanet.

Chauncy [chän′sĭ or chaun′sĭ], **Charles.** *E.*, 1592–1672. A Puritan clergyman, vicar of Ware, 1627–35. He came to America in 1638, and was 13 years minister at Scituate. He was the second president of Harvard College, succeeding Henry Dunster in 1654. His most important work is a series of Twenty-Six Sermons on Justification. Antisynodalia Scripta America, a controversial pamphlet, appeared in 1662. *See Tyler's American Literature; Dictionary of National Biography, vol. 10.*

Chauncy, Charles. *Ms.*, 1705–1787. Great-grandson of C. Chauncy, *supra.* A Congregational clergyman of Boston. A vigourous, logical thinker, who exercised a great influence upon colonial thought. Seasonable Thoughts on the State of Religion in New England; Discourse on Enthusiasm, directed against Whitefield, of whose teachings he was a strong opponent; Letters to Whitefield; Complete View of Episcopacy; The Mystery hid from the Ages; Benevolence of the Deity; Five Dissertations on the Fall and its Consequences; Validity of Presbyterian Ordination, comprise his principal works. *See Tyler's American Literature; Chauncy Memorials.*

Chauvenet [shō-ve-nay′], **William.** *Pa.*, 1820–1870. A mathematician who was chancellor of Washington University, St. Louis, 1862–69. Binomial Theorem and Logarithms; Plane and Spherical Trigonometry; Manual of Spherical and Practical Astronomy; Elementary Geometry. *See Memoir, 1877. Lip.*

Checkley, John. *Ms.*, 1680–1753. An Episcopal clergyman of Rhode Island, noted in his day for his witty, reckless attacks on his theological opponents. Choice Dialogues about Predestination.

Cheetham, James. *E.*, 1772–1810. An English journalist who came to America in 1798, and became editor of The American Citizen. Nine Letters on Burr's Defection; Reply to Aristides; Life of Thomas Paine, a work written from a hostile point of view.

Cheever, Ezekiel. *E.*, 1615–1708. A colonial educator of Boston, who was master of the Latin School for many years. Scripture Prophecies Explained, an essay on the millennium; Latin Accidence, for a century a standard introductory Latin text-book in New England.

Cheever, George Barrell. *Me.*, 1807–1890. A noted Congregational clergyman of New York city. Deacon Giles's Distillery; Studies in Poetry; Wanderings of a Pilgrim in the Shadow of Mont Blanc; Lectures on Pilgrim's Progress; Journal of the Pilgrims at Plymouth; God Against Slavery; Incidents and Memories of the Christian Life; The Guilt of Slavery; The Republic or the Oligarchy, Which?; Faith, Doubt, and Evidence; God's Timepiece for Man's Eternity; Lectures on Cowper; Windings of the River of the Water of Life, include his principal writings. *Ran. Wi.*

Cheever, Henry Theodore. *Me.*, 1814–1897. Brother of G. B. Cheever, *supra.* A Congregational clergyman. Way Marks in the Moral War with Slavery; Correspondences of Faith and Views of Madame Guyon; The Island World of the Pacific; Life in the Sandwich Islands; The Whale and his Captors; The Pulpit and the Pew; Life of Nathaniel Cheever; Life of Walter Colton, *infra;* Captain Caugar. *Har.*

Chellis, Mary Dwinell. *See Lund, Mrs.*

Cheney, Mrs. Ednah Dow [Littlehale]. *Ms.*, 1824——. A Boston writer, associated in early life with the prominent New England transcendentalists, who has been active in the woman suffrage movement, and whose writing has had more or less to do with philosophical themes. Her principal works comprise Hand-book of American History for Coloured People; Faithful to the Light, and Other Tales; Stories of the Olden Time; Gleanings in the Fields of Art; Life of Louisa Alcott, *supra;* Life of Christian Daniel Rauch, Sculptor; Memoir of John Cheney, Engraver; Memoir of Dr. Susan Dimock; Nora's Return, a sequel to Ibsen's Doll's House; Sally Williams, the Mountain Girl.

Cheney, Mrs. Harriet Vaughan [Foster]. *Ms., c.* 1815——. Daughter of Hannah Foster, *infra.* Confessions of an Early Martyr; A Peep at the Pilgrims in 1636; The Rivals of Arcadia; Sketches from the Life of Christ; The Sunday School, or Village Sketches (with her sister, Mrs. Cushing).

Cheney, John Vance. *N. Y.*, 1848——. Son of S. P. Cheney, *infra.* A poet and essayist, for some years at the head of the public library in San Francisco, and now (1897) librarian of the Newberry Library in Chicago. His work in verse includes Thistle Drift; Wood Blooms; Queen Helen, and Other Poems. In prose, The Old Doctor, a Romance of Queer Village; The Golden Guess, a series of critical essays; That Dome in Air, a similar collection of critical studies. *Ap. Cop. Le. Mg. Sto. Wy.*

Cheney, Simon Pease. *N. H.*, 1818–1890. A once noted musical educator of Vermont. The American Singing Book; Wood Notes Wild, notations of Bird Music. *Le.*

Cheney, Theseus Apoleon. *N. Y.*, 1830–1878. A writer who devoted his attention to the history of the western portion of his native State. Report on the Ancient Monuments of Western New York; Historical Sketch of the Chemung Valley; Historical Sketch of 18 Counties of Central and Southern New York; Laron; Relations of Government to Science; Antiquarian Researches.

Chenoweth, Mrs. Caroline [Van Dusen]. *Ind.*, 1846——. A teacher of literature in Boston and New York. Stories of the Saints. *Hou.*

Chesebro [cheez'brō], **Caroline.** *N. Y.*, 1825–1873. A writer of stories and sketches who was during the latter part of her life a teacher in the Packer Institute of Brooklyn. Her writing displays much individuality, and the novel, The Foe in the Household, her finest work, is a careful study of some unfamiliar phases of Pennsylvania life. Her other works include The Beautiful Gate and Other Sketches; Peter Carradine; The Children of Light; Susan the Fisherman's Daughter; The Little Cross Bearers; Dream-Land by Daylight; Philly and Kit; Victoria; Amy Carr; The Glen Cabin.

Chester, Albert Huntington. *N. Y.*, 1843——. A professor of chemistry and metallurgy at Hamilton College. Dictionary of the Names of Minerals; Catalogue of Minerals with their Chemical Composition and Synonyms. *Wil.*

Chester, Frederick Dixon Walthall. *W. I.*, 1861——. A geologist of Delaware who has written many monographs upon local state geology.

Chester, Joseph Lemuel. *Ct.*, 1821–1882. A Philadelphia journalist who went to England in 1858, living in London, and devoting himself to antiquarian research till he became one of the most famous genealogists of his day. His own writings include Greenwood Cemetery and Other Poems; Treatise on the Laws of Repulsion; Educational Laws of Virginia: the personal narrative of Margaret Douglass, imprisoned for the crime of teaching free coloured children to read; John Rogers, the Compiler of the English Bible; Preliminary Investigation of the Alleged Ancestry of George Washington. His most important antiquarian work is an edition of the Marriage, Baptismal, and Burial Registers of Westminster Abbey, with notes, on which he spent 17 years' labour. He edited also the parish registers of six London city churches. *See Dictionary of National Biography, vol. x.*

Chickering, Jesse. *N. H.*, 1797–1855. A Boston physician who was a Unitarian minister in his earlier career, and later became a noted writer on political economy. Statistical View of the Population of Massachusetts, 1765–1840; Emigration into the United States; Reports on the Census of Boston; Letter to the President on Slavery in Relation to Constitutional Government in Great Britain and the United States.

Chickering, John White. *Ms.*, 1808–1888. A Congregational clergyman of Portland, Maine, 1835–65. What it is to Believe in Christ, a very widely circulated tract; The Hillside Church.

Child, Francis James. *Ms.*, 1825–1896. A professor at Harvard University, 1851–96, and the foremost authority upon all matters pertaining to ballad literature. He edited the American edition of The British Poets, in 130 volumes; English and Scottish Popular Ballads; The Debate between the Body and the Soul, and other specimens of mediæval literature. As a Chancerian scholar he had few equals. Observations on the Language of Chaucer; Observations on the Language of Gower's Confessio Amantis. *See Atlantic Monthly, December, 1896. Hou.*

Child, Mrs. Lydia Maria [Francis]. *Ms.*, 1802–1880. A once famous writer whose literary career began with the publication of Hobomok, a Tale of Early Times, in 1821, and closed with Aspirations of the World, in 1878. In 1833 she sacrificed much of her popularity by her Appeal for that Class of Americans Called Africans, and was ever after prominent as an abolitionist, assisting her husband in editing the National Anti-Slavery Standard.

Among her other works are included The Rebels, a novel in which occur a speech by James Otis and a sermon by Whitefield, long supposed to be real and not imaginary; The First Settlers of New England; The Mother's Book; The Girl's Book; Philothea, a Greek romance; The Power of Kindness; Isaac T. Hopper, a True Life, a popular biography of a noted Quaker abolitionist; The Progress of Religious Ideas; Autumnal Leaves; Looking Toward Sunset; The Freedman's Book; Miria, a Romance of the Republic. *See Letters of; Lowell's Fable for Critics. Hou. Rob.*

Childs, George William. *Md.*, 1829–1894. A noted journalist of Philadelphia who established the Public Ledger in 1864. Recollections of General Grant; Personal Recollections. *Lip.*

Chiles, Mrs. Mary Eliza [Hicks] [Hemdin]. *Ky.*, 1820——. Among her writings are Louisa Elton, a reply to "Uncle Tom;" Bandits of Italy; Oswyn Dudley; Select Poems.

Chipman, Nathaniel. *Ct.*, 1752–1843. A Vermont jurist who was professor of law at Middlebury College, 1816–43. Sketches of the Principles of Law; Reports and Dissertations. *See Life, by D. Chipman, 1846.*

Chittenden, Lucius Eugene. *Vt.*, 1824——. A lawyer of New York city. Personal Reminiscences, 1840–1890; Recollections of Lincoln and his Administration; An Unknown Heroine, an historical episode of the War between the States; The Capture of Ticonderoga. *Do. Har.*

Chittenden, Russell Henry. *Ct.*, 1856——. A professor of chemistry in the Sheffield Scientific School at Yale University. Studies from the Laboratory of Physiology and Chemistry in Sheffield Scientific School; On Digestive Proteolysis.

Chivers, Thomas Holley. 1807–1858. A Georgia physician and versifier. Virginalia, or Songs of my Summer Nights; Atlanta, a Paul Epic in Three Lustra; Eonchs of Ruby.

Choate, Isaac Bassett. *Me.*, 1833——. An educator of Boston. Elements of English Speech; Wells of English. *Ap. Rob.*

Choate, Rufus. *Ms.*, 1799–1859. A lawyer of Boston and member of Congress, 1841–45, famous for his gifts as an orator, a distinguishing feature of his style being an extravagant use of long sentences. Addresses and Orations. *See Memoir, by S. G. Brown, supra, 1862; Some Recollections of, by E. P. Whipple; Memoirs, by Neilson, 1884. Lit.*

Chopin, Mrs. Kate [O'Flaherty]. *Mo.*, 1851——. A writer of St. Louis. Bayou Folk; At Fault, a novel. *Hou.*

Choules [chōlz], **John Overton.** *E.*, 1801–1856. A Baptist clergyman of Newport. History of Missions; Christian Offering; Young Americans Abroad; Cruise of Steam Yacht North Star.

Church, Albert Ensign. *Ct.*, 1807–1878. A mathematical professor at West Point, 1833–78. Elements of Differential Calculus; Elements of the Calculus of Variations; Elements of Analytical Geometry; Elements of Descriptive Geometry; Elements of Analytical Trigonometry.

Church, Benjamin. *Ms.*, 1639–1718. A famous colonial soldier, the conqueror of King Philip, and the founder of Little Compton, Rhode Island. Entertaining Passages Relating to Philip's War is a personal narrative of his adventures. *See edition by Dexter, 1867; History of the Eastern Expeditions against the Indians and French.*

Church, Benjamin. *R. I.*, 1734–1776. A Boston physician of considerable note as a political satirist and versifier. The Times, a political satire; Elegy on Dr. Mayhew; Address to a Provincial Bashaw; Elegy on the Death of Whitefield, comprise his chief poems.

Church, Mrs. Ella Rodman [MacIlvane]. *N. Y.*, 1831——. A popular and prolific writer of miscellaneous works, among which are Flights of Fancy; Grandmother's Recollections; The Catanese; Christmas Wreath; Golden Days; Flyers and Crawlers, or Talks about Insects; Talks by the Seashore; Among the Trees at Elmridge; Flower Talks at Elmridge; Home Animals; Some Useful Animals; How to Furnish a Home; Money-Making for Ladies. *Ap. Har.*

Church, Irving Porter. *Ct.*, 1851——. A professor of engineering at Cornell University. Statics and Dynamics for Engineering Students; Mechanics of Materials; Hydraulics and Pneumatics, three works which were afterwards published as Mechanics of Engineering; Notes and Examples in Mechanics. *Wil.*

Church, John Adams. *N. Y.*, 1843——. Son of P. Church, *infra.* A mining engineer of note. The Mining Schools of the United States; Notes on a Metallurgical Journey in Europe; The Comstock Lode; Report on the Striking of Artesian Water, Arizona.

Church, Pharcellus. *N. Y.*, 1801-1886. A Baptist clergyman of prominence. Philosophy of Benevolence; Religious Dissensions, their Cause and Cure; Antioch, or Increase of Moral Power in the Church; Mapleton, or More Work for the Maine Law; Seed-Truths; Theodosia.

Church, Samuel Harden. *Pa.*, 1858——. A Pittsburg writer, the author of Oliver Cromwell, a careful historical study. *Put.*

Chute, Horatio Nelson. *Ont.*, 1847——. A mathematical educator of Michigan. Complete School Register; Arithmetical Cabinet; Manual of Practical Physics.

Cist, Henry Martyn. *O.*, 1839——. A Cincinnati lawyer who served in the Federal army during the Civil War and became brigadier-general. The Army of the Cumberland.

Cist, Lewis Jacob. *O.*, 1818-1885. Brother of H. M. Cist, *supra.* A banker of St. Louis and Cincinnati who published Trifles in Verse.

Claflin, Mrs. Mary Bucklin [Davenport]. *Ms.*, 1825-1896. A Boston writer, the wife of ex-Governor Claflin, of Massachusetts. Brampton Sketches; Personal Recollections of Whittier; Real Happenings; Under the Elms. *Cr.*

Claiborne [klā'burn], John Francis Hamtramck. *Mi.*, 1809-1884. A journalist of New Orleans. Mississippi as a Province, Territory, and State; Life of General Dale, the Mississippi Partisan; Life of General Quitman. *Har.*

Claiborne, John Herbert. *Va.*, 1828——. A physician of Virginia. Diphtheria; Dysmenorrhea; Clinical Reports from Private Practice.

Claiborne, Nathaniel Herbert. *Va.*, 1777-1859. Uncle of J. F. H. Claiborne, *supra.* A Virginia congressman. Notes on the War in the South (1819).

Clap, Nathaniel. *Ms.*, 1669-1745. A clergyman of Newport, of some distinction in his day. Advice to Children; The Lord's Voice Crying to the People in some Extraordinary Dispensations.

Clap, Roger. *E.*, 1609-1691. A colonist of Dorchester, whose Memoirs, written for his children, have been several times reprinted, and possess considerable historical value. They were first edited and published by Thomas Prince, *infra*, 1731.

Clap, Thomas. *Ms.*, 1703-1767. A Congregational clergyman of distinction, president of Yale College, 1740-66. The Nature and Foundation of Moral Virtue and Obligation; History of Yale College; Vindication of the Doctrines of New England Churches; Nature and Motion of Meteors; The Religious Constitutions of Colleges, especially Yale, comprise his chief works. *See Sprague's Annals of the American Pulpit.*

Clap, Theodore. *Ms.*, 1792-1866. A Unitarian minister of New Orleans for many years. Autobiographical Sketches of 35 Years' Residence in New Orleans; Theological Views; Slavery, a Sermon.

Clark, Alexander. *O.*, 1834-1879. A Methodist Protestant clergyman of Pittsburg. The Old Log Schoolhouse; Workaday Christianity; The Red Sea Freedman; School Day Dialogues; The Gospel in the Trees; Rambles in Europe; Starting Out, a Story of the Ohio Hills; Ripples on the River, a collection of verses.

Clark, Alonzo Howard. *Ms.*, 1850——. A naturalist in the United States National Museum at Washington, who has published Statistics of Fisheries of New Hampshire, Rhode Island, and Connecticut; Statistics of Fisheries of Massachusetts; History of the Mackerel Fishery.

Clark, Charles Cotesworth Pinckney. *Vt.*, 1822——. A physician, at one time collector of customs at Oswego. The Commonwealth Reconstructed is his only book.

Clark, Charles Heber. "Max Adeler." 18——. A Philadelphia journalist who has written several works of a humourous character which have been popular, though their literary merit is slight. Out of the Hurly Burly; Elbow Room, a Novel without a Plot; Random Shots; Fortunate Island and Other Stories.

Clark, Davis Wasgatt. *Me.*, 1812–1871. A Methodist bishop of some note as a preacher. Mental Discipline; Death-Bed Scenes; Man all Immortal; Life of Bishop Hedding; Sermons; Elements of Algebra. *Meth.*

Clark, Edson Lyman. *Ms.*, 1827——. A Congregational clergyman of Massachusetts. The Arabs and the Turks; The Races of European Turkey; Turkey; Fundamental Questions chiefly relating to Genesis and the Hebrew Scriptures. *Do.*

Clark, Francis Edward. *Q.*, 1851——. A Congregational minister who during his pastorate in Portland, Maine, in 1881, established the Christian Endeavour Society. Danger Signals, the Enemies of Youth; Looking out on Life, a book for girls; Our Vacations, where to Go, etc.; Young People's Prayer Meeting in Theory and Practice; The Children and the Church; Mossback Correspondence; Our Business Boys; Ways and Means, a history of the Christian Endeavour movement. *Fu. Lo.*

Clark, George Hunt. *Ms.*, 1809–1881. An iron merchant of Hartford, of local fame as a verse-writer. Now and Then; The News; Undertow of a Trade Wind Surf.

Clark, George Whitfield. *N. J.*, 1831——. A Baptist clergyman of New Jersey. Harmony of the Four Gospels in English; Notes on Matthew, Mark, Luke, and John; Harmonic Arrangement of the Acts of the Apostles; Brief Notes on the New Testament; History of the First Baptist Church in Elizabeth; New Jersey.

Clark, Henry James. *Ms.*, 1826–1873. A naturalist of Cambridge. Mind in Nature; A Claim for Scientific Property.

Clark, James Gowdy. *N.Y.*, 1830——. A verse-writer and composer of San Francisco. Poetry and Song.

Clark, James Henry. *N. Y.*, 1814–1869. A physician of Newark, New Jersey. History of the Cholera in Newark in 1847; Sight and Hearing, how Preserved, how Lost; Medical Topography of Newark; The Medical Men of New Jersey in Essex District, 1666–1866.

Clark, John Alonzo. *Ms.*, 1801–1843. An Episcopal clergyman of Philadelphia. The Young Disciple; The Pastor's Testimony; A Walk about Zion; Gathered Fragments; Awake, Thou Sleeper; Glimpses of the Old World.

Clark, John Bates. *R. I.*, 1847——. A political economist, professor of political economy in Columbia College. Capital and its Earnings; The Philosophy of Wealth. *Gi.*

Clark, Mrs. Kate [Upson]. *Al.*, 1851——. A journalist of Brooklyn, who has written mainly for young people. That Mary Ann. *Lo.*

Clark, Lewis Gaylord. *N. Y.*, 1810–1873. A once prominent magazinist of New York city, and editor of the Knickerbocker Magazine. Knick-Knacks is a collection of brief sketches contributed to that periodical.

Clark, Mrs. Mary [Latham]. *Me.*, 1831——. A New England writer of religious juveniles, among which are The Mayflower Series; Daisy's Mission.

Clark, Nathaniel George. *Vt.*, 1825–1896. The foreign secretary of the American Board of Foreign Missions from 1866. In earlier life he was of some note as an educator, and published Elements of the English Language. *Scr.*

Clark, Rufus Wheelwright. *Ms.*, 1813–1886. Brother of Thomas M. Clark, *infra*. A Reformed Dutch clergyman of Albany. Among his more than a hundred publications are Lectures to Young Men; Heaven and its Scriptural Emblems; Life Scenes of the Messiah; Romanism in America; The African Slave Trade; Heroes of Albany.

Clark, Simon Tucker. *Ms.*, 1836——. A physician of Lockport, and professor of medical jurisprudence in Niagara University. My Garden.

Clark, Mrs. Susanna Rebecca Graham. *N. S.*, 1848——. A writer of Portland, Maine, who has written much juvenile literature. Yensie Walton; Our Street; The Triple E.; Achor; Herbert Gardenell's Children; Tom's Street; Go's Goings. *Lo.*

Clark, Theodore Minot. *Ms.*, 1845——. An architect in Boston, formerly instructor in the Massachusetts Institute of Technology. Architect, Owner and Builder before the Law; Building Superintendence; Rural School Architectnre. *Mac.*

Clark, Thomas. *Pa.*, 1787–1866. An educator of Philadelphia. Naval History of the United States from the Commencement of the Revolutionary War, 1814; Sketches of United States Naval History.

Clark, Thomas March. *Ms.*, 1812——. The second Protestant Episcopal bishop of Rhode Island, and prominent among theologians of the Broad Church school. Primary Truths; The Dew of Youth and Other Lectures to Young Men and Women; Early Discipline and Culture; The Efficient Sunday School Teacher; Reminiscences. *Ap. Wh.*

Clark, Willis Gaylord. *N. Y.*, 1810–1841. Twin brother of L. G. Clark, *supra.* A now forgotten verse-writer. *See Literary Remains, with Memoir by L. G. Clark; Griswold's Poets and Poetry of America.*

Clarke, Dorus. *Ms.*, 1799–1884. A Congregational clergyman of Boston. Letters to Horace Mann; Oneness of the Christian Church; Orthodox Congregationalism and the Sects; Saying the Catechism 75 Years Ago and the Historical Results; Review of the Oberlin Council; Letters to Young People in Manufacturing Villages; Revision of the English Version of the Bible; Essay on the Tri-Unity of God.

Clarke, Edward Hammond. *Ms.*, 1820–1877. A prominent physician and medical writer of Boston. Sex in Education; The Building of a Brain; Visions: a Study of False Sight; Nature and Treatment of Polypus of the Ear. *Hou.*

Clarke, Frank Wigglesworth. *Ms.*, 1847——. Chief chemist of the United States Geological Survey at Washington. Weights, Measures, and Money of All Nations; Elements of Chemistry. *Ap.*

Clarke, Isaac Edwards. *Ms.*, 1830——. A lawyer in the United States Civil Service since 1871. Tribute to Bayard Taylor; Industrial and High Art Education in the United States.

Clarke, James Freeman. *N. H.*, 1810–1888. A Unitarian clergyman of Boston, who founded there the Church of the Disciples, and was its pastor from 1841 till his death. He was especially prominent among Unitarian writers of the latter half of the century, the tone of his thought being that of the liberal conservative. His first important work was Orthodoxy: its Truths and Errors (1866). Other works of his include Ten Great Religions, Part I, an Essay in Comparative Theology; Ten Great Religions, Part II, a Comparison of all Religions; Christian Doctrine of Prayer; Thomas Didymus; Common Sense in Religion; Steps of Belief; Events and Epochs in Religious History; Self-Culture; Every Day Religion; The Ideas of the Apostle Paul; Memorial and Biographical Sketches; Vexed Questions in Theology; Anti-Slavery Days. *See Autobiography, Diary and Correspondence, edited by E. E. Hale; Memoir by H. P. Peabody, 1889. A. U. A. Hou. Le.*

Clarke, MacDonald. *Ct.*, 1798–1842. An eccentric, unbalanced verse-writer of New York city, who was commonly styled "the Mad Poet." Poems; Sketches in Verse; Death in Disguise, a Temperance poem; The Gossip; Afara, or the Belles of Broadway; A Cross and a Coronet; Elixir of Moonshine; Review of the Eve of Eternity.

Clarke, Mrs. Mary Bayard [Devereux]. *N. C.*, 1830——. A writer of Raleigh, North Carolina, who has published Reminiscences of Cuba; Mosses from a Rolling Stone; Clytie and Zenobia, a poem; Wood Notes, a compilation of North Carolina verse.

Clarke, Rebecca Sophia. "Sophie May." *Me.*, 1833——. A popular writer of stories for children and young people, who was born and has always lived at Norridgewock, Maine. Of the former class are the Little Prudy Books; Dotty Dimple Series; Flaxie Frizzle Stories. Of the latter class are Her Friend's Lover; Janet; The Asbury Twins; In Old Quinnebasset; Quinnebasset Girls; The Doctor's Daughter. *Le.*

Clarke, Richard H. *D. C.*, 1827——. A prominent Roman Catholic lawyer of Washington, and, later, of New York, who has written many controversial papers, and published Illustrated History of the Catholic Church in the United States; Lives of Deceased Roman Catholic Bishops of the United States.

Clay, Cassius Marcellus. *Ky.*, 1810——. A Kentucky congressman noted as a strong opponent of slavery, who was minister to Russia 1861–69. *See Life and Memoirs, compiled by Himself.*

Clay, Henry. *Va.*, 1777–1852. A Kentucky statesman and orator, who was in public life for half a century, and was several times an unsuccessful candidate for the presidency. He is known in literature by his Speeches, several collections of which were published in his lifetime. *See Parton's Famous Americans; Lives by G. D. Prentice, 1831; Swaim, 1843; Mallory, 1844; Sargent and Greeley, 1852; Colton, 1857; Carl Schurz, 1887.*

Cleaveland, John. *Ct.*, 1722–1799. A Congregational minister of Massachusetts. The Work of God at Chebacco (now Essex) in 1763; Essay to Defend Christ's Sacrifice and Atonement against Aspersions cast on the Same by Dr. Mayhew; Reply to Dr. Mayhew's Letter of Reproof; Treatise on Infant Baptism.

Cleaveland, Nehemiah. *Ms.*, 1796–1877. Grandson of J. Cleaveland, *supra.* An educator of Massachusetts, who published a History of Bowdoin College, with Biographical Sketches of its Graduates, 1806–79, edited and completed by A. S. Packard, *infra.*

Cleaveland, Parker. *Ms.*, 1780–1858. Grandson of J. Cleaveland, *supra.* A professor in Bowdoin College, 1805–58, whose Mineralogy and Geology, 1816, gained for him the title of "the father of American mineralogy."

Cleland, Thomas. *Va.*, 1778–1858. A Presbyterian clergyman of Kentucky, much inclined to controversy, who published Letters on Campbellism; The Socini-Arian Detected; Unitarianism Unmasked.

Clemens, Jeremiah. *Al.*, 1814–1865. An Alabama statesman who won some notice as a novelist. Bernard Lyle; Mustang Gray; The Rivals, a Tale of the Times of Burr and Hamilton; Tobias Wilson, a Tale of the Great Rebellion.

Clemens, Samuel Langhorne. "Mark Twain." *Mo.*, 1835——. A celebrated humourist, who, after an eventful experience as a journalist, rose to fame by the publication of The Innocents Abroad, a volume of extravagantly humourous travels, which still remains his most popular book. Only a very small portion of his writing has any place as literature, but as an author he is one of the most popular and successful of his time. Other works of his are, A Tramp Abroad; Roughing It; Tom Sawyer; The Gilded Age (with C. D. Warner, *infra*); The Jumping Frog; Life on the Mississippi; Huckleberry Finn; Merry Tales; A Connecticut Yankee at King Arthur's Court; Tom Sawyer Abroad; Pudd'nhead Wilson; The American Claimant. The Prince and the Pauper; Joan of Arc, are works in a serious vein, the first being his most finished production. *See Haweis's American Humourists; Steuart's Letters to Living Authors, 1890; Vedder's American Writers.*

Clemens, William M. 1850——. Cousin of S. L. Clemens. A journalist of Cleveland. Life and Times of John Brown; The Nemesis of Passion.

Clement, Mrs. Clara Erskine. *See Waters, Mrs.*

Clemmer, Mrs. Mary. *See Hudson, Mrs.*

Cleveland, Aaron. *Ct.*, 1744–1815. A verse-writer who late in life became a Congregational minister. He was the great-grandfather of President Cleveland. The Philosopher and Boy; Slavery Considered, both productions in verse.

Cleveland, Charles Dexter. *Ms.*, 1802–1869. Grandson of A. Cleveland, *supra.* An educator of Philadelphia, who published Compendiums of English, American, and Classical Literature; English Literature of the 19th Century; critical edition of Milton, with notes and life. *Bar.*

Cleveland, Cynthia Eloise. *N. Y.*, 1845——. A Washington writer employed in the civil service. See Saw, or Civil Service in the Departments, a political novel; Is it Fate?

Cleveland, Henry Russell. 1801–1843. Son of R. J. Cleveland, *infra.* The Classical Education of Boys; Life of Henry Hudson.

Cleveland, Horace William Shaler. *Ms.*, 1814——. Son of R. J. Cleveland, *infra.* A noted landscape gardener of Minneapolis. Hints to Riflemen; Landscape Architecture; Voyages of a Merchant Navigator. *Har.*

Cleveland, Richard Jeffry. *Ms.*, 1773–1860. Cousin of A. Cleveland, *supra.* Voyages and Commercial Enterprises; Voyages of a Merchant Navigator of the Days that are Past.

Cleveland, Rose Elizabeth. *N. Y.*, 1846——. Great-granddaughter of A. Cleveland, *supra*, and the only sister of President Cleveland. During the first year of her brother's first administration she was the mistress of the White House. George Eliot's Poetry and Other Studies; The Long Run, a novel. *Fu.*

Clevenger, Shobal Vail. *Iy.*, 1843——. A physician of Chicago, and son of the noted sculptor of the same name. Treatise on Government Surveying; Comparative Physiology and Psychology; Lectures on Artistic Anatomy and Sciences Useful to the Artist.

Clifford, Nathan. *N. H.*, 1803–1881. A noted jurist of Maine, who was attorney-general during Polk's administration, and published United States Circuit Court Reports.

Clingman, Thomas Lanier. *N. C.*, 1812–1897. A North Carolina congressman who served during the Civil War as brigadier-general in the Confederate army. The two Carolina mountains, Clingman's Peak and Clingman's Dome, were named in his honour, he having been the first to measure their height. Speeches; Follies of the Positivist Philosophers.

Clinton, De Witt. *N. Y.*, 1769–1828. A famous statesman and politician of New York state. Memoir of Antiquities of Western New York; Natural History and Internal Revenues of New York; Speeches to the Legislature. *See Lives, by Hosack, 1829; Renwick, 1840; Campbell, 1849.*

Clymer, Mrs. Ella Maria [Dietz]. 185——. A New York writer, once an actress, and for some time the president of the woman's club of New York, Sorosis. She has written three volumes of verse: The Triumph of Love; The Triumph of Time; The Triumph of Life.

Clymer, Meredith. *Pa.*, 1817——. A distinguished physician and medical writer of New York city. Diseases of the Respiratory Organs (with Williams); Pathology, Diagnosis, and Treatment of Fevers; Physiology and Pathology of the Nervous System; Palsies and Kindred Disorders; Ecstasy and Other Dramatic Disorders of the Nervous System; Hereditary Genius; Cerebro-Spinal Meningitis; Legitimate Influence of Epilepsy on Criminal Responsibility.

Coan, Titus. *Ct.*, 1801–1882. A missionary of note in the Sandwich Islands who wrote Life in Hawaii; Adventures in Patagonia. *Do. Ran.*

Coan, Titus Munson. *H. I.*, 1836——. Son of T. Coan, *supra.* A New York littérateur. Ounces of Prevention; Topics of the Times (edited).

Cobb, Cyrus. *Ms.*, 1834——. Son of S. Cobb, 1st, *infra.* An artist and sculptor of Boston who, besides writing much occasional verse, has published Veterans of the Grand Army, a novel.

Cobb, Howell. *Ga.*, 1795–18—. A Georgia lawyer. Penal Code of Georgia.

Cobb, Jonathan Holmes. *Ms.*, 1799–1882. A manufacturer of Dedham, who founded the silk industry in the United States, and whose Manual of the Mulberry Tree and the Culture of Silk was once well known.

Cobb, Joseph Beckham. *Ga.*, 1819–1858. A Southern author whose writings include The Creole, or the Siege of New Orleans, a novel; Mississippi Scenes; Leisure Labours.

Cobb, Lyman. *Ms., c.* 1800–1864. A once prominent educator who, besides many text-books on spelling and mathematics, published The Evil Tendency of Corporal Punishment; Just Standard for Pronouncing the English Language. *Har.*

Cobb, Sylvanus. *Me.*, 1799–1866. A Universalist clergyman of Massachusetts, editor for many years of The Christian Freeman. The New Testament, with Explanatory Notes; Compend of Divinity; Discussions. *See Autobiography, and Memoir by his son, S. Cobb, 1867.*

Cobb, Sylvanus. *Me.*, 1823–1887. Son of S. Cobb, *supra.* A prolific writer of sensational tales quite without literary value. Among them are The King's Talisman; The Patriot Cruiser; Ben Hamed.

Cobb, Thomas Read Rootes. *Ga.*, 1823–1862. A Georgia lawyer who served as brigadier-general in the Confederate army during the Civil War, and was killed in the battle of Fredericksburg. Digest of the Laws of Georgia; Historical Sketch of Slavery from the Earliest Periods; Inquiry into the Law of Negro Slavery in the United States.

Cobbett, Thomas. *E.*, 1608–1685. A nonconformist English clergyman who came to America in 1637, and was minister at Ipswich from 1656 till his death. Infant Baptism; Civil Magistrate's Power in Matters of Religion; Practical Discourse of Prayer; The Honour due from Children to their Parents.

Cocke [cōke], **James Richard.** 1863–——. A physician of Boston. Hypnotism; Blind Leaders of the Blind, a novel. *Ar. Le.*

Cocke, Zitella. *Al.*, 183——. A verse-writer whose contributions to periodicals have been collected in a volume of verse entitled A Doric Reed. *Cop.*

Cocker, William Johnson. *E.*, 1846——. An educator of Michigan. Handbook of Punctuation; The Government of the United States. *Har.*

Coddington, William. *E.*, 1601–1678. The first governor of Rhode Island. Demonstrations of True Love unto the Rulers of Massachusetts.

Codman, John. *Ms.*, 1782–1847. A Congregational clergyman of Dorchester. Sermons; Visit to England. *See Memoir, by W. A. Allen, 1853.*

Codman, John. *Ms.*, 1814——. Son of J. Codman, *supra.* A noted captain in the merchant marine. Sailors' Life and Sailors' Yarns; Ten Months in Brazil; The Mormon Country; The Round Trip by Way of Panama; A Solution of the Mormon Problem; Winter Sketches from the Saddle.

Coffin, Charles Carleton. *N. H.*, 1823–1896. A Boston journalist who became famous as the war correspondent of the Boston Journal during the Civil War, over the signature "Carleton." His writings, mainly though not exclusively for young people, include My Days and Nights on the Battlefield, a narrative of personal experience; Following the Flag; Winning his Way; Building the Nation; Old Times in the Colonies; The Boys of '76; The Story of Liberty; The Drumbeat of the Nation; Marching to Victory; Redeeming the Republic; Freedom Triumphant; Abraham Lincoln; Our New Way Round the World; Daughters of the Revolution. *See Life of, by Griffis. Est. Har. Hou.*

Coffin, Isaac Foster. *Me.*, 1787–1861. An educator of Roxbury, Massachusetts. Journal of a Residence in Chili during the revolutionary scenes of 1817–19.

Coffin, James Henry. *Ms.*, 1806–1873. A meteorologist who was professor of astronomy at Lafayette College. Solar and Lunar Eclipses Illustrated and Explained; Winds of the Northern Hemisphere; Psychometrical Table; Orbit and Phenomena of a Meteoric Fire Ball; Elements of Conic Sections and Analytical Geometry; Winds of the Globe. *See Life, by J. C. Clyde, 1882.*

Coffin, John Huntington Crane. *Me.*, 1815–1890. A mathematician of distinction. Observations with the Mural Circle at the United States Naval Observatory; The Compass; Navigation and Nautical Astronomy.

Coffin, Joshua. *Ms.*, 1792–1864. A Massachusetts antiquary prominent among the abolitionists, and one of the poet Whittier's early instructors. He published a History of Ancient Newbury; The Toppans of Toppan's Lane, a genealogy.

Coffin, Robert Allen. *Ms.*, 1801–1878. Brother of J. H. Coffin, *supra.* An instructor in western Massachusetts. Compendium of Natural Philosophy; Town Organization; History of Conway, Massachusetts.

Coffin, Robert Barry. "Barry Gray." *N. Y.*, 1826–1886. A New York journalist and littérateur, whose books, popular at one time, are now nearly forgotten. Their humour is somewhat forced, and the style has no very marked merits. Matrimonial Infelicities; Who is the Heir?; Out of Town, a Rural Episode; Cakes and Ale at Woodbine; Castles in the Air; Left in the Lurch; The Home of Cooper.

Coffin, Robert Stevenson. *Me.*, 1797–1827. A verse-writer of Boston who published The Oriental Harp; Poems of the Boston Bard. *See Autobiography, 1825.*

Coffin, Roland Folger. *N. Y.*, 1826–1888. A marine reporter in New York city. An Old Sailor's Yarns; The America's Cup; History of American Yachting. *Fu. Scr.*

Coffin, Selden Jennings. *N. Y.*, 1838——. Son of J. H. Coffin, *supra.* He succeeded his father as professor of astronomy at Lafayette College in 1873, and completed the latter's Winds of the Globe. He has also published Record of the Men at Lafayette.

Coggeshall, George. *Ct.*, 1784–18—. A sea captain of some prominence as a writer. Voyages to Various Parts of the World, 1799–1844; History of American Privateers and Letters of Marque during our War with England, 1812–14; Historical Sketch of Commerce and Navigation from the Christian Era to 1860; Religious and Miscellaneous Poetry.

Coggeshall, William Turner. *Pa.*, 1824–1867. A journalist of Cincinnati, whose principal writings include Signs of the Times, a work on spirit rappings; Home Hits and Hints; Stories of Frontier Adventure.

Cogswell, Jonathan. *Ms.*, 1782–1864. A noted Congregational clergyman of New England and New Jersey. The Necessity of Capital Punishment; Discourses; Hebrew Theocracy; Calvary and Sinai; Godliness a Great Mystery; The Appropriate Work of the Holy Spirit. *See E. O. Jameson's Cogswells of America.*

Cogswell, William. *N. H.*, 1787–1850. A Congregational clergyman of New Hampshire, among whose works are, Manual of Theology and Devotion; Assistant to Family Religion; Christian Philanthropist; Theological Class Book; Harbinger of the Millennium; Letters to Young Men Preparing for the Ministry.

Cohen, Jacob Da Silva Solis. *N. Y.*, 1838——. A Philadelphia physician and medical lecturer of prominence. Treatise on Inhalations; Diseases of the Throat; Croup in its Relations to Tracheotomy; The Throat and the Voice.

Coit, James Milnor. *Pa.*, 1845——. An instructor in chemistry at St. Paul's School, Concord. Elements of Chemical Arithmetic; Short Manual of Qualitative Analysis.

Coit, Thomas Winthrop. *Ct.*, 1803–1885. An Episcopal clergyman, professor in Berkeley Divinity School at Middletown from 1872 to 1885. Necessity of Preaching Doctrine; Theological Commonplace Book; Puritanism in New England and the Episcopal Church; Lectures on the Early History of Christianity in England.

Colburn, Warren. *Ms.*, 1793–1833. A noted mathematician of Massachusetts, whose First Lessons in Intellectual Arithmetic was translated into many languages. *Hou.*

Colburn, Zerah. *N. Y.*, 1832–1870. A nephew of the famous calculator of the same name. He was a well-known mechanical engineer who published The Locomotive Engine; Steam Boiler Explosions; Nature of Heat and its Mode of Action in the Phenomena of Combustion, etc.; Treatise on the Principles of the Locomotive Engine. *Bai. Vn.*

Colby, Frederick Myron. *N. H.*, 1848——. A journalist of New Hampshire. The Daughter of Pharaoh, a Tale of the Exodus; Brave Lads and Bonnie Lassies, a juvenile.

Colden, Cadwallader. *S.*, 1688–1776. A colonial physician, lieutenant-governor of the province of New York, 1761–76, and a prominent loyalist of his day. The History of the Five Indian Nations is his chief work. Among his many lesser writings is Principles of Actions on Matter. *See Tyler's American Literature.*

Colden, Cadwallader David. *L. I.*, 1769–1834. Nephew of C. Colden, *supra.* A commercial lawyer of prominence in New York who published Life of Robert Fulton; Vindication of the Steamboat Right granted by the State of New York.

Coleman, Leighton. *Pa.*, 1837——. The second Protestant Episcopal bishop of Delaware. The Church in America, a history of the American Episcopal Church.

Coleman, Lyman. *Ms.*, 1796–1882. A Congregational clergyman who was a classical professor at Lafayette College, 1861–82. Ancient Christianity Exemplified; Prelacy and Ritualism; The Apostolical and Primitive Church; Historical Geography of the Bible; Text-Book and Atlas of Bible Geography; Genealogy of the Lyman Family.

Coles, Abraham. *N. J.*, 1813–1891. A New Jersey physician who published a volume containing thirteen original translations of the Dies Irae. His other works include Stabat Mater Dolorosa; Stabat Mater Speciosa; Old Gems in New Settings; The Microcosm, a psychological poem; The Evangel in Verse; The Light of the World; The Psalms in Verse, with notes. *See Biographical Sketch, edited by J. A. Coles, 1892. Ap.*

Coles, George. *E.*, 1792–1858. A Methodist clergyman who published The Antidote, or Revelation Defended; Concordance of the Scriptures; Heroines of Methodism.

Colesworthy, Daniel Clement. *Me.*, 1810–1893. A once noted bookseller of Boston, who was also a writer. Some of his poems for children, like "Don't Kill the Birds" and "Little Words of Kindness," have been extremely popular. Sunday School Hymns; Advice to an Apprentice; Opening Buds; Chronicles of Casco Bay; A Group of Children, and Other Poems; School is Out; The Year; A Day in the Woods, in verse, comprise the most of his writings.

Collens, Thomas Wharton. *La.*, 1812–1879. A well-known jurist of New Orleans, who wrote The Martyr Patriots, a tragedy; Humanics; Views of the Labour Movement; The Eden of Labour.

Collier, Mrs. Ada [Langworthy]. *Ia.*, 1843——. A writer of Dubuque, whose Lilith, the Legend of the First Woman, is a poem of not a little merit.

Collier, Joseph Avery. *Ms.*, 1828–1864. A Reformed Dutch clergyman of Kingston, New York. The Right Way, or the Gospel Applied to the Intercourse of Individuals and Nations; The Christian Home; The Young Men of the Bible; Pleasant Paths for Little Feet; Little Crowns; Dawn of Heaven.

Collier, Peter. *N. Y.*, 1835——. A chemist of distinction for several years attached to the Department of Agriculture at Washington. Sorghum, its Culture and Manufacture Economically Considered; Investigations of Sorghum as a Sugar Producing Plant. *Clke.*

Collier, Robert Laird. *Md.*, 1837–1890. A Unitarian clergyman who in his later years was a London correspondent of the New York Herald. Every-Day Subjects in Sunday Sermons; Meditations on the Essence of Christianity; Henry Irving: a Sketch and a Criticism; English Home Life. *A. U. A. Hou. Rob.*

Collier, Thomas Stephens. *N.Y.*, 1842–1893. A physician and poet whose home was at New London, Connecticut. Song Spray, a collection of poems, 1889.

Collins, Charles. *Me.*, 1813–1875. A Methodist preacher and educator of Tennessee, who published Methodism and Calvinism Compared.

Collyer, Robert. *E.*, 1823——. A Unitarian clergyman of New York, and one of the leading men among the clergy of his faith. He was born in Yorkshire, and learned the blacksmith's trade, which he still followed after coming to America in 1849. He was then a Wesleyan local preacher, but his views changing he became a Unitarian, and in 1860 founded Unity Church in Chicago, over which he remained pastor till he went to New York in 1879. His influence, both within and without the Unitarian body, has been very great. The Life That Now Is; Nature and Life; A Man in Earnest; The Simple Truth, a Home Book; Lectures to Young Men and Women; History of Ilkley, in Yorkshire. *Dut. Le.*

Colman, Benjamin. *Ms.*, 1673–1747. A famous Congregational minister of Boston, whose theological views were much more liberal than those of his contemporaries, and whose literary style was far more polished and flexible. Evangelical Sermons Collected; Twenty Sacramental Sermons. *See Life by E. Turell, 1749; Tyler's American Literature; Sprague's Annals of the American Pulpit.*

Colman, Henry. *Ms.*, 1785–1849. An agricultural writer of Massachusetts, who was a Congregational minister at Hingham, 1807–20, and afterwards a Unitarian minister at Salem. Report on Silk Culture; European Agriculture and Rural Economy; Agriculture and Rural Economy of France, Belgium, Holland, and Switzerland; European Life and Manners.

Colton, Calvin. *Ms.*, 1789–1857. An Episcopal clergyman of some note in his day as a political writer. Manual for Emigrants to America; History of American Revivals; Protestant Jesuitism; Public Economy for the United States, a plea for protection; Life of Henry Clay; Junius Tracts.

Colton, George Hooker. *N. Y.*, 1818–1847. A verse-writer whose Tecumseh is a poem as ambitious in conception as it is mediocre in execution.

Colton, Walter. *Vt.*, 1797–1851. Brother of C. Colton, *supra.* A journalist and educator who established the first newspaper in California, and built the first schoolhouse there. As chaplain in the United States navy he visited many parts of the world. Visit to Athens and Constantinople; Land and Lee in the Bosphorus and Ægean; Ship and Shore; Deck and Port; The Sea and the Sailor.

Colwell, Stephen. *Va.*, 1800–1871. An iron merchant of Philadelphia, who wrote much on current topics, especially matters relating to political economy. Ways and Means of Commercial Payment; Money on Account; Removal of the Deposits from the Bank of the United States; Domestic Production and Internal Trade; Hints to Laymen; Charity and the Clergy; Politics for American Christians; New Themes for Protestant Clergy, include the more important of his writings.

Coman, Katherine. *O.*, 1857——. A professor of history at Wellesley College. Outlines in Constitutional History of England; Outlines in Industrial History; The Growth of the English Nation.

Comegys, Benjamin Bartis. *Del.*, 1819——. A banker of Philadelphia. Tour Round My Library, and Other Papers; Advice to Young Men and Boys; A Primer of Ethics; Talks with Boys and Girls; How to Get On, a Book for Boys; Turn Over a New Leaf; An Order of Worship; Old Stories with New Lessons. *Hou. Rev.*

Comfort, Mrs. Anna [Manning]. *N. J.*, 1845——. Wife of G. F. Comfort, *infra.* A physician of Syracuse, who has written Woman's Education and Woman's Health, a reply to Dr. Clarke's once famous Sex in Education.

Comfort, George Fisk. *N.Y.*, 1833——. A professor at Syracuse University since 1872. He has published a series of German text-books and The Land Troubles in Ireland. *Har.*

Comly, John. *Pa.*, 1774–1850. A Pennsylvania educator among the Friends, who prepared a speller that was phenomenally popular, and also a grammar and other text-books. *See Journal of John Comly of Ryberry, 1853.*

Comstock [kŭm'stŏk], **Cyrus Ballou.** *Ms.*, 1831——. A colonel of the Engineer Corps in the United States army, and brevet major-general of U. S. Volunteers, who has made a number of important government surveys. Notes on European Surveys; Surveys of the Northwestern Lakes; Primary Triangulation of United States Lake Survey.

Comstock, John Henry. *Wis.*, 1849——. A professor of entomology and general invertebrate zoölogy at Cornell University. Notes on Entomology; Report on Cotton Insects; Introduction to Entomology.

Comstock, John Lee. *Ct.*, 1789–1858. An educational compiler of Hartford, among whose many scientific text-books are The Elements of Chemistry; Introduction to Mineralogy; System of Natural Philosophy; History of the Precious Minerals; Natural History of Quadrupeds. He wrote also A History of the Greek Revolution.

Comstock, Theodore Bryant. *O.*, 1849——. A geologist of distinction, professor in Illinois University. Outlines of General Geology; Classification of Rocks.

Conant, Albert Jasper. *Vt.*, 1821——. A naturalist who was for some time curator in the University of Wisconsin. Footprints of Vanished Races in the Valley of the Mississippi.

Conant, Mrs. Hannah O'Brien [Chaplin]. *Ms.*, 1809–1865. Wife of T. J. Conant, *infra*, and daughter of J. Chaplin, *supra*. An Oriental scholar who assisted her husband in his literary work, made important translations from the German of Strauss, Neander, and Uhden, and was the author of History of the English Bible; Popular History of English Bible Translation; The Earnest Man, a sketch of Judson the missionary.

Conant, Mrs. Helen [Steevens]. *Ms.*, 1839——. Wife of S. S. Conant, *infra*. A magazinist of New York city. The Butterfly Hunters; Primers of German and Spanish Literature. *Har.*

Conant, Samuel Stillman. *Me.*, 1831–1885. Son of T. J. Conant, *infra*. A journalist of New York, managing editor of Harper's Weekly, 1869–85, and translator of Lermontoff's Circassian Boy.

Conant, Thomas Jefferson. *Vt.*, 1802–1891. A Baptist clergyman who was one of the foremost Hebrew scholars of his time. Baptism, its Meaning and its Use Philologically and Historically Considered. His editions of The Book of Job; The Book of Proverbs; Genesis; Psalms; Prophecies of Isaiah; Historical Books of the Old Testament from Joshua to Second Kings; The Gospel by Matthew, constitute a scholar's version of the Scriptures, amply illustrated with critical and philological notes. *Fu.*

Condie, Daniel Francis. *Pa.*, 1796–1875. A physician and medical writer of Philadelphia. Course of Examination for Medical Students; Catechism of Health; Epidemic Cholera; Diseases of Children.

Cone, Helen Gray. *N. Y.*, 1859——. An instructor in the Normal College of New York city, whose writing has been mainly in verse. Oberon and Puck, verses Grave and Gay; The Ride to the Lady and Other Poems. *Hou.*

Congdon, Charles Taber. *Ms.*, 1821–1891. A journalist of New York city for some years on the staff of the Tribune. Tribune Essays; Reminiscences of a Journalist; Recollections of a Reader; Autobiographical Papers.

Conkling, Alfred. *N. Y.*, 1789–1874. A jurist of New York whose son was the noted statesman, Roscoe Conkling. Treatise on Organization and Jurisdiction of Superior, Circuit, and District Courts; Admiralty Jurisdiction; Powers of the Executive Department of the United States; Young Citizen's Manual.

Conkling, Alfred Ronald. *N. Y.*, 1850——. Grandson of A. Conkling, *supra*. A lawyer of New York city. Appleton's Guide to Mexico; City Government in the United States; Handbook for Voters in New York city; Life of Roscoe Conkling. *Ap.*

Conn, Herbert William. *Ms.*, 1859——. A biologist whose specialty is the bacteriology of milk; instructor and professor of biology at Wesleyan University from 1884. Evolution of To-Day; The Living World: Whence it Came and Whither it is Drifting. *Put.*

Connelly, Mrs. Celia [Logan]. *Pa.*, 1839——. A journalist and playwright of Washington. An American Marriage is one of her plays.

Connelly, Emma M. *Ky.*, 18—. A writer of New York city. Under the Surface; Tilting at Wind Mills, a Story of the Blue Grass Country; The Story of Kentucky. *Lo.*

Conrad, Frederick William. *Pa.*, 1816——. A Lutheran clergyman of Philadelphia, editor of The Lutheran Observer from 1867. The Lutheran Doctrine of Baptism; Analysis of Luther's Small Catechism; The Evangelical Luthernn Church; The Call to the Ministry; The Liturgical Question.

Conrad, Robert Taylor. *Pa.*, 1810–1858. A lawyer of Philadelphia and mayor of that city in 1854, who was once noted as a dramatic poet. Aylmere, or the Bondman of Kent, is a tragedy in which Jack Cade is the chief figure, a rôle in which Edwin Forrest was very successful. Conrad of Naples, another tragedy, had also a measure of popularity.

Conrad, Timothy Abbott. *N. J.*, 1803–1877. A conchologist who published Fossil Shells of the Tertiary Formations of North America; New Fresh-Water Shells of the United States; Miocene Shells of the United States; Palæontology of State of New York.

Converse, Mrs. Harriet [Maxwell]. *N. Y.*, 184——. A writer of verse and prose in New York city. Sheaves, a collection of verses; The Religious Festivals of the Iroquois Indians; Mythology and Folk-Lore of the North American Indian.

Conway, Katherine Eleanor. *N. Y.*, 1853——. A journalist of Boston, on the editorial staff of The Pilot. Songs of the Sunrise Slope; A Dream of Lilies, a volume of poems; A Lady and Her Letters; Making Friends and Keeping Them.

Conway, Moncure Daniel. *Va.*, 1832——. A Unitarian clergyman of extremely radical views, who has for many years been in charge of a congregation in London. He has been a prolific writer in several fields, the larger number of his writings being The Rejected Stone; Idols and Ideals; Demonology and Devil Lore; The Wandering Jew; Sketch of Carlyle; The Earthward Pilgrimage; Sacred Anthology, a compilation; Emerson at Home and Abroad; George Washington and Mount Vernon; Omitted Chapters in Life and Letters of Edmund Randolph; Life of Thomas Paine; Tracts for To-Day; Natural History of the Devil; The Golden Hour; Testimonies Concerning Slavery; Human Sacrifices in England; Lessons for the Day; Travels in South Kensington; A Necklace of Stories; Pine and Palm, a novel; Prisms of Air, a novel. *Har. Ho.*

Conwell, Russell H. *Ms.*, 1842——. A Baptist minister of Philadelphia. Why the Chinese Emigrate; Woman and the Law; Life of President Hayes; Life of Bayard Taylor; Life of President Garfield; Joshua Giavencola, the Captain of the Vineyards of Lucerna. *Lo. Mer.*

Conyngham, David Power. *I.*, 1840–1883. A New York journalist, editor of The Tablet. Sherman's March Through the South; Lives of the Irish Saints and Martyrs; The Irish Brigade and its Campaigns. In fiction: Sarsfield, or the Last Great Struggle for Ireland; The O'Donnells of Glen Cottage; O'Mahoney, Chief of the Commeraghs; Rose Parnell, the Flower of Avondale.

Cook, Albert John. *Mch.*, 1842——. A professor of zoölogy at Michigan Agricultural College. Injurious Insects of Michigan; Manual of the Apiary.

Cook, Albert Stanborough. *N. J.*, 1853——. A professor of English at Yale University, who has edited Siever's Old English Grammar; Judith, an Old English Epic Fragment; Sidney's Defence of Poesy. *Gi.*

Cook, Clarence Chatham. *Ms.*, 1828——. An art critic of New York city, and editor of The Studio. He has edited Lübke's History of Art, and published also The House Beautiful; Essays on Beds and Tables, Stools and Candlesticks; The Central Park. *Scr.*

Cook, George Hammell. *N. J.*, 1818–1889. A professor of geology at Rutgers College and State geologist, whose only published work is The Geology of New Jersey.

Cook, Joel. *Pa.*, 1842——. A Philadelphia journalist, financial editor of the Public Ledger. Brief Summer Rambles near Philadelphia; An Eastern Tour at Home; A Holiday Tour in Europe; England, Picturesque and Descriptive; The Siege of Richmond. *My.*

Cook, Joseph. *N. Y.*, 1838——. A Boston lecturer whose Monday morning lectures at Tremont Temple were at one time very popular, but whose shallow, pretentious thought provoked much criticism from scholarly, accurate minds. Boston Monday Lectures, in ten volumes; Current Religious Perils, with Other Addresses on Leading Reforms. *Hou.*

Cook, Marc. *R. I.*, 1854–1882. A journalist of New York. The Wilderness Cure; Vandyke Brown Poems.

Cook, Richard Briscoe. *Md.*, 1838——. A Baptist clergyman of Wilmington, Delaware. The Story of the Baptists in all Ages and Countries.

Cook, Theodore Pease. *Ms.*, 1844——. Brother of M. Cook, *supra*. A journalist of Utica, who published a Life of Samuel J. Tilden. *Ap.*

Cooke, George Willis. *Mch.*, 1848——. A Unitarian clergyman of Lexington, Massachusetts, who has done much excellent work in criticism. George Eliot: a Critical Study; Ralph Waldo Emerson: his Life, Writings, and Philosophy; Poets and Problems, Studies of Tennyson, Ruskin, and Browning; Guide Book to Browning; The Clapboard Trees Parish, Dedham, a History. *Hou.*

Cooke, John Esten. *Va.*, 1830–1886. A noted Virginia author who served in the Confederate army during the Civil War. He wrote much historical fiction, The Virginia Comedians being the most famous of his romances. Leather Stocking and Silk; The Youth of Jefferson; Surry of Eagle's Nest; Wearing the Gray; My Lady Pokahontas; Henry St. John, reissued as Bonnybel Vane; Mohun, or the Last Days of Lee and his Paladins; Her Majesty the Queen; Pretty Mrs. Gaston; Stories of the Old Dominion; The Maurice Mystery; Mr. Grantley's Idea; Professor Pressensee; Virginia Bohemians; Hammer and Rapier; Hilt to Hilt, include the greater part of his work in fiction. He wrote also Life of General Lee; Stonewall Jackson, a Biography; Virginia, a History of the People. *Ap. Har. Hou. Lip.*

Cooke, Josiah Parsons. *Ms.*, 1827–1894. A chemist of distinction who was professor of chemistry at Harvard University from 1850, and lectured in many places on scientific topics. Religion and Chemistry; Scientific Culture; Elements of Chemical Physics; Chemical Problems and Reactions; Principles of Chemical Philosophy; The New Chemistry; The Credentials of Science the Warrant of Faith; Laboratory Practice. *Ap. Scr.*

Cooke, Nicholas Francis. *R. I.*, 1829–1885. A once prominent physician of Chicago. Satan in Society; Antiseptic Medication.

Cooke, Parsons. *Ms.*, 1800–1864. A Congregational clergyman of Lynn, strongly Calvinistic in doctrine and controversially inclined. History of German Anabaptism; A Century of Puritanism and a Century of its Opposites.

Cooke, Philip Pendleton. *Va.*, 1816–1850. Brother of J. E. Cooke, *supra*. A Virginia lawyer whose verse was once very much admired, and whose Florence Vane still lingers in the anthologies. The Froissart Ballads, and Other Poems. *See Griswold's Poets and Poetry of America; Hart's American Literature.*

Cooke, Philip St. George. *Va.*, 1809–1895. Uncle of J. E. Cooke, *supra*. A brigadier-general in the United States army who retired in 1873. Scenes and Adventures in the Army; Handy Book for United States Cavalry; Cavalry Tactics; Conquest of New Mexico and California.

Cooke, Mrs. Rose [Terry]. *Ct.*, 1827–1892. A New England writer well known both as a poet and a writer of short stories of notable excellence. Poems by Rose Terry; Happy Dodd; Somebody's Neighbors; The Sphinx's Children and Other People's; Steadfast; Huckleberries. In 1888 a complete collection of her poems was made, including the contents of her early volume and her later work in verse. The Two Villages is her best known poem, as it is one of her best. *Hou.*

Cookman, Alfred. 1828–1871. A Methodist clergyman who published Stayed on God. *See Life by H. B. Ridgaway, 1871.*

Coolbrith, Ina Donna. *Il.*, 18——. A California poet, formerly librarian of the Oakland Public Library. Her work, though uneven in quality, is nearly always musical. The Perfect Day and Other Poems; Songs of the Golden Gate. *Hou.*

Cooley, Le Roy Clark. *N. Y.*, 1833——. A professor of physics at Vassar College. Text-Book of Physics; Text-Book of Chemistry; Easy Experiments in Physical Science; Natural Philosophy; Elements of Chemistry; Students' Guide Book; Beginners' Guide to Chemistry; Laboratory Studies in Elementary Chemistry.

Cooley, Thomas McIntyre. *N. Y.*, 1824——. A jurist of prominence in Michigan, professor of history in the University of Michigan. Law of Taxation; Law of Torts; General Principles of Constitutional Law in the United States; Treatise on Constitutional Limitations of the Legislative Power in the Several States; annotated editions of Blackstone's Story's Commentaries; Michigan, a History of Governments. *Hou. Lit.*

Coolidge, Susan. *See Woolsey, Sarah.*

Coombs, Mrs. Annie [Sheldon]. *N. Y.*, 1858–1890. A novelist of New York city. As Common Mortals; A Game of Chance; The Garden of Armida. *Ap.*

Cooper, Ellwood. *Pa.*, 1820——. A horticulturist of southern California, president of the State board of horticulture. Statistics of Trade with Hayti; Forest Culture and Eucalyptus Trees; Treatise on Olive Culture.

Cooper, James Fenimore. *N. J.*, 1789–1851. The first American writer to gain general European recognition, and the first native novelist who won a national reputation. Although much that he wrote is nearly forgotten, the best of his work survives and is still popular. His first novel, Precaution, a conventional, mediocre piece of writing, appeared in 1820, and was followed, in 1821, by The Spy, the most famous of all his books, having been translated into all the principal languages of Europe. Almost as famous is The Last of the Mohicans, a much greater work. Among his tales of the sea, The Pilot and The Red Rover are the best, as the five Leather Stocking tales — The Deerslayer, The Last of the Mohicans, The Pathfinder, The Pioneers, The Prairie, — are the best of his stories of Indian life. His other fictions include The Bravo; Lionel Lincoln, or The Leaguer of Boston; The Water-Witch; The Two Admirals; The Wept of Wish-ton-Wish; The Heidenmauer; The Headsman; Homeward Bound; Home as Found; The Monikins, the weakest of all his works; Mercedes of Castile; Wing-and-Wing; Wyandotté; Afloat and Ashore; Satanstoe; The Chainbearer; The Red Skins; Jack Tier; The Crater; The Oak Openings; The Sea Lions; The Ways of the Hour; Miles Wallingford. He wrote, also, History of the United States Navy; Sketches of Switzerland; Gleanings in Europe; Notions of the Americans. *See Lowell's Fable for Critics; Bryant's Memorial Discourse, 1852; Coffin's Home of Cooper, 1872; Life, by Lounsbury, 1882; Bryant and his Friends, 1886; Richardson's American Literature; The Bookman, March, 1897. Ap. Hou. Put.*

Cooper, Myles. *E.*, 1735–1785. An Episcopal clergyman who came to America in 1762, and was president of King's (now Columbia) College, 1763–1775. Being an ardent loyalist, he was obliged to leave the colony, and returned to England. Friendly Advice to all Reasonable Americans on our Political Confusions; Poems on Several Occasions; Address to the Episcopalians of Virginia; The American Querist.

Cooper, Peter. *N. Y.*, 1791–1883. A famous philanthropist of New York city who founded the Cooper Institute. Ideas for a System of Good Government; Financial Opinions, with Autobiography.

Cooper, Susan Fenimore. *N. Y.*, 1813–1894. Daughter of J. F. Cooper, *supra.* A writer of rural sketches, whose life was passed at Cooperstown, New York. Rural Hours; Country Rambles; Rhyme and Reason; Country Life; The Shield, a Narrative;

Mount Vernon and the Children of America. *Hou.*

Cooper, Thomas. *E.*, 1759–1840. A noted scientist who came to America in 1795 with Dr. Priestley, *infra*, and was president of the College of South Carolina, 1820–34. Letters on the Slave Trade; Tracts Ethical, Theological, and Political; Information concerning America; The Bankrupt Law of America compared with that of England; Tracts on Medical Jurisprudence; Elements of Political Economy; An English Version of the Institutes of Justinian.

Cooper, William. *Ms.*, 1694–1743. A once famous Congregational minister of Boston. Tract Defending Inoculation for the Small Pox, 1720; The Doctrine of Predestination unto Life.

Cope, Edward Drinker. *Pa.*, 1840–1897. A noted Philadelphia naturalist. Origin of Genera; Extinct Batrachia and Reptilia of North America; Primary Groups of Batrachia Anura; Systematic Relations of the Fishes; Vertebrate Palæontology of New Mexico; Tertiary Vertebrata of the West; The Origin of the Fittest, include the more important of his writings. *Ap.*

Cope, Gilbert. *Pa.*, 1840——. A genealogist of Pennsylvania. Record of the Cope Family; The Browns of Nottingham; Genealogy of the Dutton Family; Genealogy of the Sharpless Family; History of Chester County, Pennsylvania.

Coppée, Henry. *Ga.*, 1821–1895. A prominent educator, president of Lehigh University, 1866–75, and professor there until his death. During the Mexican War he served as an officer in the American army. His most important work is a History of the Conquest of Spain by the Arab Moors, which takes up the narrative at the period reached at the close of Irving's "Mahomet and his Successors." His other works comprise Elements of Logic; Elements of Rhetoric; Grant and his Campaigns; Manual of Battalion Drill; Evolutions of the Line; Manual of Court Martial. *Lit.*

Copway, George, or **Kah-ge-ga-gah-bowh.** *Mch.*, 1818–*c.* 1869. An Indian of the Ojibway tribe who was a journalist in New York City, and was well known as a lecturer. Recollections of a Forest Life; Copway's "American Indian;" The Traditional History of the Ojibway Nation; The Ojibway Conquest, a poem; Running Sketches of Men and Places in Europe, include the most of his writings.

Corbin, Mrs. Caroline Elizabeth [Fairfield]. *Ct.*, 1835——. A Chicago writer of fiction and other works. Rebecca; His Marriage Vow; Belle and the Boys; A Woman's Philosophy of Love, a psychological treatise. *Le.*

Corbin, John. *Il.*, 1870——. Son of Mrs. Corbin, *supra.* The Elizabethan Hamlet. *Scr.*

Cornelius, Elias. *N. Y.*, 1794–1852. A missionary to the Cherokee Indians who wrote The Little Osage Captive, an Authentic Narrative.

Cornell, Alonzo Barton. *N. Y.*, 1832——. A governor of New York, 1880–83, and a son of the founder of Cornell University. His only publication is True and Firm, a Biography of Ezra Cornell: a Filial Tribute. *Bar.*

Cornell, John Henry. *N. Y.*, 1828–1894. A musician and organist of New York City. Primer of Modern Musical Tonality; Practice of Sight Singing; Easy Method of Modulation; Theory and Practice of Musical Form; A Manual of Roman Chant; Congregational Tune Book.

Cornell, William Mason. *Ms.*, 1802–1895. A physician of Boston and elsewhere. Robert Raikes, the Founder of Sunday Schools; Life of Horace Greeley; Grammar of the English Language; Consumption Prevented; Treatise on Epilepsy; History of Pennsylvania, include the most of his writings. *Fu. Lo.*

Cornwall, Henry Bedinger. *Ct.*, 1844——. A professor of mineralogy at Princeton College since 1873, who has published A Manual of Blow-Pipe Analysis.

Cornwallis, Kinahan. *E.*, 1835——. A New York journalist who came to America about 1860. His more important works are Yarra Yarra, or the Wandering Aborigine, a Poetical Narrative; The New Eldorado of British Columbia; Wreck and Ruin, or Modern Society; My Life and Adventures, an Autobiography; Adrift with a Vengeance; Pilgrims of Fashion; The Gold Room and the New York Stock Exchange. *Har.*

Cornwell, Henry Sylvester. *N.H.*, 1831–1886. A physician of New London, Connecticut, who wrote much thoughtful verse. The Land of Dreams and Other Poems (1879), is the only collection that has been made of his poems.

Corson, Hiram. *Pa.*, 1828——. A Chaucerian and Early English scholar, professor at Cornell University since 1870. The Voice and Spiritual Education; Elocutionary Manual; Jottings on the Text of Hamlet; Introduction to the Study of Browning; Lectures on English Language and Literature; The Aims of Literary Study; Vocal Culture in Relation to Literary Study; Thesaurus of Early English; Handbook of Anglo-Saxon and Early English. He has also edited Chaucer's Legende of Goode Women. *Gi. Ho. Mac.*

Corson, Juliet. *Ms.*, 1842–1897. A cooking instructor of New York, founder of the School of Cooking there in 1876. Cooking Manual; Cooking School Text-Book; Twenty-Five Cent Dinners for Families of Six; Meals for the Million; Practical American Cookery; Family Living on Five Hundred Dollars a Year; Diet for Invalids and Children. *Do. Har.*

Corthell, Elmer Lawrence. *Ms.*, 1840——. A civil engineer of distinction. History of the Jetties at the Mouth of the Mississippi.

Corwin, Edward Tanjore. *N.Y.*, 1834——. A Reformed Dutch clergyman of New Jersey, among whose works are Manual of the Reformed Protestant Dutch Church in North America; Manual of the Reformed Church in America; Corwin Genealogy.

Cossett, Franceway Ranna. *N.H.*, 1790–1863. A Cumberland Presbyterian clergyman of Tennessee. He published The Life and Times of Ewing, which gives a history of the beginnings of the Cumberland Presbyterian denomination.

Cotheal, Alexander Isaac. *N.Y.*, 1804–1894. An Oriental scholar of New York City who published Sketch of the Language of the Mosquito Indians; Atoff the Generous, a translation from the Arabic.

Cotting, John Ruggles. *Ms.*, 1783–1867. A once noted Georgia scientist. Introduction to Chemistry; Lectures on Geology; Soils and Manures.

a **Cotton, John.** *E.*, 1585–1652. The foremost clergyman of his century in New England. He came to the Massachusetts colony in 1633, having been for 20 years vicar of St. Botolph's church in Boston, Lincolnshire. He was at once made teacher of the church in the new settlement of Boston, and until his death exercised an influence in church and state unequalled by any one since in New England. He was a prolific writer, but his writings have no charm of style, and the power which he wielded was a force that lay in the man himself, not in his books. His principal works comprise The Bloody Tenet Washed and made White in the Blood of the Lamb, a reply to Roger Williams's famous "Bloody Tenet of Persecution"; A Brief Exposition upon Ecclesiastes; The Covenant of Grace; The Keys of the Kingdom of Heaven; The Way of the Congregational Churches Cleared; The Way of Life; Treatise concerning Predestination; The New Covenant; Meat for Strong Men, Spiritual Milk for Babes. *See Cotton Mather's Magnalia; Lives by Norton, 1653; McClure, 1843; Tyler's American Literature.*

Coues [kŏwz], **Elliott.** *N.H.*, 1842——. An eminent naturalist connected with the Smithsonian Institution. Key to North American Birds; Field Ornithology; Birds of the Northwest; Fur-Bearing Animals; Check List of North American Birds; Birds of the Colorado Valley; New England Bird Life (with W. A. Stearns); Biogen, a Speculation on the Origin of Life; The Dæmon of Darwin; Our Native Birds. *Est. Le. Wn.*

Coulter, John Merle. *Ch.*, 1851——. A botanist who was president of the Indiana State University, 1891–93. Synopsis of the Flora of Colorado (with T. C. Porter); Manual of Rocky Mountain Botany; Manual of Texan Botany;

Text-Book of Western Botany (with Asa Gray, *infra*).

Councilman, William Thomas. *Md.*, 1854——. A physician and instructor at the Harvard Medical School. Contribution to the Study of Inflammation; On Arterio Sclerosis; Syphilis of the Lungs; On the Ætiology of Malaria, and other works.

Courtenay [kŭrt'ni], **Edward Henry.** *Md.*, 1803–1853. A civil engineer who was professor of mathematics in the University of Virginia, 1842–53, and published a Treatise on Differential Calculus and the Calculus of Variations.

Covell, James. *Ms.*, 1796–1845. A Methodist clergyman of New York and Vermont who published a Dictionary of the Bible. *Meth.*

Cowan, Frank. *Pa.*, 1844——. A Pennsylvania lawyer and journalist, who has travelled extensively and who entered Corea before that country had made any treaties with foreign nations. Curious Facts in the History of Insects; Zomara, a Romance of Spain; Southwestern Pennsylvania in Song and Story; The City of the Royal Palm, and Other Poems; A Visit in Verse to Honolulu; Fact and Fancy in New Zealand.

Cowdin, Jasper Barnett. 18——. Esther's Wedding and Other Poems.

Cowell, Benjamin. *Ms.*, 1781–1860. A jurist of Providence who published an historical work, The Spirit of '76.

Cowen, Patrick H. ——18—. Digest of Criminal Decisions of the Court of New York; Reports of Criminal Cases; The Poor Laws of the State of New York.

Cowles [kōlz], **Henry.** *Ct.*, 1803–1881. A Congregational clergyman who was professor of theology at Oberlin College, 1835–48. Gospel Manna for Christian Pilgrims; Hebrew History; Critical Notes on the Old and New Testament, in 16 volumes. *Ap.*

Cowley, Charles. *E.*, 1832——. A lawyer of Lowell. Memories of the Indians and Pioneers of Lowell; Illustrated History of Lowell; Famous Divorces of all Ages; Our Divorce Courts.

Cox, Edward Travers. *Va.*, 1821——. A geologist of New York City who made a number of important surveys, and published Annual Reports of the Geological Survey of Indiana.

Cox, Jacob Dolson. *O.*, 1828——. An Ohio lawyer who served in the Union army during the Civil War as major-general, was governor of Ohio, 1866–67, Secretary of the Interior, 1869–1870, and president of Cincinnati University, 1885. Atlanta; The March to the Sea; The Second Battle of Bull Run as connected with the Fitz-John Porter Case. *Scr.*

Cox, Palmer. *Q.*, 1840——. An artist of New York City widely known by the various volumes of the Brownie Books, a series of juveniles consisting of very original humourous pictures and somewhat indifferent verses. Other works of his include Squibs, or Every-Day Life Illustrated; Hans Von Petter's Trip to Gotham; How Columbus Found America; That Stanley; Queer People, such as Goblins, etc.; Queer People with Claws and Wings; Queer People with Wings and Stings. *Cent.*

Cox, Samuel Hanson. *N. J.*, 1793–1880. A Presbyterian clergyman of the New School party noted for his eccentricities and fondness for controversy. Quakerism not Christianity; Theopneuston, or Select Scriptures Considered; Interviews Memorable and Useful, are his most important writings.

Cox, Samuel Sullivan. *O.*, 1824–1889. A noted Democratic Congressman from Ohio, and later from New York, who was a popular lecturer, humourist, and writer of travels. He was minister to Turkey, 1885–86. Eight Years in Congress; Why We Laugh; Three Decades of Federal Legislation; Diversions of a Diplomat in Turkey; A Buckeye Abroad; Search for Winter Sunbeams in the Riviera, Corsica, Algiers, and Spain; Arctic Sunbeams; Orient Sunbeams; Free Land and Free Trade. *Har.*

Coxe, Arthur Cleveland. *N. J.*, 1818–1896. The second Protestant Episcopal bishop of Western New York. A son of S. H. Cox, *supra*, having adopted an older spelling of his surname. A writer of much force and originality, holding opinions with great tenacity and much given to controversy. Christian Ballads; Halloween; Athanasius and Other Poems; Advent, a Mystery; Saul, a Mystery; Athwold, a Romaunt; St. Jonathan, the Lay of a Scald, include his writings in verse. His other works comprise Impressions of England; Thoughts on the Services; Apollos, or the Way of God; The Criterion, a Means of Distinguishing Truth from Error; Institutes of Christian History; Signs of the Times; L'Episcopat de l'Occident, a defence of Anglican theology; The Penitential. *Ap. Dut. Lip.*

Coxe, Eckley Brinton. *Pa.*, 1839——. A Pennsylvania mining engineer who has published Theoretical Mechanics.

Coxe, John Redman. *N. J.*, 1773–1864. A noted physician who was the first to introduce the practice of vaccination in Philadelphia. Inflammation; Importance of Medicine; Vaccination; Combustion; American Dispensatory; Recognition of Friends in Another World; Agaricus Atramentarius; The Writings of Hippocrates and Galen Epitomized; Refutation of Harvey's Claim to the Discovery of the Circulation of the Blood; Appeal to the Public.

Coxe, Margaret. *N. J.*, 1800–18—. Claims of the Country on American Females; Wonders of the Deep; Ladies' Companion.

Coxe, Tench. *Pa.*, 1755–1824. A once noted Philadelphia writer on commerce and political economy. Inquiry into the Principles of a Commercial System for the United States; View of the United States; On the Navigation Act; Thoughts on Naval Power; Address on American Manufactures.

Coyle, John Patterson. *Pa.*, 1852–1895. A Congregational clergyman formerly of North Adams, Massachusetts, but settled in Denver at the time of his death. The Imperial Christ, with a Biographical Introduction by George A. Gates; The Spirit in Literature and Life. *Hou.*

Cozzens, Frederick Swartwout. *N. Y.*, 1818–1869. A wine merchant of New York City, once noted as a humourist, but now neglected. The Sparrowgrass Papers; Acadia, or a Sojourn among the Blue Noses; Sayings of Dr. Bushwhacker and Other Learned Men; Stone House on the Susquehanna; Prismatics; Fitz-Greene Halleck, a Memorial.

Cozzens, Issachar. *R. I.*, 1781–18—. Uncle of F. S. Cozzens, *supra.* A mineralogist who published History of New York Island.

Cozzens, Samuel Woodworth. *Ms.*, 1834–1878. A lawyer of Arizona. Nobody's Husband; The Marvellous Country, or Three Years in Arizona; The Young Trail Hunters; The Young Silver Seekers; Crossing the Quicksands. *Le.*

Craddock, Charles Egbert. *See Murfree, Mary Noailles.*

Crafts, Wilbur Fisk. *Me.*, 1850——. A Congregational clergyman of New York City and elsewhere. Through the Eye to the Heart; Childhood; The Ideal Sunday-School; The Rescue of Child Soul; Must the Old Testament Go? The Sabbath for Man; Talks to Boys and Girls about Jesus; Successful Men of To-Day; Practical Christian Sociology, include the larger number of his writings. *Fu. Le.*

Crafts, William. *S. C.*, 1787–1826. A once noted lawyer and journalist of Charleston. *See Poems, Essays, and Orations, with Memoir, by S. Gilman, infra, 1828.*

Crafts, William Augustus. 1819——. A Boston writer. Life of General Grant; History of the United States; Pioneers in the Settlement of America.

Cram, Ralph Adams. *N. H.*, 1863——. An architect of Boston. The Decadent, being the Gospel of Inaction; Black Spirits and White, a book of ghost stories; In the Island of Avalon, a book of verse. *Cop. St.*

Cranch, Christopher Pearse. *Va.*, 1813–1892. Son of W. Cranch, *infra.* He was ordained as a Unitarian minister, but after a few years in the ministry gave up his profession and devoted himself to art. For many years he lived in Italy and Paris, but his later years were spent in Cambridge, Massachusetts. His early sympathies were with the New England Transcendentalists, and his best known poem, Thought, was written for The Dial. His work as a poet is uneven, but at its best is excellent. It never strongly appealed to popular tastes, but was always appreciated by thoughtful minds. Poems, 1844; The Bird and the Bell, and Other Poems; Ariel and Caliban, and Other Poems; Satan: a Libretto; The Æneid in English Blank Verse. The Last of the Huggermuggers; Kobboltzo, are juvenile prose tales. *Hou. Le.*

Cranch, Richard. *E.*, 1726–1811. A lawyer of Braintree, Massachusetts, who published Views of the Prophets concerning Anti-Christ.

Cranch, William. *Ms.*, 1769–1855. Son of R. Cranch, *supra*. A noted jurist who was chief justice of the District of Columbia, 1805–55. Reports of Cases in the United States District Court of the District of Columbia, 1801–41; Supreme Court Reports, 1800–1815.

Crandall, Charles Henry. *N. Y.*, 1858——. A littérateur of Springdale, Connecticut. Wayside Music, a book of verse. *Put.*

Crane, Cephas Bennett. 1833——. A Baptist clergyman of Boston. The Spiritual Court of the Christian Church.

Crane, Jonathan Townley. *N. J.*, 1819–1880. A Methodist clergyman of New Jersey. Methodism and its Methods; The Right Way; Essay on Dancing; Popular Amusements; Arts of Intoxication; Holiness the Birthright of all God's Children.

Crane, Oliver. *N. J.*, 1822–1896. A Presbyterian clergyman who lived in Boston during his latest years. Minto and Other Poems; Virgil's Aeneid translated literally into English dactylic hexameter.

√ **Crane, Stephen.** *N. J.*, 1870——. A popular novelist of New York City. George's Mother; The Black Riders and Other Lines, a collection of wilfully eccentric verse; The Red Badge of Courage, a striking historical romance of the Civil War in America; Maggie, a story of slum life. *Ap. Cop.*

Crane, Thomas Frederick. *N. Y.*, 1844——. A professor of Romance languages at Cornell University. Italian Popular Tales; The Exempla, or Illustrative Stories from the Sermones of Jacques de Vitry; Tableaux de la Revolution Française; Le Romantisme Française; La Société Française au Dix-septiéme Siècle; Chansons Populaires de la France.

Crane, William Carey. *Va.*, 1816–1885. A Baptist clergyman of Texas, president of Baylor University, 1863–1885, which was renamed Crane College in his honour, 1885. Discourses; Life of Sam. Houston, and lesser works.

Crawford, Mrs. Alice [Arnold]. *Wis.*, 1850–1874. A Milwaukee writer who published A Few Thoughts for a Few Friends, a collection of verse.

Crawford, Francis Marion. *Iy.*, 1854——. A son of the noted sculptor, Crawford. His life has been mainly spent in Italy, where he has devoted himself to novel-writing with great perseverance. His novels are of varying degrees of excellence and always entertaining, but none of them reach the high-water mark of enduring excellence. Mr. Isaacs; Dr. Claudius; A Roman Singer; To Leeward; An American Politician; Zoroaster; Adam Johnstone's Sin; A Tale of a Lonely Parish; Saracinesca; Marzio's Crucifix; Paul Patoff; With the Immortals; Greifenstein; Sant' Ilario; A Cigarette-maker's Romance; Khaled; The Witch of Prague; The Three Fates; Don Orsino; Children of the King; Pietro Ghisleri; Marion Darche; The Ralstons; Katherine Lauderdale; Casa Braccio; Love in Idleness, a Tale of Bar Harbour; The Novel: What it Is; Constantinople, a book of travels; Taquisara. *See Vedder's American Writers. Mac. Mer. Scr.*

Crawford, Nathaniel Morton. *Ga.*, 1811–1871. A Baptist minister of Kentucky, president of Georgetown College, Kentucky, 1865–71, and the author of Christian Paradoxes.

Crayon, Porte. *See Strother.*

Creswell, Mrs. Julia [Pleasants]. *Al.*, 1827–1886. A Southern writer who published Aphelia and Other Poems by Two Cousins; Callamura, an allegorical novel.

Crocker, George Glover. *Ms.*, 1843——. A lawyer of Boston. Principles of Procedure in Deliberative Assemblies.

Crocker, Mrs. Hannah [**Mather**]. *Ms.*, 1765–1847. A granddaughter of Cotton Mather, *infra.* Letters on Free Masonry; The School of Reform; Observations on the Rights of Woman.

Crocker, Uriel Haskell. *Ms.*, 1832——. Brother of G. G. Crocker, *supra.* A lawyer of Boston. The Cause of Hard Times; Notes on Common Forms; Book of Massachusetts Law; Excessive Saving a Cause of Commercial Distress; Notes on General Statutes of Massachusetts (with G. G. Crocker). *Lit.*

Crockett, David. *Tn.*, 1786–1836. A noted hunter and pioneer who enlisted in the Texan army in the revolt against Mexico, and was slain in the massacre at the Alamo, in San Antonio. Tour to the North and Down East; Life of David Crockett, by Himself (1834); Colonel Crockett's Exploits in Texas; Life of Martin Van Buren, Heir Apparent; Leisure Hour Musings in Rhyme. *See Life by E. S. Ellis; Bibliography of Texas.*

Croffut, William Augustus. *Ct.*, 1835——. A well-known journalist attached to many journals, East and West, and connected with the United States Geological Survey since 1888. The War History of Connecticut; A Helping Hand; Bourbon Ballads; Deseret, an Opera; A Midsummer Lark, a humourous volume of travels; The Vanderbilts; The Folks Next Door; The Prophecy and Other Poems.

Croly, David Goodman. *N. Y.*, 1829–1889. A journalist of New York City. Life of Horatio Seymour; History of Reconstruction; The Positivist Primer; Glimpses of the Future.

Croly, Mrs. Jane Cunningham. "Jennie June." *E.*, 1831——. Wife of D. G. Croly, *supra.* The founder of Sorosis, and editor of Demorest's Magazine, 1860–87. The originator of duplicate correspondence. Talks on Women's Topics; For Better or Worse; Knitters and Crochet; Letters and Monograms; Cookery Book for Young Beginners; Thrown upon her Own Resources. *Cr.*

Crooks, George Richard. *Pa.*, 1822–1897. A Methodist clergyman and religious journalist. Life of John McClintock, *infra;* Life of Matthew Simpson; First Books in Latin and Greek (with J. McClintock); Latin-English Lexicon (with A. J. Schem). *Fu. Har.*

Crosby, Alpheus. *N. H.*, 1810–1874. An educator of Massachusetts who published Greek Lessons; Greek Fables; Greek Tables; First Lessons in Geometry; an edition of Xenophon's Anabasis.

Crosby, Howard. *N. Y.*, 1826–1891. A Presbyterian clergyman long prominent in New York City who was chancellor of the University of New York city, 1870–81. The Christian Preacher; Notes on the New Testament; Life of Jesus; Christ and Science; At the Lord's Table; Sermons; Lands of the Moslem; Œdipus Tyrannus of Sophocles, with Notes; Bible Manual; Bible Companion; Bible View of the Jewish Church; The Seven Churches of Asia, or Worldliness in the Church; Thoughts on the Pentateuch; Commentary on the New Testament, include his principal works. *Fu. Ran.*

Crosby, Nathan. *N. H.*, 1798–1885. Brother of A. Crosby, *supra.* A prominent lawyer of Lowell, who published First Half Century of Dartmouth College.

Crosby, William Otis. *O.*, 1850——. A professor of geology in the Massachusetts Institute of Technology who has published Common Minerals and Rocks; Contributions to the Geology of Eastern Massachusetts.

Cross, Charles Robert. *N. Y.*, 1848——. A professor of physics in the Massachusetts Institute of Technology. Course in Elementary Physics; Lecture Notes on Mechanics and Optics.

Cross, David W. *N. Y.*, 1814——. A Cleveland lawyer of local fame as a sportsman. Fifty Years with the Rod and Gun.

Cross, Joseph. *E.*, 1813–1893. An Episcopal clergyman who from 1829–1856 was a prominent Methodist divine. The more important of his writings include Headlands of Faith; Pisgah Views of the Promised Inheritance; A Year in Europe; Coals from the Altar; Pauline Charity; Prelections on Charity; Old Wine and New.

Cross, Mrs. Jane Tandy [Chinn] [Harding]. *Ky.*, 1817–1870. Wife of J. Cross, *supra*. Wayside Flowerets; Heart Blossoms for my Little Daughters; Bible Gleanings; Driftwood; Gonzalo de Cordova, a translation from the Spanish; Duncan Adair, a novel.

Croswell, Andrew. 1709–1785. A Boston clergyman, very active as a controversialist. The Apostle's Advice to the Jailor Improved; Heaven shut against Arminians and Antinomians.

Croswell, Harry. *Ct.*, 1778–1858. An Episcopal clergyman who was rector of Trinity Church, New Haven, 1816–58, but in earlier life was a political journalist noted for his scathing editorials. Young Churchman's Guide; Manual of Family Prayers; Guide to the Holy Sacrament.

Croswell, William. *Ms.*, 1804–1851. Son of H. Croswell, *supra*. An Episcopal clergyman of Boston, the first rector of the Church of the Advent. Some of his hymns appear in various religious anthologies and hymnals. Poems Sacred and Secular.

Crowe, Winfield Scott. *Ind.*, 1850–——. A Universalist clergyman, of Newark, New Jersey, editor of the Universalist Monthly. The Man of Evolution; The God of Evolution; The Lordship of Jesus.

Crowell, Eugene. *N. Y.*, 1817–1894. A writer of San Francisco, and later of New York city, who was a zealous defender of Spiritualism. The Identity of Primitive Christianity with Modern Spiritualism; The Spirit World; The Philosophy of Death; Spiritualism and Insanity; The Religion of Spiritualism.

Crowell, William. *Ms.*, 1806–1871. A Baptist clergyman who published The Church Member's Manual of Ecclesiastical Principles; Church Member's Handbook; History of Baptist Literature for Fifty Years.

Cruger, Mrs. Julia Grinnell [Storrow]. "Julien Gordon." *F.*, 18——. A popular novelist of New York city. A Diplomat's Diary; Poppaea; A Successful Man; A Wedding and Other Stories; Mademoiselle Réséda; A Puritan Pagan. *Lip.*

Cruger, Mary. *N. Y.*, 1834——. A writer of Montrose, New York. Hyperæsthesia; A Den of Thieves, or the Lay Reader of St. Mark's; The Vanderheyde Manor House; How She Did It; Brotherhood. *Fo. Lo.*

Crummell, Alexander. *N. Y.*, 1819–——. A coloured Episcopal clergyman of Washington. The Future of Africa; Greatness of Christ, and Other Sermons; Africa and America.

Cruse, Christian Frederick. *Pa.*, 1794–1864. An Episcopal clergyman of New York city whose translation of the Ecclesiastical History of Eusebius is a standard English version.

Cruse, Mary Anne. *Al.*, 18——. A writer and educator of Huntsville, Alabama. Besides a novel of the Civil War, Cameron Hall, she has written several popular Sunday-school books, such as The Little Episcopalian; Bessie Melville.

Cruttenden, Daniel Henry. *N. Y.*, 1816–1874. An educator of New York city, among whose text-books are Systematic Arithmetic Series; The Philosophy of Language; Rhetorical Grammar.

Crynkle, Nym. *See Wheeler, A. C.*

Culbertson, Matthew Simpson. *Pa.*, 1818–1862. A Presbyterian missionary to China. Darkness in the Flowery Kingdom, or Religious Notions in North China.

Cullum, George Washington. *N. Y.*, 1809–1892. A brevet major-general in the United States army. Military Bridges with India-Rubber Pontoons; Biographical Register of the Officers and Graduates of the U. S. Military Academy at West Point, 1802–90; System of Military Bridges. *Hou.*

Cumming, Kate. *Al.*, c. 1835——. A resident of Mobile, prominent during the Civil War as an organizer of field hospitals in the Confederate army. Hospital Life in Tennessee from the Battle of Shiloh to the End of the War.

Cummings, Amos Jay. *N. Y.*, 1842–——. A journalist of New York city. Horace Greeley Campaign Songster; Sayings of Uncle Rufus; Ziska Letters.

Cummings, Jeremiah W. *D. C.*, 1823–1866. A once popular Roman Catholic clergyman of New York city. Italian Legends; Songs for Catholic Schools; Spiritual Progress; The Silver Stole.

Cummings, Thomas Seir. *E.*, 1804–1894. A New York artist who was author of the Historic Annals of the National Academy from its Foundation to 1865.

Cummins, Ebenezer Harlow. *N. C.*, 1790–1835. A clergyman and magistrate of Baltimore. Geography of Alabama; History of the Late War (1820).

Cummins, Maria Susanna. *Ms.*, 1827–1866. A once famous novelist of Massachusetts, whose first book, The Lamplighter, enjoyed for a time a phenomenal popularity. Her subsequent stories include El Fureidîs, a tale of Palestine; Haunted Hearts; Mabel Vaughan. *Cr. Hou.*

Curry, Daniel. *N. Y.*, 1809–1887. A Methodist divine of note. New York, an Historical Sketch; Life Story of Rev. D. W. Clark, *supra;* Fragments, Religious and Theological; Platform Papers.

Curry, Jabez Lamar Monroe. *Ga.*, 1825——. A Baptist clergyman who served in the Confederate army during the Civil War, has been prominent as an educator, and was United States Minister to Spain in 1885. Baptists and Pedobaptists, their Radical Differences in Faith and Practice; Constitutional Government in Spain; Gladstone, a Study; Southern States of the American Union.

Curry, Otway. *O.*, 1804–1855. An Ohio journalist who published Love of the Past, a poem.

Curry, Samuel Silas. *Tn.*, 1847——. An educator of Boston whose specialty is the culture of expression. The Province of Expression; Lessons in Vocal Expression; Imagination and Dramatic Instinct.

Curtin, Jeremiah. *Wis.*, 1838——. Myths and Folk-Lore of Ireland; Hero Tales of Ireland; Tales of the Fairies and the Ghost World, collected from Oral Tradition in South Munster; Myths and Folk-Tales of the Russians, Western Slavs, and Magyars. His translations include Tales of Three Centuries, from the Russian of Zagoskin; The Romances of Sienkiewicz, from the Polish. *Lit.*

Curtis, Alva. *N. H.*, 1797–1881. An Ohio physician and medical writer. Medical Discussions; Lectures on Midwifery; Theory and Practice of Medicine; Medical Criticisms.

Curtis, Benjamin Robbins. *Ms.*, 1809–1874. A noted jurist of Boston. Reports of Cases in the Circuit Courts of the United States; United States Supreme Court Decisions; Digest and Decisions of United States Supreme Court. *See Memoir by G. T. Curtis. Lit.*

Curtis, Benjamin Robbins, Jr. *Ms.*, 1855–1891. Son of B. R. Curtis, *supra.* A municipal court judge of Boston. Dottings Round the Circle, a volume of travels.

Curtis, Mrs. Caroline Gardiner [Cary]. "Carroll Winchester." *N. Y.*, 1827——. A novelist of Boston. From Madge to Margaret; The Love of a Lifetime.

Curtis, Edward. *R. I.*, 1838——. Brother of G. W. Curtis, *infra.* A physician of New York who has published Manual of General Medical Technology.

Curtis, George Ticknor. *Ms.*, 1812–1894. Brother of B. R. Curtis, *supra.* An eminent lawyer of New York city, well known as a legal writer and biographer. Digest of English and American Admiralty Decisions; Digest of Decisions of Courts of Common Law and Admiralty in the United States; American Conveyancer; Law of Patents; Equity Precedents; Inventor's Manual; Law of Copyright; Rights and Duties of Merchant Seamen; Commentaries on the Jurisprudence, Practice, and Peculiar Jurisdiction of United States Courts; A History of the Constitution of the United States; Life of James Buchanan; Life of Daniel Webster; Creation or Evolution; Last Years of Daniel Webster; John Charaxes, a novel. *Har. Lit.*

Curtis, George William. *R. I.*, 1824–1892. One of the foremost of

American essayists, and a writer whose influence was as helpful as it was widespread. In boyhood he was one of the members of the famous Brook Farm Association at West Roxbury. To Putnam's Monthly he contributed The Potiphar Papers, a spirited satire upon society; and Prne and I, a story far superior to his more ambitious novel, Trumps. For thirty-five years he filled the Easy Chair department of Harper's Monthly, and from 1863-92 he was the political editor of Harper's Weekly. He was zealous in the cause of civil service reform, and by his efforts as writer and lecturer accomplished very much in that direction. Beside the volumes already named, his writings include Nile Notes of a Howadji; Lotus Eating; The Howadji in Syria; James Russell Lowell, an Address; Eulogy on Wendell Phillips; From the Easy Chair; Speeches, Addresses, &c., edited by C. E. Norton, *infra;* Literary and Social Essays. *See Life by E. Cary, 1895; Address by J. W. Chadwick, supra; Century Magazine, February, 1883; Smalley's Studies of Men.*

Curtis, Moses Ashley. *Ms.*, 1808–1872. A botanist and Episcopal clergyman of North Carolina. Edible Fungi of North Carolina; Contributions to Mycology of North America; Catalogue of the Plants of North Carolina; Esculent Fungi; Indigenous and Native Plants of North Carolina.

Curtis, Samuel Ives. *Ct.*, 1844——. A Congregational clergyman, professor in the Theological Seminary of Chicago. The Name Maccabee; The Levitical Priests; Ingersoll and Moses; The Date of our Gospels. *Rev.*

Curtis, Thomas F. *E.*, 1815–1872. A Baptist divine who was for some years president of Lewisburg University, Pennsylvania. Progress of Baptist Principles in the Last Hundred Years (1857); The Human Element in the Inspiration of the Sacred Scriptures, a work which occupies the Colenso position on the subject and is in places more advanced.

Curtis, William Eleroy. *O.*, 1850——. A prominent Washington journalist. The United States and Foreign Powers; Life of Zachariah Chandler; The Capitals of Spanish America; The Land of the Nihilist; Venezuela; The Yankees of the East: Japan Sketches. *Har. St.*

Curtiss, Mrs. Abby [Allin]. *Ct.*, 1820——. A verse-writer of Madison, Wisconsin, who published Home Ballads (1850).

Curwen, Samuel. *Ms.*, 1715–1802. A loyalist who lived in England during the American Revolution, but returned after its close to his native town of Salem. While an exile he kept a journal which contains much valuable information concerning loyalist exiles. It was first published in 1842, with the title Journal and Letters of the Late Samuel Curwen, Judge of Admiralty, an American Refugee in England, 1775–1884.

Cushing, Caleb. *Ms.*, 1800–1879. A Massachusetts statesman and diplomatist, who was attorney-general of the United States, 1853–57. Historical and Political Review of the Late Revolution in France, 1833; Practical Principles of Political Economy; Life of William Henry Harrison; Growth and Territorial Progress of the United States, 1837; Reminiscences of Spain; History of Newburyport; The Treaty of Washington. *See Appleton's American Biography. Har.*

Cushing, Luther Stearns. *Ms.*, 1803–1856. A well-known authority on parliamentary practice and a Massachusetts jurist who was lecturer on Roman Law in Harvard University, 1848–56. Massachusetts Reports, 1848–53; Manual of Parliamentary Practice; Trustee Process; Remedial Law; Reports of Controverted Election Cases in Massachusetts; Introduction to the study of Roman Civil Law; Elements of the Law and Practice of Legislative Assemblies in the United States; Lex Parliamentaria Americana; Rules of Proceeding and Debates in the Deliberative Assemblies. *Lit.*

Cushing, William. *Ms.*, 1811–1895. Brother of L. S. Cushing, *supra.* A Unitarian clergyman of Massachusetts who, after retiring from the ministry, devoted himself to literary research, and published Anonyms; Initials and

Pseudonyms, useful guide-books of literary information. *Cr.*

Custer, Mrs. Elizabeth [Bacon]. *Mch.*, 184——. Wife of G. A. Custer, *infra.* Boots and Saddles, or Life in Dakota with General Custer; Tenting on the Plains, or General Custer in Kansas and Texas; Following the Guidon. *Har.*

Custer, George Armstrong. *O.*, 1839–1876. A famous general in the Federal army during the Civil War, who afterwards became noted in campaigns against the Indians, and was killed with his entire command in a battle with the Sioux in the Black Hills. My Life on the Plains was his only publication.

Custis, George Washington Parke. *Va.*, 1781–1857. An adopted son of General Washington. He published Recollections of Washington.

Cuthbert, James Hazard. *S. C.*, 1822——. A Baptist divine of Washington. Our Mission as Baptists; Life of Richard Fuller, *infra.*

Cutler, Elbridge Jefferson. *Ms.*, 1831–1870. A professor of modern languages at Harvard University, 1865–1870. War Poems; Stella. *See Memoir by A. P. Peabody, infra, 1872.*

Cutler, Mrs. Hannah Maria [Tracy] [Conant]. *Ms.*, 1815——. A prominent woman suffragist who became a physician in 1879, and practiced in Cobden, Illinois. Woman as She Was, Is, and Should Be; Phillipia, or A Woman's Question; The Fortunes of Michael Doyle, or Home Rule for Ireland.

Cutler, Jervis. *Ms.*, 1768–1844. A Western pioneer who published Topographical Description of the Western Country (1812). *See Life and Times of Ephraim Cutler.*

Cutler, Mrs. Lizzie [Petit]. *Va.*, 1836——. A novelist of New York City. Light and Darkness; Household Mysteries, a romance of Southern life; The Stars of the Crowd, or Men and Women of the Day.

Cutter, George Washington. *Ms.*, 1801–1865. A verse-writer of Washington. Buena Vista, and Other Poems; Song of Steam; Poems National and Patriotic.

Cutting, Hiram Adolphus. *Vt.*, 1832——. A State geologist of Vermont. Mining in Vermont; Climatology of Vermont; Microscopic Revelations; Farm Pests; Notes on Building Stones; Lectnres on Plants, Fertilization, etc.; Lectures on Milk, etc.; Farm Lectures; Vermont Agricultural Reports.

Cutting, Sewall Sylvester. *Vt.*, 1813–1882. A Baptist clergyman and religious journalist. Historical Vindications; Struggles and Triumphs of Religious Liberty; Ancient Baptistries.

Cuyler [ky'ler], Theodore Ledyard. *N. Y.*, 1822——. A Presbyterian clergyman of note, formerly pastor of Lafayette Avenue Church of Brooklyn. Stray Arrows; Cedar Christian; The Empty Crib; Wayside Springs; Right to the Point; Thought Hives; God's Light on Dark Clouds; Pointed Papers; Heart Life; From the Nile to Norway; Newly Enlisted, or Talks to Young Converts; The Young Preacher; Stirring the Eagle's Nest; How To Be a Pastor; Christianity in the Home, comprise the greater number of his works. *Rev.*

D

Dabney, Richard. *Va.*, 1787–1825. A once noted instructor in Richmond, Virginia, whose Poems, Original and Translated, contain scholarly translations from Euripides, Alcæus, and other classic poets.

Dabney, Richard Heath. *Va.*, 1859——. The Causes of the French Revolution. *Ho.*

Dabney, Robert Lewis. *Va.*, 1820–1898. Nephew of R. Dabney, *supra.* A Presbyterian clergyman, from 1882 professor of moral philosophy in the University of Texas. Life of T. S. Sampson; Life and Campaigns of General Stonewall Jackson; Sacred Rhetoric, or Lectures on Preaching; Defence of Virginia and the South; The Sensualistic Philosophy of the 19th Century; A Course of Systematic and Polemic Theology; The Christian Sabbath; Collected Discussions. *Ran.*

Dabney, Virginius. *Va.*, 1835——. A staff officer in the Confederate service during the Civil War, who published Don Miff, a Symphony of Life; Gold That Did Not Glitter. *Lip.*

Daboll [da'bōl], **Nathan.** *Circa* 1750–1818. A once famous instructor of Connecticut. He prepared The Schoolmaster's Assistant, long a standard text-book on arithmetic, and The Practical Navigator.

Daboll, Nathan. *Ct.*, 1782–1863. Son of N. Daboll, *supra.* A probate judge of Connecticut. The author, with his son, of Daboll's New Arithmetic, and compiler of the New England Almanac, begun by the father in 1773. The second of the name continued its preparation from 1818 to the year of his own death.

Da Costa, Jacob Mandes. *W. I.*, 1833——. A Philadelphia physician connected with Jefferson Medical College since 1864, and a specialist in diseases of the throat and lungs. Epithelial Tumours and Cancers of the Skin; The Pathological Anatomy of Acute Pneumonia; The Physicians of the Last Century; Serous Apoplexy; Medical Diagnosis; Inhalation in Treatment of Diseases of the Respiratory Passages; Strain and Over-action of the Heart; Harvey and his Discovery. *Lip.*

Dadd, George H. *E.*, *c.* 1813——. A veterinary surgeon who has published The Modern Horse Doctor; Manual of Veterinary Science; Anatomy and Physiology of the Horse; The American Cattle Doctor.

Dagg, John Leadley. *Va.*, 1794–1884. A Baptist clergyman who retired from the ministry in 1833, and was president of Mercer University, Georgia, 1844–56. Manual of Theology; Elements of Moral Science; Evidences of Christianity; English Grammar. *Bap.*

Dahlgren, John Adolph. *Pa.*, 1809–1870. A famous United States naval officer, made admiral in 1863, who invented the cannon bearing his name, and conducted the siege of Charleston during the Civil War. Thirty-Two Pounder Practice for Rangers; System of Boat Armament in the United States Navy; Naval Percussion Locks and Primers; Ordnance Memoranda; Shells and Shell Guns; Memoir of Ulric Dahlgren; Notes on Maritime International Law, edited by Charles Cowley, *supra. See Memoir by Mrs. Dahlgren, infra.*

Dahlgren, Mrs. Madeleine [Vinton] [Goddard]. *Circa* 1835——. Second wife of J. A. Dahlgren, *supra*, to whom she was married in 1865. A novelist of Washington. Idealities; Thoughts on Female Suffrage; South Sea Sketches; Etiquette of Social Life in Washington; Memoir of Admiral Dahlgren; South Mountain Magic, a Narrative; A Washington Winter, a Society Novel; The Lost Name; Divorced; Lights and Shadows of a Life. *Lip.*

Dalcho, Frederick. *E.*, 1777–1836. An Episcopal clergyman of Charleston, rector of St. Michael's Church there, 1819–36, but in earlier life successively a physician and journalist. The Evidence of the Divinity of Our Saviour; Historic Account of the Episcopal Church in South Carolina; Ahiman Rezon, a work for freemasons.

Dale, James Wilkinson. *Del.*, 1812–1881. A clergyman of eastern Pennsylvania. The Cup and the Cross, or the Baptism of Calvary; Classic Baptism; Judaic Baptism; Johannic Baptism; Christic and Patristic Baptism.

Dales, John Blakely. *N. Y.*, 1815——. A United Presbyterian clergyman of Philadelphia, whose principal writings include Roman Catholicism; Dangers and Duties of Young Men; The Gospel Minister.

Dall, Mrs. Caroline Wells [Healey]. *Ms.*, 1822——. Wife of C. H. A. Dall, *infra.* A Washington writer whose early efforts were mainly in the line of social reforms, while her later works were concerned with general literature. Essays and Sketches; Historical Pictures Retouched; Life of Dr. Marie Zakrzewski; Woman's Rights under the Law; The Romance of the Association, or one Last Glimpse of Charlotte Temple and Eliza Wharton; What we Really Know about Shakespeare; Woman's Place in History; Life of Dr. Anandabai Joshee; College, Market and Court; Woman's Right to Labor; Essays on Confucius; Patty Gray's Journey to the Cotton

Islands; My First Holiday, or Letters from Colorado; Egypt's Place in History, include her principal works. *Le. Rob.*

Dall, Charles Henry Appleton. *Md.*, 1816–1886. A Unitarian missionary to Calcutta. The Temperance Movement in Modern Times; Theism, in Questions and Answers.

Dall, William Healey. *Ms.*, 1845——. Son of C. H. and C. W. Dall, *supra.* A naturalist of distinction who has been connected with the United States Coast Survey and the Geological Survey. Alaska and its Resources (1870); Tribes of the Extreme Northwest; Scientific Results of the Exploration of Alaska; Coast Pilot of Alaska; Pacific Coast Pilot; Reports on the Mollusca of the Blake Expedition. *Le.*

Dallas, Alexander James. *F.*, 1759–1817. A noted statesman who was secretary of state, 1796–1801, and secretary of the treasury under Madison. Features of Jay's Treaty; Speeches on the Trial of Blount; Address to Constitutional Republicans; Causes and Character of the Late War (1815); Reports of Cases. *See Life and Writings of, by G. M. Dallas, infra.*

Dallas, George Mifflin. *Pa.*, 1792–1864. Son of A. J. Dallas, *supra.* A statesman who was minister to Russia, 1837–39, vice-president of the United States, 1845–49, minister to England, 1856–61. Series of Letters from London; Eulogy on Andrew Jackson, as well as many single speeches and addresses. *Lip.*

Dalton [dawl'ton], **John Call.** *Ms.*, 1825–1889. A physician of note who was a professor in various medical colleges. Observations on Trichina Spiralis; The Experimental Method in Medical Science; Doctrines of the Circulation; Topographical Anatomy of the Brain; History of the College of Physicians and Surgeons in New York city; Treatise on Human Physiology; Treatise on Physiology and Hygiene.

Daly, Charles Patrick. *N. Y.*, 1816——. A prominent jurist of New York City. Historical Sketch of the Judicial Tribunals of New York, 1823–46; Reports of Cases in Court of Common Pleas, City and County of New York; First Settlement of Jews in North America; What we Knew of Maps and Map Drawing before Mercator.

Daly, John Augustin. *N. C.*, 1838——. A dramatist and theatrical manager of New York City who, besides adapting many plays from the German and French, has written Divorce; Pique; Horizon; Under the Gaslight, and other plays, as well as Peg Woffington, a Tribute to the Actress and the Woman.

Damon, Howard Franklin. *Ms.*, 1833–1884. A hospital physician of Boston. Leucocythæmia; Neurosis of the Skin; General Remarks on the Frequency of Skin Diseases. *Lip.*

Dana, Alexander Hamilton. *E.*, 1807–1887. A lawyer of New York State. Ethical and Physiological Inquiries; Inductive Inquiries in Physiology; Ethics and Ethnology; Enigmas of Life, Death, and the Future State.

Dana, Charles Anderson. *N. H.*, 1819–1897. A distinguished journalist of New York City. He was assistant secretary of war 1863–65, and since 1868 the editor of The New York Sun. His political writing is noted for its bitter partisanship, but the literary quality of his work is admirable. With J. G. Wilson, *infra*, he prepared a Life of General Grant, and was co-editor with George Ripley, *infra*, of the American Cyclopædia. The Household Book of Poetry was edited by him. *Ap.*

Dana, Charles Louis. *Vt.*, 1852——. A physician of note as a neurologist, who has published a Text-Book on Nervous Diseases.

Dana, Edward Salisbury. *Ct.*, 1849——. Son of J. D. Dana, *infra*, assistant professor of natural philosophy at Yale University since 1879, and curator of the mineral cabinet in the Peabody Museum there. Since 1875 he has been one of the editors of Silliman's Journal. Text-Book of Mineralogy; Text-Book of Elementary Mechanics; Appendix II. (1875) and Appendix III. (1883) of Dana's System of Mineralogy. *Wil.*

Dana, James. *Ms.*, 1735–1812. A once famous Congregational clergyman of New Haven, who wrote An Examination of Edwards on the Will.

Dana, James Dwight. *N. Y.*, 1813–1895. A celebrated geologist, professor at Yale University from 1850. System of Mineralogy; Manual of Mineralogy; Text-Book of Geology; Corals and Coral Islands; The Geological Story Briefly Told. *Am. Do. Wil.*

Dana, James Freeman. *N. H.*, 1793–1827. A chemist and physician, the first professor of chemistry at Dartmouth College. Epitome of Chemical Philosophy; Outlines of the Mineralogy and Geology of Boston and its Vicinity (with S. L. Dana, *infra*).

Dana, Mrs. Katharine [Floyd]. *L. I.*, 1835–1886. A writer of New York City. Our Phil and Other Stories. *Hou.*

Dana, Mrs. Mary. *See Shindler, Mrs.*

Dana, Richard Henry. *Ms.*, 1787–1879. A poet and critic who was one of the founders of the North American Review in 1815. As a critic his Lectures on Shakespeare represent him fairly, and it must not be forgotten that he was one of the earliest in America to appreciate the genius of Wordsworth. The Idle Man, a publication begun in 1821 and extending to six numbers, includes his two novels, Tom Thornton; Paul Felton. His later publications include The Buccaneer, and Other Poems; Poems and Prose Writings. His verse is both imaginative and original, but at the same time unmelodious. *See Atlantic Monthly, April, 1879; Harper's Magazine, April, 1879; Lowell's Fable for Critics; Bryant and his Friends.*

Dana, Richard Henry, Jr. *Ms.*, 1815–1882. Son of R. H. Dana, *supra*. A noted lawyer of Boston, best known in literature by the famous Two Years before the Mast, a narrative of personal adventure, which first appeared in 1840, and was re-issued, enlarged, in 1869. His other works include The Seaman's Friend, known in England as The Seaman's Manual; Letters on Italian Unity; To Cuba and Back; Letters on the Somers Mutiny; Life of Major Vinton; Enemy Property and Enemy Territory. *See Life by C. F. Adams, 1891.*

Dana, Samuel Luther. *N. H.*, 1795–1868. Brother of J. F. Dana, *supra*. A noted chemist of Lowell, who made many improvements in cotton-printing, and was one of the foremost agricultural writers of his time. Chemical Changes in the Manufacture of Sulphuric Acid; Muck Mineral for Manures; Essay on Manures. *See American Journal of Science, May, 1868.*

Dana, William Coombs. *Ms.*, 1810–1873. A Presbyterian clergyman of Charleston. Hymns for Public Worship; A Transatlantic Tour; Life of Samuel Dana.

Dana, Mrs. William Starr. *See Parsons, Mrs. Frances.*

Dandridge, Mrs. Danske [Bedinger]. *Dk.*, 1858——. A verse-writer of Shepherdstown, West Virginia. Joy, and Other Poems.

Dane, Nathan. *Ms.*, 1752–1835. A very prominent lawyer of Massachusetts, who founded the Dane professorship at the Harvard University Law School. He published an Abridgment and Digest of American Law [in nine volumes].

Danenhower, John Wilson. *Il.*, 1849–1887. An Arctic explorer who was second in command of the De Long Expedition in 1879, and published The Narrative of the Jeannette, 1882.

Danforth, John. *Ms.*, 1660–1730. Son of S. Danforth, *infra*. A once noted Congregational clergyman of Dorchester, Massachusetts, who published many single sermons and occasional poems.

Danforth, Joshua Noble. *Ms.*, 1798–1861. A Congregational minister of Massachusetts and Virginia, who published Gleanings and Groupings from a Pastor's Portfolio.

Danforth, Samuel. *E.*, 1626–1674. A once famous Puritan clergyman of Roxbury, Massachusetts, 1650–74. An Astronomical Description of the Comet of 1664; An Election Sermon; The Cry of Sodom Inquired Into.

Danforth, Samuel. *Ms.*, 1666–1727. Son of S. Danforth, *supra*. A Congregational clergyman of Taunton, Massachusetts, famous for his great learning and wide influence. Eulogy on Thomas Leonard; Essay Concerning the Singing of Psalms. The MS. of his Indian Dictionary is now the property of the Massachusetts Historical Society.

Dangé, Henri. *See Hammond, Mrs.*

Daniel, John Moncure. *Va.*, 1825–1865. A once noted Virginia journalist who edited The Richmond Examiner, and was minister to Italy 1853–60. *See Writings of, with Memoir by his brother, 1868.*

Daniel, John Warwick. *Va.*, 1842–——. A prominent Virginia lawyer who was an adjutant-general in the Confederate army during the Civil War. Attachments under the Code of Virginia; Negotiable Instruments.

Daniels, Mrs. Cora [Linn]. *Ms.*, 1852——. A novelist of Franklin, Massachusetts. Sardia, a Story of Love; As It Is to Be. *Ban. Le.*

Daniels, William Haven. *Ms.*, 1836–——. A Methodist clergyman, prominent as an evangelist. D. L. Moody and his Work; That Boy, who Shall Have Him ?; The Temperance Reform and its Great Reformers; Moody, his Words, Work, and Workers; Illustrated History of Methodism in the United States; Graduated with Honour; Memorials of Gilbert Haven; Short History of the People called Methodists. *Meth.*

Dannelly, Mrs. Elizabeth Otis [Marshall]. *Ga.*, 1838——. A Texas writer of verse. Cactus, or Thorns and Blossoms; Wayside Flowers.

Da Ponte, Lorenzo. *Iy.*, 1749–1838. An Italian dramatist who furnished libretti for Mozart's operas, Don Giovanni and Nozze di Figaro. He came to America in 1805, and after 1828 was professor of Italian in Columbia College. He published his own Life (1823); History of the Florentine Republic and the Medici (1833).

Darby, John. *See Garretson.*

Darby, John. *Ms.*, 1804–1877. An educator who was connected with various colleges North and South. Manual of Botany; The Botany of the Southern States; Chemistry, are some of his publications.

Darby, William. *Pa.*, 1755–1834. A geographer who published Geographical Dictionary of Louisiana; Plan of Pittsburg and Adjacent Country; Emigrant's Guide to the Western Country; Tour from New York to Detroit (1819); Geography and History of Florida; View of the United States (1823); Lectures on the Discovery of America; Mnemonica, a Register of Events from the Earliest Period; Geographical Dictionary.

Darden, Mrs. Fannie [Baker]. *Al.*, 1829——. Romances of the Texas Revolution; Poems.

Dargan, Clara Victoria. *See Maclean, Mrs.*

Darley, Felix Octavius Carr. *Pa.*, 1822–1888. A well-known artist and illustrator whose home was at Claymont, Delaware. His only writing is included in Sketches Abroad with Pen and Pencil.

Darling, Mrs. Flora [Adams]. *N. H.*, 1840——. A writer of fiction whose writings include Mrs. Darling's Letters, or Memoirs of the Civil War; A Wayward Winning Woman; The Bourbon Lily; Was it a Just Verdict ?; A Social Diplomat; From Two Points of View; The Senator's Daughter.

Darling, Henry. *Pa.*, 1823–1891. A Presbyterian clergyman who was president of Hamilton College, 1881–1891. The Close Walk; Slavery and the War; Conformity to the World; Not Doing but Receiving.

Darling, Mary Greenleaf. 18——. Battles at Home; In the World; Gladys, a Romance. *Le. Lo.*

Darling, William. *S.*, 1815–1884. A distinguished New York physician who published Anatmography, or Graphic Anatomy; Essentials of Anatomy (with A. L. Ranney).

Darlington, William. *Pa.*, 1782–1863. A famous botanist of West Chester, Pennsylvania, in whose honour Darlingtonia, a genus of pitcher-plants, was named. Mutual Influence of Habits and Disease; Agricultural Botany; Flora Cestrica; Memorials of John Bartram, *supra*, and Humphrey Marshall.

D'Arusmont, Madame Frances [Wright]. *S.*, 1795–1852. A very energetic and versatile Scottish reformer who came several times to America, and finally settled in Cincinnati. Her attacks on social institutions aroused much hostility, her opposition to slavery making her the object of especial dislike. Popular Lectures on Free Inquiry; Biographical Notes and Political Letters of Fanny Wright D'Arusmont (1844); Altorf: a tragedy; Views of Society and Manners in America; A Few Days in Athens, include her principal works. *See Gilbert's The Pioneer Woman, 1855; Dictionary of National Biography, vol. 14.*

Daveiss, Mrs. Maria [Thompson]. *Ky.*, 1814——. A Kentucky author who has written much for agricultural journals, and has published Roger Sherman, a Tale of '76; Woman's Love; History of Mercer and Boyle Counties, Kentucky; Cultivation and Uses of the Chinese Sugar Cane.

Davenport, John. *E.*, 1597–1670. A famous Puritan divine who, before coming to America in 1637, was a celebrated London preacher. In 1638 he was one of the founders of New Haven, and in 1660 concealed the noted regicides, Goffe and Whalley, from their pursuers. In 1666 he became pastor of the First Church in Boston. Instructions to Elders of the English Church; Catechism containing the Chief Heads of the Christian Religion; Discourse about Civil Government in New England. *See Sprague's Annals of the American Pulpit; Dictionary of National Biography, vol. 14.*

David, Jean Baptist. *F.*, 1761–1841. A Roman Catholic bishop of Bardstown, Kentucky. Among his many works are Vindication of Catholic Doctrine concerning Images; Address to Brethren of Other Professions; On the Rule of Faith; True Piety.

Davidson, Charles. *O.*, 1852——. An instructor of Belmont, California. The Phonology of the Stressed Vowels of Beowulf; Studies in the English Mystery Plays.

Davidson, George. *E.*, 1825——. An astronomer of distinction, founder of the Davidson Observatory in San Francisco. The United States Coast Survey of the Pacific Coast; Coast Pilot of Alaska; Voyages of Discovery on the Northwest Coast of America, 1539–1603.

Davidson, James Wood. *S. C.*, 1829——. An educator of South Carolina and elsewhere, whose Living Writers of the South is quite wanting in discrimination and critical ability. His other works include School History of South Carolina; The Correspondent; The Poetry of the Future; Florida of To-Day. *Ap.*

Davidson, Lucretia Maria. *N. Y.*, 1808–1825. A precocious verse-writer now quite forgotten. Amir Khan and Other Poems was issued in 1829. *See Memoir by S. F. B. Morse, and Life by C. M. Sedgwick, infra.*

Davidson, Margaret Miller. *N. Y.*, 1823–1838. Sister to L. M. Davidson, and, like her, a juvenile prodigy whose immature verses were extravagantly lauded by contemporary writers, but by no critics of a later day. *See Memoir by Washington Irving.*

Davidson, Robert. *Md.*, 1750–1812. A Presbyterian clergyman who was president of Dickinson College, Carlisle, Pennsylvania, 1804–09. Epitome of Geography in Verse for Schools; The Christian's A, B, C, or the 119th Psalm in Metre; New Metrical Version of the Psalms, with Notes.

Davidson, Robert. *Pa.*, 1808–1876. Son of R. Davidson, *supra*. A Presbyterian minister in Kentucky and other States, among whose writings are Elijah, a Sacred Drama, and Other Poems; The Christ of God, or the Relation of Christ to Christianity.

Davidson, Thomas. *S.*, 1840——. A writer on art and philosophy who came to the United States in 1866 and settled at Cambridge. The Parthenon Frieze and Other Essays; The Place of Art in Education; Giordano Bruno and the Relation of his Philosophy to Free Thought; Handbook of Dante, from the Italian of Scartazzini, with Notes and Additions; Prolegomena to Tennyson's "In Memoriam;" Aristotle, and Ancient and Modern Educational Ideals; The Education of the Greek People and its Influence on Civilization. *Ap. Gi. Hou.*

Davies, Charles. *Ct.*, 1798–1876. A noted professor of mathematics in Columbia College from 1857. Beside a notable series of mathematical text-books, from A Primary Table Book to Elementary Geometry and Trigonometry, he published also editions of Legendre's Geometry and Bourdon's Algebra. Other works by him comprise Practical Mathematics; Elements of

Surveying; Analytical Geometry; Differential and Integral Calculus; Logic and Utility of Mathematics; The Metric System; Mathematical Dictionary (with W. G. Peck).

Davies, Samuel. *Del.*, 1724–1761. A Presbyterian clergyman of great renown in his day as a preacher, and the fourth president of Princeton College. He wrote a number of hymns still in use, and his Sermons in 5 volumes appeared in London in 1767. *See Sermons, 1851, with Memoir by Albert Barnes, supra.*

Davies, Thomas Alfred. *N. Y.*, 1809——. Brother of C. Davies, *supra.* A Federal officer in the Civil War. Cosmogony, or Mysteries of Creation; Adam and Ha-Adam; Genesis Disclosed; Answer to Hugh Miller and Theoretical Geologists; How to Make Money and how to Keep It.

Davis, Andrew Jackson. *N. Y.*, 1826——. A noted spiritualist of Poughkeepsie, among whose many mystical rhapsodical writings the following may be considered the most important: The Great Harmonia; Harmonial Man; Present Age and Inner Life; Philosophy of Spiritual Intercourse; The Principles of Nature; The Penetralia; Genesis and Ethics of Conjugal Love; Autobiography, 1885. *Ban.*

Davis, Andrew McFarland. *Ms.*, 1833——. Brother of H. Davis, *infra.* An antiquarian writer of Cambridge who has published a number of valuable historical monographs.

Davis, Asahel. *Ms.*, 1791–18—. A Massachusetts antiquary who published Ancient America and Researches of the East (1847); History of New Amsterdam.

Davis, Augusta Cordelia. *Me.*, 1836——. Poems from Yare.

Davis, Mrs. Caroline E—— [Kelly]. *N. H.*, 1831——. A prolific writer of Sunday-school tales. Among her fifty or more volumes are, No Cross, No Crow; Little Conqueror Series; Miss Wealthy's Hope; That Boy. *Lo.*

Davis, Charles Henry. *Ms.*, 1807–1877. Son of D. Davis, *infra.* A rear-admiral in the United States navy, and a noted hydrographer. Besides editing the American Nautical Almanac, he published Law of Deposit of Flood Tide; Geological Action of Tidal and Other Ocean Currents; and translated Gauss's Theoria Motus Corporum Cœlestium. *See Harvard Register, April, 1881.*

Davis, Charles Henry. *Ms.*, 1845——. Son of C. H. Davis, *supra.* A United States naval officer. Chronometer Rates as Affected by Temperature and Other Causes; Telegraphic Determination of Longitudes.

Davis, Charles Henry Stanley. *Ct.*, 1840——. A physician of Meriden, Connecticut. History of Wallingford and Meriden; The Voice as a Musical Instrument; Education and Training of Feeble Minded Children; Index to Periodical Literature.

Davis, Cushman Kellogg. *N. Y.*, 1838——. A prominent Minnesota lawyer who has written The Law in Shakespeare.

Davis, Daniel. *Ms.*, 1762–1835. A Massachusetts jurist who was solicitor-general of his State, 1800–32. Criminal Practice; Precedents of Indictments.

Davis, Edwin Hamilton. *O.*, 1811–1888. An archæologist whose chief work is Monuments of the Mississippi.

Davis, Emerson. *Ms.*, 1798–1866. A Congregational clergyman who was president of Williams College, 1861–68. Historical Sketch of Westfield, Massachusetts; The Teacher Taught; The First Half Century, or Events and Changes, 1800–50.

Davis, George Thomas. *Ms.*, 1810–1877. A Massachusetts lawyer whose speeches in Congress were published in 1852.

Davis, Henry Winter. *Md.*, 1817–1865. A Maryland statesman and lawyer, conspicuously loyal to the Union during the Civil War. The War of Ormuzd and Ahriman in the 19th Century (1853); Speeches and Addresses in Congress (1867). *Har.*

Davis, Horace. *Ms.*, 1831——. Nephew of G. Bancroft, *supra.* A manufacturer of California. Dolor Davis, a Sketch of his Life; American Constitutions and the Relation of the Three Departments as adjusted by a Century; Shakespeare's Sonnets, an Essay.

Davis, Jefferson. *Ky.*, 1808–1889. President of the Confederate States. After the fall of the Confederacy, in 1865, he was confined as a prisoner of war in Fortress Monroe, and upon his release, in 1867, he lived in retirement in Mississippi. His history, which appeared in 1881, The Rise and Fall of the Confederate Government, is a valuable commentary on the Civil War as it appeared to one of the chief figures of the time, but it is as narrowly conceived as it is diffuse in statement and bitter in tone. *See Lives, by Alfriend, 1868; E. A. Pollard, infra, 1869; Prison Life of, by Craven, 1866; Memoir by his Wife, 1890; London Times Biographies of Eminent Persons, 4th Series. Ap.*

Davis, John A. G. *Va.*, 1801–1840. A Virginia lawyer, professor of law in the University of Virginia, 1830–40. Estates Tail, Executive Devises, and Contingent Remainders under Virginia Statutes; Treatise on Criminal Law.

Davis, John Chandler Bancroft. *Ms.*, 1822——. Brother of H. Davis, *supra.* A diplomatist who was agent for the United States before the Geneva conrt of arbitration on the Alabama claims, and afterwards, 1873–77, minister to Germany. The Massachusetts Justice; The Case of the United States before the Tribunal of Arbitration at Geneva; Treaties of the United States, with Notes; United States Supreme Court Reports; Mr. Fish and the Alabama Claims. *Hou.*

Davis, John Woodbridge. *N. Y.*, 1854——. Son of E. H. Davis, *supra.* A civil engineer who, besides contributing much to engineering journals, has published Formulæ for the Calculation of Railroad Earth Work and Average Haul (1876), which speedily came into use as a text-book.

Davis, Lemuel Clarke. *Md.*, 1835——. A Philadelphia journalist, editor of The Inquirer, and author of The Stranded Ship, a Story of Sea and Shore.

Davis, Mrs. Mary Evelyn [Moore]. *Al.*, 1852——. A prominent writer of New Orleans, on the editorial staff of the Picayune. Minding the Gap, and Other Poems; In War Times at La Rose Blanche, sketches for young people; Under the Man-Fig, a novel; An Elephant's Track and Other Stories. *Har. Hou. Lo.*

Davis, Matthew L. *N. Y.*, 1766–1850. A Washington journalist who published a Life of Aaron Burr.

Davis, Nathan Smith. *N. Y.*, 1817——. A Chicago physician, dean of the Northwestern University, whose principal writings include Lectures on Various Important Diseases; Principles and Practice of Medicine; Verdict of Science concerning the Effects of Alcohol on Man; Medical Education and Reform.

Davis, Noah Knowles. *Pa.*, 1838——. A professor of moral science in the University of Virginia since 1873. The Theory of Thought, a Treatise on Deductive Logic; the Elements of Inductive Logic; the Elements of Deductive Logic. *Har.*

Davis, Peter Seifert. *Md.*, 1828——. A German Reformed divine who has written The Young Parson.

Davis, Mrs. Rebecca Blaine [Harding]. *Pa.*, 1831——. Wife of L. C. Davis, *supra.* A novelist whose first story, Life in the Iron Mills, a powerful but sombre study of labouring-class life, attracted great attention in the earlier pages of The Atlantic Monthly. Her later works in fiction include Margret Howth; Waiting for the Verdict; Dallas Galbraith; A Law unto Herself; Kitty's Choice; John Andross; Doctor Warrick's Daughters; Silhouettes of American Life; Kent Hampden, a Story of a Boy; Natasqua; The Faded Leaf of History; Frances Waldeaux. *Har. Lip. Scr.*

Davis, Reuben. *Tn.*, *c.* 1810–1890. A Mississippi lawyer and a general in the Confederate service, who was the author of Recollections of Mississippi and the Mississippians. *Hou.*

Davis, Richard Bingham. *N. Y.*, 1771–1799. A verse-writer of New York city. *See Poems, with Memoir edited by John T. Irving, 1807.*

Davis, Richard Harding. *Pa.*, 1864——. Son of L. C. and R. H. Davis, *supra.* A popular New York writer whose first book, Gallegher and Other Stories, brought him very suddenly into notice in 1890. His work is always characterized by dash and spirit, but exhibits some defects of style, and touches scarcely more than the superficial side of life. Van Bibber and Others; The Princess Aline; The Exiles; The West from a Car Window; Our English Cousins; About Paris; The Rulers of the Mediterranean; Three Gringos in Venezuela; Stories for Boys. *Har. Scr.*

Davis, Varina Anne Jefferson. *Va.*, 1864——. Daughter of Jefferson Davis, *supra.* An Irish Knight of the 19th Century, a Sketch of Robert Emmet; The Veiled Doctor. *Har.*

Davis, William Bramwell. *O.*, 1832——. A physician and surgeon of Cincinnati. Report on Vaccination; Consumption and Life Insurance; Revaccination; Intestinal Obstruction; Progress of Therapeutics; The Alcohol Question.

Davis, William Morris. *Pa.*, 1850——. A professor of physical geography in Harvard University since 1890. Nimrod of the Sea, or the American Whaleman; Whirlwinds, Cyclones, and Tornadoes; Elementary Meteorology. *Gi. Har. Le.*

Davis, William Watts Hart. 18———. El Gringo, or New Mexico and her People; History of the 104th Pennsylvania Regiment; The Spanish Conquest of New Mexico; History of the Doylestown Guards. *Har.*

Dawes, Anna Laurens. *Ms.*, 1851——. A daughter of Senator Dawes of Massachusetts, who has written much for journals and periodicals. How we are Governed; The Modern Jew, his Present and Future; Biography of Charles Sumner. *Do. Gi.*

Dawes, Rufus. *Ms.*, 1803–1859. A witty jurist of Massachusetts, who won notice both as orator and poet. The Valley of the Nashaway, and Other Poems; Athena of Damascus, a tragedy; Nix's Mate, an Historical Romance; Miscellaneous Poems.

Dawson, George. *S.*, 1813–1883. A once influential Albany journalist, editor of the Evening Journal, 1846–77, and author of The Pleasures of Angling.

Dawson, Henry Barton. *E.*, 1821–1889. An historical writer of New York city, editor of the Historical Magazine, 1866–77, and editor of The Federalist, reprinted from the original text. Battles of the United States by Sea and Land; Current Fictions tested by Uncurrent Facts; Rutgers against Waddington; Westchester County in the Revolution. *Scr.*

Day, Henry. *Ms.*, 1820——. A lawyer of New York city. The Lawyer Abroad; From the Pyrenees to the Pillars of Hercules, a volume of Spanish travels.

Day, Henry Noble. *Ct.*, 1808–1890. Nephew of J. Day, 2d. A Congregational clergyman, for many years a Western railway president, and president of Ohio Female College, 1858–64. The Art of Rhetoric, reprinted as Art of Discourse; Elements of Logic; Science of Æsthetics; The Art of Elocution; Rhetorical Praxis; Logical Praxis; Science of Thought; Elements of Mental Science; The Logic of Sir William Hamilton; Introduction to the Study of English Literature, include the greater number of his writings. *Scr.*

Day, Jeremiah. *Ct.*, 1738–1806. A Congregational clergyman of Connecticut, whose Sermons Collected were issued in 1797.

Day, Jeremiah. *Ct.*, 1773–1867. Son of J. Day, *supra.* A noted mathematician who was president of Yale College, 1817–46. Introduction to Algebra; Mensuration of Superficies and Solids; Examination of Edwards's Freedom of the Will; Plane Trigonometry; Navigation and Surveying; Inquiry Respecting the Self-Determining Power of the Will and Contingent Volition.

Day, Richard Edwin. *N. Y.*, 1852——. A journalist of Syracuse. Lines in the Sand; Thor, a Drama; Lyrics and Satires; Poems.

Dayton, Amos Cooper. *N. J.*, 1813–1865. A Baptist clergyman and physician of Tennessee, whose novel Theodosia, or the Heroine of Faith, was very popular. His other works comprise The Infidel's Daughter, a novel; Baptist Facts and Methodist Fiction; Baptist Question Book; Children brought to Christ; Pedobaptist and Campbellite Immersion.

Dean, Amos. *Vt.*, 1803–1868. A jurist of Albany. Lectures on Phrenology; Manual of Law; Philosophy of Human Life; Medical Jurisprudence; Bryant and Stratton's Commercial Law; History of Civilization.

Dean, John. *Ms.*, 1831–1888. A physician who published Microscopic Anatomy of the Lumbar Enlargement of the Spinal Cord; Gray Substance of the Medulla Oblongata.

Dean, John Ward. *Me.*, 1815——. A noted antiquarian of Boston, editor of the New England Historical and Genealogical Register, and one of the founders of the Prince Society. Memoir of Nathaniel Ward, *infra;* Memoir of Michael Wigglesworth, *infra;* Life of John H. Sheppard; Life of William Blanchard Towne; Brief Memoir of Giles Firmin; The Embarkation of Cromwell for New England.

Dean, Paul. *Vt.*, 1789–1860. A Unitarian clergyman, pastor in Boston, 1813–40, who was author of Lectures on Final Restoration.

Deane, Charles. *Me.*, 1813–1889. An antiquarian writer of Cambridge, who published Some Notices of Samuell Gorton, with Memoir; First Plymouth Patent; and edited Bradford's History of Plymouth Plantation; John Smith's True Relation of Virginia, and other specimens of early American literature.

Deane, Margery. *See Pitman, Mrs.*

Deane, Samuel. *Ms.*, 1784–1834. A Baptist clergyman of Scituate, Massachusetts. The Populous Village, a poem; History of Scituate.

Deane, Silas. *Ct.*, 1737–1789. A diplomatist who, with Franklin and Lee, negotiated a treaty of peace and amity between France and the United States. He was subjected to much misrepresentation, and died abroad in poverty and exile. Letters to Robert Morgan; Paris Papers, or Mr. Silas Deane's late Intercepted Letters to his Brother and Other Friends.

Deane, William Reed. *Ms.*, 1809–1879. An antiquary of Mansfield, Massachusetts, who published genealogies of the families of Deane, Leonard, and Watson.

Dearborn, Henry Alexander Scammell. *N. H.*, 1783–1851. A lawyer and public-spirited citizen of Boston, a son of Commodore Dearborn. Commerce of the Black Sea; Biography of Commodore Bainbridge; History of Navigation and Naval Architecture.

De Bow, James Dunwoody Brownson. *S. C.*, 1820–1867. A noted statistician of New Orleans, who founded De Bow's Review. Industrial Resources of the South and West; Statistical View of the United States; The Southern States, their Agriculture, Commerce, etc. (1850).

De Charms, Richard. *Pa.*, 1796–1864. A Swedenborgian divine of Baltimore and New York city. Freedom and Slavery in the Light of the New Jerusalem; The New Churchman Extra; Lectures at Charlestown.

De Costa, Benjamin Franklin. *Ms.*, 1831——. A prominent Episcopal clergyman of New York city, well known as an historical writer. The Pre-Columbian Discovery of America, illustrated by translations from the Icelandic Sagas; The Northmen in Maine; The Moabite Stone; Verrazano, the Explorer; The Rector of Roxburgh, a novel; and a number of historical monographs. *See Bibliography of Maine.*

Deems, Charles Force. *Md.*, 1820–1893. A Methodist clergyman, prominent for many years in New York city as pastor of the Church of the Strangers.. Triumphs of Peace, and Other Poems; Home Altar; Twelve College Sermons; Life of Dr. Adam Clarke; Devotional Melodies; Weights and Wings; The Light of the Nations; The Gospel of Common Sense as Contained in the Epistle of James; The Gospel of Spiritual Insight; A Scotch Verdict in re-Evolution; My Septuagint, comprise the larger number of his writings. *Cas. Fu.*

Deering, Nathaniel. *Me.*, 1791–1881. A writer of Portland, Maine, whose work enjoyed a local fame. Carabasset, a tragedy; The Clairvoyants, a comedy performed both in Portland and Boston; Bozzaris, a tragedy. *See Biographical Encyclopedia of Maine.*

De Forest, John William. *Ct.*, 1826——. A novelist of New Haven who was a Federal officer in the Civil War. His stories are skillfully constructed, and the characterization is strong, but they have hardly won the reputation that, as a whole, they deserve. History of the Indians of Connecticut to 1850; Oriental Acquaintances, or Travels in Asia Minor; European Acquaintances; Witching Times; The Lauson Tragedy; Seacliff, Miss Ravenel's Conversion from Secession to Loyalty; Overland; Kate Beaumont; Honest John Vane; The Bloody Chasm; The Wetherel Affair; Justine Vane; Irene Vane; Irene the Missionary; Playing the Mischief. *Ap. Har.*

De Hart, William Chetwood. *N. Y.*, 1800–1848. An officer in the United States army who published Observations on Military Law and Constitution and Practice of Courts Martial.

Dehon, Theodore. *Ms.*, 1776–1817. The second Protestant Episcopal bishop of South Carolina. A once popular preacher. Ninety Sermons on the Public Means of Grace.

De Kay, Charles. *D. C.*, 1849——. Grandson of J. R. Drake, *infra.* A New York journalist and poet, literary editor of The Times since 1877. Hesperus; Vision of Nimrod; Vision of Esther; Love Poems of Louis Barnaval; The Bohemians, a Tragedy of Modern Life; Barye, his Life and Works. *Ap.*

De Kay, James Ellsworth. *Pl.*, 1792–1851. A physician and naturalist of Oyster Bay, Long Island. Sketches of Turkey; Natural History of New York.

De Koven, James. *Ct.*, 1831–1879. An Episcopal clergyman of Wisconsin, very prominent at one time as a leader of ritualistic thought, whose views more than once prevented his elevation to the episcopate. Sermons Preached on Various Occasions was issued after his death. *Ap.*

De Kroyft, Mrs. Sarah Helen [Aldrich]. *N. Y.*, 1818——. A writer living in Dansville, New York, who became blind soon after her marriage in 1845, her husband having died on their wedding day. A Place in thy Memory, a very popular collection of letters; Darwin and Moses, a lecture; Little Jakey, a story.

Delafield, Francis. *N. Y.*, 1841——. A physician and surgeon of New York city, who was the first president of the Association of American Physicians and Pathologists. Handbook of Post Mortem Examinations and Morbid Anatomy; Studies in Pathological Anatomy; Handbook of Pathological Anatomy.

De Lancey, William Floyd. *N. Y.*, 1821——. A lawyer and historical writer of New York city. Memoir of James De Lancey; The Capture of Fort Washington the Result of Treason; Memoir of James W. Beekman; Memoir of William Allen, Chief Justice of Pennsylvania; Origin and History of Manors in the Province of New York; History of Mamaroneck, New York.

Deland, Ellen Douglass. *N. Y.*, 1860——. A popular writer of stories for young people. Oakleigh; In the Old Herrick House; Malvern, a Neighbourhood Story. *Har. We.*

Deland, Mrs. Margaret Wade [Campbell]. *Pa.*, 1857——. A novelist and poet of Boston who became suddenly famous on the publication of John Ward, Preacher, a story upon lines similar to Mrs. Ward's "Robert Elsmere." Other works by her include The Old Garden and Other Verses; Sydney; The Story of a Child; Mr. Tommy Dove and Other Stories; Philip and his Wife; Florida Days, a volume of travels. *Hou. Lit.*

Delano, Amasa. *Ms.*, 1763–1817. A once noted Massachusetts sea captain who was an extensive traveller, and published Narrative of Voyages and Travels.

Delavan, Edward Cornelius. *N. Y.*, 1793–1871. A retired wine-merchant of Schenectady, conspicuous as a temperance reformer. Adulterations of Liquors; Temperance in Wine Countries.

De Leon, Edwin: *S. C.*, 1828–1891. A Washington journalist who was European diplomatic agent of the Confederacy during the Civil War period. Thirty Years of my Life on Three Continents; The Khedive's Egypt; Askaros Kassis, the Captain, a novel; Under the Star and Under the Crescent. *Lip.*

De Long, George Washington. *N. Y.*, 1844–1881. An Arctic explorer who was a lieutenant-commander in the United States navy. The Voyage of the Jeannette, including his journals of his latest expedition, edited by his wife, appeared in 1884.

Delmar, Alexander. *N. Y.*, 1836——. A New York writer on political economy. Gold Money and Paper Money; Essays on Political Economy; The Great Paper Bubble; What is Free Trade?; Resources, Productions, and Social Condition of Egypt; Why Should the Chinese Go?; History of the Precious Metals; History of Money in China; History of Money in Various Countries; The Science of Money; Money and Civilization; Statistical Handbook; The National Banking System.

Demarest, David D. *N. J.*, 1819——. A Dutch Reformed clergyman, professor in the Theological Seminary at New Brunswick, New Jersey. History and Characteristics of the Reformed Protestant Dutch Church; Practical Catechetics; The Huguenots on the Hackensack.

Demarest, John Terhune. *N. J.*, 1813——. A Dutch Reformed clergyman. Exposition of the Efficient Cause of Regeneration; Exposition of the First Epistle of Peter; Commentary on Second Epistle of Peter; Commentary on the Catholic Epistles; Christocracy (with W. R. Gordon).

Demarest, Mrs. Mary Augusta [Lee]. *N. Y.*, 1838–1888. A writer of popular, unpretentious verse, who published My Ain Countree and Other Poems.

Deming, Henry Champion. *Ct.*, 1815–1872. A prominent lawyer of Hartford who published translations of the novels of Eugène Sue and a Life of General Grant.

Deming, Philander. *N. Y.*, 1829——. A stenographic court reporter of Albany until 1882, whose sketches are characterized by much originality. Adirondack Stories; Tompkins and Other Folks. *Hou.*

Dempster, John. *Fl.*, 1794–1863. A noted Methodist preacher and educator, and one of the founders of the theological school of Boston University. Lectures and Addresses was issued in 1864. *Meth.*

Denio [de-ni'o], **Hiram.** *N. Y.*, 1799–1871. A Utica jurist who published Reports of Cases in the Supreme Court, and the Court for Correction of Errors.

Denison, Charles Wheeler. *Ct.*, 1809–1881. A clergyman who as a young man was editor of The Emancipator, an anti-slavery journal of New York. During the Civil War he served as chaplain in the Federal army. The American Village and Other Poems; Paul St. Clair, a temperance tale; Antonio, the Italian Boy; The Child Hunters, an exposure of the padrone system; Life of General Grant; Out at Sea, a volume of verse; Sunshine Castle, a tale. The Tanner Boy; The Bobbin Boy; Winfield, the Lawyer's Son, form a series of biographies of noted men for juvenile reading.

Denison, Daniel. *E.*, 1613–1682. A famous colonial soldier of Massachusetts. Irenicon, or Salve for New England's Sore.

Denison, Frederic. *Ct.*, 1819——. A Baptist divine of Rhode Island. The Supper Institution; The Sabbath Institution; History of the First Rhode Island Cavalry; Westerly and its Witnesses, 1626–1876; Picturesque Narragansett; Picturesque Rhode Island, are his principal writings.

Denison, John Henry. *Ms.*, 1841——. A Congregational clergyman retired from active service, but at one time college pastor at Williamstown, Massachusetts. Christ's Idea of the Supernatural. *Hou.*

Denison, John Ledyard. *Ct.*, 1826——. Brother of F. Denison, *supra*. A publisher of Norwich, Connecticut. Picturesque History of the Wars of the United States; Illustrated History of the New World.

Denison, Mrs. Mary [Andrews]. *Ms.*, 1826——. Wife of C. W. Denison, *supra*. A prolific author of tales, mainly of home life, some of them to be classed as Sunday-school literature, while others are of a more ambitious character. Among them are Opposite the Jail; That Husband of Mine, which was issued anonymously and enjoyed an extraordinary popularity for a short time; That Wife of Mine; Rothmell; His Triumph; Old Slip Warehouse; Home Pictures; Like a Gentleman; If She Will, She Will. *Har. Le. Lip.*

Dennie, Joseph. *Ms.*, 1768–1812. A journalist and essayist of Philadelphia, whose reputation in his day vastly exceeded his deserts. The Lay Preacher, or Short Sermons for Idle Readers, is his only literary legacy. *See A. H. Smyth's Philadelphia Magazines, 1892.*

Denton, Franklin Evert. *O.*, 1859–——. A journalist of Cleveland who published in 1883 The Early Poems of Franklin Denton.

Depew, Chauncey Mitchell. *N. Y.*, 1834——. A very prominent lawyer and railway president of New York city, of wide fame as a ready after-dinner speaker. He has published Orations and After-Dinner Speeches; Later Speeches. *Cas.*

De Peyster, John Watts. *N. Y.*, 1821——. An historical writer of New York city, and a general of the State militia. Life of Torstenson; The Dutch at the North Pole and the Dutch in Maine; Decisive Conflicts of the Late Civil War; Personal and Military History of General Kearney; Life of Sir John Johnston; Mary, Queen of Scotts, a Study; The Character of Mary and a Justification of Bothwell; Bothwell, a drama; The Thirty Years' War; Before, At, and After Gettysburg; Life of Baron Cohorn; Carausius, the Dutch Augustus; The Real Napoleon Bonaparte.

De Puy, Henry Walter. *N. Y.*, 1820——. A lawyer and journalist. Kossuth and his Generals; Louis Napoleon and his Times; Ethan Allen and the Green Mountain Boys of '76.

De Puy, William Harrison. *N. Y.*, 1821——. A Methodist clergyman of western New York. Threescore Years and Beyond; Statistics of the Methodist Episcopal Church; Home and Health; Home Economics, a very popular book. *Meth.*

Derby, Elias Hasket. *Ms.*, 1803–1880. A noted railway attorney of Boston. Two Months Abroad; Catholic Letters; The Overland Route to the Pacific; Position and Prospects of the United States with Respect to Finance, Commerce, and Prosperity.

Derby, George. *Ms.*, 1819–1874. Cousin of E. H. Derby, *supra.* A physician of Boston, prominent as a sanitarian, who published Anthracite and Health.

Derby, George Horatio. "John Phœnix." *Ms.*, 1823–1861. Son of J. B. Derby, *infra.* A topographical engineer in the United States army who was a popular humourist in his day. Phœnixiana; Squibob Papers.

Derby, James Cephas. *N. Y.*, 1818–1892. A noted publisher of New York and San Francisco, and author of Fifty Years Among Authors, Books, and Publishers.

Derby, John Barton. *Ms.*, 1792–1867. Half-brother of G. Derby, *supra.* A verse-writer whose later years were spent in Boston. Musings of a Recluse; The Sea; The Village.

De Saussure, Henry William. *S. C.*, 1763–1839. A jurist of South Carolina, who was director of the United States Mint in 1794, and published Reports of the Courts of Chancery and Equity in South Carolina from the Revolution to 1813.

Deshon, George. *Ct.*, 1823——. A Roman Catholic priest of the Redemptorist order, whose Guide for Young Catholic Women has had a very extended circulation.

De Smet, Peter John. *Bm.*, 1801–1872. A noted Roman Catholic missionary to the Indians, who came to the United States in 1821. His writings, originally published in French, include The Oregon Missions and Travels over the Rocky Mountains; Indian Letters and Sketches; Western Missions and Missionaries; New Indian Sketches.

De Trobriand [trō-brē-ăn′], **Philip Regis.** *F.*, 1816–1897. A military writer who came to the United States in 1841, entered the army, and, after serving through the Civil War, retired from active service in 1879, and resided in New Orleans. Les Gentilshommes de l'Ouest, a novel; Quatre ans de Campagnes à armée du Potomac.

De Vere, Mary Ainge, "Madeline Bridges." *N. Y.*, 18——. A writer of Brooklyn, Long Island. Love Songs and Other Poems; Poems.

De Vere, Maximilian Schele. *Sn.*, 1820——. A philologist of note who came from Sweden to the United States in 1843, and since 1844 has been a professor in the University of Virginia. Outlines of Comparative Philology; Studies in English; Americanisms; Wonders of the Deep; Grammar of the Spanish Language; Stray Leaves from the Book of Nature; Romance of American History, include the most important of his works. *Lip. Put. Scr.*

Devereux, Thomas Pollock. *N. C.*, 1793–1869. A North Carolina lawyer who published Reports of North Carolina Supreme Court, 1826–34; Reports in the Superior Court, 1834–40; Equity Reports, 1826–40.

De Vinne, Daniel. *I.*, 1793–1883. A Methodist clergyman of New York city. The Methodist Episcopal Church and Slavery; Recollections of Fifty Years in the Ministry; Irish Primitive Church.

De Vinne, Theodore Low. *Ct.*, 1828——. Son of D. De Vinne, *supra*. A noted printer of New York city. Printer's Price List; Invention of Printing; Historic Types.

Dew, Thomas Roderick. *Va.*, 1802–1846. An educator of Virginia, president of William and Mary College, 1836–46. A Digest of the History and Laws of Ancient and Modern Nations is his chief work. Other writings of his include The Policy of the Government; Lectures on History; Usury; Essay in Favour of Slavery, which had a great influence in turning popular sentiment against emancipation. *Ap.*

De Walden, Thomas Blaides. *E.*, 1811–1873. A New York actor of some note as an author and adapter of many plays, among which are The Upper Ten and the Lower Twenty; Kit; The Jesuit.

Dewees, William Potts. *Pa.*, 1768–1841. A once popular physician of Philadelphia, professor of obstetrics in the University of Pennsylvania. His literary style was bad, yet his writings were widely circulated in the profession and highly valued. Medical Essays; Physical and Medical Treatment of Children; System of Midwifery; Practice of Medicine. *See Gross's Sketches of Contemporaries.*

Dewey, Chester. *Ms.*, 1783–1867. A botanist who as an educator was connected with various colleges, and lastly with the University of Rochester. Besides a History of Herbaceous Plants of Massachusetts, he wrote an elaborate monograph on the Carices of North America, the result of many years' labour.

Dewey, Melvil. *N. Y.*, 1851——. The librarian of Columbia College and director of the New York State library. Library School Rules; The Decimal Classification and Relation Index.

Dewey, Orville. *Ms.*, 1794–1882. A Unitarian clergyman of conservative opinions, once prominent as a pastor in New York and Boston. Unitarian Belief; Discourses on Human Life; The Old World and the New; Letters on Revivals; Problems of Human Life and Destiny; Education of the Human Race, comprise his principal writings. *See Autobiography and Letters, 1883. A. U. A.*

De Witt, Benjamin. 1774–1819. A New York physician and scientist who published Oxygen; Minerals in New York.

De Witt, John. *N. Y.*, 1821——. A Reformed Dutch clergyman, professor in the Theological Seminary at New Brunswick, New Jersey, 1863–92. The Sure Foundation and how to Build on It; The Psalms, a New Translation (1891); What is Inspiration? *Rev.*

De Witt, John. *Pa.*, 1842——. A Presbyterian clergyman, professor at Princeton Theological Seminary since 1892, and the author of Sermons on the Christian Life.

De Witt, Simeon. *N. Y.*, 1756–1834. A once famous surveyor who is commonly held responsible for the classical nomenclature of places in central and western New York. He published Elements of Perspective.

Dexter, Henry Martyn. *Ms.*, 1821–1890. A Congregational clergyman of prominence in Boston as editor of The Congregationalist, 1867–90. He was a positive, dogmatic writer, much addicted to historical and religious controversy. His most important work is The Congregationalism of the Last Three Hundred Years. Handbook of Congregationalism; Pilgrim Memoranda; The Verdict of Reason; As to Roger Williams and his Banishment, a marked example of special pleading; History of the Old Plymouth Colony; History and the Study of History; The Right Use of Books; The Study of Politics, include the greater number of his other works. *C. P. S. Har.*

Dexter, Samuel. *Ms.*, 1761–1816. A jurist of Boston who was secretary of war under President John Adams. Letters on Free Masonry; Progress of Science, a poem; Speeches and Political Papers.

Diaz, Mrs. Abby [Morton]. *Ms.*, 1821——. A Boston writer who in youth was one of the famous company at Brook Farm, and has since been prominent in relation to social reforms. Her books for juvenile readers, which are characterized by a strong vein of humour, include The William Henry Letters; William Henry and his Friends; Chronicles of the Stimpcett Family; The Cats' Arabian Nights; The John Spicer Lectures; Lucy Maria; Polly Cologne; Jimmyjohns; A Story-book for Children. Other works are Bybury to Beacon Street, a discussion of social topics; Domestic Problems; Only a Flock of Women. *Lo.*

Dibble, Sheldon. *N. Y.*, 1809–1845. A missionary to the Sandwich Islands who published History of the Sandwich Island Missions.

Dickenson, Baxter. *Ms.*, 1795–1875. A Congregational clergyman of Boston, author of Letters to Students.

Dickinson, Anna Elizabeth. *Pa.*, 1842——. A once famous lecturer on politics and woman suffrage who, after a short and unsuccessful career as an actress, has since lived in retirement. A Paying Investment, a Plea for Education; A Ragged Register of People, Places, and Opinions; What Answer? a novel; and two plays, Mary Tudor; The Crown of Thorns. *Har. Hou.*

Dickinson, Charles Monroe. *N. Y.*, 1842——. A journalist of Binghamton, New York, who published The Children, and Other Verses.

Dickinson, Daniel Stevens. *Ct.*, 1800–1866. A Democratic politician, long prominent in the State of New York. Speeches and Correspondence, with a biography of him by his brother, appeared in 1867.

Dickinson, Emily. *Ms.*, 1830–1886. A poet whose entire life was passed in Amherst, Massachusetts, in great seclusion, and who rarely published any of her work. Since her death attention has been drawn to the strikingly original nature of her poetry by the publication of three volumes of Poems, selected from her manuscripts. They display an utter disregard of technique as well as an almost startling originality of conception. *See Letters of, 1847–1886, edited by Mrs. Todd. Rob.*

Dickinson, John. *Md.*, 1732–1808. A political writer of great influence during the period of the Revolution. Dickinson College, which he helped to found, was named in his honour. He wrote vigourously against the Stamp Act, and his various state papers display both eloquence and dignity. Petition to the King; Second Petition to the King; Letters from a Pennsylvania Farmer; Letters of Fabius.

Dickinson, Jonathan. *E.*, 16——1722. A chief justice of Pennsylvania who came to the colony in 1696. His book, entitled God's Protecting Providence Man's Surest Help in Times of Danger, is a narrative of personal adventure, and has been several times reprinted since its first appearance in 1699.

Dickinson, Jonathan. *Ms.*, 1688–1747. A Presbyterian clergyman of Elizabethtown, New Jersey, who was one of the chief American theologians of his day, and the first president of the College of New Jersey (now Princeton College). He was a voluminous writer, and much given to controversy of a theological nature. Among his many works are included Familiar Letters upon Important Subjects in Religion; Reasonableness of Christianity; True Scripture Doctrine. *See Tyler's American Literature.*

Dickinson, Richard William. *N. Y.*, 1804–1874. A Presbyterian clergyman of New York city. Scenes from Sacred History; Responses from the Sacred Oracles; Religious Teaching by Example; Life and Times of John Howard; The Resurrection of Christ Historically and Logically Viewed.

Dickinson, Rodolphus. *Ms.*, 1787–1863. An Episcopal clergyman in Deerfield, Massachusetts, who published a much criticised New and Corrected Version of the New Testament; Geographical and Statistical View of Massachusetts.

Dickson, Andrew Flinn. *S. C.*, 1825–1879. A Presbyterian clergyman of Alabama. Plantation Sermons; The Temptation in the Desert; The Light, is it Waning?

Dickson, John. *N. H.*, 1783–1852. A New York congressman, early prominent in opposition to slavery. Remarks on the Presentation of Petitions for the Abolition of Slavery in the District of Columbia.

Dickson, Samuel Henry. *S. C.*, 1798–1872. A physician of eminence in Charleston, and afterwards in Philadelphia, where from 1858 to 1872 he was a professor in the Jefferson Medical College. He wrote much on medical and other topics, his literary style being greatly admired. Essays on Life, Sleep, Pain, and Death; On the Correlation of Forces; Æsthetics of Suicide; Elements of Medicine; Dengue, its History, Pathology, and Treatment; Manual of Pathology; Practice of Medicine; Essays on Pathology and Therapeutics; Studies in Pathology and Therapeutics. *See Allibone's Dictionary; Gross's Sketches of Contemporaries.*

Didier [dy'deer], **Eugene Lemoine.** *Md.*, 1838——. Son of F. J. Didier, *infra.* A Baltimore littérateur whose style as a critic is somewhat aggressive. Life of Poe; Life and Letters of Madame Bonaparte; Primer of Criticism; The Political Adventures of James G. Blaine (1884). *Scr.*

Didier, Franklin James. *Md.*, 1794–1840. A Baltimore physician who was the author of Didier's Letters from Paris; Franklin's Letters to his Kinsfolk.

Dillaye, Stephen Devalson. *N. Y.*, 1820–1884. The Money and Finances of the French Revolution of 1789.

Dillon, John Forrest. *N. Y.*, 1831–——. A noted jurist of Iowa, and, since 1879, of New York city. United States Circuit Court Reports; Municipal Corporations; Removal of Causes from State to Federal Courts; Municipal Bonds; Laws and Jurisprudence of England and America. *Lit.*

Diman, Jeremiah Lewis. *R. I.*, 1831–1881. A Congregational clergyman who was professor of history and political economy in Brown University from 1864. Orations and Essays; The Theistic Argument as Affected by Recent Theories. *See Memoirs by Caroline Hazard, infra. Hou.*

Dimitry, Charles Patton. *D. C.*, 1837——. A novelist and journalist of New Orleans. Guilty or not Guilty; Angela's Christmas; The Alderly Tragedy; The House in Balfour Street.

Dimitry, John Bull Smith. *D. C.*, 1835——. Brother of C. P. Dimitry, *supra.* A journalist of New York city. History and Geography of Louisiana from its Earliest Settlement to the Close of the Civil War.

Dimmock, George. *Ms.*, 1852——. A naturalist of Cambridge, at one time editor of Psyche, a journal of entomology. Anatomy of Mouth Parts of Some Insects of the Order of Diptera.

Dinnies, Mrs. Anna Peyre [Shackelford]. *S. C.*, 1816——. A verse-writer of New Orleans who published The Floral Year, a collection of one hundred poems.

Dinsmore, Robert. *N. H.*, 1757–1836. A homely verse-writer of Windham, New Hampshire, who was known as "The Rustic Bard," and published Incidental Poems, strongly imitative of Burns. *See Whittier's Old Portraits and Modern Sketches.*

Dirck, Cornelius Lansing. *N. Y.*, 1785–1857. A Presbyterian clergyman for many years connected with Auburn Theological Seminary, who published Sermons on Important Subjects.

Disosway, Gabriel Poillon. *N.Y.*, 1798–1868. An antiquary of New York city. The Children's Book of Sermons; The Earliest Churches of New York and its Vicinity.

Disturnell, John. *N. Y.*, 1801–1877. A map-publisher of New York city who was an industrious compiler of guide-books and similar literature. New York as it Was and Is, 1876; Influence of Climate in North and South America; The Great Lakes of America; Traveller's Guide to Hudson River; Tourist's Guide to the Upper Mississippi, include some of his more important works.

Ditson, George Leighton. *Ms.*, 1812——. A noted traveller who published Circassia, or a Tour to the Caucasus; Crimora; The Para Papers, or France, Egypt, and Ethiopia; The Crescent and the French Crusaders; The Fedariti of Italy, a Romance of Circassian Captivity.

Dix, Dorothea Lynde. *Me.*, 1802–1887. A famous Massachusetts philanthropist the greater part of whose life was spent in efforts to improve the condition of the insane. The present enlightened treatment of the insane throughout the world is due in large measure to the impetus given in that direction by her labours in America and Europe. Her writings, except Prisons and Prison Discipline, are intended for children, and include The Garland of Flora; Conversations about Common Things; Alice and Ruth; Evening Hours. *See Life by F. Tiffany, infra.*

Dix, John Adams. *N. H.*, 1798–1879. A general and statesman who while secretary of the treasury in 1861 issued the celebrated order, "If any one attempts to tear down the American flag, shoot him on the spot." A Winter in Madeira, and A Summer in Spain and Florence; Speeches and Occasional Addresses; Resources of the State of New York. *See Memoir, by Morgan Dix, infra. Ap.*

Dix, John Homer. *Circa* 1810–1884. An oculist and aurist of Boston who published Changes of the Blood, a translation from the French of Gibert; Treatise on Strabismus; Morbid Sensibility of the Retina; The Opthalmoscope and its Uses.

Dix, Morgan. *N. Y.*, 1827——. Son of J. A. Dix, *supra*. A prominent Episcopal clergyman of New York city conspicuous among High Church theologians, and rector of Trinity Church since 1859. Sermons, Doctrinal and Practical; Lectures on the Calling of a Christian Woman; Memoir of J. A. Dix, *supra;* Gospel and Philosophy; The Sacramental System; The Seven Deadly Sins; Lectures on the First Prayer Book of King Edward VI.; The Two Estates, — Wedded in the Lord, Single for the Kingdom of Heaven's Sake. *Ap. Dut. Har.*

Dixon, James Main. *S.*, 1856——. A professor of English literature in Washington University, St. Louis, since 1892, and the author of A Dictionary of Idiomatic English Phrases.

Doane, George Hobart. *Ms.*, 1830——. Son of G. W. Doane, *infra*. A prelate of the papal household at Rome since 1886, with the title of Monsignore. First Principles; Exclusion of Protestant Worship from Rome; Manual of Instructions and Prayers.

Doane, George Washington. *N. J.*, 1799–1859. The second Protestant Episcopal bishop of New Jersey; consecrated bishop in 1832. Songs by the Way; Sermons on Various Occasions. The familiar hymn beginning "Softly now the light of day" is one of his most noted poems. *See Life and Writings of, by W. C. Doane, infra.*

Doane, William Croswell. *N. J.*, 1832——. Son of G. W. Doane, *supra*. The first Protestant Episcopal bishop of Albany. He has contributed much to reviews and other periodicals on topics of the day, is the author of a number of poems, among which The Sculptor Boy is often quoted, and has published several works, including Sermons; Mosaics, or the Harmony of Collect Epistle and Gospel for the Sundays of the Christian Year. As a theologian his place is amongst liberal High Churchmen.

Dod, Albert Baldwin. *N. J.*, 1805–1845. A Presbyterian clergyman, professor of mathematics at Princeton College, 1830–45. Theological Essays was his only published work.

Dodd, Mrs. Anna Bowman [Blake]. *L. I.*, 185——. A New

York writer whose volumes of travels have been very popular. The Republic of the Future, or Socialism a Reality; Cathedral Days; Glorinda: a Story; Three Normandy Inns; In the Norfolk Broads. *Cas. Rob.*

Dodd, Stephen. *N. J.*, 1777–1856. A Presbyterian minister of Connecticut, who published History of East Haven; Revolutionary Memorials.

Doddridge, Joseph. *Pa.*, 1769–1826. An Episcopal clergyman of western Virginia. Logan, a drama; Notes on the Settlement and Indian Wars of the Western Country, 1763–83.

Dodge, David Low. *Ct.*, 1774–1852. A New York merchant who was the first president of the New York Peace Society. The Mediator's Kingdom not of this World; War Inconsistent with the Religion of Jesus Christ. *See Memorials of, 1854.*

Dodge, Ebenezer. *Ms.*, 1819–1890. A Baptist clergyman, president of Madison (now Colgate) University, 1868–90. Evidences of Christianity; Christian Theology.

Dodge, Mary Abby. "Gail Hamilton." *Ms.*, 1838–1896. A noted essayist and magazinist of Hamilton, Massachusetts, whose aggressive, pungent style made her writings at one time extremely popular. Much of her work is ephemeral in its nature, but it is always readable and often brilliant. A New Atmosphere; Gala Days; Woman's Wrongs; Red-Letter Days; Summer Rest; Battle of the Books; Twelve Miles from a Lemon; Sermons to the Clergy; First Love is Best; What Think ye of Christ?; Country Living and Country Thinking; Skirmishes and Sketches; Wool-Gathering; Woman's Worth and Worthlessness; Little Folk Life; Nursery Noonings; Our Common School System; Divine Guidance; The Insuppressible Book; A Washington Bible Class; Biography of James G. Blaine. *Ap. Har.*

Dodge, Mrs. Mary Barker [Carter]. *Pa.*, 18——. Belfry Voices; The Gray Masque and Other Poems. *Lo.*

Dodge, Mrs. Mary [Mapes]. *N. Y.*, 1838——. A writer of New York city who has edited the Saint Nicholas Magazine since 1873. Her writings for young people include Hans Brinker; Donald and Dorothy; Rhymes and Jingles; Irvington Stories; A Few Friends; The Land of Pluck; When Life is Young, poems for young people. She has also written Theophilus and Others; Along the Way: a volume of Short Poems. *Scr.*

Dodge, Nathaniel Shatswell. *Ms.*, 1810–1874. A Boston littérateur who was the author of Stories of a Grandfather about American History. *Le.*

Dodge, Richard Irving. *N.C.*, 1827–1895. A colonel in the United States army who saw much service in Indian campaigns, and made careful study of the Indian character. The Black Hills; The Plains of the Great West; Our Wild Indians; A Living Issue.

Dodge, Theodore Ayrault. *Ms.*, 1842——. A captain and brevet lieutenant-colonel in the United States army, prominent as a military historian. The Campaign of Chancellorsville; A Bird's-Eye View of our Civil War; Great Captains; Alexander, a History of the Origin and Growth of the Art of War from the Earliest Times to the Battle of Ipsus, B. C. 301, with a detailed account of the Campaigns of the Great Macedonian; Hannibal; Cæsar; Gustavus Adolphus; Patroclus and Penelope, a Chat in the Saddle; Riders of Many Lands. *Har. Hou.*

Dods, John Bovee. *N. Y.*, 1795–1872. A clergyman of New York city whose published works include Thirty Sermons; Philosophy of Mesmerism; Philosophy of Electrical Psychology; Immortality Triumphant; Spirit Manifestations Examined and Explained.

Doe, Charles Henry. *Ms.*, 1838——. A journalist of Worcester, Massachusetts. Buffets, a novel.

Doesticks, Q. K. Philander. *See Thomson, Mortimer.*

Doggett, David Seth. *Va.*, 1810–1880. A Methodist bishop who lived at Richmond, Virginia, and published The War and its Close.

Dolbear, Amos Emerson. *Ct.*, 1837——. A professor of physics and astronomy at Tufts College since 1874. The Art of Projecting; The Speaking

Telephone; Sound and its Phenomena. Matter, Ether, and Motion. *Le.*

Dole, Charles Fletcher. *Me.*, 1845–——. A Unitarian clergyman of Boston. The Citizen and the Neighbour; Jesus and the Men about Him; A Catechism of Liberal Faith; The American Citizen.

Dole, Edmund Pearson. *Me.*, 1850–——. Cousin of C. F. Dole, *supra.* Assistant attorney-general of the Hawaiian Islands. Talks About Law. *Hou.*

Dole, Nathan Haskell. *Ms.*, 1852–——. Brother of C. F. Dole, *supra.* A littérateur of Boston who, besides publishing translations from the Russian of Tolstoï and other writers, is the author of A Score of Famous Composers; The Hawthorn Tree and Other Poems, a collection of pleasing, unpretentious verse; Not Angels Quite; History of the Turko-Russian War of 1877–1878; On the Point, a Summer Idyl; Flowers from Foreign Gardens. One of his most important works is a variorum edition of the Rubáiyát of Omar Khayyám. *Cr. Est. Kt. Mer.*

Donald, Elijah Winchester. *Ms.*, 1848——. An Episcopal clergyman of Boston, rector of Trinity Church from 1892. The Expansion of Religion. *Hou.*

Donaldson, Frank. *Md.*, 1822–1891. A Baltimore physician, professor of hygiene in the University of Maryland since 1866. Influence of City Life and Occupations in Consumption.

Donaldson, James Lowry. *Md.*, 1814–1885. A colonel and brevet major-general in the United States army who published Sergeant Atkins, a tale of the Florida War.

Donnelly, Eleanor Cecilia. *Pa.*, 1838——. Sister of I. Donnelly, *infra.* A Philadelphia writer of religious verse, the greater part of which is occupied with Roman Catholic themes. Among her many volumes are Domus Dei; Out of Sweet Solitude; Hymns of the Sacred Heart; Children of the Golden Sheaf and Other Poems.

Donnelly, Ignatius. *Pa.*, 1831——. A Minnesota writer who, besides publishing An Essay on the Sonnets of Shakespeare; Atlantis: the Antediluvian World; Cæsar's Column; Ragnarok: the Age of Fire and Gravel, is the author of The Great Cryptogram. In this work he claims to have discovered a cipher in the plays of Shakespeare which sufficiently establishes the fact that they were written by Lord Bacon, an eccentric exercise of ingenuity that has not been taken seriously by scholars. *Ap. Har.*

Doolittle, Benjamin. *Ms.*, 1695–1749. A clergyman of Northfield, Massachusetts, 1718–49. Narrative of the Mischief of the French and Indians, 1744–48; Inquiry into Enthusiasm.

Dorchester, Daniel. *Ms.*, 1827——. A prominent Methodist clergyman of Pittsburg. Concessions of Liberalists to Orthodoxy; Problem of Religious Progress; Latest Drink Sophistries; The Liquor Problem in All Ages; The Why of Methodism; Christianity in the United States; Romanism versus the Public Schools. *Meth.*

Dorgan, John Aylmer. 1836–1866. A lawyer and verse writer of Philadelphia, whose only publication was a collection of verse entitled Studies. *See Manhattan Magazine, June, 1883.*

Dorr, Benjamin. *Ms.*, 1796–1869. An Episcopal clergyman who was rector of Christ Church, Philadelphia, 1837–69. The Churchman's Manual; The History of a Pocket Prayer-Book; Recognition of Friends in Another World; Sunday-School Teacher's Encouragement; Prophecies and Types Relative to Christ; Memorials of Christ Church; Travels in the East; Memoir of John Fanning Watson, *infra.*

Dorr, Mrs. Julia Caroline [Ripley]. *S. C.*, 1825——. A poet and novelist of Rutland, Vermont. Her verse, much of which reaches a high degree of excellence, includes Daybreak, an Easter Poem; Vermont; Friar Anselmo; Afternoon Songs; Legend of the Baboushka; Poems (complete edition). Her other writings comprise four novels: Lanmere; Sibyl Huntington; Expiation; Farmingdale; Bermuda, a volume of travel; Bride and Bridegroom, or Letters to a Young Married Couple; The Flower of England's Face; A Cathedral Pilgrimage. *Lip. Mac. Meth. Ran. Scr.*

Dorsey, Mrs. Anna Hanson. *D. C.*, 1815–1896. A prolific writer of dramas, novels, poems, and essays, long resident in Washington, and from 1840 an ardent Roman Catholic. Among her works are May Brooke; Guy the Leper, an epic poem; The Old House at Glenarra; Palms; Warp and Woof.

Dorsey, Ella Loraine. *D. C.*, 185—. Daughter of Mrs. Anna Dorsey, *supra*. A Washington writer of stories for boys. Midshipman Bob; Saxty's Angel; The Two Tramps.

Dorsey, James Owen. *Md.*, 1848–1895. An ethnologist who for a time was an Episcopal missionary to the Ponka Indians, but for many years has been engaged in linguistic studies for the Bureau of Ethnology. Omaha Sociology; Osage Traditions; Kansas Mourning and War Customs; The Dhegiha Language, are among his writings.

Dorsey, Mrs. Sarah Anne [Ellis]. *Mi.*, 1829–1879. A Mississippi author who was the amanuensis of Jefferson Davis, *supra*, to whom she bequeathed her estate of Beauvoir on the Gulf of Mexico, where he died. Lucia Dare; Agnes Graham, both stories of the Civil War; Panola, a tale of Louisiana; Atalie, or a Southern Villeggiatura; Life of Governor Allen of Louisiana.

Dorsheimer, William. *N. Y.*, 1832–1888. A prominent citizen of Buffalo who was twice lieutenant-governor of New York, and published A Life of Grover Cleveland (1884).

Doten, Lizzie. *Ms.*, 1829——. A Boston spiritualist trance medium whose verses are claimed to be inspired by the spirits of Shakespeare, Burns, Poe, and other poets of the past. Poems of Progress; Poems from the Inner Life. *Ban.*

Doubleday, Abner. *N. Y.*, 1819–1893. A colonel and brevet major-general in the United States army who retired from active service in 1873. Reminiscences of Forts Sumter and Moultrie; Chancellorsville and Gettysburg; Gettysburg made Plain. *Har. Scr.*

Doubleday, Charles William. *E.*, 1829——. A soldier who accompanied Walker on the famous Nicaragua expedition, and later served as acting brigadier-general in the United States army. Reminiscences of the Filibuster War in America.

Douglas, Alice May. *Me.*, 1865——. A writer of verse and juvenile tales whose home is at Bath, Maine. Her verse includes Phlox; May Flowers; Gems Without Polish. Jewel Gatherers; The Peacemaker; Self-Exiled from Russia, are among her tales for young readers.

Douglas, Amanda Minnie. *N. Y.*, 1837——. A popular novelist of Newark, New Jersey, whose more than thirty works of fiction have obtained a wide circulation. They are readable, and not without skill in construction, but are not particularly strong on the literary side. Among them are In Trust; Stephen Dane; Clandia; With Fate Against Him; Sherburne House; In Wild Rose Time; Seven Daughters; Larry; Hope Mills. *Do. Le.*

Douglas, Marian. *See Robinson, Mrs. A.*

Douglas, Silas Hamilton. *N. Y.*, 1816——. A professor of chemistry at the University of Michigan, 1844–79. Tables for Qualitative Chemical Analysis; Qualitative Chemical Analysis (with A. R. Prescott).

Douglass, Frederick. *Md.*, 1817–1895. A famous orator and the most distinguished member of the African race in America. He was born in slavery, but escaped to the North in 1838, educated himself, and soon became prominent as an anti-slavery speaker. As time went on, his style, always picturesque and eloquent, became polished and elegant. My Bondage and My Freedom; Narrative of My Experience in Slavery; Life and Times of Frederick Douglass (1881). *See Life by Holland, 1891.*

Douglass, William. *S.*, *c.* 1691–1752. A Scottish physician who came to America and settled in Boston in 1718. He was a man of very positive views, most of which were opposed to those of the age and the community in which he lived, and his time was well filled in controversies with the clergy, physicians, magistrates, and colonial governors. His principal work is a Summary, Historical and Political, of the British Settlements in America. Others of less note are Mercurius Novanglicanus, an almanac; Treatise on Small Pox; Midwifery; Practical History of a New, Eruptive, Miliary Fever. *See Tyler's American Literature.*

Dow, Daniel. *Ct.*, 1772–1849. A Congregational clergyman of Thompson, Connecticut. Familiar Letters to Rev. John Sherman; The Pedobaptist Catechism; The Sinaitic and Abrahamic Covenants; Free Inquiry Recommended on the Subject of Free Masonry.

Dow, Lorenzo. *Ct.*, 1777–1834. An eccentric Methodist travelling preacher, especially vehement against the Jesuits. Polemical Works; The Stranger in Charleston, or the Trial and Confession of Lorenzo Dow; A Short Account of a Long Travel; Journal and Miscellaneous Writings; History of a Cosmopolite, an autobiographic work.

Dowd, Mary Alice. *W. Va.*, 1855——. An educator of Stamford, Connecticut, who has published Vacation Verses.

Dowling, John. *E.*, 1807–1878. A Baptist clergyman of New York city whose writings had a large circulation. Vindication of the Baptists; History of Romanism; Defence of the Protestant Scriptures; Power of Illustration; Nights and Mornings; Judson Offering; Exposition of the Prophecies concerning the Second Coming of Christ.

Downes, John. *N. Y.*, 1799–1882. A mathematician of Washington. Peter Parley's Almanacs for Old and Young; Logarithms and Logarithmic Sines and Tangents; United States Almanac Complete, or Ephemeris.

Downes, William Howe. *Ct.*, 1854——. A Boston journalist, for many years on the staff of the Transcript, and an art critic. Spanish Ways and By-Ways; The Tin Army of the Potomac, or a Kindergarten of War.

Downie, David. *S.*, 1838——. A Baptist missionary to India who has published a History of the Telugu Mission.

Downing, Andrew Jackson. *N. Y.*, 1815–1852. A once noted horticulturist and landscape gardener of New York who did much to popularize a knowledge of rural art. Theory and Practice of Landscape Gardening; Fruit and Fruit Trees of America; Architecture of Country Houses; Cottage Residences; Rural Essays. *See Garden and Forest, vol. 8. Wil.*

Downing, Mrs. Frances [Murdaugh]. *Circa* 1835–1894. A writer of Charlottesville, North Carolina, who has published Pluto, or the Origin of Mint Julep, a story in verse after the manner of the "Ingoldsby Legends;" and several novels, including Nameless; Perfect Through Suffering; Florida; Five Little Girls and Two Little Boys.

Downing, Jack. *See Smith, Seba.*

Drake, Benjamin. *Ky.*, 1794–1841. A Cincinnati journalist whose writings include Cincinnati in 1820; Tales and Sketches from the Queen City; Life of Black Hawk; Life of William Henry Harrison; Life of Tecumseh.

Drake, Charles Daniel. *O.*, 1811–1892. Son of Daniel Drake, *infra.* An eminent lawyer of St. Louis who published Law of Attachments; Life of Daniel Drake. *Lit.*

Drake, Daniel. *N. J.*, 1785–1852. Brother of B. Drake, *supra.* A distinguished physician of Cincinnati and Philadelphia who is best known by his valuable work on The Diseases of the Interior Valley of North America, which embodies a vast amount of patient research. His other works include Pictures of Cincinnati and the Miami Country (1815); History of the Prevention and Treatment of Epidemic Cholera; Essays on Medical Education; Discourses; Pioneer Life in Kentucky. *See Lives by Mansfield, 1855, C. D. Drake, supra, 1871; Gross's Sketches of Contemporaries. Clke.*

Drake, Francis Samuel. *Ms.*, 1828–1885. Son of S. G. Drake, *infra.* A bookseller of Boston whose Dictionary of American Biography is incorporated in Appleton's Cyclopedia of Biography. Other works of his are Life of General Knox; The Town of Roxbury; Tea Leaves; Indian History for Young Folks. *Har. Lip.*

Drake, Joseph Rodman. *N. Y.*, 1795–1820. A talented physician of New York city, co-author with Halleck, *infra*, of The Croaker Papers in the Evening Post. His poetical fame rests on The Culprit Fay, a delicate, fanciful creation, and the often-quoted poem The American Flag. His poetry was once extremely popular, but has failed to interest the readers of the latter half of the 19th century. A selection from his poems was made by his daughter and published in 1836.

Drake, Samuel Adams. *Ms.*, 1833——. Son of S. G. Drake, *infra.* A littérateur of Boston whose histories and books of home travel have been deservedly popular. Around the Hub, a Boy's Book About Boston; The Heart of the White Mountains; Old Landmarks and Historic Personages of Boston; Nooks and Corners of the New England Coast; Old Landmarks and Historic Fields of Middlesex; Captain Nelson; The Watch Fires of '76; Burgoyne's Invasion of 1777; The Taking of Louisburg; The Battle of Gettysburg; Our Colonial Homes; New England Legends and Folk-Lore; The Making of New England, 1580–1643; The Making of Virginia and the Middle Colonies, 1578–1701; The Making of the Ohio Valley States, 1660–1837; The Making of the Great West, 1512–1853; History of Middlesex County; The Pine-Tree Coast. *Est. Har. Le. Rob. Scr.*

Drake, Samuel Gardiner. *N. H.*, 1798–1875. A Boston bookseller of antiquarian tastes who, beside editing several historical works, was the author of Memoir of Cotton Mather; Entertaining History of King Philip's War; Book of the Indians; Old Indian Chronicle; Account of the Family of Drake; Memoir of Walter Raleigh; History and Antiquities of Boston; Indian Biography; Indian Captivities; Annals of Witchcraft in the United States; History of the French and Indian War. *See Bibliography of Maine.*

Draper, Andrew Sloan. *N. Y.*, 1848——. A lawyer and educator of Albany, and, since 1894, president of the University of Illinois. What Ought the Common Schools to Do?; How to Improve the Country Schools; Powers and Obligations of Teachers; School Administration in Large Cities; Origin of the New York Common School System; A Teaching Profession; Authority of the State in Education; Legal Status of the Public Schools; Normal and Training School System of New York; Responsibility and Authority of Trustees; American Schools and American Citizenship; Public School Pioneering in New York and Massachusetts.

Draper, Henry. *Va.*, 1837–1882. Son of J. W. Draper, *infra.* A professor in the University of New York. The Construction of a Silvered Glass Telescope; Text-Book of Chemistry.

Draper, John Christopher. *Va.*, 1835–1885. Son of J. W. Draper, *infra.* A New York physician, professor in the University of New York. Text-Book in Anatomy; Physiology and Hygiene; Practical Laboratory Course in Physics; Text-Book of Medical Physics.

Draper, John William. *E.*, 1811–1882. A distinguished scientist who came from England to the United States in 1832, and from 1839 to 1881 was connected with the University of New York. History of the Civil War in America; History of the Intellectual Development of Europe; The Future Civil Policy of America; Human Physiology; Elements of Chemistry; Text-Book of Natural Philosophy; Text-Book on Physiology; Researches in Actino-Chemistry; Scientific Memoirs; History of the Conflict between Religion and Science. *See Dictionary of National Biography, vol. 16.*

Draper, Lyman Copeland. *N. Y.*, 1815–1891. An antiquarian writer of Madison, Wisconsin. Madison, the Capital of Wisconsin; King's Mountain and its Heroes.

Drayton, John. *S. C.*, 1766–1822. Son of W. H. Drayton, *infra.* A South Carolina statesman, twice governor of his State. View of South Carolina; Letters written during a Tour through the Northern and Eastern States.

Drayton, William Henry. *S. C.*, 1742–1779. A prominent figure among statesmen of the Revolution and a member of the Continental Congress. A History of the American Revolution, which he left in manuscript, was afterwards published by his son.

Drinker, Mrs. Anna. "Edith May." *Pa.*, 1827——. A verse-writer of Montrose, Pennsylvania. Poems by Edith May; Tales and Verses for Children; Katy's Story.

Drisler, Henry. *N. Y.*, 1818-1897. A classical scholar of distinction, professor at Columbia College from 1843, whose Greek-and-English Lexicon has long been a standard authority.

Droch. *See Bridges, Robert.*

Drone, Eaton Sylvester. *O.*, 1842——. legal writer on the staff of the New York Herald. The Law of Property in Intellectual Productions, embracing Copyright and Playright. *Lit.*

Drummond, Josiah Hayden. *Me.*, 1827——. A lawyer who was attorney-general of Maine for some years, and published Maine Masonic Text-Book for Use of Lodges; History of Masonic Jurisprudence.

Drury, Augustus Waldo. 1851——. A clergyman of the sect of United Brethren in Christ who has written a Life of Otterbein, the founder of the sect.

Drury, John Benjamin. *N. Y.*, 1838——. A Dutch Reformed clergyman of Ghent, New York, who has published Truths and Untruths of Evolution. *Ran.*

Duane, James Chatham. *N. Y.*, 1824——. A retired brigadier-general of the United States army, author of A Manual for Engineer Troops.

Duane, William. *N. Y.*, 1760-1835. A once prominent journalist and politician of Philadelphia. Military Dictionary; The Mississippi Question; An Epitome of the Arts and Sciences; Visit to Colombia in 1822; American Military Library; Handbook for Riflemen; Handbook for Infantry.

Duane, William. *Pa.*, 1807——. Son of W. J. Duane, *infra.* A Philadelphia writer who published Relation of Landlord to Tenant in Pennsylvania; Law of Roads, etc., in Pennsylvania; Canada and the Continental Congress; Ligan, a collection of Tales and Essays.

Duane, William John. *I.*, 1780-1865. Son to W. Duane, *supra.* An eminent lawyer of Philadelphia who was secretary of the treasury in 1833, and was dismissed from office by President Jackson for declining to order the deposits removed from the Bank of the United States. The Law of Nations Investigated; Letters on Internal Improvement; Narrative and Correspondence Concerning the Removal of the Deposits, 1838.

Dubbs, Joseph Henry. *Pa.*, 1838——. A German Reformed clergyman, professor of history in Franklin and Marshall College, Lancaster, Pennsylvania, since 1875. Otterbein and the Reformed Church; Historic Manual of the Reformed Church; Home Ballads and Metrical Versions; Why Am I Reformed?

Du Bois, Augustus Jay. *O.*, 1849——. A professor of engineering at Yale University since 1877. Elements of Graphical Statics; The New Method of Graphical Statics; Strains in Framed Structures; Mechanics. *Wil.*

Du Bois, William Edward Burghardt. *Ms.*, 1868——. An educator of African descent, assistant professor of sociology in the University of Pennsylvania. The Suppression of the African Slave Trade to the United States, 1638-1810. *Lgs.*

Du Bois, William Ewing. *Pa.*, 1810-1881. A Philadelphia numismatist, assayer at the Mint. Manual of Gold and Silver Coins of All Nations; Pledges of History, an account of the Antique Coins in the United States Mint.

Du Bose, Mrs. Catherine Anne [Richards]. *E.*, 1826——. A Georgia writer who published The Pastor's Household, or Lessons on the Eleventh Commandment, a juvenile tale.

Ducatel, Julius Timoleon. *Md.*, 1796-1849. A chemist of Baltimore, professor in the University of Maryland and author of a Manual of Toxicology.

Du Chaillu [dü-chä-yü'], **Paul Belloni.** *F.*, 1835——. A noted French traveller who has become a naturalized citizen of the United States. Ivar the Viking; Explorations and Adventures in Equatorial Africa; A Journey to Ashango Land; My Apingi Kingdom; Wild Life under the Equator; Lost in the Jungle; The Country of the Dwarfs; Land of the Midnight Sun; Age of the Vikings; Stories of the Gorilla Country. The greater number of his works are intended for juvenile reading. *Har.*

Duché, Jacob. *Pa.*, 1737-1798. An Episcopal clergyman of Philadelphia who made the prayer at the opening of the Continental Congress. Becoming discouraged at the want of success of the colonists, he urged Washington to abandon the cause. He was thereupon considered an enemy of the country and his property was confiscated. Caspipina's Letters; Discourses on Various Subjects.

Dudley, Dean. *Me.*, 1823——. A Boston lawyer of antiquarian tastes. Pictures of Life in England and America; The Dudley Genealogies; Social and Political Aspects of England and the Continent; History of the First Council of Nice; Officers of the Army and Navy; History of the Dudley Family.

Dudley, Thomas Underwood. *Va.*, 1837——. The second Protestant Episcopal bishop of Kentucky. He served in the Confederate army as a colonel, and afterwards entered the ministry. A Wise Discrimination the Church's Need.

Dudley, William Russell. *Ct.*, 1849——. A professor of botany at Cornell University, who has published The Cayuga Flora.

Duer, Edward Louis. *N. J.*, 1836——. A physician of Philadelphia. Post Mortem Discoveries; Treatment of Diphtheria.

Duer, John. *N. Y.*, 1782–1858. A once prominent New York jurist whose specialty was insurance law. Duer's Reports; Laws and Practice of Marine Insurance.

Duer, William Alexander. *N. Y.*, 1780–1858. Brother of J. Duer, *supra*, and like him a prominent jurist. He was president of Columbia College, 1829–42. Constitutional Jurisprudence of the United States.

Duff, Peter. *N. B.*, 1802–1869. An educator of Pittsburg, where he founded Duff's Mercantile College, one of the earliest institutions of the kind. The North American Accountant was his only publication of note.

Duffel, Mary Gordon. *Al.*, *c.* 1840——. A resident of Alabama, who published A History of Alabama; Guide to the Mammoth Cave.

Duffield, George. *Pa.*, 1794–1869. A Presbyterian clergyman, once prominent in Detroit as a leader among New School Presbyterians. Dissertations on the Prophecies; Regeneration; Travels in the Holy Land; Claims of Episcopal Bishops Examined, include his most important writings.

Duffield, George. *Pa.*, 1818–1888. Son of G. Duffield, *supra*. A Presbyterian clergyman of some note as a hymn-writer, one of his most popular hymns being "Stand up for Jesus."

Duffield, John Thomas. *Pa.*, 1823——. A Presbyterian clergyman who was professor of mathematics in Princeton College for many years, and published The Princeton Pulpit and many religious monographs.

Duffield, Samuel Augustus Willoughby. *L. I.*, 1843–1887. Son of G. Duffield, 2d. A Presbyterian clergyman of Bloomfield, New Jersey. English Hymns, their Authors and History; Latin Hymn-Writers and their Hymns; Warp and Woof, a Book of Verse. *Fu.*

Duffield, William Ward. *Pa.*, 1823——. An engineer of Kentucky who was a brigadier-general in the Federal army during the Civil War. School of the Brigade and Evolutions of the Line.

Duganne, Augustine Joseph Hickey. *Ms.*, 1823–1884. A journalist of New York city chiefly known as a poet. During the Civil War he served in the Federal army, and was for some time a captive in Southern prisons. Among his writings are Prison Life in the South; Camps and Prisons; History of Governments; The Lydian Queen, a tragedy; Home Poems; Parnassus in Pillory, a satire.

Dugdale, Richard L. *F.*, 1841–1883. A writer on sociology. The Jukes, or Heredity in Crime; Further Studies of Criminals.

Duhring, Julia. *Pa.*, 1836——. An essayist who has published Philosophers and Fools; Gentlefolks and Others; Amor in Society; Mental Life and Culture. *Lip.*

Duhring, Louis Adolphus. *Pa.*, 1845——. Brother of J. Duhring, *supra*. A physician of Philadelphia, prominent as a dermatologist. Atlas of Skin Diseases; Practical Treatise on Diseases of the Skin; Epitome of Skin Diseases; Cutaneous Medicine. *Lip.*

Duke, William. *Md.*, 1757–1840. An Episcopal clergyman and educator of Maryland who published A Clew to Religious Truth.

Dulany, Daniel. *Md.*, 1721–1797. A noted Maryland statesman. Considerations on the Propriety of Imposing Taxes on the British Colonies.

Dulles, Charles Winslow. *E. I.*, 1850——. A surgeon of Philadelphia. What to Do First in Accidents or Poisoning; What to Do First in Accidents and Emergencies; Accidents and Emergencies.

Dulles, John Welsh. *Pa.*, 1823–1887. A Presbyterian clergyman of Philadelphia, at one time a missionary to India. The Soldier's Friend; Life in India; The Ride Through Palestine.

Dummer, Jeremiah. *Ms.*, *c.* 1680–1739. A noted scholar who was colonial agent for Massachusetts in London, 1710–21, and was a political friend of Bolingbroke. A Letter to a Noble Lord concerning the Late Expedition to Canada; A Defence of the New England Charters, — both excellent specimens of literary skill as well as patriotism. *See Tyler's American Literature.*

Dumont, Mrs. Julia Louisa [Carey]. *O.*, 1794–1857. A once noted educator of Vevay, Indiana. Life Sketches from Common Paths.

Dunbar, Charles Franklin. *Ms.*, 1830——. A professor of political economy at Harvard University from 1871. Chapters on The Theory and History of Banking. *Put.*

Dunbar, Paul Laurence. *O.*, 1872——. A verse-writer of Dayton, Ohio, of African descent. Lyrics of Lowly Life. *Do.*

Duncan, William Cecil. *N. Y.*, 1824–1864. A Baptist clergyman of New Orleans. Life of John the Baptist; History of the Baptists for the First Two Centuries of the Christian Era; The Years of Jesus; Brief History of the Baptists.

Duncan, William Stevens. *Pa.*, 1834——. A physician of Brownsville, Pennsylvania. Medical Delusions; Physiology of Death.

Dunglison [dŭng′glĭ-son], **Richard James.** *Md.*, 1834——. Son of R. Dunglison, *infra.* A physician of Philadelphia who has issued Practitioner's Reference Book; Elementary Physiology.

Dunglison, Robley. *E.*, 1798–1869. An eminent Philadelphia physician, professor in Jefferson Medical College from 1836, and one of the most learned men of his profession. His most important work is his Medical Dictionary, which has a very wide reputation. Other works are, Human Physiology; Elements of Hygiene; General Therapeutics; The Medical Student; The Practice of Medicine; Commentaries on Diseases of the Stomach and Bowels in Children. *See Gross's Sketches of Contemporaries.*

Dunham, Carroll. *N. Y.*, 1828–1877. A once prominent homœopathic physician of New York. Homœopathy the Science of Therapeutics; Lectures in Materia Medica.

Dunham, William Russell. *N. H.*, 1833——. A physician of Keene, New Hampshire, who has published Theory of Medical Science.

Dunlap, Andrew. *Ms.*, 1794–1835. A lawyer of Boston, and author of Admiralty Practice in Cases of Maritime Jurisdiction.

Dunlap, John A. *Circa* 1793–c. 1858. A justice of the peace in New York city. Practice of the Superior Court of New York in Civil Actions; Abridgement of the 13th and 14th books of Coke's Reports.

Dunlap, Samuel Fales. *Ms.*, 1825——. Son of A. Dunlap, *supra*, and, like him, a lawyer of Boston. Origin of Ancient Names; Vestiges of the Spirit History of Man.

Dunlap, William. *N. J.*, 1766–1839. A once prominent artist, dramatist, and theatrical manager of New York city. Life of George Frederick Cooke; Life of Charles Brockden Brown; The American Theatre; History of New York; History, Rise, and Progress of the Arts of Design in the United States; Thirty Years Ago, a novel; New Netherlands, Province of New York; The Father, a comedy; Leicester, a tragedy, include the greater part of his writings.

Dunlop, James. *Pa.*, 1795–1856. A Pittsburg lawyer prominent as an opponent of slavery. Laws of Pennsylvania, 1700–1853; Digest of the General Laws of the United States.

Dunn, Jacob Piatt. 18——. The State librarian of Indiana. History of Indiana; Massacres of the Mountains, a History of Indian Wars in the Far West. *Har. Hou.*

Dunn, Lewis Romaine. *N. J.*, 1822–1876. A Methodist divine of New Jersey. Lizzie Hagar, the Orphan Girl; The Mission of the Spirit; Angels of God; Sermons on the Higher Life.

Dunning, Albert Elijah. *Ct.*, 1844——. A Congregational clergyman of Boston, editor of the Congregationalist. The Sunday-School Library; Bible Studies; Congregationalists in America. *C. P. S. Hi.*

Dunning, Mrs. Annie [Ketchum]. "Nellie Grahame." *N. Y.*, 1831——. A prolific writer of Sunday-school tales, mainly for the Presbyterian Board of Publication. Among them are Clementina's Mirrour; A Story of Four Lives; Broken Pitchers; Contradictions. *Lo.*

Dunning, Charlotte. *See Morse, Mrs.*

Duponceau [du-pŏn'sō or dü'poɴ'so'], **Pierre Etienne.** *F.*, 1760–1844. A Frenchman who came to America as aid to Baron Steuben, settled in Philadelphia, and became eminent as a lawyer. He was president of the American Philosophical Society, and his Memoir on the Indian Languages of North America attracted much attention amongst scholars.

Dupuy [dü-pwe'], **Eliza Ann.** *Va.*, 1814–1881. A sensational novelist of Kentucky, for many years a regular contributor of serial stories to the New York Ledger. Among them are The Conspirator, a story of Aaron Burr; The Huguenot Exiles; The Concealed Treasure. *Har.*

Durbin, John Price. *Ky.*, 1800–1876. A Methodist clergyman noted for his eloquence, who was missionary secretary of the Methodist Episcopal Church, 1850–72. Observations in Europe; Observations in Egypt, Palestine, Syria, and Asia Minor. *See Life by J. A. Roche, 1879. Har.*

Durfee, Job. *R. I.*, 1790–1847. A Rhode Island jurist who was chief justice of his State, 1835–47. What Cheer, or Roger Williams in Exile; Panidea, a philosophical treatise. *See Complete Works, with Memoir by his son, 1849.*

Durivage, Francis Alexander. *Ms.*, 1813–1881. Nephew to Edward Everett, *infra.* A magazinist of Boston, among whose writings are The Fatal Casket; Life Scenes from the World Around Us; Cyclopedia of History.

Durrie, Daniel Steele. *N. Y.*, 1819——. An antiquarian writer of Madison, Wisconsin, who has published Bibliographia Genealogica Americana; History of Madison.

Dutcher, Addison Porter. *N. Y.*, 1818–1884. A physician of Cleveland. Selections from my Portfolio, essays on Popular and Scientific Subjects; Pulmonary Tuberculosis; Sparks from the Forge of a Rough Thinker; Two Voyages to Europe. *Lip.*

Dutcher, Jacob C. *Circa* 1820——. A Dutch Reformed clergyman of New York. Requisites of National Greatness; The Prodigal Son; Our Fallen Heroes; The Old Home by the River; Frank Lyttleton, or Winning his Way.

Dutton, Clarence Edward. *Ct.*, 1841——. An officer in the United States army associated with the Geological Survey. Geology of the High Plateaus of Utah; Tertiary History of the Grand Cañon District; Hawaiian Volcanoes; Mount Taylor and the Zuñi Plateau; The Charleston Earthquake of 1886.

Dutton, Henry. *Ct.*, 1796–1869. A prominent jurist of Connecticut who issued a Digest of the Connecticut Reports.

Duval, John Pope. *Va.*, 1790–*c.* 1855. A Florida lawyer who published in 1840 A Digest of the Laws of Florida.

Duyckinck [dī'kiŋk], **Evert Augustus.** *N. Y.*, 1816–1878. A literary critic of New York city, who with his brother George, *infra*, was the author of an Encyclopædia of American Literature, first issued in 1855. Its estimates were sometimes over-indulgent, but on the whole the work gave a fairly just view of the subject at that time. Other works by the elder Duyckinck are History of the War for the Union; Biography of Eminent Men and Women of Europe and America.

Duyckinck, George Long. *N. Y.*, 1823–1863. Brother of E. A. Duyckinck, *supra*. A writer of New York city who, beside his share in The Encyclopædia of American Literature, was the author of Lives of George Herbert; Bishop Ken; Jeremy Taylor; Bishop Latimer.

Dwight, Benjamin Woodbridge. *Ct.*, 1816–1880. Grandson of Timothy Dwight, *infra*. An educator of New York city. The Higher Christian Education; Modern Philosophy; Modern Philology; Woman's Higher Culture; The True Doctrine of Divine Providence; History of the Dwight Family in America; History of the Strong Family.

Dwight, Edwin Welles. *Ms.*, 1789–1841. A Congregational clergyman of Richmond, Massachusetts, whose only publication was a History of Berkshire County.

Dwight, Harrison Gray Otis. *Ms.*, 1803–1862. A Congregational missionary to Armenia. Researches of Smith and Dwight in Armenia; Christianity Revived in the East; Catalogue of Armenian Literature in the Middle Ages.

Dwight, Henry Edwin. *Ct.*, 1797–1832. The eighth son of Timothy Dwight, *infra*. An educator of New Haven who published Travels in the North of Germany.

Dwight, Henry Otis. *Ty.*, 1843——. Son of H. G. O. Dwight, *supra*. A Federal officer during the Civil War, who was a correspondent of the New York Tribune from Constantinople, 1876–79. Turkish Life in War Times. *Scr.*

Dwight, John Sullivan. *Ms.*, 1813–1893. A distinguished musical critic of Boston, editor of Dwight's Journal of Music, an outspoken, fearless, high-class critical periodical, 1852–81. In earlier life he spent five years at Brook Farm, and was a contributor to The Dial. He was the author of a History of Music in Boston and the poem God Save the State.

Dwight, Mary Ann. *Ms.*, 1806–1858. A teacher of drawing and painting in New York city. Grecian and Roman Mythology; Introduction to the Study of Art; Art as a Branch of Education.

Dwight, Nathaniel. *Ms.*, 1770–1831. Brother of Timothy Dwight, *infra*. A physician and clergyman of Rhode Island and Connecticut, who published the first school geography in America, and was author also of The Great Question Answered; A Compendious History of the Signers of the Declaration of Independence. *Bar.*

Dwight, Sereno Edwards. *Ct.*, 1786–1850. The fifth son of Timothy Dwight, *infra*. A Congregational clergyman and educator. Life of David Brainerd; The Hebrew Wife, an argument in opposition to marriage with a deceased wife's sister; Select Discourses. He edited the Works of Jonathan Edwards, *infra*, in ten volumes, with Life. *See Memoir by W. T. Dwight.*

Dwight, Theodore. *Ms.*, 1764–1846. Brother of Timothy Dwight, *infra*. A once famous journalist of New York city, and a member of Congress, well known as a Federalist. History of the Hartford Convention; Character of Thomas Jefferson. *See Life and Writings, 1840.*

Dwight, Theodore. *Ct.*, 1796–1866. Son of T. Dwight, *supra*. A New York littérateur whose varied writings include Tour in Italy; New Gazetteer of the United States; History of Connecticut; Summer Tour of New England; The Northern Traveller; The Roman Republic of 1849; The Kansas War; Life of Garibaldi; The Father's Book; First Lessons in Modern Greek; School Dictionary of Roots and Derivatives.

Dwight, Theodore William. *N. Y.*, 1822-1892. Grandson of Timothy Dwight, *infra*. A jurist of note who was professor of municipal law in Columbia College. Argument in the Rose Will Case; Trial by Impeachment; Prisons and Reformatories (with E. C. Wines, *infra*).

Dwight, Thomas. *Ms.*, 1843——. A physician of Boston, successor to O. W. Holmes, *infra*, as professor of anatomy in the Harvard Medical School. Anatomy of the Head; The Intracranial Circulation. *Hou.*

Dwight, Timothy. *Ms.*, 1752–1817. A Congregational clergyman who was a very prominent figure in the early history of the republic, and as president of Yale College, 1795–1817, of great influence as an educator as well. His most important work is Theology Explained and Defended in a Course of 173 Sermons, which has gone into more than one hundred editions. Other prose works are Genuineness and Authenticity of the Old Testament; Observations on Language; Essay on Light; Travels in New England and New York, which still furnishes entertaining reading. His writings in verse include The Conquest of Canaan, a very ponderous epic; Greenfield Hill, a pastoral; The Triumph of Infidelity, a satire. *See Sparks's American Biography; Allibone's Dictionary; Tyler's Three Men of Letters, 1895.*

Dwight, Timothy. *Ct.*, 1822——. Grandson of Timothy Dwight, *supra.* A Congregational clergyman, president of Yale University from 1886, and one of the members of the New Testament Revision Company. The True Ideal of an American University.

Dwight, William Buck. *Ty.*, 1833-——. Son of H. G. O. Dwight, *supra.* A scientist who has been curator of Vassar College Museum for many years.

Dyckman, Jacob. *N. Y.*, 1788–1822. A physician of New York city who was the author of Pathology of Human Fluids.

Dyer, Mrs. Catherine Cornelia [Joy]. 18——. Wife of H. Dyer, *infra.* Henry and the Bird's Nest; Sunny Days Abroad; Brief History of the Joy Family; Records of the Dyer Family.

Dyer, Heman. *Vt.*, 1810——. An Episcopal clergyman of New York city. Voice of the Lord upon the Waters; Records of an Active Life, an autobiography.

Dyer, Sidney. *N. Y.*, 1814——. A Baptist clergyman of Philadelphia, well known as a song-writer. Voices of Nature and Thoughts in Rhyme; Psalmist for Use of Baptist Churches; Songs and Ballads; The Drunkard's Child; Ruth, a Cantata; Black Diamonds; Home and Abroad; Hoofs and Claws; Ocean Gardens and Palaces; Elmdale Lyceum; The Beautiful Ladder, or the Two Students.

E

Eads, James Buchanan. *Ind.*, 1820–1887. A civil engineer of distinction and the designer of the Mississippi jetties. System of Naval Defence; Mouth of the Mississippi, the Jetty System Explained; Discussion on Upright Bridges.

Eames, Mrs. Jane [Anthony]. *Ms.*, 1816–1894. A writer of Concord, New Hampshire. A Budget of Letters; The Budget Closed; My Mother's Jewel; The Christmas Gift; Letters from Bermuda, comprise the most of her writing.

Earle, Mrs. Alice [Morse]. *Ms.*, 1851——. A writer on American antiquarian themes. Curious Punishments of Bygone Days; Margaret Winthrop, a biography; Costume of Colonial Times; Customs and Fashions in Old New England; The Sabbath in Puritan New England; China-Collecting in America; Colonial Dames and Goodwives; Colonial Days in Old New York. *Hou. S. Scr.*

Earle, Pliny. *Ms.*, 1809–1892. A son of the inventor of the same name, and a prominent physician, who was superintendent of the State Insane Hospital at Northampton, Massachusetts, 1864–1885. Marathon and Other Poems; Institutions for the Insane in Prussia, Germany, and Austria; Visits to Thirteen Insane Asylums in Europe; The Curability of Insanity; Blood-Letting in Disorders; The Earle Family: Ralph Earle and his Descendants.

Earle, Thomas. *Ms.*, 1796–1849. Brother of P. Earle, *supra.* A lawyer and philanthropist of Philadelphia. Essay on Penal Law; Right of States to Alter and Annul their Charters; Railroads and Internal Communications (1830); Life of Benjamin Lundy.

Early, Jubal Anderson. *Va.*, 1816–1894. A distinguished general in the Confederate army who settled in New Orleans after the close of the Civil War. Memoir of the Last Year of the War for Independence in the Confederate States; Campaigns of General Lee; Jackson's Campaign against Pope.

Eastburn, James Wallis. *E.*, 1797–1819. An Episcopal clergyman remembered as co-author with R. C. Sands of the once noted poem Yamoyden.

Eastburn, Manton. *E.*, 1801-1872. The fourth Protestant Episcopal bishop of Massachusetts, and somewhat prominent as a dogmatic, aggressive Low Churchman. Lectures on Hebrew, Latin, and Greek Poetry; Lectures on the Epistles to the Philippians; Essays and Dissertations on Biblical Literature.

Eastman, Charles Gamage. *Me.*, 1816-1861. A verse-writer of Montpelier, Vermont, who published in 1848 a volume of Poems, descriptive of rural life in New England, that was popular for a time.

Eastman, Mrs. Elaine [Goodale]. *Ms.*, 1863——. A writer who, with her younger sister, Dora Goodale, *infra*, attracted much attention, when both were children, by the publication of several volumes of poems, of which the literary quality was very marked. She afterward became a teacher at various Indian schools, and in 1891 married Dr. Charles Eastman, a Sioux Indian, educated at the Boston University; she now lives in South Dakota. Journal of a Farmer's Daughter; The Coming of the Birds. *See Goodale, D. R.*

Eastman, Julia Arabella. *N. Y.*, 1837——. A Massachusetts teacher who has written a number of juvenile tales, among which are Short Comings and Long Goings; Young Rick; Kitty Kent's Trouble. *Lo.*

Eastman, Mrs. Mary [Henderson]. *Va.*, 1818——. Wife of S. Eastman, *infra*. Romance of Indian Life; Dacotah, or Life and Legends of the Sioux; American Aboriginal Portfolio; Chicora and other Regions of the Conquerors and the Conquered; Tales of Fashionable Life; Aunt Phillis's Cabin, a reply to Uncle Tom's Cabin.

Eastman, Philip. *N. H.*, 1799-1869. A jurist of Maine. General Statutes of Maine; Digest of Maine Law Reports.

Eastman, Seth. *Me.*, 1808-1875. An officer in the United States army stationed at Fort Snelling and other places on the Western frontier; afterwards a lieutenant-colonel and brevet brigadier-general. History, Condition, and Future Prospects of the Indians of the United States; Topographical Drawing.

Eaton, Amos. *N. Y.*, 1776-1842. A once prominent scientist whose writings include Index to Geology of the Northern States; Natural History of New York; Geological Survey of the Erie Canal District; Philosophical Instructor; Manual of Botany of North America.

Eaton, Arthur Wentworth Hamilton. *N. S.*, 1849——. An Episcopal clergyman and instructor of New York city. The Heart of the Creeds, a notable contribution to Broad church literature; Acadian Legends and Lyrics; Letter-Writing: its Ethics and Etiquette; The Church of England in Nova Scotia; Tales of a Garrison Town (with C. L. Betts, *supra*).

Eaton, Cyrus. *Me.*, 1784-1875. An educator of Maine who was totally blind for the last thirty years of his life. Annals of Warren, Maine; Woman, a poem; History of Thomaston, Maine.

Eaton, Daniel Cady. *Mch.*, 1834-1895. Grandson of Amos Eaton, *supra*. A professor of botany at Yale University. The Ferns of North America; Ferns of the Southwest. *Wn.*

Eaton, Daniel Cady. *N. Y.*, 1837——. Cousin of D. C. Eaton, *supra*. A professor of the history of art at Yale University, 1869-76. Handbook of Greek and Roman Sculpture. *Hou.*

Eaton, Dorman Bridgeman. *Vt.*, 1823——. A jurist of New York city, prominent in civil service reform, who has published Civil Service in Great Britain, and edited the seventh edition of Kent's Commentaries. *Har.*

Eaton, John Henry. *Tn.*, 1790-1856. A once noted politician who was secretary of war, 1829-31, and minister to Spain, 1836-40. He wrote a Life of Andrew Jackson.

Eaton, Samuel John Mills. *Pa.*, 1820——. A Presbyterian clergyman of Franklin, Pennsylvania, 1848-82. Petroleum; History of Venango County, Pennsylvania; Lake Side; Jerusalem, the Holy City; Palestine.

Eaton, Thomas Treadwell. *Tn.*, 1845——. A Baptist minister of Louisville. My Angels; Talks to Children; Marriage and Law; Talks on Getting Married.

Eberle, John. *Pa.*, 1787-1838. A noted physician of Philadelphia, and later of Cincinnati. Botanical Terminology; Diseases and Physical Education of Children; Therapeutics and Materia Medica; Notes on Theory and Practice of Medicine. *Lip.*

Eckard, James Read. *Pa.*, 1805-1887. A Presbyterian missionary to India. Faith and Justification (in the Tamil language); The Hindoo Traveller; Outline of English Law from Blackstone.

Eddy, Ansel Doane. *Ms.*, 1798-1875. A Presbyterian clergyman of New York who published the Christian Citizen; Duties, Dangers, and Securities of Youth.

Eddy, Clarence. *Ms.*, 1851——. An organist of Chicago. The Church and Concert Organist; The Organ in Church.

Eddy, Daniel Clark. *Ms.*, 1823-1896. A Baptist clergyman of Boston, and subsequently of Brooklyn, who wrote extensively, some of his books having been very popular. Among them are The Percy Family, and Walter's Tour in the East, two series of volumes for young readers; Young Man's Friend; Young Woman's Friend; The Burman Apostle, a life of Judson; Roger Williams and the Baptists; The Unitarian Apostasy; Europa, or Scenes in the Old World; Waiting at the Cross; Angel Whispers.

Eddy, Henry Turner. *Ms.*, 1844——. A mathematician, since 1874 a professor in the University of Cincinnati. Analytical Geometry; Researches in Graphical Statics; Thermodynamics; Maximum Stress under Concentrated Loads.

Eddy, Mrs. Mary Baker [Glover]. *N. H.*, 18——. A resident of Concord, New Hampshire, widely known as the founder of the sect of Christian Scientists. Besides Christian Science; Science and Health, she has published a number of pamphlets on the general subject of Christian Science. *See Carol Norton's Woman's Cause, 1895.*

Eddy, Richard. *R. I.*, 1828——. A Universalist clergyman of Melrose, Massachusetts. Universalism in America; History of the Sixtieth New York Regiment; The Martyr to Liberty.

Eddy, Thomas. *Pa.*, 1758-1827. A philanthropist whose efforts were chiefly in the direction of prison reform, and who was the author of The State Prisons of New York. *See Life by S. L. Knapp, 1834.*

Eddy, Thomas Mears. *O.*, 1823-1874. A Methodist minister of Chicago, who published Patriotism of Illinois, a history of that State during the Civil War.

Eddy, Zachary. *Vt.*, 1815-1891. A Presbyterian minister of Augusta, Georgia. Immanuel, or the Life of Christ; Hymns of the Church; Songs of the Church.

Edes, Henry Herbert. *Ms.*, 1849——. A Boston merchant of antiquarian tastes, who has published Charlestown's Historic Points; Memorial of Josiah Barker.

Edes, Robert Thaxter. *Me.*, 1838——. A physician of Washington. Nature and Time in the Cure of Diseases; Physiology and Pathology of the Sympathetic or Ganglionic Nervous System; Therapeutical Handbook of United States Pharmacopœia; Text Book of Therapeutics and Materia Medica.

Edgar, Cornelius Henry. *N. J.*, 1811-1884. A Dutch Reformed clergyman of Easton, Pennsylvania. Lectures on Slavery; Discourses on the Death of Lincoln; Curse of Canaan Rightly Interpreted; Exposition of the Nine Last Wars (1867).

Edgren, August Hjalmar. *Sn.*, 1840——. A Swedish scholar who came to the United States in 1862, and served for a time in the Federal army, and afterwards in the Swedish army. Since 1884 he has been professor of languages in the University of Nebraska. Complete Sanskrit Grammar; German and English Dictionary (with W. D. Whitney, *infra*); The Literature of America (in Swedish); Public Schools and Colleges of the United States; Swedish Literature in America; American Antiquities.

Edmonds, John Worth. *N. Y.*, 1799-1874. A prominent jurist of New York city, noted as an ardent defender of Spiritualism. Spiritualism (with G. T. Dexter); Reports of Select Law

Cases; Letters and Tracts on Spiritualism.

Edwards, Bela Bates. *Ms.*, 1802–1852. A Congregational clergyman, professor in Andover Theological Seminary, and editor of the Bibliotheca Sacra. He published an Eclectic Reader; Biography of Self-made Men; Memoirs of E. Cornelius; but his principal work was in the line of religious editorship. *See Memoir by E. A. Parks, infra.*

Edwards, Charles. *E.*, 1797–1868. A New York lawyer who was counsel to the British consulate. The Juryman's Guide; Parties to Bills and Other Pleadings; Feathers from my Own Wings; Receivers in Chancery; Reports of Chancery Cases; Receivers in Equity; Referees; History and Poetry of Finger Rings; Pleasantries about Courts and Lawyers.

Edwards, Emory. *Va.*, 1841——. A naval engineer who served in the United States navy as assistant engineer, 1864–68, and was subsequently employed in a similar capacity in the merchant marine service. A Catechism of the Marine Steam Engine; Modern American Locomotive Engines; Modern American Marine Engines, Boilers, and Screw Propellers; The Practical Steam Engineer's Guide. *Bai.*

Edwards, George Wharton. *Ct.*, 1860——. An artist and writer of short stories living at Plainfield, New Jersey. P'tit Matinic', and Other Monotones; Thumb-Nail Sketches; The Rivalries of Long and Short Codiac; Break o' Day and Other Stories. *Cent.*

Edwards, Harry Stillwell. *Ga.*, 1854——. A littérateur and journalist of Macon, Georgia. Two Runaways and Other Stories; Sons and Fathers. *Cent. Ra.*

Edwards, James Thomas. *N. J.*, 1838——. A Methodist clergyman and educator of Baltimore. The Grass Family; The Voice Tree; The Silva of Chautauqua Lake.

Edwards, John. *W.*, 1806–1887. A Welsh poet who came to America in 1828, and settled in central New York. He was long prominent amongst Welsh residents in the United States, and published two volumes of verse, The Crucifixion; The Omnipresence of God.

Edwards, John Ellis. *N. C.*, 1814——. A Methodist clergyman of Richmond, Virginia. Life of John Wesley Childs; Random Sketches and Notes of European Travel; The Confederate Soldier; Log Meeting-House.

Edwards, Jonathan. *Ct.*, 1703–1757. A Congregational clergyman who must be called the most subtle reasoner the New World has ever produced. He was the son of Timothy Edwards, a Congregational minister of East Windsor, Connecticut, and was minister at Northampton, Massachusetts, 1727–50. From 1751 to 1758 he served as missionary to the Stockbridge Indians, and the last month of his life was president of the College of New Jersey (now Princeton University). He was the greatest defender of Calvinism that has ever lived, and as a preacher had an extraordinary influence. His famous sermon, "Sinners in the Hands of an Angry God," is the best example of the pitiless, ferocious realism of his style. His chief work is the celebrated Inquiry into the Freedom of the Will, a masterpiece of acute, precise, and original thinking. His other works include Notes on the Mind and Natural Science, written when he was between 15 and 16 years of age; The Religious Affections; Distinguishing Marks of a Work of the Spirit; Nature of True Virtue; God's Last End in the Creation; Treatise on Grace; Doctrine of Original Sin Defended; Inquiry into the Qualifications for Communion; Thoughts for the Revival of Religion; History of the Redemption; Life of David Brainerd. *See Lives by S. E. Dwight, supra; S. Hopkins, infra; A. V. G. Allen, 1889, supra; Sparks's American Biography, vol. 8; Tyler's American Literature; Duyckinck's Cyclopedia; Allibone's Dictionary.*

Edwards, Jonathan, Jr. *Ms.*, 1745–1801. Son of Jonathan Edwards, *supra*. A Congregational clergyman of great ability who was president of Union College. Treatise on Liberty and Necessity; Discourses on the Atonement. *See Memoir by Tryon Edwards, infra; Sprague's Annals of the American Pulpit.*

Edwards, Justin. *Ms.*, 1787–1853. A Congregational clergyman, prominent in the temperance movement. Beside a Sabbath Manual; Temperance Manual, he published a great number of tracts. *See Memoir by W. Hallock, 1854.*

Edwards, Morgan. *W.*, 1722–1795. A Welsh Baptist clergyman who came to America in 1761, and was the foremost colonial minister of his faith. He was one of the founders of Brown University. Materials Toward a History of the Baptists in Pennsylvania; Materials Toward a History of the Baptists in New Jersey.

Edwards, Ninian Wirt. *Ky.*, 1809——. A prominent jurist of Illinois, son of Ninian Edwards, governor of that State. History of Illinois and Ninian Edwards.

Edwards, Tryon. *Ct.*, 1809–1894. A grandson of Jonathan Edwards, Jr. A Congregational clergyman who edited the Works of Joseph Bellamy, *supra*, with Memoir; the Works of his grandfather; and published, among other works, Christianity a Philosophy of Principles; Self-Cultivation; Light for the Day; Wonders of the Word; Anecdotes for the Family.

Edwards, William Emory. *Va.*, 1842——. Son of J. E. Edwards, *supra*. A Methodist clergyman of Virginia who is the author of John Newson, a Tale of College Life.

Edwards, William Henry. *N. Y.*, 1822——. A naturalist of Coalburgh, West Virginia. The Butterflies of North America; Voyage up the Amazon. *Hou.*

Egan, Maurice Francis. *Pa.*, 1852——. A journalist and littérateur, now professor at the Roman Catholic University of Notre Dame, Indiana. His prose writings include That Girl of Mine; That Lover of Mine; A Garden of Roses; Stories of Duty; The Life Around Us; The Theatre and Christian Parents; Modern Novelists; Lectures on English Literature; The Disappearance of Mr. Longworthy; A Primer of English Literature; A Gentleman; A Marriage of Reason; The Success of Patrick Desmond; The Flower of the Flock. In verse he has published Preludes; Songs and Sonnets, and Other Poems. *Mg.*

Egar, John Hodson. *E.*, 1832——. An Episcopal clergyman of Rome, New York. The Threefold Grace of the Holy Trinity; Christendom, Ecclesiastical and Political.

Eggleston, Edward. *Ind.*, 1837——. A novelist now (1897) living near Lake George, New York, who, in the early part of his career, was a Methodist minister. He has been especially successful in depicting life in southern Indiana in pioneer days, his first important work, The Hoosier Schoolmaster, attracting widespread notice. Other fictions by him include The End of the World; The Circuit Rider; Roxy; The Graysons, a story of Illinois; The Faith Doctor; The Hoosier Schoolboy; Queer Stories for Boys and Girls; Schoolmasters' Stories; Mr. Blake's Walking Stick; Duffels. Still other works are, Sunday-school Manual; Counsel for Teachers; School History of the United States; Household History of the United States; First Book in American History; Stories of Great Americans; The Beginners of a Nation, the first volume in a History of Life in the United States. With his daughter, Mrs. Seelye, *infra*, he has written Tecumseh and the Shawnee Prophet; Pocahontas; Brandt and Red Jacket; Montezuma. *See Vedder's American Writers. Am. Ap. Cent. Do. Scr.*

Eggleston, George Cary. *Ind.*, 1839——. Brother of E. Eggleston, *supra*. During the Civil War he served in the Confederate army, and afterwards filled several journalistic positions in New York city, becoming editor of the Commercial Advertiser in 1886. His writings are mainly for young people. How to Educate Yourself; A Man of Honor; A Rebel's Recollections; How to Make a Living; How to Make Money; The Big Brother, or a Story of the Indian War; Captain Sam; Signal Boys; The Wreck of the Red Bird; Strange Stories from History for Young People; Red Eagle; Juggernaut: a Veiled Record (with Dolores Marbourg). *Do. Fo. Har. Put.*

Egle, William Henry. *Pa.*, 1830——. A physician and local historian of Harrisburg, Pennsylvania. History of Pennsylvania; History of Dauphin

County; History of Lebanon County; Historical Register; Pennsylvania Genealogies, Scotch-Irish and German; Pennsylvania in the Revolution; Notes and Queries relative to Interior Pennsylvania; Pennsylvania Archives (edited with J. B. Linn, *infra*), in 12 volumes.

Egleston, Thomas. *N. Y.*, 1832——. A metallurgist of note, professor of mineralogy at Columbia College from 1864. Metallurgy of Silver; Catalogue of Minerals; Lectures on Mineralogy; Life of John Patterson, Major-General in the Army of the Revolution. *Wil.*

Eidlitz, Leopold. *Bo.*, 1823–189–. An architect of New York city. The Nature and Function of Art.

Elder, Cyrus. *Pa.*, 1833——. Nephew of W. Elder, *infra*. A revenue commissioner of Pennsylvania. Dream of a Free-Trade Paradise; Man and Labor; Short Studies; May Gift, in verse.

Elder, George A. M. *Ky.*, 1794–1838. A Roman Catholic priest who founded the College of St. Joseph, at Bardstown, Kentucky, and was its first president. He wrote Letters to Brother Jonathan.

Elder, Mrs. Susan [Blanchard]. *La.*, 1835——. A littérateur of New Orleans who has written extensively for Roman Catholic periodicals. The Loss of the Papacy; James the Second; Savonarola; Ellen Fitzgerald, a Southern tale.

Elder, William. *Pa.*, 1806–1885. A Philadelphia physician, prominent as an abolitionist. Periscopics, a volume of miscellanies; The Enchanted Beauty; Life of Dr. Kane, *infra;* The Debt and Resources of the United States (1863); Questions of the Day, Economic and Social; Conversations on the Principal Subjects of Political Economy. *Bai.*

Eliot, Charles William. *Ms.*, 1834——. Son of S. A. Eliot, *infra*. A distinguished educator who has been president of Harvard University since 1869. Manual of Qualitative Chemical Analysis; Manual of Inorganic Chemistry (with Storer).

Eliot, Jared. *Ct.*, 1685–1763. Grandson of John Eliot, 1st, *infra*. A Congregational clergyman of Killingworth, Connecticut, 1707–63, famous in his day as an agriculturist, physician, and scientist. He was awarded a medal by the London Institute in 1786 "for producing malleable iron from American Black Sand." Essays upon Field and Husbandry, and many single sermons.

Eliot, John. *E.*, 1604–1690. A Puritan minister of Roxbury who came to America in 1631, and is famous in history as the "Indian Apostle." He is chiefly remembered for his famous translation of the Bible into the Indian language, but he was the author of other works, among which are the Communion of Churches; The Harmony of the Gospels; Dying Speeches of Several Indians; The Indian Primer; Indian Logic Primer. *See Sparks's American Biography; Life by R. B. Caverly; Appleton's American Biography; Hart's American Literature.*

Eliot, John. *Ms.*, 1754–1813. A clergyman of Boston, pastor of the New North Congregational church, 1779–1813, and author of the New England Biographical Dictionary.

Eliot, Samuel Atkins. *Ms.*, 1798–1862. A citizen of Boston who was mayor 1837–39, and published Observations on the Bible for the Use of Young Persons; Sketch of the History of Harvard College.

Eliot, Samuel. *Ms.*, 1821——. A New England educator of prominence, at one time president of Trinity College. History of Liberty; Manual of United States History; Life and Times of Savonarola.

Eliot, William Greenleaf. *Ms.*, 1811–1887. A Unitarian clergyman of St. Louis, chancellor of Washington University there, 1872–87. Doctrines of Christianity; Early Religious Education; Lectures to Young Men; Lectures to Young Women; Discipline of Sorrow; Manual of Prayer; The Unity of God; The Story of Archer Alexander from Slavery to Freedom; Home Life and Influence. *A. U. A.*

Ellet, Charles. *Pa.*, 1810–1862. An engineer of note who built the first wire suspension bridge in America. He served during the Civil War as a colonel in the Federal army, and was killed in an engagement on the Mississippi. Physical Geography of the Mississippi Valley; Coast and Harbor Defences;

The Mississippi and Ohio Rivers, with Plans for Protecting the Delta from Inundation. *Lip.*

Ellet, Mrs. Elizabeth Fries [Lummis]. *N. Y.*, 1818–1877. A once popular miscellaneous writer whose historical works were the outcome of a good deal of research and are not without value, but whose productions as a whole have little of the quality of permanence. They include Domestic History of the American Revolution; Women of the American Revolution; Court Circles of the Republic; Queens of American Society; Pioneer Women of the West; Novelettes of the Musicians; Rambles in the West; The Practical Housekeeper; Family Pictures from the Bible; Evenings at Woodlawn; Poems, Original and Selected; Teresa Contarini, a tragedy; Scenes in the Life of Joanna of Sicily; The Characters of Schiller; Women Artists in All Ages. *Har.*

Ellinwood, Frank Fields. *N. Y.*, 1826——. A Presbyterian clergyman, secretary of the Presbyterian Board of Foreign Missions. The Great Conquest; Oriental Religions and Christianity. *Scr.*

Elliot, Benjamin. *S. C.*, 1786–1836. A South Carolina jurist who published Refutation of Calumnies respecting the Institution and Existence of Slavery; The Militia System of South Carolina.

Elliot, George Henry. *Ms.*, 1831——. A military engineer in the service of the United States. European Light-House Systems; The Presidio of San Francisco.

Elliot, Henry Rutherford. 1849——. A journalist of New York city. The Basset Claim, a Story of Life in Washington; The Common Chord, a Story of the Ninth Ward. *Cas.*

Elliot, Samuel Hayes. *Vt.*, 1809–1869. A Congregational clergyman of New Haven. Rolling Ridge, or the Book of Four-and-Twenty Chapters; The Parish Side; Dreams and Realities; New England's Chattels, or Life in a Northern Poor-House; The Attractions of New Haven.

Elliott, Charles. *I.*, 1792–1869. A Methodist clergyman, at one period president of Iowa Wesleyan University. Treatise on Baptism; Delineation of Roman Catholicism; Life of Bishop Roberts; History of the Great Secession from the Methodist Episcopal Church; Political Romanism; Reminiscences of the Wyandotte Mission; Southwestern Methodism; The Bible and Slavery; Sinfulness of American Slavery. *Meth.*

Elliott, Charles. *S.*, 1815–1892. A Presbyterian minister, professor of Hebrew at Lafayette College, Easton, Pennsylvania. The Sabbath; The Inspiration of the Holy Scriptures; Vindication of the Mosaic Authorship of the Pentateuch.

Elliott, Charles Wyllys. *Ct.*, 1817–1883. A New York writer, at one time a landscape gardener of note. The Book of American Interiors; Pottery and Porcelain; Remarkable Characters and Places in the Holy Land; Cottages and Cottage Life; Mysteries, or Glimpses of the Supernatural; St. Domingo, its Revolution and its Hero, Toussaint l'Ouverture; New England History, from its Discovery by the Northmen; Wind and Whirlwind, a novel. *Ap. Hou.*

Elliott, Ezekiel Brown. *Sn.*, 1823–1888. A government statistician of note. Unification of International Coinage.

Elliott, Franklin Reuben. *Ct.*, 1817–1878. A horticulturist of Cleveland. The Western Fruit Book; Popular Deciduous and Evergreen Trees; Handbook for Fruit Growers; Handbook of Practical Landscape Gardening.

Elliott, Henry Wood. *O.*, 1846——. Son of F. R. Elliott, *supra*. An artist in the employ of the Smithsonian Institution. Monograph of the Seal Islands of Alaska; Our Arctic Provinces. *Scr.*

Elliott, John. *Ct.*, 1768–1824. A Congregational minister at Madison, Connecticut, 1791–1824, co-author with S. Johnson of the first American dictionary of the English language.

Elliott, Jonathan. *E.*, 1784–1846. A publicist of Washington who published American Diplomatic Code; Debate on Adoption of the Constitution; Funding System of the United States; Statistics of the United States; The

Comparative Tariffs; Sketches of the District of Columbia. *Lip.*

Elliott, Mrs. Maud [Howe]. *Ms.*, 1855——. Daughter of S. G. Howe, *infra*. A fiction writer of Chicago. Atalanta in the South; Mammon; A Newport Aquarelle; The San Rosario Ranch; Honor; Phyllida. *Mer. Rob.*

Elliott, Sarah Barnwell. 18—— ——. Granddaughter of S. Elliott, *infra*. Jerry; John Paget, a novel of New York and Newport; The Felmeres. *Ho.*

Elliott, Stephen. *S. C.*, 1771–1830. A naturalist of South Carolina, and a professor in the State Medical College. His son Stephen, 1800–1866, was the first Episcopal bishop of Georgia, and his grandson, Robert Woodward Barnwell Elliott, 1840–1887, the first bishop of Western Texas. The Botany of South Carolina and Georgia.

Elliott, William. *S. C.*, 1788–1863. Nephew of S. Elliott, *supra*. A politician of Beaufort, South Carolina, who published the tragedy of Fiesco; Carolina Sports by Land and Water.

Ellis, Charles Mayo. *Ms.*, 1818–1878. A Boston lawyer of prominence as an abolitionist, who published a History of Roxbury.

Ellis, Edward Sylvester. *O.*, 1840——. A popular writer of school text-books and juvenile tales, who was for a number of years an instructor in Trenton, New Jersey. Among his numerous writings are included The People's Standard History of the United States; several school histories of the United States; From the Throttle to the President's Chair; Lost in Samoa; The Camp Fires of General Lee; The Hunters of the Ozark; The Last War Trail; Righting the Wrong; Up the Tapajos; Down the Mississippi; Life of Daniel Boone; Storm Mountain. *Am. Cas. Co. Mer.*

Ellis, George Edward. *Ms.*, 1814–1894. A Unitarian clergyman of Boston who was pastor of the Harvard Church in Charlestown, 1840–69, and for many years president of the Massachusetts Historical Society. He was an enthusiastic historical student with positive convictions. They were, however, held without bitterness or prejudice. A Half Century of the Unitarian Controversy; Evidences of Christianity; The Red Man and the White in North America; The Organ and Church Music; Aims and Purposes of the Founders of Massachusetts; Memoirs of Count Rumford, Jared Sparks, Jacob Bigelow, Luther Bell, and others; Lives of John Mason, Anne Hutchinson, and William Penn, in Sparks's American Biography; History of the Battle of Bunker Hill. The Puritan Age and Rule in the Colony of the Massachusetts Bay is his most important work. *Hou. Lit.*

Ellis, Sumner. *Ms.*, 1828–1886. A Universalist clergyman of Boston and Chicago. At Our Best, and Other Essays; Life of E. H. Chapin, *supra;* Hints on Preaching. *See Memorial by C. R. Moor, 1887. Meth.*

Ellsworth, Erastus Wolcott. *Ct.*, 1822——. An inventor of Connecticut who published in 1855 a volume of poems of very uneven excellence, some of which were popular for a time.

Ellsworth, Henry Leavitt. *Ct.*, 1791–1858. A commissioner of patents who was a son of the noted jurist, Oliver Ellsworth. Digest of Patents from 1770 to 1859.

Ellsworth, Henry William. *Ct.*, 1814–1864. Son of H. L. Ellsworth. A lawyer of Indiana. Sketch of the Upper Mississippi Valley; American Swine-Breeder.

Ellsworth, Mrs. Mary Wolcott [Janvrin]. *N. H.*, 1830–1870. A writer for periodicals. Peace, or the Stolen Will; An Hour with the Children; Smith's Saloon.

Ellwanger, George Herman. *N. Y.*, 1848——. Brother of H. B. Ellwanger, *infra*. A writer of Rochester, New York. The Garden's Story; The Story of My House; In Gold and Silver; Idyllists of the Country-Side. Love's Demesne, a Garland of Contemporary Love Poems. *Ap. Do.*

Ellwanger, Henry Brooks. *N. Y.*, 1851–1883. A horticulturist of Rochester, New York. The Rose, a Treatise on Cultivation, History, etc., of Roses. *Do.*

Elmendorf, John James. *N. Y.*, 1827–1896. An Episcopal clergyman, professor of philosophy in Racine College, Wisconsin, 1867–88, and later connected with the Western Theological Seminary at Chicago. Manual of Rites and Ritual; History of Philosophy; Outlines of Logic; Aspects of Modern Philosophy; Moral Philosophy.

Elmer, Lucius Quintus Cincinnatus. *N. J.*, 1793–1883. A jurist of Bridgeton, New Jersey, who published a Digest of the Laws of New Jersey, commonly styled "Nixon's Digest;" Genealogy of the Elmer Family; History of Cumberland County; History of New Jersey.

Elsberg, Louis. *P.*, 1836–1885. A physician of New York city. Laryngoscopal Medication; The Throat and its Functions.

Elson, Louis Charles. *Ms.*, 1848——. A Boston journalist, editor of the Vox Humana. History of Music; History of German Song; Curiosities of Music. *Dit.*

Elton, Romeo. *Ct.*, 1790–1870. A once prominent clergyman of the Baptist faith, at one time a professor in Brown University, who was author of a Life of Roger Williams.

Elwell, Edward Henry. *Me.*, 1825–1890. A journalist of Portland, Maine. Portland and Vicinity; The Boys of Thirty-Five, a Story of a Seaport Town.

Elwyn, Alfred Langdon. *N. H.*, 1804–1884. A noted Philadelphia philanthropist. Bonaparte, a poem; Glossary of Supposed Americanisms; Melancholy and its Musings; Hints to the City on Intemperance.

Ely, Ezra Stiles. *Ct.*, 1780–1861. A Presbyterian minister of Philadelphia. Contrast between Calvinism and Hopkinsianism; Endless Punishment; The Science of the Human Mind; Sermons on Faith; Visits of Mercy; Memoir of Zebulon Ely; The Contrast; Ely's Journal.

Ely, Richard Theodore. *N. Y.*, 1854——. A political economist of distinction, professor of political economy at Wisconsin University since 1892. French and German Socialism in Modern Times; The Past and Present of Political Economy; Taxation in American States and Cities; Problems of To-Day; Political Economy; Social Aspects of Christianity; Outlines of Economics. *See Bibliography of Wisconsin. Fl. Har. Meth.*

Embury, Mrs. Emma Catharine [Manly]. *N. Y.*, 1806–1863. A writer of verse and prose whose home was in Brooklyn. Her various works include Guido and Other Poems; The Blind Girl and Other Tales; The Waldorf Family, a Fairy Tale; Female Education; Glimpses of Home Life; Pictures of Early Life; Poems; Token of Flowers; Nature's Gems, or American Wild Flowers; Love's Token Flowers, a collection of verse.

Emerson, Alfred. *Pa.*, 1859——. An archæologist, professor at Cornell University since 1891. Dissertatio de Hercule Homerico.

Emerson, Charles Noble. *Ms.*, 1821–1869. A Massachusetts lawyer, commissioner of revenue, who published Internal Revenue Guide; Handbook of Internal Revenue for Popular Use.

Emerson, Edward Waldo. *Ms.*, 1844——. Son of R. W. Emerson, *infra.* An instructor in art anatomy, living at Concord, Massachusetts. Emerson in Concord. *Hou.*

Emerson, Mrs. Ellen [Russell]. *Ms.*, 1837——. A Boston writer upon art and Indian mythology. Indian Myths; Masks, Heads, and Faces, with Considerations Respecting the Rise and Development of Art. *Hou.*

Emerson, Frederick. *N. H.*, 1788–1857. A once prominent Boston educator who published a series of popular arithmetics, chief among which was the North American Arithmetic.

Emerson, George Barrell. *Me.*, 1797–1881. An educator of Boston of much prominence and wide influence. Lectures on Education; The School and the Schoolmaster (with A. Potter, *infra*); Manual of Agriculture (with C. L. Flint); Report on the Trees and Shrubs of Massachusetts; Reminiscences of an Old Teacher. *See Harvard Register, May, 1881. Lit.*

Emerson, Joseph. *N. H.*, 1777–1833. A New England clergyman and educator, author of Lectures on the Millennium. *See Life by R. Emerson, infra.*

Emerson, Ralph. *N. H.*, 1787–1862. Brother of J. Emerson, *supra.* A Congregational clergyman, professor in Andover Theological Seminary, 1829–53, and author of Life of Joseph Emerson, and translation of Wisgon's Augustinianism and Pelagianism.

Emerson, Ralph Waldo. *Ms.*, 1803–1882. The most distinguished of American essayists, and by some critics ranked as the foremost American poet when the substance of his poetry is considered apart from its form. He was ordained in 1829 as a Unitarian minister in Boston, but retired from the profession in 1833, and the next year settled in Concord, Massachusetts, where the remainder of his life was spent. He succeeded Margaret Fuller as editor of The Dial, and was the most prominent figure among the Transcendentalists. As a lecturer he was frequently before the public, and in his writings faced a world-wide public as a philosophical thinker. His first volume of Poems appeared in 1847, followed in 1867 by May-Day and Other Pieces. His prose writings are comprised in Nature; Essays, first and second series; Representative Men; English Traits; Conduct of Life; Society and Solitude; Letters and Social Aims; Lectures and Biographical Sketches; Miscellanies; Natural History of Intellect, and Other Papers. *See Scribner's Magazine, February, 1879; Century Magazine, April, 1883; Fraser's Magazine, May, 1867; Harper's Magazine, February, 1884; Conway's Emerson at Home and Abroad; Correspondence between Carlyle and Emerson; Benton's Emerson as a Poet; Emerson in Concord; Appletons' American Biography; Stedman's American Poets; Lives by Cabot (1887), Garnett, Ireland, Holmes, Cooke; Guernsey's Emerson as Poet and Philosopher; Nichol's American Literature; Richardson's American Literature; New England Magazine, December, 1896; Emerson-Stirling Letters; Atlantic Monthly, January, and February, 1897; Peterson's Magazine, February, 1897; The Forum, November, 1896; The Arena, March, 1896. Hou.*

Emerton, Ephraim. *Ms.*, 1851——. A professor of history at Harvard University. Introduction to the Study of Mediæval History; Synopsis of the History of Continental Europe; The Practical Method in Higher Historical Instruction; Sir William Temple und die Tripleallianz vom Jahre 1668; Mediæval Europe, 814–1300. *Gi.*

Emerton, James Henry. *Ms.*, 1847——. A naturalist of eminence. Structure and Habits of Spiders; Life on the Seashore. *Wn.*

Emmerton, James Arthur. *Ms.*, 1834——. A New England genealogist and physician. Eighteenth Century Baptisms in Salem, Massachusetts; Record of the 23d Massachusetts Regiment; Materials towards an Emmerton Genealogy.

Emmet, Thomas Addis. *I.*, 1764–1827. An Irish patriot who came to the United States in 1804 and settled in New York city, where he practiced law. He was a brother of the famous Robert Emmet. Pieces of Irish History. *See Memoir by C. G. Haynes.*

Emmet, Thomas Addis. *Va.*, 1828——. Grandson of T. A. Emmet, *supra.* A physician and surgeon of New York city, whose chief work is The Principles and Practice of Gynecology.

Emmons, Ebenezer. *Ms.*, 1799–1863. A noted geologist who in the latter part of his life was attached to the State geological survey of North Carolina. Manual of Mineralogy and Geology; American Geology.

Emmons, George Foster. *Vt.*, 1811–1884. A rear-admiral in the United States service who wrote The Navy of the United States from 1775 to 1853.

Emmons, Nathanael. *Ct.*, 1745–1840. A once noted Congregational minister at Franklin, Massachusetts, 1773–1840. His theological works in six volumes, with Memoir by J. Ide, appeared in 1842. A later edition contains a Memoir by E. H. Park, *infra. See Sprague's Annals of the American Pulpit.*

Emmons, Samuel Franklin. *Ms.*, 1841——. A geologist in government service. Descriptive Geology; Geological and Mining Industries of Leadville; Statistics and Technology of the Precious Metals (with G. F. Becker, *supra*).

Emory, John. *Md.*, 1789–1835. A Methodist bishop of prominence in his denomination. The Divinity of Christ Vindicated; Defence of Our Fathers. *See Life by R. Emory, infra. Meth.*

Emory, Robert. *Pa.*, 1814–1848. Son of J. Emory, *supra*. A Methodist minister and educator who was president of Dickinson College, Carlisle, Pennsylvania, 1842–48. Life of Bishop Emory; History of the Discipline of the Methodist Episcopal Church. *Meth.*

Emory, William Helmsley. *Md.*, 1811——. Cousin of J. Emory, *supra*. An army officer who retired from the United States service in 1876 with the rank of brigadier-general. Notes of a Military Reconnoissance in Missouri and California, 1848; Report on the United States and Mexican Boundary Commission.

Endicott, Charles Moses. *Ms.*, 1793–1863. A writer of Salem, Massachusetts, who was at one time commander of a merchantman. Life of John Endicott; The Persian Poet, a tragedy; Rights and Duties of Nations; Three Orations.

Endress, Christian. *Pa.*, 1755–1827. A Lutheran clergyman of Lancaster, Pennsylvania, who published in German The Kingdom of Heaven not Susceptible of Union with Temporal Monarchy and Aristocracy.

Engelmann, George Julius. *Mo.*, 1847——. A St. Louis physician, founder of the Polyclinic School of Medicine in that city. Labor among Primitive Peoples, or the Development of Obstetric Science.

England, John. *I.*, 1786–1842. A Roman Catholic prelate who was appointed bishop of Charleston in 1820, and came to America in that year. He was eminent as a lecturer and orator, whose influence both within and without his church was widespread and beneficent. Letters on Slavery are among his writings. *See Works, 8 vols., 1849.*

Engles, William Morrison. *Pa.*, 1797–1867. A Presbyterian minister of Philadelphia, for many years editor of The Presbyterian. Records of the Presbyterian Church; English Martyrology; Sick-Room Devotion; Bible Dictionary; Sailor's Companion; Soldier's Pocket Book.

English, George Bethune. *Ms.*, 1787–1828. A versatile adventurer who wrote The Grounds of Christianity Examined, which was answered by Edward Everett, and this brought a rejoinder from English entitled Five Smooth Stones out of the Brook. He published also Narrative of the Expedition to Dongola and Sennaar.

English, Thomas Dunn. *Pa.*, 1819——. A physician and poet of Newark, New Jersey, widely known by his famous song Ben Bolt, first published in 1843. His various writings include Walter Woolfe, a novel; Poems; 1844, or the Power of the S. F., a political satire; Ambrose Fecit, or the Peer and the Painter; American Ballads; Book of Battle Lyrics; Jacob Schuyler's Millions. *Har.*

Errett, Isaac. *N. Y.*, 1820–1888. A Campbellite clergyman of Cincinnati. Debate on Spiritualism; Brief View of Missions; Walks about Jerusalem; Talks to Bereans; Letters to Young Christians; Evenings with the Bible, comprise the most of his writing.

Esling, Mrs. Catherine Harbeson [Waterman]. *Pa.*, 1812——. A verse-writer of Philadelphia who published The Broken Bracelet and Other Poems in 1850.

Esling, Charles Henry Augustine. *Pa.*, 1845——. A lawyer of Philadelphia, author of Life of Saint Germaine Cousin, the Shepherdess of Pibrac.

Espy, James Pollard. *Pa.*, 1785–1860. A meteorologist of Philadelphia, sometimes called "the storm king," who published The Philosophy of Storms (1841).

Evans, Augusta Jones. *See Wilson, Mrs. Augusta.*

Evans, Edward Payson. *N. Y.*, 1833——. An Oriental scholar who has lived chiefly in Europe. Abriss der deutschen Literaturgeschichte; Progressive German Reader; translation of Stahr's Life and Works of Lessing.

Evans, Mrs. Elizabeth Edson [Gibson]. *R. I.*, 1833——. Wife of E. P. Evans, *supra.* The Abuse of Maternity; Laura, an American Girl; The Story of Kaspar Hauser; The Story of Louis XVII. of France.

Evans, Frederick William. *E.*, 1808–1893. An elder among the Shakers of Lebanon, New York, from 1838. He wrote and lectured much, and possessed great influence in his sect. Compendium of Origin, History, and Doctrines of Shakers; Shaker Communism; Autobiography of a Shaker; Second Appearing of Christ; Test of Divine Inspiration, are his chief works.

Evans, Hugh Davy. *Md.*, 1792–1868. A Baltimore lawyer, conspicuous for loyalty to the Union during the Civil War, who wrote on legal and High Church topics. Essay on Pleading; Maryland Common Law Practice; Essay on the Episcopate; Treatise on the Christian Doctrine of Marriage; Essays on the Validity of Anglican Ordination; Theophilus Americanus. *Hou.*

Evans, Lewis. *Circa* 1700–1756. A surveyor and geographer of Philadelphia who published Geographical, Historical, Political, and Mechanical Essays.

Evans, Mrs. Lizzie Phelps [Esterbrook]. *Ms.*, 1846——. A writer of Somerville, Massachusetts. Aunt Nabby; From Summer to Summer.

Evans, Nathaniel. *Pa.*, 1742–1767. An Episcopal clergyman stationed as a missionary in Gloucester County, New Jersey. Poems on Several Occasions, with Memoir by Wm. Smith, appeared in 1772.

Evans, Oliver. *Del.*, 1755–1819. A once famous inventor who constructed the first high-pressure steam-engine. The Young Engineer's Guide; Miller and Millwright's Guide.

Evans [ĭv'anz], **Thomas.** *Pa.*, 1798–1868. A Quaker controversialist of Philadelphia who was an active opponent of the doctrines of Thomas Hicks, *infra*, and published an Exposition of the Faith of the Religious Society of Friends.

Evans, Thomas Wiltberger. *Pa.*, 1823–1897. A famous dentist, resident in Paris from 1848, through whose aid the Empress Eugénie escaped from that city in 1870. History of the American Ambulance in Paris during the Siege, 1870–71; Sanitary Institutions during the Austro-Prussian-Italian Conflict, 1868; Lettres sur le Gouvernement des États Unis; La Commission Sanitaire des États Unis.

Eve, Paul Fitzsimmons. *Ga.*, 1806–1877. A distinguished surgeon of Nashville during the Civil War, surgeon-general of the Confederate army of Tennessee. Collection of Remarkable Cases in Surgery; One Hundred Cases of Lithotomy; The Inhumanity of Capital Punishment by Hanging.

Everest, Harvey William. *N. Y.*, 1831——. A clergyman and educator of the Christian denomination. The Divine Demonstration: a Text-Book of Christian Evidence.

Everett, Alexander Hill. *Ms.*, 1792–1847. Brother of E. Everett, *infra.* An able member of the diplomatic service of the United States who was minister to Spain, 1825–29, and to the Chinese Empire at the time of his death. Critical anq Miscellaneous Essays; Poems; Europe: a General Survey; America: a General Survey. *See Allibone's Dictionary.*

Everett, Charles Carroll. *Me.*, 1829——. A Unitarian clergyman of Cambridge, dean of the theological faculty of Harvard University from 1878, and a profound and independent philosophical thinker. The Science of Thought; Religions before Christianity; Fichte's Science of Knowledge, a Critical Exposition; Poetry, Comedy, and Duty; Ethics for Young People; The Gospel of Paul. *Gi. Hou. Sc.*

Everett, David. *Ms.*, 1770–1813. A Boston journalist who wrote the famous lines beginning, —

> "You 'd scarce expect one of my age
> To speak in public on the stage."

Common Sense in Déshabillé, or the Farmer's Monitor; Daranzel, or the Persian Poet, a tragedy.

Everett, Edward. *Ms.*, 1794–1865. A distinguished Massachusetts statesman famous for his oratory. He was ordained to the Unitarian ministry in 1813, but soon retired from the profession and entered political life, becoming a congressman in 1825. After that date he was successively governor of Massachusetts, president of Harvard College, and secretary of state. He achieved a wide popularity, and his literary style was greatly admired. His work has, however, failed to retain its hold upon attention, and his polished sentences now find a constantly lessening circle of readers. Defence of Christianity; Orations and Speeches; Mount Vernon Papers; Importance of Practical Education. *See Whipple's Character and Characteristic Men; Allibone's Dictionary; Appleton's American Biography. Lit.*

Everett, Edward Franklin. *Ms.*, 1840——. A Boston genealogist who has published genealogies of the families of Capen and Everett.

Everett, Erastus. *Ms.*, 1813——. An educator once prominent in Brooklyn. System of English Versification; Progress, a poem.

Everett, William. *Ms.*, 1839——. Son of E. Everett, *supra*. At one time an instructor in Harvard University, afterward master of the Adams Academy at Quincy, Massachusetts, member of Congress in 1893, and an active political speaker. College Essays; On the Cam: Lecture on Cambridge University; the poem Hesione, or Europe Unchained; School Sermons. His books for boys include Thine not Mine; Changing Base; Double Play. *Rob.*

Everhart, Benjamin Mablack. *Pa.*, 1818——. A Pennsylvania botanist, co-author with J. B. Ellis of The North American Pyrenomycetes.

Everhart, James Bowen. *Pa.*, 1821——. Brother of B. M. Everhart, *supra*. A Pennsylvanian politician and congressman who published Miscellanies; Poems; The Fox Chase, a Poem.

Everts, Orpheus. *Ind.*, 1826——. A physician of Cincinnati. Giles & Co., or Views and Interviews concerning Civilization; What Shall we Do with the Drunkard? *Clke.*

Everts, William Wallace. *N. Y.*, 1814——. A Baptist clergyman of Chicago, and later of Jersey City, among whose many published works are included The Pastor's Hand-Book; Bible Prayer-Book; The Voyage of Life; Manhood, its Duties and Responsibilities; Promise and Training of Childhood; Words in Earnest; The Baptist Layman's Book; The Sabbath; The Christian Apostolate; Life of John Foster. *Bap. Fu. Rev.*

Ewbank, Thomas. *E.*, 1792–1870. A scientist of New York, at one period commissioner of patents. Thoughts on Matter and Force; Hydraulics; The World a Workshop; Life in Brazil; Experiments in Marine Propulsion; Reminiscences in the Patent Office. *Har. Scr.*

Ewell, Marshall Davis. *Mch.*, 1844——. A lawyer of Chicago, and professor of law in Union College of Law in Chicago. Blackwell on Tax Titles; Treatise on the Law of Fixtures; Essentials of the Law; Manual of Medical Jurisprudence.

Ewer, Ferdinand Cartwright. *Ms.*, 1826–1883. An Episcopal clergyman of New York city of the extreme ritualistic school, whose Sermons on the Failure of Protestantism attracted much attention at the time of their delivery. His other writings include The Operation of the Holy Spirit; Grammar of Theology; Two Eventful Nights, or the Fallibility of Spiritualism Exposed; Sanctity and Other Sermons. *See American Church Review, December, 1883; Sermons of, with Memoir by C. T. Congdon, supra.*

Ewing, Finis. *Va.*, 1773–1841. A Presbyterian clergyman who with two others organized the Cumberland Presbyterian church in 1810. Lectures on Divinity is an exposition of the doctrines of the sect.

Ewing, Hugh Boyle. *O.*, 1826——. A general in the Federal army during the Civil War, and minister to the Netherlands, 1866–70. A Castle in the Air; Ladron, a Tale of Early California.

Ewing, John. *Md.*, 1732–1802. A Presbyterian clergyman of Philadelphia, provost of the University of Pennsylvania, 1777–1802, and eminent in his day as a scientific observer. He published an Account of the Transit of Venus, and his Lectures on Natural Philosophy were issued after his death.

Eyster, Mrs. Nellie [Blessing]. *Md.*, 1831——. A writer for young people, formerly living in Pennsylvania, now in

California. Sunny Hours; Chincapin Charlie; Tom Harding; Lionel Wintour's Diary; A Colonial Boy. *Lo.*

F

Fabbri, Cora Randall. *N. Y.*, 1871-1892. A verse-writer of Italian descent whose volume of Lyrics was published but a few days before her death. *Har.*

Fabens, Joseph Warren. *Ms.*, 1821-1875. A native of Salem, Massachusetts, who was an envoy extraordinary and minister plenipotentiary of the Dominican republic. The Camel Hunt, a Narrative of Personal Adventure; Story of Life on the Isthmus; Facts about Santo Domingo; The Last Cigar, and Eight Other Poems; In the Tropics (probably).

Fairbairn, Robert Brinckerhoff. *N. Y.*, 1818——. An Episcopal clergyman, warden of St. Stephen's College, Annandale, New York. The Child of Faith; Sermons Preached at St. Stephen's; Morality in its Relation to the Grace of Redemption; Unity of Faith as Influenced by Speculative Philosophy. *Wh.*

Fairbanks, George Rainsford. *N. Y.*, 1820——. A Confederate officer during the Civil War; since 1880 a resident of Fernandina, Florida. History and Antiquities of St. Augustine; History of Florida, 1512-1842.

Fairchild, Ashbel Green. *N. J.*, 1795-1864. A Presbyterian clergyman of Pennsylvania, among whose writings are The Great Supper, long a popular defence of Calvinism; Baptism; Faith and Works; Confession of Faith.

Fairchild, Herman Le Roy. *Pa.*, 1850——. A lecturer on natural science who has written a History of the New York Academy of Sciences.

Fairchild, James Harris. *Ms.*, 1817——. A Congregational clergyman, president of Oberlin College, 1866-89. Moral Philosophy; Needed Phases of Christianity; Oberlin, the Colony and the College; Elements of Theology; Woman's Right to the Ballot.

Fairfield, Francis Gerry. *Ct.*, 1844-1887. A New York city journalist who was in early life a Lutheran minister. The Clubs of New York; Ten Years with Spiritual Mediums. *Ap.*

Fairfield, Genevieve Genevra. *N. Y.*, 1832——. Daughter of S. L. Fairfield, *infra*. Genevra, or the History of a Portrait; The Vice-President's Daughter; The Wife of Two Husbands; The Innkeeper's Daughter; Irene.

Fairfield, Mrs. Jane Frazee. *N. J.*, 18——. Wife of S. L. Fairfield, *infra*, of whom she wrote a Life in 1846. She afterwards published an Autobiography.

Fairfield, Sumner Lincoln. *Ms.*, 1803-1844. An educator of Philadelphia and elsewhere, and an ambitious versifier, whose work received very little attention from the public. Abaddon, the Spirit of Destruction; Lays of Melpomene; The Sisters of St. Clara; Cities of the Plain; The Heir of the World; The Last Night of Pompeii; Poems and Prose Writings; Select Poems (1860). *See Griswold's Poets and Poetry of America.*

Fales, Edward Lippitt. 18——. Underneath the Mistletoe, and Other Poems; Songs and Song Legends of Dahkotah Land.

Fall, Charles Gershom. *Ms.*, 1845——. A lawyer of Boston. Dreams, a volume of verse; A Village Sketch and Other Poems; Employers' Liability for Personal Injuries to their Employés.

Fallows, Samuel. *E.*, 1835——. A bishop of the Reformed Episcopal faith. In early life he was a Methodist minister, and during the Civil War a brigadier-general in the Federal army. He left Methodism for the Reformed Episcopal church in 1875, and was advanced to the episcopate the next year. The Bible Story for Young People; Complete Hand-Book of Synonyms and Antonyms; Hand-Book of Abbreviations and Contractions; Hand-Book of Briticisms, Americanisms, etc.; The Home Beyond, or Views of Heaven; Past Noon; Complete Dictionary of Synonyms and Antonyms. He has edited a Supplemental Dictionary of the English Language. *Meth. Rev.*

Fanning, David. *N. C.*, *c.* 1756-1825. A once famous freebooter who acted with the royalists during the American Revolution, and was one of those persons exempted by name from benefits of the general pardon. He was the author of a Narrative of Adventures in North Carolina, edited by J. H. Wheeler, and printed privately in 1861.

Fanning, John Thomas. *Ct.*, 1837-——. A distinguished civil engineer of Minneapolis, whose Treatise on Water Supply Engineering has had wide circulation.

Farley, Harriet. *N. H.*, *c.* 1815——. A factory operative of Lowell who, in 1841 and subsequently, edited The Lowell Offering, a periodical to which she and her companions in the mills were the contributors. It attracted much attention, from its literary character. A selection from its pages, Mind among the Spindles, was published in London in 1849. Shells from the Strand of Genius is partly original and partly selected. Fancy's Frolics, a juvenile work, appeared many years later.

Farlow, William Gilson. *Ms.*, 1844-——. A professor of botany in Harvard University since 1874, and the foremost American authority on cryptogamic botany. Marine Algæ of New England; The Black Knot; The Gymnosporangia of the United States; Index of Fungi; The Potato Rot; Diseases of Orange and Olive Trees.

Farman, Ella. *See Pratt, Mrs.*

Farmer, Henry Tudor. *E.*, 1782-1828. A writer of English birth who came to America in early life and settled in Charleston. He published Imagination (1819); The Maniac's Dream, and Other Poems.

Farmer, John. *Ms.*, 1789-1838. A genealogist of New England, whose Genealogical Register of the First Settlers of New England is a much valued work. His other writings include History of Billerica; History of Amherst; Gazetteer of New Hampshire; and an edition, with notes, of Belknap's History of New Hampshire. *See Savage's edition of the Register, 1862; Memorial by Le Bosquet.*

Farmer, John. *N. Y.*, 1798-1859. A noted cartographer of Detroit who published A Gazetteer of Michigan.

Farmer, Mrs. Lydia [Hoyt]. *O.*, 1842——. A miscellaneous writer of Cleveland. Aunt Belindy's Points of View; Boys' Book of Famous Rulers; A Story Book of Science; Girls' Book of Famous Queens; The Prince of the Flaming Star, an Operetta; Life of Lafayette; A Short History of the French Revolution; A Knight of Faith; A Moral Inheritance; The Doom of the Holy City. *Cr. Lo. Mer. Ran.*

Farmer, Silas. *Mch.*, 1839——. Son of J. Farmer, *supra.* A publisher and antiquarian of Detroit. History of Detroit and Michigan.

Farnam, Henry Wolcott. *Ct.*, 1853-——. A professor of political economy at Yale University. Die Innere Französische Gewerpolitik von Colbert bis Turgot.

Farnham, Mrs. Eliza Woodson [Burhans]. *N. Y.*, 1815-1864. Wife of T. J. Farnham, *infra.* A philanthropist who from 1844 to 1848 was matron at the prison of Sing Sing, and later a resident of California. Woman and her Era is her most important work. Others are Life in Prairie Land; My Early Days; The Ideal Attained; California Indoors and Out.

Farnham, John Marshall Willoughby. *Me.*, 1829——. A Presbyterian missionary to China; Homeward; Farnham Genealogy; The Missionary Complaint and Appeal.

Farnham, Thomas Jefferson. *Vt.*, 1804-1848. A lawyer who in 1839 headed an expedition to Oregon. Travels in Oregon Territory (1842); Travels in California; Memorial of the Northwest Boundary Line; Mexico, its Geography, People, and Institutions (1846).

Farquharson, Martha. *See Finley, Martha.*

Farrar, Charles A. J. 18—-1893. A New England writer who published Moosehead Lake and the North Maine Wilderness; Camp Life in the Wilderness; The Lake and Forest Series; Wild-Woods Life; From Lake to Lake. *Le.*

Farrar, Mrs. Eliza Ware [Rotch]. *Bm.*, 1791-1870. A writer of Cambridge who was the wife of a professor of mathematics in Harvard University. She was educated in England, where her first book, Congo in Search of his Master, was written. Her other works include The Children's Robinson Crusoe; The Young Lady's Friend; Life of Howard; The Story of Lafayette; Youth's Love-Letters; Recollections of Seventy Years.

Farrar, Timothy. *N. H.*, 1788–1874. A New Hampshire jurist. Report of Dartmouth College Case; Reviews of the Dred Scott Decision; Manual of the United States Constitution.

Farrington, Margaret Vere. *See Livingston, Mrs. Margaret.*

Farrow, Edward Samuel. *Md.*, 1855——. An army officer and engineer. West Point and the Military Academy; A Military System of Gymnastic Exercises; Mountain Scouting; Pack Mules and Packing; Farrow's Military Encyclopædia.

Fasquelle, Jean Louis. *F.*, 1808–1862. A French educator who came to America in 1834, and was professor of modern languages at Michigan University, 1846–62. Lessons in French; French Course; Télémaque, with Notes and Grammatical References; General and Idiomatic Dictionary of the French and English Languages. *Cas.*

Faunce, David Worcester. *Ms.*, 1829——. A Baptist minister of New England. Words and Works of Jesus; Words and Acts of the Apostles; The Christian in the World; A Young Man's Difficulties with his Bible; The Resurrection in Nature and Revelation. *Ran.*

Fawcett, Edgar. *N. Y.*, 1847——. A New York author who has written much fiction, more or less ephemeral in its nature, but whose work as a poet takes far higher rank, some of it in the realm of pure fancy standing quite alone in excellence. His novels include An Ambitious Woman; Fabian Dimitry; A Gentleman of Leisure; A Hopeless Case; Olivia Delaplaine; Asses' Ears; A New York Family; The Confessions of Claude; Purple and Fine Linen; A Mild Barbarian; The House at High Bridge; Social Silhouettes; The Adventures of a Widow; Tinkling Cymbals; Rutherford; Douglas Duane; Ellen Story; A Demoralizing Marriage; A Man's Will; Miriam Balestier. In verse he has published Short Poems for Short People; The Buntling Ball, a satire; Poems of Fantasy and Passion; Romance and Revery; Song and Story; Songs of Doubt and Dream; The New King Arthur. He has also written Agnosticism, and Other Essays. *Ap. Cas. Fu. Hou. Lip. Ra.*

Fay, Amy. *La.*, 1844——. A Chicago musician. Music Study in Germany. *Mg.*

Fay, Theodore Sedgwick. *N. Y.*, 1807——. A writer who belongs to the generation of literary New Yorkers which included Halleck, Willis, and Bryant. He was secretary of legation at Berlin, 1837–53; minister to Switzerland, 1853–61. He has since lived in Berlin. The novel Norman Leslie is his best known work. Others are, Dreams and Reveries of a Quiet Man; The Minute Book, a record of travel; Countess Ida; Hoboken, a romance of New York; Sidney Clifton; Robert Rueful; Ulric, a volume of verse; Views of Christianity; Great Outlines of Geography; History of Switzerland; History of the Three Germanys. *Bar.*

Fearing, Lilian Blanche. *Ia.*, 1863——. A lawyer of Chicago. The Sleeping World and Other Poems; In the City by the Lake (verse); Roberta. *Ke.*

Fellows, John. *Ms.*, 1760–1844. The Veil Removed; Mysteries of Free Masonry.

Felt, Joseph Barlow. *Ms.*, 1780–1869. A Congregational minister of Massachusetts who, after retiring from the ministry, devoted himself to antiquarian research at Salem. Annals of Salem; History of Ipswich, Essex, and Hamilton; Historical Account of Massachusetts Currency; Memoirs of Hugh Peters; The Customs of New England; Ecclesiastical History of New England, include the most of his writings.

Felton, Cornelius Conway. *Ms.*, 1807–1862. A Greek scholar of eminence who was president of Harvard College, 1860–62. Besides his many translations from the Greek, among which The Clouds and The Birds of Aristophanes are the most noteworthy, he published Selections from Modern Greek Writers, with Notes; Familiar Letters from Europe; Greece, Ancient and Modern. *Hou.*

Fenner, Cornelius George. *R. I.*, 1822–1847. A Unitarian clergyman at one time in charge of a church at Cincinnati. Poems of Many Moods.

Fern, Fanny. *See Parton, Mrs.*

Fernald, Charles Henry. *Me.*, 1838–——. A naturalist who has been professor of zoölogy at Massachusetts Agricultural College since 1886. Tortricidæ of North America; Butterflies of Maine; Grasses of Maine; Sphingidæ of New England.

Fernald, Chester Bailey. 1868–——. A littérateur of San Francisco. The Cat and the Cherub, and Other Stories. *Cent.*

Fernald, James Champlin. *Me.*, 1838——. The Economics of Prohibition; The New Womanhood.

Ferrel, William. *Pa.*, 1817–1891. A distinguished meteorologist employed at various times in the Coast Survey and the Signal Service. Recent Advances in Meteorology; Popular Treatise on the Winds; Motions of Fluids and Solids on the Earth's Surface. *Wil.*

Ferris, George Titus. 18——. Great German Composers; Great Italian and French Composers; Great Singers; Great Violinists and Pianists; Great Leaders. *Ap.*

Fessenden, Thomas Green. *N. H.*, 1771–1837. An agricultural writer of Boston who edited the New England Farmer and similar journals, but in earlier life won considerable attention as a satirical poet under the name of Christopher Caustic. Country Lovers and The Terrible Tractoration are the poems by which he is remembered. He published Original Poems; The Ladies' Monitor; American Clerk's Companion; Democracy Unveiled; Pills, Poetical, Political, and Philosophical; Laws of Patents for New Inventions. *See Hawthorne's Fanshawe, and Other Pieces.*

Festetitts, Mrs. Kate [Neely]. *Va.*, 1837——. A writer of children's books whose home has been in Washington since 1885. Ellie Randolph; A Year at Dangerfield.

Feuchtwanger, Lewis. *G.*, 1805–1876. A once noted chemist of New York city who came to America from Germany in 1829. Popular Treatise on Gems; Elements of Mineralogy; Treatise on Fermented Liquors; Practical Treatise on Soluble or Water Glass.

Fewkes, Jesse Walter. *Ms.*, 1850–——. An ethnologist of Boston who has written valuable professional monographs and edited the Journal of American Ethnology and Archæology. *Hou.*

Ficklin, Joseph. *Ky.*, 1833 ——. A professor of mathematics in the University of Missouri who has published The Complete Algebra; Elements of Algebra, and a series of arithmetical text-books.

Field, Mrs. Caroline Leslie [Whitney]. *Ms.*, 18——. Daughter of Mrs. A. D. T. Whitney, *infra*. A writer of Guilford, Connecticut. High Lights, a novel; The Unseen King, and Other Verses. *Hou.*

Field, David Dudley. *Ct.*, 1781–1867. A Congregational clergyman of Stockbridge, Massachusetts. History of Pittsfield; Genealogy of the Brainerd Family; Histories of the Counties of Berkshire and Middlesex.

Field, David Dudley. *Ms.*, 1805–1894. Son of D. D. Field, *supra*. A distinguished jurist of New York city. His Speeches, Arguments, and Miscellaneous Papers have been edited by A. P. Sprague in three volumes. Speeches and Arguments before United States Supreme Court; The Electoral Votes of New York; Miscellaneous Papers. *Ap.*

Field, Eugene. *Mo.*, 1850–1895. A journalist and author of Chicago whose writing has received much undiscriminating and damaging praise. The greater part of his work is purely ephemeral, but his poems for and about children possess both originality and beauty. The Denver Tribune Primer; Culture's Garland; A Little Book of Profitable Tales; A Little Book of Western Verse; Second Book of Verse; Love Songs of Childhood; With Trumpet and Drum (verse); Echoes from the Sabine Farm (with R. M. Field); Songs and Other Verse; A Second Book of Verse; The Holy Cross, and Other Tales. *Hou. Scr.*

Field, George Washington. 18——1889. Iowa County and Township Officers; Law of Damages; Private Corporations for Pecuniary Gain; Law of Private Corporations; Constitution and Jurisdiction of United States Supreme Courts; Field's Lawyers' Briefs; Field's Medico-Legal Guide for Doctors and Lawyers; Legal Relations of Infants in the State of New York.

Field, Henry Martyn. *Ms.*, 1822——. Son of D. D. Field, 1st, *supra.* A Congregational clergyman, and editor of the New York Evangelist, whose writings are chiefly concerned with his extensive travels. From the Lakes of Killarney to the Golden Horn; From Egypt to Japan; Story of the Atlantic Telegraph; Among the Holy Hills; Our Western Archipelago; The Barbary Coast; On the Desert; Old Spain and New Spain; Gibraltar; Bright Skies and Dark Shadows; Summer Pictures, from Copenhagen to Venice; Blood is Thicker than Water; The Irish Confederates, or the Rebellion of 1798. *Har. Scr.*

Field, Henry Martyn. *Ms.*, 1837——. A physician, professor in Dartmouth Medical School. Evacuant Medication is his only publication.

Field, Mrs. James A. *See Field, Mrs. Caroline Leslie.*

Field, Joseph M.* *E.*, 1810–1856. An actor and dramatist of St. Louis. The Drama in Pokerville, and Other Stories.

Field, Kate. *See Field, Mary.*

Field, Mary Katherine Kemble. *Mo.*, 1838–1896. Daughter of J. M. Field, *supra.* A journalist of Washington. Planchette's Diary; Ten Days in Spain; Pen Photographs of Dickens's Readings; Hap-Hazard, Travel Sketches; History of Bell's Telephone; Adelaide Ristori, a Biography; Life of Fechter. *See The Arena, November, 1896. Hou.*

Field, Maunsell Bradhurst. *N. Y.*, 1822–1875. A lawyer of New York city. Adrian (with G. P. R. James); Poems; Memories of Many Men and Some Women, a volume of entertaining gossip.

Field, Thomas Warren. *N. Y.*, 1810–1881. An educator of Brooklyn who was superintendent of public schools there, 1873–81. Pear Culture; Historic and Antiquarian Scenes in Brooklyn; Essay Toward an Indian Bibliography. *Scr.*

* A distinguishing initial only.

Fields, Mrs. Annie [Adams]. *Ms.*, 1834——. Wife of J. T. Fields, *infra.* A Boston littérateur. Under the Olive, a volume of verse; The Singing Shepherd, and Other Poems; A Shelf of Old Books; Whittier, Notes of his Life and Friendships; Memoir of J. T. Fields; How to Help the Poor; Authors and Friends. *Har. Hou. Scr.*

Fields, James Thomas. *N. H.*, 1816–1881. A well-known publisher of Boston who edited the Atlantic Monthly, 1862–70. Yesterdays with Authors; Underbrush, a collection of essays; Ballads, and Other Verses. *See Memoir by Mrs. Fields. Hou.*

Fillmore, John Comfort. *Ct.*, 1843——. A musician of Milwaukee. History of Piano-Forte Music; New Lessons in Harmony; Lessons in Musical History.

Filson, John. *Pa.*, 1747–1788. An early explorer of the Western country. The Discovery, Settlement, and Present State of Kentucky; Map of Kentucky; Topographical Description of the Western Territory. *See Life by R. T. Durret, 1884.*

Finch, Francis Miles. *N. Y.*, 1827——. A New York jurist, dean of the law school of Cornell University since 1892. He has published a number of poems, among which Nathan Hale and The Blue and the Gray are well known.

Finck, Henry Theophilus. *Mo.*, 1854——. A musical journalist of New York city. Wagner and Other Musicians; Romantic Love and Personal Beauty; Chopin, and Other Musical Essays; Lotos-Time in Japan; The Pacific Coast Scenic Tour; Spain and Morocco. *Scr.*

Findley, Samuel. *Pa.*, 1818——. An Associate Reformed clergyman and educator. Rambles Among the Insects.

Findley, William. *I., c.* 1750–1821. A once noted Pennsylvania politician. Review of the Funding System; History of the Insurrection of the Four Western Counties of Pennsylvania.

Finley, James Bradley. *N. C.*, 1781–1856. A Methodist clergyman of Ohio, at one time chaplain in the state penitentiary. History of the Wyandot Mission; Memorials of Prison Life; Sketches of Western Methodism; Life Among the Indians. *See Autobiography. Bibliography of Ohio. Meth.*

Finley, John. *Va.*, 1796–1866. A journalist of Richmond, Indiana, mayor of that town for a number of years. The Hoosier's Nest and Other Poems were once widely circulated.

Finley, John Park. *Mch.*, 1854——. A lieutenant in the signal service. Tornadoes; Manual of Instruction in Optical Telegraphy; Sailors' Handbook of Storm Track, Fog and Ice Charts of the North Atlantic and Gulf of Mexico.

Finley, Martha. "Martha Farquharson." *O.*, 1828——. A voluminous writer of religious and moral tales for girls, including more than twenty Elsie Books; The Mildred Books; Casella; Wanted — a Pedigree; and others. *Do. Lip.*

Finney, Charles Grandison. *Ct.*, 1792–1875. A Congregational clergyman famous during his earlier career as a revivalist. He was president of Oberlin College, 1852–66. Lectures on Revivals; Systematic Theology; Lectures to Professing Christians; Character of Free Masonry; Sermons on Gospel Themes. *See Autobiography; Life by G. F. Wright, 1890. Bar.*

Finotti, Joseph Maria. *Iy.*, 1817–1879. A Roman Catholic clergyman who was in charge of a Colorado parish at the time of his death. French Grammar; A Month of Mary; Life of Blessed Paul of the Cross; Italy in the Fifteenth Century; Diary of a Soldier; The French Zouave; Herman the Pianist; The Spirit of St. Francis de Sales. Bibliographia Catholica Americana, his most important work, was never completed.

Fish, Henry Clay. *Vt.*, 1820–1877. A Baptist clergyman of Newark, New Jersey. Primitive Piety Revived; The Price of Soul Liberty; Harry's Conversion; Harry's Conflicts; Handbook of Revivals; Bible Lands Illustrated, and several compilations. *Bar. Do.*

Fisher, Ebenezer. *Me.*, 1815–1879. A Universalist clergyman who was the first president of the theological seminary at Canton, New York. The Christian Salvation. *See Life, 1880.*

Fisher, Frances. "Christian Reid." *See Tiernan, Mrs. F.*

Fisher, George Judson. *N.Y.*, 1825——. A physician for many years medical director at Sing Sing prison. Biographical Sketches of Distinguished Physicians of Westchester County, New York. Animal Substances Employed as Medicines by the Ancients; Diploteratology.

Fisher, George Park. *Ms.*, 1827——. A Congregational clergyman, professor of ecclesiastical history at Yale University since 1861. The Supernatural Origin of Christianity; The Reformation; The Beginnings of Christianity; Faith and Rationalism; Discussions in History and Theology; Life of Benjamin Silliman, *infra;* The Grounds of Theistic and Rationalistic Belief; History of the Christian Church; The Christian Religion; Manual of Natural Theology; Manual of Christian Evidences; Outlines of Universal History; Nature and Method of Revelation; The Colonial Era. *Fl. Scr.*

Fisher, Joshua Francis. *Pa.*, 1807–1873. A municipal reformer of Philadelphia. The Degradation of our Representative System and its Reform; Reform of Municipal Elections; Nomination of Candidates.

Fisher, Michael Montgomery. *Ind.*, 1834——. A Presbyterian clergyman and educator, professor of Latin at the University of Missouri since 1871. The Three Pronunciations of Latin; Education.

Fisher, Samuel Reed. *Pa.*, 1810–1881. A German Reformed clergyman of Chambersburg, Pennsylvania. Exercises in the Heidelberg Catechism; The Rum Plague, a translation from Zschokke; The Family Assistant; Heidelberg Catechism Simplified.

Fisher, Samuel Ware. *Pa.*, 1814–1874. A Presbyterian clergyman and educator, who was president of Hamilton College, 1858–67. Three Great Temptations of Young Men; Occasional Sermons and Addresses.

Fisher, Sydney George. *Pa.*, 1856——. A lawyer of Philadelphia. The

Evolution of the Constitution of the United States; The Making of Pennsylvania; Pennsylvania: Colony and Commonwealth. *Co. Lip.*

Fisher, Theodore Welles. *Ms.*, 1837——. A physician, since 1881 clinical instructor in mental disease at Harvard University. Plain Talks About Insanity.

Fisher, Thomas. *Pa.*, 1801-1856. A Philadelphia writer who published Dial of the Seasons; Song of the Sea Shells; Mathematics Simplified and Made Attractive.

Fisk, Samuel. *Ms.*, 1828-1864. A Congregational clergyman who served as a soldier in the Federal army, and was killed at the Battle of the Wilderness. Mr. Dunn Browne's Experiences in the Army.

Fisk, Wilbur. *Vt.*, 1792-1839. A Methodist clergyman once famous as a pulpit orator, and the first president of Wesleyan University, 1831-39. Calvinistic Controversy; Travels in Europe; Sermons on Universalism. *See Lives by G. Prentice, 1889, J. Holdich, 1890. Meth.*

Fiske, John. *Ct.*, 1842——. A philosopher and historian of Cambridge, who has lectured extensively upon American history, and is a thinker of the school of Darwin and Spencer. Myths and Myth-Makers; Outlines of Cosmic Philosophy; The Unseen World; Darwinism and Other Essays; Tobacco and Alcohol; Excursions of an Evolutionist; The Destiny of Man; The Idea of God as Affected by Modern Knowledge; American Political Ideas from the Standpoint of Universal History; The Critical Period of American History, 1783-89; The Beginnings of New England; Civil Government in the United States; The War of Independence, a work for young readers; The American Revolution; The Discovery of America; United States History for Schools; Life of Edward L. Youmans, *infra;* Virginia and Her Neighbours. *Ap. Har. Hou.*

Fiske, Nathan. *Ms.*, 1733-1799. A Congregational clergyman of Brookfield, Massachusetts, who was a prolific author of essays and addresses. Beside separate sermons, his published works include Sermons (1794); The Moral Monitor, a collection of essays once very popular as a school reader.

Fiske, Nathan Welby. *Ms.*, 1798-1847. Son of N. Fiske, *supra.* A Congregational clergyman, professor at Amherst College, 1824-47. He was the father of Mrs. Helen Jackson, "H. H.," *infra.* Manual of Classical Literature; Sermons; Young Peter's Tour Around the World; Story of Aleck, or the History of Pitcairn's Island. *See Biography by H. Humphrey, 1850.*

Fitch, Elijah. 1745-1788. A Congregational minister of Hopkinton, Massachusetts. The Beauties of Religion, a Poem Addressed to Youth; The Choice, a Poem. *See Duyckinck's American Literature.*

Fitch, William Clyde. 1865——. A dramatist of New York city, the author of Beau Brummell and other plays; The Knighting of the Twins, and Ten Other Tales; Some Correspondence and Six Conversations. *Rob. St.*

Fitzgerald, Oscar Penn. *N. C.*, 1820——. A bishop of the Methodist Church South, living at Atlanta. California Sketches; Christian Growth; Centenary Cameos; Bible Nights; The Class Meeting; Life of Judge Longstreet, *infra.*

Fitzhugh, George. *Va.*, 1807-1881. A lawyer of Port Royal, Virginia, noted as an advocate of slavery as the proper condition for the mass of mankind. Sociology for the South; Cannibals All, or Slaves without Masters.

Flagg, Edmund. *Me.*, 1815——. A lawyer and journalist of St. Louis and elsewhere, living in West Salem, Virginia, in recent years. Venice, the City of the Sea, a history, is his most important work. Other writings of his include North Italy since 1849; Commercial Relations of the United States; Blanche of Artois; Edmond Dantes, a sequel to Monte Christo.

Flagg, Isaac. *Ms.*, 1843——. Son of W. Flagg, *infra.* A professor of Greek at Cornell University, 1871-88, and professor at the University of California since 1891. The Hellenic Orations of Demosthenes; Versicles; The Seven Against Thebes, of Æschylus; Iphigenia among the Taurians, of Euripides. *Gi.*

Flagg, John Foster Brewster. *Ms.*, 1804–1872. A Philadelphia physician. Ether and Chloroform and their Employment in Surgery, Dentistry, Midwifery, etc.

Flagg, Wilson. *Ms.*, 1805–1884. A naturalist of Cambridge. Studies in the Field and Forest; Woods and By-Ways of New England; Halcyon Days; A Year among the Trees; A Year among the Birds.

Flanders, Henry. *N. H.*, 1826——. A lawyer of Philadelphia. Maritime Law; The Law of Shipping; Lives of the United States Chief Justices (1858); Memoirs of Cumberland; Exposition of the United States Constitution; The Law of Fire Insurance; Adventures of a Virginian.

Flash, Henry Lynden. *O.*, 1835——. An officer in the Confederate army during the Civil War. Since 1887 he has lived in Los Angeles. He published a volume of Poems (1860).

Fleeta. *See Hamilton, Kate.*

Fleming, Mrs. May Agnes [Early]. *N. B.*, 1840–1880. A prolific author of sensational romances, some of which were issued under the pseudonyn "Cousin May Carleton." Among them are Guy Earlscourt's Wife; Lost for a Woman; Pride and Passion.

Fleming, George. *See Fletcher, Julia.*

Fletcher, James Cooley. *Ind.*, 1823——. A Presbyterian clergyman, missionary to Brazil, 1851–54, author with D. P. Kidder of the once very popular work Brazil and the Brazilians, which first appeared in 1857, and reached an eighth edition in 1868. *See Hart's American Literature.*

Fletcher, Julia Constance. "George Fleming." *B.*, *c.* 1850——. Daughter of J. C. Fletcher, *supra*. A novelist whose home is in Rome. Kismet; The Head of Medusa; Mirage; Vestigia; Andromeda; The Truth About Clement Ker; For Plain Women Only. *Rob.*

Fletcher, Robert. *E.*, 1823——. An eminent anthropologist of Washington. Paul Broca and the French School of Anthropology; Prehistoric Trephining and Cranial Amulets; Human Proportion in Art and Anthropometry; Some Recent Experiments in Serpent Venom; The New School of Criminal Anthropology; Tattooing among Civilized People.

Fletcher, William Baldwin. *Ind.*, 1837——. A physician, since 1883 superintendent of the Indiana Hospital for the Insane. Cholera, its Characteristics, History, etc. *Clke.*

Flickinger, Daniel Krumler. *O.*, 1824——. A clergyman belonging to the sect of United Brethren, and since 1885 a foreign missionary bishop of that faith. Off-hand Sketches of Men and Things in Western Africa; Ethiopia; The Churches, Marching Orders.

Flint, Abel. *Ct.*, 1765–1825. A Congregational clergyman of Hartford who published a Geometry and Trigonometry with a Treatise on Surveying.

Flint, Austin. *Ms.*, 1812–1886. A distinguished physician of New York city who held professorships in several New York medical colleges. Practice of Medicine; Continued Fever; Chronic Pleurisy; Dysentery; Physical Explanation and Diagnosis of Diseases of the Respiratory Organs; Diseases of the Heart; Essays on Conservative Medicine; Phthisis; Clinical Medicine; Manual of Auscultation and Percussion; Medical Ethics and Etiquette; Medicine of the Future. *Ap.*

Flint, Austin, Jr. *Ms.*, 1836——. Son of Austin Flint, *supra*, and like his father an eminent physician of New York city, connected with several hospitals and medical colleges. Text-Book of Human Physiology; Manual of Chemical Examinations of Urine in Disease; Physiological Effects of Severe and Protracted Muscular Exercise; The Source of Muscular Power; Physiology of Man. *Ap.*

Flint, Charles Louis. *Ms.*, 1824——. The secretary of the Massachusetts Board of Agriculture, 1853–81, and one of the founders of the Massachusetts Agricultural College. The Agriculture of Massachusetts; Grass and Forage Plants; Milch Cows and Dairy Farming; Manual of Agriculture (with G. B. Emerson, *supra*). *Le.*

Flint, Henry Martyn. *Pa.*, 1829–1868. A journalist of Chicago. Life of Stephen A. Douglas; History and

Statistics of United States Railroads; Mexico under Maximilian.

Flint, Joshua Barker. *Ms.*, 1801–1864. A surgeon of Boston and subsequently of Louisville, where he was professor of surgery in the Kentucky school of medicine from 1849 till his death. He published The Practice of Medicine.

Flint, Micah P. *Ms.*, 1807–1830. Son of T. Flint, *infra.* The Hunter and Other Poems (1826). *See Coggeshall's Poets of the West.*

Flint, Timothy. *Ms.*, 1780–1840. A Congregational clergyman of New England who after some years of missionary labour in the Ohio Valley devoted himself to literary pursuits in Cincinnati, New York, and elsewhere. His most important work in some respects, the Geography and History of the Mississippi Valley, materially advanced the settlement of that region. His other works include Recollections of Ten Years in the Valley of the Mississippi; Indian Wars in the West; Memoir of Daniel Boone; Lectures on Natural History, etc. *Fiction:* Francis Berrian; Arthur Clenning; George Mason; The Shoshonee Valley. *See Bibliography of Ohio.*

Flower, Benjamin Orange. *Il.*, 1859——. Formerly the editor and publisher of The Arena at Boston. Civilization's Inferno, or Studies in the Social Cellar; Lessons Learned from Other Lives; The New Time; Persons, Places, and Ideas; The Century of Sir Thomas More; Gerald Massey, Poet, Prophet, and Mystic. *Ar.*

Flower, Frank Abial. *N. Y.*, 1854——. A Wisconsin statistician, curator of the state historical society. Old Abe, the Wisconsin War Eagle; Life of Matthew H. Carpenter; History of the Republican Party.

Floy, James. *N. Y.*, 1806–1863. A Methodist clergyman of New York city, prominent as a botanist and as an anti-slavery leader. Guide to the Orchard and Fruit Garden; Occasional Sermons, etc.; Literary Remains (1870).

Folger, Peter. *E.*, 1617–1690. Grandfather of Benjamin Franklin. An emigrant from Norwich, England, in 1635. He settled successively at Watertown, Martha's Vineyard, and in 1663 at Nantucket. He is remembered as the author of A Looking-Glass for the Times, a spirited doggerel ballad without literary merit, but a very manly appeal for religious toleration. *See Tyler's American Literature.*

Follen, Charles Theodore Christian. *G.*, 1796–1840. A German scholar who came to America in 1824. He was German instructor at Harvard University, 1830–34, but lost his position on account of his anti-slavery opinions, and in 1836 was ordained as a Unitarian clergyman. He published a German Reader; Practical German Grammar. *See Works in five volumes, with Memoir, edited by Mrs. Follen.*

Follen, Mrs. Eliza Lee [Cabot]. *Ms.*, 1787–1859. Wife of C. Follen, *supra.* A popular author for many years. Sketches of Married Life; Twilight Stories, a volume of excellent juvenile tales; The Well-spent Hour; The Skeptic; Poems; To Mothers in the Free States; Anti-Slavery Hymns and Songs; Home Dramas; Little Songs for Little People; The Old Garret Stories. *Le.*

Folsom, Charles Follen. *Ms.*, 1842——. A physician of Boston, professor in the Harvard Medical School, 1877–1885. Mental Diseases; Present Aspect of the Sewage Question Applied to Boston (1877).

Folsom, George. *Me.*, 1802–1869. An antiquarian writer of New York city. Sketches of Saco and Biddeford; Dutch Annals of New York; Letters and Dispatches of Cortés, translated from the Spanish; Political Condition of Mexico.

Folwell, William Watts. *N. Y.*, 1833——. An educator of Minnesota. Public Instruction in Minnesota; Lectures on Political Economy.

Fontaine, Edward. *Va.*, 1814–1884. An Episcopal clergyman of Mississippi. How the World was Peopled, a series of ethnological lectures.

Fontaine, Francis. 18—. The Exile; Etowah, a Romance of the Confederacy.

Foote, Andrew Hull. *Ct.*, 1806–1863. A rear-admiral of the United States navy. Africa and the American

Flag (1854). *See Life by J. M. Hoppin, infra.*

Foote, Henry Stuart. *Va.*, 1800–1880. A prominent Mississippi politician. He was governor of his State, 1853–54, and, though opposed to secession, a member of the Confederate Congress, where he was noted for his strong opposition to Jefferson Davis. Texas and the Texans; The War of the Rebellion, or Scylla and Charybdis; Bench and Bar of the South and Southwest; Personal Reminiscences.

Foote, Henry Wilder. *Ms.*, 1838–1889. A Unitarian clergyman of Boston, minister of King's Chapel from 1861 till his death. Annals of King's Chapel; Thy Kingdom Come, ten sermons on the Lord's Prayer; The Insight of Faith. *El. Rob.*

Foote, Mrs. Mary [Hallock]. *N.Y.*, 1847——. A novelist and illustrator whose married life has been passed chiefly in the Rocky Mountain country, in which region the scene of much of her work is laid. The Led Horse Claim, a Romance of a Mining Camp; In Exile, and Other Stories; John Bodewin's Testimony; The Chosen Valley; Cœur d'Alene; The Last Assembly Ball; The Cup of Trembling, and Other Stories. *Hou.*

Foote, William Henry. *Ct.*, 1794–1869. A Presbyterian clergyman and educator of West Virginia. Sketches of North Carolina; Sketches of the Presbyterian Church in Virginia; The Huguenots, or Reformed French Church; Sketches of Virginia.

Forbes, Mrs. Harriette [Merrifield]. *Ms.*, 1856——. A writer of Westborough, Massachusetts. The Hundredth Town, a series of historical sketches of Westborough; A Lily Stalk, studies of child life.

Forbes, Robert Bennet. *Ms.*, 1804–1889. A sea captain who was subsequently a Boston merchant. China and the China Trade (1844); Construction of Ships for the Merchant Service; Life Boats, Projectiles, and Other Means for Saving Life; Seamen Past and Present; Rambling Reminiscences; Notes on Some Few Wrecks and Rescues.

Forbes, Stephen Alfred. *Il.*, 1844——. A professor of zoölogy in the University of Illinois and State entomologist. Studies of the Food of Birds, Fishes, and Insects; Contagious Diseases of Insects.

Force, Manning Ferguson. *O.*, 1824——. Son of P. Force, *infra.* A brigadier-general in the Federal army during the Civil War, and subsequently a prominent jurist of Cincinnati. From Fort Henry to Corinth; Marching Across Carolina; The Mound Builders; Prehistoric Man; Recollections of the Vicksburg Campaign, include the most of his writings. *Clke. Scr.*

Force, Peter. *N. J.*, 1790–1868. A journalist and historian of Washington who began in 1833 a documentary history of the American colonies. Thirty years' labour was spent upon the task, and nine volumes completed, entitled American Archives. His other works include Tracts and Other Papers relating to the Origin of the North American Colonies; Grinnell Land. His immense and valuable library was purchased by Congress in 1867.

Force, William Quereau. *D. C.*, 1820–1880. Son of P. Force, *supra.* A meteorologist of Washington who assisted his father in preparing American Archives, and published Builder's Guide; The Picture of Washington.

Ford, Corydon La. *N. Y.*, 1813——. A physician of note who has held several medical professorships, and since 1880 has been professor emeritus in the Long Island College hospital. Questions on Anatomy, etc.; Questions on the Structure and Development of the Human Teeth; Syllabus of Lectures on Odontology, Human and Comparative.

Ford, Mrs. Emily Ellsworth [Fowler]. *Ms.*, 1826——. Daughter of W. C. Fowler, *infra*, and grand-daughter of Noah Webster. A Brooklyn writer who has published My Recollections, a volume of verse.

Ford, James Lauren. *Mo.*, 1854——. A journalist and littérateur of New York city. Dr. Dodd's School; The Third Alarm, are tales for juvenile readers. Other works of his are Hypnotic Tales; The Literary Shop; Bohemia Invaded; Dolly Dillenback. *Ric. Sto.*

Ford, Paul Leicester. *L. I.*, 1865——. Son of Mrs. Emily Ford, *supra.* A resident of Brooklyn. Bibliotheca Hamiltonia; Franklin Bibliography; The Honorable Peter Stirling, a novel of New York Society; The True George Washington. *Ho. Lip.*

Ford, Mrs. Sallie [Rochester]. *Ky.*, 1828——. Wife of S. H. Ford, *infra.* A St. Louis writer whose early writings were very popular, Grace Truman, her first book, having an extensive sale. Other works of hers are, Romance of Freemasonry; Raids and Romance of Morgan and his Men; Mary Bunyan, the Dreamer's Blind Daughter; Evangel Wiseman; Ernest Quest.

Ford, Samuel Howard. *Mo.*, 1823——. A Baptist clergyman of Memphis, Mobile, and elsewhere, living in retirement in St. Louis since 1887. The Origin of the Baptists; Servetus, Hero and Martyr.

Ford, Thomas. *Pa.*, 1800–1850. An Illinois jurist who was governor of his State, 1842–46. History of Illinois from 1818 to 1847.

Ford, William Henry. *Pa.*, 1830——. A Philadelphia surgeon twice president of the municipal board of health. He has published Healthy Dwelling-Houses and How to Build Them.

Ford, Worthington Chauncey. *L. I.*, 1858——. Son of Mrs. Emily Ford, *supra.* A government statistician at Washington. American Citizens' Manual; The Standard Silver Dollar.

Forester, Frank. *See Herbert, W. H.*

Forestier, Auber. *See Moore, Mrs. Annie.*

Forney, John Weiss. *Pa.*, 1817–1881. A journalist of Philadelphia and Washington, of prominence as a politician, and secretary of the United States Senate, 1861–68. Life of General Hancock; Anecdotes of Public Men; The New Nobility, a story of England and America; What I Saw in Texas; A Centennial Commissioner in Europe; Letters from Europe; Forty Years of American Journalism. *Ap. Har. Lip.*

Forrester, Fanny. *See Judson, Mrs.*

Forrester, Francis. *See Wise, David.*

Forry, Samuel. *Pa.*, 1811–1844. A physician and surgeon of New York city. The Climate of the United States and its Endemic Influences; Meteorology.

Fort, George Franklin. *N. J.*, 1809–1872. A governor of New Jersey, 1850–1854. Early History and Antiquities of Freemasonry.

Fortier, Alcée. *La.*, 1856——. An educator of Louisiana, professor of Romance languages in Tulane University. Le Château de Chambord; Gabriel d'Ennerich, an historical novelette; Bits of Louisiana Folk-Lore; Sept Grands Auteurs de xixe Siècle; Histoire de la Littérature Française; Louisiana Studies; Louisiana Folk Tales. He has also annotated college editions of several French texts. *He. Ho. Hou.*

Forwood, William Stump. *Md.*, 1830——. A physician of Darlington, Maryland. History and Descriptive Account of Mammoth Cave, with Full Scientific Details of the Eyeless Fishes.

Fosdick, Charles Austin. "Harry Castlemon." *N. Y.*, 1842——. A voluminous author of juvenile books, among which The Gunboat Series; Rocky Mountain Series; Roughing It Series; The Steel Horse, or the Rambles of a Bicycle, are but a few of the whole number. *Co.*

Fosdick, William Whiteman. *O.*, 1825–1862. A lawyer of Cincinnati, who published Malmiztic the Toltec, a novel; Ariel and Other Poems.

Foss, Samuel Walter. *N. H.*, 1858——. A writer of popular dialect and other poems, whose home is in Somerville, Massachusetts. Back Country Poems; Whiffs from Wild Meadows (verse). *Le.*

Foster, Charles Hubbs. *N. Y.*, 1833–1895. An actor and playwright of New York city, who wrote more than seventy-five plays, mostly melodramas, among which are, Twins of London; Twenty Years Dead; The Chain Gang.

Foster, Mrs. Hannah [Webster]. *Ms.*, 1759–1840. A writer who was the wife of John Foster, minister at Brighton, Massachusetts, 1784–1827, and after his death a resident of Montreal. She was the daughter of Grant Webster, a merchant of Boston, and was probably born in that city. She wrote The Boarding School; Letters of a Preceptress; but is remembered chiefly for having been the author of the once famous story, The Coquette, or the History of Eliza Wharton, which was largely based upon fact, and passed through more than thirty editions.

Foster, John Wells. *Ms.*, 1815–1873. A geologist employed by the United States in a geological survey of the Lake Superior region, and subsequently a resident of Chicago. The Mississippi Valley; Mineral Wealth and Railroad Development; Prehistoric Races of the United States; Geology and Topography of the Lake Superior Land District (with J. D. Whitney, *infra*). *Sc.*

Foster, Mrs. Judith Ellen [Horton]. *Ms.*, 1840——. A lawyer and prominent temperance advocate of Iowa. The Crime Against Ireland; Amendment Manual (Prohibition); The American Renaissance; Republican Contentions and Supreme Court Decisions.

Foster, Randolph Sinks. *O.*, 1820——. A Methodist bishop of much prominence in his denomination. Objections to Calvinism; Christian Purity; Ministry Needed for the Times; Theism; Beyond the Grave; Centenary Thoughts; Studies in Theology. *Meth.*

Foster, Robert Verrell. *Tn.*, 1845——. A Cumberland Presbyterian clergyman and educator, professor of Hebrew in the Theological Seminary at Lebanon, Tennessee, since 1877. Introduction to the Study of Theology; Old Testament Studies; Commentary on the Epistle to the Romans.

Foster, Stephen Collins. *Pa.*, 1826–1864. A famous song-writer and composer of Pittsburg and New York city. He set to music 125 or more songs, the words in nearly all cases being his own. Some of them, like the Suwanee River, My Old Kentucky Home, Nelly Bly, are known in all English-speaking lands. *See Atlantic Monthly, November, 1867.*

Foster, Stephen Symonds. *N.H.*, 1809–1881. A noted anti-slavery agitator of Worcester, Massachusetts. He married in 1845 Abby Kelly, also noted as an abolitionist. The Brotherhood of Thieves, a True Picture of the American Church and Clergy.

Foster, Mrs. Theodosia Maria [Toll]. "Faye Huntington." *N. Y.*, 1838——. An educator of Verona, New York, who has written much for young people. In Earnest; What Fide Remembers; A Baker's Dozen; A Modern Exodus, are among her works. *Lo.*

Foster, William Eaton. *Vt.*, 1851——. A librarian of Providence. The Civil Service Reform Movement; The Literature of Civil Service Reform in the United States; Stephen Hopkins, a Rhode Island Statesman; Town Government in Rhode Island.

Fowler, Henry. *Ms.*, 1824–1872. A Presbyterian clergyman of Auburn, New York. The American Pulpit, a collection of sketches of American preachers.

Fowler, Lorenzo Niles. *N.Y.*, 1811–1896. A lecturer, editor, and publisher of New York city who settled in London in 1863, and lectured frequently in England from that period. Marriage, its History and Ceremonies; Lectures on Man.

Fowler, Mrs. Lydia [Folger]. *Ms.*, 1823–1879. Wife of L. N. Fowler, *supra.* A practicing physician for some years. Nora, the Lost and Redeemed; The Pet of the Household and How to Save It; Familiar Lessons on Phrenology and Physiology; Familiar Lessons on Astronomy.

Fowler, Orin. *Ct.*, 1791–1852. A Congregational clergyman of Fall River, noted as a temperance and anti-slavery orator, who was a member of Congress, 1848–52. Treatise on Baptism; Historical Sketch of Fall River.

Fowler, Orson Squire. *N.Y.*, 1809–1887. Brother of L. N. Fowler, *supra*, and with him a member of the New York publishing house of Fowler & Wells, 1844–63. He was an ardent phrenologist, and wrote much on his favourite topic. Memory and Intellectual Improvement; Physiology, Animal and Mental; Matrimony; Self-Culture; Hereditary Descent; Love and Parentage; Sexual Science; Amativeness; Human Science; Creative Science; The Self-Instructor in Phrenology (with L. N. Fowler).

Fowler, Philemon Halstead. *N. Y.*, 1814——. A Presbyterian clergyman of Utica. History of Presbyterianism in central New York; The Presbyterian Element in our National Life and History.

Fowler, William Chauncey. *Ct.*, 1793–1881. A Congregational clergyman and educator of New England, who married a daughter of Noah Webster, *infra*. Memorials of the Chaunceys; The Sectional Controversy, or Passages in United States Political History; History of Durham, Connecticut; Local Law in Massachusetts and Connecticut; Essays; English Grammar; The English Language in its Elements and Forms. *Har.*

Fowler, William Worthington. *Vt.*, 1833–1881. Son of W. C. Fowler, *supra*. He was successively a lawyer, broker, and journalist of New York city. Ten Years in Wall Street; Fighting Fire, the Great Fires of History (1873); Woman on the American Frontier; Twenty Years of Inside Life in Wall Street.

Fox, Ebenezer. *Ms.*, 1763–1843. A Bostonian who was postmaster of his city 1830–36, and the author of The Revolutionary Adventures of Ebenezer Fox (1848).

Fox, John [William]. *Ky.*, 186——. A Cumberland Vendetta. *Har.*

Fox, Norman. *N. Y.*, 1836——. A Baptist minister of New York and Missouri. George Fox and the Early Friends; Rise of the Use of Pouring and Sprinkling for Baptism; A Layman's Ministry; Inspiration of the Apostles in Speaking and Writing.

Foxton, E. *See Palfrey, Sarah.*

Foye, James Clark. *N. H.*, 1841——. An educator who has been professor of chemistry at Lawrence University since 1867. Chemical Problems; Handbook of Mineralogy; Tables for Determination of United States Minerals.

France, Lewis B——. *D. C.*, 18——. A lawyer and littérateur of Denver. Over the Old Trail; Pine Valley, a volume of short stories; Mountain Trails and Parks in Colorado. *Cr.*

Francis, Convers. *Ms.*, 1795–1863. Brother of Mrs. Lydia Child, *supra*. A Unitarian clergyman of Watertown, Massachusetts, and subsequently Parkman professor of pulpit eloquence at Harvard University, 1843–63. Life of John Eliot (*supra*); Historical Sketch of Watertown; Errors of Education, include his principal writings.

Francis, James Bicheno. *E.*, 1815–1892. A noted hydraulic engineer of Lowell. Lowell Hydraulic Experiments; The Strength of Cast Iron Columns.

Francis, John Wakefield. *N. Y.*, 1789–1861. A physician of much prominence at one time in medical and literary circles of New York city. Use of Mercury; Cases of Morbid Anatomy; Febrile Contagion; The Anatomy of Drunkenness; Old New York, a volume of pleasant reminiscences, comprise his principal writings. *See Life by Tuckerman.*

Francis, Samuel Ward. *N. Y.*, 1835–1886. Son of J. W. Francis, *supra*. A physician of New York city and subsequently of Newport, Rhode Island. Mott's Clinics; Water; Inside and Out; Biographical Sketches of New York Surgeons and Physicians; Life and Death; Curious Facts Concerning Man and Nature.

Francis, Valentine Mott. *N. Y.*, 1834. Son of J. W. Francis, *supra*. A physician of Newport who has published Hospital Hygiene.

Francke, Kuno. *Sg.*, 1855——. A professor in Harvard University. Social Forces in German Literature: a Study in the History of Civilization. *Ho.*

Franklin, Benjamin. *Ms.*, 1706–1790. A celebrated philosopher, statesman, and scientist who was born in Boston but went to Philadelphia in 1723, where he worked as a journeyman printer. In 1729 he became the proprietor of The Pennsylvania Gazette, and after that date his rise in life was rapid. He established the Philadelphia Library in 1731, the American Philosophical Society in 1744, and was one of the founders in 1749 of the institution which in 1753 became the University of Pennsylvania. In 1753 he was appointed, jointly with William Hunter, postmaster-general of the colonies. He was twice sent to London as colonial agent for Pennsylvania, and in 1770 was appointed agent for Massachusetts in England. In 1776 he helped draft the Declaration of Independence. During the next nine years he was first commissioner, then minister, to France; and was also a member of the commission which negotiated the treaty of peace with England. He was the discoverer of the identity of lightning with electricity, and the inventor of the lightning-rod. As a writer his influence has been felt throughout the world, his works including essays on politics, religion, commerce, science, and philosophy. The Busybody is a series of papers of the type of those in The Spectator, but furnishing much more lively reading. Poor Richard's Almanac, published 1732–57, was everywhere popular, and had a great influence over the mass of readers. The work by which he is best known, however, is his famous Autobiography, which has been one of the most widely read books ever printed. His Complete Works in ten volumes have been edited by J. Bigelow, *supra. See Edinburgh Review, July, 1806, and August, 1817; Contemporary Review, July, 1879; Harper's Magazine, July, 1880; Godey's Magazine, 1896; Appleton's American Biography; Parker's Historic Americans; Hale's Franklin in France; Lives by Parton, McMaster, H. Mayhew, Morse; Mignet's Vie de Franklin, 1873; Wetzel's Franklin as an Economist. Put.*

Franklin, Benjamin. *R. I.*, 1819——. An Episcopal clergyman of Shrewsbury, New Jersey. The Creed and Modern Thought; The Church and the Era.

Franklin, Thomas Levering. *Pa.*, 1820——. An Episcopal clergyman of western New York, and more recently of Philadelphia. His writings include an important work on The Creed, and several tractates on Divorce.

Frazer, Persifor. *Pa.*, 1844——. A distinguished geologist attached to the State geological survey of Pennsylvania who has published Tables for the Determination of Minerals; The Geology of Lancaster County. *Lip.*

Frederic, Harold. *N. Y.*, 1856——. A novelist and journalist who has been the London correspondent of the New York Times since 1884. The scenes of several of his novels are placed in small American communities. Marsena, and Other Stories; The Copperhead; The Lawton Girl; In the Valley; Seth's Brother's Wife; The Damnation of Theron Ware; March Hares. *Ap. Scr. St.*

Fredet, Peter. *F.*, 1801–1856. A Roman Catholic priest who came from France to America in 1831, and was professor in St. Mary's Seminary at Baltimore from that date until his death. Ancient History; Modern History; Original Texts and Translations of the Bible; Treatise on the Eucharistic Mystery; Lay Baptism; Inspiration and Canon of Scripture; Interpretation of Scripture; Doctrine of Exclusive Salvation; Necessity of Baptism; Effect of Baptism.

Freedley, Edwin Troxell. *Pa.*, 1827——. A Philadelphia writer and compiler of books of useful information, but of small literary value. The Business Man's Legal Adviser; Leading Pursuits of Leading Men; Philadelphia and its Manufactures; Opportunities for Industry; History of American Manufactures; Common Sense in Business; Home Comforts. *Lip.*

Freeman, Barnardus. *G.*, 1660–1743. A Dutch Reformed clergyman of Long Island who came to America in 1700 and was especially noted for his influence over the Indians. De Spizel der Self Kennis (Mirror of Self-Knowledge); De Weegshale der Gerade Gods (Balance of God's Grace).

Freeman, Frederick. *Ms.*, 1800–1883. An Episcopal clergyman and educator who was a Presbyterian minister in the earlier portion of his career. History of Cape Cod; Annals of Barnstable County; Freeman Genealogy; Civilization and Barbarism illustrated by Especial Reference to Metacomet and the Extinction of his Race.

Freeman, James. *Ms.*, 1759–1835. The first clergyman in the United States to bear the name Unitarian. While a lay reader at King's Chapel in Boston, in 1782, he became a Unitarian in his views, and was ordained in 1787 minister of that church, the members of which adopted Mr. Freeman's theology as their own, and he continued in that office until his death. The oldest Episcopal church in New England thus became the first Unitarian church in America. Mr. Freeman's Sermons and Charges were published in 1832.

Freeman, James Midwinter. "Robert Ranger." *N. Y.*, 1827——. A Methodist clergyman of New York city who published many books for children under the pseudonym "Robert Ranger." Other works of his include Illustration in Sunday-School Teaching; Handbook of Bible Manners and Customs; Short History of the English Bible; Book of Books. *Meth.*

Freeman, Samuel. *Me.*, 1743–1831. A jurist of Portland, Maine. The Massachusetts Justice; Probate Directory; The Town Officer. *See Bibliography of Maine.*

Frémont, Mrs. Jessie [Benton]. *Va.*, 1824——. Wife of J. C. Frémont, *infra*, and daughter of T. H. Benton, *supra*. A resident of Los Angeles. The Story of the Guard, a Chronicle of the War; A Year of American Travel; Souvenirs of My Time; Sketch of Senator Benton; Far West Sketches; Will and the Way Stories. *Lo.*

Frémont, John Charles. *Ga.*, 1813–1890. A famous soldier and politician who in 1856 was the first Republican candidate for the presidency, and served during the Civil War as a major-general in the Federal army. Report of the Exploring Expedition to the Rocky Mountains in 1842, and to Oregon and Northern California in 1843–44; Frémont's Explorations; Memoirs of My Life. *See Appleton's American Biography; Lives by J. Bigelow, supra, C. Upham.*

French, Alice. "Octave Thanet." *Ms.*, 1850——. A writer of novels and short stories whose home has been in Davenport, Iowa, and also in Arkansas. Knitters in the Sun; Otto the Knight, and other Trans-Mississippi Stories; Stories of a Western Town; An Adventure in Photography; Expiation. *Hou. Scr.*

French, Benjamin Franklin. *Va.*, 1799–1877. A writer of New Orleans and subquently of New York city. Biographia Americana; Memoirs of Eminent Female Writers; Historical Collections of Louisiana; History of the Iron Trade in the United States; Historical Annals of North America.

French, Henry Willard. *Ct.*, 1853——. A lecturer and miscellaneous writer of Boston. Art and Artists in Connecticut; Our Boys in China; Our Boys in India; Through Arctics and Tropics; Gems of Genius; Nuna the Brahmin Girl; Lance of Kehama; Oscar Peterson; Colonel Thorndike's Adventures; and the novels, The Only One; Castle Foam; Ego. *Le. Lo.*

French, John William. *Ct.*, 1809–1871. An Episcopal clergyman of Washington, 1842–56, and from the latter date till his death professor of ethics at West Point. He was the author of a work on Practical Ethics.

French, Mrs. L. Virginia [Smith]. *Va.*, 1830–1881. A writer and educator of Memphis. Wind Whispers, a collection of poems; Legend of the South; Iztalixo, a Tragedy; My Roses, the Romance of a June Day.

French, William Henry. *Md.*, 1815–1881. An officer who served in the army of the United States during the Mexican, Seminole, and Civil wars. His only published work is a manual of Instruction for Field Artillery.

Freneau [frē-nō′], **Philip.** *N. Y.*, 1752–1832. A journalist of New York city who, during the Revolution, produced much patriotic verse that was very effective as well as popular, though none of it is marked by any high degree of excellence. Poems of Philip Freneau, written chiefly during the Late War (1786); Poems Written between the Years 1768 and 1794; Poems Written and Published during the American Revolution; Collection of Poems on American Affairs. Among his prose writings are, The Philosopher of the Forest; Essays by Robert Slender. *See American Literatures by Hart, Nichol, and Richardson. Cr.*

Frey, Albert Romer. *N. Y.*, 1858——. A writer of New York city upon Shakesperean and dramatic topics, who has also published a work upon Sobriquets and Nicknames. *Hou.*

Frey, Joseph Samuel Christian Frederick. *G.*, 1773–1850. A clergyman of Jewish descent who became a

Christian in 1798, and, after coming to America in 1816, was for some ten years a Presbyterian minister and subsequently a Baptist preacher, especially active as a missionary to the Jews. Narrative of My Life; Hebrew Bible; Hebrew Grammar; Judah and Israel; Joseph and Benjamin; The Passover; Scripture Types.

Frieze, Henry Simmons. *Ms.*, 1817–1889. A professor of Latin in the University of Michigan from 1854 until his death. He published editions of Quintilian and Virgil's Æneid, and was the author of The Story of Giovanni Dupré.

Frisbie, Levi. *Ct.*, 1748–1806. A Congregational clergyman of Ipswich, Massachusetts, who published Sermons and Orations.

Frisbie, Levi. *Ms.*, 1783–1822. Son of L. Frisbie, *supra.* A tutor and professor at Harvard College from 1805 till his death. Miscellaneous Writings of Professor Frisbie, edited with Memoir by Andrews Norton, *infra*, appeared in 1823.

Fritschel, Gottfried Leonhard Wilhelm. *G.*, 1836——. A Lutheran clergyman who came from Germany to the United States in 1857, and has been professor of theology in the seminary at Mendota, Illinois, since that time. He has published (in German) Meditations on the Passion of Christ; History of Protestant Missions among North American Indians in the 17th and 18th Centuries.

Frost, John. *Me.*, 1800–1859. An educator of Philadelphia who was a prolific writer and compiler of historical and other works of indifferent merit. Their number was very great, and the sale of some of them extensive. Among them are, Beauties of English History; Beauties of French History; Wild Scenes in a Hunter's Life; Pioneer Mothers in the West; The Presidents of the United States; Pictorial History of the United States; History of the World. *Har. Le.*

Frothingham, Ellen. *Ms.*, 1835——. Daughter of N. L. Frothingham, *infra.* A Bostonian who has published several fine translations from Lessing (The Laocoön); Auerbach; Goethe (Hermann and Dorothea); Grillparzer (Sappho). *Rob.*

Frothingham, Nathaniel Langdon. *Ms.*, 1793–1870. A Unitarian clergyman of Boston whose writing displays singular grace and refinement. Deism or Christianity; Sermons in the Order of a Twelvemonth; Metrical Pieces, Original and Translated.

Frothingham, Octavius Brooks. *Ms.*, 1822–1895. Son of N. L. Frothingham, *supra.* A Unitarian clergyman of extremely radical views who resigned his charge in New York city in 1879, and returned to Boston the next year, devoting the remainder of his life to literary pursuits. He was at one period art critic for the New York Tribune. Stories from the Lips of the Teacher; Stories from the Old Testament; The Religion of Humanity; The Cradle of the Christ; Memoir of W. H. Channing, *supra;* The Safest Creed; Beliefs of the Unbelievers; Creed and Conduct; The Spirit of the New Faith; The Rising and the Setting Faith; Visions of the Future; Lives of Gerrit Smith, George Ripley, Theodore Parker; History of New England Transcendentalism; Boston Unitarianism; Recollections and Impressions. *Hou. Put.*

Frothingham, Richard. *Ms.*, 1812–1880. A journalist and local historian of Charlestown, Massachusetts. History of the Siege of Boston; The Rise of the Republic; History of Charlestown; Life of General Joseph Warren; The Command in the Battle of Bunker Hill. *Lit.*

Frothingham, Washington. *N. Y.*, 1828——. A Presbyterian clergyman of Albany. Atheos, or Tragedies of Unbelief; The Martel Papers: Scenes in the Reign of Terror.

Fry, James Barnet. *Il.*, 1827–1894. A colonel and brevet major-general in the United States army who was retired from active service in 1881, and thereafter lived in New York city. Sketch of the Adjutant-General's Department, 1775–1875; Historical and Legal Effects of Brevets in Great Britain and the United States from their Origin in 1692; Army Sacrifices; McDowell and Tyler in the Campaign of Bull Run; Operations of the Army under Buell; New York and Conscription.

Fuller, Andrew S——. *N.Y.*, 1828–1896. A horticultural writer and journalist of New York city, editor of Woodward's Record of Horticulture. The Fruit Tree Culturist; The Grape Culturist; The Small Fruit Culturist; The Strawberry Culturist; Practical Forestry; The Propagation of Plants; The Nut Culturist.

Fuller, Anna. *Ms.*, 1853——. A Boston novelist. Pratt Portraits; A Literary Courtship; Peak and Prairie; A Venetian June. *Put.*

Fuller, Edward. *N. Y.*, 1860——. A Boston journalist, subsequently on the staff of the Providence Journal. The Complaining Millions of Men, a novel of social conditions in Boston.

Fuller, Henry Blake. *Il.*, 1857——. A novelist of Chicago. The Chevalier of Pensieri-Vani; The Chatelaine of La Trinité; The Cliff Dwellers; With the Procession; The Puppet-Booth, twelve one-act plays. *Cent. Har.*

Fuller, Hiram. *Ms.*, c. 1815–1880. A journalist of New York city who at the outset of the Civil War supported the Confederate cause, and emigrated to England on that account. Subsequently he became an adventurer in Paris. The Groton Letters; Belle Brittan on a Tour; Sparks from a Locomotive; Grand Transformation Scenes in the United States.

Fuller, Margaret. *See Ossoli.*

Fuller, Richard. *S. C.*, 1804–1876. A Baptist clergyman of Charleston, and subsequently of Baltimore. Argument on Baptist Close Communion; Sermons; Scriptural Baptism.

Fuller, Richard Frederick. *Ms.*, 1821–1869. Brother of M. Fuller, *supra.* A lawyer of Boston who published Visions in Verse; Chaplain Fuller, a life of his brother Arthur.

Fuller, Samuel. *N. Y.*, 1802–1895. An Episcopal clergyman, professor at the Berkeley Divinity School, Middletown, Connecticut. Confirmation, its Authority and Nature; The Revelation of St. John Self-Interpreted.

Fuller, Samuel Richard. *Ms.*, 1850——. Son of S. Fuller, *supra.* An Episcopal clergyman of Massachusetts. Personality, a volume of Sermons. *Hou.*

Fullerton, George Stuart. *E. I.*, 1859——. An Episcopal clergyman, professor of moral philosophy in the University of Pennsylvania. The Conception of the Infinite and the Solution of the Mathematical Antinomies, a psychological treatise; A Plain Argument for God. *Lip.*

Fullerton, William Morton. *Ct.*, 1865——. A journalist in Boston for several years, and since 1890 a member of the Paris staff of the London Times. Cairo, a descriptive essay; Patriotism and Science, a collection of essays. *Mac. Rob.*

Fulton, John. *S.*, 1834——. An Episcopal clergyman noted as an able exponent of canon law, and professor of that subject at the Episcopal Divinity School in Philadelphia. Letters on Christian Unity; Index Canonum; The Laws of Marriage; Documentary History of the Episcopal Church in the Confederate States; The Beautiful Land, a description of Palestine; The Chalcedonian Decree. *Wh.*

Fulton, Justin Dewey. *N. Y.*, 1828——. A Baptist clergyman, prominent in Boston and Brooklyn for his continued and violent attacks upon the Roman Catholic Church. The Roman Catholic Element in American History; The True Woman; Show Your Colors, a story of Boston Life; The Way Out; Witnessing for the Truth, or the Overthrow of the Papacy; Rome in America, include the most of his work, which is of interest as an example of religious bigotry if for no other reason.

Furness, Mrs. Helen Kate [Rogers]. 1837–1883. Wife of H. H. Furness, *infra.* A Shakespearean scholar of Philadelphia who published A Concordance to the Poems of Shakespeare. *Lip.*

Furness, Horace Howard. *Pa.*, 1833——. Son of W. H. Furness, *infra.* A distinguished Shakespearean scholar of Philadelphia, widely known in the literary world for his scholarly and exhaustive variorum editions of King Lear, Hamlet, Macbeth, Romeo and Juliet, Othello, Merchant of Venice, As You Like It, Midsummer Night's Dream. The edition of Hamlet fills two volumes. *Lip.*

Furness, William Henry. *Ms.*, 1802–1896. A Unitarian clergyman of Philadelphia, from 1825 to 1875 pastor of the Unitarian church in that city. A theologian of radical views, but reverent temper. The Unconscious Truth of the Four Gospels; Jesus and his Biographers; History of Jesus; Thoughts on the Life and Character of Jesus; The Story of the Resurrection Told Once More; The Power of Spirit; Discourses; The Veil Lifted and Jesus becoming Visible; Verses: Translations and Hymns; The Faith of Jesus; a much-admired translation of Schiller's Song of the Bell. *See Harvard Graduates' Magazine, June, 1896. El. Lip.*

Futhey, John Smith. *Pa.*, 1820–1888. A lawyer and antiquarian of Eastern Pennsylvania. History of Chester County; Historical Collections of Chester County.

G

Gage, Mrs. Frances Dana [Barker]. *O.*, 1808–1884. A prominent advocate of woman suffrage who lectured much on that subject as well as upon temperance and anti-slavery. Elsie Magoon, a temperance story; Poems; Gertie's Sacrifice; Nightcaps, a Series of Books; Sparks Upward. She wrote much over the signature "Aunt Fanny." *Lip.*

Gage, Mrs. Matilda Joslyn. *N. Y.*, 1826——. A noted woman suffragist of Fayetteville, New York. Woman's Rights Catechism; Woman as an Inventor; Woman, Church, and State; History of Woman Suffrage (with Miss Anthony and Mrs. Stanton). *Ke.*

Gage, Simon Henry. *N. Y.*, 1851——. A physiologist who has been professor of physiology at Cornell University. The Microscope and Histology; Anatomical Technology (with B. G. Wilder, *infra*).

Gage, William Leonard. *N. H.*, 1832–1889. A Unitarian clergyman of Hartford, 1868–84. Trinitarian Sermons to a Unitarian Congregation; Songs of War Time; Light in Darkness; Life of Carl Ritter; Studies in Bible Lands; Verses; The Home of God's People; A Leisurely Journey; Palestine, Historic and Descriptive; The Salvation of Faust; a number of translations from the German. *Lo.*

Gallagher [găl'a-ger], **William Davis.** *Pa.*, 1808–1894. A journalist of Cincinnati prominent in the early literary annals of the Ohio Valley, whose home in later years was near Louisville. Miami Woods and Other Poems; A Golden Wedding, and Other Poems; Erato (verse). *See Griswold's Poets and Poetry of America. Clke.*

Gallatin, Albert. *Sd.*, 1761–1849. A financier of distinction. He came to America from Switzerland in 1780, and was active in political affairs. He was secretary of the treasury under President Jefferson; an associate of Adams and Clay in negotiating the Treaty of Peace with Great Britain in 1815; minister to France 1816–23; subsequently minister to Great Britain. After his retirement from public life he became a banker in New York city. Considerations on the Currency and Banking System of the United States; Synopsis of the Indian Tribes; Notes on the Semi-Civilized Nations of Mexico, Yucatan, and Central America; Peace with Mexico; War Expenses. His writings have been edited in six volumes by H. Adams, *supra. See Lives by H. Adams, J. A. Stevens. Lip.*

Gallaudet [găl-aw-dĕt'], **Edward Miner.** *Ct.*, 1837——. Son of T. H. Gallaudet, *infra.* Popular Manual of International Law; Life of T. H. Gallaudet, *infra.*

Gallaudet, Thomas Hopkins. *Pa.*, 1787–1851. A celebrated educator of deaf mutes, who was superintendent of the institution for deaf mutes at Hartford, the first in the United States, 1817–30. Child's Book of the Soul; The Youth's Book of Natural Theology; Sermons Preached to an English Congregation in Paris; Bible Stories for the Young. *See Lives by H. Humphrey, E. M. Gallaudet.*

Gallitzin, Demetrius Augustine. Prince. *Md.*, 1770–1841. The son of the Russian ambassador to France, he came to America in 1792, was educated as a Sulpitian priest, and founded the Roman Catholic colony of Loretto in Pennsylvania in 1803. Defence of

Catholic Principles; Appeal to the Protestant Public; Six Letters of Advice; Letter to a Protestant Friend on the Holy Scripture. *See Lives by Lemcke, Heyden, Brownson.*

Galloway, Charles Betts. *Mi.*, 1849——. A bishop of the Methodist Church South. Methodism a Child of Providence; Aaron's Rod in Public Morals.

Galloway, Joseph. *Md.*, 1731–1803. A Philadelphia lawyer who was a noted loyalist, and went to England after the evacuation of the city by the English. Historical and Political Reflections on the American Rebellion; The Prophetic History of the Church of Rome.

Gallup, Joseph Adams. *Ct.*, 1769–1849. A Vermont physician, professor in Vermont Medical College, which he founded. Epidemic Diseases in Vermont; Outlines of the Institutes of Medicine.

Gammell, William. *Ms.*, 1812–1889. An educator of Rhode Island, professor at Brown University, 1835–64. Life of Roger Williams; History of American Baptist Missions.

Gannett, Ezra Stiles. *Ms.*, 1801–1871. A Unitarian clergyman of prominence in Boston for many years, who published a great number of single sermons and addresses. *See Memoir by W. C. Gannett.*

Gannett, Henry. *Me.*, 1846——. The chief topographer of the United States Geological Survey since 1882. Boundaries of the United States; The Building of a Nation; Dictionary of Altitudes in the United States; Results of Primary Triangulation; Manual of Topographical Methods; Geographic Dictionaries of Massachusetts, Connecticut, Rhode Island, New Jersey.

Gannett, William Channing. 1840——. Son of E. S. Gannett, *supra*. A Unitarian clergyman of Minneapolis, and subsequently of Rochester, New York. A Year of Miracle, a poem in Four Sermons; Memoir of E. S. Gannett, *supra;* The Thought of God in Hymns and Poems (with F. L. Hosmer). *A. U. A. El. Rob.*

Garden, Alexander. *S., circa* 1685–1750. An Episcopal clergyman of Charleston remembered for his vigorous opposition to Whitefield. Six Letters to the Reverend George Whitefield; Two Sermons. *See Tyler's American Literature.*

Garden, Alexander. *S.*, 1728–1791. A botanical writer of Charleston for whom Linnæus named the genus Gardenia. He went to England as a loyalist in 1783, and became vice-president of the Royal Society.

Garden, Alexander. *S. C.*, 1757–1829. Son of A. Garden, 2d. An officer in the American army during the Revolution. Anecdotes of the Revolutionary War (1822). *See edition of 1865.*

Gardener, Mrs. Helen. *See Smart, Mrs.*

Gardiner, Frederick. *Me.*, 1822–1889. An Episcopal clergyman, professor in the Berkeley Divinity School at Middletown from 1869. The Island of Life, an Allegory; Commentary on Epistle of Jude; Harmony of the Four Gospels in Greek; Harmony of the Four Gospels in English; Diatessaron; The Principles of Textual Criticism; The Old and New Testament in their Mutual Relations; Aids to Scripture Study. *Hou.*

Gardner, Augustus Kinsley. *Ms.*, 1812–1876. Son of S. J. Gardner, *infra.* A physician of New York city. The French Metropolis; Causes of Sterility; Conjugal Sins; Our Children, a Handbook for Parents; Old Wine in New Bottles; Ships and Shipbuilders of New York; translation of Scanonzi's Diseases of Females.

Gardner, Charles Kitchell. *N. J.*, 1787–1869. A United States army officer who was postmaster of Washington in President Polk's administration. Dictionary of United States Army Commissioned Officers from 1789 to 1853; Compendium of Military Tactics; Permanent Designation of Companies, and lesser works.

Gardner, Dorsey. *Pa.*, 1842–1894. A journalist of New York city who was one of the revisers of the Webster International Dictionary. Quatre Bras, Ligny, and Waterloo; Condensed Etymological Dictionary of the English Language.

Gardner, Eugene C. *Ms.*, 1836——. An architect of Springfield, Massachusetts. Homes and All About Them; The House that Jill Built; Homes and How to Make Them; Illustrated Homes; Home Interiors; Common Sense in Church-Building; Town and Country School Buildings.

Gardner, Samuel Jackson. *Ms.*, 1788–1864. A lawyer of Boston, and subsequently a journalist of Newark, New Jersey, whose essays over the signature "Decius" were issued in book form with the title Autumn Leaves.

Garfield, James Abram. *O.*, 1831–1881. The twentieth president of the United States. A statesman of Ohio, prominent as a general in the Federal army during the Civil War, and subsequently as a congressman till his elevation to the presidency. In July, 1881, he was mortally wounded by an assassin, and died in the September following. His Complete Works have been edited by B. A. Hinsdale, *infra*. *See Appleton's American Biography; Life by J. R. Gilmore, infra, 1880; Eulogy by G. F. Hoar.*

Garland, Hamlin. *Wis.*, 1860——. A novelist who was for some years a resident of Boston, and then returned to the Western States, in which the scenes of his realistic fictions are mainly laid. Main Travelled Roads; A Spoil of Office; Prairie Folks; Prairie Songs; Crumbling Idols; Rose of Dutcher's Coolly; Little Norsk. *St.*

Garland, Landon Cabell. *Va.*, 1810——. A mathematician who held professorships in several Southern colleges, and published Trigonometry, Plane and Spherical.

Garman, Samuel. *Pa.*, 1846——. A naturalist of Cambridge, assistant in the Agassiz Museum there. The Reptiles and Batrachians of North America; Reptiles and Batrachians of Bermuda. *Clke.*

Garnett, James Mercer. *Va.*, 1840——. A professor of English literature at the University of Virginia since 1882. Translation of Beowulf; Anglo-Saxon Poems; Translations of Elene, Judith, Athelstan, and Byrhtnoth.

Garretson, James Edmund. "John Darby." *Del.*, 1828——. A physician of Philadelphia, dean of the dental college there from 1879. System of Oral Surgery; Odd Hours of a Physician; Thinkers and Thinking; Two Thousand Years Ago; Hours with John Darby; Brushland; 19th Century Common Sense. *Lip.*

Garrett, Alexander Charles. *I.*, 1832——. The first Protestant Episcopal bishop of Northern Texas. Historical Continuity, a series of Sketches on the Church. *Wh.*

Garrigues, Henry Jacques. *Dk.*, 1831——. A Danish physician who came to America in 1875, and since 1886 has been professor of practical obstetrics in the post-graduate medical school of New York city. Gastro-Elytrotomy; Practical Guide in Antiseptic Midwifery.

Garrison, James Harney. *Mo.*, 1842——. A clergyman and editor of religious journals. Heavenward Way; Alone With God.

Garrison, Joseph Fithian. *N. J.*, 1823–1892. An Episcopal clergyman of Camden, New Jersey, professor of canon law at the Philadelphia Episcopal Divinity School for some years. The Formation of the Protestant Episcopal Church in the United States; The American Prayer Book.

Garrison, William Lloyd. *Ms.*, 1805–1879. A very celebrated anti-slavery journalist of Boston who established The Liberator in 1831, and was its editor for the thirty-five years of its existence. His uncompromising attitude roused the fiercest opposition in both North and South, and he was at one time dragged through the streets of Boston by a mob who intended to hang him for his newspaper utterances, but he fortunately lived to see the triumph of his ideas and the liberation of the slave. Thoughts on African Colonization; Sonnets and Other Poems. *See Johnson's Garrison and his Times; Life by his Sons.*

Gath. *See Townsend, G. A.*

Gay, Ebenezer. *Ms.*, 1696–1787. A Unitarian clergyman of Hingham from 1718 until his death. The Old Man's Calendar, a sermon preached on his eighty-fifth birthday, went through several editions in America and England,

and was translated into several continental languages.

Gay, Eben Howard. *Ms.*, 1858——. Nephew of S. H. Gay, *infra.* A banker of Boston who has published A Treatise on Municipal Bonds.

Gay, Sydney Howard. *Ms.*, 1814–1888. Great-grandson of E. Gay, *supra.* A journalist of New York and Chicago, during the Civil War the managing editor of the New York Tribune. Life of James Madison; Bryant and Gay's Popular History of the United States, of which the preface only was the work of Mr. Bryant. *Hou. Scr.*

Gayarré, Charles Étienne Arthur. *La.*, 1805–1895. A jurist of New Orleans, profoundly versed in the history of his State. Histoire de la Louisiane; Romance of the History of Louisiana; Colonial History of Louisiana; Louisiana as a French Colony; The Spanish Domination in Louisiana; Philip the Second, a Biography; Louisiana Supreme Court Reports; School for Politics, a drama; Fernando de Lemos, a novel; Aubert Dubayet, a sequel to the preceding; School for Politics, a Dramatic Novel.

Gayler, Charles. *N. Y.*, 1820–1892. A dramatist of New York city among whose many plays are, The Gold Hunters; Taking the Chances; Fritz. Among his various novels are, The Romance of a Poor Young Man; Out of the Streets, both of which were dramatized by their author.

Gaylord, Glance. *See Bradley, Warren.*

Geer, George Jarvis. *Ct.*, 1821–1885. An Episcopal clergyman, long rector of St. Timothy's Church, New York city, and the author of The Conversion of St. Paul, a series of Discourses.

Gemünder, George. *Wg.*, 1816——. A violin-maker who came to America from Würtemberg in 1847, and settled in New York city, 1852. He published Progress in Violin-Making.

Genin, John Nicholas. *N. Y.*, 1819–1878. A noted hatter of New York city who wrote a History of the Hat from the Earliest Ages.

Genth, Frederick Augustus Louis Charles William. *G.*, 1820–1893. A professor of chemistry at the University of Pennsylvania from 1872. Ammonia Cobalt Bases (with O. W. Gibbs, *infra*); Minerals of North Carolina; First and Second Preliminary Reports on the Mineralogy of Pennsylvania.

Genung [je-nŭng'], **John Franklin.** *N. Y.*, 1850——. A professor at Amherst College. A Study of In Memoriam; The Epic of the Inner Life, an annotated translation of Job; Practical Elements of Rhetoric; The Study of Rhetoric in College Courses. *Gi. Hou.*

George, Henry. *Pa.*, 1839–1897. A very widely known political economist of New York city whose radical views upon economic and social topics have met with much criticism both in America and Europe. Progress and Poverty; Our Land and Land Policy; The Subsidy Question and the Democratic Party; Protection or Free Trade; The Irish Land Question; The Land Question; Social Problems.

George, Nathan Dow. *N. H.*, 1808–1896. A Methodist clergyman, long prominent in Maine, and subsequently in Massachusetts. An Examination of Universalism; Universalism Not of God; Materialism Anti-Scriptural; Annihilation Not of the Bible. *Meth.*

Gerard, James Watson. *N. Y.*, 1822——. A lawyer of New York city. The Pelican Papers, a satire; Titles to Real Estate in New York City; Title of the Corporation and Others to the Streets, Wharves, Lands, and Franchises in New York City; The Peace of Utrecht; Aquarelles (verse); Ostrea, or the Loves of the Oysters, a collection of humourous verse. *Put.*

Gerhard, William Paul. *G.*, 1854——. A sanitary engineer of New York city. Theatre Fires and Panics; Anlagen von Haus-Erwässerungen; Diagram for Sewer Calculations; House Drainage and Sanitary Plumbing; Guide to General House Inspection; Domestic Sanitary Appliances; Prinzipien der Haus-Kanalization, include his principal writings. *Wil.*

Gerhard, William Wood. *Pa.*, 1809–1872. A Philadelphia physician. Diagnosis of Chest Diseases; Spotted Fever; Fevers; Clinical Guide.

Gerhart [gair'hart], **Emmanuel Vogel.** *Pa.*, 1817——. A German Reformed clergyman of Lancaster, Pennsylvania, professor of theology in Franklin and Marshall College. Philosophy and Logic; Monograph of the Reformed Church; Child's Heidelberg Catechism; Institutes of the Christian Religion.

Gerrish, Theodore. 1846——. A clergyman of Portland, Maine. Army Life; Will Newton, the Young Volunteer; Life in the World's Wonderland; The Blue and the Gray, an army history (with J. Hutchinson).

Gholson, William Yates. *O.*, 1807-1870. An Ohio jurist who published Speeches on Payment of the Public Debt of the United States.

Gianque, Florien. *O.*, 1843——. A Cincinnati lawyer of Swiss descent. Laws of Election in Ohio; Election and Naturalization Laws of the United States; Manual for Ohio Road Supervisors; Manual for Guardians and Trustees; Manual for Assignees, Insolvent Debtors, etc.; Laws of Ohio relating to Roads, Ditches, Bridges, and Water-Courses; Manual for Notaries, etc.; Appendix to Ohio Revised Statutes. *Clke.*

Gibbes [gĭbz], **Robert Wilson.** *Ms.*, 1809-1866. A physician, educator, and journalist of Columbia, South Carolina. Monograph of the Squalidæ; Typhoid Pneumonia; Documentary History of South Carolina; Documentary History of the American Revolution.

Gibbon, John [Oliver]. *Pa.*, 1827-1896. A major-general in the Federal army during the Civil War who published The Artillerist's Manual.

Gibbons, Henry. *Del.*, 1808-1848. Son of W. Gibbons, *infra*. A physician of San Francisco, professor in the Pacific Medical College who was the author of an anti-tobacco treatise, Tobacco and its Effects.

Gibbons, James. *Md.*, 1834——. A cardinal of the Roman Catholic church since 1886. The Faith of Our Fathers; Our Christian Heritage; The Ambassador of Christ.

Gibbons, James Sloan. *Del.*, 1810-1892. Son of W. Gibbons, *infra*. A prominent financier and philanthropist of New York city. He was a noted abolitionist, and was a pioneer in the movement for preserving the forests. The Banks of New York; The Public Debt of the United States. He wrote the popular war song, "We are Coming, Father Abraham."

Gibbons, Mrs. Phœbe [Earle]. *Pa.*, 182——. An author of Lancaster County, Pennsylvania. Pennsylvania Dutch, and Other Essays; French and Belgians. *Lip.*

Gibbons, William. *Pa.*, 1781-1845. A philanthropist and scientist of Wilmington, Delaware. He wrote Truth Vindicated, a notably clear exposition of the principles of the Friends.

Gibbs, George. *L. I.*, 1815-1873. A lawyer and antiquarian of New York city. The Judicial Chronicle; Dictionary of the Chinook Jargon or Trade Language of Oregon; Comparative Vocabulary; Research relative to the Ethnology and Philology of America; Suggestions relating to Scientific Observation in Russian America.

Gibbs, Josiah Willard. *Ms.*, 1790-1861. A philologist who was professor of sacred literature at Yale University, 1824-61. Philological Studies; New Latin Analyst; Teutonic Etymology.

Gibbs, Josiah Willard. *Ct.*, 1839——. Son of J. W. Gibbs, *supra*. A professor of physics at Yale University, and the author of scientific papers and monographs.

Gibbs, [Oliver] Wolcott. *N. Y.*, 1822——. Brother of G. Gibbs, *supra*. A chemist of distinction, Rumford professor at Harvard University, and author of scientific papers.

Gibson, Louis Henry. *Ind.*, 1854——. An architect of Indianapolis. Beautiful Houses, a Study in House-building; Convenient Houses; Gradual Reduction Milling; Artistic Houses at Moderate Cost. *Cr.*

Gibson, William. *Md.*, 1788-1868. A once famous physician of Philadelphia, professor of surgery in the University of Pennsylvania, 1819-55. Principles and Practice of Surgery; Rambles in Europe. *See Gross's Sketches of Contemporaries.*

Gibson, William. *Md.*, 182—1887. A United States naval officer retired in 1879. Sailing Directions for the Kattegat, etc.; Poems of Many Years; Vision of Faery Land, and Other Poems; a translation of the Miscellaneous Poems of Goethe. *Le.*

Gibson, William Hamilton. *Ct.*, 1850–1896. An artist and author of New York city who has illustrated his own writings. The Complete American Trapper; Pastoral Days; Highways and Byways; Strolls by Starlight and Sunshine; Happy Hunting-Grounds; Sharp-Eyes, a Rambler's Calendar; Camp Life in the Woods; Our Edible Toadstools and Mushrooms. *See New England Magazine, February, 1897. Har.*

Giddings, Franklin Henry. *Ct.*, 1855——. A lecturer on sociology at Columbia University since 1891. Report on Profit Sharing; The Modern Distributive Process (with J. B. Clark); The Principles of Sociology. *Mac.*

Giddings, Joshua Reed. *Pa.*, 1795–1864. A once noted anti-slavery statesman and congressman of Ohio. The Exiles of Florida; The Rebellion: its Authors and its Causes; Speeches in Congress; Essays of Pacificus. *See Life by G. W. Julian, infra.*

Gihon, Albert Leary. *Pa.*, 1833——. A United States naval surgeon. Practical Suggestions in Naval Hygiene; Need of Sanitary Reform in Ship Life; Sanitary Commonplaces Applied to the Navy; Prevention of Venereal Disease by Legislation.

Gilbert, Benjamin. *Pa.*, 1711–1780. A miller of Northumberland, Pennsylvania, who wrote on theological themes. Truth Defended; Discourses on Perfection; Further Discourses on Sin, Election, Reprobation, and Baptism.

Gilbert, Charles Henry. *Il.*, 1859——. An ichthyologist, professor of zoölogy at Stanford University. Synopsis of the Fishes of North America (with D. S. Jordan).

Gilbert, David McConaughy. *Pa.*, 1836——. A Lutheran clergyman of Virginia. The Lutheran Church in Virginia, 1776–1876; The Synod of Virginia; The Annihilation Theory Briefly Examined; Muhlenberg's Ministry in Virginia.

Gilbert, Grove Karl. *N. Y.*, 1843——. A geologist attached to the United States Geological Survey. Geology of the Henry Mountains; Topographical Features of Lake Shores; Geology of Nevada, Utah, etc.; Lake Bonneville.

Gilder, Richard Watson. *N. J.*, 1844——. A writer of New York City well known both as a poet and as the editor of The Century Magazine, of which, with its predecessor, Scribner's Monthly, he has been editor-in-chief since 1881. The New Day, The Poet and his Master, Lyrics; The Celestial Passion; Two Worlds; The Great Remembrance, and Other Poems; Five Books of Song (1894), include all of his collected poems up to the year of issue. *Cent.*

Gilder, William Henry. *Pa.*, 1835——. Brother of R. W. Gilder, *supra.* An Arctic explorer. Schwatka's Search; Ice Pack and Tundra. *Scr.*

Gildersleeve, Basil Lanneau. *S. C.*, 1831——. A professor of Greek at Johns Hopkins University from 1876, and editor of the American Journal of Philology from its establishment. He is the author of Essays and Studies, and has published a Latin Grammar, and editions of Justin Martyr and the Odes of Pindar. *Gi. Har.*

Giles, Chauncey. 1813–1893. A Swedenborgian clergyman of Philadelphia, and of much prominence in his denomination. The Nature of Spirit; The Second Coming of our Lord; Perfect Prayer; Man as a Spiritual Being; The Incarnation; The Wonderful Pocket; The Magic Spectacles, a fairy tale; The Gate of Pearl; The Magic Shoes, and Other Stories; Heavenly Blessedness; The New Jerusalem; The Spiritual World; The Valley of the Diamonds, and Other Stories. *Lip.*

Giles, Ella Augusta. *Wis.*, 1851——. A writer of Madison, Wisconsin. Bachelor Ben; Out from the Shadows; Maiden Rachel; Flowers of the Spirit (verse). *See Bibliography of Wisconsin.*

Giles, Henry. *I.*, 1809–1882. A Unitarian minister of Liverpool, England, and after 1840 a literary lecturer in the United States. Lectures and Essays;

Christian Thought on Life; Illustrations of Genius; Human Life in Shakespeare; Lectures on the Irish, and Other Subjects. *See Hart's American Literature.*

Gill, Theodore Nicholas. *N. Y.*, 1837——. A naturalist, professor of zoölogy in the Columbian University, Washington, District of Columbia. Arrangement of the Families of Mollusks; Arrangement of the Families of Fishes; Arrangement of the Families of Mammals; Catalogue of the Fishes of the East Coast of North America; Scientific and Popular Views of Nature Contrasted.

Gill, William Fearing. 18——. The Martyred Church (verse); Home Recreations; Life of Poe.

Gill, William Ireland. 18——. Evolution and Progress; Analytical Processes; Christian Conception and Experience.

Gillespie, George. *S.*, 1683–1760. A Presbyterian clergyman, once prominent in Delaware. Treatise Against Deists and Free Thinkers; Letters to the Presbytery of New-York; Remarks upon Mr. George Whitefield.

Gillespie, William Mitchell. *N. Y.*, 1816–1868. A professor of civil engineering at Union College, 1845–68. Rome as seen by a New Yorker; Roads and Railroads; Manual for Road-making; Principles and Practice of Land Surveying; Levelling; Topography and Higher Surveying; Philosophy of Mathematics (from Comte). *Ap.*

Gillet, Ransom H——. *N. Y.*, 1800–1876. A lawyer of Ogdensburg, New York. History of the Democratic Party; The Federal Government; Life of Silas Wright.

Gillett [jĭl-lĕt'], **Ezra Hall.** *Ct.*, 1823–1875. A Presbyterian clergyman of New York city, professor of political economy in the University of New York from 1868. History of the Presbyterian Church in the United States; Life of John Huss; God in Human Thought; The Moral System; Life Lessons in the School of Christianity; What Then? or the Soul's To-Morrow; Ancient Cities and Empires. *Scr.*

Gillette, Mrs. L—— Fidelia [Woolley]. *N. Y.*, 1827——. A Universalist minister who published Pebbles from the Shore (verse); Editorials and Other Waifs.

Gillette, William Hooker. *Ct.*, 1853——. An actor and playwright, among whose plays are Held by the Enemy; The Professor; Esmeralda; The Private Secretary.

Gilliss, James Melville. *D. C.*, 1811–1865. An astronomer of distinction in charge of the naval observatory at Washington. United States Astronomical Expedition to the Southern Hemisphere; Observations at the Naval Observatory. *Lip.*

Gillmore, Quincy Adams. *O.*, 1825–1888. A military engineer in charge of the Federal bombardment of Charleston in 1863. He was a major-general of volunteers in the Civil War, and a high authority on engineering matters. Siege and Reduction of Fort Pulaski; Limes, Hydraulic Cements, and Mortars; Engineer and Artillery Operations Against the Defences of Charleston; Compressive Strength, etc., of Building Stones of the United States.

Gilman, Arthur. *Il.*, 1837——. An educator of Cambridge, and the organizer of Radcliffe College (long known as "the Harvard Annex"). First Steps in English Literature; Seven Historic Ages; First Steps in English History; History of the American People; Rome from the Earliest Times; Tales of the Pathfinders; Short Stories from the Dictionary; The Saracens; Colonization of America; The Discovery of America; The Making of the American Nation. He has also edited the Riverside Chaucer. *Lo.*

Gilman, Mrs. Caroline [Howard]. *Ms.*, 1794–1888. Wife of S. Gilman, *infra.* A writer whose married life was passed in Charleston. Among her writings are included Recollections of a Southern Matron; Recollections of a New England Housekeeper; The Sibyl, or New Oracles from the Poets; Verses of a Lifetime; Poetry of Travelling in the United States; Ruth Raymond; Stories and Poems. *Le.*

Gilman, Chandler Robbins. *O.*, 1802–1865. A physician of New York City, professor from 1841 in the College of Physicians and Surgeons. Legends of a Log Cabin; Life on the Lakes; Life of J. B. Beck, *supra;* The Relations of the Medical to the Legal Profession; Tracts on Generation.

Gilman, Daniel Coit. *Ct.*, 1831——. An educator of prominence, President of Johns Hopkins University from 1875. Our National Schools in Science; Life of James Monroe.

Gilman, Nicholas Paine. *Il.*, 1849——. A Unitarian clergyman, formerly of Massachusetts, prominent as a writer upon economics and since 1895 professor of sociology at the Meadville Theological Seminary. Profit Sharing between Employer and Employee; The Laws of Daily Conduct; Socialism and the American Spirit. *Hou.*

Gilman, Samuel. *Ms.*, 1791–1858. A Unitarian clergyman of Charleston, 1819–58. He published Memoirs of a New England Choir; The History of a Ray of Light; Pleasures and Pains of a Student's Life; Contributions to Literature, and was the author of the noted college song, "Fair Harvard."

Gilman, Mrs. Stella [Scott]. *Al.*, 18——. Wife of A. Gilman, *supra.* Mothers in Council.

Gilmer, George Rockingham. *Ga.*, 1790–1859. A Georgia lawyer who was governor of his State, 1829–31, and three times a representative in Congress. The Georgians, an historical work (1855).

Gilmore, James Roberts. "Edmund Kirke." *Ms.*, 1823——. In earlier life a shipping merchant in New York city, but during and since the Civil War a journalist and miscellaneous writer. Among the Pines; My Southern Friends; Down in Tennessee; Life of Garfield; Among the Guerillas; Adrift in Dixie; On the Border; Patriot Boys; The Rear Guard of the Revolution; John Sevier as a Commonwealth Builder; The Advance Guard of Western Civilization. *See Hart's American Literature. Ap.*

Gilmore, Joseph Henry. *Ms.*, 1834——. A Baptist minister of Rochester, New York, professor of rhetoric in the University of Rochester since 1867. Outlines of the Art of Expression; Outlines of Logic; English Language and its Early Literature; English Literature; He Leadeth Me, and Other Poems.

Gilpin, Henry Dilwood. *E.*, 1801–1860. Son of J. Gilpin, *infra.* A jurist of Pennsylvania who was attorney-general of the United States, 1840–41. He edited The Atlantic Souvenir, the first American literary annual, and published Reports of Cases in the United States District Court for Eastern Pennsylvania; Opinions of the Attorneys-General. He also edited the Papers of President Madison in three volumes.

Gilpin, Joshua. *Pa.*, 1765–1840. A Philadelphia writer who published Verses at the Fountain of Vaucluse; Farm of Virgil, and Other Poems; Memoir on a Canal from the Chesapeake to the Delaware.

Girard, Charles. *F.*, 1822——. A naturalist who came to the United States with Agassiz in 1847. Life in its Physical Aspects; Contributions to the Fauna of Chili; Herpetology of the Wilkes Expedition, are his more important publications. *Lip.*

Girardeau, John L. *S. C.*, 1825——. A Presbyterian clergyman of South Carolina, professor of systematic theology in Columbia Theological Seminary from 1876. Calvinism and Evangelical Arminianism Compared; The Will in its Theological Relations.

Gladden, Washington. *Pa.*, 1836——. A Congregational clergyman of Columbus, Ohio, of prominence as a writer upon social reforms. The Lord's Prayers: Seven Homilies; The Christian League of Connecticut; Things New and Old; Amusements, their Uses and Abuses; Plain Thoughts on the Art of Living; From the Hub to the Hudson; Being a Christian; Working-People and their Employers; The Christian Way; The Young Man and the Church; Applied Christianity; Parish Problems; Tools and the Man; Who Wrote the Bible?; Ruling Ideas of the Present Age; The Cosmopolis City Club; Burning Questions, a volume of sermons. *Cent. Co. Hou.*

Glazier, Willard. *N. Y.*, 1841——. A captain in the Federal army during the Civil War. His works have been widely circulated, but are of purely ephemeral interest. Capture, Prison-

Pen, and Escape; Three Years in the Federal Cavalry; Battles for the Union; Heroes of Three Wars; Peculiarities of Great Cities; Down the Great River. *See Life by Owens, "Sword and Pen," 1881.*

Gleason, Mrs. Rachel Brooks. *Vt.*, 1820——. A physician of Elmira, New York, for many years in charge of the Gleason Sanitarium. She has published Talks to My Patients.

Glisan, Rodney. *Md.*, 1827——. A physician of Portland, Oregon, emeritus professor of obstetrics in Willamette University. Journal of Army Life; Modern Midwifery; Two Years in Europe.

Glyndon, Howard. *See Searing, Mrs.*

Gmeiner, John. *Bv.*, 1847——. A Roman Catholic priest of Milwaukee, professor of homiletics in St. Francis de Sales Seminary. Die Katholische Kirche in den Vereinigten Staaten; Sind wir den Weltende nahe?; Modern Scientific Views and Christian Doctrines Compared; The Spirits of Darkness and their Manifestations on Earth; The Church and the Various Nationalities in the United States.

Godfrey, Thomas. *Pa.*, 1736–1763. A lieutenant in the colonial militia who possessed much poetic ability, and was the first dramatic author in America. The Court of Fancy; Juvenile Poems on Various Subjects, with The Prince of Parthia, a Tragedy. *See Tyler's American Literature.*

Godkin, Edwin Lawrence. *I.*, 1831——. A prominent journalist of New York city. He came to America in 1856, and since 1865 has been editor of The Nation, and from 1881 of the Evening Post. Government; History of Hungary; Reflections and Comments; Problems of Democracy. *Scr.*

Godman, John D. *Md.*, 1794–1830. A physician and naturalist of Cincinnati and New York. A man of great natural gifts whose career was one of failure and disappointment. Rambles of a Naturalist; American Natural History; Irregularities of Structure and Morbid Anatomy; Anatomical Investigations. *See North American Review, January, 1835; Gross, Lives of Eminent American Physicians, 1861, and Autobiography, vol. 1.*

Godwin, Parke. *N. Y.*, 1816——. A journalist of New York city, the son-in-law of the poet Bryant, whose writings he has edited. He was long connected with the Evening Post, and was the editor of Putnam's Monthly Magazine, 1853–55 and 1867–70. Pacific and Constructive Democracy; Popular View of the Doctrines of Fourier; Vala, a mythological tale; Political Essays; History of France; Life of William Cullen Bryant; Out of the Past, a collection of essays; Commemorative Addresses; Handbook of Universal Biography (edited). *Har.*

Goebel, Julius. *G.*, 1857——. A philologist, professor at Leland Stanford Junior University from 1892. Ueber die Zukunft unseres Volkes in Amerika; Ueber Fragische Schuld und Sühne; Zur deutschen Frage in Amerika; Poetry in the Limburger Chronik.

Goff, Mrs. Harriet Newell [Kneeland]. *N. Y.*, 1828——. A noted reformer of Brooklyn and elsewhere, prominent in the temperance, woman-suffrage, and other movements. Was it an Inheritance?; Who Cares?; Episodes in the Life of Mary Campbell.

Gooch, Mrs. Fannie. *See Inglehart, Mrs.*

Good, James Isaac. *Pa.*, 1850——. A German Reformed clergyman and educator of Reading, Pennsylvania, professor in Ursinus Theological Seminary, 1890–93. Origin of the Reformed Church of Germany; Rambler Around Reformed Lands.

Goodale, Dora Reed. *Ms.*, 1866——. Sister of Mrs. E. G. Eastman, *supra*, and author with her in their childhood of Verses from Sky-Farm; Apple Blossoms; In Berkshire with the Wild Flowers. She has contributed much verse to The Century and other periodicals, and has also published Heralds of Easter. *Put.*

Goodale, Elaine. *See Eastman, Mrs. Elaine.*

Goodale, George Lincoln. *Me.*, 1839——. A botanist of prominence, professor of botany at Harvard University from 1878. The Wild Flowers of America; Physiological Botany;

Concerning a Few Common Plants; Useful Plants of the Future. *Wn.*

Goode, George Brown. *Ind.*, 1851–1896. An ichthyologist in the government service. Catalogue of the Fishes of the Bermudas; Annual Resources of the United States; Game Fishes of the United States; Beginnings of Natural History in America; Britons, Saxons, and Virginians; American Fishes, a popular treatise; Fisheries and Fishing Industries of the United States; Oceanic Ichthyology (with T. H. Bean). *Est.*

Goodell, William. *Malta*, 1829–1894. A Philadelphia physician, medical professor in the University of Pennsylvania, and author of Lessons in Gynæcology.

Goodhue, Bertram Grosvenor. *Ct.*, 1869——. An architect of Boston whose border designs and initials for book illustration are of notable excellence. Mexican Memories.

Goodenow, John M. *Ms.*, 1782–1838. An Ohio jurist who published American Jurisprudence in Contrast with the Doctrine of English Law.

Goodnow, Frank Johnson. *L. I.*, 1859——. A professor of administrative law in Columbia University from 1884. Comparative Administrative Law; Municipal Home Rule. *Mac.*

Goodrich, Aaron. *N. Y.*, 1807——. A Minnesota jurist, secretary of legation at Brussels 1861–68. He published A History of the So-called Christopher Columbus. *Ap.*

Goodrich, Charles Augustus. *Ct.*, 1790–1862. Brother of S. G. Goodrich, *infra*. A Congregational clergyman of Hartford. Lives of the Signers of the Declaration of Independence; History of the United States; View of Religions; Family Tourist; Great Events of American History; Outlines of Geography; Universal Traveller. He assisted his brother in the preparation of a number of works.

Goodrich, Chauncey Allen. *Ct.*, 1790–1860. A Congregational clergyman, professor at Yale University, 1817–60. He published Greek and Latin Lessons; A Greek Grammar; was the editor and reviser of Webster's Dictionary, and also edited Select British Eloquence, with careful critical notes. *Har.*

Goodrich, Frank Boot. "Dick Tinto." *Ms.*, 1826–1894. Son to S. G. Goodrich, *infra*. A dramatist and miscellaneous writer of New York city. The Court of Napoleon; Man upon the Sea; Tri-Colored Sketches of Paris; The Tribute Book; World-Famous Women; Women of Beauty and Heroism; History of Maritime Adventure. *Lip.*

Goodrich, Samuel Griswold. "Peter Parley." *Ct.*, 1793–1863. Brother of Charles A. Goodrich, *supra*. A once famous writer and compiler of Boston and New York. He published nearly two hundred volumes, mainly juvenile and educational, some of which achieved a wide popularity. Among them are, History of All Nations; Tales of Peter Parley about America; Recollections of a Lifetime, an autobiography. *See Allibone's Dictionary.*

Goodwin, Daniel. *N. Y.*, 1832——. A lawyer of Chicago. James Pitts and his Sons in the American Revolution; The Dearborns; The Lord's Table; Provincial Pictures.

Goodwin, Daniel Raynes. *Me.*, 1811–1890. An Episcopal clergyman who was a professor in the Philadelphia Divinity School, and of much prominence as a Low Churchman. Southern Slavery in its Present Aspects; Christianity Neither Ascetic nor Fanatic; The Christian Ministry; Shall we Return to Rome?; The Perpetuity of the Sabbath; The New Ritualistic Divinity; Christian Eschatology. *See Bibliography of Maine.*

Goodwin, Mrs. Hannah Elizabeth [Bradbury]. *Ms.*, 1827–1893. A Boston writer for young people, among whose works are Madge; Christine's Fortune; Dorothy Gray; Dr. Howells's Family; Fortunes of Miss Follen. *Ap.*

Goodwin, Isaac. *Ms.*, 1786–1832. A writer of Worcester, Massachusetts, and the father of Mrs. Jane Goodwin Austin, *supra*. History of the Town of Stirling; The Town Officer; The New England Sheriff.

Goodwin, John Abbott. *Ms.*, 1824–1884. Son of I. Goodwin, *supra*. A Lowell writer who published The Pilgrim Fathers Neither Puritans nor Persecutors; The Pilgrim Republic, an historical review of the Plymouth colony. *Hou.*

Goodwin, Mrs. Lavinia Stella [Tyler]. *Vt.*, 1833——. The Mysterious Miner; The Little Helper; Little Folks' Own. *Le.*

Goodwin, Mrs. Maud [Wilder]. *N. Y.*, 1856——. An historical novelist of New York city. The Colonial Cavalier, or Southern Life before the Revolution; The Head of a Hundred; White Aprons, an historical romance; Dolly Madison, a biography. *Lit. Scr.*

Goodwin, Nathaniel. *Ct.*, 1782–1855. A Hartford genealogist and probate judge. Genealogical Notes of Some of the First Settlers of Connecticut and Massachusetts.

Goodwin, William Watson. *Ms.*, 1831——. Nephew of I. Goodwin, *supra.* An eminent Greek scholar, Eliot professor of Greek at Harvard University from 1860. He has published Syntax of Moods and Tenses of the Greek Verb; A Greek Grammar. *Gi.*

Goodyear, William Henry. *Ct.*, 1846——. An art educator of New York city, the son of the noted inventor, Charles Goodyear. Roman and Mediæval Art; Renaissance and Modern Art; History of Art; The Grammar of the Lotus; Ancient and Modern History. *Bar. Fl.*

Gookin, Daniel. *E.*, *c.* 1612–1687. A colonial writer of Massachusetts, the friend of John Eliot, the "Indian apostle," and a man far in advance of the general sentiment of his time and country in regard to the treatment of the Indians. For the last thirty years of his life he was superintendent of the Indians in Massachusetts. His writings include Historical Collections of the Indians in New England; Account of the Doings and Sufferings of the Christian Indians in New England. The first of these remained in manuscript until 1792, and the second until 1836. *See Tyler's American Literature.*

Gordon, Adoniram Judson. *N. H.*, 1836–1895. A Baptist clergyman of Boston, pastor of the Clarendon Church from 1869 until his death. Grace and Glory; In Christ; Ministry of Healing; The Ministry of the Spirit; The Life that Now Is and That to Come; The Holy Spirit in Missions; Ecce Venit. *See Life of, by E. B. Gordon, 1896. Bap. Rev.*

Gordon, Archibald D. *I.*, 1848–1895. A dramatic critic and playwright of New York city. The Ugly Duckling; Is Marriage a Failure?; That Girl from Mexico, are among his plays.

Gordon, Armistead Churchill. *Va.*, 1855——. A lawyer of Staunton, Virginia, co-author with T. N. Page, *infra*, of a volume of verse entitled Befo' the War; Echoes in Negro Dialect; Congressional Currency. *Put.*

Gordon, Clarence. "Vieux Moustache." *N. Y.*, 1835——. A writer of Newburg, New York. His writings, intended for juvenile reading, include Christmas at Under Tor; Our Fresh and Salt Tutors; Two Lives in One; Boarding-School Days.

Gordon, George Angier. *S.*, 1853——. A prominent Congregational clergyman of Boston, pastor of the Old South Church from 1884. The Christ of To-Day; The Witness to Immortality in Literature, Philosophy, and Life; Immortality and the New Theodicy. *Hou.*

Gordon, George Henry. *Ms.*, 1823–1886. A lawyer of Boston who served as a brigadier-general in the Federal army during the Civil War. History of the Second Massachusetts Infantry; The Campaign of the Army of Virginia under General Pope; War Diary of Events in the War of the Great Rebellion; Brook Farm to Cedar Mountain. *Hou.*

Gordon, Julien. *See Cruger, Mrs. Julia.*

Gordon, M Lafayette. *Pa.*, 1843——. A Congregational clergyman and physician, formerly a missionary to Japan, and subsequently a professor in Dōshisha University, Kyōto. An American Missionary in Japan. *Hou.*

Gordon, Thomas F——. *Pa.*, 1787–1860. A Philadelphia lawyer and antiquarian. Digest of the Laws of the United States; History of Pennsylvania to 1776; History of New Jersey to 1789; History of America; Cabinet of American History; History of Ancient Mexico; Gazetteers of New York, New Jersey, and Pennsylvania.

Gordon, William Robert. *N. Y.*, 1811——. A Dutch Reformed clergyman of New York and New Jersey. Supreme Godhead of Christ; Particular Providence, A Threefold Test of Modern Spiritualism; The Peril of our Ship of State; Revealed Truth Impregnable; The Reformed Church in America; Christocracy (with J. T. Demarest, *supra*), include his principal writings.

Gore, James Howard. *Va.*, 1856——. A professor of mathematics in Columbian University, Washington, District of Columbia. Geodesy; Elements of Geodesy; and several annotated editions of German works for college study. *Gi. Hou. Wil.*

Gorgas, Ferdinand J—— S——. *Va.*, 1834——. A Baltimore dentist, professor in the College of Dental Surgery from 1860. Lectures on Dental Science and Therapeutics; Dental Materia Medica.

Gorrie, Peter Douglas. *S.*, 1813–1884. A Methodist clergyman of New York. Churches and Sects in the United States; Episcopal Methodism as it Was and Is; Lives of Eminent Methodists.

Gorringe, Henry Honeychurch. *W. I.*, 1841–1885. A United States naval officer who superintended the removal of the obelisk from Egypt to New York, and after leaving the navy engaged in ship-building. His only publication is a work on Egyptian Obelisks.

Gorton, David Allyn. *N. Y.*, 1832——. Descendant of S. Gorton, *infra*. A physician of Brooklyn. The Monism of Man, or the Unity of the Divine and Human; The Principles of Mental Hygiene; The Drift of Medical Philosophy; Neurasthenia. *Put.*

Gorton, Samuell. *E.*, 1592–1677. The founder of a small sect sometimes called "Nothingarians," which survived him for about a century. Simplicitie's Defence against Seven Headed Policy; An Incorruptible Key composed of the CX. Psalm; Saltmarsh Returned from the Dead; An Antidote Against the Common Plague of the World; Certain Copies of Letters. *See Life of, by L. G. Janes, 1896; Bibliography of Rhode Island.*

Goss, Warren Lee. *Ms.*, 1838——. A writer of Norwich, Connecticut, and more recently of Rutherford, New Jersey. The Soldier's Story of the Captivity at Andersonville; Jack Alden; Tom Clifton; Jed; Recollections of a Private. *Cr. Le.*

Gouge, William M——. *Pa.*, 1796–1863. A financial writer, for thirty years in the Treasury Department at Washington. History of the American Banking System (1835); Expediency of Dispensing with Bank Paper; Fiscal History of Texas.

Gough [gŏf], **John Ballentine.** *E.*, 1817–1880. A celebrated temperance lecturer. He came to America in 1829, fell into habits of dissipation, but reformed and signed the pledge in 1842. Entering into the temperance movement as a lecturer, he soon rose to fame. Autobiography (1846); Temperance Lectures; Sunlight and Shadow, or Gleanings from my Life Work; Temperance Dialogues; Platform Echoes. *See Life, by Carlos Martyn, infra.*

Gould [goold], **Augustus Addison.** *N. H.*, 1805–1866. Son of N. D. Gould, *infra*. A conchologist of Boston. System of Natural History; Mollusca and Shells; Olia Conchologia; The Mollusca of the North Pacific Expedition; The Invertebrata of Massachusetts.

Gould, Benjamin Apthorp. *Ms.*, 1787–1859. An educator of Massachusetts who published The Prize Book; Adam's Latin Grammar; and editions of Horace, Ovid, and Virgil.

Gould, Benjamin Apthorp. *Ms.*, 1824–1896. Son of B. A. Gould, *supra*. A distinguished astronomer, from 1868–1885 director of the Argentine Republic national observatory at Cordova, and subsequently a resident of Cambridge. Uranometry of the Southern Heavens; Trans-Atlantic Longitude as Determined by the Coast Survey.

Gould, Edward Sherman. *Ct.*, 1808–1885. Son of J. Gould, *infra*. A merchant and author of New York city. The Sleep Rider; The Very Age, a comedy; John Doe and Richard Roe, a tale of New York life; Classified Elocution; Good English.

Gould, Ezra Palmer. *Ms.*, 1841——. An Episcopal clergyman, professor of New Testament literature in the Philadelphia Episcopal Divinity School. Commentary on Corinthians; Notes on the Lessons of 1885.

Gould, Hannah Flagg. *Vt.*, 1789–1865. Sister of B. A. Gould, 1st, *supra.* A verse-writer of Newburyport whose work was simple in conception but not unpleasing. The Snow Flake and the Frost still find a place in anthologies, and afford a fair example of her style. Hymns and Poems for Children; The Golden Vase; The Youth's Coronal; Mother's Dream, and Other Poems; Diosma, poems original and selected; Gathered Leaves, a volume of prose. *See North American Review, October, 1835.*

Gould, James. *Ct.*, 1770–1836. A jurist of Connecticut who published The Principles of Pleading in Civil Actions.

Gould, John W* *Ct.*, 1814–1838. Son of J. Gould, *supra.* Forecastle Yarns; Private Journal of Voyage from New York to Rio Janeiro.

Gould, Nathaniel Duren. *Ms.*, 1781–1864. A musician and penman of Boston who published A History of Church Music.

Goulding, Francis Robert. *Ga.*, 1810–1881. A Presbyterian clergyman of Georgia whose Young Marooners on the Florida Coast, a tale for boys, has long been popular. Other works of his include Marooner's Island; Frank Gordon; Fishing and Fishes; Woodruff Stories; Little Josephine; Cousin Aleck; Adventures among the Indians; Boy Life on the Water. *Do.*

Gouley, John William Severin. *La.*, 1832——. A physician, professor in the University of New York. External Périneal Urethrotomy; Diseases of the Urinary Organs; Diseases of Man. *Ap.*

Graebner, Augustus L——. *Mch.*, 1849——. A Lutheran clergyman, professor in the Theological Seminary at St. Louis from 1887. Half a Century of Sound Lutheranism in America.

Grafton, Charles Chapman. *Ms.*, 1832——. The second Protestant Episcopal bishop of Fond du Lac, and, prior to his consecration in 1889, rector of the Church of the Advent in Boston. Vocation, or the Call of the Divine Master to a Sister's Life.

* A distinguishing initial only.

Graham, David. *E.*, 1808–1852. A lawyer of New York city. Practice of the Supreme Court of New York State; New Trials; Courts of Law and Equity in New York State.

Graham, John Andrew. *Ct.*, 1764–1841. A lawyer of Rutland, Vermont. Descriptive Sketch of Present State of Vermont (1797); Speeches; Memoirs of Horne Tooke.

Graham, Mrs. Margaret [Collier]. *Ia.*, 1850——. A California writer who has published Stories of the Foot-Hills. *Hou.*

Graham, Sylvester. *Ct.*, 1794–1851. A once well-known vegetarian and lecturer upon temperance. He advocated the use of unbolted wheat, since called Graham flour. Lectures on the Science of Human Life; Bread and Breadmaking; Philosophy of Sacred History.

Grahame, Nellie. *See Dunning, Mrs.*

Granbery, John Cowper. *Va.*, 1829——. A bishop of the Methodist Church South who published a Bible Dictionary.

Grant, Asahel. *N. Y.*, 1807–1844. A physician who was a missionary in Persia. The Nestorians, or the Lost Tribes. *See Memoir, 1847; Grant and the Nestorians, 1853.*

Grant, Robert. *Ms.*, 1852——. A lawyer of Boston well known as a littérateur; from 1893 a judge of probate and insolvency for Suffolk County, Massachusetts. He has written several satirical works, including The Little Tin Gods on Wheels; The Lambs; Yankee Doodle; and the juvenile tales, Jack Hall; Jack in the Bush. In fiction he has published Confessions of a Frivolous Girl; The Carletons; Mrs. Harold Stagg; An Average Man; The Knave of Hearts; A Romantic Young Lady; Face to Face; The Bachelor's Christmas, and Other Stories; The Opinions of a Philosopher; Reflections of a Married Man. Other works of his are, The Art of Living; The Oldest School in America. *Hou. Scr.*

Grant, Ulysses Simpson. *O.*, 1822–1885. The eighteenth president of the United States. He served in the Mexican War as lieutenant, and in the Civil War as major-general, 1861–64, and subsequently became lieutenant-general in command of the entire army. Report of the Armies of the United States; Personal Memoirs. *See Military Life of, by A. Badeau, supra; Life by J. G. Wilson; Appleton's American Biography. Cent.*

Gratacap, Louis Pope. *N. Y.*, 1850–——. A naturalist connected with the American Museum of Natural History in New York city who has published Philosophy of Ritualism, or Apologia Pro Ritu.

Graves, Mrs. Adelia Cleopatra [Spencer]. "Aunt Alice." *O.*, 1821–——. An educator of Tennessee. Life of Columbus; Poems for Children; Seclusarval, or the Arts of Romanism; Jephtha's Daughter, a drama.

Graves, James Robinson. *Vt.*, 1820–——. Brother-in-law of Mrs. A. C. Graves, *supra*. A Baptist clergyman of Nashville, prominent as a controversialist. The Great Iron Wheel, or Republicanism Backward; The Little Iron Wheel; The Intermediate State; Old Landmarks; Intercommunion of Churches; The Redemptive Work of Christ; The New Great Iron Wheel; Denominational Sermons; Parables and Prophecies of Christ.

Gray, Albert Zabriskie. *N. Y.*, 1840–1889. An Episcopal clergyman and educator, warden of Racine College, Wisconsin, 1882–88. Racine and her Labour of Love; The Land and the Life; Jesus Only, and Other Devotional Poems; Mexico as it Is. *Ran.*

Gray, Asa. *N. Y.*, 1810–1888. An eminent botanist of Cambridge, and one of the highest authorities in his department. He was professor at Harvard University 1842–88, and was in charge of the botanical garden at Cambridge. Elements of Botany, now called Structural and Systematic Botany; How Plants Grow; A Free Examination of Darwin's "Origin of Species;" Darwiniana; Natural Science and Religion; Manual of the Botany of the Northern United States; Synoptical Flora of North America; How Plants Behave; Field, Forest, and Garden Botany; Lessons in Botany; School and Field Book of Botany; Botany of the United States Pacific Exploring Expedition (1854); Scientific Papers selected by C. S. Sargent. *See Letters of, edited by Mrs. Gray. Am. Ap.*

Gray, Barry. *See Coffin, R. B.*

Gray, David. *S.*, 1836–1888. A journalist of Buffalo, on the editorial staff of The Courier, 1856–82. *See Letters, Poems, and Selected Writings.*

Gray, Elisha. *O.*, 1835–——. An electrician and inventor who has published Experimental Researches in Electric Harmonic Telegraphy.

Gray, Francis Calley. *Ms.*, 1790–1856. A Boston lawyer prominent as an enlightened patron of arts and education who published a work on Prison Discipline.

Gray, George Seaman. *N. Y.*, 1835–1885. A Presbyterian clergyman who, after retiring from the ministry, engaged in business in Cincinnati. Eight Studies of the Lord's Day. *Hou.*

Gray, George Zabriskie. *N. Y.*, 1838–1889. Brother of A. Z. Gray, *supra*. An Episcopal clergyman of Cambridge, dean of the Theological School, 1876–89, and prominent among Broad Church thinkers. The Scripture Doctrine of Recognition; The Children's Crusade: An Episode of the Thirteenth Century; Husband and Wife; The Church's Certain Faith. *Hou. Wh.*

Gray, John Chipman. *Ms.*, 1839–——. A lawyer of Boston. Royall professor of law at Harvard University from 1883. Restraints on the Alienation of Property; Rule against Perpetuities; Select Cases. *Lit.*

Graydon, Alexander. *Pa.*, 1752–1818. A citizen of Harrisburg who published Memoirs of a Life Passed Chiefly in Pennsylvania within the last Sixty Years (1811), a lively, entertaining autobiography.

Graydon, William. *Pa.*, 1759–1840. Brother of A. Graydon, *supra*. A lawyer of Harrisburg. Digest of the Laws of the United States; Justice and Constable's Assistant; Forms of Conveyancing.

Grayson, William John. *S. C.*, 1788–1863. A South Carolina statesman. Chicora, and Other Poems; The Hireling and Slave, a poem; The Country, a poem; Life of James Petigru. *Har.*

Greeley, Horace. *N. H.*, 1811-1872. A famous journalist of New York city, founder and editor of The Tribune. In 1872 he was the unsuccessful candidate of the Democratic party for the presidency. For a generation he was one of the most influential leaders of American public opinion. Letters from Texas; Glances at Europe; Essays in Political Economy; What I Know About Farming; The American Conflict; Recollections of a Busy Life. *See Lives by Parton, 1868; Reavis, Ingersoll; Appleton's American Biography.*

Greely, Adolphus Washington. *Ms.*, 1844——. An arctic explorer in the United States service. In 1887 he was appointed chief of the signal service corps, with the rank of brigadier-general, and was thus at the head of the Weather Bureau until its transfer to the Department of Agriculture in 1891. Three Years of Arctic Service; American Weather; Handbook of Arctic Discoveries; Explorers and Travellers. *Do. Rob. Scr.*

Green, Alexander Little Page. *Tn.*, 1806-1874. A Methodist clergyman of Nashville who was the author of The Church in the Wilderness.

Green, Anna Katharine. *See Rohlfs, Mrs.*

Green, Ashbel. *N. J.*, 1762-1848. A Presbyterian clergyman, president of Princeton College, 1812-22. Sermons from 1790 to 1836; Sermons on the Assembly's Catechism; History of Presbyterian Missions. *See Autobiography and Memoir by J. H. Jones, 1849. Ran.*

Green, Beriah. *N. Y.*, 1794-1874. A reformer and anti-slavery leader of Ohio and New York. History of the Quakers; Sermons and Discourses.

Green, Duff. *Ga.*, 1780-1875. A Washington lawyer and journalist. Facts and Suggestions; How to Pay off the National Debt.

Green, Francis Matthews. *Ms.*, 1835——. A United States naval commander. The Navigation of the Caribbean Sea; Telegraphic Determination of Longitudes; List of Geographical Positions.

Green, George Walton. *N. Y.*, 1854——. A New York city lawyer and politician. Repudiation.

Green, Horace. *Vt.*, 1802-1866. A physician of New York city, president of the New York Medical College, 1850-60. Diseases of the Air Passages; Pathology and Treatment of Croup; Surgical Treatment of the Polypi of the Larynx; Report of a Hundred Cases of Pulmonary Diseases.

Green, Jacob. *Pa.*, 1790-1841. Son of Ashbel Green, *supra*. A Philadelphia scientist who was professor of chemistry in Jefferson Medical College. Chemical Diagrams; Chemical Philosophy; Astronomical Recreations; Trilobites; The Botany of the United States; Notes of a Traveller; Diseases of the Skin.

Green, Joseph. *Ms.*, 1706-1780. A Boston loyalist, widely known in his day for his political lampoons and his ready wit. He went to England in 1775, and never returned. The Wonderful Lament of Old Mr. Tanner; Poems and Satires. *See Tyler's American Literature; Hart's American Literature.*

Green, Mrs. Julia [Boynton]. *N. Y.*, 1861——. A verse-writer of Rochester, New York, who has published Lines and Interlines.

Green, Rufus Smith. *N. Y.*, 1848——. A Presbyterian minister, president of Elmira College for Women since 1893. History of Morristown, New Jersey; Our Church at Work; The Christian Steward; Both Sides, or Jonathan and Absalom.

Green, Samuel Abbott. *Ms.*, 1830——. A physician and antiquarian of Boston. Groton during the Indian Wars; History of Medicine in Massachusetts; Groton Historical Series.

Green, Seth. *N. Y.*, 1817-1888. A noted pisciculturist, from 1870 until his death the superintendent of the New York Fish Commission. Trout Culture; Home Fishing and Home Waters; Fish Hatching and Fish Catching.

Green, William Henry. *N. J.*, 1825——. A Presbyterian clergyman, professor of biblical literature at Princeton College from 1851. The Pentateuch Vindicated; Grammar of the Hebrew Language; A Hebrew Chrestomathy; Argument of Job Unfolded; Moses and the Prophets; Newton Lectures for 1885; The Hebrew Feasts; The Higher Criticism of the Pentateuch; The Unity of the Book of Genesis. *Scr. Wil.*

Green, William Mercer. *N. C.*, 1798–1887. The first Protestant Episcopal bishop of Mississippi. His only publications were Lives of Bishop Ravenscroft and Bishop Otey.

Greene, Aella. *Ms.*, 1838——. A journalist of Springfield, Massachusetts. Rhymes of Yankee Land; Into the Sunshine, and Other Poems; Stanza and Sequel, and Other Poems; John Peters; Gathered from Life.

Greene, Albert Gorton. *R. I.*, 1802–1868. A lawyer of Providence who is chiefly remembered for his humourous poem, Old Grimes. He published Canonchet.

Greene, Asa. *Ms.*, 1788–1837. A bookseller of New York city of note among his contemporaries as a humourist. Life and Adventures of Dr. Dodimus Duckworth; Perils of Pearl Street; A Yankee Among the Nullifiers; A Glance at New York; Debtor's Prison; Travels of Ex-Barber Fribbleton in America.

Greene, Belle C. *See Greene, Mrs. Isabella.*

Greene, Charles Ezra. *Ms.*, 1842——. A professor of civil engineering in the University of Michigan from 1872. Graphical Method for Analysis of Bridge Trusses; Trusses and Arches; Notes on Rankine's Civil Engineering. *Wil.*

Greene, Charles Warren. *Ms.*, 1840——. Nephew of S. S. Greene, *infra.* A Massachusetts physician who has written upon natural science. Animals, their Homes and Habits; Birds, their Homes and Habits.

Greene, Edward Lee. *R. I.*, 1843——. A professor of botany in the University of California. Illustrations of West American Oaks; Flora Franciscanæ.

Greene, Mrs. Frances Harriet [Whipple]. *See McDougal, Mrs.*

Greene, Francis Vinton. *R. I.*, 1850——. A captain in the United States army who resigned in 1886. The Russian Army and its Campaigns in Turkey in 1877–78; Sketches of Army Life in Texas; The Mississippi, a military work; Life of General Greene. *Ap. Scr.*

Greene, George Washington. *R. I.*, 1811–1883. An historian who was professor of American history at Cornell University from 1872. Historical Studies; The German Element in the American War of Independence; Short History of Rhode Island; Historical View of the American Revolution; Life of General Nathanael Greene; Biographical Studies; History and Geography of the Middle Ages. *Hou.*

Greene, Homer. *Pa.*, 1853——. A story-writer of Honesdale, Pennsylvania. The Blind Brother; Burnham Breaker; Coal and the Coal Mines; The Riverpark Rebellion. *Cr. Hou.*

Greene, Mrs. Isabella Catherine [Colton]. *Vt.*, 1844——. A novelist and writer for young people, long a resident of Nashua, New Hampshire. A New England Conscience; Adventures of an Old Maid; A New England Idyl; The Hobbledehoy. *Lo.*

Greene, Nathaniel. *N. H.*, 1797–1877. A Boston journalist, postmaster of Boston 1829–40 and 1845–49. He published a translation of Sforzosi's History of Italy; Tales from the German; Tales and Sketches from the German, Italian, and French.

Greene, Samuel Stillman. *Ms.*, 1810–1883. An educator of Providence, professor at Brown University, 1851–83, who published Analysis of the English Language and several text-books on English Grammar.

Greene, Mrs. Sarah Pratt [McLean]. *Ct.*, 1858——. A writer whose first novel, Cape Cod Folks, was widely popular, while the fact that certain of the dramatis personæ were portraits of living people gave rise to much litigation. Her other works include Towhead; Some Other Folks; Peter Patrick; Vesty of the Basins. *Har.*

Greene, William Batchelder. *Ms.*, 1819–1878. Son of N. Greene, *supra.* In early life a member of the noted Brook Farm Community. He was subsequently a Unitarian minister, and during the Civil War served as colonel of a Massachusetts regiment. Remarks on the Science of History; Theory of the Calculus; Socialistic, etc., Fragments; Reflections and Modern Maxims. *Put.*

Greene, William Houston. *Pa.*, 1854——. A Philadelphia chemist, professor in the Central High School from 1880. Medical Chemistry; Lessons in Chemistry. *Lip.*

Greenhow, Robert. *Va.*, 1800–1854. A surgeon and scholar whose latest years were spent in California. History of Tripoli; History of Oregon and California (1840).

Greenleaf, Benjamin. *Ms.*, 1786–1864. An educator of Bradford, Massachusetts, who published a popular series of text-books on arithmetic and the higher mathematics.

Greenleaf, Jonathan. *Ms.*, 1785–1865. A Presbyterian clergyman of Brooklyn. Sketches of Ecclesiastical History of Maine; History of New York Churches; Genealogy of the Greenleaf Family.

Greenleaf, Moses. *Ms.*, 1788–1834. Brother of J. Greenleaf, *supra.* Statistical View of Maine (1816); Survey of Maine (1829).

Greenleaf, Simon. *Ms.*, 1783–1853. Brother of B. Greenleaf, *supra.* A distinguished jurist of Massachusetts, and professor of law at Harvard University from 1833 till his death. His greatest work, A Treatise on the Laws of Evidence, has passed into fifteen editions. His other writings include Origin and Principles of Freemasonry; Full Collection of Cases Overruled, etc.; Reports of Cases in the Supreme Court of Maine, 1820–31; Examination of the Testimony of the Four Evangelists by the Rules of Evidence. *See Bibliography of Maine.*

Greenough [green'o], **Henry.** *Ms.*, 1807–1883. An architect of Cambridge whose writings include the novels Ernest Carroll; Apelles and his Contemporaries, and various essays on art.

Greenough, James Bradstreet. *Me.*, 1833——. A professor of Latin at Harvard University from 1873, who has published with J. H. Allen, *supra*, a series of classical text-books. Other works of his are, Special Vocabulary to Virgil; The Queen of Hearts, a Dramatic Fantasia. *Gi.*

Greenough, Mrs. Richard. *See Greenough, Mrs. Sarah.*

Greenough, Mrs. Sarah Dana [**Loring**]. 1827–1885. The wife of the noted sculptor Richard Greenough. In Extremis, a Story of a Broken Law; Arabesques, four stories of the supernatural; Mary Magdalene, and Other Poems. *Rob.*

Greenwald, Emanuel. *Md.*, 1811–1885. A Lutheran clergyman of Lancaster, Pennsylvania. Order of Family Prayer; The Lutheran Reformation; The Baptism of Children; Meditations for Passion Week; Romanism and the Reformation; The True Church; Meditations for the Closet, include the most of his controversial and other writings. *See Life by Haupt, 1889.*

Greenwood, Francis William Pitt. *Ms.*, 1797–1843. A Unitarian clergyman of Boston, pastor of King's Chapel, 1824–43. History of King's Chapel; Sermons to Children; Sermons of Consolation; Sermons on Various Subjects; Essays; Lives of the Apostles; Miscellaneous Writings. *A. U. A.*

Greenwood, Grace. *See Lippincott, Mrs. Sarah.*

Greenwood, James M——. *Il.*, 1836——. An educator and school superintendent of Kansas City who has published Principles of Education Practically Applied. *Ap.*

Greer, David Hummell. *W. Va.*, 1844——. A prominent Episcopal clergyman of New York city of Broad Church views. The Preacher and his Place; From Things to God. *Scr. Wh.*

Greey [gree], **Edward.** *E.*, 1835–1888. An English writer of French descent who came to America in 1868, and was for many years a dealer in Japanese curios in New York city. His writings include the dramas, Vendome, and Mirah; Blue Jackets, a novel; The Golden Lotus; the juvenile tales Young Americans in Japan; The Wonderful City of Tokio; The Bear Worshippers of Yezo; and translations from the Japanese of the novels, The Loyal Ronins; The Captive of Love. *Le.*

Gregg, Alexander. *S. C.*, 1819–1893. The first Protestant Episcopal bishop of Texas. History of the Old Cheraws, an Account of the Indian Tribes in the Valley of the Pedee.

Gregory, Daniel Seeley. *N. Y.*, 1832——. A Presbyterian clergyman, president of Lake Forest University, Illinois, 1878–86. Christian Ethics; Why Four Gospels; Practical Logic; The Tests of Philosophic Systems; Christ's Trumpet Call to the Ministry. *Fu.*

Gregory, John Milton. *N. Y.*, 1822——. A Baptist clergyman and educator of Michigan and Illinois. Handbook of History; New Political Economy; The Seven Laws of Teaching.

Greylock, Godfrey. *See Smith, J. E. A.*

Griffin, Edward Dorr. *Ct.*, 1777–1837. A Congregational clergyman of Boston and elsewhere who was president of Williams College, 1821–36. Lectures in Park Street Church, Boston; Sixty Sermons on Practical Subjects. *See Recollections of, by P. Cooke, 1856.*

Griffin, George. *Ct.*, 1778–1860. Brother of E. D. Griffin, *supra.* A lawyer of New York city. Sufferings of Our Saviour; Evidences of Christianity; The Gospel its Own Evidence.

Griffin, Gilderoy Wells. *Ky.*, 1840——. A journalist who has been consul in Australia and elsewhere. Studies in Literature; Danish Days; Visit to Stratford; New Zealand, her Commerce and Resources; Life of George Prentice, *infra.*

Griffin, Solomon Bulkley. *Ms.*, 1852——. A journalist of Springfield, Massachusetts, who has published Mexico of To-Day (1886). *Har.*

√ **Griffis, William Elliot.** *Pa.*, 1843——. A Dutch Reformed clergyman, pastor at Schenectady 1877–86, in charge of the Shawmut Congregational Church in Boston 1886–92, and subsequently settled at Ithaca, New York. An authority upon Japanese topics. The Mikado's Empire; Japanese Fairy World; Corea: the Hermit Nation; The Tokio Guide; The Yokohama Guide; Japan in History, Folk-Lore, and Art; The Religions of Japan; Brave Little Holland and What She Taught Us; The Lily Among Thorns, a biblical study; Life of Matthew Calbraith Perry; Sir William Johnson and the Six Nations; Townsend Harris, first American Envoy in Japan; Honda the Samurai: a Story of Modern Japan. *Do. Har. Hou. Scr.*

Griffith, Robert Eglesfield. *Pa.*, 1798–1850. A physician and botanist who was from 1838 a medical professor in the University of Virginia. Medical Botany; Universal Formulary.

Griffiths, John Willis. *N. Y.*, 1809–1882. A naval architect of New York city. Treatise on Marine and Naval Architecture, a work of great value; The Ship Builders' Manual; The Progressive Ship Builder.

Grimke [grim'ke], **Archibald Henry.** *S. C.*, 184——. A Massachusetts lawyer of African descent. Eulogy on Wendell Phillips; Charles Sumner, the Scholar in Politics; William Lloyd Garrison, the Abolitionist. *Fu.*

Grimke, Frederick. *S. C.*, 1791–1863. Son of J. F. Grimke, *infra.* An Ohio jurist. Ancient and Modern Literature; Nature and Tendencies of Free Institutions. *Clke.*

Grimke, John Faucheraud. *S. C.*, 1752–1819. A jurist of South Carolina. Revised Edition of Laws of South Carolina; Law of Executors of South Carolina; Public Law of South Carolina; Probate Directory; Duty of Justices of the Peace.

Grimke, Sarah Moore. *S. C.*, 1792–1873. Daughter of J. F. Grimke, *supra.* A reformer who was very prominent in the anti-slavery movement. Epistle to the Clergy of the Southern States; Letters on the Condition of Women.

Grimke, Thomas Smith. *S.C.*, 1786–1834. Son of J. F. Grimke, *supra.* A reformer of Charleston, active in temperance and in the promotion of peace societies, who published Addresses on Science, Education, and Literature.

Grimshaw, Robert. *Pa.*, 1850——. A civil engineer, lecturer on physics at the Franklin Institute of Philadelphia. History, etc., of Saws; Saw Filing; Steam Engine Catechism; Pump Catechism; Steam Boiler Catechism; Record of Scientific Progress; Hints to Power Users; Fifty Years Hence. *Bai. Cas. Wil.*

Grimshaw, William. *I.*, 1782–1852. A Philadelphia writer who published a once popular series of school histories, and also Etymological Dictionary; Gentlemen's Lexicon; Ladies' Lexicon; The American Chesterfield; Life of Napoleon. *Lip.*

Grinnell [grin'el], **George Bird.** *N. Y.*, 1849——. An ornithologist and the editor of "Forest and Stream" of New York city. He has enjoyed a long and friendly acquaintance with the Indians of the Great Plains. The Story of a Prairie People; The Story of the Indian; Pawnee Hero Stories and Folk Tales. *Ap. Scr.*

Grinnell, Josiah Bushnell. *Vt.*, 1821——. A distinguished citizen of Iowa; in early life a Presbyterian minister. He founded the Iowa town of Grinnell in 1854, and was president of Iowa College, formerly Grinnell University. It was to him that Horace Greeley is said to have made the famous remark, "Go West, young man, go West." Home of the Badgers; Cattle Industries of the United States; Men and Events of Forty Years. *Lo.*

Griscom, John. *N. J.*, 1774–1852. A once noted educator who was professor of chemistry at Rutgers College, 1812–28. A Year in Europe; Monitorial Instruction. *See Memoirs of, by his Son.*

Griscom, John Hawkins. *N. Y.*, 1809–1874. Son of J. Griscom, *supra.* An eminent physician of New York city. Animal Mechanism and Physiology; Prison Hygiene; Use and Abuses of Air; Use of Tobacco and Evils Resulting Therefrom; Physical Indications of Longevity. *Har.*

Griswold, Alexander Viets. *Ct.*, 1766–1843. Third Protestant Episcopal bishop of Massachusetts. Discourses on the Most Important Doctrines; The Reformation and the Apostolic Office; Remarks on Prayer Meetings. *See Memoirs, by J. S. Stone, infra.*

Griswold, Mrs. Frances Irene [Burge] [Smith]. *R. I.*, 1826——. A Brooklyn writer of Sunday-school tales, among which are The Bishop and Nannette Series; Miriam's Reward.

Griswold, Mrs. Harriet [Tyng]. *Ms.*, 1842——. In early life a school-teacher in Columbus, Wisconsin, who has published Apple Blossoms, a volume of poems; Home Life of Great Authors; Waiting on Destiny; Lucille and her Friends. Her poem, Under the Daisies, has had a wide popularity as a song. *Mg.*

Griswold, Rufus Wilmot. *Vt.*, 1815–1857. An industrious compiler and literary editor who possessed but a slight amount of critical insight and discrimination. His best known publications are, Female Poets of America; Prose Writers of America; Poets and Poetry of America; Sacred Poets of England and America. His other works include Washington and the Generals of the Revolution; The Republican Court; Scenes in the Life of the Saviour; Napoleon and the Marshals of the Empire (with H. B. Wallace, *infra*). *See Lowell's Fable for Critics. Ap. Co.*

Griswold, William Macrillis. *Me.*, 1853——. Son of R. W. Griswold, *supra.* A literary worker of Cambridge who has published A Manual of Misused Words, and many valuable indexes to periodicals.

Gronlund, Laurence. *Dk.*, 1847——. A lecturer upon socialistic topics in many cities of the United States. The Coöperative Commonwealth in its Outlines; Ca Ira, or Danton in the French Revolution; Our Destiny. *Le.*

Gross, Joseph B——. 18—1891. Brother of S. D. Gross, *infra.* A Lutheran clergyman, among whose writings are The Heathen Religion in its Symbolical Development; Teachings of Providence; Truth in Religion; Belief in Immortality on Purely Logical Principles; Old Faith and New Thoughts.

Gross, Samuel David. *Pa.*, 1805–1884. A distinguished surgeon of Philadelphia who was professor of surgery in Jefferson Medical College 1856–82, and a member of many medical associations in America and Europe. A System of Surgery; Lives of Eminent American Physicians and Surgeons of the 19th Century; Manual of Military Surgery; History of American Medical Literature; John Hunter and his Pupils; Pathological Anatomy; Wounds of the Intestines; Diseases of the Urinary

Organs. He also edited American Medical Biography. *See Autobiography, edited by his sons, 1887.*

Gross, Samuel Weissell. *O.*, 1837–1889. Son of S. D. Gross, *supra.* A surgeon of Philadelphia who succeeded his father as professor of surgery in Jefferson Medical College in 1882. Tumors of the Mammary Gland; Treatise on Impotence, Sterility, and Allied Disorders. *Ap.*

Grosvenor, Edwin Augustus. *Ms.*, 1845——. A professor of European History at Amherst College, and from 1873–90 professor of history at Roberts College, Constantinople. Constantinople. *Rob.*

Grote, Augustus Radcliffe. 18——. A scientist, formerly of Buffalo, but now (1897) living in Bremen, Germany. Notes on the Bombycidæ of Cuba; Notes on the Sphingidæ of Cuba; Notes on the Zygænidæ of Cuba; Genesis; The New Infidelity; Notes of the Lepidoptera of America (with C. T. Robinson); Rip Van Winkle, a Sun Myth, and Other Poems.

Grubé, Bernhard Adam. *G.*, 1715–1808. A Moravian missionary who came to America in 1746 and settled in Pennsylvania. He published Delaware Indian Hymn Book; Harmony of the Gospels.

Grund, Francis Joseph. *Bo.*, 1805–1863. A journalist of Philadelphia who published Exercises in Arithmetic; Americans in their Moral, Religious, and Social Relations; Aristocracy in America; Life of General Harrison (in German); Thoughts and Reflections on the Present Position of Europe (1860).

Guernsey, Alfred Hudson. *Vt.*, 1825——. A writer of New York city, at one period editor of Harper's Monthly. The Spanish Armada; The World's Opportunities; Carlyle, his Life, Books, and Theories; Emerson, Poet and Philosopher. *Ap.*

Guernsey, Clara Florida. *N. Y.*, 1836——. A Rochester writer of juvenile tales, among which are, The Boys of Eaglewood School; The Silver Library; Friends in Need; The Merman and the Figure Head. *Lip.*

Guernsey, Egbert. *Ct.*, 1823——. A homœopathic physician of New York city, editor of The Medical Times from 1872. History of the United States; Homœopathic Domestic Practice; The Gentleman's Book of Homœopathy.

Guernsey, Henry Newell. *Vt.*, 1817–1885. A homœopathic physician of Philadelphia. Application of Homœopathy to Obstetrics; Plain Talks on Avoided Subjects; The Keynote System; Obstetrics and Diseases of Women and Children; Lectures on Materia Medica.

Guernsey, Lucy Ellen. *N. Y.*, 1826——. Sister of C. F. Guernsey, *supra.* A writer of Rochester, New York, who has published more than fifty juvenile tales, some of which are, Old Stanfield House; Through Unknown Ways; Winifred; Agnes Warrington's Mistake. *Do.*

Guernsey, Rocellus S. 18——. Juries and Physicians on Insanity; Mechanics' Lien Laws for New York city; Municipal Law and its Relations to the Constitution of Man; Key to Story's "Equity Jurisprudence;" Living Authors at the New York Bar; Suicide, a History of the Penal Laws Relating to It; New York City and Vicinity during the War of 1812.

Guild, Mrs. Caroline Snowden [Whitmarsh]. *Ms.*, 1827——. A religious writer of Boston. Violet; Daisy; Never Mind the Face; Some House Songs. Compiler of Hymns of the Ages; Prayers of the Ages.

Guild, Curtis. *Ms.*, 1828——. A journalist of Boston, founder and editor of The Commercial Bulletin. Over the Ocean, a popular book of travels; Abroad Again; Britons and Muscovites; From Sunrise to Sunset, a volume of verse; A Chat About Celebrities. *Le.*

Guild, Reuben Aldridge. *Ms.*, 1822——. A librarian of Brown University, 1848–93. Librarian's Manual; Rhode Island in the Continental Congress (edited); History of Brown University; Chaplain Smith and the Baptists; Footprints of Roger Williams; Roger Williams, the Pioneer Missionary to the Indians.

Guiney [gĭ'nĭ], **Louise Imogen.** *Ms.*, 1861——. A writer of Newton, Massachusetts, whose published works include

Goose-Quill Papers; Brownies and Bogles; Three Heroines of New England Romance (with Mrs. Spofford and Alice Brown); Monsieur Henri, a Footnote to French History; A Little English Gallery; Lovers' Saint Ruths, and Three Other Tales; Patrins, a collection of essays; Verse: Songs at the Start; The White Sail; A Roadside Harp. She has edited the select poems of Mangan, with a study of his life and work. *Cop. Har. Hou. Lam. Lo. Rob.*

Gummere [gŭm'ery], **Francis Barton.** *N. J.*, 1855——. A professor of English in Haverford College, Pennsylvania. The Anglo-Saxon Metaphor; Handbook of Poetics; Germanic Origins, a study in Primitive Culture. *Gi. Scr.*

Gummere, John. *Pa.*, 1784–1845. A once noted educator of Burlington, New Jersey. Treatise on Surveying; Theoretical and Practical Astronomy.

Gummere, Samuel R. *Pa.*, 1789–1866. Brother of J. Gummere, *supra*, and also an educator of Burlington. Treatise on Geography; Compendium of Elocution.

Gunnison, Almon. *Me.*, 1844——. A Universalist clergyman of prominence. Rambles Overland, a Trip Across the Continent; Wayside and Fireside Rambles.

Gunnison, Elisha Norman. *Ms.*, 1837–1880. A journalist of York, Pennsylvania, who published One Summer Dream, and Other Poems; Our Stars.

Gunnison, John Williams. *N. H.*, 1812–1853. A civil engineer killed by Mormons and Indians while making railway surveys in Utah. A History of the Mormons was his only published work.

Gunsaulus, Frank Wakeley. *O.*, 1856——. A Congregational clergyman of Chicago. The Metamorphosis of a Creed; The Transfiguration of Christ; Monk and Knight, an Historical Study in Fiction; Phidias, and Other Poems; October at Eastwood; Songs of Night and Day. *Hou. Mg.*

Gunter, Archibald Clavering. 18———. A writer of popular sensational romances quite destitute of literary merit. Mr. Barnes of New York; Mr. Potter of Texas; The First of the English; The Ladies' Juggernaut.

Gurowski, Adam. *Po.*, 1805–1866. A Polish count who came to the United States in 1849, and was employed as a translator in the state department at Washington. La Civilisation et la Russie; Pensées sur l'Avenir des Polonais; Aus meinem Gedankenbuche; Eine Tour durch Belgien; Impressions et Souvenirs; Die letzen Ereignisse in den drei Theilen des alten Polen; Le Panslavisme; Russia as It Is; The Turkish Question; A Year of the War (1855); America and Europe; Slavery in History; My Diary, 1861–66.

Gurteen, Stephen Humphreys Villiers. *E.*, 1840——. An Episcopal clergyman of Buffalo, Toledo, and elsewhere, prominent as an organizer of charities. Phases of Charity; Provident Schemes; What is Charity Organization; How Paupers are Made; Casuistry; The Arthurian Epic; Epic of the Fall of Man. *Put.*

Gustafson, Axel. "Carl Johan." *Sn.*, c. 1847——. A Swedish writer who came to the United States in 1868, and has published The Foundation of Death: a Study of The Drink Question; The Drink Problem; Some Thoughts on Moderation. *Fu.*

Gustafson, Mrs. Zadel [Barnes] [Buddington]. *Ct.*, 1841——. Wife of A. Gustafson, *supra*. Meg: a Pastoral, and Other Poems; Can the Old Love? a novel; Genevieve Ward, a Biography. *Le.*

Gutheim, James Koppel. *Wa.*, 1817–1886. A Jewish clergyman of New Orleans who published The Temple Pulpit, a volume of sermons; and a translation of Gratz's History of the Jews.

Guyot [gē-o'], **Arnold Henry.** *Sd.*, 1807–1884. A geographer of distinction who came to America in 1849, and from 1854 until his death was professor of geography at Princeton College. He was the founder of the Princeton Museum. Earth and Man; Creation, or the Biblical Cosmogony in the Light of Modern Science; Physical Geography; Social Economy. *See Memoir by J. A. Dana, supra. Scr.*

H

Habberton, John. *L. I.*, 1842——. A journalist of New York city whose first book, Helen's Babies, enjoyed a popularity out of all proportion to its literary merit. His subsequent writings include Other People's Children; The Barton Experiment; The Jericho Road; Who was Paul Grayson?; The Scripture Club of Valley Rest; The Bowsham Puzzle; Brueton's Bayou; Country Luck; Grown-Up Babies; Life of Washington; Some Folks; My Mother-in-Law; Mrs. Mayburn's Twins; The Worst Boy in Town; The Chautauquans; All He Knew; Honey and Gall; The Lucky Lover. *Fl. Fu. Har. Ho. Lip.*

Habersham, Alexander Wylly. *N. Y.*, 1826–1883. A naval officer who in later life was a tea merchant in Japan, and the author of My Last Cruise, an Account of the United States North Pacific Exploring Expedition. *Lip.*

Hackett, Horatio Balch. *Ms.*, 1808–1875. A Baptist clergyman, professor at Newton Seminary, Massachusetts, 1839–70, and from 1870 till his death professor in Rochester Seminary, New York. He was one of the American Revisers of the Bible, and editor of Smith's Bible Dictionary. A Commentary on the Original Text of the Acts of the Apostles is his chief work. Others are, Memorials of Christian Men in the War; Illustrations of Scriptnre by a Tour in the Holy Land. *See Memorials of, 1876.*

Hackett, James Henry. *N. Y.*, 1800–1871. A popular actor, noted for his impersonation of Falstaff. Notes and Comments on Shakespeare.

Hackley, Charles William. 1808–1861. An Episcopal clergyman who was professor of mathematics at Columbia College from 1843 until his death. Treatise on Algebra; Elementary Course in Geometry; Elements of Trigonometry.

Haddock, Charles Brickett. *N. H.*, 1796–1861. Nephew of D. Webster, *infra.* A professor of rhetoric at Dartmouth College, 1819–50, and chargé d'affaires in Portugal, 1850–54. He originated the railway system of New Hampshire, and also the system of common schools in that State. His Addresses and Miscellaneous Writings appeared in 1840.

Hadley, Arthur Twining. *Ct.*, 1856——. Son of J. Hadley, *infra.* A professor of political science at Yale University from 1886. Private Property and Public Welfare; Railroad Transportation, its History and Laws; Report on the System of Weekly Payments. *Put.*

Hadley, James. *N. Y.*, 1821–1872. A philologist who was Greek professor at Yale University, 1848–72. Lectures on Roman Law; A Greek Grammar; Elements of the Greek Language; Essays, Philological and Critical; Brief History of the English Language. *See The New Englander, January, 1873. Ap.*

Hageman, Samuel Miller. *N. J.*, 1848——. Grandson of S. Miller, *infra.* A Presbyterian clergyman who has published Once, a novel; and several volumes of poems, including Vesper Voices; Greenwood, and Other Poems; Silence; Saint Paul.

Hagen, Hermann August. *P.*, 1817–1893. An entomologist of prominence who came to Cambridge from Königsberg in 1870, and was professor of comparative zoölogy at Harvard University. Catalogue of Neuropterous Insects in the British Museum; Synopsis of the Neuroptera of North America; North American Astacidæ; Some Insect Deformities.

Hagen, Theodor von. *G.*, 1823–1871. A musician who came to New York city from Germany in 1854. Civilisation und Musik; Musikalische Novellen.

Hager, Albert David. *Vt.*, 1817——. A geologist, since 1877 librarian of the Chicago Historical Society. Geology of Vermont (with C. H. Hitchcock, *infra*); Economic Geology of Vermont.

Hager, Mrs. Lucie Caroline [Gilson]. *Ms.*, 1853——. A Massachusetts writer who has published Boxborough, a New England Town and its People.

Hagert, Henry Schell. *Pa.*, 1826–1885. A noted *nisi prius* lawyer of

Philadelphia. Poems, with Memoir by C. A. Lagen (1886).

Hague, Arnold. *Ms.*, 1840——. Son of W. Hague, *infra*. A geologist in the government service. Volcanoes of California, Oregon, and Washington; Volcanic Rocks of the Great Basin; Nevada, with Notes on the Geology of the District; Volcanic Rocks of Salvador; Crystallization in the Igneous Rocks of Washoe.

Hague, James Duncan. *Ms.*, 1836——. Son of W. Hague, *infra*. An engineer attached to the United States Geological Survey who has published a work on Mining Industry.

Hague, Mrs. Parthenia Antoinette [Vardaman]. *Ga.*, 1838——. A Florida writer. A Blockaded Family; Life in Southern Alabama during the Civil War. *Hou.*

Hague, William. *N. Y.*, 1808–1887. A Baptist clergyman of Boston and elsewhere. Christianity and Statesmanship; The Baptist Church Transplanted from the Old World to the New; Guide to Conversion; Home Life; Authority of the Christian Sabbath; Self-Witnessing Character of the New Testament; Ralph Waldo Emerson; Life Notes, or Fifty Years' Outlook. *Le.*

Haldeman [hŏl′de-man], **Samuel Stehman.** *Pa.*, 1812–1880. A professor of comparative philology in the University of Pennsylvania, 1869–81. Zoölogical Contributions; Analytical Orthography; Word-Building; Tours of a Chess Knight; Elements of Latin Pronunciation; Pennsylvania Dutch; Outlines of Etymology; Affixes in their Origin and Application; Rhymes of the Poets. *Lip.*

Hale, Benjamin. *Ms.*, 1797–1863. An Episcopal clergyman and educator, president of Hobart College, Geneva, New York, 1836–58. Introduction to the Mechanical Principles of Carpentry; Scriptural Illustrations of the Liturgy; Education in its Relations to a Free Government; Historical Notices of Geneva College (1849). *See Life of, by Malcolm Douglass, 1883.*

Hale, Charles Reuben. *Pa.*, 1837——. The Protestant Episcopal coadjutor bishop of Springfield, Illinois, with the title of Bishop of Cairo. The Mozarabic Liturgy; The Universal Episcopate; Speeches and Addresses.

Hale, Edward Everett. *Ms.*, 1822——. A prominent Unitarian clergyman of Boston, widely known as a writer, whose literary activity covers a wide field. Since 1856 he has been pastor of the South Congregational Church, and his influence in civic life has been extensive. As a writer of short stories he will, perhaps, be longest remembered, his work in this direction including The Man Without a Country; Ten Times One is Ten; In His Name; Mrs. Merriam's Scholars; His Level Best; The Ingham Papers; Four and Five; Crusoe in New York; Christmas Eve and Christmas Day; Christmas in Narragansett; Our Christmas in a Palace. Longer essays in fiction are, Margaret Percival in America; Mr. Tangier's Vacations; Ups and Downs; Philip Nolan's Friends; The Fortunes of Rachel. Other works of his are, Sketches in Christian History; Kansas and Nebraska; How To Do It; What Career?; Gone to Texas; Seven Spanish Cities; June to May, a collection of sermons; Boys' Heroes; The Story of Massachusetts; Sybaris and Other Homes; Sunday-School Stories on the Golden Texts of 1889; For Fifty Years, a collection of poems; A New England Boyhood, an autobiographic work; Chautauquan History of the United States; If Jesus Came to Boston. *See Vedder's American Writers. See, also, Hale, Susan. A. U. A. Cas. Fu. Lam. Rob. Scr.*

Hale, Edwin Moses. *N. H.*, 1826——. Nephew of Mrs. Sarah Hale, *infra*. A Chicago physician, professor in the Homœopathic College. Pocket Manual of Domestic Practice; Homœopathic Materia Medica; Treatment of Diseases of Women; Treatise on Cerebro-Spinal Meningitis.

Hale, Enoch. *Ms.*, 1790–1848. A physician in Boston, and a nephew of the patriot Nathan Hale. History of the Spotted Fever at Gardiner, Maine, in 1814; Typhoid Fever.

Hale, Horatio. *R. I.*, 1817–1896. Son of Mrs. Sarah Hale, *infra*. A lawyer and ethnologist of prominence who lived in Clinton, Ontario, from 1856.

Ethnology and Philology; Indian Migrations as Evidenced by Language; Report on the Blackfeet Tribes. He has edited the Iroquois Book of Rites.

Hale, Lucretia Peabody. *Ms.*, 1820——. Sister of E. E. Hale, *supra.* A writer who is best known by her humourous juvenile books. The Peterkin Papers; The Last of the Peterkins. Her other works comprise The Lord's Supper and its Observance; The Service of Sorrow; Sunday-School Stories for Little Children; Fagots for the Fireside, a collection of games; The Struggle for Life, a Story of Home; Art Needle Work; An Uncloseted Skeleton (with E. L. Bynner, *supra*); The New Harry and Lucy (with E. E. Hale). *Hou. Rob.*

Hale, Robert Beverly. *Ms.*, 1869–1895. Son of E. E. Hale, *supra.* Elsie and Other Poems; Six Stories and Some Verses.

Hale, Salma. *N. H.*, 1787–1866. Brother-in-law of Mrs. Sarah Hale, *infra.* A New Hampshire jurist who represented his State in Congress in 1816. History of the United States; Annals of the Town of Keene. *Har.*

Hale, Mrs. Sarah Josepha [Buell]. *N. H.*, 1788–1879. A once well-known writer of Philadelphia who was editor of The Lady's Book for forty years. It was largely through her influence that Thanksgiving became a national festival. Among her numerous books Woman's Record, a large biographical and critical work, is the most important. Others are, The Genius of Oblivion, and Other Poems; Northwood, a novel; Sketches of American Character; Traits of American Life; Flora's Interpreter; The Way to Live Well; Grosvenor, a Tragedy; Manners, or Happy Homes; Love, or Woman's Destiny, with Other Poems; The White Veil; The Judge, a drama; Three Hours, or the Vigil of Love; Harry Gray, a Sea Story; Alice Ray, a Romance in Rhyme. She also edited cookery books, compilations, annuals, and the letters of Madame de Sévigné and Lady Mary Wortley Montagu. *See Allibone's Dictionary. Har.*

Hale, Susan. *Ms.*, 1838——. Sister of E. E. Hale, *supra*, and co-author with him of the Family Flight series of travels for young people. She has also published The Life and Letters of Thomas Gold Appleton, *supra. Ap. Lo. Rob.*

Hall, Abraham Oakey. *N. Y.*, 1826——. A once prominent Tammany politician of New York city, of which he was at one time mayor. He was subsequently on the staff of The World, but for many years has lived in Europe. The Manhattaner in New Orleans; The Congressman's Christmas Dream; Ballads; Old Whitey's Christmas Trot, a story for the holidays. *Har.*

Hall, Arethusa. *Ms.*, 1802–1891. An educator in New England, and subsequently in the Packer Institute, Brooklyn. The poet Whittier was one of her early pupils. Manual of Morals; Life of Sylvester Judd; Memorials of S. Judd, Senior; Thoughts of Pascal, a translation. *See Memorial of, edited by F. E. Abbot, 1892.*

Hall, Arthur Crawshay Alliston. *E.*, 1847——. The third Protestant Episcopal bishop of Vermont. He was for many years in charge of the mission of the Cowley Fathers in Boston. Confession and the Lambeth Conference; Meditations on the Creed; Meditations on the Collects; The Example of the Passion.

Hall, Baynard Rust. *Pa.*, 1798–1863. An educator of New Jersey and New York. A Latin Grammar; The New Purchase of Life in the Far West, long a very popular book; Something for Everybody; Teaching a Science; The Teacher an Artist; Frank Freeman's Barber's Shop.

Hall, Benjamin Franklin. *N. Y.*, 1814–1891. A New York jurist, chief justice of Colorado, 1861–64. The Land Owner's Manual; The Republican Party; Methodism, its Source and Power.

Hall, Benjamin Homer. *N. Y.*, 1830–1893. Brother of Fitzedward Hall, *infra.* A lawyer of Troy, New York. College Words and Customs; History of Eastern Vermont; Bibliography of the United States: Vermont.

Hall, Charles Cuthbert. *N. Y.*, 1852——. A Presbyterian clergyman of New York city, pastor of the First Presbyterian Church, Brooklyn, 1877–97; from 1897 president of Union Theological Seminary. Does God Send

Trouble ?; Into His Marvellous Light; The Children, the Church, and the Communion; Qualifications for Ministerial Power; The Gospel of the Divine Sacrifice. *Do. Hou.*

Hall, Charles Francis. *N. H.*, 1821-1871. An Arctic explorer. The Arctic Regions; Life Among the Esquimaux; Narrative of the Second Arctic Expedition. *Har.*

Hall, Charles Henry. *Ga.*, 1820-1895. An Episcopal clergyman of Brooklyn, rector of Holy Trinity Church, 1869-95. Commentaries on the Gospel; Protestant Ritualism; Spina Christi; The Church of the Household; Valley of the Shadow.

Hall, Charles Winslow. 184——. A lawyer of Minnesota. Arctic Rovings; Twice Taken; Adrift in the Ice-Fields; Drifting Around the World. *Le.*

Hall, Christopher W. *Vt.*, 1845-——. A professor of geology and mineralogy in the University of Minnesota, at Minneapolis, from 1878, and dean of the College of Engineering, Metallurgy, and Mechanic Arts. He has written many valuable professional papers, and a History of the University of Minnesota.

Hall, Edward Henry. *O.*, 1831-——. Son of Mrs. Louisa Hall, *infra.* A Unitarian clergyman of Worcester, and subsequently of Cambridge. Orthodoxy and Heresy in the Christian Church; Lessons on the Life of Saint Paul; Discourses. *A. U. A. El.*

Hall, Edwin. *N. Y.*, 1802-1877. A Congregational clergyman, professor of theology in Auburn Seminary, 1854-77. The Law of Baptism; The Puritans and their Principles; Historical Records of Norwalk; Shorter Catechism with Proofs.

Hall, Fitzedward. *N. Y.*, 1825——. A philologist of distinction who was inspector of schools in India, 1846-62, and in the latter year became professor of Sanskrit in King's College, London. Recent Exemplifications of False Philology; Modern English; English Adjectives in -able with Special Reference to Reliable; Lectures on the Nyâya Philosophy; and several works in Sanskrit. *Scr.*

Hall, Mrs. Florence [Howe]. *Ms.*, 1845——. Daughter of Mrs. J. W. Howe, *infra.* A writer of Plainfield, New Jersey. Social Customs; The Correct Thing in Good Society. *Est.*

Hall, Frederick. *Vt.*, 1780-1843. An educator who was professor of chemistry in Columbian College, Washington, at the time of his death. He published Letters from the East and from the West.

Hall, Gertrude. 186——. A Boston writer of short stories and poems. Far From To-Day, a collection of strikingly original stories; Allegretto, a volume of verse; Foam of the Sea, and Other Tales; Verses. *Rob.*

Hall, Granville Stanley. *Ms.*, 1845-——. An educator of note, president of Clark University, Worcester, Massachusetts, from 1888. Aspects of German Culture; Hints Toward a Bibliography of Education (with J. M. Mansfield); How to Teach Reading.

Hall, Harrison. *Md.*, 1785-1866. Son of Mrs. Sarah Hall, *infra.* A scientist of Philadelphia who in 1815 published a work on Distillation that was much commended in its day.

Hall, Hiland. *Vt.*, 1795-1885. A jurist of Vermont and governor of that State, 1858-60, who wrote a History of Vermont to 1791.

Hall, Isaac Hollister. *Ct.*, 1837-1896. Son of E. Hall, *supra.* A lawyer and Oriental scholar, lecturer on New Testament Greek in Johns Hopkins University, 1884-96. He published American Greek Testaments, a critical Bibliography.

Hall, James. *Pa.*, 1744-1826. A Presbyterian clergyman in the Southern States. Narrative of a Most Extraordinary Work of Religion in North Carolina; Missionary Tour through the Mississippi and Southwest Country.

Hall, James. *Pa.*, 1793-1868. Son of Mrs. Sarah Hall, *infra.* Letters from the West; Legends of the West; Tales of the Border; Sketches of the West; Notes on the Western States; Life of General Harrison; History of the Indian Tribes (with McKinney); The Wilderness and the War Path; The Harpe's Head, a Legend of Kentucky; Romance of Western History.

See Allibone's Dictionary; Bibliography of Ohio. *Clke.*

Hall, James. *Ms.*, 1811——. A paleontologist of distinction, professor of geology at the Troy Polytechnic School from 1836, and State geologist of New York from 1837. Geology of the Fourth District of New York; Paleontology of New York; Geological Survey of Wisconsin; and many scientific monographs.

Hall, John. *Pa.*, 1806–1894. A Presbyterian clergyman, pastor of the First Church in Trenton, New Jersey, from 1841, among whose writings are, Translation of Milton's Latin Letters; History of the Presbyterian Church in Trenton; Forty Years' Familiar Letters of James W. Alexander, *supra;* Sabbath-School Theology.

Hall, John. *I.*, 1829——. A Presbyterian clergyman who came from Dublin to America in 1867, and became pastor of the Fifth Avenue Presbyterian Church in New York city. All the Way Across; The Chief End of Man; Familiar Talks to Boys; Questions of the Day; God's Word through Preaching; A Christian Home; Foundation Stones for Young Builders, include his principal writings. *Bar. Ran.*

Hall, John Elihu. *Pa.*, 1783–1829. Son of Mrs. Sarah Hall, *infra.* A lawyer and author of Philadelphia who edited The Portfolio, 1817–27. Memoirs of Eminent Persons; Practice and Jurisdiction of the Court of Admiralty; Life of Dr. John Shaw; Tracts on Constitutional Law. *See A. H. Smyth's Philadelphia Magazines, 1892.*

Hall, Mrs. Louisa Jane [Park]. *Ms.*, 1802–1892. A writer of Providence. Miriam, a dramatic poem; Joanna of Naples, a tale; Life of Elizabeth Carter. *See Griswold's Female Poets of America.*

Hall, Samuel Read. *N. H.*, 1795–1877. An educator of Vermont who organized the first training-school for teachers in the United States. The Instructor's Manual; Lectures on Education; Geography for Children.

Hall, Mrs. Sarah [Ewing]. *Pa.*, 1761–1830. A Philadelphia writer well known at one time as the author of Conversations on the Bible. Selections from her work were published in 1833, with Memoir by Harrison Hall, *supra.*

Hall, Thomas Mifflin. *Pa.*, 1798–1828. A Philadelphia littérateur. Son of Mrs. Sarah Hall, *supra.*

Hall, William Whitty. *Ky.*, 1810–1876. A physician of New York city, the founder of Hall's Journal of Health. Health and Good Living; Health and Disease as Affected by Constipation; Fun Better than Physic; Consumption; Sleep; Guide-Board to Health; Coughs and Colds; Health at Home; How to Live Long; Dyspepsia; Treatise on Cholera; Bronchitis and Kindred Diseases. *Hou.*

Hallam, Robert Alexander. *Ct.*, 1807–1877. An Episcopal clergyman who was rector of St. James's Church, New London, Connecticut, from 1835 till his death. Lectures on the Morning Prayer; Lectures on Moses; Sovereigns of Judah; Sermons; Annals of St. James's.

√**Halleck, Fitz-Greene.** *Ct.*, 1790–1867. A poet who was for many years a clerk in a New York banking-house, and subsequently confidential adviser to John Jacob Astor. His verse has grace and sweetness, but is wanting in positive qualities, and has already largely passed out of remembrance. Marco Bozzaris is his most famous poem. Fanny; Alnwick Castle, and Other Poems. *See Life and Letters, by Grant Wilson; Lowell's Fable for Critics; Bryant and his Friends; Appleton's American Biography.* *Ap. Cr.*

Halleck, Henry Wager. *N. Y.*, 1816–1872. A major-general who was general-in-chief of the armies of the United States, 1862–64. Bitumen, its Varieties, Properties, and Uses; Mining Laws of Spain and Mexico; Elements of International Law (1866); Treatise on International Law (1861); Elements of Military Art and Science. *See Appleton's American Biography.* *Lip.*

Halliday, Samuel Byram. *N. J.*, 1812–1897. A Congregational clergyman of Brooklyn, assistant of Henry Ward Beecher at Plymouth Church for nearly twenty years. The Little Street Sweeper; The Lost and Found, or Life Among the Poor; Winning Souls; The

Church in America and Its Baptisms of Fire (with D. S. Gregory, *supra*). *Fu.*

Hallock, Charles. *N. Y.*, 1834——. A journalist of New York city, founder of Forest and Stream. The Fishing Tourist; Camp Life in Florida; The Sportsman's Gazetteer; Our New Alaska. *Har.*

Hallock, Mrs. Julia Isabel [Sherman]. *Ct.*, 1846——. A Connecticut writer. Broken Notes from a Gray Nunnery, a study of country life. *Le.*

Hallock, Mrs. Mary Angelina [Ray] [Lathrop]. *Ms.*, 1810——. Wife of W. A. Hallock, *infra.* A writer of Sunday-school books, including That Sweet Story of Old; Child's History of the Fall of Jerusalem; Child's Life of Daniel; The Story of Moses; Bethlehem and her Children; Beasts and Birds; Child's History of Solomon; Life of the Apostle Paul.

Hallock, William Allen. *Ms.*, 1794–1880. A Congregational clergyman, secretary of the American Tract Society, 1825–70. Life of Harlan Page; Moses Hallock; Justin Edwards, *supra*, and several very popular tracts.

Hallowell, Richard Price. *Pa.*, 1835——. A wool merchant of Boston who has written The Quaker Invasion of Massachusetts; The Pioneer Quakers. *Hou.*

Halpine, Charles Graham. "Miles O'Reilly." *I.*, 1829–1868. A journalist of New York city who came to America in 1852 and served during the Civil War as a colonel in the Federal army. Lyrics; Poems; Miles O'Reilly Papers; Life and Adventures of Private Miles O'Reilly; Baked Meats of the Funeral. His Poetical Works, edited by R. B. Roosevelt, *infra*, appeared in 1869. *See Dictionary of National Biography, vol. 24; Appleton's American Biography. Har.*

Halsey, Leroy Jones. *Va.*, 1812——. A Presbyterian clergyman, from 1859 professor in Chicago Theological Seminary. The Literary Attractions of the Bible; The Life and Pictures of the Bible; The Beauty of Emmanuel; Living Christianity; Scotland's Influence on Civilization.

Halstead, Murat. *O.*, 1829——. A journalist of note, editor and proprietor of The Commercial of Cincinnati, and since 1890 of The Standard Union, Brooklyn. Caucuses of 1860; Life of William McKinley.

Halsted, Byron David. *N. Y.*, 1852——. An agricultural writer, since 1884 professor of botany in Iowa Agricultural College. A Century of American Weeds; The Vegetable Garden; Farm Conveniences; Household Conveniences.

Halsted, George Bruce. *N. J.*, 1853——. Grandson of O. S. Halsted, *infra.* A professor of mathematics in the University of Texas from 1887, and a mathematician of prominence. Metrical Geometry, a Treatise on Mensuration; Elements of Geometry; Synthetic Geometry; Number, Discrete and Continuous. *See Bibliography of Texas. Gi. Wil.*

Halsted, Oliver Spencer. *N. J.*, 1792–1877. A jurist of Newark, New Jersey. The Theology of the Bible; The Book called Job.

Ham, Charles Henry. *N. H.*, 1831——. A lawyer and journalist of Chicago. Manual Training: the Solution of Social and Industrial Problems. *Har.*

Ham, Marion Franklin. *O.*, 1867——. A verse-writer of Chattanooga. The Golden Shuttle, and Other Poems.

Hamersley, Lewis Randolph. *D. C.*, 1847——. A lieutenant in the United States marine corps. Records of Living Officers of the United States Navy and Marine Corps (1890); Naval Encyclopædia.

Hamilton, Alexander. *W. I.*, 1757–1804. A statesman who ranks as the ablest political writer of his day in America. In 1789 he became the first secretary of the United States Treasury, and his first Report on the Public Credit was one of the most notable of national state papers. He was the principal contributor to The Federalist, 51 of its 85 articles being by him alone, and he assisted Washington in preparing the latter's Farewell Address. *See Complete Works, including The Federalist, edited by H. C. Lodge, infra, 1885; Lives, by Williams, 1804; J. C. Hamilton, infra, 1840; Renwick,*

1841; Smucker, 1856; J. T. Morse, Jr., 1876; Shea, 1879; Lodge, 1882; Hamilton and his Contemporaries, Richtmueller; Shea's Historical Study of Hamilton; Bibliotheca Hamiltoniana, Ford, 1886. Ap. Put.

Hamilton, Alice King. 18——. A novelist. Mildred's Cadet; One of the Duanes. *Lip.*

Hamilton, Allen McLane. *N. Y.*, 1828——. A physician of New York city. Clinical Electro-Therapeutics; Nervous Diseases; Medical Jurisprudence; Types of Insanity; The Modern Treatment of Headaches. *Ap.*

Hamilton, Edward John. *I.*, 1834——. A Presbyterian clergyman, professor of philosophy in the State University of Washington. The general system of philosophy advocated by him is best defined by the term Perceptional. The Human Mind; Mental Science; The Modalist, or the Laws of Rational Thought; A New Analysis in Fundamental Modes, a short treatise in ethics. *Gi.*

Hamilton, Frank Hastings. *Vt.*, 1813–1886. A distinguished surgeon of New York city, for many years professor in Bellevue Hospital. Strabismus; Fractures and Dislocations; Military Surgery; Principles and Practice of Surgery; Surgical Memories of the War of the Rebellion.

Hamilton, Gail. *See Dodge, Abigail.*

Hamilton, James Alexander. *N. Y.*, 1788–1878. Third son of A. Hamilton, *supra*. A lawyer of New York city. Reminiscences during Three Quarters of a Century; Martin Van Buren's Calumnies Repudiated.

Hamilton, John Church. *Pa.*, 1792–1882. The fourth son of A. Hamilton, *supra*. A lawyer in New York city. Memoirs of Alexander Hamilton; History of the Republic; The Prairie Province. He edited his father's works.

Hamilton, John William. *W. Va.*, 1845——. A Methodist clergyman who founded the People's Church in Boston. Memorials of Jesse Lee; Lives of the Methodist Bishops; People's Church Pulpit.

Hamilton, Kate Waterman. "Fleeta." *N. Y.*, 18——. An Illinois writer of Sunday-school and other fictions. Among them are, The Old Brown House; Frederick Gordon; Wood, Hay, and Stubble; Rachel's Share of the Road, a Novel; The Parson's Proxy. *Hou.*

Hamilton, Robert S——. 18——. Present Status of Social Science; Present Status of the Philosophy of Society.

Hamilton, Schuyler. *N. Y.*, 1822——. Son of J. C. Hamilton, *supra.* A major-general in the Federal army during the Civil War. History of the American Flag; Our National Flag.

Hamlin, Alfred Dwight Foster. *Ty.*, 1855——. Son of Cyrus Hamlin, *infra*. An architect, professor of architecture in Columbia College from 1889. Handbook of the History of Ornament.

Hamlin, Augustus Choate. *Me.*, 1829——. A surgeon of Bangor. Martyria, or Andersonville Prison; The Tourmaline; Leisure Hours Among the Gems. *Hou.*

Hamlin, Charles. *Me.*, 1837——. Cousin of A. C. Hamlin, and son of Hannibal Hamlin, who was vice-president of the United States, 1861–65. He was an officer in the Federal army during the Civil War, and has published The Insolvent Laws of Maine.

Hamlin, Cyrus. *Me.*, 1811——. A Congregationalist missionary in Turkey, 1837–60, president of Robert College, Constantinople, 1860–76, and of Middlebury College, Vermont, 1880–85. Papists and Protestants; Arithmetic for Americans; Cholera and Its Treatment; Among the Turks; My Life and Times (1893). *C. P. S.*

Hamlin, Teunis Slingerland. *N. Y.*, 1847——. A Presbyterian clergyman of Washington. Denominationalism versus Christian Union. *Rev.*

Hamline, Leonidas Lent. *Ct.*, 1797–1865. A Methodist bishop prominent in Ohio. Sermons; Works, edited by F. G. Hibbard.

Hammett, Samuel A——. "Philip Paxton." *Ct.*, 1816–1865. A journalist of New York city. A Stray Yankee in Texas; The Wonderful Adventures of Captain Priest, are among his works.

Hammond, Anthony. 18——. Law of Nisi Prius; Parties to Actions; Principles of Pleading; Reports in Equity; Criminal Code: Forgery; Practice and Proceedings in Parliament; Index to Tennessee Reports; Criminal Code: Simple Larceny.

Hammond, Edward Payson. *Ms.*, 1831——. A noted evangelist who has been a prolific author of religious books and tracts. Among his hundred or more publications are, Good Will to Men; Sketches of Palestine; The Conversion of Children; Gathered Lambs. *See Reaper and Harvest, by P. C. Headley, infra. Fu. Rev.*

Hammond, Mrs. Henrietta [Hardy]. "Henri Dangé." *Va.*, 1854–1883. A Southern writer of fiction. The Georgians; A Fair Philosopher; Her Waiting Heart; Woman's Secrets, or How to be Beautiful. *Hou.*

Hammond, Jabez D. *Ms.*, 1778–1855. A jurist of New York State. The Political History of New York; Life of Julius Melbourn; Life of Silas Wright; Evidence of the Immortality of the Soul.

Hammond, James Henry. *S. C.*, 1807–1864. A South Carolina politician, governor of his State, 1842–47, and United States Senator, 1857–60. Owing to a speech of his in Congress in which the term "mudsills" was used, he was afterwards known as "Mudsill Hammond." He published The Pro-Slavery Argument.

Hammond, Marcus Claudius Marcellus. *S. C.*, 1814–1876. Brother of J. H. Hammond, *supra*. A United States army officer whose home was in South Carolina, and who published A Critical History of the Mexican War.

Hammond, William Alexander. *Md.*, 1828——. An eminent physician of New York city, surgeon-general of the United States army, 1862–64; now on the retired list as brigadier-general and surgeon-general. His medical writings include Military Hygiene; Physiological Essays; Sleep and its Derangements; Nervous Derangements; Physiological Memoirs; Lectures on Venereal Diseases; Wakefulness; Insanity in its Medico-Legal Relations; Physics and Physiology of Spiritualism; Diseases of the Nervous System; Insanity and its Medical Relations; Sexual Impotence in the Male; Cerebral Hyperæmia; Neurological Contributions. His novels include Robert Severne; Lal; Dr. Grattan; Mr. Oldmixon; A Strong-Minded Woman; On the Susquehanna. *Ap. Lip.*

Hanaford, Mrs. Phebe Ann [Coffin]. *Ms.*, 1829——. A Universalist minister, the first woman to enter the ministry in the Universalist denomination. Since 1887 she has been in charge of a church at New Haven. Life of Abraham Lincoln; Life of George Peabody; Lucretia the Quakeress; Leonette, or Truth Sought and Found; The Best of Books and its History; Frank Nelson the Runaway Boy; The Soldier's Daughter; Field, Gunboat, and Hospital; Women of the Century; The Captive Boy of Tierra del Fuego; Life of Dickens; From Shore to Shore, and Other Poems. *Mer.*

Hancock, Anson Uriel. 18——. The Genius of Galilee, an historical novel; John Auburntop, Novelist; Old Abraham Jackson, a Nebraska Story. *Ke.*

Hanson, Edgar Filmore. *Me.*, 1853——. Demonology or Spiritualism, Ancient and Modern.

Hanson, John Wesley. *Ms.*, 1823——. A Universalist clergyman, pastor of the Church of the Covenant, Chicago, 1869–84. Histories of Danvers, Norridgewock, and Gardiner, in Maine; Bible Threatenings Explained; Cloud of Witnesses, a compilation; Aion Aionos; Bible Proofs of Universal Salvation; Sermons on the Lord's Prayer; The Leaven at Work; The New Covenant, a translation of the New Testament.

Hapgood, Isabel Florence. *Ms.*, 1851——. A writer and translator of New York city. The Epic Songs of Russia; Russian Rambles; translations of Gogol and Victor Hugo. *Hou. Scr.*

Harbaugh [har'baw], **Henry.** *Pa.*, 1817–1867. A German Reformed clergyman of Pennsylvania, professor in Mercersburg Seminary, whose principal writings include Fathers of the German Reformed Church in Europe and America; The Heavenly Home; Christological Theology; The True Glory of Woman; Heaven, or the Sainted Dead; Birds of the Bible; The Golden Censer; Union with the Church.

Harbaugh, Thomas Chalmers. *Md.*, 1849——. A popular verse-writer of Casstown, Ohio, whose only published collection of poems is entitled Maple Leaves.

Harby, Isaac. *S. C.*, 1788–1828. A dramatist of Charleston whose plays include Alexander Severus; The Gordian Knot; Alberti. *See Life by H. L. Pinckney, 1829.*

Harby, Mrs. Lee [Cohen]. *S. C.*, 1849——. A New York writer, formerly of Texas, who has published Christmas Before the War. *See Bibliography of Texas.*

Hardee, William Joseph. *Ga.*, 1815–1873. A Confederate general who was the author of a well-known work on Rifle and Light Infantry Tactics. *See Southern Generals, by W. P. Snow.*

Hardie, James. *S.*, *c.* 1750–1832. An educator of New York city. Corderii Colloquia; Epistolary Guide; Freeman's Monitor; Wonders of Art and Nature, especially in America; Biographical Dictionary; Malignant Fevers in New York; Viris Illustribus Urbis Romæ; Description of New York City.

Hardy, Arthur Sherburne. *Ms.*, 1847——. A professor of mathematics at Dartmouth College 1878–93, well known both as novelist and mathematician. Elements of Quaternions; New Methods in Surveying; Elements of Analytic Geometry; Elements of Calculus; But Yet A Woman; The Wind of Destiny; Passe Rose; Joseph Hardy Neesima, a biography. *See London Academy, June 30, 1883. Gi. Hou.*

Hare, George Emlen. *Pa.*, 1808–1892. Son of R. Hare, *infra.* An Episcopal clergyman, professor of biblical learning in the Philadelphia Divinity School from 1852. Christ to Return; Visions and Narratives of the Old Testament, a volume of sermons. *Dut.*

Hare, John Innes Clark. *Pa.*, 1816——. Son of R. Hare, *infra.* A noted Philadelphia jurist. Treatise on Contracts; New England Exchequer Reports; American Constitutional Law. *Lit.*

Hare, Robert. *Pa.*, 1781–1858. A once prominent Philadelphia scientist who made a number of important discoveries, and contributed frequently to scientific journals. Brief View of Policy and Resources of the United States; Spiritualism Scientifically Demonstrated; Chemical Apparatus and Scientific Manipulations.

Hargrove, Robert Kenyon. *Al.*, 1829——. A bishop of the Methodist Church South from 1882. Laws of the Methodist Episcopal Church South as Interpreted by the College of Bishops.

Hark, J[oseph] Max[imilian]. *Pa.*, 1849——. A Moravian clergyman and educator of Bethlehem, Pennsylvania. The Unity of Truth in Christianity and Evolution. He has translated and edited from the German The Chronicon Ephratense.

Harkey, Sidney Levi. *N. C.*, 1827——. A Lutheran clergyman whose writings include The Signs of the Times; The Faith Once Delivered to the Saints; Thorough Education; Agnosticism; National Blessings and Dangers.

Harkey, Simon Walcher. *N. C.*, 1811–1889. A Lutheran clergyman of Illinois. True Wisdom Triumphant; Justification by Faith; The Church's Best State, are among his writings.

Harkness, Albert. *Ms.*, 1822——. An educator of Providence, professor of Greek in Brown University from 1855. He has published Complete Latin Course for the First Year, and many Greek and Latin text-books.

Harkness, James. *S.*, 1803–1878. A Presbyterian clergyman who emigrated from Scotland in 1839, and was a pastor in Jersey City, 1862–78. Messiah's Throne and Kingdom was his only published work.

Harkness, William. *S.*, 1837——. Son of J. Harkness, *supra.* A mathematician of distinction who has published Magnetic Observations on the Monadnock.

Harlan, George Cuvier. *Pa.*, 1835——. Son of R. Harlan, *infra.* A Philadelphia physician who has made a specialty of diseases of the eye, and is the author of Eyesight and How to Take Care of It.

Harlan, Richard. *Pa.*, 1796–1843. A physician and naturalist of Philadelphia. Observations on the Genus Salamandra; Fauna Americana; American Herpetology; Medical and Physical Researches.

Harland, Henry. "Sidney Luska." *N. Y.*, 1861——. A novelist of New York city who removed to London, and has there edited The Yellow Book. Grandison Mather; Mea Culpa; As It Was Written; Mrs. Peixada; The Land of Love; The Yoke of the Thorah; My Uncle Florimond; Grey Roses. *Cas. Rob.*

Harland, Marion. *See Terhune, Mrs.*

Harman, Henry Martyn. *Md.*, 1822–1897. A Methodist clergyman, professor in Dickinson College, Carlisle, Pennsylvania, from 1870. Journey to Egypt and the Holy Land; Introduction to Study of the Scriptures. *Meth.*

Harney, John Milton. *Del.*, 1789–1825. A Savannah journalist who became a Dominican monk. He published Crystallina, a fairy tale in verse, and his other poems appeared posthumously in periodicals.

Harney, William Wallace. *Ia.*, 1831——. A journalist and verse-writer of Florida whose poems have appeared in magazines and anthologies, but have not been gathered into book form.

Harper, Robert Goodloe. *Va.*, 1765–1825. A once noted South Carolina and Maryland statesman. Letters on the Proceedings of Congress; Letters to Constituents. His Select Works appeared in 1814.

Harper, William Rainey. *O.*, 1856——. A Baptist clergyman, president of the University of Chicago. Elements of Hebrew; Elements of Hebrew Syntax; Hebrew Vocabularies; An Introductory New Testament, Greek Method (with R. F. Weidner). *Scr.*

Harrigan, Edward. *N. Y.*, 1845——. An actor and playwright of New York city among whose many plays of low life in the metropolis are, Squatter Sovereignty; Cordelia's Aspirations.

Harriman, Walter. *N. H.*, 1817–1884. A New Hampshire politician, governor of his state, 1867–68, and during the Civil War a Federal officer. History of Warner, New Hampshire; Travels and Observations in the Orient. *See Life by Amos Hadley. Le.*

Harrington, Mark Walrod. *Il.*, 1848——. A scientist, professor of astronomy in the University of Michigan. The Analysis of Plants; Identification of Crude Drugs.

Harris, Amanda Bartlett. *N. H.*, 1824——. A writer whose life has been mainly spent at her birthplace, Warner, New Hampshire. Christ our Friend; Thy Will be Done; The Duty of Uniting with the Church; Summer's Autographs; How we went Birds'-Nesting, republished as Field, Wood, and Meadow Rambles; Wild Flowers and Where They Grow; Door-yard Folks; Pleasant Authors for Young Folks; American Authors for Young Folks; The Luck of Edenhall. She has contributed much to periodical literature, and has written reviews for The (Boston) Literary World from 1877. *Lo.*

Harris, Chapin A——. *N. Y.*, 1806–1860. A dentist of Baltimore, founder of the Baltimore Dental College. Principles of Dental Surgery; Characteristics of the Human Teeth; Diseases of the Maxillary Sinus; Dictionary of Dental Science.

Harris, George. *Me.*, 1844——. A Congregational clergyman of Massachusetts, professor of Christian theology in Andover Theological Seminary since 1883, and one of the editors of "The Andover Review," 1884–93. Editor (with W. J. Tucker and E. K. Glezen) of Hymns of the Faith. Author of Moral Evolution. *Hou.*

Harris, George Washington. *Pa.*, 1814–1869. A Tennessee River steamboat captain who contributed humourous and political articles to newspapers. Sut Lovengood's Yarns were published in 1867.

Harris, Joel Chandler. *Ga.*, 1848——. An Atlanta journalist, editor of The Constitution, celebrated as the author of Uncle Remus, a unique character study of the Southern negro as well as a notable contribution to the literature of folk-lore. His writings include Uncle Remus: his Songs and his Sayings; Nights with Uncle Remus; Uncle Remus and his Friends; Mingo, and Other Sketches in Black and White; Balaam and his Master, and Other Sketches; Little Mr. Thimblefinger, a juvenile; Mr. Rabbit at Home, a juvenile; The Story of Aaron, a juvenile; Free Joe, and Other Georgian Sketches; Evening Tales, from the French of Fréderic Ortoli; Stories of Georgia; Sister Jane, her Friends and Acquaintances; Georgia, from the Invasion of De Soto to Recent Times. *See Chautauquan, October, 1896. Ap. Hou. Scr.*

Harris, Mrs. Miriam [Coles]. *L. I.*, 1834——. A novelist of New York city whose first story, Rutledge, was very popular. Later works are, Richard Vandermarck; The Sutherlands; St. Philip's; Happy-Go-Lucky; Missy; Frank Warrington; A Perfect Adonis; Phœbe; An Utter Failure; Louie's Last Term at St. Mary's; The Rosary for Lent, a compilation. *Ap. Hou.*

Harris, Samuel. *Me.*, 1814——. A Congregational clergyman, professor of systematic theology at Yale University from 1871. Zaccheus, or the Scriptural Plan of Benevolence; The Kingdom of Christ on Earth; The Philosophic Basis of Theism; The Self-Revelation of God; Christ's Prayer for the Death of His Redeemed; God: Creator and Lord of All. *See Andover Review, February, 1884. Scr.*

Harris, Samuel Smith. *Al.*, 1841-1888. The second Protestant Episcopal bishop of Michigan. The Dignity of Man; Christianity and Civil Society; Thoughts on Life, Death, and Immortality; Shelton, a novel. *Mg. Wh.*

Harris, Thaddeus Mason. *Ms.*, 1768-1842. A Unitarian clergyman of Dorchester from 1793 until his death. Discourses in Favor of Freemasonry; Journal of a Tour in the Northwest Territory (1805); Memorials of the First Church at Dorchester; Biographical Memoirs of James Oglethorpe; Natural History of the Bible.

Harris, Thaddeus William. *Ms.*, 1795-1856. Son of T. M. Harris, *supra.* An entomologist and physician who was librarian of Harvard University from 1831. He published Systematic Catalogue of the Insects of Massachusetts, and a valuable work on Insects Injurious to Vegetation.

Harris, Thomas Lake. *E.*, 1823-——. A mystical philosopher who founded the Brotherhood of the New Life, which had its home at Salem-on-Erie, near Brocton, New York. He has since lived in California. Among his writings are included Epics of the Starry Heavens; Modern Spiritualism; Lyric of the Morning Land; Truth and Life in Jesus; The Millennium Age; Arcana of Christianity; The Wisdom of the Adepts; God's Breath in Man. *See Life of Laurence Oliphant, by Mrs. M. O. W. Oliphant.*

Harris, William Logan. *O.*, 1817-1887. A Methodist bishop of prominence as educator and missionary. The Powers of the General Conference; Ecclesiastical Law (with W. J. Henry); Relation of Episcopacy to the General Conference. *Meth.*

Harris, William Torrey. *Ct.*, 1835-——. A speculative philosopher and educator of Washington city, a translator of Hegel, and editor of The Journal of Speculative Philosophy; since 1889 United States commissioner of education. The Spiritual Sense of Dante's Divina Commedia; Method of Study of Social Science; How to Teach Social Science; Hegel's Logic, a critical exposition; Introduction to the Study of Philosophy. *Ap. Hou. Sc.*

Harrison, Mrs. Burton. *See Harrison, Mrs. Constance.*

Harrison, Mrs. Constance [Cary]. *Va.*, 1835——. A novelist and miscellaneous writer of New York city. Story of Helen Troy; Woman's Handiwork in Modern Homes; An Edelweiss of the Sierras, and Other Tales; Bar Harbor Days; The Old-Fashioned Fairy Book; Folk and Fairy Tales; Anglomania; An Errant Wooing; A Virginia Cousin; Bric-a-Brac Stories; A Bachelor Maid; Sweet Bells Out of Tune; Crow's Nest and Belhaven Tales; Externals of Modern New York. *Bar. Cent. Har. Scr.*

Harrison, Gabriel. *Pa.*, 1825——. A Brooklyn dramatist and instructor in elocution. Life of John Howard Payne; The Stratford Bust, a Critical Inquiry as to its Authenticity; Melanthia; Dartmore, are among his writings.

Harrison, George Leib. *Pa.*, 1811–1885. A philanthropist of Philadelphia. Chapters on Social Science; Legislation on Insanity, a compilation of lunacy laws.

Harrison, Gessner. *Va.*, 1807–1862. A once noted educator of Virginia. Exposition of some Laws of Greek Grammar; On Greek Prepositions.

Harrison, Hall. *Md.*, 1837——. An Episcopal clergyman and educator. From 1865 to 1879 he was a master in St. Paul's School at Concord, and since the latter date rector of St. John's church at Ellicott City, Maryland. Life of Hugh Davy Evans, *supra;* Life of Bishop Kerfoot.

Harrison, James Albert. *Mi.*, 1848——. An educator in Virginia, since 1876 a professor of languages at Washington and Lee University. Greek Vignettes; Spain in Profile; The Rhine; French Syntax; The History of Spain; The Story of Greece; Autrefois, tales of Old New Orleans and Elsewhere; A Group of Poets and Their Haunts; Dictionary of Anglo-Saxon Poetry (with W. M. Baskerville); Exodus and Daniel (with T. W. Hunt). *Hou. Lip..Lo. Mer. Put.*

Harrison, Jonathan Baxter. *O.*, 1835——. A Unitarian clergyman of New Hampshire. Certain Dangerous Tendencies in American Life; The Latest Studies on Indian Reservations. *Hou.*

Harrison, Joseph. *Pa.*, 1810–1874. A Philadelphia engineer and inventor, from 1843–52 employed in locomotive construction by the Russian government. Essay on the Steam Boiler; The Locomotive Engine and Philadelphia's Share in its Early Improvements; The Iron Worker and King Solomon, a poem.

Harrison, William Pope. *Ga.*, 1830——. A prominent clergyman of the Methodist Church South. Theophilus Walton, a controversial work; Lights and Shadows of Forty Years; The Living Christ; The High Churchman Disarmed; Methodist Union; The Gospel among the Slaves.

Harrisse [har-ēs'], **Henri.** *F.*, 1830——. A bibliographer of New York city, of French birth, but long a citizen of the United States. Bibliotheca Americana Vetustissima; Christophe Colombe; Jean et Sebastian Cabot; The Discovery of North America. *Do.*

Harsha, David Addison. *N. Y.*, 1827——. A writer in Argyle, New York. The Heavenly Token; The Star of Bethlehem; Manual of Sacred Literature; Lives of Charles Sumner, Doddridge, Baxter, Bunyan, Addison, James Hervey, Watts, Whitefield, Abraham Booth; Eminent Orators and Statesmen. *Co.*

Hart, Albert Bushnell. *Pa.*, 1854——. A professor of history in Harvard University. Coercive Powers of the United States Government; Introduction to the Study of Federal Government; Formation of the Union, 1750–1829; Studies in Education; Life of Salmon Chase; Practical Essays on American Government. *Fl. Hou. Lgs.*

Hart, Charles Henry. *Pa.*, 1847——. A lawyer and antiquarian of Philadelphia. Memoir of W. H. Prescott, *infra:* Biographical Sketch of Abraham Lincoln; Turner, the Dream Painter; Remarks on Tabasco, Mexico; Bibliographia Websteriana.

Hart, James Morgan. *N. J.*, 1839——. Son of J. S. Hart, *infra.* A professor of Germanic languages at Cornell University from 1868. Handbook of English Composition; Syllabus of Anglo-Saxon Literature; German Universities. *Put.*

Hart, John Seely. *Ms.*, 1810–1877. An educator of New Jersey who was professor of rhetoric at Princeton College, 1872–77. Manuals of English and American Literature; Composition and Rhetoric; In the Schoolroom.

Hart, Samuel. *Ct.*, 1845——. An Episcopal clergyman, professor in Trinity College from 1868, who has published editions of Juvenal and Persius. Historical Sermons of Bishop Seabury.

Harte, [Francis] Bret. *N. Y.*, 1839——. A Californian writer who first drew public attention in 1868 by a short story called The Luck of Roaring Camp, published in The Overland

Monthly, which he edited. This tale, and the now famous poem, Plain Language from Truthful James, established his reputation. From 1871 to 1878 he resided in New York, and since that date he has lived abroad, but mainly in London from 1885. His writings include, Condensed Novels; The Luck of Roaring Camp, and Other Sketches; Mrs. Skaggs's Husbands; Tales of the Argonauts; Gabriel Conroy; Two Men of Sandy Bar, a play; The Story of a Mine; Drift from Two Shores; Thankful Blossom; The Twins of Table Mountain; By Shore and Sedge; Flip, and Found at Blazing Star; In the Carquinez Woods; On the Frontier; Maruja; Snow-Bound at Eagle's; The Queen of the Pirate Isle, a Child's Story; A Millionaire of Rough-and-Ready; The Crusade of the Excelsior; A Phyllis of the Sierras; The Argonauts of North Liberty; Cressy; The Heritage of Dedlow Marsh; A Waif of the Plains; A Ward of the Golden Gate; A Sappho of Green Springs; Colonel Starbottle's Client; A First Family of Tasajara; Susy; A Protégée of Jack Hamlin's; Sally Dows; The Bell-Ringer of Angel's; Clarence; In a Hollow of the Hills; Barker's Luck. In verse he has published East and West Poems; Echoes of the Foot Hills. *See Haweis's American Humourists; Nichol's American Literature; Vedder's American Writers; Atlantic Monthly, November, 1896. Hou.*

Harte, Walter Blackburn. *Ont.*, 1866——. A littérateur who has published Meditations in Motley. *Ar.*

Hartley, Cecil B——. 18—18—. Louis Wetzel, the Virginia Ranger; lives of Empress Josephine, Francis Marion, Daniel Boone; Hunting Spots in the West; Lives of the Three Mrs. Judsons; Pictorial Teaching and Bible Illustration. *Co.*

Hartley, Isaac Smithson. *N. Y.*, 1830——. Son of R. M. Hartley, *infra*. A Dutch Reformed clergyman of Utica since 1871. Prayer and its Relation to Modern Criticism; Old Fort Schuyler in History, are his principal works.

Hartley, Robert Milham. *E.*, 1796–1881. A philanthropist who founded in 1842 the New York Association for Improving the Condition of the Poor. History, Science, and Practical Essay on Milk; Temperance in Large Cities and Towns.

Hartshorne, Edward. *Pa.*, 1818–1885. A Philadelphia physician. Separate System for Criminals; Ophthalmic Medicine and Surgery; an edition of Taylor's Medical Jurisprudence, with Notes.

Hartshorne, Henry. *Pa.*, 1823–1897. Brother of E. Hartshorne, *supra*. A Philadelphia physician, professor of organic science at Haverford College, 1867–97. Memoranda Medica; Essentials of Principles and Practice of Medicines; Family Adviser; Our Homes; Cholera; Household Manual; Handbook of Human Anatomy; Conspectus of the Medical Sciences; Glycerin and its Uses; Woman's Witchcraft, a dramatic romance; Summer Songs. *Lip.*

Hartzell, J—— Hazard. *Pa.*, 1830–1890. An Episcopal clergyman of Waverly, New York, but prior to 1881 a noted clergyman in the Universalist faith, for fourteen years a pastor in Buffalo. Wanderings on Parnassus, a collection of verse; Application and Achievement.

Hartt, Charles Frederick. *N. B.*, 1840–1878. A professor of geology at Cornell University, 1868, and chief of the geological surveys in Brazil at the time of his death. Geology and Physical Geography of Brazil; Contributions to the Geology of the Lower Amazons; Amazonian Tortoise Myths.

Harvey, William Hope. *W. Va.*, 1851——. A writer on financial topics whose theories regarding unlimited coinage of silver have been popular with superficial thinkers. Coin's Financial School; A Tale of Two Nations, a financial novel.

Harwood, Andrew Allen. *Pa.*, 1802–1884. Son of J. E. Harwood, *infra*. A rear-admiral in the United States navy. Summary Courts Martial; Law and Practice of the United States Navy Courts Martial.

Harwood, John Edmund. *E.*, 1771–1809. An English actor who came to the United States in 1793, and published a collection of Poems the year of his death.

Hascall, Daniel. *Vt.*, 1782–1852. A Baptist clergyman of Hamilton, New York. Baptism; Elements of Theology; Analysis of Divine Revelation.

Haskell, Daniel. *Ct.*, 1784–1848. A Congregational clergyman of Burlington, Vermont, who was subsequently a writer in Brooklyn. Gazetteer of the United States (with J. C. Smith); Chronological View of the World.

Haskins, David Greene. *Ms.*, 1818–1896. An Episcopal clergyman and educator of Cambridge. Selections from the Old and New Testament for Use in Families and Schools; French and English First Book; Maternal Ancestors of Ralph Waldo Emerson (his cousin).

Hassard, John Rose Greene. *N. Y.*, 1836–1888. A New York journalist who was a literary critic on the staff of The Tribune. The King of the Nibelung; School History of the United States; Life of Archbishop Hughes, *infra;* Life of Pope Pius Ninth; A Pickwickian Pilgrimage. *Hou.*

Hassaurek, Friedrich. *A.*, 1832–1885. A journalist and lawyer of Cincinnati. Four Years Among the Spanish-Americans; The Secret of the Andes. *Clke.*

Hassler, Ferdinand Rudolph. *Sd.*, 1770–1843. A noted surveyor in the government service who published System of the Universe and a series of works on astronomy, arithmetic, geometry, and trigonometry.

Hastings, Horace Lorenzo. *Ms.*, 1831——. A Boston writer. Signs of the Times; Reasons for My Hope; Thessalonica; Atheism and Arithmetic, are his principal writings.

Haswell, Charles Haynes. *N. Y.*, 1809——. A civil engineer of much prominence. Mechanics' and Engineers' Pocket Book; Mechanics' Tables; Mensuration and Practical Geometry; Book-keeping; History of the Steam Boiler; Reminiscences of New York from 1816 to 1855. *Ap. Har.*

Hatfield, Edwin Francis. *N. J.*, 1807–1883. A Presbyterian clergyman of St. Louis, and subsequently of New York city. Universalism As It Is; History of Elizabeth, New Jersey; St. Helena and the Cape of Good Hope; The Poets of the Church. *Rev.*

Hathaway, Benjamin. *N. Y.*, 1822——. A verse-writer who was for many years a nurseryman and farmer. Art Life, and Other Poems; The League of the Iroquois; The Finished Creation, and Other Poems. *Ar.*

Haupt [howpt], **Herman.** *Pa.*, 1817——. An engineer of distinction who has held many important posts, and is the inventor of a drilling engine. Since 1875 the chief engineer of the Tide Water Pipe Line Company. Hints on Bridge Building; General Theory of Bridge Construction; Plan for Improvement of the Ohio River; Military Bridges; Street Railway Motors. *Ap. Bai.*

Haupt, Lewis Muhlenberg. *Pa.*, 1844——. Son of H. Haupt, *supra.* An engineer of Philadelphia, since 1872 professor of civil engineering in the University of Pennsylvania. Engineering Specifications and Contracts; Working Drawings and How to Make Them; The Topographer: his Methods and Instruments; Essays on Road Making. *Bai.*

Haven, Mrs. Alice [Bradley] [Neal]. "Cousin Alice." *N. Y.*, 1828–1863. A writer of juvenile tales which were very popular. Her later years were spent in New York city, but she formerly lived in Philadelphia, her first husband being J. C. Neal, *infra.* Among her writings are, No Such Word as Fail; Contentment Better than Wealth; Patient Waiting No Loss. *See Memoir; Harper's Magazine, October, 1863. Ap.*

Haven, Erastus Otis. *Ms.*, 1820–1881. A Methodist bishop, chancellor of Syracuse University from 1874, and from 1863–69 president of the University of Michigan. Pillars of Truth; Young Man Advised; Rhetoric; American Progress. *Har. Meth.*

Haven, Gilbert. *Ms.*, 1821–1880. A Methodist bishop whose official residence was in Atlanta. National Sermons; The Pilgrim's Wallet; Our Next-Door Neighbor, or Mexico of To-Day; Life of Father Taylor, the Sailor Preacher; Christus Consolator. *Meth.*

Haven, Joseph. *Ms.*, 1816–1874. A Congregational clergyman, a professor in the Chicago Theological Seminary,

1858–70. Mental Philosophy; Moral Philosophy; History of Ancient and Modern Philosophy; Studies in Philosophy and Theology; Systematic Theology.

Haven, Samuel Foster. *Ms.*, 1806–1881. An archæologist who was librarian of the American Antiquarian Society at Worcester. Archæology of the United States; History of the Grants Under the Great Council for New England.

Hawes, Joel. *Ms.*, 1789–1867. A prominent Congregational clergyman of Hartford, 1818–67. Lectures to Young Men; The Religion of the East; Looking-Glass for Ladies; Washington and Jay; Experimental and Practical Sermons; Tribute to the Pilgrims; Character Everything to the Young.

Hawes, William Post. *N. Y.*, 1803–1842. A lawyer of New York city, author of Sporting Scenes and Sundry Sketches, published, with Memoir, by H. W. Herbert, *infra*.

Hawkins, Benjamin Waterhouse. *E.*, 1807–1889. An English anatomist who removed to the United States in 1868. Popular Comparative Anatomy; Elements of Form; Comparative View of the Human and Animal Frame; Artistic Anatomy of the Horse; Artistic Anatomy of Cattle and Sheep; Artistic Anatomy of the Dog and Deer; Atlas of Comparative Osteology (with Huxley).

Hawkins, Dexter Arnold. *Me.*, 1825–1886. A lawyer of New York city, an advocate of protection and similar political measures. Among his writings are, Traditions of Overlook Mountain; Free Trade and Protection; The Roman Catholic Church in New York City.

Hawkins, Rush Christopher. *Ct.*, 1831——. Cousin of D. A. Hawkins, *supra*. A New York city lawyer who served as a colonel in the Federal army during the Civil War, and has since been a prominent advocate of political reforms. He has published The First Books and Printers of the 15th Century.

Hawkins, William George. *Md.*, 1823——. An Episcopal clergyman of Nebraska, prominent in the field of domestic missions. Life of J. H. Hawkins, his father, a noted temperance reformer; Lunsford Lane; History of the New York Freedmen's Association.

Hawks, Francis Lister. *N. C.*, 1798–1866. A once noted Episcopal clergyman, rector of churches in New York, New Orleans, and Baltimore. History of North Carolina; Reports of Cases in North Carolina Supreme Court; History of the Episcopal Church in Virginia and Maryland; The Romance of Biography; Cyclopædia of Biography; Egypt and its Monuments; Documentary History of the Episcopal Church.

Hawley, Bostwick. *N. Y.*, 1814——. A Methodist clergyman of New York State. Close Communion; Manual of Methodism; The Shield of Faith; Dancing as an Amusement; The Lenten Season; Methodist Episcopacy Valid, include his chief works. *Meth.*

Hawley, Charles. *N. Y.*, 1819–1885. A Presbyterian clergyman of Auburn, New York. Early Chapters of Cayuga History; Sanitary Reforms; Memorial Discourses; Early Chapters of Seneca History.

√**Hawthorne, Julian.** *Ms.*, 1846——. Son of N. Hawthorne, *infra*. A novelist who has inherited much of his father's originality, but whose work is often careless and hasty in construction and of ephemeral interest only. Bressant; Garth; Dust; Idolatry; Fortune's Fool; Beatrix Randolph; Saxon Studies; Archibald Malmaison; Sebastian Strome; Noble Blood; Love, or a Name; Mrs. Gainsborough's Diamonds; David Poindexter's Disappearance, and Other Tales; A Dream and a Forgetting; Confessions and Criticisms; Constance; Nathaniel Hawthorne and his Wife; American Literature; The Trial of Gideon; Prince Saroni's Wife; Love is a Spirit. *Ap. Fu. He. Hou.*

√**Hawthorne, Nathaniel.** *Ms.*, 1804–1864. A celebrated romancer, born at Salem, Massachusetts. From 1838 to 1841 he held a position in the Boston custom-house, was next a member of the Brook Farm Association, and after 1843 a resident at Concord, Massachusetts, from time to time until his death, though within that period he was surveyor of the port of Salem, 1846–50, and from

1853 to 1857 consul at Liverpool. Fanshawe; Twice-Told Tales; Grandfather's Chair; Mosses from an Old Manse; Famous Old People; Liberty Tree; Biographical Stories for Children; The Scarlet Letter; True Stories; The House of the Seven Gables; A Wonder-Book; The Snow Image, and Other Twice-Told Tales; The Blithedale Romance; Tanglewood Tales; The Marble Faun, known in England as Transformation; Our Old Home; Passages from American Note-Books; English Note-Books; French and Italian Note-Books; Septimius Felton; The Dolliver Romance; Dr. Grimshawe's Secret. *See North American Review, July, 1837, July, 1850, January, 1852; Blackwood's Magazine, November, 1863; Atlantic Monthly, May, 1860; Lathrop's Study of Hawthorne; James's Hawthorne; Hawthorne Index; Lowell's Fable for Critics; Personal Recollections of, by H. N. Bridge; Nathaniel Hawthorne and His Wife, by J. Hawthorne; Some Memories of Hawthorne, by Mrs. R. H. Lathrop; Appleton's American Biography; Nichol's American Literature; Richardson's American Literature. Hou.*

Hawthorne, Mrs. Sophia [Peabody]. *Ms.*, 1810–1871. Wife of N. Hawthorne, *supra*, sister of Elizabeth Peabody, *infra*. Her only publication was Notes in England and Italy. *Hou.*

Hay, John. *Ind.*, 1838——. A writer who was Lincoln's private secretary, adjutant, and aide-de-camp during the Civil War, and also served under Generals Hunter and Gillmore as major and assistant adjutant-general, being brevetted colonel. He was subsequently in the diplomatic service. Life of Abraham Lincoln (with J. G. Nicolay, *infra*); Pike County Ballads, and Other Poems; Castilian Days, a volume of travels. Of his dialect poems, Jim Bludso and Little Breeches are the best known. *Cent. Hou.*

Hayden, Ferdinand Vanderveer. *Ms.*, 1827–1880. A professor of geology in the University of Pennsylvania. Origin and Progress of the United States Geological Survey of the Territories; The Yellowstone National Park.

Hayden, Horace H——. *Ct.*, 1769–1844. A once noted Baltimore dentist who published Geological Essays.

Hayden, William Benjamin. *N.Y.*, 1816–1893. A Swedenborgian clergyman. Science and Revelation; Phenomena of Modern Spiritualism; The Apocalyptic Dispensation; Light on the Last Things; Dangers of Modern Spiritualism, include the greater portion of his work. *See Selected Essays and Memorials of his Life, 1894. Lip.*

Hayes, Augustus Allen. 1837–1892. A novelist of Brookline, Massachusetts. New Colorado and the Santa Fé Trail; The Jesuit's Ring, a Romance; The Denver Express. *Har. Scr.*

Hayes, Henry. *See Kirk, Mrs. Ellen.*

Hayes, Isaac Israel. *Pa.*, 1832–1881. An Arctic explorer whose first voyage was made with Dr. Kane, *infra*. The Open Polar Sea; An Arctic Boat Journey; Cast Away in the Cold; The Land of Desolation; Pictures of Arctic Travel. *Har. Hou. Le.*

Haygood, Atticus Green. *Ga.*, 1839–1896. A Methodist clergyman of much prominence in the South. The Monk and the Prince, a Critical Study of Savonarola and Lorenzo de' Medici; Our Keep-Sake; Our Children; Our Brother in Black; Speeches and Sermons; Jackknife and Brambles, a discussion of the authorship and meaning of the books of the Bible; Pleas for Progress; The Man of Galilee. *Meth.*

Hayne, Paul Hamilton. *S. C.*, 1830–1886. A lyric poet whose verse has much melody. He served as a colonel in the Confederate army, and at the close of the Civil War, broken in health and fortunes, retired to the small village of Grovetown, Georgia, where the rest of his life was passed. Avolio; The Mountain of the Lovers; Legends and Lyrics; Sonnets and Other Poems; Lives of Robert Hayne and Hugh Legare, *infra*. A complete edition of his Poems appeared in 1883. *Lip. Lo.*

Hayne, William Hamilton. *S. C.*, 1856——. Son of Paul Hayne, *supra*, and a popular lyrist of the South. Sylvan Lyrics. *Sto.*

Haynes, Emory Judson. *Vt.*, 1846——. A Methodist clergyman of Boston and elsewhere. Are These Things So?; Fairest of Three, a Tale of American Life; Dollars and Duties; A Farmhouse Cobweb, a Vermont novel. *Har.*

Hays, George Peirce. *Pa.*, 1838——. A Presbyterian clergyman of Kansas City. Everyday Reasoning; The Honest Book; May Women Speak? ; Presbyterians.

Hays, William Shakespeare. *Ky.*, 1837——. A popular ballad and song composer of Louisville. Mollie Darling is one of his best known songs. He has published a volume of Poems and Songs.

Hayward, Edward Farwell. *Ms.*, 1851——. A Unitarian clergyman for some years pastor of a church in Boston. Willoughby; Patrice; Ecce Spiritus.

Hayward, George. *Ms.*, 1781–1862. A Boston writer who published View of the United States; Religious Creeds of the United States; Book of Religions, and several gazetteers.

Hayward, George. *Ms.*, 1791–1863. A Boston physician of note. Outlines of Physiology; Surgical Records.

Haywood, John. *N. C.*, 1753–1826. A jurist of Tennessee. Manual of Laws of North Carolina; Haywood's Justice; Tennessee Reports; History of Tennessee; Statute Laws of Tennessee (with R. L. Cutts).

Hazard, Caroline. *R. I.*, 1856——. Granddaughter of R. G. Hazard, *infra.* Narragansett Ballads; Thomas Hazard, a Study of Life in Narragansett in the XVIIIth Century; Memoirs of J. L. Diman, *supra.* She has edited, with introductions, the works of R. G. Hazard.

Hazard, Ebenezer. *Pa.*, 1744–1817. A Philadelphia writer who was postmaster-general, 1782–89. Historical Collections, the beginnings of a United States history; Remarks on a Report Concerning the Western Indians.

Hazard, Rowland Gibson. *R. I.*, 1801–1888. A woolen manufacturer of Peace Dale, Rhode Island. Essays on Finance; Resources of the United States; Essay on Language, and Other Essays and Addresses; Freedom of Mind in Willing; Causation and Freedom in Willing; Man a Creative First Cause. *See Works, in four volumes, edited by C. Hazard. Hou.*

Hazard, Samuel. *Pa.*, 1784–1870. Son of E. Hazard, *supra.* An archæologist of Philadelphia. Annals of Pennsylvania, 1609–82; Register of Pennsylvania, 1828–36; Pennsylvania Archives, 1682–1790; United States Commercial and Statistical Register.

Hazard, Samuel. *Pa.*, 1834–1876. Son of S. Hazard, *supra.* An officer in the United States army. Santo Domingo Past and Present; Cuba with Pen and Pencil. *Har.*

Hazard, Thomas Robinson. *R. I.*, 1784–1876. Brother of R. G. Hazard, *supra*, and like him a manufacturer at Peace Dale. He was an ardent Spiritualist, and wrote much in defence of his beliefs. Facts for the Laboring Man; The Ordeal of Life; Capital Punishment; Mediums and Mediumship; Recollections of Olden Time.

Hazard, Willis Pope. *Al.*, 1825——. Son of S. Hazard, *supra.* A retired bookseller of Westchester, Pennsylvania. The Art of Pleasing, a work on etiquette; The Jersey, Alderney, and Guernsey Cow; Butter and Butter-making; Annals of Philadelphia, a continuation of Watson's Annals. *Co.*

Hazelius, Ernest Lewis. *P.*, 1777-1853. A Lutheran clergyman who was professor in a South Carolina theological seminary. Life of Luther; Church History; History of the Lutheran Church in America.

Hazeltine, Mayo Williamson. *Ms.*, 1841——. A New York journalist, since 1878 the literary editor of the New York Sun. Chats About Books; British and American Education; The American Woman in Europe. *Scr.*

Hazen, William Babcock. *Vt.*, 1830–1887. A general in the Federal army during the Civil War, and from 1880 chief officer of the Signal Service. The School and the Army in Germany and France; Barren Lands in the Interior of the United States; A Narrative of Military Service. *Clke. Har. Hou.*

Head, Franklin H. *N. Y.*, 1835——. A Chicago Writer who has published Shakespeare's Insomnia and the Causes thereof, an ingenious burlesque. *Hou.*

Headley, Joel Tyler. *N. Y.*, 1813–1897. An historical writer of Newburg, New York, whose work is usually strongly partisan in character, though nearly always as entertaining as it is undiscriminating. Napoleon and his Marshals; The Old Guard of Napoleon; Life of Oliver Cromwell; The Great Rebellion; Sacred Scenes and Characters; Washington and his Generals; Life of Washington; Grant and Sherman; Life of General Grant; Life of Havelock; Achievements of Stanley and Other Explorers; The Adirondacks, or Life in the Woods; Farragut and Our Naval Commanders; Chaplains of the Revolution; Sacred Heroes and Martyrs; Letters from Italy and the Alps; The Second War with England. *Scr.*

Headley, Phineas Camp. *N. Y.*, 1819——. Cousin of J. T. Headley, *supra.* A Congregational clergyman. Women of the Bible; The Island of Fire; Young Folks' Heroes of the Rebellion; Lives of Josephine, Lafayette, Napoleon, Mary Queen of Scotts; Half-Hours in Bible Lands; Evangelists in the Church. *Le.*

Heap, Gwynn Harris. *Pa.*, 1817-1887. A diplomatist who was consul-general at Constantinople from 1878. He published Central Route to the Pacific.

Heap, David Porter. *Ty.*, 1843——. A major of engineers in government service. History of Application of Electric Light to the Courts of France; Ancient and Modern Lights; Electrical Appliances of the Present Day (1884).

Heard, Franklin Fiske. *Ms.*, 1825-1889. A Boston lawyer who was a high authority on pleading. Criminal Law; Criminal Pleading; Civil Pleading; Shakespeare as a Lawyer; Libel and Slander; Leading Cases in Criminal Law (with E. H. Bennett, *supra*); Curiosities of the Law Reporters; Oddities of the Law; Precedents of Equity Pleadings; Precedents of Pleadings in Special Actions. *Lit.*

Hearn, Lafcadio. *Ion.*, 1850——. A writer of Irish and Greek parentage long a resident of New Orleans, later of New York city, and more recently of Japan. Stray Leaves from Strange Literature; Some Chinese Ghosts; Chita; Two Years in the French West Indies; Youma, the Story of a West Indian Slave; Glimpses of Unfamiliar Japan; Out of the East: Reveries and Studies in New Japan; Kokoro: Hints and Echoes of Japanese Inner Life. *Har. Hou.*

Hebbard, Stephen Southwick. 1841——. A Universalist clergyman. The Secret of Christianity; History of Wisconsin under the Dominion of France. *See Bibliography of Wisconsin.*

Hecker, Isaac Thomas. *N.Y.*, 1819-1888. A Roman Catholic clergyman who in early life was one of the noted Brook Farm community. Becoming a Roman Catholic he founded the Order of the Paulists in 1858. In 1865 he established The Catholic World, of which he remained the editor till his death. Questions of the Soul; Aspirations of Nature; Catholicity in the United States; Catholics and Protestants agreeing on the School Question; The Church and the Age.

Heckewelder [hĕk'e-wel-der], **John Gottlieb Ernest.** *E.*, 1743-1823. A Moravian missionary who made extended studies of Indian customs. His views were vehemently attacked by Lewis Cass, and stoutly defended by Nathan Hale. History, etc., of the Pennsylvania Indians; Mission of the United Brethren among the Delawares; Names which the Delawares Gave to Rivers and Streams, etc., with their Signification. *See Life by E. Rondthaler, 1847; Bibliography of Ohio.*

Hedge, Frederic Henry. *Ms.*, 1805-1890. Son of L. Hedge, *infra.* A Unitarian clergyman, professor of German language and literature at Harvard University, 1872-81. Reason in Religion; The Primeval World of Hebrew Tradition; A Christian Liturgy; Prose Writers of Germany; Ways of the Spirit and Other Essays; Atheism in Philosophy; Sermons; Hours with German Classics; Martin Luther and Other Essays; Metrical Translations and Poems (with Mrs. A. L. Wister, *infra*). *Co. Hou. Rob.*

Hedge, Levi. *Ms.*, 1767-1843. An educator of Massachusetts, professor of logic in Harvard University, 1810-27, and author of A System of Logic.

Heilprin, Angelo. *Hy.*, 1853——. Son of M. Heilprin, *infra.* A Philadelphia naturalist and artist, professor of geology at Wagner Free Institute from 1885. Contributions to the Tertiary Geology and Palæontology of the United States; Town Geology, the Lesson of the Philadelphia Rocks; Geographical and Geological Distribution of Animals; Explorations on the West Coast of Florida; Animal Life of Our Seashore; Geological Evidences of Evolution; The Arctic Problem. *Ap. Lip.*

Heilprin, Louis. *Hy.*, 1851——. Son of M. Heilprin, *infra*. A writer of New York city. The Story of Hungary (with A. Vambéry); Historical Reference Book; Chronological Table of Universal History. *Ap. Put.*

Heilprin, Michael. *Po.*, 1823–1888. A Polish refugee and scholar who supported Kossuth in Hungary in 1848, and came to the United States in 1850. He published Historical Poetry of the Hebrews Critically Examined. *Ap.*

Heitzman, Charles. *Hy.*, 1836——. A physician who came to New York city from Vienna in 1874, and is of prominence as a dermatologist. Chirurgische Pathologie und Therapie; Descriptive and Topographical Anatomy of Man; Microscopic Morphology of the Animal Body.

Helmuth, Justus Christian Henry. *G.*, 1745–1825. A Lutheran clergyman who came to America in 1769, and was pastor of St. Michael's Lutheran Church in Philadelphia, 1779–1820, and for eighteen years professor of languages in the University of Pennsylvania. Taufe und heilige Schrift; Unterhalten mit Gott; Geistliche Lieder; and several works for children.

Helmuth, William Tod. *Pa.*, 1833——. A surgeon of New York city. Treatise on Diphtheria; Medical Pomposity; System of Surgery; Scratches of a Surgeon; Suprapubic Lithotomy; With the "Pousse Café," postprandial verses.

Helper, Hinton Rowan. *N. C.*, 1829——. A Southern writer long resident in New York city. The Impending Crisis of the South, a once famous work, which appeared shortly before the opening of the Civil War; Nojoque; The Negroes in Negroland; The Land of Gold; Oddments of Andean Diplomacy; The Three Americas Railway.

Hempel, Charles Julius. *P.*, 1811–1879. A physician of Grand Rapids, Michigan, who came to America from Prussia in 1835. Christendom and Civilization; System of Materia Medica and Therapeutics; The Science of Homœopathy; Homœopathic Theory and Practice in Surgical Diseases (with J. Beakley); True Organization of the New Church; Life of Christ (in German); several important translations from the German.

Henck, John Benjamin. *Pa.*, 1816——. A professor of engineering in the Massachusetts Institute of Technology, 1865–81, and the author of a Field Book for Railway Engineers.

Henderson, Ernest Flagg. *N. Y.*, 1861——. An instructor in Wellesley College. A History of Germany in the Middle Ages; Historical Documents of the Middle Ages (edited); collaborator in Larned's History for Ready Reference. *Mac.*

Henderson, Isaac. *N. Y.*, 1850——. A New York city journalist, 1872–81, who has since lived abroad. The Prelate; Agatha Page. The second of these two novels has been dramatized. *Hou.*

Henderson, Mrs. Mary Foote. *N. Y.*, *c.* 1835——. A writer of St. Louis who organized the Industrial Art School in that city. Practical Cooking and Dinner-Giving; Diet for the Sick. *Har.*

Henderson, Peter. *S.*, 1823–1890. A noted seedsman of New York city. Gardening for Profit; Practical Floriculture; Gardening for Pleasure; Handbook of Plants; How the Farm Pays; Garden and Farm Topics. *Ju.*

Henderson, William James. *N. J.*, 1855——. A journalist on the staff of the New York Times. The Story of Music; Preludes and Studies; Sea Yarns for Boys; Afloat with the Flag; Elements of Navigation. *Har.*

Hendrix, Eugene Russell. *Mo.*, 1847——. A bishop of the Methodist Church South, whose official residence is at Kansas City. He has written Around the World.

Hening, William Waller. 17—1828. A legal writer of Virginia. The American Pleader and Lawyer's Guide; The New Virginia Justice; The Statutes of Virginia, 1691–1792; Reports of Cases in the Supreme Court of Appeals of Virginia and in the Supreme Court of Chancery for Richmond District (with W. Munford, *infra*).

Henkle, Moses Montgomery. *Va.*, 1798–1864. A Methodist clergyman of Baltimore and elsewhere. Masonic Addresses; Primary Platform of Methodism; Analysis of Church Government; Life of Bishop Bascom; Primitive Episcopacy.

Hennequin [en′-cǎn], **Alfred.** *F.*, 1846——. A dramatist and educator who beside several Anglo-French text-books has published The Art of Play-writing. *Hou.*

Henningsen, Charles Frederick. *E.*, 1815–1877. A soldier of Swedish descent and English birth who served with the Carlists in Spain in 1834, and subsequently joined Kossuth in Hungary. He came to America in 1856, was with Walker in Nicaragua, entered the Confederate army in 1861, and became a general. The Last of the Sophis, a Poem; Twelve Months' Campaign with Zumalacarregui; The White Slave, a novel; Eastern Europe; Sixty Years Hence, a novel of Russian life; Scenes from the Belgian Revolution; Analogies and Contrasts; Personal Recollections of Nicaragua; The Past and Future of Hungary.

Henry, Alexander. *N. J.*, 1739–1824. A once noted traveller in northwest America who published Travels and Adventures in Canada between 1760–76.

Henry, Caleb Sprague. *Ms.*, 1804–1884. An Episcopal clergyman of New York and Connecticut who held professorships in several colleges, and was at one time a journalist in New York city. Moral and Philosophical Essays; Satan as a Moral Philosopher; About Men and Things; Dr. Oldham at Greystones and his Talk There; Social Welfare and Human Progress; Household Liturgy; The Endless Future of the Human Race; Epitome of the History of Philosophy. He was the translator of Guizot's History of Civilization and other works. *Ap. Har.*

Henry, Guy Vernor. *N. J.*, 1839——. Son of W. S. Henry, *infra*. An officer in the United States army who served during the Civil War, and in Indian wars subsequently. Military Record of Civilian Appointments in the United States Army; Army Catechism for Non-Commissioned Officers; Manual of Target Practice.

Henry, James. *Pa.*, 1809–1895. A rifle manufacturer of Boulton, Pennsylvania, who was president of the Moravian Historical Society, and published Sketches of Moravian Life and Character.

Henry, John Flournay. *Ky.*, 1793–1873. A physician of Burlington, Iowa, who published a Treatise on Causes and Treatment of Cholera.

Henry, John Joseph. *Pa.*, 1758–1811. A jurist of Lancaster, Pennsylvania, who was author of the Accurate and Interesting Account of Arnold's Campaign Against Quebec.

Henry, Joseph. *N. Y.*, 1797–1878. A scientist of eminence who was director of the Smithsonian Institution from 1846 till his death. Syllabus of Lectures on Physics; Scientific Writings of Joseph Henry, 1886. *See Memorial, 1880; Appleton's American Biography.*

Henry, Patrick. *Va.*, 1736–1799. A celebrated Virginia patriot and orator known to literature by his speeches. *See Lives by William Wirt, H. H. Everett, M. C. Tyler, W. W. Henry; Appleton's American Biography.*

Henry, Mrs. Sarepta M—— [**Irish**]. *Pa.*, 1839——. A temperance reformer of Evanston, Illinois. Victoria, with Other Poems; After the Truth; The Voice of the Home; Mabel's Work; Beforehand; One More Chance.

Henry, Thomas Chalmers. *Pa.*, 1790–1827. A Presbyterian clergyman of South Carolina. Consistency of Popular Amusements for Professing Christians; Moral Etchings from the Religious World; Letters from an Anxious Believer. *See Memoir by T. Lewis, 1829; Allibone's Dictionary.*

Henry, William Seaton. *N. Y.*, 1816–1851. An officer in the United States army who published Campaign Sketches of the War with Mexico.

Henry, William Wirt. *Va.*, 1831——. A Virginia lawyer and historical writer who has published Life, Correspondence, and Speeches of Patrick Henry.

Hensel, William Uhler. *Pa.*, 1851——. A politician and journalist of Lancaster, Pennsylvania, author of Lives of T. A. Hendricks and Grover Cleveland.

Henshaw, David. *Ms.*, 1791–1852. A politician who was secretary of the navy in 1843, and wrote Letters on the Internal Improvement and Commerce of the West.

Henshaw, John Prentiss Kewley. *Ct.*, 1792–1852. The first Protestant Episcopal bishop of Rhode Island. Theology for the People; Lessons in Elocution; On Confirmation; The Work of Christ's Living Body, are his principal works.

Henshaw, Joshua Sidney. *Ms.*, 1811–1859. A lawyer in Utica from 1848, but previously an instructor in the United States navy. Incitements to Well Doing; Life of Father Matthew; United States Manual for Consuls; Around the World (1840); Philosophy of Human Progress.

Hentz, Mrs. Caroline Lee [Whiting]. *Ms.*, 1800–1856. Wife of N. M. Hentz, *infra*. A popular Southern writer of many sensational romances of ephemeral interest. Among them are, Lovell's Folly; Rena; The Planter's Northern Bride; Linda. *Pet.*

Hentz, Nicholas Marcellus. *F.*, 1797–1856. A French educator well known as an entomologist. He came to America in 1816, and taught in the University of North Carolina and elsewhere in the South.

Hepburn, James Curtis. *Pa.*, 1815——. A missionary to Japan of note as a lexicographer. A Japanese and English Dictionary; A Japanese-English and English-Japanese Dictionary, an abridgment of the earlier work.

Hepworth, George Hughes. *Ms.*, 1833——. A New York journalist since 1887 on the editorial staff of the Herald. From 1855–72 he was a Unitarian clergyman, but subsequently entered the Presbyterian ministry. Rocks and Shoals; Brown Studies; Hiram Golf's Religion; The Life Beyond; They Met in Heaven; Herald Sermons; Starboard and Port, a summer's yacht cruise; a book entitled ! ! !. *Dut. Har.*

Herbermann, Charles George. *Wa.*, 1840——. A professor of Latin in the College of the City of New York from 1869, author of Business Life in Ancient Rome. *Har.*

Herbert, Henry William. "Frank Forester." *E.*, 1807–1858. A versatile, gifted writer who came to America in 1831, and lived near Newark, New Jersey. His writings in historical fiction include Cromwell; Marmaduke Nyvil; The Puritans of New England, issued later as The Puritan's Daughter; The Fronde; Sherwood Forest. In history: Captains of the Old World; Cavaliers of England; Knights of England; Chevaliers of France; Persons and Pictures from French and English History; Captains of the Great Roman Republic; Henry VIII. and his Six Wives. As "Frank Forester" he published Field Sports of the United States and British Provinces; Fish and Fisheries of the United States; Frank Forester and his Friends; Warwick Woodlands; My Shooting Box; The Deer Stalkers; Manual for Young Sportsmen; Horse and Horsemanship; Fugitive Sporting Sketches. He also made a number of translations from the French, while a collection of his Poems, edited by M. Herbert, appeared in 1888. *See Life by T. Picton, 1881; Allibone's Dictionary; Appleton's American Biography. Co. Lip.*

Hering, Constantin. *Sxy.*, 1800–1880. A German physician who came to Philadelphia in 1833 and founded there the first homœopathic school in America. Among his writings are, Rise and Progress of Homœopathy; Condensed Materia Medica; Effects of Snake Poison; American Drug Provings; Domestic Physician. *See Allibone's Dictionary.*

Hering, Rudolph. *Pa.*, 1847——. A civil engineer of prominence and an authority upon sewerage and the water supply of cities, upon which topics he has written valuable reports.

Herndon, Mrs. Mary. *See Chiles, Mrs.*

Herndon, William Henry. *Ky.*, 1818-1891. A lawyer of Springfield, Illinois, and a law partner of Abraham Lincoln, of whom he published a Life in 1891.

Herndon, William Lewis. *Va.*, 1813-1857. A naval officer sent by government to explore the Amazon. The results of his expedition are detailed in his Exploration of the Valley of the Amazon (1853). His daughter became the wife of President Arthur.

Herrick, Mrs. Christine [Terhune]. *N. J.*, 1859——. Daughter of Mrs. Mary Terhune, *infra*. A writer of New York city who has written much upon housekeeping themes. Housekeeping Made Easy; The Chafing-Dish Supper; The Little Dinner; What to Eat, how to Serve It; Cradle and Nursery; Liberal Living upon Narrow Means. *Har. Hou. Scr.*

Herrick, John Russell. *Vt.*, 1822——. A Congregational clergyman, president of Dakota University since 1883, and the author of Lectures on Positivism.

Herrick, Samuel Edward. *L. I.*, 1841——. A Congregational clergyman of Boston. Some Heretics of Yesterday. *Hou.*

Herrick, Mrs. Sophie McIlvaine [Bledsoe]. *O.*, 1837——. Daughter of A. T. Bledsoe, *supra*. A New York writer on The Century staff, and well known as a microscopist. Wonders of Plant Life; Chapters in Plant Life; The Earth in Past Ages. *Har. Put.*

Herron, George Davis. *Ind.*, 1862——. A Congregational clergyman of Iowa, since 1893 professor of applied Christianity in Iowa College, very prominent as a writer and lecturer upon Christian Socialism. The Christian Society; The Call of the Cross; The Larger Christ; The Message of Jesus to Men of Wealth; The Christian State; Social Meanings of Religious Experiences. *See The Arena, April, 1896. Ar. Cr. Rev.*

Hewett, Waterman Thomas. *Mo.*, 1846——. An educator who has held the chair of German literature at Cornell University from 1883. The Frisian Language and Literature; Aims and Efforts of Collegiate Study of Modern Languages; Mutual Relations of High Schools and Colleges.

Hewit, Nathaniel Augustus. *Ct.*, 1820-1897. A Roman Catholic clergyman who, previous to 1846, was successively a Congregational and Episcopal clergyman. In 1858 he entered the Paulist order, taking the name of Augustine Francis, and since 1865 has been a professor in the Paulist Seminary. Reasons for Submitting to the Catholic Church; Life of Princess Borghese; Life of a Modern Martyr, — Dumoulin-Borie; Problems of the Age; The King's Highway; Light in Darkness.

Hewitt, Edward Crawford. *Ms.*, 1828——. An educator of Illinois, president of the State Normal University from 1876, and author of Pedagogy for Young Teachers.

Hewitt, Mrs. Emma [Churchman]. *La.*, 1850——. A writer of Philadelphia. Ease in Conversation; Hints to Ballad Singers; Queens of Home, a book for the household.

Hewitt, John Hill. *N. Y.*, 1801-1890. A Baltimore author, once a rival of Poe. He wrote many ballads, among which is The Minstrel's Return from the War; The Governess, a comedy; Washington, a play; Shadows on the Wall, a collection of reminiscences.

Hewitt, Mrs. Mary. *See Stebbins, Mrs.*

Hibbard, Freeborn Garretson. *N. Y.*, 1811——. A Methodist clergyman of western New York. Christian Baptism; Geography and History of Palestine; The Religion of Childhood; Life of L. L. Hamline, *supra*; Eschatology; Commentary on the Psalms. *Meth.*

Hibbard, George Abiah. *N. Y.*, 1858——. A Buffalo writer of short stories, notable for excellence of workmanship. Iduna, and Other Stories; Nowadays, and Other Stories; The Governor, and Other Stories. *See The Book-Buyer, August, 1895. Har. Scr.*

Hickok [hĭk'ŏk], Laurens Perseus. *Ct.*, 1798-1888. A Congregational clergyman who held several college professorships, and was president of Union College, 1866-68. He subsequently lived at Amherst. Logic of Reason; Moral Science; Empirical Psychology;

Rational Psychology; Rational Cosmology; Creator and Creation; Humanity Immortal. *Gi.*

Hickox, John Howard. *N. Y.*, 1832——. The State librarian of New York, 1848–63, and subsequently employed in the Congressional Library. Historical Acconnt of American Coinage; History of New York Paper Money, 1709–89; Catalogue of United States Government Publications.

Hicks, Elias. *L. I.*, 1748–1830. A famous Quaker controversialist, and founder of the sect known as Hicksite Quakers. He was an early and very active opponent of slavery. Observations on Slavery; Journal of Life and Religious Labours of Elias Hicks; Doctrinal Epistle. *See Letters of; History of the Friends, by S. Janney, infra.*

Higginson, Mrs. Ella [Rhoads]. *Kan.*, 1862——. A druggist of New Whatcom, Washington, who has written much verse of a popular character, and The Flower that Grew in the Sand, and Other Stories.

a **Higginson, Francis.** *E.*, 1588–1630. A Puritan clergyman of Salem who emigrated to America in 1629. True Relation of the Last Voyage to New England; New England's Plantation. *See Life, by T. W. Higginson, infra; Tyler's American Literature; Sprague's Annals of the American Pulpit.*

Higginson, John. *E.*, 1616–1708. Son of F. Higginson, *supra.* A Congregational clergyman of Salem, from 1659 till his death in charge of the church founded by his father, and widely popular in New England. The Cause of God and His People in New England; Attestation to Cotton Mather's Magnalia. *See Tyler's American Literature.*

Higginson, Mrs. Mary Potter [Thacher]. *Me.*, 1844——. Wife of T. W. Higginson, *infra.* Seashore and Prairie, stories and sketches.

Higginson, Mrs. Sarah Jane [Hatfield]. *Pa.*, 1840——. A writer of New York city. A Princess of Java, a tale of the Far East; Java: the Pearl of the East; The Bedouin Girl. *Hou.*

Higginson, Stephen. *Ms.*, 1743–1828. A descendant of J. Higginson, *supra.* A merchant of Boston of note in his day as a political writer. Essays by Laco, reprinted as Ten Chapters in the Life of John Hancock; Defence of Jay's Treaty.

Higginson, Thomas Wentworth. *Ms.*, 1823——. Grandson of S. Higginson, *supra.* An essayist and littérateur of Cambridge. In early life he was a Unitarian clergyman of a radical type, and prominent among anti-slavery thinkers. During the Civil War he commanded a regiment of freedmen. He has since been particularly active as an advocate of suffrage for women. His writings include, The Birthday in Fairy Land; Woman and her Wishes; Out-Door Papers; a translation of Epictetus; Malbone, a romance; Army Life in a Black Regiment; Atlantic Essays; Sympathy of Religions; Oldport Days; Young Folks' History of the United States; Young Folks' Book of American Explorers; Short Studies of American Authors; Common Sense about Women; Life of Margaret Fuller; Larger History of the United States; Travellers and Outlaws; Women and Men; The Afternoon Landscape, a collection of poems; Life of Francis Higginson; The New World and the New Book; Concerning All of Us; Such as They Are; The Monarch of Dreams; Hints on Writing and Speech-Making; Cheerful Yesterdays; English History for Americans (with E. Channing, *supra*); Book and Heart. *Do. Har. Hou. Le. Lgs.*

Hildeburn, Charles Swift Riche. *Pa.*, 1855——. The librarian of the Philadelphia Athenæum from 1876. A Century of Printing, or the Issues of the Press in Pennsylvania, 1685–1784; Printers and Printing in Colonial New York. *Do.*

Hildeburn, Mrs. Mary Jane [Reed]. *Pa.*, 1821–1882. A Philadelphia writer of Sunday-school tales, among which are, Day Dreams; Archy and Pussy Series; Dr. Leslie's Boys; Gaffney's Tavern.

Hildreth, Charles Lotin. *N. Y.*, 1856–1896. A journalist of New York city. Judith, a novel; The New Symphony, and Other Stories; The Masque of Death, and Other Poems.

Hildreth, Ezekiel. *Ms.*, 1784–1856. An educator of Ohio and Virginia. Logopolis, a grammatical treatise; A Key to Knowledge.

Hildreth, Richard. *Ms.*, 1807–1865. A Boston journalist and historian who was consul at Trieste in his latest years. Archy Moore, an anti-slavery novel; History of Banks; Theory of Politics; Despotism in America; Japan as it Was and Is; History of the United States from the Discovery of the Continent to the Close of the 16th Congress in 1820, a work which has few charms of style, though its general merit is unquestioned. *Har.*

Hildreth, Samuel Prescott. *Ms.*, 1783–1863. A physician once prominent in Marietta, Ohio, where he settled in 1806. History of the Diseases and Climate of Southeastern Ohio; Lives of the Early Settlers of Ohio; Contributions to the Early History of the North-West; Meteorological Observations (with J. Wood); Pioneer History of the Ohio Valley (1848); Biographical and Historical Memoirs of Early Pioneer Settlers of Ohio. *See Bibliography of Ohio. Meth.*

Hilgard, Eugene Waldemar. *Bv.*, 1831——. A professor of agricultural chemistry at the University of California from 1875. Geology and Agriculture of Mississippi; Geology of Lower Louisiana; Cotton Production in the United States; Climatic Features, etc., of the Arid Regions of the Pacific Slope (with T. C. Jones).

Hilgard, Julius Erasmus. *Bv.*, 1825–1891. Brother of E. W. Hilgard, *supra*. A civil engineer of note who was superintendent of the United States Coast Survey, 1881–85, who published many valuable professional papers.

Hill, Adams Sherman. *Ms.*, 1833——. The Boylston professor of rhetoric at Harvard University from 1876. Our English; The Principles of Rhetoric; The Foundation of Rhetoric. *Har.*

Hill, Mrs. Agnes Leonard [Scanland]. "Mollie Myrtle." *Ky.*, 1842——. Myrtle Blossoms; Vanquished, a novel; Heights and Depths.

Hill, Benjamin Dionysius. *E.*, 1842——. A Roman Catholic clergyman and educator, for some time at Notre Dame University, who has published Poems Devotional and Occasional.

Hill, Benjamin Harvey. *Ga.*, 1823–1882. A noted Georgia statesman. Notes on the Situation (1867–68); Address to the People of Georgia.

Hill, Britton Armstrong. *N. J.*, *c.* 1818——. A prominent lawyer of St. Louis. Liberty and Law under Federative Government; Absolute Money; Specie Resumption and National Bankruptcy Identical.

Hill, Daniel Harvey. *S. C.*, 1821–1889. A noted mathematician who held professorships in several Southern colleges before and since the Civil War, but during that conflict was a general in the Confederate army. Elements of Algebra; Consideration of the Sermon on the Mount; The Crucifixion of Christ.

Hill, David Jayne. *N. J.*, 1850——. An educator of note, president of the Lewisburg University, Pennsylvania, from 1879, and subsequently of the University of Rochester, New York. Science of Rhetoric; Elements of Rhetoric; Life of Washington Irving; Life of Bryant; Principles and Fallacies of Socialism; Social Influences of Christianity; The Elements of Psychology; Genetic Philosophy.

Hill, Edward Judson. *N.Y.*, 183——. A lawyer of Chicago. Common Law Jurisdiction in Illinois; Chancery Jurisdiction in Illinois; Probate Jurisdiction in Illinois; Municipal Offices in Illinois.

Hill, Frederic Stanhope. *Ms.*, 1829——. A journalist of Cambridge. Twenty Years at Sea, or Leaves from my Old Log-Books; Historical Continuity of the Anglican Church. *Hou.*

Hill, George. *Ct.*, 1796–1871. A verse-writer who held several government clerkships, and after 1835 lived at Guilford, his native town. Ruins of Athens, and Other Poems; Titania's Banquet, and Other Poems. *See Griswold's Poets of America.*

Hill, George Canning. *Ct.*, 1825——. Lives of Captain John Smith, Israel Putnam, Benedict Arnold, Daniel Boone; Homespun, or Five and Twenty Years Ago; Our Parish, or Pen Paintings of Village Life.

Hill, Hamilton Andrews. *E.*, 1827–1895. A Boston writer who published History of the Old South Church, Boston, 1669–1884; Memoir of Abbot Lawrence. *Hou. Lit.*

Hill, Henry Barker. *Ms.*, 1849——. Son of T. Hill, *infra*. A professor of chemistry at Harvard University from 1870, and author of Notes on Qualitative Analysis. *Put.*

Hill, Theophilus Hunter. *N. C.*, 1836——. A lawyer of Raleigh, North Carolina. Hesper, and Other Poems, the first book copyrighted by the Confederate government; Passion Flower, and Other Poems.

Hill, Thomas. *N. J.*, 1818–1891. A Unitarian clergyman and educator and a mathematician of eminence. He was president of Harvard University, 1862–1868, and held pastorates at Waltham, Massachusetts, and Portland, Maine. He invented several mathematical instruments, one of which is the occultator. The Postulates of Religion and Ethics; The Stars and the Earth; The True Order of Studies; Geometry and Faith; Curvature; Jesus the Interpreter of Nature; Christmas, and Poems on Slavery; The Natural Sources of Theology; In the Woods and Elsewhere, containing notable experiments in classic metres; and several text-books on arithmetic and geometry. *See Bibliography of Maine. El. Le. Put.*

Hill, Walter Henry. *Ky.*, 1822——. A Roman Catholic clergyman and educator of Chicago, a professor in St. Louis University, 1864–65 and 1871–1884. Elements of Philosophy; Ethics, or Moral Philosophy; Historical Sketch of St. Louis University.

Hillard, George Stillman. *Me.*, 1808–1879. A lawyer of Boston. Life of General McClellan; Life of George Ticknor (with Mrs. Ticknor); Six Months in Italy. He also published a series of school readers and an edition of Spenser. *Hou.*

Hillhouse, James Abram. *Ct.*, 1789–1841. A dramatic poet of New Haven. His ambitious, heavy dramas, Percy's Masque, Hadad, Demetria, were once extravagantly praised, but have long been hopelessly dead. Dramas, Discourses, and Other Pieces, appeared in 1839. *See North American Review, January, 1840.*

Hilliard [hil'yärd], **Francis.** *Ms.*, 1808–1878. A jurist of Boston. The Law of Taxation; The Law of Vendors and Purchasers; The Law of Mortgages; The Law of Torts; Law of Injunctions; Law of New Trials; Law of Contracts; Law of Bankruptcy; American Jurisprudence; American Law, a Comprehensive Summary. *Lip.*

Hilliard, Henry Washington. *N. C.*, 1808——. A lawyer and congressman of Alabama. In 1841 he was chargé d'affaires to Belgium. During the Civil War he served in the Confederate army, and subsequently practiced law in Atlanta, serving as minister to Brazil, 1877–81. Speeches and Addresses; De Vane, a Story of Plebeians and Patricians; Politics and Pen Pictures. *Har.*

Hills, George Morgan. *N. Y.*, 1825–1890. An Episcopal clergyman, rector of St. Mary's Church, Burlington, New Jersey, 1870–90. History of the Church in Burlington; John Talbot, the First Bishop in North America; Church of England Missions in New Jersey; Transfer of the Church from Colonial Dependence to the Freedom of the Republic.

Hinkel, Charles John. *E.*, 1817–1894. A German educator who came to America in 1855, and was professor of Greek and Latin at Vassar College, 1869–90. Die Speculative Analysis des Begriffs Geist; Leitfaden bei dem Unterreicht in der deutschen Grammatik; Allegemeine Aesthetik für gebildete Leser.

Hinman, Royal Ralph. *Ct.*, 1785–1868. A lawyer and antiquarian of New Hampshire, and subsequently of New York city. Historical Recollections of Connecticut in the American Revolution; Catalogue of the First Puritan Settlers of Connecticut.

Hinrichs, Carl Detlef. *Dk.*, 1836——. A Danish educator who came to America in 1860, and was professor of physical sciences in Iowa University, 1863–85. Elements of Physics; Elements of Atom Mechanics; Principles of Pure Crystallography; Principles of Physical Sciences; First Course in Qualitative Analysis.

Hinsdale, Burke Aaron. *O.*, 1837——. An Ohio educator, president of Hiram College, 1870–82, and for four years subsequently superintendent of schools in Cleveland. Genuineness and Authenticity of the Gospels; President Garfield and Education; Schools and Studies; The Old Northwest; How to Study and Teach History; editor Life and Works of Garfield. *Ap. Hou. Sil.*

Hinton, Isaac Taylor. *E.*, 1799–1847. A Baptist clergyman who came to America from England in 1822, and was pastor in Richmond, Virginia, and in New Orleans, in which latter city he died. History of Baptism; Lectures on the Prophecies.

Hirst, Henry Beck. *Pa.*, 1813–1874. A lawyer and verse-writer of Philadelphia. His poetical writings comprise Endymion, a Tale of Greece; The Penance of Roland; The Coming of the Mammoth, and Other Poems. He also published a Poetical Dictionary.

Hitchcock, Alfred. *Vt.*, 1813–1874. A surgeon of Fitchburg, Massachusetts, who published Christianity and Medical Science.

Hitchcock, Charles Henry. *Ms.*, 1836——. Son of Edward Hitchcock, *infra.* The State geologist of New Hampshire. Natural History and Geology of Maine; New Hampshire Geological Survey; The Geology of New Hampshire.

Hitchcock, Edward. *Ms.*, 1793–1864. A Congregational clergyman, State geologist of Massachusetts, 1833–1844, and president of Amherst College, 1845–54. Religion of Geology; Illustrations of Surface Geology; Fossil Footprints in the United States; Ichnology of New England; Dyspepsia Forestalled and Resisted; Religious Truth Illustrated from Science; Elementary Geology; Reminiscences of Amherst College. *See Allibone's Dictionary.*

Hitchcock, Edward. *Ms.*, 1828——. Son of E. Hitchcock, *supra.* A physician, professor of hygiene in Amherst College from 1861. Anatomy and Physiology.

Hitchcock, Enos. *Ms.*, 1744–1803. A Congregational clergyman of Providence once famous as a preacher. Treatise on Education; Sermons; Catechetical Instruction for Children and Youth.

Hitchcock, Ethan Allen. *Vt.*, 1798–1870. A general in the Federal army during the Civil War. He was a grandson of Ethan Allen, the noted patriot, and was an ardent advocate of the doctrines of Swedenborg. Alchemy and the Alchemists; Swedenborg, a Hermetic Philosopher; Christ the Spirit, an argument for the symbolic exposition of the Gospels; Remarks on the Sonnets of Shakespeare; Spenser's Colin Clout Explained; Notes on Dante's "Vita Nuova."

Hitchcock, James Ripley Wellman. *Ms.*, 1857——. Son of A. Hitchcock, *supra.* A littérateur of New York city. The Western Art Movement; A Study of George Jenness; Etchings in America; Madonnas by Old Masters; Notable Etchings by American Artists; Some American Painters in Water Colors; The Future of Etching.

Hitchcock, Roswell Dwight. *Me.*, 1817–1887. A Congregational clergyman who was president of Union Seminary from 1880. Life of Edward Robinson, *infra;* Complete Analysis of the Bible; The New Testament, with Readings Preferred by the American Committee Incorporated into the Text; Eternal Atonement (with Francis Brown, the editor of The Teaching of the Twelve Apostles). *Scr.*

Hittell, John Shertzer. *Pa.*, 1825——. A journalist of San Francisco. Evidences against Christianity; Mining in the Pacific States; Brief History of Culture; History of San Francisco; The Spirit of the Papacy; History of Mental Growth of Mankind in Ancient Times; Resources of California. *Ap. Ho.*

Hittell, Theodore Henry. *Pa.*, 1830——. Brother of J. S. Hittell, *supra.* A prominent lawyer and historian of San Francisco. Adventures of Captain Capen Adams; General Laws of California, 1850–64, commonly called Hittell's Digest; Codes and Statutes of California; History of California, a work of great value, the first two volumes, appearing in 1885, carrying the narrative as far as the close of the Mexican War, the remaining two volumes, issued in 1897, bringing it to 1887. Goethe's Faust, a critical review, was issued in 1870. *Se.*

Hobart, John Henry. *Pa.*, 1775–1830. The third Protestant Episcopal bishop of New York, and a leader of Church thought in his day. Companion for the Altar; State of Departed Spirits; Festivals and Fasts; Apology for Apostolic Order. *See Early and Professional Years of Bishop Hobart, 1834–36. Dut.*

Hobart, John Henry. *N. Y.*, 1817–1889. Son of J. H. Hobart, *supra.* An Episcopal clergyman of New York city. Instruction and Encouragement for Lent; Church Reform in Mexico; Mediæval Papal and Ritual Principles Stated and Contrasted.

Hobby, William. *Ms.*, 1707–1765. A Congregational clergyman of Reading, Massachusetts. Vindication of Whitefield; Self-Examination.

Hodge, Archibald Alexander. *N. J.*, 1823–1886. Son of C. Hodge, *infra.* A Presbyterian clergyman, professor of theology at Princeton College from 1877. Outlines of Theology; Life of Charles Hodge, *infra;* The Atonement; Commentary on the Confession of Faith; Popular Lectures on Theological Themes. *Scr.*

Hodge, Charles. *Pa.*, 1797–1878. A Presbyterian clergyman, for nearly forty years editor of The Princeton Review, which he founded, and to which he was the chief contributor. Systematic Theology; Commentaries on the Epistles; Constitutional History of the Presbyterian Church in the United States; What is Darwinism?; Discussions in Church Polity; Conference Papers. *See Life by A. A. Hodge; Princetoniana, by Charles Salmond. Scr.*

Hodge, Frederick Webb. *E.*, 1864——. An ethnologist at the Smithsonian Institution. Architecture of the Prehistoric Pueblos of Southern Arizona; Methods of Irrigation of the Ancient Inhabitants of the Salado Valley.

Hodge, Hugh Lenox. *Pa.*, 1796–1873. Brother of C. Hodge, *supra.* A physician who was professor of obstetrics in the University of Pennsylvania from 1835. Principles and Practice of Obstetrics; Diseases Peculiar to Women.

Hodge, John Aspinwall. *Pa.*, 1831——. A Presbyterian clergyman in Hartford, 1866–92. What is Presbyterian Law?; Theology of the Shorter Catechism (second part); Recognition After Death.

Hodges, George. *N. Y.*, 1856——. An Episcopal clergyman, dean of the Theological School at Cambridge from 1894, and prominent among Broad Church thinkers. The Heresy of Cain; Christianity Between Sundays; Faith and Social Service. *Wh.*

Hodgkin, Louise Manning. *Ms.*, 1846——. An educator who was from 1876 to 1891 professor of English Literature in Wellesley College. Guide to the Study of Nineteenth Century Literature.

Hodgson, Francis. *E.*, 1805–1877. A Methodist minister in Pennsylvania and other States. Examination into the System of New Divinity; Ecclesiastical Policy of Methodism Defended; Calvinistic Doctrine of Predestination Examined and Refuted. *Meth.*

Hoffman, Charles Fenno. *N. Y.*, 1806–1884. Half brother of M. Hoffman, *infra.* A once popular poet and story-writer of New York city who from 1850 lived in absolute retirement by reason of mental disorder. He excelled as a song-writer, his best known songs being, Sparkling and Bright, and The Myrtle and Steel. A Winter in the West; Wild Scenes in the Forest and Prairie; The Vigil of Faith, and Other Poems; The Echo, or Borrowed Notes for Home Circulation (verse). Love's Calendar, and Other Poems; Grayslaer, a novel. *See Poems of, edited by E. Hoffman, 1874.*

Hoffman, David. *Md.*, 1784–1854. A lawyer who was professor of law in the University of Maryland. A Course of Legal Study; Legal Outlines; Legal Hints; Miscellaneous Thoughts on Men and Things; Chronicles Selected from the Originals of Cartaphilus, the Wandering Jew; Viator, a Peep into my Notebook.

Hoffman, David Bancroft. *N. Y.*, 1827——. A politician and physician of San Diego who has published Medical History of San Diego County, California.

Hoffman, Eugene Augustus. *N. Y.*, 1829——. An Episcopal clergyman of New York city, dean of the General Theological Seminary from 1879, and a prominent benefactor of that institution. Free Churches; The Ritualistic Week; Manual of Devotion for Communicants.

Hoffman, John N——. *Pa.*, 1804–1857. A Lutheran clergyman of Lebanon, Pennsylvania. Evangelical Hymns, Original and Selected; A Collection of Tests; The Broken Platform, a Defence of the Symbolical Books of the Lutheran Church.

Hoffman, Murray. *N. Y.*, 1791–1878. A once prominent jurist of New York city. Office and Duties of Masters in Chancery; Estate and Rights of the Corporation of New York as Proprietors; Law of the Protestant Episcopal Church in the United States; Ecclesiastical Law in the State of New York; Law and Practice as to References.

Hoffman, Wickham. *N. Y.*, 1821——. Son of M. Hoffman, *supra*. A diplomatist who, after serving as secretary of legation at Paris, London, and St. Petersburg successively, was minister to Denmark, 1883–85. Camp, Court, and Siege, a Narrative of Personal Adventure during Two Wars; Leisure Hours in Russia.

Hogan, John. *I.*, 1805–1892. A politician and banker of St. Louis. Thoughts about St. Louis; Resources of Missouri; Sketches of Early Western Pioneers; History of Western Methodism.

Hoge [hōg], **Moses.** *Va.*, 1752–1820. A Presbyterian clergyman and educator of Virginia, president of Hampden and Sidney College, 1806–20, and widely known as an eloquent preacher. Christian Panoply, a Reply to Paine's "Age of Reason;" Sermons.

Hoge, William James. *Va.*, 1821–1864. A Presbyterian clergyman of New York city, and subsequently of Petersburg, Virginia, very popular in his day, and the author of Blind Bartimeus, or the Sightless Sinner.

Hogg, Wilson Thomas. *N. Y.*, 1852——. A Free Methodist clergyman, president of Greenville College from 1893. Handbook of Homiletics and Pastoral Theology; Revivals and Revival Work.

Hoke, Jacob. 18——. The Age we Live In; Holiness, or the Higher Christian Life; Clusters from Eshcol; Guide to the Battle Field of Gettysburg; The Great Invasion of 1863.

Holbrook, Alfred. *Ct.*, 1816——. An educator of Lebanon, Ohio. The Normal, or Methods of Teaching; An English Grammar Conformed to Present Usage.

Holbrook, James. 1812–1864. From 1845 a special agent of the United States Post Office. He published Ten Years Among the Mailbags.

Holbrook, John Edwards. *S. C.*, 1794–1871. A physician and naturalist, professor of anatomy at the Medical College in Charleston for more than thirty years. American Herpetology; Ichthyology of South Carolina.

Holbrook, Martin Luther. *O.*, 1831——. A physician of New York city, professor of hygiene in the New York Medical College and Hospital for Women, and editor of The Herald of Health and Journal of Hygiene. Parturition Without Pain; Eating for Strength; Hygiene of Brain and Nerves; Marriage and Parentage; How to Strengthen the Memory; Hygienic Treatment of Consumption.

Holbrook, Silas Pinckney. *S. C.*, 1796–1835. Brother of J. E. Holbrook, *supra*. A lawyer of Medfield, Massachusetts. Sketches by a Traveller is a collection of his contributions to the Boston Courier and the New England Galaxy.

Holcombe, Henry. *Va.*, 1762–1826. A Baptist clergyman of Philadelphia. Lectures on Primitive Theology; First Fruits.

Holcombe, Hosea. *S. C.*, 1780–1841. A Baptist clergyman of Alabama. Collection of Sacred Hymns; Anti-Mission Principles Exposed; History of Alabama Baptists.

Holcombe, James Philemon. *Va.*, 1820–1873. A lawyer and educator of Virginia, professor of law in the University of Virginia, 1852–60, and member of the Confederate Congress, 1861–1863. Law of Debtor and Creditor; Literature and Letters; Introduction to Equity Jurisprudence; Leading Cases upon Commercial Law; Digest of

United States Supreme Court Decisions; Merchants' Book of Reference. *Ap.*

Holcombe, William Frederick. *Ms.*, 1827——. A physician of New York city, professor of eye and ear diseases in several medical institutions. History of Mount Sterling, Kentucky; History of the Holcombes in America; Family Records, their Importance and Value.

Holcombe, William Henry. *Va.*, 1825–1894. Brother of J. P. Holcombe, *supra.* A homœopathic physician of New Orleans, who was well known as a Swedenborgian writer. Our Children in Heaven; Lost Truths of Christianity; The Other Life; Southern Voices, a volume of verse; Scientific Basis of Homœopathy; How I Became a Homœopath; Poems; The Sexes Here and Hereafter; In Both Worlds; The End of the World; The New Tenant; Letters on Spiritual Subjects; Condensed Thoughts About Christian Science. *Lip.*

Holden, Edward Singleton. *Mo.*, 1846——. An astronomer, president of the University of California since 1880, and director of the Lick Observatory. Astronomy for Students (with S. Newcomb, *infra*); Life of Sir William Herschel; Monograph of the Central Parts of the Nebula of Orion; Notes on the Bastion System of Fortification; Astronomical Bibliography; Handbook of Lick Observatory; The Mogul Emperors of Hindustan. *Scr.*

Holden, George Henry. *Ms.*, 1848——. The proprietor of a bird store in Boston who has published Canaries and Cage Birds. *Ju.*

Holden, Luther Loud. 18——. Persis, a Tale of the White Mountains; A Summer Jaunt through the Old World.

Holder, Charles Frederick. *Ms.*, 1851——. Son of J. B. Holder, *infra.* A naturalist of New York city, and a popular writer upon natural history topics. Elements of Zoölogy (with J. B. Holder); Marvels of Animal Life; The Ivory King; Living Lights; Wonder Wings; A Strange Company; A Frozen Dragon, and Other Tales; All About Pasadena; Along the Florida Reef; Life of Agassiz; Young Folks' Story Book of Natural History. *Ap. Do. Le. Lo. Put. Scr.*

Holder, Joseph Bassett. *Ms.*, 1824–1888. A zoölogist who was a curator in the American Museum of Natural History, New York city. History of the North American Fauna; History of the Atlantic Right Whales; The Living World.

Holdich, Joseph. *E.*, 1804——. A Methodist clergyman who was secretary of the American Bible Society, 1849–78. Bible History; Life of A. H. Hurd; Life of Wilbur Fisk, *supra. Har. Meth.*

Holland, Edward Clifford. *S. C.*, 1794–1824. A journalist of Charleston who was the author of a volume of Odes, Naval Songs, and Other Poems.

Holland, Frederick May. *Ms.*, 1836——. Son of F. W. Holland, *infra.* A Unitarian clergyman of Massachusetts. The Reign of the Stoics; Stories from Robert Browning; The Rise of Intellectual Liberty from Thales to Copernicus; Life of Frederick Douglass. *Fu. Ho.*

Holland, Frederick West. *Ms.*, 1811–1895. A Unitarian clergyman of Concord, Massachusetts. Scenes in Palestine; Sinai and Jerusalem, or Scenes from Bible Lands.

Holland, Henry Ware. *N. Y.*, 1844——. Son of F. W. Holland, *supra.* A Boston lawyer and journalist. William Dawes and his Ride with Paul Revere.

Holland, Josiah Gilbert. "Timothy Titcomb." *Ms.*, 1819–1881. A popular author and lecturer whose writings met with severe criticism as literary productions without being materially affected in popularity. They were addressed to average commonplace humanity, and exerted a wide and helpful influence. He was editor of The Springfield Republican, 1849–66, and of Scribner's Magazine from 1870 until his death. His writings in verse include, Kathrina; Bitter Sweet; The Mistress of the Manse; The Marble Prophecy; Garnered Sheaves, including all his poems up to 1873; The Puritan's Guest, and Other Poems. In fiction: The Bay Path; Arthur Bonnicastle; Sevenoaks; Miss Gilbert's Career; Nicholas Minturn. His other works comprise, Gold Foil Hammered from Popular Proverbs; History of Western Massachusetts; Letters to Young People; Lessons in Life; Concerning the Jones Family; Plain Talks on Familiar Subjects; Life of Abraham Lincoln, which had an enormous sale. *See Century Magazine, December, 1881; Memoir by Mrs. H. M. Plunkett. Scr.*

Holland, Robert Afton. *Tn.*, 1844——. An Episcopal clergyman of St. Louis, but formerly a clergyman of the Methodist faith. The Philosophy of the Real Presence; Relations of Philosophy to Agnosticism and Religion; The Proof of Immortality; Midsummer Night's Dream, an Interpretation; Democracy in the Church; What is the Use of Going to Church?

Holley, Alexander Lyman. *Ct.*, 1832–1882. An engineer of eminence who was a lecturer on iron and steel manufacture in the Columbia School of Mines from 1879, and an inventor of prominence. Railway Economics (with Zerah Colburn, *supra*); Treatise on Ordnance and Armor. *See Memorial of, 1884.*

Holley, Marietta. "Josiah Allen's Wife." *N. Y.*, 1844——. A well-known and popular humourous writer whose home has always been at Ellisburg, New York. Her writings contain much real wit and shrewd sense, but the effect is often marred by extravagance and faults of taste. My Opinions and Betsey Bobbet's; My Wayward Pardner; Josiah Allen's Wife as a P. A. and a P. I.; Samantha at the World's Fair; Samantha in Europe; Samantha Among the Brethren; Samantha at Saratoga; Samantha at the Centennial; Poems; Sweet Cicely; Josiah's Alarm. *Fu. Lip.*

Holley, Mrs. Mary Austin. 17—1846. The wife of Horace Holley, a Unitarian clergyman of Kentucky. Texas: Observations Historical, Geographical, and Descriptive (1833); Memoir of Horace Holley.

Holley, Orville Luther. *Ct.*, 1791–1861. Brother-in-law of Mrs. Holley, *supra*. A lawyer and journalist of New York city. Description of New York City; Life of Benjamin Franklin.

Hollister, Gideon Hiram. *Ct.*, 1817–1881. A lawyer of Litchfield, Connecticut, who was minister to Hayti, 1868–69. Mount Hope, an historical romance; History of Connecticut; Thomas à Becket, a Tragedy, and Other Poems; Kinley Hollow.

Holloway, Mrs. Laura [Carter]. *Tn.*, 1848——. A writer who was for ten years on the editorial staff of The Brooklyn Eagle. Ladies of the White House; An Hour with Charlotte Brontë; The Hearthstone, or Life at Home; The Mothers of Great Men and Women; Chinese Gordon; Howard, the Christian Hero; Life of Adelaide Neilson; The Buddhist Diet Book. *Fu.*

Holly, Henry Hudson. *N. Y.*, 1834–1892. An architect of New York city. Country Seats; Church Architecture; Modern Dwellings in Town and Country.

Holm, Saxe. *See Jackson, Mrs. Helen.*

Holmes, Abiel. *Ct.*, 1763–1837. A Unitarian clergyman of Cambridge, pastor of the First Church there, 1792–1832. Life of Ezra Stiles, *infra*; History of Cambridge; American Annals; Memoir of the French Protestants. *See Life by W. Jenks.*

Holmes, Daniel. *N. Y.*, 1810–1873. A Methodist preacher in Michigan and Indiana. Pure Gold, or Truth in its Native Loveliness; The Wesley Offering; Discussion on the Atonement.

Holmes, Mrs. Georgiana [Klingle]. "George Klingle." *Pa.*, 185——. A verse-writer of Philadelphia. Make Thy Way Mine; In the Name of the King. *Sto.*

Holmes, John. *Ms.*, 1773–1843. A once prominent senator in Congress from Massachusetts, and subsequently from Maine, who was the author of The Statesman, or Principles of Legislation.

Holmes, Mrs. Mary Jane [Hawes]. *Ms.*, 18———. A voluminous author of popular fiction of a domestic kind, the literary merit of which is slight. She has for many years lived at Brockport, New York. Among her writings are, Lena Rivers; Tempest and Sunshine; Marian Grey; Gretchen. *Dil.*

Holmes, Nathaniel. *N. H.*, 1814——. A jurist of St. Louis in earlier life, but from 1868–72 Royall professor of law in Harvard University, and for many years a resident of Cambridge. He is an ardent advocate of the Baconian theory of the authorship of Shakespeare's plays. The Authorship of Shakespeare; Realistic Idealism in Philosophy Itself. *Hou.*

Holmes, Oliver Wendell. *Ms.*, 1809–1894. Son of A. Holmes, *supra.* A famous physician of Boston, widely known as poet, novelist, and essayist. He was born in Cambridge, and there and in Boston his life was almost entirely passed. From 1847 to 1882 he was professor of anatomy in Harvard University. His popularity dates from the founding of The Atlantic Monthly in 1857, in the earliest number of which he began the publication of the articles entitled The Autocrat of the Breakfast Table. Much of his verse was composed for especial occasions, and is more or less ephemeral in its nature; but his serious verse and his essays entitle him to a high place among American writers. The Autocrat of the Breakfast Table; The Professor at the Breakfast Table; The Poet at the Breakfast Table; Mechanism in Thought and Morals; Memoir of Motley; Over the Teacups; Our Hundred Days in Europe; Life of Emerson; Medical Essays; Elsie Venner; The Guardian Angel; A Mortal Antipathy; Currents and Counter Currents; Pages from an Old Volume of Life, comprise his prose works. In verse his publications include, Urania; Astræa; Songs in Many Keys; Songs of Many Seasons; The Iron Gate; The School-Boy; Before the Curfew. *See Lives by W. Kennedy, E. E. Brown, J. T. Morse; Haweis's American Humourists; Nichol's American Literature; Richardson's American Literature; Stedman's Poets of America; O. W. Holmes, by Walter Jerrold; Ashcroft Noble's Impressions and Memories; Steuart's Letters to Living Authors, 1890; Harper's Monthly, December, 1896. Hou.*

Holmes, Oliver Wendell, Jr. *Ms.*, 1841——. Son of O. W. Holmes, *supra.* A jurist of Boston who has published The Common Law and edited Kent's Commentaries. *Lit.*

Holst, Hermann Eduard von. *Livonia*, 1841——. An historian who first came to America in 1866 and engaged in lecturing and writing, but returned to Europe in 1872 and was successively professor of history in the University of Strassburg, 1872–74, and at Freiburg, 1874–92. In 1892 he became professor of history at the University of Chicago. His greatest work is Verfassung und Demokratie der Vereinigten Staaten von Amerika, the translation of which is entitled The Constitutional and Political History of the United States. His other works are, Life of Calhoun; Life of John Brown; Constitutional Law of the United States. *Hou.*

Holt, John Saunders. *Al.*, 1826–1886. A lawyer of New Orleans. Life of Abraham Page, a Novel; What I Know About Ben Eccles; The Quines. *Lip.*

Homes, Henry Augustus. *Ms.*, 1812–1888. A Congregational clergyman who was a missionary at Constantinople, 1836–50, and subsequently in the diplomatic service there. From 1854 he was employed as librarian in the State library at Albany. The Need of Yezedees of Mesopotamia; Design and Import of Medals; Our Knowledge of California; The Palatine Emigration to England in 1709; The Water Supply of Constantinople, comprise his principal works.

Homes, Mrs. Mary Sophie [Shaw] [Rogers]. *Md.*, 1830——. A writer of New Orleans. Carrie Harrington, or Scenes in New Orleans; Progression, or the South Defended, a volume of verse; A Wreath of Rhymes.

Honeywood, Saint John. *Ms.*, 1763–1798. A lawyer of Salem, New York, whose political Poems were published in 1801.

Hood, George. *Circa* 1815–1869. A Philadelphian who was manager of the Academy of Music in his city, and author of a History of Music in New England (1846).

Hood, John Bell. *Ky.*, 1831–1879. A noted general in the Confederate army. Advance and Retreat: Personal Experience in the United States and Confederate Armies, a careful defence of his military movements.

Hood, Samuel. *I.*, *c.* 1800–1875. A Philadelphia lawyer, author of A Practical Treatise on the Law of Decedents in Pennsylvania.

Hooke, William. *E.*, 1601–1678. A Puritan clergyman who was a cousin of Oliver Cromwell. He came to America about 1636; was for some seven years minister at Taunton, and for twelve years following pastor at New Haven. Returning to England in 1656, he became chaplain to Cromwell. New England's Teares for Old England's Feares is the best known of his writings. *See Tyler's American Literature; Sprague's Annals of the American Pulpit.*

Hooker, Edward William. *Ct.*, 1794–1875. A Congregational clergyman of Vermont who was a descendant of T. Hooker, *infra.* A Plea for Sacred Music; Life of Thomas Hooker.

Hooker, Herman. *Vt.*, 1804–1865. An Episcopal clergyman who retired from the ministry and became a bookseller in Philadelphia. Family Book of Devotion; The Uses of Adversity; Thoughts and Maxims; The Portion of the Soul; Popular Infidelity; The Christian Life a Life of Faith.

Hooker, Horace. *Ct.*, 1793–1864. A Congregational clergyman of Hartford. Youth's Book of Natural Theology; Bible History.

Hooker, Mrs. Isabella [Beecher]. *Ct.*, 1822——. The youngest daughter of Lyman Beecher, *supra.* A philanthropist of Hartford, prominent as an advocate of spiritualism and woman-suffrage. Womanhood: its Sanctities and Fidelities.

Hooker, Thomas. *E.*, 1586–1647. A Puritan clergyman who came to America in 1633, and was for three years minister at Cambridge, then called Newtowne. In 1636 he led a large portion of his flock to the Connecticut valley, where they founded the town of Hartford. A theologian of great influence in his century. Survey of the Summe of Church Discipline (with John Cotton); Application of Redemption; The Poore Doubting Christian drawne to Christ. *See Tyler's American Literature; Palfrey's History of New England; Allibone's Dictionary; Dictionary of National Biography, vol. 27.*

Hooker, Worthington. *Ms.*, 1806–1867. A physician of Norwich, Connecticut, who was professor of medicine at Yale University, 1852–67. Physician and Patient; An Examination of Homœopathy; Human Physiology for Schools; Rational Therapeutics; Child's Book of Nature; Child's Book of Common Things; Lessons from the History of Medical Delusions; Science for the School and Family; The Medical Profession and the Community. *Har.*

Hooper, Edward James. *E.*, 1803——. A once prominent agriculturist in the West who published a Dictionary of Agriculture.

Hooper, Johnson. *N. C.*, *c.* 1815–1863. A lawyer of Alabama. Adventures of Captain Simon Suggs; Widow Rugby's Husband, and Other Alabama Tales.

Hooper, Lucy. *Ms.*, 1816–1841. A verse-writer of much promise whose home was in Brooklyn. Scenes from Real Life, a collection of prose Sketches, appeared during her lifetime, and her Complete Poems in 1848. *See Griswold's Female Poets of America.*

Hooper, Mrs. Lucy Hamilton [Jones]. *Pa.*, 1835–1893. A Philadelphia author who lived in Europe after 1870, and was Paris correspondent for several American papers. Poems, with translations from the German; Under the Tri-Color, a Novel; The Tsar's Window, a Novel. *Lip. Rob.*

Hope, James Barron. *Va.*, 1827–1887. A lawyer and journalist of Norfolk. Leoni di Monti, and Other Poems; An Elegiac Ode; Under the Empire, or the Story of Madelon; Arms and the Man, and Other Poems.

Hopkins, Alphonso Alvah. *N. Y.*, 1843——. A journalist, educator, and lecturer. His Prison Bars, a Temperance Tale; Newspaper Poets; Our Sabbath Evenings; Sinner and Saint, a Novel; Life of General Clinton Fisk; Asleep in the Sanctum, and Other Poems; Waifs and their Authors; Wealth and Waste; Geraldine, a novel in verse on the model of Lucile. *Fu. Hou.*

Hopkins, Caspar Thomas. *Vt.*, 1826——. Son of Bishop Hopkins, *infra.* A Californian journalist who established the first insurance company on the Pacific coast. He published a Manual of American Ideas.

Hopkins, Edward Washburn. *Ms.*, 1857——. A professor of Sanskrit in Yale University. Mutual Relations of the Four Castes in Manu; Translation of Laws of Manu; Social and Military Position of the Ruling Caste in Ancient ndia; The Religions of India. *Gi.*

Hopkins, Erastus. *Ms.*, 1810–1872. A Presbyterian clergyman, long a resident of Northampton, Massachusetts, and the author of The Family a Religious Institution.

Hopkins, John Henry. *I.*, 1792–1868. The first Protestant Episcopal bishop of Vermont. A writer of vigour and versatility, prominent both as a High Churchman and a controversialist. History of the Confessional; The End of Controversy Controverted; The Primitive Church; Essay on Gothic Architecture; The Church of Rome in her Primitive Purity; Scriptural View of Slavery, a defence of the institution; Law of Ritualism; Lectures on the Reformation; Twelve Canzonets, words and music; History of the Church in verse, include his principal writings. *See Life by his son, J. H. Hopkins, infra.*

Hopkins, John Henry. *Pa.*, 1820–1891. Son of J. H. Hopkins, *supra.* An Episcopal clergyman who founded The Church Journal, of which he was long the editor. Among his writings are included Carols, Hymns, and Songs; Poems by the Wayside; Life of Bishop Hopkins; Faith and Order of the Protestant Church in the United States; and a translation of Goethe's Autobiography. *See C. F. Sweet's Champion of the Cross, 1894. Wh.*

Hopkins, Lemuel. *Ct.*, 1750–1801. A political writer of note in his day, author of satires, poems, and a favourite version of Psalm cxxxii. With Barlow and others he wrote the Anarchiad, a plea for an efficient federal constitution.

Hopkins, Mrs. Louisa Parsons [Stone]. *Ms.*, 1834–1895. An educator of Boston, for some years a member of the Boston School Board. How Shall my Child be Taught?; Practical Pedagogy; Educational Psychology; Observation Lessons in Primary Schools; Cosmic Geography; Handbook of the Earth; Parables of Nature and Life. In verse she wrote, Motherhood; Breath of the Field and Shore; Easter Carols. *Le.*

Hopkins, Mrs. Louisa [Payson]. *Me.*, 1812–1862. A writer of religious works for young people, the wife of Professor Albert Hopkins, Williamstown, Massachusetts. The Pastor's Daughter; Lessons on the Book of Proverbs; Henry Langdon; The Guiding Star; The Silent Comforter; Select Thoughts. *See Sewall's Memoirs of Albert Hopkins.*

Hopkins, Mark. *Ms.*, 1802–1887. A Congregational clergyman who was president of Williams College, 1836–1872, and a man of wide influence as an educator and a religious writer. Lectures on Moral Science; The Law of Love and Love as a Law; Discourses and Essays; Outline Study of Man; The Scriptural Idea of Man; Teachings and Counsels; Evidences of Christianity. *See Life by F. Carter, supra. Rev. Scr.*

Hopkins, Mark. *Ms.*, 1851——. Son of M. Hopkins, *supra.* A journalist in London. The World's Verdict, a novel. *Hou.*

Hopkins, Samuel. *Ct.*, 1721–1803. A Congregational clergyman of Newport, Rhode Island, the founder of what has been called Hopkinsian Divinity, which differed from Calvinism in maintaining the free agency of sinners, the moral inability of the unregenerate, and ascribing the essence of sin to the disposition and purpose of the mind. His views had great influence in the modification of contemporary thought. He was a strong opponent of slavery, and his influence procured the passage of a law prohibiting the importation of slaves into Rhode Island. The System of Doctrine contained in Divine Revelation is his principal work. Others are, The True State of the Unregenerate; Nature of True Holiness; The Duty and Interest of American States to Emancipate their Slaves. *See Life by Park; Mrs. Stowe's Minister's Wooing; Sprague's Annals of the American Pulpit.*

Hopkins, Samuel. *Ms.*, 1807-1887. Cousin of M. Hopkins, 1st, *supra*. A Congregational clergyman of New England, long a resident of Northampton, Massachusetts. The Puritans and Queen Elizabeth; Lessons at the Cross; Youth of the Old Dominion.

Hopkins, Samuel Miles. *Ct.*, 1772-1837. A jurist of New York State. Chancery Reports; Treatise on Temperance.

Hopkins, Samuel Miles. *N. Y.*, 1813——. Son of S. M. Hopkins, *supra*. A Presbyterian clergyman, professor in Auburn Theological Seminary from 1847. Manual of Church Polity; Liturgy and Book of Common Prayer.

Hopkins, Stephen. *R. I.*, 1707-1785. One of the signers of the Declaration of Independence, and ten times governor of Rhode Island. He was the author of Rights of the Colonies Examined; History of the Planting and Growth of Providence. *See Life by W. E. Foster, 1884; Bibliography of Rhode Island.*

Hopkinson, Francis. *Pa.*, 1737-1791. A once famous political writer and lawyer of Philadelphia, among whose political writings are, The Pretty Story; The Prophecy; The Political Catechism; The New Roof. He is best known by his humourous poem, The Battle of the Kegs. Three volumes of his Miscellaneous Writings were published in 1792.

Hopkinson, Joseph. *Pa.*, 1770-1842. Son of F. Hopkinson, *supra*. A jurist of Philadelphia who is chiefly remembered as the author of the poem, Hail Columbia.

Hoppin, Augustus. *R. I.*, 1828-1896. An artist and illustrator. On the Nile; Ups and Downs on Land and Water; Jubilee Days; Hay Fever; Recollections of Auton House, a novel; A Fashionable Sufferer; Two Compton Boys; Married for Fun, a romance. *Hou.*

Hoppin, James Mason. *R. I.*, 1820——. Cousin of A. Hoppin, *supra*. A Congregational clergyman, professor of homiletics at Yale University, 1861-1879, and subsequently of the history of art. Notes of a Theological Student; Old England; Life of Admiral Foote; Memoirs of Henry Armitt Brown, *supra*; Homiletics; Pastoral Theology; Office and Work of the Christian Minister; Sermons on Faith, Hope, Love, etc.; The Early Renaissance; Greek Art on Greek Soil. *Do. Fu. Har. Hou. Lip.*

Horn, Edward Traill. *Pa.*, 1850——. A Lutheran clergyman of Charleston. The Christian Year; Old Matin and Vesper Services of the Lutheran Church; Outlines of Liturgics; The Evangelical Pastor.

Hornaday, William Temple. *Ind.*, 1854——. A naturalist of Washington, for eight years chief taxidermist of the National Museum. Two Years in the Jungle; The Buffalo Hunt; Canoe and Rifle on the Orinoco; Free Rum on the Congo; Taxidermy and Zoölogical Collecting. *Scr.*

Horner, William Edmunds. *Va.*, 1793-1853. A physician of Philadelphia, professor of anatomy in the University of Pennsylvania, 1819-53. Special Anatomy and Histology; United States Dissector; Anatomical Atlas; Pathological Anatomy. *See Gross's Sketches of Contemporaries.*

Horsfield, Thomas. *Pa.*, 1773-1859. A naturalist and traveller who was a native of Philadelphia, but was in the employ of the East India Company, and lived in England after 1820. Lepidopterous Insects; Zoölogical Researches in Java. *See Dictionary of National Biography, vol. 27.*

Horsford, Eben Norton. *N. Y.*, 1818-1893. A chemist of Cambridge who was Rumford professor at Harvard University, 1847-63. He was the discoverer of acid phosphate, and one of the founders of the Lawrence Scientific School at Harvard. Theory and Art of Breadmaking; The Army Ration; Discovery of America by Northmen. *Hou.*

Horsford, Mrs. Mary L'Hommedieu [Gardiner]. *N.Y.*, 1824-1855. Wife of E. N. Horsford, *supra*, and author of Indian Legends and Other Poems.

Horsmanden, Daniel. *E.*, 1691-1778. A jurist of New York city. The New York Conspiracy, or the History of the Negro Plot; Letters to Governor Clinton.

Horton, George Forman. *Pa.*, 1808–1888. A lawyer of Terrytown, Pennsylvania. Geology of Bradford County, Pennsylvania; The Horton Genealogy.

Horton, Samuel Dana. *O.*, 1844–1895. A publicist of Pomeroy, Ohio, eminent as an advocate of bimetallism. Silver and Gold; The Silver Pound and England's Monetary Position since the Restoration, with a History of the Guinea; Silver in Europe. *Clke. Mac.*

Hosack, David. *N. Y.*, 1769–1835. An eminent physician and scientist of New York city who founded the first botanic garden in America. Contagious Diseases; Vision; Hortus Elginensis; Memoir of Hugh Williamson; Memoirs of De Witt Clinton; Essays on Medical Science; Theory and Practice of Medicine.

Hoskins, Nathan. *Vt.*, 1795–1869. A lawyer of Vermont and Massachusetts. History of Vermont; Notes in the West; The Bennington Court Controversy.

Hosmer, Frederick Lucian. *Ms.*, 1846——. A Unitarian clergyman of Chicago. The Way of Life; The Thought of God in Hymns and Poems (with W. C. Gannett, *supra*). *Rob.*

Hosmer, George Washington. 184——. A physician. The People and Politics; As We Went Marching On, a Story of the War. *Har. Hou.*

Hosmer, James Kendall. *Ms.*, 1834——. A professor in Washington University of St. Louis, 1874–92, and since the latter date public librarian of Minneapolis. Short History of Anglo-Saxon Freedom; The Story of the Jews; Life of Sir Henry Vane; Life of Samuel Adams; Thomas Hutchinson, Royal Governor of the Province of Massachusetts Bay; The Color Guard, a narrative of personal experience; The Thinking Bayonet, a novel; A Short History of German Literature; How Thankful was Bewitched. *Hou. Put. Scr.*

Hosmer, Mrs. Margaret [Kerr]. *Pa.*, 1830–1897. A Philadelphia writer of Sunday-school tales, among which are, A Chinaman in California; The Chinese Boy; The Little Captives; Lonny the Orphan. She wrote, also, three novels, Blanche Gilroy; The Morrisons; Ten Years of a Life Time. *Co. Lip.*

Hosmer, William Henry Cuyler. *N. Y.*, 1814–1877. A lawyer of western New York who wrote much in verse, the greater part of which is concerned with Indian legends. Fall of Tecumseh; Legends of the Senecas; The Themes of Song; The Months; Yonnondio; Bird Notes; Indian Traditions and Songs; The Pioneers of Western New York. *See Griswold's Poets and Poetry of America.*

Hotchkiss, James Harvey. *Ct.*, 1781–1851. A Presbyterian minister of Prattsburg, New York, the author of History of the Churches of Western New York.

Hough [hŭff], **Franklin Benjamin.** *N. Y.*, 1820–1885. A physician whose later years were passed in Lowville, New York, in scientific and historical study. Among his works are, Catalogue of Plants in Lewis and Franklin Counties; History of St. Lawrence and Franklin Counties; The Siege of Charleston in 1780; Duty of Government in the Preservation of Forests; Report on Forestry; Elements of Forestry; American Constitutions. *Clke.*

Hough, George Washington. *N. Y.*, 1836——. An astronomer of Chicago, director of the Dearborn Observatory. Annals of Dudley Observatory; Report of Dearborn Observatory; The Galvanic Battery, are among his writings.

Houghton [ho′ton], **George Washington Wright.** *Ms.*, 1850–1891. A journalist and verse-writer of New York city. His published volumes of verse include, Songs from Over the Sea; Album Leaves; Drift from York Harbor, Maine; The Legend of St. Olaf's Kirk; Niagara, and Other Poems. *Hou.*

Houghton, Henry Clark. *Ms.*, 1837——. A physician of New York city, dean of the ophthalmic hospital. Lectures on Clinical Otology.

House, Edward Howard. *Ms.*, 1836——. A journalist and critic of Boston and New York, long resident in Japan. The Simonoseki Affair; The Kagosima Affair; The Japanese Expedition to Formosa; Japanese Episodes; Yone Santo, a Child of Japan; The Midnight Warning, and Other Stories. *Har.*

Houston, Daniel Franklin. 18——. A professor of political economy in the University of Texas. A Critical History of Nullification in South Carolina. *Lgs.*

Hovey [hŭv′ĭ], **Alvah.** *N. Y.*, 1820——. A Baptist clergyman, professor in Newton Theological Seminary from 1849, and since 1868 its president. The Miracles of Christ; The Scriptural Law of Divorce; Life of Isaac Backus; State of the Impenitent Dead; Christian Teaching and Life; God With Us; Systematic Theology; Biblical Eschatology; Studies in Ethics and Religion, include his principal works. *Bap.*

Hovey, Charles Mason. *Ms.*, 1810–1887. A noted horticulturist of Cambridge, editor of Hovey's Magazine of Horticulture, which reached its thirty-fourth volume, and author of Fruits of America.

Hovey, Horace Carter. *Ind.*, 1833——. A Congregational clergyman of Bridgeport, Connecticut. Celebrated American Caverns.

Hovey, Richard. *Il.*, 1864——. A verse-writer of Washington. The Laurel, an Ode; Launcelot and Guenevere, a Poem in Dramas, republished as The Marriage of Guenevere; Seaward, an Elegy on the Death of Thomas William Parsons, *infra;* Gandelfo, a tragedy; Songs from Vagabondia, and More Songs from Vagabondia (with W. B. Carman, *supra*). *Cop. Lo. St.*

Howard, Blanche Willis. *See Teuffel, von.*

Howard, Bronson. *Mch.*, 1842——. A prominent dramatist of New York city. Saratoga, produced in London as Brighton, and in Berlin as Eine Erste und Einzige Liebe; Diamonds; The Banker's Daughter; Old Love Letters; Young Mrs. Winthrop; One of Our Girls; The Henrietta; Shenandoah; Aristocracy; Moorcroft; Hurricanes; Wives; Met by Chance; Greenroom Fun.

Howard, Oliver Otis. *Me.*, 1830——. A major-general in the United States army who served during the Civil War and in several Indian campaigns; in command of the Division of the Atlantic from 1888. Donald's School Days; a translation of Agenor's Life of Count de Gasparin; Chief Joseph, or the Nez Percés in Peace and War; Isabella of Castile. *Fu. Le.*

Howarth, Mrs. Ellen Clementine [Doran]. *N. Y.*, 1827——. A verse-writer of Trenton, New Jersey. Poems; Poems edited by R. W. Gilder, (1868). 'Tis but a Little Faded Flower, and Thou Wilt Never Grow Old, are well-known poems of hers.

Howe, Edgar Watson. *Ind.*, 1854——. A journalist of Atchison, Kansas, editor of The Daily Globe. His first novel, The Story of a Country Town, attracted much attention. Later stories include, The Mystery of The Locks; A Moonlight Boy; A Man Story.

Howe, Fisher. *Vt.*, 1798–1871. A philanthropist of Brooklyn. Oriental and Sacred Scenes; The True Site of Calvary. *Ran.*

Howe, Frederic Clemson. *Pa.*, 1867——. Taxation and Taxes in the United States under the Internal Revenue System, 1791–1895. *Cr.*

Howe, George. *Ms.*, 1802–1883. A Presbyterian clergyman, professor of biblical literature in the Theological Seminary at Columbia, South Carolina, from 1831. Theological Education; History of the Presbyterian Church in South Carolina.

Howe, Henry. *Ct.*, 1816——. An historical writer and compiler of Cincinnati. Historical Collections of New Jersey (with J. W. Barber, *infra*); Our Whole Country; The Great West; Historical Collections of Virginia and Ohio; Over the World; Adventures and Achievements of Americans; Times of the Rebellion in the West, are among his works.

Howe, Henry Marion. *Ms.*, 1848——. Son of S. G. and J. W. Howe, *infra.* A metallurgist who has published The Metallurgy of Steel; Copper Smelting.

Howe, Herbert Alonzo. *N. Y.*, 1858——. An astronomer of Colorado, director of Chamberlin Observatory, University of Denver. A Study of the

Sky; Elements of Descriptive Astronomy. *Fl. Sil.*

Howe, John Badlam. *Ms.*, 1813–1882. A publicist of Indiana whose works upon finance have had much influence. Monetary and Industrial Fallacies; Mono-Metalism and Bi-Metalism; The Political Economy of Great Britain, the United States, and France in the Use of Money; The Common Sense of Money; Replies to Criticisms. *Hou.*

Howe, Mrs. Julia [Ward]. *N. Y.*, 1819——. Wife of S. G. Howe, *infra*. A writer of Boston long prominent in philanthropic movements, and as a lecturer upon the enfranchisement of women. The Battle Hymn of the Republic is her finest effort. Her writings include, Passion Flowers; Words for the Hour; The World's Own; A Trip to Cuba; From the Oak to the Olive; Later Lyrics; Sex and Education; Memoir of S. G. Howe, *infra;* Modern Society; Life of Margaret Fuller; Is Polite Society Polite? and Other Essays. *Lam. Le.*

Howe, Mark Antony De Wolfe. *R. I.*, 1809–1895. The first Protestant Episcopal bishop of Central Pennsylvania. Domestic Slavery, a Reply to Bishop Hopkins; Life of Alonzo Potter, *infra.*

Howe, Maud. *See Elliott, Mrs.*

Howe, Samuel Gridley. *Ms.*, 1801–1876. A physician of Boston, the first superintendent of the Perkins Institution for the Blind, and a man of prominence in the anti-slavery movement. Reader for the Blind; Historical Sketch of the Greek Revolution. *See J. F. Clarke's Memorial and Biographical Sketches; Memoir by Mrs. Howe.*

Howell, Robert Boyte Crawford. *N. C.*, 1801–1868. A once noted Baptist clergyman of Nashville. Terms of Sacramental Communion; The Way of Salvation; Evils of Infant Baptism; The Cross; The Covenant; Early Baptists of Virginia.

Howells, William Cooper. *W.*, 1807–1894. Life in Ohio from 1813 to 1840. *Clke.*

Howells, William Dean. *O.*, 1837——. Son of W. C. Howells, *supra*. A novelist of much prominence who at nineteen was a printer on a Cincinnati journal, and in 1860 published with J. J. Piatt, *infra*, Poems of Two Friends. In the same year he wrote a Life of Abraham Lincoln, and from 1861–65 was consul at Venice. Venetian Life, and Italian Journeys, date from this portion of his career. From 1872–81 he was editor of The Atlantic Monthly, and since then has devoted his time wholly to literature in Boston and New York. His writings since 1869 include: The Day of Their Wedding; At the Sign of the Lion's Head; No Love Lost; Suburban Sketches; Their Wedding Journey; A Chance Acquaintance; A Foregone Conclusion; The Lady of the Aroostook; The Undiscovered Country; A Modern Instance; A Woman's Reason; The Minister's Charge; Indian Summer; A Fearful Responsibility, and Other Stories; Doctor Breen's Practice; The Rise of Silas Lapham; April Hopes; Annie Kilburn; A Hazard of New Fortunes; The Shadow of a Dream; An Imperative Duty; The Quality of Mercy; The World of Chance; The Coast of Bohemia; A Traveller from Altruria; Christmas Every Day, and Other Stories for Children; A Parting and a Meeting; The Sleeping-Car, and Other Farces; The Mouse-trap, and Other Farces; Out of the Question, a comedy; A Counterfeit Presentment, a comedy; A Sea Change, or Love's Stowaway; Poems; Stops from Various Quills, a book of verse. Among miscellaneous writings of his are, Three Villages (Shirley, Lexington, Gnadenhütten); Modern Italian Poets; A Boy's Town; Tuscan Cities; My Year in a Log Cabin; Criticism and Fiction; My Literary Passions. *Steuart's Letters to Living Authors; Century Magazine, March, 1882; Vedder's American Writers; New England Magazine, October, 1893; The Bookman, February, 1897. Har. Hou.*

Howison, George Holmes. *Md.*, 1834——. A mathematician who has published a Treatise on Analytic Geometry.

Howison, Robert Reid. *Va.*, 1820——. A lawyer of Richmond. History of Virginia; History of the American Civil War; Fredericksburg; Lives of Generals Morgan, Marion, Gates; God and Creation.

Howland, George. *Ms.*, 1824——. An educator of Illinois, president of the State board of education, 1882. Grammar of the English Language; Little Voices, a book of verse; an hexameter translation of the Æneid; Practical Hints for the Teachers of Public Schools. *Ap.*

Hows, John William Stanhope. *E.*, 1797–1871. A journalist and educator of New York city who published The Practical Elocutionist, and edited a number of school books.

Hoyt, Epaphras. *Ms.*, 1765–1850. A major-general of the Massachusetts militia, who lived in Deerfield. Treatise on the Military Art; Military Instructions; Cavalry Discipline; Antiquarian Researches.

Hoyt, Henry Martyn. *Pa.*, 1830–1892. A Pennsylvania lawyer, governor of his State, 1878–83. Controversy between Connecticut and Pennsylvania; Protection versus Free Trade. *Ap.*

Hoyt, John Wesley. *O.*, 1831–1892. An educator of distinction, governor of Wyoming, 1878–82, and president of Wyoming University from 1887. Resources and Progress of Wisconsin; Resources and Progress of Wyoming.

Hoyt, Ralph. *N. Y.*, 1806–1878. An Episcopal clergyman of New York city. The Chant of Life, and Other Poems; Echoes of Memory and Emotion; Sketches of Life and Landscape. *See Duyckinck's American Literature.*

Hoyt, Wayland. *O.*, 1838——. A popular Baptist minister of Brooklyn. Hints and Helps for the Christian Life; Present Lessons from Distant Days; Gleams from Paul's Prison; The Brook in the Way; Saturday Afternoon; Light on Life's Highway. *Ran.*

Hubbard, Bela. *N. Y.*, 1814–1896. A prominent lawyer and geologist of Detroit, author of Memorials of a Half Century; Ancient Garden-Beds of Michigan.

Hubbard, Elbert. *Il.*, 1856——. A littérateur of East Aurora, New York, editor of The Philistine. No Enemy but Himself; Little Journeys; The Legacy, a novel; Forbes of Harvard; One Day, a Tale of the Prairies. *Put.*

Hubbard, Lucius Lee. *O.*, 1849——. The State geologist of Michigan from 1893. Summer Vacations at Moosehead Lake; Woods and Lakes of Maine. *Hou.*

Hubbard, William. *E.*, 1621–1704. A colonial historian who was a Congregational clergyman of Ipswich, and a member of the first graduating class at Harvard College, 1642. Narrative of Troubles with the Indians; Sermons; Present State of New England. He also wrote a History of New England, for which the colony paid him £50, and which was printed by the Massachusetts Historical Society in 1815. *See Tyler's American Literature.*

Hubbell, Mrs. Martha [Stone]. *Ct.*, 1814–1856. A writer of religious juveniles, and of The Shady Side, or Life in a Country Parsonage, which for a time enjoyed an extraordinary popularity.

Hubner, Charles William. *Md.*, 1835——. A journalist of Atlanta. Souvenirs of Luther; Poems and Essays; Modern Communism; Wild Flowers, a book of verse; Cinderella, and Prince and Fairy, two lyrical dramas. *Meth.*

Hudson, Charles. *Ms.*, 1795–1881. A Universalist clergyman in charge of a parish at Westminster, Massachusetts, 1819–41, and subsequently a resident of Lexington in the same State. Letters to Reverend Hosea Ballou; History of Westminster; History of Lexington; Doubts Concerning the Battle of Bunker Hill; History of Marlborough.

Hudson, Erasmus Darwin. *Ct.*, 1805–1880. A surgeon of New York city. Resections; Essay on Temperance; Immobile Apparatus for Ununited Fractures.

Hudson, Erasmus Darwin. *Ms.*, 1843–1887. Son of E. D. Hudson, *supra*. A physician of New York city. Doctors' Hygiene and Therapeutics; Home Treatment of Consumptives; Physical Diagnosis of Thoracic Diseases; Methods of Examining Weak Chests; Diagnosis of the Relations of Weak Digestions.

Hudson, Frederick. *Ms.*, 1819–1875. A journalist connected with The New York Herald in various capacities for nearly thirty years, who after 1866 lived at Concord, Massachusetts. History of Journalism in the United States, 1690-1872. *Har.*

Hudson, Henry Norman. *Vt.*, 1814-1886. An Episcopal clergyman who was a Shakespearean scholar of eminence. He served as chaplain in the Federal army during the Civil War, and in his later years was professor of Shakespeare study in Boston University. Lectures on Shakespeare; Sermons; Studies in Wordsworth; A Chaplain's Campaign with General Butler; Shakespeare: his Life and Characters; Essays on Education. He edited the Harvard and the University editions of Shakespeare. His criticisms are helpful, but are somewhat dogmatic in tone. *Est. Gi. Lit.*

Hudson, James Fairchild. *O.*, 1846——. A journalist of Pittsburg for many years. The Railways and the Republic. *Har.*

Hudson, Mrs. Mary [Clemmer] [Ames]. *N. Y.*, 1839-1884. A journalist of Washington, well known at one period by her Woman's Letters from Washington in The Independent. Eirene; His Two Wives; Victoria (three novels); Ten Years in Washington; Men, Women, and Things; Poems of Life and Nature; Memorials of Alice and Phœbe Cary. *See Memorial Biography, by E. Hudson.*

Hudson, Thomson Jay. *O.*, 1834——. The Law of Psychic Phenomena; A Scientific Demonstration of the Future Life. *Mg.*

Hudson, William Henry. *E.*, 1863——. A professor of English literature at Leland Stanford Junior University from 1892. The Church and the Stage; Introduction to Study of Herbert Spencer.

Hughes, John. *I.*, 1797-1864. A noted Roman Catholic archbishop of New York, 1850-64. He was prominent as a controversialist, and a controversy which he held with Erastus Brooks on the church property question attracted much attention. He collected the letters on both sides in a volume entitled Brooksiana. His writings were published in 1865. He founded St. John's College, Fordham, New York, in 1830. *See Life by Hassard; Appleton's American Biography.*

Hughes, Robert William. *Va.*, 1821——. A jurist of Richmond, Virginia. Reports of Cases; The Currency Question from a Southern Point of View; Transcript of United States Supreme Court Decisions; The American Dollar; Lives of Generals Floyd and Johnston. *Ap.*

Huidekoper, Frederic. *Pa.*, 1817——. A Unitarian theologian and philanthropist of Meadville, Pennsylvania. Belief of the First Three Centuries concerning Christ's Mission to the Underworld; Judaism at Rome; Indirect Testimony of History to the Genuineness of the Gospels.

Huidekoper, Henry Shippen. *Pa.*, 1839——. A soldier in the Federal army during the Civil War who afterwards attained the rank of major-general in the Pennsylvania militia. He was postmaster of Philadelphia, 1880-1885, and author of a Manual of Military Service.

Hull, William. *Ct.*, 1753-1825. A famous general court-martialed in 1812 for his surrender of Detroit to the English. His defence of his action appears in his book, The Campaign of the Northwest Army (1824). *See Life by Maria Campbell and James Freeman Clarke* (1848).

Humes, Thomas William. *Tn.*, 1815-1892. An Episcopal clergyman and educator of Tennessee who published The Loyal Mountaineers of Tennessee.

Humphrey, Edward Porter. *Ct.*, 1809-1887. Son of H. Humphrey, *infra.* A Presbyterian clergyman of Louisville. Our Theology in its Development; Sacred History from the Creation to the Giving of the Law.

Humphrey, Heman. *Ct.*, 1779-1861. A Congregational clergyman who was president of Amherst College, 1823-1845. Tour in France, etc.; Domestic Education; Sketches and History of Revivals; Essays on the Sabbath; Life of Nathan Fiske; Letters to a Son in the Ministry.

Humphreys, Andrew Atkinson. *Pa.*, 1810-1883. A general in the Federal army during the Civil War, subsequently Chief of Engineers of the United States Army. The Virginia

Campaigns of 1864 and 1865; From Gettysburg to the Rapidan. *Scr.*

Humphreys, David. *Ct.*, 1752–1818. A colonel who was aide-de-camp to Washington. His miscellaneous works, of which two collections appeared in his lifetime, include articles in both prose and verse, and he was also the author of a Life of General Putnam.

Humphreys, Edward Rupert. *I.*, 1820–1893. An educator of Boston who came thither from England in 1859. Lessons on the Liturgy of the Protestant Episcopal Church; Education of Military Officers; The Higher Education of Europe and America; Manual of Political Science, include his principal works.

Humphreys, Milton Wylie. *W. Va.*, 1844——. A professor of Greek at the University of Virginia from 1887. He has published scholarly translations, with notes, of the Antigone of Sophocles and The Clouds of Aristophanes.

Hunnewell, James Frothingham. *Ms.*, 1832——. A resident of Charlestown, Massachusetts. Bibliography of the Hawaiian Islands; The Lands of Scott; The Historical Monuments of France; The Imperial Island: England's Chronicle in Stone; Bibliography of Charlestown and Bunker Hill; A Century of Town Life, a History of Charlestown. *Hou. Lit.*

Hunt, Ezra Mundy. *N. J.*, 1830——. A physician of Trenton, New Jersey. Patients' and Physicians' Assistant; Physicians' Counsels; Alcohol as Food and Medicine; Principles of Hygiene, are among his writings.

Hunt, Freeman. *Ms.*, 1804–1858. A publisher of New York city who was the founder of Hunt's Merchants' Magazine. Lives of American Merchants; Sketches of Female Character; Letters About the Hudson River.

Hunt, Harriot Kezia. *Ms.*, 1805–1875. A physician of Boston who lectured upon woman-suffrage and sanitary reforms. She published Glances and Glimpses, or Fifty Years' Social and Twenty Years' Professional Life.

Hunt, Helen. *See Jackson, Mrs. Helen.*

Hunt, Henry Jackson. *Mch.*, 1819–1889. A brigadier-general in the Federal army during the Civil War, brevetted major-general at its close. He was the author of Instructions for Field Artillery.

Hunt, Jedediah. *N. Y.*, 1815——. A verse-writer of Chilo, Ohio. The Cottage Maid, a Tale in Rhyme.

Hunt, Samuel. *Ms.*, 1810–1878. A Congregational clergyman of Franklin, Massachusetts. He assisted Henry Wilson, *infra*, in writing The Rise of the Slave Power, and completed the work after Mr. Wilson's death. He was author of Political Duties of Christians; Letter to the Avowed Friends of Missions.

Hunt, Theodore Whitefield. *N. Y.*, 1844——, An educator, professor of English literature in Princeton College. Principles of Written Discourse; English Prose and Prose Writers; Ethical Teachings in Old English Literature. *Fu.*

Hunt, Thomas Poage. *Va.*, 1794–1876. A clergyman and temperance lecturer of Pennsylvania. History of Jesse Johnson and his Times; Death by Measure; Liquor Selling, a History of Fraud, include the most of his works.

Hunt, Thomas Sterry. *Ct.*, 1826–1892. A geologist who was professor in the Massachusetts Institute of Technology, 1872–78. Chemical and Geological Essays; Azoic Rocks; Mineral Physiology; New Basis for Chemistry.

Hunter, John Dunn. *Circa* 1798–1827. An adventurer whose Manners and Customs of the Indian Tribes West of the Mississippi once attracted much attention.

Huntington, Faye. *See Foster, Mrs. Theodosia.*

Huntington, Frederic Dan. *Ms.*, 1819——. The first Protestant Episcopal bishop of Central New York. He was in earlier life a Unitarian clergyman, and in 1842 was professor of Christian morals in Harvard University. He entered the Episcopal ministry in 1860, and was consecrated bishop in 1864. Christian Believing and Living; Sermons for the People; Christ in the Christian Year; Steps to a Living Faith; Lessons on the Parables; Helps to a Holy Lent; Christ in the World;

Forty Days with the Master, The Fitness of Christianity to Man; Human Society, include the larger part of his works. *Dut. Wh.*

Huntington, Jedediah Vincent. *N. Y.*, 1815–1862. A writer who was once an Episcopal clergyman, but became a Roman Catholic layman. He was a journalist in St. Louis for some years, and died in France. America Discovered: a Poem; Alban, or the History of a Young Puritan; Poems; Lady Alice, or the New Una; Blonde and Brunette; Rosemary, or Life and Death.

Huntington, William Reed. *Ms.*, 1838——. An Episcopal clergyman of prominence as a Broad Churchman. He was rector of All Saints church at Worcester, 1862–83, and since 1883 has been rector of Grace church, New York city. The Church Idea; Conditional Immortality; The Peace of the Church; The Church Porch; Questions on the Fourth Gospel; The Causes of the Soul; Short History of the Book of Common Prayer; Quinquaginta, a book of fifty poems. *Dut. Scr. Wh.*

Hurd, John Codman. *Ms.*, 1816–1892. A writer of Boston. The Law of Freedom and Bondage in the United States; The Theory of Our National Existence. *Lit.*

Hurlburt, William Henry. *S. C.*, 1827–1895. A journalist of New York city of much prominence at one time as one of the editors of The World. His latest years were spent in Europe. Gan Eden, or Pictures of Cuba; General McClellan and the Conduct of the War. *See Hart's American Literature.*

Hurlbut, Jesse Lyman. *N. Y.*, 1843——. A Methodist clergyman of prominence in New York and New Jersey. Manual of Biblical Theology; Studies in the Four Gospels; Outlines in Old Testament History. *Meth.*

Hurst, John Fletcher. 1834——. A Methodist bishop of much prominence as a writer. Literature of Theology; History of Rationalism; Martyrs to the Tract Cause; Life and Literature in the Fatherland; Outline of Church History; Our Theological Century; Bibliotheca Theologica; Short Histories of the Church; Short History of the Christian Church; Indika, the Country and People of India and Ceylon, include the greater part of his original works. He is also the translator of Hagenbach's History of the Church in the 18th and 19th Centuries; of Van Oosterzee's Lectures on John's Gospel; and of Lange's Commentary on the Epistle to the Romans, with additions. *Har. Meth. Ran. Scr.*

Hutchins, Thomas. *N. J.*, 1730–1789. A noted geographer of the colonial period. Topographical Description of Virginia, etc.; History, Narrative, and Topographical Description of Louisiana and West Florida.

Hutchinson, Ellen Mackay. *N. Y.*, 18———. A literary journalist of New York city, on The Tribune staff, and editor with E. C. Stedman of The Library of American Literature, in eleven volumes. She has published Songs and Lyrics. *Hou.*

Hutchinson, Thomas. *Ms.*, 1711–1780. The last royal governor of Massachusetts. An historian of great ability but whose merits as such were not recognized by his contemporaries. His History of the Colony of Massachusetts Bay, the third and last volume of which was not published till nearly fifty years after his death, begins with the year 1628, and closes with the year 1774. He published also a Collection of Original Papers relating to the same subject. *See Diary and Letters of, edited by P. O. Hutchinson, 1884–86; Life by J. K. Hosmer, supra; Dictionary of National Biography, vol. 28; Appleton's American Biography.*

Hutchison, Joseph Chrisman. *Ms.*, 1822–1867. A noted physician of Brooklyn. History of Asiatic Cholera in Brooklyn; Physiology and Hygiene; Contributions to Orthopædic Surgery; Acupressure.

Hutson, Charles Woodward. 18———. Out of a Beleaguered City, a Tale of the Revolution; Beginnings of Civilization; History of French Literature; The Story of Beryl, a novel.

Hutton, Laurence. *N. Y.*, 1843——. A littérateur of prominence in New York city. Other Times and Other Seasons; Plays and Players; Artists of the 19th Century (with Mrs. Waters, *infra*); Literary Landmarks of London; Literary Landmarks of Edinburgh; Curiosities of the American Stage; From the Books of Laurence Hutton; Portraits in Plaster; Edwin Booth; Literary Landmarks of Jerusalem; Literary Landmarks of Venice; Literary Landmarks of Florence; Literary Landmarks of Rome. *Har.*

Hyatt, Alpheus. *D. C.*, 1838——. A professor of zoölogy in the Massachusetts Institute of Technology and curator of the Boston Society of Natural History. Observations on Fresh Water Polyzoa; About Pebbles; Commercial and Other Sponges; Common Hydroids; Worms and Crustacea; Guides to Science Teaching; The Oyster, Clam, and other Common Mollusks.

Hyde, Edward Wyllys. *Mch.*, 1843——. A professor of mathematics and civil engineering in the University of Cincinnati from 1875, and author of Skew Arches; Directional Calculus. *Gi. Vn.*

Hyde, James Nevins. *Ct.*, 1840——. A surgeon of Chicago. Early Medical Chicago; Diseases of the Skin.

Hyde, Thomas Worcester. *Iy.*, 18———. A brigadier-general in the Army of the Potomac in the Civil War. At present (1897) a builder of steel ships at Bath, Maine. Following the Greek Cross, or Memories of the Sixth Army Corps. *Hou.*

Hyde, William De Witt. *Ms.*, 1858——. A Congregational clergyman, president of Bowdoin College from 1885. Practical Ethics; Outlines of Social Theology. *Ho. Mac.*

Hylton, John Dunbar. *W. I.*, 1837——. A physician of Palmyra, New Jersey, whose writings are wholly in verse of a very ambitious but unpoetical character. They include The Bride of Gettysburg; Betrayed, a Northern Tale; The Heir of Liolyn; Above the Grave of John Odenswurge; Artaloisi, a Romance of King Arthur.

Hyneman, Leon. *Pa.*, 1805–1879. An editor of New York city. The Fundamental Principles of Science; Freemasonry in England from 1567 to 1813.

Hyslop, James Hervey. *O.*, 1854——. An instructor in Columbia College. The Elements of Ethics; The Elements of Logic; The Ethics of Hume. *Gi. Scr.*

I

Ide, George Barton. *Vt.*, 1804–1872. A Baptist clergyman, of Springfield, Massachusetts. Green Hollow; Bible Echoes, or Lessons from the War; The Power of Kindness, a juvenile tale; Bible Pictures.

Ilsley, Charles Parker. *Me.*, 1807–1887. A writer whose home was in Portland, Maine, till 1866. The Island Fête, a poem; The Liberty Pole, a tale of Machias; Forest and Shore, subsequently published as The Wrecker's Daughter.

Ingalls, Joshua King. 18———. Social Wealth; Economic Equities.

Ingalls, William. *Ms.*, 1769–1851. A physician who was professor of anatomy at Brown University, 1811–23, and author of a treatise on Malignant Fevers.

Ingersoll, Charles Jared. *Pa.*, 1782–1862. A political writer and statesman of Philadelphia who filled several diplomatic positions abroad. History of the War of 1812–15; Chiomara, a Poem; Edwy and Elgiva, a Tragedy; Inchiquin, the Jesuit's Letters in American Literature and Politics; Recollections, etc., a volume of personal reminiscences. *See Duyckinck's American Literature; Life by W. M. Meigs, 1897.*

Ingersoll, Edward. *Pa.*, 1817——. Son of C. J. Ingersoll, *supra.* History and Law of Habeas Corpus and Grand Juries; Personal Liberty and Martial Law.

Ingersoll, Ernest. *Mch.*, 1852——. A naturalist of New York city whose writing is mainly for young people and of a popular character. Friends Worth Knowing; Natural History of Insects; Knocking Around the Rockies; Nests and Eggs of American Birds; The Crest of the Continent; Strange Adventures of a Stowaway; Down East Latch Strings; The Ice Queen, a story; Birds'-Nesting; Country Cousins, or Short Studies in Natural History; Old Ocean; To the Shenandoah and Beyond; Habits of Animals. *Har. Lo. Mer. Wn.*

Ingersoll, Luther Dunham. 18——. The librarian of the War Department at Washington. Iowa and the Rebellion; Life of Horace Greeley; History of the War Department.

Ingersoll, Joseph Reed. *Pa.*, 1786–1868. Brother of C. J. Ingersoll, *supra*. A lawyer of Philadelphia who was minister to England in 1852. Secession a Folly and a Crime; Memoir of Samuel Breck.

√ **Ingersoll, Robert Green.** *N. Y.*, 1833——. A noted lawyer and politician of Peoria, Illinois, and more recently of New York city, famous also as a lecturer and writer strongly opposed to the Christian religion. The Gods; Ghosts; Some Mistakes of Moses; Complete Lectures; Prose Poems. *Ban.*

Inglehart, Mrs. Frances [Chambers] [Gooch]. *Ts.*, 18——. A writer of Austin, Texas, author of Face to Face with the Mexicans. *Fo.*

Inglis, David. *S.*, 1825–1877. A Presbyterian clergyman of Brooklyn who published Systematic Theology in Relation to Modern Thought.

Ingraham, Edward Duncan. *Pa.*, 1793–1854. A lawyer of Philadelphia. English Ecclesiastical Reports; A View of the Insolvent Laws of Pennsylvania.

Ingraham, Joseph Holt. *Me.*, 1809–1866. An Episcopal clergyman of Holly Springs, Mississippi. In the earlier portion of his career he wrote a number of wildly sensational romances, among them Lafitte: the Pirate of the Gulf; Captain Kyd; The Dancing Feather, all of which were very popular and quite worthless as literature. The Southwest, by a Yankee, was another work of this period. He entered the Episcopal ministry in 1855, and afterwards wrote three religious romances as popular as the others and almost as valueless. They are, The Prince of the House of David; The Pillar of Fire; The Throne of David. *Rob.*

Innsley, Owen. *See Jennison, Lucia.*

Inskip, John Swannell. *E.*, 1816–1884. A Methodist clergyman who was a noted camp-meeting conductor. Life of Rev. William Summers; Methodism Explained and Defended; Remarkable Display of the Mercy of God.

Iredell, James. *N. C.*, 1788–1853. A lawyer of Raleigh who was governor of North Carolina, 1827. Laws of North Carolina; North Carolina Reports; Equity Reports; Law of Executors; Digest of Reported Cases.

Ireland, Joseph Norton. *N. Y.*, 1817——. A merchant of New York city. Records of the New York Stage, 1750–1860; Memories of Mrs. Duff; Professional Life of Thomas Cooper.

Irving, John Treat, Jr. 1812——. Nephew of Washington Irving, *infra*. A lawyer of New York city. Indian Sketches; Hawk Chief; The Attorney; Harry Harson; The Van Gelder Papers. *Put.*

Irving, Peter. *N. Y.*, 1771–1838. Brother of Washington Irving, *infra*. A journalist of New York city, who published Giovanni Sbogarra, a Venetian Tale.

Irving, Pierre Munroe. *N. Y.*, 1803–1876. Son of William Irving, *infra*, and the author of a Life of Washington Irving. *Put.*

Irving, Roland Duer. *N. Y.*, 1847——. A professor of geology in the University of Wisconsin from 1870. Geology of Central Wisconsin; Geology of Lake Superior; Copper-Bearing Rocks of Lake Superior, are among his writings.

Irving, Theodore. *N. Y.*, 1809–1880. Nephew of Washington Irving, the son of his brother Ebenezer. An Episcopal clergyman and educator. The Fountain of Living Waters; Tiny Footfalls; More than Conqueror; The History of De Soto's Conquest of Florida. *Put. Ran.*

√ **Irving, Washington.** *N. Y.*, 1783–1859. The most popular of the earlier American writers of the 19th century. He was born in New York city, and his earliest work was Salmagundi, written with his brother William and J. K. Paulding, *infra*. Diedrich Knickerbocker's History of New York, his next work, and the one by which he will be longest remembered, appeared in 1809. Irving spent the years from 1815 to 1832 abroad, a portion of the time as secretary of the United States Legation at London, and from 1842 to 1846 as minister to Spain. The rest of his life was spent at his home in Tarrytown on the

Hudson. His writings not already named include, The Sketch Book; Bracebridge Hall; Tales of a Traveller; Life and Voyages of Columbus; Conquest of Grenada; The Companions of Columbus; The Alhambra; Crayon Miscellanies; Astoria; Adventures of Captain Bonneville; Life of Oliver Goldsmith; Mahomet and his Successors; Wolfert's Roost; Life of Washington; Spanish Papers. *See Life and Letters of, by Pierre Irving; Atlantic Monthly, November, 1860, and June, 1864; Haweis's American Humourists; Irvingiana; Life by C. D. Warner; Allibone's Dictionary; Appleton's American Biography; Nichol's American Literature; The Bookman, February, 1897. Cr. Har. Kt. Lip. Mac. Put.*

Irving, William. *N. Y.*, 1766–1821. Brother of Washington Irving, *supra*. A merchant of New York city who was in Congress, 1814–18. He was author of the poetical portion of Salmagundi.

Ives, Levi Silliman. *Ct.*, 1797–1867. The second Protestant Episcopal bishop of North Carolina, consecrated in 1832 and deposed in 1853, he having become a Roman Catholic at the close of 1852. After that period he lectured in convents of the Sacred Heart. Trials of a Mind in its Progress to Catholicism; The Obedience of Faith; Manual of Devotion; Humility a Ministerial Qualification.

J

Jackson, Abraham Reeves. *Pa.*, 1827——. A noted surgeon of Chicago, who has published many valuable professional papers.

Jackson, Abraham Willard. *Me.*, 1842——. A Unitarian clergyman who was formerly a pastor in New Hampshire and California, but has since devoted himself to study and literary work at Concord, Massachusetts. The Immanent God, and Other Essays. *Hou.*

Jackson, Charles. *Ms.*, 1775–1855. A jurist of Boston who published a valued Treatise on Real Actions.

Jackson, Charles Davis. *Ms.*, 1811–1871. An Episcopal clergyman of Westchester, New York, 1843–71, whose only published work is Suffering Here and Glory Hereafter. *Ran.*

Jackson, Charles Thomas. *Ms.*, 1805–1880. A Boston scientist whose laboratory for research in analytical chemistry was the first of its kind in the United States. Report on the Geology of Maine; Mineral Lands in Michigan; Manual of Etherization.

Jackson, Edward Payson. *Ty.*, 1840——. An educator of Boston, master in the Latin School from 1877. Mathematic Geography; A Demigod, a novel; The Earth in Space; Character Building. *Har. Hou.*

Jackson, Francis. *Ms.*, 1789–1861. A once prominent reformer who was president of the Anti-Slavery Society for many years, and published a History of Newton, Massachusetts (his home), from 1639 to 1800.

Jackson, George Anson. *Ms.*, 1846——. A Congregational clergyman of Swampscott, Massachusetts. The Son of a Prophet, an historical novel; Apostolic Fathers; Fathers of the Second Century; Post-Nicene Greek Fathers; Post-Nicene Latin Fathers, four works which form a series of early Christian literature primers. *Hou.*

Jackson, George Thomas. *N. Y.*, 1852——. A noted dermatologist of New York city. Diseases of the Hair and Scalp; Baldness; Handbook of Diseases of the Skin.

Jackson, Mrs. Helen [Fiske] [Hunt]. "H. H." *Ms.*, 1831–1885. A novelist and poet whose greatest achievement is Ramona, a powerful romance of Indian life in southern California. To her is usually attributed the authorship of the "Saxe Holm" stories. Her other works include, Verses; Bits of Travel; Bits of Talk; A Century of Dishonor; Bits of Talk in Verse and Prose; Bits of Travel at Home; The Story of Boon, a Poem; Sonnets and Lyrics; Nelly's Silver Mine; Cat Stories; Mercy Philbrick's Choice; Hetty's StrangeHistory; Zeph; Glimpses of Three Coasts; Between Whiles, a collection of short stories; The Procession of Flowers in Colorado; Condition and Needs of the Mission Indians of California (with K. Abbot). *See Allibone's Dictionary, Supplement. Kt. Rob.*

Jackson, Henry Rootes. *Ga.*, 1820——. A Georgia jurist who was minister to Austria, 1854–58, and to Mexico 1885–86. During the Civil War he was a general in the Confederate army. Tallulah, and Other Poems, was published in 1850. *See Griswold's Poets and Poetry of America.*

Jackson, Isaac W——. *N.Y.*, 1805–1877. An educator who was professor of mathematics in Union College from 1826, and did much toward developing the arts of landscape gardening and horticulture. Elements of Conic Sections; Treatise on Optics.

Jackson, James. *Ms.*, 1777–1867. Son of C. Jackson, *supra.* The first physician of the Massachusetts General Hospital at Boston, and professor of medicine at Harvard University from 1810 until his death. On the Brunonian System; Medical Effects of Dentition; Syllabus of Lectures; Text-Book of Lectures; Letters to a Young Physician.

Jackson, James Caleb. *N. Y.*, 1811——. The founder of a popular hydropathic institution at Dansville, New York, called "Our Home." Hints on the Reproductive Organs; The Sexual Organism and its Healthful Management; Consumption; Tobacco and its Effect; How to Treat the Sick without Medicine; Dancing, its Evils and Benefits; American Womanhood; Training of Children; Debilities of Our Boys; Christ as a Physician; Morning Watches.

Jackson, Sheldon. *N. Y.*, 1834——. A Presbyterian missionary, government general agent of education in Alaska since 1885. Alaska and Missions on the North Pacific Coast; Education in Alaska. *Do.*

Jacobi [yä-kō'bē], **Abraham.** *Wa.*, 1830——. A New York city physician, professor in the College of Physicians since 1870. Dentition and its Derangements; Infant Hygiene; Diphtheria; Pathology of the Thymus Gland; Therapeutics of Infancy and Childhood; Contributions to Midwifery (with E. Noeggereth); Infant Diet. *Lip. Put.*

Jacobi, Mrs. Mary [Putnam]. *E.*, 1842——. Wife of A. Jacobi, *supra*, and daughter of George P. Putnam, a noted publisher of New York, *infra.* A physician of prominence in New York city, and the first woman to enter and graduate from the Ecole de Médecine in Paris. The Value of Life; Cold Pack and Anæmia; Hysteria, and Other Essays; The Martyr to Science; Studies in Primary Education; Common Sense Applied to Woman Suffrage; Manual of Nursing; Found and Lost. *Put.*

Jacobs, Henry Eyster. *Pa.*, 1844——. Son of M. Jacobs, *infra.* A Lutheran clergyman of Philadelphia, professor in the Lutheran Seminary from 1883, and editor of the Lutheran Review from 1882. The Lutheran Movement in England; The Lutherans; several translations of religious works from the German; History of the Evangelical Lutheran Church in the United States. *Fu.*

Jacobs, John Adamson. *Va.*, 1806–1869. An educator who was forty-five years superintendent of the deaf and dumb institution at Danville, Kentucky, his nephew of the same name succeeding him at his death. He published Primary Lessons for Deaf Mutes.

Jacobs, Michael. *Pa.*, 1808–1871. An educator who was professor in Pennsylvania College at Gettysburg, 1852–1871, and published Notes on the Rebel Invasion and the Battle of Gettysburg.

Jacobs, Michael William. *Pa.*, 1850——. Son of M. Jacobs, *supra.* A lawyer of Harrisburg, and the author of a Treatise on the Law of Domicile. *Lit.*

Jacobs, Sarah Sprague. *R. I.*, 1813——. A writer of Cambridge. Nonantum and Natick, a juvenile giving an account of the labours of John Eliot among the New England Indians; White Oak and its Neighbors.

Jacobus, Melancthon Williams. *N. J.*, 1816–1876. A Presbyterian clergyman of Brooklyn and Pittsburg, professor of Oriental literature in the theological seminary at Allegheny City, 1851–76. Letters on the Public School Question; Notes on the New Testament, a very popular work; Notes on Genesis.

Jacoby, Ludwig Sigismund. *Mg.*, 1811–1874. A Methodist clergyman of German birth who as general foreign agent of the Methodist church resided at Bremen, 1849–72. On his return to the United States he lived in St. Louis. Geschichte des Methodismus; Letzte Stunden; Kurzer Inbegriff der christlichen Glaubenlehre; Biblische Hand-Concordanz.

Jacques, Daniel Harrison. *Circa* 1825–1877. A Southern physician who edited The Rural Carolinian. Hints about Physical Perfection; The Garden; The Farm; The Barnyard; The House; Florida as a Permanent Home; How to Grow Handsome; The Temperaments; How to Behave; How to Talk.

James, Edmund Janes. *Il.*, 1855——. An educator well known as a political economist, since 1883 professor in the Wharton School of Finance in the University of Pennsylvania. Studien über den amerikanischen Zolltarif; Our Legal Tender Decisions; The Education of Business Men; The Relation of the Modern Municipality to the Gas Supply; with several translations from the German, comprise his more important works.

James, Edwin. *Vt.*, 1797–1861. A geologist and botanist whose later years were spent in Burlington, Iowa. Expedition from Pittsburg to the Rocky Mountains, 1818–19; Narrative of John Tanner; a translation of the New Testament into the Ojibway language.

James, Henry. *N. Y.*, 1811–1882. A Swedenborgian writer of Cambridge who was a thinker of marked spirituality and originality. Spiritual Creation, which he did not live to complete, affords the best example of his felicitous style and matured thought. His other works include, Society the Redeemed Form of Man; Remarks on the Gospels; Moralism and Christianity; The Nature of Evil; Substance and Shadow; The Secret of Swedenborg; What Is the State?; The Church of Christ; Christianity the Lyric of Creation; Literary Remains, edited by W. James, *infra. Hou.*

James, Henry. *N. Y.*, 1843——. Son of H. James, *supra.* A novelist and critic who since 1869 has resided in Europe, and mainly in London. He has been a prolific writer whose works have been much discussed by critics and general readers. In fiction his writings include, Roderick Hudson; The American; The Europeans; A Passionate Pilgrim, and Other Tales; Confidence; Washington Square; The Portrait of a Lady; Watch and Ward; Daisy Miller; An International Episode; The Siege of London; The Author of Beltraffio, and Other Tales; The Bostonians; The Princess Casamassima; The Reverberator; The Aspern Papers, and Other Stories; A London Life; The Tragic Muse; The Lesson of the Master, and Other Tales; The Spoils of Poynton; What Maisie Knew; The Other House; The Private Life; The Wheel of Time; Terminations; Embarrassments; Theatricals, two comedies; The Real Thing, and Other Tales; Tales of Three Cities. Other works by Mr. James are, Transatlantic Sketches; French Poets and Novelists; Portraits of Places; Life of Hawthorne; The Madonna of the Future; A Little Tour in France; Picture and Text; Essays in London; Partial Portraits. *See Hazeltine's Chats About Books; Allibone's Dictionary, Supplement; Vedder's American Writers. Har. Hou. Mac. S.*

James, Henry Ammon. *Md.*, 1854——. A lawyer of New York city who has published Communism in America.

James, William. *N. Y.*, 1842——. Son of H. James, 1st, *supra.* A psychologist of distinction, professor at Harvard University from 1872. Principles of Psychology; Psychology, a briefer study of the subject. *Ho.*

Jameson, John Alexander. *Vt.*, 1824——. A jurist of Chicago, for many years an assistant editor of The American Law Register. The Constitutional Convention, its History, Power, and Modes of Proceeding.

Jameson, John Franklin. *Ms.*, 1859——. A professor of history in Brown University. William Usselinx, Founder of the Dutch and Swedish West India Companies; The History of Historical Writing in America; Dictionary of United States History. *Hou.*

Jamison, Mrs. Cecile Viets [Hamilton]. *N. S.*, 18——. The Story of an Enthusiast; Toinette's Philip; Lady Jane; Seraph, the Little Violiniste. *Cent. Hou. We.*

Janes, Edwin Lines. *Ms.*, 1807–1875. A Methodist clergyman. Wesley his

Own Historian; Character and Career of Bishop Asbury; Memento of Edward Payson. *Meth.*

Janes, Lewis George. *R. I.*, 1844——. A lecturer of Brooklyn, for twelve years president of the Brooklyn Ethical Association. A Study of Primitive Culture; Samuell Gorton, a Forgotten Founder of Our Liberties. *Pr.*

Janeway, Jacob. *N. Y.*, 1774–1858. A Presbyterian clergyman who held several pastorates in Pennsylvania and New Jersey, and was engaged in general mission work. Exposition of the Acts, Romans, and Hebrews; Internal Evidences of the Holy Bible; Unlawful Marriage; Review of Dr. Schaff on Protestantism; The Abrahamic Covenant. *See Memoir by T. L. Janeway.*

Janney, Samuel Macpherson. *Va.*, 1801–1880. A preacher among the Hicksite Friends who in 1869 was appointed one of the government superintendents of Indian affairs. Lives of William Penn and George Fox; Conversations on Religious Subjects; The Last of the Lenape, and Other Poems; Historical Sketch of the Christian Church; Summary of Christian Doctrines Held by Friends; Peace Principles Exemplified in the Early History of Pennsylvania; History of the Religious Society of Friends from its Rise to 1828.

Janvier, Francis de Haes. *Pa.*, 1817–1885. Cousin of T. A. Janvier, *infra.* The Skeleton Monk, and Other Poems; The Sleeping Sentinel (verse); Patriotic Poems. *Lip.*

Janvier, Margaret Thomson. "Margaret Vandegrift." *La.*, 1845——. Sister of T. A. Janvier, *infra.* A Philadelphia writer of children's books, among which are, Clover Bank; Under the Dog Star; Little Helpers; A Dead Doll, and Other Verses. *Hou.*

Janvier, Thomas Allibone. *Pa.*, 1849——. A journalist and littérateur of Philadelphia, and subsequently of New York. An Embassy to Provence, a volume of travel; Color Studies: Four Stories; The Mexican Guide; Stories of Old New Spain; The Aztec Treasure House, a Romance; The Uncle of an Angel, and Other Stories; In Old New York. *Ap. Cent. Har. Scr.*

Jarves, James Jackson. *Ms.*, 1820–1888. An art connoisseur who lived in Hawaii, 1838–49, and subsequently for many years in Florence. Why and What Am I?; Art Studies; History of the Sandwich Islands (1843); Scenes and Scenery in the Sandwich Islands; Parisian Sights and French Principles; Italian Sights and Papal Principles; Kiana, a Tradition of Hawaii; A Glimpse at the Art of Japan; Art Hints; The Art Idea; Art Thoughts; Italian Rambles; Pepero, the Boy Artist. *Har. Hou.*

Jarvis, Edward. *Ms.*, 1803–1884. A once prominent physician of Dorchester, Massachusetts. Physiology and Health; Elementary Physiology; Condition of the Insane and Idiots in Massachusetts, are his more important publications.

Jarvis, Samuel Farmar. *Ct.*, 1786–1851. An Episcopal clergyman of Connecticut. Sermons on Prophecy; No Union with Rome; Chronological Introduction to the History of the Church; The Religion of the Indian Tribes of North America.

Jay, Sir James. *N. Y.*, 1732–1815. An elder brother of J. Jay, *infra.* A physician of New York city who was knighted by George III., and who published Reflections and Observations on Gout.

Jay, John. *N. Y.*, 1745–1829. A famous New York statesman who was one of the authors of The Federalist. Of his state papers, the Address to the People of Great Britain is the most celebrated. His Correspondence and State Papers, edited by H. P. Johnston, appeared 1890–93. *See Lives by Wm. Jay, infra; Pellew; Appleton's American Biography. Put.*

Jay, John. *N. Y.*, 1817–1894. Son of W. Jay, *infra.* A lawyer and diplomat of New York who was minister to Austria, 1869–75, and a prominent opponent of slavery. Dignity of the Abolition Cause; Caste and Slavery in the American Church; America Free or America Slave, are some of his political and other pamphlets.

Jay, William. *N. Y.*, 1789–1858. Son of J. Jay, *supra.* A philanthropist of New York city who was strongly opposed to slavery. Life of John Jay;

War and Peace; Causes and Consequences of the Mexican War.

Jay, W. M. L. *See Woodruff.*

Jeffers, William Nicholson. *N. J.*, 1824–1883. A United States naval officer who became a commodore in 1878. Short Methods in Navigation; Theory and Practice of Naval Gunnery; Inspection and Proof of Cannon; Ordnance Instruction for the United States Navy.

Jefferson, Joseph. *Pa.*, 1829——. A famous actor of New York city who has published an entertaining Autobiography. He is the author of the famous play, Rip Van Winkle, in which he has long been identified with the leading rôle. *Cent. Do.*

Jefferson, Thomas. *Va.*, 1743–1826. The third president of the United States. A statesman whose literary monument is the world-famous Declaration of Independence. Other writings of his are, Notes on Virginia; Rights of British America; Manual of Parliamentary Practice. A ten-volume edition of his works was published in 1892. *See Lives by Linn, 1834; Rayner, 1834; Tucker, 1837; Dwight, 1839; Randall, 1858; Parton, 1874; J. T. Morse, 1883; Domestic Life of, by Randolph, 1871; Edinburgh Review, July, 1830, and October, 1837; North American Review, April, 1830, and January, 1835; Allibone's Dictionary; Jefferson at Monticello; Appleton's American Biography; Henry Adams's History of the Administration of Jefferson. Put.*

Jeffrey, Mrs. Rosa Vertner [Griffith] [Johnson]. *Mi.*, 1826–1894. A verse-writer of Lexington, Kentucky. Poems by Rosa; Florence Vale; The Crimson Hand, and Other Poems; Marah, a Novel; Woodburn, a Novel. *Lip.*

Jeffries, Benjamin Joy. *Ms.*, 1833——. A prominent physician of Boston. Color Blindness: its Dangers and its Detection; The Eye in Health and Disease; Diseases of the Skin.

Jenkins, John Stilwell. *N. Y.*, 1818–1852. A lawyer and journalist of Weedsport, New York. The Heroines of History; Lives of the Governors of New York; Lives of Jackson, Polk, and Calhoun; Political History of New York; History of the Mexican War; Generals of the Last War with Great Britain; Life of Silas Wright, include the larger part of his writings. *Co.*

Jenks, Jeremiah Whipple. *Mch.*, 1856——. An educator, since 1891 professor of political, municipal, and social institutions at Cornell University. Henry C. Carey als National-ökonom; Road Legislation for the American State.

Jenks, John Whipple Potter. *Ms.*, 1819–1894. A naturalist who was director of the museum of natural history at Brown University, 1872–94, and professor of agriculture and zoölogy there, 1875–94. Hunting in Florida; Jenks and Steele's Zoölogy.

Jenks, William. *Ms.*, 1778–1866. A once prominent Congregational clergyman of Boston who founded the American Oriental Society. Commentary on the Bible, long a popular work; Bible Atlas and Scripture Gazetteer.

Jenness, John Scribner. *N. H.*, 1827–1879. A lawyer of New York city. The Isles of Shoals, an Historical Sketch; The First Planting of New Hampshire. He edited Transcripts of Original Documents relating to the Early History of New Hampshire.

Jennison, Lucy White. "Owen Innsley." *Ms.*, 1850——. A verse-writer who has lived mainly in Europe. Love Poems and Sonnets.

Jervey, Mrs. Caroline H—— [Gilman] [Glover]. *S. C.*, 1823–1877. Daughter of S. Gilman, *infra.* A writer of fiction and occasional verse. Vernon Grove; Helen Courtenay's Promise.

Jervis, John Bloomfield. *N. Y.*, 1795–1885. A civil engineer of New York who designed many important works, such as the Croton Dam and High Bridge. Railway Property; Labor and Capital. *Bai.*

Jessup, Henry Harris. *Pa.*, 1832——. A Presbyterian missionary in Syria from 1856. The Women of the Arabs; The Children of the East; The Greek Church and Protestant Missions; Syrian Home Life, include his most important works. *Do.*

Jeter, Jeremiah Bell. *Va.*, 1802–1880. A Baptist clergyman prominent in the South as a preacher and controversialist. Among his writings are, Campbellism Examined; Campbellism Re-Examined; The Seal of Heaven; The Christian Mirror; Recollections of a Long Life. *See Life by W. E. Hatcher.*

Jewett, Charles Coffin. *Me.*, 1816–1868. A bibliographer who was the first superintendent of the Boston Public Library. Facts and Considerations Relative to Duties on Books; Notices of Public Libraries in the United States; Construction of Catalogues.

Jewett, George Baker. *Me.*, 1818–1880. Brother of C. C. Jewett, *supra*. A New England educator whose principal works were Baptism versus Immersion; Critique on the Greek Text of the New Testament.

Jewett, Milo Parker. *Vt.*, 1808–1882. An educator who was the first president of Vassar College. Baptism; The Relation of Boards of Health and Intemperance.

Jewett, Sarah Orne. *Me.*, 1849——. A popular writer of quiet fiction whose life has been passed mainly at her birthplace in South Berwick, Maine, and in Boston. Her painstaking, accurate studies of phases of rural New England life and character have received much well-deserved praise. Old Friends and New; Play-Days; Country By-Ways; Deephaven; The Mate of the Daylight, and Friends Ashore; A Country Doctor; A Marsh Island; A White Heron, and Other Stories; The Story of the Normans, an historical work; The King of Folly Island, and Other People; Betty Leicester, a Story for Girls; Strangers and Wayfarers; A Native of Winby, and Other Tales; The Life of Nancy; The Country of the Pointed Firs. *See Bibliography of Maine. Hou. Put.*

Johnson, Alexander Bryan. *E.*, 1786–1867. A prominent banker of Utica for nearly half a century. Treatise on Banking; The Philosophy of Human Knowledge; Religion in its Relations to the Present Life; The Physiology of the Senses; The Meaning of Words; Nature and Value of Capital; Encyclopædia of Instruction; Guide to the Right Understanding of Our American Union.

Johnson, Barton W——. *Il.*, 1833–1894. A Campbellite minister and educator of Iowa. The Vision of the Ages; Commentary on John; The People's New Testament; Young Folks in Bible Lands.

Johnson, Benjamin F., of Boone. *See Riley, James Whitcomb.*

Johnson, Charles Frederick. *N.Y.*, 1836——. A professor of English literature in Trinity College. English Words, an Elementary Study of Derivations; Three Americans and Three Englishmen, lectures. *Har.*

Johnson, Clifton. *Ms.*, 1865——. A writer and illustrator of Hadley, Massachusetts, best known by his photographic illustrations to White's Selborne and other books. What They Say in New England; A Book of Country Clouds and Sunshine; The Country School in New England; The Farmer's Boy; The New England Country. *Ap. Le.*

Johnson, Edward. *E.*, 1600–1682. The principal founder of Woburn, Massachusetts, in 1640, and a prominent citizen of that town for the rest of his life. The Wonder-Working Providence of Zion's Saviour in New England is a valuable account of New England "from the English planting in 1628 till 1652." An edition, with Introduction and Notes by W. F. Poole, *infra*, appeared in 1867. *See Tyler's American Literature; Bibliography of Rhode Island.*

Johnson, Edwin A——. *N.Y.*, 1829——. A Methodist clergyman. Half-Hour Studies of Life; The Live Boy, or Charley's Letters; Winter Greeneries at Home; The Lilyvale Club and its Doings. *Meth.*

Johnson, Francis Howe. *Ms.*, 1835——. A Congregational clergyman in Andover, Massachusetts. What is Reality? an Inquiry as to the Reasonableness of Natural Religion, and the Naturalness of Revealed Religion. *Hou.*

Johnson, Frank Grant. *Ct.*, 1835——. A physician and inventor of Brooklyn. The Water Metre and the Actual Measurement System; The Nicholson and Other Pavements; Health Lifts; Infected Air and Disinfectants.

Johnson, Franklin. 1836——. A Baptist clergyman, professor in Chicago

University, and previously pastor of a church in Cambridge. Quotations of the New Testament from the Old; True Womanhood; The New Psychic Studies in their Relation to Christian Thought; Heine's Lyrical Interludes, with introduction and notes; Dies Irae, and Stabat Mater, with introduction and notes. *Bap. Fu. Lo.*

Johnson, Mrs. Helen [Kendrick]. *N. Y.*, 1843——. Wife of Rossiter Johnson, *infra*, and daughter of A. C. Kendrick, *infra*. She has edited Our Familiar Songs; Tears for the Little Ones; The Nutshell Series, and other works; and has written Raleigh Westgate, or Epimenides in Maine; The Roddy Books; Woman and the Republic. *Ap. Ho. Hou. Put.*

Johnson, Herrick. *N.Y.*, 1832——. A Presbyterian clergyman of Chicago, professor in McCormick Theological Seminary from 1880. Christianity's Challenge; Plain Talks about Theatres; Forms for Special Occasions; Revivals. *Rev.*

Johnson, John Butler. *O.*, 1850——. A professor of civil engineering in Washington University, at St. Louis, from 1883. Theory and Practice of Surveying; Modern Framed Structures; Stadia and Earth-Work Tables. *Wil.*

Johnson, Mrs. Laura [Winthrop]. *Ct.*, 1825——. Sister of Theodore Winthrop, *infra*. A writer of New York city. Little Blossom's Reward; Poems of Twenty Years; Eight Hundred Miles in an Ambulance. *Lip.*

Johnson, Oliver. *Vt.*, 1809–1889. An editor and lecturer of New York city, successively managing editor of The Independent, editor of the Weekly Tribune, and editor of the Christian Union. William Lloyd Garrison and his Times. *Hou.*

Johnson, Richard W. *Ky.*, 1827–1897. A brigadier-general in the Federal army during the Civil War, brevetted major-general. A Soldier's Reminiscences in Peace and War; Life of Major-General George H. Thomas.

Johnson, Robert Underwood. *D. C.*, 1853——. A New York writer on the editorial staff of The Century Magazine from 1873. The Winter Hour and Other Poems. *Cent.*

Johnson, Mrs. Rosa V. *See Jeffrey, Mrs.*

Johnson, Rossiter. *N. Y.*, 1840——. A writer of New York city who has edited Appleton's Annual Cyclopædia from 1883, and also edited Famous Single Poems; Play-day Poems; Little Classics; The Authorized History of the World's Columbian Exposition, and other works. His original writings include, Phaëton Rogers, a Novel of Boy Life; History of the French War, Ending in the Conquest of Canada; History of the War of 1812–15; A Short History of the War of Secession, enlarged as Campfire and Battlefield; The End of a Rainbow, an American Story; Idler and Poet (verse); Three Decades (verse). *Ap. Do. Ho. Hou. Scr.*

Johnson, Samuel. *Ct.*, 1696–1772. An Episcopal clergyman of Stratford, Connecticut, who was president of Columbia (then Kings) College, 1753–63. A System of Morality, republished by Franklin as Elementa Philosophia; English and Hebrew Grammar. An influential writer in his day. *See Life and Correspondence by E. E. Beardsley; Life by T. B. Chandler, 1805.*

Johnson, Samuel. *Ms.*, 1822–1882. A Unitarian clergyman of radical views, pastor of an independent church in Lynn for many years. Oriental Religions; Lectures, Essays, and Sermons; The Worship of Jesus in its Past and Present Aspect. *See Memoir by S. Longfellow, infra. Hou.*

Johnson, Samuel William. *N. Y.*, 1830——. A professor of chemistry in Sheffield Scientific School at Yale University from 1856. Essays on Manures; Peat and Its Uses; How Crops Feed; Chemical Notation and Nomenclature, and several translations of German scientific works. *Wil.*

Johnson, Mrs. Sarah [Barclay]. *Va.*, 1837–1885. Daughter of J. T. Barclay, *supra*. She lived for many years in Syria, where her husband was consul-general. The Hadji in Syria was her only published work.

Johnson, Thomas Cary. *W. Va.*, 1859——. A Presbyterian clergyman, professor of ecclesiastical polity in Union Seminary, Virginia, from 1892. The History of the Southern Presbyterian Church.

Johnson, Virginia Wales. *L. I.*, 1847——. A novelist who has resided in Europe since 1875, and mainly in Italy. The Neptune Vase is her finest effort. Her other works comprise, Joseph the Jew; A Sack of Gold; The Calderwood Secret; Two Old Cats; Miss Nancy's Pilgrimage; A Foreign Marriage; An English Daisy Miller; The House of the Musician; Tulip Place; The Fainalls of Tipton; America's Godfather. *Est. Har. Hou. Scr.*

Johnson, Walter Rogers. *Ms.*, 1794–1852. A once prominent chemist of Boston and elsewhere. The Use of Anthracite; Report on Coals; Coal Trade of British America; Natural Philosophy; Memoir of L. D. von Schweinitz, *infra.*

Johnston, Alexander. *L. I.*, 1849–1889. A professor of political economy at Princeton College, 1883–89. The Genesis of a New England State; History of the United States for Schools; The United States, its History and Constitution; History of Connecticut; History of American Politics. *Ho. Hou. Scr.*

Johnston, Henry Phelps. 1842——. A professor of history in the College of the City of New York. Loyalist History of the Revolution; The Campaign of 1776 around New York; The Yorktown Campaign; Yale and her Honor Roll in the American Revolution; Observations on Judge Jones. *Har.*

Johnston, John. *Me.*, 1806–1879. An educator who was for many years professor of natural science in Wesleyan University. Manual of Chemistry; Manual of Natural Philosophy; Primer of Natural Philosophy; History of the Towns of Bristol and Bremen in Maine.

Johnston, Joseph Eggleston. *Va.*, 1807–1891. A famous general in the Confederate service who surrendered to General Sherman on April 26, 1865. He published a Narrative of Military Operations, a spirited defence of his military policy. *See Life of, by R. M. Hughes. Ap.*

Johnston, Richard Malcolm. *Ga.*, 1822——. A Baltimore writer and educator whose humourous writings are very distinctly original. Life of Alexander Stephens, *infra* (with W. H. Browne, *supra*); Dukesborough Tales; Old Mark Langston; Two Gray Tourists; Mr. Absalom Billingslea and Other Georgia Folk; Ogeechee Cross-Firings; Studies, Literary and Social; The Primes and Their Neighbors; Mr. Billy Downs and his Likes; Widow Guthrie, a Novel; The Chronicles of Mr. Bill Williams; Mr. Fortner's Marital Claims; Little Ike Templin, stories for young people; English Classics: a Historical Sketch. *Ap. Har. Lip. Lo.*

Johnston, William Preston. *Ky.*, 1831——. An educator of Louisiana, president of Tulane University from 1884. He is the son of the Confederate general, Albert Sidney Johnston, whose life he has written. He has also written The Prototype of Hamlet. *Ap.*

Johonnot, James. *Vt.*, 1823–1888. An educator of Illinois and Missouri. Principles and Practice of Teaching; Glimpses of the Animate World; Book of Cats and Dogs; Friends in Feathers and Fur; Some Curious Flyers, Creepers, and Swimmers; Schoolhouses; Schoolhouse Architecture. *Ap.*

Jones, Alexander. *N. C.*, *c.* 1802–1863. A New York journalist who was a physician in the earlier portion of his career. Cuba in 1851; Historical Sketch of the Electric Telegraph, 1852; The Cymri of Seventy-Six.

Jones, Amanda Theodosia. *O.*, 1835——. An educator and inventor of Chicago. Her writings in verse comprise Ulah, and Other Poems; Atlantis; A Prairie Idyl.

Jones, Charles Colcock. *Ga.*, 1804–1863. A Presbyterian clergyman of Georgia. Religious Instruction for Negroes; History of The Church of God.

Jones, Charles Colcock. *Ga.*, 1831–1893. Son of C. C. Jones, *supra.* A lawyer and archæologist of Augusta, Georgia. Ancient Tumuli in Georgia; Antiquities of the Southern Indians; The History of Georgia; Negro Myths from the Georgia Coast; Biographical Sketches of the Delegates from Georgia to the Continental Congress; The English Colonization of Georgia. *Ap. Hou.*

Jones, George. *Me.*, 1800–1870. An Episcopal chaplain in the United States navy. Sketches of Naval Life; Life

Scenes from the Gospels; Life Scenes from the Old Testament; Excursions to Cairo, Jerusalem, etc.

Jones, Horatio Gates. *Pa.*, 1822——. A lawyer of Philadelphia who has published many local histories and biographies, among the latter being Andrew Bradford, Founder of the Newspaper Press in the Middle States.

Jones, Hugh. *E.*, 1669–1760. An Episcopal clergyman, for sixty-five years rector of parishes in Virginia and Maryland. He was author of The Present State of Virginia, a work much valued by collectors of colonial literature.

Jones, James Athearn. *Ms.*, 1790–1853. A journalist of Philadelphia and elsewhere. Traditions of the North American Indians; Haverhill, a novel.

Jones, Jenkin Lloyd. *W.*, 1843——. A Unitarian clergyman of Chicago, editor of Unity from 1880. Practical Piety; The Faith that Makes Faithful.

Jones, Joel. *Ct.*, 1795–1860. A jurist of Philadelphia who wrote much on theological topics, and was the first president of Girard College. Manual of Pennsylvania Land Law; Jesus and the Coming Glory; Knowledge of One Another in a Future State, are among his works.

Jones, John Beauchamp. *Md.*, 1810–1866. A journalist whose books enjoyed considerable popularity at one time, but have very little literary merit. A Rebel War Clerk's Diary; Wild Western Scenes; Border War; Love and Money; Life and Adventures of a Country Merchant; War Path; Freaks of Fortune; The Rival Belles, are some of them. *Lip.*

Jones, Joseph. *Ga.*, 1833——. Son of C. C. Jones, 1st, *supra.* A physician, professor in Tulane University, New Orleans, from 1869. Among his writings are, Sanitary Memoirs of the War of the Rebellion; Surgical Memoirs of the War of the Rebellion; Hospital Construction and Organization; Medical and Surgical Memoirs.

Jones, Joseph Huntington. *Ct.*, 1797–1868. Brother of Joel Jones, *supra.* A Presbyterian clergyman of Philadelphia. The Effects of Physical Causes on Christian Experience; Life of Ashbel Green, *supra;* Revival of Religion.

Jones, Joseph Seawell. *N. C.*, c. 1811–1855. A Southern writer who published Defence of the Revolutionary History of North Carolina; Memorials of North Carolina.

Jones, Joseph Stevens. 1811–1877. An extremely prolific playwright of Boston, among whose best known productions are, Solon Shingle; Eugene Aram; The Silver Spoon; The Liberty Tree; Moll Pitcher.

Jones, Leonard Augustus. *Ms.*, 1832——. A lawyer of Boston, editor of The American Law Register. Personal Property; The Law of Mortgages of Real Property; On The Law of Pledges; Pledges and Collateral Securities; Corporate Bonds and Mortgages; Chattel Mortgages; Liens; Real Estate in Conveyancing; Forms in Conveyancing. *Hou.*

Jones, Samuel Porter. *Al.*, 1847——. A noted and eccentric revival preacher. Sam Jones's Sermons; Music Hall Sermons; Sam Jones's Own Book. *Meth.*

Jones, William Alfred. *N. Y.*, 1817——. A critic and essayist of Norwich, Connecticut. The Analyst; Essays upon Authors and Books; Characters and Criticisms; Literary Studies.

Jordan, Mrs. Cornelia Jane [Matthews]. *Va.*, 1830——. A Virginia writer of verse whose volume, Corinth, and Other Poems of the War, was publicly burnt on its appearance in 1865, by order of General Terry, as an objectionable and incendiary publication. Her other works are, Flowers of Hope and Memory; Christmas Poem for Children; Richmond, her Glory and her Graves; Useful Maxims for a Noble Life.

Jordan, David Starr. *N. Y.*, 1851——. A noted naturalist who became the first president of Leland Stanford Junior University. Besides a great number of scientific papers and monographs, he has published A Manual of the Vertebrate Animals of the Northern United States; Scientific Sketches; Contributions to American Ichthology; The Factors in Organic Evolution. *Gi. Mg.*

Jordan, Mrs. Dulcie [Mason]. *N. Y.*, 1835——. A journalist and verse-writer of Richmond, Indiana, who has published Rosemary Leaves, a volume of uneven but often pleasing verse.

Jordan, John Woolf. *Pa.*, 1840——. A Philadelphia antiquarian, editor of the Pennsylvania Magazine of History. Friedensthal and its Stockaded Mill; A Red Rose from the Olden Time; Something about Trombones; Occupation of New York by the British.

Jordan, Thomas. *Va.*, 1819——. A Confederate officer, editor of The Mining Record. The South, its Products, Commerce, and Resources (1861); Campaigns of Lieutenant-General Forrest.

Jouin, Louis. *P.*, 1818——. A Jesuit educator of note, professor at St. John's College, Fordham. Elementa Philosophiæ Moralis; Compendium Logicæ et Metaphysicæ; Evidences of Religion.

Joyce, Robert Dwyer. *I.*, 1836–1883. An Irish journalist who came to America in 1866 and settled in Boston. Ballads, Romances, and Songs; Deirdrè, a Poem; Ballads of Irish Chivalry; Irish Fireside Tales; Legends on the Wars in Ireland; Blanid; The Squire of Castleton, an historical novel. *Rob.*

Judd, Sylvester. *Ms.*, 1789–1860. An antiquarian of Northampton, Massachusetts. Thomas Judd and his Descendants; History of Hadley. *See Memorials of, by A. Hall, supra.*

Judd, Sylvester. *Ms.*, 1813–1853. Son of S. Judd, *supra.* A Unitarian clergyman of Augusta, Maine. His greatest work is the remarkable story of Margaret: a Tale of the Real and the Ideal. Other works of his include, Philo, a religious poem; Richard Edney, a novel; The Church, a series of sermons. *See Nichol's American Literature; Lowell's Fable for Critics. Rob.*

Judson, Edward Z—— C——. *Pa.*, 1822–1886. A writer of sensational non-literary stories for weekly papers which gave him a large income. He was also a temperance lecturer. Among his stories are, Rod Ralph the Ranger; The Sea Bandit; Buffalo Bill; The White Cruiser.

Judson, Mrs. Emily [Chubbuck]. "Fanny Forester." *N. Y.*, 1817–1854. A once popular writer who was the third wife of the famous Baptist missionary, Adoniram Judson. Alderbrook, a collection of stories; Trippings in Author Land; An Olio of Domestic Verses.

Judson, Harry Pratt. *N. Y.*, 1849——. A professor of political science in the University of Chicago. Europe in the Nineteenth Century; The Growth of the American Nation; Cæsar's Army, a Study of the Military Art of the Romans. *Gi. Fl.*

Judson, L—— Carroll. 18——. Biography of the Signers of the Declaration of Independence; Sages and Heroes of the American Revolution; The Moral Probe, a collection of Essays. *Le.*

Julian, George Washington. *Ind.*, 1817——. An Indiana statesman, surveyor-general of New Mexico in 1885. Speeches on Political Questions; Political Recollections from 1840–72; Life of Joshua Giddings, *supra. Mg.*

June, Jennie. *See Croly.*

Junkin, David Xavier. *Pa.*, 1808–1880. A Presbyterian clergyman of Chicago and elsewhere. The Good Steward; Life of General Hancock (with F. H. Norton); The Oath a Divine Ordinance. *Ap.*

Junkin, George. *Pa.*, 1790–1868. Brother of D. X. Junkin, *supra.* A Presbyterian clergyman once prominent among leaders of the Old School party. He was the founder of Lafayette College, Easton, Pennsylvania, and was twice its president. His more important works include, Commentary on Hebrews; Political Fallacies; The Great Apostasy; Sanctification; Justification; The Tabernacle. *See Biography by D. X. Junkin.*

Junkin, Margaret. Daughter of G. Junkin, *supra. See Preston, Mrs.*

K

Kaler, James Otis. *Me.*, 1846——. A journalist of New York city who has written much for juvenile readers. The Boy Captain; Under the Liberty Tree; A Short Cruise; The Boys' Revolt; Toby Tyler; Left Behind; Mr. Stubbs's Brother; Tom and Tip; Raising the

Pearl; Silent Pete; The Castaways; Little Joe; Stories of American History; Jerry's Family; Jenny Wren's Boarding-House. *Cr. Est. Har.*

Kalisch, Isidor. *P.*, 1816–1886. A Jewish clergyman who came to the United States in 1849, and was rabbi of congregations in Cleveland, Milwaukee, and elsewhere. He published Sketch of the Talmud, and several important translations from the German and Hebrew.

Kane, Elisha Kent. *Pa.*, 1820–1857. A surgeon in the United States navy who was famous as an Arctic explorer. The United States Grinnell Expedition of 1850; Second Grinnell Expedition. *See Lives by Elder and Schmucker.*

Kane, Thomas Leiper. *Pa.*, 1822–1883. Brother of E. K. Kane, *supra.* A lawyer of Philadelphia, and a brigadier-general in the Federal army in the Civil War. The Mormons; Alaska; Coahuila.

Kautz, August Valentine. *G.*, 1828–1895. An officer in the United States army who served in the Civil War and in several subsequent Indian campaigns, and became a colonel and brevet major-general. The Company Clerk; Customs of Service for Non-Commissioned Officers and Soldiers; Customs of Service for Officers. *Lip.*

Keating, John M——. *Pa.*, 1852-——. A Philadelphia physician. With General Grant in the East; Mothers' Guide for Management of Infants; Maternity, Infancy, and Childhood; Diseases of the Heart (with W. A. Edwards), include his principal writings. *Lip.*

Kedney, John Steinfort. *N. J.*, 1819——. An Episcopal clergyman, professor in Seabury Divinity School at Faribault, Minnesota, from 1871. Mens Christi, and Other Problems in Theology; Catawba, and Other Poems; The Beautiful and the Sublime, an Analysis of the Emotions; Hegel's Æsthetics; Christian Doctrine Harmonized. *Put. Sc.*

Keeler, Charles Augustus. *Wis.*, 1871——. An ornithologist and verse-writer of California. Evolution of Color in North American Land Birds; A Light through the Storm.

Keeler, Ralph. *O.*, 1840–1873. A journalist of California and New York. Gloverson and his Silent Partner; Vagabond Adventures.

Keen, William Williams. *Pa.*, 1837——. An eminent Philadelphia surgeon, professor of surgery at Jefferson Medical College from 1889. Reflex Paralysis; Gunshot Wounds; Clinical Chart of the Human Body; Complications and Sequels of Continuous Fever; Early History of Practical Anatomy.

Keenan, Henry Francis. *N. Y.*, 1849——. A journalist and novelist formerly of Rochester, New York. The Money-Makers, a Social Problem; Trajan, the History of a Sentimental Young Man; The Aliens; One of a Thousand; The Iron Game. *Ap. Cas.*

Keep, Josiah. *Ms.*, 1849——. An educator of California. Common Sea Shells of California; West Coast Shells.

Keep, Robert Porter. *Ct.*, 1844-——. An educator of Norwich, Connecticut. Stories from Herodotus; Essential Uses of the Moods in Greek and Latin; Greek Lessons. *Har.*

Keith, Alyn Yates. *See Morris, Mrs.*

Keller, Joseph Edward. *Bv.*, 1827–1886. A Jesuit educator, president of St. Louis University. Life and Acts of Pope Leo XIII. (1880).

Kelley, Hall Jackson. *N. H.*, 1790–1874. An educator of Boston who organized the first Sunday-school in New England, and made an unsuccessful attempt to colonize Oregon in 1830. Geographical Description of Oregon; Letters from an Afflicted Husband; History of the Settlement of Oregon.

Kelley, James Douglas Jerrold. 185——. A lieutenant in the United States navy. The Question of Ships; Our Navy; A Desperate Chance, a story. *Scr.*

Kelley, William Darrah. *Pa.*, 1814–1890. A jurist of Philadelphia who was in Congress from 1860, and was very prominent as an abolitionist and a protectionist. Speeches, Addresses, and Letters on Political Questions; Letters from Europe; Lincoln and Stanton; The Old South and the New. *Bai.*

Kellogg, Alfred Hosea. *Pa.*, 1837-——. A Presbyterian clergyman of Detroit. Abraham, Joseph, and Moses in Egypt, an attempted solution of the Exodus problem.

Kellogg, Elijah. *Me.*, 1813——. A Congregational clergyman of Harpswell, Maine, from 1844. He has written many popular juvenile books, including Elm Island Series; Forest Glen Series; Good Old Times Series; Pleasant Cove Series; Whispering Pine Series, but perhaps is best known as the author of the Address of Spartacus to the Gladiators. *See Bibliography of Maine. Le.*

Kellogg, Samuel Henry. *L. I.*, 1839——. A Presbyterian missionary to India. Grammar of the Hindi Language; The Jews, or Prediction and Fulfillment; The Light of Asia and the Light of the World; From Death to Resurrection; The Genesis and Growth of Religion. *Mac.*

Kellogg, Warren Franklin. *N. Y.*, 1860——. A Boston publisher. Recent French Art; Hunting in the Jungle, adapted from "Les Animaux Sauvages." *Est.*

Kelton, John Cunningham. *Pa.*, 1828——. A brigadier-general in the United States army. New Manual of the Bayonet; Fencing with Foils; Pigeons as Couriers; Information for Riflemen.

Kendall, Amos. *Ms.*, 1789–1869. A once famous journalist, politician, and philanthropist of Washington. Life of Andrew Jackson; Autobiography (edited by W. Stickney). *Le.*

Kendall, George Wilkins. *Vt.*, 1810——. A journalist of New Orleans. The War between the United States and Mexico; The Texan Santa Fé Expedition. *Ap.*

Kendrick, Asahel Clark. *Vt.*, 1809–1895. A noted Greek scholar who was professor of Greek at Rochester University from 1850. Echoes: metrical translations from the Greek and German; The Moral Conflict of Humanity and Other Papers; Life of Mrs. Emily Judson, *supra;* A Child's Book of Greek; Introduction to the Greek Language, are among his writings. He was one of the Revisers of the New Testament, published independent commentaries and translations, and edited Our Poetical Favorites. *Bap. Hou.*

Kenly, John Reese. *Md.*, 1822–1891. A captain and major of volunteers in the Mexican War, and brigadier-general in the Federal army in the Civil War. Memoirs of a Maryland Volunteer in the Mexican War.

Kennan, George. *O.*, 1845——. A noted traveller who made a careful investigation of the Russian exile system for The Century Magazine, and drew world-wide attention to the subject. Tent Life in Siberia; Siberia and the Exile System. *Cent. Put.*

Kennedy, Crammond. *S.*, 1842——. A lawyer of Washington. James Stanly, a Sunday-school tale; The Liberty of the Press; Corn in the Blade, a book of verse; Close Communion or Open Communion.

Kennedy, John Pendleton. *Md.*, 1795–1870. A once famous novelist who was a prominent Maryland politician and secretary of the navy in 1852. Annals of Quodlibet; At Home and Abroad; Swallow Barn; Horse-Shoe Robinson; Rob of the Bowl; Life of William Wirt. *See Life by H. T. Tuckerman, infra. Put.*

Kennedy, William Sloane. *Pa.*, 1822–1861. A Congregational clergyman of Ohio. Messianic Prophecies; Life of Christ; History of the Plan of Union; Sacred Analysis.

Kennedy, William Sloane. *O.*, 1850——. A littérateur of Belmont, Massachusetts. Lives of Longfellow, Holmes, and Whittier; Wonders and Curiosities of the Railway; Poems of the Weird and Mystical; Reminiscences of Walt Whitman; Art of Life, a Ruskin Anthology; Whittier, the Poet of Freedom; In Portia's Gardens; Bibliography and Literary History of Leaves of Grass. *Fu. Lo. Mer. Wn.*

Kenrick, Francis Patrick. *I.*, 1797–1863. The Roman Catholic archbishop of Baltimore, 1851–63. An active controversialist and a biblical scholar of distinction. Theologia Dogmatica; Theologia Moralis; The Primacy of the Apostolic See Vindicated; Vindication of the Catholic Church; End of Religious Controversy Controverted, are among his many works. He also published a translation of the Scriptures with commentary.

Kenrick, Peter Richard. *I.*, 1806–1896. Brother of F. P. Kenrick. The first Roman Catholic archbishop of St. Louis. In the Ecumenical Council of 1870 he actively opposed the dogma of papal infallibility. The Holy House of Lorretto; Anglican Ordinations; Concia in Concilio Vaticana.

Kent, James. *N. Y.*, 1763–1847. A jurist of eminence who was chancellor of New York, 1814–23, and professor of law at Columbia College, 1793–1798, and again on retiring from the chancellorship of the State. His famous Commentaries on American Law, a work of the highest authority, reached a 13th edition in 1884, that of Holmes and Barnes. He published also a treatise On the Charter of New York City. *See Duer's Discourse on Life of Kent. Lit.*

Kenyon, James Benjamin. *N. Y.*, 1858——. A Methodist clergyman of Syracuse who has written much verse of a pleasing if not very striking kind. Out of the Shadows; The Fallen, and Other Poems; Songs in All Seasons; In Realms of Gold; At the Gate of Dreams; An Oaten Pipe. *Lip.*

Ker, David. *E.*, 18——. A journalist of New York city. The Broken Image, and Other Tales; On the Road to Khiva; The Wild Horseman of the Pampas; The Boy Slave in Bokhara; From the Hudson to the Neva; Lost Among White Africans; Into Unknown Seas; The Lost City, or the Boy Explorers in Central Asia; The Wizard King. *Har. Lip. Lo.*

Kerr, Orpheus C. *See Newell, R. H.*

Kerr, Robert Pollok. *Ms.*, 1850——. Presbyterianism for the People; History of Presbyterianism; Hymns of the Ages; Voice of God in History.

Ketchum, Mrs. Annie [Chambers]. *Ky.*, 1824——. An educator and lecturer. Lotos Flowers (verse); Christmas Carillons, and Other Poems; Botany for Academies and Colleges; The Teacher's Empire; Nellie Braden, a novel; Rilla Motto, a romance. *Lip.*

Key, Francis Scott. *Md.*, 1780–1843. A lawyer of Washington whose miscellaneous poems were collected and published after his death. The Star-Spangled Banner, composed in 1814 during the bombardment of Fort McHenry by English forces in whose hands the author was a prisoner, is his only poem of note. *See Boyle's Biographical Sketches of Distinguished Marylanders.*

Keyes, Edward Lawrence. *S. C.*, 1843——. Son of E. D. Keyes, *infra.* A physician of New York city. The Tonic Treatment of Syphilis; Venereal Diseases; Genito-Urinary Diseases. *Ap.*

Keyes, Emerson Willard. 1828——. A lawyer of New York city. New York Court of Appeals Reports; History of United States Savings Banks; Laws of New York Relating to Common Schools, with Comments.

Keyes, Erasmus Darwin. *Ms.*, 1810–1895. A major-general in the Federal army in the Civil War, who resigned in 1864. Fifty Years' Observation of Men and Events. *Scr.*

Keyser, Peter Dirck. *Pa.*, 1835–1897. A surgeon of Philadelphia who has published Operations for Cataracts, and other works on diseases of the eye.

Kidder, Daniel Parrish. *N. Y.*, 1815–1891. A Methodist clergyman of prominence who held professorships in several theological institutions. Homiletics; The Christian Pastorate; Mormonism and the Mormons; Sketches of a Residence in Brazil; Helps to Prayer; co-author with J. C. Fletcher, *supra*, of Brazil and the Brazilians. *Meth.*

Kidder, Frederick. *N. H.*, 1804–1885. A Boston merchant among whose historical monographs are, The Boston Massacre; The Expeditions of Captain John Lovewell.

Kiddle, Henry. *E.*, 1824–1891. An educator who was superintendent of the schools of New York city, 1870–79. Text-Book of Physics; Elements of Astronomy; Dictionary of Education, include his most important works.

Kieffer, Henry Martyn. *Pa.*, 1845——. A German Reformed clergyman of Norristown, and subsequently of Easton, Pennsylvania. The Recollections of a Drummer Boy. *Hou.*

Kilbourne, Payne Kenyon. *Ct.*, 1815–1859. A journalist of Connecticut. The Skeptic and Other Poems; History of the County of Litchfield; Chronicles of Litchfield.

Kilgore, Damon Young. 1827–1888. A lawyer of Philadelphia. Dangers which Threaten the Republic; Questions of the Day.

Kimball, Arthur Lalanne. *N. J.*, 1856——. A professor of physics at Amherst College from 1891. The Physical Properties of Gases. *Hou.*

Kimball, Harriet McEwen. *N. H.*, 1834——. A religious verse-writer of Portsmouth, New Hampshire. Swallow Flights of Song; Hymns; The Blessed Company of All Faithful People; Complete Poems (1889). *Ran.*

Kimball, James William. *Ms.*, 1812–1885. A religious writer educated for the ministry, but whose life was spent in commercial pursuits. Heaven my Father's Home; Friendly Words with Fellow Pilgrims; Encouragements to Faith; How to See Jesus; The Christian Ministry.

Kimball, Richard Burleigh. *N. H.*, 1816–1892. A lawyer of New York city who founded the town of Kimball in Texas, and built the first railroad in that State. His novels and other writings at one time enjoyed considerable popularity. They include St. Leger; Undercurrents of Wall Street Life; Letters from Cuba; Letters from England; Cuba and the Cubans; Was He Successful?; To-day in New York; Stories of Exceptional Life; Henry Powers, Banker, a Novel; Romance of a Student Life Abroad.

King, Mrs. Anna [Eichberg]. *Sd.*, 1853——. A Boston writer of short stories. Brown's Retreat, and Other Stories; Kitwyk Stories. *Cent. Rob.*

King, Charles. *N. Y.*, 1844——. A United States army officer, retired in 1879 with the rank of captain, whose military novels and other works have been very popular. Among his many publications are, Famous and Decisive Battles; Between the Lines; Campaigning with Crook; Stories of Army Life; Cadet Days; The Colonel's Daughter; The Deserter; A War Time Wooing; Kitty's Conquest; Under Fire; Waring's Peril; Foes in Ambush; Fort Frayne; Noble Blood. *See Bibliography of Wisconsin. Har. Lip. Ne.*

King, Clarence. *R. I.*, 1842——. A geologist for a number of years in the government service. Mountaineering in the Sierra Nevada; Systematic Geology.

King, Dan. *Ct.*, 1791–1864. A Rhode Island physician. Life and Times of Governor Dorr; Quackery Unmasked; Tobacco: What it Is and What it Does.

King, David Bennett. *Pa.*, 1848——. A lawyer of New York city. Latin Pronunciation; The Irish Question. *Scr.*

King, Edward. *Ms.*, 1848–1896. A journalist who lived in Paris as correspondent for American journals. The Gentle Savage; The Golden Spike; French Leaders; My Paris, or French Character Sketches; Kentucky's Love; The Great South; Echoes from the Orient, a volume of poems; Europe in Storm and Calm; A Venetian Lover, a Poem; Joseph Zalmonah; Under the Red Flag. *Co. Hou. Le.*

King, Grace Elizabeth. *La.*, 1859——. A popular writer of New Orleans. Monsieur Motte; Tales of a Time and Place; Earthlings; New Orleans, the Place and the People; Jean Baptiste Lemoine, Founder of New Orleans; Balcony Stories. *Cent. Do. Har. Mac.*

King, Henry Melville. *Mo.*, 1838——. A Baptist clergyman. Early Baptists Defended; Mary's Alabaster Box, a collection of homilies; Our Gospels. *Bap.*

King, Horatio. *Me.*, 1811–1897. An attorney in Washington who was postmaster-general in 1861. Sketches of Travel, or Twelve Months in Europe; Turning on the Light, a Survey of the Administration of Buchanan. *Lip.*

King, Horatio Collins. *Me.*, 1837——. Son of H. King, *supra*. A journalist of New York city. Guide for Regimental Courts Martial; The Brooklyn Congregational Council; The Plymouth Silver Wedding.

King, James Wilson. *Md.*, 182——. A naval engineer, chief of the bureau of steam engineering, 1869–73. European Ships of War; The War Ships and Navies of the World.

King, Jonas. *Ms.*, 1792–1869. A Congregational missionary in Greece who lived at Athens from 1831. He was a profound Oriental scholar, and his various works were written in Modern Greek, Classical Greek, French, and Arabic. The Defence of Jonas King; Exposition of an Apostolic Church; Hermeneutics of the Sacred Scriptures; Sermons; Synoptical View of Palestine; Miscellaneous Works. *See Life, 1879.*

King, Rufus. *O.*, 1817–1891. A prominent lawyer of Cincinnati. History of Ohio. *Hou.*

King, Mrs. Sue [Petigru]. *See Bowen, Mrs.*

King, Thomas Starr. *N. Y.*, 1824–1864. A Unitarian clergyman of Boston, 1845–56, and of San Francisco for the remainder of his life. He was largely instrumental in securing the wavering allegiance of California to the general government at the opening of the Civil War, and as a religious writer his influence was widely felt. Substance and Show; Christianity and Humanity, with a Memoir by E. P. Whipple; The White Hills, a volume of travel in the White Mountains; Patriotism, and Other Papers. *Hou.*

King, William Basil. *P. E. I.*, 1859–——. An Episcopal clergyman of Cambridge. The Daily Song: Thoughts on the Offices for Morning and Evening Prayer.

King, William Rufus. *N. Y.*, 1839–——. An engineering officer in the United States army. Torpedoes, their Invention and Use; Materials for Defensive Armor.

Kingsley, Calvin. *N. Y.*, 1812–1870. A Methodist bishop. The Resurrection of the Dead; Round the World.

Kinney, Coates. *N. Y.*, 1826——. An Ohio lawyer and journalist. Keuka, and Other Poems; Lyrics of the Real and Ideal. The Rain upon the Roof is his most familiar poem. *Clke.*

Kinney, Mrs. Elizabeth Clementine [Dodge] [Stedman]. *N. Y.*, 1810–1889. Mother of E. C. Stedman, *infra.* A verse-writer of Newark, New Jersey, but resident in Italy, 1850–65. Felicitá; Poems; Bianca Capello: a Tragedy. *See Griswold's Female Poets of America.*

Kinzie, Mrs. Juliette Augusta [Magill]. *Ct.*, 1806–1870. A novelist of Chicago. Wau-bun, or the Early Day in the Northwest; Walter Ogilby; Mark Logan. *Lip.*

Kip, Leonard. *N. Y.*, 1826–18—. Brother of W. I. Kip, *infra.* A lawyer of Albany. California Sketches; The Volcano Diggings; Ænone, a Roman Tale; The Dead Marquise; Hannibal's Man, and Other Tales; Under the Bells, a romance; Nestlenook, a novel; At Cobweb and Crusty's; Thalöe; The Puntacooset Colony; Three Pines; A Tale of the Incredible.

Kip, William Ingraham. *N. Y.*, 1811–1893. The first Protestant Episcopal bishop of California, 1853–93. A popular religious writer whose works have gone into many editions. Double Witness of the Church; Lenten Fasts; Early Conflicts of Christianity; Christmas Holidays in Rome; Catacombs of Rome; Early Jesuit Missions in North America; Recantation, an Italian tale; The Unnoticed Things of Scripture; The Church of the Apostles; The Olden Time in New York. *Ap. Dut. Ran. Wh.*

Kirk, Edward Norris. *N.Y.*, 1802–1874. A Congregational clergyman of Boston, pastor of the Mount Vernon church, 1842–74. Sermons; The Parables of our Lord; Lectures on Revivals; Canon of the Holy Scripture; The Waiting Saviour; Christian Sympathy Awakened.

Kirk, Eleanor. *See Ames, Mrs. E.*

Kirk, Mrs. Ellen Warner [Olney]. "Henry Hayes." *Ct.*, 1842——. Wife of J. F. Kirk, *infra.* A popular novelist of Germantown, Philadelphia. Through Winding Ways; A Midsummer Madness; Walford; The Story of Margaret Kent; Sons and Daughters; Love in Idleness; A Lesson in Love; Fairy Gold; Queen Money; Better Times, short stories; A Daughter of Eve; Narden's Choosing; Ciphers; The Story of Lawrence Garthe. *Hou.*

Kirk, John Foster. *N. B.*, 1824–——. The secretary to the historian Prescott for eleven years, and since 1885 lecturer on European history at the University of Pennsylvania. History of Charles the Bold; Supplement to Allibone's Dictionary. *Lip.*

Kirkbride, Thomas Story. *Pa.*, 1809–1883. A physician of Philadelphia, widely known for skillful treatment of the insane, who was superintendent of the Pennsylvania Hospital for the Insane, 1840–83. Appeal for the Insane; Essays on Insanity; Construction of Hospitals for the Insane.

Kirke, Edmund. *See Gilmore.*

Kirkland, Mrs. Caroline Matilda [Stansbury]. *N. Y.*, 1801–1864. A once popular writer of New York city. A New Home, Who 'll Follow ?; Western Clearings; Fireside Talks on Morals and Manners; Holidays Abroad; A Book for the Home Circle; Forest Life, include her principal writings. *See Hart's American Literature. Cr. Scr.*

Kirkland, Elizabeth Stansbury. *N. Y.*, 1828–1896. Daughter of Mrs. Kirkland, *supra*. An educator of Chicago. Six Little Cooks; Dora's Housekeeping; Speech and Manners for Home and School; Short Histories of English Literature, France, England, Italy, for Young People. *Mg.*

Kirkland, John Thornton. *N. Y.*, 1770–1840. A Unitarian clergyman who was president of Harvard University, 1810–27. Life of Fisher Ames; Eulogy of General Washington.

Kirkland, Joseph. *N. Y.*, 1830–1894. Son of Mrs. Kirkland, *supra*. A lawyer of Chicago who was a major in the Federal army during the Civil War. His two novels of pioneer life in Illinois, Zury, and The McVeys, are notably faithful, graphic studies. His other writings include, The Captain of Company K; The Story of Chicago; Story of the Chicago Massacre of 1812. *Hou.*

Kirkman, Marshall Monroe. *Il.*, 1842——. The vice-president of the Chicago and Northwestern Railway. Railway Disbursements; Railway Revenue; Railway Service; Baggage Car Traffic; Railway Expenditures; Handling of Railway Supplies; Railway Rates and Government Control; How to Collect Railway Revenues without Loss.

Kirkwood, Daniel. *Md.*, 1814–1895. An astronomer of distinction, professor in Indiana University from 1850. Meteoric Astronomy; Comets and Meteors; Asteroids and Minor Planets between Mars and Jupiter.

Kirkwood, Robert. *S.*, 1793–1866. A Presbyterian clergyman of Yonkers. Lectures on the Millennium; Universalism Explained; A Plea for the Bible; Illustration of the Offices of Christ.

Kirwan. *See Murray, Nicholas.*

Klingle, George. *See Holmes, Mrs. Georgiana.*

Knapp, Arthur May. *Ms.*, 1841——. A Unitarian clergyman, pastor at Fall River, Massachusetts, from 1891. Feudal and Modern Japan. *Kt.*

Knapp, Samuel Lorenzo. *Ms.*, 1783–1838. A lawyer of New York city, among whose many works are, The Genius of Freemasonry; Travels in North America by Ali Bey; American Biography; Lives of Aaron Burr, Andrew Jackson, Daniel Webster; Female Biography.

Kneeland, Abner. *Ms.*, 1774–1844. A Universalist clergyman who became a free-thinker, and established The Investigator in Boston in 1832. The Deist; Universal Benevolence; Universal Salvation; Review of Evidences of Christianity.

Kneeland, Samuel. *Ms.*, 1821–1888. A naturalist and surgeon of Boston. Science and Mechanism; An American in Iceland; The Wonders of the Yo Semite; Volcanoes and Earthquakes. *Lo.*

Knight, Edward Henry. *E.*, 1824–1883. An English writer who settled in the United States in 1845, and was long connected with the patent office in Washington. American Mechanical Dictionary; New Mechanical Dictionary. *Hou.*

Knight, James. *Md.*, 1810——. A physician of New York city. Improvement of Health by Natural Means; Orthopædia; Static Electricity as a Therapeutic Agent.

Knight, Sarah Kemble. *Ms.*, 1666–1727. A teacher of Boston among whose pupils was Benjamin Franklin. Her Narrative of a Journey from Boston to New York in 1704 is a valuable historical record of contemporary manners and customs written in a graphic, entertaining style.

Knortz, Karl. *P.*, 1841——. A German writer who came to the United States in 1863, and settled in New York city. Märchen und Sagen der nordamerikanische Indianer; Amerikanische Skizzen; An American Shakespeare Bibliography; Humorische Gedichte; Longfellow: eine literarhistorische Studie; Aus der Wigwam; Kapital und Arbeit in Amerika; Aus der transatlantischen Gesellschaft; Staat und Kirche in Amerika; Shakespeare in Amerika; Amerikanische Lebensbilder; Brook Farm and Margaret Fuller, include his principal writings. *Ho.*

Knox, Mrs. Adeline [Trafton]. *Me.*, 1845——. A novelist of St. Louis. Katharine Earle; His Inheritance; An American Girl Abroad; Dorothy's Experience. *Le.*

Knox, Charles Eugene. *N.Y.*, 1833——. A Presbyterian clergyman, president of the theological seminary at Bloomfield, New Jersey, from 1863. A Year with Saint Paul; Love to the End; David the King; Graduated Sunday-school Text-Books. *Meth. Ran.*

Knox, George William. *N. Y.*, 1853——. A Presbyterian missionary in Japan, professor of ethics in the University of Japan from 1886. His writings in Japanese include: A Brief System of Theology; Outlines of Homiletics; Christ the Son of God; The Basis of Ethics. In English he has published The Japanese Systems of Ethics.

Knox, John Jay. *N. Y.*, 1828–1892. A financier of distinction, comptroller of the currency, 1867–84. He published United States Notes, a History of the Various Issues of Paper Money by the United States Government. *Scr.*

Knox, Thomas Wallace. *N. H.*, 1835–1896. A journalist and traveller whose home was in New York city. His books of travel for young people have been widely popular. Overland Through Asia; Camp-Fire and Cotton-Field; Backsheesh; Underground Life; John; The Boy Travellers Series, in sixteen volumes; How to Travel; Pocket Guide Around the World; The Voyage of the Vivian; Hunting Adventures on Land and Sea; Marco Polo for Boys and Girls; Decisive Battles since Waterloo; Life of Robert Fulton; Hunters Three; In Wild Africa; The Siberian Exiles; The Lost Army, include the greater number of his books. *Ap. Cas. Har. Mer. Put. We.*

Kobbe, Gustav. *N. Y.*, 1857——. A littérateur of New York city. Jersey Coast and Pines; Wagner's "Ring of the Nibelung;" New York City and its Environs. *Har.*

Koehler, Sylvester Rosa. *G.*, 1837——. An art critic of Boston, editor of the American Art Review. His more important publications are, American Art; Etching: an Outline of its Technical Processes and History. *Cas. Le.*

Koopman [kope'man], Harry Lyman. *Me.*, 1860——. A verse-writer, librarian of Brown University. The Great Admiral; Orestes, and Other Poems; Woman's Will, with Other Poems; What to Read.

Kouns [koonz], Nathan Chapman. *Mo.*, 1833–1890. A Missouri lawyer, State librarian at Jefferson City from 1886, who published two historical romances, Arius the Libyan; Dorcas the Daughter of Faustina. *Ap. Fo.*

Kraitsir, Charles. *Hy.*, 1804–1860. An educator and philologist of New York city. The Poles in the United States; Significance of the Alphabet; Glossology.

Krauth, Charles Porterfield. *Va.*, 1823–1883. A prominent Lutheran clergyman of Philadelphia, professor of moral science in the University of Pennsylvania, 1868–83. The Conservative Reformation and its Theology is his greatest work; and among others are, The Evangelical Mass and the Romish Mass; Sketch of the Thirty Years' War; Christian Liberty; Infant Baptism and Salvation in the Calvinistic System; Chronicle of the Augsburg Confession. *See American Lutheran Biographies. Lip.*

Krebs, John Michael. *Md.*, 1804–1867. A Presbyterian clergyman of New York city. Righteousness and National Prosperity; The American Citizen; Private, Domestic, and Social Life of Jesus; The Presbyterian Psalmist.

Krehbiel, Henry Edward. *Mch.*, 1854——. A musical critic on the staff of the New York Tribune. Notes on the Cultivation of Choral Music;

Review of the New York Musical Seasons, 1885–90; Studies in the Wagnerian Drama; How to Listen to Music. *Har. Scr.*

Kroeger, Adolph Ernst. *Sg.*, 1837–1882. A writer of St. Louis. The Minnesingers of Germany; Our Forms of Government and the Problems of the Future; translations of Fichte's Science of Knowledge and Science of Rights.

Kron, Karl. *See Bagg.*

Krotel, Gottlob Frederick. *Wg.*, 1826——. A Lutheran clergyman of New York city. Who are the Blessed?; Explanation of Luther's Small Catechism; several translations from the German.

Kunz [koonz], **George Frederick.** *N. Y.*, 1856——. A mineralogist of note, the foremost American specialist in precious stones. He has published Gems and Precious Stones of North America.

Kunze [koont-se], **John Christopher.** *Sxy.*, 1744–1807. A once famous Lutheran clergyman of New York city, professor of ancient languages in Columbia College. History of the Christian Religion and of the Lutheran Church; Catechism and Liberty.

Kunze, Richard Ernest. *G.*, 1838——. A physician of New York city who has done much to promote a knowledge of medical botany. Cactus; Cardinal Points in the Study of Medical Botany; Germination and Vitality of Seeds.

Kurtz, Benjamin. *Pa.*, 1795–1865. A Lutheran clergyman, for nearly thirty years the editor of The Lutheran Observer. Lutheran Prayer-Book; Year-Book of the Reformation; Why are You a Lutheran?; Faith, Hope, and Charity; Theological Sketch-Book, are his most important works.

L

Labagh, Isaac P——. *N. Y.*, 1804–18—. An Episcopal clergyman of Iowa, but formerly a clergyman of the Dutch Reformed faith. Great Events of Unfulfilled Prophecy; The Great Events that are Coming; The Two Witnesses, Moses and Elijah; Theoklesia.

La Borde, Maximilian. *S. C.*, 1804–1873. An educator who was professor in the University of South Carolina, 1842–73. Introduction to Physiology; Story of Lethea and Verona; History of South Carolina College.

Ladd, George Trumbull. *O.*, 1842——. A Congregational clergyman of prominence, professor of philosophy at Yale University from 1881. Principles of Church Polity; The Doctrine of Sacred Scripture; Philosophy of Mind; A Primer of Psychology; Psychology, Descriptive and Explanatory; Outlines of Psychological Psychology; Elements of Psychological Psychology; Introduction to Philosophy; What is the Bible? He has translated Lotze's Philosophical Outlines, from the German. *Gi. Scr.*

Ladd, Horatio Oliver. *Me.*, 1839——. An Episcopal clergyman, but formerly of the Congregational faith, at one period president of the University of New Mexico. History of the War with Mexico; The Story of New Mexico. *Do. Lo.*

La Farge, John. *N. Y.*, 1835——. A noted figure and landscape artist of New York city. Lectures on Art. *Mac.*

Laighton, Albert. *N. H.*, 1829–1887. A banker of Portsmouth, New Hampshire, cousin of Mrs. Thaxter, *infra.* Poems, a collection of quiet, thoughtful verse, was published in 1878.

Lamar, Mirabeau Buonaparte. *Ga.*, 1798–1859. The second of the four presidents of the Republic of Texas, 1838, and United States minister to Central America, 1857–58. Verse Memorials. *See Bibliography of Texas.*

Lamb, Mrs. Martha Joan Reade [Nash]. *Ms.*, 1829–1893. An historical writer of New York city, editor of the Magazine of American History, 1883–93. The History of the City of New York, her chief work, is the result of a vast amount of patient labour and research. Her other works include, Spicy, a novel; Play-School Stories: The Christmas Owl; Snow and Sunshine, a Story for Girls; Wall Street in History. *Bar. Do.*

Lambert, Mrs. Mary Eliza [Perine] [Tucker]. *Al.*, 1838——. A writer of Philadelphia. Poems; Loew's

Bridge, a Broadway Idyl; Life of Mark Pomeroy.

Lamon, Ward Hill. 18——. An Illinois lawyer, law partner of Abraham Lincoln; Recollections of Abraham Lincoln; Life of Abraham Lincoln. *Mg.*

Lamson, Alvan. *Ms.*, 1792-1864. A Unitarian clergyman of Dedham, Massachusetts, 1818-60. History of the First Church in Dedham; Sermons; The Church of the First Three Centuries.

Lamson, Daniel Lowell. *N. H.*, 1834——. A physician of Fryeburg, Maine. Lectures; Differential Diagnosis of Diseases.

Lamson, Mrs. Mary [Swift]. *Ms.*, 1822——. For five years a teacher of Laura Bridgman, the noted blind deaf mute, and for three years in entire charge of her education. Life and Education of Laura Dewey Bridgman. *Hou.*

Lance, William. 1791-1840. A lawyer and political writer of Charleston, who published a Life of Washington in Latin.

Lander, Meta. *See Lawrence, Mrs.*

Lander, Sarah West. *Ms.*, 1810-1872. A writer of Salem, Massachusetts, whose Spectacles for Young Eyes, a series of volumes of travel, was very popular.

Landon, Judson Stuart. *Ct.*, 1832-——. A lawyer of Schenectady, justice of the Supreme Court of the State of New York and lecturer in the Albany Law School. The Constitutional History and Government of the United States. *Hou.*

Landon, Melville De Lancey. "Eli Perkins." *N.Y.*, 1839——. A popular humourous lecturer. The Franco-Prussian War in a Nutshell; Saratoga in 1901; Eli Perkins at Large; Eli Perkins's Wit, Humor, and Pathos; Fun and Fact, Thirty Years of Wit; Money: Silver, Gold, or Bimetallism, include the most of his writing. *Cas. Ke.*

Langdell, Christopher Columbus. *N. H.*, 1826——. A legal writer of distinction, dean of the Harvard Law School. Cases on the Law of Contracts; Summary of Equity Pleading; Cases in Equity Pleading; Elementary Treatise on the Law of Contracts.

Langdon, William Chauncey. *Vt.*, 1831-1895. An Episcopal clergyman of Bedford, Pennsylvania. The Defects of our Practical Catholicity; Plain Papers for Parish Priests and Peoples; The Catholic Reform Movement in the Italian Church; Conflict of Practice and Principle in the American Church.

Langley, Samuel Pierpont. *Ms.*, 1834——. An astronomer of eminence, the secretary of the Smithsonian Institution from 1887. Researches on Solar Heat; The New Astronomy. *Hou.*

Langston, John Mercer. *Va.*, 1829-1897. A distinguished educator of African birth, minister to Hayti, 1877-85, and president of the Virginia Normal Institute at Petersburg from the latter date. He has published Freedom and Citizenship.

Lanier [la-neer′], Clifford Anderson. *Ga.*, 1844——. A Georgia writer of fiction. Two Hundred Bales; Thorn-Fruit.

Lanier, Sidney. *Ga.*, 1842-1881. Brother of C. A. Lanier, *supra*. A distinguished Southern writer over whose rank as a poet much controversy has arisen. His verse can hardly be said to appeal to many readers, and its formlessness at times repels rather than attracts. A Centennial Ode, written for the opening of the Exposition of 1876, first brought him into general notice. Subsequently he lectured upon English literature in Baltimore. Poems; Tiger Lilies, a novel; The Science of English Verse; The English Novel and its Development; Florida: its Scenery, History, and Climate. He edited The Boys' Percy; The Boys' Mabinogion; The Boys' King Arthur; The Boys' Froissart. *See Century Magazine, April, 1884; Gosse's Questions at Issue. Lip. Scr.*

Lanigan, George Thomas. *Q.*, 1845-1886. A journalist of Montreal, and subsequently of New York city. Canadian Ballads; Fables Out of the World.

Lanman, Charles. *Mch.*, 1819-1895. An artist and author of Washington, at one time the private secretary of Daniel Webster. Essays for Summer Hours; Summer in the Wilderness; Private

Life of Daniel Webster; Dictionary of Congress; The Red Book of Michigan; Leading Men of Japan; Letters from a Landscape Painter; Tour to the River Saguenay; Farthest North; Haphazard Personalities, include the most of his works. *Ap. Le. Lo.*

Lanman, Charles Rockwell. *Ct.*, 1850——. A professor of Sanskrit at Harvard University from 1880. Noun Inflection in the Vedas; A Sanskrit Reader, with Notes. *Gi.*

Lansing, John Gulian. *La.*, 1851—— A Dutch Reformed clergyman, professor of Old Testament Languages in the New Brunswick Theological Seminary, New Jersey. American Revised Version of the Book of Psalms; An Arabic Manual. *Scr.*

Lanza, Marchioness Clara [Hammond]. *Ks.*, 1858——. Daughter of W. A. Hammond, *supra.* A novelist of New York city. Tit for Tat; Mr. Perkins's Daughter; A Righteous Apostate; Tales of Eccentric Life; A Modern Marriage; David Morton's Transgression; A Golden Pilgrimage.

Lapham [lăp′ạm], **Increase Allen.** *N. Y.*, 1811–1875. A prominent scientist of Milwaukee. Antiquities of Wisconsin; Wisconsin: its Geography, Topography, History, Geology, and Mineralogy. *See Popular Science Monthly, April, 1883.*

Lapham, William Berry. *Me.*, 1828–1894. An agricultural editor of Maine, who published several histories of Maine localities, including Woodstock, Paris, Norway, Bar Harbor, and Mount Desert Island. *See Bibliography of Maine.*

Larcom, Lucy. *Ms.*, 1824–1893. A popular verse and prose writer of Beverly, Massachusetts, who in early life worked in the Lowell factories, and was a contributor to the noted Lowell Offering. Her writings in verse include, At the Beautiful Gate; Childhood Songs; Wild Roses of Cape Ann; An Idyl of Work; Easter Gleams; Complete Poems. Skipper Ben and Hannah Binding Shoes are her best known lyrics. Her original work in prose comprises, Ships in the Mist, and Other Stories; The Sunbeam; Similitudes; Leila among the Mountains; The Unseen Friend; As It is in Heaven; A New England Girlhood, an autobiographic work. *See Life by D. D. Addison. Hou.*

Larned, Augusta. *Vt.*, 1835——. A journalist of New York city. Home Story Scenes; Talks with Girls; Old Tales from Grecian Mythology; Tales from the Norse Grandmother; Village Photographs, a work of the nature of Miss Mitford's "Our Village," and with much of the same charm; In Woods and Fields, a book of verse. *Ho. Meth. Put.*

Larned, Joshua Nelson. *Ont.*, 1836——. The superintendent of the public library at Buffalo. History for Ready Reference; Talks About Labor. *Ap.*

Larned, Walter Cranston. *Il.*, 1850——. A lawyer and littérateur of Lake Forest, Illinois. Churches and Castles of Mediæval France. *Scr.*

La Roche, René. *Pa.*, 1794–1872. A Philadelphia physician. Pneumonia: its Supposed Connection with Autumnal Fevers; Treatise on Yellow Fever.

Larrabee, William Clark. *Me.*, 1802–1859. A once prominent Methodist clergyman and educator of Indiana, professor in De Pauw University for a number of years. Scientific Evidences of Natural and Revealed Religion; Wesley and his Co-Laborers; Asbury and his Co-Laborers; Rosebower, a volume of essays. *Meth.*

Latham, Charles Sterrett. *Cal.*, 1861–1890. A Translation of Dante's Eleven Letters, with Explanatory Notes and Historical Comments. *Hou.*

Lathbury, Mrs. Mary A——. 18——. That Sweet Story of Old; Bethlehem and her Children; Child's History of Paul; Fleda and the Voice; From Meadow Sweet to Mistletoe. *Meth.*

Lathrop, George Parsons. *H. I.*, 1851——. A littérateur of New York city, and more recently of New London. His writings in verse include, Rose and Rooftree; Dreams and Days. In fiction they comprise, Afterglow; An Echo of Passion; In the Distance; Newport; Would You Kill Him?; True; Two Sides of a Story; Love Wins; Gold of Pleasure; Behind Time. Other works are, A Study of Hawthorne; Spanish Vistas; A Story of

Courage: Annals of the Georgetown Convent (with Mrs. Lathrop, *infra*). *Cas. Fu. Har. Hou. Lip. Scr.*

Lathrop, Mrs. Rose [Hawthorne]. *Ms.*, 1851——. Wife of G. P. Lathrop, *supra*, and daughter of N. Hawthorne, *supra*. Along the Shore, a volume of verse; Some Memories of Hawthorne. *Hou.*

Latimer, Charles. *D. C.*, 1827——. An engineer of note who has published Roadmaster's Assistants; The Divining Rod; Battle of Standards.

Latimer, Mrs. Mary Elizabeth [Wormeley]. *E.*, 1822——. An educator of Baltimore. Familiar Talks on Shakespeare's Comedies; France in the Nineteenth Century, 1830–90; Russia and Turkey in the Nineteenth Century; England in the Nineteenth Century; Europe in Africa in the Nineteenth Century; Italy in the Nineteenth Century. *Mg. Rob.*

Latrobe, John Hazelhurst Boneval. *Pa.*, 1803–1891. A lawyer of Baltimore. Son of the architect Benjamin Latrobe. History of Mason and Dixon's Line; Three Great Battles; Justices' Practice under the Laws of Maryland; Reminiscences of West Point; Odds and Ends, a book of verse; History of Maryland in Liberia.

Latta, Samuel Arminius. *O.*, 1804–1852. A Methodist clergyman of Ohio, subsequently a physician in Cincinnati, who published The Chain of Sacred Wonders.

Laughlin, James Lawrence. *O.*, 1850——. A political economist of note, professor at Harvard University, 1883–87, and at Chicago University from 1892. Facts About Money; Study of Political Economy; Elements of Political Economy; History of Bi-Metallism in the United States. *Ap. Am.*

Lawrence, Eugene. *N. Y.*, 1823–1894. An historical writer of New York city. Lives of the British Historians; Historical Studies; Essays and Papers; Literature Primers; The Jews and their Persecutors; Columbus and his Contemporaries. *Har.*

Lawrence, Mrs. Margaret Oliver [Woods]. "Meta Lander." *Ms.*, 1813——. Daughter of L. Woods, *infra*. Light on the Dark River; Fading Flowers; L'Espérance; The Tobacco Problem; Marion Graham. *Le.*

Lawrence, William. *O.*, 1819——. A jurist of Ohio who was comptroller of the national treasury, 1880–85. Decisions of Ohio Supreme Court; The Treaty Question; Law of Religious Societies and Religious Corporations; Law of Claims Against the Government; Organization of the United States Treasury Department; Decisions of the First Comptroller of the Treasury.

Lawrence, William. *Ms.*, 1850——. The seventh Protestant Episcopal bishop of Massachusetts. Life of Amos A. Lawrence; Visions and Service, discourses in collegiate chapels. *Hou.*

Lawrence, William Beach. *N. Y.*, 1800–1881. An eminent jurist of New York city, and after 1850 of Newport, Rhode Island. Letters on the Treaty of Washington; an edition of Wheaton's Elements of International Law; Visitation and Search; Institutions of the United States; Commentaire sur les éléments du droit international; Administration of Equity Jurisprudence, include his principal writings.

Lawson, James. *S.*, 1799–1880. A New York city journalist. Tales and Sketches by a Cosmopolite; Poems; Giordana, a tragedy. *See Wilson's Poets and Poetry of Scotland.*

Lawson, John. *E.*, 16—1712. The surveyor-general of North Carolina, burned at the stake by hostile Indians. His entertaining travels were published with the title of History of North Carolina. *See Tyler's American Literature.*

Lawton, William Cranston. *Ms.*, 1853——. A classical teacher and lecturer, formerly of Cambridge, now (1897) of Brooklyn and professor in Adelphi College there. Three Dramas of Euripides; Folia Dispersa, a book of verse; Art and Humanity in Homer. *Hou. Mac.*

Lay, Henry Champlin. *Va.*, 1823–1885. The first Protestant Episcopal bishop of Easton (Maryland), but from 1859 to 1869 the third bishop of Arkansas. Studies in the Church; The Church and the Nation.

Lazarus, Emma. *N. Y.*, 1849–1887. A talented Jewish writer of New York city who wrote much in verse and prose for The Century and other periodicals. Alide, an Episode of Goethe's Life; Poems; Admetus, and Other Poems; Songs of a Semite; Poems and Ballads translated from Heine. Her Complete Poems, with a brief memoir, appeared in 1889. *Hou.*

Lazarus, Josephine. 18———. Sister of E. Lazarus, *supra*. The Spirit of Judaism; The Love-Letters of a Portuguese Nun, a translation from the French. *Cas. Do.*

Lazelle, Henry Martyn. *Ms.*, 1832——. A United States army officer, since 1887 in charge of the bureau of war records. One Law in Nature; Improvements in the Art of War.

Lea, Henry Charles. *Pa.*, 1825——. Son of I. Lea, *infra*. A prominent writer and publisher of Philadelphia. Superstition and Force; An Historical Sketch of Sacerdotal Celibacy in the Christian Church; Chapters from the Religious History of Spain; Studies in Church History; Translations, and Other Rhymes; History of the Inquisition. *See Allibone's Dictionary, Supplement; Catholic World, March,* 1897. *Har. Hou.*

Lea, Isaac. *Del.*, 1792–1886. A publisher and naturalist of Philadelphia. Contributions to Geology; Observations on the Genus Unio, in thirteen volumes; Fossil Footmarks in the Red Sandstones of Pottsville.

Lea, Matthew Carey. *Pa.*, 1823——. Son of I. Lea, *supra*. A chemist of Philadelphia whose Manual of Photography is a standard work.

Learned, Walter. *Ct.*, 1847——. A verse-writer of New London who has published Between Times, a collection of poems, and translated Ten Tales from Coppée. *Sto.*

Leaming, Jeremiah. *Ct.*, 1717–1804. An Episcopal clergyman of Connecticut. Defense of Episcopal Government; Evidences of the Truth of Christianity; Dissertations.

Leavitt, John McDowell. *O.*, 1824–1888. An Episcopal clergyman. Faith, a Poem; Afranius; The Siege of Babylon, a tragedy; Hymns to Our King; New World Tragedies from Old World Life; Reasons for Faith; Visions of Solyma.

Le Conte [le-kŏnt], **John.** *Ga.*, 1818–1891. A naturalist and physician, president of the University of California, 1875–81, and professor of physics there before and after his presidency. Philosophy of Medicine; Study of the Physical Sciences; Vital Statistics.

Le Conte, John Eaton. *N. J.*, 1784–1860. Uncle of J. Le Conte, *supra*. A naturalist who in early life served in the corps of army engineers with the rank of major. Monographs of North American Species of Utricularia, Gratiola, and Ruellia; North American Species of Viola.

Le Conte, John Lawrence. *N. Y.*, 1825–1883. Son of J. E. Le Conte, *supra*. An entomologist of distinction, author of List of Coleoptera of North America, and other technical publications.

Le Conte, Joseph. *Ga.*, 1823——. Brother of John Le Conte, *supra*. A geologist of eminence, professor of geology in the University of California from 1869. Elements of Geology; Sight; Evolution and its Relation to Religious Thought; Religion and Science. *Ap.*

Lee, Alfred. *Ms.*, 1807–1887. The first Protestant Episcopal bishop of Delaware, and prominent as a Low Churchman. The Harbinger of Christ; Life of St. Peter; Eventful Nights in Bible History; Life of St. John; Treatise on Baptism. *Har. Ran.*

Lee, Benjamin. *Ct.*, 1833——. Son of A. Lee, *supra*. A physician of Philadelphia. Treatment for Angular Curvature of the Spine; Tracts on Massage.

Lee, Benjamin Franklin. *N. J.*, 1841——. A Methodist clergyman of African birth, president of Wilberforce University from 1876. Wesley the Worker; Causes of the Success of Methodism.

Lee, Charles Alfred. *Ct.*, 1810–1872. A physician of New York city who published Elements of Geology for Popular Use; Human Physiology.

Lee, Day Kellogg. *N. Y.*, 1816–1869. A Universalist clergyman of New York city. Summerfield, or Life on a Farm; Master Builders, or Life at a Trade; Merrimack, or Life at a Loom.

Lee, Mrs. Eliza [Buckminster]. *N. H.*, 1794–1864. Sister of J. S. Buckminster, *supra*. A once popular Boston writer. Life of Richter; Sketches of a New England Village; Naomi; Florence, the Parish Orphan; Parthenia, or the Last Days of Paganism.

Lee, Mrs. Hannah Farnham [Sawyer]. *Ms.*, 1780–1865. A once prominent writer of Boston. Grace Seymour; Luther and his Times; Sculpture and Sculptors; Three Experiments in Living, which was extraordinarily popular both in America and England; Familiar Sketches of the Old Painters; The Huguenots in France and America; Memoir of Pierre Toussaint.

Lee, Henry. *Va.*, 1756–1818. A famous general in the American army during the Revolution. He published Memoirs of the War in the Southern Departments of the United States. In his oration in Congress on the death of Washington first occurs the familiar phrase, "first in war, first in peace, and first in the hearts of his countrymen."

Lee, Henry. *Va.*, 1786–1837. Son of H. Lee, *supra*. A Virginia writer who published The Campaign of 1781 in the Carolinas; Life of Napoleon.

Lee, Jesse. *Va.*, 1758–1816. A Methodist missionary, called "the Apostle of Methodism," who published a History of Methodism, which is a valuable record of the early years of that faith. *See Life and Times by L. M. Lee.*

Lee, Luther. *N. Y.*, 1800–1889. A Wesleyan clergyman of Michigan. Universalism Examined and Refuted; Church Polity; Immortality of the Soul; Slavery in the Light of the Bible; Elements of Theology.

Lee, Mrs. Mary Catherine [Jenkins], *Ms.* 18——. A novelist of Springfield, Massachusetts. A Quaker Girl of Nantucket; In the Cheering-Up Business; A Soulless Singer. *Hou.*

Lee, Mary Elizabeth. *S. C.*, 1813–1849. A writer of Charleston, author of Historical Tales for Youth, and a volume of Poems issued in 1851 with memoir by S. Gilman, *supra*.

Leech, Samuel Van Derlip. *N. Y.*, 1837——. A Methodist clergyman and temperance reformer. The Drunkard; Ingersoll and the Bible; The Inebriates. *Fu.*

Leeds, David. *E.*, 1652–1720. A prominent figure among the early settlers of Burlington, New Jersey, and a violent opponent of the Quakers. His writings, directed almost entirely against them, include The Temple of Wisdom; The News of a Trumpet; Hue and Cry against Error; A Trumpet Sounded; The Rebuker Rebuked; The Great Mystery of Fox-Craft Discovered.

Leeser [lā'zer], **Isaac.** *Wa.*, 1806–1868. A Jewish rabbi of Philadelphia who published The Jews and the Mosaic Law; Discourses on the Jewish Religion; Portuguese Forms of Prayer; a Translation of the Scriptures from the original Hebrew.

Lefferts, George Morewood. *L. I.*, 1846——. A physician of New York city. Diseases of the Nose; Diagnosis of Nasal Catarrh; Pharmacopœia for Diseases of the Throat and Nose.

Legare [lā-gree'], **Hugh Swinton.** *S. C.*, 1799–1843. A South Carolina jurist and essayist, attorney-general of the United States in 1841. Constitutional History of Greece; Essay on Classical Learning; Essay on Roman Literature.

Legare, James Matthews. *S. C.*, 1823–1859. An inventor and verse writer. Orta-Undis, and Other Poems.

Leggett, William. *N. Y.*, 1802–1839. A journalist once prominent in New York city. Leisure Hours at Sea; Tales by a Country Schoolmaster; Naval Stories; Political Writings. *See Memoir by T. Sedgwick, infra.*

Leidy [lī'dī], **Joseph.** *Pa.*, 1823–1891. A Philadelphia scientist of distinction who was a constant contributor to scientific periodicals. Among his writings are, The Extinct Species of the American Ox; Ancient Fauna of Nebraska; Cretaceous Reptiles of the United States; Elementary Text-Book on Human Anatomy. *Lip.*

Leighton [lī'ton], **William.** *Ms.*, 1833——. A writer of Wheeling, West Virginia. The Sons of Godwin, a tragedy that appeared simultaneously with Tennyson's "Harold" on the same theme; At the Court of King Edwin, a drama; Shakespeare's Dream; Change; The Subjection of Hamlet.

Leland, Charles Godfrey. "Hans Breitmann." *Pa.*, 1824——. A very versatile Philadelphia author who has lived much in Europe, and is considered an authority upon Gypsy lore. Hans Breitmann Ballads; The Music Lesson of Confucius, and Other Poems; Songs of the Sea and Lays of the Land; The English Gypsies and their Language; Origin of the Gypsies; The Gypsies; The Algonquin Legends of New England; Egyptian Sketch Book; Abraham Lincoln and the Abolition of Slavery; Practical Education; Manual of Wood Carving; Memoirs, include his more important works. *See Allibone's Dictionary and Supplement; Appletons' American Biography. Ap. Hou. Lip. Mac. Scr.*

Leland, Henry Perry. *Pa.*, 1828–1868. Brother of C. G. Leland, *supra.* A Philadelphia writer who served as lieutenant in a Pennsylvania regiment during the Civil War. The Americans in Rome; The Grey Bay Mare, and Other Humorous Sketches.

Lemmon, John Gill. *Mch.*, 1832——. A botanist attached to the California department of forestry from 1880. Ferns of the Pacific Coast; Discovery of the Potato.

Leonard, Agnes. *See Hill, Mrs. Agnes.*

Leonard, William Andrew. *Ct.*, 1848——. The fourth Protestant Episcopal bishop of Ohio. Via Sacra; The Christmas Festival, its Origin, etc.; Summary of Herbert Spencer's "First Principles;" Brief History of the Christian Church.

Leonowens, Mrs. Anna Harriette [Crawford]. *W.*, 1834——. An Englishwoman who was governess in the royal family of Siam for four years, came to New York in 1867, and has since taught there. The English Governess at the Siamese Court; The Romance of the Harem; Life and Travels in India; Our Asiatic Cousins. *Co. Lo.*

Le Plongeon, Mrs. Alice [Dixon]. *E.*, 1851——. The wife of the archæologist and explorer, Dr. Le Plongeon. Here and There in Yucatan.

Lesley, John Peter. *Pa.*, 1810——. A Philadelphia geologist of distinction. Man's Origin and Destiny from the Platform of the Sciences; Coal and its Topography; The Iron Manufacturer's Guide.

Leslie, Eliza. *Pa.*, 1787–1858. A Philadelphia writer of tales and sketches whose work was extremely popular in her day. She was a sister of the famous English artist Charles Robert Leslie. Among her writings are, Domestic Cookery; Mrs. Washington Potts; The Behaviour Book; Pencil Sketches; American Girl's Book; The Dennings. She wrote nothing that will live, but much that was of service to her generation. *See Hart's Amercan Literature. Bai.*

Lesquereux [lā-ke-rū'], **Leo.** *Sd.*, 1806–1889. A Swiss paleontologist who came to America in 1848 and settled in Columbus, Ohio. Catalogue of the Mosses of Switzerland; Musci Americani Exsiccati (with Sullivant); Icones Muscarum; Land Plants in the Lower Silurian; The Tertiary Flora; The Coal Flora; Mosses of North America (with T. P. James).

Leslie, Madeline. *See Baker, Mrs.*

Lester, Charles Edwards. *Ct.*, 1815–1890. A journalist and littérateur of New York city, at one time consul at Genoa. Life of Vespucius; The Napoleon Dynasty; Artists of America; The Glory and Shame of England; My Consulship; Condition and Fate of England; Samuel Houston and his Republic; Life of Charles Sumner; Our One Hundred Years; America's Advancement; The Mexican Republic; History of the United States; Stanhope Burleigh, a novel; with several translations of standard Italian authors, include the greater portion of his work.

Leverett, Frederick Percival. *Ms.*, 1803–1836. A once distinguished educator of Boston. Besides annotated editions of Juvenal and other classics, he prepared a much valued Lexicon of the Latin Language. *Lip.*

Le Vert, Mrs. Octavia [Walton]. *Ga.*, 1820–1877. A once prominent social leader of Mobile, whose literary reputation was greater than her actual accomplishment seemed to warrant. Souvenirs of Travel was her only published book.

Lewis, Abram Herbert. *N. Y.*, 1836——. A Seventh Day Baptist clergyman of Plainfield, New Jersey, and a writer of much prominence in his denomination. Sabbath and Sunday; Biblical Teachings Concerning the Sabbath and Sunday; Critical History of the Sabbath; Critical History of Sunday Legislation; Biography of the Puritan Sunday; Paganism in Christianity. *Ap. Put.*

Lewis, Alonzo. *Ms.*, 1794–1861. A verse-writer of Lynn, once styled "The Lynn Bard." Forest Flowers and Sea Shells; History of Lynn. A complete edition of his poems was issued in 1883.

Lewis, Charles Bertrand. "M. Quad." *O.*, 1842——. A journalist of Detroit on the staff of the Free Press for many years, and since 1891 on that of The New York World. Quad's Odds; Goaks and Tears; The Lime Kiln Club.

Lewis, Charlton Thomas. *Pa.*, 1834——. Grandson of Enoch Lewis, *infra.* A lawyer and mathematician of Morristown, New Jersey. History of the German People; Latin Dictionary for Schools; Elementary Latin Dictionary. *Har.*

Lewis, Dio. *N. Y.*, 1823–1886. A well-known Boston physician and health reformer. New Gymnastics; Our Girls; Our Digestion; Chastity; Weak Lungs and How to Make Them Strong, are among his most important works.

Lewis, Elisha Joseph. *Md.*, 1820——. A Philadelphia physician. Hints to Sportsmen; The American Sportsman. *Lip.*

Lewis, Enoch. *Pa.*, 1776–1856. An educator among the Friends of Pennsylvania. Vindication of the Society of Friends; Oaths; Baptism; Life of William Penn.

Lewis, Mrs. Estelle Anna Blanche [Robinson]. "Stella." *Md.*, 1824–1880. A Brooklyn writer whose life was largely spent in Europe. Her verse, which once received much more praise than its degree of excellence at all warranted, is now nearly forgotten. Sappho of Lesbos; Records of the Heart; Child of the Sea; Myths of the Minstrel; Helémah, or the Fall of Montezuma.

Lewis, Mrs. Harriet. 1841–1878. Amber, the Adopted; Her Double Life.

Lewis, Laurence. *Pa.*, 1857–1890. A lawyer of Philadelphia. Pennsylvania Courts in the 17th Century; History of the Bank of North America; Memoir of Edward Shippen; Original Land Titles in Philadelphia.

Lewis, Tayler. *N. Y.*, 1802–1877. An educator of note who was professor of Greek in Union College from 1849 until his death. The Platonic Theology; The Bible and Science; Six Days of Creation; Defence of Capital Punishment (with G. B. Cheever, *supra*); The Divine-Human in the Scriptures; States' Rights; Heroic Periods in the Nation's History; The Light by which we See Light.

Lieber [lee′bẹr], **Francis.** *P.*, 1800–1872. An eminent publicist, professor of political economy in the University of South Carolina, 1835–56, and subsequently at Columbia College. Reminiscences of Niebuhr; The West, and Other Poems; Manual of Political Ethics; Laws of Property; Civil Liberty and Self-Government; Legal and Political Hermeneutics; Instructions for the Armies in the Field; The Character of the Gentleman; Miscellaneous Writings. *See Life and Letters of, by T. S. Perry. Lip.*

Lieber, Oscar Montgomery. *Ms.*, 1830–1862. Son of F. Lieber, *supra.* A soldier in the Federal army during the Civil War. The Assayer's Guide; The Analytical Chemist's Assistant; The Geology of Mississippi. *Bai.*

Light, George Washington. *Me.*, 1809–1860. A journalist of Boston. Life of Timothy Claxton; Keep Cool, Go Ahead, and a Few More Poems.

Lillie, John. *S.*, 1812-1867. A Presbyterian clergyman of Kingston, New York, who published The Perpetuity of the Earth.

Lillie, Mrs. Lucy Cecil [White]. *N. Y.*, 1855——. A writer of popular juveniles. Mildred's Bargain; Nan; The Story of Music and Musicians; Rolf House; The Colonel's Money; Jo's Opportunity; The Household of Glen Holly; The Story of English Literature; Prudence, a Novel of Æsthetic London; Ruth Endicott's Way; Alison's Adventures. *Co. Har.*

Lincoln, Abraham. *Ky.*, 1809-1865. The sixteenth president of the United States. His place in literature is determined by his famous Gettysburg Address and the equally admirable Second Inaugural Address. His Complete Works are contained in two volumes, edited by Nicolay and Hay. *See Lives by Holland, 1865; Arnold, 1868; Lamon, 1872; Nicolay and Hay, 1890; Herndon, 1892; Abraham Lincoln, an Essay, by C. Schurz, 1892.*

Lincoln, Mrs. Almira. *See Phelps, Mrs. A. Cent.*

Lincoln, Daniel Francis. *Ms.*, 1841——. A physician of Boston. School Hygiene; Electro-Therapeutics; School and Industrial Hygiene.

Lincoln, Heman. *Ms.*, 1821——. A Baptist divine, professor of church history at Newton Theological Seminary from 1868. Outline Lectures in Church History; Outline Lectures in History of Doctrine.

Lincoln, Mrs. Jeanie [Gould]. *N. Y.*, 184——. Granddaughter of James Gould, *supra*. A writer of Washington city. A Chaplet of Leaves, a book of verse; Marjorie's Quest, a story for young people; Her Washington Winter; A Genuine Girl. *Hou.*

Lincoln, John Larkin. *Ms.*, 1817-1891. Brother of H. Lincoln, *supra*. A professor of Latin in Brown University, well known as a classical scholar, and editor of editions of Livy, Horace, and Cicero. *See In Memoriam: John Larkin Lincoln.*

Lincoln, Mrs. Mary Johnson [Bailey]. *Ms.*, 1844——. A Boston teacher of cookery, culinary editor of The American Kitchen Magazine. Boston Cook Book; Carving and Serving; Twenty Lessons in Cookery; Kitchen Text-Book. *Rob.*

Linderman, Henry Richard. *Pa.*, 1825-1879. The director of the United States mint at Philadelphia from 1873, whose annual report for 1877 is a powerful argument for the gold standard. Money and Legal Tender in the United States.

Lindsey, William. *Ms.*, 1858——. A Boston littérateur. Apples of Istakhar, a volume of verse; Cinder-Path Tales. *Cop.*

Linen, James. *S.*, 1808-1873. A bookbinder of New York city. Songs of the Seasons; Poetical and Prose Writings.

Lining, John. *S.*, 1708-1760. A physician and scientist of Charleston who published in 1753 a History of Yellow Fever, the earliest American treatise on the subject.

Linn, John Blair. *Pa.*, 1777-1804. Son of W. Linn, *infra*. A Presbyterian clergyman of Philadelphia. The Power of Genius, a Poem; Valerian, a Poem; The Gallic Orphan, a drama; Miscellanea.

Linn, John Blair. *Pa.*, 1831——. Grandson of W. Linn, *infra*. A Pennsylvania lawyer. Annals of Buffalo Valley; Pennsylvania Archives (with W. H. Egle); History of Centre and Clinton Counties.

Linn, William. *Pa.*, 1752-1808. A Presbyterian clergyman of Philadelphia famous in his day as a preacher. Discourses on Leading Personages of Scripture History; Signs of the Times. His sermon on the death of Washington was formerly much quoted.

Linn, William. *N. Y.*, 1790-1867. Son of W. Linn, *supra*. A lawyer of Ithaca. Life of Thomas Jefferson; The Roorback Papers; Legal and Commercial Commonplace Book.

Linton, William James. *E.*, 1812-1897. An English engraver and poet who came to the United States in 1867 and settled in New Haven. Beside ably editing several poetical anthologies, he was the author of Claribel, and Other Poems; Life of Thomas Paine; a valuable History of Wood Engraving in America; The English Republic;

The Flower and the Star, and Other Stories; Practical Hints on Wood Engraving; Wood Engraving, a Manual of Instruction; Poems and Translations; Three Score and Ten Years; Life of Whittier. *See Stedman's Victorian Poets; Atlantic Monthly, February, 1883. Le. Mac. Rob. Scr.*

Lippard, George. *Pa.*, 1822–1854. A sensational romancer of Philadelphia, among whose now nearly forgotten tales are, Blanche of Brandywine; Legends of Mexico; The Ladye Annabel.

Lippincott, Mrs. Esther J—— [Trimble]. *Pa.*, 1838–1888. An educator of Pennsylvania, professor of literature in the Westchester Normal School. Handbook of English and American Literature; Short Course in Literature.

Lippincott, Mrs. Sara Jane [Clarke]. "Grace Greenwood." *N. Y.*, 1823——. A popular littérateur of Philadelphia who has written much in the line of newspaper correspondence, but whose early fame was gained as a writer for young people. Greenwood Leaves; Records of Five Years; Poems; Life of Queen Victoria; New Life in New Lands; Recollections of My Childhood; Merrie England, include the most of her books.

Lippitt, Francis James. *R. I.*, 1812——. A soldier who served in the Federal army during the Civil War, and was brevetted brigadier-general of volunteers. A Treatise on the Tactical Use of the Three Arms; Treatise on Intrenchments; Special Operations of War; Field Service in War; Massachusetts Criminal Law; Physical Proofs of Another Life. *Hou.*

Lippmann, Julie Mathilde. *L. I.*, 1864——. A writer of Brooklyn. Through Slumbertown and Wakeland, a book for juvenile readers.

Lipscomb, Andrew Adgate. *D. C.*, 1816–1890. A Methodist clergyman and educator of Tennessee, who was professor in Vanderbilt University. Studies in the Forty Days; Supplementary Studies; Our Country; Christian Heroism, are among his works.

Litchfield, Grace Denio [dē-nī'o]. *N. Y.*, 1849——. A fiction writer of Washington. Only an Incident; The Knight of the Black Forest; Criss-Cross; A Hard-Won Victory; Little Venice, and Other Stories; Mimosa Leaves; Little He and She; In the Crucible. *Lo. Put.*

Littell, Squier. *N. J.*, 1803–1886. A Philadelphia physician. Manual of Diseases of the Eye; Illustrations of the Prayer Book.

Littell, William. *N. J.*, c. 1780–1825. Cousin of S. Littell, *supra.* A lawyer of Frankfort, Kentucky. Statute Law of Kentucky; Selected Cases; Festoons of Fancy.

Little, George. *Ms.*, 1754–1809. A United States naval officer who published The American Cruiser; Life on the Ocean.

Little, Mrs. Sophia Louise [Robbins]. *R. I.*, 1799–18—. A verse-writer of Newport, Rhode Island. The Last Days of Jesus, and Other Poems (1877), is a reprint of the contents of her several previous volumes.

Littlejohn, Abram Newkirk. *N. Y.*, 1824——. The first Protestant Episcopal bishop of Long Island. Conciones ad Clenem; Individualism; The Christian Ministry; The Philosophy of Religion.

Livermore, Abiel Abbot. *N. H.*, 1811–1892. A Unitarian clergyman who was president of the theological seminary at Meadville, Pennsylvania, from 1863 until his death. Lectures to Young Men; Discourses; Commentaries on the Gospels, Acts, Romans, Corinthians to Philemon, Hebrews to Revelation; The Marriage Offering; History of Wilton, New Hampshire. *A. U. A. El.*

Livermore, Mrs. Mary Ashton [Rice]. *Ms.*, 1821——. A noted lecturer upon temperance and woman-suffrage whose home is in Melrose, Massachusetts. Superfluous Women, and Other Lectures; Pen Pictures; Thirty Years Too Late: a Temperance Tale; What Shall we Do with Our Daughters?; My Story of the War. *Le.*

Livermore, Samuel. *Circa* 1786–1833. A lawyer of New Orleans. Treatise on Law of Principal and Agent and Sales by Auction; Contrariety of Laws of Different States and Nations.

Livingston, Edward. *N. Y.*, 1764–1836. An eminent jurist of New York city, and subsequently of New Orleans, who was secretary of state, 1831–32, and minister to France, 1833–35. System of Penal Law for Louisiana; Penal Law for the United States; Criminal Jurisprudence. *See Life by Hunt, 1864; Recollections of, by Davezac; Appletons' American Biography.*

Livingston, Mrs. Margaret Vere [Farrington]. *Me.*, 1863——. The wife of an Episcopal clergyman in Augusta, Maine. Tales of King Arthur and His Knights; Fra Lippo Lippi, a Romance of Florence. *Put.*

Livingston, Robert R* *N. Y.*, 1747–1813. Brother of E. Livingston, *supra.* The chancellor of New York, 1771–1801. He administered the oath of office to Washington at his inauguration in 1789. Essays on Agriculture; Essay on Sheep. *See Life by F. De Peyster, 1878.*

Livingston, William. *N.Y.*, 1723–1790. An eminent statesman who was governor of New Jersey, 1776–90. Philosophic Solitude, a poem; Review of the Military Operations in North America, 1757; Digest of the Laws of New York. *See Memoir by T. Sedgwick; Tyler's American Literature.*

Lloyd, David Demarest. *N. Y.*, 1851–1889. A journalist and playwright of New York city. His plays include, For Congress; The Woman Hater; The Dominie's Daughter; The Senator.

Lloyd, Henry Demarest. *N. Y.*, 1847——. Brother of D. D. Lloyd, *supra.* A writer of Winnetka, Illinois, but formerly a journalist of Chicago. A Strike of Millionaires against Miners, or the Story of Spring Valley; Wealth Against Commonwealth. *Har.*

Locke, David Ross. "Petroleum V. Nasby." *N. Y.*, 1833–1888. A widely known political humourist whose satires had much effect upon public opinion. A Paper City, a novel; Swingin' Round the Cirkle; The Moral History of America's Life Struggle; Ekkoes from Kentucky; Struggles of Petroleum V. Nasby; Nasby in Exile; Morals of Abou Ben Adhem; The Demagogue, a novel; Hannah Jane, a poem. *Le.*

* A distinguishing initial only.

Locke, Mrs. Jane Erminia [Starkweather]. *Ms.*, 1805–1859. A verse-writer of Boston. Poems; Rachel, or the Little Mourner; Boston, a Poem; Eulogy in rhyme on the Death of Webster.

Locke, John Staples. 1836——. A writer of Saco, Maine. Shores of Saco Bay; Historical Sketches of Old Orchard; The Art of Correspondence; A Brave Struggle, a novel; Pleasing Rhymes for Happy Times; Bright Hours. *Cas.*

Locke, Richard Adams. *N. Y.*, 1800–1871. A journalist of New York city who published, in 1835, Great Astronomical Discoveries lately made by Sir John Herschel, since known as "The Moon Hoax." He subsequently issued The Lost Manuscript of Mungo Park, another hoax.

Lockhart, Arthur John. *N. S.*, 1850——. A Methodist clergyman and verse-writer. The Mask of Minstrels; Beside the Narragaugus.

Lockwood, Henry Hayes. *Del.*, 1814——. A United States army officer. Manual of Naval Batteries; Exercises in Small Arms.

Lockwood, Ingersoll. *N. Y.*, 1841——. Nephew of R. I. Lockwood, *infra.* A lecturer and littérateur of New York city. The Travels of Little Baron Trump; Wonderful Deeds of Little Giant Roab; Extraordinary Experience of Little Captain Doppelkopp; Baron Trump's Journey Underground. *Le.*

Lockwood, Ralph Ingersoll. *N. Y.*, 1798–1855. A lawyer of New York city. Rosine Laval, a novel; The Insurgents, a novel; Lockwood's Reversed Cases.

Lockwood, Samuel. *E.*, 1819–1894. A Reformed Dutch clergyman who after 1867 was school superintendent of Monmouth County, New Jersey, and wrote much on scientific themes. Temperance, Fortitude, Justice; The American Oyster; Abnormal Entozoa in Man; The Life of an Oyster; Animal Memoirs.

Lodge, Giles Henry. *Ms.*, 1805–1880. A physician of Boston, the author of a scholarly translation of Winckelmann's History of Ancient Art.

Lodge, Henry Cabot. *Ms.*, 1850——. Nephew of G. H. Lodge, *supra*. A Massachusetts politician of prominence, representative in Congress, 1886–1892, and senator from 1893. Essay on Anglo-Saxon Land Law; Life and Letters of George Cabot; Short History of the English Colonies in America; Lives of Washington, Webster, Hamilton; Studies in History; Historical and Political Essays; Speeches; History of Boston; Hero Tales from American History (with T. Roosevelt, *infra*). *Cent. Har. Hou. Lit. Lgs.*

Logan, Celia. Daughter of C. A. Logan, 2d, *infra*. *See Connelly, Mrs.*

Logan, Cornelius Ambrose. *Ms.*, 1830——. Son of C. A. Logan, *infra*. A physician of Leavenworth, Kansas, minister to Chili, 1873, and 1881–1883. Sanitary Relations of Kansas; Climatology of the Missouri Valley; Physics of Infectious Diseases.

Logan, Cornelius Ambrosius. *Md.*, 1806–1853. A dramatist and theatrical manager of Cincinnati among whose plays are The Wag of Maine; The Wool Dealer; Yankee Land.

Logan, James. *I.*, 1674–1751. Chief justice of Pennsylvania, and a man of much note in the early history of that colony. He founded the Loganian Library at Philadelphia. Duties of Man; Defence of Aristotle; Experimenta de Plantarum Generatione; Essays on Languages; a translation, with notes, of Cicero's De Senectute, printed by Franklin in 1744.

Logan, John Alexander. *Il.*, 1826–1886. A major-general in the Federal army during the Civil War who was nominated as the Republican candidate for vice-president in 1884. The Great Conspiracy; The Volunteer Soldier of America.

Logan, John Henry. *S. C.*, 1822–1885. A physician who was a professor in the medical college at Atlanta. History of the Upper Country of South Carolina; Students' Manual of Chemico-Physics.

Logan, Olive. Daughter of C. A. Logan, 2d, *supra*. *See Sikes, Mrs.*

Lomax, John Tayloe. *Va.*, 1781–1862. A Virginia jurist. Digest of United States Real Property Laws; Treatise on the Law of Executors and Administrators.

Long, Charles Chaillé. *Md.*, 1842——. A soldier who served in the Federal army during the Civil War, became colonel in the Egyptian army in 1869, and in 1887 was American consul-general in Corea. Central Africa; The Three Prophets, — Chinese Gordon, the Mahdi, Arabi Pacha. *Ap. Har.*

Long, John Davis. *Me.*, 1838——. A prominent jurist of Boston who was governor of Massachusetts, 1880–82. After-Dinner and Other Speeches; a blank-verse translation of the Æneid. *Hou.*

Long, Robert Carey. *Circa* 1819–1849. An architect of New York city who published a work on Ancient Architecture in America.

Longfellow, Henry Wadsworth. *Me.*, 1807–1882. The most widely read of American poets. He was born in Portland, Maine, and graduated at Bowdoin College in 1825 in the class with Nathaniel Hawthorne. After three years of study in Europe he was professor of modern languages at Bowdoin College, 1829–35, and filled the same position at Harvard University, 1835–1854, his home being at Cambridge from 1835. The range of his thought is not wide, and his genius was rather adaptive than creative, but his poetry appeals to a larger number of readers of verse than, perhaps, any other poet of his time. Its finished execution is especially noteworthy in most of his later work, his sonnets, for example, being nearly flawless specimens of their kind. Coplas de Manrique, a verse translation from the Spanish (1833); Outre-Mer, a prose volume of travels (1835); Hyperion, a prose romance (1839); Voices of the Night (1839); Ballads, and Other Poems (1841); Poems on Slavery (1842); The Spanish Student (1843); The Belfry of Bruges, and Other Poems (1846); Evangeline (1847); Kavanagh, a prose tale (1849); Seaside and Fireside (1850); The Golden Legend (1851); Hiawatha (1855); The Courtship of Miles Standish (1858); Tales of a Wayside Inn, 1st series (1863); Flower de Luce (1867); New England Tragedies (1868); Dante's

Divina Commedia: a translation, 1867-1870; The Divine Tragedy (1872); Three Books of Song (1872); Aftermath (1874); The Masque of Pandora (1875); Kéramos (1878); Ultima Thule (1880); In the Harbor (1882); Michael Angelo (1883). *See Lives by S. Longfellow, infra, Stoddard, Underwood, Austin; Atlantic Monthly, December, 1863, and June, 1882; Scribner's Magazine, November, 1878; Harper's Magazine, June, 1882; Living Age, November 4, 1882; Fortnightly Review, January, 1883; Century Magazine, October, 1883; Hazeltine's Chats About Books; Stedman's Poets of America; Works on American Literature by Nichol, Richardson, Hawthorne; Cheney's That Dome in Air; Bibliography of Maine; Memorial Address by D. R. Goodwin. Hou.*

Longfellow, Samuel. *Me.*, 1819-1892. Brother of H. W. Longfellow, *supra.* A Unitarian clergyman who held pastorates at Fall River, Brooklyn, and Germantown, but whose latest years were spent in Cambridge. He was a poet with a very distinct individuality, and as a hymn-writer had few equals, a large number of the best of Unitarian hymns being from his pen. Life of H. W. Longfellow; Hymns and Verses; Memoir of S. Johnson; Essays and Sermons. With S. Johnson, *supra*, he edited Hymns of the Spirit. *See Memoir and Letters, edited by J. May; New England Magazine, October, 1894. Hou.*

Longfellow, William Pitt Preble. *Me.*, 1836——. Nephew of H. W. Longfellow, *supra.* An architect of note, editor of the Cyclopædia of Architecture in Italy, Greece, and the Levant. *Scr.*

Longstreet, Augustus Baldwin. *S. C.*, 1790-1870. A jurist and educator of Georgia who became a Methodist minister in 1838, and was subsequently president of several Southern colleges. He is remembered for his genuinely humourous Georgia Scenes. Among his other works are, Master William Mitten; Letters from Georgia to Massachusetts.

Longstreet, James. *S. C.*, 1821——. A noted general of the Confederate army. From Manassas to Appomattox. *Lip.*

Loomis, Alfred Lebbeus. *Vt.*, 1831——. A physician of New York city, professor in the University of the City of New York from 1865. Lessons in Physical Diagnosis; Diseases of the Respiratory Organs; Lectures on Fevers; Diseases of Old Age; Text-Book of Practical Medicine.

Loomis, Augustus Ward. *Ct.*, 1816——. A Presbyterian clergyman, for many years a missionary among the Chinese of California. Learn to Say No; Scenes in Chusan; Scenes in the Indian Country; The Profits of Godliness; Confucius and the Chinese Classics; English and Chinese Lessons.

Loomis, Eben Jenks. *N. Y.*, 1828——. An astronomer of Washington city, senior assistant in the Nautical Almanac office. Wayside Sketches; An Eclipse Party in Africa. *Rob.*

Loomis, Elias. *Ct.*, 1811-1889. An astronomer and mathematician who was professor at Yale University from 1860. He published a series of textbooks in thirteen volumes, among which are, Plane and Spherical Trigonometry; Treatise on Astronomy; Treatise on Meteorology. *Har.*

Loomis, Justin Rudolph. *N. Y.*, 1810——. An educator of Pennsylvania, president of Lewisburg University, 1858-78. Elements of Geology; Elements of Anatomy.

Loomis, Lafayette Charles. *Ct.*, 1824——. A physician and educator of Washington city. Mizpah: Prayer and Friendship; Mental and Social Culture; Summer Guide to Central Europe; Index Guide to Travel and Art Study in Europe. *Lip. Scr.*

Loomis, Samuel Lane. *Ms.*, 1856——. A Congregational clergyman of Boston. Modern Cities and their Religious Problems.

Loomis, Silas Laurence. *Ms.*, 1822——. Brother of L. C. Loomis, *supra.* A physician and educator of Washington city. Analytical Arithmetic; Normal Arithmetic. *Lip.*

Lord, David Nevins. *Ct.*, 1792-1880. A merchant and importer of New York city. Exposition of the Apocalypse; Characteristics of Figurative Language; Louis Napoleon: is he to be Anti-Christ?; Visions of Paradise, an Epic.

Lord, Eleazer. *Ct.*, 1788–1871. Brother of D. N. Lord, *supra.* A noted financier of New York city who was the founder of the Manhattan Insurance Company. Among his rather numerous writings are, Credit, Currency, and Banking; Six Letters on a National Currency; The Epoch of the Creation; Analysis of Isaiah; The Prophetic Office.

Lord, John. *N. H.*, 1809–1894. A Congregational clergyman widely known as an historical lecturer, who did much to arouse an interest in the study of history. History of the United States; Modern History; Points of History; The Old Roman World; Ancient States and Empires; Life of Emma Willard, *infra;* Beacon Lights of History; Two German Giants. *Ap. Fo.*

Lord, John Chase. *N. Y.*, 1805–1877. A prominent Presbyterian clergyman of Buffalo. The Land of Ophir, and Other Lectures; Occasional Poems. *See Memoir, 1878.*

Lord, William Wilberforce. *N. Y.*, 1819——. Brother of J. C. Lord, *supra.* An Episcopal clergyman of Vicksburg, Mississippi, and more recently of Cooperstown, New York, whose verse attracted the praise of Wordsworth simultaneously with the ridicule of Poe. Poems; Christ in Hades; André, a tragedy.

Lord, Willis. *Ct.*, 1809–1889. A Presbyterian clergyman who held several theological professorships as well as pastorates in Chicago and elsewhere. Men and Scenes Before the Flood; Christian Theology for the People; The Blessed Hope.

Lorimer, George Claude. *S.*, 1837——. A noted Baptist clergyman of Boston, pastor of Tremont Temple. Isms Old and New; Under the Evergreens; The Great Conflict; Jesus: the World's Saviour; Studies in Social Life. *Le. Sc.*

Loring, Charles Greeley. *Ms.*, 1794–1868. A lawyer of Boston. The Neutral Relations of England and the United States; English Liability for Indemnity; Life of William Sturgis.

Loring, Edward Greeley. *Ms.*, 1837–1881. A physician of New York city. Text-Book of Ophthalmoscopy: I. The Normal Eye; II. Diseases of the Retina. *Ap.*

Loring, Frederic Wadsworth. *Ms.*, 1848–1871. A Boston journalist killed by the Apaches in Arizona. Two College Friends, a novel; The Boston Dip, and Other Verses.

Loring, George Bailey. *Ms.*, 1817–1891. A noted agriculturist of Salem, Massachusetts, United States commissioner of agriculture, 1881–85, minister to Portugal, 1889–90. The Farmyard Club of Jotham.

Loring, William Wing. *N. C.*, 1818–1886. A soldier who, after serving successively in the United States and Confederate armies, served in the Egyptian army, 1869–79. A Confederate General in Egypt is a narrative of personal adventure.

Loskiel, George Henry. *R.*, 1740–1814. A Moravian bishop in Pennsylvania whose two books have been many times reprinted. Etwas fürs Herz; History of the Moravian Missions among the North American Indians.

Lossing, Benson John. *N. Y.*, 1813–1891. An artist and wood-engraver of Poughkeepsie who made many valuable contributions to American history. His later years were spent at Dover Plains, New York. The more important of his many works include, Pictorial Field-Book of the Revolution; Pictorial Field-Book of the War of 1812; Pictorial Field-Book of the Civil War; Life of General Philip Schuyler; The Two Spies: Nathan Hale and John André; Cyclopædia of United States History; Mary and Martha Washington; History of the United States Navy for Boys; Mount Vernon and its Associations; The Empire State, a History of New York; Life of Washington; Lives of the Presidents (1847). *Ap. Fu. Har. Ho.*

Lothrop, Amy. *See Warner, Anna.*

Lothrop, Mrs. Harriet Mulford [Stone]. "Margaret Sidney." *Ct.* 1844——. A popular writer of juvenile literature, living at Concord, Massachusetts. Among her many books of this character are, Five Little Peppers and How They Grew; The Pettibone Name; So as by Fire; Half Year at Bronckton; What the Seven Did; Rob; The Golden West; How they Went to Europe; Hester, and Other New England Stories. *Lo.*

Lothrop, Thornton Kirkland. *N. H.*, 1830——. A lawyer of Boston. The Life of William H. Seward, *infra.*

Loughborough [luf'boro], **Mrs. Mary Webster.** *N. Y.*, 1836–1887. A writer of Little Rock, Arkansas. My Cave Life in Vicksburg, an account of life in Vicksburg during the siege; For Better, for Worse, and Other Stories.

Loughead, Mrs. Flora [Haines]. *Wis.*, 1855——. A writer of Santa Barbara, California. The Libraries of California; The Man Who was Guilty, a novel; Quick Cookery; The Abandoned Claim, a story for young people; Practical Handbook of Science. *Hou.*

Lounsbury, Thomas Raynesford. *N. Y.*, 1838——. A professor of English at the Sheffield Scientific School of Yale University from 1871. History of the English Language; Life of James Fenimore Cooper; Studies in Chaucer. *Ho. Hou.*

Love, William De Loss. *N. Y.*, 1819——. A Congregational clergyman. Wisconsin in the War of the Rebellion.

Love, William De Loss. *Ct.*, 1851——. Son of W. D. Love, *supra.* A Congregational clergyman, pastor in Hartford, Connecticut, from 1885. The Fast and Thanksgiving Days of New England. *Hou.*

Lowe, Mrs. Martha Ann [Perry]. *N. H.*, 1820——. A verse-writer of Somerville, Massachusetts, whose husband, Charles Lowe, was a Unitarian minister of prominence. The Olive and the Pine, a book of verse; Love in Spain, and Other Poems; The Story of Chief Joseph (verse); Life of Charles Lowe.

Lowell, Abbott Lawrence. *Ms.*, 1856——. A lawyer of Boston. Essays on Government; Governments and Parties in Continental Europe. *Hou.*

Lowell, Mrs. Anna Cabot [Jackson]. *Ms.*, 1819–1874. Sister-in-law of J. R. Lowell, *infra.* Theory of Teaching; Edward's First Lessons in Grammar and Geometry; Outlines of Astronomy; Letters to Madame Pulksky; Seed Grains for Thought, and several compilations. *Rob.*

Lowell, Charles. *Ms.*, 1782–1861. A prominent Unitarian clergyman of Boston, pastor of the West Church from 1806 until his death. Occasional Sermons; Practical Sermons; Meditations for the Afflicted; Devotional Exercises for Communicants.

Lowell, Edward Jackson. *Ms.*, 1845–1894. Grandnephew of C. Lowell, *supra.* A lawyer of Boston. The Hessians and Other German Auxiliaries of Great Britain in the Revolutionary War, an exhaustive survey of the subject; The Eve of the French Revolution. *Har. Hou.*

Lowell, Francis Cabot. *Ms.*, 1855——. A Boston jurist. Joan of Arc, a valuable historical biography. *Hou.*

Lowell, James Russell. *Ms.*, 1819–1891. Son of C. Lowell, *supra.* The foremost American man of letters. He was born in Cambridge, and was graduated from Harvard University in 1839, where he succeeded Longfellow as professor of belles-lettres in 1855. He was one of the founders of The Atlantic Monthly, editing that periodical from the start in 1857 until 1862, and coeditor of The North American Review with C. E. Norton, *infra*, 1863–72. In 1877 he was appointed minister to Spain, and in 1878 transferred to England, where he remained as minister until 1885. He did much to make America and American letters respected in England, and was very popular with the English people both as a man and as a writer, a window having been placed to his memory in the chapter-house of Westminster Abbey in 1893. His work in verse includes: A Year's Life (1841); Poems (1844); The Vision of Sir Launfal (1848); A Fable for Critics (1848); The Biglow Papers (1848); Poems (editions of 1848, 1849, 1854, 1858); The Commemoration Ode (1865); The Biglow Papers, Second Series (1866); Under the Willows, and Other Poems (1869); Three Memorial Poems (1876); Heartsease and Rue (1888); Last Poems (1895). In prose his writing comprises Conversations with Some of the Old Poets (1845); Life of Keats (with an edition of his works) (1854); Fireside Travels (1864); The President's Policy (1864); Among My Books (1870); My Study Windows (1871); Among My Books, Second Series (1876); Democracy, and Other Addresses (1886); Political Essays (1888); Latest Literary Essays and Addresses (1891); The Old English Dramatists (1892); Letters, edited by C. E. Norton (1893). *See Lives by E. E. Brown, Underwood, Lowell, by G. W. Curtis; Steuart's Letters to Living Authors, 1890; Haweis's American Humourists; Stedman's Poets of America; works on American Literature, by Nichol, Richardson, Hawthorne; Cheney's That Dome in Air. Har. Hou.*

Lowell, Mrs. Josephine [Shaw]. *Ms.*, 1843——. Daughter-in-law of Mrs. Anna Lowell, *supra.* A philanthropist of New York city. Public Relief and Private Charity. *Put.*

Lowell, Mrs. Maria [White]. *Ms.*, 1821–1855. The first wife of J. R. Lowell, *supra.* A verse-writer whose only volume of poems was privately printed. The Alpine Sheep is her best known poem.

Lowell, Percival. *Ms.*, 1855——. Brother of A. L. Lowell, *supra.* A Boston writer, traveller, and astronomical investigator. Chosön, a sketch of Korea; The Soul of the Far East; Noto: an Unexplored Corner of Japan; Occult Japan; Mars. *Hou.*

Lowell, Robert Traill Spence. *Ms.*, 1816–1891. Son of C. Lowell, *supra.* An Episcopal clergyman and educator, head master of St. Mark's School, Southborough, 1869–73, and professor of Latin at Union College, 1873–79. After the latter date he continued to live at Schenectady, which is the *locale* of his book, A Story or Two from an Old Dutch Town, as Southborough suggests that of his popular story of school life, Antony Brade. His other works include The New Priest in Conception Bay, a novel of life in Newfoundland, the scene of his first rectorship; Fresh Hearts that Failed Three Thousand Years Ago, and Other Poems. The Defence of Lucknow is his most familiar poem. *Rob.*

Lowrie, John Cameron. *Pa.*, 1808——. A Presbyterian clergyman of New York city. Travels in Northern India; Two Years in Upper India; Manual of Foreign Missions; Missionary Papers; Presbyterian Missions.

Lowrie, John Marshall. *Pa.*, 1817–1867. Cousin of J. C. Lowrie, *supra.* A Presbyterian clergyman of New Jersey. Esther and Her Times; Adam and His Times; A Week with Jesus; The Translated Prophet; The Prophet Elisha; The Life of David.

Lucas, Daniel Bedinger. *W. Va.*, 1836——. A lawyer of Charlestown, West Virginia, who was a United States senator in 1887. A Wreath of Eglantine, and Other Poems; The Maid of Northumberland, a dramatic poem; Ballads and Madrigals.

Luce, Stephen Bleecker. *N. Y.*, 1827——. A rear-admiral of the United States navy, retired in 1887, who, beside publishing a treatise on Seamanship, has edited a collection of Naval Songs.

Lüders, Charles Henry. *Pa.*, 1858–1891. A verse-writer of Philadelphia. The Dead Nymph, and Other Poems; Hallo, My Fancy! a collection of verse (with S. D. Smith). *Scr.*

Ludlam, Reuben. *N. J.*, 1831——. A Chicago physician, dean of the Hahnemann Medical College. Clinical Lectures on Diphtheria; Clinical Lectures on Diseases of Women.

Ludlow, Fitzhugh. *N. Y.*, 1836–1870. A littérateur and journalist of New York city. The Hasheesh-Eater; The Opium Habit; The Heart of the Continent; Little Brother, and Other Genre Pictures; Augustus Jones, Jr. *Le.*

Ludlow, James Meeker. *N. J.*, 1841——. A Presbyterian clergyman of East Orange, New Jersey, from 1886. My Saint John; Concentric Chart of History; The Captain of the Janizaries, a tale of the times of Scanderbeg; A King of Tyre, a tale of the times of Ezra and Nehemiah; That Angelic Woman, a novel. *Fu. Har.*

Ludlow, Noah Miller. *N. Y.*, 1795–1886. An actor and theatrical manager in the Southern States. Dramatic Life as I found It.

Lukens, Henry Clay. *Pa.*, 1838——. A journalist of New York city. The Marine Circus at Cherbourg, and Other Poems; Lean Nora, a travesty; Story of the Types; Jets and Flashes.

Lum, Daniel Dyer. 18——. The Spiritual Delusion; Early Social Life of Man; Utah and its People. *Lip.*

Lummis, Charles Fletcher. *Ms.*, 1859——. A Los Angeles writer. The Land of Poco Tiempo; A Tramp Across the Continent; The Spanish Pioneers; The Man who Married the Moon: Indian folk-lore stories; Some Strange Corners of our Country; The Gold Fish of Grand Chimú; A New Mexico David, and Other Stories. *Cent. Lam. Mg. Scr.*

Lund, Mrs. Mary Dwinell [Chellis]. *N. H.*, 18——. A prolific writer of Sunday-school fiction, among whose works are, All for Money; Old Sunapee; Fife and Drum; Good Work; Mystery of the Lodge; Father Merrill. *Cr. Lo.*

Lundy, John Patterson. *Pa.*, 1823-1892. An Episcopal clergyman of New York city. Review of Bishop Hopkins's "Bible View of Slavery;" Monumental Christianity; Forestry.

Lunt, Edward Clark. 186——. A writer on economics. The Present Condition of Economic Science.

Lunt, George. *Ms.*, 1803-1885. A lawyer of Newburyport, and later a resident of Scituate, among whose writings in verse and prose are, The Age of Gold, and Other Poems; Lyric Poems: Sonnets and Miscellanies; Old New England Traits; Three Eras of New England. The latest collection of his verse was made in 1883.

Lunt, William Parsons. *Ms.*, 1805-1857. A Unitarian clergyman of Quincy, Massachusetts, from 1835 until his death, whose literary work was much admired for the beauty of its style. Union of the Human Race; Gleanings.

Lupton, Nathaniel Thomas. *Va.*, 1830——. An educator and scientist of Alabama, State chemist from 1885, and author of The Elementary Principles of Scientific Agriculture.

Lusk, William Thompson. *Ct.*, 1838——. A prominent obstetric physician of New York city. The Science and Art of Midwifery.

Luska, Sidney. *See Harland, Henry.*

Lyle, William. *S.*, 1822——. A verse-writer of Rochester, New York. The Martyr Queen, and Other Poems.

Lyman, Henry Munson. *H. I.*, 1835——. A Chicago physician, professor of medicine in Rush College. Insomnia and Other Disorders of Sleep; Artificial Anæsthesia; Practice of Medicine.

Lyman, Joseph Bardwell. *Ms.*, 1829-1872. An agricultural journalist of New York city. Philosophy of Housekeeping; Resources of the Pacific States; Women of the War; Cotton Culture.

Lyman, Theodore. *Ms.*, 1792-1849. A noted philanthropist of Boston, the founder of the Lyman School at Westborough. Three Weeks in Paris; The Political State of Italy; Account of the Hartford Convention; The Diplomacy of the United States with Foreign Nations.

Lyman, Theodore. *Ms.*, 1833-1897. Son of T. Lyman, *supra*. A scientist of note associated with the Museum of Comparative Zoölogy in Cambridge from 1860. His principal work is the Ophiuroidea of the Challenger Expedition.

Lynch, Anne C. *See Botta, Mrs.*

Lynch, James Daniel. *Va.*, 1836——. A political writer of Mississippi. Kemper County Vindicated; Bench and Bar of Mississippi; Bench and Bar of Texas.

Lynch, William Francis. *Va.*, 1801-1865. A naval officer of prominence as an explorer. Narrative of the United States Exploring Expedition to the River Jordan and the Dead Sea; Naval Life, or Afloat and Ashore.

Lyon, Anne Bozeman. *Al.*, 1860——. A Southern writer of fiction. No Saint; A Sterlings Camp.

Lyon, David Gordon. *Al.*, 1852——. An educator of Cambridge, Hollis professor of divinity at Harvard University from 1882. Keilschrifttexte Sargons Koenigs von Assyrien; An Assyrian Manual. *Scr.*

Lyon, Irving Whitall. *N. Y.*, 1840-1896. A Hartford physician who wrote

Colonial Furniture in New England. *Hou.*

Lyons, Albert Brown. *H. I.*, 1841——. A prominent chemist of Detroit who has published a Manual of Practical Assaying.

Lyttle, William Haines. *O.*, 1826–1863. A general in the Federal army during the Civil War, remembered in literature for the poem beginning, "I am Dying, Egypt, Dying." *See Poems of, edited, with Memoir, by W. Venable, infra. Clke.*

M

Mabie, Hamilton Wright. 1845——. A journalist and essayist of New York city, editor of The Outlook. Norse Stories Retold from the Eddas; My Study Fire; Under the Trees and Elsewhere; Short Studies in Literature; Essays in Literary Interpretation; Essays on Nature and Culture; Essays on Books and Culture. *Do. Rob.*

McAdoo, Mrs. Mary Faith [Floyd]. *Tn.*, 1832——. Wife of W. McAdoo, *infra.* The Nereid, a romance; Antethusia.

McAdoo, William Gibbs. *Tn.*, 1820——. A jurist of Tennessee. Poems; Elementary Geology of Tennessee (with H. C. White).

MacAfee, Mrs. Nelly Nichol [Marshall]. *Ky.*, 1845——. A Kentucky writer of fiction. Eleanor Morton, or Life in Dixie; Gleanings from Fireside Fancies; Sodom Apples; Wearing the Cross; Passion; A Criminal through Love.

McAnally, David Rice. *Tn.*, 1810——. A Methodist clergyman, prominent in St. Louis and elsewhere in the Southwest, who, besides a History of Methodism in Missouri, has written a number of lives of Methodist bishops.

MacArthur, Arthur. *S.*, 1815——. A prominent jurist of Washington. Lectures on the Law; Reports of Supreme Court Cases; Education in its Relation to Manual Industry. *Ap.*

MacArthur, Robert Stuart. *Q.*, 1841——. A distinguished Baptist clergyman of New York city, pastor of Calvary Baptist Church from 1870. Quick Truths in Quaint Texts; Calvary Pulpit, or Christ and Him Crucified; Divine Balustrades, and Other Sermons. *Bap. Fu. Re.*

McBride, James. *Pa.*, 1788–1859. A writer of Hamilton, Ohio. Pioneer Biography. *See Bibliography of Ohio.*

McCabe, James Dabney. *Va.*, 1842–1883. A versatile and prolific Southern writer whose principal work is a Life of General Robert Lee, while among his many others are, Planting the Wilderness; History of the War between France and Germany; History of the Turko-Russian War; Paris by Sunlight and Gaslight; Our Young Folks Abroad; The Great Republic; Lights and Shadows of New York Life; Centennial History of the United States. *Le. Lip.*

McCabe, William Gordon. *Va.*, 1841——. Cousin of J. D. McCabe, *supra.* A Confederate officer, since 1888 head master of a school in Petersburg, Virginia. The Defence of Petersburg; A Latin Grammar.

McCall, George Archibald. *Pa.*, 1802–1868. A soldier of Philadelphia, who served in the Mexican war, and in the Civil War was brigadier-general of volunteers in the Federal army. Letters from the Frontier.

McCall, Hugh. *S. C.*, 1767–1824. A United States army officer. History of Georgia (1811–16).

McCall, John Cadwalader. *Pa.*, 1793–1846. Cousin of G. A. McCall, *supra.* A lawyer of Philadelphia. The Troubadour, and other poems; Fleurette, and other rhymes.

McCall, Peter. *N. J.*, 1809–1880. Cousin of G. A. McCall, *supra.* An eminent lawyer of Philadelphia, mayor of that city, 1844–45. Rise and Progress of Civil Society; History of Pennsylvania Law and Equity.

MacCarroll, James. *I.*, 1815–1892. A musical and dramatic critic of New York city. Letters of Terry Finnegan to D'Arcy McGee; The New Gauger; Adventures of a Night; The New Life-Boat.

MacCarty, J—— Hendrickson. *Pa.*, 1830——. A Methodist clergyman. The Black Horse and Carry-All; Inside the Gates; Two Thousand Miles through the Heart of Mexico; Fact and Fiction in Holy Writ. *Meth.*,

Macchetta, Mrs. Blanche Roosevelt [Tucker]. *Wis.*, 18——. Home Life of Longfellow; Marked "In Haste;" Stage Struck; Life of Doré; The Copper Queen, a novel; Verdi, Milan, and Othello. *Fo.*

McClellan, Carswell. *Pa.*, 1835-1892. Brother of H. B. McClellan, *infra*. A topographical assistant on the staff of General A. A. Humphreys in the Civil War. Afterwards a civil engineer in railroad and government service. The Personal Memoirs and Military History of U. S. Grant *versus* The Record of the Army of the Potomac. *Hou.*

McClellan, Ely. 18——. Brother of C. McClellan, *supra*. Assistant medical director, United States army. The Cholera Epidemic of 1873 in the United States.

McClellan, George. *Ct.*, 1796-1847. A noted surgeon of Philadelphia, professor of surgery in Jefferson Medical College, for which institution he obtained the charter. The Principles and Practice of Surgery. *Lip.*

McClellan, George Brinton. *Pa.*, 1826-1885. Son of G. McClellan, *supra*. A distinguished soldier, general-in-chief of the armies of the United States, 1861-62; an unsuccessful candidate for the presidency in 1864; governor of New Jersey, 1878-81. His most important works include, The Armies of Europe; Organization and Campaigns of the Army of the Potomac; European Cavalry; McClellan's Own Story. *See Appletons' American Biography.*

McClellan, Henry Brainerd. *Pa.*, 1840——. Brother of C. McClellan, *supra*. A major in the Confederate service during the Civil War, who published an admirable Life of Major-General J. E. B. Stuart. *Hou.*

McClelland, Alexander. *N. Y.*, 1796-1864. A Reformed Presbyterian clergyman and educator. Canon and Interpretation of Scripture; Sermons.

MacClelland, Margaret Greenway. 18—1895. A Virginia novelist. Mammy Mystic; Old Ike's Memories, a book of verse. Princess; Oblivion; Jean Monteith; Madame Silva; Manitou Island; Burkett's Lock; St. John's Wooing; The Old Post Road. *Har. Ho. Mer.*

MacClelland, Milo Adams. *Pa.*, 1837——. A physician of Knoxville, Illinois. Civil Malpractice, a Treatise on Surgical Jurisprudence. *Hou.*

MacClenachan, Charles Thompson. *D. C.*, 1829——. A lawyer of New York city, long employed in the department of public works, among whose writings are, Law of the Fire Department; The Atlantic Cable of 1858; Book of the Ancient Accepted Rite of Scottish Freemasonry.

McClintock, John. *Pa.*, 1814-1870. A Methodist clergyman of New York city, professor in Drew Theological Seminary at the time of his death. He is best known by the Theological and Biblical Cyclopædia which he began with James Strong, *infra*, but he was the author, also, of Living Words; Lectures on Theological Encyclopædia and Methodology. *See Life by G. R. Crooks, supra. Meth.*

McClure, Alexander Kelly. *Pa.*, 1828——. A Philadelphia journalist, founder of The Times in 1873, and its editor since then. Three Thousand Miles Through the Rocky Mountains; The South: its Industrial, etc., Condition. *Lip.*

McClure, Alexander Wilson. *Ms.*, 1808-1865. A Congregational clergyman of Boston, among whose writings are, Lectures on Ultra Universalism; Life of John Cotton, *supra*.

McConnel, John Ludlam. *Il.*, 1826——. A lawyer and novelist of Jacksonville, Illinois, who was a soldier in the Mexican War. His fictions are studies of Western life. Talbot and Vernon; Grahame, or Youth and Manhood; The Glenns; Western Characters.

McConnell, Samuel D* *Pa.*, 1846——. An Episcopal clergyman of prominence as an independent thinker, rector of St. Stephen's Church in Philadelphia, 1882-96, and of Holy Trinity, Brooklyn, subsequently. Sons of God; Sermon Stuff; History of the Episcopal Church in the United States; A

* A distinguishing initial only.

Year's Sermons; An Open Secret. *Ar. Wh.*

McCook, Henry Christopher. *O.*, 1837——. A Presbyterian clergyman of Philadelphia, well known as a naturalist. Object and Outline Teaching; The Last Year of Christ's Ministry; The Last Days of Jesus; Garfield Memorial Sermons; The Women Friends of Jesus; The Gospel in Nature; The Mound-Making Art of the Alleghanies; Natural History of the Agricultural Ant of Texas; Honey Ants and Occident Ants; Tenants of an Old Farm; American Spiders. *Fu. Lip.*

McCord, Mrs. Louisa Susannah [Cheves]. *S. C.*, 1810-1880. A writer of South Carolina. Sophisms of the Protective Policy, translated from Bastral; Caius Gracchus, a tragedy; My Dreams, a volume of verse.

McCormick, Richard Cunningham. *N. Y.*, 1832——. An Arizona journalist, governor of that Territory, 1866–69. Visit to the Camp at Sebastopol; St. Paul's to St. Sophia; Arizona: its Resources (1865).

McCosh, James. *S.*, 1811-1894. A metaphysician of eminence and a Presbyterian divine of the Free Church. After being professor in Queen's College, Belfast, 1852–68, he came to America in 1868, and was president of Princeton College, 1868–88, resigning in the latter year, but holding an emeritus professorship until his death. As a philosophical thinker he exercised an extended influence. His principal writings include, Logic: the Laws of Discursive Thought; Christianity and Positivism; Scottish Philosophy; Mill's Philosophy; Method of the Divine Government; First and Fundamental Truths; Psychology; The Emotions; Our Moral Nature; Gospel Sermons; Philosophy of Reality; The Religious Aspect of Evolution; Realistic Philosophy defended; Whither? O Whither Tell Me Where; The Development of Hypotheses; Philosophic Series: I. Expository, II. Historical and Critical. *See Life of, edited by W. M. Sloane, infra. Meth. Scr.*

McCoy, Mrs. Catherine [Webb] [Towles]. *Ms.*, 1823——. A writer of Columbus, Georgia. Tales from the Freemason's Fireside; The Three Golden Links; Poor Claire, or Life Among the Queer.

McCrackan, William Denison. *Bv.*, 1864——. An author and lecturer of New York city, born in Munich of American parents. The Rise of the Swiss Republic; Romance and Teutonic Switzerland; Swiss Solutions of American Problems; Little Idyls of the Big World. *Ar. Kt.*

MacCracken, Henry Mitchell. *O.*, 1840——. A Presbyterian clergyman and educator, chancellor of the University of the City of New York from 1891. Tercentenary of Presbyterianism; Kant and Lotze; A Metropolitan University; Leaders of the Church Universal.

MacCreary, George Washington. *Ind.*, 1835–1890. An Indiana jurist. Treatise on the American Law of Elections; Reports of the Circuit Courts of the United States, Eighth District, 1879–83.

McCulloch, Hugh. *Me.*, 1808–1895. A distinguished financier, secretary of the treasury, 1865–69 and 1884–85. Men and Measures of Half a Century was his only publication. *Scr.*

McDermott, Hugh Farrar. 1833–1890. A journalist of New York city. Poems from an Editor's Table; The Blind Canary, a book of verse.

McDonald, James Madison. *Me.*, 1812–1876. A Congregational clergyman who was pastor of a church in Princeton, New Jersey, 1856–76. Credulity; My Father's House, or the Heaven of the Bible; Life and Writings of St. John; Ecclesiastes Explained; Key to the Book of Revelation. *Scr.*

McDougal, Mrs. Frances Harriet [Whipple] [Greene]. *R. I.*, 1805–1875. A Rhode Island writer who resided in California from 1862. The Original; The Mechanic; Might and Right, a History of the Dorr Rebellion; Shahmah in Pursuit of Freedom; The Dwarf Boy, and Minor Poems; Beyond the Veil.

MacDowell, Mrs. Katherine Sherwood [Bonner]. *Mi.*, 1849–1883. A writer of Holly Springs, Mississippi, from 1873 to 1878 a resident of Boston and the private secretary of Longfellow. In Mrs. Kirk's novel of "Margaret Kent" she figures as the heroine. Dialect Tales; Suwanee River Tales; Like unto Like. *Har. Rob.*

Mace, Mrs. Frances Parker [Laughton]. *Me.*, 1836——. A popular verse-writer of San José, California. The authorship of Only Waiting, her best known poem, has been claimed by several writers. Legends, Lyrics, and Sonnets; Under Pine and Palm. *Hou.*

McFadden, Bernarr Adolphus. *Mo.*, 1868——. A teacher of physical training in New York city. The Athlete's Conquest, a novel; System of Physical Training.

MacFerrin, Anderson Purdy. *Tn.*, 1818——. A Methodist clergyman in Tennessee. Sermons for the Times; Heavenly Shadows and Hymns.

MacFerrin, John Berry. *Tn.*, 1807-1887. Brother of A. P. MacFerrin, *supra.* A Methodist clergyman in Tennessee. History of Methodism in Tennessee.

McGaffey, Ernest. *O.*, 1861——. A lawyer of Chicago. Poems of Gun and Rod; Poems. *Do. Scr.*

MacGahan, Januarius Aloysius. *O.*, 1844-1878. A famous journalist and war correspondent. During the Franco-Prussian war he was the correspondent at Paris of the New York Herald, and he went through the Russo-Turkish war as the correspondent of the London Daily News. Campaigning on the Oxus, and the Fall of Khiva; Under the Northern Lights; Turkish Atrocities in Bulgaria. *Har.*

McGarvey, John William. *Ky.*, 1829——. A clergyman of the Christian denomination, professor of sacred history in the University of Kentucky from 1865. Commentary on the Acts; Commentary on Matthew and Mark; Lands of the Bible; Text and Canon; Credibility and Inspiration of the Bible.

McGiffert, Arthur Cushman. *N.Y.*, 1861——. A Presbyterian clergyman, professor of church history in Union Seminary from 1893. Dialogue of Papias and Jason. He has published a translation with prolegomena and notes of the Church History of Eusebius Pamphilus; The Apostolic Age. *Scr.*

McGill, John. *Pa.*, 1809-1872. A Roman Catholic bishop of Richmond. Our Faith the Victory; The True Church Indicated; Life of John Calvin, from the French.

McGlasson, Eva Wilder. *See Brodhead, Mrs.*

McIlvaine [mąk-il-vān'], **Charles Petitt.** *N. J.*, 1799-1873. The second Protestant Episcopal bishop of Ohio, and long a prominent figure among Low Churchmen. Evidences of Christianity; Oxford Divinity; The Holy Catholic Church; The Truth and the Life, include his chief works. *Ran.*

McIlvaine, Joshua Hall. *Del.*, 1815-1897. A Presbyterian clergyman of note in the Middle States who founded Evelyn College at Princeton, New Jersey, in 1887. He was professor of belles-lettres at Princeton College, 1860-70, and president of Evelyn College at the time of his death. The Tree of the Knowledge of Good and Evil; Elocution, the Sources and Elements of its Power; The Wisdom of Holy Scripture; The Wisdom of the Apocalypse; Pastoral Directions to Inquiring Souls. *Ran. Scr.*

McIntosh, Maria Jane. *Ga.*, 1803-1878. A New York writer whose novels and tales of domestic life enjoyed a long popularity. Her writings include, Praise and Principle; Conquest and Self-Conquest; Violet; Two Lives, or To Seem and To Be; Charms and Counter-Charms; The Lofty and the Lowly; Meta Gray; Two Pictures; Evenings at Donaldson Manor; Aunt Kitty's Tales; Woman in America, her Work and her Reward; The Cousins, a juvenile tale. *Ap.*

Mackaye, Mrs. Maria Ellery [Goodwin]. *R. I.*, 1830——. An educator of Cambridge, author of The Abbess of Port Royal, and Other French Studies. *Le.*

McKeever, Harriet Burn. *Pa.*, 1807-1886. A Philadelphia writer of Sunday-school fiction, among whose works are, Nothing but Leaves; Edith's Ministry; The Old Château; Crown Jewels. *Meth.*

McKellar, Thomas. *N. Y.*, 1812——. A prominent type-founder of Philadelphia who, beside publishing

The American Printer, has written Tam's Fortnight Ramble, and Other Poems; Droppings from the Heart; Lines for the Gentle and Loving; Rhymes Atween Times. His verse is unpretentious, and seldom more than commonplace in sentiment and execution. *Lip.*

McKenny, Thomas Lorraine. *Md.*, 1785–1859. A writer for many years in charge of the Bureau of Indian Affairs. Sketches of a Tour to the Lakes; Essays on the Spirit of Jacksonianism; History of the Indian Tribes (with J. Hall); Memoirs, Official and Personal.

McKenzie, Alexander. *Ms.*, 1830——. A Congregational clergyman of Cambridge from 1867. Cambridge Sermons; History of the First Church in Cambridge; Some Things Abroad; The Two Boys. *Lo.*

Mackenzie, Alexander Slidell. *N. Y.*, 1803–1848. A naval officer of prominence in his day. Popular Essays on Naval Subjects; The American in England; Lives of John Paul Jones, Commodore Decatur, Commodore Oliver Hazard Perry; A Year in Spain. *Har.*

Mackenzie, Robert Shelton. *I.*, 1809–1881. A journalist of London who came to America in 1852, and from 1857 was the literary editor of the Philadelphia Press. His writings include, Lives of Dickens, Scott, and Guizot; Titian: an art novel; Lays of Palestine; Partnership *en Commandité*, a work upon commercial law; Bits of Blarney; Mornings at Matlock; Tressilian and his Friends.

Mackey [măk'ee], **Albert Gallatin.** *S. C.*, 1807–1881. A physician of Charleston whose life was principally devoted to the study of freemasonry. Text-Book of Masonic Jurisprudence; Lexicon of Freemasonry; The Mystic Tie; Book of the Chapter; Manual of the Lodge; Cryptic Masonry; Masonic Ritualist; Masonic Parliamentary Law; History of Freemasonry in South Carolina; Encyclopædia of Freemasonry. He edited the Ahimon Rezon.

Mackey, John. *S. C.*, 1765–1831. A journalist and educator of Charleston whose American Teacher's Assistant (1826) was the first comprehensive work on arithmetic published in America.

Mackie, John Milton. *Ms.*, 1813–1894. A New England writer, in early life a tutor in Brown University. Cosas de España; Lives of Leibnitz, Schamyl, Samuell Gorton; Tai Ping Wang; From Cape Cod to Dixie.

McKim, Randolph Harrison. *Md.*, 1842——. An Episcopal clergyman, rector of the Church of the Epiphany at Washington. Nature of the Christian Ministry; Vindication of Protestant Principles; Futnre Punishment; Bread in the Desert, and Other Sermons; Christ and Modern Unbelief; Christianity and Buddhism. *Wh.*

McKinney, Mordecai. *Pa.*, *c.* 1796–1867. A jurist of Harrisburg. Pennsylvania Justice of the Peace; United States Constitntional Manual; Our Government; The American Magistrate and Civil Officer; Pennsylvania Tax Laws; Digest of Pennsylvania Banking Laws.

McLaren, William Edward. *N. Y.*, 1831——. The third Protestant Episcopal bishop of Chicago. He was consecrated bishop in 1875, but prior to 1872 was a Presbyterian clergyman. Catholic Dogma the Antidote of Doubt; The Practice of the Interior Life.

McLaughlin, Andrew Cunningham. *Il.*, 1861——. A professor of American history at the University of Michigan from 1891. Life of Lewis Cass, *supra.* *Hou.*

Maclean, Mrs. Clara Victoria [Dargan]. *S. C.*, *c.* 1840——. An educator of South Carolina. Her work in fiction includes Riverlands; Helen Howard.

McLellan, Isaac. *Me.*, 1806——. A verse-writer of New York city of note as a sportsman. His verse, once popular, is now nearly forgotten. The Year, and Other Poems; The Fall of the Indian; Poems of the Rod and Gun (1883), with biographical sketch.

McLeod, Alexander. *S.*, 1774–1833. A Reformed Presbyterian minister of New York city, famous as a preacher in his day. Negro Slavery Unjustifiable; The Messiah; Life and Power of True Godliness; American Christian Expositor, include his chief works.

McLeod, Xavier Donald. *N. Y.*, 1821-1865. Son of A. McLeod, *supra*. A Roman Catholic clergyman, but before 1852 an Episcopal clergyman. Pynnshurst, his Wanderings and Ways of Thinking; Life of Sir Walter Scott; Life of Mary Queen of Scots; Our Lady of Litanies; Devotion to the Blessed Virgin Mary, include the more important of his works.

McMahon, John Van Lear. *Md.*, 1800-1871. A prominent lawyer and politician of Maryland, whose Historical View of Maryland is an authority on the early history of the province.

McMaster, Gilbert. *I.*, 1778-1854. A Reformed Presbyterian clergyman of Duanesburgh, New York. The Shorter Catechism Analyzed; Apology for the Psalms; Moral Character of Civil Government.

McMaster, Guy Humphrey. *N. Y.*, 1829-1887. A jurist and verse-writer of Bath, in central New York. He wrote a History of Steuben County, but his name lingers in anthologies as author of the well-known lyric, Carmen Bellicosum.

McMaster, John Bach. *L. I.*, 1852- ——. A professor of American history at the University of Pennsylvania from 1883, and prior to that date an instructor in engineering at Princeton College. Bridge and Tunnel Centres; High Masonry Dams; History of the People of the United States; Franklin as a Man of Letters; Pennsylvania and the Federal Constitution (with F. D. Stone). *Ap. Hou.*

McMillan, Conway. *Mch.*, 1867- ——. A professor of botany in the University of Minnesota from 1891. Twenty-Two Common Insects of Nebraska; The Metaspermæ of the Minnesota Valley.

McMurtrie, Henry. *Pa.*, 1793-1865. An educator of Philadelphia. Lexicon Scientiarum is his principal work.

McMurtrie, William. *N. J.*, 1851- ——. A professor of chemistry in the University of Illinois. Culture of the Sugar Beet; Culture of Sumac; Grape Culture in the United States, are among his publications.

McNamara, John. *I.*, 1824-1885. An Episcopal clergyman of Nebraska. Three Years on the Kansas Border; The Black Code of Kansas.

McNaughton, John Hugh. *N. Y.*, 1829——. A verse-writer of Caledonia, New York, many of whose songs have been set to music, and proved extremely popular. Babble Brook Songs; Onnalinda, a romance in verse.

Macomb, Alexander. *D. C.*, 1782-1841. An officer of prominence in the American army during the War of 1812, becoming major-general in command of the army in 1828. Treatise on Martial Law; Treatise on Practice of Courts-Martial; Pontiac, a drama. *See Memoir by G. H. Richards.*

Macon, John Alfred. *Al.*, 1851- ——. A journalist of New York city. Uncle Gabe Tucker. *Lip.*

McPherson, Edward. *Pa.*, 1830-1895. A journalist of Gettysburg, editor of The Tribune Almanac from 1877, and for some years American editor of the Almanach de Gotha. Political History of the United States during the Civil War; Political History of the United States during Reconstruction; Handbook of Politics.

MacQueary, Howard. *Va.*, 1861- ——. A Universalist clergyman of Minneapolis. He was formerly an Episcopal clergyman in Ohio, but, on account of his denial of the Virgin birth of Christ, was tried for heresy in 1891, and suspended from the Episcopal ministry. Evolution of Man and Christianity; Topics of the Times, lectures on theological and sociological themes. *Ap.*

McSherry, James. *Md.*, 1819-1869. A lawyer of Frederick, Maryland. Père Jean, the Jesuit Missionary; Williloft, or the Days of James the First; History of Maryland.

McSherry, Richard. *W. Va.*, 1817-1885. A physician of prominence in Baltimore, and in early life in the naval service. Early History of Maryland, and Other Essays; El Puchero, a discursive work on Mexico; Military Life in Field and Camp; Health and How to Promote It, are his principal writings. *Ap.*

McTyeire [măk-teer′], **Holland Nimmons.** *S. C.*, 1824–1889. A Methodist bishop in Tennessee. Manual of Discipline; Duties of Masters; History of Methodism, are among his works.

McVickar, William Augustus. *N. Y.*, 1827–1877. An Episcopal clergyman who became rector of Christ Church, New York city, in 1876. Life of Rev. John McVickar; City Missions. *Hou.*

Macy, Jesse. *Ind.*, 1842——. A professor of political science in Iowa College. Our Government; The English Constitution. *Mac.*

Madison, James. *Va.*, 1751–1836. The fourth President of the United States. The Reports of the Debates in the National Convention of 1788 are the most important writings of his earlier career. His complete works have been issued in six volumes. *See Lives by Rives, J. Q. Adams, S. H. Gay; History of the United States, Madison's Administrations, by H. Adams.*

Maffit, John Newland. *I.*, 1795–1850. A once noted Methodist preacher and lecturer. Tears of Contrition; Pulpit Sketches; Poems.

Magill, Mary Tucker. *Va.*, 1832——. Granddaughter of H. St. George Tucker, *infra.* An educator and fiction-writer of Winchester, Virginia. The Holcombes; Women, or Chronicles of the Late War; School History of Virginia; Pantomimes, or Wordless Poems. *Lip.*

Magoon, Elias Lyman. *N. H.*, 1810——. An eminent Baptist clergyman of Philadelphia, well known as a lecturer and art connoisseur of liberal thought and wide attainments. Proverbs for the People; Orators of the American Revolution; Republican Christianity; Westward Empire; Eloquence of the Colonial Times; Living Orators in America.

Magruder, Allan Bowie. 18———. The Bible Defended; Life of John Marshall, *infra.* *Hou.*

Magruder, Julia. *Va.*, 1854——. A novelist. Miss Ayr of Virginia, and Other Stories; The Child Amy; Across the Chasm; At Anchor; A Magnificent Plebeian; Honored in the Breach; The Violet; Princess Sonia. *Cent. Har. Lgs. Lip. Lo. S. Scr.*

Mahan [ma-hăn′], **Alfred Thayer.** *N. Y.*, 1840——. A distinguished officer in the United States navy whose masterly works upon sea power in history have received official recognition from both home and foreign governments. The Influence of Sea Power upon History, 1600–1783; Influence of Sea Power upon the French Revolution and Empire, 1783–1812; The Gulf and Inland Waters; Life of Admiral Farragut; Life of Nelson, the Embodiment of the Sea Power of Great Britain. *Ap. Lit. Scr.*

Mahan, Asa. *N. Y.*, 1799–1889. A Congregational clergyman and educator, president of Adrian College, 1860–1871, and after the latter date resident in England. Critical History of Philosophy; The Science of Intellectual Philosophy; Science of Moral Philosophy; The Doctrine of the Will; The Scripture Doctrine of Christian Perfection; Logic; Theism and Anti-Theism in their Relations to Science; Critical History of the American Civil War. *Bar. Meth.*

Mahan, Dennis Hart. *N. Y.*, 1802–1871. A military engineer of distinction whose text-books have been widely used. Treatise on Field Fortifications; Elementary Course of Civil Engineering; Elementary Treatise on Advanced Guard, etc.; Industrial Drawing; Descriptive Geometry; Philosophy of Engineering; Permanent Fortifications; an edition of Moseley's Mechanical Principles of Engineering and Architecture, with additions. *Wil.*

Mahan, Milo. *Va.*, 1819–1870. Brother of D. H. Mahan, *supra.* An Episcopal clergyman of Baltimore. The Exercise of Faith; History of the Church; Reply to Colenso; Palmoni, a Free Inquiry; Comedy of Canonization.

Malcom, Howard. *Pa.*, 1799–1879. A Baptist clergyman and educator at one time prominent in Philadelphia. Nature and Extent of the Atonement; Bible Dictionary; Christian Rule of Marriage; Travels in Southeastern Asia.

Mallery, Garrick. *Pa.*, 1831–1894. An army officer in charge of the bureau of ethnology from its foundation in 1879. Calendar of the Dakota Language; Introduction to the Study of Sign Language among North American Indians; Greeting by Gesture; Israelite and Indian, a Parallel in Planes of Culture; Picture Writing of the American Indians, are among his important contributions to ethnology.

Malone, Walter. *Mi.*, 1866——. A verse-writer of Memphis, Tennessee. Songs of Dark and Dawn.

Maltby, Isaac. *Ct.*, 1767–1819. A Boston author who was general of militia. Elements of War; Courts-Martial and Military Law; Military Tactics.

Manly, Basil. *S. C.*, 1825–1892. A Baptist clergyman and educator, professor in the Southern Baptist Seminary at Louisville. Kind Words Teacher; A Call to the Ministry; Bible Doctrine of Inspiration Defended.

Manly, John Matthews. *Al.*, 1865——. Pre-Shakesperean Drama.

Mann, Cyrus. *N. H.*, 1785–1850. A Congregational clergyman of Westminster, Massachusetts, 1815–41. Epitome of the Evidences of Christianity; History of the Temperance Reformation.

Mann, Horace. *Ms.*, 1796–1859. A famous Massachusetts educator and philanthropist, president of Antioch College, Ohio, 1852–59, and for twelve years secretary of the Massachusetts Board of Education. He entirely remodelled the school system of his State. Beside his twelve important annual reports on education, he published Lectures on Education; An Educational Tour; Thoughts for a Young Man; Slavery: Letters and Speeches; Lectures on Intemperance; Powers and Duties of Women. *See Life by Mrs. Mann; Boone's Education in the United States; Gordey's Rise and Growth of the Normal School System; Horace Mann, the Educator, by A. Winship. Le.*

Mann, Mrs. Mary Tyler [Peabody]. *Ms.*, 1806–1887. Wife of H. Mann, *supra*, and sister of Elizabeth Peabody, *infra*. Flower People; Christianity in the Kitchen; Culture in Infancy (with E. Peabody); Life of Horace Mann; Juanita, a Romance of Real Life in Cuba. *Le. Lo.*

Mann, Matthew Derbyshire. *N. Y.*, 1845——. A physician, professor of gynæcology in the University of Buffalo, who has published a Text-Book on Prescription Writing, and edited The American System of Gynæcology.

Mann, William Julius. *G.*, 1819–1892. A Lutheran clergyman of Philadelphia, author of Life and Times of Henry Muhlenberg. *See Memoir by E. T. Mann, 1893.*

Manning, Jacob Merrill. *N. Y.*, 1824–1882. A Congregational clergyman of Boston, pastor of the Old South Church, 1857–82. Helps to a Life of Prayer; Half Truths and the Truth; Not of Man, but of God; Sermons. *Hou.*

Mansfield, Edward Deering. *Ct.*, 1801–1880. Son of J. Mansfield, *infra*. A lawyer and journalist of Cincinnati. Utility of Mathematics; Treatise on Constitutional Law; Political Grammar of the United States; Legal Rights, etc., of Married Women; Life of General Scott; History of the Mexican War; American Education; Memoirs of D. Drake, *supra*; Popular Life of General Grant; Personal Memories. *Clke.*

Mansfield, Jared. *Ct.*, 1759–1830. A mathematician, professor at West Point, 1812–28, who published Essays: Mathematical and Physical.

Mansfield, Lewis William. *Ct.*, 1816——. A writer of Cohoes, New York. The Morning Watch, a book of verse; Up-Country Letters; Country Margins.

Manship, Andrew. *Md.*, 1824——. A Methodist evangelist of Philadelphia. Thirteen Years in the Itineracy; Cherished Memories; Reminiscences from the Saddle-Bags of a Methodist Preacher; History of Gospel Tents and Experience.

Manville, Mrs. Helen Adelia [Wood]. *N. Y.*, 1839——. A verse-writer of La Crosse, Wisconsin. Heart Echoes, a volume of verse.

Manville, Marion. Daughter of Mrs. Manville, *supra*. *See Pope, Mrs.*

Marble, Manton. *Ms.*, 1835——. A journalist of New York city, editor and proprietor of The World, 1862–76, and author of A Secret Chapter of Political History.

March, Alden. *Ms.*, 1795–1869. A once prominent surgeon of Albany. Wounds of the Abdomen; Improved Forceps for Harelip Operations.

March, Charles Wainright. *N. H.*, 1815–1864. A journalist and essayist of New York city. Daniel Webster and His Contemporaries; Sketches in Madeira, Portugal, and Spain.

March, Daniel. *Ms.*, 1816——. A Congregational clergyman. Walks and Homes of Jesus; Night Scenes in the Bible; Our Father's House; From Dark to Dawn; Home Life in the Bible; The First Khedive, or Lessons in the Life of Joseph; Morning Light in Many Lands. *C. P. S.*

March, Francis Andrew. *Ms.*, 1825——. A philologist of distinction, professor at Lafayette College from 1856, and the successor of James Russell Lowell in 1891 as president of the American Language Association. Relation of the Study of Jurisprudence to the Roman Period; Hamilton's Theory of Perception; Method of Philological Study of the English Language; Comparative Grammar of the Anglo-Saxon Language; Anglo-Saxon Reader. *Har.*

Marcy, Erastus Edgerton. *Ms.*, 1815——. A physician of New York city. Theory and Practice of Medicine; Theory and Practice of Homœopathy; Christianity and its Conflicts; Life Duties.

Marcy, Henry Orlando. *Ms.*, 1837——. A physician of Cambridge. Anatomy and Surgical Treatment of Hernia; professional translations from the Italian of Ercolani. *Ap.*

Marcy, Randolph Barnes. *Ms.*, 1812–1887. Brother of E. E. Marcy, *supra.* A brigadier-general in the United States army. Exploration of the Red River in 1852; Thirty Years of Army Life on the Border; The Prairie Traveller; Border Reminiscences. *Har.*

Marden, Orison Swett. *N. H.*, 1848——. A Boston writer whose collections of brief biographies, comprise Pushing to the Front; Architects of Fate. *Hou.*

Marguerittes, Julie de. *See Rea, Mrs.*

Markell, Charles Frederick. *Md.*, 1855——. A Maryland lawyer and journalist. Charmodine, a volume of verse.

Markham, Charles Edwin. *Or.*, 1852——. An educator and verse-writer of California. In Earth's Shadow, a book of verse; Songs of a Dream Builder.

Markham, Jared Clark. *Ms.*, 1816——. An architect who designed the Saratoga monument. Appeal in Behalf of National Monuments; Monumental Art; Historic Sculpture.

Markoe, Thomas Masters. *Pa.*, 1819——. A surgeon of New York city, professor in Columbia College from 1860, and author of a Treatise on Diseases of the Bones. *Ap.*

Marsh, Mrs. Caroline [Crane]. *Ms.*, 1816——. Wife of G. P. Marsh, *infra.* The Hallig, or the Sheepfold in the Waters, from the German of Biernatzki; Wolfe of the Knoll, and Other Poems; Life of George P. Marsh. *Scr.*

Marsh, George Perkins. *Vt.*, 1801–1882. A philologist of distinction who was minister to Italy, 1861–82. Lectures on the English Language; Man and Nature, re-written and enlarged with the title, The Earth as Modified by Human Action; Icelandic Grammar; Origin and History of the English Language; Mediæval and Modern Saints and Miracles. *See Life by Mrs. Marsh, supra. Har. Scr.*

Marsh, John. *Ct.*, 1788–1864. A Congregational clergyman long prominent as a temperance lecturer. Epitome of Ecclesiastical History; Half Century Tribute to Temperance; Temperance Recollections.

Marsh, Othniel Charles. *N. Y.*, 1831——. A palæontologist, professor at Yale University from 1866. Odontornithes; Dinocerata; Sauropoda, are among valuable scientific monographs by him.

Marshall, Edward Chauncey. *N. Y.*, 1824——. An educator, inventor, and journalist. Book of Oratory; History of the United States Naval Academy; Ancestry of General Grant.

Marshall, Humphrey. *Pa.*, 1722–1801. A famous botanist of Marshallton, Pennsylvania. Arboretum Americanum, a very valuable work of his, was translated into a number of foreign languages.

Marshall, John. *Va.*, 1755–1835. Chief Justice of the United States from 1801 until his death. The Life of Washington; Writings upon the Federal Constitution. *See Lives by Van Santvord, 1854, Flanders, 1858, Magruder, 1885; Appletons' American Biography.*

Martin, Edward Sandford. *N. Y.*, 1856——. A journalist of New York city. Sly Ballades in Harvard China; A Little Brother of the Rich, and Other Poems; Cousin Anthony and I, some Views of Ours; Windfalls of Observation. *Scr.*

Martin, François Xavier. *F.*, 1764–1846. A New Orleans jurist, chief justice of Louisiana, 1837–45. General Digest of Louisiana Laws; Reports of Louisiana Supreme Court, 1813–30; History of Louisiana to 1814.

Martin, Henry Newell. *I.*, 1848–1896. A biologist of note, professor of biology at Johns Hopkins University from 1876. The Human Body; Practical Biology (with T. H. Huxley); Handbook of Vertebrate Dissection (with W. A. Moale). *Ho.*

Martin, John Hill. *Pa.*, 1823——. A lawyer of Philadelphia, legal editor of The Intelligencer from 1881. Bethlehem and the Moravians; The Bench and Bar of Philadelphia; Chester and its Vicinity; Delaware County.

Martin, Mrs. Margaret [Maxwell]. *S.*, 1807——. An educator of Columbia, South Carolina. Day Spring; Christianity in Earnest; Religious Poems; Scenes and Scenery of South Carolina, include the larger part of her writings.

Martin, William Alexander Parsons. *N. Y.*, 1827——. A Presbyterian clergyman and missionary, president of the Tungwen College, Peking. Among his writings in Chinese are, Evidences of Christianity; The Three Principles; Religious Allegories. In English he has published The Chinese: their Education, Philosophy, and Letters. *Har.*

Martyn, Mrs. Sarah Towne [Smith]. *N. H.*, 1805–1879. A writer of Sunday-school semi-historical fiction whose home was in New York city. Among her many works are comprised Huguenots of France; William Tyndale; Lady Alice Lisle.

Martyn, William Carlos. *N. Y.*, 1841——. Son of Mrs. Martyn, *supra.* A Presbyterian clergyman of New York city. History of the Huguenots; History of the English Puritans; The Pilgrim Fathers of New England; History of the Dutch Reformation; Lives of John Milton, John B. Gough, Wendell Phillips, William E. Dodge. *Fu.*

Marvel, Ik. *See Mitchell, D. G.*

Marvin, Enoch Mather. *Mo.*, 1823–1877. A bishop of the Methodist Church South. The Work of Christ; Sermons; To the East by Way of the West.

Mason, Mrs. Caroline Atherton [Briggs]. *Ms.*, 1823–1890. A verse-writer of Fitchburg, Massachusetts, whose poem, Do They Miss Me at Home, was long a popular song. Utterance, a Collection of Home Poems; The Lost Ring, and Other Poems; Rose Hamilan, a tale. *Hou.*

Mason, Mrs. Clara Stevens Arthur. *Me.*, 1844–1884. The Cherry Blooms of Yeddo, a volume of verse. *Lo.*

Mason, David Hastings. *Pa.*, 1828——. A Chicago journalist who has published a Short Tariff History of the United States. *Bai.*

Mason, Emily Virginia. *Ky.*, 1815——. A nurse in Confederate hospitals, and after the Civil War an educator in Paris. She edited a collection of Southern Poems of the War, and wrote a Popular Life of General Robert E. Lee.

Mason, George Champlin. *R. I.*, 1820–1894. An architect of Newport, Rhode Island. Newport and its Environs; Application of Art to Manufactures; The Old House Altered; Life and Works of Gilbert Stuart; Reminiscences of Newport.

Mason, John. *E.*, 1600–1672. A Puritan soldier who held a place in the estimation of the Massachusetts Bay Puritans corresponding to that filled by Miles Standish among the Pilgrims. History of the Pequot War is a vigourous narrative, first printed by Increase Mather in 1677. *See Tyler's American Literature; Life by G. E. Ellis, supra.*

Mason, John Mitchell. *N. Y.*, 1770-1829. A Presbyterian clergyman of New York city, long famous as a pulpit orator, his Oration on the Death of Alexander Hamilton being especially noted. Letters on Frequent Communion; Plea for Sacramental Communion on Catholic Principles. *See Works in four volumes; Memoirs by Van Vechten, 1856.*

Mason, Otis Tufton. *Me.*, 1838——. An anthropologist of note. The Hupa Indian Industries; Woman's Share in Primitive Culture; The Origins of Invention; The Land Problem; Cradles of the North American Indians; The Antiquities of Guadeloupe. *Ap. Scr.*

Mather, Cotton. *Ms.*, 1663-1728. Son of I. Mather, *infra.* A famous Congregational clergyman of Boston, pastor of the North Church, 1683-1728, and his father's colleague for the greater part of that period. He was a prolific author, publishing nearly four hundred works, large and small, but it is upon the Magnalia Christi Americana that his reputation rests. Among other works are Wonders of the Invisible World; Christian Philosopher; Psalterium Americanum; Manductio ad Ministerium; Memorable Providences Relating to Witchcraft; Essays to Do Good; The Armour of Christianity; Batteries Upon the Kingdom of the Devil; Death made Easie and Happy. His style is disfigured by pedantry and strained analogies, and is at all times far removed from simplicity, but the author is nevertheless easily seen to be intensely in earnest in his endeavours to be of service to his generation. *See Lives by S. Mather, 1729, W. B. O. Peabody, A. P. Marvin, 1889. B. Wendell, 1892; North American Review, July, 1840, April, 1869; Tyler's American Literature; Pond's The Mather Family; Old Colony Days, by Mrs. May Alden Ward.*

Mather, Fred. *N. Y.*, 1833——. A pisciculturist of note, author of Ichthyology of the Adirondacks.

Mather, Increase. *E.*, 1639-1723. Son of R. Mather, *infra.* A Congregational clergyman of Boston, pastor of the North Church, and president of Harvard College, 1685-1701. Of his nearly one hundred printed works, the most noted is the Remarkable Providences, which was entitled by its author An Essay for the Recording of Illustrious Providences, an effort to prove by induction the existence of mundane supernatural forces. His style is much superior to that of his son. *See Tyler's American Literature; Sprague's Annals of the American Pulpit.*

Mather, Moses. *Ct.*, 1719-1806. A Congregational clergyman of Darien, Connecticut, from 1744 till his death, who was of much prominence in his day as a controversialist. Systematic View of Divinity; Infant Baptism Defended; Election Sermons. *See Sprague's Annals of the American Pulpit.*

Mather, Richard. *E.*, 1596-1669. A Puritan clergyman who came from England in 1635, and was minister at Dorchester, 1636-69. He was a man of large influence in the colony, and was one of the three divines who prepared The Bay Psalm Book. A Treatise on Justification is as important as any of his many writings. *See Life by I. Mather; Tyler's American Literature.*

Mather, Samuel. *Ms.*, 1706-1785. Son of C. Mather, *supra.* A Congregational clergyman of Boston who succeeded his father and grandfather as pastor of the North Church, but in 1741 became the head of a new church, of which he was pastor till his death. Among his writings are, Life of Cotton Mather, *supra;* Essay on Gratitude; America Known to the Ancients, an attempt to prove the Japhetic origin of the first inhabitants of the American continent. *See Sprague's Annals of the American Pulpit.*

Mather, William Williams. *Ct.*, 1804-1859. A geologist of Ohio. Geology of the First Geological District.

Mathews, Albert. *N. Y.*, 1820——. A lawyer of New York city. Walter Ashwood, a Love Story; A Bundle of Papers, by Paul Siegvolk; Thoughts on Codification of the Common Law; Ruminations, and Other Essays. *Put.*

Mathews, Cornelius. *N. Y.*, 1817-1889. Cousin of A. Mathews, *supra.* An author and playwright of New York city, among whose non-dramatic works are, Indian Book of Fairy Tales; The Enchanted Moccasins, and Other Legends; Money-Penny: a romance. Jacob Leisler; The Politicians; Witchcraft, comprise some of his plays.

Mathews, James McFarlane. *N. Y.*, 1785–1870. A Reformed Dutch clergyman of New York city, at one period chancellor of the University of the City of New York. What is Your Life?; The Bible and Men of Learning; Fifty Years in New York.

Mathews, Joanna H——. 18———. Daughter of J. M. Mathews, *supra*. A writer of Sunday-school tales, among which are, The Bessie Books; The Sunbeams. *Cas.*

Mathews, Julia A——. 183———. Daughter of J. M. Mathews, *supra*. A writer of Sunday-school fiction, among which are, Bessie Harrington's Venture; Jack Granger's Cousin; Drayton Hall Series. *Ran.*

Mathews, William. *Me.*, 1818——. An educator and essayist of Chicago, and later of Boston. Hours with Men and Books; Getting on in the World; The Great Conversers; Literary Style; Men, Places, and Things; Oratory and Orators; Wit and Humor, their Use and Abuse; Nugæ Litterariæ. *Rob. Sc.*

Mathews, William Smith Babcock. *N. H.*, 1837——. A musical critic of Chicago. Outline of Musical Form; Dictionary of Music and Musicians; How to Understand Music; New Musical Miscellanies.

Matthews, [James] Brander. *La.*, 1852——. A littérateur of New York city. Among his many writings the more important are, The Theatres of Paris; French Dramatists of the 19th Century; Margery's Lovers, a Comedy; The Last Meeting, a Story; The Secret of the Sea, and Other Stories; A Family Tree, and Other Stories; The Story of a Story; Tom Paulding; Studies of the Stage; Americanisms and Briticisms; Vignettes of Manhattan; His Father's Son; Introduction to the Study of American Literature; The Royal Marine; Tales of Fantasy and Fact. *Har. Scr.*

Matthews, James Newton. *Ind.*, 1852——. A physician and verse-writer of Mason, Illinois. Tempe Vale, and Other Poems, includes many of his contributions to The Century and other periodicals. *Ke.*

Matthews, Stanley. 1824–1889. A Cincinnati jurist, associate justice of the United States Supreme Court from 1881. A Summary of the Law of Partnership for the Use of Business Men. *Clke.*

Matthews, Washington. *I.*, 1843——. A surgeon in the regular army, well known as an ethnologist. Among his writings are included a Grammar of the Language of the Hidatsa; Ethnography and Philology of the Hidatsa Indians; Gentile Organization of the Navajo Indians.

Mattison, Hiram. *N. Y.*, 1811–1868. A Methodist clergyman of New York city, active as a controversialist. Bible Doctrine of Immortality; The Trinity and Modern Arianism; Tracts for the Times; Impending Crisis; Defence of American Methodism; Popular Amusements, include his chief works. *Meth.*

Maturin [măt′u-rĭn], **Edward.** *I.*, 1821–1881. An educator of New York city. Beside Lyrics of Spain and Erin, he was the author of several historical novels, comprising Eva; Bianca; Montezuma; Benjamin: the Jew of Grenada. *Har.*

Maury [maw′rĭ], **Ann.** *E.*, 1803–1876. Cousin of M. F. Maury, *infra*. Memoirs of a Huguenot Family.

Maury, Dabney Herndon. *Va.*, 1822——. Nephew of M. F. Maury, *infra*. A Confederate major-general in the Civil War. Skirmish Drill for Mounted Troops; Recollections of a Virginian in the Mexican, Indian, and Civil Wars. *Scr.*

Maury, Matthew Fontaine. *Va.*, 1806–1873. A once famous scientist, for many years in charge of the Hydrographical Office at Washington, as well as of the Naval Observatory. During the Civil War he entered the Confederate service, and from 1868–73 was a professor in the Virginia Military Institute at Lexington. Treatise on Navigation; Physical Geography of the Sea; Wind and Current Charts; Physical Geography for Schools; The World we Live In. *See North British Review,*

May, 1858; Life by his daughter, Mrs. Corbin; Manly's Southern Literature.

Maury, Mrs. Sarah Mytton [Hughes]. *E.*, 1808–1849. Sister-in-law of A. Maury, *supra.* Etchings from the Caracci; The Englishwoman in America; The Statesmen of America; Progress of the Catholic Church in America.

May, Caroline. *E.*, c. 1820——. A writer of New York city. American Female Poets; The Woodbine, a Holiday Gift; Poems; Hymns on the Collects; Lays of Memory and Affection.

May, Edith. *See Drinker, Mrs.*

May, John Wilder. *Ms.*, 1819–1883. A jurist of Boston. The Law of Insurance; Law of Crimes; Criminal Law. *Lit.*

May, Margaret. *See Tucker, Mrs.*

May, Samuel. *Ms.*, 1810——. A retired Unitarian clergyman of Leicester, Massachusetts, of prominence in the anti-slavery movement, and author of The Fugitive Slave Law and its Victims.

May, Samuel Joseph. *Ms.*, 1797–1871. Cousin of S. May, *supra.* A Unitarian clergyman of Syracuse prominent in the anti-slavery cause, and also in educational reforms. Education of the Faculties; Revival of Education; Recollections of the Anti-Slavery Conflict. *See Memoir, 1873.*

May, Sophie. *See Clarke, Rebecca.*

Mayer, Alfred Marshall. *Md.*, 1836–1897. Nephew of B. Mayer, *infra.* An astronomer, professor of physics in Stevens Institute at Hoboken, New Jersey, from 1871. Light (with C. Barnard); Notes on Physics; The Earth a Great Magnet; Sound; Sport with Gun and Rod in American Woods and Waters (edited.) *Ap. Cent.*

Mayer, Brantz. *Md.*, 1809–1879. A lawyer and journalist of Baltimore, and an officer in the Federal army during the Civil War. Mexico as It Was and as It Is; Mexico: Aztec, Spanish, and Republican; Observations on Mexican History and Archæology; Mexican Antiquities; Captain Canot, or Twenty Years of an African Slaver; Memoir of Jared Sparks, *infra.*

Mayer, Lewis. *Pa.*, 1783–1849. A German Reformed clergyman of eastern Pennsylvania. Lectures on Scriptural Subjects; The Sin Against the Holy Ghost; History of the German Reformed Church.

Mayhew, Experience. *Ms.*, 1673–1758. A missionary to the Indians of Martha's Vineyard. Indian Converts; Grace Defended.

Mayhew, Jonathan. *Ms.*, 1720–1766. Son of Experience Mayhew, *supra.* A Congregational clergyman of Boston, pastor of the West Church, 1747–66. He was a bold thinker both in religion and politics, and his influence over the colonial mind at an eventful period was very great. He was as eloquent as he was original and independent. A noted Sermon on the Repeal of the Stamp Act is an effective example of his style. Seven Sermons; Sermons to Young Men. *See Memoir by Alden Bradford, 1838.*

Maynard, Charles Johnson. *Ms.*, 1845——. A naturalist of Newton, Massachusetts. The Naturalist's Guide; The Birds of Florida; The Birds of Eastern North America; A Manual of Taxidermy; The Butterflies of New England.

Mayo, Amory Dwight. *Ms.*, 1823——. A Unitarian clergyman, prominent since the Civil War in educational matters in the Southern States. Graces and Powers of the Christian Life; Symbols of the Capitol; Religion in Common Schools; Talks with Teachers.

Mayo, Robert. *Va.*, 1784–1864. A writer long in the civil service at Washington. View of Ancient Geography and History; New System of Mythology; United States Pension Laws; Synopsis of the Commercial and Revenue System; The Treasury Department, its Origin and Operations.

Mayo, Mrs. Sarah Carter [Edgarton]. *Ms.*, 1819–1848. Wife of A. D. Mayo, *supra.* The Palfreys; Ellen Clifford, and several compilations of verse and prose.

Mayo, William Starbuck. *N. Y.*, 1812–1895. A novelist and physician of New York city. Kaloolah; The Berber; Never Again; Flood and Field; Romance Dust, a collection of short stories. *Put.*

Mead, Charles Marsh. *Vt.*, 1836——. A Congregational clergyman, professor at Andover Seminary, 1866–1882, and since the latter date a resident in Germany. He published The Soul Here and Hereafter, a Biblical Study; Christ and Criticism; Supernatural Revelation. *Ran.*

Mead, Edwin Doak. *N. H.*, 1849–——. A Boston writer and lecturer upon social and historical topics, and editor of The New England Magazine (1897). Martin Luther: a Study of the Reformation; The Philosophy of Carlyle; The Roman Church and the Public Schools. *El.*

Meade, William. *Va.*, 1789–1862. The third Protestant Episcopal bishop of Virginia. Family Prayers; Old Churches of Virginia; Lectures on the Pastoral Office; Reasons for Loving the Episcopal Church. *See Memorial by J. Johns.*

Mears, John William. *Pa.*, 1825–1881. A Presbyterian clergyman, professor in Hamilton College, 1870–81. The Bible in the Workshop; The Martyrs of France; The Beggars of Holland; The Story of Madagascar; The Heroes of Bohemia; From Exile to Overthrow.

Meehan, Thomas. *E.*, 1826——. A botanist and nurseryman of Germantown, Philadelphia, editor and publisher of "Meehan's Monthly," a popular journal devoted to botany and floriculture. American Handbook of Ornamental Trees; Flowers and Ferns of the United States.

Meek, Alexander Beaufort. *S. C.*, 1814–1865. An Alabama jurist and journalist. Red Eagle; Songs and Poems of the South; Romantic Passages in Southern History.

Meek, Fielding Bradford. *Ind.*, 1817–1876. A palæontologist in government service. Palæontology of the Upper Missouri; Check List of North American Invertebrate Fossils; Report on Fossils of the Upper Missouri Country.

Megapolensis, Johannes. *Hd.*, 1603–1670. A Dutch clergyman of the New Amsterdam colony, the first Protestant missionary to the Indians. His Short Account of the Mohawk Indians appeared in 1651.

Meigs [mĕgs], **Charles Delucena.** *Ba.*, 1792–1869. A noted Philadelphia physician, professor in Jefferson Medical College, 1841–61. Philadelphia Practice of Midwifery; Science and Art of Obstetrics; Treatment of Child-Bed Fevers; Acute and Chronic Diseases of the Neck of the Uterus, and several translations from French medical writers. *See Memoir by J. F. Meigs, infra; Allibone's Dictionary; Gross's Sketches of Contemporaries.*

Meigs, James Aitkin. *Pa.*, 1829–1879. A physician and naturalist of Philadelphia, author of Cranial Characteristics, and other scientific monographs. *See Gross's Sketches of Contemporaries.*

Meigs, John Forsyth. *Pa.*, 1818–1882. Son of C. D. Meigs, *supra.* A Philadelphia physician. Memoir of C. D. Meigs, *supra;* Diseases of Children.

Meigs, Return Jonathan. *Ct.*, 1734–1823. A noted soldier in the American Revolution. Journal of Occurrences during the Expedition to Quebec.

Meigs, Return Jonathan. *Ky.*, 1801–1891. Grand-nephew of R. J. Meigs, *supra.* A noted lawyer of Tennessee. Reports of Tennessee Supreme Court Cases; Digest of Tennessee Decisions; The Code of Tennessee.

Meline, James Florant. *N. Y.*, 1811–1873. A New York writer, an officer in the Federal army during the Civil War. Two Thousand Miles on Horseback; Commercial Travelling; Mary Queen of Scots and her Latest English Historian, an attack upon Froude's view of the subject; Life of Sixtus V. *Clke.*

Melish, John. *S.*, 1771–1822. A once noted traveller of Scottish birth. Travels in the United States, etc.; Description of the Roads, etc.; Description of the United States (1816); Necessity of Protecting Manufactures; Information for Emigrants; Statistical View of the United States.

Mell, Patrick Hues. *Ga.*, 1811–1888. A Baptist clergyman and educator of Georgia, vice-chancellor of the University of Georgia. Baptism; Corrective Church Discipline; Parliamentary Practice; The Philosophy of Prayer; Church Polity; Predestination.

Mellen, Grenville. *Me.*, 1799–1841. A lawyer and littérateur of New York city, whose verse was once very popular and much praised by critics, but is now forgotten. Our Chronicle of '26, a satire; The Martyr's Triumph, and Other Poems; The Passions; Glad Tales and Sad Tales, a collection of tales in prose; The Rest of the Nations. *See Griswold's Poets and Poetry of America.*

Mellick, Andrew D——. *N. J.*, 1844–1895. A lawyer of Plainfield, New Jersey. The Story of an Old Farm; The Hessians in New Jersey.

Melville, George Wallace. *N. Y.*, 1841——. Chief of the Bureau of Steam-Engineering in the United States navy from 1887. A survivor of the ill-fated "Jeannette," of which he was engineer. In the Lena Delta, a Narrative of the Search for Lieut.-Commander De Long and his Companions. *Hou.*

Melville, Herman. *N.Y.*, 1819–1891. A novelist of New York city, for many years employed in the custom-house. His earliest writings were very popular, but had nearly passed out of remembrance before the author's death. Typee; Omoo; White Jacket; Redburn; Mardi; Pierre; Israel Potter; The Piazza Tales; Moby Dick; The Confidence Man; Battle Pieces, a volume of verse; Clarel, a poem; John Marr and Other Sailors; Timoleon, a collection of poems. *Har.*

Mendenhall, James William. *O.*, 1844–1892. A Methodist clergyman, editor of The Methodist Review from 1888. Echoes from Palestine; Plato and Paul. *Meth.*

Mendenhall, Thomas Corwin. *O.*, 1841——. A prominent scientist, president of the Worcester Polytechnic Institute from 1894, and author of A Century of Electricity. *Hou.*

Menken, Adah Isaacs. *La.*, 1835–1868. An actress of Jewish birth whose name originally was Dolores Adios Fuertes. She was several times married and divorced, but is known by the name of her first husband. Her verse is morbid, but still finds occasional readers. Memories; Infelicia. *See Every Saturday, September 12, 1868.* *Lip.*

Mercein, Thomas Fitz Randolph. *N. Y.*, 1825–1856. A Methodist clergyman of New York State. Natural Goodness; The Wise Master Builder; Childhood and the Church. *Meth.*

Mercer, Charles Fenton. *Va.*, 1778–1858. A congressman from Virginia, 1816–40, prominent as an opponent of slavery. The Weakness and Inefficiency of the Government of the United States was not published until 1863.

Mercur, James. *Pa.*, 1842–1896. A scientist and army officer, professor at West Point from 1884. Elements of the Art of War; Military Mines, Blasting, and Demolitions. *Wil.*

Meriwether, Mrs. Elizabeth [Avery]. *Tn.*, 1832——. A novelist of Memphis, Tennessee. The Master of Red Leaf; Black and White; The Ku Klux Klan; My First and Last Love.

Meriwether, Lee. *Mi.*, 1862——. Son of Mrs. Meriwether, *supra.* A special agent of the United States Bureau of Labor. A Tramp Trip: how to See Europe on Fifty Cents a Day; The Tramp at Home; Afloat and Ashore on the Mediterranean. *Har. Scr.*

Merriam, Augustus Chapman. *N. Y.*, 1843–1895. A Greek scholar, adjunct professor of Greek at Columbia College. Law Code of Gortynia in Crete; Inscriptions on the Obelisk Crab; The Phæacians of Homer; Sixth and Seventh Books of Herodotus. *Har.*

Merriam, Clinton Hart. *N.Y.*, 1855——. A naturalist of note, chief of the United States Biological Survey. Vertebrates of the Adirondack Region; Mammals of the Adirondacks. *Ho.*

Merriam, Florence Augusta. *N.Y.*, 1863——. Sister of C. H. Merriam, *supra.* A Washington writer. A-Birding on a Bronco; My Summer in a Mormon Village; Birds Through an Opera Glass. *Hou.*

Merriam, George Spring. *Ms.*, 1843——. A littérateur of Springfield, Massachusetts. A Living Faith; Life and Times of Samuel Bowles, *supra;* The Way of Life; The Story of William and Lucy Smith; A Symphony of the Spirit; The Chief End of Man; Reminiscences and Letters of Caroline C. Briggs. *Cent. El. Hou.*

Merrill, Ayres Phillips. *Ms.*, 1793–1873. A physician of Memphis, and subsequently of New York city. Lectures on Fevers.

Merrill, George Perkins. *Me.*, 1854——. A geologist, professor in Columbian University, Washington, from 1893. Stones for Building and Decoration; Handbook of the Geological Department, Smithsonian Institution.

Merrill, Selah. *Ct.*, 1837——. A Congregational clergyman and archæologist, United States consul at Jerusalem, 1882–86. East of the Jordan; Galilee in the Time of Christ; Greek Inscriptions Collected in 1875–77 East of the Jordan; The Site of Calvary. *Scr.*

Merrill, Stephen Mason. *O.*, 1825——. A Methodist bishop in Ohio. Christian Baptism; New Testament Idea of Hell; The Second Coming of Christ; Aspects of Christian Experience; Digest of Methodist Law; Outlines of Thought on Probation; Mary of Nazareth and Her Family. *Meth.*

Merrill, William Emory. *Wis.*, 1837——. A military engineer in the United States army. Iron Truss Bridges; Improvement of Tidal Rivers.

Merriman, Mansfield. *Ct.*, 1841——. A civil engineer, professor at Lehigh University from 1881. Continuous Bridges; Elements of the Method of Least Squares; The Figure of the Earth; Mechanics of Materials; Treatise on Hydraulics; Text-Book on Retaining Walls and Masonry Dams; Introduction to Geodetic Surveying; Text-Book on Roofs and Bridges.

Merritt, Timothy. *Ct.*, 1775–1845. A Methodist clergyman and journalist. Christian Manual; Convert's Guide; Discussion against Universal Salvation; Validity of Infant Baptism; Lectures on Universal Salvation (with W. Fiske, *supra*).

Merwin, Elias. *Ct.*, 1825–1891. A Boston lawyer, professor of equity in Boston University from 1854. The Principles of Equity and Equity Pleading. *Hou.*

Merwin, Henry Childs. *Ms.*, 1853——. Son of E. Merwin, *supra*. A Boston lawyer living in Concord, Massachusetts. The Patentability of Inventions; Road, Track, and Stable, a book about Horses. *Lit.*

Messenger, Mrs. Lilian Roselle. *Ky.*, 1853——. In the Heart of America (verse); The Vision of Gold, and Other Poems.

Metcalf, Richard. *R. I.*, 1820–1881. A Unitarian clergyman, pastor at Winchester, Massachusetts, 1866–81. Letter and Spirit; The Abiding Memory, a collection of Sermons. *A. U. A.*

Metcalf, Theron. *Ms.*, 1784–1875. A jurist of Massachusetts. Principles of the Law of Contracts; Digest of Massachusetts Supreme Court Cases, 1816–1823; Reports, 1840–1849.

Metcalfe, Henry. *N. Y.*, 1847——. An instructor of ordnance at West Point who has published The Cost of Manufactures; Ordnance and Gunnery. *Wil.*

Metcalfe, Samuel L——. *Va.*, 1798–1856. A physician and scientist of New York city. Narratives of Indian Warfare in the West; New Theory of Terrestrial Magnetism; Caloric. *Lip.*

Michie [my'key], **Peter Smith.** *S.*, 1839——. A military engineer, professor of mathematics at West Point from 1871. Wave Motion Relating to Sound and Light; Life of General Upton, *infra*; Analytical Mechanics; Hydromechanics; Practical Astronomy (with Harlow). *Wil.*

Middleton, Henry. *F.*, 1797–1876. A once prominent writer of Charleston. Prospects of Disunion; The Government and the Currency; Economical Causes of Slavery in the United States, and Obstacles to its Abolition; The Government of India; Universal Suffrage.

Milburn, William Henry. *Pa.*, 1823——. A Methodist clergyman, famous as "the blind preacher," who has been six times chaplain of the United States House of Representatives. Rifle, Axe, and Saddle-Bags; Ten Years of Preacher Life; Pioneers and People of the Mississippi Valley.

Miles, George Henry. *Md.*, 1824–1871. A Maryland lawyer and educator, professor of English literature at Mount St. Mary's College, Emmettsburg, Maryland, popular at one period as a verse-writer and dramatist. Besides his dramas, Cromwell; Mahomet; De Soto, he published Christine, and Other Poems; Abu Hassan the Wag, or the Sleeper Awakened; A Review of Hamlet; The Truce of God.

Miles, Henry Adolphus. *Ms.*, 1809–1895. A Unitarian clergyman of Eastern Massachusetts. Lowell as It Was and Is (1845); Grains of Gold; Gospel Narratives; Words of a Friend; Modern Ideas of the Birth of Jesus; Traces of Picture Writing in the Bible. *El.*

Miles, James Warley. *S. C.*, 1818–1875. An Episcopal clergyman of Charleston. Philosophic Theology, or Ultimate Grounds of all Religious Belief based on Reason (1849).

Miles, Nelson Appleton. *Ms.*, 1839——. A noted soldier of the United States army who served as a brigadier-general of volunteers during the Civil War. He became a major-general in 1890. Personal Recollections.

Miles, Pliny. *N. Y.*, 1818–1865. A traveller who made his home in London in his later years. Statistical Register; Elements of Mnemotechny, or Art of Memory; Northufari, or Rambles in Iceland; Ocean Steam Navigation; Postal Reform.

Miley, John. *O.*, 1813–1895. A Methodist minister and educator, professor of systematic theology in Drew Seminary, Madison, New Jersey, from 1873. The Atonement in Christ; Systematic Theology.

Millard, David. *N. Y.*, 1794–1873. A minister of the Christian denomination, professor at Meadville Seminary, Pennsylvania, 1845–67. The True Messiah Exalted; Journal of Travels in Egypt, etc., 1841. *See Life by D. E. Millard, 1874.*

Miller, Mrs. Annie [Jenness]. *N. H.*, 1859——. A dress reformer of New York city, publisher of The Jenness Miller Magazine. Physical Beauty; Mother and Babe; Barbara Thayer, a novel. *Le.*

Miller, Charles Henry. *N. Y.*, 1842——. An art critic of New York city. The Philosophy of Art in America.

Miller, Cincinnatus Hiner. "Joaquin Miller." *Ind.*, 1841——. A poet and prose-writer who, after a life of adventure in California, went to London in 1870, and speedily became famous as the author of Songs of the Sierras. For a time his work continued popular, but his fame has since greatly declined, though his writings continue to be read. Since 1887 he has lived in Oakland, California. His more important works include, Songs of the Sierras; The Ship of the Desert; Songs of the Sunland; in prose: The Danites in the Sierras; Shadows of Shasta; Memorie and Rime; '49, or the Gold Seekers of the Sierras; The One Fair Woman; The Destruction of Gotham; The Building of the City Beautiful, a poetic romance. *See Allibone's Dictionary, Supplement; Vedder's American Writers. Fu. St.*

Miller, Elihu Spencer. *N. J.*, 1817–1879. Son of S. Miller, *infra*. A lawyer of Philadelphia, professor in the University of Pennsylvania. Treatise on the Law of Partition by Writ in Pennsylvania; Caprices, a volume of verse.

Miller, Mrs. Emily Huntington. *Ct.*, 1833——. An educator of Evanston, Illinois, president of the Woman's College of the Northwestern University, and a popular writer of semi-religious fiction for young people. Among her various writings are, From Avalon, and Other Poems; The Royal Road to Fortune; The Kirkwood Series; Captain Fritz; Little Neighbors. *Dut.*

Miller, Mrs. Harriet Mann. "Olive Thorne Miller." *N. Y.*, 1831——. A writer of Brooklyn whose books and magazine articles upon birds have been widely popular. A Bird-Lover in the West; Little Brothers of the Air; Bird-Ways; In Nesting Time; Four-Handed Folk; Little Folks in Feathers and Fur; Nimpo's Troubles; Queer Pets at Marcy's; Our Home Pets; Little People of Asia. *Dut. Har. Hou.*

Miller, James Russell. *Pa.*, 1840——. A Presbyterian clergyman of Philadelphia. Week Day Religion; Home Making; In His Steps; Silent Time; Come Ye Apart; The Marriage Altar; Practical Religion; Bits of Pasture; Making the Most of Life; Mary of Bethany; The Dew of Thy Youth; The Every Day of Life. *Rev.*

Miller, Joaquin. *See Miller, C. H.*

Miller, John. *N. J.*, 1819–1895. Son of S. Miller, *infra*. A Presbyterian clergyman who was a colonel in the Confederate army during the Civil War, and who lived in Princeton, New Jersey, from 1871. He was tried for heresy, but allowed to withdraw from the Presbytery, and subsequently established several independent churches in the vicinity of Princeton. Design of the Church; Commentary on the Proverbs; Fetich in Theology; Metaphysics; Are Souls Immortal?; Was Christ in Adam?; Is God a Creed?; Theology; Commentary on Romans. *Ran.*

Miller, Mrs. Minnie [Willis] [Baines]. *N. H.*, 1845——. A religious writer of Springfield, Ohio. The Silent Land; His Cousin the Doctor; The Pilgrim Vision.

Miller, Olive Thorne. *See Miller, Mrs. Harriet.*

Miller, Samuel. *Del.*, 1769–1850. A Presbyterian clergyman, pastor of the Brick Church, New York city, 1793–1813, and professor of ecclesiastical history at Princeton Theological Seminary for the remainder of his life. Presbyterianism the Truly Primitive and Apostolic Constitution of the Church of Christ; Letters on Clerical Habits and Manners; Letters on Unitarians; Life of Jonathan Edwards; Letters on the Christian Ministry; Letters on Church Government, include his more important writings. *See Life by his son.*

Miller, Samuel Freeman. *Ky.*, 1816–1890. A jurist of Kentucky, and after 1850 of Iowa; a strong opponent of slavery. The Supreme Court of the United States, a series of Biographies; Reports of Supreme Court Decisions.

Miller, Stephen Franks. *N. C.*, *c.* 1810–1867. A once noted Georgia lawyer. Bench and Bar of Georgia; Wilkins Wylder, or the Successful Man; Memoir of General Blackshear and the War in Georgia, 1813–14. *Lip.*

Millet, Francis Davis. *Ms.*, 1846——. An artist and littérateur of New York city. A Capillary Crime, and Other Stories; The Danube from the Black Forest to the Black Sea. *Har.*

Milligan, Robert. *I.*, 1814–1875. A Campbellite clergyman and educator, president of Kentucky University, 1859–66. Brief Treatise on Prayer; Reason and Revelation; Scheme of Redemption; The Great Commission; Analysis of the New Testament Commentary on Hebrews.

Mills, Abraham. *N. Y.*, 1769–1867. A once popular educator of New York city who, besides editing a number of text-books, was author of Literature and Literary Men of Great Britain and Ireland; Outlines of Rhetoric; Poets and Poetry of the Ancient Greeks; Compendium of the History of the Ancient Hebrews. *Har.*

Mills, Charles Karsner. *Pa.*, 1845——. A physician of Philadelphia, a specialist in nervous diseases. The Nursing and Care of the Nervous and Insane.

Mills, Robert. *S. C.*, 1781–1855. An architect of Washington, the original designer of the Washington Monument. Statistics of South Carolina; American Pharos, or Lighthouse Guide; Guide to the National Executive Offices.

Miner, Alonzo Ames. *N. H.*, 1814–1896. A prominent Universalist clergyman of Boston. Bible Exercises; Right and Duty of Prohibition; Old Forts Taken. *See Life by Emerson, 1896.*

Miner, Charles. *Ct.*, 1780–1865. A journalist of the Wyoming Valley, Pennsylvania. History of Wyoming; Essays from the Desk of Poor Robert.

Mines, John Flavel. *F.*, 1835–1891. A journalist of New York city. The Heroes of the Last Lustre, a poem; A Tour Around New York by Mr. Felix Oldboy. *Har.*

Minifie, William. *E.*, 1805–1880. An architect and educator of Baltimore. Text-Book of Mechanical Drawing; Text-Book of Geometrical Drawing; Theory and Application of Color; Popular Lectures on Drawing and Design.

Minor, John Barbee. *Va.*, 1813–1895. A professor of law in the University of Virginia. Virginia Report of 1799–1800; Synopsis of the Law of Crimes and Punishments; Institutes of Common and Statute Law.

Minor, Lucian. *Va.*, 1802–1858. Brother of J. B. Minor, *supra*. A lawyer of Williamsburg, Virginia. Reasons for Abolishing the Liqnor Traffic; Travels in New England.

Minot, Henry Davis. *Ms.*, 1859–1890. At the time of his death a railway president in Minnesota. While a schoolboy of Roxbury, Massachusetts, he wrote at the age of sixteen The Land-Birds and Game-Birds of New England. *Hou.*

Minot, William. *Ms.*, 1840——. A Boston lawyer. Taxation in Massachusetts (1877); Local Taxation and Municipal Extravagance.

Minturn, Robert Bowne. *N. Y.*, 1836——. From New York to Delhi, a popular book of travels.

Mitchel, Frederick Augustus. 1839——. A son of O. M. Mitchel, *infra.* Fiction editor of the American Press Association. Chattanooga, a Romance of the American Civil War; Chickamauga, a Romance of the American Civil War; Ormsby MacKnight Mitchel, Astronomer and General. *Hou.*

Mitchel, Ormsby MacKnight. *Ky.*, 1810–1862. An astronomer of distinction, director of the Dudley Observatory at Albany, and a prominent Union general in the Civil War. Planetary and Stellar Worlds; The Orbs of Heaven; Elementary Treatise on the Sun, Planets, etc.; Astronomy of the Bible. *See Headley's Old Stars; Popular Science Monthly, March, 1884; Life by F. A. Mitchel.*

Mitchell, Annie Maria. *Ms.*, 1847——. A writer of religious juveniles, among which are Martha's Gift; Freed Boy in Alabama.

Mitchell, Donald Grant. "Ik Marvel." *Ct.*, 1822——. A littérateur of New Haven, who is best known by his earlier and still popular works, Dream Life; Reveries of a Bachelor, books of a pleasantly sentimental cast. His other works include, My Farm at Edgewood; Dr. Johns, a novel; Rural Studies; Fresh Gleaning from the Old Fields of Europe; The Battle Summer, or Paris in 1848; The Lorgnette; Fudge Doings; Seven Stories; Wet Days at Edgewood; About Old Story-Tellers; The Woodbridge Record, a genealogy; Bound Together: a Sheaf of Papers; Out of Town Places, a revision of Rural Studies; English Lands, Letters, and Kings; American Lands and Letters. *Scr.*

Mitchell, Edward Coppée. *Ga.*, 1836–1887. A real estate lawyer of Philadelphia. Separate Use in Pennsylvania; Contracts for Land Sales in Pennsylvania; Equitable Relations of Buyer and Seller.

Mitchell, Edward Cushing. *Ms.*, 1829——. Grandson of N. Mitchell, *infra.* A Baptist clergyman and educator, president of Leland University, New Orleans, from 1887. Les Sources du Nouveau Testament; Hebrew Introduction; Gnide to the Authenticity, Canon, and Text of the New Testament; The Critical Handbook.

Mitchell, Elisha. *Ct.*, 1793–1857. An educator of note, professor of geology in the University of North Carolina from 1825. While exploring the mountain region of North Carolina, he lost his life. He is buried on the summit of the mountain bearing his name. Elements of Geology; Reports on North Carolina Geology.

Mitchell, Henry. *Ms.*, 1830——. A hydrographer of prominence, among whose scientific monographs are, Physical Hydrography of the Maine Coast; The Estuary of the Delaware; Reclamation of Tide Lands.

Mitchell, Hinckley Gilbert. *N. Y.*, 1846——. A Methodist clergyman and educator, professor at Wesleyan University from 1884. Final Constructions of Biblical Hebrew; Hebrew Lessons; Amos, an Essay in Exegesis; The Pentateuch.

Mitchell, James Tyndale. *Il.*, 1834——. A jurist of Philadelphia. History of the District Court; Mitchell on Motions and Rules.

Mitchell, John. *Ct.*, 1794–1870. A Congregational minister of Stratford, Connecticut. Letters to a Disbeliever in Revivals; Notes from Over the Sea; Reminiscences of College Scenes and Characters; My Mother; Rachel Kell, or the Diamond.

Mitchell, John Ames. *Ms.*, 1845——. A journalist of New York city, founder of Life in 1883, and its editor from that date. The Summer School of Philosophy at Mount Desert; The Romance of the Moon; The Last American; Amos Judd, a novel; That First Affair, and Other Stories. *Ho. Scr.*

Mitchell, John Kearsley. *W. Va.*, 1798–1858. A physician of Philadelphia, of eminence as a medical lecturer. Indecision, and Other Poems; St. Helena: a poem; Remote Consequences of Injuries of Nerves; Cryptogamic Origin of Malarious and Epidemic Fevers; Five Essays on Fevers. *See Gross's Sketches of Contemporaries. Lip.*

Mitchell, Langdon Elwyn. "John Philip Varley." *Pa.*, 1862——. Son of S. W. Mitchell, *infra.* A verse-writer of promise. Sylvian, a Tragedy; Poems; Love in the Backwoods, prose stories. *Har. Hou.*

Mitchell, Mrs. Lucy Myers [Wright]. *Per.*, 1845–1888. An archæologist (the wife of S. S. Mitchell, an artist), who spent much of her life abroad. Her only writing, a History of Ancient Sculpture, is one of the best books in English upon Greek art. *Do.*

Mitchell, Maria. *Ms.*, 1818–1889. Sister of H. Mitchell, *supra.* A distinguished astronomer, professor at Vassar College from 1865. Her scientific papers have not [1897] been collected. *See Mrs. Hale's Woman's Record; Life by Mrs. Kendall.*

Mitchell, Nahum. *Ms.*, 1769–1853. An eminent jurist of Massachusetts, well known in his day as a musical composer. History of the Early Settlement of Bridgewater; Grammar of Music.

Mitchell, Samuel Augustus. 1792–1888. A noted geographer of Philadelphia who besides publishing a series of geographies was author also of General View of the World; New Traveller's Guide.

Mitchell, Silas Weir. *Pa.*, 1829——. Son of J. K. Mitchell, *supra.* A distinguished physician of Philadelphia, well known also as novelist and poet. His professional writings include Wear and Tear, or Hints for the Overworked; Injuries of the Nerves; Nurse and Patient; Fat and Blood; Doctor and Patient. In fiction he has published Hugh Wynne, Free Quaker; Hephzibah Guinness; In War Time; Roland Blake; Far in the Forest; Philip Vernon; Prince Little Boy, and Other Tales out of Fairy Land; Characteristics; A Madeira Party; When all the Woods are Green; and, in verse, Francis Drake, a Tragedy of the Sea; The Mother, and Other Poems; The Cup of Youth; The Hill of Stones, and Other Poems; A Psalm of Death; A Masque, and Other Poems. *See Allibone's Dictionary, Supplement. Cent. Hou. Lip.*

Mitchell, Walter. *Ms.*, 1826——. An Episcopal clergyman of New York city. Two Strings to His Bow; Bryan Maurice, a novel; Poems. Tacking Ship off Shore is the poem by which he is best known. *Hou. Wh.*

Mitchell, William. *Ct.*, 1793–1867. Brother of John Mitchell, *supra.* A Congregational minister of Texas who published A Doctrinal Guide for Young Christians; Coleridge and the Moral Tendency of his Writings.

Mitchill, Samuel Latham. *L. I.*, 1764–1831. A once famous physician and man of letters of New York city who filled there a position very similar to that of Oliver Wendell Holmes in Boston at a later day, the two men having many points of resemblance. He was long a professor of chemistry in Columbia College, and for more than a generation one of the prominent literary and social figures of the metropolis. Among his writings are: Life of Tammany, the Indian Chief; Picture of New York; Description of Schooley's Mountain. *See Reminiscences of, by J. W. Francis, 1859; Allibone's Dictionary.*

Moak, Nathaniel Cleveland. *N. Y.*, 1833–1892. An Albany lawyer. Albany Penitentiary Statutes; English Reports; English Digest.

Moffat, James Clement. *S.*, 1811–1890. A Presbyterian clergyman and educator, professor at Princeton Theological Seminary, 1853–90. Comparative History of Religions; Life of Dr. Chalmers; Song and Scenery, or a Summer Ramble in Scotland; Alwyn, a Romance of Study (verse); The Church in Scotland; Church History in Brief; Rhyme of the North Countrie; The Story of a Dedicated Life. *Do. Ran.*

Mombert, Jacob Isidor. *G.*, 1829——. An Episcopal clergyman of

Paterson, New Jersey. Faith Victorious; Handbook of the English Versions of the Bible; Great Lives; History of Lancaster County, Pennsylvania; History of Charles the Great; Short History of the Crusades. *Ap. Ran.*

Monfort, Francis Cassette. *Ind.*, 1844——. A Presbyterian minister and editor of Cincinnati. Sermons for Silent Sabbaths; Socialism and City Evangelization.

Monroe, Harriet. *Il.*, 1860——. A verse-writer of Chicago. Valeria, and Other Poems; Life of John Wellborn Root. *Hou. Mg.*

Monroe, James. *Va.*, 1758–1831. The fifth President of the United States. An able though not brilliant statesman. State Papers; Tour of Observation in 1817; The People: the Sovereigns; View of the Conduct of the Executive in the Foreign Affairs of the United States. *See Lives by J. Q. Adams, 1850, D. C. Gilman, 1885; Concise History of the Monroe Doctrine by G. F. Tucker, 1885; Appletons' American Biography.*

Montague, Charles Howard. *Ms.*, 1858–1889. A journalist of Boston, city editor of The Globe. The Romance of the Lilies; The Face of Rosenfel; Two Strokes of the Bell; The Doctor's Mistake; The Countess Muta.

Montague, William Lewis. *Ms.*, 1831——. A Congregational clergyman, professor of modern languages at Amherst College from 1862. Comparative Spanish Grammar; Manual of Italian Grammar; Introduction to Italian Literature.

Montefiore, Joshua. *E.*, 1762–1843. A Hebrew lawyer, brother of Sir Moses Montefiore, who came to the United States, and settled in St. Albans, Vermont. Commercial and Notatorial Precedents; Commercial Dictionary; Traders' Compendium; United States Traders' Compendium; Law and Treatise on Bookkeeping; Laws of Land and Sea.

Montgomery, George Washington. *Sp.*, 1804–1841. A United States consul at Tampico. Tarcas de un Solitario, a collection of tales; El Bastarde de Catilla; Journey to Guatemala in 1838.

Montgomery, George Washington. *Me.*, 1810——. A Universalist clergyman of Rochester, New York. Illustrations of the Law of Kindness; Sermons.

Montgomery, Marcus Whitman. *N. Y.*, 1839–1894. A Congregational clergyman, instructor in Chicago Theological Seminary from 1890. History of Jay County, Indiana; A Wind from the Holy Spirit; The Mormon Delusion.

Monti, Luigi. *Sy.*, 1830——. An educator of New York city who appears in Longfellow's Tales of a Wayside Inn as "The Young Sicilian." An American Consul Abroad; Leone, a novel. *Le.*

Mooar, George. *Ms.*, 1830——. A Congregational clergyman, professor in Pacific Theological Seminary at Oakland, California, from 1870. The Religion of Loyalty; Prominent Characteristics of Congregational Churches.

Moody, Dwight Lyman. *Ms.*, 1837——. A celebrated evangelist. Among his more important writings are The Second Coming of Christ; The Way and the Word; Secret Power; The Way to God; Glad Tidings; Great Joy; To All People; Bible Characters; How to Study the Bible. *Ran. Rev.*

Moody, James. *N. J.*, 1744–1809. A New Jersey farmer, active as a Royalist spy during the Revolution. Lieutenant James Moody's Narrative of his Exertions and Sufferings in the Cause of Government.

Moody, Samuel. *Ms.*, 1676–1747. A once famous Congregational clergyman. The Doleful State of the Damned; Judas Hung in Chains.

Moore, Mrs. Annie Aubertine [Woodward]. "Auber Forestier." *Pa.*, 1841——. A Wisconsin translator of note from the Norse; co-translator with Anderson of Björnson's novels, and editor of Echoes from Mist Land. *See Bibliography of Wisconsin. Sc.*

Moore, Mrs. Bloomfield. *See Bloomfield-Moore, Mrs. Clara.*

Moore, Charles Herbert. *N. Y.*, 1840——. A professor of art at Harvard University. The Development and Character of Gothic Architecture, a work of much value; Examples for

Elementary Practice in Delineation. *Hou. Mac.*

Moore, Charles Leonard. *Pa.*, 1854——. A lawyer and verse-writer of Philadelphia. Poems Antique and Modern; Banquet of Palacios, a Comedy; A Book of Day Dreams (verse). *Ho.*

Moore, Clement Clarke. *N. Y.*, 1779–1863. An educator of New York city, professor of Oriental literature in the General Theological Seminary, 1821–63. He published a Hebrew-English Lexicon and a volume of Poems, but is more widely known as the author of the famous poem, The Visit of St. Nicholas.

Moore, David Albert. "Paul Wright." *N. Y.*, 1814——. A physician of Syracuse. A Panorama of Time; How She Won Him.

Moore, Erasmus Darwin. *Ct.*, 1802–1889. A Congregational minister and editor of Boston. Life Scenes in Mission Fields; The New Heart.

Moore, Frank. *N. H.*, *c.* 1828——. Son of J. B. Moore, *infra.* A writer of New York city who has edited a Cyclopædia of American Eloquence; The Rebellion Record, and other compilations. Women of the War is one of his original works.

Moore, George Henry. *N. H.*, 1823–1892. Son of J. B. Moore, *infra.* The superintendent of the Lenox Library, New York city, from 1872 till his death. History of the Jurisprudence of New York; Treason of Charles Lee; Notes on the History of Slavery in Massachusetts; Washington as an Angler; Employment of Negroes in the Revolutionary Army.

Moore, Horatio Newton. *N. J.*, 1814–1859. Orlando, a Tragedy; The Regicide, a drama; Memoir of the Duanes; Mary Morris, a novel; Lives of Marion and Wayne.

Moore, Jacob Bailey. *N. H.*, 1797–1853. A journalist who was postmaster of San Francisco, 1849–53. Laws of Trade in the United States; Gazetteer of New Hampshire; Annals of Concord, New Hampshire.

Moore, John Weeks. *N. H.*, 1807–1889. Brother of J. B. Moore, *supra.* Historical Gatherings relating to Printers, Printing, and Publishing (1820–86).

Moore, Joseph West. 18——. Picturesque Washington; The American Congress: a History of National Legislation and Political Events, 1774–1895. *Har.*

Moore, Mrs. Susan Teackle [Smith]. *Md.*, 18——. Sister of F. H. Smith, *infra.* A novelist of Brooklyn. Ryle's Open Gate. *Hou.*

Moore, Thomas Vernon. *Pa.*, 1818–1881. A Presbyterian minister of Nashville. Last Words of Jesus; God's University, or the World a School; The Culdee Church; Corporate Life of the Church; The Last Days of Jesus.

Moore, William Eves. *Pa.*, 1823——. A Presbyterian clergyman of Columbus, Ohio, from 1872. New Digest of the General Assembly; The Presbyterian Digest.

Moorehead, Warren King. *Iy.*, 1866——. An archæologist of Italian birth, but American parentage, curator of the Ohio State Archæological Museum at Columbus. Primitive Man in Ohio; Fort Ancient: the Great Prehistoric Earthwork of Warren County, Ohio; Wanneta the Sioux, a Story of Indian Life; Field Work. *Clke. Do. Put.*

Mordecai, Alfred. *N. C.*, 1804–1887. A soldier and military engineer, secretary of the Pennsylvania Canal Company from 1867. Digest of Military Laws; Ordnance Manual; Reports of Gunpowder Experiments; Artillery for United States Land Service.

More, Paul Elmer. *Mo.*, 1864——. An instructor in Sanskrit and Greek at Bryn Mawr College. The Great Refusal: Being Letters of a Dreamer in Gotham. *Hou.*

Morfit, Campbell. *Md.*, 1820–1897. A chemist who lived in London from 1861. Practical Treatise on the Making of Soaps; Pure Fertilizers and Phosphates; Arts of Tanning and Currying; Use and Manufacture of Perfumery, are among his works.

Morford, Henry. *N. J.*, 1823–1881. A journalist of New York city who wrote a number of novels, dramas, and poems of ephemeral merit. The Bells of Shandon is his best-known play, and among his novels are, Shoulder Straps; Days of Shoddy; Only a Commoner. Other works are, Rhymes of Twenty Years; Rhymes of an Editor; Sprees and Splashes.

Morgan, Abel. *W.*, 1673–1722. A Welsh Baptist minister who came to Philadelphia from Wales in 1712. He was the author of Cyd Gordiad, a Scripture concordance published in 1730, the second Welsh book printed in America.

Morgan, Henry. *Ct.*, 1823–1884. A once prominent Methodist minister and lecturer of Boston. Ned Nevins, the Newsboy; The Fallen Priest; Sketches and Sermons; The Shadowy Hand, or Life Struggles; Boston Inside Out.

Morgan, [James] Appleton. *Me.*, 1849——. A lawyer of New York city. Laws of Literature; The Shakespearean Myth; A History of the Shakespeare Text; Some Shakespearean Commentators; Shakespeare in Fact and Criticism; Venus and Adonis: a Study in Warwickshire Dialect; English Version of Legal Maxims. *Clke.*

Morgan, Lewis Henry. 1819–1881. A lawyer of Rochester, New York, widely known as an ethnologist. League of the Iroquois; Systems of Consanguinity and Affinity of the Human Family; The American Beaver and his Works; Ancient Society; Horses and Horse Life of the American Aborigines. *See Allibone's Dictionary, Supplement. Ho.*

Morgan, Morris Hicky. *R. I.*, 1859——. A professor of Greek and Latin at Harvard University. De ignis eliciendi modis apud antiquos; Dictionary to Xenophon's Anabasis; The Art of Horsemanship by Xenophon, a translation with Essays and Notes. *Gi.*

Moriarty, James Joseph. *I.*, 1843–1887. A Roman Catholic clergyman of New York state. Wayside Pencillings; Stumbling Blocks made Stepping Stones on the Way to the Catholic Faith; All for Love; The Keys of the Kingdom.

Moriarty, Patrick Eugene. *I.*, 1804–1875. An Augustinian priest of Philadelphia, father superior of his order in the United States. Life of St. Augustine.

Morrell, Benjamin. *Ms.*, 1795–1839. A navigator who published a noted Narrative of Four Voyages to the South Seas.

Morrill, Justin Smith. *Vt.*, 1810——. A distinguished Vermont statesman, a member of Congress from 1855, and a senator from 1867. Self-Consciousness of Noted Persons.

Morris, Caspar. *Pa.*, 1805–1884. A noted Philadelphia physician. Life of William Wilberforce; Lectures on Scarlet Fever; Hospital Construction; Heart Voices and Home Songs.

Morris, Charles. *Pa.*, 1833——. A Philadelphia author and compiler. Manual of Classical Literature; The Aryan Race; The Stolen Letter; The Detective's Crime; Broken Fetters, an historical review of the drinking habit. *Lip. Sc.*

Morris, Charles D'Urban. *E.*, 1827–1886. An educator who was professor of Latin and Greek in Johns Hopkins University from 1876. A Compendious Grammar of Attic Greek; Compendious Grammar of the Latin Language; Principia Latina.

Morris, Edmund. *N. J.*, 1804–1874. A journalist and agricultural writer of Burlington, New Jersey. Ten Acres Enough; How to Get a Farm and Where to Find One; Farming for Boys.

Morris, Edward Joy. *Pa.*, 1817–1881. A diplomatist who was minister to Turkey, 1861–70. He published A Tour Through Turkey; The Turkish Empire; Afraja, or Life and Love in Norway; Corsica, Social and Political, all but the first-named being translations from the German.

Morris, Edwin Dafydd. *N. Y.*, 1825——. A Presbyterian minister and educator, professor of theology in Lane Seminary from 1874. Outlines of Christian Doctrine; Ecclesiology; Salvation After Death; A Defence of Lane Seminary.

Morris, Mrs. Eugenia Laura [Tuttle]. "Alyn Yates Keith." *Ct.*, 1833——. A writer of New Haven. A Spinster's Leaflets; A Hilltop Summer; Aunt Billy. *Le.*

Morris, George Pope. *Pa.*, 1802–1864. A journalist of New York city, long famous as a song-writer, and now chiefly remembered for such poems as My Mother's Bible; Woodman, Spare that Tree. He was for many years editor of The Home Journal, and one of the prominent literary figures of the metropolis. Briarcliff, a drama; The Little Frenchman; Poems.

Morris, George Sylvester. *Vt.*, 1840–1889. An educator and philosophical writer, who was professor at the University of Michigan from 1870. British Thought and Thinkers; Kant's Critique of Pure Reason, a Critical Exposition; Philosophy and Christianity; Hegel's Philosophy of the State and of History. *Sc.*

Morris, Gouverneur. *N. Y.*, 1752–1816. A New York statesman of distinction, prominent in the formative period of the republic. Observations on the American Revolution. *See Sparks's Memoirs of, with Selections from his Papers and Correspondence; Diary and Letters, edited by Annie Cary Morris; Life by T. Roosevelt, infra, 1888.*

Morris, Harrison Smith. *Pa.*, 1856——. A littérateur of Philadelphia. A Duet in Lyrics (verse, with J. A. Henry); Madonna, and Other Poems. He has edited Tales from Ten Poets; In the Yule Log Glow; Where Meadows Meet the Sea, and an edition of Lamb's Tales from Shakespeare with a continuation and completion. *Lip.*

Morris, Herbert William. *W.*, 1818——. A Presbyterian clergyman, since 1877 retired from the ministry and devoted to literary pursuits. Science and the Bible; Present Conflict of Science with Religion; The Testimony of the Ages; The Celestial Symbol Interpreted; Natural Law and Gospel-Teachings.

Morris, James Cheston. *Pa.*, 1831——. Son of Caspar Morris, *supra.* A Philadelphia physician. The Milk Supply of Large Cities; The Water Supply of Philadelphia; Annals of Hygiene.

Morris, John Gottlieb. *Pa.*, 1803–1895. A noted Lutheran divine of Baltimore, founder of The Lutheran Observer, and long professor of natural history in the University of Maryland. Catechumen's and Communicant's Companion; Popular Exposition of the Gospels; Life of John Arndt; Life of Catherine de Bora; The Blind Girl of Wittenberg; Fifty Years in the Lutheran Ministry; The Diet of Augsburg; Journeys of Luther; Luther at Wartburg and Coburg; Lutheran Doctrine of the Lord's Supper, comprise his chief works.

Morris, Phineas Pemberton. *Pa.*, 1817–1888. A lawyer of Philadelphia, professor of law in the University of Pennsylvania from 1862. The Law of Replevin; Mining Rights in Pennsylvania.

Morris, Ramsay. *N. Y.*, 1858——. An actor and playwright of New York city. He dramatized his own novel, Crucify Him, with the title, The Tigress.

Morris, Robert. *Ms.*, 1818–1888. A writer of Lagrange, Kentucky. History of the Morgan Affair; Lights and Shadows of Freemasonry; Code of Masonic Law; History of Freemasonry in Kentucky; Freemasonry in the Holy Land; The Poetry of Freemasonry.

Morris, Thomas Asbury. *W. Va.*, 1794–1874. A Methodist bishop in Ohio. Church Polity; Essays, etc.; Sketches of Western Methodism. *Meth.*

Morris, William Hopkins. *N. Y.*, 1820——. Son of G. P. Morris, *supra.* A brigadier-general of United States volunteers in the Civil War, brevetted major-general. Field Tactics for Infantry; Infantry Tactics.

Morrison, Charles Robert. *N. H.*, 1819——. A jurist of Concord, New Hampshire. Digest of New Hampshire Reports; Probate Directory; Justice and Sheriff and Attorney's Assistant; Town Officer; Digest of Common-School Laws; Proofs of Christ's Resurrection from a Lawyer's Standpoint.

Morrison, Leonard Allison. *N. H.*, 1843——. A New Hampshire antiquarian. History of the Morison or Morrison Family; History of Wyndham in New Hampshire; Rambles in Europe, with Historical Facts Relating to Scotch-American Families.

Morse, Abner. *Ms.*, 1793–1865. A Congregational clergyman and genealogist of Sharon, Massachusetts. Memorial of the Morses; Genealogy of

Early Planters in Massachusetts; Descendants of Several Ancient Puritans, are his more important publications.

Morse, Mrs. Charlotte Dunning [Wood]. "Charlotte Dunning." *N. Y.*, 1858——. A novelist. Upon a Cast, a society novel; A Step Aside; Cabin and Gondola. *Har. Hou.*

Morse, Edward Sylvester. *Me.*, 1838——. An eminent biologist of Salem, Massachusetts, who has published First Book on Zoölogy; Japanese Homes, and many scientific papers. *Har.*

Morse, James Herbert. *Ms.*, 1841——. An educator and verse-writer of New York city. Summer Haven Songs.

Morse, Jedidiah. *Ct.*, 1761–1826. A Congregational clergyman of New England, very active as a controversialist and eminent as a geographer. He is sometimes styled the "Father of American Geography," his being the first school text-books in America of any importance. Elements of Geography; American Gazetteer; Annals of the American Revolution; Compendious History of New England; Geography Made Easy; American Geography. *See Life by W. Sprague, infra.*

Morse, John Torrey. *Ms.*, 1840——. Nephew of the wife of O. W. Holmes, *supra*. A lawyer of Boston. Lives of Hamilton, J. Q. Adams, Jefferson, John Adams, Oliver Wendell Holmes, Lincoln, Franklin; Banks and Banking; Arbitration and Award; Famous Trials. *Hou. Lit.*

Morse, Mrs. Lucy [Gibbons]. *N. Y.*, 1839——. A novelist of New York city. Rachel Stanwood, a Story; The Chezzles, a Story of Young People. *Hou.*

Morse, Samuel Finley Breese. *Ms.*, 1791–1872. Son of J. Morse, *supra*. The inventor of the electro-magnetic telegraph. Foreign Conspiracies against the Liberties of the United States; Our Liberties Defended; Imminent Dangers through Foreign Immigration.

Morse, Sidney Edwards. *Ms.*, 1794–1871. Son of J. Morse, *supra*. A journalist and geographer of New York city. System of Modern Geography; Premium Questions on Slavery. With a younger brother he founded The New York Observer in 1823.

Morton, Charles. *E.*, 1620–1698. A Puritan clergyman who came to New England in 1686, and was minister at Charlestown and vice-president of Harvard College. The Ark: its Loss and Recovery; System of Logic, long a text-book at Harvard.

Morton, Henry. *N. Y.*, 1836——. A noted physicist, president of the Stevens Institute of Technology at Hoboken, New Jersey, from 1870. The Student's Practical Chemistry (with A. R. Leeds) and many valuable scientific monographs. *Lip.*

Morton, James St. Clair. *Pa.*, 1829–1864. Son of S. G. Morton, *infra*. A Federal officer killed in the attack upon Petersburg. Instruction in Engineering; New System of Fortifications; Memoir on Fortification; Dangers and Defences of New York City.

Morton, Nathaniel. *H.*, 1613–1685. The secretary of the Plymouth Colony from 1647 till his death, whose New England's Memoriall is well known among colonial annals. *See Tyler's American Literature. C. P. S.*

Morton, Oliver Throck. *Ind.*, 1860——. A lawyer of Chicago. The Southern Empire, with Other Papers. *Hou.*

Morton, Samuel George. *Pa.*, 1799–1851. A once prominent Philadelphia physician and scientist, and president of the Academy of Natural Sciences. Crania Americana; Crania Egyptica; Illustrated System of Human Anatomy.

Morton, Mrs. Sarah Wentworth [Apthorpe]. *Ms.*, 1759–1846. A verse-writer of Quincy, Massachusetts. Ouabi, an Indian Tale in four cantos; My Mind and its Thoughts.

Morton, Thomas. *E.*, c. 1575–1646. A famous adventurer who, settling himself at Mount Wollaston, which he termed Ma-re Mount, scandalized the colonists at Plymouth and Boston by his sports and carousals. The New English Canaan is a sarcastic and humourous description of his pious neighbours and their country. *See Motley's Morton's Hope and Merry Mount; Hawthorne's Merry Mount; Mrs. Jane Aus-*

tin's Betty Alden, chapters 8 and 9; Dictionary of National Biography, vol. 39.

Morton, Thomas George. *Pa.*, 1835–——. Son of S. G. Morton, *supra*. A Philadelphia physician. Surgery in the Pennsylvania Hospital: an Epitome of Practice from 1756; Transfusion of Blood and its Practical Application.

Mosby, John Singleton. *Va.*, 1833–——. A famous Confederate cavalry leader, consul at Hong Kong, 1878–85, and subsequently a lawyer in San Francisco. War Reminiscences. *See Scott's Partisan Life with Mosby; Crawford's Mosby and his Men. Do.*

Motley, John Lothrop. *Ms.*, 1814–1877. A distinguished historian, born in Dorchester, Massachusetts, who was minister to Austria, 1861–67, and to England, 1869–70. His writings are remarkable for colour and dramatic vigour, while his estimates are tinged more or less with personal feeling. But though not a dispassionate historian, he is nevertheless quite removed from a spirit of blind partisanship. His work evinces immense research, but the main lines of the narrative are always clear. Morton's Hope, a romance; Merry Mount, a romance; The Rise of the Dutch Republic; The History of the United Netherlands; Life and Death of John of Barneveld. *See Correspondence of, edited by G. W. Curtis, supra; Life, by O. W. Holmes; Allibone's Dictionary, Supplement. Har.*

Mott, George Scudder. *N. Y.*, 1829–——. A Presbyterian minister of Flemington, New Jersey. The Prodigal Son; The Resurrection of the Dead; The Perfect Law. *Ran.*

Mott, Henry Augustus. *S. I.*, 1852–1896. Grandson of V. Mott, *infra*. A chemist of New York city. The Chemist's Manual; Was Man Created?; The Air We Breathe; Fallacy of the Present Theory of Sound. *Wil.*

Mott, Valentine. *L. I.*, 1785–1865. A celebrated surgeon of New York city. Travels in Europe and the East; Mott's Cliniques; a translation of Velpeau's Operative Surgery, and surgical papers. *See Lives by S. D. Gross and S. W. Francis; Appletons' American Biography.*

Moulton, Mrs. Ellen Louise [Chandler]. *Ct.*, 1835——. A prominent poet and prose-writer of Boston. Her verse is characterized by a great degree of feeling, and her sonnets display a remarkable mastery of technique. Her volumes of verse include, Poems; Swallow Flights; In the Garden of Dreams; In Childhood's Country. Her prose comprises, This, That, and the Other; Juno Clifford; My Third Book; three collections of Bed-Time Stories; Some Women's Hearts; Random Rambles, a volume of travel sketches; Ourselves and Our Neighbors; Miss Eyre from Boston; Firelight Stories; Stories Told at Twilight; Lazy Tours in Spain; Life of Arthur O'Shaughnessy. *Cop. Har. Rob. St.*

Moulton, Joseph White. *Ct.*, 1789–1875. An antiquarian writer of Roslyn, Long Island. History of the State of New York (with J. Yates); Chancery Practice of New York.

Moulton, Richard Green. *E.*, 1849–——. An educator of note, professor in the University of Chicago. Ancient Classical Drama; The University Extension Movement; Shakespeare as a Dramatic Artist. *Mac. Rev.*

Moultrie, William. *S. C.*, 1731–1805. A soldier of distinction in the American army during the Revolution, made major-general in 1782. He was governor of South Carolina, 1785–87 and 1794–1796. Memoirs of the Revolution (1802).

Mountford, William. *E.*, 1816–1885. A Unitarian clergyman of Boston who became a spiritualist in his later years. Martyria; Euthanasy, or Happy Talk Toward the End of Life; Christianity the Deliverance of the Soul; Minutes Past and Present; Thorpe, a Quiet English Town. *Hou.*

Moustache, Vieux. *See Gordon, C.*

Mowatt, Mrs. *See Ritchie, Mrs.*

Mowry, Sylvester. *R. I.*, 1830–1871. An army officer who resigned in 1858. Arizona and Sonora: the Geography, History, and Resources of the Silver Regions of North America.

Mowry, William Augustus. *Ms.*, 1829–——. An educator of Boston. Talks with My Boys; Studies in Civil Government; Elements of Civil Government; School History of the United States (with A. M. Mowry). *Rob. Sil.*

Mudge, Enoch. *Ms.*, 1776–1850. A once noted Methodist itinerant preacher of New England. Notes on the Parables; Lynn, a Poem; The Juvenile Expositor; Lectures to Seamen.

Mudge, Zachariah Atwell. *Me.*, 1813–1888. Nephew of E. Mudge, *supra*. A Methodist clergyman of Massachusetts. Among his miscellaneous writings are, The Christian Statesman; Views from Plymouth Rock; Witch Hill, a History of Salem Witchcraft; Life of Abraham Lincoln; Footprints of Roger Williams; Arctic Heroes; Fur-clad Adventurers; History of Suffolk County, Massachusetts; The Luck of Alden Farm. *Lo. Meth.*

Muhlenberg, Gotthilf Henry Ernst. *Pa.*, 1753–1815. A Lutheran divine of Philadelphia, famous as a botanist in his day. Catalogus Plantarum Americæ Septentrionalis; Descriptio uberior Graminum et Plantarum Calamiarum Americæ Septentrionalis; English and German Lexicon and Grammar. *See G. H. E. Muhlenberg als Botaniker, by Maisch, 1886.*

Muhlenberg, William Augustus. *Pa.*, 1796–1877. A distinguished Episcopal clergyman, rector of the Church of the Holy Communion, in New York city, 1846–77. He was the founder of St. Luke's Hospital, and organized the first Protestant Sisterhood in America. His hymn, "I would not live alway," is widely known. Church Poetry; Music of the Church; People's Psalter; Evangelical Catholic Papers; Christ and the Bible; Family Prayers; Letters on Protestant Sisterhoods; St. Johnland; Ideal and Actual. *See Lives by Anne Ayres, supra, W. W. Newton, infra; Atlantic Monthly, October, 1880. Ran. Wh.*

Muir, James. *S.*, 1757–1820. A Presbyterian clergyman of Alexandria, Virginia. An Examination of the Principles in the "Age of Reason" in Ten Discourses; Sermons.

Muir, John. *S.*, 1838——. A noted California scientist and explorer, discoverer of the Muir Glacier in Alaska. The Mountains of California. *Cent.*

Mulford, Elisha. *Pa.*, 1833–1885. An Episcopal clergyman of Cambridge, lecturer in the Episcopal Theological School there, and prominent among Broad Church thinkers. The Nation; The Foundations of Civil Order and Political Life in the United States; The Republic of God. *Hou.*

Mulford, Prentice. *L. I.*, 1834–1891. A journalist of New York city and San Francisco. The Swamp Angel; Life by Land and Sea; Your Forces and How to Use Them.

Mullany, Patrick Francis. "Brother Azarias." *I.*, 1847–1893. A Roman Catholic educator of the order of Brothers of the Christian Schools; president of Rock Hill College, 1878–89, and subsequently a resident of New York city. The Development of English Literature: Old English Period; Philosophy of Literature; Psychological Aspects of Education; Address on Thinking; Aristotle and the Christian Church; Culture of the Spiritual Sense; Phases of Thought and Criticism. *Ap. Hou.*

Müller, Nikolaus. *G.*, 1809–1873. A German poet who emigrated to New York city in 1853 and established himself there as a printer. Zehn gepanzerte Sonette; Neuere Gedichte; Frische Blätter auf die Wunden deutscher Krieger.

Munday, John William. "Charles Sumner Seeley." *Ind.*, 1844——. A lawyer of Chicago. The Spanish Galleon; The Lost Canyon of the Toltecs, both tales of adventure for boys. *Mg.*

Munde, Paul Fortunatus. *Sxy.*, 1846——. A prominent New York physician. Obstetric Palpation; Minor Surgical Gynæcology; Management of Pregnancy.

Munford, William. *Va.*, 1775–1825. A lawyer of Richmond, Virginia, who, beside several volumes of Law Reports, published a volume of Poems (1798) and a scholarly blank-verse translation of the Iliad. *See Griswold's Poets and Poetry of America.*

Munger, Theodore Thornton. *N. Y.*, 1830——. A Congregational clergyman of New Haven, prominent among liberal thinkers of that faith. On the Threshold; The Freedom of Faith; Lamps and Paths; The Appeal to Life. *See Atlantic Monthly, July, 1883. Hou.*

Munkittrick, Richard Kendall. *E.*, 1853——. A humourous writer of

New York city, on the editorial staff of Puck. The Moon Prince, a juvenile; Farming; The Acrobatic Muse, a collection of humourous verse. *Har. Wy.*

Munroe, [Charles] Kirk. *Wis.*, 1850——. A popular writer, now resident in Florida, whose writings are mainly for juvenile readers. Wakulla; Life of Mrs. Stowe (with her son); The Flamingo Feather; Derrick Sterling; Chrystal Jack and Co.; The Golden Days of '49; Dorymates; Under Orders; Prince Dusty; Campmates; Canoemates; Cab and Caboose; Raftmates; The Coral Ship; The White Conquerors; The Fur Seal's Tooth; Big Cypress; Snow-Shoes and Sledges; Totem of the Bear; Rick Dale; A Young War Chief; At War with Pontiac. *Do. Har. Put. Scr.*

Munsell, Franklin. *N.Y.*, 1857——. Son of J. Munsell, *infra.* A publisher of Albany. Chips for the Chimney Corner; The Bibliography of Albany.

Munsell, Joel. *Ms.*, 1808–1880. A printer and publisher of Albany. Outlines of the History of Printing; Every-Day Book of History and Chronology; Chronology of Paper and Paper-Making.

Munsey, Frank Andrew. *Me.*, 1854——. A prominent magazine publisher of New York city. Afloat in a Great City; The Boy Broker; Deringforth.

Munson, James Eugene. *N. Y.*, 1835——. A phonographer of New York city. The Complete Phonographer; Dictionary of Practical Phonography; Phrase Book of Practical Phonography. *Har.*

Murat, Napoléon Achille. *F.*, 1801–1847. The son of Joachim Murat, King of Naples. In his youth he bore the title of Prince of the Two Sicilies. He came to the United States in 1821, was naturalized and settled at Tallahassee, Florida. He was mayor of that place in 1824, and postmaster, 1826–28. Lettres d'un citoyen des États Unis à ses amis d'Europe; Esquisses morales et politiques sur les États Unis d'Amérique; Exposition des principes du gouvernement republicain tel qu'il à été perfectionné en Amérique, which went through more than fifty editions.

Murdoch, James Edward. *Pa.*, 1811–1893. A noted actor and lecturer. Orthophony (with W. Russell); The Stage; Plea for Spoken Language; Analytic Elocution. *Clke. Lip.*

Murdock, Harold. *Ms.*, 1862——. A bank cashier of Boston. The Reconstruction of Europe, a Sketch of the Diplomatic and Military History of Continental Europe from the Rise to the Fall of the Second French Empire. *Hou.*

Murdock, James. *Ct.*, 1776–1856. A Congregational clergyman and educator of New Haven. He was the author of Sketches of Modern Philosophy, and translator of Mosheim's Ecclesiastical History, and other works, as well as of a Literal Translation of the New Testament from the Ancient Syriac.

Murfree, Fanny Noailles Dickinson. *Tn.*, 185——. Sister of M. N. Murfree, *infra.* Felicia, a Novel. *Hou.*

Murfree, Mary Noailles. "Charles Egbert Craddock." *Tn.*, 1850——. A novelist of Tennessee whose stories are all concerned with the life of the mountaineers in North Carolina and Tennessee. They display close, sympathetic observation and strong, vivid characterization. In the Tennessee Mountains; Where the Battle was Fought; The Prophet of the Great Smoky Mountains; Down the Ravine; His Vanished Star; In the Clouds; The Story of Keedon Bluffs; The Despot of Broomsedge Cove; In the "Stranger People's" Country; The Phantoms of the Footbridge; The Mystery of Witch-Face Mountain, and Other Stories; The Juggler. *See Allibone's Dictionary, Supplement.* *Har. Hou.*

Murphy, Lady Blanche Elizabeth Mary Annunciata [Noel]. *E.*, 1846–1881. The eldest daughter of the Earl of Gainsborough. She married her father's organist, came to America, and wrote stories and sketches for the magazines. On the Rhine, and Other Sketches.

Murphy, Henry Cruse. *L. I.*, 1810–1882. A lawyer and journalist of Brooklyn. The Voyage of Verrazano; Henry Hudson in Holland; Anthology of the New Netherlands.

Murphy, Thomas. *I.*, 1823——. A Presbyterian clergyman of Philadelphia. Pastoral Theology; Pastor and People; Duties of Church Members.

Murray, David. *N. Y.*, 1830——. An educator of New York city, foreign adviser to the Japanese government on education. Manual of Land Surveying; Outline History of Japanese Education; The Story of Japan.

Murray, James Ormsbee. 1827-——. An educator, professor of English literature in Princeton College, and dean of the college from 1886. Life of Francis Wayland, *infra.*

Murray, John O'Kane. *I.*, 1847-1885. A physician and author of New York city. Popular History of the Catholic Church in the United States; Catholic Pioneers of America; Lessons in English Literature; The Prose and Poetry of Ireland; Little Lives of the Great Saints; Catholic Heroes and Heroines of America.

Murray, Lindley. *Pa.*, 1745-1826. A famous grammarian whose life after 1784 was passed near York, England. Grammar of the English Language; Power of Religion on the Mind; Compendium of Religious Faith and Practice. *See Memoirs written by Himself, with continuation by E. Frank, 1826; Dictionary of National Biography, vol. 39; Allibone's Dictionary; Bibliography of Maine. Lip.*

Murray, Nicholas. "Kirwan." *I.*, 1802-1861. A Presbyterian clergyman of Elizabeth, New Jersey, famous in his day as a controversialist. Letters by Kirwan to Bishop Hughes; Romanism at Home; Men and Things; The Happy Home; Preachers and Preaching; Parish and Other Pencillings. *See Life by Prime. Har.*

Murray, William Henry Harrison. *Ct.*, 1840——. A noted Congregational minister, pastor of Park Street Church, Boston, 1868-74. Adventures in the Wilderness; Adirondack Tales; Deacons; Music Hall Sermons; The Perfect Horse; Sermons from Park Street Pulpit; How Deacon Tubner Kept New Year's; The Doom of Mamelons; Daylight Land; Words Fitly Spoken. *Le.*

Murray, William Vans. *Md.*, 1762-1803. A Maryland statesman who was minister to the Netherlands from 1793 till his death, and author of a treatise on The Constitution and Laws of the United States.

Musick, John Roy. *Mo.*, 1849——. A novelist and historian of Kirksville, Missouri. The Banker of Bedford; History Stories of Wisconsin; Calamity Row; Brother Against Brother; Mysterious Mr. Howard; and a series of twelve Columbian historical novels, including Columbia; Estevan; St. Augustine; Pocahontas; The Pilgrims; A Century Too Soon, a story of Bacon's Rebellion; The Witch of Salem; Braddock; Independence; Sustained Honor; Humbled Pride; Union. *Fu. Lo.*

Mussey, Reuben Dimond. *N. H.*, 1780-1866. A Boston physician who published Health: its Friends and its Foes.

Muzzey, Artemas Bowers. *Ms.*, 1802-1892. A Unitarian clergyman of Massachusetts who retired from active ministry in 1865. The Blade and the Ear; Prime Movers of the Revolution; The Young Men's Friend; Moral Teacher; Christ in the Will, the Heart, and Life; The Higher Education; Immortality in the Light of Scripture and Science; Truths Consequent upon Belief in God; Education of Old Age, comprise his chief works. *A. U. A. Le. Lo.*

Myer, Albert James. *N. Y.*, 1827-1880. A brigadier-general in the United States army, for some years chief signal officer and author of Manual of Signals for Use in the Field.

Myers, Peter Hamilton. *N. Y.*, 1812-1878. A lawyer and romancer of Brooklyn. The First of the Knickerbockers, a tale; The Young Patroon; The King of the Hurons; The Prisoner of the Border.

Myers, Philip Van Ness. *N. Y.*, 1846——. An educator of Cincinnati, professor of history and political economy in the University of Cincinnati from 1890, and dean of the University from 1895. Life and Nature under the Tropics; Remains of Lost Empires; Outlines of Ancient History; Outlines of Mediæval and Modern History; A History of Greece; The Eastern Nations and Greece; A History of Rome; General History. *Gi. Har.*

Myers, Mrs. Sarah Ann [**Irwin**]. *Del.*, 1800–1876. A writer and artist of Carlisle, Pennsylvania. Among her many contributions to juvenile literature are, Margaret Gordon; Impatient Ellen; The Silk-Weaver of Lyons.

Myrtle, Mollie. *See Hill, Mrs. Agnes.*

N

Nack, James. *N. H.*, 1809–1879. A deaf and dumb verse-writer of New York city. The Legend of the Ark; Earl Rupert; The Immortal, a dramatic romance; The Romance of the King, and Other Poems. *See Duyckinck's American Literature.*

Nadal, Bernhard Harrison. *Md.*, 1812–1870. A Methodist clergyman and educator of Virginia who published New Life Dawning. *Meth.*

Nadal, Ehrman Syme. *W. Va.*, 1843——. Son of B. H. Nadal, *supra.* A journalist who has lived much in London as secretary of legation, 1870–1871, and 1877–1884. Essays at Home and Elsewhere; Impressions of London Social Life; Zweiback, or Notes of a Professional Exile. *Cent. Scr.*

Naphegi, Gabor. *Hy.*, 1824–1884. A native of Buda-Pesth who became a naturalized American citizen in 1868. Ghardia, or Ninety Days in the Desert; The Album of Language; Hungary; Among the Arabs; The Grand Review of the Dead (verse). *Lip.*

Napheys [nā'feez], **George Henry.** *Pa.*, 1842–1876. A prominent physician and medical writer of Philadelphia. The Body and its Ailments; Modern Medical Therapeutics; Modern Surgical Therapeutics; The Transmission of Life; Physical Life of Woman; Prevention and Cure of Disease; Personal Beauty (with D. G. Brinton, *supra*). *My.*

Nasby, Petroleum Vesuvius. *See Locke, D. R.*

Nash, Simeon. *Ms.*, 1804–1879. A jurist of Gallipolis, Ohio. Digest of Ohio Reports; Pleading and Practice under the Civil Code; Morality and the State; Crime and the Family. *Clke.*

Nason, Elias. *Ms.*, 1811–1887. A Congregational minister of North Billerica, Massachusetts, among whose numerous religious biographical and historical writings are, Gazetteer of Massachusetts; Life of John A. Andrew; Lives of Moody and Sankey; Life of Charles Sumner; Life of Henry Wilson, *infra;* History of Middlesex County; Originality; Thou Shalt Not Steal; Fountains of Salvation. *Lo.*

Nason, Mrs. Emma [**Huntington**]. *Me.*, 1845——. A verse-writer of Augusta, Maine. White Sails (verse); The Tower, with Legends and Lyrics. *Hou. Lo.*

Nason, Henry Bradford. *Ms.*, 1831–1895. Cousin of Elias Nason, *supra.* A professor of chemistry in the Troy Polytechnic Institute. Table of Reactions for Qualitative Analysis; Table for Qualitative Analysis in Colors, are among his published works.

Nast, William. *G.*, 1807——. A Methodist minister of Cincinnati, editor of The Christian Apologist for many years. Christological Meditations; Gospel Records; A German Commentary on the New Testament; Das Christenthum und seine Gegensätze.

Nauman, Mary. *See Robinson, Mrs. Mary.*

Navarro, Madame Mary Antoinette [**Anderson**] **de.** *Cal.*, 1859——. A once popular actress who retired from the stage in 1890, was married to M. de Navarro soon after, and has since lived in England. A Few Memories, an autobiography. *See Lives by Farrar, 1884, Winter, 1886.*

Nead, Benjamin Matthias. *Pa.*, 1847——. A lawyer and journalist of Harrisburg. Sketches of Early Chambersburg; Guide to County Officers; Early Government of Pennsylvania; Brief Review of the Financial History of Pennsylania.

Neal, Alice B. Wife of J. C. Neal, *infra.* *See Haven, Mrs.*

Neal, John. *Me.*, 1793–1876. A once famous littérateur of Portland, Maine, who early gained a hearing, and, as poet, novelist, dramatist, and magazinist, was constantly before the public for the rest of his long life, though little of his work can be said to survive, able as some of it is. The more important of his writings include, Keep Cool, a novel; The Battle of Niagara, a poem; Goldau, and Other Poems; Rachel Dyer, a novel; Downeasters, a novel; True Womanhood; Bentham's Morals and Legislation; Great Mysteries and Little Plagues; Wandering Recollections of a Somewhat Busy Life (1870). *See Duyckinck's American Literature; Lowell's Fable for Critics; Allibone's Dictionary; Appletons' American Biography; Bibliography of Maine.*

Neal, Joseph Clay. *N. H.*, 1807–1847. A journalist of Philadelphia who founded The Saturday Gazette, and was a popular humourist in his day. Charcoal Sketches; Peter Ploddy, and Other Oddities. *See Griswold's American Prose Writers; Hart's American Literature.*

Neeley, Thomas B——. 18——. A Methodist clergyman. Young Workers in the Church; The Church Lyceum; Parliamentary Practice; Evolution of Episcopacy and Organic Methodism; The Parliamentarian; The Governing Conference in Methodism. *Meth.*

Neill, Edward Duffield. *Pa.*, 1823–1893. A Reformed Episcopal clergyman of St. Paul, but formerly a Presbyterian clergyman. History of Minnesota; Terra Mariæ, or Threads of Maryland History; The Fairfaxes of England and America; History of the Virginia Company; English Colonization of America in the 17th century; Founders of Virginia; Virginia Vetusta; Virginia Carolorum; Concise History of Minnesota. *Lip.*

Neill, John. *Pa.*, 1819–1880. Brother of E. D. Neill, *supra*. A Philadelphia physician. Neill on the Veins; Compend of Medicine (with F. G. Smith).

Neill, William. *Pa.*, 1778–1860. A Presbyterian minister of Philadelphia, president of Dickinson College, 1824–1829. Lectures on Bible History; Divine Origin of the Christian Religion; Ministry of Fifty Years.

Neilson, Joseph. *N. Y.*, 1813–1888. Memoirs of Rufus Choate, with some Consideration of his Studies, Opinions, and Style. *Hou.*

Nelson, David. *Ind.*, 1793–1844. A Presbyterian minister and educator of Missouri and Illinois. His principal work, Cause and Cure of Infidelity, has been widely read.

Nelson, Harry Leverett. *Ms.*, 1858–1880. A lawyer of Worcester, Massachusetts. Bird Songs About Worcester, a collection of nature studies. *Lit.*

Nelson, Henry Addison. *Ms.*, 1820——. A Presbyterian clergyman, professor at Lane Seminary, 1868–74, and from 1886 editor of The Church at Home and Abroad. Seeing Jesus; Sin and Salvation; Home Whispers. *Ran.*

Nelson, Henry Loomis. *N. Y.*, 1846——. A journalist of New York city, now (1897) editor-in-chief of Harper's Weekly. The Money We Need; Our Unjust Tariff Law; John Rantoul, a novel. *Har. Hou.*

Nesmith, James Ernest. *Ms.*, 1856——. An artist and verse-writer of Lowell, Massachusetts. Monadnoc, and Other Sketches in Verse; Philoctetes, and Other Poems; Life and Addresses of Governor Greenhalge.

Nevin, Alfred. *Pa.*, 1816–1890. A prominent Presbyterian clergyman and religious editor of Philadelphia. His more important writings include, Words of Comfort for Doubting Hearts; The Voice of God; The Man of Faith; Letters to Colonel Ingersoll; Christian's Rest; Guide to the Oracles; Triumph of Truth.

Nevin, Edwin Henry. *Pa.*, 1814——. Brother of A. Nevin, *supra*. A German Reformed clergyman of Philadelphia. The City of God; Humanity and its Responsibilities; Thoughts About Christ; The Minister's Handbook.

Nevin, John Williamson. *Pa.*, 1803–1886. Cousin of A. Nevin, *supra*. An eminent German Reformed clergyman of Lancaster, Pennsylvania, president of Franklin and Marshall College, 1866–76. Prior to his presidency he had been active as a theologian at Mercersburgh, and his works form the basis of what is styled the "Mercersburgh Theology." Among his writings are, History and Genesis of the Heidelberg Catechism; The Mystical Presence; Anti-Christ; The Anxious Bench; Biblical Antiquities. *See Life by T. Appel. 1889.*

Nevin, William Channing. *O.*, 1844——. Nephew of A. Nevin, *su-*

pra. A lawyer of Philadelphia. History of All Religions; Life of Albert Barnes, *supra;* The Blue Ray of Sunlight; A Slight Misunderstanding; A Wild Goose Chase; In the Nick of Time; Joshua Whitcomb's Tribulations; A Summer School Adventure.

Nevin, William Wilberforce. *Pa.*; 1836——. Son of J. W. Nevin, *supra.* A journalist and railway director of Philadelphia who has published Vignettes of Travel.

Nevins, William. *Ct.*, 1797–1835. A Presbyterian minister of Baltimore. Thoughts on Popery; Practical Thoughts; Select Remains, with Memoir.

Nevius, Mrs. Helen S—— [Coan]. *N. Y.*, 1832——. Wife of J. L. Nevius, *infra.* A Catechism of Christian Doctrine (in Chinese); Our Life in China; Life of J. P. Nevius. *Rev.*

Nevius, John Livingston. *N. Y.*, 1829–1893. A Presbyterian missionary in Ningpo. China and The Chinese; San-Poh, or North of the Hills; Methods of Missionary Work; Demon Possession; and a number of works in Chinese. *See Life by his wife. Rev.*

Newberry, John Strong. *Ct.*, 1822–1892. A geologist who was professor of geology in the School of Mines of Columbia College, 1866–92, and State geologist of Ohio from 1869. He published nine volumes of reports relating to the geological survey of Ohio; Paleozoic Fishes of North America, and many scientific papers.

Newcomb, Harvey. *Ms.*, 1803–1863. A Congregational clergyman of Western Pennsylvania and other localities among whose many moral and religious works, mainly juvenile in character, are, Young Lady's Guide; How to be a Man; How to be a Lady; Manners and Customs of North American Indians.

Newcomb, Simon. *N. S.*, 1835——. An astronomer of distinction, superintendent of the Nautical Almanac, issued by the Navy Department, from 1877, and professor of astronomy and mathematics at Johns Hopkins University, 1884–93. Popular Astronomy; School Astronomy; Geometry; Analytic Geometry; Essentials of Trigonometry; Calculus; A Plain Man's Talk on the Labor Question; Principles of Political Economy; The A, B, C, of Finance, include his most important publications. *Har. Ho.*

Newell, Robert Henry. "Orpheus C. Kerr." *N. Y.*, 1836——. A journalist of New York city, at one time popular as a humourist. Versatilities, a collection of humourous and other verses; The Palace Beautiful, and Other Poems; Avery Glibun, an American romance; The Walking Doll, a novel; There Was Once a Man; Studies in Stanzas. *Fo. Le.*

Newell, Samuel. *Me.*, 1784–1821. A noted Baptist missionary in Bombay. The Conversion of the World (1818); Life of Harriet Newell (his first wife) which was widely popular.

Newell, William Wells. *Ms.*, 1839——. A folk-lore scholar of Cambridge, editor of The Journal of American Folk-Lore from 1888. Games and Songs of American Children; Words for Music, a collection of verse. *Har.*

Newhall, Charles Stedman. *Ms.*, 1842——. A clergyman and educator of Asbury Park, New Jersey. The Trees of Northeastern America; The Shrubs of Northeastern America; The Vines of Northeastern America; The Leaf-Collector's Handbook and Herbarium. His writings for young people include Harry's Trip to the Orient; Joe and the Howards; Ruthie's Story. *Put.*

Newman, John Philip. *N. Y.*, 1826——. A Methodist bishop at Omaha, at one time a prominent Washington pastor. From Dan to Beersheba; Thrones and Palaces of Babylon and Nineveh; Christianity Triumphant; America for Americans; The Supremacy of Law. *Fu. Meth.*

Newman, Samuel Phillips. *Ms.*, 1796–1842. An educator who was a classical professor in Bowdoin College. Practical System of Rhetoric, long a popular work; Elements of Political Economy.

Newton, Richard. *E.*, 1812–1887. An Episcopal clergyman of Philadelphia, long prominent among extreme Low Churchmen. The King's Highway; The Great Pilot; Rills from the Fountain of Life; Bible Promises; Natural History of the Bible, are among his writings. *Rev.*

Newton, Richard Heber. *Pa.*, 1840——. Son of R. Newton, *supra.* An Episcopal clergyman of New York city, rector of All-Souls Church, and prominent as a very Broad Church theologian. Among more conservative thinkers his views have excited much opposition and needless alarm. Womanhood; The Morals of Trade; The Right and Wrong Uses of the Bible; The Book of the Beginnings; Philistinism; Social Studies; Church and Creed; The Children's Church. *Put. Ran.*

Newton, Robert Safford. *O.*, 1818–1881. A surgeon of New York city. Eclectic Treatise in the Practice of Medicine; Antiseptic Surgery.

Newton, William. *E.*, *c.* 1820–189–. Brother of R. Newton, *supra.* A Reformed Episcopal clergyman of West Chester, Pennsylvania. The First Two Visions of the Book of Daniel; The Morning Star, and Other Poems; Nature's Testimony to Nature's God.

Newton, William Wilberforce. *Pa.*, 1843——. Son of R. Newton, *supra.* An Episcopal clergyman of Pittsfield, Massachusetts. Essays of To-Day, Religious and Theological; The Legend of St. Telemachus; The Voice of St. John, and Other Poems; Summer Sermons; The Voice Out of Egypt; Ragnar, the Sea King; Paradise; The Priest and the Man, or Abelard and Héloise, an historical novel; Life of W. A. Muhlenberg, *supra;* and several collections of sermons to children, including, The Wicket Gate; The Interpreter's House; Little and Wise; A Father's Blessing. *Hou. Ran. Wh.*

Nichols, Edward Leamington. *E.*, 1854——. A professor of physics at Cornell University from 1887. Laboratory Manual of Physics and Applied Mechanics; The Galvanometer. *Mac.*

Nichols, George Ward. *Me.*, 1831–1885. A writer on art and music who was president of the Cincinnati College of Music. The Story of the Great March; Art Education Applied to Industry; Pottery; Sanctuary, a story of the Civil War. *Har.*

Nichols, Ichabod. *N. H.*, 1784–1859. A Unitarian minister of Portland, Maine, 1814–55, and from the latter date a resident of Cambridge. Natural Theology; Hours with the Evangelists; Remembered Words. *A. U. A.*

Nichols, James Robinson. *Ms.*, 1819–1888. A manufacturing chemist of Boston who founded The Journal of Chemistry (now The Popular Science News) in 1866. What, When, and Where?; Fireside Science; Chemistry of the Farm; The New Agriculture.

Nichols, Mrs. Mary Sargeant [Neal] [Gove]. "Mary Orme." *N. H.*, 1810——. A hydropathic physician. Lectures on Anatomy and Physiology; Experience in Water Cure; A Woman's Work in Water Cure and Sanitary Education. As "Mary Orme" she published the novels, Uncle John; Agnes Norris; The Two Loves, Eros and Anteros.

Nichols, Mrs. Rebecca S—— [Reed]. *Ms.*, 1820——. A verse-writer of Cincinnati. Bernice, and Other Poems; Songs of the Heart.

Nichols, Starr Hoyt. *Ct.*, 1834——. A broker of New York city, in earlier life a Unitarian minister. He has published Monte Rosa, the Epic of an Alp.

Nichols, Thomas L——. *Circa* 1820——. An American physician who settled in Malvern, England, near the opening of the Civil War. Women in All Ages; Esoteric Anthropology; Forty Years of American Life; How to Cook; How to Behave; How to Live on Sixpence a Day; Human Physiology the Basis of Sanitary Reforms.

Nichols, Walter Ripley. *Ms.*, 1847–1886. A professor of chemistry in the Massachusetts Institute of Technology, who published Water Supply from a Chemical and Sanitary Standpoint, and many scientific papers.

Nicholson, Mrs. Eliza [Poitevent]. "Pearl Rivers." *Mi.*, 1849–1896. A journalist of New Orleans, owner and editor of The Picayune, and the first woman in the world to own and manage a great daily paper. Lyrics.

Nicholson, James Bartram. *Mo.*, 1820——. A prominent bookbinder of Philadelphia, author of a Manual of Bookbinding, an exhaustive treatise on the subject. *Bai.*

Nicholson, William Rufus. *Mi.*, 1822——. A Reformed Episcopal bishop, dean of the theological seminary of that faith in Philadelphia. The Blessedness of Heaven; Why I Became a Reformed Episcopalian; The Real Presence; The Call to the Ministry.

Nicolay, John George. *Bv.*, 1832——. The private secretary of President Lincoln, and marshal of the United States Supreme Court, 1872–87. The Outbreak of the Rebellion; Abraham Lincoln, a History (with J. Hay, *supra*). *Cent. Scr.*

Nicum, John. *Wg.*, 1851——. A prominent Lutheran minister of Rochester, New York, who has published History of the New York Ministerium; Gleichuiss - Reden Jesu; Weihnachts Andacht; and a translation of Wolf's Lutherans in America.

Nieriker, Mrs. May [Alcott]. *Ms.*, 1840–1879. Daughter of A. B. Alcott, *supra*. An artist who published Concord Sketches; Studying Art Abroad. *Rob.*

Niles, Hezekiah. *Del.*, 1777–1839. A journalist of Baltimore, founder of Niles's Register. The towns of Niles, Michigan, and Niles, Ohio, were named in his honour. Quill Driving; Principles and Acts of the Revolutionary Period. *Bar.*

Niles, John Milton. *Ct.*, 1787–1856. A journalist of Hartford who was postmaster-general in 1840. Lives of Perry, Laurence, Pike, Harrison; The Civil Officer; History of the Revolution in Mexico and Central America.

Niles, Samuel. *R. I.*, 1674–1762. A Congregational clergyman who was pastor of the church at Braintree, Massachusetts, from 1711 till his death. Tristitiæ Ecclesiarum, a Brief and Sorrowful Account of the Churches in New England; God's Wonder-Working Providence for New England in the Reduction of Louisburg; Vindication of the Doctrine of Original Sin; The True Scripture Doctrine of Original Sin; History of the French and Indian Wars.

Nipher, Francis Eugene. *N. Y.*, 1847——. A professor of physics in Washington University at St. Louis from 1874, who has published Theory of Magnetic Measurement.

Nitsch, Mrs. Helen Alice [Matthews]. "Catherine Owen." *E.*, 18——1889. A writer on domestic science whose home was at Plainfield, New Jersey. Choice Cookery; Culture and Cooking; Ten Dollars Enough; Perfect Bread; Gentle Bread-Winners; Molly Bishop's Family; Progressive Housekeeping. *Har. Hou.*

Noah, Mordecai Manuel. *Pa.*, 1785–1851. A once noted journalist of New York city, who endeavoured unsuccessfully to found a Jewish colony on Grand Island, in the Niagara River. Travels in England, France, and Spain; Gleanings from a Gathered Harvest. He wrote several successful plays, among which are, The Siege of Tripoli; The Fortress of Sorrente.

Noble, Annette Lucile. *N. Y.*, 1844——. A fiction-writer of Albion, New York, among whose works are, Uncle Jack's Executors; Eunice Lathrop, Spinster; Love and Shawl-Straps; After the Failure; The Silent Man's Legacy. *Put.*

Noble, Lucretia Gray. *Ms.*, 18————. A writer of Wilbraham, Massachusetts, whose only novel, A Reverend Idol, was very popular. *Hou.*

Noble, Edmund. *S.*, 18———. A journalist who travelled in Russia, 1882–1884, and since 1884 has lived in Boston. The Russian Revolt (1885). *Hou.*

Noble, Louis Legrand. *N. Y.*, 1813–1882. An Episcopal clergyman who held various rectorships successively in the State of New York. Ne-Ma-Nin, an Indian story in verse; The Course of Empire, a work relating to the artist Cole; The Lady Angeline, and Other Poems; A Voyage to the Arctic Seas.

Nordheimer, Isaac. *G.*, 1809–1842. An educator of New York city, instructor in sacred literature at Union Theological Seminary, 1838–42. Hebrew Grammar; Grammatical Analysis of Select Portions of Scripture.

Nordhoff, Charles. *P.*, 1830——. A littérateur and journalist of New York city. Man-of-War Life; The Merchant Vessel; Whaling and Fishing; Man-of-War Yarns; Cape Cod and All Along Shore; Peninsular California; Northern California; Secession is Rebellion; Communistic Societies of the United States; Politics for Young Americans; God and the Future

Life, include his more important works. *Do. Har.*

Norman, Benjamin Moore. *N. Y.*, 1809–1860. A bookseller of New Orleans. Rambles in Yucatan; New Orleans and its Environs; Rambles by Land and Water.

Norman, Henry. *Ms.*, 1858——. A journalist of prominence. The Peoples and Politics of the Far East; The Real Japan. *Scr.*

Norris, George Washington. *Pa.*, 1808–1875. A Philadelphia physician. Contributions to Practical Surgery; Early History of Medicine in Philadelphia.

Norris, Thaddeus. *Pa.*, 1811–1877. A Philadelphia business man who wrote much on sporting topics. American Angler's Book; American Fish Culture. *Co.*

North, Elisha. *Ct.*, 1771–1843. A physician of New London, Connecticut. Treatise on Spotted Fever; Outlines of the Science of Life; Uncle Toby's Pilgrim's Progress in Phrenology. *See Life and Writings of, 1837.*

Northend, Charles. *Ms.*, 1814–1895. A prominent educator of Connecticut. Teacher and Parent; Teachers' Associations; Annals of American Institutes of Instruction; Life of Elihu Burritt, *supra*.

Northend, William Dummer. *Ms.*, 1823——. Brother of C. Northend, *supra*. A lawyer of Salem, Massachusetts. Speeches and Essays on Political Subjects; The Bay Colony. *Est.*

Northrop, Birdsey Grant. *Ct.*, 1817——. A prominent Connecticut educator, secretary of the State Board of Education, 1869–82. Education Abroad; Rural Improvement; Tree-Planting.

Northrup, Ansel Judd. *N. Y.*, 1833——. A lawyer of Syracuse. Camps and Tramps in the Adirondacks; Grayling Fishing in Northern Michigan; Sconset Cottage Life.

Norton, Andrews. *Ms.*, 1786–1853. A Unitarian clergyman of Cambridge, professor of sacred literature in Harvard University, 1819–30, and prominent among conservative theologians of his faith. Historical Evidences of the Genuineness of the Gospels; Internal Evidences of the Genuineness of the Gospels; Tracts Concerning Christianity; Reasons for not Believing the Doctrines of the Trinitarians. *See Memoir by W. Newell. A. U. A.*

Norton, Augustus Theodore. *Ct.*, 1808–1884. A Presbyterian clergyman of Alton, Illinois, author of a History of the Presbyterian Church in Illinois.

Norton, Charles Eliot. *Ms.*, 1827——. Son of A. Norton, *supra*. A distinguished Dante scholar and a high authority on the history of art, since 1875 professor of the history of art in Harvard University. He has edited the Letters of J. R. Lowell, *supra*; the Writings of G. W. Curtis, *supra*; the Goethe and Carlyle Correspondence; the Letters of Carlyle; and has translated Dante's Vita Nuova and Divina Commedia. His other works include, Historical Studies of Church-Building in the Middle Ages; Notes of Travel and Study in Italy; Considerations of Some Recent Social Theories. *Har. Hou.*

Norton, Charles Ledyard. *Ct.*, 1837——. A journalist of New York city, at one time editor of Outing. Handbook of Florida; Political Americanisms; Jack Benson's Log; A Medal of Honor Man, a book for boys. *Lgs. We.*

Norton, Frank Henry. *Ms.*, 1836——. A journalist of New York city. Lives of General Hancock, Alexander Stephens; Daniel Boone, a romance.

Norton, George Habley. *N. Y.*, 1824–1893. An Episcopal clergyman of Alexandria, Virginia, who published Inquiry into the Nature and Extent of the Holy Catholic Church.

Norton, Herman. *N. Y.*, 1799–1855. A Presbyterian evangelist in New York State. The Christian and Deist in Contrast; Signs of Danger and Promise; Startling Facts for American Protestants.

Norton, John. *E.*, 1606–1663. A Puritan clergyman who came to New England in 1635, and in 1653 succeeded John Cotton as teacher of the church at Boston. He wrote much, and was a strenuous advocate of religious persecution. Among his writings are, The Heart of New England Rent at the Blasphemies of the Present Generation; Life of Mr. John Cotton. *See Sprague's Annals of the American Pulpit; Longfellow's New England Tragedies.*

Norton, John. *Ms.*, 1651–1716. Nephew of J. Norton, *supra*. A Congregational clergyman, pastor of the church at Hingham, 1678–1716, who is remembered for his Elegy on Anne Bradstreet, a poem of some force and merit. *See Tyler's American Literature.*

Norton, John Nicholas. *N. Y.*, 1820–1881. Brother of G. H. Norton, *supra*. An Episcopal clergyman of Louisville, among whose many works are, Lives of Bishops White, Seabury, Bowen, Freeman, Provost, Stewart, Wilson, Claggett, Henshaw; Short Sermons for Families; The King's Ferry-Boat; Lives of Washington, Franklin, Bishop Berkeley, Archbishop Cranmer. *Wh.*

Norton, Mrs. Minerva [Brace]. *N. Y.*, 1837——. An educator of Beloit, Wisconsin. In and Around Berlin; Service in the King's Gardens. *Mg.*

Norton, Sidney Augustus. *O.*, 1835. A scientist who has been professor of chemistry in Ohio University from 1873. Elements of Natural Philosophy; Elements of Physics; Elements of Inorganic Chemistry; Organic Chemistry.

Norton, William Augustus. *N.Y.*, 1810–1883. A professor of civil engineering in Sheffield Scientific School, Yale University, from 1852. Elementary Treatise on Astronomy; First Book of Natural Philosophy and Astronomy.

Nott, Eliphalet. *Ct.*, 1773–1866. A Presbyterian clergyman of note, president of Union College, 1804–66. Counsels to Young Men; Lectures on Temperance. *See Memoir by Van Santvoord, 1876.*

Nott, Josiah Clark. *S. C.*, 1804–1873. A physician of Mobile, who wrote The Physical History of the Jewish Race, and was co-author with Gliddon of the once famous Types of Mankind, and of Indigenous Races of the Earth. *Lip.*

Nourse, James Duncan. *Ky.*, 1817–1854. A journalist of St. Louis. The Forest Knight, a novel; Leavenworth, a story of the Mississippi; God in History.

Nourse, Joseph Everett. *D.C.*, 1819——. Cousin of J. D. Nourse, *supra*. A professor in the Naval Academy, 1850–81. The Maritime Canal of Suez; Astronomical and Meteorological Observations; American Explorations in the Ice Zones. *Lo.*

Noyes, Arthur Ames. *Ms.*, 186——. A professor of chemistry in the Massachusetts Institute of Technology who has published a treatise on Qualitative Chemical Analysis.

Noyes, Charles Henry. "Charles Quiet." *Mch.*, 1849——. A lawyer and verse-writer of Warren, Pennsylvania, who has published Studies in Verse. *Lip.*

Noyes, George Rapall. *Ms.*, 1798–1868. A Unitarian clergyman eminent as a biblical scholar, and professor of Hebrew in Harvard University from 1840. He published translations with notes of the Psalms, Job, Ecclesiastes, Canticles, the Prophets, and Proverbs; and a translation of the New Testament. *A. U. A.*

Noyes, Henry Drury. *N. Y.*, 1832——. An ophthalmologist of New York city. Treatise on Diseases of the Eye; Text-Book on Diseases of the Eye.

Noyes, James. *E.*, 1608–1656. A Puritan clergyman of Newbury, Massachusetts, pastor of the church there, 1635–56. The Temple Measured; Moses and Aaron, or the Rights of Church and State.

Noyes, James Oscar. *N. Y.*, 1829–1872. A physician and journalist of New Orleans. Roumania; The Gypsies: their History, Origin, and Manner of Life.

Noyes, John Humphrey. *Vt.*, 1811–1886. A noted religionist who founded the Oneida Community, and other associations of socialists. The Second Coming of Christ; Salvation from Sin the End of Christian Faith; History of American Socialisms; House Talks. *Lip.*

Nuttall [nŭt'al], **Thomas.** *E.*, 1786–1859. A noted ornithologist and botanist, of English birth, whose life was mainly spent in the United States, but who returned to England in 1842. The Genera of North American Plants; Travels in Arkansas in 1819; The North American Sylva; Manual of the Ornithology of the United States and Canada (1832 and 1834); Geological

Sketch of the Valley of the Mississippi; A Popular Handbook of the Ornithology of Eastern North America, being a new edition of the Manual of Ornithology revised and annotated by Montague Chamberlain. *See Popular Science Monthly, March, 1895. Lit.*

Nye, Bill. *See Nye, Edgar.*

Nye, Edgar Wilson. *Me.*, 1850–1896. A humourous journalist whose writing, though very popular, is ephemeral in its nature and of little or no literary value. Bill Nye and the Boomerang; Forty Liars, and Other Lies; Baled Hay; Bill Nye's Blossom Rock; Remarks; Bill Nye's Thinks; The Cadi, a comedy; Comic History of the United States; A Guest at the Ludlow, and Other Stories; Comic History of England. *Lip.*

Nystrom, John William. 18—1885. An engineer in the United States navy. Treatise on Parabolic Construction of Ships; Technological Education; The Force of Falling Bodies; Treatise on the Elements of Mechanics; New Treatise on Steam Engineering; Pocket Book of Mechanics and Engineering; Principles of Dynamics; Treatise on Screw Propellers. *Bai. Lip.*

O

Oakes, Urian. *E.*, 1631–1681. A Congregational clergyman, pastor of the church in Cambridge, and president of Harvard College, 1675–81. He is chiefly remembered for his Elegy upon the Death of Thomas Shepard, a notable poem in six-lined stanzas, but his sermons, in point of style, are the best which were written in America during the colonial period. *See Tyler's American Literature.*

Oakey, Alexander F. *N. Y.*, 1850——. An architect of Buffalo. Building a Home; Home Grounds; The Art of Life and the Life of Art. *Ap. Har.*

Oakey, Emily Sullivan. *N. Y.*, 1829–1883. An educator of Albany. Dialogues and Conversations; At the Foot of Parnassus, a collection of verse.

Ober, Frederick Albion. *Ms.*, 1849——. A writer of Beverly, Massachusetts, well known as a traveller. Camps in the Caribbees; Young Folks' History of Mexico; The Silver City; Travels in Mexico; Mexican Resources and Guide to Mexico; Montezuma's Gold Mines; The Knockabout Club in the Antilles; The Knockabout Club in the Everglades; In the Wake of Columbus; Josephine, Empress of the French. *Est. Le. Lo. Mer.*

Oberholtzer, Ellis Paxon. *Pa.*, 1868——. Son of Mrs. Oberholtzer, *infra.* A Philadelphia journalist. The Referendum in America, a Discussion of Law-Making by Popular Vote.

Oberholtzer, Mrs. Sara Louisa [Vickers]. *Pa.*, 1841——. A verse-writer of Norristown, Pennsylvania. Violet Lee, and Other Poems; Come for Arbutus; Hope's Heart Bells, a novel; Daisies of Verse; Souvenirs of Occasions. *Lip.*

O'Brien, Fitz James. *I.*, 1828–1862. A brilliant but erratic journalist of New York city. Poems and Stories; The Diamond Lens, and Other Stories. *See Memoir by W. Winter, infra. Scr.*

O'Brien, John. *I.*, 1841–1879. A Roman Catholic clergyman and educator, professor of ecclesiastical history and sacred theology in Mount St. Mary's College, Emmittsburg, Maryland, from 1877. He published, in 1879, A History of the Mass and its Ceremonies in the Eastern and Western Churches, which has since passed through fourteen editions. It is non-controversial in character, and is clear and forcible in its style.

O'Callaghan, Edmund Bailey. *I.*, 1797–1880. An historical writer of Albany, and subseqnently of New York city. History of New Netherlands; Jesuit Relations; Docnmentary History of New York. He edited many volumes of State and colonial records.

O'Connell, Jeremiah Joseph. *I.*, 1821——. A Roman Catholic priest of the Benedictine order in North Carolina. Catholicity in the Carolinas and Georgia; Conferences on the Blessed Trinity.

O'Connor, Joseph. *N. Y.*, 1841——. A journalist of Rochester, New York, whose collected Poems appeared in 1895. *Put.*

O'Connor, William Douglas. *Ms.* 1832–1889. A clerk in the civil service at Washington. Harrington, a novel; The Good Gray Poet, a defence of Walt Whitman; The Ghost; Three Tales; Hamlet's Note-Book. *Hou.*

O'Conor, John Francis Xavier. *N. Y.*, 1852——. A Roman Catholic clergyman of the Society of Jesus, a professor in Boston College. Something Real; Lyric and Dramatic Poetry; Reading and the Mind.

Odenheimer, William Henry. *Pa.*, 1817–1879. The third Protestant Episcopal bishop of New Jersey, 1859–74, becoming bishop of Northern New Jersey in the latter year. Origin of the Prayer-Book; Essay on Canon Law; The Sacred Scriptures the Imperial Record of the Glory of the Holy Trinity; Jerusalem and its Vicinity; The Devout Churchman's Companion; The True Catholic no Romanist; Thoughts on Immersion; Bishop White's Opinions; Sermons, with Memoir. *Dut.*

Odiorne, Thomas. *N. H.*, 1769–1851. An iron manufacturer of Malden, Massachusetts. The Progress of Refinement, a Poem; Fame and Miscellanies.

O'Donnell, Daniel Kane. *Pa.*, 1838–1871. A Philadelphia journalist who published The Song of Iron and the Song of Slaves, with Other Poems.

O'Donnell, Jessie Fremont. *N. Y.*, 1860——. A writer of Lowville, New York. 'Heart Lyrics; Horseback Sketches.

Officier, Morris. *O.*, 1823–1874. A Lutheran missionary. Plea for a Lutheran Mission in Africa; Western Africa a Mission Field; African Bible Pictures.

O'Hara, Theodore. *Ky.*, 1820–1867. An officer in the United States army during the Mexican War, and subsequently in the Confederate army. He is remembered for his poem, The Bivouac of the Dead, stanzas from which have been inscribed on tablets in several of the national cemeteries.

Olin, Mrs. Julia Matilda [Lynch]. *N. Y.*, 1814–1879. Wife of S. Olin, *infra.* Words of the Wise; Four Days in July; Curious and Useful Questions on the Bible; The Perfect Light, comprise her most important writings.

Olin, Stephen. *Vt.*, 1797–1851. A Methodist clergyman and educator, president of Wesleyan University from 1842. Travels in Egypt, Arabia Petræa, and the Holy Land; Greece and the Golden Horn; College Life, its Theory and Practice; Youthful Piety. *See Life and Letters, 1857. Meth. Har.*

Oliver, Benjamin Lynde. *Ms.*, 1788–1843. A lawyer of Boston. Hints on the Pursuit of Happiness; Rights of an American Citizen; Law Summary; Practical Conveyancing; Forms of Practice; Forms of Chancery. *Lit.*

Oliver, Mrs. Grace Atkinson [Little] [Ellis]. *Ms.*, 1844——. A littérateur of Salem, Massachusetts. Lives of Mrs. Barbauld, Maria Edgeworth, Theodore Parker, Dean Stanley. She has edited Tales of Maria Edgeworth; Essays of Mrs. Barbauld; Tales and Poems of Ann and Jane Taylor.

Oliver, Mrs. Martha [Capps]. *Il.*, 1845——. A writer of Jacksonville, Illinois. Her writings in verse for juvenile readers comprise, The Story of Columbus; In Slavery Days; The Far West.

Oliver, Peter. *N. H.*, 1822–1855. Nephew of B. L. Oliver, *supra.* A lawyer of Boston whose Puritan Commonwealth, an historical review of the Puritan government of Massachusetts, presents a not altogether favourable picture of the period under discussion. *Lit.*

Olmsted [ŭm'sted or ŏm'sted], **Alexander Fisher.** *N. C.*, 1822–1853. Son of D. Olmsted, *infra.* A professor of chemistry in the University of North Carolina who published Elements of Chemistry.

Olmsted, Denison. *Ct.*, 1791–1859. A scientist who was professor of natural philosophy at Yale College from 1825. Letters on Astronomy; Compendium of Natural Philosophy; Students' Commonplace Book; Introduction to Natural Philosophy.

Olmsted, Francis Allyn. *N. C.*, 1819–1844. Son of D. Olmsted, *supra.* A physician who published Incidents of a Whaling Voyage.

Olmsted, Frederick Law. *Ct.*, 1822——. A celebrated landscape architect of Boston. He designed the

Central Park of New York city and the park systems of Boston, Buffalo, and many other American cities. Walks and Talks of an American Farmer; A Journey in the Seaboard Slave States; A Journey through Texas; A Journey in the Back Country.

Olney, Jesse. *Ct.*, 1798-1872. A noted educator of Connecticut. The National Preceptor; Geography and Atlas (1828), a standard work for a generation; History of the United States.

Olssen, William Whittingham. *N. Y.*, 1827——. An Episcopal clergyman and educator, professor of mathematics in St. Stephen's College, Annandale, New York, from 1871. Personality, Human and Divine; Revelation, Universal and Special.

Olsson [ōl'sŭn], **Olof.** *Sn.*, 1841——. A Lutheran clergyman, president of Augustana College, Rock Island, Illinois, from 1891. At the Cross; Greetings from Afar, a volume of travel; The Christian Hope.

Onderdonk, Henry. *L. I.*, 1804-1886. Nephew of H. U. Onderdonk, *infra*. An educator of Long Island, principal of Union Hall Academy, 1832-1865. Queens County in Olden Times; Annals of Hempstead, 1643-1832; Long Island and New York in Olden Times.

Onderdonk, Henry Ustick. *N. Y.*, 1789-1858. The second Protestant Episcopal bishop of Pennsylvania. Episcopacy Tested by Scripture, republished as Episcopacy Examined and Re-Examined; Essay on Regeneration; Sermons and Charges; Family Devotions.

O'Neall, John Belton. *S. C.*, 1793-1863. A South Carolina jurist. Digest of the Negro Law; Annals of Newberry District; Bench and Bar of South Carolina.

Opdyke, George. *N. J.*, 1805-1880. A banker of New York city, and mayor of that city, 1862-63. Treatise on Political Economy; Report on the Currency; Official Documents and Addresses.

Optic, Oliver. *See Adams, W. T.*

O'Reilly, Henry. *I.*, 1800-1886. A journalist of Rochester, New York. Sketches of Rochester; American Political Anti-Masonry.

O'Reilly, John Boyle. *I.*, 1844-1890. A noted journalist of Boston, editor of The Pilot. In his youth he was concerned in a Fenian outbreak in Ireland, and banished to Australia. Escaping thence he came to America in 1869 and settled in Boston, where his talents speedily secured recognition. Much of his work in verse is ephemeral, but his best lines have the ring of true poetry. Songs, Legends, and Ballads; Moondyne; The Statues in the Block, and Other Poems; Songs of the Southern Seas; In Bohemia. In prose he published, Stories and Sketches; The Ethics of Boxing. *See Life by J. J. Roche, infra; Dictionary of National Biography, vol. 42.*

O'Reilly, Miles. *See Halpine.*

Orme, Mary. *See Nichols, Mrs.*

Ormond, Alexander Thomas. *Pa.*, 1847——. Stuart professor of mental science and logic at Princeton University from 1883. Basal Concepts in Philosophy. *Scr.*

Orne, Mrs. Caroline [Chaplin]. *Ms.*, 18—1882. Niece of J. Chaplin, 1st, *supra*. A once popular magazinist, who was the author of more than two hundred and fifty stories.

Orne, Caroline Frances. *Ms.*, 1818——. A Cambridge writer of verse, and also of stories for children. Her life has all been passed in Cambridge, her native place. A Day in the Woodlands; Lucy's Party, and Other Tales; Sweet Auburn and Mount Auburn, with Other Poems; Morning Songs of American Freedom.

Orton, Edward. *N. Y.*, 1829——. The State geologist of Ohio from 1883. Economic Geology of Ohio; Petroleum and Inflammable Gas. *Clke.*

Orton, James. *N. Y.*, 1830-1877. A Congregational clergyman, well known as a naturalist, who was professor of natural history at Vassar College, 1869-1877. Comparative Zoölogy; The Andes and the Amazon; Underground Treasures; Liberal Education of Women. *Bai. Har.*

Orton, James Rockwood. *N. Y.*, 1800-1867. A littérateur of New York city. Poetical Sketches; Arnold, and Other Poems; Camp Fires of the Red Men; Confidential Experiences of a Spiritualist. *Mac.*

Osborn, Henry Fairfield. *Ct.*, 1857——. A professor of biology at Columbia College. From the Greeks to Darwin, an outline of the evolution idea. *Mac.*

Osborn, Henry Stafford. *Pa.*, 1823——. A Presbyterian clergyman and educator, professor in Miami University, Ohio, 1871–73. Palestine Past and Present; Fruits and Flowers of the Holy Land; Scientific Metallurgy of Iron and Steel in the United States; Manual of Bible Geography; Ancient Egypt in the Light of Recent Discoveries; Little Pilgrims in the Holy Land; New Descriptive Geography of Palestine; The Prospector's Field Book and Guide; A Practical Manual of Minerals, Mines, and Mining. *Bai. Clke.*

Osborn, John. *Ms.*, 1713–1753. A physician of Middletown, Connecticut, whose Whaling Song was long popular among sailors.

Osborn, Laughton. *N. Y.*, 1809–1878. An artist and littérateur of New York city. Confessions of a Poet; Sixty Years of the Life of Jeremy Levis; The Vision of Rubeta; Arthur Carryl; Handbook of Oil Painting; Travels by Sea and Land, and a number of comedies and tragedies, include the most of his writing.

Osborn, Selleck. *Ct.*, 1783–1826. A journalist, once popular as a poet, who published Poems, Moral, Sentimental, and Satirical.

Osborne, [Samuel] Duffield. *L. I.*, 1858——. A littérateur of New York city. The Spell of Ashtaroth; The Robe of Nessus. *Scr.*

Oscanyan, Hatchik. *Ty.*, 1818——. An Armenian writer of New York city who took the name of Christopher. Acaby, a satirical romance; Veronica, a novel; Bedig, a work for young readers; The Sultan and His People, once a very popular work.

Osgood, Mrs. Frances Sargent [Locke]. *Ms.*, 1811–1850. A verse-writer whose poems were for a time extremely popular. She was the wife of an artist, and lived some years in London. The Casket of Fate; A Wreath of Wild Flowers from New England; The Happy Release, a play written for Sheridan Knowles; Poems. *See Life by Griswold; Allibone's Dictionary.*

Osgood, Samuel. *Ms.*, 1748–1813. A statesman who was a member of the Continental Congress, 1780–84, and naval officer of the port of New York, 1803–13. Letter on Episcopacy; Remarks on Daniel and Revelation; Theology and Metaphysics.

Osgood, Samuel. *Ms.*, 1812–1880. A Unitarian clergyman, pastor of the Church of the Messiah in New York city, 1849–69. In 1870 he entered the Episcopal ministry, but assumed no parochial duties. Studies in Christian Biography; God with Men; Mile-Stones in our Life Journey; The Hearthstone; Student Life; The Gospel Among the Animals; American Leaves; The New Hampshire Book (with C. J. Fox). His published orations upon patriotic events, notable men, and historic themes, are numerous. *Har.*

Osler, William. *Ont.*, 1849——. A physician, professor in Johns Hopkins University from 1889. Clinical Notes on Small-Pox; Histology Notes for Students; Cerebral Palsies of Children; Principles and Practice of Medicine; Diagnosis of Abdominal Tumors. *Ap.*

Osmun, Thomas Embley. "Alfred Ayres." *O.*, 1826——. An author of New York city. The Verbalist; The Orthoepist; an annotated edition of Cobbett's Grammar; The Mentor; Acting and Actors; The Essentials of Elocution. *Ap. Fu.*

Ossoli [ŏs'o-lee], **Sarah Margaret [Fuller], Marchioness d'.** *Ms.*, 1810–1850. A once famous writer of Boston whose personality was more than anything she ever wrote, and who is little more than a name to the present generation. She was a gifted woman, and as a teacher in Boston, editor of The Dial, and literary critic for The New York Tribune, was a prominent figure. In 1845 she went to Italy, and there was married to the Marquis d'Ossoli. Woman in the Nineteenth Century; Art, Literature, and the Drama; At Home and Abroad; A Summer on the Lakes. *See Memoir by Emerson, W. H. Channing, and J. F. Clarke; Lives by Higginson, Mrs. J. W. Howe; Galaxy Magazine, May, 1878; Lowell's Fable for Critics.*

Oswald, Felix Leopold. *Bm.*, 1845——. A naturalist of Tennessee. Physical Education; Summerland Sketches; Zoölogical Sketches; Household Remedies; The Secret of the East, or the Origin of the Christian Religion; Days and Nights in the Tropics; The Bible of Nature; The Poison Problem. *Ap. Lip. Lo.*

Otis, Mrs. Eliza [Henderson]. *Ms.*, 1796–1873. Wife of H. G. Otis, *infra.* A once prominent philanthropist and social leader in Boston who wrote The Barclays of Boston, a novel.

Otis, Elwell Stephen. *Md.*, 1838——. A United States army officer. The Indian Question.

Otis, Fessenden Nott. *N. Y.*, 1825——. A physician of New York city. Lessons in Drawing; Tropical Journeyings; History of the Panama Railroad; Stricture of the Male Urethra; Clinical Lessons on Syphilis; Physiology of Syphilitic Infection.

Otis, George Alexander. *Ms.*, 1830–1881. A surgeon who was curator of the Army Medical Museum at Washington. Report of Surgical Cases Treated in the United States Army, 1867–71; Amputation at the Hip Joint.

Otis, Harrison Gray. *Ms.*, 1765–1848. Son of J. Otis, *infra.* A prominent citizen of Boston famous for his eloquence. Letters in Defence of the Hartford Convention; Orations and Addresses.

Otis, James. *Ms.*, 1725–1783. A celebrated orator and politician, and one of the most active advocates of American independence. He was an impetuous, vehement speaker, and seldom failed to carry his hearers with him. Rights of the British Colonies Asserted and Approved; Vindication of the British Colonies; Considerations on Behalf of the Colonists; A Vindication of the Rights of the House of Representatives of Massachusetts Bay. *See Life by Tudor.*

Otis, James. *See Kaler.*

Ott, Isaac. *Pa.*, 1847——. A physician who has published Cocaine, Veratria, and Gelseminum; Action of Medicines; Physiology and Pathology of the Nervous System.

Otts, John Martin Philip. *S. C.*, 1838——. A Presbyterian minister of Talladega, Alabama. Nicodemus with Jesus; Light and Life for a Dead World; The Southern Pen and Pulpit; Inter-denominational Literature; The Gospel of Honesty; Laconisms; The Fifth Gospel; Unsettled Questions; At Mother's Knee. *Rev.*

Overman, Frederick. *G.*, *c.* 1810–1852. A mining engineer of Philadelphia. The Manufacture of Iron; The Manufacture of Steel; Political Mineralogy; Moulder's and Founder's Pocket Guide; Mechanics for the Millwright, etc.; Treatise on Metallurgy. *Ap. Bai.*

Owen, Catherine. *See Nitsch, Mrs.*

Owen, David Dale. *S.*, 1807–1860. Brother of R. D. Owen, *infra.* The State geologist of Indiana. Report of a Geological Survey of Kentucky; Geological Survey of Wisconsin; Report of a Geological Reconnoissance.

Owen, John Jason. *N. Y.*, 1803–1869. A Presbyterian clergyman and educator of New York city. Commentary on the Gospels; Acts of the Apostles in Greek, with Lexicon; and text-book editions of Xenophon, Thucydides, and Homer.

Owen, Richard. *S.*, 1810–1890. Brother of R. D. Owen, *infra*, and of D. D. Owen, *supra.* A geologist of New Harmony, Indiana. He succeeded his brother David as State geologist in 1860, and was author of a Key to the Geology of the Globe.

Owen, Robert Dale. *S.*, 1801–1877. A prominent writer of New Harmony, Indiana, the son of Robert Owen, the noted Scottish socialist. He was active in political life, and was an ardent advocate of Spiritualism. Outlines of the System of Education at New Lanark; Moral Physiology; Popular Traits; Pocahontas, a drama; Hints on Public Architecture; The Wrong of Slavery and the Right of Freedom; Footfalls on the Boundary of Another World; Beyond the Breakers, a novel; Threading my Way; Debatable Land between this World and the Next. *See Woollen's Biographical Sketches of Early Indiana; Dictionary of National Biography, vol. 42. Lip.*

P

Packard, Alpheus Spring. *Me.*, 1839——. A naturalist of eminence, professor of geology and zoölogy in Brown University from 1878. Zoölogy; Life Histories of Animals, or Comparative Embryology; Guide to the Study of Insects; Half-Hours with Insects; Our Common Insects; Entomology for Beginners; A Naturalist on the Labrador Coast; Observations on the Glacial Phenomena of Labrador and Maine. *Est. Ho.*

Packard, Frederick Adolphus. *Ms.*, 1794–1867. A Philadelphia writer, editor for nearly forty years of the publications of the American Sunday School Union. The Teacher Taught; Life of Robert Owen; Visit to European Hospitals; The Teacher Teaching; Union Bible Dictionary, include his most important writings.

Packard, John Hooker. *Pa.*, 1832——. Son of F. A. Packard, *supra.* A surgeon of Philadelphia, surgeon to the Pennsylvania Hospital from 1884. Manual of Minor Surgery; Lectures on Inflammation; Handbook of Operative Surgery; Sea Air and Sea Bathing. *Lip.*

Packard, Lewis Richard. *Pa.*, 1836–1884. Son of F. A. Packard, *supra.* An educator who was professor of Greek at Yale University from 1866, and author of Studies in Greek Thought.

Packard, Silas Sadler. *Ms.*, 1826——. An educator who founded a business college in New York city. Bryant and Stratton's Bookkeeping Series; Complete Course of Business Training; Commercial Arithmetic; New Manual of Bookkeeping.

Paddock, Benjamin Henry. *Ct.*, 1828–1891. The fifth Protestant Episcopal bishop of Massachusetts, 1873–1891. Ten Years in the Episcopate; The First Century of the Diocese of Massachusetts; The Pastoral Relation; The Foundation of Religious Belief. *Ap.*

Paddock, Mrs. Cornelia. 18———. In the Toils; The Fate of Madame la Tour, a Tale of Great Salt Lake. *Fo.*

Page, Charles Edward. *Me.*, 1840——. A physician of Boston. How to Treat the Baby; Natural Cure of Consumption; Horses: their Feed and Feet; Pneumonia and Typhoid Fever.

Page, Charles Grafton. *Ms.*, 1812–1868. An examiner in the Patent Office at Washington from 1840, who published Psychomancy, Spirit Rappings, and Table Tippings Exposed.

Page, David Perkins. *N. H.*, 1810–1845. A once prominent educator of Albany whose Theory and Practice of Teaching was long popular.

Page, Emily Rebecca. *Vt.*, 1834–1862. A verse-writer of Vermont whose work, which enjoyed local fame, is included in the volume, Lily of the Valley.

Page, Richard Channing Moore. *Va.*, 1841——. A physician of New York city, but during the Civil War a Confederate officer. Genealogy of the Page Family of Virginia; Sketch of Page's Battery, Lee's Army; Chart of Physical Diagnosis.

Page, Thomas Jefferson. *Va.*, 1808——. A naval officer in the service of the Southern Confederacy, 1861–62. La Plata, the Argentine Confederation, and Paraguay.

Page, Thomas Nelson. *Va.*, 1853——. A lawyer of Richmond, Virginia, whose studies of Southern life are notable for a singular charm of style. In Old Virginia; Two Little Confederates; On Newfound River; Elsket, and Other Stories; The Old South; Pastime Stories; Essays, Social and Political; Unc' Edinburg, a Plantation Echo; The Burial of the Guns; Polly; Among the Camps; Meh Lady; Marse Chan; Befo' de War (with A. C. Gordon, *supra*). *Har. Scr.*

Paige, Lucius Robinson. *Ms.*, 1802–1896. A Universalist clergyman who retired from the ministry in 1839, and subsequently filled several offices of trust in Cambridge. Commentary on the New Testament; History of Cambridge, 1630–1877, with Genealogical Register; History of Hardwick, Massachusetts. *Hou.*

Paine, Elijah. *Vt.*, 1796–1853. A jurist and legal writer of New York city. Paine's Reports; Practice in Civil Actions and Proceedings in the State of New York (with W. Duer, *supra*).

Paine, Halbert Eleazar. *O.*, 1826–——. A Federal army officer during the Civil War, and subsequently a lawyer in Washington, whose Treatise on the Law of Elections to Public Offices is a much-valued work. *Lit.*

Paine, Harriet Eliza. "E. Chester." *Ms.*, 18———. A Boston educator. Girls and Women, a helpful book for girls. *Hou.*

Paine, Martyn. *Vt.*, 1794–1877. A physician of New York city. Medical and Physiological Commentaries; Institutes of Medicine; The Cholera Asphyxia of New York (1832); Physiology of Digestion; Physiology of the Soul and Instinct as distinguished from Materialism; Review of Theoretical Geology; The Philosophy of Vitality; Defence of the Medical Profession of the United States; A Therapeutical Arrangement of Materia Medica; Organic Life Distinguished from Chemical and Physical Doctrines. *See Gross's Sketches of Contemporaries.*

Paine, Robert. *N. C.*, 1799–1882. A prominent Methodist bishop whose Life and Times of Bishop McKendree was once a popular biography.

Paine, Robert Treat. *Ms.*, 1773-1811. A once noted verse-writer of Boston whose spirited song, Adams and Liberty, has preserved his memory. He gave up his profession of law for literary pursuits, and received large sums for his poems, among which are, The Invention of Letters, and The Ruling Passion. His work was stilted and conventional, with the exception of the song named above. His collected Verse and Prose, edited by Prentiss, appeared in 1812. *See Allibone's Dictionary.*

Paine, Thomas. *E.*, 1737–1809. A celebrated political and deistical writer of English birth who came to America in 1774, and in 1776 issued his famous pamphlet, Common Sense, which was of great service to the American cause. In the American Crisis, pnblished in numbers, 1776–83, he continued his defence of America. His other works include, The Rights of Man, a reply to Burke's "Reflections on the French Revolution"; The Age of Reason, a work inferior to his other writings in matter and style, and fiercely assailed by the religious sentiment of his day. His works have been ably edited by M. D. Conway (1894–95), *supra. See Lives by Chatham, Cobbett, Rickman, G. Chalmers, G. Vale, Sherwin, M. D. Conway; Atlantic Monthly, July, November, and December, 1859; Nineteenth Century, March, 1879; McMaster's History of the People of the United States, Watson's Men and Times of the Revolution; Allibone's Dictionary; Dictionary of National Biography, vol. 43. Put.*

Paine, Timothy Otis. *Me.*, 1824–1895. A Swedenborgian clergyman of Elmwood, Massachusetts. Solomon's Temple and Capitol; Idolatrous High Places. *Hou.*

Palfrey [pawl′fri], **Francis Winthrop.** *Ms.*, 1831–1889. Son of J. G. Palfrey, *infra.* An officer in the Federal army during the Civil War, and from 1872 register of bankruptcy in Boston. Antietam and Fredericksburg; Memoir of William Francis Bartlett. *Hou. Scr.*

Palfrey, John Gorham. *Ms.*, 1796–1881. A Unitarian clergyman in Cambridge, professor of sacred literature in Harvard University, 1831–37, subsequently a member of Congress, and postmaster of Boston, 1861–67. His literary reputation rests upon his History of New England, a painstaking, accurate work, but not especially attractive in style, and marred by want of perspective. Other works by him are, Lectures on the Jewish Scriptures; The Relation between Judaism and Christianity. *Hou. Lit.*

Palfrey, Sarah Hammond. "E. Foxton." *Ms.*, 1823——. Daughter of J. G. Palfrey, *supra.* A novelist and verse-writer of Cambridge. Her work in verse comprises, Prémices; Sir Pavon and St. Pavon; The Chapel; The Blossoming Rod; Agnes Wentworth. In fiction she has published Katharine Morne; Herman, or Young Knighthood. *Le.*

Palmer, Alonzo Benjamin. *N. Y.*, 1815–1887. A physician who was medical professor in the University of Michigan from 1852. Homœopathy, What Is It?; The Treatment of the Science and Practice of Medicine; Epidemic Cholera; Temperance Teachings of Science; Diarrhœa and Dysentery.

Palmer, Mrs. Anna [Campbell]. "Mrs. George Archibald." *N. Y.*, 1854——. A writer of Elmira, New York. The Summerville Prize; Little Brown Seed; Lally Gay; Lally Gay and her Sister; Verses from a Mother's Corner.

Palmer, Benjamin Morgan. *S. C.*, 1818——. A Presbyterian minister of New Orleans. Life and Letters of James Thornwell, *infra*; Sermons; The Family in its Civil and Churchly Aspects; Formation of Character; The Broken Home; Theology of Prayer.

Palmer, Elihu. *Ct.*, 1764–1806. A writer of New York city who was in his early career a Congregational minister, but became a deist and a political agitator. The Principles of Nature; Prospect or View of the Moral World from 1804.

Palmer, Mrs. Frances [Purdy]. *N. Y.*, 1839——. A journalist and lecturer of Providence who has published A Dead Level, and Other Episodes.

Palmer, George Herbert. *Ms.*, 1842——. Alford professor of natural religion, moral philosophy, and civil polity at Harvard University. He has published The New Education, and an English translation of the Odyssey in rhythmic prose. *Hou. Lit.*

Palmer, Mrs. Henrietta [Lee]. *Md.*, 1834——. Wife of J. W. Palmer, *infra*. The Stratford Gallery, or the Shakespeare Sisterhood; Home Life in the Bible; The Heroines of Shakespeare.

Palmer, Horatio Richmond. *N. Y.*, 1834——. Elements of Musical Composition; Theory of Music.

Palmer, John Williamson. *Md.*, 1825–1896. A physician and littérateur of Baltimore and subsequently of New York city. The Queen's Heart: a Comedy; The Beauties and Curiosities of Engraving; After His Kind, a novel; The Golden Dagon, or Up and Down the Irrawaddi; The New and the Old, or California and India.

Palmer, Julius Auboineau. *Ms.*, 1840——. About Mushrooms; Memories of Hawaii; One Voyage and its Consequences; Mushrooms of America; Again in Hawaii. *Le. Lo. Wn.*

Palmer, Lynde. *See Peebles, Mrs.*

Palmer, Mrs. Phœbe Worrell. *N. Y.*, 1807–1874. A Wesleyan evangelist of New York city, whose writing is mainly concerned with the doctrine of perfection. The Way of Holiness; Entire Devotion; Faith and its Effect; Promises of the Father; Four Years in the Old World; Pioneer Experiences. *See Life and Letters of, 1876.*

Palmer, Ray. *R. I.*, 1808–1887. A Congregational clergyman of Albany, widely known as a writer of hymns, the most famous of which is, "My Faith Looks up to Thee." Home, or the Unlost Paradise; Spiritual Improvement; Closet Hours; Hymns and Poems; Hymns of My Holy Hours; Remember Me; Voices of Hope and Gladness. *Bar. Le. Ran.*

Palmer, William Pitt. *Ms.*, 1805–1884. An insurance president of New York city known also as a verse-writer. Light; Echoes of Half a Century, a collection of poems.

Pancoast, Joseph. *N. J.*, 1805–1882. An eminent surgeon of Philadelphia, professor of surgery in Jefferson Medical College, 1838–74. Operative Surgery; Essays and Lectures; System of Anatomy. *See Gross's Sketches of Contemporaries.*

Pancoast, Seth. *Pa.*, 1823–1889. A Philadelphia physician, professor in Pennsylvania Medical College, 1854–62. The Cabala; Consumption; Ladies' Medical Guide; Boyhood's Perils; Bright's Disease.

Pansy. *See Alden, Mrs.*

Parish, Elijah. *Ct.*, 1762–1825. A Congregational minister, pastor at Byfield, Massachusetts, 1787–1825. He was co-author with Jedediah Morse, *supra*, of several geographical works, and wrote a New System of Modern Geography. *See Sermons of, with Memoir, 1826.*

Park, Edwards Amasa. *R. I.*, 1808——. A Congregational clergyman in Andover, Massachusetts, professor in the Theological Seminary there, 1835–1881. Discourses and Treatises on the Atonement; Discourses on Some Theological Doctrines as Related to the Religious Character; Lives of S. Hopkins, *supra*, N. Emmons, *supra*, B. B. Edwards, *supra*, S. H. Taylor, *infra*, W. B. Homer.

Park, Roswell. *Ct.*, 1807–1869. An Episcopal clergyman and educator, president and chancellor of Racine College, 1852–63. Sketch of the History of West Point; Jerusalem, and Other Poems; Pantology, or Systematic Survey of Human Knowledge.

Park, Roswell. *Ct.*, 1852——. A professor of surgery in the University of Buffalo from 1883 who has published Lectures on Surgical Pathology.

Parke, John. *Del.*, 1754–1789. An officer in the American army during the Revolution, who published The Lyric Works of Horace. The translation, in rhymed verse, was dedicated to Washington, and in it the names of American patriots were substituted for those of the Roman worthies.

Parke, John Grubb. *Pa.*, 1827——. A soldier of distinction who was superintendent of the United States Military Academy in 1887, and was retired from active service in 1889. United States Laws Relating to Public Works; Laws Relating to the Construction of Bridges over Navigable Waters.

Parker, Edward Griffin. *Ms.*, 1825–1868. A lawyer of New York city. The Golden Age of American Oratory; Reminiscences of Rufus Choate.

Parker, Edwin Pond. *Me.*, 1836——. A Congregational clergyman of Hartford, pastor of the South Church from 1860. Book of Praise; Memorial of H. Bushnell, *supra;* The Ministry of Natural Beauty.

Parker, Mrs. Elizabeth Lowber [Chandler]. "Bessie Chandler." *N. Y.*, 1856——. A writer of Batavia, New York, who has contributed much to magazines. A Woman who Failed and Others. *Rob.*

Parker, Foxhall Alexander. *N. Y.*, 1821–1879. A commodore in the United States navy. Fleet Tactics under Steam; The Naval Howitzer Afloat; The Naval Howitzer Ashore; The Fleets of the World; The Battle of Mobile Bay; Elia, or Spain Fifty Years Ago, a translation from the Spanish.

Parker, Francis Wayland. *N. H.*, 1837——. A prominent educator of Chicago, principal of Cook County Normal School, and formerly supervisor of the Boston schools. Talks on Teaching; The Practical Teacher; Course in Arithmetic; How to Teach Geography. *Ap.*

Parker, Gilbert. *Ont.*, 1861——. A popular Canadian novelist now living in the United States. Pierre and His People: Tales of the Far North; An Adventurer of the North; A Romany of the Snows; A Lover's Diary; When Valmond Came to Pontiac; The Seats of the Mighty; The Pomp of the Lavillettes. *Lam. St.*

Parker, Mrs. Helen Fitch. *N. Y.*, 1827–1874. Wife of H. W. Parker, *infra.* Sunrise and Sunset; Morning Stars of the New World; Rambles After Land Shells; Missions and Martyrs of Madagascar; Frank's Search for Sea Shells; Constance of Aylmer, a tale; Blind Florette; Arthur's Aquarium.

Parker, Henry Webster. *N. Y.*, 1824——. Son of S. Parker, *infra.* A Presbyterian clergyman and educator, professor of mental science in Iowa College from 1879. The Story of a Soul, a poem; Verse.

Parker, James Cutter Dunn. *Ms.*, 1828——. Nephew of R. G. Parker, *infra.* A Boston musician. Manual of Harmony; Theoretical and Practical Harmony.

Parker, Joel. *N. H.*, 1795–1875. A jurist of Massachusetts, professor of law at Harvard University, 1847–75. The War Power of Congress; The Right of Secession; The Non-Extension of Slavery; Constitutional Law; Revolution and Construction; The Three Powers of Government; Conflict of Decisions.

Parker, Joel. *Vt.*, 1799–1873. A Presbyterian clergyman of New York city. Lectures on Unitarianism; Invitations to True Happiness; Reasonings of a Pastor; Sermons; Notes on Twelve Psalms, include his principal writings. *Har.*

Parker, Nathan Howe. 18——. Iowa as it is in 1855; Kansas and Nebraska Handbook for 1857–58; The Missouri Handbook (1865); Missouri as it is in 1867, are among his various statistical works.

Parker, Mrs. Permelia Jane [Marsh]. *N. Y.*, 1830——. A writer of Rochester, New York. Toiling and Hoping, a novel; The Boy Missionary; Losing the Way; Under His Banner; The Midnight Cry, a novel of the Millerite delusion; Rochester, a Story Historical; Life of S. F. B. Morse, *supra;* The Morgan Boys; Around the Manger; Andy, the Story of a Troublesome Boy. *Cas. Do.*

Parker, Peter. *Ms.*, 1804–1888. A Congregational missionary and diplomat in China, and after 1857 a resident of Washington. Journal of an Expedition from Singapore to Japan; Statement respecting Hospitals in China.

Parker, Richard Green. *Ms.*, 1798–1869. An educator of Boston. Natural Philosophy; Aids to English Composition.

Parker, Samuel. *Ms.*, 1799–1866. A Congregational clergyman of New York State, said to have been the first who suggested the possibility of a railway through the Rocky Mountains to the Pacific Ocean. He published, Exploring Tour Beyond the Rocky Mountains.

Parker, Theodore. *Ms.*, 1810–1860. A famous Unitarian clergyman of West Roxbury, Massachusetts, whose extremely radical views excited great opposition in his denomination, and resulted in his becoming pastor of an independent congregation in Boston. He was very outspoken in his championship of freedom for the slave, temperance, and the rights of labour, and rapidly came to be a controlling influence in contemporary thought. Since his death his influence has deepened both in America and Europe. He was a prolific writer, but the purely literary value of his work is not great. Miscellaneous Writings; Sermons on Theism, Atheism, and Popular Theology; Occasional Sermons and Speeches; Matters Pertaining to Religion; Additional Sermons and Speeches; Sermons for the Times; Experience as a Minister; West Roxbury Sermons; Prayers; Lessons from the World of Matter and the World of Mind; Historic Americans; Views of Religion. His complete works, as edited by Frances Power Cobbe, fill twelve volumes. *See Lives by John Weiss, 1864, Réville, 1865, O. B. Frothingham, 1874; The Story of Theodore Parker, by Miss Cobbe; Atlantic Monthly, October, 1860; North American Review, April, 1864. A. U. A. Rob.*

Parker, Thomas. *E.*, 1595–1677. A learned Puritan clergyman who was one of the founders of Newbury, Massachusetts, and its first pastor. Parker River, in that region, is named in his honour. Letter on Church Government; Prophecies of Daniel Expounded; Methodus Gratiæ Diviniæ; Theses de Traductione Peccatoris ad Vitam.

Parker, Willard. *N. H.*, 1800–1884. A distinguished surgeon of Philadelphia, professor of surgery in the College of Physicians and Surgeons, 1839–1869. Cystotomy; Spontaneous Fractures; The Concussion of Nerves, are among his professional monographs.

Parker, William Harwar. *N. Y.*, 1826——. Brother of F. Parker, *supra.* An officer in the Confederate navy during the Civil War. Instruction for Naval Light Artillery; Recollections of a Naval Officer. *Scr.*

Parkhurst, Charles Henry. *Ms.*, 1842——. A Presbyterian clergyman of New York city, pastor of the Madison Square Church from 1880, and very prominent as a municipal reformer. Forms of the Latin Verb Illustrated by the Sanskrit; The Blind Man's Creed; The Pattern on the Mount; Three Gates on a Side; What Would the World Be Without Religion?; The Swiss Guide; Our Fight with Tammany. *Ran. Rev. Scr.*

Parkinson, William. *Md.*, 1774–1848. A Baptist clergyman of New York city. Ecclesiastical History; Public Ministry of the Word; Sermons on Deuteronomy xxxii. *See Sprague's Annals of the American Pulpit.*

Parkman, Ebenezer. *Ms.*, 1703–1780. A Congregational pastor in Westborough, Massachusetts, from 1724 till his death. Reformers and Intercessors.

Parkman, Francis. *Ms.*, 1788–1852. Grandson of E. Parkman, *supra.* A Unitarian clergyman of Boston, author of The Offering of Sympathy.

Parkman, Francis. *Ms.*, 1823–1893. Son of F. Parkman, *supra.* The foremost of American historians. He was born in Boston, was a graduate of Harvard in 1844, and in 1846 explored the wilderness beyond the Rocky Mountains, The Oregon Trail resulting from this journey. For many years he was partially blind, but as far as possible continued the historical work which he was meditating, while as a relaxation he devoted much time to horticulture and published a Book of Roses in 1866. The work of his life was the series of historical narratives called France and England in North America, begun in 1864 and completed in 1892. The work includes, in their order, Pioneers of France in the New World; The Jesuits in North America; La Salle and the Discovery of the Great West; The Old Régime in Canada; Count Frontenac and New France under Louis XIV.; A Half Century of Conflict; Montcalm and Wolfe. The Conspiracy of Pontiac forms a sequel to the work, though first issued in 1857. The picturesque charm of his style has been widely acknowledged, while his scholarship has never been questioned. *See Life and Uncollected Papers, by Farnham; Atlantic Monthly, November, 1874, May, 1894; Canadian Magazine, October, 1894; Macmillan's Magazine, April, 1894; Harvard Graduates' Magazine, June, 1895; Vedder's American Writers. Lit.*

Parkman, George. *Ms.*, 1791–1849. Grandson of E. Parkman, *supra*. A Boston physician who published Insanity and the Management of the Insane. *See Trial of Webster for the Murder of Dr. Parkman, 1850.*

Parks, Leighton. *N. Y.*, 185——. An Episcopal clergyman of Boston, rector of Emmanuel Church from 1878. His Star in the East; Winning of the Soul, and Other Sermons. *Dut. Hou.*

Parley, Peter. *See Goodrich, S. G.*

Parloa, Maria. *Ms.*, 1843. A lecturer and writer upon domestic economy, especially upon the science of food preparation. First Principles of Household Management and Cookery; Kitchen Companion; The Young Housekeeper; New Cook Book and Marketing Guide. *Est. Hou.*

Parrish, Edward. *Pa.*, 1822–1872. Son of Joseph Parrish, 1st, *infra*. An educator and pharmacist of Philadelphia, and president of Swarthmore College, 1868–70. Introduction to Practical Pharmacy; The Phantom Bouquet, a Treatise on Skeletonizing Leaves; Essay on Education in the Society of Friends.

Parrish, John. *Md.*, 1729–1807. A Quaker preacher of Pennsylvania noted as an early opponent of slavery, who published Remarks on the Slavery of the Black Race.

Parrish, Joseph. *Pa.*, 1779–1840. Nephew of J. Parrish, *supra*. An eminent Philadelphia physician who was the author of Practical Observations on Strangulated Hernia. *See Memoir by G. B. Wood.*

Parrish, Joseph. *Pa.*, 1811–1891. Son of Joseph Parrish, *supra*. A physician of Burlington, New Jersey, famous as an authority upon the treatment of inebriates. Alcoholic Inebriety from the Medical Standpoint.

Parry, Charles Christopher. *E.*, 1823–1890. A botanist of Davenport, Iowa, among whose writings are, Botanical Observations in Western Wyoming; Botanical Observations in Southern Utah.

Parsons, Mrs. Frances Theodora [Smith] [Dana]. *N. Y.*, 1861——. A writer of Albany whose books were published under the name of Mrs. William Starr Dana. How to Know the Wild Flowers; According to Season; Plants and Their Children. *Am. Scr.*

Parsons, Frank. *N. J.*, 1855——. A lawyer of Boston. The World's Best Books; Our Country's Need, or the Development of a Scientific Industrial System. He has edited several legal works.

Parsons, George Frederic. *E.*, 1840——. A journalist of New York city. Life of J. W. Marshall, Discoverer of Gold in California; Middle Ground, a novel.

Parsons, Jonathan. *Ms.*, 1705–1776. A Presbyterian minister of Newburyport, who adopted the views of Whitefield, and in whose house that famous preacher died. Lectures on Justification; Good News from a Far Country, said to be the first book published in New Hampshire; Sixty Sermons;

Freedom from Ecclesiastical and Civil Slavery the Purchase of Christ. *See Sprague's Annals of the American Pulpit.*

Parsons, Theophilus. *Ms.*, 1750–1813. A jurist of Newburyport and after 1800 of Boston, and chief justice of Massachusetts from 1801. Commentaries on the Law of the United States; The Essex Result, a famous political pamphlet of 1777. *See Memoir by his son.*

Parsons, Theophilus. *Ms.*, 1797–1882. Son of T. Parsons, *supra.* A noted legal writer, Dane professor of Law in Harvard University from 1847, and an eminent Swedenborgian thinker. Treatise on the Law of Contracts; Elements of Mercantile Law; The Laws of Business; Maritime Law; Law of Promissory Notes; Principles of the Law of Partnership; The Law of Marine Insurance; Treatise on the Law of Partnership; Political, Personal, and Property Rights of a United States Citizen; Memoir of Chief Justice Parsons, *supra*; The Ministry of Sorrow; Deus Homo; The Infinite and the Finite; Essays; Outlines of the Religion and Philosophy of Swedenborg; The Mystery of Life. *Lip. Lit.*

Parsons, Thomas William. *Ms.*, 1819–1892. A poet of Boston who for some years practised his profession of dentistry there. The quality of his writing is uneven, but in such poems as the Lines on a Bust of Dante, and When Francesca Sings, he is at his best. His work includes a much-admired though incomplete translation in English verse of Dante's Divina Commedia, of which an edition was issued in 1893, with introduction by C. E. Norton, *supra*, and memorial sketch by Miss Guiney, *supra*; Ghetto di Roma; The Magnolia; The Old Home at Sudbury; The Shadow of the Obelisk, and Other Poems; Poems (1893). *See Atlantic Monthly; Stedman's Poets of America; Hovey's Seaward, an Elegy. Hou.*

Parsons, Usher. *Me.*, 1788–1868. A surgeon of Providence. The Art of Making Anatomic Preparations; Prize Dissertations; Sailors' Physician; History of the Battle of Lake Erie; Life of Sir William Pepperell.

Partington, Mrs. *See Shillaber.*

Parton, James. *E.*, 1822–1891. A popular littérateur of English birth who came to America when very young and for the latter part of his life resided in Newburyport. The permanent value of his writing is not great, with the possible exception of his Life of Voltaire. His other works include, Lives of Greeley, Aaron Burr, Andrew Jackson, Franklin, Jefferson; General Butler in New Orleans; Famous Americans of Recent Times; Smoking and Drinking; Captains of Industry; Triumphs of Enterprise; Noted Women of America and Europe; The People's Book of Biography; Caricature and Other Comic Art; Topics of the Times (1871). *See New England Magazine, January, 1893. Cr. Har. Hou.*

Parton, Mrs. Sarah Payson [Willis] [Eldridge]. "Fanny Fern." *Me.*, 1811–1872. Wife of J. Parton, *supra*, and sister of N. P. Willis, *infra.* A once popular but now neglected writer who for some sixteen years contributed a weekly article to The New York Ledger. Her writing was fresh and piquant in style, but wholly ephemeral in character. Rose Clark, a novel; Ruth Hall, a novel more or less autobiographic; Fern Leaves; Folly as it Flies; Ginger Snaps; Caper Sauce. *See Memoir by J. Parton, supra.*

Partridge, William Ordway. *F.*, 1861——. A sculptor of Milton, Massachusetts. Art for America; The Technique of Sculpture; The Song Life of a Sculptor. *Gi. Rob.*

Parvin, Theodore Sutton. *N. J.*, 1817——. An educator of Iowa, professor in Iowa University, 1859–70. History of Iowa; History of Templary in Iowa.

Parvin, Theophilus. *Ar.*, 1829——. A Philadelphia physician, professor in Jefferson Medical College, who has published The Science and Art of Obstetrics.

Paschall, George Washington. *Ga.*, 1812–1878. A jurist of Texas, and later of Washington, where he was professor of jurisprudence in Georgetown College. Annotated Digest of Texas Laws; Decisions of Texas Supreme Court; Annotated Constitution of the United States.

Patten, Claudius Buchanan. 1828–1886. A banker of Boston who published, in 1885, England as Seen by an American Banker. *Lo.*

Patten, George Washington. *R. I.*, 1808–1882. Son of W. Patten, *infra.* An officer in the United States army who wrote the noted lyrics, The Seminole's Reply; Joys that We've Tasted. His published books include, Army Manual; Infantry Tactics; Cavalry Drill; Voices of the Border, a volume of verse.

Patten, Simon Nelson. *Il.*, 1852——. A professor of political economy in the University of Pennsylvania from 1888. The Stability of Prices; The Consumption of Wealth; Economic Basis of Protection; Principles of Rational Taxation; Educational Value of Political Economy; Theory of Dynamic Economics; The Premises of Political Economy; The Theory of Social Forces.

Patten, William. *Ms.*, 1763–1839. A Congregational clergyman of Newport, Rhode Island. Christianity the True Religion; Reminiscences of Samuel Hopkins, *supra.*

Patterson, Christopher Stuart. *Pa.*, 1842——. A lawyer of Philadelphia, professor of the law of real estate in the University of Pennsylvania from 1887. Memoir of Theodore Cuyler; Railway Accident Law; Federal Restraints on State Action; The United States and the State under the Constitution.

Patterson, Robert. *I.*, 1743–1824. A professor of mathematics in the University of Pennsylvania, 1779–1814, and director of the Philadelphia Mint. The Newtonian System; Treatise on Arithmetic.

Patterson, Robert. *I.*, 1829——. A Presbyterian clergyman of Brooklyn, California, from 1880. The Fables of Infidelity and the Facts of Faith; The American Sabbath; The Sabbath: Scientific, American, and Christian; Christianity the Only Republican Religion; Christ's Testimony to the Scriptures; Egypt's Place in History.

Patterson, Robert Mayne. *Pa.*, 1832——. A Presbyterian clergyman of Philadelphia. History of Presbyterianism in Philadelphia; Paradise; Visions of Heaven; Elijah the Favored Man; History of the Synod of Pennsylvania.

Patton, Alfred Spencer. *E.*, 1825–1888. A Baptist minister of Utica, and subsequently editor, in New York city, of The Baptist Weekly. Light in the Valley; My Joy and Crown; Kincaid, the Hero Missionary; The Losing and Taking of Mansoul.

Patton, Francis Landey. *Ba.*, 1843——. A Presbyterian clergyman and educator, president of Princeton College from 1888. Inspiration of the Scriptures; Summary of Christian Doctrine.

Patton, Jacob Harris. *Pa.*, 1812——. An historical writer of New York city. Concise History of the American People; Yorktown, 1781–1881; The Democratic Party: its History and Influence; Brief History of the Presbyterian Church in the United States; Natural Resources of the United States; Political Economy for American Youth; Four Hundred Years of American History; Political Parties in the United States. *Fo. Lov.*

Patton, William. *Pa.*, 1798–1879. A Presbyterian clergyman of New York city, founder of the Union Theological Seminary. The Laws of Fermentation and the Wines of the Ancients; The Judgment of Jerusalem Predicted in Scripture; Jesus of Nazareth; Bible Principles and Bible Characters.

Patton, William Weston. *N. Y.*, 1821–1889. Grandson of W. Patton, *supra.* A Congregational clergyman in New York city, and president of Howard University from 1877. Spiritual Victory; Prayer and its Remarkable Answers; The Young Man's Friend; Conscience and Law; Slavery and Infidelity. *Fa.*

Paul, John. *See Webb, C. H.*

Paulding, James Kirke. *Md.*, 1779–1860. A versatile and once popular writer of New York city, the friend of Irving, and co-author with him of The Salmagundi Papers in 1807. He was secretary of the navy, 1837–41. His various writings include: The Diverting History of John Bull and Brother Jonathan, his most successful work; Salmagundi, a second series, 1819; Koningsmarke, the Long Finne, a novel; John Bull in America; The Dutchman's Fireside; Lay of the Scottish Fiddle, a travesty of the Lay of the Last Minstrel; Westward Ho; Merry Tales of the Three Wise Men of Gotham; The Puritan and his Daughter; The New Mirror for Travellers; The Backwoodsman, a poem; The Bucktails, a Comedy; Letters from the South; Life of George Washington; Slavery in America, a spirited defence of that institution. *See Literary Life of Paulding by his son; Appletons' American Biography. Scr.*

Payne, Charles Henry. *Ms.*, 1830——. A Methodist clergyman and educator, president of Ohio Wesleyan University, 1876-88. The Social Glass and Christian Obligation; Daniel, the Uncompromising Young Man; Guides and Guards in Character-Building; Methodism, its History and Results; Temperance; Women and their Work in Methodism. *Meth.*

Payne, Daniel Alexander. *S. C.*, 1811——. A Methodist bishop of African descent, president of Wilberforce University, 1865-76. Domestic Education; History of the African Methodist Church; Recollections of Men and Things.

Payne, John Howard. *N. Y.*, 1792-1852. A dramatist and actor of New York city in whose drama of Clari, the Maid of Milan, occurs the famous lyric, Home, Sweet Home, his chief claim to remembrance. From 1841 till his death he was United States consul at Tunis, his remains being removed from there to Washington in 1883. His best plays include, Brutus; Virginius; Charles II. *See American Magazine of History, May, 1881; Biographical Sketch by Brainard, 1885.*

Payne, William Harold. *N. Y.*, 1836——. An educator of Tennessee, chancellor of the University of Nashville, and president of Peabody Normal College from 1888. School Supervision; Outlines of Educational Doctrine; Contributions to the Science of Education; Lectures on Pedagogy. *Ap.*

Payne, Will[iam Hudson]. *Il.*, 1865——. A journalist of Chicago. Jerry the Dreamer, a novel. *Har.*

Payne, William Morton. *Ms.*, 1858——. An educator and literary critic of Chicago, professor of physical science in the High School. Our New Education; Little Leaders. *Wy.*

Payson, Edward. *N. H.*, 1783-1827. A Congregational clergyman of Portland, Maine, whose three volumes of Sermons were for a long time widely popular in the religious world. *See Bibliography of Maine.*

Payson, Edward. 1814-1890. A writer of Deering, Maine. The Law of Equivalents in its Relations to Political and Social Ethics; Doctor Tom; The Maine Law in the Balance. *Hou. Le.*

Peabody, Andrew Preston. *Ms.*, 1811-1893. A Unitarian clergyman of eminence, pastor of a church at Portsmouth, New Hampshire, 1833-60, and Plummer professor of Christian morals at Harvard University, 1860-81. A conservative, tolerant thinker, greatly beloved by all within the sphere of his influence. Sermons of Consolation; Lectures on Christian Doctrine; Christianity the Fruit of Nature; Moral Philosophy; Faults and Graces of Conversation; Sermons for Children; Christianity and Science; King's Chapel Sermons; Reminiscences of European Travel; Christian Belief and Life; Baccalaureate Sermons; Building a Character; Harvard Graduates Whom I Have Known; Harvard Reminiscences; translations of the ethical writings of Cicero and Plutarch's Delay of Divine Justice. *A. U. A. Hou. Lit. Rob.*

Peabody, Elizabeth Palmer. *Ms.*, 1804-1894. A noted educator of Boston, very active in awakening American interest in the kindergarten system, and in her early life associated in teaching with A. B. Alcott, *supra*, as related in her Record of a School. Her other works include: Chronological History of the United States; Kindergarten Guide; Æsthetic Papers; Letters to Kindergarteners; First Steps to History; Reminiscences of Dr. Channing; Last Evening with Allston, and Other Papers. *Le. Rob.*

Peabody, Ephraim. *N. H.*, 1807-1856. Cousin of A. P. Peabody, *supra*. A Unitarian clergyman of Boston, rector of King's Chapel, 1846–56. Christian Days and Thoughts; Sermons (with Memoir by S. A. Eliot), 1857.

Peabody, Francis Greenwood. *Ms.*, 18——. Son of E. Peabody, *supra.* A Unitarian clergyman of Cambridge, Parkman professor of theology at Harvard University, 1880–86, and Plummer professor of Christian morals from 1886. Mornings in the College Chapel. *Hou.*

Peabody, Oliver William Bourne. *N. H.*, 1799–1848. A lawyer and journalist of Boston, subsequently a Unitarian clergyman and pastor of a church in Burlington, Vermont, 1845–48. He published Lives of Generals Sullivan and Putnam, in Sparks's American Biography, and an edition of Shakespeare with Life and Notes.

Peabody, William Bourne Oliver. *N. H.*, 1799–1847. Twin brother of O. W. B. Peabody, *supra.* A Unitarian clergyman, pastor of a church in Springfield, Massachusetts, 1820–47. He was the author of Lives of A. Wilson, Cotton Mather, Brainerd, and Oglethorpe, in Sparks's American Biography; and Report on Birds of the Commonwealth. As a verse-writer he is best represented by such poems as Monadnock; Hymn of Nature; Winter Night.

Peacock, Thomas Brower. *O.*, 1852——. A verse-writer of Topeka, whose ambitious lines are quite without poetic merit. The Rhyme of the Border War; The Vendetta; Poems of the Plains. *Put.*

Peale, Charles Wilson. *Md.*, 1741–1827. An artist, inventor, and miscellaneous writer of Philadelphia, among whose works are, On Building Wooden Bridges; Domestic Happiness; Economy in Fuel. *See Tuckerman's Book of the Artists; Biography of, by R. Peale, infra; Boyle's Distinguished Marylanders.*

Peale, Rembrandt. *Pa.*, 1778–1860. Son of C. W. Peale, *supra.* An artist of Philadelphia. Notes on Italy; Portfolio of an Artist; Graphics. *See Tuckerman's Book of the Artists.*

Pearson, Jonathan. *N. H.*, 1813——. A genealogist who was professor of chemistry and subsequently of botany at Union College from 1839. Early Records of the County of Albany; Genealogy of the First Settlers of Albany; Genealogies of the First Settlers of Schenectady.

Pease, Theodore Claudius. *N. Y.*, 1853–1893. A Congregational clergyman of Malden, Massachusetts. The Christian Ministry. *Hou.*

Peaselee, Edmund Randolph. *N. H.*, 1814–1878. A physician of New York city, medical professor in several institutions. Human Histology; Ovarian Tumors. *Ap.*

Peattie, Mrs. Elia Wilkinson. *Mch.*, 1862——. A journalist of Chicago. The Judge, a novel; A Trip through Wonderland, a volume of Alaska travel; With Scrip and Staff, a story of the Children's Crusade; A Mountain Woman. *Wy.*

Peck, George. *N. Y.*, 1797–1876. A Methodist clergyman of prominence who was editor of several denominational journals. Christian Perfection; Early Methodism; Wyoming and its History; Universalism Examined; History of the Apostles and Evangelists; Rule of Faith; Manly Character, include his chief works. *See Life and Times of, by himself. Meth.*

Peck, George Washington. *Ms.*, 1817–1859. A journalist of Boston and New York. Melbourne and the Chincha Islands.

Peck, George Wesley. *Pa.*, 1849——. Great-nephew of J. T. Peck, *infra.* A Methodist clergyman of Western New York. The Realization and Benefit of Ideals; Walk in the Light.

Peck, George Wilbur. *N. Y.*, 1840——. A Wisconsin politician, successively mayor of Milwaukee and governor of Wisconsin. Peck's Bad Boy; Compendium of Fun, and other works of his, represent almost the lowest depths of vulgarity to which American humour has descended.

Peck, Harry Thurston. *Ct.*, 1856——. A professor of Latin at Columbia College and a literary critic. Latin Pronunciation; The Semitic Theory of Creation; The Personal Equation. *Har.*

Peck, Jesse Truesdell. *N. Y.*, 1811–1883. Brother of G. Peck, *supra.* A bishop in the Methodist church. The Central Idea of Christianity; The True

Woman; What Must I Do to be Saved?; The Great Republic. *Meth.*

Peck, John Lord. 18——. The Ultimate Generalization of Science; The Political Economy of Democracy and Capital and Labor.

Peck, John Mason. *Ct.*, 1789–1858. A Baptist general missionary in the Western States. New Guide for Emigrants to the West (1836); Father Clark, or the Pioneer Preacher.

Peck, Samuel Minturn. *Al.*, 1854——. A popular lyric poet and physician of Tuscaloosa, Alabama. Cap and Bells; Rings and Love Knots; Rhymes and Roses; Fair Women of To-Day. *Sto.*

Peck, William Guy. *Ct.*, 1820–1892. A soldier and mathematician, professor in Columbia College from 1857. Elementary Mechanics; Popular Astronomy; and a complete course of mathematical text-books.

Peck, William Henry. *Ga.*, 1830——. An educator of Georgia and a prolific writer of sensational novels remarkable for an entire absence of any literary quality. Among them are The McDonalds, or the Ashes of Southern Homes; The Confederate Flag of the Ocean; The Brother's Vengeance. *See Davidson's Living Writers of the South.*

Pedder, James. *E.*, 1775–1859. An agricultural writer who came to America in 1832, and settled in Philadelphia as a sugar manufacturer. From 1844 to 1859 he edited The Boston Cultivator. The Farmer's Land Measure; The Yellow Shoestrings; Frank.

Peebles, Mrs. Mary Louise [Parmelee]. "Lynde Palmer." *N. Y.*, 1833——. A writer of religious juvenile tales and other works, among them being The Little Captain; Helps Over Hard Places; The Good Fight; Where Honour Leads; A Question of Honour, a story; The Magnet Stones; The Two Blizzards. *Do. Kt.*

Peers, Benjamin Orrs. *Va.*, 1800–1842. An Episcopal clergyman and educator of Kentucky, founder of the common school system of Kentucky. American Education.

Peet, Harvey Prindle. *Ct.*, 1794–1873. A noted educator of deaf-mutes in New York city. Course of Instruction for the Deaf and Dumb; Legal Rights of the Deaf and Dumb; History of the United States, include his most important writings.

Peet, Stephen Denison. *O.*, 1830——. A Congregational minister, eminent as an anthropologist. The Ashtabula Disaster; History of Ashtabula County, Ohio; Ancient Architecture in America; History of Early Missions in Wisconsin; Picture Writing; Primitive Symbolisms; The Effigy Mounds of Wisconsin. *See Bibliography of Wisconsin.*

Peffer, William Alfred. *Pa.*, 1831——. A prominent lawyer and journalist of Kansas, and well known as a Populist Congressman. Tariff Manual; The Way Out.

Peirce [pêrss], **Benjamin.** *Ms.*, 1778–1831. A merchant of Salem, Massachusetts, subsequently librarian of Harvard University, who published a History of Harvard University from 1636 to the American Revolution.

Peirce, Benjamin. *Ms.*, 1809–1880. Son of B. Peirce, *supra.* An eminent mathematician, professor of mathematics and astronomy at Harvard University, 1833–67. Elementary Treatise on Plane and Spherical Trigonometry; Elementary Treatise on Sound; Curves, Functions, and Forces; Ideality in the Physical Sciences, compromise his most important works.

Peirce, Benjamin Osgood. *Ms.*, 1854——. Kinsman of preceding. A professor of physics at Harvard University from 1884, and author of Theory of the Newtonian Potential Functions. *Gi.*

Peirce, Bradford Kinney. *Vt.*, 1819–1889. A Methodist clergyman and journalist, editor of Zion's Herald, 1872–88. Bible Scholar's Manual; The Eminent Dead; Notes on the Acts; The Word of God Opened; A Half Century with Juvenile Delinquents; Trials of an Inventor; Audubon's Adventures; Stories from Life which the Chaplain Told; The Chaplain with the Children; The Young Shetlander and His Home; Hymns of the Higher Life. *Meth.*

Peirce, Charles Sanders. *Ms.*, 1839——. Son of B. Peirce, 2d, *supra.* A physician and lecturer on logic. Studies in Logic.

Peirce, Ebenezer Weaver. *Ms.*, 1822——. An officer in the Federal army during the Civil War. The Peirce Family of the Old Colony; Indian History, Biography, and Genealogy; Contributions, Biographical, etc.

Peirce, James Mills. *Ms.*, 1834——. Son of B. Peirce, 2d, *supra*. An educator of Cambridge, professor of mathematics in Harvard University from 1867. Text-Book of Analytical Geometry; Elements of Logarithms, are among his technical works. *Gi.*

Peirson, Mrs. Lydia Jane [Wheeler]. *Ct.*, 1802–1862. A verse-writer of Adrian, Michigan. Forest Leaves, and Other Poems; The Forest Minstrel. *See Griswold's Female Poets of America.*

Pellew, [William] George. *E.*, 1859–1892. A littérateur of New York city. Jane Austen's Novels, a Dissertation; In Castle and Cabin, or Talks in Ireland; Woman and the Commonwealth; Life of John Jay. *Hou.*

Pemberton, Ebenezer. *Ms.*, 1704–1777. A Presbyterian clergyman prominent as a loyalist in Boston at the opening of the Revolution. Sermons on Several Subjects; Practical Discourses; Salvation by Grace; Occasional Sermons. *See Sprague's Annals of the American Pulpit.*

Pendleton, Edmund Monroe. 1815–1884. A physician who published Scientific Agriculture (1876).

Pendleton, James Madison. *Va.*, 1811–1891. A Baptist clergyman of Upland, Pennsylvania. Three Reasons Why I Am a Baptist; Church Manual; Christian Doctrines; Sermons; Distinctive Principles of Baptists; Atonement of Christ. *Bap.*

Pendleton, Louis [Beauregard]. *Ga.*, 1861——. A novelist of Philadelphia. Bewitched, and Other Stories; In the Wire Grass, a novel of Southern Georgia; King Tom and the Runaways, a juvenile tale; The Wedding Garment, a Tale of the Life to Come; The Sons of Ham; Corona of the Nantahalas; In the Okefenokee, a juvenile tale. *Ap. Cas. Mer. Rob.*

Pendleton, William Nelson. *Va.*, 1809–1883. An Episcopal clergyman and educator of Virginia, a Confederate officer during the Civil War, and subsequently rector of Grace Church, Lexington, Virginia. Science a Witness for the Bible. *See Memoirs of, by E. P. Lee. Lip.*

Penhallow, Samuel. *E.*, 1665–1726. A citizen of Portsmouth, New Hampshire, chief justice of New Hampshire, 1717–26. He published in 1726 a realistic and valuable History of the Wars of New England with the Eastern Indians. *See Tyler's American Literature.*

Penick, Charles Clifton. *Va.*, 1843——. The third Protestant Episcopal bishop of the West African Mission. He was consecrated in 1877, resigned in 1883, and is now (1897) a general agent at Baltimore of the commission on work among the coloured people. More than a Prophet, or Chapters on St. John the Evangelist.

Penn, Arthur. *See Matthews, J. B.*

Pennell, Mrs. Elizabeth [Robins]. 18——. Niece of C. G. Leland, *supra*, and wife of J. Pennell, *infra*. A writer who has lived in London for many years. Life of Mary Wollstonecraft; A Canterbury Pilgrimage; Two Pilgrims' Progress; Our Sentimental Journey through France and Italy; Our Journey to the Hebrides; To Gipsyland; Play in Provence; The Feasts of Autolycus. *Cent. Har. Mer. Rob. Scr.*

Pennell, Joseph. *Pa.*, 1859——. An artist living in London who has illustrated his wife's books, and published Pen Drawing and Pen Draughtsmen; The Jew at Home; Modern Illustration. *Ap. Mac.*

Penny, Virginia. *Ky.*, 1826——. An educator who has written much in relation to wider opportunities for women. The Employment of Women; Five Hundred Occupations Adapted to Women; Think and Act.

Pennypacker, Isaac Rusling. *Pa.*, 1852——. A journalist and verse-writer of Philadelphia. Gettysburg, and Other Poems.

Pennypacker, Samuel Whitaker. *Pa.*, 1843——. A jurist of Philadelphia. Annals of Phœnixville; Pennsylvania Supreme Court Reports; Historical and Biographical Sketches.

Pentecost, George Frederick. *Il.*, 1843——. A Congregational minister in Brooklyn, 1881–90, and subsequently an evangelist in America and England. The Angel in the Marble; In the Volume of the Book; Out of Egypt; The Christian and the Modern Dance; Bible Studies; The Gospel of Luke; Grace Abounding in the Forgiveness of Sins. *Bar. Rev.*

Pepper, George Dana Boardman. *Ms.*, 1833——. A Baptist clergyman and educator, president of Colby University from 1882. Outlines of Theology.

Pepper, William. *Pa.*, 1843——. An eminent Philadelphia physician, provost of the University of Pennsylvania, 1881–94. Higher Medical Education; Diseases of Children (with J. F. Meigs, *supra*). *Lip.*

Perce, Elbert. *N.Y.*, 1831–1869. A littérateur of New York city. Old Carl the Cooper; The Last of His Name; The Battle Roll; Gulliver Joi: his Three Voyages; and several translations from the Swedish of Carlén.

Percival, James Gates. *Ct.*, 1795–1856. A verse-writer once popular, but now wholly neglected. His verse is not unmusical, but seldom rises much above mediocrity. Seneca Lake and The Coral Grove are still found lingering in anthologies. Prometheus; Clio; Dream of a Day; Poems, include his poetical works. He was a geologist of some reputation, and published Geological Surveys of Connecticut and Wisconsin. *See Life and Letters, by Julius Ward, infra; Allibone's Dictionary.*

Percy, Florence. *See Allen, Mrs. Elizabeth.*

Perkins, Charles Callahan. *Ms.*, 1823–1886. A prominent art patron and critic of Boston. Raphael and Michael Angelo; Tuscan Sculptors; Italian Sculptors; Historical Handbook of Italian Sculpture; Ghiberti et son école; Art in Education; History of the Boston Handel and Haydn Society. *Hou. Scr.*

Perkins, Eli. *See Landon.*

Perkins, Mrs. Elmira [Johnson]. *Me.*, 1814–1896. A missionary among the Indians in Oregon. Her later life was passed in Boston. Harp of the Willows, a volume of verse.

Perkins, Frederic Beecher. *Ct.*, 1828——. Grandson of Lyman Beecher, *supra.* A librarian. Scrope, or the Lost Library, a novel; Devil Puzzlers, and Other Studies; My Three Conversations with Miss Chester; Life of Dickens; Check List of American Local History, include the more important of his writings.

Perkins, George Henry. *Ms.*, 1844——. A naturalist, State entomologist of Vermont. The Injurious Insects of Vermont; The Flora of Vermont.

Perkins, George Roberts. *N. Y.*, 1812–1876. An educator of New York State, who published Plane and Solid Geometry, and other mathematical text-books.

Perkins, James Breck. *Wis.*, 1847——. A lawyer of Rochester, New York. France Under Mazarin; France Under the Regency; France under Louis XV. *Hou. Put.*

Perkins, James Handasyd. *Ms.*, 1810–1849. A Unitarian clergyman of Cincinnati, very active in the cause of prison discipline reform. Annals of the West. *See Memoir by his cousin, W. H. Channing, supra.*

Perkins, Justin. *Ms.*, 1805–1869. A Congregational missionary in Persia. Residence of Eight Years in Persia; Missionary Life in Persia.

Perkins, Maurice. *Ct.*, 1836——. A professor of chemistry at Union College from 1865, author of a Manual of Qualitative Analysis.

Perkins, Samuel. *Ct.*, 1767–1850. A lawyer of Windham, Connecticut. History of the Late War between the United States and Great Britain (1825); General Jackson's Conduct in the Seminole War; Historical Sketches of the United States.

Perkins, William Rufus. *Pa.*, 1847–1895. An educator and poet, professor of history in the Iowa State University, 1887–95. He was the author of two careful historical monographs, History of the Trappist Abbey of New Melleray; and History of the Amana Society; and of Eleusis and Lesser Poems, a striking collection of musical meditative verse. *Mg.*

Perrin, Mrs. Martha Chamberlin [Drinker]. *Pa.*, 186——. Chansons du Matin. *Put.*

Perrin, Raymond S——. *N. Y.*, 1849——. The Student's Dreams; The Religion of Philosophy, or the Unification of Knowledge. *Put.*

Perrine, William Henry. *N. Y.*, 1827–1880. A Methodist clergyman, professor for some years in Albion College, Michigan. The Principles of Church Government with Special Application to the Polity of Episcopal Methodism.

Perry, Amos. *Ms.*, 1812——. A Providence writer who was superintendent of the State census in 1865. Carthage and Tunis is his only work of importance.

Perry, Arthur Latham. *N.H.*, 1830——. A professor of history and political economy at Williams College from 1853, and a prominent advocate of free trade. Elements of Political Economy; Introduction to Political Economy; Principles of Political Economy; Origins of Williamstown. *Scr.*

Perry, Benjamin Franklin. *S. C.*, 1805–1886. A lawyer of South Carolina, provisional governor of his State at the close of the Civil War. Reminiscences of Public Men; Sketches of Eminent Statesmen (1887).

Perry, Bliss. *Ms.*, 1860——. Son of A. L. Perry, *supra.* A professor of oratory and æsthetic criticism at Princeton College. The Plated City; Salem Kittredge, and Other Stories; The Broughton House. He has edited Selections from Burke, and Scott's Woodstock and Ivanhoe. *Ho. Lgs. Scr.*

Perry, Carlotta. *See Perry, Charlotte.*

Perry, Charlotte Augusta. "Carlotta Perry." *Wis.*, 1848——. A popular verse-writer of Milwaukee. Carlotta Perry's Poems.

Perry, Edward Delevan. *N. Y.*, 1854——. A professor of Sanskrit in Columbia College. Indra in the Rig-veda; A Sanskrit Primer.

Perry, Mary Alice. *Ms.*, 1854–1883. A writer of fiction. Esther Pennefather; More Ways Than One. *Har.*

Perry, Nora. *Ms.*, 1832–1896. A poet and littérateur of Boston. Her verse was popular, and had not unfrequently the genuine poetic ring, while her stories for girls were animated and fresh. Her verse includes, After the Ball, and Other Poems; Her Lover's Friend, and Other Poems; New Songs and Ballads; Legends and Lyrics. Her prose work comprises, The Tragedy of the Unexpected, and Other Stories; For a Woman, a novel; The Youngest Miss Lorton, and Other Stories; A Book of Love Stories; A Rosebud Garden of Girls; A Flock of Girls and their Friends; A Flock of Girls and Boys; Another Flock of Girls; Three Little Daughters of the Revolution; Hope Benham. *Hou. Lit.*

Perry, Rufus Lewis. *Tn.*, *c.* 1833–1895. A Baptist clergyman of African descent, widely known as a linguist. Among his various writings is The Cushite, or the Children of Ham as seen by Ancient Historians and Poets.

Perry, Thomas Sergeant. *R. I.*, 1845——. An educator of Boston. English Literature in the Eighteenth Century; Life of Lieber; From Opitz to Lessing, a Study of Pseudo-Classicism in Literature; The Evolution of the Snob; History of Greek Literature. *Ho. Hou.*

Perry, William Stevens. *R. I.* 1832——. The second Protestant Episcopal bishop of Iowa, prominent among High Churchmen. The Documentary History of the Protestant Episcopal Church; The History of the American Episcopal Church; Life Lessons from the Book of Proverbs; Some Summer Days Abroad; The General Ecclesiastical Constitution of the American Church; The American Episcopate. *Wh.*

Peters, Christian Henry Frederick. *Sd.*, 1813–1890. A German astronomer, director of the observatory at Hamilton College, 1858–90, who discovered over forty asteroids. Celestial Charts.

Peters, Edward Dyer. *Ms.*, 1849——. A metallurgist who has published Modern American Methods of Copper Smelting.

Peters, George Nathaniel Henry. *Pa.*, 1825——. A Lutheran minister of Ohio. The Theocratic Kingdom of Christ.

Peters, John Charles. *N. Y.*, 1819–1893. A physician of New York city of note as a bacteriologist. Diseases of the Brain and Nervous System; Diseases of Women; Diseases of the Eye; Notes on Asiatic Cholera; A New Materia Medica, are among his works.

Peters, Mrs. Phillis [Wheatley]. *Sl.*, 1754–1784. A verse-writer of African birth brought to Boston in childhood as a slave. Poems on Various Occasions, Religious and Moral, appeared in London in 1772, and won a fleeting popularity there, the author being regarded as a prodigy. But there is little in her work that should keep it in remembrance. *See Griswold's Female Poets of America.*

Peters, Samuel Andrew. *Ct.*, 1735–1826. An Episcopal clergyman of Hartford who published a famous General History of Connecticut by a Gentleman of that Province, a curious satirical production, to which may be traced the well-known fable of the Connecticut Blue Laws. Other works of his include a Life of Rev. Hugh Peters; History of Hebron, Connecticut.

Peterson, Arthur. *Pa.*, 1851——. Son of H. Peterson, *infra.* A naval officer who has published Songs of New Sweden.

Peterson, Charles Jacobs. *Pa.*, 1818–1887. A Philadelphia publisher and novelist, the founder of Peterson's Magazine. Kate Aylesford; Cruising in the Last War; Military Heroes of the United States; Grace Dudley, or Arnold at Saratoga; Mabel, or Darkness and Dawn; The Old Stone Mansion, include his principal writings.

Peterson, Frederick. *Min.*, 1859——. A physician and verse-writer. Poems and Swedish Translations; In the Shade of Ygdrasil (verse).

Peterson, Mrs. Hannah [Bouvier]. *Pa.*, 1811–1870. First wife of R. E. Peterson, *infra.* Familiar Astronomy.

Peterson, Henry. *Pa.*, 1818–1891. Cousin of C. J. Peterson, *supra.* A Philadelphia verse-writer, and editor for many years of The Saturday Evening Post. The Modern Job, and Other Poems; Faire-Mount; Bessie's Lovers; Cæsar, a Dramatic Study.

Peterson, Robert Evans. *Pa.*, 1812–1894. Brother of H. Peterson, *supra.* A Philadelphia writer whose principal work is The Roman Catholic not the Only True Religion. *Lip.*

Pettingill, Amos. *N. H.*, 1780–1830. A Methodist clergyman and educator of Connecticut. View of the Heavens; The Spirit of Methodism. *See Memoir of, by Hart, 1832.*

Pettingill, John Hancock. *Vt.*, 1815–1887. A Congregational clergyman in Ohio, widely known as an earnest believer in conditional immortality. The Theological Trilemma; Platonism *versus* Christianity; Bible Terminology; Life Everlasting; The Unspeakable Gift; Views and Reviews in Eschatology.

Peyton, John Lewis. *Va.*, 1824—— A lawyer of Staunton, Virginia, who served as an officer in the Confederate service. Adventures of my Grandfather; History of Augusta County, Virginia; The American Crisis; Over the Alleghanies; Memorials of Nature and Art.

Phelan, James. *Mi.*, 1856–1891. A Memphis lawyer and journalist. Philip Massinger and his Plays; History of Tennessee. *Hou.*

Phelps, Mrs. Almira [Hart] [Lincoln]. *Ct.*, 1793–1884. A noted educator of Baltimore who published many text-books on the natural sciences. Among her works are, Geology for Beginners; Christian Households; Ida Norman, a tale; Familiar Lectures on Botany; Hours with my Pupils. *See Mrs. Hale's Woman's Record. Lip.*

Phelps, Austin. *Ms.*, 1820–1890. A Congregational clergyman of Andover, Massachusetts, professor of sacred rhetoric in the Theological Seminary there, 1848–79. The Still Hour; The New Birth; The Theory of Preaching; English Style in Public Discourse; The Solitude of Christ; Studies of the Old Testament; Men and Books; My Study, and Other Essays; My Portfolio; My Note-Book. *See Life by his daughter, Mrs. Ward, 1891. C. P. S. Lo. Scr.*

Phelps, Mrs. Elizabeth [Stuart]. *Ms.*, 1815–1853. Wife of A. Phelps, *supra.* A writer whose Sunnyside, and A Peep at Number Five, stories descriptive of clerical life, were once widely popular. She wrote, also, Last Sheaf from Sunnyside, and a number of Sunday-school tales, the latter over the signature "H. Trusta."

Phelps, Elizabeth Stuart. Daughter of A. and E. S. Phelps, *supra*. *See Ward, Mrs. Elizabeth.*

Phelps, John Wolcott. *Vt.*, 1813–1885. Stepson of Mrs. Almira Phelps, *supra*. A writer of Brattleboro, Vermont, who was an officer in the United States army in the Mexican War and became a brigadier-general of United States volunteers in the Civil War. In 1880 he was the presidential nominee of the American party. Sibylline Leaves; Good Behavior; History of Madagascar; The Fables of Florian in English Verse.

Phelps, Sylvanus Dryden. *Ct.*, 1816——. A Baptist clergyman of New Haven, and subsequently of Hartford. Eloquence of Nature, and Other Poems; Sunlight and Heartlight, and Other Poems; The Poet's Song for Heart and Home; Bible Lands; Sermons in the Four Quarters of the Globe.

Phelps, Thomas Stowell. *Me.*, 1822——, A rear-admiral in the United States navy who retired in 1885. Reminiscences of Washington Territory (1882).

Phelps, William Lyon. *Ct.*, 1865——. An instructor at Yale University. The Beginnings of the English Romantic Movement. *Gi.*

Philbrick, Edward Southwick. *Ms.*, 1827–1889. A sanitarian who published American Sanitary Engineering, 1881.

Philbrick, John Dudley. *N. H.*, 1818–1886. A prominent educator of Boston who published nearly fifty valuable public-school reports, and City School Systems in the United States.

Philips, Samuel. *Md.*, 1823——. A German Reformed clergyman, professor in Muhlenberg College, Allentown, Pennsylvania, from 1866. Gethsemane and the Cross; The Christian Home; The Voice of Blood; The Communion of Saints.

Phillips, Barnet. *Pa.*, 1828——. A journalist of New York city, on the staff of The Times from 1872. The Struggle, a novel; Burning their Ships.

Phillips, George. *E.*, 1593–1644. A Puritan clergyman, minister at Watertown, Massachusetts, from 1630 till his death. He was a noted controversialist of his day, and published a treatise on Infant Baptism.

Phillips, George Searle. "January Searle." *E.*, 1818–1889. A writer and lecturer of Yorkshire, England, who, after some years of literary work in the United States, became, in 1873, an inmate of an insane asylum in New Jersey. Chapters in the History of a Life; Life of Ebenezer Elliott; Memoirs of Wordsworth; The Gypsies of the Dane's Dyke; Chicago and Her Churches.

Phillips, Henry. *Pa.*, 1838——. A lawyer of Philadelphia. History of American Colonial Paper Currency; History of American Continental Paper Money; Pleasures of Numismatic Science; Poems from the Spanish and German; Faust, from the German of Chamisso.

Phillips, Maude Gillette. *Ms.*, 1860——. An educator who has published A Popular Manual of English Literature. *Har.*

Phillips, Wendell. *Ms.*, 1811-1884. A celebrated orator of Boston, a vehement opponent of slavery, and an active champion of labor reform and woman suffrage. The Constitution a Pro-Slavery Contract; Lectures, Orations, and Letters to 1861; Speeches, Lectures, and Addresses; The Scholar in a Republic. *See Lives by G. L. Austin, C. Martyn; Appletons' American Biography.*

Phillips, Willard. *Ms.*, 1784–1873. A lawyer of Boston. Treatise on the Law of Insurance; Manual of Political Economy; The Law of Patents; The Inventor's Guide; Protection and Free Trade. *See Allibone's Dictionary.*

Phin, John. *S.*, 1832——. A New York publisher of technical journals, Open-Air Grape Culture; Chemical History of the Creation; Practical Treatise on Lightning Rods; How to Use the Microscope; Workshop Companion; Preparation and Use of Cements and Glue; Dictionary of Practical Agriculture; Trade Secrets and Private Recipes; A Pocket Dictionary of Monetary and Coinage Terms.

Phœnix, John. *See Derby, George.*

Phyfe, William Henry Pinkney. *N. Y.*, 1855——. An author of New York city. How Should I Pronounce? The School Pronouncer; Seven Thousand Words Often Mispronounced; The Test Pronouncer; Five Thousand Words Commonly Misspelled. *Put.*

Piatt [pē-ăt′], **Donn.** *O.*, 1819–1891. A lawyer and journalist of Washington, and during the Civil War a Federal officer. Sunday Meditations; Memories of the Men who Saved the Union; Poems and Plays; Life of General George H. Thomas; The Lone Grave of the Shenandoah (verse). *See Life of, by C. G. Miller, 1893. Clke.*

Piatt, John James. *Ind.*, 1835——. Nephew of D. Piatt, *supra.* A poet who was consul at Cork, 1882–93. He has been a prolific writer of verse, but The Morning Street, one of his earlier poems, still ranks as his finest effort. Landmarks; Western Windows; Poems of House and Home; Idyls and Lyrics of the Ohio Valley; Poems in Sunshine and Firelight; The Lost Farm, and Other Poems; At the Holy Well; A Dream of Church Windows (a revised edition of Poems of House and Home); The Lost Hunting Ground; Little New World Idyls; Poems by Two Friends (with W. D. Howells, *supra*); The Children Out of Doors; and Nests at Washington (with Mrs. Piatt). His prose is included in Penciled Fly-Leaves; A Return to Paradise. *Clke. Hou. Ls.*

Piatt, Mrs. Sarah Morgan [Bryan]. *Ky.*, 1836——. Wife of J. J. Piatt, *supra.* A poet whose range of expression is not very wide, but, within its limits, genuine and original. A Woman's Poems; A Voyage to the Fortunate Isles, and Other Poems; That New World, and Other Poems; Dramatic Persons and Moods; An Irish Garland; In Primrose Time; The Witch in the Glass; Complete Poems (1894); An Enchanted Castle; Child's World Ballads. *See Wide-Awake Magazine, November, 1876. Clke. Hou. Lgs.*

Picard, George Henry. *O.*, 1850——. A physician and novelist of New York city. A Matter of Taste; A Mission Flower; Old Boniface.

Pick, Bernhard. *P.*, 1842——. A Lutheran clergyman of Pennsylvania, prior to 1884 a Presbyterian minister. Luther as a Hymnist; Historical Sketch of the Jews; Life of Christ according to Extra Canonical Sources; Index to the Ante-Nicene Fathers; The Talmud: What It Is.

Pickard, Samuel Thomas. *Ms.*, 1828——. A writer who for many years edited the Portland (Maine) Transcript. Life and Letters of John Greenleaf Whittier. *Hou.*

Pickering, Charles. *Pa.*, 1805–1878. A grandson of Timothy Pickering, the noted statesman. A naturalist of eminence. Races of Men and their Geographical Distribution; Geographical Distribution of Animals and Men; Chronological History of Plants. *See Allibone's Dictionary.*

Pickering, Edward Charles. *Ms.*, 1846——. Son of C. Pickering, *supra.* The director of Harvard Observatory at Cambridge, and author of Elements of Physical Manipulation. *Hou.*

Pickering, Henry. *N. Y.*, 1781–1831. The third son of the statesman, Timothy Pickering. A verse-writer of New York who published Ruins of Pæstum; Athens, and Other Poems; The Buckwheat Cake.

Pickering, John. *Ms.*, 1777–1846. The eldest son of Timothy Pickering. A lawyer of Boston and a linguist of eminence. Greek and English Lexicon; Collection of Words and Phrases Supposed to be Peculiar to the United States; Remarks on the Indian Languages of North America. *See Allibone's Dictionary. Lip.*

Pickering, Octavius. *Pa.*, 1791–1868. Brother of J. Pickering, *supra.* A Boston lawyer who published Reports of Cases in the Supreme Judicial Court of Massachusetts, 1822–40; and Life of Timothy Pickering (completed by Upham).

Pickering, William Henry. *Ms.* 1858——. Son of C. Pickering, *supra.* An astronomer, professor in Harvard University from 1887. Walking Guide to the White Mountain Range.

Pickett, Albert James. *N. C.*, 1810–1858. A writer of Montgomery, Alabama, who published a History of Alabama.

Pierce, Edward Lillie. *Ms.*, 1829–1897. A prominent Boston lawyer. American Railroad Law; Life of Charles Sumner; The Law of Railroads; Enfranchisement and Citizenship. *Lit. Rob.*

Pierce, Frederick Clifton. *Ms.* 1856——. An Illinois writer who has written town histories of Barre and Grafton, Massachusetts, and of Rockford, Illinois; The Harwood Genealogy; Pierce History and Genealogy; Peirce History and Genealogy; Pearse and Pearce Genealogy.

Pierce, Henry Niles. *R. I.*, 1820——. The fourth Protestant Episcopal bishop of Arkansas, consecrated in 1870. The Agnostic, and Other Poems. *Wh.*

Pierpont, John. *Ct.*, 1785–1866. A Unitarian clergyman of Boston, pastor of the Hollis Street Church, 1819–45. He wrote a volume of sacred verse, Airs of Palestine, and a number of domestic lyrics, which were very popular, Passing Away being the best known of any. He compiled several school readers, the most noted of which was The American First-Class Book. *See Atlantic Monthly, December, 1866. Lip.*

Pierrepont, Edward Willoughby. *N. Y.*, 1860–1885. A chargé d'affaires at Rome at the time of his death. From Fifth Avenue to Alaska.

Pierson, Arthur Tappan. *N. Y.*, 1837——. A Congregational clergyman of note. Acts of the Holy Spirit; Many Infallible Proofs; The Crisis of Missions; The Miracles of Missions; The Divine Art of Preaching; The Heart of the Gospel; Keys to the Word; Lessons on Prayer, comprise his more important works. *Fu. Ran. Rev.*

Pierson, Mrs. Cornelia [Tuthill]. *Ct.*, 1820–1870. Daughter of Mrs. Tuthill, *infra.* Our Little Comfort; Wreaths and Blossoms for the Church; When are we Happiest?; The Belle, the Blue, and the Bigot, are among her works.

Pierson, Hamilton Wilcox. *N. Y.*, 1817——. A Presbyterian clergyman in Kentucky. Thomas Jefferson at Monticello; In the Brush, or Old-Time Social, Political, and Religious Life in the Southwest. *Ap.*

Pike, Albert. *Ms.*, 1809–1891. A lawyer and journalist of Little Rock, Memphis, and Washington successively, who served as an officer in the Confederate army. His writings include, Hymns to the Gods; Prose Sketches and Poems; Nugæ, a collection of Poems; Arkansas Supreme Court Reports, 1840–45. *See Griswold's Poets and Poetry of America.*

Pike, James Shepherd. *Me.*, 1811–1882. A journalist of New York city who was minister to the Netherlands, 1861–66. A Prostrate State; The Restoration of the Currency; The Financial Crisis; Horace Greeley in 1872; The First Blows of the Civil War; The New Puritan: New England Two Hundred Years Ago. *Har.*

Pike, Mrs. Mary Hayden [Green]. *Me.*, 1825——. A once popular novelist. Ida May; Caste; Agnes; Bond and Free.

Pilcher, Elijah Homes. *O.*, 1810–1887. A Methodist clergyman of Michigan who wrote a History of Protestantism in Michigan.

Pilling, James Constantine. *D. C.*, 1840–1895. An ethnologist of distinction in the government service, among whose writings are Bibliographies of the Languages of the North American Indians, of the Eskimoan Languages, of the Siouan, of the Iroquoian, and others.

Pillsbury, Parker. *Ms.*, 1809——. A noted anti-slavery agitator. Acts of the Anti-Slavery Apostles.

Pinckney, Charles Cotesworth. *S. C.*, 1812——. An Episcopal clergyman of Charleston. Life of General Thomas Pinckney. *Hou.*

Pindar, Susan. *N. Y.*, *c.* 1820——. Susan Pindar's Story Books; Legends of the Flowers.

Pinkerton, Allan. *S.*, 1819–1884. A Chartist who came to America in 1842 and settled in Chicago, where he founded a famous detective agency. Among his many detective stories are, The Molly Maguires and the Detectives; Criminal Reminiscences; The Spy of the Rebellion; Thirty Years a Detective; Railroad Forgers and the Detectives.

Pinkney, Edward Coate. *E.*, 1802–1828. A lyric poet of Baltimore who published his Poems in 1825. *See Griswold's Poets and Poetry of America.*

Piper, Richard Upton. *N. H.*, 1818——. A Chicago physician. Operative Surgery; The Trees of America.

Pise [pize], **Charles Constantine.** *Md.*, 1802–1866. A once prominent Roman Catholic clergyman of Brooklyn. History of the Church to the Reformation; The Acts of the Apostles in Blank Verse; Father Rowland; Indian Cottage, a Unitarian Story; The Pleasures of Religion, and Other Poems; Horæ Vagabundæ; Alethia; Zenosius; Letters to Ada; Lives of St. Ignatius and his First Companions; Notes on a Protestant Catechism; Christianity and the Church.

Pitkin, Timothy. *Ct.*, 1766–1847. A lawyer and politician of Connecticut, prominent as a Federalist congressman. A Statistical View of the Commerce of the United States; Political and Civil History of the United States, 1763–1847.

Pitman, Benn. *E.*, 1822——. A stenographer of Cincinnati, and in his later years an art instructor of the school of design at the University of Cincinnati. The Reporter's Companion; Manual of Phonography; Phonographic Dictionary (with J. B. Howard).

Pitman, Mrs. Marie J—— [Davis]. *N. Y.*, 1850–1888. A journalist and correspondent of Boston who published European Breezes and a number of juvenile stories.

Pittenger, William. *O.*, 1840——. A Methodist clergyman and educator of Philadelphia, a Federal soldier during the Civil War. Daring and Suffering; Oratory, Sacred and Secular; Extempore Speech.

Pitzer, Alexander White. *Va.*, 1834——. A Presbyterian clergyman of Washington, professor of biblical literature in Howard University from 1875. Ecce Deus Homo; Christ the Teacher of Men; The New Life and Not the Higher Life.

Platt, Franklin. *Pa.*, 1844——. A Pennsylvania geologist, president of the Rochester and Pittsburg Coal Company from 1881. Coke Manufacturing; Waste in Mining Anthracite, and other volumes of geological reports.

Platt, William Henry. *N. Y.*, 1821——. An Episcopal clergyman of Rochester, New York, and more recently of Petersburg, Virginia. Influence of Religion in the Development of Jurisprudence; After Death — What?; God Out and Man In; The Philosophy of the Supernatural.

Pleasanton, Augustus James. *D. C.*, 1808–1894. An army officer prominent for a short time as the author of a work on the Influence of the Blue Ray in Developing Animal and Vegetable Life.

Plumer [plŭm'er], **William.** *N. H.*, 1789–1854. A New Hampshire lawyer who was an active congressional opponent of slavery. Lyra Sacra; A Pastoral on the Story of Ruth.

Plumer, William Swan. *Pa.*, 1802–1880. A Presbyterian clergyman of extreme Calvinistic views, professor of theology in the Theological Seminary at Columbia, South Carolina, 1856–80. His principal writings include, Pastoral Theology; Jehovah-jireh; Studies in the Book of Psalms; The Book of Our Salvation; Words of Truth and Love; The Saint and the Sinner; Vital Godliness; Commentary on Romans; A Word to the Weary. *Har. Lip. Ran.*

Plympton, George Washington. *Ms.*, 1827——. A civil engineer of note, editor of Van Nostrand's Engineering Magazine, 1870–86. The Blowpipe; The Starfinder; The Aneroid.

Poe, Edgar Allan. *Ms.*, 1809–1849. A poet and romancer who is pronounced by some critics the foremost of American poets so far as melody and technique are concerned. He was born in Boston, his parents being actors then playing in that city, and, left an orphan at an early age, was adopted and educated by Mr. Allan, a Virginia merchant. At nineteen he published his first volume, Tamerlane, and Other Poems. He led a wandering, dissipated life, editing at various times Graham's Magazine, The Southern Literary Messenger, and other periodicals, and died of delirium tremens in Baltimore. He criticized the work of his contemporaries with severity, yet in the main with justice, but in so doing raised up a host of literary enemies. Among his prose tales, The Gold Bug; The Fall of the House of Usher; Ligeia, are especially characteristic of his genius, while such poems as The Bells, The Raven, Annabel Lee, display wonderful melody and perfect mastery of metre. Beside Tamerlane, his writings include, The Conchologist's First Book; Eureka, a Prose Poem; The Raven, and Other Poems; Tales of the Grotesque and Arabesque; The Narrative of Arthur Gordon Pym. The best edition of Poe is that edited by E. C. Stedman and G. E. Woodberry, in ten volumes (1895). *See Lives by Stoddard, Didier, Ingram, Woodberry; Fortnightly Review, July, 1880; Poe and his Critics by Mrs. Whitman; Stedman's Poets of America. Co. Cr. Har. Kt. Lip. Mac. Sto.*

Poinsett, Joel Roberts. *S. C.*, 1779–1851. A South Carolina statesman, sent on a special mission to Mexico in 1822, minister to that country 1825–29, and secretary of war under President Van Buren. He was a botanist of some note, the genus Poinsettia having been named in his honour. Notes on Mexico, made in 1822.

Pollard, Edward Albert. *Va.*, 1828–1872. A once noted journalist of Richmond, Virginia, and an active opponent of the policy of Jefferson Davis during the Civil War. Black Diamonds; Letters of the Southern Spy; Southern History of the War; Observations in the North; The Lost Cause; The Lost Cause Regained; Lee and his Lieutenants; Life of Jefferson Davis, with the Secret History of the Confederacy; The Virginia Tourist. *Lip.*

Pollard, Josephine. *N. Y.*, 1843–1892. A littérateur of New York city, whose work was mainly intended for juvenile readers. The Gypsy Books; A Piece of Silver; Elfin Land; Vagrant Verses; Songs of Bird Life; The Decorative Sisters; The Boston Tea Party; Gellivor, a Christmas Legend. *Meth. Ran.*

Pomeroy, Brick. *See Pomeroy, Marcus.*

Pomeroy, John Norton. *N. Y.*, 1828–1885. A lawyer of Rochester, New York, but subsequently professor of law in the University of California, 1878–85. Introduction to Municipal Law; Remedies and Remedial Rights; Specific Performance of Contract; Equity Jurisprudence; Riparian Rights; Introduction to United States Constitutional Law; Lectures on International Law in Time of Peace. *Hou. Lit.*

Pomeroy, Marcus Mills. "Brick Pomeroy." *N. Y.*, 1833–1896. A journalist successively of La Crosse, Wisconsin, New York city (where he established Brick Pomeroy's Democrat), and Chicago. Sense; Nonsense; Gold Dust; Brick Dust; Our Saturday Nights; Home Harmonies; Perpetual Money.

Pond, Enoch. *Ms.*, 1791–1882. A Congregational clergyman, professor in the Theological Seminary at Bangor, Maine, from 1832, and its president from 1856. Text-Book of Ecclesiastical History; Pastoral Theology; Memoir of Zinzendorf; Life of Increase Mather; Plato: his Life, Works, Opinions, and Influence; Christian Theology; History of God's Church, are among his works. *See Autobiography; Bibliography of Maine. C. P. S.*

Pond, Frederick Eugene. "Will Wildwood." *Wis.*, 1856——. A sporting writer and editor of Chicago. Handbook for Young Sportsmen; Memoirs of Eminent Sportsmen; Gun Trial and Field Records of America.

Pond, George Edward. *Ms.*, 1837——. A journalist of New York and Philadelphia, editor of The Army and Navy Journal. The Shenandoah Valley in 1864. *Scr.*

Pond, Samuel William. *Ct.*, 1808——. A Congregational missionary to the Indians in Minnesota. History of Joseph in the Dakota Language; Wonapi Inonpa, the Second Dakota Reading Book.

Pool, Maria Louise. *Ms.*, 1845——. A novelist of Rockland, Massachusetts, for many years a writer for the New York Tribune. In Buncombe County; A Vacation in a Buggy; Tenting at Stony Beach; Dolly; Roweny in Boston; Mrs. Keats Bradford; Out of Step; The Two Salomes; Katharine

North; Mrs. Gerald; Against Human Nature; In a Dike Shanty; In the First Person; Boss and Other Dogs. *Har. Hou. S. St.*

Poole, Mrs. Hester Martha [Hunt]. *Vt.*, 1843——. A writer living at Metuchen, New Jersey, who has written much for periodicals on social and domestic topics. Fruits and How to Use Them.

Poole, Willard Henry. *Ms.*, 1864——. An educator of Fall River, Massachusetts. Elementary Course in Experimental Physics.

Poole, William Frederick. *Ms.*, 1821–1894. A bibliographer of Chicago, librarian of the Public Library there, 1874–87, and, from the latter date, of the Newberry Library, Chicago; best known as compiler (with W. I. Fletcher) of Poole's Index to Periodical Literature. Two supplementary volumes carry the work forward to January, 1892. Other works of his are, Anti-Slavery Opinions before 1800; The Battle of the Dictionaries; Websterian Orthography; Cotton Mather and Salem Witchcraft. *Clke. Hou.*

Poore, Benjamin Perley. *Ms.*, 1820–1887. A once well-known journalist of Washington. Campaign Life of Zachary Taylor; Early Life of Napoleon; Rise and Fall of Louis Philippe; Agricultural History of Essex County, Massachusetts; Life of Burnside; Political Register and Congressional Directory, 1776–1878; Perley's Reminiscences of Sixty Years. *Hou.*

Pope, Franklin Leonard. *Ms.*, 1840–1895. An electrical engineer of New York city. Modern Practice of the Electric Telegraph; Life and Work of Joseph Henry, *supra.*

Pope, John. *Ky.*, 1822–1892. A prominent general in the Federal army during the Civil War. The Virginia Campaign of July and August, 1862.

Pope, Mrs. Marion [Manville]. *Wis.*, 1859——. A verse-writer whose home in recent years has been in Valparaiso, Chili. Over the Divide, and Other Verses. *Lip.*

Porcher, Francis Peyre. *S. C.*, 1825–1895. A physician and botanist of Charleston. Sketch of the Medical Botany of South Carolina; Resources of the Southern Fields and Forests, are among his writings.

Porter, Benjamin Fickling. *S. C.*, 1808——. A lawyer of Alabama. Alabama Supreme Court Reports; Offices of Executors and Administrators.

Porter, Charles Talbot. *N.Y.*, 1826——. A mechanical engineer of prominence. Mechanics and Faith, a Study of the Spiritual Truths in Nature.

Porter, David. *Ms.*, 1780–1843. A once noted commodore in the United States navy. Journal of a Cruise to the Pacific Ocean in 1812–15; Constantinople and its Environs. *See Life of, by his son.*

Porter, David Dixon. *Pa.*, 1813–1891. Son of D. Porter, *supra.* An admiral of the Federal navy who commanded the fleet at the storming of Fort Fisher, and amused his latest years by the composition of sensational romances. Life of Commodore Porter, *supra;* Allan Dare and Robert le Diable; Adventures of Harry Marline; Arthur Merton, a romance; Incidents and Anecdotes of the Civil War; History of the Navy in the War of the Rebellion. *Ap.*

Porter, Ebenezer. *Ct.*, 1772–1834. A Congregational clergyman and educator, of contemporary renown as a preacher. He was professor of sacred rhetoric at Andover Theological Seminary, 1812–32, and president of that institution from 1827 till his death. Among his publications are, The Young Preacher's Manual; A Rhetorical Reader, which reached its 300th edition; Lectures on Homiletics; Lectures on Eloquence and Style. *See Memoir of, by Matthews, 1837.*

Porter, Fitz-John. *N. H.*, 1822——. A brevet brigadier-general dismissed from the service in 1863, reinstated by act of Congress, 1886. Narrative of the Services of the Fifth Army Corps in 1862 in Northern Virginia.

Porter, James. *Ms.*, 1800–1888. A once prominent Methodist clergyman of Boston. History of Methodism; The Winning Worker; Hints to Self-Educated Ministers; Compendium of Methodism, comprise a portion of his writings. *Meth.*

Porter, John Addison. *N.Y.*, 1822–1866. A professor of chemistry at Yale College, 1852–64. Principles of Chemistry; First Book of Chemistry.

Porter, John Addison. *Ct.*, 1856——. Son of J. A. Porter, *supra*. The Corporation of Yale College; Administration of the City of Washington; Sketches of Yale Life.

Porter, Linn Boyd. "Albert Ross." 184——. A novelist of Cambridge whose writings have been extremely popular, although severely criticised from a literary point of view as well as from an ethical standpoint. Among them are, Thou Shalt Not; Speaking of Ellen; A Black Adonis; Out of Wedlock. *Dil.*

Porter, Mrs. Lydia Ann [Emerson]. *Ms.*, 1816——. Cousin of R. W. Emerson, *supra*. An educator of Springfield, Vermont. Uncle Jerry's Letters to Young Mothers; The Lost Will, are among her writings.

Porter, Noah. *Ct.*, 1811–1892. A Congregational clergyman of Connecticut, president of Yale College, 1871–85, and a metaphysician of distinction. The Human Intellect; Books and Reading; Elements of Intellectual Science; Elements of Moral Science; The American Colleges and the American Public; Science and Sentiment; Bishop Berkeley; Fifteen Years in Yale College Chapel, a volume of sermons; The Science of Nature and the Science of Man. *Scr.*

Porter, Rose. *N. Y.*, *c.* 1845——. An author of New Haven who has written and compiled a large number of religious books. Among her original works are, Summer Driftwood for the Winter Fire; A Modern St. Christopher; Our Saints, a Family Story; My Son's Wife. *Lo. Ran. Rev.*

Porter, Thomas Conrad. *Pa.*, 1822——. A German Reformed clergyman famous as a botanist, and professor of botany at Lafayette College, Easton, Pennsylvania, from 1866. Sketch of the Flora of Pennsylvania; Sketch of the Botany of the United States; Synopsis of the Flora of Colorado (with J. M. Coulter); The Carices of Pennsylvania; The Grasses of Pennsylvania.

Posse, Nils. Baron Posse. *Sn.*, 1862–1895. A Boston instructor in gymnastics. Special Kinesiology of Educational Gymnastics; Medical Gymnastics; Scientific Aspect of Swedish Gymnastics. *Le.*

Post, Truman Marcellus. *Vt.*, 1810–1866. A Congregational clergyman and editor of St. Louis, professor of history in Washington University. The Skeptical Era in Modern History. *See Life of, by T. H. Post.*

Post, Waldron Kintzing. *N. Y.*, 1868——. A lawyer of New York city. Harvard Stories. *Put.*

Potter, Alonzo. *N. Y.*, 1800–1865. The third Protestant Episcopal bishop of Pennsylvania and an active promoter of educational movements. The Principles of Science Applied to Domestic and Mechanic Arts; Religious Philosophy; Political Economy; co-author with G. B. Emerson, *supra*, of The School and the Schoolmaster. *See Memoirs of, 1870.*

Potter, Burton Willis. *N. Y.*, 1843——. A lawyer of Worcester, Massachusetts. The Road and Roadside, a legal treatise. *Lit.*

Potter, Eliphalet Nott. *N. Y.*, 1836——. Son of A. Potter, *supra*. An Episcopal clergyman and educator, president of Hobart College, Geneva, New York, 1884–96. Parochial Sermons; Christian Evidences.

Potter, Henry Codman. *N. Y.*, 1835——. Son of A. Potter, *supra*. The sixth Protestant Episcopal bishop of New York, and prominent among Broad Church thinkers. Sermons of the City; The Gates of the East; a Winter in Egypt and Syria; Sisterhoods and Deaconesses; Waymarks. *Dut.*

Potter, Platt. *N. Y.*, 1800–1891. A jurist of Schenectady. Potter's Dwarris; Treatise on Corporations; Equity Jurisprudence.

Potter, William James. *Ms.*, 1830–1894. A Unitarian clergyman of New Bedford for many years, prominent as a radical thinker. Twenty-Five Sermons of Twenty-Five Years; Lectures and Sermons. *El.*

Potts, James Henry. *Ont.*, 1848——. A Methodist clergyman, editor of The Michigan Christian Advocate from 1877. Methodism in the Field;

Golden Dawn; Spiritual Life; Our Thorns and Crowns; Faith Made Easy.

Potts, Stacey Gardner. *Pa.*, 1799–1865. A jurist of Trenton, New Jersey. Village Tales; Precedents and Notes of Practice in the New Jersey Chancery Court.

Powell, Edward Payson. *N. Y.*, 1833——. A clergyman who has held pastorates in Congregational and Unitarian churches successively, and has long been resident in Clinton, New York. Our Heredity from God; Liberty and Life. *Ap.*

Powell, John Wesley. *N. Y.*, 1834——. An eminent geologist, director of the United States Geological Survey, 1879–94. Exploration of the Uinta Mountains; The Arid Regions of the United States; Introduction to the Study of the Indian Languages; Studies in Sociology; Canyons of the Colorado. *Am. Fl.*

Powell, Thomas. *E.*, 1809–1887. An English writer who came to America in 1849, and was for many years connected with the Frank Leslie publications. He wrote a number of plays, among which are, True at Last; The Shepherd's Well. Other works of his are, Florentine Tales; Tales from Boccaccio; Living Authors of England; Living Authors of America.

Powers, Edward. *N. Y.*, 1830——. Brother of H. N. Powers, *infra.* A civil engineer who published a work entitled War and the Weather, or the Artificial Production of Rain.

Powers, Horatio Nelson. *N. Y.*, 1826–1890. An Episcopal clergyman of Chicago, Bridgeport, and, in his latest years, of Piermont, New York, who was favourably known as a poet. His writings include, Early and Late; Poems; Ten Years of Song; Lyrics of the Hudson; Through the Year, a volume of religious essays. *Lo. Rob.*

Poyas, Catherine Gendron. *S. C.*, 1813–1882. A verse-writer of Charleston. Huguenot Daughters, and Other Verses; A Year of Grief.

Pratt, Daniel Johnson. *N. Y.*, 1827–1884. Annals of Public Education in the State of New York, 1626–1746.

Pratt, Mrs. Ella [Farman]. *N. Y.*, 18——. A popular writer for young people, long the editor of The Wide Awake, and more recently of Our Little Men and Women. Among her writings are, Good-for-Nothing Polly; A Girl's Money; A Little Woman; A White Hand; Happy Children. *Cr. Lo.*

Pratt, Jacob Loring. 1835–1891. A clergyman of Maine. Evening Rest; Branches of Palm; Broken Fetters; The Mask Lifted; Bonnie Aerie; Mecca; The Crown of Silver. *Lo.*

Pratt, Orson. *N. Y.*, 1811–1881. A Mormon apostle and educator, professor of mathematics in Deseret University. Divine Authenticity of the Book of Mormon; Cubic and Bi-Quadratic Equations; The Great First Cause; The Absurdities of Immaterialism.

Pratt, Parley Parker. *N. Y.*, 1807–1857. Brother of O. Pratt, *supra.* A Mormon apostle and missionary. Voice of Warning and Instruction to All People; History of the Persecutions of Missouri; Key to the Science of Theology.

Pratt, Samuel Wheeler. *N. Y.*, 1838——. A Presbyterian clergyman at Monroe, Michigan, from 1883. A Summer at Peace Cottage, or Talks About Home Life; The Gospel of the Holy Spirit; Life of St. Paul. *Ran.*

Pray, Isaac Clark. *Ms.*, 1813–1869. A journalist, playwright, and theatrical manager of New York city. Prose and Verse; The Book of the Drama; Memoirs of James Gordon Bennett, are among his miscellaneous works. Virginius; Hermit of Malta; Giulietta Gordoni, and the first and last acts of The Corsican Brothers, are a portion of his dramatic writings.

Pray, Lewis Glover. *Ms.*, 1793–1882. A Boston philanthropist who published Child's First Book of Thought; History of Sunday-Schools; The Sylphid's School, and Other Pieces in Verse.

Preble, George Henry. *Me.*, 1816–1885. A rear-admiral in the United States navy. History of the American Flag; Chronological History of Steam Navigation; The Preble Family in America.

Preble, Henry. *Me.*, 1853——. An educator who was professor of Latin at Harvard University. He has edited a revised edition of Andrews and Stoddard's Latin Grammar, and several volumes of Latin classics, and has published (with C. Parker) a Handbook of Latin Writing; and Latin Lessons (with L. C. Hull). *Gi. Hou.*

Prentice, George. *Ms.*, 1834–18—. A Methodist clergyman, professor of modern languages at Wesleyan University. Life of Bishop Gilbert Haven, *supra;* Rome and Italy at the Opening of the Œcumenical Council, from the French of Pressensé; Life of Wilbur Fisk, *supra. Hou.*

Prentice, George Denison. *Ct.*, 1802–1870. A once famous Kentucky journalist who was editor of The Louisville Journal, 1831–70, and widely known for his witticisms. Life of Henry Clay; Prenticeana. *See Poems, with Memoir of, by J. J. Piatt; Lippincott's Magazine, November, 1869; Harper's Magazine, January, 1875. Clke.*

Prentiss, Charles. *Ms.*, 1774–1820. A journalist of Washington. Fugitive Essays in Prose and Verse; Poems; History of the United States; Trial of Calvin and Hopkins; Lives of Robert Treat Paine and General William Eaton.

Prentiss, Mrs. Elizabeth [Payson]. *Me.*, 1818–1878. Wife of G. L. Prentiss, *infra.* A popular writer of religious fiction whose Stepping Heavenward has been widely read. Among her many other works are, Pemaquid; The Home at Graylock; Aunt Jane's Hero; The Flower of the Family; Little Susy Series; Fred, Maria, and Me. *See Life by her husband. Ran. Scr.*

Prentiss, George Lewis. *Me.*, 1816——. A Presbyterian clergyman of New York city, professor of pastoral theology in Union Seminary from 1873. Memoir of Sargent Prentiss; Life of Elizabeth Prentiss, *supra;* Our National Bane; The Problem of the Veto Power; The Argument between Union Seminary and the General Assembly; Fifty Years of Union Seminary. *Ran.*

Prescott, Albert Benjamin. *N. Y.*, 1832——. A chemist who has been dean of the school of pharmacy at Michigan University from 1876. Outlines of Proximate Organic Analysis; Chemical Examination of Alcoholic Liquors; Organic Analysis; Qualitative Analysis (with S. Douglas).

Prescott, George Benjamin. *N. H.*, 1830–1894. A prominent electrician of New York city. History of the Electric Telegraph; Dynamo Electricity; Invention of Bell's Telephone, are his principal writings.

Prescott, Mary Newmarch. *Me.*, 1849–1888. Sister of Mrs. H. Spofford, *infra.* A popular magazine-writer of Newburyport who published Matt's Follies, a juvenile tale.

Prescott, William Hickling. *Ms.*, 1796–1859. A celebrated historian of Boston. While a student at Harvard College, he lost the use of one eye and not long afterwards the free use of the other, and, until in later life his eyesight improved, he was obliged to depend upon the reading of others in his historical researches. In 1837 his History of the Reign of Ferdinand and Isabella appeared and brought him instant fame. It was followed by The Conquest of Mexico; The Conquest of Peru; an edition of Robertson's Charles V., with Prescott's own work on the cloister life of that monarch; History of Philip II.; Biographical and Critical Miscellanies. *See Life by Ticknor, infra; Allibone's Dictionary; Appletons' American Biography. Lip.*

Preston, Harriet Waters. *Ms.*, c. 1843——. A high authority upon Provençal literature and a writer of literary criticism and historical studies who has lived much in Europe. Her writings include, Aspendale; Love in the Nineteenth Century; Troubadours and Trouvères; A Year in Eden; Is That All? a novel; The Georgics of Vergil in English Verse; and a translation from the Provençal of Frédéric Mistral's Mirèio.

Preston, Mrs. Margaret [Junkin]. *Va.*, c. 1825–1897. A poet and prose-writer of Lexington, Virginia, and later of Baltimore. Old Song and New; Beechenbrook, a Rhyme of the War; Colonial Ballads, Sonnets, and Other Verse; For Love's Sake; The Young Ruler's Question; Silverwood, a novel; A Handful of Monographs. *Hou.*

Preston, Thomas Scott. *Ct.*, 1824–1891. A Roman Catholic clergyman, but prior to 1849 in orders in the Episcopal Church. From 1881 he was a domestic prelate of the papal household with the title of Monsignore. Protestantism and the Bible; Reason and Revelation; Christ and the Church; The Ark of the Covenant; Sermons for the Seasons; Life of St. Mary Magdalene; Life of St. Vincent de Paul; Christian Unity; Purgatorian Manual.

Price, Bruce. *N. Y.*, 1845——. An architect of New York city. A Large Country House.

Price, Eli Kirk. *Pa.*, 1797-1884. A Philadelphia lawyer of eminence. Law of Limitations and Liens against Real Estate. *See Memoir of, by Rothrock, 1880.*

Price, Ira Maurice. *O.*, 1856——. An educator of Chicago, professor of Semitic languages in the University of Chicago from 1892. Syllabus of Old Testament History. *Rev.*

Price, Thomas Randolph. *Va.*, 1839——. A professor of English literature at Columbia College from 1882. The Teaching of the Mother Tongue; Shakespeare's Verse Construction.

Priest, Josiah. *N. Y.*, *c.* 1790–*c.* 1850. A harness-maker of New York State, some of whose books were very popular. Wonders of Nature; View of the Millennium; Stories of the Revolution; American Antiquities; Slavery in the Light of History and Scripture.

Prime, Benjamin Young. *L. I.*, 1733-1791. A physician of Huntington, Long Island, who wrote patriotic verses during the Revolutionary period. The Patriot Muse, published in 1764, includes his earlier poems. Columbia's Glory, or British Pride Humbled, is a long poem printed in 1791.

Prime, Edward Dorr Griffin. *N. Y.*, 1814-1891. Son of N. S. Prime, *infra.* A Presbyterian clergyman who was one of the editors of The New York Observer, to which he contributed the Letters of Eusebius. Around the World; Forty Years in the Turkish Empire, or Memoirs of Reverend William Goodell.

Prime, Nathaniel Scudder. *L. I.*, 1785-1856. Son of B. Y. Prime, *supra.* A Presbyterian clergyman of Newburgh, New York. Familiar Illustration of Christian Baptism; History of Long Island.

Prime, Samuel Irenæus. *N. Y.*, 1812-1885. Son of N. S. Prime, *supra.* A Presbyterian clergyman, editor of The New York Observer for forty-five years. Among his many works are, Fifteen Years of Prayer; Irenæus Letters; The Old White Meeting-House; Life in New York; Annals of the English Bible; Songs of the Soul; Life of S. B. F. Morse, *supra;* Prayer and its Answer; Walking with God; Travels in Europe and the East; The Bible in the Levant; The Alhambra and the Kremlin; Under the Trees. *See Autobiography, 1886. Ap. Har. Ran. Scr.*

Prime, William Cowper. *N. Y.*, 1825——. Son of N. S. Prime, *supra.* A lawyer and journalist, professor of the history of art at Princeton College from 1884. Boat Life in Egypt; Tent Life in the Holy Land; Pottery and Porcelain; The Owl Creek Letters; Coins, Medals, and Seals; I Go A-Fishing; Holy Cross; Along New England Roads; Among the Northern Hills. *Har. Ran.*

Prince, Mrs. Helen Choate [Pratt]. *Ms.*, 1857——. A granddaughter of R. Choate, *supra.* A novelist now living in France. The Story of Christine Rochefort; A Transatlantic Chatelaine. *Hou.*

Prince, Le Baron Bradford. *L. I.*, 1840——. Son of W. R. Prince, *infra.* A jurist of New Mexico. Agricultural History of Queen's County, Long Island; E Pluribus Unum, or American Nationality; General Laws of New Mexico; History of New Mexico; The American Church and its Name.

Prince, Thomas. *Ms.*, 1687-1758. A Congregational minister, pastor of the Old South Church in Boston, 1718-58, and one of the most fair-minded, accurate historical writers that America has had. His library now forms a separate collection in the Boston Public Library. Earthquakes of New England (1755); Chronological History of New England. *See Tyler's American Literature; Allibone's Dictionary.*

Prince, William. *L. I.*, 1766-1842. A horticulturist of Flushing, Long Island, whose Treatise on Horticulture

(1826) was the first comprehensive work on the subject published in the United States.

Prince, William Robert. *L. I.*, 1795–1869. Son of W. Prince, *supra.* A horticulturist of Flushing. History of the Vine (with W. Prince); Pomological Manual; Manual of Roses.

Proctor, Edna Dean. *N. H.*, 1838–——. A littérateur formerly of Brooklyn, New York, now (1897) of South Framingham, Massachusetts. Poems; A Russian Journey; The Song of the Ancient People.

Proctor, Lucien Brock. *N. H.*, 1826–——. A legal writer of Albany. The Bench and Bar of the State of New York; Lives of the State Chancellors; Life of Thomas Emmet; Lawyer and Client; Bench and Bar of King's County; Legal History of Albany and Schenectady Counties.

Proudfit, Alexander Moncrief. *Pa.*, 1770–1843. An Associate Reformed Presbyterian clergyman. Discourses on the Parables; Theological Works (four volumes, 1815). *See Life of, by Forsyth.*

Proudfit, David Law. "Peleg Arkwright." *N. Y.*, 1842–1897. A Federal officer during the Civil War, and subsequently a resident of New York city. Love Among the Gamins, and Other Poems; Mask and Domino (verse). *Co.*

Proudfit, John Williams. *N. Y.*, 1803–1870. Son of A. M. Proudfit, *supra.* A Dutch Reformed clergyman, professor of Greek in Rutgers College, 1840–64. Man's Two-Fold Life.

Prudden, Theophile Mitchell. *Ct.*, 1849——. A New York physician, professor of pathology in the College of Physicians and Surgeons. Manual of Normal Histology (with Delafield); Dust and its Dangers; Water and Ice; Handbook of Pathological Anatomy; Story of the Bacteria. *Put.*

Pugh [pew], **Mrs. Eliza Lofton** [**Phillips**]. "Arria." *La.*, 1841——. A novelist of Assumption Parish, Louisiana. Not a Hero; In a Crucible.

Pulte, Joseph Hippolyt. *G.*, 1811–1884. A physician of Cleveland. The Homœopathic Domestic Physician; The Science of Medicine; The Woman's Medical Guide.

Pumpelly [pum-pĕl'ly], **Mrs. Mary Hollenback** [**Welles**]. *Pa.*, 1803–1879. A verse-writer whose religious historical Poems were collected in a volume in 1852.

Pumpelly, Raphael. *N. Y.*, 1837–——. Son of Mrs. Pumpelly, *supra.* A geologist of note, professor of mining engineering at Harvard University from 1866. Geological Researches in China; Aross America and Asia; Notes of a Five-Years' Journey Around the World. *Ho.*

Punchard, George. *Ms.*, 1806–1881. A Boston journalist, for many years editor of The Traveller, but who, prior to 1845, was a Congregational clergyman in New Hampshire. History of Congregationalism from A. D. 250; View of Congregationalism. *C. P. S.*

Purinton, Daniel Boardman. *Pa.*, 1850——. A Baptist clergyman and educator of Ohio, president of Denison University from 1889. Christian Theism; The Battle of the Frogs, a poem. *Put.*

Purple, Samuel Smith. *N. Y.*, 1822–——. A physician of New York city. The Corpus Luteum; Menstruation; Contributions to the Practice of Midwifery; Observations on Wounds of the Heart.

Purves, George Tybout. *Pa.*, 1852–——. A Presbyterian clergyman, professor of New Testament literature at Princeton College from 1892. The testimony of Justin Martyr to Early Christianity. *Ran.*

Putnam, Albigence Waldo. *O.*, 1799–1869. A lawyer of Nashville; History of Middle Tennessee; Life and Times of General James Robertson; Life of General John Sevier.

Putnam, Eleanor. *See Bates, Mrs. H.*

Putnam, George Haven. *E.*, 1844–——. Son of G. P. Putnam, *infra.* A prominent publisher of New York city. Authors and Publishers; International Copyright; Authors and their Public in Ancient Times. *Put.*

Putnam, George Palmer. *Me.*, 1814–1872. A well-known publisher of New York city, the founder of the present publishing house of G. P. Putnam's Sons. The Tourist in Europe; American Facts; The World's Progress. *See Allibone's Dictionary. Put.*

Putnam, Mrs. Katharine Hunt [Palmer]. *Ms.*, 1792–1869. A Boston writer. Scripture Text Book; The Old Testament Unveiled.

Putnam, James Osborne. *N. Y.*, 1818——. A Buffalo lawyer who was minister to Belgium in 1880. Addresses, Speeches, and Miscellanies.

Putnam, Mrs. Mary [Lowell]. *Ms.*, 1810——. Sister of J. R. Lowell, *supra.* A life-long resident of Boston. Fifteen Days; History of the Court of Hungary; Records of an Obscure Man; Tragedy of Errors; Tragedy of Success.

Putnam, Ruth. 18——. Daughter of G. P. Putnam, *supra.* Life of William the Silent. *Put.*

Putnam, Mrs. Sarah A. —— Brock. *Va.*, c. 1845——. A writer of New York city. Richmond During the War; The Southern Amaranth; Kenneth, My King; Myra, a novel.

Pyle, Howard. *Del.*, 1853——. Artist and littérateur of Wilmington, Delaware. The Merrie Adventures of Robin Hood; Within the Capes: a novel; Otto of the Silver Hand; Twilight Land; The Garden Behind the Moon; Pepper and Salt, or Seasoning for Young Folk; A Modern Aladdin; The Rose of Paradise; Men of Iron, a romance of chivalry; Jack Ballister's Fortunes. *Cent. Har. Scr.*

Pynchon, Thomas Ruggles. *Ct.*, 1823——. Descendant of W. Pynchon, *infra.* An Episcopal clergyman and educator, president of Trinity College, 1874–83, and professor of chemistry there. Bishop Butler: a Religious Philosopher for All Time; Introduction to Chemical Physics. *Ap.*

Pynchon, William. *E.*, 1590–1662. A noted colonist of New England who founded the town of Springfield, Massachusetts, in 1636. In 1652 he returned to England. The Meritorious Price of Our Redemption, first published in 1650, excited a storm of controversy, and was publicly burned on Boston Common as an heretical book. It was reprinted in 1655 as The Meritorious Price of Man's Redemption, or Christ's Satisfaction discussed and explained, with a rejoinder to Rev. John Norton's Answer; The Jewes Synagogue; How the First Sabbath was Ordained; The Covenant of Nature made with Adam.

Q

Quackenbos, George Payn. *N. Y.*, 1826–1881. An educator of New York city. School History of the United States; Natural Philosophy; a series of English grammars; An Advanced Course of Rhetoric.

Quackenbos, John Duncan. *N. Y.*, 1848——. Son of G. P. Quackenbos, *supra.* An adjunct professor of English literature at Columbia College from 1884. Illustrated History of the World; History of the English Language; History of Ancient Literature; Practical Rhetoric. *Har.*

Qualtrough, Edward F——. *N. Y.*, 1850——. A United States naval officer who has published The Sailor's Handy Book and Yachtsman's Manual; The Boat Sailor's Manual. *Scr.*

Quiet, Charles. *See Noyes, C. H.*

Quinby, George Washington. *Me.*, 1810–1884. A Universalist clergyman in Maine and Ohio. The Salvation of Christ; Brief Exposition of Universalism; Marriage and Its Duties; The Gallows, the Prison, and the Poor House; Heaven Our Home.

Quincy, Edmund. *Ms.*, 1703–1788. A Boston merchant who wrote a Treatise on Hemp Husbandry. One of his daughters married John Hancock.

Quincy, Edmund. *Ms.*, 1808–1877. Son of J. Quincy, 2d, *infra.* A Boston writer whose literary fame was hardly proportioned to his deserts. Wensley, and Other Stories; The Haunted Adjutant, and Other Stories; Life of President Josiah Quincy. *Hou. Lit.*

Quincy, Josiah. *Ms.*, 1744–1775. Nephew of E. Quincy, 1st. A famous Boston lawyer and patriot, very prominent at the opening of the Revolutionary period. Observations on the Boston Port Bill. *See Life of, by his son.*

Quincy, Josiah. *Ms.*, 1772–1864. Son of J. Quincy, *supra.* An eminent Massachusetts statesman, mayor of Boston, 1823–29; president of Harvard University, 1829–45; representative in Congress, 1805–13. History of Harvard University; Speeches and Orations in Congress; History of Boston; Life of Josiah Quincy, Jr. *See Life by E. Quincy; Duyckinck's American Literature; Lowell, My Study Windows. Lit.*

Quincy, Josiah. *Ms.*, 1802–1882. Son of J. Quincy, 2d, *supra*. A citizen of Boston, and mayor of that city, 1845–1849. Figures of the Past. *Rob.*

Quincy, Josiah Phillips. *Ms.*, 1829——. Son of J. Quincy, 3d, *supra*. A littérateur of Boston. Charicles, a drama; Lyteria, a drama; The Peckster Professorship, a Story; The Protection of Majorities, and Other Papers. *Hou. Rob.*

Quincy, Samuel Miller. *Ms.*, 1833–1887. Son of J. Quincy, 3d. A Boston lawyer who served in the Federal army during the Civil War. The Man Who was Not a Colonel; A Prisoner's Diary.

Quint, Alonzo Hall. *N. H.*, 1828–1896. A prominent Congregational clergyman of Boston. The Potomac and the Rapidan, or Army Notes; Records of the Second Massachusetts Infantry, 1861–65.

Quitman, Frederick Henry. *Wa.*, 1760–1832. A Lutheran clergyman of Rhinebeck, New York. Treatise on Magic; Sermons on the Reformation, are his more important writings.

R

Raff, George Wertz. *O.*, 1825–1888. A savings bank president of Canton, Ohio. Guide to Executors and Administrators in Ohio; Manual of Pensions; The Law Relating to Roads in Ohio; War Claimant's Guide.

Rafinesque, Constantine Smaltz. *Ty.*, 1784–1842. An eccentric naturalist and botanist of French parentage who, after years of travel, settled in Philadelphia. The value of his work is impaired as much by his inaccuracy as by his very eccentric methods. Among his many works are, Medical Flora of the United States; A Life of Travel and Researches; Annals of Kentucky; Recent and Fossil Conchology (edited by Binney and Tryon, 1864). *See Silliman's Journal, 1841; Life by R. E. Call. Mor.*

Ragozin, Madame Zénaïde Alexeïevna. *R., c.* 1835——. A Russian historical writer, naturalized in the United States in 1874. The Story of Chaldea; The Story of Assyria; The Story of Media and Babylon; The Story of Vedic India. *Put.*

Raguet [ra-gā'], **Condy.** *Pa.*, 1784–1842. A merchant and lawyer of Philadelphia. The Principles of Free Trade; Currency and Banking; An Inquiry into the Present State of the Circulating Medium of the United States (1815).

Rains, George Washington. *N. C.*, 1817——. A Confederate army officer, professor of chemistry at the University of Georgia from 1867. Steam Portable Engines; Rudimentary Course of Analytical and Applied Chemistry; Chemical Qualitative Analysis.

Rainsford, William Stephen. *I.*, 1850——. A prominent Episcopal clergyman of New York city, rector of St. George's Church from 1883, and an active worker in philanthropic and other reforms. Sermons Preached in St. George's; The Church's Opportunity in the City of To-Day. *Do.*

Ralph, Julian. *N. Y.*, 1853——. A popular journalist and littérateur. On Canada's Frontier; Dixie; Our Great West; Chicago and the World's Fair; People We Pass; Alone in China, and Other Stories. *Har.*

Ralston, Samuel. I., 1756–1851. A Presbyterian clergyman in what is now Monongahela City, Pennsylvania, from 1796 till his death. On Baptism; The Last Plagues; The Currycomb, are among his writings.

Ralston, Thomas Neely. *Ky.*, 1806——. A Methodist clergyman and religious editor of Kentucky. Elements of Divinity; Evidences of Christianity; Ecce Unitas; Bible Truths.

Ramsay, David. *Pa.*, 1749–1815. A physician of Charleston, eminent among early American historians. History of the American Revolution; History of the United States; Life of Washington; History of South Carolina, include his chief works. *See Tuckerman's Sketch of American Literature; Allibone's Dictionary.*

Ramsay, Mrs. Vienna G—— [Morrell]. *Me.*, 1817——. Facts on Missions; Evenings With the Children; A Legend of the White Hills, and other Poems. *Lo.*

Rand, Asa. *N. H.*, 1783–1871. A Congregational clergyman in Maine and New York prominent as an opponent of slavery. Teachers' Manual in English Grammar; The Slave-Catcher Caught in the Meshes of Eternal Law.

Rand, Benjamin. *N. S.*, 1856——. An instructor in philosophy at Harvard University. Economic History Since 1763; A Bibliography of Economics; and also bibliographies of æsthetics, ethics, psychology, metaphysics, logic, history of philosophy, philosophy of religion.

Rand, Benjamin Howard. *Ms.*, 1792–1862. A Philadelphia teacher of penmanship who published The American Penman and similar works.

Rand, Benjamin Howard. *Pa.*, 1827–1883. Son of B. H. Rand, *supra.* A physician of Philadelphia. Outlines of Medical Chemistry; Elements of Medical Chemistry. *Lip.*

Rand, Edward Augustus. *N. H.*, 1837——. An Episcopal clergyman, rector at Watertown, Massachusetts, from 1883. Christmas Jack; Behind Manhattan Gables; School and Camp Series; Sailor Boy Bob; Pushing Ahead; Fighting the Sea Series, are among his many books for juvenile readers. *Lo. Meth. Wh.*

Rand, Edward Sprague. *Ms.*, 1834–1897. Formerly a floriculturist of Dedham, Massachusetts. Garden Flowers; Complete Manual of Orchid-Culture; Popular Flowers; Rhododendrons; Flowers for the Parlor and Garden; The Window Gardener; Life Memoirs, and Other Poems. *Hou.*

Rand, Mrs. Mary Frances [Abbott]. *Me.*, 1840——. Wife of E. A. Rand, *supra.* Holly and Mistletoe; Home-Spun Yarns for Christmas Stockings.

Randall, David Austin. *Ct.*, 1813–1884. A Baptist clergyman and religious editor of Ohio. God's Handwriting in Egypt; The Wonderful Tent, or the Mosaic Tabernacle. *Clke.*

Randall, Henry Stephens. *N. Y.*, 1811–1876. A once prominent advocate of public instruction in New York State. Sheep Husbandry; Fine Wool Sheep Husbandry; Practical Shepherd; Life of Thomas Jefferson. *Lip.*

Randall, James Ryder. *Md.*, 1839——. A journalist of Augusta, Georgia, and elsewhere in the South, who has written a number of spirited lyrics, the best known of which is the famous song, Maryland, My Maryland.

Randall, Samuel Sidwell. *N. Y.*, 1809–1881. Cousin of H. S. Randall, *supra.* A superintendent of public schools in New York city, 1854–70. History of the State of New York; Mental and Moral Culture; Principles of Popular Education; Incitements to the Study of Geology, include his more important works. *Har.*

Randolph, Anson Davies Fitz. *N. J.*, 1820–1896. A publisher and religious verse-writer of New York city. Hopefully Waiting; Verses; At the Beautiful Gate; The Palace of the King; Unto the Desired Haven. *Ran.*

Randolph, Sarah Nicholas. *Va.*, 1839——. A great-granddaughter of Thomas Jefferson. An educator of Baltimore. The Domestic Life of Thomas Jefferson; The Lord Will Provide; The Life of Stonewall Jackson. *Har. Lip. Ran.*

Ranger, Robert. *See Freeman, J. M.*

Rankin, Jeremiah Eames. *N. H.*, 1828——. A Presbyterian clergyman, president of Howard University. Auld Scotch Mither, and Other Poems; Subduing Kingdoms; The Hotel of God, and Other Sermons; Atheism of the Heart; Christ His Own Interpreter; Ingleside Rhaims.

Rankin, John. *Tn.*, 1793–1886. A Presbyterian clergyman of Ripley, Ohio, famous as an abolitionist, and many times mobbed for his anti-slavery zeal. Letters on American Slavery; The Covenant of Grace. *See Ritchie's Life of, entitled The Soldier, the Battle, and the Victory.*

Rankin, John Chambers. *N. C.*, 1816——. A Presbyterian clergyman of Baskingridge, New Jersey, from 1851. The Coming of the Lord.

Ranney, Ambrose Loomis. 184——. A physician, professor of nervous diseases in the University of the City of New York. A Practical Treatise on Surgical Diagnosis; Applied Anatomy of the Nervous System; Practical Medical Anatomy; Lectures on Nervous Diseases, include his principal writings. *Ap.*

Rapelje, Stewart. *N. Y.*, 1842–1896. A legal writer of New York city. Digest of Decisions of New York Courts to 1881; Digest of Federal Decisions and Statutes from the Earliest Period to 1880; Treatise on the Law of Witnesses; Dictionary of American and English Decisions.

Raphall, Morris Jacob. *Sn.*, 1798–1868. A Jewish clergyman once prominent in New York city. Post-Biblical History of the Jews; Literature of the Jews in Spain; Social Condition of the Jews; Festivals of the Lord; The Path to Immortality. *Ap.*

Rarey, John S——. *O.*, 1828–1866. A famous horse-tamer who wrote a Treatise on Horse-Taming that was very extensively circulated.

Rau, Charles. *Bm.*, 1826–1887. An archæologist of distinction of Belgian birth who settled in the United States in 1848, and was curator of antiquities in the United States National Museum, 1875–87. Early Man in Europe; Prehistoric Fishing. *Har.*

Rauch, Friedrich Augustus. *G.*, 1806–1841. A psychologist of Mercersburg, Pennsylvania, prominent among thinkers of the German Reformed faith. Psychology: a View of the Human Soul; The Inner Life of the Christian.

Raum, Green Berry. *Il.*, 1829——. A commissioner of internal revenue, 1870–83; later United States commissioner of pensions. The Existing Conflict between Republican Government and Southern Oligarchy (1884).

Ravenel, Henry William. *S. C.*, 1814–1887. A botanist of Aiken, South Carolina, distinguished for his knowledge of fungi. Fungi Caroliniani Exsiccati; Fungi Americani Exsiccati (with Cooke).

Rawle, Francis. *E.*, *c.* 1660–1727. A Quaker colonist of Pennsylvania whose Ways and Means for the Inhabitants of Delaware to become Rich is said to have been the first book printed by Franklin.

Rawle, William. *Pa.*, 1759–1836. Great-grandson of F. Rawle, *supra.* A distinguished lawyer of Philadelphia. View of the Constitution of the United States; The Study of the Law. *See Memoir of, by Wharton, 1840; Allibone's Dictionary.*

Rawle, William Brooke. *Pa.*, 1843——. Grand-nephew of W. Rawle, *supra.* A lawyer of Philadelphia who has published The Right Flank at Gettysburg; With Gregg in the Gettysburg Campaign.

Rawle, William Henry. *Pa.*, 1823–1889. Grandson of W. Rawle, *supra.* A prominent lawyer of Philadelphia. Law of Covenants for Title; Some Contrasts in the Growth of Pennsylvania in English Law; Equity in Pennsylvania. *Lit.*

Rawson, Albert Leighton. *Vt.*, 1829——. A traveller of note who has published Histories of All Religions; Antiquities of the Orient; The Unseen World, and a number of dictionaries and vocabularies of Oriental tongues.

Ray, Anna Chapin. *Ms.*, 1865——. A writer of West Haven, Connecticut, whose tales for juvenile reading have been popular. Cadets of Fleming Hall; Half a Dozen Boys; Half a Dozen Girls; In Blue Creek Cañon; Dick; Margaret Davis Tutor. *Cr.*

Ray, Isaac. *Ms.*, 1807–1881. A physician of Philadelphia. Conversations on Animal Economy; Education in Relation to the Health of the Brain; Mental Hygiene; Medical Jurisprudence of Insanity.

Ray, Joseph. *Va.*, 1807–1855. A mathematician and educator of Cincinnati, who published an Eclectic Series of Arithmetics long popular in the Western States.

Raymond, George Lansing. *Il.*, 1839——. A professor of oratory at Princeton College from 1881. His writings in verse include, Colony Ballads; A Life in Song; Ballads of the Revolution, and Other Poems; Sketches in Song; Pictures in Verse. Other works of his are, The Orator's Manual; Modern Fishers of Men, a novel; Poetry as a Representative Art; The Genesis of Art Form; Art in Theory;

Painting, Sculpture, and Architecture as Representative Arts; Rhythm and Harmony in Poetry and Music; Ideals Made Real. *Put.*

Raymond, Henry Jarvis. *N. Y.*, 1820–1869. A journalist who founded and edited The New York Times. Life of Lincoln; Political Lessons of the Revolution; History of the Administration of Lincoln; Letters to Mr. Yancey. *See Maverick's Raymond and the New York Press.*

Raymond, Miner. *N. Y.*, 1811–1897. A Methodist clergyman of Illinois, theological professor in Garrett Biblical Institute at Evanston, Illinois, from 1864. Systematic Theology. *Meth.*

Raymond, Rossiter Worthington. *O.*, 1840——. A mining engineer of Brooklyn, editor of The Engineering and Mining Journal from 1868. Among his technical and other writings are included, Mines and Mining of the Rocky Mountains; Mines, Mills, and Furnaces of the Pacific Slope; Silver and Gold; Brave Hearts, a novel; The Man in the Moon, and Other People; The Book of Job; Essays and a Metrical Paraphrase; The Merry-Go-Round; Two Ghosts, and Other Tales. *Lo.*

Rea, Mrs. Julie [de Marguerittes] [Foster]. *E.*, 1814–1866. An opera singer and dramatic critic of Philadelphia. The Ins and Outs of Paris; Italy and the War of 1859; Parisian Pickings.

Read, Hollis. *Vt.*, 1802–1887. A Presbyterian foreign missionary who after 1835 was settled over various New Jersey parishes. Journal in India; The Hand of God in History, a very popular book at one time; The Palace of the Great King; India and its People; The Coming Crisis of the World; The Negro Problem Solved; The Devil in History.

Read, Jane Maria. *Ms.*, 1853——. A verse-writer of Colebrook Springs, Massachusetts, who has published, Between the Centuries, and Other Poems.

Read, John Meredith. *Pa.*, 1837–1896. A lawyer of Albany who was minister to Greece 1873–79, and subsequently filled other important diplomatic positions. An Historical Inquiry Concerning Hendrick Hudson.

Read, Opie. *Tn.*, 1852——. A journalist now living in Chicago who edited The Arkansaw Traveller for some years, and whose studies of Arkansas life have been widely read. My Young Master; An Arkansaw Planter; Len Gansett; Up Terrapin River; A Kentucky Colonel; On the Suwannee River; Miss Polly Lopp, and Other Stories; The Captain's Romance; The Jucklins, a novel.

Read, Thomas Buchanan. *Pa.*, 1822–1872. A poet and artist of Philadelphia whose later years were spent in Florence and Rome. As a poet he is best known by the famous Sheridan's Ride; Drifting; and The Closing Scene, and it is by these poems that he will continue to be remembered. Poems; Lays and Ballads; The Pilgrims of the Great St. Bernard, a prose romance; The New Pastoral; The House by the Sea; The Wagoner of the Alleghanies, in which occurs the fine lyric beginning, "The maid who binds her warrior's sash;" Sylvia; A Voyage to Iceland; A Summer Story; Sheridan's Ride, and Other Poems. His complete poems were issued in 1882. *See Allibone's Dictionary. Lip.*

Realf [rĕlf], **Richard.** *E.*, 1834–1878. A journalist and verse-writer of Pittsburg who was a Federal officer during the Civil War. Guesses at the Beautiful. *See Lippincott's Magazine, February, 1879.*

Reavis [rĕv'is], **Logan Uriah.** *Il.*, 1831–1889. A St. Louis journalist, who published St. Louis the Future Great City of the World; Life of Horace Greeley; Thoughts for the Young Men and Women of America; Life of General Harney; Railway and River System.

Redden, Laura. *See Searing, Mrs.*

Redfield, Amasa Angell. *N. Y.*, 1837——. A lawyer of New York city. Handbook of United States Tax Laws; Law and Practice of Surrogates' Courts; Reports of Surrogates' Courts of New York State, 1864–82; The Law of Negligence (with Shearman).

Redfield, Isaac Fletcher. *Vt.*, 1804–1876. A lawyer who was chief justice of Vermont, 1852–60, and a resident of Boston after the latter date. The Law of Railways; The Law of Wills; Law of Carriers and Bailments; Leading American Railway Cases; Civil Pleading (with Herrick). *Lit.*

Redfield, William Charles. *Ct.*, 1789–1857. A once noted meteorologist. On Whirlwind Storms, and many monographs upon meteorology. *See Biography of, by D. Olmsted.*

Redpath, James. *E.*, 1833–1891. A New York journalist for many years on the staff of The Tribune, and prominent as an abolitionist. The Roving Editor; Handbook of Kansas Territory; Public Life of Captain John Brown; Echoes of Harper's Ferry; Guide to Hayti; Talks About Ireland.

Redway, Jacques Wardlaw. *Tn.*, 1849——. A geographer and educator of California. Complete Geography; Manual of Physical Geography; Manual of Geography and Travel.

Reed, Edwin. *Me.*, 1835——. A Shakespearean scholar who has published Bacon *vs.* Shakspere, a history of the controversy, with arguments pro and con. *Kt.*

Reed, Henry. *Pa.*, 1808–1854. An educator of Philadelphia, professor of English literature in the University of Pennsylvania. Lectures on English History; Lectures on English Literature; Lectures on the British Poets. *See Memoir, by W. B. Reed, infra.*

Reed, Henry. *Pa.*, 1846——. Son of H. Reed, *supra.* A Philadelphia jurist who has published The Law of the Statute of Frauds.

Reed, Hugh. *Ind.*, 1850——. A military educator of Virginia. Signal Tactics; Cadet Regulations; Military Science and Tactics; Broom Tactics.

Reed, James. *Ms.*, 1834——. Son of S. Reed, *infra.* A Swedenborgian clergyman of Boston from 1858. Men and Women; Religion and Life; Swedenborg and the New Church. *Hou.*

Reed, John. *Pa.*, 1786–1850. A Pennsylvania jurist, professor of law in Dickinson College, Carlisle, Pennsylvania, 1834–50, and author of The Pennsylvania Blackstone.

Reed, Sampson. *Ms.*, 1800–1880. A Swedenborgian writer of Boston, editor of The New Church Magazine for Children. Observations on the Growth of the Mind. *Hou.*

Reed, William Bradford. *Pa.*, 1806–1876. Brother of H. Reed, 1st, *supra.* A lawyer of Philadelphia, minister to China, 1857–58. Life and Correspondence of Joseph Reed; Memoir of Henry Reed, *supra.*

Rees, John Krom. *N.Y.*, 1851——. An astronomer, professor at Columbia College, and director of the Observatory from 1881. Report on the Solar Eclipse, 1878; International Time System; Observations of the Transit of Venus, 1882.

Reese, David Meredith. *Pa.*, 1800–1861. An eminent physician of New York city, superintendent of the city public schools at one period. Strictures on Health; Review of the Anti-Slavery Society's First Annual Report; Quakerism *versus* Calvinism; Phrenology Known by its Fruits; Medical Lexicon of Modern Terminology; Humbugs of New York.

Reese, John James. *Pa.*, 1818–1892. A Philadelphia physician, professor of jurisprudence in the University of Pennsylvania. American Medical Formulary; Analysis of Physiology; Manual of Toxicology; Text-Book of Medical Jurisprudence.

Reese, Lizette Woodworth. *Md.*, 1856——. A verse-writer and educator of Baltimore. A Branch of May; A Handful of Lavender; A Quiet Road. *Hou.*

Reeve, James Knapp. *N. Y.*, 1856——. A novelist of Franklin, Ohio. Vawder's Understudy; The Three Richard Whalens. *Sto.*

Reeve, Tapping. *L. I.*, 1744–1823. An eminent jurist of Litchfield, Connecticut. Law of Baron and Femme, of Parent and Child, of Guardian and Ward, of Servant and Master; Treatise on the Law of Descents in the Several United States.

Reeves, Marian Colhoun Legaré. *S. C.*, *c.* 1854——. A novelist of Washington. Ingemisco; Randolph Honor; Sea Drift; A Little Maid of Arcadie; Wearithorne; and with Emily Read, Old Martin Boscawen's Jest; Pilot Fortune. *Hou.*

Reichel, William Cornelius. *N. C.*, 1824–1876. A Moravian clergyman and educator of Bethlehem, Pennsylvania, among whose writings are Moravianism in New York and Connecticut; Memorials of the Moravian Church; A Red Rose from the Olden Time.

Reichert, Edward Tyson. *Pa.*, 1855——. A Philadelphia physician and educator, professor of physiology in the University of Pennsylvania from 1886. A Text-Book of Physiology.

Reid, Christian. *See Tiernan, Mrs. Frances.*

Reid, David Boswell. *S.*, 1805–1863. A chemist who came to America in 1856, and was director of the medical inspection of the United States Sanitary Commission. Introduction to the Study of Chemistry; Rudiments of Chemistry of Daily Life; Ventilation for American Dwellings, are among his writings.

Reid, John Morrison. *N. Y.*, 1820——. A Methodist clergyman and editor of religious journals who secured the library of Von Ranke for Syracuse University. Missions of the Methodist Church; Doomed Religions (edited). *Meth.*

Reid, Samuel Chester. *N. Y.*, 1818——. A lawyer of New Orleans. The United States Bankrupt Law of 1841; The Battle of Chickamauga.

Reid, Whitelaw. *O.*, 1837——. A journalist of prominence in New York city and editor of The Tribune from 1872. After the War, a Southern Tour; Ohio in the War; Schools of Journalism; Newspaper Tendencies. *See Hart's American Literature. Clke.*

Reid, William James. *N. Y.*, 1834——. A United Presbyterian clergyman, pastor at Pittsburg from 1880. Lectures on the Revelation; United Presbyterianism.

Reily, William McClellan. *Pa.*, 1837——. A German Reformed clergyman and educator of Allentown, Pennsylvania, president of the Female College there from 1888. The Artist and his Mission.

Reimensnyder, Junius Benjamin. *Va.*, 1841——. A Lutheran clergyman of New York city from 1880. Heavenward; Doom Eternal; Lutheran Literature: its Distinctive Traits; Work and Personality of Luther; Six Days of Creation; Lutheran Manual. *Fu.*

Remington, Frederic. *N. Y.*, 1861——. A popular artist and illustrator, whose work in the main reflects the life of the far West. Pony Tracks. *Har.*

Remington, Joseph Price. *Pa.*, 1847——. A professor of pharmacy in the Philadelphia College of Pharmacy from 1874. The Practice of Pharmacy. *Lip.*

Remington, Stephen. *N. Y.*, 1803–1869. A Baptist minister, but prior to 1845 a preacher of the Methodist faith. Reasons for Becoming a Baptist; A Defence of Restricted Communion.

Remsen, Ira. *N. Y.*, 1846——. An eminent chemist, professor of chemistry at Johns Hopkins University from 1876. Chemical Experiments (with W. Randall). *Ho.*

Reno, Conrad. *Al.*, 1859——. A lawyer of Boston. Employers' Liability Act. *Har.*

Renwick, James. *N. Y.*, 1792–1863. A once prominent scientist of New York city, professor of natural and experimental philosophy and chemistry at Columbia College from 1820 to 1853. Lives of Rittenhouse, Fulton, Count Rumford, in Sparks's American Biography; Outlines of Natural Philosophy; Treatise on the Steam Engine; Elements of Mechanics; Lives of Jay, Hamilton, De Witt Clinton, include the greater number of his works. *Har.*

Repplier, Agnes. *Pa.*, 1859——. A popular essayist of Philadelphia. Books and Men; Points of View; In the Dozy Hours, and Other Papers; Essays in Idleness; Essays in Miniature; Varia. *Hou.*

Requier, Augustus Julian. *S. C.*, 1825–1887. A lawyer of Mobile prior to the Civil War, and subsequently of New York city. The Old Sanctuary, a romance; Poems; and the dramas, Marco Bozzaris; The Spanish Exile.

Revere, Joseph Warren. *Ms.*, 1812–1880. A grandson of Paul Revere, and an officer in the Federal army during the Civil War. Keel and Saddle: Retrospect of Forty Years' Military Service (1872).

Rexdale, Robert (*pseud.*). *Me.*, 1859——. A journalist and verse-writer of

Portland, Maine. Drifting Songs and Sketches; Saved by the Sword, a novel; The Cuban Liberated.

Rexford, Eben Eugene. *N. Y.*, 1848——. A popular verse and song writer of Shiocton, Wisconsin, whose poem Silver Threads Among the Gold has been set to music and widely sung. Brother and Lover; Grandmother's Garden; John Fielding and his Enemy.

Reynolds, Elmer Robert. *N. Y.*, 1846——. An ethnologist in the United States civil service from 1877. A Scientific Visit to the Caverns of Luray; Shell Mounds, etc., of the Choptank Indians; Aboriginal Soapstone Quarries in the District of Columbia, are among his professional monographs.

Reynolds, John. *Pa.*, 1789–1865. An Illinois lawyer and journalist, governor of Illinois, 1832–34. Pioneer History of Illinois; Glance at the Crystal Palace; My Life and Times.

Reynolds, William Morton. *Pa.*, 1812–1876. An Episcopal clergyman, but prior to 1864 a Lutheran clergyman. Discourse on the Swedish Churches. He translated, from the Swedish of Israel Acrelius, A History of New Sweden, with introduction and notes.

Rhees, William John. *Pa.*, 1830–——. The chief clerk of the Smithsonian Institution from 1852, who has published, among other works, The Smithsonian Institution; James Smithson and His Bequest.

Rhodes, Albert. *Pa.*, 1840——. A writer who was successively United States consul at Jerusalem, Rotterdam, Rouen, and Elberstadt, and since 1885 has been a resident of Paris. Jerusalem as It Is; The French at Home; Monsieur at Home.

Rhodes, James Ford. *O.*, 1848–——. An historian, of Boston. History of the United States from the Compromise of 1850. *Har.*

Rhodes, Mosheim. *Pa.*, 1837——. A Lutheran clergyman of St. Louis from 1874. Life Thoughts for Young Men; Life Thoughts for Young Women; Recognition in Heaven; Vital Questions; The Throne of Grace; Expository Lectures on Philippians.

Rice, David Hall. *Ms.*, 1841——. A lawyer of Boston, living in Brookline, Massachusetts. Protective Philosophy; Digest of Decisions of Commissioner of Patents, 1869–80 (with C. Lepine).

Rice, Edwin Wilbur. *N. Y.*, 1831–——. A Congregational clergyman connected with the Sunday-School Union from 1871. People's Lesson Book in Matthew; Stories of Great Painters; Historical Sketch of the United States; People's Commentary on the Acts.

Rice, George Edward. *Ms.*, 1822–1861. A verse-writer of Boston. Ephemeral; Nugamenta; A New Play in an Old Garb, a fanciful adaptation of Hamlet.

Rice, Harvey. *Ms.*, 1800–1891. A prominent lawyer of Cleveland. Mount Vernon, and Other Poems; Select Poems; Nature and Culture; Pioneers of the Western Reserve; Sketches of Western Life; The Founder of the City of Cleveland. *Le.*

Rice, Isaac Leopold. *Bo.*, 1850——. A lawyer of New York city who has written What Is Music?

Rice, Nathan Lewis. *Ky.*, 1807–1877. A Presbyterian clergyman of note who held pastorates in St. Louis, Cincinnati, and New York city, and was an active controversialist. Romanism the Enemy of Free Institutions; The Signs of the Times; Baptism; The Pulpit; Discourses.

Rich, Mrs. Helen [Hinsdale]. *N. Y.*, 1827——. A verse-writer of Chicago. A Dream of the Adirondacks, and Other Poems; Madame de Staël. *S.*

Richards, Mrs. Cornelia Holroyd [Bradley]. *N. Y.*, 1822——. Wife of W. C. Richards, *infra*, and sister of Mrs. Alice Haven, *supra*. At Home and Abroad, or How to Behave; Pleasure and Profit, or Lessons on the Lord's Prayer; Hester and I; Memoir of Mrs. Haven.

Richards, Mrs. Ellen Henrietta [Swallow]. *Ms.*, 1842——. An instructor in sanitary chemistry in the Massachusetts Institute of Technology, wife of Professor Richards of the same institution. Chemistry of Cookery and Cleaning; Food Materials and their Adulterations; First Lessons in Minerals. *Est.*

Richards, Mrs. Laura Elizabeth [Howe]. *Ms.*, 1850——. Daughter of Mrs. J. G. Howe, *supra*. A writer of juvenile books, whose home is in Gardiner, Maine. The Joyous Story of Toto; Toto's Merry Winter; In My Nursery; Five Mice; Captain January; Jim of Hellas; Queen Hildegarde, are among her books. *Est. Rob.*

Richards, Mrs. Maria [Tolman]. *Ms.*, 1821——. An educator and lecturer of Providence. Life in Judea; Life in Israel.

Richards, William Carey. *E.*, 1818–1892. A Baptist minister of Chicago, widely known as a lecturer upon physical science. Baptist Banquets; The Lord is My Shepherd; The Mountain Anthem; Our Father in Heaven, a series of sonnets; Science in Song. *Le.*

Richardson, Mrs. Abby [Sage]. 1835——. Wife of A. D. Richardson, *infra*. An educator and lecturer upon literature. Familiar Talks on English Literature; Stories from Old English Poetry; History of Our Country; Abelard and Heloise, a Mediæval Romance. She has edited Songs from the Old Dramatists, and other works. *Hou. Mg.*

Richardson, Albert Deane. *Ms.*, 1833–1869. A journalist of New York city, famous as the war correspondent of The Tribune during the Civil War. Beyond the Mississippi; Personal History of Ulysses Grant; The Field, the Dungeon, and the Escape; Garnered Sheaves. *See Memoir.*

Richardson, Charles Francis. *Me.*, 1851——. A professor of English literature at Dartmouth College from 1882. Primer of American Literature; The Cross, a collection of verse; American Literature, 1607–1885; The Choice of Books. Co-editor with H. A. Clark of The College Book. *Hou. Lip. Put.*

Richardson, Hobart Wood. 1831–1889. A journalist of Portland, Maine. Paper Money; The National Banks; The Standard Dollar. *Ap. Har.*

Richardson, Nathaniel Smith. *Ct.*, 1810–1883. An Episcopal clergyman who was editor of The American Church Review. Reasons Why I Am a Churchman; Reasons Why I Am Not a Papist; Evidences of Natural and Revealed Religion, are among his writings.

Richardson, William Adams. *Ms.*, 1821–1896. A Massachusetts jurist, chief justice of the United States Court of Claims from 1885, and secretary of the United States Treasury, 1873–74. The Banking Laws of Massachusetts; History of the Court of Claims; Practical Information concerning the United States Public Debt; National Banking Laws.

Richardson, William Merchant. *N. H.*, 1774–1838. Chief justice of New Hampshire, 1816–38. The New Hampshire Justice; The Town Officer.

Richmond, Mrs. Euphemia Johnson [Guernsey]. *N. Y.*, 1825——. A writer of Upton, New York. Hope Raymond; Two Paths; The McAllisters, a temperance tale; The Jewelled Serpent; The Fatal Dower; Anna Maynard, the King's Daughter, form a portion of her writings. *Meth.*

Ricord [rē-cor′], **Mrs. Elizabeth [Stryker].** *L. I.*, 1788–1865. Wife of J. B. Ricord, *infra*. An educator of Geneva, New York, and after 1845 a resident of Newark, New Jersey. Philosophy of the Mind; Zamba, or the Insurrection, a Dramatic Poem.

Ricord, Frederick William. *W. I.*, 1819——. Son of J. B. Ricord, *infra*. A lawyer and educator of Newark, New Jersey. History of Rome; The Youth's Grammar; English Songs from Foreign Tongues; The Self-Tormentor, from the Latin of Terentius, with More English Songs.

Ricord, Jean Baptiste. *F.*, 1777–1837. A French physician and naturalist who settled in New York city. Improved French Grammar; Recherches et expériences sur les poissons d'Amérique.

Riddle, Albert Gallatin. *Ms.*, 1816——. A lawyer of Washington who has written a number of romances of early life in Ohio. The House of Ross; Bart Ridgeley; Alice Brand; The Tory's Daughter; Mark Loan; The Portrait; Personal Recollections of War Times; Students and Lawyers; Life of Benjamin Wade; Life of Garfield; Speeches and Arguments, include his principal works. *Put.*

Rideing, William Henry. *E.*, 1853——. A Boston littérateur on the editorial staff of The Youth's Companion. Pacific Railway Illustrated; A Saddle in the Wild West; Boys in the Mountains and on the Plains; Boys Coastwise; Stray Moments with Thackeray; Alpenstock; Young Folks' History of London; The Boyhood of Living Authors; Thackeray's London; A Little Upstart, a novel; In the Land of Lorna Doone; The Captured Cunarder. *Ap. Cop. Cr. Est.*

Ridgaway, Henry Bascom. *Md.*, 1830–1895. A Methodist clergyman and educator of Illinois, president of Garrett Biblical Institute at Evanston, Illinois, from 1882. Life of Alfred Cookman; The Lord's Land, or Travels in Sinai and Palestine; Lives of Bishops Janes, Waugh, Simpson. *Meth.*

Ridgway, Robert. *O.*, 1850——. An eminent ornithologist of Washington, curator of the department of birds in the National Museum from 1879. The Birds of Colorado; Ornithology of the Fortieth Parallel; Manual of North American Birds; History of North American Birds (with Baird and Brewer, *supra*). *Lip.*

Ridpath, John Clark. *Il.*, 1840——. A professor of belles-lettres at De Pauw University. Popular and Academic Histories of the United States; History of Texas; Life of Garfield; History of the World; Christopher Columbus; Columbia, a Quadricentennial Story; Great Races of Mankind; Epic of Life, a poem. *Meth.*

Riggs, Elias. *N. J.*, 1810——. A Congregational missionary in Constantinople, famous as a linguist, among whose writings are, Manual of the Chaldee Language; Grammar of the Modern Armenian Language; Notes of Difficult Passages of the New Testament; A Harmony of the Gospels, in Bulgarian. *Ran.*

Riggs, James Stevenson. *N. Y.*, 1853——. A Presbyterian clergyman, professor in Auburn Theological Seminary from 1881, who has published The Bible in Art.

Riggs, Mrs. Kate Douglas [Smith] [Wiggin]. *Pa.*, 18——. A popular writer of New York city. Timothy's Quest; Polly Oliver's Problem; The Birds' Christmas Carol; The Story of Patsy; A Summer in a Cañon; Children's Rights; A Cathedral Courtship, and Penelope's English Experiences; The Village Watch-Tower; Marm Lisa; Nine Love Songs and a Carol. She has also written in collaboration with her sister, Nora Archibald Smith, The Story Hour; and The Republic of Childhood, a work on the kindergarten. *Hou.*

Riggs, Stephen Return. *O.*, 1812–1883. A missionary to the Indians in Minnesota and Dakota. Forty Years Among the Sioux; The Bible in Dakota (with Williamson); and many translations and other writings relating to the Dakota Indians.

Riis, Jacob August. *Dk.*, 1849——. A New York writer on social problems. How the Other Half Lives; The Children of the Poor; Nibsy's Christmas. *Scr.*

Riley, Charles Valentine. *E.*, 1843–1895. A distinguished entomologist of Washington, at one period State entomologist of Missouri, and from 1881 till his death in charge of the entomological division of the United States Department of Agriculture. The Locust Plague in the United States; Potato Pests; Noxious, Beneficial, and Other Insects of Missouri.

Riley, Henry Hiram. *Ms.*, 1813–1888. A lawyer of Constantine, Michigan, once known as a humourous writer. Paddleford and Its People; The Paddleford Papers, or Humors of the West. *Le.*

Riley, James. *Ct.*, 1777–1840. A mariner who was enslaved by the Arabs of Africa in 1815 and ransomed by Mr. Willshire, the British consul, at Mogadore. In 1821 he settled in Ohio and founded the town of Willshire, named in honour of the consul. From his journals was prepared, in 1816, the Authentic Narrative of the Loss of the American Brig Commerce on the West Coast of Africa, with a Description of Timbuctoo.

Riley, James. *I.*, 1848——. A verse-writer of Boston whose unpretentious Poems, published in 1886, reached a third edition in 1888.

Riley, James Whitcomb. *Ind.*, 1852——. A very popular poet of Indianapolis whose dialect poems of Hoosier life have been greatly praised. His earliest work appeared over the signature "Benjamin F. Johnson of Boone." His dialect and other poems display much real feeling and originality. The Old Swimmin' Hole and 'Leven More Poems; The Boss Girl, and Other Sketches; Afterwhiles; Old-Fashioned Roses; Pipes o' Pan at Zekesbury; Rhymes of Childhood; Flying Islands of the Night; Neighborly Poems; An Old Sweetheart of Mine; Green Fields and Running Brooks; Poems Here at Home; Armazindy; A Child World. *Bo. Cent. Lgs.*

Riley, John Campbell. *D. C.*, 1828–1879. A Washington physician who wrote a Compend of Materia Medica and Therapeutics. *Lip.*

Rimmer, Caroline Hunt. *Ms.*, 1851–——. Daughter of W. Rimmer, *infra*. Animal Drawing. *Hou.*

Rimmer, William. *E.*, 1816–1879. A Boston painter, sculptor, and teacher of art anatomy, who also practiced medicine, but gave up his profession to devote himself to art. Art Anatomy; Elements of Design. *Hou.*

Riordan, Roger. *I.*, 1848——. A New York city journalist. A Score of Etchings; Sunrise Stories, a Glance at the Literature of Japan. *Scr.*

Ripley, George. *Ms.*, 1802–1880. A Unitarian clergyman who was pastor in Boston, 1826–41, and then for several years the chief promoter of the famous Brook Farm experiment. In 1849 he became literary editor of The New York Tribune, and continued in that position until his death. With C. A. Dana, *supra*, he edited the American Cyclopædia, 1857–63, and also the revised edition of the same, 1873–76. His literary criticisms exerted a wide and beneficial influence. Discourses on the Philosophy of Religion; Letters to Andrews Norton, *supra*, on the Latest Form of Infidelity. *See Modern Review, July, 1883; Appletons' American Biography; Life by O. B. Frothingham, supra.*

Ripley, Henry Jones. *Ms.*, 1798–1875. A Baptist clergyman who held a pastorate in Georgia, 1819–26, and from 1826 to 1860 was a professor in the Theological Seminary at Newton, Massachusetts. Notes on the Gospels, Acts, Hebrews; Christian Baptism; Church Polity; The Exclusiveness of the Baptists.

Ripley, Roswell Sabine. *O.*, 1823–1887. A Confederate army officer of prominence who wrote a History of the Mexican War.

Ritchie, Mrs. Anna Cora [Ogden] [Mowatt]. *F.*, 1822–1870. A once popular actress who retired from the stage in 1854, and for the last ten years of her life lived in Florence and London. Her writings include several novels, The Fortune Hunter; The Mute Singer; Fairy Fingers; Evelyn; The Twin Roses; The Clergyman's Wife; two successful plays, Fashion and Armand; Mimic Life, or Before and Behind the Curtain; Autobiography of an Actress, the last named an exceedingly popular book.

Ritter, Abraham. *Pa.*, 1792–1860. A merchant of Philadelphia. History of the Moravian Church in Philadelphia; Philadelphia and her Merchants.

Ritter, Mrs. Fanny Raymond. 18——. Wife of F. L. Ritter, *infra*. Woman as a Musician; Some Famous Songs, an Art Historical Sketch; Songs and Ballads.

Ritter, Frederick Louis. *F.*, 1834–1891. A musician of Alsace who came to the United States in 1856, and, becoming professor of music at Vassar College in 1867, retained that position until his death. Music in England; Music in America; History of Music in the Form of Lectures; Manual of Musical History. *Dit. Scr.*

Rivers, Pearl. *See Nicholson, Mrs.*

Rivers, Richard Henderson. *Tn.*, 1814–1894. A Methodist clergyman and educator of Alabama, for many years pastor in Louisville, 1883–87. Mental Philosophy; Moral Philosophy; Our Young People; Life of Robert Paine; Arrows From Two Quivers.

Rivers, William James. *S. C.*, 1822–——. An educator of South Carolina and Maryland, professor in Washington College in the latter State from 1873. History of South Carolina to the Close of the Proprietary Government in 1719; Catechism of the Constitution of South Carolina.

Rives [reevz], **Amélie.** Granddaughter of W. C. Rives, *infra. See Troubetzkoy.*

Rives, Mrs. Judith Page [Walker]. *Va.*, 1802–1882. Wife of W. C. Rives, *infra.* Souvenirs of a Residence in Europe; Home and the World; The Canary Bird; Epitome of the Bible.

Rives, William Cabell. *Va.*, 1793–1868. A prominent Virginia statesman, twice minister to France, and during the Civil War a member of the Confederate Congress. Lives of John Hampden, James Madison; Ethics of Christianity.

Robbins, Chandler. *Ms.*, 1810–1882. A Unitarian clergyman of Boston, pastor of the Second Church, 1833–74. Liturgy for the Use of a Christian Church; History of the Second or Old North Church; Memoir of Benjamin Curtis, *supra;* Portrait of a Christian Drawn from Life. *See Frothingham's Boston Unitarianism. A. U. A.*

Robbins, Eliza. *Ms.*, 1786–1853. An educator in Boston for many years. Elements of Mythology; Grecian History; Tales from American History, are among her published works.

Robbins, Mrs. Mary Caroline [Pike]. *Me.*, 1842——. Daughter of J. S. Pike, *supra.* The wife of a physician of Hingham, Massachusetts. A writer for the magazines on art, landscape gardening, and kindred topics. The Rescue of An Old Place. *Hou.*

Robbins, Royal. *Ct.*, 1787–1861. A Congregational clergyman, pastor at Kensington, Connecticut, 1816–61. Outlines of Ancient History; The World Displayed.

Roberts, Mrs. Anna Smith [Rickey]. *Pa.*, 1827–1858. Wife of S. W. Roberts, *infra.* A verse-writer who published Forest Flowers of the West.

Roberts, Benjamin Titus. *N. Y.*, 1823–1893. A Free Methodist clergyman of North Chili, New York, founder of Chesbrough Academy there in 1865, and president of that institution, 1869–1893. Fishers of Men; Why Another Sect; First Lessons on Money; Ordaining Women.

Roberts, Charles George Douglas. *N. B.*, 1860——. A popular Canadian poet and littérateur, formerly a professor of literature in King's College, Windsor, Nova Scotia, and in recent years a resident of New York city. His work in verse includes, Orion, and Other Poems; In Divers Tones; The Book of the Native. His prose comprises, Earth's Enigmas, a collection of short stories; The Forge in the Forest, an Acadian Romance; A History of Canada; Around the Camp Fire; Canadian Guide Book; Reube Dare's Shad Boat; Raid from Beausejour, and How the Carter Boys Lifted the Mortgage. *Ap. Cr. Lam. Lo. Meth.*

Roberts, Edmund Quincy. *N. H.*, 1784–1836. A diplomatist who did much to promote trade in Farther India. Embassy to the Eastern Courts (1857).

Roberts, Ellis Henry. *N. Y.*, 1827——. Formerly a journalist of Utica; now (1897) president of a national bank in New York city. He was a member of Congress from 1871 to 1875. Government Revenue; New York: the Planting and Growth of the Empire State. *Hou.*

Roberts, John Bingham. *Pa.*, 1852——. A Philadelphia physician. Paracentesis of the Pericardium; Compendium of Anatomy.

Roberts, Oran Milo. *S. C.*, 1815——. A Texas jurist who was governor of Texas, 1879–83, and professor of law in the University of Texas from 1883. He wrote a description of his State, entitled Governor Robinson's Texas.

Roberts, Robert Ellis. *N. Y.*, 1809–1888. A prominent merchant and citizen of Detroit. Sketches of Detroit; The City of the Straits.

Roberts, Solomon White. *Pa.*, 1811–1882. A distinguished civil engineer of Pennsylvania. The Destiny of Pittsburg.

Roberts, William. *W.*, 1809–1887. A Welsh Presbyterian clergyman of Utica from 1875. He published, in Welsh, The Abrahamic Covenant; The Election of Grace.

Roberts, William Henry. *W.*, 1844——. A Presbyterian clergyman, professor of theology in Lane Seminary, 1886–93, and stated clerk of the General Assembly from 1884. History of the Presbyterian Church in the United

States; Ecclesiastical Status of Theological Seminaries; The Presbyterian System.

Robertson, John. *Va.*, 1787–1873. A Virginia jurist. Riego, or the Spanish Martyr, a tragedy; Opuscula, a book of verse.

Robinson, Mrs. Annie Douglas [Green]. "Marian Douglas." *N. H.*, 1842——. A writer of Bristol, New Hampshire. Picture Poems for Young Folks; Peter and Polly, or Home Life in New England One Hundred Years Ago. *Do.*

Robinson, Charles. *Ms.*, 1818——. A noted Kansas politician, three times governor of the State as candidate of the Free State party, 1856–59. The Kansas Conflict (1892). *Har.*

Robinson, Charles Seymour. *Vt.*, 1829——. A Presbyterian clergyman of prominence in New York city, well known as an hymnologist. Besides Laudes Domini, and other hymnals, he has published Church Work, a volume of sermons; Studies on the New Testament; Studies of Neglected Texts; The Pharaohs of the Bondage and the Exodus; Simon Peter, his Life and Work; Studies in Mark's Gospel; Simon Peter's Later Life and Labors; Sermons in Songs; Sabbath Evening Sermons. *Fu.*

Robinson, Edith. *Ms.*, 1858——. A Boston novelist. A Forced Acquaintance; Penhallow Tales; A Loyal Little Maid. *Cop. Hou. Kt.*

Robinson, Edward. *Ct.*, 1794–1863. A distinguished Congregational clergyman and Biblical scholar of New York city, a professor in Union Seminary, 1837–63, and the founder of the Bibliotheca Sacra. Harmony of the Four Gospels, in Greek; Harmony of the Four Gospels, in English; Biblical Researches in Palestine; Physical Geography of the Holy Land; A Greek and English Lexicon of the New Testament. *See Life by R. D. Hitchcock; Allibone's Dictionary. Hou. Rev.*

Robinson, Ezekiel Gilman. *Ms.*, 1815–1894. A Baptist clergyman and educator, president of Brown University, 1872–89. Yale Lectures on Preaching; Principles and Practice of Morality; Christian Evidences. *Ho. Sil.*

Robinson, Fayette. *Va.*, ——1859. Mexico and her Military Chieftains; Account of the Organization of the United States Army; California and the Gold Regions (1849); Spanish Grammar; Wizard of the Wave, a romance; and a number of translations from the French.

Robinson, Frank Torrey. *Ms.*, 1845——. A journalist and art critic of Boston, and more recently one of the curators of the Metropolitan Museum of New York city. Quaint New England; Living New England Artists; History of the Fifth Massachusetts Regiment of Volunteer Militia.

Robinson, Mrs. Harriet Jane [Hanson]. *Ms.*, 1825——. Wife of W. S. Robinson, *infra*. A prominent woman-suffragist of Malden, Massachusetts. In her early life she was one of the contributors to the noted Lowell Offering. Massachusetts in the Woman Suffrage Movement; Captain Mary Miller, a drama; Early Factory Labor in New England; The New Pandora, a drama in blank verse. *Put. Rob.*

Robinson, Harry Perry. *E. I.*, 1860——. An English littérateur resident in the United States from 1883, and now (1897) living in Chicago. A brother of Philip Robinson, the English writer. Men Born Equal, a novel; monographs on railway topics. *Har.*

Robinson, Horatio Nelson. *N. Y.*, 1806–1867. A mathematician and educator of Cincinnati, Ohio, after 1854 a resident of Eldridge, New York. University Algebra; Mathematical Recreations; Treatise on Surveying and Navigation; Treatise on Astronomy; Analytical Geometry and Conic Sections, include the greater number of his writings. *Am.*

Robinson, John Hovey. *Me.*, 1825——. A physician who wrote a large number of sensational romances of slight literary merit, among which are, White Rover; Nightshade; Silver-Knife.

Robinson, Mrs. Leora [Bettison]. *Ark.*, 1840——. A writer and educator of Tallahassee. House with Spectacles; Than; Patsy.

Robinson, Mrs. Martha Harrison. *Va.*, 18——. A writer of Philadelphia who has published a number of translations from the French, and Helen Erskine, an original novel. *Lip.*

Robinson, Mrs. Mary Dommet [Nauman]. *Pa.*, 185——. A novelist of Lancaster, Pennsylvania. Twisted Threads; Sidney Elliot; The Enchanted Princess; Clyde Wardleigh's Promise; Eva's Adventures in Shadowland. *Lip.*

Robinson, Rowland Evans. *Vt.*, 1833——. A farmer of Ferrisburgh, Vermont. Danvis Folks, a novel; Vermont: a Study of Independence; Uncle 'Lisha's Shop; In New England Fields and Woods. *Hou.*

Robinson, Mrs. Sarah Tappan Doolittle [Lawrence]. *Ms.*, 1827——. Wife of C. Robinson, *supra.* A writer of Lawrence, Kansas, who published, in 1856, Kansas: its Exterior and Interior Life, a work giving valuable information concerning a critical period in the history of the State.

Robinson, Solon. *Ct.*, 1803–1880. A journalist of New York city long known as an agricultural writer for The Tribune, and after 1870 a resident of Jacksonville, Florida. Hot Corn, or Life Scenes in New York, a very popular book for a short period; Facts for Farmers, which was extensively circulated; How to Live, or Domestic Economy Illustrated; Me-won-i-toc.

Robinson, Stillman Williams. *Vt.*, 1838——. A civil engineer, professor of physics at Ohio State University from 1878. Practical Treatise on the Teeth of Wheels; Railroad Economics; Strength of Wrought Iron Bridge Materials.

Robinson, Stuart. *I.*, 1816–1881. A Presbyterian clergyman of prominence in Louisville. Discourses of Redemption; The Church of God. *Ap.*

Robinson. Mrs. Therese Albertine Luise [Von Jakob]. "Talvi." *G.*, 1797–1869. Wife of E. Robinson, *supra.* An able and learned author who wrote both in English and German, using the pseudonym Talvi in the latter case. Characteristik der Volkslieder germanischen Nationen; Die Unechtheit der Lieder Ossians; Aus der Geschichte der ersten Ansiedelungen in den Vereinigten Staaten; Die Colonisation von New England; Fifteen Years, a Picture from the Last Century; Historical View of the Language and Literature of the Slavic Nations. She also wrote a number of stories which her daughter translated from the German, including Psyche; Heloise; Life's Discipline; The Exiles.

Robinson, Tracy. *N. Y.*, 183——. An official of the Panama Railway, 1861–74, and subsequently a resident of New York city. Song of the Palm, and Other Poems.

Robinson, William Stevens. "Warrington." *Ms.*, 1818–1876. A journalist of Boston long known as the Boston correspondent of the New York Tribune and the Springfield Republican. The Salary Grab; Manual of Parliamentary Practice; Warrington's Pen Portraits; Personal and Political. *See Memoir by Mrs. Robinson. Le.*

Roche, James Jeffrey. *I.*, 1847——. A popular Boston journalist, since 1890 the editor of The Pilot. Songs and Satires; Ballads of Blue Water; Life of John Boyle O'Reilly, *supra;* The Story of the Filibusters; Her Majesty the King. *Hou. St.*

Rochester, Thomas Fortescue. *N. Y.*, 1823–1887. A once prominent physician of Buffalo. The Army Surgeon; Medical Men and Medical Matters in 1776.

Rockwell, Alphonso David. *Ct.*, 1840——. A physician of New York city. Relation of Electricity to Medicine and Surgery; Medical and Surgical Uses of Electricity (with G. M. Beard, *supra*).

Rockwell, Charles. *Ct.*, 1806–1882. A Congregational clergyman who held pastorates in the New England and other States. Sketches of Foreign Travel and Life at Sea; The Catskill Mountains and the Region Around.

Rockwell, Joel Edson. *Vt.*, 1816–1882. A Presbyterian clergyman of Stapleton, Staten Island. Sketches of the Presbyterian Church; The Young Christian Warned; Scenes and Impressions Abroad; My Sheet Anchor; Seed Thoughts.

Rockwell, John Arnold. *Ct.*, 1803–1861. A jurist of Norwich, Connecticut. Spanish and American Law in

Relation to Mines and Titles to Real Estate.

Rodenbough, Theophilus Francis. *Pa.*, 1838——. A Federal army officer, assistant inspector-general of New York State, 1880–83. From Everglade to Cañon with the Second United States Cavalry; Afghanistan and the Anglo-Russian Dispute; Uncle Sam's Medal of Honor.

Rodman, Thomas Jefferson. *Ind.*, 1815–1871. An army officer, brevetted brigadier-general in 1865. He invented the method of hollow casting. Report of Experiments on Metals for Cannon and Cannon Powder.

Rodney, Cæsar Augustus. *Del.*, 1772–1824. A noted Delaware jurist, prominent in Congress, and the first United States minister to Argentina. Reports on the Present State of the United Provinces of South America (with T. Graham) (1824).

Roe, Azel Stevens. *N. Y.*, 1798–1886. A once popular novelist who was for many years a wine merchant of New York city. True to the Last; A Long Look Ahead; Time and Tide; To Love and To Be Loved; James Montjoy; True Love Rewarded; How Could He Help It?; Looking Around; Woman Our Angel; The Cloud in the Heart.

Roe, Edward Payson. *N. Y.*, 1838–1888. A Presbyterian clergyman who retired from the ministry, and, living at Cornwall-on-the-Hudson, devoted himself to novel-writing. His stories, which are nearly all of a semi-religious character, have been extraordinarily popular, but it must be admitted that their literary merit is very slight, the style being weak and inflated and the construction poor. The best that can be said in their favour is that they are well-intentioned. Barriers Burned Away; Opening a Chestnut Burr; A Face Illumined; His Sombre Rivals; What Can She Do?; Near to Nature's Heart; From Jest to Earnest; A Knight of the Nineteenth Century; A Day of Fate; Without a Home; A Young Girl's Wooing; An Original Belle; Driven Back to Eden; Nature's Serial Story; The Earth Trembled; Miss Lou; Taken Alive, and Other Stories. He also published two horticultural books, The Home Acre; Success with Small Fruits. *Do.*

Roe, Edward Reynolds. 18——. A novelist of Chicago. Brought to Bay; The Grey and the Blue; God Reigns: Lay Sermons; From the Beaten Path; May and June.

Roebling, John Augustus. *P.*, 1800–1869. A civil engineer of note who built the suspension bridge across the Ohio between Cincinnati and Covington, and was the designer of the Brooklyn Bridge. Long and Short Span Railway Bridges.

Roebling, Washington Augustus. *P.*, 1837——. Son of J. A. Roebling, *supra*. A famous civil engineer of Brooklyn who completed the Brooklyn Bridge. He has published Military Suspension Bridges. *See Schuyler's Studies in American Architecture.*

Roemer, Jean. *E.*, 1806–1892. An educator of New York city, vice-president of the College of the City of New York from 1869. Dictionary of English-French Idioms; Polyglot Readers; Cavalry; Principles of General Grammar; Cours de lecture et de traduction; Origins of the English People and Language; Left in the Wilderness. *Ap.*

Rogé, Mrs. Charlotte Fiske [Bates]. *N. Y.*, 1838——. An educator and verse-writer of Cambridge and New York city who has written Risk, and Other Poems, and edited The Cambridge Book of Poetry and other works. *Cr. Hou.*

Rogers, Fairman. *Pa.*, 1833——. A professor of civil engineering in the University of Pennsylvania, 1855–70. The Magnetism of Iron Vessels.

Rogers, Henry Darwin. *Pa.*, 1808–1866. A noted geologist who was professor in the University of Pennsylvania, 1835–46, and held the chair of natural history in the Scottish University of Glasgow from 1857 till his death. The Geology of Pennsylvania; Geological Map of Pennsylvania. *Lip.*

Rogers, Henry Wade. *N. Y.*, 1853——. A lawyer and educator, president of Northwestern University from 1890. Illinois Citations; Expert Testimony.

Rogers, Horatio. *R. I.*, 1836——. A Providence jurist who has published The Private Libraries of Providence; Mary Dyer of Rhode Island, the Quaker Martyr; and edited Hadden's Journal and Orderly Books. *Pr.*

Rogers, James Webb. *N. C.*, 1822——. A writer who in early life was an Episcopal clergyman in Tennessee, and during the Civil War a Confederate officer. He became a Roman Catholic in 1878 and settled in Washington as a lawyer. Lafitte, or the Greek Slave; Arlington, and Other Poems; Parthenon.

Rogers, Robert Cameron. *N. Y.*, 1862——. A littérateur of Buffalo. The Wind in the Clearing, and Other Poems; Will of the Wasp, a yarn of the War of 1812; Old Dorset, a collection of short stories. *Put.*

Rogers, Robert William. *Pa.*, 1864——. A Methodist clergyman and educator, professor of Hebrew in Drew Theological Seminary, Madison, New Jersey, from 1893. Two Texts of Esarhaddon; Unpublished Inscriptions of Esarhaddon; The Inscriptions of Sennacherib.

Rogers, William Barton. *Pa.*, 1804–1882. Brother of H. D. Rogers, *supra*. An eminent scientist of Boston, the founder of the Massachusetts Institute of Technology, in 1862, and its president, 1862–70, and again, 1878–81. The Geology of the Virginias; Elements of Mechanical Philosophy; The Strength of Materials. *See The Brothers Rogers, by W. Ruschenberger, infra, 1885; Life by E. Rogers, 1896. Ap.*

Rohlfs, Mrs. Anna Katharine [Green]. *L. I.*, 1846——. A very popular novelist of Buffalo whose detective romances display much inventive skill. The Sword of Damocles; The Leavenworth Case; A Strange Disappearance; Hand and Ring; The Mill Mystery; Behind Closed Doors; Cynthia Wakeham's Money; Marked "Personal"; Miss Hurd; An Enigma; Dr. Izard; Old Stone House, and Other Stories; 7 to 12; X, Y, Z; The Doctor, His Wife, and the Clock; That Affair Next Door; Risifi's Daughter, a Drama; The Defence of the Bride, and Other Poems. *Put.*

Rolfe, John Carew. *Ms.*, 1859——. Son of W. J. Rolfe, *infra*. A professor of Latin in the University of Michigan. Heanton Timorumenos of Terence. *Gi.*

Rolfe, William James. *Ms.*, 1827——. A distinguished Shakespearean scholar and educator of Cambridge. He has published Shakespeare the Boy; two annotated editions of Shakespeare, the Friendly Edition in twenty volumes, and a School Edition in forty volumes; and a series of annotated editions of selections from Tennyson, Browning, Wordsworth, Gray, Goldsmith, Scott, and other English poets. He has also edited Craik's English of Shakespeare; and is co-author with J. H. Hanson of several classical text-books, and with J. A. Gillet of The Cambridge Physics. *Har. Hou.*

Rollins, Mrs. Alice Marland [Wellington]. *Ms.*, 1847–1897. A littérateur of New York city. My Welcome Beyond, and Other Poems; The Ring of Amethyst, and Other Poems; The Story of a Ranch; All Sorts of Children; The Three Tetons; From Palm to Glacier; Uncle Tom's Tenement, a study of New York tenement-house life. *Put.*

Rollins, Mrs. Ellen Chapman [Hobbs]. "E. H. Arr." *N. H.*, 1831–1881. A writer of Philadelphia. New England Bygones; Old-Time Child-life. *See Memoir by Gail Hamilton, 1882. Lip.*

Ronayne, Maurice. *I.*, 1828——. A Roman Catholic clergyman and educator of New York city, professor of history at St. Francis Xavier's College from 1888. Religion and Science; God Knowable and Known.

Rood, Ogden Nicholas. *Ct.*, 1831——. A physicist of note, professor of physics at Columbia College from 1863, and author of Modern Chromatics. *Ap.*

Roosa [ro'zah], **Daniel Bennett St. John.** *N. Y.*, 1838——. A prominent physician of New York city, and a professor at the University of the City of New York, 1863–82. Treatise on the Ear; A Doctor's Suggestions; On the Necessity of Wearing Glasses.

Roosevelt, Blanche. *See Machetta, Mrs.*

Roosevelt, Robert Barnwell. *N. Y.*, 1829——. A lawyer of New York city who was minister to the Netherlands, 1888–89. The Game Fish of North America; Coast and Game Birds of the Northern States; Florida and the Game Water Birds; Love and Luck; Progressive Petticoats; Five Acres Too Much, a Satire. *Har.*

Roosevelt, Theodore. *N. Y.*, 1858——. Nephew of R. B. Roosevelt, *supra*. A politician and municipal reformer. President of the board of police commissioners of New York city from 1895 to 1897, when he resigned that position to become assistant secretary of the navy. The Naval War of 1812; Hunting Adventures of a Ranchman; Ranch Life and the Hunting Trail; The Winning of the West; The Wilderness Hunter; Essays on Practical Politics; History of the City of New York; Lives of Thomas H. Benton, *supra*, and Gouverneur Morris. *Cent. Har. Lgs. Put.*

Ropes, John Codman. *R.*, 1836——. A lawyer of Boston well known as a military historian. The Army under Pope; The Campaign of Waterloo; Atlas of Waterloo; The First Napoleon; The Story of the Civil War. *Hou. Put. Scr.*

Rose, Aquila. *E.*, 1695–1723. A printer and verse writer of Philadelphia whose Poems on Several Occasions were collected after his death.

Rosengarten, Joseph George. *Pa.*, 1835——. A lawyer of Philadelphia. The German Soldier in the Wars of the United States. *Lip.*

Rosenthal, Lewis. *Md.*, 1856——. A journalist who has published America and France: the Influence of the United States on France in the Eighteenth Century. *Ho.*

Ross, Albert. *See Porter, L. B.*

Ross, Clinton. *N. Y.*, 1861——. A novelist of New York city. The Silent Workman; The Countess Bettina; The Speculator; Adventures of Three Worthies; Improbable Tales; Two Soldiers and a Politician; The Puppet; The Scarlet Coat; Battle Tales; Bobbie McDuff; The Meddling Hussy; Zuleika. *Lam. Put. St.*

Ross, Frederick Augustus. *Va.*, 1796–1883. A Presbyterian clergyman of Huntsville, Alabama. Slavery as Ordained of God.

Rosser, Leonidas. *Va.*, 1815–1892. A Methodist clergyman of Virginia. Baptism; Experimental Religion; Class Meetings; Recognition in Heaven; Open Communion; Initial Life; Reply to Howell's "Evils of Baptism."

Rotch [rōch], **Abbott Lawrence.** *Ms.*, 1861——. A meteorologist who founded the Blue Hill meteorological observatory in Milton, Massachusetts, in 1885, and who has published many valuable meteorological papers.

Rothrock, Joseph Trimble. *Pa.*, 1839——. A professor of botany in the University of Pennsylvania from 1877. Botany of the Wheeler Expedition; Vacation Cruisings; Flora of Alaska; Revision of the North American Gaurineæ, include his principal publications. *Lip.*

Round, William Marshall Fitz. *R. I.*, 1845——. A writer active in prison reforms. His books for juvenile readers include, Achsah; Child Marion Abroad; Torn and Mended; Hal; Rosecroft. *Le.*

Rouquette [roŏ-ket′], **Adrien Emmanuel.** *La.*, 1813–1887. A Roman Catholic clergyman and educator of New Orleans, known as the Abbé Rouquette. Les Savannes; Poésies américaines; Wild Flowers; Sacred Poetry; Le Thébaïde en Amérique; L'Antoniade, ou la Solitude avec Dieu; Poëmes patriotiques.

Rouquette, François Dominique. *Pa.*, 1810——. Brother of A. E. Rouquette, *supra*. A lawyer who resided in France for the greater part of his life. Les Meschacébéennes; Fleurs d'Amérique; and a work in French and English on the Choctaw Indians.

Rowe, Mrs. Harriet Gould. *Me.*, 1854——. A writer of Bangor, Maine. Re-told Tales of the Hills and Shores of Maine; Queenshithe.

Rowland, Henry Augustus. *Ct.*, 1804–1859. A Congregational clergyman of Newark, New Jersey. Common Maxims of Infidelity; The Path of Life; Light in a Dark Valley; The

Way of Peace. *See Memorial of, by Fairchild, 1860.*

Rowson, Mrs. Susanna [Haswell]. *E.*, 1762–1824. A once famous novelist whose Charlotte Temple was the most popular tale of its day. Born in England, she came to Boston as a child, but returned to England in 1784 and there married. In 1793 she came again to America, and after a short career as an actress opened a school in Boston, which was very successful. Her writings include Victoria; Mary, or the Test of Honour; The Fille de Chambre; The Inquisitor; The Trials of the Heart; Reuben and Rachel; Lucy Temple, a sequel to Charlotte Temple; Miscellaneous Poems; The Slaves of Algiers, an opera; The Volunteers, a farce; The French Patriot, a comedy. *See Memoir by E. Nason, supra, 1870.*

Royall, Mrs. Anne. *Va.*, 1769–1854. A once well-known and unpopular Washington journalist, editor of the Washington Paul Pry, whose literary style was quite devoid of merit. The Black Book; The Tennessean, a novel; Sketches of History, Life, and Manners in the United States; A Southern Tour: Letters from Alabama.

Royce, Josiah. *Cal.*, 1855——. A professor of the history of philosophy at Harvard University. The Religious Aspect of Philosophy; California: a Study of American Character; The Feud of Oakfield Creek, a novel; Primer of Logical Analysis; The Spirit of Modern Philosophy. *Hou.*

Rudder, William. *B. G.*, 1820–1880. An Episcopal clergyman of Philadelphia, rector of St. Stephen's Church. Sermons; A Rationale of the Church's Liturgic Worship. *Co. Lip.*

Rude, Mrs. Ellen [Sergeant]. *N. Y.*, 1838——. A verse-writer of Duluth who has published Magnolia Leaves (verse).

Ruffner, Henry. *Va.*, 1798–1861. A Presbyterian clergyman of Virginia, and a noted opponent of slavery. Fathers of the Desert: a History of Monachism; Future Punishment.

Ruffner, William Henry. *Va.*, 1824——. Son of W. Ruffner, *supra.* A Presbyterian clergyman of Philadelphia, and from 1870 State superintendent of public instruction in Virginia. Charity and the Clergy.

Ruggles, Henry Joseph. *N. Y.*, 181——. A lawyer of New York city. The Method of Shakespeare as an Artist; The Plays of Shakespeare founded on Literary Forms. *Hou.*

Rumford, Benjamin Thompson, Count. *Ms.*, 1753–1814. A statesman and philosopher. After serving Great Britain in the War of the Revolution, he entered the service of the Elector of Bavaria, rose to the position of minister of war, and was created Count of the Holy Roman Empire, taking his title Rumford from Rumford, now Concord, New Hampshire. Essays: Political, Economical, and Philosophical, 1798–1806. *See Cuvier's Éloge de Rumford; Sparks's American Biography; Life by G. E. Ellis, supra; Atlantic Monthly, April, 1871.*

Runcie, Mrs. Constance [Faunt Le Roy]. *Ind.*, 1836——. A writer whose home was many years at St. Joseph, Missouri. Divinely Led; Poems, Dramatic and Lyric; Woman's Work; Felix Mendelssohn; Children's Stories and Fables.

Runkle, John Daniel. *N. Y.*, 1822——. A noted mathematician, professor of mathematics in the Massachusetts Institute of Technology, 1870–78. Elements of Plane and Solid Analytic Geometry. *Gi.*

Rupp, Isaac Daniel. *Pa.*, 1803–1878. An industrious local historian of Pennsylvania, who, besides writing histories of nearly thirty counties in his State, published also Events in Indian History; History of Religious Denominations in the United States; Early History of Western Pennsylvania; Thirty Thousand Names of German Emigrants.

Ruschenberger [roo'shĕn-ber-ger], **William S. W.** *N. Y.*, 1807–1895. A noted naval surgeon and naturalist of Philadelphia. Elements of Natural History; A Voyage Around the World; Three Weeks in the Pacific; Notes and Commentaries during Voyages to Brazil and China; Lexicon of Natural History Terms; Account of the College of Physicians and Surgeons in Philadelphia, 1787–1887; The Brothers Rogers.

Rush, Benjamin. *Pa.*, 1745–1813. An eminent physician of Philadelphia who was one of the signers of the Declaration of Independence and treasurer of the United States Mint, 1799–1813. Treatise on Diseases of the Mind; Essays, Literary, Moral, and Philosophical; Sixteen Introductory Lectures. *See Thacher's Medical Biography; Allibone's Dictionary; Appletons' American Biography.*

Rush, Benjamin. *Pa.*, 1811–1877. Son of R. Rush, *infra.* A lawyer of Philadelphia. Appeal for the Union; Letters on the Rebellion, 1862.

Rush, Jacob. *Pa.*, 1746–1820. Brother of B. Rush, 1st. A Philadelphia jurist. Charges on Moral and Religious Subjects; Character of Christ; Christian Baptism.

Rush, James. *Pa.*, 1786–1869. Son of B. Rush, 1st. A distinguished Philadelphia citizen, the founder of the Ridgeway Library, to which he left one million dollars. He was a physician by profession, but lived the life of a recluse. The Philosophy of the Human Voice; Analysis of the Human Intellect; Rhymes of Contrast on Wisdom and Folly. *Lip.*

Rush, Richard. *Pa.*, 1780–1859. Son of B. Rush, 1st, *supra.* A Philadelphia statesman who was secretary of the treasury, 1825–29. Codification of the Laws of the United States (1815); Court of London (1819–25); Washington in Domestic Life; Occasional Productions. *See Allibone's Dictionary.*

Russell, Addison Peale. *O.*, 1826——. An Ohio journalist and essayist, now (1897) living in retirement in Wilmington, Ohio. Half Tints; Library Notes; Thomas Corwin, a Sketch; Characteristics; A Club of One; In a Club Corner; Sub-Cœlum. *Clke. Hou.*

Russell, Francis Thayer. *Ms.*, 1828——. Son of W. Russell, *infra.* An Episcopal clergyman and educator of Waterbury, Connecticut, rector of St. Margaret's School there, and voice instructor in the General Theological Seminary in New York city. The Use of the Voice.

Russell, Irwin. *Mi.*, 1853–1879. A Southern writer of dialect verse. Dialect Poems. *Cent.*

Russell, Israel Cook. *N. Y.*, 1852——. A professor of geology in the University of Michigan from 1892, and a geologist in the United States Geological Survey, 1880–92. Lakes of North America; Lake Lahontan; Quarternary History of Moro Valley; Glaciers of North America; Present and Extinct Lakes of Nevada; Volcanoes of North America, and many geological reports. *Am. Gi.*

Russell, William. *S.*, 1798–1873. An elocutionist of note, widely known in his day as a teacher. Orthophony, or Vocal Culture; Pulpit Elocution; Lessons in Enunciation; Grammar of Composition. *Hou.*

Russell, William Eustis. *Ms.*, 1857–1896. A popular Massachusetts statesman, mayor of his native city of Cambridge, 1884–88, and governor of Massachusetts, 1890–93. Speeches and Messages. *Lit.*

Rutherford, Mildred. *Ga.*, 1852——. An educator of Athens, Georgia. Her series of literary text-books includes, English Authors; American Authors; Classic Authors; French and German Authors.

Rutledge, Edward. *S. C.*, 1797–1832. An Episcopal clergyman who was professor of moral philosophy at the University of Pennsylvania. The Family Altar; History of the Church of England.

Ruttenber, Edward Manning. *Vt.*, 1824——. An antiquary of Newburg, New York, who has published a History of Newburg; History of Orange County; History of the Hudson River Tribes.

Ryan, Abram Joseph. "Father Ryan." *Va.*, 1839–1888. A Roman Catholic priest and verse-writer of the South whose verse has been much overpraised in some quarters. It is spirited and fluent, but has not the literary quality needful to preserve it. Poems, Patriotic, Religious, and Miscellaneous; The Conquered Banner, and Other Poems; A Crown for Our Queen.

Ryan, Father. *See Ryan, Abram.*

Ryan, Mrs. Marah Ellis [Martin]. *Pa.*, 1860——. An actress and novelist living at Fayette Springs, Pennsylvania. A Pagan of the Alleghanies;

Merze; On Love's Domains; Told in the Hills; Squaw Eloise.

Ryan, Patrick John. *I.*, 1831——. A Roman Catholic archbishop of Philadelphia. What Catholics do Not Believe; Some of the Causes of Modern Religious Scepticism.

Ryan, Stephen Vincent. *Ont.*, 1825–1896. The Roman Catholic bishop of Buffalo from 1860. The Claims of a Protestant Episcopal Bishop to Apostolical Succession and Valid Orders Disproved.

Rylance, Joseph Hine. *E.*, 1862——. An Episcopal clergyman of New York city, rector of St. Mark's in the Bowery from 1871, and prominent among Broad Churchmen. Preachers and Preaching; Essays on Miracles; Social Questions; Pulpit Talks on Topics of the Time.

S

Sabin, Elijah Robinson. *Ct.*, 1776–1818. A Methodist evangelist of New England. The Road to Happiness; Charles Observator.

Sabin, Joseph. *E.*, 1821–1881. An English publisher and bibliophile who came to America in 1848, and finally, settling in New York city, became widely known as a bookseller and collector of rare books. The Thirty-Nine Articles of the Church of England, with Scriptural Proofs; Bibliotheca Americana; Bibliography of Bibliographies.

Sabine, Lorenzo. *N. H.*, 1803–1877. Son of E. R. Sabin, *supra*, but choosing another spelling of his surname. A secret government agent in relation to the Ashburton Treaty, and secretary of the Boston Board of Trade in his later years, as well as member of Congress from Massachusetts. The American Loyalists; Life of Commodore Edward Preble, in Sparks's American Biography; Notes on Duels and Duelling; Report on the Principal Fisheries of the American Seas. *Lit.*

Sachs, Bernard. *Md.*, 1858——. A physician of New York city, well known as a neurologist. Nervous and Mental Diseases of Childhood, and many professional monographs.

Sachse, Julius Friedrich. *Pa.*, 1842——. A journalist of Philadelphia. The German Pietists of Provincial Pennsylvania; The Genesis of the Lutheran Church in Pennsylvania.

Sadlier [săd-leer′], **Anna Teresa.** *Q.*, 1850——. Daughter of Mrs. Sadlier, *infra.* Seven Years and Mair; The King's Page; Ethel Hamilton; Names that Live: a volume of biographies; Women of Catholicity; The Silent Woman of Alood; and many translations from the French, Italian, and German. *Har. Sad.*

Sadlier, Mrs. Mary Anne [Madden]. *I.*, 1820——. A prominent writer of Roman Catholic Sunday-school tales, wife of J. Sadlier, a New York publisher. Among her many writings are, Alice Riordan; Red Hand of Ulster; The Daughter of Tyrconnell; The Old House by the Boyne.

Sadtler, Samuel Philip. *Pa.*, 1847——. A chemist of Philadelphia, professor in the University of Pennsylvania from 1875. Chemical Experimentation; Handbook of Industrial Organic Chemistry; A Text-Book of Chemistry (with H. Trimble). *Lip.*

Safford, James Merrill. *O.*, 1822——. The State geologist of Tennessee from 1854, professor in Vanderbilt University from 1875. A Geological Reconnoissance of Tennessee; Geology of Tennessee.

Safford, Truman Henry. *Vt.*, 1836——. An astronomer of note, famous in childhood as a mathematician, and professor of astronomy at Williams College from 1876. Mathematical Teaching and its Modern Methods.

Safford, William Harrison. *W. Va.*, 1821——. A lawyer of Chillicothe, Ohio. Life of Blennerhasset; The Blennerhasset Papers. *Clke.*

Salisbury, Edward Elbridge. *Ms.*, 1814——. A philologist of distinction, professor of Arabic at Yale University, 1841–56. General and Biographical Monographs (1885).

Saltus, Edgar Evertson. *N. Y.*, 1858——. A novelist of New York city. Balzac: a Study; The Philosophy of Disenchantment; The Anatomy of Negation; Mr. Incoul's Misadventure; The Truth about Tristram Varick;

Eden; A Transaction in Hearts; When Dreams Come True; The Pace that Kills. *Hou.*

Saltus, Francis Saltus. *N.Y.*, 1849–1889. Brother of E. E. Saltus, *supra.* An erratic verse-writer, much of whose life was passed abroad. His verse is not without a certain luxurious power, but it is wilful in the extreme, diffuse, and unpruned. Honey and Gall; Shadows and Ideals; The Witch of Endor; The Bayadere, and Other Sonnets. *Lip. Put.*

Sampson, Ezra. *Ms.*, 1749–1823. A Congregational clergyman at Plympton, Massachusetts, 1775–95, subsequently a journalist in Hartford. Beauties of the Bible; The Historical Dictionary; The Sham Patriot Unmasked; The Brief Remarker on the Ways of Men. *See Sprague's Annals of the American Pulpit. Har.*

Sampson, John Patterson. *N. C.*, 1837——. A minister of the African Methodist church, prior to 1882 a lawyer in Washington. Common Sense Physiology; The Disappointed Bride; Temperament and Phrenology of Mixed Races; Jolly People; Illustrations in Theology.

Sampson, William. *I.*, 1764–1836. A once famous lawyer of New York city who came to America in 1798, having previously been a barrister in Dublin. Sampson Against the Philistines, or the Reform of Lawsuits; Memoir of William Sampson, are his chief works.

Samson, George Whitefield. *Ms.*, 1819–1896. A Baptist clergyman and educator of New York city, president of Rutgers Female College from 1871. A voluminous writer whose principal works comprise, Elements of Art Criticism; Physical Media in Spiritual Manifestations; The Atonement; The Divine Law as to Wines; Idols of Fashion and Culture; Tested Truths as to Relations of Capital and Labor; Outlines of the History of Ethics; Spiritualism Tested, originally issued as To Daimonion; Guide to Self-Education; The Bible Revisers' Greek Text; Guide to Bible Interpretation. *Lip.*

Samuels, Adelaide Frances. *Ms.*, 1845——. Sister of E. A. Samuels, *infra.* A writer for juveniles. Dick and Daisy Series; Dick Travers Abroad Series; Daisy Travers. *Le.*

Samuels, Edward Augustus. *Ms.*, 1836——. A Boston naturalist. Ornithology and Oölogy of New England; Among the Birds; Mammalogy of New England; The Living World (with A. Arnold).

Samuels, Samuel. *Pa.*, 1825——. A noted seaman and inventor who organized the Steam Heating Company of New York city in 1881. From Forecastle to Cabin. *Har.*

Samuels, Mrs. Susan Blagge [Caldwell]. *Ms.*, 1848——. Wife of E. A. Samuels, *supra.* A popular writer for juveniles. The Golden Rule Series. *Le.*

Sanborn, Alvan Francis. *Ms.*, 1866. ——. Moody's Lodging House, and Other Tenement Sketches; Meg McIntyre's Raffle, and Other Stories. *Cop.*

Sanborn, Edwin David. *N. H.*, 1808–1885. An educator who was professor of literature at Dartmouth College, 1863–85, and author of a History of New Hampshire.

Sanborn, Franklin Benjamin. *N. H.*, 1831——. A noted journalist and reformer living at Concord, Massachusetts, and connected with The Springfield Republican from 1868. Life of Thoreau; Life and Letters of John Brown; Life of Dr. S. E. Howe, *supra. Fu. Hou. Rob.*

Sanborn, Helen Josephine. *Me.*, 1857——. A Winter in Central America, a volume of travels. *Le.*

Sanborn, Kate. *See Sanborn, Katherine.*

Sanborn, Katherine Abbott. *N. H.*, 1839——. Daughter of E. D. Sanborn, *supra.* A popular and versatile writer of ephemeral books, who was professor of English literature at Smith College prior to 1886. Home Pictures of English Poets; Vanity and Insanity of Genius; Adopting an Abandoned Farm; Abandoning an Adopted Farm; A Truthful Woman in Southern California; My Literary Zoo, and a number of compilations. *Ap. Fu. Hou.*

Sanborn, Mrs. Mary [Farley]. 18———. A novelist of Boston. Sweet and Twenty; It Came to Pass; Paula Ferris. *Le.*

Sandeman, Robert. *S.*, 1718 or 1723–1771. The founder of the Sandemanian sect, who came to America in 1764 and gathered a church at Danbury, Connecticut, where he died. Letters on Theron and Aspasio; Thoughts on Christianity.

Sanders, Daniel Clarke. *Ms.*, 1768–1850. A Congregational clergyman and educator, president of the University of Vermont, 1800–14, subsequently pastor at Medfield, Massachusetts. A History of the Indian Wars with the First Settlers of the United States, which he published in 1812, is now a very rare book. *See Sprague's Annals of the American Pulpit.*

Sanders, Mrs. Elizabeth [Elkins]. *Ms.*, 1762–1851. A writer of Salem, Massachusetts. Conversations, principally on the Aborigines of North America; First Settlers of New England; Reviews.

Sanderson, John. *Pa.*, 1783–1844. An educator of Philadelphia, classical professor in the High School, 1836–44, and of some note in his day as a humourist. The American in Paris; The American in England; and the first two volumes of the Biography of the Signers of the Declarations of Independence. *See Hart's American Literature.*

Sanderson, John Philip. *Pa.*, 1818–1864. An officer in the Federal army. Views and Opinions of American Statesmen on Foreign Immigration; Republican Landmarks.

Sanderson, Joseph. *I.*, 1823——. A Presbyterian clergyman in New York and other localities. Jesus on the Holy Mount; Memorial Tributes; The Bow in the Cloud.

Sands, Alexander Hamilton. *Va.*, 1828–1887. A lawyer of Richmond, Virginia, who entered the Baptist ministry not long before his death. History of a Suit in Equity; Recreations of a Southern Barrister; Practical Law Forms; Sermons by a Village Pastor.

Sands, Robert Charles. *N. Y.*, 1799–1832. A journalist and verse-writer of New York city who wrote a Life of Paul Jones; The Talisman (with Bryant and Verplanck); co-author with Eastburn of the once noted poem Yamoyden. *See Life by Verplanck; Griswold's Poets and Poetry of America.*

Sanford, Henry Shelton. *Ct.*, 1823——. A diplomatist who was secretary of the United States legation at Paris, 1849–53, chargé d'affaires there till April, 1854, and minister to Belgium, 1861–69; and who founded the town of Sanford, Florida, in 1870. Penal Codes in Europe; The Avendslood Correspondence.

Sangster, Mrs. Margaret Elizabeth [Munson]. *N. Y.*, 1838——. A journalist of New York city, editor of Harper's Bazar from 1889, and a popular verse-writer whose domestic poems display sentiment of a very genuine kind. Her writings in verse comprise, On the Road Home; Easter Bells; Poems of the Household; Home Fairies and Heart Flowers. She has also written a Manual of Missions of the Reformed Church, and several books for girls, including Hours with Girls; Home and Heaven; Splendid Times; Five Happy Weeks; May Stanhope and her Friend; Miss Dewbury's School; Little Knights and Ladies. Maidie's Problem. *Har. Hou. Meth. Wh.*

Santayana, George. *Sp.*, 1863——. An instructor in philosophy at Harvard University. Sonnets and Other Poems; The Sense of Beauty: being the Outlines of Æsthetic Theory. *St.*

Sargent, Charles Sprague. *Ms.*, 1841——. Grand-nephew of L. M. Sargent, *infra*. A botanist of eminence, Arnold professor of arboriculture at Harvard University from 1870, editor of Garden and Forest from 1888. The Silva of North America; Report on the Forests of North America; The Woods of the United States; Notes on the Forest Flora of Japan. *Ap. Hou.*

Sargent, Epes. *Ms.*, 1813–1880. A once prominent Boston journalist and littérateur, who perhaps will be longest remembered by the familiar poem, Life on the Ocean Wave. His verse includes, Songs of the Sea; Poems; The Woman who Dared. In fiction he published, Wealth and Worth; What 's to be Done?; Fleetwood; Peculiar, a tale of the Great Rebellion. He wrote the dramas, Bride of Genoa; Velasco;

Change Makes Change; The Priestess. His miscellaneous writings comprise, Life of Henry Clay; American Adventures by Land and Sea; Arctic Adventures by Sea and Land; Original Dialogues; Planchette, the Despair of Science; Memoir of Franklin. He edited a popular series of school and critical editions of many English poets, and Harper's Cyclopedia of Poetry. *Co. Har. Le. Rob.*

Sargent, Fitzwilliam. *Ms.*, 1820–——. Grand-nephew of W. Sargent, 1st, and father of John Singer Sargent, the artist. A Philadelphia surgeon who went to live in Switzerland in 1854. Bandaging and Other Operations of Minor Surgery.

Sargent, Henry Winthrop. *Ms.*, 1810–1882. A noted horticulturist of Fishkill, New York. Skeleton Routes through England, etc.; Treatise on Landscape Gardening. *Ap.*

Sargent, John Osborne. *Ms.*, 1811–1891. Brother of E. Sargent, *supra*. A lawyer and journalist of New York city. He translated Grün's Last Knight; and published, also, Papers for the Times by a Berkshire Farmer; and Horatian Echoes: Translation of the Odes of Horace. *Hou.*

Sargent, Lucius Manlius. *Ms.*, 1786–1867. Brother of H. W. Sargent, *supra*, and a distant cousin of W. Sargent, 1st, *infra*. A once prominent temperance advocate of Boston. Temperance Tales, a very popular work; Dealings with the Dead; The Irrepressible Conflict; Hubert and Ellen, and Other Poems; Translations from the Minor Latin Poets. *See Reminiscences of, by Sheppard, 1889.*

Sargent, Nathan. *Vt.*, 1794–1875. A journalist and politician. Life of Henry Clay; Public Men and Events (1875).

Sargent, Winthrop. *Ms.*, 1753–1820. A patriot soldier in the Revolutionary War, governor of Northwest Territory, 1798–1800, and of Mississippi Territory, 1790 and 1801. Papers Relating to Certain American Antiquities; Boston, a poem.

Sargent, Winthrop. *Pa.*, 1825–1870. Grandson of W. Sargent, *supra*. A lawyer of New York city. Life of Major André, a work displaying much research. He also edited the History of Braddock's Expedition, from Original Papers.

Sartwell, Henry Parker. *Ms.*, 1792–1867. A botanist and physician of Penn Yan, New York, who from 1840 devoted his attention to the genus Carex. His herbarium of more than eight thousand specimens is in Hamilton College. Carices Americanæ Exsiccatæ.

Satterlee, Henry Yates. *N. Y.*, 1843——. The first Protestant Episcopal bishop of Washington, prior to 1896 a prominent clergyman of New York city. A Creedless Gospel and the Gospel Creed. *Scr.*

Saunders, Frederick. *E.*, 1807–——. The librarian of the Astor Library, New York city, 1859–96. New York in a Nut-Shell; Salad for the Solitary and Salad for the Social; Memoirs of the Great Metropolis; The Story of Some Famous Books; Story of the Discovery of the New World by Columbus (1892); Pastime Papers; Stray Leaves of Literature; Character Studies. *Ran. Wh.*

Savage, Edward Hartwell. *N. H.*, 1812–1893. A Boston policeman and justice of the peace. Boston Police Recollections; Five Thousand Boston Events, 1630–1880.

Savage, James. *Ms.*, 1784–1873. A Boston lawyer eminent as a genealogist. He is best known as the author of a Genealogical Dictionary of the First Settlers of New England, upon which twenty years of labour were expended.

Savage, John. *I.*, 1828–1888. A journalist of New York city, and subsequently of Washington. Poems; Picturesque Ireland; Lays of the Folkstead; Modern Revolutionary History of Ireland; Our Living Representative Men; Life of Andrew Johnson; Fenian Heroes and Martyrs; Sibyl, a tragedy; and several other plays.

Savage, Minot Judson. *Me.*, 1841–——. A Unitarian clergyman of prominence among radical thinkers, pastor of Unity Church, Boston, 1874–96, and, since the latter year, of the Church of the Messiah in New York city. Christianity the Science of Manhood; Beliefs About Man; Belief in God; Life Questions; Poems; The Religion of Evolution; The Religion of Morals; Talks About Jesus; The Modern Sphinx; Man, Woman, and Child; Social Problems; My Creed; Religious Reconstruction; Signs of the Times; Helps for Daily Living; Four Great Questions Concerning God; The Evolution of Christianity; Is This a Good World?; Jesus and Modern Life; A Man; Light on the Cloud; Bluffton, a novel; The Minister's Handbook. *See Men of Progress of Massachusetts. El.*

Savage, Philip Henry. *Ms.*, 1868——. Son of M. J. Savage, *supra.* A Boston littérateur. First Poems and Fragments. *Cop.*

Savage, Richard Henry. *N. Y.*, 1846——. A novelist. My Official Wife; For Life and Love; A Daughter of Judas; The Anarchist; Delilah of Harlem; In the Old Chateau; The Little Judge of Lagunitas; The Masked Venus; The Flying Halcyon; Miss Devereux of the Mariquita; After Many Years, and Other Poems. *Ne.*

Sawtelle, Henry Allen. *Me.*, 1832–1885. A Baptist clergyman of San Francisco and elsewhere. Open Communion; Things to Think Of. *Ne.*

Sawyer, Mrs. Catharine Mehetabel [Fisher]. *Ms.*, 1812——. Wife of T. J. Sawyer, *infra.* The Poetry of Hebrew Tradition.

Sawyer, Frederick William. *Me.*, 1810–1875. A Boston lawyer. Merchant's and Shipmaster's Guide; Plea for Amusements; Hits at American Whims.

Sawyer, Leicester Ambrose. *N. Y.*, 1807——. A Presbyterian clergyman and educator, after 1860 a resident of Whitesboro, New York, prominent as a biblical scholar. Elements of Biblical Interpretation; Mental Philosophy; Moral Philosophy; A Critical Exposition of Baptism; Organic Christianity; Reconstruction of Bible Theories. He made a translation of the Scriptures, of which the New Testament was published.

Sawyer, Lemuel. *N. C.*, 1777–1852. A North Carolina lawyer. Life of John Randolph; Autobiography.

Sawyer, Thomas Jefferson. *Vt.*, 1804——. A Universalist clergyman and educator, after 1869 a professor of theology at Tufts College. Doctrine of Eternal Salvation; Who Is God,— the Son or the Father?; Endless Punishment in the Very Words of its Advocates.

Saxe, John Godfrey. *Vt.*, 1816–1887. A lawyer and littérateur of Vermont and subsequently of New York, widely known as a humorous poet. Progress; A New Rape of the Lock; The Proud Miss McBride; The Money King; Clever Songs of Many Nations; The Masquerade; Leisure Day Rhymes; Fables and Lyrics in Rhyme. *Hou.*

Say, Thomas. *Pa.*, 1787–1834. A zöologist who was the first curator of the Philadelphia Academy of Natural Sciences. In 1825 he removed to New Harmony, Indiana, and was the agent of the Owen socialist colony there. Vocabularies of Indian Languages; American Conchology; American Entomology. His Complete Writings on Conchology have been edited by Binney, and those on Entomology by Le Conte. *See Memoir by Ord.*

Sayles, John. *N. Y.*, 1825–1897. A Texas jurist, professor in Baylor University from 1880. Practice in the District and Supreme Courts of Texas; Civil Jurisdiction of Justices of the Peace in the State of Texas; Principles of Pleading in Civil Actions in the Courts of Texas; Probate Laws of Texas; Laws of Business; Constitution of Texas, with Notes; Notes on Texan Reports, include the larger number of his professional writings. *See Bibliography of Texas.*

Sayre, Lewis Albert. *N. J.*, 1820——. A distinguished surgeon of New York city, professor of orthopædic surgery in Bellevue Hospital College. Practical Manual of the Treatment of Club-Foot; Lectures on Orthopædic Surgery; Spinal Curvature and its Treatment. *Ap.*

Scarborough, William Saunders. *Ga.*, 1852——. An educator of African descent, professor of ancient languages in Wilberforce University, Ohio, from 1877. First Lessons in Greek; Theory and Functions of the Thematic Vowel in the Greek Verb.

Schaeffer [shā'fẹr], Charles Frederick. *Pa.*, 1807–1879. Son of F. D.

Shaeffer, *infra*. A Lutheran clergyman and educator, professor of systematic theology in the Lutheran Theological Seminary at Philadelphia, 1864–76. A System of Lutheran Theology is one of several important works which he translated from the German. *See American Lutheran Biographies.*

Schaeffer, Charles William. *Md.*, 1813–1896. Nephew of C. F. Schaeffer, *supra*. A Lutheran clergyman and educator of eminence, professor of church history in the Philadelphia Lutheran Seminary from 1864. History of the Lutheran Church in the United States; Family Prayers.

Schaeffer, Frederick David. *G.*, 1760–1836. A once prominent Lutheran clergyman of Philadelphia. Antwort auf eine Vertheidigung der Methodisten; Eine herzliche Anrede.

Schaff [shäf], **Philip.** *Sd.*, 1819–1893. A distinguished German Reformed divine who came to the United States in 1844, and was professor of church history in the seminary at Mercersburg, Pennsylvania, 1844–63. In 1873 he became professor of sacred literature in Union Seminary in New York city. Principles of Protestantism; History of the Christian Church; Creeds of Christendom; Theological Propædeutics; Christ and Christianity; Critical Edition of the Heidelberg Catechism; Bible Revision; Through Bible Lands; Progress of Religious Freedom; Church and State in the United States; The Person of Christ; Literature and Poetry; A Companion to the Greek Testament and the English Version, include his principal original works. He has edited the Schaff-Herzog Encyclopædia of Religious Knowledge; Lange's Commentary, and other important works. *Fu. Har. Ran. Scr. Wh.*

Scharf, John Thomas. *Md.*, 1843——. An historical writer of Baltimore. Chronicles of Baltimore; History of Maryland; History of Baltimore; History of Western Maryland; History of the City of St. Louis; History of Philadelphia; History of the Confederate Navy; History of Delaware.

Schauffler [show'fler] **William Gottlieb.** *G.*, 1798–1883. A Congregational missionary in Turkey well known as a linguist. He translated the Bible into Hebrew-Spanish and Turkish, and also wrote Essay on the Right Use of Property; Meditations on the Last Days of Christ. *See Autobiography, 1887. Ran.*

Schayer, Mrs. Julia [Thompson] [von Storch]. *Me.*, 1840——. A Washington writer. The Tiger Lily, and Other Stories.

Schem [shem], **Alexander Jacob.** *G.*, 1826–1881. A statistician of note who was assistant superintendent of schools in New York city, 1874–81. Latin-English Dictionary (with G. Crooks, *supra*); Statistics of the World; Cyclopædia of Education (with H. Kiddle, *supra*).

Schenck, William Edward. *N. J.*, 1819——. A Presbyterian minister of Philadelphia. Children in Heaven; Nearing Home; The Fountain for Sin; Church Extension in Cities.

Schereschewsky, Samuel Isaac Joseph. *R.*, 1831——. The third Protestant Episcopal bishop of the China Mission. He was consecrated in 1877, but resigned his office in 1883 and lived for some years in Cambridge, but since 1895 has lived at Shanghai. He is the author of a translation of the Bible into Chinese.

Schieffiin [shĕf'lin], **Samuel Bradhurst.** *N. Y.*, 1811——. A business man of New York city who wrote on religious topics. Message to the Ruling Elders; Foundations of History; Words to Christian Teachers; The Church in Ephesus and the Presbyterian and Reformed Churches.

Schindler, Solomon. *Sil.*, 1842——. A Hebrew clergyman now (1897) living in Cambridge but formerly in charge of Temple Adath Israel, Boston. Young West, a sequel to "Looking Backward;" Messianic Exhortations and Modern Judaism; Dissolving Views on the History of Judaism. *Ar. Le.*

Schley, Winfield Scott. *Md.*. 1839——. A naval officer and explorer who published (with J. R. Soley, *infra*) The Rescue of Greeley. *Scr.*

Schmauk [shmowk], **Theodore Emmanuel.** *Pa.*, 1860——. A Lutheran clergyman of Lebanon, Pennsylvania, editor of The Lutheran from 1889, and author of The Negative Criticism.

Schmidt, Henry Immanuel. *Pa.*, 1806–1889. A Lutheran clergyman and educator of New York city, professor of German in Columbia College, 1848–80. History of Education; The Lutheran Doctrine of the Lord's Supper; Course of American Geography.

Schmucker, Beale Melanchthon. *Pa.*, 1827–1888. Son of S. S. Schmucker, *infra.* A Lutheran clergyman of Pittsville, Pennsylvania, 1881–88. A liturgical scholar of note, editor of The Church Book of the General Council, and of The Church Service, 1888.

Schmucker, Samuel Mosheim. *Va.*, 1823–1863. Son of S. S. Schmucker, *infra.* A Philadelphia author who was in the early part of his career a Lutheran minister. His various writings, which display industry rather than original talent, comprise for the most part Errors of Modern Infidelity; The Spanish Wife, a play; History of the Four Georges; History of All Religions; Court and Reign of Catharine II.; Lives of Washington, Hamilton, Jefferson, Webster, Clay, Dr. Kane, Frémont; Memorable Scenes in French History; History of the Modern Jews; History of Napoleon Third; Arctic Explorations; History of the Civil War in the United States (1863). *Co.*

Schmucker, Samuel Simon. *Md.*, 1799–1873. A Lutheran clergyman and educator, professor in the Theological Seminary at Gettysburg, 1826–64. He was an advocate of American Lutheranism as characterized by indifference to the distinctive doctrines of Lutheranism. Elements of Popular Theology; Psychology; Lutheran Manual; Lutheran Symbols, or American Lutheranism Vindicated; Church of the Redeemer; The Unity of Christ's Church, are his chief works. *Ran.*

Schneck, Benjamin Shroder. *Pa.*, 1806–1874. A Lutheran clergyman, pastor at Chambersburg from 1855. Die deutsche Kanzel; The Burning of Chambersburg; Mercersburg Theology.

Schodde, George Henry. *Pa.*, 1854——. A Lutheran clergyman and educator of Ohio, professor at Capitol University from 1880. The Book of Enoch translated from the Ethiopic, with Notes; A Day in Capernaum, from the German of Delitzsch.

Schoolcraft, Henry Rowe. *N. Y.*, 1793–1864. An eminent ethnologist and geologist, thirty years of whose life were spent among the Indians, chiefly at Mackinaw. His later life was passed in Washington. He discovered the source of the Mississippi. Among his many works are included, View of the Lead Mines of Missouri; Algic Discoveries; Historical Information Concerning the Indian Tribes; Narrative of an Expedition to Itasca Lake; Oneota, re-issued as The Indian and His Wigwam; The Myth of Hiawatha; Personal Memoirs of Thirty Years' Residence with Indian Tribes; Scenes and Adventures in the Ozark Mountains; Life of General Cass, and several volumes of verse. His talents lay rather in accumulating facts than in perceiving their relations to each other. *Lip.*

Schoolcraft, Mrs. Mary [Howard]. *S. C.*, ———. Wife of H. R. Schoolcraft, *supra.* The Black Gauntlet, a Tale of Plantation Life. *Lip.*

Schouler [skool'er], **James.** *Ms.*, 183——. Son of W. Schouler, *infra.* A lawyer and historian of Boston, professor in the law school of Boston University. The Law of Bailments; The Law of Personal Property; The Law of Husband and Wife; Law of Executors and Administrators; Law of Wills; A History of the United States under the Constitution; Life of Thomas Jefferson; Historical Briefs. *Do. Lit.*

Schouler, William. *S.*, 1814–1872. A journalist of Boston who published A History of Massachusetts during the Civil War.

Schroeder, John Frederick. *Md.*, 1800–1857. An Episcopal clergyman and educator of Flushing, Long Island. Life of Washington; Maxims of Washington; Class Book of Astronomy; Sunday Addresses. *Ap.*

Schuette, Conrad Herman Louis. *G.*, 1843——. A Lutheran clergyman and educator of Ohio, professor in Capitol University from 1872. Church Member's Manual; The State, the Church, and the School.

Schulte, Mrs. Mary Jemima [McColl]. *E.*, 1847——. A verse-writer of Jersey City. Bide a Wee, and Other Poems.

Schurman, Jacob Gould. *P. E. I.*, 1854——. A Canadian educator, since 1892 president of Cornell University. Kantian Ethics and the Ethics of Evolution; The Ethical Import of Darwinism; Belief in God; Agnosticism and Religion. *Scr.*

Schurz [shoorts], **Carl.** *P.*, 1829——. A statesman of eminence, active in the support of civil service reform. He came to America in 1852; settled in Missouri, from which he went to Congress as senator; served as general in the Union army during the Civil War; removed to New York city in 1875, and was editor of The Evening Post, 1881–84. Speeches; Life of Henry Clay; Abraham Lincoln: an Essay. *Hou. Le. Lip.*

Schuyler [sky'lẹr], **Aaron.** *N. Y.*, 1828——. A mathematician who was professor in Baldwin University and president of that institution, 1875–81, and since 1885 a professor in Kansas Wesleyan University. The Human Soul; Higher Arithmetic; Principles of Logic; Surveying and Navigation; Elements of Geometry; Empirical and Rational Psychology.

Schuyler, Anthony. *N. Y.*, 1816——. An Episcopal clergyman, rector of Grace Church at Orange, New Jersey, from 1868, and author of Household Religion.

Schuyler, Eugene. *N. Y.*, 1840–1890. Son of G. W. Schuyler, *infra.* A diplomatist who was United States secretary of legation at St. Petersburg, 1870–76, secretary of legation and consul-general at Constantinople, 1876–78, and minister to Greece, 1882–84. Peter the Great as Ruler and Reformer; Turkistan; American Diplomacy and the Furtherance of Commerce. *Scr.*

Schuyler, George Washington. *N. Y.*, 1810–1888. A prominent State official of New York for many years. Colonial New York; Philip Schuyler and his Family. *Scr.*

Schuyler, Montgomery. *N. Y.*, 1814–1896. Cousin of Anthony Schuyler, *supra.* An Episcopal clergyman of St. Louis, rector of Christ Church from 1854. The Church: its Ministry and Worship; The Pioneer Church.

Schuyler, Montgomery. *N. Y.*, 1843——. Son of Anthony Schuyler, *supra.* A journalist of New York city on the staff of The Times. Studies in American Architecture. *Har.*

Schwatka, Frederick. *Ill.*, 1849–1892. A naval officer and explorer. In the Land of Cave and Cliff Dwellers; Nimrod in the North; Along Alaska's Great River; The Children of the Cold. *See Schwatka's Search, by W. H. Gilder, supra.* *Cas.*

Schweinitz, Edmund Alexander de. *Pa.*, 1825–1887. Son of L. D. de Schweinitz, *infra.* A Moravian bishop in Pennsylvania, president of the Moravian College, 1867–84. The Moravian Manual; The Moravian Episcopate; Life of Zeisberger, the Western Pioneer and Apostle to the Indians; Some of the Fathers of the American Moravian Church; History of the Church known as the Unitas Fratrum; Systematic Benevolence.

Schweinitz, George Edmund de. *Pa.*, 1858——. Son of E. A. de Schweinitz, *supra.* A Philadelphia physician of note as an ophthalmologist who has written Diseases of the Eye, and professional monographs and papers.

Schweinitz, Lewis David de. *Pa.*, 1780–1834. A Moravian clergyman of Bethlehem, Pennsylvania, famous in his day as a botanist. Conspectus Fungorum Lusatiæ; Synopsis Fungorum Carolinæ Superioris; Synopsis Fungorum in America; Boreali Media Digentium. *See Memoir of, by W. R. Johnson, supra.*

Scollard, Clinton. *N. Y.*, 1860——. An educator of Clinton, New York, professor of English literature and Anglo-Saxon at Hamilton College, 1888–1896, and a well-known poet of the day. His writings in verse include, Pictures in Song; With Reed and Lyre; Old and New World Lyrics; Giovio and Giulia; Songs of Sunrise Lands; Hills of Song; Skenandoa; A Boy's Book of Rhyme. In prose he has published, Under Summer Skies; On Sunny Shores. *Cop. Hou. Lo. Sto.*

Scott, Charles. *Tn.*, 1811–1861. Son of E. Scott, *infra.* A lawyer of Jackson, Mississippi. Analogy of Ancient Craft Masonry to Natural and Revealed Religion; The Keystone of the Masonic Arch.

Scott, Eben[ezer] Greenough. *Pa.*, 1836——. A writer of Wilkesbarre, Pennsylvania. Development of Constitutional Liberty in the English Colonies of America; Commentaries upon the Intestate System of Pennsylvania; Reconstruction During the Civil War in the United States of America. *Hou. Put.*

Scott, Edward. *Va.*, 1774–1852. A Tennessee lawyer, prominent in the State's early history, who published Laws of the State of Tennessee, in 1822.

Scott, Henry Lee. *N. C.*, 1814–1886. Son-in-law of Winfield Scott, *infra.* An army officer who served in the Mexican and Civil Wars, and was the author of A Military Dictionary.

Scott, John. *Pa.*, 1820——. A Methodist Protestant clergyman of Cincinnati. Pulpit Echoes; The Land of Sojourn.

Scott, Mrs. Julia H—— [Kinney]. *Pa.*, 1809–1842. A verse-writer of Towanda, Pennsylvania, whose Poems, with Memoir, were posthumously published.

Scott, Robert Nicholson. *Tn.*, 1838–1887. Son of W. A. Scott, *infra.* An army officer, in charge of the publication of war records at Washington, 1877–87, who published a Digest of the Military Laws of the United States.

Scott, William Anderson. *Tn.*, 1813–1885. A Presbyterian clergyman of San Francisco, professor in the Theological Seminary there from 1871. The Bible and Politics; Strauss and Renan; Daniel: a Model for Young Men; Achan in El Dorado; The Giant Judge; The Church in the Army; The Christ of the Apostles' Creed; Trade and Letters, include his chief work.

Scott, Winfield. *Va.*, 1786–1866. A famous general who served in the War of 1812, and was commander-in-chief of the American army during the war with Mexico. General Regulations of the Army; System of Infantry and Rifle Tactics; Autobiography (1864). *See Lives by Mansfield, 1846, Headley, 1852, Victor, 1861; and United States histories.*

Scouller, James Brown. *Pa.*, 1820——. A prominent United Presbyterian clergyman. Manual of the United Presbyterian Church; History of the United Presbyterian Church; Calvinism: its History and Influence.

Scoville, Joseph A——. "Walter Barrett." *Ct.*, 1811–1864. A journalist of New York city, clerk of the Common Council, and at one period private secretary to Calhoun. Adventures of Clarence Bolton, or Life in New York; The Old Merchants of New York; Vigor, a novel; Marion.

Scripture, Edward Wheeler. *N. H.*, 1864——. A scientist, director of the physical laboratory of Yale University. Thinking, Feeling, Doing, a popular psychology; The New Psychology; Studies from the Yale Physical Laboratory. Among his various monographs the more important are those on the association of ideas and the measurement of hallucinations. *Fl.*

Scudder, Eliza. *Ms.*, 1821–1896. Cousin of H. E. Scudder, *infra.* A hymn-writer of Massachusetts. Hymns and Sonnets. *Hou.*

Scudder, Henry Martyn. *Cy.*, 1822–1895. Son of J. Scudder, *infra.* A Presbyterian clergyman and missionary, pastor in Chicago, 1883–87, and from 1887 a missionary in Japan. He published, in the Tamil language, Liturgy of the Dutch Reformed Church; The Bazaar Book; Sweet Savors of Divine Truth; Spiritual Teaching.

Scudder, Horace Elisha. *Ms.*, 1838——. A Boston littérateur, editor of The Atlantic Monthly from 1890. Seven Little People and Their Friends; Dream Children; Stories from my Attic; The Dwellers in Five-Sisters' Court; Stories and Romances; Boston Town; Life of Noah Webster; A History of the United States; A Short History of the United States; The Book of Fables; The Book of Folk Stories; Fables and Folk Stories; George Washington: an Historical Biography; Men and Letters, a volume of essays; Childhood in Literature and Art; Recollections of Samuel Breck; The Bodley Books, a series of popular juveniles. *Co. Hou. Scr. Sh.*

Scudder, John. *N. J.*, 1793–1855. A Dutch Reformed missionary and physician in Ceylon, 1820–39. Letters from the East; Letters to Pious Young Men; Promises for Passing Over Jordan. *See Memoir by J. B. Waterbury, 1856.*

Scudder, John Milton. *O.*, 1829–1894. A Cincinnati physician and educator, long a professor in the Eclectic Medical Institute. Diseases of Women; Principles of Medicine; Specific Medication; The Reproductive Organs; Specific Diagnosis.

Scudder, Moses Lewis. *Ms.*, 1843–——. A broker of Chicago. Brief Honors, a romance; Almost an Englishman; National Banking; Congested Prices; The Labor Value Prophecy.

Scudder, Samuel Hubbard. *Ms.*, 1837-——. Brother of H. E. Scudder, *supra.* A naturalist of Cambridge. The Butterflies of the Eastern United States and Canada; Butterflies, their Structure, Changes, and Life Histories; Brief Guide to the Commoner Butterflies; The Life of a Butterfly; Frail Children of the Air: Excursions into the World of Butterflies; A Century of Orthoptera; The Fossil Insects of North America. *Ho. Hou. Mac.*

Scudder, Vida Dutton. *E. I.*, 1861–——. Niece of H. E. Scudder, *supra.* An educator of Massachusetts, professor in Wellesley College. How the Rain Sprites were Freed; The Life of the Spirit in the Modern English Poets; The Witness of Denial; The Prometheus Unbound of Shelley. *Dut. He. Hou.*

Seabury, Samuel. *Ct.*, 1729–1796. The first Protestant Episcopal bishop of Connecticut. He was the first American bishop and the first presiding bishop. Being refused consecration by the Anglican Church, he was consecrated at Aberdeen, Scotland, and through him the Episcopal Church in the United States derives its succession from the Church in Scotland. During the early days of the American Revolution he attracted much attention by his pamphlets signed A. W. Farmer, which sharply criticised the actions of the patriots. They include, Free Thoughts on the Proceedings of the Continental Congress; The Continental Congress Canvassed; View of the Controversy between Great Britain and her English Colonies. His Sermons have been issued in three volumes. *See Life by E. E. Beardsley, 1881; Seabury Centennial Commemoration.*

Seabury, Samuel. *Ct.*, 1801–1872. Grandson of S. Seabury, *supra.* An Episcopal clergyman of New York city, prominent among High Churchmen, and professor in the General Theological Seminary. Continuity of the Church of England; Mary the Virgin; Historical Sketch of Augustine of Hippo; Supremacy of Conscience; American Slavery Justified; Theory and Use of the Calendar; Discourses on the Holy Calendar.

Seabury, William Jones. *N. Y.*, 1837——. Son of Samuel Seabury, 2d. An Episcopal clergyman of New York city, rector of the Church of the Annunciation from 1868, and professor in the General Seminary from 1873. Suggestions in Aid of Devotion; Introduction to the Study of Ecclesiastical Polity. *See American Church Review, July, 1885.*

Seaman, Ezra Champion. *N. Y.*, 1805–1880. The comptroller of the treasury, 1849–53, and subsequently inspector of the Michigan State prisons. Essays on the Progress of Nations; Commentaries on the Constitution, Laws, People, and History of the United States; The American System of Government; Views of Nature.

Seaman, Valentine. *L. I.*, 1770–1817. A once prominent physician of New York city, active in introducing the practice of vaccination. Waters of Saratoga; Midwife's Monitor; On Vaccination.

Searing, Mrs. Laura Catherine [Redden]. "Howard Glyndon." *Md.*, 1840——. A verse-writer and journalist now living in California, but from 1868–76 on the staff of The New York Mail. Sounds from Secret Chambers; Poems; Idylls of Battle; Brother and Sister. *Hou.*

Searle, Arthur. *E.*, 1837-——. A professor of astronomy at Harvard University from 1887, who has published Outlines of Astronomy.

Searle, January. *See Phillips, E. S.*

Searles, William Henry. *O.*, 1837–——. A civil engineer. Field Engineering; The Railroad Spiral. *Wil.*

Sears, Barnas. *Ms.*, 1802–1880. A Baptist clergyman and educator of prominence in his day. He was professor at Newton Theological Seminary, 1836–48, and president of Brown University, 1855–47. Life of Luther; The Ciceronian or Prussian Mode of Instruction in Latin; Essays on Classical Literature (with B. B. Edwards, *supra*, and C. C. Felton, *supra*.

Sears, Edmund Hamilton. *Ms.*, 1810–1876. A Unitarian clergyman and religious poet, pastor at Weston, Massachusetts, 1865–76. He wrote the familiar Christmas hymn, "Calm on the listening ear of night." Regeneration; Foregleams and Foreshadows of Immortality, originally published as Athanasia; The Fourth Gospel the Heart of Christ; Christ in the Life; Sermons and Songs of the Christian Life; Pictures of the Olden Time; That Glorious Song of Old. *A. U. A. Le.*

Sears, George W——. *Ms.*, 1821–——. A writer of Wellsboro, Pennsylvania, who served in the Federal army during the Civil War. Woodcraft; Forest Runes (verse).

Sears, [Joseph] Hamblen. *Ms.*, 1865——. A writer of New York city. The Governments of the World To-Day. *Fl.*

Seawell, Molly Elliott. *Va.*, 1860–——. A Washington writer and newspaper correspondent. The Sprightly Romance of Marsac; Hale Weston, a novel; The Berkeleys and their Neighbors; Throckmorton; Maid Marian, and Other Stories; Children of Destiny; Little Jarvis; Midshipman Paulding; Paul Jones; Decatur and Somers; Through Thick and Thin; A Strange, Sad Comedy; Quarterdeck and Fok'sle. *Ap. Lo. We.*

Seccomb, John. *Ms.*, 1708–1792. A Congregational minister at Harvard, Massachusetts, 1733–57, and after 1763 at Chester, Nova Scotia. He was the author of Father Abbey's Will, a once extremely popular piece of doggerel, which was followed by The Letter to the Widow Abbey, a work as destitute of genuine wit and worth as its predecessor. *See Tyler's American Literature; Hart's American Literature.*

Seccomb, Joseph. *Ms.*, 1706–1760. Brother of J. Seccomb, *supra*. A Congregational minister at Kingston, New Hampshire, from 1737, and author of A Plain and Brief Rehearsal of the Operations of Christ as God.

Sedgwick, Arthur George. *N. Y.*, 1844——. Son of T. Sedgwick, 2d, *infra*. A lawyer of New York city. Principles and Practices Governing the Trial of Title to Land (with F. S. Wait); Elements of Damages. *Lit.*

Sedgwick, Catharine Maria. *Ms.*, 1789–1867. A once famous novelist whose name was for a time the foremost among those of American literary women. Her work has very real excellence, but its merits were hardly of a quality to preserve it, and it is now superseded by the writings of others who have cultivated the same field with even more skill. Hope Leslie; Redwood; The New England Tale; The Traveller; Clarence; Le Bossu; The Linwoods; Married or Single (1857), include her novels. Other works for older readers are, Letters from Abroad; Historical Sketches of the Old Painters. Her juvenile moral tales, of which Live and Let Live; Poor Rich Man and Rich Poor Man; Means and Ends; Morals and Manners, are good examples, are as entertaining as they were popular. For a half century she was principal of a school for girls in Stockbridge, Massachusetts, her native town. *See Life and Letters, 1871. Har.*

Sedgwick, Mrs. Elizabeth Buckminster [Dwight]. *Ms.*, 1791–1864. Sister-in-law of C. M. Sedgwick, *supra*, and a teacher for many years. Beatitudes and Pleasant Sundays; Lessons Without Books; A Talk with My Pupils; Stories of the Spanish Conquest.

Sedgwick, Henry Dwight. *Ms.*, 1785–1831. Brother of C. M. Sedgwick, *supra*. An eminent lawyer of New York city who was a noted opponent of slavery, and author of English Practice of the Common Law.

Sedgwick, Mrs. Susan Livingston [Ridley]. 1789–1867. Wife of T. Sedgwick, 1st, *infra*. A writer for young people. Walter Thornley; The Morals of Pleasure; The Young Emigrants; Allen Prescott; Alida, or Town and Country. *Har.*

Sedgwick, Theodore. *Ms.*, 1780–1839. Brother of C. M. Sedgwick, *supra*.

A lawyer of Albany, and from 1819 a resident of Stockbridge, Massachusetts. Public and Private Economy; Hints to my Countrymen.

Sedgwick, Theodore. *N. Y.*, 1811–1859. Son of T. Sedgwick, *supra*. A lawyer of New York city. Rules which Govern the Interpretation and Application of Statutory and Court Law; Treatise on the Measure of Damages, a work of much importance.

Seeley, Charles Sumner. *See Munday, J. W.*

Seely, [Edward] Howard. *N. Y.*, 1856–1894. A littérateur of New York city. A Lone Star Bo-peep, and Other Tales of Texan Ranch Life; A Ranchman's Stories; A Nymph of the West; The Jonah of Lucky Valley, and Other Stories; A Border Leander. *Ap. Do. Har.*

Seelye [see'le], **Mrs. Elizabeth [Eggleston].** *Min.*, 1858——. Daughter of E. Eggleston, *supra*. A writer living at Lake George, New York. The Story of Columbus; Montezuma; Brandt and Red Jacket; Pocahontas; Tecumseh (with E. Eggleston); The Story of Washington. *Ap. Do.*

Seelye, Julius Hawley. *Ct.*, 1824–1895. A Congregational clergyman long prominent as an educator. He was a professor of Amherst College from 1850, and its president, 1876–90. Natural Religion; The Way, the Truth, and the Life; Christian Missions; Duty. *Do.*

Seemuller, Mrs. Annie Moncure [Crane]. *Md.*, 1838–1872. A novelist of New York city whose somewhat striking fictions were popular for a brief period. Emily Chester; Reginald Archer; Opportunity. *See Boyle's Distinguished Marylanders.*

Seguin [sā-gwin'], **Edouard.** F., 1812–1880. A French physician who came to the United States in 1848 and whose specialty was the training of idiots. Among his many works on this and other professional topics are, New Facts Concerning Idiocy; Family Thermometer; Medical Thermometry; Théorie et practique de l'éducation des idiots; Traitement moral, hygiène et éducation des idiots et des antre enfants arriérés; Idiocy and its Treatment by the Physiological Methods.

Segur, Seth Willard. *Vt.*, 1831–1875. A Congregational clergyman of Ohio and subsequently of Massachusetts. Relation and Responsibilities of Pastor and People; The True Manhood; The Nation's Hope; National Blessings and Duties.

Seiss [seess], **Joseph Augustus.** *Md.*, 1823——. An eminent Lutheran clergyman of Philadelphia, pastor of the Church of the Holy Communion, and a voluminous writer on religious themes. Among his many works are, The Gospel in the Stars; The Miracle in Stone, a re-statement of Piazzi Smyth's famous theory of the Pyramid; Lectures on the Apocalypse; Lectures on the Epistle to the Hebrews; Luther and the Reformation; The Lutheran Church; Recreation Songs; Life After Death; Right Life; The Children of Silence, the Story of the Deaf; Christ's Descent into Hell; The Last Times; Voices from Babylon. *See American Lutheran Biographies. Co. Lip.*

Seligman, Edwin Robert Anderson. *N. Y.*, 1861——. A professor of political economy and finance in Columbia College. Chapters on Mediæval Guilds in England; Owen and the Christian Socialists; Railway Tariffs; Shifting and Incidence of Taxation; Progressive Taxation in Theory and Practice; Essays on Taxation. *Mac.*

Selyns, Henricus. *H.*, 1636–1701. A Dutch clergyman who came to New York in 1660, remaining four years as pastor in Brooklyn before returning to Holland. Settling permanently in New York in 1682, he was pastor of the First Dutch Reformed Church for the rest of his life. His Poems, written in Dutch, have been translated by H. C. Murphy, *supra*.

Semmes, Alexander Jenkins. *D. C.*, 1828——. Cousin of R. Semmes, *infra*. A surgeon in the Confederate navy who became a Roman Catholic clergyman, president of Pio Nono College, Macon, Georgia, from 1886. Medical Sketches of Paris; Gunshot Wounds; Notes from a Surgical Diary, are among his writings.

Semmes, Raphael. *Md.*, 1809–1877. A celebrated naval officer in the Confederate service during the Civil War as commander of the Alabama. Service Afloat and Ashore during the Mexican War; Campaign of General Scott in the Valley of Mexico; The Cruise of the Alabama; Memoirs of Service Afloat during the War between the States. *See Sinclair's Two Years in the Alabama, 1895.*

Sergeant, Thomas. *Pa.*, 1782–1860. A Philadelphia jurist. Treatise on the Law of Pennsylvania relating to Proceedings by Foreign Attachment; Constitutional Law; View of the Land Laws of Pennsylvania; Sketch of the National Judiciary Powers.

Seth, James. *S.*, 1860——. A professor of moral philosophy in Cornell University from 1896. A Study of Ethical Principles. *Scr.*

Seton, Mrs. Elizabeth Ann [Bayley]. *N. Y.*, 1774–1821. The founder and first superior of the order of Sisters of Charity in the United States. After the death of her husband she became a Roman Catholic, took the veil as a Sister of Charity in 1809, and in 1812 founded at Emmettsburg, Maryland, the first American house of the order. A volume entitled Memoirs of Mrs. Seton, written by Herself: a Fragment of Real History, was published in 1817. *See Life by White; Vie de Madame Seton by Madame de Barbary.*

Seton, Robert. *I.*, 1839——. A grandson of Mrs. Seton, *supra.* A Roman Catholic clergyman of Jersey City, dean of the monsignori in the United States. Memoirs, Letters, and Journal of E. Seton; Essays on Various Subjects, principally Roman.

Seton, William. *N. Y.*, 1835——. A grandson of Mrs. E. Seton, *supra.* A naval officer of the United States. Romance of the Charter Oak; The Pride of Lexington; Rachel's Fate, and Other Tales; The Poor Millionaire; The Shamrock Gone West; Moida, a Tale of the Tyrol; The Pioneer, a poem.

Severance, Mark Sibley. *O.*, 1846——. Hammersmith: his Harvard Days, a novel. *Hou.*

Sewall, Frank. *Me.*, 1837——. A Swedenborgian clergyman of Washington. Moody Mike, or the Power of Love; The Hem of his Garment; The Pillow of Stones; The New Ethics; The New Metaphysics; Angelo and Ariel, are among his writings. *Lip. Ran.*

Sewall, Mrs. Harriet [Winslow]. *Me.*, 1819–1889. A religious verse-writer of Boston, some of whose lyrics are found in the anthologies. A collection of her Poems, with Memoir by Mrs. E. Cheney, *supra*, appeared in 1889.

Sewall, Jonathan Mitchell. *Ms.*, 1748–1808. A lawyer of Portsmouth, New Hampshire, popular in his own day as a verse-writer. His verse is for the most part forgotten, but his song, War and Washington, is yet remembered, and in his Epilogue to Cato occurs the famous couplet: —

"No pent-up Utica contracts your powers,
But the whole boundless continent is yours."

Miscellaneous Poems, 1801.

Sewall, Rufus King. *Me.*, 1814——. A lawyer of Wiscasset, Maine. Lectures on the Holy Spirit; Sketches of St. Augustine; Ancient Dominions of Maine.

Sewall, Samuel. *E.*, 1652–1730. A noted jurist of Boston, best remembered for his connection with the Salem witchcraft trials. The Selling of Joseph; Answer to Queries Respecting America; Accomplishment of Prophecies; Memorial Relating to the Kennebec Indians; Description of the New Heaven. *See Diary of, Tyler's American Literature; Whittier's Prophecy of Samuel Sewall.*

Sewall, Stephen. *Me.*, 1734–1804. A grand-nephew of S. Sewall, *supra.* A Hebrew scholar, professor of Hebrew at Harvard College, 1765–85, among whose writings are, Hebrew Grammar; Scripture Account of the Shechinah; Carmina Sacra quæ Latine Græceque condidit America.

Sewall, Thomas. *Me.*, 1786–1845. A Washington physician, professor of anatomy in Columbian University from 1821, who is chiefly remembered for his work, The Pathology of Drunkenness, which had a wide circulation.

Seward, George Frederick. *N.Y.*, 1840——. A nephew of W. H. Seward, *infra*, and minister to China, 1876–80. Chinese Immigration in its Social and Economical Aspects.

Seward, Theodore Frelinghuysen. *N. Y.*, 1835——. Cousin of W. H. Seward, *infra.* A musical educator of note. Hadrian Theology; The School of Life; A Plea for the Christian Year.

Seward, William Henry. *N. Y.*, 1801–1872. A statesman of distinction, secretary of state during the Civil War period. Diplomatic History of the Civil War; Orations and Speeches; Life of J. Q. Adams, *supra*; Travels Round the World. His complete works in five volumes have been edited by G. E. Baker. *See Autobiography; North American Review, October, 1866; Bartlett's Modern Agitators; Life by Lothrop; and Histories of the Civil War. Ap. Co. Hou.*

Seybert, Adam. *Pa.*, 1773–1825. A Philadelphia chemist who published The Statistical Annals of the United States, 1789–1818. It was in a notice of this book for The Edinburgh Review that Sydney Smith made the famous query, "Who reads an American book?"

Seyffarth [zif'fǎart], **Gustav.** *Sxy.*, 1796–1885. A German scientist who was professor of Oriental archæology at Leipzig University, 1825–55, and, coming to America in the latter year, was professor at Concordia Seminary, in St. Louis, 1855–71. The remainder of his life was passed in New York city. He was distinguished for the extremely literal nature of his biblical interpretations. Among his voluminous writings are, Rudimenta Hieroglyphica; Grammatica Ægyptiaca; Egyptian Theology according to a Paris Mummy Coffin. *See Literary Life of, an autobiography, 1886.*

Seymour, George Franklin. *R. I.*, 1829——. The first Protestant Episcopal bishop of Springfield, and prominent among extreme High Churchmen. Modern Romanism not Catholicism.

Seymour, Mrs. Mary [Harrison]. *Ct.*, 1835——. A writer of Hartford whose writings are mainly for juvenile readers. Among them are, Mollie's Christmas Stocking; Sunshine and Starlight; Recompense; Through the Darkness; Ned, Nellie, and Amy. *Dut. Ran. Wh.*

Seymour, Thomas Day. *O.*, 1840——. A professor of Greek at Yale University from 1880. Homeric Vocabulary; School Iliad; Selected Odes of Pindar, with Notes; Introduction to the Language and Verse of Homer; Homer's Iliad, books i.–vi. *Gi.*

Shaffner, Taliaferro Preston. *Va.*, 1818–1881. An inventor of note. The Telegraph Companion; The Telegraph Manual; The Secession War in America; History of America; Odd Fellowship.

Shaler, Nathaniel Southgate. *Ky.*, 1841——. An eminent geologist, professor of paleontology at Harvard University, 1868–87, and of geology from 1887. Kentucky Geological Reports; Kentucky, a Pioneer Commonwealth; The Nature of Intellectual Property and its Importance to the State; The Interpretation of Nature; The Story of Our Continent; Illustrations of the Earth's Surface: Glaciers (with W. M. Davis); The United States of America: a study of the American Commonwealth; First Book in Geology; Nature and Man in America; Sea and Land: Features of Coasts and Oceans; Aspects of the Earth; Fossil Branchiopods of the Ohio Valley; American Highways; Domesticated Animals: their Relation to Man. *Am. Ap. Clke. Gi. Hou. Scr.*

Shanks, William Franklin Gore. *Ky.*, 1837——. A journalist of New York city. Recollections of Distinguished Generals; A Noble Treason, a tragedy. *Har.*

Shanly, Charles Dawson. *I.*, 1811–1875. A journalist and verse-writer of New York city. The Walker in the Snow is his best-known poem. A Jolly Bear and His Friends; The Monkey of Porto Bello; The Truant Chicken.

Shapley, Rufus Edmond. *Pa.*, 1840——. A Philadelphia lawyer, author of Solid for Mulhooly, a political satire.

Sharswood, George. *Pa.*, 1810–1883. An eminent Philadelphia jurist. Professional Ethics; Popular Lectures on Common Law; Lectures on Commercial Law; Sharswood's Blackstone. *Lip.*

Shattuck, Mrs. Harriette [Robinson]. *Ms.*, 1850——. Daughter of W. S. Robinson, *supra*. A writer of Malden, Massachusetts, who has published The Story of Dante's Divine Comedy; Little Folks East and West;

Woman's Manual of Parliamentary Law.

Shaw, Albert. *O.*, 1857——. A journalist of New York city, the American editor of The Review of Reviews from 1891, and a recognized authority on such themes as municipal government and municipal reforms. Icaria: a Chapter in the History of Communism; Local Government in Illinois; Coöperation in a Western City; Municipal Government in Great Britain; Municipal Government in Continental Europe. *Cent.*

Shaw, Charles. *Me.*, 1782–1828. A lawyer of Montgomery, Alabama, who published A Topographical Description of Boston from its First Settlement (1817).

Shaw, Henry Wheeler. "Josh Billings." *Ms.*, 1818–1885. A noted humourist whose shrewd, sensible sayings have been hardly appraised at their full value owing to the laboriously bad spelling in which they have been given to the world. Josh Billings's Sayings; Everybody's Friend; Josh Billings's Trump Kards; Josh Billings's Spice Box. *See Life by F. S. Smith, 1883.*

Shaw, Thomas. *Ont.*, 1843——. A Canadian educator, since 1893 professor of animal husbandry at the Minnesota Agricultural Experiment Station. The First Principles of Agriculture; Weeds and How to Eradicate Them.

Shea [shā], **George.** *I.*, 1827–1895. Son of J. A. Shea, *infra.* A jurist who was chief justice of the City Court of New York. Alexander Hamilton: a Historical Study; Nature and Form of the American Government. *Hou.*

Shea, John Augustus. *I.*, 1802–1845. An Irish verse-writer who came to America in 1827, and was a journalist in New York city. His writings include, Adolph; Parnassian Wild Flowers; Ruddeki, an Eastern Romance, in verse; Clontarf, a Poem.

Shea, John Dawson Gilmary. *N. Y.*, 1824–1892. An historical writer of note, for a number of years editor of Frank Leslie's Chimney Corner, in New York city. The Catholic Church in the United States; Legendary History of Ireland; History of Catholic Indian Missions; Discovery and Exploration of the Mississippi Valley; Early Voyages Up and Down the Mississippi; Novum Belgium, an Account of New Netherlands, 1633–44; The Operations of the French under De Grasse; Life of Pius Ninth; The Catholic Church in Colonial Days; The Catholic Hierarchy of the United States; Life and Times of Archbishop Carroll, include his principal original works.

Shearman [sher'man], **Thomas Gaskell.** *E.*, 1834——. A lawyer and political economist of New York city. Law of Practice and Pleadings; Law of Negligence; Talks on Free Trade; Does Protection Protect?; Pauper Labor of Europe; The Single Tax; National Taxation; Henry George's Mistake; Crooked Taxation.

Shecut, John Linnæus Edward Whitridge. *S. C.*, 1770–1836. A once eminent physician and scientist of Charleston. Flora Carolinensis; Medical and Philosophical Essays; Elements of Natural Philosophy; A New Theory of the Earth, comprise his chief works.

Shedd, Joel Herbert. *Ms*, 1834——. An eminent civil engineer of Providence whose most important professional labour is the Providence Water Works. He has written a work on Landscape Gardening (with Follen), and many important professional papers.

Shedd, Mrs. Julia Ann [**Clark**]. *Me.*, 1834–1897. Wife of J. H. Shedd, *supra.* Famous Painters and Paintings; Famous Sculptors and Sculpture; The Ghiberti Gates; Raphael: his Madonnas and Holy Families. *Hou.*

Shedd, William Greenough Thayer. *Ms.*, 1820–1894. A Presbyterian clergyman of New York city, professor in Union Seminary, 1863–90, and a theologian of a very conservative type. History of Christian Doctrine; Sermons to the Natural Man; Homiletics and Pastoral Theology; Theological Essays; Sermons to the Spiritual Man; Endless Punishment; Dogmatic Theology; The Pro-Revision of the Westminster Standards; Calvinism Pure and Mixed; Literary Essays. *Ran. Scr.*

Sheeleigh, Matthias. *Pa.*, 1821——. A Lutheran minister at Fort Washington, near Philadelphia, from

1869. American Ecclesiad; A Gettysburgiad; Luther: a Song Tribute; Brief History of Luther; Outlines of Old and New Testament History.

Sheldon, David Newton. *Ct.*, 1807–1889. A Baptist clergyman who became a Unitarian in 1856. He was president of Colby University, 1843–1853. Sin and Redemption.

Sheldon, Edward Austin. *N. Y.*, 1823–1897. A noted educator of Oswego, principal of the Normal School there from 1862. Manual of Elementary Training; Lessons on Objects, are his principal works.

Sheldon, Edward Stevens. *Me.*, 1851——. A professor of Romance philology at Harvard University from 1883. Short German Grammar and monographs.

Sheldon, George William. *S. C.*, 1843——. A journalist and art critic of New York city, now (1897) in charge of the London office of D. Appleton and Company, publishers. American Painters; The Story of the Volunteer Fire Department of New York City; Hours with Art and Artists; Artistic Homes; Artistic Country Seats; Selections in Modern Art; Recent Ideals of American Art. *Har.*

Sheldon, Henry Clay. *N. Y.*, 1845——. A Methodist clergyman, professor of historic theology in Boston University from 1882. History of Christian Doctrine; History of the Christian Church. *Cr. Har.*

Sheldon, Mary Downing. Daughter of E. A. Sheldon, *supra*. *See Barnes, Mrs.*

Shelton, Frederick William. *L. I.*, 1814–1881. An Episcopal clergyman of Carthage Landing, New York, who wrote in both prose and verse a number of humourous and satirical books. The Trollopiad, or the Travelling Gentleman in America; The Rector of St. Bardolph's; Peeps from the Belfry, or the Parish Sketch-Book; Salander and the Dragon, a romance; Up the River, a collection of rural sketches; Chrystalline, a romance; The Gold Mania; Use and Abuse of Reason.

Shepard, Charles Upham. *R. I.*, 1804–1886. A geologist, professor of geology at Amherst College, who published a valuable Report on the Geology of Connecticut.

Shepard, Edward Morse. *N. Y.*, 1850——. A lawyer of Brooklyn, author of a Life of Martin Van Buren. *Hou.*

Shepard, Elihu Hotchkiss. *Vt.*, 1795–1876. An educator of St. Louis. Autobiography (1869); Early History of St. Louis and Missouri.

Shepard, Isaac Fitzgerald. *Ms.*, 1816–1889. A Federal officer in the Civil War who was consul at Swatow and Hankow, 1874–80. Pebbles from Castalia; Poetry of Feeling; Scenes and Songs of Social Life; Household Tales.

Shepard, Thomas. *E.*, 1605–1649. A Puritan clergyman who came to America in 1635, and from 1636 until his death was minister of what is now the Shepard Church in Cambridge. He won great renown as a preacher, and as a theologian was a Calvinist of the extremest type. New Englands Lamentations for Old Englands present Errours; The Sound Beleever; The Clear Sunshine of the Gospel; Theses Sabbaticæ; Subjection to Christ; The Parable of the Ten Virgins Opened and Applied; Autobiography. His Sermons, with Memoir by Alger, were printed in three volumes in 1853. *See Tyler's American Literature; Memoir by S. Mather and Greenhill, 1652; Life by Cotton Mather in the Magnalia.*

Shepard, William. *See Walsh, W. S.*

Shepherd, William Robert. 18——. History of Proprietary Government in Pennsylvania. *Mac.*

Sheppard, Furman. *N. J.*, 1823——. A Philadelphia lawyer who has published a Constitutional Text-Book.

Sheppard, Nathan. *Md.*, 1834–1888. A journalist and educator who was a special correspondent of The Cincinnati Gazette during the Franco-German war. Shut up in Paris during the Siege; Darwinism Stated by Himself; Before an Audience; Saratoga Chips. *Ap. Fu.*

Sherburne, John Henry. *N. H.*, 1794–*c.* 1850. A register of the navy in Washington. Osceola, a tragedy; Erratic Poems; Life of John Paul Jones; The Tourist's Guide in Europe;

A Suppressed History of the Administration of John Adams.

Sheridan, Philip Henry. *N. Y.*, 1831–1888. A famous soldier, lieutenant-general of the United States army, 1869–88, and general for the two months preceding his death. Personal Memoirs (1888). *See Appletons' American Biography; Life by H. E. Davies; histories of the Civil War.*

Sherman, Frank Dempster. *N.Y.*, 1860——. A lyrist of New York city, adjunct professor of architecture at Columbia College, who has written much pleasing *vers de société* as well as other verse. Madrigals and Catches; Lyrics for a Lute; Little-Folk Lyrics; New Waggings of Old Tales (with J. K. Bangs, *supra*). *Hou. Sto.*

Sherman, Henry. *N. Y.*, 1808–1879. A Hartford lawyer, author of An Analytical Digest of the Laws of Marine Insurance to the Present Time (1841); The Governmental History of the United States; Slavery in the United States.

Sherman, John. *Ct.*, 1772–1828. A Unitarian clergyman of Trenton Falls, New York, where he conducted an academy. From 1797 to 1805 he was a Congregational minister at Mansfield, Connecticut, but resigned his charge on account of his becoming a Unitarian. One God in One Person Only, the first noteworthy defence of Unitarianism in America; Philosophy of Language Illustrated; A Description of Trenton Falls. *See Sprague's Annals of the American Pulpit.*

Sherman, John. *O.*, 1823——. Brother of W. T. Sherman, *infra*. A noted statesman of Ohio; United States senator, 1861–77 and 1881–97; secretary of the treasury, 1877–1881; and secretary of state from 1897. Recollections of Forty Years in the House, Senate, and Cabinet; Selected Speeches and Reports on Taxation, 1859–78. *See Life by Bronson, 1880.*

Sherman, William Tecumseh. *O.*, 1820–1891. A distinguished soldier who was general of the United States army, 1869–84. The Military Lessons of the War; Memoirs by Himself. *See Appletons' American Biography; Johnson's Universal Cyclopædia; The Sherman Letters; and histories of the Civil War. Ap.*

Sherwin, Thomas. *N. H.*, 1799–1869. A noted educator of Boston, master of the High School, 1838–69, and author of treatises on algebra.

Sherwood, Adiel. *N. Y.*, 1791–1879. A Baptist minister and educator of Georgia. Gazetteer of Georgia; Christian and Jewish Churches; Notes on the New Testament. *See Memoir by his daughter, 1884.*

Sherwood, Mrs. Emily [Lee]. *Ind.*, 1843——. A Washington journalist who has published Willis Peyton, a novel.

Sherwood, James Manning. *N. Y.*, 1814——. A Presbyterian clergyman and editor of religious journals. A Plea for the Old Foundations; The History of the Cross; Books and Authors. *Fu.*

Sherwood, Mrs. John. *See Sherwood, Mrs. Mary.*

Sherwood, John D* *N. Y.*, 1818–1891. Cousin of J. M. Sherwood, *supra*. A writer whose home was at Englewood, New Jersey. Comic History of the United States; The Case of Cuba.

Sherwood, Mrs. Katherine Margaret [Brownlee]. *Pa.*, 1841——. A verse-writer and journalist of Canton, Ohio, who has been especially successful as a writer of army lyrics and poems for military occasions. Camp Fire and Memorial Poems; Columbia.

Sherwood, Mrs. Mary Elizabeth [Wilson]. *N. H.*, 1830——. A Washington novelist and miscellaneous writer, prominent as a social leader. The Sarcasm of Destiny; A Transplanted Rose· Amenities of Home; Home Amusements; Manners and Social Usages; Royal Girls and Royal Courts; Sweet Brier; Roxobel; The Art of Entertaining. *Ap. Do. Har. Lo.*

Shew, Joel. *N. Y.*, 1816–1855. A hydropathic physician of New York State among whose writings are, Hydropathy, or the Water Cure; Cholera Treated by Water; The Hydropathic Family Physician.

Shields, Charles Woodruff. *Ind.*, 1825——. A Presbyterian clergy-

* A distinguishing initial only.

man, professor of the harmony of science and revealed religion at Princeton College from 1865, and active in behalf of church unity. The Presbyterian Book of Common Prayer according to the Revision of the Westminister Divines; Philosophia Ultima, or Science of the Sciences; The Order of the Sciences; Religion and Science in their Relations to Philosophy; Essays on Church Unity; The Historic Episcopate; The Question of Unity; The United Church of the United States. *Scr.*

Shields, Mrs. Sarah Annie [Frost]. 18——. Parlor Charades and Proverbs; Laws and By-Laws of American Society; The Art of Dressing Well; Almost a Woman; Sunshine for Rainy Days, are among her works.

Shillaber, Benjamin Penhallow. "Mrs. Partington." *N. H.*, 1814–1890. A journalist of Boston, once widely known as a humourist, whose latest years were spent in Chelsea, Massachusetts. Life and Sayings of Mrs. Partington; Partingtonian Patchwork; Mrs. Partington's Mother Goose; Ike Partington Stories; Lines in Pleasant Places; Wide Swath, a volume of collected verse; Rhymes with Reason; Cruises with Captain Bob; The Double-Runner Club. *See New England Magazine, June, 1891. Le.*

Shimeall [shim'e-all], **Richard Cunningham.** *N. Y.*, 1803–1874. An Episcopal clergyman who adopted Reformed Dutch tenets in 1834, and subsequently became a Presbyterian. He was a noted biblical scholar of millenarian views. The End of Prelacy; Christ's Second Coming; Prophetic Career and Destiny of Napoleon III.; Unseen World; Political Economy of Prophecy, are his principal works.

Shindler, Mrs. Mary Stanley Bunce [Palmer] [Dana]. *S. C.*, 1810–1883. A once popular South Carolina verse-writer whose home was at Nacogdoches, Texas, after 1869. In 1844 she became a Unitarian, and published the next year Letters on the Trinity. In 1848 she married her second husband, an Episcopal clergyman, and was received into his church. The Northern Harp; The Southern Harp; The Parted Family, and Other Poems; The Temperance Lyre; and several prose works, including Charles Martin, or the Young Patriot; The Young Sailor; Forecastle Tom; A Southerner Among the Spirits. *See Bibliography of Texas.*

Shinn, Asa. *N. J.*, 1781–1853. A Methodist Protestant minister in Ohio. Essay on the Plan of Salvation; Benevolence and Rectitude of the Supreme Being.

Shinn, Charles Howard. *Ts.*, 1852–——, A California writer who has published Mining Camps, a Study in American Frontier Government; The Story of the Mine. *Ap. Scr.*

Shinn, Earl. "Edward Strahan." *Pa.*, 1837–1886. A New York journalist, at one period art critic of The Nation. The New Hyperion: from Paris to Marly by Way of the Rhine; Studies in Modern French Art. *Lip.*

Shinn, George Wolfe. *Pa.*, 1839–——. An Episcopal clergyman, rector of Grace Church, Newton, Massachusetts, from 1875. Friendly Talks About Marriage; Manual of the Prayer Book; Manual of Church History; Questions about Our Church; Questions that Trouble Beginners in Religion; Stories for Christmas Time; Some Modern Substitutes for Christianity. *Kt. Wh.*

Shipp, Albert Micajah. *N. C.*, 1819–1887. A Methodist clergyman and educator, professor of theology in Vanderbilt University from 1874, and author of The History of Methodism in South Carolina.

Shipp, Bernard. *Mi.*, 1813——. A verse-writer of Natchez, and subsequently of Louisville. Fame, and Other Poems; Progress of Freedom, and Other Poems.

Shippen, Edward. *N. J.*, 1827——. An eminent naval surgeon of Philadelphia who published Thirty Years at Sea.

Shirley, John Milton. *N. H.*, 1831–1887. A lawyer of Andover, New Hampshire. The Early Jurisprudence of New Hampshire; Complete History of the Dartmouth College Case; Reports of Cases in Supreme Judicial Court.

Shirley, William. *E.*, 1693–1771. A noted colonial soldier who planned the conquest of Cape Breton, and was governor of Massachusetts, 1741–45. Electra, a tragedy; The Birth of Hercules, a masque; Letter to the Duke of Newcastle, with Journal of the Siege of Louisburg; The Conduct of General Shirley Briefly Stated.

Shock, William Henry. *Md.*, 1821–——. A United States naval officer whose Steam Boilers: their Design, Construction, and Management, is a standard authority.

Shoemaker, Michael Myers. *Ky.*, 1853——. A writer of travels. Eastward to the Land of Morning; The Kingdom of the White Woman, a volume of Mexican travel; Trans-Caspia: the Sealed Provinces of the Czar. *Clke.*

Shoup, Francis Asbury. *Ind.*, 1834–1896. An Episcopal clergyman and educator of Sewanee, Tennessee, professor of metaphysics in the University of the South, and a Confederate officer in the Civil War. Infantry Tactics; Artillery Division Drill; Elements of Algebra.

Shreve, Samuel Henry. *N. J.*, 1829–1884. A civil engineer of New York city. The Strength of Bridges and Roofs.

Shreve, Thomas H——. *D. C.*, 1808–1853. Cousin of S. H. Shreve, *supra*. A journalist of Louisville. Drayton, an American tale; Poems.

Shuck [shook], **Mrs. Henrietta [Hall].** *Va.*, 1817–1844. The wife of a missionary in China. Scenes in China (1852). *See Life by Jeter, 1848.*

Shurtleff, Ernest Warburton. *Ms.*, 1862——. A Congregational clergyman and verse-writer of Plymouth, Massachusetts. Poems; Easter Gleams; Song of Hope; When I was a Child; New Year's Peace.

Shurtleff, Nathaniel Bradstreet. *Ms.*, 1810–1874. An antiquarian of Boston. Elements of Phrenology; A Perpetual Calendar of Old and New Style; Topographical Description of Boston; Passengers of the Mayflower in 1620, comprise his principal writings. With D. Pulsifer he edited The Records of the Colony of New Plymouth, in twelve volumes.

Sibler, Wilhelm. *P.*, 1801–1885. A Lutheran clergyman of Missouri. Sermons on the Epistles and Gospels of the Christian Year. *See Biography (Lebeslauf), 1880.*

Sibley, John Langdon. *Me.*, 1804–1885. The librarian of Harvard University, 1841–77. History of the Town of Union, Maine; Biographical Sketches of Harvard University Graduates.

Sidney, Margaret. *See Lothrop, Mrs.*

Sigourney [sig'or-nī], **Mrs. Lydia Howard [Huntly].** *Ct.*, 1791–1865. One of the most popular of the earlier American writers, but now quite neglected. Her fifty-three volumes of prose and verse were adapted to an uncritical audience that demanded only gentle feeling and excellence of intention, and they served their purpose well in their day. Her verse is not without sweetness, but it never strays far beyond the realm of the commonplace. She was nearly all her life a resident of Hartford. Among her prose writings are, Myrtis; Post Meridian; Letters to My Pupils; Letters to Young Ladies; Traits of the Aborigines in America; Letters of Life (1866). Other works are, Pocahontas; Moral Pieces in Prose and Verse; Poetry for Children; Zinzendorf, and Other Poems. *See Griswold's Female Poets of America; Allibone's Dictionary; Stone's First Editions of American Authors. Har.*

Sikes, Mrs. Olive [Logan]. *N. Y.*, 1841——. Wife of W. W. Sikes, *infra*. An actress and author, popular at one period as a lecturer. Photographs of Paris Life; Chateau Frissac, or Home Scenes in France; John Morris's Money; Somebody's Stockings; Apropos of Women and Theatres; Before the Footlights and Behind the Scenes; The Mimic World; Get Thee Behind Me, Satan; They Met by Chance, a novel.

Sikes, William Wirt. *N. Y.*, 1836–1883. A journalist of New York city who was consul at Cardiff, Wales, 1876–1883. British Goblins: Welsh Folk-Lore; One Poor Girl; Rambles and Studies in Old South Wales; Studies of Assassination.

Sill, Edward Rowland. *Ct.*, 1841–1887. A poet and educator of Cuyahoga Falls, Ohio, professor in the University of California, 1874–82. His verse is small in quantity, but of rare quality. The Hermitage, and Other Poems; The Hermitage, and Later Poems; Poems (containing The Venus of Milo, and other poems). *See Mrs. E. Ward's Chapters from a Life. Ho. Hou.*

Sill, John Mahelon Berry. *N. Y.*, 1831——. A Michigan educator of prominence, principal of the State Normal School. Synthesis of the English Sentence; Practical Lessons in English.

Silliman, Augustus Ely. *R. I.*, 1807–1884. Cousin of B. Silliman, 2d, *infra*. A banker of New York city who published A Gallop Among American Scenery.

Silliman, Benjamin. *Ct.*, 1779–1864. A chemist of distinction, professor of chemistry at Yale University, 1802–55, and the founder in 1818 of Silliman's Journal of Science and Art. Journal of Travels in England (1810); Narrative of a Visit to Europe (1853); Elements of Chemistry; Consistency of Modern Geology with Sacred History. *See Life by G. P. Fisher; American Journal of Science, May, 1865; Popular Science Monthly, June, 1883.*

Silliman, Benjamin. *Ct.*, 1816–1885. Son of B. Silliman, *supra*. A professor of chemistry at Yale University from 1846 until his death, and editor of Silliman's Journal. First Principles of Chemistry; American Contributions to Chemistry; Principles of Physics.

Silloway, Thomas William. *Ms.*, 1828——. A Boston architect who became a Universalist minister in 1862. Theogonis; Text-Book of Modern Carpentry; Warming and Ventilation; Cathedral Towns of England (with L. Powers).

Silsbee, Mrs. Marianne Cabot [Devereux]. 1812–1889. A Boston writer who published A Half Century in Salem, and several compilations of poems. *Hou.*

Silver, Thomas. *N. J.*, 1813–1888. A civil engineer well known as an inventor. A Trip to the North Pole, or Theory of the Origin of Icebergs.

Simmons, William Johnson. *S. C.*, 1849——. A Baptist minister of African birth who has published Men of Mark.

Simms, Jeptha Root. *Ct.*, 1807–1883. A once popular writer of Fort Plain, New York. History of Schoharie County; The American Spy: Nathan Hale; The Frontiersman; Trappers of New York.

Simms, Joseph. *N. Y.*, 1833——. Nephew of J. R. Simms, *infra*. A writer on physiognomy. Nature's Revelations of Character; Book of Scientific Lectures; Health and Character; Practical and Scientific Physiognomy; Human Faces: What They Mean.

Simms, William Gilmore. *S. C.*, 1806–1870. A voluminous romancer and verse-writer of Charleston, long popular but now little read. Among his thirty romances, The Partisan; The Yemassee; Guy Rivers; Martin Faber; Border Beagles; Beauchampe, are as well known as any; and of some twelve volumes of verse, Atalantis; Lays of the Palmetto; Areytos, or Songs and Ballads of the South, are the most characteristic. Other works of his include, A History of South Carolina; Lives of Marion, General Greene, Captain John Smith, Chevalier Bayard. *See Allibone's Dictionary; Life by Trent. Stone's First Editions of American Authors. Lov.*

Simonds, William. "Walter Aimwell." *Ms.*, 1822–1859. A Boston journalist who was a very popular writer for young people. The Aimwell Stories; The Boys' Own Guide; Boys' Book of Morals and Manners.

Simpson, Edward. *N. Y.*, 1824–1888. A naval officer of prominence, rear-admiral from 1884. Ordnance and Naval Gunnery; The Naval Mission to Europe; Report of the Gun Foundry Board.

Simpson, Henry. *Pa.*, 1790–1868. A Philadelphia author who published Lives of Eminent Philadelphians.

Simpson, James Hervey. *N. J.*, 1813–1883. A colonel of engineers and brevet brigadier-general in the United States army. A Military Reconnoissance from Sante Fé to the Navajo Country in 1849. The Shortest Route to California; Coronado's March in Search of the Seven Cities of Cibola. *Lip.*

Simpson, Matthew. *O.*, 1811–1884. A Methodist bishop famous as a pulpit orator. Lectures on Preaching; A Hun.

dred Years of Methodism; Sermons; Cyclopædia of Methodism. *See Life of, by G. R. Crooks, supra. Har. Meth.*

Sims, Clifford Stanley. *Pa.*, 1839–1896. A lawyer of Arkansas, and latterly of New Jersey, whose principal work is The Origin and Signification of Scottish Surnames.

Sims, James Marion. *S. C.*, 1813–1883. A celebrated surgeon of New York city to whose influence is due the establishment of gynæcology as a department of medicine. Clinical Notes on Uterine Surgery; Ovariotomy; The Story of My Life. *See Life of, by T. A. Emmet, supra. Ap.*

Sinclair, Carrie Bell. *Ga.*, 1837–——. A verse-writer of Philadelphia. Poems; Heart Whispers, or Echoes of Song.

Skene, Alexander Johnston Chalmers. *S.*, 1837–——. A Brooklyn physician, professor of gynæcology in Long Island College Hospital from 1884. Diseases of the Bladder in Women; Diseases of Women from the Standpoint of the Physician. *Ap.*

Skinner, Charles Montgomery. *N. Y.*, 1852–——. A journalist and littérateur of Brooklyn, associate editor of The Eagle. Villon the Vagabond, and other plays; Myths and Legends of Our Own Land; Nature in a City Yard. *Cent. Lip.*

Skinner, Otis Ainsworth. *Ms.*, 1807–1861. A Universalist minister of Boston and elsewhere. Family Prayer Book; Sermons on Doctrinal Subjects; Universalism Defended; Letters on Revivals; Moral Duties of Parents, are his principal works. *See Life of, by T. B. Thayer, infra.*

Skinner, Thomas Harvey. *N. C.*, 1791–1871. A Presbyterian clergyman of New York city, professor of sacred rhetoric in Union Seminary, 1848–71. Religion of the Bible; Aids to Preaching and Hearing; Discussions in Theology; Thoughts on Evangelizing the World. *Ran.*

Slade, Daniel Denison. *Ms.*, 1823–——. A physician and scientist, professor of zöology at Harvard University from 1871. Diphtheria: its Nature and Treatment; Twelve Days in the Saddle, a Journey in New England in 1883. Evolution of Horticulture in New England. *Put.*

Slaughter, Philip. *Va.*, 1808–1890. Cousin of W. B. Slaughter, *infra*. An Episcopal clergyman of Virginia, historiographer of the diocese. The Colonial Church in Virginia; Man and Woman, are his most important writings.

Slaughter, William Bank. *Va.*, 1798–1879. A Wisconsin lawyer of note who published Reminiscences of Distinguished People I Have Met.

Sleeper, John Sherburne. *Ms.*, 1794–1878. A shipmaster and subsequently a journalist of Boston, editor of The Journal, 1834–54. Tales of the Ocean; Salt-Water Bubbles; Jack in the Forecastle; Mark Rowland, a Tale of the Sea.

Slenker, Mrs. Emma [Drake]. *N. Y.*, 1827–——. A writer living at Snowville, Virginia. Studying the Bible; John's Way; The Darwins; Mary Jones; Little Lessons for Little Folks.

Slicer, Henry. *Md.*, 1801–1874. A Methodist clergyman, eight times chaplain of the United States Senate. Appeal on Christian Baptism; Discourse on Duelling, which materially helped forward the passage of the anti-duelling law in Congress.

Sloan, Samuel. *N. C.*, 1815–1884. An architect of Philadelphia. City and Suburban Architecture; Constructive Architecture; The Model Architect; Homestead Architecture. *Bai. Lip.*

Sloane, Thomas O'Conor. *N. Y.*, 1851–——. A chemist of New York city, on the editorial staff of The Scientific American. Home Experiments in Science; Standard Electrical Dictionary.

Sloane, William Milligan. *O.*, 1850–——. A professor of history at Columbia College. The French War and the Revolution; Life of James M'Cosh, *supra*; Life of Napoleon Bonaparte. *Cent. Scr.*

Slosson, Mrs. Annie [Trumbull]. *Ct.*, 184–——. An author of New York city noted for the excellence of her short stories, and also known as an entomologist whose specialty is the study of moths. Aunt Liefy; Fishin' Jimmy; Seven Dreamers; The Heresy of Mehetabel Clark; Anna Malann; The China Hunter's Club. *Har. Ran.*

Sluter, George Ludewig. *G.*, 1837-——. A Lutheran clergyman, pastor at Arlington, New Jersey, from 1881. History of Our Beloved Church; Life of Tiberius; The Religion of Politics, are his principal writings.

Smalley, Eugene Virgil. *O.*, 1841-——. A journalist of St. Paul. History of the Northern Pacific Railroad; History of the Republican Party.

Smalley, George Washburn. *Ms.*, 1833-——. A noted journalist who was the London correspondent of The New York Tribune, 1867-95, and from 1895 American correspondent of The London Times. London Letters, and Some Others; Studies of Men. *Har.*

Smalley, John. *Ct.*, 1734-1820. A Congregational clergyman, pastor at New Britain from 1758 till his death. National and Moral Inability; Universal Salvation.

Smart, Mrs. Helen Hamilton [Gardener]. *Va.*, 1853——. A Boston novelist whose writings are mainly concerned with the furtherance of social reforms. An Unofficial Patriot; Is This Your Son, My Lord?; Facts and Fictions of Life; Pray You, Sir, Whose Daughter?; Pushed by Unseen Hands; A Thoughtless Yes; The Fortunes of Margaret Weld. *Ar.*

Smedes, Mrs. Susan [Dabney]. *Mi.*, 1840——. A Mississippi writer now living in Washington, whose Memorials of a Southern Planter is much valued as an accurate picture of Southern life.

Smith, Arthur Donaldson. *Pa.*, 1864——. An African explorer. Through Unknown African Countries.

Smith, Ashbel. *Ct.*, 1805-1886. A Texas politician and physician. Account of the Geography of Texas; Permanent Identity of the Human Race.

Smith, Augustus William. *N. Y.*, 1802-1866. An educator who was professor of mathematics at Wesleyan University, 1831-51, and president of that institution from 1851. Elementary Treatise on Mechanics.

Smith, Buckingham. *Ga.*, 1810-1871. A Spanish-American scholar and antiquary of note, twice secretary of the United States legation at Mexico, and after 1850 a lawyer in Florida. Among his many publications are, Grammatical Sketch of the Heve Language; Grammar of the Pima, or Nevome; Coleccion de Varios Documentos para la Historia de la Florida; Narratives of the Career of Hernando de Soto in the Conquest of Florida.

Smith, Charles. *Pa.*, 1765-1836. Son of William Smith, 1st, *infra.* A Philadelphia lawyer who published a Treatise on the Land Laws of Philadelphia.

Smith, Charles Adam. *N. Y.*, 1809-1879. A Lutheran clergyman, pastor at Rhinebeck, New York, and elsewhere. The Catechumen's Guide; Men of the Olden Time; Before the Flood and After; Among the Lilies; Inlets and Outlets; Stoneridge, pastoral sketches; Popular Exposition of the Gospels (with J. Morris). *Lip.*

Smith, Charles Henry. "Bill Arp." *Ga.*, 1826——. A lawyer and journalist of Rome, Georgia, well known as a humourous contributor to The Atlanta Constitution. Bill Arp's Letters; Bill Arp's Scrap Book: The Farm and the Fireside; A Side Show of the Southern Side of the War; Georgia as a Colony and State, 1733-1893. *Gi.*

Smith, Daniel. *Ct.*, 1806-1852. A Methodist clergyman of New York State very active in the temperance cause. Wisdom in Miniature; Gems of Female Biography; Anecdotes for the Young; Teachers' Assistant; Lectures to Young Men; Book of Manners; Anecdotes of the Christian Ministry. *Meth.*

Smith, Edward Delafield. *N. Y.*, 1826-1878. A lawyer of New York city. Avidæ, a poem; Destiny, a poem; Oratory, a poem; Reports of Cases in the New York Court of Common Pleas; Addresses to Juries in Slave Trade Trials.

Smith, Eli. *Ct.*, 1801-1857. A Congregational missionary at Beirut. Missionary Researches in Armenia (1853); and an Arabic translation of the Bible.

Smith, Elias. *Ct.*, 1769-1846. A Congregational clergyman of Massachusetts. The Clergyman's Looking-Glass; History of Anti-Christ; Sermons on the Prophecies, are among his writings.

Smith, Elihu Hubbard. *Ct.*, 1771-1798. A physician and verse-writer of New York city. Edwin and Angelina, an opera; American Poems, Original and Selected.

Smith, Mrs. Elizabeth Oakes [Prince]. *Me.*, 1806-1893. Wife of Seba Smith, *infra*. A once prominent writer of prose and verse, who was the first woman lecturer in America. Her later years were passed in Hollywood, South Carolina. Among her many works are, The Sinless Child, and Other Poems; The Newsboy, which first directed public attention to a hitherto neglected class; Riches Without Wings; Old New York, or Jacob Leisler, a tragedy; Woman and Her Needs; Bertha and Lily; The Western Captive.

Smith, Erasmus Peshine. *N. Y.*, 1814-1882. A jurist and political economist. Manual of Political Economy.

Smith, Mrs. Erminnie Adelle [Platt]. *N. Y.*, 1837-1886. An ethnologist who published an Iroquois-English dictionary. *See Memorial, 1890.*

Smith, Ethan. *Ms.*, 1762-1849. A Congregational clergyman, city missionary of Boston, 1832-49. A View of the Trinity; A View of the Hebrews, in which the origin of the American Indians was traced to the ten tribes of Israel. *See Sprague's Annals of the American Pulpit.*

Smith, Mrs. Eugenia M. [Bryce]. *Vt.*, 1852——. A fiction-writer of Dubuque. Winsome but Wicked; The Parson's Sin; Our Money-Makers, a poultry book.

Smith, Florence. *N. Y.*, 1845-1871. A verse-writer of New York city who published Piero's Painting, and Other Poems.

Smith, Mrs. Frances Irene [Burge]. *See Griswold, Mrs. Frances.*

Smith, Francis Henney. *Va.*, 1812-1890. A Confederate officer who was professor of mathematics at Hampden Sidney College, Virginia, 1837-39, and superintendent of the Virginia Military Institute, 1839-61 and 1865-90. Best Methods of Conducting Common Schools; College Reform; and a series of algebras.

Smith, Francis Hopkinson. *Md.*, 1838——. An artist, civil engineer, and popular littérateur of New York city. Well-Worn Roads of Spain, Holland, and Italy; Old Lines in New Black and White; A White Umbrella in Mexico; Colonel Carter of Cartersville, a novel; A Day at Laguerre's, and Other Days; American Illustrators; Venice of To-Day; A Gentleman Vagabond, and Some Others; Tom Grogan; Gondola Days. *Hou. Scr.*

Smith, Gerrit. *N. Y.*, 1797-1874. A famous philanthropist of Peterboro, New York, who was an ardent opponent of slavery. Speeches in Congress; Sermons and Speeches; The Religion of Reason; The Theologies; Nature the Basis of a Free Theology. *See Life of, by O. B. Frothingham, supra.*

Smith, Gertrude. *Cal.*, 186——. Sister of M. C. Smith, *infra*. A Boston writer, whose early life was spent in the West. The Rousing of Mrs. Potter, and Other Stories; The Arabella and Araminta Stories; Dedora Heywood. *Cop. Do. Hou.*

Smith, Gustavus Woodson. *Ky.*, 1822-1896. A Confederate general who lived in New York city from 1876. Notes on Life Insurance; Confederate War Papers.

Smith, Hamilton Lanphere. *Ct.*, 1819——. An educator who has been professor of natural philosophy at Hobart College from 1868. Natural Philosophy; First Lessons in Astronomy and Geology.

Smith, Henry Boynton. *Me.*, 1815-1877. A Presbyterian clergyman of eminence as a theologian, and professor of systematic theology in Union Seminary, New York city, 1854-74. Faith and Philosophy; Apologetics; Chronological History of the Church of Christ; Introduction to Christian Theology; System of Christian Theology. *See Life and Work of, 1881; Life by Stearns, 1892. Scr.*

Smith, Henry Hollingsworth. *Pa.*, 1815——. A surgeon of Philadelphia. Minor Surgery; System of Operative Surgery; Practice of Surgery; Professional Visit to London and Paris.

Smith, Herbert Huntington. *N.Y.*, 1851——. A scientist who has been engaged upon geological surveys in

Ohio, New York, and Brazil. Brazil, the Amazons, and the Coast. *Scr.*

Smith, Horace Wemyss. *Pa.*, 1825–——. Son of R. P. Smith, *infra.* A Philadelphia journalist whose principal works include, Nuts for Future Historians to Crack; Yorktown Orderly Book; Life of Reverend William Smith, *infra.*

Smith, James. *I.*, *c.* 1720–1806. A lawyer of York, Pennsylvania, who was one of the signers of the Declaration of Independence. He wrote The Constitutional Power of Great Britain over the Colonies in America, which materially aided the cause of the patriots.

Smith, James. *Pa.*, 1737–1812. A once noted Kentucky pioneer. Shakerism Developed; Shakerism Detected; Remarkable Adventures in the Life of Colonel James Smith; Mode and Manner of Indian War. *See Bibliography of Ohio.*

Smith, Jerome Van Crowninshield. *N. H.*, 1800–1879. A physician of Boston, where he was mayor in 1854, and subsequently of New York city. Class Book of Anatomy; Life of Andrew Jackson; Natural History of the Fishes of Massachusetts; Pilgrimage to Palestine; Turkey and the Turks; The Ways of Women.

Smith, Job Lewis. *N.Y.*, 1827——. A physician of New York city who wrote a Treatise on Diseases of Children.

Smith, John. *E.*, 1579–1631. A celebrated sea captain and adventurer who was one of the founders of Virginia, and of the company who settled at Jamestown in 1607. He was a forcible, vigourous writer, much given to magnifying his own exploits, and not always to be trusted in the absence of other testimony. A True Relation of Virginia; The Generall Historie of Virginia, which is partly original and partly compiled; A Map of Virginia, with a Description of the Country; A Description of New England (1616); An Accidence, or Pathway to Experience; A Sea Grammar; The True Travels of Captain John Smith, a work in which his imagination is under very little restraint as regards facts. *See Lives by Hillard in Sparks's American Biography, Mrs. Robinson, 1845, Simms, 1846, Deane, 1859, Warner, 1881, True, 1882; Tyler's American Literature; North American Review, January, 1867; Appletons' American Biography.*

Smith, John. *N. H.*, 1752–1809. A Congregational minister and educator, professor of languages at Dartmouth College and college pastor, 1778–1809, as well as librarian of the college for some thirty years. He was the author of Hebrew, Greek, and Latin Grammars, as well as some minor publications. *See Memoir by his Wife, 1815.*

Smith, John Augustine. *Va.*, 1782–1865. A physician of New York city, previously president of William and Mary College, 1814–26. Mutations of the Earth; Moral and Physical Science; Functions of the Nervous System.

Smith, John Cotton. *Ms.*, 1826–1882. An Episcopal clergyman of New York city, rector of the Church of the Ascension, 1860–82. The Church's Law of Development; Certain Aspects of the Church; Miscellanies; Old and New; The Liturgy as a Basis of Union.

Smith, John Hyatt. *N. Y.*, 1824–1886. A prominent Baptist clergyman of Brooklyn, a member of Congress, 1880–82. Gilead; The Open Door.

Smith, John Jay. *N. J.*, 1798–1881. A librarian of Philadelphia who edited many works, and was author of Notes for a History of the Library Company of Philadelphia; A Summer's Jaunt Across the Water; Historical and Literary Curiosities (with J. F. Watson).

Smith, John Lawrence. *S. C.*, 1818–1883. A chemist of note who was professor of chemistry in the University of Louisville. Mineralogy and Chemistry: Original Researches.

Smith, John Talbot. *N. Y.*, 1855–——. A Roman Catholic clergyman in the diocese of Ogdensburg. History of Ogdensburg Diocese; A Woman of Culture, a novel; Solitary Island, a novel; Prairie Boy, a juvenile tale; Our Seminaries: an essay on Clerical Training.

Smith, Joseph. *Pa.*, 1796–1868. A Presbyterian clergyman, once prominent in western Pennsylvania. History of Jefferson College; Old Redstone, or Historical Sketches of Western Presbyterianism.

Smith, Joseph Edward Adams. "Godfrey Greylock." 1822–1896. A writer of Pittsfield, Massachusetts. Taghconic: the Romance and Beauty of the Hills; A History of Paper.

Smith, Joseph Mather. *N.Y.*, 1789–1866. A physician of New York city. Elements of the Etiology and Philosophy of Epidemics; Illustrations of Medical Phenomena in Public Life.

Smith, Judson. *Ms.*, 1837——. A Congregational clergyman and educator, secretary of the American Board of Commissioners for Foreign Missions from 1884. Lectures in Church History; Lectures on Modern History.

Smith, Justin Almerin. *N.Y.*, 1819–1896. A Baptist clergyman of Chicago, editor of The Standard from 1853. The Martyr of Vilvorde; Sinclair Thompson, the Shetland Apostle; The Spirit in the Word; Modern Church History; Patmos.

Smith, Mrs. Luella [Dowd]. *Ms.*, 1847——. A verse-writer of Hudson, New York. Wayside Leaves; Wind Flowers.

Smith, Mrs. Lura Eugenie [Brown]. *N. Y.*, 1864——. A journalist of Little Rock. On the Track and Off the Train.

Smith, Mrs. Margaret [Bayard]. *Pa.*, 1778–1844. Wife of S. H. Smith, *infra*, and once a social leader in Washington. A Winter in Washington; What is Gentility?

Smith, Mrs. Mary Louise [Riley]. *N. Y.*, 1842——. A popular verse-writer of New York city. Sometime, and Other Poems; The Inn of Rest; A Gift of Gentians, and Other Verses; Cradle and Armchair. *Ran.*

Smith, Mrs. Mary Prudence [Wells]. "P. Thorne." *N.Y.*, 1840——. A Cincinnati writer for young people. The Browns; Child Life on a Farm; Jolly Good Times at School; Jolly Good Times at Hackmatack; More Good Times at Hackmatack; Miss Ellis's Mission. *A. U. A. Rob.*

Smith, Mrs. Mary Stuart [Harrison]. *Pa.*, 1834——. The wife of a professor at the University of Virginia. She has made many translations from the German and French, and has also published, Heirs of the Kingdom; Virginia Cookery Book. *Har.*

Smith, Matthew Hale. *Me.*, 1810–1879. Son of Elias Smith, *supra*. A clergyman of the Universalist and subsequently of the Presbyterian and other faiths, who was also a lawyer and a brilliant journalist, known as "Burleigh." Universalism Examined, Renounced, and Exposed; Universalism not of God; Sabbath Evenings; Mount Calvary; Sunshine and Shadow in New York; Bulls and Bears of Wall Street, include his chief works.

Smith, Minna Caroline. *Cal.*, 1860——. A journalist of Boston. The Boys of Cary Farm, a juvenile tale; Trilby, the Fairy of Argyle, from the French of Nodier. *Lam. Lo.*

Smith, Nathan. *N. H.*, 1762–1828. A physician who was a medical professor in Dartmouth College, 1798–1813. Practical Essays on Typhus Fever; Medical and Surgical Memoirs.

Smith, Nathan Ryno. *N. H.*, 1797–1877. Son of N. Smith, *supra*. A professor of surgery in the University of Maryland, 1840–70. Surgical Anatomy of the Arteries; Legends of the South, are among his works.

Smith, Oliver Hampton. *N. J.*, 1794–1859. A once prominent United States senator from Indiana. Recollections of a Congressional Life; Early Indian Trials.

Smith, Persifor Frazer. *Pa.*, 1808–1882. A lawyer of Philadelphia. Forms of Procedure in Pennsylvania Courts; Pennsylvania Supreme Court Reports, 1865–82.

Smith, Richard Penn. *Pa.*, 1790–1854. Grandson of William Smith, 1st, *infra*. A lawyer and dramatist of Philadelphia, fifteen of whose plays were placed on the stage, and were once popular, Caius Marius being one of the best. He wrote also The Forsaken, a novel; The Actress of Padua, and Other Tales; Lives of Crockett and Martin Van Buren. His complete works in four volumes were issued in 1888.

Smith, Richard Somers. *Pa.*, 1813–1877. A soldier and educator, president of Girard College, 1863–68, and for the last seven years of his life in charge of the department of drawing at the United States Naval Academy. Manual of Topographical Drawing; Manual of Linear Perspective.

Smith, Richmond Mayo. *O.*, 1854——. A professor of political economy at Columbia College from 1883. Statistics and Economics; Emigration and Immigration; Statistics and Sociology. *Mac. Scr.*

Smith, Samuel. *N. J.*, 1720–1766. A colonial treasurer of the province of West Jersey, who published a History of Nova Cæsarea, or New Jersey, from its Settlement to 1721.

Smith, Samuel Francis. *Ms.*, 1808–1895. A Baptist clergyman near Boston, who wrote much religious verse, but will probably be longest remembered for the familiar "My Country, 'tis of thee." He published, for juvenile readers and others, Knights and Sea Kings; Mythology and Early Greek History; Noble Workers; Poor Boys who Became Great; Rambles in Mission Fields. *Lo.*

Smith, Samuel Stanhope. *Pa.*, 1750–1819. A Presbyterian divine, president of Princeton College, 1794–1812. Lectures on the Evidences of the Christian Religion; Moral and Political Philosophy; Sermons; Comprehensive View of Natural and Revealed Religion; On the Variety of Complexion and Figure of the Human Species, which was much noticed in its day.

Smith, Mrs. Sarah Louisa [Hickman]. *Mch.*, 1811–1832. A Cincinnati verse-writer whose Poems appeared in 1829.

Smith, Seba. "Jack Downing." *Me.*, 1792–1868. A journalist of Portland, Maine, and, after 1842, of New York city, very popular as a humourist in the earlier part of his career. The Letters of Major Jack Downing; Powhatan, a metrical romance; New Elements of Geometry; Way Down East, or Portraitures of Yankee Life; My Thirty Years Out of the Senate; Dew-Drops of the Nineteenth Century.

Smith, Sebastian Bach. *G.*, 1845–1895. A Roman Catholic clergyman at Paterson, New Jersey. Elements of Ecclesiastical Law; New Procedure in Criminal and Disciplinary Causes of Ecclesiastics in the United States.

Smith, Solomon Franklin. *N. Y.*, 1801–1869. A once popular low comedian who left the stage in 1853, and was afterward a noted lawyer of St. Louis. Theatrical Apprenticeship; Theatrical Journey Work; Autobiography (1868). *Har.*

Smith, Stephen. *N. Y.*, 1823——. A New York surgeon, professor of clinical surgery in the University of the City of New York from 1874. Handbook of Surgical Operations; Principles of Operative Surgery.

Smith, Uriah. *N. H.*, 1832——. A Seventh Day Adventist writer of Battle Creek, Michigan. Looking Unto Jesus; Here and Hereafter; The Destiny of the Wicked; Nature and Destiny of Man; A Word for the Sabbath (verse); The United States in the Light of Prophecy; Daniel and the Revelation, a very popular work, the sale of which has reached 72,000 copies; The Sure Foundation; Scripture Pathways Cleared of Stumbling-Stones.

Smith, William. *S.*, 1721–1803. An Episcopal clergyman of Philadelphia who came to America from Scotland in 1751, and in 1754 was made first provost of the University of Pennsylvania. A General Idea of the College of Mirania first brought him to the knowledge of Franklin, who was then laying plans for the university. He was author, also, of Brief Account of the Province of Pennsylvania; Sermons; Discourses on Public Occasions. *See Tyler's American Literature; Life and Correspondence of H. W. Smith, supra; Fisher's Pennsylvania: Colony and Commonwealth.*

Smith, William. *N. Y.*, 1728–1793. A jurist of New York city who was a loyalist during the Revolution, and in 1786 was appointed chief justice of Canada. History of the Province of New York from its Discovery to 1732. *See Tyler's American Literature.*

Smith, William. *S.*, 1754–1821. Nephew of W. Smith, 1st, *supra.* An Episcopal clergyman of Newport, Rhode Island, and elsewhere, of some note as an educator in his day. Essays on the Christian Ministry. *See Sprague's Annals of the American Pulpit.*

Smith, William Andrew. *Va.*, 1802–1870. A Methodist clergyman of Virginia whose Lectures on the Philosophy and Practice of Slavery are considered the ablest presentation of the pro-slavery side of the question.

Smith, William Farrar. *Vt.*, 1824——. A brevet major-general in the United States army who resigned in 1867. From Chattanooga to Petersburg under Generals Grant and Butler. *Hou.*

Smith, William Henry. *O.*, 1833-1896. A journalist of Cincinnati, subsequently collector of Chicago. The St. Clair Papers; Political History of the United States.

Smith, William Loughton. *S. C.*, 1758-1812. A diplomatist who was minister to Portugal (1797-1800) and to Spain (1800-01), and an active Federalist politician. Speeches; Comparative View of the Constitutions of the States; American Arguments for British Rights.

Smith, William L—— G——. *Vt.*, 1814——. Uncle Tom's Cabin as It Is.

Smith, William Rudolph. *Pa.*, 1787-1868. A Wisconsin lawyer, author of Observations on Wisconsin Territory, 1831; History of Wisconsin.

Smith, William Russell. *Al.*, 1813——. A lawyer of Tuscaloosa, Alabama, who was a congressman prior to the Civil War, and during that period sat in the Confederate congress. The Alabama Justice; The Uses of Solitude, a poem; As It Is, a novel; Condensed Alabama Reports.

Smith, Worthington. *Ms.*, 1795-1856. A Congregational clergyman of Vermont, pastor at St. Albans, 1823-1849, and president of the University of Vermont, 1849-56. His Select Sermons were much read. *See Memoir by Torrey, 1861.*

Smith, Zachariah Frederick. *Ky.*, 1827——. An educator who was superintendent of public instruction in Kentucky for four years and author of a History of Kentucky.

Smock, John Conover. *N. J.*, 1842——. A geologist, assistant in charge of the New York State Museum from 1885. Report on Clay Deposits; On Building-Stones in New York.

Smyth, Albert Henry. *Pa.*, 1863——. An educator of Philadelphia, professor of English at the Central High School from 1886. Life of Bayard Taylor. *Hou.*

Smyth, Egbert Coffin. *Me.*, 1829——. Son of W. Smyth, *infra*. A Congregational clergyman prominent among liberal thinkers in his denomination, and professor of ecclesiastical history at Andover Seminary from 1863. The Value of the Study of Church History in Ministerial Education; translation of Uhlhorn's Conflict of Christianity and Heathenism (with W. Ropes).

Smyth, Herbert Weir. *Del.*, 1857——. A professor of Greek in Bryn Mawr College from 1888. Der Diphthong EI in Griech; Sounds and Inflections of the Greek Dialects. *Mac.*

Smyth, Julian Kennedy. *N. Y.*, 1856——. A Swedenborgian clergyman of Boston. Footprints of the Saviour; Holy Names as Interpretations of the Story of the Manger and the Cross. *Rob.*

Smyth, [Samuel] Newman [Phillips]. *Me.*, 1843——. Son of W. Smyth, *infra*. A Congregational clergyman of prominence and of liberal theology, pastor of the First Church at New Haven from 1882. Old Faiths in New Light; The Orthodox Theology of To-Day; The Religious Feeling; The Morality of the Old Testament; Personal Creeds; Christian Ethics; Dorner on the Future State; the Reality of Faith. *Cas. Scr.*

Smyth, Thomas. *I.*, 1808-1873. A Presbyterian clergyman of Charleston, pastor of the Second Church, 1832-73, and very active as a controversialist, among whose many writings are, Lectures on the Prelatical Doctrine of the Apostolical Succession; History of the Westminster Assembly; Why Do I Live?; Solace for Bereaved Parents; Calvin and his Enemies; Ecclesiastical Republicanism.

Smyth, William. *Me.*, 1797-1868. An educator who was professor of mathematics at Bowdoin College from 1825. Elements of Algebra; Treatise on Algebra; Trigonometry, Surveying, and Navigation; Elements of Analytical Geometry; Elements of the Differential and Integral Calculus; Lectures on Modern History.

Snead, Thomas Lowndes. *Va.*, 1828-

1890. A St. Louis lawyer who served in the Confederate army, and after 1865 resumed his profession in New York city. The Fight for Missouri in 1861. *Scr.*

Snelling, Henry Hunt. *N.Y.*, 1817——. Brother of W. J. Snelling, *infra.* A writer living at Cornwall, New York, from 1871. History and Practice of Photography; Dictionary of the Photographic Art.

Snelling, William Joseph. *Ms.*, 1804–1848. A journalist of Boston. The Polar Regions of the Western Continent Explored; Truth: a Satirical Poem; Six Months in a House of Correction.

Snethen, Nicholas. *L. I.*, 1769–1845. A Methodist itinerant preacher, active in the formation of the Methodist Protestant denomination. Preaching the Gospel; Lay Representation; Lectures on Biblical Subjects. *See Sprague's Annals of the American Pulpit.*

Snider, Denton Jaques. *O.*, 1841——. A literary lecturer of St. Louis. System of Shakespeare's Dramas; A Walk in Hellas; Delphic Days, an idyl in the elegiac distich; Agamemnon's Daughter, a classic romantic poem; An Epigrammatic Voyage; Goethe's Faust: a Commentary; The Shakespearean Drama.

Snively, William Andrew. *Pa.*, 1833——. An Episcopal clergyman of Louisville. Family Prayers for the Christian Year; Testimonies to the Supernatural; Parish Lectures on the Prayer Book; Æsthetics in Worship; The Oberammergau Passion Play. *Wh.*

Snow, Caleb Hopkins. *Ms.*, 1796–1835. A Boston physician who published A History of Boston; Geography of Boston and Adjacent Towns.

Snow, Marshall Solomon. *Ms.*, 1842——. A professor of history in Washington University, author of The City Government of St. Louis. *J. H. U.*

Snowden, James Ross. *Pa.*, 1810–1878. A numismatist who was director of the mint, 1856–61. The Mint at Philadelphia; The Mint Manual of Coins; The Coins of the Bible and its Money Terms; Medals; The Cornplanter Memorial. *Lip.*

Soley, James Russell. *Ms.*, 1850——. An educator, professor at the Naval Academy, 1871–82, and lecturer on international law at Newport Naval College from 1885. The Rescue of Greeley (with W. Schley, *supra*); Foreign Systems of Education; The Blockade and the Cruisers; The Boys of 1812 and Other Naval Heroes; History of the Naval Academy; The Sailor Boys of '61. *Est. Scr.*

Somerville, William Clarke. *Md.*, 1790–1826. A writer who was appointed minister to Sweden, but died before reaching there and was buried at the Marquis Lafayette's home at Lagrange. Letters from Paris on the Causes of the French Revolution.

Sophocles, Evangelinus Apostolides. *Gr.*, 1807–1883. A Greek scholar of distinction, professor at Harvard University, 1849–83. His chief work is a Greek Lexicon of the Roman and Byzantine Periods; and among his other publications are, Greek Grammar for Learners; History of the Greek Alphabet. *Scr.*

Sotheran, Charles. *E.*, 1847——. An English lithographer who came to America in 1874, and, settling in New York city, engaged in journalism. Alessandro di Cagliostro: Impostor or Martyr; Shelley as Philosopher and Reformer.

Soule [soo'lay], **Mrs. Caroline Augusta [White].** *N. Y.*, 1824——. The widow of a Universalist minister who entered the ministry herself, was the first foreign missionary of that denomination, and in 1888 was in charge of a congregation in Glasgow, Scotland. House Life; The Pet of the Settlement; Wine or Water.

Soule [sole], **Richard.** *Ms.*, 1812–1877. A lexicographer of Boston. Manual of English Pronunciation (with W. H. Wheeler, *infra*); Dictionary of English Synonyms; Pronouncing Handbook (with L. Campbell). *Le.*

Southgate, Horatio. *Me.*, 1812–1894. The first and only Protestant Episcopal bishop of Constantinople. He was consecrated in 1844, but resigned his office in 1850, and held various rectorships subsequently, including that of Zion Church, New York city, 1859–72, in which latter year he retired from active duties. The Cross Above the Crescent; Parochial Sermons; Narrative of a Tour Through Armenia, etc.; The War in the

East; Practical Directions for the Observance of Lent.

Southworth, Mrs. Emma Dorothy Eliza [**Nevitte**]. *D. C.*, 1818——. A voluminous writer of sensational romances, mainly of Southern life and some sixty in number, for many years a resident of Washington, but since 1876 of Yonkers, New York. The literary merit of her works is very slender. They were in nearly every case first issued serially in The New York Ledger, and have been very popular amongst uncritical readers. Among them are, Ishmael; The Widow's Son; Retribution; The Family Doom. *See Hart's American Literature.*

Spaeth [spāt], **Adolph.** *Wg.*, 1839——. A prominent Lutheran clergyman of Philadelphia, pastor of St. John's Church from 1867. Die Evangelien des Kirchenjahrs; Brosamen von des Herrn Tische; Saarkörner; Luther in Lied seiner Zeitgenossen; Phœbe the Deaconess; Liederlust; Faith and Life Represented by Luther; Annotations on the Gospel according to St. John.

Spahr, Charles Barzillai. *O.*, 1860——. A political economist, associate editor of The Outlook from 1886. The Distribution of American Wealth. *Cr.*

Spalding, John Franklin. *Me.*, 1828——. The first Protestant Episcopal bishop of the diocese of Colorado. The Threefold Ministry; Manual of Prayers; The Church and its Apostolic Ministry.

Spalding, John Lancaster. *Ky.*, 1840——. Nephew of M. T. Spalding, *infra*. The Roman Catholic bishop of Peoria, and widely known as a thoughtful essayist and educator. Life of Archbishop Spalding; Essays and Reviews; Religious Mission of the Irish People and Catholic Colonization; Lectures and Discourses; America, and Other Poems; The Poet's Praise; Education and the Higher Life; Means and Ends of Education; Things of the Mind; Songs, chiefly from the German. *Mg.*

Spalding, Lyman. *N. H.*, 1775–1821. A physician at Portsmouth, in his native State, and subsequently of New York city, who was one of the early advocates of vaccination. Reflections on Fever; Reflections on Yellow Fever Periods.

Spalding, Martin John. *Ky.*, 1810–1872. A Roman Catholic archbishop of Baltimore, 1864–72, active as a controversialist. Review of D'Aubigné's History of the Reformation; Modern Civilization; Evidences of Catholicity; Life of Bishop Flaget; Early Catholic Missions in Kentucky; Miscellanea. *See Life by J. L. Spalding, supra; Gross's Sketches of Contemporaries.*

Spalding, Mrs. Susan [**Marr**]. *Me.*, 18——. A verse-writer of Philadelphia whose poems are much above the level of average verse. The Wings of Icarus, and Other Poems. *Rob.*

Sparhawk, Frances Campbell. *Me.*, 1847——. A novelist and philanthropist of Newton, Massachusetts, who has written much in behalf of the Indian cause. A Chronicle of Conquest, a romance of the Indian school at Carlisle; Little Polly Blatchley; Miss West's Class in Geography; Elizabeth, a colonial romance; The Query Club; A Lazy Man's Work; Onoqua, an Indian Story; Senator Intrigue and Inspector Nosely. *Le. Lo.*

Sparks, Jared. *Ct.*, 1789–1866. A Unitarian clergyman, pastor at Baltimore, 1819–23, professor of history at Harvard University, 1839–49, and president of Harvard University, 1849–53. He is best known by the American Biography which he edited, and of which he was in part the author. It includes sixty lives, of which he wrote those of Ethan Allen; Benedict Arnold; Marquette; La Salle; Pulaski; Ribault; Charles Lee; Ledyard. He was also author of a Life of Gouverneur Morris. He published editions of the works of Franklin and Washington, with notes and life of each; and also Correspondence of the American Revolution. His editing has been sometimes criticised because he occasionally toned down passages of unorthodox vigour and corrected the spelling of his subjects, but his eminent merits in other respects have been generally recognized. *See Lives by Mayer, supra, 1867; G. E. Ellis, supra, 1869; Herbert Adams, supra. Har.*

Sparks, William Henry. *Ga.*, 1800–1882. A Mississippi planter, after 1850 a lawyer of New Orleans, who published Memories of Fifty Years. He was a popular verse-writer, his best-known poems being, Somebody's Darling; The Dying Year.

Spaulding, Elbridge Gerry. *N. Y.*, 1809–1897. A banker of Buffalo, author of a History of Legal Tender Money During the Great Rebellion.

Spaulding, Henry George. *Ms.*, 1837——. A Unitarian clergyman of Massachusetts, among whose writings are, The Teachings of Jesus; Later Heroes of Israel; Forty Hymns and their Authors.

Spaulding, Solomon. *Ct.*, 1761–1816. A Congregational clergyman of New England who left the ministry in 1795 and was subsequently an iron-founder at Conneaut, Ohio, where he wrote a romance called The Manuscript Found, published in 1812, and sometimes asserted to be the basis of the Mormon Bible. *See Patterson's, Who Wrote the Mormon Bible? 1882.*

Spear, Charles. *Ms.*, 1801–1863. A Universalist minister of Boston active in prison reform. Names and Titles of Christ; Essays on the Punishment of Death; Plea for Discharged Convicts; Voices from Prison.

Spear, Samuel Thayer. *N. Y.*, 1812–1891. A Presbyterian clergyman of Brooklyn, editor of The New York Independent from 1871. Family Power; Religion and the State; Constitutionality of the Legal Tender Act; The Law of the Federal Judiciary; The Law of Extradition; The Bible Heaven. *Fu.*

Spears, John Randolph. *O.*, 1850——. A journalist of New York city. The Gold Diggings of Cape Horn; The Port of Missing Ships, and Other Stories of the Sea. *Mac. Put.*

Speed, John Gilmer. *Ky.*, 1853——. A journalist of New York city. Life of Keats.

Speer, William. *Pa.*, 1822——. A Presbyterian missionary in China. China and the United States; The Great Revival of 1800; God's Rule for Christian Giving.

Spencer, Mrs. Bella Zilfa. *E.*, 1840–1867. A novelist who was the first wife of General George E. Spencer, formerly of the United States army. Ora, the Lost Wife; Tried and True; Surface and Depth.

Spencer, Mrs. Cornelia [Phillips]. *N. Y.*, 1825——. A North Carolina writer who published The Last Ninety Days of the War in North Carolina; History of North Carolina.

Spencer, Ichabod Smith. *Vt.*, 1798–1854. A Presbyterian clergyman prominent in Brooklyn for many years. A Pastor's Sketches; Sermons; Sacramental Discourses; Evidences of Divine Revelation.

Spencer, Jesse Ames. *N. Y.*, 1816——. An Episcopal clergyman and educator, professor in the College of the City of New York, 1869–83, and editor of many valuable classical text-books. His other works include, History of the English Reformation; History of the United States, a very popular work; Sermons; Discourses; The East: Sketches of Travel in Egypt and the Holy Land; Greek Praxis; Five Last Things; Studies in Eschatology; Papalism *vs.* Catholic Truth; Memorabilia of Sixty-Five Years, 1820–86. *Wh.*

Spencer, Mrs. Sara [Andrews]. *N. Y.*, 1837——. A prominent woman-suffragist of Washington, proprietor of the Spencerian Business College. Problems on the Woman Question; Lessons in the English Language.

Spencer, Thomas. *Ms.*, 1793–1857. A physician who was medical professor at Hobart College, 1835–57. Lectures on Vital Chemistry; Practical Observations on Epidemic Diarrhœa known as Cholera. *See Memoir of, by S. Willard, 1858.*

Spencer, Mrs. William Loring [Nuñez]. *Fl.*, 18———. A writer who is the second wife of General George E. Spencer, formerly of the United States army. Salt Lake Fruit; The Story of Mary, republished as Dennis Day; A Plucky One; Calamity Jane. *Cas.*

Spitzka, Edward Charles. *N. Y.*, 1852——. A physician of New York city eminent as a neurologist. Insanity, its Classification, Diagnosis, and Treatment.

Spofford, Ainsworth Rand. *N. H.*, 1825——. The librarian of Congress, and editor of The American

Almanac and Treasury of Facts. Library of Choice Literature; Library of Historical Characters.

Spofford, Mrs. Harriet Elizabeth [Prescott]. *Me.*, 1835——. A novelist and poet of Newburyport whose best work in both prose and verse is markedly original, and characterized by striking luxuriance of description. Azarian; Sir Rohan's Ghost; The Amber Gods, and Other Stories; New England Legends; The Thief in the Night; The Marquis of Carabas, a romance; A Lost Jewel; Hester Stanley at St. Mark's, a story for girls; The Scarlet Poppy, and Other Stories; Art Decoration Applied to Furniture; Home and Hearth; Essays on the Domestic Relations; Three Heroines of New England (with Alice Brown, *supra*, and L. Guiney, *supra*); The Servant Girl Question; A Master Spirit; Ballads About Authors; Poems; In Titans' Garden, and Other Poems. *See Atlantic Monthly, April, 1882. Cop. Do. Har. Hou. Le. Rob. Scr.*

Spooner, Lysander. *Ms.*, 1808–1887. A lawyer of Boston prominent as an abolitionist. Our Finances; The Deist's Reply to the Alleged Supernatural Evidences of Christianity; A Defence for Fugitive Slaves; Unconstitutionality of Slavery; The Law of Prices; Poverty: Causes and Cure.

Spooner, Shearjashub. *Vt.*, 1809–1859. A dentist of New York city. Guide to Sound Teeth; Surgical and Mechanical Dentistry; Biographical and Critical Dictionary of Painters, Engravers, Sculptors, and Architects; Anecdotes of Painters.

Sprague, Alfred White. *Sh.*, 1821——. A Boston chemist who published Chemical Experiments; Elements of Natural Philosophy.

Sprague, Charles. *Ms.*, 1791–1875. A cashier of the Globe Bank, Boston, 1825–65, well known in his life-time as a verse-writer, and still pleasantly remembered for the genuine sentiment in such poems as The Family Meeting and The Winged Worshippers, though an Ode to Shakespeare was once much praised. His poems first appeared in 1841, the latest edition being that of 1876. *See Griswold's Poets and Poetry of America.*

Sprague, Charles Ezra. *N. Y.*, 1842——. The secretary of the Dime Savings Institution in New York city from 1878. Logical Symbolism; Handbook of Volapük.

Sprague, John Titcomb. *Ms.*, 1810–1888. An officer of the United States army who was military governor of Florida in 1865. Origin, etc., of the Florida War (1848).

Sprague, Mary Aplin. *O.*, 1849——. A novelist of Newark, Ohio. An Earnest Trifler. *Hou.*

Sprague, Peleg. *Ms.*, 1793–1880. A once noted jurist of Boston. Speeches and Addresses; Decisions in Admiralty and Maritime Cases.

Sprague, William Buell. *Ct.*, 1795–1875. A Presbyterian clergyman of Albany whose Annals of the American Pulpit in ten volumes is the work by which he is best known. Other works of his include, Letters to a Daughter; The Daughter's Own Book; Letters from Europe; Letters on Revivals; True Christianity, and Other Systems; Life of Edward Dorr Griffin, *supra;* Letters to Young Men; Women of the Bible; Visits to European Celebrities; Life of Jedidiah Morse, *supra;* Aids to Early Religion.

Sprecher, Samuel. *Md.*, 1810——. A Lutheran clergyman, president of Wurtemburg Seminary at Springfield, Ohio, 1849–74, and author of The Groundwork of a System of Lutheran Theology.

Spring, Gardiner. *Ms.*, 1785–1873. A Presbyterian clergyman, long prominent in New York city as pastor of the Brick Church, 1810–73. Power of the Pulpit; The Church in the Wilderness; Sermons; Distinguishing Traits of Christian Character; Pulpit Ministrations; Attractions of the Cross; The Bible Not of Man; The Mercy Seat, comprise his chief works. *See Personal Reminiscences of. C. P. S.*

Spring, Leverett Wilson. *Vt.*, 1840——. A Congregational clergyman and educator, professor of English literature at the University of Kansas, 1881–86, and professor of rhetoric at Williams College from 1886. History of Kansas; Mark Hopkins: Teacher. *Hou.*

Springer, Mrs. Rebecca [Ruter]. *Ind.*, 1832——. The wife of an Illinois senator, and author of Songs of the Sea, and two novels, Beechwood; Self.

Sproull [sprowl], **Thomas.** *Pa.*, 1803–1892. A Reformed Presbyterian clergyman of Pittsburg, who published Prelections on Theology.

Squier [skwīr], **Ephraim George.** *N. Y.*, 1821–1888. An archæologist and diplomatist, consul to Peru, 1863–1865, and consul-general of Honduras at New York in 1868. Nicaragua; Mexican Hieroglyphics; Ancient Monuments of the Mississippi Valley (with E. H. Davis, *supra*); Antiquities of the State of New York; Waikna, or Adventures on the Mosquito Coast; The States of Central America; Serpent Symbols; Peru. *Ho.*

Squier, Miles Powell. *Vt.*, 1792–1866. A Presbyterian clergyman of Geneva, New York. The Problem Solved, or Sin Not of God; Reason and the Bible; Miscellaneous Writings; Autobiography.

Staley, Cady. *N. Y.*, 1840——. A civil engineer, president of the Case School of Applied Science at Cleveland, and author of The Separate System of Sewerage (with G. S. Pierson).

Stall, Sylvanus. *N. Y.*, 1847——. A Lutheran clergyman of Lancaster, Pennsylvania, 1880–87, and since then editor of Stall's Lutheran Year Book. Methods of Church Work; Pastor's Record; Talks to the King's Children; Five-Minute Object Sermons to Children. *Fu.*

Stallo, John Bernhard. *G.*, 1823——. A Cincinnati lawyer, minister to Italy in 1885. Concepts and Theories of Modern Physics; General Principles of the Philosophy of Nature. *Ap.*

Stanley, Anthony Dumond. *Ct.*, 1810–1853. An educator who was a professor of mathematics at Yale University, 1830–53. Elementary Treatise of Spherical Geometry and Trigonometry; Tables of Logarithms.

Stanley, Henry Morton, originally John Rowlands. *W.*, 1840——. A celebrated African explorer. In 1855 he was adopted by a New Orleans merchant whose name he took. He was sent by the New York Herald in search of Livingstone in 1870, and was again sent to Africa by the Herald in 1874. In 1879 he accompanied an African expedition sent by the King of the Belgians, which resulted in the establishment of the Congo Free State. How I Found Livingstone; My Kalulu, Prince, King, and Slave, a Study of Central Africa; Coomassie and Magdala; Through the Dark Continent; The Congo and the Founding of its Free State; In Darkest Africa; My Dark Companions; My Early Travels in America and Asia; Slavery and the Slave Trade in India. *See Stanley and Africa, 1890; Headley's Adventures of Stanley; Lives by Montefiore, 1889, Little, 1890, Reddall, 1890; Packard's Stanley and the Congo; Stanley and his Heroic Relief of Emin Pasha, by E. P. Scott; Wauters's Stanley's Emin Pasha Expedition; With Stanley's Rear Column. Har.*

Stansbury, Howard. *N. Y.*, 1806–1863. An explorer who was a topographical engineer in the United States army, and published An Expedition to Great Salt Lake (1852). *Lip.*

Stanton, Mrs. Elizabeth [Cady]. *N. Y.*, 1815——. Wife of H. B. Stanton, *infra.* A celebrated woman-suffragist and reformer who has devoted the larger part of her life to suffrage and other reforms, and (with S. Anthony and F. Gage) has published a History of the Woman Suffrage Movement.

Stanton, Frank Lebby. *Ga.*, 1858——. A journalist and popular verse-writer of Atlanta. Songs of the Soil. *Ap.*

Stanton, Henry Brewster. *Ct.*, 1805–1887. A journalist and reformer of New York city. Sketches of Reforms and Reformers in Great Britain and Ireland; Random Recollections. *Har.*

Stanton, Henry Thompson. *Va.*, 1834——. Son of R. H. Stanton, *infra.* An officer in the United States army and an Indian commissioner who has written much humourous verse. The Moneyless Man, and Other Poems; Jacob Brown, and Other Poems. *Clke.*

Stanton, Richard Henry. *Va.*, 1812——. A jurist of Kentucky. Code of Civil and Criminal Practice in

Kentucky; Practical Treatise for Justices of the Peace; Manual for Kentucky Executors.

Stanton, Robert Livingstone. *Ct.*, 1810——. A Presbyterian clergyman in Ohio who published The Church and the Rebellion.

Stanton, Theodore. *N. Y.*, 1851——. Son of H. B. and E. Stanton, *supra*. A journalist living in Paris. The Woman Question in Europe. *Put.*

Stanwood, Edward. *Me.*, 1841——. A Boston journalist, managing editor of The Youth's Companion. A History of Presidential Elections; History of Cotton Manufacture in New England. *Hou.*

Starr, Eliza Allen. *Ms.*, 1824——. An art lecturer in Chicago. Patron Saints; Pilgrims and Shrines; Songs of a Lifetime.

Starr, Frederic Ratchford. *N. S.*, 1821——. A noted dairy farmer of Litchfield, Connecticut. Didley Dumps, the Newsboy; May I Not?; What Can I Do?; Farm Echoes; From Shore to Shore.

Starr, Moses Allen. *N. Y.*, 1854——. A physician of New York city, prominent as a neurologist. Familiar Forms of Nervous Diseases; Lectures on Insanity; Brain Surgery.

Stauffer, Francis Henry. *Pa.*, 1832——. A sensational novelist of Philadelphia, long a contributor to the Saturday Night. Among his serials published in that paper, none of them of much literary merit, are Ruth Brandon; Lucy Darrel; Devona the Dauntless.

Staunton, William. *E.*, 1803-1889. An Episcopal clergyman of New York city who published an Ecclesiastical Dictionary, and wrote much on musical topics.

Stearns, Asahel. *Ms.*, 1774-1839. A Massachusetts lawyer and Congressman, professor of law at Harvard University, 1817-29. Summary of the Law and Practice of Real Actions; General Laws, 1780-1822 (with L. Shaw).

Stearns, Charles. *Ms.*, 1753-1826. A Unitarian clergyman, pastor at Lincoln, Massachusetts, from 1785 till his death. The Ladies' Philosophy of Love, a Poem; Principles of Morality and Religion.

Stearns, Charles Woodward. *Ms.*, 181—1887. A physician and surgeon of note as a Shakespearean scholar. Shakespeare's Medical Knowledge; Shakespeare Treasury of Wisdom and Knowledge; Concordance of the Constitution of the United States; The Black Men and the South and the Rebels.

Stearns, Edward Josiah. *Ms.*, 1810-1890. An Episcopal clergyman and educator in Maryland. A Platform for All Parties; Notes on Uncle Tom's Cabin; Practical Guide to English Pronunciation; The Faith of Our Forefathers, an Examination of Archbishop Gibbons's "Faith of Our Fathers;" The Archbishop's Champion Brought to Book. *Wh.*

Stearns, Frank Preston. *Ms.*, 1846——. Great-nephew of L. M. Child, *supra*. A Boston writer upon art, literature, and history. The Real and Ideal in Literature; Life of Tintoretto; The Midsummer of Italian Art; Sketches from Concord and Appledore; Modern English Prose; Summer Travel in Europe. *Put.*

Stearns, John Glazier. *N. H.*, 1795-1874. A Baptist clergyman once prominent in central New York. The Primitive Church; Letters on Freemasonry; The Sovereignty of God and Free Agency; The Influence of the Spirit and the Word in Regeneration.

Stearns, John William. *Ms.*, 1829——. A professor in the University of Wisconsin from 1884. The History of Education in Wisconsin.

Stearns, Lewis French. *Ms.*, 1847-1892. A Presbyterian clergyman, afterwards professor of systematic theology in Bangor Theological Seminary, 1880-92. The Evidence of Christian Experience; Present Day Theology, with Biographical Sketch by G. L. Prentiss, *supra*; Life of Henry Boynton Smith, *supra*. *Hou. Scr.*

Stearns, Oakman Sprague. *Me.*, 1817-1893. A Baptist clergyman of Massachusetts, professor of biblical interpretation at Newton Theological Seminary from 1868. A Syllabus of Messianic Passages in the Old Testament; Introduction to the Books of the Old Testament.

Stearns, Samuel. *Ms.*, 1747–1819. A physician and astronomer of Worcester, New York city, and lastly of Brattleboro, Vermont. Tour to London and Paris; Mystery of Animal Magnetism; American Oracle; The American Herbal or Materia Medica.

Stearns, William Augustus. *Ms.*, 1805–1876. A Congregational clergyman, president of Amherst College, 1854–76. Infant Church Membership; A Plea for the Nation.

Stearns, Winfrid Alden. 185——. Son of W. A. Stearns, *supra*. Labrador: a Sketch of its Peoples, etc.; Wrecked on Labrador; New England Bird Life (with E. Coues, *supra*).

Stebbins, Giles Badger. 181——. After Dogmatic Theology, What?; The American Protectionist's Manual; Chapters from the Bible of the Ages; Facts and Opinions Touching the American Colonization Society; Progress from Poverty.

Stebbins, Emma. *N. Y.*, 1815–1882. A sculptress who lived many years in Rome, where she formed a friendship with Charlotte Cushman. Charlotte Cushman: Her Letters and Memories of her Life. *Hou.*

Stebbins, Mrs. Mary Elizabeth [Moore] [Hewitt]. *Ms.*, 1818——. Memorial of F. S. Osgood, *supra*; Songs of Our Lord; Heroines of History; Poems: Sacred, Passionate, and Legendary.

Stebbins, Rufus Phineas. *Ms.*, 1810–1885. A Unitarian clergyman of Ithaca, New York, and subsequently of Newton Centre, Massachusetts. A Study of the Pentateuch; A Common Sense View of the Books of the Old Testament.

Stedman, Edmund Clarence. *Ct.*, 1833——. A poet and literary critic of New York city, for many years a member of the Stock Exchange there. His volumes of verse include, Poems: Lyric and Idyllic; The Prince's Ball; The Battle of Bull Run; Alice of Monmouth; Idyl of the Great War, and Other Poems; The Blameless Prince; Hawthorne, and Other Poems; Lyrics and Idyls; Poems, Household Edition; The Star Bearer. His other works comprise, Octavius Brooks Frothingham and the New Faith; Victorian Poets; Poets of America; The Nature and Elements of Poetry. His most important labours as editor have been, A Library of American Literature (with E. M. Hutchinson, *supra*); The Works of Poe (with G. E. Woodberry, *infra*); A Victorian Anthology. *See Vedder's American Writers; Foley's American Authors, 1897. Hou.*

Steele, Daniel. *N.Y.*, 1824——. A Methodist clergyman and educator of note. Commentary on Joshua; Love Enthroned; Milestone Papers; Antinomianism Revived; Commentary on Leviticus and Numbers; Bible Readings; Sermons and Essays. *Meth.*

Steele, David. *I.*, 1827——. A Reformed Presbyterian clergyman of Philadelphia from 1861. The Times in Which we Live, and the Ministry they Require; The Apologetics of History.

Steele, Mrs. Esther [Baker]. *N. Y.*, 1835——. Wife of J. D. Steele, *infra*, and co-author with him of a General History and school histories of the United States; France; Ancient Peoples; Mediæval and Modern Peoples; Greece; Rome.

Steele, George McKendree. *N. Y.*, 1823——. A Methodist clergyman and educator, principal of Wilbraham Academy, Massachusetts. Outline Study of Political Economy. *Meth.*

Steele, Joel Dorman. *N. Y.*, 1836–1886. A prominent educator of Elmira, New York, who published Barnes's History of the United States and a series of text-books on the sciences, each intended for a course of study of fourteen weeks, including Natural Philosophy; Geology; Human Physiology; Zoölogy; Chemistry.

Steele, Mrs. Margaret. *See Conkling, Mrs.*

Steele, Thomas Sedgwick. *Ct.*, 1845——. Canoe and Camera: a Tour Through the Maine Forests; Paddle and Portage from Moosehead Lake to the Aroostook River; A Voyage to Vikingland. *Est.*

Steendam, Jacob. *H.*, 1616–16—?. The earliest verse-writer of New York. He was in the employ of the Dutch West India Company, and lived in New Amsterdam, now New York, from 1650 to 1663, about which time he returned to Holland. The place and date of his death are unknown. His four small volumes of verse include, Der Distelvink (The Thistle Finch); Klacht van Nieuw Amsterdam (The Complaint of New Amsterdam); Tlof van Nieuw Nederland (The Praise of New Netherland; Prichel Vaarsen (Spurring Verses). The literary merit of his work is small.

Steenstra, Peter Henry. *H.*, 1833——. An Episcopal clergyman of Cambridge, Massachusetts, professor of Old Testament criticism and interpretation in the Episcopal Theological School from 1867. The Being of God as Unity and Trinity. *Hou.*

Steiger, Ernst. *Sxy.*, 1832——. A bibliographer and publisher of New York city. Der Nachdruck in Nordamerika; Das Copyright Law in den Vereinigten Staaten; Periodical Literature, a bibliography.

Stella. *See Lewis, Mrs.*

Stellhorn, Frederick William. *G.*, 1841——. A Lutheran clergyman of Ohio, professor of theology in Capitol University, who has published a Lexicon of New Testament Greek; Annotations on the Acts of the Apostles; Annotations on the Gospels.

Stephen, Mrs. Elizabeth [Willison]. *Al.*, 1856——. The wife of a Presbyterian clergyman in Rockport, Illinois. The Confessions of Two, a novel.

Stephens, Alexander Hamilton. *Ga.*, 1812–1883. A distinguished Georgia statesman who was a representative in Congress from his State, 1843–59, vice-president of the Confederacy, subsequently a member of Congress, and in 1882 governor of Georgia. School History of the United States; History of the War between the States; Compendium of United States History. *See Carroll's Twelve Americans; Life by F. H. Norton; Life by Johnston and Browne; Harper's Magazine. February, 1870; Appletons' American Biography; Trent's Southern Statesmen. Lip.*

Stephens, Mrs. Ann Sophia [Winterbotham]. *Ct.*, 1813–1886. A novelist and littérateur of New York city whose books were at one time much read. Among them are, Fashion and Famine, her best work; A Story of Western Life; The Old Homestead; Myra, the Child of Adoption; The Heiress; Wives and Widows; The Curse of Gold; A Popular History of the United States. She wrote not a little verse, her best known poem being the familiar Polish Boy.

Stephens, Charles Asbury. *Me.*, 1845——. A writer of Norway, Maine. Camping Out; Off the Geysers; Left on Labrador; Fox Hunting; On the Amazon; The Young Moose-Hunters; The Knockabout Club in the Woods and in the Tropics. *Co. Est.*

Stephens, Harriet Marion. 1823–1850. Home Scenes and Home Sounds; Hagar the Martyr, a novel.

Stephens, John Lloyd. *N. J.*, 1805–1852. A traveller of note. Incidents of Travel in Central America; Yucatan; Egypt, Arabia, and the Holy Land; Greece, Turkey, and Russia. *See Allibone's Dictionary. Har.*

Stephens, William. *E.*, 1671–1753. A colonial governor of Georgia, 1743–1750, who published a Journal of the Proceedings in Georgia. *See Biography by his son, entitled The Castle Builder, or the History of William Stephens of the Isle of Wight.*

Stern, Simon Adler. *Pa.*, 1838——. Florentine Nights; Excerpts; Jottings of Travel in China and Japan.

Sternberg, George Miller. *N. Y.*, 1838——. A surgeon in the United States army. Photo-Micrographs; Malaria and Malarial Diseases; Bacteria, from the French of Maguin; Immunity: Protective Inoculations in Infectious Diseases; Manual of Bacteriology. *Hou.*

Sterne, Simon. *Pa.*, 1839——. A prominent politician of New York city. Popular Government and Personal Representation; Constitutional History and Development of the United States; Suffrage in Cities; Hindrances to Prosperity. *Lip. Put.*

Sterne, Stuart. *See Bloede.*

Sterrett, John Robert Sitlington. *Va.*, 1851——. A professor of Greek at Amherst College from 1892. Qua in re Hymni Homerici quinque majores inter se differunt; Inscriptions of Assos; Epigraphical Journey in Asia Minor; The Wolfe Expedition to Asia Minor.

Stevens, Abel. *Pa.*, 1815-1897. A Methodist clergyman of New York city of prominence as a writer, and long connected with the Methodist Book Concern. History of the Methodist Episcopal Church in the United States; History of Methodism; Life of Madame de Staël; Life of Nathan Bangs, *supra;* Character Sketches; Women of Methodism; Christian Work and Consolation; Church Polity; Tales from the Parsonage, are among his many publications. *Har. Meth.*

Stevens, Alexander Hodgdon. *N. Y.*, 1789-1869. A surgeon of New York city, whose chief works are, Inflammation of the Eye; Lectures on Lithotomy; First Lines of Surgery.

Stevens, Benjamin. *Vt.*, 1833——. Brother of H. Stevens, *infra.* A bibliographer who has edited Campaign in Virginia in 1781; Facsimiles of MSS. in European Archives Relating to America, 1773-83.

Stevens, Charles Ellis. *Ms.*, 1853-——. An Episcopal clergyman of Philadelphia. The Sources of the Constitution of the United States in Relation to Colonial and English History. *Mac.*

Stevens, George Barker. *N. Y.*, 1854——. A Congregational clergyman and educator of New Haven, professor in Yale Divinity School from 1886. Commentary on Galatians; The Pauline Theology; The Johannine Theology; Doctrine and Life. *Scr.*

Stevens, Henry. *Vt.*, 1819-1886. A bibliographer of prominence, who lived in London after 1845. Historical Nuggets; Historical Collections; Recollections of James Lenox; The Tehuantepec Railway; Historical and Geographical Notes; The Bibles in the Caxton Exhibition; Catalogue of the American Books in the British Museum; and indexes to state papers in London relating to Virginia, Maryland, Rhode Island, and New Jersey.

Stevens, John Austin. *N.Y.*, 1827-——. An author of New York city, and later of Newport, Rhode Island, who founded the Magazine of American History; The Valley of the Rio Grande; The Expedition of Lafayette against Arnold; Life of Albert Gallatin, *supra. Hou.*

Stevens, John Leavitt. *Me.*, 1820-1895. A diplomatist who was minister to Uruguay and Paraguay, 1870-73, to Sweden, 1877-83, to Hawaii, 1889-93. History of Gustavus Adolphus.

Stevens, Thomas. *E.*, 1855——. A noted cyclist who has published, Scouting for Stanley in East Africa; Around the World on a Bicycle: From San Francisco to Teheran, From Teheran to Yokohama; Through Russia on a Mustang. *Cas. Scr.*

Stevens, William Bacon. *Me.*, 1815-1887. The fourth Protestant Episcopal bishop of Pennsylvania, consecrated in 1862. History of Georgia; The Bow in the Cloud; Sermons; Sabbaths of Our Lord; Parables of the New Testament Unfolded; History of Silk Culture in Georgia; The Sunday at Home. *Co.*

Stevenson, E[dward] Irenæus. *N. J.*, 1858——. A littérateur of New York city, since 1881 the editor of The New York Independent, and for many years an editor of Harper's Weekly. He has been the musical editor of several journals for a number of years. White Cockades, an Incident of the "Forty-five;" Janus, reissued as A Matter of Temperament, a musical novel; Left to Themselves, reissued as Philip and Gerald; Mrs. Dee's Encore; A Square of Sevens. *Har. Meth. Scr.*

Stevenson, Sarah Hackett. *Il.*, 1843——. A physician of Chicago. Boys and Girls in Biology; The Physiology of Woman.

Steward, Theophilus Gould. *N. J.*, 1843——. A clergyman of African descent. Death, Hades, and the Resurrection; The End of the World; Genesis Re-read.

Stewart, Austin. *Va.*, c. 1793-186-. An author and educator of African descent who published, Twenty-Two Years a Slave and Forty Years a Freeman.

Stewart, Charles Samuel. *N. J.*, 1795-1870. A Presbyterian clergyman, chaplain in the navy. Residence at the Sandwich Islands in 1822-23; Visit to the South Seas in the Ship Vincennes; Sketches of Society in Great Britain and Ireland in 1832; Brazil and La Plata in 1850-63; Personal Record of a Cruise.

Stewart, Mrs. Electra Maria [Sheldon]. *N. Y.*, 1817——. A writer of Detroit. Early History of Michigan; The Clevelands, a religious juvenile tale.

Stewart, Ferdinand Campbell. *Va.*, 1815——. A physician of New York city who removed to England in 1855. Hospitals and Surgeons of Paris.

Stewart, James. *N. Y.*, 1799-1864. A physician of New York city. Diseases of Children; The Lungs.

Stewart, Thomas McCants. *S. C.*, 1854——. A New York city lawyer of African descent. Liberia: the Americo-African Republic; Perils of a Great City.

Stickney, Albert. *Ms.*, 1839——. A lawyer of New York city. The Lawyer and his Clients; A True Republic; Democratic Government: a Study of Politics; The Political Problem. *Har.*

Stickney, Mrs. Julia Granby [Noyes]. *Ms.*, 1830——. A verse-writer of Groveland, Massachusetts. Poems on Lake Winnepesaukee.

Stiles, Ezra. *Ct.*, 1727-1795. A Congregational clergyman, famous in colonial days, who was president of Yale College, 1778-95. Account of the Settlement of Bristol, Rhode Island; History of Three of the Judges of Charles the First, Whalley, Goffe, and Dixwell. *See Life, by Abiel Holmes, supra; Life by Kingsley in Sparks's American Biography; Sprague's Annals of the American Pulpit.*

Stiles, Henry Reed. *N. Y.*, 1832——. Kinsman of E. Stiles, *supra*. A prominent physician of Brooklyn. History and Genealogies of Ancient Windsor, Connecticut; History of Brooklyn, Long Island; The Wallabout Prison Ship.

Stiles, Joseph Clay. *Ga.*, 1795-1875. A Presbyterian clergyman, after 1860 an evangelist in the South. Modern Reform Examined, or the Union of North and South on Slavery; The National Controversy.

Stiles, William Henry. *Ga.*, 1808-1865. Brother of J. C. Stiles, *supra*. A Savannah lawyer who was an officer in the Confederate army. History of Austria.

Still, William. *N. J.*, 1821——. A noted Philadelphia philanthropist of African descent. The Underground Railroad; Voting and Laboring; Struggle for the Rights of Colored People in Philadelphia.

Stillé [stĭl'le], **Alfred.** *Pa.*, 1813——. A physician of Philadelphia. Elements of General Pathology; The Unity of Medicine; Humboldt's Life and Character; War as an Element of Civilization; Othello and Desdemona: their Characters; The National Dispensatory (with Maisch); Therapeutics and Materia Medica; Epidemic Meningitis; Epidemic or Malignant Cholera. *Lip.*

Stillé, Charles Janeway. *Pa.*, 1819——. Brother of A. Stillé, *supra*. A Philadelphia educator, provost of the University of Pennsylvania, 1868-80. Historical Development of American Civilization; Studies in Mediæval Civilization; Beaumarchais and the Lost Million, a chapter of the Secret History of the American Revolution; History of the United States Sanitary Commission; How a Free People Conduct a Long War; Northern Interest and Southern Independence; Life and Times of John Dickinson; General Anthony Wayne and the Pennsylvania Line. *Lip.*

Stillé, Moreton. *Pa.*, 1822-1855. Brother of A. Stillé, *supra*. A Philadelphia physician, co-author with F. Wharton of a Treatise on Medical Jurisprudence.

Stillman, Samuel. *Pa.*, 1738-1807. A Baptist clergyman, pastor of the First Baptist Church in Boston from 1765 till his death, and a man of prominence in his day. His Select Sermons were published in 1808. *See Sprague's Annals of the American Pulpit.*

Stillman, William James. *N. Y.*, 1828——. A littérateur and artist who was consul at Rome, 1861-65, and in Crete, 1865-69. He has lived at Rome from 1886 as the correspondent of The London Times for Italy and Greece. History of the Cretan Insurrection; Poetic Localities of Cambridge; Herzegovina and the Late Uprising; Turkish Rule and Warfare; On the Track of Ulysses; Manual of Photography. *Hou.*

Stimpson, William. *Ms.*, 1830–1872. A naturalist of eminence. Descriptiones Animalium Evertebratorum; Notes on North American Crustacea; Crustacea Dredged in the Gulf Stream.

Stimson, Alexander Lovett. *Ms.*, 1816——. A lawyer and journalist. History of the Express Companies; New England Boys; Waifwood, a novel.

Stimson, Frederick Jesup. "J. S. of Dale." *Ms.*, 1855——. A lawyer and popular novelist of Boston. Labor in its Relations to Law; Handbook of the Labor Law of the United States; American Statute Law; Glossary of Technical Terms of the Common Law; Uniform State Legislation. In fiction he has published, Guerndale; The Crime of Henry Vane; The King's Men; The Residuary Legatee; The Sentimental Calendar; In the Three Zones; First Harvests; Pirate Gold; King Noanett; Rollo's Journey to Cambridge (with J. T. Wheelwright, *infra*). *Hou. Lam. Lit. Scr.*

Stimson, John Ward. *N. J.*, 1850——. An artist of New York city, four years superintendent of the Metropolitan Museum art schools. The Law of Three Primaries.

Stimson, Lewis Atterbury. *N. J.*, 1844——. A physician of New York city, professor of surgery in the University of the City of New York. Manual of Operative Surgery; Practical Treatise on Fractures; Treatise on Dislocations.

Stith, William. *Va.*, 1689–1785. An Episcopal clergyman of Virginia, president of William and Mary College, 1752–55. He wrote a History of Virginia, which though diffuse is not without interest and dignity of style. *See Tyler's American Literature.*

Stockton, Francis Richard. *Pa.*, 1834——. A widely popular humourist and novel-writer who first attracted general notice by his now famous Rudder Grange, a thoroughly original piece of humour. In the same vein are, The Rudder Grangers Abroad, and Other Stories; Pomona's Travels; The Casting Away of Mrs. Lecks and Mrs. Aleshine. His other works, which all display original inventive humour, are, Tales Out of School; The Ting-a-Ling Stories; Roundabout Rambles; What Might Have Been Expected; A Jolly Fellowship; The Floating Prince; The Story of Viteau; The Late Mrs. Null; The Lady or the Tiger?, his most celebrated work; The Christmas Wreck, and Other Stories; The Hundredth Man; The Bee Man of Orn; The Dusantes; Amos Kilbright; Ardis Claverden; The Great War Syndicate; The Stories of the Three Burglars; The Merry Chanter; The House of Martha; Kobel Land; The Clocks of Rondaine; The Watchmaker's Wife; The Adventures of Captain Horn; A Chosen Few; Personally Conducted; A Story-Teller's Pack, a volume of short stories; Stories of New Jersey; Captain Chap, or the Rolling Stones. *See Vedder's American Writers. Am. Cent. Do. Hou. Lip. Scr.*

Stockton, Thomas Hewlings. *N. J.*, 1808–1868. Half brother of F. R. Stockton, *supra*. A Methodist preacher of Baltimore and Philadelphia, chaplain to both houses of Congress successively, and famous for his eloquence. Floating Flowers from a Hidden Brook; Poems; Stand Up for Jesus, and Other Poems; The Book Above All. *See Life by Wilson, 1869.*

Stoddard, Amos. *Ct.*, 1762–1813. Great-grandson of S. Stoddard, *infra*. A soldier of note in the early days of the Republic. Sketches of Louisiana (1812); The Political Crisis.

Stoddard, Charles Augustus. *Ms.*, 1833——. A Presbyterian clergyman of New York city, editor of The Observer from 1885. Across Russia; Spanish Cities; Beyond the Rockies; Cruising Among the Caribbees. *Scr.*

Stoddard, Charles Warren. *N. Y.*, 1840——. A lecturer on English literature in the Catholic University of America at Washington. Poems; Mashallah: a Flight into Egypt; South Sea Idyls; Summer Cruising in the South Seas; The Lepers of Molokai. *Scr.*

Stoddard, Mrs. Elizabeth Drew [Barstow]. *Ms.*, 1823——. Wife of R. H. Stoddard, *infra*. A novelist and poet whose work in verse and fiction shows much individuality. The

Morgesons; Temple House; Two Men; Lolly Dinks's Doings, a juvenile tale; Poems. *Cas. Hou.*

Stoddard, John F——. *N.Y.*, 1825–1873. An educator of New York State who published a Universal Algebra, and a widely circulated series of arithmetics.

Stoddard, John Lawson. *Ms.*, 1850——. A popular stereopticon lecturer. Red Letter Days Abroad; Napoleon from Corsica to St. Helena. *Hou. Mer.*

Stoddard, Richard Henry. *Ms.*, 1825——. A poet, journalist, and critic of New York city, literary editor of The Mail and Express from 1880. His verse is unequal in merit, but his best work has always won the praise of the discriminating few, though never much heeded by the average reader. He has edited the Bric-a-Brac Series and other volumes, while his own writings include, Poems; Adventures in Fairy Land; Footprints; Life of Humboldt; Songs of Summer; The King's Bell; The Book of the East; Abraham Lincoln: a Horatian Ode; Putnam the Brave; A Century After; Life of Washington Irving; The Lion's Cub, with Other Verse; Under the Evening Lamp, a collection of essays on literary topics. *See Stedman's Poets of America; Vedder's American Writers. Scr.*

Stoddard, Solomon. *Ms.*, 1643–1720. A Congregational clergyman, pastor at Northampton, Massachusetts, from 1669 until his death. Appeal to the Learned; Guide to Christ; Safety in the Righteousness of Christ; Doctrine of Instituted Churches Explained, a reply to Increase Mather's "Order of the Gospel," and one which occasioned much exciting controversy.

Stoddard, William Osborn. *N. Y.*, 1835——. A journalist and inventor whose writings have been largely though not entirely for juvenile readers, and have been very popular. Little Smoke; The Windfall; Esau Hardery; Dab Kinzer; Saltillo Boys; Wrecked; Verses of Many Days; The Heart of It; The White Cave, an Australian Story; The Red Mustang; Two Arrows; Among the Lakes; The Quartet; Winter Fun; Men of Business; The Talking Leaves; The Volcano Under the City, a story of the draft riots in New York; Lives of the Presidents; Gid Granger; Chuck Purdy, comprise the greater part of his works. *Ap. Cent. Fo. Har. Lo. Mer. Scr. Sto.*

Stoever, Martin Luther. *Pa.*, 1820–1870. A Pennsylvania educator, a professor in the college at Gettysburg, 1840–70. Brief Sketch of the Lutheran Church in the United States; Life and Times of Henry Muhlenberg.

Stone, Andrew Leete. *Ct.*, 1815–1892. A Congregational clergyman in San Francisco from 1866. Service the End of Living; Ashton's Mothers; Memorial Discourses; Leaves from a Finished Pastorate.

Stone, David Marvin. *Ct.*, 1817–1895. Brother of A. L. Stone, *supra*. A noted journalist of New York city, editor of The Journal of Commerce, 1849–93. He published Frank Forrest (1850), a work that passed into twenty editions.

Stone, Ebenezer Whitten. *Ms.*, 1801–1880. An adjutant-general of the Massachusetts militia from 1851. Digest of Massachusetts Militia Laws; Compend of Instructions in Military Tactics; Manual of Percussion Aim.

Stone, Edwin Martin. *Ms.*, 1805–1883. A Congregational clergyman of Providence. Life of Elhanan Winchester; History of Barre, Massachusetts, 1630–1842; The Invasion of Canada in 1775; Our French Allies in the Revolution.

Stone, Edwin Winchester. *Ms.*, 1835–1878. Son of E. M. Stone, *supra*. A soldier in the Federal army during the Civil War. He was the war correspondent of The Providence Journal, and author of Rhode Island in the Rebellion.

Stone, James Kent. *Ms.*, 1840——. Son of J. S. Stone, *infra*. A Roman Catholic clergyman of the order of Passionists, and known as Father Fidelis. He was formerly an Episcopal clergyman and president of Hobart College. The Invitation Heeded, issued in 1870, and giving his reasons for his recent change of faith, was widely read.

Stone, James Samuel. *E.*, 1852——. An Episcopal clergyman of Chicago. Simple Sermons on Simple Subjects; The Heart of Merrie England; Readings in Church History; Woods and Dales of Derbyshire. *Co.*

Stone, John Augustus. *Ms.*, 1801–1834. A dramatist and actor. He is best remembered by Metamora, a play written for Edwin Forrest, for whom he also wrote The Ancient Briton; and Fauntleroy. Other dramas by him are, Tancred; The Demoniac; La Roque.

Stone, John Seely. *Ms.*, 1795–1882. An Episcopal clergyman of Cambridge, dean of the Episcopal Theological School there, 1867–72, and prominent among the Low Churchmen of his day. The Living Temple; The Christian Sacraments; Sermons; Memoir of Bishop Griswold; The Christian Sabbath; The Contrast, or the Evangelical and Tractarian Systems Compared. *Ran.*

Stone, Thomas Treadwell. *Me.*, 1801–1895. A Unitarian clergyman of Bolton, Massachusetts. Sermons on War; Sermons; The Rod and Staff; Sketches of Oxford County, Maine.

Stone, William Leete. *N. Y.*, 1792–1844. A journalist of prominence in New York city, and the first superintendent of public schools there. History of the Albany Constitutional Convention of 1821; Tales and Sketches; Matthias and his Impostures; Maria Monk and the Nunnery of the Hotel Dieu; Ups and Downs of a Distressed Gentleman, a social satire; Letters on Animal Magnetism; Poetry and History of Wyoming; Lives of Brant, Red Jacket; Letters on Masonry. *See Life by his son.*

Stone, William Leete. *N. Y.*, 1835——. Son of W. L. Stone, *supra.* A lawyer and historical writer of Jersey City. History of New York City; Life of Sir William Johnson; Burgoyne's Campaigns; Life and Military Journals of General Riedesel; Reminiscences of Saratoga and Ballston; Life of William Leete Stone, *supra;* Visits to Saratoga Battle Grounds, include his principal publications.

Storer, David Humphreys. *Me.*, 1804–1891. A Boston physician, dean of the Harvard Medical School, 1854–1868. Ichthyology and Herpetology of Massachusetts; Synopsis of North American Fishes; History of the Fishes of Massachusetts.

Storer, Francis Humphreys. *Me.*, 1832——. Son of D. H. Storer, *supra.* An eminent chemist, professor of agricultural chemistry at Harvard University from 1870, and dean of the Bussey Institute. Alloys of Copper and Zinc; Manufacture of Paraffin Oils; First Outlines of a Dictionary of the Solubilities of Chemical Substances; Manual of Inorganic Chemistry (with C. W. Eliot, *supra*); Manual of Qualitative Chemical Analysis; Agriculture in Some of its Relations with Chemistry. *Scr.*

Storer, Horatio Robinson. *Ms.*, 1830——. Son of D. H. Storer, *supra.* A surgeon of note. Why Not? a Book for Every Woman; Is It I? a Book for Every Man; Nurses and Nursing; Criminal Abortion (with F. F. Heard, *supra*). *Le. Lit.*

Storey, Moorfield. *Ms.*, 1845——. A Boston lawyer living in Brookline, Massachusetts. Life of Charles Sumner. *Hou.*

Stork, Charles Augustus. *Md.*, 1838–1883. Son of T. Stork, *supra.* A Lutheran clergyman, professor of theology at Gettysburg, 1881–83. Light on the Pilgrim's Way. *See the Stork Family in the Lutheran Church, 1886.*

Stork, Theophilus. *N. C.*, 1814–1874. A Lutheran clergyman of Philadelphia. Life of Luther; Luther's Christmas Tree; Luther and the Bible; Afternoon; Home Scenes in the New Testament; The Unseen World, are his principal works. *Lip.*

Storrs, Richard Salter. *Ms.*, 1821——. A distinguished Congregational clergyman of Brooklyn, pastor of the Church of the Pilgrims from 1846. The Constitution of the Human Soul; Historical Addresses; Divine Origin of Christianity; Conditions of Success in Preaching without Notes; John Wycliffe and the First English Bible; Manliness in the Scholar; Love to Christ; Recognition of the Supernatural; Bernard of Clairvaux; Forty Years of Pastoral Life. *Do. Ran. Scr.*

Story, Isaac. *Ms.*, 1774–1803. Cousin of J. Story, *infra.* A lawyer and verse-writer of Castine, Maine. An Epistle from Tarico to Inkle; Consolatory Odes; A Parnassian Shop.

Story, Joseph. *Ms.*, 1779–1845. A jurist of eminence, Dane professor of law at Harvard University, 1829–45. His earliest work was The Power of Solitude, with Fugitive Poems, a somewhat callow performance; and his first legal production, which appeared in 1805, was a Selection of Pleadings in Civil Actions. His subsequent works include, Commentaries on the Constitution of the United States; The Conflict of Laws, his most able effort; Equity Jurisprudence; The Law of Agency; Law of Bailments; Equity Pleadings; Law of Partnership; Law of Promissory Notes; Miscellaneous Writings. *See Allibone's Dictionary; Life by W. W. Story; Biographical Encyclopædia of Massachusetts. Har. Lit.*

Story, William Wetmore. *Ms.*, 1819–1895. Son of J. Story, *supra*. A poet, sculptor, and essayist. He studied law and practised at the bar in Boston for a short time, but after 1848 lived in Rome and became widely known as a sculptor. His prose writings include, The Law of Contracts; The Law of Sales; Life of Joseph Story; Proportions of the Human Figure; Roba di Roma; The American Question; Fiammetta, a novel; Conversations in a Studio; Excursions in Art and Letters. The Castle of St. Angelo; A Roman Lawyer in Jerusalem; Nero, an Historical Play; and a two-volume edition of Poems, comprise his verse. He and She: a Poet's Portfolio; and A Poet's Portfolio: Later Readings, contain both poetry and prose. *See Appletons' Annual Cyclopædia, 1895. Hou. Lip. Lit.*

Stow, Baron. *N. H.*, 1801–1869. A Baptist clergyman of Boston, of much prominence in his day, among whose writings are, Helen's Pilgrimage; History of the English Baptist Mission to India; Christian Brotherhood; First Things. *See Life by Neale, 1870; Memoir of by J. C. Stockbridge, 1895.*

Stowe, Calvin Ellis. *Ms.*, 1802–1886. A Congregational clergyman and educator who held successive professorships at Dartmouth College, Lane Seminary, Bowdoin College, and Andover Seminary. While at Lane Seminary he married his second wife, Harriet Beecher, the daughter of Lyman Beecher, *supra*. Origin and History of the Books of the Bible; Elementary Instruction in Europe; Lectures on the Sacred Poetry of the Hebrews; Introduction to Biblical Criticism.

Stowe, Mrs. Harriet Elizabeth [Beecher]. *Ct.*, 1811–1896. Wife of C. E. Stowe, *supra*, and daughter of Lyman Beecher, *supra*. In 1836 she was married to Professor Stowe at Cincinnati, and, in frequent visits to the slave States at that period, acquired a knowledge of Southern customs. In 1850 she removed to Brunswick, Maine, and, having by this time become deeply impressed with the wrong of slavery, she wrote Uncle Tom's Cabin for The National Era at Washington, in which paper it appeared serially from June, 1851, till April, 1852. It was then published in book form and speedily became world-famous, five hundred thousand copies being sold in America within five years, while translations of it appeared in twenty languages. As a moral agent few books have been of so much importance. From a literary point of view there is less to be said of it; and The Minister's Wooing, a novel of the early days of the republic, must rank as her finest work. The quality of her other work is uneven, its highest level being represented by Oldtown Folks; The Pearl of Orr's Island; Dred; The Chimney Corner; Religious Poems, among which is the well-known hymn, "Still, still with Thee." Her lesser works comprise, My Wife and I; Sam Lawson's Fireside Stories; We and Our Neighbors; Little Foxes; The Mayflower, and Other Sketches; Sunny Memories of Foreign Lands; Our Charley; Agnes of Sorrento, an Italian novel; House and Home Papers; Stories about Our Dogs; Queer Little People; Daisy's First Winter; Men of Our Times, biographical sketches; The American Woman's Home (with Catherine Beecher); Little Pussy Willow; Pink and White Tyranny; Palmetto Leaves; Betty's Bright Idea; Footsteps of the Master; Bible Heroines; Poganuc People; A Dog's Mission. *See Life of, by her Son; Atlantic Monthly, July, 1882, August and September, 1896; The Century Magazine, September, 1896; New England Magazine, September, 1896; The Forum, August, 1896; The Outlook, July 25, 1896; Life of, by Mrs. Fields, supra. Fo. Hou.*

Stowell, Charles Henry. *N. Y.*, 1850——. A microscopist, professor of histology in the University of Michigan. Students' Manual of Microscopy; Physiology and Hygiene; The Microscopical Structure of the Human Tooth; A Primer of Health; A Healthy Body; Essentials of Health. *Sil.*

Stowell, Mrs. Louisa Maria [Reed]. *Mch.*, 1850——. Wife of C. H. Stowell, *supra.* An instructor in microscopical botany at the University of Michigan for twelve years. Microscopical Structure of Wheat; Microscopic Diagnosis (with C. H. Stowell).

Strachey, William. *E.*, *c.* 1585–16—. The first secretary of the Virginia colony. He was the author of A True Repertory of the Wracke and Redemption of Sir Thomas Gates upon and from the Islands of the Bermudas, supposed to have been the inspiration of Shakespeare's Tempest; Historie of Travaile into Virginia Britannia; For the Colony in Virginia Britannia: Lawes Divine, Morall, and Martiall, a compilation. *See Tyler's American Literature.*

Strahan, Edward. *See Shinn, Earl.*

Stranahan, Mrs. Clara Cornelia [Harrison]. *Ms.*, 183——. An art writer of Brooklyn. A History of French Painting from its Earliest to its Latest Practice. *Scr.*

Straus, Oscar Solomon. *Bv.*, 1850——. A municipal reformer of New York city, minister to Turkey in 1887. The Origin of Republican Government in the United States; Roger Williams, the Pioneer of Religious Liberty. *Cent. Put.*

Street, Alfred Billings. *N. Y.*, 1811–1882. A verse-writer of Albany, and State librarian of New York from 1848. His verse is chiefly nature poetry and was popular for a time. His writings include, Frontenac; Woods and Waters; Forest Pictures; The Burning of Schenectady, and Other Poems; Drawings and Tintings; Fugitive Poems; Digest of Taxation in the United States. *See Griswold's Poets and Poetry of America.*

Strickland, William. *Pa.*, 1787–1854. A Philadelphia architect whose chief professional work was the Capitol at Nashville, Tennessee. Triangulation of the Entrance into Delaware Bay; Report on Canals and Railways; Public Works of the United States (with Gill and Campbell).

Strickland, William Peter. *Pa.*, 1809–1884. A Methodist clergyman, pastor of a Presbyterian church at Bridgehampton, Long Island, 1865–77, whose principal writings comprise, Pioneers of the West; History of the American Bible Society; The Genius of Methodism; Light of the Temple; Old Mackinaw, or the Fortress of the Lakes; Christianity Demonstrated by Facts; The Astrologer of Chaldea, or the Life of Faith. *Meth.*

Strohm, Gertrude. *O.*, 1843——. A writer living near Dayton, Ohio. Word Pictures; Universal Cookery Book; Flower Idyls; The Young Scholar's Companion.

Strong, Augustus Hopkins. *N. Y.*, 1836——. A Baptist clergyman of Rochester, New York, president of Rochester Theological Seminary from 1872. Systematic Theology; Philosophy and Religion.

Strong, George Crockett. *Vt.*, 1832–1863. A general in the Federal army during the Civil War who fell in the assault on Fort Wagner. Cadet Life at West Point.

Strong, James. *N. Y.*, 1822–1894. A Methodist clergyman and educator of eminence, professor in Drew Seminary at Madison, New Jersey, from 1868. With T. McClintock, *supra*, he edited a Biblical Encyclopædia, continuing the work alone after 1870. His other writings include, English Harmony of the Gospels; Greek Harmony of the Gospels; Irenics; The Tabernacle of Israel; Sacred Idyls; Future Life; Jewish Life; Our Lord's Life; Commentary on Ecclesiastes; Concordance of the Bible. *Meth.*

Strong, Josiah. *Il.*, 1847——. A Congregational clergyman, general agent of the Evangelical Alliance in America after 1886. Our Country; The New Era of the Coming Kingdom.

Strong, Latham Cornell. *N. Y.*, 1845–1879. A journalist and verse-writer of Troy, New York. Castle Windows; Pots of Gold; Poke o' Moonshine; Midsummer Dreams.

Strong, Nathan. *Ct.*, 1748–1816. A Congregational clergyman of Hartford. Sermons; The Doctrine of Eternal Misery Consistent with the Infinite Benevolence of God.

Strong, Theodore. *Ms.*, 1790–1869. A professor of mathematics at Rutgers College, 1827–63. Treatise on Elementary Algebra; On Differential and Integral Calculus.

Strong, Titus. *Ms.*, 1787–1855. An Episcopal clergyman of Greenfield, Massachusetts. Tears of Columbia, a Political Poem; Candid Examination of the Episcopal Church; The Deerfield Captive; The Young Scholar's Manual.

Strother [strŭth'ẽr], **David Hunter.** "Porte Crayon." *Va.*, 1816–1888. An artist of Berkeley Springs, West Virginia, once popular as a magazinist. During the Civil War he was a colonel in the Union army, and in 1865 he was brevetted brigadier-general. The Blackwater Chronicle; Virginia Illustrated. *See Hart's American Literature.*

Stroud, George McDowell. *Pa.*, 1895–1875. A Philadelphia jurist who published Sketch of Laws Relating to Slavery in the Several States.

Stryker, Melanchthon Woolsey. *N. Y.*, 1851———. A Presbyterian clergyman and educator, president of Hamilton College from 1892. Beside several hymnals, he has published Miriam, and Other Verse; Hamilton, Lincoln, and Other Addresses; The Letter of James the Just. *Gi.*

Stuart, Charles Beebe. *N. H.*, 1814–1881. A military engineer in government service. Naval Dry Docks of the United States; Water Works of the United States; Civil and Military Engineers of the United States.

Stuart, Moses. *Ct.*, 1780–1852. A Congregational clergyman and educator of Massachusetts, professor of sacred literature at Andover Seminary, 1809–1848. Among his writings are, Commentaries on the Epistles to the Romans and the Hebrews; Hints on the Prophecies; Conscience and the Constitution; Critical History and Defence of the Old Testament Canon.

Stuart, Mrs. Ruth McEnery. *La.*, 18———. A Golden Wedding, and Other Tales; Carlotta's Intended, and Other Stories; The Story of Babette; Sonny; Solomon Crow's Christmas Pockets. *Cent. Har.*

Stuckenberg, John Henry Wilburn. *G.*, 1835———. A Lutheran clergyman, professor of theology at Wittenberg College, Springfield, Ohio, 1873–80, and minister in charge of the American chapel at Berlin from 1880. Christian Sociology; Life of Kant; Introduction to the Study of Philosophy.

Sturges, Mrs. Mary Jane [Upshur] [Stith]. *Va.*, 1828———. A writer of New York city. Confederate Notes, a novel; Poems.

Sturgis, Frederick Russell. *Ph.*, 1844———. A prominent physician and surgeon of New York city. Human Cestoids; Students' Manual of Venereal Diseases.

Sturgis, Russell. *Md.*, 1836———. An architect of New York city, a valued authority upon art, architecture, and archæology. European Architecture. *Mac.*

Sturtevant, Julian Monson. *Ct.*, 1805–1886. A prominent educator of Jacksonville, Illinois, professor in Illinois College, 1830–86. Economics, or the Science of Wealth; Keys of Sect. *Le. Put.*

Sullivan, James. *Me.*, 1744–1808. An eminent Boston jurist who was governor of Massachusetts, 1807–08. History of Land Titles of Massachusetts; Observations on the Government of the United States; The Path to Riches, or a Dissertation on Banks; The Altar of Baal Thrown Down, or the French Nation Defended; Impartial Review of Causes of the French Revolution. *See Life by Amory, 1859.*

Sullivan, James William. *Pa.*, 1848———. A journalist of New York city, editor of social reform journals, 1893–96. Tenement Tales of New York; So the World Goes; Direct Legislation through the Initiative and Referendum, a widely circulated work. *Ho.*

Sullivan, Mrs. Margaret Frances [Buchanan]. *I.*, 18———. A journalist of Chicago. Ireland of To-Day (1881).

Sullivan, Thomas Russell. *Ms.*, 1799–1862. Grandson of J. Sullivan, *supra.* A Unitarian clergyman of Keene, New Hampshire, 1825–35, and from 1835 till his death an educator in Boston. Letters Against the Immediate Abolition of Slavery; Limits of Responsibility in Reforms.

Sullivan, Thomas Russell. *Ms.*, 1849——. A novelist of Boston. Tom Sylvester; Roses of Shadow; Day and Night Stories; and several plays. *Scr.*

Sullivan, William. *Me.*, 1774–1839. Son of J. Sullivan, *supra.* A lawyer of Boston. Familiar Letters on Public Men of the Revolution; Historical Causes and Effects; Sea Life.

Sullivant, William Starling. *O.*, 1803–1873. A botanist of Ohio. Musci Alleghanienses; Musci Cubenses; Icones Muscorum; Musci and Hepaticæ of the United States East of the Mississippi.

Sully, Thomas. *E.*, 1783–1872. A distinguished portrait painter of Philadelphia. Hints to Young Painters.

Summerfield, John. *E.*, 1798–1825. A Methodist clergyman, renowned for eloquence in his day. His Sermons and Sketches of Sermons were posthumously published. *See Lives by Holland, 1829, Willett, 1857. Har.*

Summers, Thomas Osmond. *E.*, 1812–1882. A Methodist clergyman of Nashville. Commentary on the Gospels, Acts, and Ritual of the Methodist Church South; Treatise on Baptism; On Holiness; Talks Pleasant and Profitable, include his principal writings. *See Life of, by Fitzgerald, 1884.*

Sumner, Charles. *Ms.*, 1811–1874. Son of C. P. Sumner, *infra.* A distinguished Massachusetts statesman who succeeded Daniel Webster in 1851 in the Senate of the United States. He was a fearless opponent of slavery, and, in consequence of this attitude of his, was assaulted in the Senate Chamber by Preston Brooks, of South Carolina, in 1856, and severely injured. The True Grandeur of Nations; Prophetic Voices Concerning America. His Complete Works, including his many orations and speeches, have been issued in fifteen volumes. *See Lives by Pierce, Storey. Le.*

Sumner, Charles Allen. *Ms.*, 1835——. A stenographer of San Francisco. Shorthand and Reporting; Golden Gate Sketches; Travel in Southern Europe; Poems (with R. Sumner).

Sumner, Charles Pinckney. *Ms.*, 1766–1839. A lawyer of Boston, high sheriff of Suffolk County from 1825 till his death. Eulogy on Washington; The Compass (verse); Letters on Speculative Masonry.

Sumner, George. *Ct.*, 1793–1855. A Hartford physician, professor of botany at Trinity College, 1824–55. Compendium of Physiological and Systematic Botany.

Sumner, William Graham. *N. J.*, 1840——. An Episcopal clergyman, prominent as a political economist, professor of political and social science at Yale University from 1872. A History of American Currency; What Social Classes Owe to Each Other; Problems in Political Economy; Collected Essays in Political and Social Science; Protectionism; Lives of Andrew Jackson, Alexander Hamilton, Robert Morris; The Financier and the Finances of the Revolution, a more extended life of Robert Morris. *Do. Har. Ho. Hou.*

Sunderland, Jabez Thomas. *E.*, 1842——. A Unitarian clergyman, editor of The Unitarian from 1880. A Rational Faith; What is the Bible?; The Liberal Christian Ministry; Home Travel in Bible Lands; The Bible: its Origin and Place among the Sacred Books of the World; Orthodoxy and Revivalism. *El. Put.*

Sunderland, La Roy. *R. I.*, 1802–1885. A writer who in early life was a zealous Methodist preacher, and after 1845 an equally zealous opponent of Christianity, slavery, Spiritualism, and Mormonism. Among his writings are, History of South America; Book of Human Nature; Book of Psychology; The Trance, and How Introduced; Anti-Slavery Manual; Mormonism Exposed.

Suplée [su-play′], **Thomas Danly.** *Pa.*, 1848——. An educator of New Jersey. Frank Muller, or Labor and its Fruits; Pebbles from the Fountain of Castalia; Poems; Plain Talks; Riverside, a romance; Civil Government under the United States Constitution.

Suydam, John Howard. *N. Y.*, 1832——. A Dutch Reformed clergyman of Jersey City from 1869. The Cruger Family; Cruel Jim; The Wreckmaster.

Swain, David Lowry. *N. C.*, 1801-1868. A governor of North Carolina, 1832-35, who wrote a Revolutionary History of North Carolina.

Swain, James Barrett. *N. Y.*, 1820-1895. A journalist of New York city, post-office inspector, 1881-85. Life and Speeches of Henry Clay; Historical Notes to Speeches of Henry Clay; A Military History of New York State.

Swan, James. *S.*, 1754-1831. A soldier in the American army during the Revolution, afterwards adjutant-general of Massachusetts. The last fifteen years of his life were passed in a debtors' prison in Paris. Dissuasion to Great Britain and the Colonies from the Slave Trade to Africa (1772); Causes qui sont opposées au Progrès du commerce entre la France et les États-Unis de l'Amérique (1790); On the Fisheries; Fisheries of Massachusetts; National Arithmetick; Address on Agriculture, Manufactures, and Commerce.

Swan, Josiah Rockwell. *N. Y.*, 1802-1884. A prominent jurist of Columbus, Ohio. Treatise on Justices of the Peace and Constables in Ohio; Manual for Executors and Administrators; Pleading and Practice; Commentaries on Pleadings under the Ohio Code, constitute his principal writings.

Swan, William Draper. *Ms.*, 1809-1864. An educator and bookseller of Boston. He published a popular series of school readers, and (with R. Swan and D. Leach) a series of widely used arithmetics.

Swank, James Moore. *Pa.*, 1832-——. The general manager of the American Iron and Steel Association since 1885. History of the Department of Agriculture; Iron Making and Coal Mining in Pennsylvania; Iron Manufacture in All Ages.

Swartz, Joel. *Va.*, 1827——. A Lutheran clergyman, pastor at Gettysburg from 1881. Dreamings of the Waking, with Other Poems; Lyra Lutherana.

Sweat, Mrs. Margaret Jane [Muzzey]. *Me.*, 1823——. Ethel's Love Life; Highways of Travel, or a Summer in Europe.

Sweet, Alexander Edwin. *N. B.*, 1841——. A Texas journalist who served in the Confederate army. Three Dozen Good Stories from Texas Siftings.

Sweet, Homer De Lois. *N. Y.*, 1826——. A civil engineer of Syracuse. The Averys of Groton, a genealogy; Twilight Hours in the Adirondacks.

Sweetser, Charles Humphreys. *Ms.*, 1841-1871. A journalist of New York city and subsequently of Chicago. Songs of Amherst; History of Amherst College; Tourist's and Invalid's Guide to the Northwest.

Sweetser, Moses Foster. *Ms.*, 1848-1897. A Boston writer who has published Europe for Two Dollars a Day; Artist Biographies; Summer Days Down East; guide-books to New England, the Middle States, the White Mountains, and the Maritime Provinces; In Distance and in Dream, a story. *Hou. Kt.*

Sweetser, William. *Ms.*, 1797-1875. A physician who was professor of medicine at Bowdoin College, 1845-61. Treatise on Consumption; Digestion and its Disorders; Mental Hygiene; Human Life.

Swenson, Carl Aaron. *Pa.*, 1857-——. A Lutheran clergyman, founder and president of Bethany College in Lindsborg, Kansas, editor of several Swedish journals, and author of Sondagsskolboken; Minnen från Kyrkan; Vid Hemmets Härd.

Swett, John Appleton. *Ms.*, 1808-1854. A physician of New York city. Diseases of the Chest. *Ap.*

Swett, Josiah. *N. H.*, 1814-1890. An Episcopal clergyman long prominent in Vermont. English Grammar; Pastoral Visiting; Family Prayer; The Firmament in the Midst of the Waters.

Swett, Samuel. *Ms.*, 1782-1866. A once prominent citizen of Boston who during the War of 1812 served in the American army as a topographical engineer. History and Topographical

Sketch of Bunker Hill Battle; Who was Commander at Bunker Hill?; Sketches of Distinguished Men of Newbury and Newburyport.

Swett, Sophia Miriam. *Me.*, 186— ——. A writer of short stories and juvenile books, now (1897) living at Arlington, Massachusetts. Pennyroyal and Mint; The Lollipops' Vacation; Captain Polly; Flying Hill Farm; The Mate of the Mary Ann; Cap'n Thistletop; The Ponkaty Branch Road. *Est. Har. Lo. We.*

Swett, Susan Hartley. *Me.*, 186— ——. Sister of S. M. Swett, *supra.* A writer of Arlington, Massachusetts. Field Clover and Beach Grass, a volume of short stories. *Est.*

Swett, William. *N. H.*, 1825–1884. A deaf-mute who founded the Deaf-Mute Industrial School at Beverly, Massachusetts. Adventures of a Deaf-Mute in the White Mountains.

Swift, John Lindsay. *Ms.*, 1828–1895. A Boston lawyer and journalist, deputy collector of the port of Boston from 1890. About Grant. *Le.*

Swift, Zephaniah. *Ms.*, 1759–1823. A noted Connecticut jurist. System of the Laws of Connecticut; Digest of the Laws of Evidence; Digest of the Laws of Connecticut, a standard authority.

Swinburne, Louis Judson. *N. Y.*, 1855–1887. A Colorado writer who was in Paris during the siege in 1871, and published a volume of observations on the subject entitled Paris Sketches.

Swing, David. *O.*, 1830–1894. A Presbyterian clergyman of Chicago, tried for heresy in 1874, and acquitted, subsequently pastor of the Central Church there until his death. Sermons; Club Essays; Truths for To-day; Motives of Life; Old Pictures of Life, a collection of essays. *Mg. St.*

Swinton, John. *S.*, 1830——. Brother of W. Swinton, *infra.* A journalist of New York city whose principal work is John Swinton's Travels.

Swinton, William. *S.*, 1833–1892. A journalist and educator, long prominent in New York city. Rambles Among Words; Twelve Decisive Battles of the War; Campaigns of the Army of the Potomac; The "Times's" Review of McClellan; History of the New York Seventh Regiment; Word Analysis; Bible Word Book; Studies in English Literature. *Har. Scr.*

Swisher, Mrs. Bella [French]. *Ga.*, 1837–1894. A writer who resided in Texas from 1877. Struggling up to the Light, a novel; Rocks and Shoals; Florecita, a romance; History of Brown County, Wisconsin; Cassie; Homeless Though at Home; The Story of a Woman's Love.

Swisshelm, Mrs. Jane Gray [Cannon]. *Pa.*, 1815–1884. A journalist of Pittsburg, and subsequently of St. Cloud, Minnesota, prominent as an abolitionist. Letters to Country Girls; Half a Century, an autobiography. *See Hart's American Literature. Mg.*

Sylvester, Herbert Milton. *Ms.*, 1849——. A Boston lawyer who has published two volumes of sympathetic nature studies. Prose Pastorals; Homestead Highways. *Hou.*

Sylvester, Nathaniel Bartlett. *N. Y.*, 1825——. A lawyer of Troy, New York. Historical Sketches of Northern New York; History of the Connecticut Valley of Massachusetts; Indian Legends of Saratoga; Historical Narratives of the Upper Hudson; Histories of Saratoga, Rensselaer, and Ulster Counties, New York.

Symmes, John Cleves. *N. J.*, 1780–1829. A soldier of Newport, Kentucky. He was the author of The Theory of Concentric Spheres, an attempt to prove that the earth is hollow, open at the poles, and habitable in the interior. *See Harper's Magazine, October, 1882; Atlantic Monthly, April, 1873; McBride's Pioneer Biography.*

Sypher, Josiah Rinehart. *Pa.*, 1832— ——. A journalist and lawyer of Philadelphia, war correspondent of The New York Tribune, 1862–65. History of the Pennsylvania Reserve Corps; School History of Pennsylvania; The Art of Teaching School; School History of New Jersey (with E. A. Apgar). *Lip.*

Szabad, Emeric. *Hy.*, c. 1822——. A soldier under Garibaldi who came to America in 1861, and served in the Federal army. Hungary Past and

Present; State Policy of Modern Europe; Modern War: its Theory and Practice.

T

Tabb, John Banister. *Md.*, 1845——. A Roman Catholic clergyman and educator, professor of English literature in St. Charles's College, Ellicott City, Maryland. His verse has received much well merited praise. Poems; Lyrics; An Octave to Mary. *Cop.*

Tafel, Johann Friedrich Leonhard. *Wg.*, 1800——. A German educator who removed to the United States in 1853, and lived in St. Louis. Staat und Christenthum; Der Christ und der Atheist; A German-English and English-German Pocket Dictionary (with his son Ludwig Tafel).

Tafel, Rudolph Leonhard. *Wg.*, 1831——. Son of J. F. L. Tafel, *supra.* Formerly an educator of St. Louis, but since 1868 a Swedenborgian minister in London, England. Emanuel Swedenborg as Philosopher and Man; Our Heavenward Journey; Authority in the New Church; The Preaching Gift; Investigation as to the Laws of English Pronunciation and Prosody.

Talbot, Charles Remington. 1851–1891. A writer of juvenile books who was an Episcopal clergyman at Wrentham, Massachusetts. Honor Bright; Miltiades Peterkin Paul; Royal Louise; Romulus and Remus, a dog story; A Midshipman at Large; The Impostor; A Romance of the Revolution. *Lo.*

Talbot, Henry Paul. *Ms.*, 1864——. An associate professor of analytical chemistry in the Massachusetts Institute of Technology. An Introductory Course of Quantitative Chemical Analysis. *Mac.*

Talmage [tăl-mĭj or tăm-ĭj], **Thomas De Witt.** *N. J.*, 1832——. A Presbyterian clergyman of Brooklyn, 1869–1894, and subsequently of New York, widely known as a preacher. He has been a prolific writer, but the literary worth of his books is very slight. Crumbs Swept Up; Sermons; From Manger to Throne; Sports that Kill; Social Dynamite; The Pathway of Life; The Marriage Ring; Old Wells Dug Out; Every-Day Religion; Sundown; Fishing Too Near Shore, include his principal works. *Fu.*

Talvi. *See Robinson, Mrs. Thérèse.*

Tannehill, Wilkins. *Pa.*, 1787–1858. A journalist of Nashville. Freemasons' Manual; Sketches of the History of Literature; Sketches of the History of Roman Literature.

Tanner, Benjamin Tucker. *Pa.*, 1835——. A bishop of the African Methodist Church. Paul *vs.* Pius Ninth; The Negro's Origin, and Is the Negro Cursed?; Outline of the History and Government of the African Methodist Episcopal Church.

Tanner, Henry S——. *N. Y.*, 1786–1858. A geographer of Philadelphia. Memoir on the Recent Surveys in the United States (1830); View of the Valley of the Mississippi; American Traveller; Central Traveller; New Picture of Philadelphia; Description of Canals and Railways in the United States (1840).

Tappan, David. *Ms.*, 1752–1803. A Congregational clergyman, pastor at Newbury, Massachusetts, 1774–92, and Hollis professor of divinity at Harvard University from 1792 until his death. Sermons on Important Subjects; Lectures on Jewish Antiquities. *See Memoir by Abiel Holmes, supra.*

Tappan, Eli Todd. *O.*, 1824——. A professor of mathematics at Kenyon College, Gambier, Ohio, 1875–87, and since then Ohio commissioner of common schools. Plane and Solid Geometry; Elements of Geometry; Treatise on Geometry and Trigonometry.

Tappan, Henry Philip. *N. Y.*, 1805–1881. A Dutch Reformed clergyman, professor of philosophy in the University of the City of New York, chancellor of the University of Michigan, 1852–1863. Elements of Logic; Treatise on Universal Education; Review of Edwards's "Inquiry into the Freedom of the Will;" The Doctrine of the Freedom of the Will Determined by an Appeal to Consciousness: The Doctrine of the Freedom of the Will Applied to Moral Agency; A Step from the Old World to the New and Back Again; Introductions to Illustrious Personages of the Nineteenth Century.

Tappan, Lewis. *Ms.*, 1788–1873. A

merchant of New York city, proprietor of The Journal of Commerce, and active as an abolitionist. Life of Arthur Tappan, by his brother, a valuable contribution to anti-slavery literature.

Tappan, William Bingham. *Ms.*, 1794–1849. A verse-writer and educator of Philadelphia and Boston. Poetry of the Heart; Poetry of Life; New England, and Other Poems; Songs of Judah; Lyrics; Sacred and Miscellaneous Poems; The Sunday School, and Other Poems; Early and Late Poems. *See Griswold's Poets and Poetry of America; Duyckinck's American Literature.*

Tarbell, Frank Bigelow. *Ms.*, 1853——. A professor of Greek in the University of Chicago from 1892. A History of Greek Art; The Philippics of Demosthenes, with Introduction and Notes. *Fl. Gi.*

Tarbell, Ida M——. 18———. Madame Roland; Early Life of Abraham Lincoln (with J. M. Davis). *Scr.*

Tarbell, John Adams. *Ms.*, 1810–1864. A homœopathic physician of Boston. Sources of Health; Homœopathy Simplified.

Tarbox, Increase Niles. *Ct.*, 1815–1888. A Congregational clergyman who was secretary of the American College and Education Society, 1851–84. Winnie and Walter Stories; When I was a Boy; Nineveh, or the Buried City; Uncle George's Stories; Journeys and Labors of St. Paul; Life of General Israel Putnam; Sir Walter Raleigh and His Colony in America; Songs and Hymns for Common Life. *Lo.*

Tarr, Ralph Stockman. *Ms.*, 1864——. A geologist, assistant professor of geology at Cornell University, 1892–1897, professor of dynamic geology and physical geography there from 1897. Elementary Geology; Economic Geology of the United States; Elementary Physical Geography. *Mac.*

Tatham, William. *E.*, 1752–1819. An engineer and lawyer of Virginia who served in the American army during the Revolution. An Analysis of the State of Virginia; Remarks on Inland Canals; National Irrigation, are among his writings.

Taussig [tŏw′sig], **Frank William.** *Mo.*, 1859——. A professor of political economy at Harvard University. Protection to Young Industries as Applied in the United States; The History of the Present Tariff, 1860–83; The Tariff History of the United States; The Silver Situation in the United States (1892); Wages and Capital. *Ap. Put.*

Taylor, Alfred. *Pa.*, 1831——. A Presbyterian clergyman of Philadelphia. Peeps at Our Sunday-Schools; Sunday-School Photographs; Hints about Sunday-School Work. *Meth.*

Taylor, Bayard. *See Taylor,* [*James*] *Bayard.*

Taylor, Benjamin Franklin. *N.Y.*, 1819–1887. A popular verse-writer of Chicago whose work is always pleasing, though it never reaches a very high plane of inspiration. Songs of Yesterday; Old Time Pictures, and Sheaves of Rhyme; Dulce Domum; Between the Gates; Summer Savory; The River of Time; Pictures of Life in Camp and Field; Complete Poems (1887); Theophilus Trent, a novel. *Ap. Sc.*

Taylor, Charles. *Ms.*, 1819——. A Methodist clergyman who was a missionary to China, 1848–54. Five Years in China; Baptism in a Nutshell.

Taylor, Charles Fayette. *Vt.*, 1827——. A surgeon of New York city. Theory and Practice of the Movement Cure; Spinal Irritation; Sensation and Pain; Mechanical Treatment of Angular Curvature of the Spine; Treatment of Disease of the Hip Joint; Infantile Paralysis. *Lip.*

Taylor, Fitch Waterman. *Ct.*, 1803–1865. An Episcopal chaplain in the United States navy. The Flag Ship, or a Voyage Around the World; The Broad Pennant, a work of similar nature.

Taylor, George Boardman. *Va.*, 1832——. A Baptist missionary in Rome since 1873. Oakland Stories; Costar Grew; Roger Bemant, the Pastor's Son; Walter Ennis, a tale of the Early Virginia Baptists; Life of J. B. Taylor, *infra. Bap.*

Taylor, George Henry. *Vt.*, 1821——. Brother of C. F. Taylor, *supra.* A physician of New York city, among whose writings are, Exposition of the

Swedish Movement Cure; Health for Women; Massage; Pelvic and Hernial Therapeutics.

Taylor, George Lansing. *N. Y.*, 1835——. A Methodist clergyman of eastern New York. Elijah the Reformer, a Ballad Epic; Grant: an Elegy, and Other Poems; What Shall we Do with the Sunday-School?; The New Africa. *Fu. Meth.*

Taylor, Hannis. *N. C.*, 1851——. A lawyer of Mobile, minister to Spain, 1893–97. The Origin and Growth of the English Constitution. *Hou.* .

Taylor, Henry Osborn. *N. Y.*, 1856——. A legal writer of New York city. Treatise on the Law of Private Corporations, a standard work much used as a text-book in law schools; Ancient Ideals. *Put.*

Taylor, Hobart Chatfield. *See Chatfield-Taylor.*

Taylor, James Barnett. *E.*, 1819–1871. A Baptist missionary in Virginia. Life of Lot Cary; Lives of Virginia Baptist Ministers. *See Life, by G. B. Taylor, supra. Bap.*

Taylor, [James] Bayard [bi'ard]. *Pa.*, 1825–1878. An author well known as poet, novelist, translator, and traveller. It was as a poet that he most desired to be remembered, but except in a few instances his verse does not reach a very lofty level of attainment, and, while often excellent in quality, lacks usually the element of spontaneity. His volumes of verse comprise, Ximena, and Other Poems; Rhymes of Travel; Poems and Ballads; Poems of Home and Travel; Poems of the Orient, his most original work; The Picture of St. John; The Poet's Journal; Lars; The Masque of the Gods; Home Pastorals; Prince Deukalion; The Prophet, a tragedy; Centennial Ode. In fiction he published, Beauty and the Beast; Hannah Thurston; The Story of Kennett; John Godfrey's Fortune; Joseph and his Friend. His travels include, Views Afoot; Eldorado; By-ways of Europe; Central Africa; Egypt and Iceland; Greece and Russia; At Home and Abroad; India, China, and Japan; The Lands of the Saracen; Colorado. The translation of Faust is his greatest work, and the one on which his fame will most securely rest. Other works of his are, School History of Germany; Literary Essays and Notes; Studies in German Literature; The Echo Club, and Other Literary Diversions. *See Catholic World, April, 1879; Lippincott's Magazine, August, 1879; Stedman's Poets of America; Life and Letters of, by Marie Hansen-Taylor and H. E. Scudder; Life by Smyth; Allibone's Dictionary. Ap. Hou. My. Put.*

Taylor, James Monroe. *N. Y.*, 1848——. A Baptist clergyman and educator, president of Vassar College from 1886. Psychology.

Taylor, James Wickes. *N. Y.*, 1819–1893. A United States consul at Winnipeg, Manitoba, from 1870. The Victim of Intrigue, a Tale of Burr's Conspiracy; History of Ohio, First Period: 1620–1787; Manual of Ohio School System; Forest and Fruit Culture in Manitoba; Mineral Resources of the United States (with Browne).

Taylor, John. *Va.*, 1750–1824. A politician of prominence in his day as a senator from Virginia. Inquiry into the Principles and Polity of the United States Government; Agricultural Essays; Construction Construed; Tyranny Unmasked; New Views of the United States Constitution.

Taylor, John Louis. *E.*, 1769–1829. A former chief justice of North Carolina, 1810–29. Superior Court Cases in Law and Equity; The North Carolina Law Repository; Term Reports; Duties of Executors and Administrators.

Taylor, John Neilson. *N. J.*, 1805–1878. A lawyer of Brooklyn. American Law of Landlord and Tenant; The Law of Executors and Administrators in New York State. *Lit.*

Taylor, John Orville. *N. Y.*, 1807–1890. An educational writer and reformer long prominent in New York State, and after 1879 a resident of New Brunswick, New Jersey. The District School, or Popular Education.

Taylor, Marshall William. *Ky.*, 1846–1887. A Methodist clergyman of African descent in Kentucky. Handbook for Schools; The Negro in Methodism.

Taylor, Nathaniel William. *Ct.*, 1786–1858. A Congregational clergyman prominent in his day as the exponent of the New Haven type of theology, who was Dwight professor at Yale University, 1822–38. Practical Sermons; Moral Government of God; Essays, etc., upon Select Topics in Revealed Theology.

Taylor, Oliver Alden. *Ms.*, 1801–1851. A Congregational clergyman of Manchester, Massachusetts. Brief Views of the Saviour; Life of Jesus. *See Memoir by A. A. Taylor.*

Taylor, Richard. *La.*, 1826–1879. A son of President Taylor, and a Confederate officer. Destruction and Reconstruction. *Ap.*

Taylor, Richard Cowling. *E.*, 1789–1851. An English geologist who came to America in 1830, among whose publications are, Geology and Natural History of the Northeast Extremity of the Alleghany Mountains; History and Description of Fossil Fuel; Statistics of Coal. *Bai.*

Taylor, Rufus. *Ms.*, 1811——. Brother of O. A. Taylor, *supra.* A Congregational minister of Massachusetts, whose home was at Beverly, New Jersey, after 1878. Union to Christ; Love to God; Thoughts on Prayer; Cottage Piety Exemplified. *Lip.*

Taylor, Samuel Harvey. *N. H.*, 1807–1871. An educator long prominent in Massachusetts, principal of Phillips Academy, Andover, 1837–71. Method of Classical Study. *See Memorial compiled by his last class.*

Taylor, Thomas House. *S. C.*, 1799–1869. An Episcopal clergyman, prominent in New York city as the rector of Grace Church, 1834–67, and active as a Low Church controversialist. Sermons Preached in Grace Church.

Taylor, Walter Herron. *Va.*, 1838——. A Confederate officer during the Civil War, and subsequently a banker in Norfolk. The Book of Travels of a Doctor of Physic; Four Years with General Lee. *Ap.*

Taylor, William. *Va.*, 1821——. A noted Methodist missionary and evangelist, appointed bishop in Africa in 1884, among whose writings are, California Life Illustrated; Seven Years' Street Preaching in San Francisco; Pauline Methods of Missionary Work; The Model Preacher; Reconciliation; The Election of Grace; Christian Adventures in South Africa; Our South American Cousins.

Taylor, William Mackergo. *S.*, 1829–1895. A Presbyterian clergyman of eminence. He came from Scotland to New York city in 1871, and was pastor of the Broadway Tabernacle, 1871–1893. Contrary Winds; The Limitations of Life; The Lost Found; The Gospel Miracles; Prayer and Business; Life Truths; John Knox; Joseph the Prime Minister; Ruth the Gleaner and Esther the Queen; David, King of Israel; Elijah the Prophet; Peter the Apostle; Daniel the Beloved; Moses the Law-Giver; Paul the Missionary; The Scottish Pulpit from the Reformation, comprise his most important works. *Har. Ran. Scr.*

Tefft, Benjamin Franklin. *N. Y.*, 1813–1885. A Methodist clergyman of Maine. The Shoulder-Knot, a Story of the 17th Century; Memorials of Prison Life; Methodism Successful; Our Political Parties; Evolution and Christianity; Hungary and Kossuth; Life of Daniel Webster. *Co. Le.*

Tennent, Gilbert. *I.*, 1703–1764. A Presbyterian clergyman of Philadelphia, active in his day as a controversialist. XXIII Sermons; Discourses on Several Subjects; Sermons on Important Subjects.

Tenney, Edward Payson. 1835——. A Congregational clergyman of New England, at one time President of Colorado College. Agamenticus; Constance of Acadia, a novel. *Le. Rob.*

Tenney, Sanborn. *N. H.*, 1827–1877. A naturalist who was professor of natural history at Williams College from 1868. Elements of Zoölogy; Manual of Zoölogy; Geology for Teachers.

Tenney, Mrs. Sarah [Brownson]. *Ms.*, 1839–1876. Wife of W. J. Tenney, *infra*, and daughter of O. Brownson, *supra.* Marion Elwood, or How Girls Live; At Anchor; Life of Demetrius Gallitzin, Prince and Priest.

Tenney, Mrs. Tabitha [Gilman]. *N. H.*, 1762–1837. The wife of a noted physician of Exeter, New Hampshire. She wrote Female Quixotism, an amusing satirical novel, which was long popular.

Tenney, William Jewett. *R. I.*, 1814–1883. A writer who lived at Elizabeth, New Jersey, for many years. He edited Appletons' Annual Cyclopedia, 1861–82, and wrote a Military and Naval History of the Rebellion.

Terhune, Albert Payson. *N. J.*, 1868——. Son of Mrs. Terhune, *infra*. A journalist and author of New York city. Syria from the Saddle, a volume of travels; Columbia Stories, a collection of sketches; The Great Cedarhurst Mystery. *Sil.*

Terhune, Mrs. Mary Virginia [Hawes]. "Marion Harland." *Va.*, 1835——. A popular novelist, lecturer, and writer on domestic topics, the wife of a Dutch Reformed clergyman of New York city. Her work in fiction includes, Alone; Moss-Side; Beechdale; Judith; The Hidden Path; Handicapped; Nemesis; At Last; Helen Gardner's Wedding-Day; Jessamine; With the Best Intentions; True as Steel; Sunnybank; From My Youth Up; My Little Love; A Gallant Fight; The Royal Road; His Great Self; Mr. Wayt's Wife's Sister; Eve's Daughters; Marion. Other works of hers are, Common Sense in the Household, a widely known manual of housewifery; Common Sense in the Nursery; The Cottage Kitchen; The Dinner Year-Book; Breakfast, Luncheon, and Tea; The Story of Mary Washington; Loitering in Pleasant Paths. *Cas. Do. Hou. Scr.*

Terry, Adrian Russell. *Ct.*, 1808–1864. A physician and educator who was for some years professor in Bristol College, Pennsylvania, and author of Travels in the Equatorial Regions of South America in 1832.

Terry, John Orville. *L. I.*, 1796–1860. A rural versifier of Orient, Long Island, who published The Poems of J. O. T., consisting of Song, Satire, and Pastoral Descriptions.

Terry, Milton Spenser. *N. Y.*, 1840——. A Methodist clergyman and educator, since 1884 a professor in Garrett Biblical Institute at Evanston, Illinois. Commentary on Judges, Ruth, and Samuel; Commentary on Kings, Chronicles, Ezra, and Nehemiah; Commentary on Genesis and Exodus; Biblical Hermeneutics; Sibylline Oracles (from the Greek); The Song of Songs; Prophecies of Daniel Expounded; Rambles in the Old World. *Meth.*

Teuffel, Mrs. Blanche Willis [Howard] von. *Me.*, 1847——. A novelist who has lived in Stuttgart, Germany, since 1875. One Summer; Aulnay Tower; Aunt Serena; Guenn; The Open Door; No Heroes, a Story for Boys; A Fellowe and His Wife (with William Sharp); Seven on the Highway, short stories; One Year Abroad: European Travel Sketches. *Hou.*

Thacher, James. *Ms.*, 1754–1844. A physician of Plymouth, Massachusetts, prominent in his youth as a military surgeon in the battles of the American Revolution. American Medical Biography; History of Plymouth; Essay on Demonology; American New Dispensatory; Observations on Hydrophobia; A Military Journal during the American Revolution, a work of great value; The Management of Bees; American Orchardist; Observations Relating to the Execution of Major André.

Thacher, John Boyd. *N. Y.*, 1847——. A critical scholar and bibliographer of Albany, mayor of that city in 1897. Charlecote, a drama; The Continent of America, its Discovery and its Baptism; Little Speeches. *Do.*

Thacher, Mary Potter. *See Higginson, Mrs. Mary.*

Thacher, Samuel Cooper. *Ms.*, 1785–1818. A Unitarian clergyman of Boston, pastor of the New South Church, 1811–15. An Apology for Rational and Evangelical Christianity; The Unity of God; Sermons; Evidences Necessary to Establish the Doctrine of the Trinity.

Thacher, Thomas. *E.*, 1620–1678. A Puritan clergyman, pastor and physician at Weymouth, Massachusetts, 1644–66, and pastor of the Old South Church in Boston from 1666. He published, in 1677, A Brief Rule to Guide the Common People of New England How to Order Themselves and Theirs in the Small Pocks or Measels, supposed to be the first medical work published in New England. *See Sprague's Annals of the American Pulpit.*

Thanet, Octave. *See French, Alice.*

Tharin, Robert Seymour Symmes. *Al.*, 1830——. A lawyer of Alabama who was prominent as a Unionist during the Civil War, and has since been employed in the auditor's office in Washington. Arbitrary Arrests in the South; Letters on the Political Situation.

Thatcher, Benjamin Bussey. *Me.*, 1809–1840. A Boston lawyer and littérateur. Indian Biography; Indian Traits; Traits of the Boston Tea Party; Tales of the American Revolution; Memoir of Phillis Wheatley. *Har.*

Thatcher, Oliver Joseph. *O.*, 185——. A Presbyterian clergyman, assistant professor of mediæval and English history in the University of Chicago from 1893. A Sketch of the History of the Apostolic Church; Europe in the Middle Age (with F. Schwill); A Short History of Mediæval Europe. *Hou. Scr.*

Thaxter, Adam Wallace. *Ms.*, 1832–1864. A dramatist of Boston among whose plays are, The Sculptor; Olympia; Mary Tudor; The Painter of Naples. He published, also, The Grotto Nymph.

Thaxter, Mrs. Celia [Laighton]. *N. H.*, 1835–1894. A poet whose childhood and much of whose later life was spent in the Isles of Shoals. Her verse is distinctly original and is largely the poetry of the shore, such poems as The Sandpiper; Courage; Kittery Church-Yard; The Spaniards' Graves; The Watch of Boon Island, being characteristic of her work in verse. Her volumes of verse comprise, Drift-Weed; The Cruise of the Mystery; Idyls and Pastorals; Verses; Poems for Children; Poems, Appledore Edition (1896). She wrote, also, An Island Garden; Among the Isles of Shoals. *See Letters of; Appletons' Annual Cyclopedia, 1894. Hou. Lo.*

Thayer, Alexander Wheelock. *Ms.*, 1817–1897. A writer whose later life was spent abroad, and who was consul at Trieste, 1859–82. His most important work, a Life of Beethoven, the third volume of which was published in Berlin in 1887, has not been printed in English. It was unfinished in 1897. The Hebrews and the Red Sea; Signor Masoni, and Other Papers of the late J. Brown.

Thayer, Eli. *Ms.*, 1819——. An educator of Worcester, Massachusetts, very prominent in the history of the settlement of Kansas. A History of the Kansas Crusade: its Friends and its Foes. *Har.*

Thayer, Mrs. Emma [Homan] [Graves]. *N.Y.*, 1842——. A writer and artist of Salida, Colorado. Wild Flowers of Colorado; Wild Flowers of the Pacific Coast; An English American, a novel.

Thayer, James Bradley. *Ms.*, 1831——. A professor in the Harvard Law School at Cambridge. A Western Journey with Mr. Emerson; Cases on Constitutional Law; A Preliminary Treatise on Evidence at the Common Law.

Thayer, Joseph Henry. *Ms.*, 1828——. A Congregational clergyman, professor of New Testament criticism and interpretation in the Divinity School of Harvard University from 1884. Books and Their Use; The Change of Attitude Toward the Bible; A Greek-English Lexicon of the New Testament. *Har. Hou.*

Thayer, Martin Russell. *Va.*, 1819——. A jurist of Philadelphia. The Duties of Citizenship; The Great Victory: its Cost and Value; The Law as a Progressive Science; On Libraries; Life and Works of Francis Lieber; The Battle of Germantown.

Thayer, Stephen Henry. *N. H.*, 1839——. A banker of New York city living at Tarrytown, New York, who has published Songs of Sleepy Hollow.

Thayer, Sylvanus. *Ms.*, 1785–1872. Cousin of M. R. Thayer, *supra.* A military engineer of distinction, superintendent of West Point Academy, 1817–1833, and from 1836–68 in charge of the military defences of Boston. Papers on Practical Engineering.

Thayer, Thomas Baldwin. *Ms.*, 1812–1882. A Universalist clergyman of Lowell. Over the River; Christianity *vs.* Infidelity; Historical Doctrine of Endless Punishment; Bible Class Assistant; Theology of Universalism.

Thayer, William Makepeace. *Ms.*, 1820——. A Congregational clergyman who retired from the ministry, and, living at Franklin, Massachusetts, devoted himself to authorship. His books, which have been extraordinarily popular, are mainly intended for juvenile reading. Among them are, Youths' History of the Rebellion; The Bobbin Boy; The Pioneer Boy; The Printer Boy; The Poor Boy and the Merchant Prince; Turning Points in Successful Careers; Marvels of the New West; The White House Series; Aim High: Hints for Young Men; Life of Garfield; Men Who Win; Women Who Win. *Cr. Wh.*

Thayer, William Roscoe. *Ms.*, 1859——. Formerly an instructor at Harvard University. His writings in verse include, The Confessions of Hermes; Hesper; Poems, New and Old. He has published, also, The Dawn of Italian Independence; The Best Elizabethan Plays. *Gi. Hou.*

Thébaud [tay-bo'], **Augustine J——.** *F.*, 1807–1885. A Roman Catholic clergyman and educator of New York city. The Irish Race in the Past and Present; Louisa Kirkbride, a tale of New York; The Church and the Moral World; The Twit-Twats, a bird allegory.

Theller, Edward Alexander. *Q.*, *c.* 1810–1859. A Canadian physician who, for his activity in the Canadian rebellion of 1837, was imprisoned and sentenced to death. He escaped to the United States, and was subsequently a journalist in California and superintendent of schools in San Francisco. Canada in 1837–38.

Thieblin, Nicolas Leon. *Iy.*, 1834–1889. A journalist of London, and, after 1874, of New York city. He was Spanish correspondent of The Herald in the Carlist war. A Little Book About Great Britain; Spain and the Spaniards. *Le.*

Thoburn, James Mills. *O.*, 1836——. A Methodist missionary, bishop in India and Malaysia since 1888. Missionary Addresses; My Missionary Apprenticeship in New York; India and Malaysia; Light in the East; The Deaconess and Her Vocation; Christless Nations. *Meth.*

Thomas, Abel Charles. *Pa.*, 1807–1880. A Universalist clergyman of Philadelphia, and for a short time in Lowell, where he established the Lowell Offering, a periodical written by the factory operatives. Allegories and Divers Day Dreams; Centenary of Universalism; Discussions on Universalism; The Christian Helper; Autobiography.

Thomas, Amos Russell. *N.Y.*, 1826——. A Philadelphia physician, dean of Hahnemann Medical College. Post Mortem Examinations and Morbid Anatomy.

Thomas, Benjamin Franklin. *Ms.*, 1813–1878. Grandson of I. Thomas, *infra*. A jurist of Worcester, Massachusetts. Digest of Laws of Massachusetts in Relation to Powers, Duties, and Liabilities of Towns and Town Officers; Life of Isaiah Thomas, *infra*.

Thomas, Cyrus. *Tn.*, 1825——. A noted ethnologist and entomologist in the government service. Actididæ of North America; Noxious and Beneficial Insects of Illinois; Study of the Manuscript Troano; Notes on Certain Maya and Mexican Manuscripts; Aids to the Study of the Maya Chronicles; The Cherokees and Shawnees in Pre-Columbian Times; Catalogue of Prehistoric Works East of the Rocky Mountains; Mound Exploration of the Bureau of Ethnology.

Thomas, David. *Pa.*, 1776–1859. A pomologist and engineer, once prominent in western New York. Travels in the West (1819).

Thomas, Ebenezer Smith. *Ms.*, 1780–1844. Nephew of I. Thomas, *infra*. A Cincinnati journalist who published Reminiscences of the Last Sixty-Five Years (1840); Reminiscences of South Carolina.

Thomas, Mrs. Edith [Carpenter]. *N. H.*, 18——. A writer of Millville, New Jersey. Lorenzo Di Medici: an Historical Portrait; Your Money or Your Life, a novel. *Put. Scr.*

Thomas, Edith Matilda. *O.*, 1854——. A poet and prose-writer, formerly of Geneva, Ohio, but since 1888 of New York city and its vicinity. The best of her poems are marked by great refinement of expression as well as subtlety of thought. Beside a volume of prose papers, The Round Year, she has published in verse, A New Year's Masque; A Winter Swallow, with Other Verse; Fair Shadow Land; Lyrics and Sonnets; The Inverted Torch; In Sunshine Land; In the Young World, the two last named being intended for juvenile reading. *Hou. Scr.*

Thomas, Frederick William. *R. I.*, 1811–1864. Son of E. S. Thomas, *supra*. A journalist, novelist, and educator who was also a Methodist clergyman. The Emigrant, a Poem; The Beechen Tree, and Other Poems; Sketches of Character; Randolph of Roanoke. His novels include, Clinton Bradshaw; East and West; Howard Pinckney.

Thomas, Isaiah. *Ms.*, 1749–1831. A noted printer of Worcester, Massachusetts, who was the founder of the American Antiquarian Society at Worcester. He published The Massachusetts Spy till 1801; The New England Almanac; and wrote a valuable History of Printing. *See Life of, by B. F. Thomas, supra.*

Thomas, Jesse Burgess. *Il.*, 1832–——. A Baptist clergyman, professor in the Theological Seminary at Newton, Massachusetts, from 1887. The Old Bible and the New Science; The Mould of Doctrine; Significance of the Historical Element in Scripture.

Thomas, John J——. *N. Y.*, 1810–1895. Son of D. Thomas, *supra*. An agricultural writer of Albany, long on the editorial staff of The Country Gentleman. He edited Rural Affairs, and was author of The American Fruit Culturist; Farm Implements: their Construction and Use; Farm Implements and Farm Machinery. He was a much-esteemed authority in his department.

Thomas, Joseph. *N. Y.*, 1811–1891. Son of D. Thomas, *supra*. An eminent lexicographer of Philadelphia. A Pronouncing Gazetteer and Dictionary of the World; Gazetteer of the United States; Medical Dictionary; Universal Pronouncing Dictionary of Biography and Mythology; First Book of Etymology; Travels in Egypt and Palestine. *Lip.*

Thomas, Lewis Foulke. *Md.*, 1815–1868. Son of E. S. Thomas, *supra*. A lawyer and verse-writer of Washington. India, and Other Poems; Cortez the Conqueror, a drama; Osceola, a drama; Rhymes of the Routes.

Thomas, Martha McCannon. *Md.*, 1823——. Daughter of E. S. Thomas, *supra*. Life's Lessons, a Tale; Captain Phil, a story of the Civil War. *Ho.*

Thomas, Mary von Erden. *S. C.*, 1825——. Daughter of E. S. Thomas, *supra*. A computer in the Coast Survey Office at Washington from 1854. Winning the Battle, a novel.

Thomas, Reuen. *E.*, 1840——. A Congregational clergyman, pastor of the Harvard Church at Brookline, Massachusetts, from 1875. Through Death to Life; Divine Sovereignty; Grafenburg People; Leaders of Thought in the Modern Church. *Lo.*

Thomas, Robert Baily. *Ms.*, 1766–1846. Editor for fifty-three years of The Farmer's Almanack, which he first published in 1793 and which is still issued yearly.

Thomas, Theodore Gaillard. *S. C.*, 1832——. An eminent physician of New York city who has published Diseases of Women; Abortion and its Treatment. *Ap.*

Thomas, William Henry. *Me.*, 1824–1895. A journalist and traveller. Life in the East Indies; A Whaleman's Adventures; A Slaver's Adventures; Running the Blockade; The Belle of Australia; On Land and Sea; Lewey and I; Ocean Rovers.

Thompson, Alexander Ramsey. *N. Y.*, 1822–1895. A Presbyterian clergyman of New York city who published Christianity and Patriotism; Casting Down Imaginations, and was the author of many hymns.

Thompson, Augustus Charles. *Ct.*, 1812——. A Congregational clergyman, pastor of the Eliot Church at Roxbury, Massachusetts, from 1842. Lyra Cœlestis, or Hymns on Heaven; Christian's Consolation; Songs in the Night; The Mercy Seat; Foreign Missions; Moravian Missions; Future Probation and Foreign Missions; Our Birthdays; Protestant Missions. *Cr. Scr.*

Thompson, Benjamin. *See Rumford.*

Thompson, Charles Lemuel. *Pa.*, 1839——. A Presbyterian clergyman of New York city. Times of Refreshing: a History of American Revivals; Etchings in Verse. *Ran.*

Thompson, Charles Miner. *Vt.*, 1864——. Grandson of D. P. Thompson, *infra.* A Boston writer on the editorial staff of The Youth's Companion. The Nimble Dollar, with Other Stories; Life of Ethan Allen. *Hou.*

Thompson, Daniel Greenleaf. *Vt.*, 1850–1897. Son of D. P. Thompson, *infra.* A lawyer of New York city. First Book in Latin; A System of Psychology; The Problem of Evil; The Religious Sentiments of the Human Mind; Social Progress; Philosophy of Fiction in Literature; Politics in a Democracy; Woman's New Opportunity. *Lgs.*

Thompson, Daniel Pierce. *Ms.*, 1795–1868. A lawyer of Montpelier, Vermont, whose semi-historical fictions, though somewhat artless in construction, are vigorously conceived narratives of early life in Vermont, and have been very popular. Gaut Gurley; May Martin; Green Mountain Boys; Locke Amsden; Lucy Hosmer; The Doomed Chief; The Rangers; Tales of the Green Mountains; Centeola, and Other Tales; History of Montpelier. *Cr. Le.*

Thompson, Hugh Miller. *I.*, 1830——. The second Protestant Episcopal bishop of Mississippi. Unity and its Restoration; Copy, a collection of essays; Sin and its Penalty; First Principles; The World and the Logos; The World and the Kingdom; The World and the Man; The World and the Wrestlers; Absolution. *Wh.*

Thompson, [James] Maurice. *Ind.*, 1844——. A writer of Crawfordsville, Indiana, who was a Confederate soldier during the Civil War, and State geologist of Indiana, 1885–89. His work in fiction includes, A Tallahassee Girl; His Second Campaign; At Love's Extremes; A Fortnight of Folly; The Ocala Boy; King of Honey Island. Other Works are, Hoosier Mosaics, a volume of sketches; The Witchery of Archery; Songs of Fair Weather; Byways and Bird Notes; Sylvan Secrets; The Story of Louisiana; Poems (1892); Lincoln's Grave, a Poem. *Hou. Lo. Scr. St.*

Thompson, John Reuben. *Va.*, 1823–1873. A journalist and lawyer of Richmond, Virginia, editor of The Southern Literary Messenger, 1847–59, and very popular in the South as a lyrist. *See Manly's Southern Literature.*

Thompson, Joseph Parrish. *Pa.*, 1819–1879. An eminent Congregational clergyman of New York city, pastor of the Broadway Tabernacle, 1845–71, and from 1872 a resident in Berlin, Germany. The Theology of Christ; Man in Genesis and Geology; Lectures to Young Men; Church and State in the United States; The United States as a Nation; Egypt Past and Present; The Workman: his False Friends and his True Friends; Life of Christ; American Comments on European Questions; Christianity and Emancipation; The Holy Comforter, include his principal works. *Ran.*

Thompson, Lewis O——. *N.*, 1830–1887. A Presbyterian clergyman of Peoria, Illinois. The Presidents and their Administrations; Nothing Lost; How to Conduct Prayer Meetings; The Prayer Meeting and its Improvement; Nineteen Christian Centuries in Outline. *Lo.*

Thompson, Maurice. *See Thompson, J. M.*

Thompson, Mortimer. "Q. K. Philander Doesticks." 1830–1875. A once popular humourous writer and lecturer. Doesticks: What he Says; Plu-Ri-Bus-Tah, a travesty of "Hiawatha;" The Witches of New York; Nothing to Say; History and Records of the Elephant Club.

Thompson, Richard Wigginton. *Va.*, 1809——. An Indiana jurist who was secretary of the United States navy, 1877–81. The Papacy and the Civil Power; Footprints of the Jesuits; History of Protective Tariff Laws. *Cr. Har. Meth.*

Thompson, Robert Ellis. *I.*, 1844——. A political economist of Philadelphia. He was editor of The Penn Monthly, 1870–80; professor in the University of Pennsylvania, 1870–92; president of the Central High School from 1894. History of the Presbyterian Churches in the United States; Elements of Political Economy; Social Science and National Economy; Hard Times and What to Learn from Them; Protection to Home Industry; De Civitate Dei. *Ap. Bai. Gi. Wat.*

Thompson, William Tappan. *O.*, 1812–1882. A prominent journalist of Savannah, the rough, extravagant humour of whose studies of Georgia life was once popular. Major Jones's Courtship; Major Jones's Sketches of Travel; Major Jones's Characters of Pineville; The Live Indian, a Farce; John's Alive. *See Manly's Southern Literature. Ap.*

Thompson, Seymour Dwight. 18——. A lawyer of Saint Louis. On the Liability of Stockholders in Corporations; Charging the Jury; The Law of Carriers of Passengers; The Law of Negligence in Relations not resting in Contract; Liabilities of Directors.

Thompson, Zadock. *Vt.*, 1796–1856. An Episcopal clergyman, professor of natural history in the University of Vermont, and State geologist, 1845–48. History of Vermont, Natural, Civil, and Statistical; Gazetteer of Vermont; Geography and Geology of Vermont; Guide to Lake George.

Thomson, Charles. *I.*, 1729–1824. A writer of Lower Merion, Pennsylvania, who was secretary of the first Continental Congress. He published Inquiry into the Causes of the Alienation of the Delaware and Shawanese Indians; Synopsis of the Four Evangelists; a noted translation of the Bible, that of the Old Testament being the earliest English version of the Septuagint.

Thomson, Charles West. *Pa.*, 1798–1879. An Episcopal clergyman at York, Pennsylvania, 1849–66, who wrote The Limner, in prose; and in verse, The Phantom Barge; The Sylph; Elinor; The Love of Home.

Thomson, Edward. *E.*, 1810–1870. A Methodist clergyman, president of Ohio Wesleyan University, 1846–60. Evidences of Revealed Religion; Our Oriental Missions; Educational Essays; Moral and Religious Essays; Biographical Sketches; Letters from Europe; Letters from India. *See Life of, by his son. Meth.*

Thomson, Edward William. *Ont.*, 1849——. A civil engineer of Boston who was for some years editor-in-chief of The Toronto Globe. Old Man Savarin, and Other Stories, a striking collection of short stories; Walter Gibbs, a book for boys; and the metrical portions of M. S. Henry's version of Aucassin and Nicolette. *Cop. Cr.*

Thomson, James Bates. *Vt.*, 1808–1883. An educator of Brooklyn who was a mathematician and conchologist. He published a School Algebra; Arithmetical Analysis, and a popular series of arithmetics.

Thomson, Samuel. *N. H.*, 1769–1843. A physician of Boston who originated the Thomsonian school of medicine, so called. Materia Medica and Family Physician; New Guide to Health; Life and Medical Discoveries.

Thomson, Samuel Harrison. *Ky.*, 1813–1882. Cousin of W. M. Thomson, *infra.* A Presbyterian clergyman and educator. The Mosaic Account of the Creation; Geology an Interpreter of Scripture.

Thomson, William Hanna. *Sa.*, 1833——. Son of W. M. Thomson, *infra.* A physician of New York city. The Great Argument, or Jesus Christ in the Old Testament; The Parables and Their Home; Materialism and Modern Physiology of the Nervous System. *Har. Put.*

Thomson, William McClure. *O.*, 1806–1894. A Presbyterian missionary in Beyrout, 1833–76, widely known as author of The Land and the Book. He wrote also The Land of Promise. *Har.*

Thorburn, Grant. "Lawrie Todd." *S.*, 1773–1863. A Scottish nail-maker who came to America in 1794, and subsequently established himself in New York city as a seedsman. He was a noted figure in his day, not only as the hero of Galt's novel, Lawrie Todd, but because of his eccentricities. Lawrie Todd's Notes on Virginia; Fifty Years' Reminiscences of New York; Men and Manners in Great Britain; Hints to Merchants, Married Men, and Bachelors; Forty Years' Residence in America. *See Autobiography.*

Thoreau [thō'rō], **Henry David.** *Ms.*, 1817–1862. A unique figure in literature, whose fame, circumscribed in his lifetime, has steadily widened since his death. He was all his life a resident of Concord, Massachusetts, devoting himself to the study of nature, and occasionally working at his trade of pencil-making, surveying, or lecturing, for his support. A Week on the Concord and Merrimac Rivers, and Walden were the only works by him which were published in his lifetime. Those since issued include, Excursions; Maine Woods; Cape Cod; A Yankee in Canada. Early Spring in Massachusetts; Summer; Autumn; Winter, are selections from Thoreau's Journal edited by H. G. O. Blake. Still other works are, Miscellanies; Letters to Various Persons; Familiar Letters; Poems of Nature. *See North American Review, October, 1865; Fraser's Magazine, April, 1866; Memoir by Emerson in Thoreau's Miscellanies; Thoreau: the Poet Naturalist, by W. E. Channing, 1873; Life and Aims of, by Page, 1877; Encyclopædia Britannica, ninth edition; Harvard Register, April, 1881; Life by Sanborn, 1882; Thoreau: a Glimpse, by S. H. Jones, 1890; Life by Salt, 1890; Atlantic Monthly, December, 1896; Foley's American Authors, 1897. Hou.*

Thorne, P. *See Smith, Mrs. Mary.*

Thorne, William Henry. *E.*, 18——. An aggressive essayist and critic, editor of The Globe Review from 1880. He came to the United States from England in 1855, and after some years spent in the Presbyterian ministry became a Roman Catholic layman. Modern Idols: Studies in Biography and Criticism; Quintets, and Other Verses. *Lip.*

Thornton, Jessy Quinn. *W. Va.*, 1810–1888. An Oregon jurist of note. Oregon and California in 1848; History of the Provisional Government of Oregon; The Gold Mines of California.

Thornton, John Wingate. *Me.*, 1818–1878. A Boston lawyer of genealogical tastes. Colonial Schemes of Popham and Gorges; The Landing at Cape Anne; First Records of Anglo-American Civilization; The Pulpit of the American Revolution; Historical Relation of New England to the English Commonwealth, include his principal publications.

Thornton, William. *W. I.*, 17—1827. A physician and architect of Philadelphia who removed to Washington, where he drew the plans of the first Capitol building, and was at the head of the Patent Office, 1802–27. Cadmus, or the Elements of Written Language.

Thornton, William. *E.*, 1840——. A physician of Boston. The Origin, Purpose, and Destiny of Man.

Thornwell, James Henley. *S. C.*, 1812–1862. A Presbyterian clergyman, professor in the theological seminary at Columbia, South Carolina, prominent alike for his rigid Calvinism and his extreme pro-slavery opinions. Arguments of Romanists Discussed and Refuted; Discourses on Truth; Rights and Duties of Masters; The State of the Country.

Thorpe, Francis Newton. *Ms.*, 1857——. A lawyer of Philadelphia. The Government of the People of the United States; The Story of the Constitution. *Meth.*

Thorpe, Kamba. *See Bellamy, Mrs.*

Thorpe, Mrs. Rosa [Hartwick]. *Ind.*, 1850——. A verse-writer chiefly known as the author of Curfew Must Not Ring Tonight. Temperance Poems; Ringing Ballads; and several juvenile prose works, including The Year's Best Days; The Chester Girls; Fred's Dark Days; The Fenton Family; Minna Bruce. *Le.*

Thorpe, Thomas Bangs. *Ms.*, 1815–1878. An artist and author of New Orleans, 1836–53, and in later life of New York city. Niagara as It Is is his finest painting. His writings include, The Hive of the Bee Hunter; Tom Owen the Bee Hunter; Mysteries of the Backwoods; Our Army of the Rio Grande; Our Army at Monterey; A Voice to America; Scenes in Arkansas; Lynde Weirs, an Autobiography.

Throop, Montgomery Hunt. *N. Y.*, 1827——. A lawyer of New York city. The Future: a Political Essay; Validity of Verbal Agreements; Annotated Code of Civil Procedure; The New York Justices' Manual; Digest of Massachusetts Supreme Judicial Court Decisions; Revised Statutes of the State of New York.

Thurber, Charles Herbert. *N. Y.*, 1864——. An educator of Chicago, a professor in the University of Chicago from 1895. In and Out of Ithaca; The Higher Schools of Prussia.

Thurber, George. *R. I.*, 1821–1890. A botanist who edited The American Agriculturist, 1863–90. He published American Weeds and Useful Plants, a revision of Darlington's Agricultural Botany.

Thurston, Robert Henry. *R. I.*, 1839——. An eminent mechanical engineer and inventor, professor in Stevens Technological Institute at Hoboken, 1871–85, and director of Sibley College, Cornell University, from 1885. Friction and Lubrication; Manual of the Steam Engine; Manual of Steam Boilers; Engine and Boiler Trials; History of the Growth of the Steam Engine; Materials of Engineering; Friction and Lost Work; Steam-Boiler Explosions in Theory and Practice; Heat as a Form of Energy; Robert Fulton, his Life and its Results, include his most important works. *Ap. Do. Hou. Wil.*

Thwaites, Reuben Gold. *Ms.*, 1853——. An historical writer in Wisconsin, and secretary of the State Historical Society. Historic Waterways: Six Hundred Miles of Canoeing down the Rock, Fox, and Wisconsin Rivers; The Story of Wisconsin; Our Cycling Tour in England; The Colonies, 1492–1750. He is also the editor of the Jesuit Relations and Allied Documents. *See Bibliography of Wisconsin. Bur. Le. Lgs. Mg.*

Thwing [twing], **Charles Franklin.** *Me.*, 1853——. A Congregational clergyman of Minneapolis from 1886. American Colleges; The Reading of Books; The Working Church; The Family: an Historical and Social Study (with Mrs. Thwing); The College Woman. *Le. Put.*

Thwing, Edward Payson. *Mo.*, 1830–1893. A Congregational clergyman and professor of vocal culture. The Preacher's Cabinet; Out-Door Life in Europe; Windows of Character; The King in His Beauty; Ex-Oriente; Drill Book in Vocal Culture. *Fu.*

Ticknor, Caleb B——. *Ct.*, 1805–1840. A homœopathic physician of New York city. Medical Philosophy; Guide to Mothers and Nurses.

Ticknor, Caroline. *Ms.*, 18——. A Boston writer of short stories. A Hypocritical Romance, and Other Stories; Miss Belladonna, a Child of To-day. *Kt. Lit.*

Ticknor, Francis Orrery. *Ga.*, 1822–1874. A physician near Columbus, Georgia. Virginians of the Valleys, and Other Poems, edited by Paul Hayne, *supra*, appeared in 1879. *Lip.*

Ticknor, George. 1791–1871. A noted Boston historian who was professor of modern languages at Harvard University, 1820–35. A History of Spanish Literature, the fruit of many years' study and research, is his principal work. It is a recognized authority in its department, but is cold and lifeless in its treatment of the subject. Other works by him are, Life of W. H. Prescott, *supra*; Life of Lafayette. *See London Quarterly Review, October, 1850; Lippincott's Magazine, May, 1876; Life, Letters, and Journals; Allibone's Dictionary and Supplement. Foley's American Authors, 1897. Hou. Lip.*

Tidball, John Caldwell. *W. Va.*, 1825——. A Federal officer during the Civil War who has published a Manual of Heavy Artillery Service.

Tidball, Mrs. Mary Langdon. 18——. Wife of J. C. Tidball, *supra*. A novelist of Virginia. Barbara's Vagaries. *Har.*

Tidball, Thomas Allen. *Va.*, 1847——. Cousin of J. C. Tidball, *supra*. An Episcopal clergyman of Philadelphia, rector of the Church of the Epiphany. Christ in the New Testament; The Character of Christ its Own Witness; The Holy Spirit as Energizing the Sacrament. *Wh.*

Tiedeman, Christopher Gustavus. *S. C.*, 1857——. A legal writer, professor of law in the University of Missouri, 1881–91, and from 1891 professor of constitutional law in the University of the City of New York. The Law of Real Property; Limitations of the Police Power; Commercial Paper; The Unwritten Constitution of the United States; Law of Sales; Law of Municipal Corporations. *Put.*

Tiernan, Mrs. Frances [Fisher]. "Christian Reid." *N. C.*, 18——. A popular novelist whose writings include, Valerie Aylmer; Mabel Lee; Morton House; A Daughter of Bohemia; Miss Churchill; Bonny Kate; Ebb Tide; Nina's Atonement, and Other Stories; After Many Days; Heart of Steel; Hearts and Hands; A Question of Honor; A Summer Idyl; A Gentle Belle; Roslyn's Fortune; A Comedy of Elopement; The Picture of Las Cruces; The Land of the Sun; A Woman of Fortune. *Ap.*

Tiernan, Mrs. Mary Spear [Nicholas]. 1836–1891. A Georgia novelist. Homoselle; Suzette; Jack Horner. *Ho. Hou.*

Tiffany, Alexander Ralston. *Ont.*, 1796–1868. A jurist of Palmyra, Michigan. The Justices' Guide; Criminal Law; Form Book for Michigan Attorneys.

Tiffany, Charles Comfort. *Md.*, 1829——. An Episcopal clergyman of New York city, but prior to 1866 a Congregational clergyman. Expression in Church Architecture; History of the Protestant Episcopal Church in the United States.

Tiffany, Francis. *Md.*, 1827——. A Unitarian clergyman living in Cambridge, pastor at West Newton, Massachusetts, 1865–82. Life of Dorothea Lynde Dix, *supra;* Bird Bolts; Life of Charles Francis Barnard; This Goodly Frame, the Earth, a volume of travels in America, Japan, Egypt, Palestine, and Greece. *El. Hou.*

Tiffany, Joel. 18——. Treatise on Government and Constitutional Law; Man and His Destiny; Reports of Cases Argued and Determined in the Court of Appeals of the State of New York; The Book of Forms (with H. Smith); Laws of Trusts and Trustees (with E. Bullard); Treatise on Practice and Pleadings in the Courts of Record (with H. Smith).

Tiffany, Osmond. *Md.*, 1823——. A custom-house clerk in Baltimore from 1869. The Canton Chinese; Brandon, a Tale of the American Revolution; Life of General Otho Williams.

Tiffany, Otis Henry. *Md.*, 1825——. A Methodist clergyman of prominence. Pulpit and Platform Addresses and Sermons. *Meth.*

Tigert, John James. *Ky.*, 1856——. A Methodist clergyman and educator in Nashville. Handbook of Logic; The Preacher Himself; A Voice from the South; Constitutional History of American Episcopal Methodism.

Tilden, Samuel Jones. *N. Y.*, 1814–1886. A distinguished lawyer and statesman, governor of New York in 1874, and the Democratic candidate for the presidency in 1876. Writings and Speeches, edited by John Bigelow. *See Lives of, by Cook, 1876, J. Bigelow. 1895. Har.*

Tilden, William Phillips. *Ms.*, 1811–1890. A Unitarian clergyman of Boston. The Work of the Ministry; Buds for the Bridal Wreath. *See Autobiography. El. Le.*

Tillett, Wilbur Fisk. *N. C.*, 1854——. A Methodist clergyman and educator, vice-chancellor of Vanderbilt University, Nashville. 1882–95. Our Hymns and their Authors; Discussions in Theology.

Tillinghast, Nicholas. *Ms.*, 1804–1856. A Massachusetts educator, principal of the Normal School at Bridgewater, 1840–53. Elements of Plane Geometry; Prayers for Schools.

Tillman, Samuel Dyer. *N. Y.*, 1815–1875. A lawyer who practiced in Seneca Falls, New York, and, removing to New York city in 1850, devoted himself to scientific pursuits, and published a Treatise on Musical Sounds.

Tillman, Samuel Escue. *Tn.*, 1847——. A soldier and educator, professor of chemistry at West Point from 1880. Elementary Lessons in Heat; Essential Principles of Chemistry.

Tilton, Benjamin Trowbridge. *R. I.*, 1868——. Brother of W. F. Tilton, *infra.* A physician of New York city, translator of Die Specielle Chirurgie, in two volumes, and Allgemeine Chirurgie from the German of Tillmanns. *Ap.*

Tilton, Theodore. *N. Y.*, 1835——. A journalist and verse-writer who was editor of The New York Independent, 1863–72, and since 1883 has lived in Europe. The American Board and Slavery; The King's Ring; Sanctum Sanctorum or an Editor's Proof Sheets; Life of Victoria Woodhull; Tempest-Tossed, a novel; Swabian Stories; The

Sexton's Tale, and Other Poems; Thou and I, a volume of verse.

Tilton, William Frederic. *Ms.*, 1867——. An historical writer. Die Spanische Armada; The Life of Philip the Second.

Timayenis, Telemachus Thomas. *A. M.*, 1853——. A writer of New York city of Greek parentage, resident in the United States from 1870. The Modern Greek, its Pronunciation and Relations to Ancient Greek; A History of Greece; Greece in the Times of Homer; Contes Tirés de Shakespeare; Talks with Æsop; In Search of Happiness, a play. *Ap. Scr.*

Timrod, Henry. *S. C.*, 1829–1867. Son of W. H. Timrod, *infra*. A poet and journalist of Charleston, and, in his last years, of Columbia, South Carolina, whose verse has very real merit. Spring in Carolina is one of his best poems. *See Poems (1873), with Memoir by Paul Hayne, supra; Manly's Southern Literature.*

Timrod, William Henry. *S. C.*, 1792–1838. A bookbinder of Charleston who published a volume of Lyrics.

Tincker, Mary Agnes. *Me.*, 1833——. A popular novelist who lived in Italy, 1873–87, and subsequently in Boston. Signor Monaldini's Niece; The Jewel in the Lotus; Aurora; Two Coronets; By the Tiber; The House of Yorke; A Winged Word; Grapes and Thorns; Six Sunny Months; San Salvador. *Hou. Lip. Rob.*

Tinto, Dick. *See Goodrich, F. B.*

Titchener, Edward Bradford. *E.*, 1867——. A professor of psychology at Cornell University from 1892, and Sage professor of psychology there from 1895; the American editor of Mind, and co-editor of The American Journal of Psychology. Beside translating Kuelpe's Outlines of Psychology and other German works, he has published An Outline of Psychology. *Mac.*

Titcomb, Sarah Elizabeth. *Ms.*, 1841–1895. A Boston writer who published Early New England People; Mind-Cure on a Material Basis; Aryan Sun Myths the Origin of Religions.

Titcomb, Timothy. *See Holland, J. G.*

Todd, Albert. *R. I.*, 1854——. A lieutenant in the United States army who has published The Campaigns of the Rebellion.

Todd, Charles Burr. *Ct.*, 1849——. A magazinist of Redding, Connecticut. Life and Letters of Joel Barlow, *supra*; General History of the Burr Family; History of Redding, Connecticut; Story of the City of New York; The Story of the City of Washington. *Put.*

Todd, David Peck. *N. Y.*, 1855——. Son of S. E. Todd, *infra*. A professor of astronomy at Amherst College from 1881. Stars and Telescopes (with W. T. Lynn); Astronomy for Beginners, and many scientific papers. *Am. Rob.*

Todd, John. *Vt.*, 1800–1873. A Congregational clergyman, pastor of the First Church in Pittsfield, Massachusetts, 1842–72. Among his many popular works are included, Lectures to Children; Student's Manual; Truth Made Simple; Hints to Young Men; The Daughter at School; Mountain Gems; Woman's Rights; Sunset Land; Old-Fashioned Lives; Future Punishment. *See Life; Harper's Magazine, February, 1876. Le. Ran.*

Todd, Lawrie. *See Thorburn, Grant.*

Todd, Mrs. Mabel [Loomis]. *Ms.*, 1858——. Wife of D. P. Todd, *supra*, and daughter of E. J. Loomis, *supra*. She has edited The Poems and Letters of Emily Dickinson, *supra*; A Cycle of Sonnets, and is the author of a work on Total Eclipses of the Sun. *Rob.*

Todd, Mrs. Marion. *N. Y.*, 1841——. A lawyer and lecturer of Eaton Rapids, Michigan. Railways of Europe and America, or Government Ownership; Protective Tariff Delusion. *Ar.*

Todd, Sereno Edwards. *N. Y.*, 1820——. A journalist of New York city, at one period agricultural editor of The Times, now (1897) living at Orange, New Jersey. The Apple Culturist; Young Farmer's Manual; The American Wheat Culturist; Country Homes; Rural Poetry and Country Lyrics. *Har.*

Toland, Mrs. Mary B—— M——. 18———. Sir Rae; Stella; Iris; Onti Ora; Aegle and the Elf; Eudora; Legend Layamone; Tisáyac of the Yosemite; Atlina, the Queen of the Floating Isle. *Lip.*

Tomes, Robert. *N. Y.*, 1817–1882. A physician and littérateur. Panama in 1855; Bourbon Prince; My College Days; Richard the Lion-Hearted; Oliver Cromwell; The Americans in Japan; Battles of America by Sea and Land; The War with the South; The Champagne Country. *Har.*

Tomlinson, Everett Titsworth. N. J., 1859——. A Baptist clergyman of Elizabeth, New Jersey, popular as a writer of juvenile tales, among which are, The Search for Andrew Field; The Boy Soldiers of 1812; The Boy Officers of 1812; Three Colonial Boys; Tecumseh's Young Braves; Three Young Continentals. *Le. We.*

Tompson, Benjamin. *Ms.*, 1642–1714. A colonial educator, the master of a preparatory school in Cambridge for nearly forty years from 1670, and a satirical verse-writer of some merit. New England's Crisis, a poem on King Philip's War. *See Tyler's American Literature.*

Tone, William Theobald Wolfe. *I.*, 1791–1828. A son of Wolfe Tone, the Irish patriot and French general. After serving in the French army he came to America in 1816 and was in the artillery service of the United States for ten years. L'État civil et politique de l'Italie sous la domination des Goths; School of Cavalry, a proposed system for the United States cavalry. He also edited his father's autobiography.

Toner, Joseph Meredith. *Pa.*, 1825–1896. An eminent physician of Washington city, among whose writings are, Abortion in its Medical and Moral Aspects; Maternal Instinct; Medical Men of the Revolution.

Toppan, Robert Noxon. *Pa.*, 1836——. A lawyer of Cambridge, Massachusetts. Historical Summary of Metallic Money; Biographical Sketches of Old Newbury. *Lit.*

Torrey, Bradford. *Ms.*, 1843——. An essayist of Boston, a member of the editorial staff of The Youth's Companion. Birds in the Bush; The Foot-Path Way; A Rambler's Lease; A Florida Sketch-Book; Spring Notes from Tennessee. *Hou.*

Torrey, Charles Turner. *Ms.*, 1813–1846. An anti-slavery reformer who was imprisoned in Baltimore for aiding in the escape of slaves, and died in imprisonment. Memoir of William Sarton; Home, or the Pilgrim's Faith Reward. *See Memoir of the Martyr Torrey, 1847.*

Torrey, John. *N. Y.*, 1796–1873. A distinguished botanist and physician of New York city, professor in the College of Physicians and Surgeons, 1827–55, and United States assayer, 1853–73. Catalogue of Plants Growing Spontaneously Within Thirty Miles of New York; Flora of the Northern and Middle States; Flora of New York State.

Torrey, Joseph. *Ms.*, 1797–1867. A Congregational clergyman and educator, professor in the University of Vermont, 1827–67. A Theory of Art; translation of Neander's History of the Christian Religion. *Scr.*

Totten, Benjamin J——. *W. I.*, 1806–1877. A naval officer of New Bedford. Totten's Naval Text-Book.

Totten, Charles Adelle Lewis. *Ct.*, 1851——. A military inventor. Strategos, the American War Game; Yale Military Lectures; Nativity: its Facts and Fancies. *Ap.*

Totten, Joseph Gilbert. *Ct.*, 1788–1864. A military engineer of distinction, brevetted major-general in 1864. Essays on Hydraulic and Other Cements.

Totten, Silas. *N. Y.*, 1804–1873. An Episcopal clergyman, president of Trinity College, 1837–48. New Introduction to Algebra; The Analogy of Truth.

Toucey, Sinclair. *Ct.*, 1818–1887. A publisher of New York city, president of the American News Company, 1864–87. Papers from Over the Water.

Toulmin, Henry. *E.*, 1767–1823. A jurist who was the Kentucky secretary of state, 1796–1804, and president of Transylvania University, and subsequently lived in Alabama. A Description of Kentucky; Magistrate's Assistant; Collection of the Acts of Kentucky; Review of the Criminal Law of Kentucky (with J. Blair); Digest of the Territorial Laws of Alabama.

Tourgée [toor-zhay′], **Albion Winegar.** *O.*, 1838——. A writer who settled in North Carolina at the close of the Civil War and practised law there, becoming a member of the judiciary. Some of his experiences are related in his novel, A Fool's Errand, which made a great sensation when first issued. He was subsequently editor of Our Continent, in Philadelphia, and in 1897 became consul at Bordeaux. His other works include, Bricks Without Straw; Figs and Thistles; Hot Plowshares; An Appeal to Cæsar; Black Ice; With Gauge and Swallow; Pactolus Prime; Mervale Eastman; Button's Inn; An Outing with the Queen of Hearts; Letters to a King; John Eax; A Royal Gentleman; The Mortgage on the Hip-Roof House. *Cas. Fo. Lip. Meth. Rob.*

Towle [tōle], **George Makepeace.** *D. C.*, 1841–1893. A Boston journalist and littérateur. History of Henry V.; Glimpses of History; Modern France; Certain Men of Mark; American Society; Beaconsfield; England and Russia in Asia; England in Egypt; Young People's History of England; Young People's History of Ireland; The Nation in a Nutshell; Heroes of History; The Literature of the English Language; Heroes and Martyrs of Invention. *Ap. Har. Hou. Le. Rob.*

Towler, John. *E.*, 1811——. An English educator who settled in America in 1850, was a professor in Hobart College, Geneva, New York, 1853–82, and subsequently lived at Orange, New Jersey. Beside publishing a number of works on photography, he wrote Der Kleine Engländer, and was co-editor of Hilpert's German and English Dictionary.

Towles, Catherine. *See McCoy, Mrs.*

Town, Ithiel. *Ct.*, 1784–1844. An architect of New York city who built the State capitols of North Carolina and Indiana. School-House Architecture; Atlantic Steamships; Improvement in Construction of Bridges.

Town, Salem. *Ms.*, 1779–1864. A once noted educator of New York and Indiana. System of Speculative Masonry; Analysis of English Derivatives; and, with N. Holbrook, a popular series of readers.

Towne, Edward Cornelius. *Ms.*, 1834——. A Congregational clergyman of New Haven. The Question of Hell; Electricity and Life.

Townsend, Calvin. 18———. Analysis of the United States Constitution; Compendium of Commercial Law; Analysis of Letter-Writing; Shorter Course in Civil Government. *Am.*

Townsend, Charles. 18———. Essays on Mind, Matter, Force, etc.; Primordial Principles of the Universe.

Townsend, Edward Davis. *Ms.*, 1817–1893. An adjutant-general of the United States army, at the time of his death on the retired list as brigadier-general. He was chief executive officer of the war department in Washington during the Civil War. Catechism of the Bible; Anecdotes of the Civil War in the United States. *Ap.*

Townsend, Edward Waterman. *O.*, 1855——. A journalist of New York city whose studies of Bowery life and dialect have been widely popular. Chimmie Fadden, Major Max, and Other Stories; Chimmie Fadden Explains, Major Max Expounds; A Daughter of the Tenements, a novel; Near a Whole City Full, a collection of short dramatic stories. In collaboration he has written several plays, including Chimmie Fadden; A Daughter of the Tenements; The Marquis of Michigan. *Ll.*

Townsend, Eliza. *Ms.*, 1789–1854. A verse-writer of Boston whose collected Poems and Miscellanies appeared in 1856. *See Griswold's Female Poets of America.*

Townsend, George Alfred. "Gath." *Del.*, 1841——. A journalist of New York city and Chicago famous as a war correspondent, among whose writings are, Washington Outside and Inside; Tales of the Chesapeake; Bohemian Days; Campaigns of a Non-Combatant; The Entailed Hat, a novel; Poems; Life of Garibaldi; The Real Life of Abraham Lincoln; Katy of Catoctin, a National Romance; Mrs. Reynolds and Hamilton. *See Hart's American Literature. Ap. Har.*

Townsend, Howard. *N. Y.*, 1823–1867. A physician of Albany. The Sunbeam and the Spectroscope; Food and its Digestion; Sinai Bible.

Townsend, John Kirk. *Pa.*, 1809–1851. A naturalist of Washington. A Journey to the Columbia River (1839), republished in London as Sporting Adventures in the Rocky Mountains.

Townsend, Luther Tracy. *Me.*, 1838——. A Methodist clergyman and educator of prominence, professor in Boston University, 1873–93, a pastor in Baltimore from 1893. God-Man; Credo; The Fate of Republics; Outlines of Christian Theology; Sword and Garment; The Arena and the Throne; The Intermediate World; Search and Manifestations; The Mosaic Record and Modern Science; Bible Miracles and Modern Thought; Outlines of Theology; The Supernatural Factor in Religious Revivals; Real and Pretended Christianity; The Bible and Other Ancient Literature in the Nineteenth Century; The Chinese Problem; The Intermediate World; The Art of Speech. *Ap. Le. Meth.*

Townsend, Mrs. Mary Ashley [Van Voorhees]. "Xariffa." *N.Y.*, 1836——. A popular verse-writer of New Orleans. Xariffa's Poems; Down the Bayou, and Other Poems; Distaff and Spindle; The Captain's Story, a Poem; The Brother Clerks. *Lip.*

Townsend, Virginia Frances. *Ct.*, 1836——. Kinswoman to L. T. Townsend, *supra.* A novelist. A Woman's Word; One Woman's Two Lovers; Lenox Dare; Protestant Queen of Navarre; Only Girls; Sirs, Only Seventeen; A Boston Girl's Ambition; Six in All; But a Philistine; That Queer Girl, are a few of her works. *Le. Lip. Meth.*

Toy, Crawford Howell. *Va.*, 1836——. A Unitarian clergyman, professor of Hebrew in Harvard University Divinity School. Quotations in the New Testament; History of the Religion of Israel; Judaism and Christianity, the Progress of Thought from the Old Testament to the New. *Lit. Scr.*

Tracy, Charles Chapin. *Pa.*, 1838——. A Presbyterian foreign missionary. Letters to Members of Oriental Families; Myra, or a Child's Story of Missionary Life.

Tracy, Ira. *Vt.*, 1806–1875. Brother of J. Tracy, *infra.* A Congregational missionary in the East Indies, author of Duty to the Heathen.

Tracy, Joseph. *Vt.*, 1794–1874. A Congregational clergyman, secretary of the Massachusetts Colonization Society. Three Last Things; The Great Awakening, a History of the Revival of Religion in the Time of Edwards and Whitefield.

Tracy, Roger Sherman. *Vt.*, 1841——. A physician of New York city. Handbook of Sanitary Information for Householders; Essentials of Anatomy; Physiology and Hygiene; The New Liber Primus. *Ap.*

Trafton, Adeline. Daughter of M. Trafton, *infra.* *See Knox, Mrs.*

Trafton, Mark. *Me.*, 1810——. A Methodist clergyman of prominence in his day, member of Congress, 1855–57. Rambles in Europe; Safe Investment; Baptism: its Subjects and Mode; Scenes in My Life. *Meth.*

Train, Elizabeth Phipps. *Ms.*, 1857——. A novelist of Duxbury, Massachusetts. Dr. Lamar; Autobiography of a Professional Beauty; A Social Highwayman; A Marital Liability. Her translations from the French include, The Apostate; The Shadow of Dr. Laroque; Recollections of the Court of the Tuileries. *Cr. Lip.*

Train, George Francis. *Ms.*, 1830——. A lecturer of New York city widely known for his eccentricities. An American Merchant in Europe; Young America Abroad; Young America in Wall Street; Spread Eagleism; Union Speeches; Irish Independency, include his chief writings.

Trall, Russell Thacher. *Ct.*, 1812–1877. A homœopathic physician of New York city, and subsequently of Florence, New Jersey. The Bath: the History and Uses of, in Health and Disease; Digestion and Dyspepsia; The Mother's Hygienic Handbook; The Human Voice; Popular Physiology; The True Temperance Platform; Encyclopedia of Hydropathy; Uterine Diseases, include most of his writing.

Trautwine, John Cresson. *Pa.*, 1810–1883. A civil engineer of eminence. Method of Calculating Cubic Contents of Excavations and Embankments; Field Practice of Laying out Railroad Curves; Civil Engineer's Pocket-Book. *Wil.*

Treadwell, Daniel. *Ms.*, 1791–1872. The inventor of the power-press, and Rumford professor at Harvard University, 1834–45. The Relations of Science to the Useful Arts; The Practicability of Constructing Cannon of Great Calibre; Construction of Hooped Cannon.

Treadwell, Seymour Boughton. *C.*, 1795–1867. A politician of Jackson, Michigan. American Liberties and American Slavery Politically Illustrated (1838).

Treat, John Harvey. *N. H.*, 1839——. A business man and writer of Lawrence, Massachusetts. Notes on the Rubric of the Communion Office; Truro Baptisms, 1711–1800; The Catholic Faith; Genealogy of the Treat Family.

Treat, Mrs. Mary Lua Adelia [Davis] [Allen]. 18——. A naturalist of Vineland, New Jersey. Chapters on Ants; Injurious Insects of the Farm and Garden; Home Studies in Nature; My Garden Pets. *Am. Ju. Lo.*

Tremain, Henry Edwin. *N. Y.*, 1840——. A lawyer of New York city who was an officer in the Federal army during the Civil War. Sailor's Creek to Appomattox Court House, or the Last Hours of Sheridan's Cavalry.

Trent, William Peterfield. *Va.*, 1862——. A professor of English and history at the University of the South, Sewanee, Tennessee, from 1888. English Culture in Virginia; Life of William Gilmore Simms, *supra;* Southern Statesmen of the Old Régime. *See The Bookman, May, 1897. Hou. J. H. U.*

Trescot, William Henry. *S. C.*, 1822——. A lawyer and diplomatist of Washington. Diplomacy of the Revolution; Diplomatic History of the Administrations of Washington and Adams.

Trott, Nicholas. *E.*, 1663–1740. A Charleston jurist, very eminent in the Carolinas in his day. Laws of South Carolina (1734); Clavis Linguæ Sanctæ; Laws relating to the Church and Clergy in America.

Troubat, Francis Joseph. *Pa.*, 1802–1868. A lawyer of Philadelphia. Practice in Civil Actions in Pennsylvania Supreme Court (with W. Haley); The Law of Limited Partnership in the United States; Treatise on the Law of Partnerships.

Troubetzkoy, Mrs. Amélie [Rives] [Chanler]. *Va.*, 1863——. A novelist whose second husband is a Russian prince. Though her work excited much unfavourable criticism, yet it enjoyed a sudden brief popularity. The Quick or the Dead; A Brother to Dragons; Virginia of Virginia; Barbara Dering; The Witness of the Sun; Athelwold, a tragedy; Herod and Marianne, a drama. *Har. Lip.*

Trowbridge, Catherine Maria. *Ct.*, 1818——. A writer of South Manchester, Connecticut, who has made many contributions to juvenile literature, a few among them being, Christian Heroism; Victory at Last; Will and Will Not; Snares and Safeguards; Changing Paths.

Trowbridge, John. *Ms.*, 1843——. A physicist of note, professor at Harvard University from 1880, Rumford professor of the application of science to the useful arts there from 1888. What is Electricity?; The New Physics; Three Boys on an Electrical Boat; The Electrical Boy. *Ap. Hou. Rob.*

Trowbridge, John Townsend. *N. Y.*, 1827——. A popular writer of Arlington, Massachusetts, whose work in verse and prose reaches a high grade of excellence. His novel, Neighbor Jackwood, when first issued in 1857, was a strong moral agent in stimulating anti-slavery sentiment. His other fictions include, Lucy Arlyn; Coupon Bonds, and Other Stories; Farnell's Folly; Neighbors' Wives; Martin Merrivale; Cudjo's Cave; Three Scouts. Among his very many juvenile tales are, The Drummer Boy; The Prize Cup; The Lottery Ticket; The Tide-Mill Stories; The Toby Trafford Series; The Little Master; Jack Hazard Series. His published volumes of verse include, The Vagabonds (his best known poem), and Other Poems; The Emigrant's Story, and Other Poems; A Home Idyl, and Other Poems; The Lost Earl; The Book of Gold, and Other Poems. At Sea and Midsummer are two of his finest poems. *Cent. Co. Har. Hou. Le. Lo.*

Trowbridge, William Petit. *Mch.*, 1828–1892. An engineer and scientist in charge of the engineering department of the School of Mines, Columbia College, 1877–92. Steam Generator; Heat as a Source of Power; Turbine Wheels; Stationary Steam Engines. *Wil.*

True, Charles Kittridge. *Me.*, 1809–1878. A Methodist clergyman and educator, professor at Wesleyan University, 1849–60. Elements of Logic;

Shawmut, or the Settlement of Boston; John Winthrop and the Great Colony; Lives of Raleigh, John Knox, John Harvard, Captain John Smith; The Thirty Years' War; Heroes of Holland. *Meth.*

True, John Preston. *Me.*, 1859——. A Boston writer. Their Club and Ours, a popular juvenile tale; Shoulder Arms, a tale of life in a military school. *Lo. Meth.*

Truman, Benjamin Cummings. *R. I.*, 1835——. A California writer, military governor of Tennessee during the Civil War. The South During the War; Semi-Tropical California; Occidental Sketches; Winter Resorts of California; From the Crescent City to the Golden Gate; Homes and Happiness in the Golden Gate; The Field of Honor, a history of duelling. *Fo.*

Trumbull, Benjamin. *Ct.*, 1735–1820. A Congregational clergyman, pastor at North Haven, Connecticut, for sixty years. Plea in Vindication of the Connecticut Title to the Contested (Western) Lands; Divine Origin of the Holy Scriptures; General History of the United States (1810); A Complete History of Connecticut, 1630–1764.

Trumbull, Gurdon. *Ct.*, 1841——. Brother of J. H. Trumbull, *infra.* An artist and ornithologist who has published, American Game Birds, or Names and Portraits of Birds which Interest Gunners, with Descriptions. *Har.*

Trumbull, Henry Clay. *Ct.*, 1830——. Brother of J. H. Trumbull, *infra.* A Congregational clergyman of Philadelphia, editor of The Sunday-School Times. A Model Superintendent; The Threshold Covenant; The Knightly Soldier; Kadesh-Barnea; Teaching and Teachers; The Blood Covenant, a Primitive Rite; The Sunday-School, its Origin, Methods, and Auxiliaries; Children in the Temple; Some Army Sermons; The Worth of an Historic Consciousness; Principles and Practice; Friendship the Master Passion; Studies in Oriental Social Life. *Wat.*

Trumbull, James Hammond. *Ct.*, 1821–1897. A Hartford philologist, an acknowledged authority upon Indian languages. The Composition of Indian Geographical Names; Best Method of Studying the Indian Languages; Indian Names of Places; On the Algonkin Verb; The True Blue-Laws of Connecticut. He had edited The Colonial Records of Connecticut; Roger Williams's Key to the Languages of North America, and other works.

Trumbull, John. *Ct.*, 1750–1831. A noted jurist of Hartford, famous in his day as a satirical poet. With Barlow and others he published The Anarchiad, a series of satirical essays, and he was the author of The Progress of Dulness; but MacFingal, a Hudibrastic poem, the first canto of which appeared in 1775, is his best title to remembrance. It bristles with sharp points of satire, and quite deserved the extensive popularity it for a time enjoyed. *See Stedman's Poets of America; Tyler's Literary History of the American Revolution.*

Tryon, George Washington. *Pa.*, 1838–1888. A conchologist of Philadelphia. Land and Fresh-Water Shells of North America; Marine Conchology; Structural and Systematic Conchology; Manual of Conchology.

Tucker, George. *Ba.*, 1775–1861. Kinsman of Saint George Tucker, *infra.* A Virginia lawyer and educator, professor of moral philosophy and political economy in the University of Virginia, 1825–45. Among his writings are included, Life of Jefferson; Political History of the United States; Essays Moral and Philosophical; Theory of Money and Banks; Essays on Subjects of Taste; Principles of Rent, Wages, and Profits; The Valley of the Shenandoah, a novel; A Voyage to the Moon, a satirical romance.

Tucker, George Fox. *Ms.*, 1852——. A lawyer of New Bedford, Massachusetts. Manual of Wills; Manual of Business Corporations; Manual of the Constitution of Massachusetts, the Interpretation of Statutes, Special Writs, and Motions for New Trials; The Monroe Doctrine; Notes on the United States Revised Statutes (with J. M. Gould); A Quaker Home, a novel; Uncle Calup's Christmas Dinner; Your Will: how to Make It. *Hou. Lit.*

Tucker, Henry Holcombe. *Ga.*, 1819–1890. A Baptist clergyman and educator of Georgia, editor of The Christian Index, at Atlanta, from 1878. Religious Liberty; The Gospel in Enoch; The Old Theology Restated in Sermons. The Position of Baptism in the Christian System is a noted sermon by him.

Tucker, Henry Saint George. *Va.*, 1780–1848. Son of Saint George Tucker, *infra.* An eminent Virginia lawyer. Lectures on Natural Law and Government; Lectures on Constitutional Law; Commentaries on the Law of Virginia.

Tucker, Henry Saint George. *Va.*, 1828–1863. Grandson of Saint George Tucker, *infra.* A lieutenant-colonel in the Confederate army. Hansford, a Tale of Bacon's Rebellion; The Southern Crop.

Tucker, Joshua Thomas. *Ms.*, 1812–1897. A Congregational clergyman of Boston. The Sinless One, a life of Christ; Christ's Infant Kingdom.

Tucker, Mrs. Margaretta [Ames]. "Margaret May." *N. H.*, 1836——. A verse-writer of Boston. For My Friend, a collection of verses; Driftwood, and Other Poems, are among her writings, some of which have been set to music.

Tucker, Mrs. Mary Eliza. *See Lambert, Mrs.*

Tucker, Nathaniel Beverly. *Va.*, 1784–1851. Son of Saint George Tucker, *infra.* A Virginia jurist, professor of law at William and Mary College, 1834–51. The Partisan Leader (1836) is his most noted book. It is a political novel, having for its theme the revolt of the Southern States, and in 1861 it was republished as A Key to the Southern Conspiracy. Other works of his are, George Balcombe, a novel; Principles of Pleading.

Tucker, Pomeroy. *N.Y.*, 1802–1870. A Canandaigua journalist who published a work on The Origin of Mormonism.

Tucker, Saint George. *Ba.*, 1752–1828. The stepfather of John Randolph the statesman. A Virginia jurist who published Letters on the Alien and Sedition Laws; The Probationary Odes of Jonathan Pindar, a collection of political satires; an annotated Blackstone; but is known to general literature only by the lyric beginning, "Days of my Youth, ye have Glided Away." *See Griswold's Poets and Poetry of America.*

Tucker, William Jewett. *Ct.*, 1839——. A Congregational clergyman and educator. He was professor in Andover Theological Seminary, 1879–93, and has been president of Dartmouth College from 1893. The New Movement in Humanity. *Hou.*

Tuckerman, Arthur Lyman. *N.Y.*, 1861–1892. Son of C. K. Tuckerman, *infra.* An architect of New York city, superintendent of the Metropolitan Museum Art Schools in 1888. A Short History of Architecture. *Scr.*

Tuckerman, Bayard. *N. Y.*, 1855——. A writer of New York city. History of English Prose Fiction; Life of Lafayette; Life of William Jay, *supra;* Life of Peter Stuyvesant. *Do. Put.*

Tuckerman, Charles Keating. *Ms.*, 1821–1896. Brother of H. T. Tuckerman, *infra.* A diplomat who was minister to Greece, 1868–72, and lived in Europe subsequently. The Greeks of To-Day (1872); Poems; Personal Recollections of Notable People. *Do.*

Tuckerman, Edward. *Ms.*, 1817–1886. Nephew of J. Tuckerman, *infra.* A professor of botany at Amherst College, 1858–86. Genera Lichenum; Synopsis of the North American Lichens; Catalogue of Plants Growing Wild within Thirty Miles of Amherst. *See Memoir of, by Farlow.*

Tuckerman, Frederick Goddard. *Ms.*, 1821–1877. Brother of E. Tuckerman, *supra.* A lawyer and littérateur of Boston whose only published book was a volume of poems.

Tuckerman, Henry Theodore. *Ms.*, 1813–1871. Nephew of J. Tuckerman, *infra.* A writer once ranked among the first of American essayists, but whose criticisms, though delicate and discriminating, lack the force and originality of many later writers in the same field. Much of his life was spent abroad, largely in Italy, his intimate acquaintance with Italian affairs appearing in his earliest works, The Italian Sketch-Book; Isabel, or Sicily, a Pilgrimage (1839), republished as Sicily and Pilgrimage (1852). His subsequent writings include, Thoughts on the Poets; The Book of the Artists; Essays Biographical and Critical; Artist Life; Rambles and Reveries; Characteristics of Literature; The Criterion; Maga Papers about Paris; Leaves from the Diary of a Dreamer; Life of J. P. Kennedy, *supra;* America and Her Commentators; The Optimist, a series of essays; A Sheaf of Verse; Poems; Mental Portraits; The Collector, a volume of essays. *See Allibone's Dictionary; Foley's American Writers.*

Tuckerman, Joseph. *Ms.*, 1778–1840. A Unitarian clergyman, minister at Chelsea, Massachusetts, 1801–28, long eminent as a philanthropist. Gleams of Truth; Principles and Results of the Ministry at Large in Boston. Elevation of the Poor (1874), is a collection of his most important writings. *See Memoir by Mary Carpenter; Allibone's Dictionary. Rob.*

Tudor, William. *Ms.*, 1779–1830. A Boston merchant who founded the ice trade with the tropics. Gebel Teir; Life of James Otis, *supra;* Letters on the Eastern States; Miscellanies.

Tully, William. *Ct.*, 1785–1859. A noted New England botanist and physician, medical professor at Yale University, 1829–42. Essays upon Fever (with T. Miner); Materia Medica, or Pharmacology; Therapeutics.

Tunis, John. *N. Y.*, 1858–1896. An Episcopal clergyman of Millbrook, New Jersey, but prior to 1892 in the Unitarian ministry. The Faith By Which We Stand.

Tuomy, Michael. *I.*, 1808–1857. A professor of geology in the University of Alabama, 1847–57, State geologist of South Carolina from 1844, and of Alabama from 1848. Geological and Agricultural Survey of South Carolina; Report on the Geology of South Carolina; Fossils of South Carolina (with F. Holmes); First and Second Biennial Reports on the Geology of Alabama.

Tupper, Henry Allen. *S. C.*, 1828——. A Baptist clergyman of Richmond, Virginia. Foreign Missions of the Southern Baptist Convention; Truth in Romance. *Bap.*

Turchin, John Basil (Ivan Vasilevitch Turchinoff). *R.*, 1822——. A Russian soldier who came to America in 1856, served in the Federal army during the Civil War, and in 1873 established the Polish colony of Radone in Illinois. The Campaign and Battle of Chickamauga.

Turnbull, Laurence. *S.*, 1821——. An eminent physician of Baltimore. Hints and Observations on Military Hygiene; Imperfect Hearing; Clinical Manual of Diseases of the Ear; Advantages and Disadvantages of Artificial Anæsthesia; The Electro-Magnetic Telegraph. *Lip.*

Turnbull, Robert. *S.*, 1809–1877. A Baptist clergyman of Hartford, 1845–1869. The Theatre; Olympia Morata; The Genius of Scotland; The Genius of Italy; Pulpit Orators of France and Switzerland; The Student Preacher; Theophany; The World We Live In; Life Pictures; Christ in History.

Turnbull, Robert James. *Fl.*, 1775–1833. A lawyer and political writer of Charleston. A Visit to the Philadelphia Penitentiary, much noticed at the time of its appearance in 1797; The Crisis, a work on nullification; The Principle of Dernier Ressort.

Turnbull, William Paterson. *S.*, 1830–1871. A Philadelphia ornithologist. Birds of East Lothian; Birds of East Pennsylvania and New Jersey.

Turner, Mrs. Eliza [Sproat]. *Pa.*, 1826——. A verse-writer of Pennsylvania. Out-of-Door Rhymes.

Turner, Henry McNeal. *S. C.*, 1833——. A bishop of the African Methodist Church, author of a work on Methodist Polity.

Turner, Samuel Epes. *Md.*, 1846——. A Sketch of the Germanic Constitution from Early Times to the Dissolution of the Empire. *Put.*

Turner, Samuel Hulbeart. *Pa.*, 1790–1861. An Episcopal clergyman, professor in the General Theological Seminary in New York city, 1818–61, best known by his Commentaries on Hebrews, Romans, Ephesians, and Galatians. Other works by him are, Companion to the Book of Genesis; Thoughts on Scripture Prophecy; Comparing Spiritual Things with Spiritual;

Biographical Notices of Jewish Rabbis. *See Autobiography; Allibone's Dictionary.*

Turner, Thomas Sloss. *Ky.*, 1860——. A Texas journalist and verse-writer. Life's Brevity, and Other Poems; Heart Melodies; A Dream of Bachelors.

Tuthill [tŭt'il], **Cornelia.** Daughter of Mrs. L. Tuthill, *infra. See Pierson, Mrs.*

Tuthill, Mrs. Louisa Caroline [Huggins]. *Ct.*, 1798–1879. A once popular writer of moral tales for young people, whose home was at Princeton, New Jersey, from 1849. Among her many publications are, I Will be a Gentleman; I Will be a Lady; Tales for the Young; True Manliness; I Will be a Sailor; I Will be a Soldier; Onward, Right Onward; Romantic Belinda; Ancient Architecture. *See Hart's Female Prose-Writers of America.*

Tuttle, Charles Richard. *N.S.* 1850——. General History of Michigan; Border Wars of Two Centuries; History of Indiana; History of Canada; History of Wisconsin (with D. Durrie); The Boss Devil of America (verse).

Tuttle, Mrs. Emma [Rood]. *O.*, 1839——. Wife of Hudson Tuttle, *infra.* A lecturer and verse-writer of Berlin Heights, Ohio. Blossoms of Our Spring; Gazelle; From Soul to Soul, Poems; Stories for Our Children; The Lyceum Guide.

Tuttle, Herbert. *Vt.*, 1846–1894. A professor at Cornell University, 1883–1894, occupying the chair of modern European history from 1891. The History of Prussia; German Political Leaders. *See Biographical Sketch, by H. B. Adams, supra, in vol. iv. of The History of Prussia. Hou.*

Tuttle, Hudson. *O.*, 1836——. A spiritual medium of Berlin Heights, Ohio. Life in the Spheres; Arcana of Nature; Career of the God Idea; Career of the Christ Idea; Career of Religious Ideas; Origin and Development of Man; Clair, a Tale; Camile, or Love and Labor; Heloise; Love or Religion. *Ban.*

Tuttle, Joseph Farrand. *N. J.*, 1818——. A Presbyterian clergyman. Life of William Tuttle; The Way Lost and Found; Annals of Morris County, New Jersey.

Twain, Mark. *See Clemens.*

Twichell, Joseph Hopkins. *Ct.*, 183——. A Congregational clergyman of Hartford from 1865. Life of John Winthrop, *infra;* Some Old Puritan Love Letters (edited). *Do.*

Tyler, Bennet. *Ct.*, 1783–1858. A Congregational clergyman, president of Dartmouth College, 1822–28, and subsequently minister at Portland, Maine. History of New Haven Theology; The Sufferings of Christ; New England Revivals; Lectures on Christian Nurture, include his principal works.

Tyler, John Mason. 18——. Son of W. S. Tyler, *infra.* A professor of biology at Amherst College. The Whence and the Whither of Man. *Scr.*

Tyler, Joseph. 18—1895. Son of B. Tyler, *supra.* A Congregational missionary in South Africa for forty years, for the last ten years of his life a resident of St. Johnsbury, Vermont. Forty Years Among the Zulus. *C. P. S.*

Tyler, Lyon Gardiner. *Va.*, 1853——. A son of President John Tyler and president of William and Mary College from 1888. The Letters and Times of the Tylers; Parties and Patronage in the United States.

Tyler, Moses Coit. *Ct.*, 1835——. A professor of American history at Cornell University from 1881. From 1860 to 1881 he was a member of the Congregational ministry, but in the latter year took orders in the Episcopal Church. He is best known by an admirable History of American Literature During the Colonial Period, 1606–1765, which is as readable as it is scholarly, the style being both vigourous and original. Other works of his are, The Brawnville Papers; Life of Patrick Henry; Three Men of Letters (Berkeley, Dwight, Joel Barlow); The Literary History of the American Revolution, 1763–1783; Manual of English Literature. *Hou. Put. Sh.*

Tyler, Ransom Hebbard. *Ms.*, 1813–1881. A lawyer and bank president of Fulton, New York. The Bible and Social Reform; American Ecclesiastical Law; Commentaries on the Law of Infancy and Covertures; Ejectment and Adverse Enjoyment; Usury; Pawns and Loans; Fixtures; Boundaries, Fences, and Window Lights.

Tyler, Robert. *Va.*, 1818–1877. The eldest son of President John Tyler. A lawyer of Philadelphia, and after the Civil War a journalist in Montgomery, Alabama. Ahasuerus, a Poem; Death, a Poem; Is Virginia a Repudiating State?

Tyler, Royall. *Ms.*, 1757–1826. A Vermont jurist, chief justice of the supreme court of his State from 1800. Reports of Vermont Supreme Court Cases; The Contrast, a brilliant comedy, the first American play acted by regular comedians, and the earliest in which "Yankee dialect" is employed; May Day, a comedy; The Georgia Speculator, or Land in the Moon; The Algerine Captive; Moral Tales for American Youths; The Yankey in London.

Tyler, Samuel. *Md.*, 1809–1878. A jurist of Frederick, Maryland. The Progress of Philosophy; Discourse on the Baconian Philosophy; Burns as a Poet and as a Man; Memoir of Chief Justice Taney; Commentary on the Law of Partnership.

Tyler, William Seymour. *Pa.*, 1810–1897. A Congregational clergyman and educator, professor at Amherst College from 1836; latterly professor emeritus of the Greek language and literature. Prayer for Colleges; Theology of the Greek Poets; editions of Tacitus and the Iliad of Homer; History of Amherst College, 1821 to 1891. *Har.*

Tyng, Dudley Atkins. *Md.*, 1825–1858. Son of S. H. Tyng, *infra*, 1st. An Episcopal clergyman of Philadelphia. Vital Truth and Deadly Error; Children of the Kingdom; Our Country's Troubles.

Tyng, Stephen Higginson. *Ms.*, 1800–1885. An Episcopal clergyman of New York city, rector of St. George's Church, 1844–85, and long prominent among Low Churchmen. Among his works are, The Christian Pastor; Family Commentary on the Gospels; Lectures on the Law and the Gospel; The Israel of God; Christ is All; The Rich Kinsman, the history of Ruth; The Prayer-Book Illustrated by Scripture; The Captive Orphan; Esther the Queen of Persia; Forty Years' Experience in Sunday Schools. *See Life of, by C. R. Tyng. Har.*

Tyng, Stephen Higginson. *N. Y.*, 1839——. Son of S. H. Tyng, *supra*. An Episcopal clergyman of New York city, for a number of years subsequent to 1881 the manager of an insurance company in Paris. The Square of Life; He Will Come; Our Church Work.

Tyson, James. 1841——. A Philadelphia physician, medical professor in the University of Pennsylvania from 1870. Manual of Physical Diagnosis; The Cell Doctrine; Introduction to Practical Histology; Practical Examination of the Urine; Treatise on Bright's Disease. *Lip.*

Tyson, Job Roberts. *Pa.*, 1804–1858. A lawyer of Philadelphia. Essay on the Penal Laws of Pennsylvania; The Lottery System of the United States; Social and Intellectual State of Pennsylvania prior to 1743; Resources and Commerce of Philadelphia.

U

Underwood, Benjamin Franklin. 1839——. Formerly the editor of The Index in Boston. Influence of Christianity upon Civilization; Essays and Lectures.

Underwood, Francis Henry. *Ms.*, 1825–1894. A Boston littérateur, the organizer of The Atlantic Monthly. He was American consul at Glasgow, 1885–89, and subsequently at Leith, where he died. Handbooks of English Literature: British Authors, and American Authors; Builders of American Literature; biographies of Lowell, Longfellow, and Whittier; The Poet and the Man, Recollections of James Russell Lowell; Cloud Pictures; and the novels, Lord of Himself; Man Proposes; Dr. Gray's Quest; Quabbin. *Hou. Le.*

Underwood, Lucien Marcus. *N. Y.*, 1853——. Cousin of F. H. Underwood, *supra*. A professor of botany at Syracuse University from 1883. Systematic Plant Record; Our Native Ferns and How to Study Them; Our Native Ferns and Their Allies; North American Hepaticæ. *Ho. Wh.*

Upham, Charles Wentworth. *N. B.*, 1802–1875. A Unitarian clergyman, pastor of the First Church in Salem, Massachusetts, 1824–44, subsequently prominent as a politician in his city and State. Lectures on the Logos; Prophecy as an Evidence of Christianity; Salem Witchcraft and Cotton Mather; Life of Timothy Pickering; Life of Sir Henry Vane; Lectures on Witchcraft; Principles of Congregationalism.

Upham, Francis William. *N. H.*, 1817–1895. Brother of T. C. Upham, *infra.* An educator of New York city, whose writings were chiefly a defence of the Scriptures as opposed to "the higher criticism." The Debate Between the Church and Science; The Wise Men: Who They Were; The Star of Our Lord; Thoughts on the Gospels; St. Matthew's Witness; The First Words from God.

Upham, Mrs. Grace Le Baron [Locke]. "Grace Le Baron." *Ms.*, 1845——. A Boston writer of popular juvenile tales. The Rosebud Club; Little Miss Faith; Little Daughter. *Le.*

Upham, Thomas Cogswell. *N. H.*, 1799–1872. A professor of philosophy at Bowdoin College, 1824–72. Elements of Moral Philosophy; Treatise on the Will; Life of Madame Guyon; Principles of the Hidden Life; Disordered Mental Action; Elements of Intellectual Philosophy; Ratio Disciplinæ; Christ in the Soul; The Life of Faith; The Manual of Peace; Divine Union; American Cottage Life, a book of verse; Life of Madame Catherine Adorna; View of the Absolute Religion. *See Allibone's Dictionary; Bibliography of Maine. Hur.*

Upshur, Abel Parker. *Va.*, 1790–1844. A Virginia lawyer and Congressman, secretary of the navy, 1841–1843, and of State, 1843–44. Inquiry into the Nature and Character of Our Federal Government.

Upshur, Mary. Niece of A. P. Upshur, *supra. See Sturges, Mrs.*

Upton, Emory. 1839–1881. An officer with the rank of major-general in the Federal army during the Civil War. Infantry Tactics; The Armies of Asia and Europe; Tactics for Non-Military Bodies. *See Life of, by Michie. Ap.*

Upton, Francis Henry. *Ms.*, 1814–1876. An eminent lawyer of New York city. Treatise on the Law of Trade-Marks; The Law of Nations affecting Commerce During War.

Upton, George Putnam. *Ms.*, 1834——. A Chicago journalist. Letters of Peregrine Pickle; The Great Fire; Woman in Music; The Standard Operas; The Standard Oratorios; The Standard Cantatas; The Standard Symphonies; Lives of Haydn, Liszt, and Wagner, from the German of Nohl; Memories, from the German of Max Müller. *Mg.*

Upton, Jacob Kendrick. *N. H.*, 1837——. The assistant secretary of the treasury in 1880. Money in Politics; A Coin Catechism. *Lo.*

Urmy, Clarence [Thomas]. *Cal.*, 1858——. An organist and verse-writer of San José, California. A Rosary of Rhyme; A Vintage of Verse. He has been a contributor to magazines.

Usher, Edward Preston. *Ms.*, 1851——. A Boston lawyer living in Grafton, Massachusetts. Sales of Personal Property; Protestantism, a Study in the Direction of Religious Truth. *Le.*

Utter, Mrs. Rebecca [Palfrey]. *Ms.*, 1844——. Daughter of C. Palfrey, *supra*, and wife of a Unitarian clergyman. The King's Daughter, and Other Poems.

V

Vachell, Horace Annesley. *E.*, 1861——. A novelist now (1897) resident in California, but in 1883 an English lieutenant in the Rifle Brigade. The Romance of Judge Ketchum; The Model of Christian Gay; The Quicksands of Pactolus; An Impending Sword. *Ho. Lip.*

Vail, Alfred. *N. J.*, 1807–1859. A scientist who was one of the inventors of the telegraph. He published a work on The American Electro-Magnetic Telegraph.

Vail, Stephen Montford. *N. Y.*, 1818–1880. A Methodist clergyman, at one time tried by his church for advocating an educated ministry. Outlines of Hebrew Grammar; Education in the Methodist Church; The Bible Against Slavery. *Meth.*

Vail, Thomas Hubbard. *Va.*, 1812–1889. The first Protestant Episcopal bishop of Kansas, consecrated bishop in 1864. Hannah, a Sacred Drama; The Comprehensive Church.

Vale, Gilbert. *E.*, 1788–1866. A Brooklyn writer prominent as a freethinker. Fanaticism; Life of Thomas Paine, *supra.*

Valentine, David Thomas. *N. Y.*, 1801–1869. The clerk of the New York Common Council, 1831–69, and author of a Manual of the Corporation of New York City; History of New York City.

Valentine, Milton. *Md.*, 1825——. A Lutheran clergyman, professor of systematic theology at Gettysburg Theological Seminary from 1884. Natural Theology, or Rational Theism; The Relations of the Family to the Church; The Dynamics of Success; Knowledge by Service; Absolute Christianity; Truth's Testimony to its Servants: Is the Lord's Day only a Human Institution? *Sil.*

Valentini, Philipp Johann Joseph. *P.*, 1828——. A New York archæologist among whose writings upon Mexican archæology are, The Landa Alphabet: a Spanish fabrication; Mexican Copper Tools; The Olmecas and theTultecas.

Vallentine, Benjamin Bennaton. *E.*, 1843——. A journalist of New York city, dramatic critic of The Herald. The Fitznoodle Papers; Fitznoodle in America; The Lost Train.

Van-Anderson, Mrs. Helen [Van Metre]. *Ia.*, 1859——. A minister and lecturer of Boston. The Right Knock; It is Possible; The Story of Teddy; Journal of a Live Woman. *Le.*

Van Brunt, Henry. *Ms.*, 1832——. An architect of note, the designer of Memorial Hall at Cambridge. Greek Lines, and Other Architectural Essays. *Hou.*

Van Buren, John Desh. *N.Y.*, 1838——. A civil engineer of New York city. Investigation of Formulas for the Strength of Iron Parts of Steam Machinery; Quay and Other Retaining Walls.

Van Buren, Martin. *N. Y.*, 1782–1862. The eighth President of the United States. An Inquiry into the Origin and Causes of Political Parties in the United States is his only writing of importance, except state papers. *See Lives by Emmons, 1835, Grund (in German), 1835, Holland, 1836, Crockett, 1836, Mackenzie, 1846, Butler, 1862, Shepard, 1888, Bancroft, 1889; Allibone's Dictionary.*

Van Buren, William Holme. *Pa.*, 1819–1883. An eminent surgeon of New York city. Contributions to Practical Surgery; Diseases of the Rectum; Diseases of the Genito-Urinary Organs (with Keyes); The Principles of Surgery. *Ap.*

Vandegrift, Margaret. *See Janvier, Margaret.*

Vandenhoff, George. *E.*, 1820——. An actor and elocutionist of note. Plain System of Elocution; Leaves from an Actor's Note Book; Dramatic Reminiscences; Clerical Assistant, or Elocutionary Guide; Common Sense; The Art of Reading Aloud.

Van Deusen, Mrs. Mary [Westbrook]. *N. Y.*, 1829——. A writer of Rondout, New York, whose principal works include, Rachel Du Mont; Gertrude Willoughby, a novel; Colonial Dames of America; Voices of My Heart, a book of verse.

Van Dyke, Henry Jackson. *Pa.*, 1822–1891. A Presbyterian clergyman of Brooklyn. The Lord's Prayer; The Church: Her Ministry and Sacraments.

Van Dyke, Henry Jackson. *Pa.*, 1852——. Son of H. J. Van Dyke, *supra.* A Presbyterian clergyman of New York city, pastor of the Brick Church from 1882. The Reality of Religion; The Story of the Psalms; The National Sin of Literary Piracy; The Poetry of Tennyson; Historic Presbyterianism; Straight Sermons to Young Men; The Christ Child in Art; Little Rivers; The Story of the Other Wise Man; God and Little Children; The Gospel for an Age of Doubt; The Builders, and Other Poems. *Har. Mac. Ran. Scr.*

Van Dyke, John Charles. *N. J.*, 1856——. An art critic, librarian of the Sage Library at New Brunswick, New Jersey. Books and How to Use Them; Principles of Art; How to Judge a Picture; Serious Art in America; Art for Art's Sake; History of Painting; Old Dutch and Flemish Masters. *Cent. Fo. Lgs. Scr. Meth.*

Van Dyke, Joseph Smith. *N. J.*, 1832——. A Presbyterian clergyman, minister at Cranbury, New Jersey, from 1869. Popery the Foe of the Church; Prohibition of the Liquor Traffic; Through the Prison to the Throne; From Gloom to Gladness; Giving or Entertainment,—Which? ; Theism or Evolution. *Fu.*

Van Dyke, Theodore Strong. *N. J.*, 1842——. Brother of J. C. Van Dyke, *supra*. A lawyer and sportsman of Southern California. Rifle, Rod, and Gun in California; Southern California; The Still Hunter; Game Birds at Home; Southern California the Italy of America. *Fo.*

Van Horne, Thomas B——. 18———. A clergyman, chaplain in the Federal army during the Civil War. History of the Army of the Cumberland; Life of Major-General Thomas. *Clke. Scr.*

Van Lennep, Henry John. *A. M.*, 1815–1889. A Congregational missionary in Asia Minor, 1839–69. Ten Days Among Greek Brigands; Bible Lands; Travels in Little Known Parts of Asia Minor; The Oriental Album. *Har. C. P. S.*

Vannah, Letitia Catharine. *Me.*, 1857——. A verse-writer of Gardiner, Maine, who has published a volume of Verses.

Van Ness, Thomas. *Md.*, 1859——. A Unitarian clergyman of Boston, pastor of the Second Church. The Coming Religion; The Ideal Commonwealth; My Visit to Count Tolstoi. *Rob.*

Van Ness, William Peter. *N. Y.*, 1778–1826. A jurist of New York city. Examination of Charges against Aaron Burr; Laws of New York (with Woodworth); Concise Narrative of Jackson's First Invasion of Florida.

Van Nest, Abraham Rynier. *N. Y.*, 1823–1892. A Dutch Reformed clergyman in charge of American chapels abroad, and pastor in Philadelphia, 1878–86. Signs of the Times; Life of G. Bethune, *supra*.

Van Norden, Charles. *Ct.*, 1843——. A Congregational clergyman at Suffield, Connecticut. The Outermost Rim and Beyond; The Psychic Factor. *Ap. Ran.*

Van Rensselaer [rĕn′sĕl-ar], **Cortland.** *N. Y.*, 1808–1860. A Presbyterian clergyman who was secretary of the Presbyterian Board of Education, 1846–60. Miscellaneous Sermons, Essays, and Addresses; Essays and Discourses.

Van Rensselaer, Mrs. Mariana [Griswold]. *N. Y.*, 1851——. An art critic of New York city. Art Out of Doors, a work on gardening; English Cathedrals; Six Portraits; Handbook of English Cathedrals; Henry Hobson Richardson; One Man who was Content, and Other Stories. *Cent. Hou. Scr.*

Van Rensselaer, Maunsell. *N. Y.*, 1819——. An Episcopal clergyman of New York city. Sister Louise: her Life Book; Annals of the Van Rensselaers in the United States.

Van Santvoord, Cornelius. *N. J.*, 1816–1892. A Dutch Reformed clergyman of New York State. Memoir of Eliphalet Nott, *supra;* Limitation of the Liabilities of Ship Owners Under United States Laws.

Van Santvoord, George. *N. J.*, 1819–1863. Brother of C. Van Santvoord, *supra*. A lawyer of Kinderhook, New York. Life of Algernon Sidney; Lives of the Chief Justices of the United States; The Indiana Justice; Principles of Pleading in Civil Actions; Precedents of Pleading; Practice in Equity Actions in New York Supreme Court.

Van Santvoord, Harold. *N. Y.*, 1854——. Son of G. Van Santvoord, *supra*. A New York littérateur. Half Holidays, a volume of essays.

Van Schaack, Henry Cruger. *N. Y.*, 1802–1887. Son of P. Van Schaack, *infra*. A lawyer of Manlius, New York. History of Manlius Village; An Old Kinderhook Mansion; Captain Thomas Morris; Life of Peter Van Schaack, *infra*.

Van Schaack, Peter. *N. Y.*, 1747–1832. A once famous jurist of Kinderhook, New York. Laws of the Colony of New York; Conductor Generalis. *See Life of, by his son, with Journal, Diary, and Letters.*

Vanuxem, Lardner. *Pa.*, 1792–1848. A scientist who was State geologist of New York, 1836–42. Geology of New York, Third District; Essay on the Ultimate Principles of Chemistry, Natural Philosophy, and Physiology (1827), an early declaration of the qualitative interconvertibility of heat, light, electricity, and magnetism.

Van Zile, Edward Sims. *N. Y.*, 1863——. A novelist and journalist of New York city on the staff of The World. Wanted, a Sensation; The Last of the Van Slacks; A Magnetic Man, and Other Stories; Don Miguel, and Other Stories; The Manhattaners; A Crown Prince. *Cas. Lov.*

Varley, John Philip. *See Mitchell, L. E.*

Varney, George Jones. *Me.*, 1836——. Young People's History of Maine; Gazetteer of Maine; A Brief History of Maine; The Story of Patriot's Day. *Le.*

Varnum, Joseph Bradly. *D. C.*, 1818–1874. A lawyer and littérateur of New York city. The Seat of Government of the United States; The Washington Sketch-Book.

Vasey, George. *E.*, 1822–1893. A physician and botanist who was botanist of the Department of Agriculture at Washington, 1872–93. Beauties and Utilities of a Library; The Philosophy of Laughing and Smiling; A Descriptive Catalogue of Native Forest Trees of the United States; Grasses of the United States; Agricultural Grasses of the United States; Grasses of the South; Grasses of the Arid Districts; Descriptive Catalogue of the Grasses of the United States; Individual Liberty.

Vassar, John Guy. *N. Y.*, 1811–1888. A philanthropist of Poughkeepsie, nephew of the founder of Vassar College. Twenty Years Around the World.

Vassar, Thomas Edwin. *N. Y.*, 1834——. Cousin of J. G. Vassar, *supra.* A Baptist clergyman, author of Uncle John Vassar, or The Fight of Faith, a very popular work.

Vaughan [vawn], **John.** *Pa.*, 1775–1807. A physician of Wilmington, Delaware, very eminent in his day. Chemical Syllabus; Observations on Animal Electricity.

Vaux [vauks], **Calvert.** *E.*, 1824–1895. An English architect and landscape gardener who settled in the United States in 1851. With F. L. Olmsted, *supra*, he designed Central Park in New York city, and he was associated with him in many similar works throughout the country. He published Villas and Cottages in the earlier part of his career. *See Annual Cyclopædia, 1895.*

Vaux, Richard. *Pa.*, 1816–1895. Son of R. Vaux, *infra.* A distinguished penologist of Philadelphia. His writings include every annual report of the Eastern Penitentiary for more than fifty years; Recorders' Decisions; and many volumes on the subject of penology.

Vaux, Roberts. *Pa.*, 1786–1836. A jurist and penologist of Philadelphia, prominent in all local philanthropic enterprises throughout his life. Memoirs of Benjamin Lay, Ralph Sandiford, and Anthony Benezet; Efforts to Improve the Discipline of the Prison at Philadelphia.

Vedder, Henry Clay. *N. Y.*, 1853——. A journalist for many years, and subsequently professor of church history at Crozer Theological Seminary, Upland, Pennsylvania. American Writers of To-day; A Short History of the Baptists. *Bap. Sil.*

Veeder, Mrs. Emily Elizabeth [Ferris]. *N. Y.*, 1841——. A novelist and verse-writer of St. Louis. Her Brother Donnard; Entranced; The Unexpected; In the Garden, and Other Poems. *Lip.*

Venable, Charles Scott. *Va.*, 1827——. A Confederate army officer, professor of mathematics in the University of Virginia from 1865, and author of a series of popular mathematical text-books.

Venable, Frank Preston. *Va.*, 1856——. Son of C. S. Venable, *supra.* A professor of chemistry at the University of North Carolina from 1880. A Short Course in Qualitative

Own Historian; Character and Career of Bishop Asbury; Memento of Edward Payson. *Meth.*

Janes, Lewis George. *R. I.*, 1844——. A lecturer of Brooklyn, for twelve years president of the Brooklyn Ethical Association. A Study of Primitive Culture; Samuell Gorton, a Forgotten Founder of Our Liberties. *Pr.*

Janeway, Jacob. *N. Y.*, 1774–1858. A Presbyterian clergyman who held several pastorates in Pennsylvania and New Jersey, and was engaged in general mission work. Exposition of the Acts, Romans, and Hebrews; Internal Evidences of the Holy Bible; Unlawful Marriage; Review of Dr. Schaff on Protestantism; The Abrahamic Covenant. *See Memoir by T. L. Janeway.*

Janney, Samuel Macpherson. *Va.*, 1801–1880. A preacher among the Hicksite Friends who in 1869 was appointed one of the government superintendents of Indian affairs. Lives of William Penn and George Fox; Conversations on Religious Subjects; The Last of the Lenape, and Other Poems; Historical Sketch of the Christian Church; Summary of Christian Doctrines Held by Friends; Peace Principles Exemplified in the Early History of Pennsylvania; History of the Religious Society of Friends from its Rise to 1828.

Janvier, Francis de Haes. *Pa.*, 1817–1885. Cousin of T. A. Janvier, *infra.* The Skeleton Monk, and Other Poems; The Sleeping Sentinel (verse); Patriotic Poems. *Lip.*

Janvier, Margaret Thomson. "Margaret Vandegrift." *La.*, 1845——. Sister of T. A. Janvier, *infra.* A Philadelphia writer of children's books, among which are, Clover Bank; Under the Dog Star; Little Helpers; A Dead Doll, and Other Verses. *Hou.*

Janvier, Thomas Allibone. *Pa.*, 1849——. A journalist and littérateur of Philadelphia, and subsequently of New York. An Embassy to Provence, a volume of travel; Color Studies: Four Stories; The Mexican Guide; Stories of Old New Spain; The Aztec Treasure House, a Romance; The Uncle of an Angel, and Other Stories; In Old New York. *Ap. Cent. Har. Scr.*

Jarves, James Jackson. *Ms.*, 1820–1888. An art connoisseur who lived in Hawaii, 1838–40, and subsequently for many years in Florence. Why and What Am I?; Art Studies; History of the Sandwich Islands (1843); Scenes and Scenery in the Sandwich Islands; Parisian Sights and French Principles; Italian Sights and Papal Principles; Kiana, a Tradition of Hawaii; A Glimpse at the Art of Japan; Art Hints; The Art Idea; Art Thoughts; Italian Rambles; Pepero, the Boy Artist. *Har. Hou.*

Jarvis, Edward. *Ms.*, 1803–1884. A once prominent physician of Dorchester, Massachusetts. Physiology and Health; Elementary Physiology; Condition of the Insane and Idiots in Massachusetts, are his more important publications.

Jarvis, Samuel Farmar. *Ct.*, 1786–1851. An Episcopal clergyman of Connecticut. Sermons on Prophecy; No Union with Rome; Chronological Introduction to the History of the Church; The Religion of the Indian Tribes of North America.

Jay, Sir James. *N. Y.*, 1732–1815. An elder brother of J. Jay, *infra.* A physician of New York city who was knighted by George III., and who published Reflections and Observations on Gout.

Jay, John. *N. Y.*, 1745–1829. A famous New York statesman who was one of the authors of The Federalist. Of his state papers, the Address to the People of Great Britain is the most celebrated. His Correspondence and State Papers, edited by H. P. Johnston, appeared 1890–93. *See Lives by Wm. Jay, infra; Pellew; Appleton's American Biography. Put.*

Jay, John. *N. Y.*, 1817–1894. Son of W. Jay, *infra.* A lawyer and diplomat of New York who was minister to Austria, 1869–75, and a prominent opponent of slavery. Dignity of the Abolition Cause; Caste and Slavery in the American Church; America Free or America Slave, are some of his political and other pamphlets.

Jay, William. *N. Y.*, 1789–1858. Son of J. Jay, *supra.* A philanthropist of New York city who was strongly opposed to slavery. Life of John Jay;

War and Peace; Causes and Consequences of the Mexican War.

Jay, W. M. L. *See Woodruff.*

Jeffers, William Nicholson. *N. J.*, 1824–1883. A United States naval officer who became a commodore in 1878. Short Methods in Navigation; Theory and Practice of Naval Gunnery; Inspection and Proof of Cannon; Ordnance Instruction for the United States Navy.

Jefferson, Joseph. *Pa.*, 1829——. A famous actor of New York city who has published an entertaining Autobiography. He is the author of the famous play, Rip Van Winkle, in which he has long been identified with the leading rôle. *Cent. Do.*

Jefferson, Thomas. *Va.*, 1743–1826. The third president of the United States. A statesman whose literary monument is the world-famous Declaration of Independence. Other writings of his are, Notes on Virginia; Rights of British America; Manual of Parliamentary Practice. A ten-volume edition of his works was published in 1892. *See Lives by Linn, 1834; Rayner, 1834; Tucker, 1837; Dwight, 1839; Randall, 1858; Parton, 1874; J. T. Morse, 1883; Domestic Life of, by Randolph, 1871; Edinburgh Review, July, 1830, and October, 1837; North American Review, April, 1830, and January, 1835; Allibone's Dictionary; Jefferson at Monticello; Appleton's American Biography; Henry Adams's History of the Administration of Jefferson. Put.*

Jeffrey, Mrs. Rosa Vertner [Griffith] [Johnson]. *Mi.*, 1826–1894. A verse-writer of Lexington, Kentucky. Poems by Rosa; Florence Vale; The Crimson Hand, and Other Poems; Marah, a Novel; Woodburn, a Novel. *Lip.*

Jeffries, Benjamin Joy. *Ms.*, 1833——. A prominent physician of Boston. Color Blindness: its Dangers and its Detection; The Eye in Health and Disease; Diseases of the Skin.

Jenkins, John Stilwell. *N. Y.*, 1818–1852. A lawyer and journalist of Weedsport, New York. The Heroines of History; Lives of the Governors of New York; Lives of Jackson, Polk, and Calhoun; Political History of New York; History of the Mexican War; Generals of the Last War with Great Britain; Life of Silas Wright, include the larger part of his writings. *Co.*

Jenks, Jeremiah Whipple. *Mch.*, 1856——. An educator, since 1891 professor of political, municipal, and social institutions at Cornell University. Henry C. Carey als National-ökonom; Road Legislation for the American State.

Jenks, John Whipple Potter. *Ms.*, 1819–1894. A naturalist who was director of the museum of natural history at Brown University, 1872–94, and professor of agriculture and zoölogy there, 1875–94. Hunting in Florida; Jenks and Steele's Zoölogy.

Jenks, William. *Ms.*, 1778–1866. A once prominent Congregational clergyman of Boston who founded the American Oriental Society. Commentary on the Bible, long a popular work; Bible Atlas and Scripture Gazetteer.

Jenness, John Scribner. *N. H.*, 1827–1879. A lawyer of New York city. The Isles of Shoals, an Historical Sketch; The First Planting of New Hampshire. He edited Transcripts of Original Documents relating to the Early History of New Hampshire.

Jennison, Lucy White. "Owen Innsley." *Ms.*, 1850——. A verse-writer who has lived mainly in Europe. Love Poems and Sonnets.

Jervey, Mrs. Caroline H—— [Gilman] [Glover]. *S. C.*, 1823–1877. Daughter of S. Gilman, *infra*. A writer of fiction and occasional verse. Vernon Grove; Helen Courtenay's Promise.

Jervis, John Bloomfield. *N. Y.*, 1795–1885. A civil engineer of New York who designed many important works, such as the Croton Dam and High Bridge. Railway Property; Labor and Capital. *Bai.*

Jessup, Henry Harris. *Pa.*, 1832——. A Presbyterian missionary in Syria from 1856. The Women of the Arabs; The Children of the East; The Greek Church and Protestant Missions; Syrian Home Life, include his most important works. *Do.*

Jeter, Jeremiah Bell. *Va.*, 1802–1880. A Baptist clergyman prominent in the South as a preacher and contro-

Manual for Railway Engineers; Bridge Disasters in America; A Graphic Method for Solving Algebraic Problems; Elementary Course of Geometric Drawing; Life of G. W. Whistler, Civil Engineer. *Le.*

Vose, John. *N. H.*, 1766–1840. An educator of Atkinson, New Hampshire, prominent in his day, and author of System of Astronomy; Compendium of Astronomy.

W

Wackerhagen, Augustus. *G.*, 1774–1865. A Lutheran clergyman of Columbia County, New York. Inbegriff des Glaubens und Sittenlehre.

Wade, William P——. 18———. Treatise on the Law of Notice; On the Operation and Construction of Retroactive Laws; Manual of American Mining Laws in the Western States; The Laws of Notice as Affecting Civil Rights and Remedies; The Law of Attachment and Garnishment.

Wadsworth, Marshman Edward. *Me.*, 1847——. The State geologist of Michigan from 1888. Geology of the Iron and Copper Districts of Lake Superior; The Azoid System (with J. D. Whitney, *infra*); Lithological Studies, are among his writings.

Wagner, Arthur Lockwood. *Il.*, 185———. An officer in the United States army. Catechism of Outpost Duty; Organization and Tactics; The Service of Security and Information; The Campaign of Königgrätz.

Wainwright, Jonathan Mayhew. *E.*, 1792–1854. A provisional Protestant Episcopal bishop of New York, 1852–54. The Land of Bondage; Short Family Prayers; The Pathway and Abiding Places of Our Lord; Lessons on the Church Religious Education; Selected Sermons. *See Lives by Doane, 1856, Norton, 1858. Ap. Dut.*

Wait, William. *N. Y.*, 1821–1880. An eminent lawyer of Fulton County, New York. Law and Practice in Civil Actions; New York Annotated Code of Procedure; Actions and Defences at Law and in Equity; Treatise on General Principles of the Law.

Waite, Charles Burlingame. *N. Y.*, 1824——. A Chicago jurist, author of The Christian Religion to A. D. 200.

Waite, Mrs. Catherine [Van Valkenburg]. *Ont.*, 1829——. Wife of C. B. Waite, *supra*. A Chicago lawyer, founder of The Chicago Law Times, and an active advocate of woman-suffrage. The Mormon Prophet and his Harem.

Waite, Henry Randall. *N.Y.*, 1845——. A Presbyterian clergyman who has published The Motive of St. Paul's Life; Illiteracy and the Mormon Problem; A Boy's Workshop. *Lo.*

Wakefield, Mrs. Nancy Amelia Woodbury Priest. *N. H.*, 1836–1870. A verse-writer remembered for her poem, Over the River. *See Poems of, with Memoir, 1871.*

Wakeley, Joseph Beaumont. *Ct.*, 1804–1876. A Methodist clergyman of New York city among whose writings are, The Heroes of Methodism; Lost Chapters Recovered from Early American Methodism; Reminiscences; The American Temperance Cyclopedia. *Meth.*

Walcott, Charles Doolittle. *N. Y.*, 1850——. A geologist of note, director of the United States Geological Survey from 1894. The Trilobite; Paleontology of the Eureka District; The Cambrian Faunas of North America; The Fauna of the Lower Cambrian or Olinus Zone; Correlation Papers.

Walcott, Charles Melton. *E.*, 1815–1868. An actor and playwright of Philadelphia among whose plays are, The Course of True Love; Hoboken; Washington, or Valley Forge; A Good Fellow.

Walden, Treadwell. *N. Y.*, 1830——. An Episcopal clergyman of Washington. Sunday-School Prayer Book; Our English Bible and its Ancestors; The Great Meaning of Metanoia. *Co. Wh.*

Waldo, Frank. *O.*, 1857——. A meteorologist of Princeton, New Jersey, formerly a junior professor in the United States signal service. Beside a number of scientific monographs, he has published Modern Meteorology; Elementary Meteorology. *Am.*

Waldo, Samuel Putnam. *Ct.*, 1780–1826. A writer of Hartford, Connecticut. Tour of President Monroe in 1818; Memoirs of General Andrew Jackson; Life of Stephen Decatur; Biographical Sketches.

Waldstein, Charles. *N. Y.*, 1856——. An eminent archæologist, the director of the American School of Archæology at Athens from 1888. Excavations at the Heraion of Argos; The Balance of Emotion and Intellect; Essays on the Art of Pheidias; The Work of John Ruskin; Study of Art in Universities. *Gi. Har.*

Wales, Philip Skinner. *Md.*, 1837——. A United States naval officer who has published a Treatise on Mechanical Therapeutics.

Walke, Henry. *Va.*, 1808–1896. A naval officer appointed rear-admiral in 1870, and the author of Naval Scenes and Reminiscences of the Civil War.

Walker, Alexander Joseph. *Va.*, 1819–1893. A lawyer and journalist of New Orleans. Jackson and New Orleans; History of the Battle of Shiloh; Butler at New Orleans; Duelling in Louisiana; Life of General Andrew Jackson.

Walker, Amasa. *Ct.*, 1799–1875. A political economist of Boston. The Science of Wealth; The Nature and Uses of Money. *Lip.*

Walker, Charles Manning. *O.*, 1834——. A journalist of Indianapolis. History of Athens County, Ohio; First Settlement of Ohio at Marietta; Lives of Oliver Martin and Alvin Hovey. *Clke.*

Walker, Cornelius. *Va.*, 1819——. An Episcopal clergyman, professor in the Virginia Theological Seminary from 1866. Sorrowing Not Without Hope; Outlines of Christian Theology; Lectures on Christian Ethics. *Wh.*

Walker, Edward Dwight. *L. I.*, 1859–1890. A journalist and littérateur of New York city. Reincarnation, a Study of Forgotten Truth.

Walker, Francis Amasa. *Ms.*, 1840–1897. Son of A. Walker, *supra.* The president of the Massachusetts Institute of Technology from 1881, and during the Civil War a Federal officer, rising to the rank of colonel, and brevetted brigadier-general in 1865. A distinguished authority on financial topics; an advocate of bi-metallism. Wages; Money; Money in its Relations to Trade and Industry; Political Economy; The Indian Question; Land and its Rent; History of the Second Army Corps; Life of General Hancock; The Making of the Nation; Double Taxation in the United States; International Bimetallism. *See Review of Reviews, February, 1897. Ap. Ho. Lit. Mac. Scr.*

Walker, George Leon. *Vt.*, 1830——. A Congregational clergyman, pastor of a church in Hartford, Connecticut, from 1879. History of the First Church in Hartford, 1633–1883; Thomas Hooker: Preacher, Founder, Democrat; Some Aspects of the Religious Life of New England. *Do. Sil.*

Walker, James. *Ms.*, 1794–1874. A Unitarian clergyman, minister at Charlestown, Massachusetts, 1818–38, president of Harvard University, 1853–60. Lectures on Natural Religion; Lectures on the Philosophy of Religion; Sermons Preached in the College Chapel; Discourses. *A. U. A.*

Walker, James Barr. *Pa.*, 1805–1887. A popular Presbyterian clergyman in Ohio and Illinois. Philosophy of the Plan of Salvation; Poetry of Reason and Conscience; Pioneer Life in the West; God Revealed in Nature and in Christ; Philosophy of Skepticism and Ultraism; The Divine Operation in the Redemption of Man; Living Questions of the Age; Doctrine of the Holy Spirit; Poems. *Meth.*

Walker, James Bradford Richmond. *Ms.*, 1821——. A Congregational clergyman of Massachusetts. Comprehensive Concordance to the Holy Scriptures. *C. P. S.*

Walker, James Murdock. *S. C.*, 1813–1854. A South Carolina lawyer. The Theory of Common Law; Tract on Government; The State *versus* Bank of South Carolina; Roman Jurisprudence in the Law of Real Estate.

Walker, James Perkins. *N. H.*, 1829–1868. A Boston publisher. Faith and Patience, a story for boys; Book of Raphael's Madonnas; Sunny-Eyed Tim. *See Memoir of, 1869.* .

Walker, Joseph Burbeen. *N. H.*, 1822——. An agriculturist of New

Hampshire. Land Drainage; Forests of New Hampshire; Prospective Agriculture in New Hampshire; Oats; Rogers the Ranger; Birth of the Federal Constitution.

Walker, Joseph Henry. *Ms.*, 1820——. A Republican Congressman from Massachusetts whose home is in Worcester. A Few Facts and Suggestions on Money, Trade, and Banking. *Hou.*

Walker, Mrs. Katherine Kent [Child]. *Vt.*, 1840——. A writer who is best known by a famous paper in The Atlantic Monthly on The Total Depravity of Inanimate Things. Bible Stories for the Young; Life of Christ; From the Crib to the Cross. *Ran.*

Walker, Mrs. Mary Spring. 18—-A Boston writer. Wife of J. B. R. Walker, *supra*. The Family Doctor, or Mrs. Barry and her Bourbon; Rev. Dr. Willoughby and his Wine; Both Sides of the Street; Down in a Saloon; White Robes.

Walker, Robert James. *Pa.*, 1801-1869. The secretary of the United States Treasury, 1845-49, and author of Letters on the Finances and Resources of the United States.

Walker, Sears Cook. *Ms.*, 1805-1853. Brother of T. Walker, *infra*. An astronomer who published a number of professional monographs.

Walker, Timothy. *Ms.*, 1806-1856. A jurist of Cincinnati. Elements of Geometry; Introduction to American Law. *Lit.*

Walker, William. *Tn.*, 1824-1860. A famous adventurer who led a filibustering expedition into Nicaragua in 1855, and was afterwards court-martialled and shot by the authorities of Honduras. The War in Nicaragua. *See Walker's Expedition to Nicaragua, by W. V. Wells, 1856; Reminiscences of the Filibuster War by Doubleday, 1886; Joaquin Miller's Walker in Nicaragua.*

Walker, William McCreary. *Md.*, 1813-1866. A United States naval officer who published a work on Screw Propulsion.

Walker, Williston. *Me.*, 1860——. Son of G. L. Walker, *supra*. A Congregational clergyman, professor of Germanic and Western Church History in Hartford Theological Seminary from 1889. The Creeds and Platforms of Congregationalism; On the Increase of Royal Power under Philip Augustus; A History of the Congregational Church in the United States. *Scr.*

Wallace, Horace Binney. *Pa.*, 1817-1852. Son of J. B. Wallace, *infra*. A lawyer and littérateur of Philadelphia. Literary Criticisms; Art and Scenery in Europe. *See Allibone's Dictionary.*

Wallace, John Bradford. *N. J.*, 1778-1837. A lawyer of Philadelphia. Remarks on the Law of Bailment; Reports of Cases of the Third Circuit Court. *See Memoir by his wife, 1848.*

Wallace, John William. *Pa.*, 1815-1884. Son of J. B. Wallace, *supra*. A master in chancery of the Pennsylvania Supreme Court. The Reporters, Chronologically Arranged; Cases in the Circuit Court of the United States for the Third Circuit; Cases Argued and Adjudged in the Supreme Court of the United States, 1863-1874; An Old Philadelphian: Colonel William Bradford, the Patriot Printer of 1776. *See Allibone's Dictionary.*

Wallace, Lew[is]. *Ind.*, 1827——. A Federal major-general during the Civil War, subsequently a lawyer of Crawfordsville, Indiana, and minister to Turkey, 1881-85. Ben Hur, a Tale of the Christ, has been extremely popular, but neither this nor his other romances have met the entire approval of literary critics. His other works include, The Fair God, an Aztec Story; The Prince of India; The Boyhood of Christ; Life of General Benjamin Harrison. *Har.*

Wallace, Mrs. Susan Arnold [Elston]. *Ind.*, 1830——. Wife of L. Wallace, *supra*. The Storied Sea; Ginevra, a Christmas Story; The Land of the Pueblos; The Repose in Egypt. *Har.*

Wallace, William Ross. *Ky.*, 1819-1881. A lawyer and verse-writer of New York city. Perdita; Alban; Meditations in America, and Other Poems. The Liberty Bell is his best-known poem. *See Griswold's Poets and Poetry of America.*

Wallack, Lester (real name John Johnstone Wallack). *N. Y.*, 1820-

1888. A noted comedian and dramatist of New York city. The Veteran; Rosedale. *See Galaxy Magazine, October, 1868; Autobiography of, 1889. Scr.*

Wallis, Severn Teackle. *Md.*, 1816–1894. A lawyer of Baltimore. Glimpses of Spain; Spain: her Institutions, Politics, and Public Men. A memorial edition of his writings in four volumes was published in 1896. *Har.*

Waln, Robert. *Pa.*, 1765–1836. A Philadelphia merchant. Answer to the Anti-Protection Report of Henry Lee; Seven Letters to Elias Hicks, widely read at the time of their appearance.

Waln, Robert. *Pa.*, 1794–1825. Son of R. Waln, *supra*. A Philadelphia littérateur. The Hermit in America; American Bards, a satire; Sisyphi Opus, with Other Poems; Life of Lafayette.

Walsh, Michael. *I.*, 1763–1840. A once popular educator of Massachusetts who published a Mercantile Arithmetic, and a New System of Bookkeeping.

Walsh, Robert. *Md.*, 1784-1859. A prominent Philadelphian who was United States consul at Paris, 1845–51. In 1811 he established the American Review of History and Politics, the first quarterly in the United States. An Appeal from the Judgments of Great Britain; Letter on the Genius and Disposition of the French Government; Correspondence Respecting Russia; Didactics; The Museum of Foreign Literature and Science. *See Edinburgh Review, May, 1820; North American Review, April, 1820.*

Walsh, William Shepard. "William Shepard." *F.*, 1854–189–. Grandson of R. Walsh, *supra*. A Philadelphia littérateur, editor of Lippincott's Magazine, 1886–90. Authors and Authorship; Pen Pictures of Earlier Victorian Authors; Faust: the Legend and the Poem; Paradoxes of a Philistine; Pen Pictures of Modern Authors; Our Young Folks' History of the Roman Empire.

Walter, Nehemiah. *I.*, 1663–1750. A Congregational clergyman, pastor at Roxbury, Massachusetts, from 1688 until his death. The Sense of Indwelling Sin in the Unregenerate; Sermons; Practical Discourses on the Holiness of Heaven.

Walter, Thomas. *Ms.*, 1696–1725. Son of N. Walter, *supra*. A Congregational clergyman, the colleague of his father. Grounds and Rules of Music Explained; Infallibility May Sometimes Mistake.

Walter, William Bicker. *Ms.*, 1796–1822. Great-grandnephew of T. Walter, *supra*. A verse-writer who published Poems; Sukey, suggested by Halleck's "Fanny."

Walters, William Thompson. *Pa.*, 1820–1891. A merchant of Baltimore, long prominent as an art patron. Antoine Louis Barye, from the French of Various Critics; The Percheron Horse, from the French of Du Hays; Notes upon Certain Masters of the Nineteenth Century.

Walther, Carl Ferdinand Wilhelm. *Sxy.*, 1811–1887. A Lutheran clergyman who came to America in 1839, and was president of the Lutheran Theological Seminary at St. Louis, 1849–1887. Dr. Luther's kleiner Katechismus ausgelegt von Dr. J. C. Dietrich, mit Zusätzen; Amerikanisch - Lutherische Evangelien-Postille; Amerikanisch - Lutherische Epistel - Postille; Amerikanisch - Lutherische Pastoraltheologie. He was the leader of what are known as Missouri Lutherans. *See Biography of, by Günther (Lebensbild), 1890; Brömel's Homiletische Characterbilder, 1874.*

Walton, George Edward. *O.*, 1839–——. A Cincinnati physician, professor of medicine in Cincinnati College from 1880. The Mineral Springs of the United States and Canada.

Walworth [wŏl'wŭrth], **Clarence Alphonsus.** *N. Y.*, 1820-——. Son of Reuben Walworth, *infra*. A Roman Catholic clergyman who was one of the founders of the Paulist order in the United States, a prominent temperance advocate, and since 1864 rector of St. Mary's, Albany. The Gentle Sceptic; The Doctrine of Hell; Andiatorocté, and Other Poems.

Walworth, Mrs. Ellen [Hardin]. *Il.*, 1832——. Wife of M. T. Walworth, *infra*. A Saratoga writer who has published Saratoga, the Battle Ground.

Walworth, Ellen Hardin. *N. Y.*, 1858——. Daughter of M. T. Walworth, *infra.* An Old World as Seen Through Young Eyes.

Walworth, Mrs. Jeanette Ritchie [Hadermann]. *Pa.*, 1837——. A novelist of New York city. Dead Men's Shoes; The Bar Sinister; The Man at Rossmere; At Bay; Southern Silhouettes; Forgiven at Last; Baldy's Point; The Silent Witness; Heavy Yokes; An Old Fogy; The Little Radical; Uncle Scipio, are among her numerous fictions. *Cas. Ho.*

Walworth, Mansfield Tracy. *N. Y.*, 1837–1873. Son of Reuben H. Walworth, *infra.* A lawyer once well known as a writer of extremely sensational romances. Among them are, Beverly; Warwick; Lulu; Delaplene; Stormcliff; Mission of Death; Tahara, a Leaf from Empire.

Walworth, Reuben Hyde. *Ct.*, 1787–1867. An eminent jurist of Saratoga, the last Chancellor of the State of New York. Rules and Orders of the New York Court of Chancery; The Hyde Genealogy.

Walworth, Reubena Hyde. *Ky.*, 1867——. Daughter of M. T. Walworth, *supra.* Where was Elsie?, a comedietta.

Ward, Aaron. *N. Y.*, 1790–1867. A New York congressman and major-general of militia, the author of Around the Pyramids, a volume of travel.

Ward, Andrew Henshaw. *Ms.*, 1784–1864. A lawyer of Shrewsbury, Massachusetts, and subsequently of Newton in the same State. History of Shrewsbury; Genealogy of the Rice Family; The Ward Family.

Ward, Artemus. *See Browne, C. F.*

Ward, Mrs. Elizabeth Stuart [Phelps]. *Ms.*, 1844——. Wife of Herbert D. Ward, *infra*, daughter of A. Phelps, *supra.* A popular New England novelist whose life was mainly passed at Andover and Gloucester until her marriage in 1888. She has more recently lived in Newton, Massachusetts. The publication in 1869 of The Gates Ajar, a tale whose theme is the life of departed spirits in the next world, aroused much discussion, and instantly made its author famous. She has since pursued the same motive in Beyond the Gates, and The Gates Between. Her latest works, as a whole, show an increase of power and a higher level of literary excellence. Hedged in; The Silent Partner; Sealed Orders, and Other Stories; Men, Women, and Ghosts; Friends: a Duet; Dr. Zay; The Story of Avis; An Old Maid's Paradise, and Burglars in Paradise; Fourteen to One, a book of short stories; Donald Marcy; Jack the Fisherman; The Madonna of the Tubs; A Singular Life; The Supply at St. Agatha's; The Master of the Magicians (with H. D. Ward); Come Forth (with H. D. Ward); What to Wear?; The Struggle for Immortality, a collection of essays; Chapters from a Life, an autobiography. Less widely known as a poet, her Poetic Studies, and Songs of the Silent World, perhaps represent her highest point of attainment. Her juvenile books include, Gypsey's Rainy Day Book; My Cousin and I; The Trotty Book; Trotty's Wedding Tour and Story Book. *See Vedder's American Writers. Hou.*

Ward, Ferdinand De Wilton. *N. Y.*, 1812——. A Presbyterian missionary in India, 1836–47, and subsequently a minister in Geneseo, New York. India and the Hindoos; Christian Gift, or Pastoral Letters Upon Character; Summer Vacation Abroad; History of the Churches of Rochester, New York.

Ward, Henry Augustus. *N. Y.*, 1834——. Nephew of F. Ward, *supra.* A naturalist of note, professor in the University of Rochester, 1860–75. Notices of the Megatherium Cuvieri; Description of the Most Celebrated Fossil Animals in Royal Museums of Europe.

Ward, Henry Dana. *Ms.*, 1797–1884. A Baptist clergyman prominent as an opponent of freemasonry. Freemasonry: its Pretensions; The Gospel of the Kingdom; The History of the Cross; The Faith of Abraham and Christ.

Ward, Herbert Dickinson. *Ms.*, 1861——. Son of W. H. Ward, *infra.* The Captain of the Kittie Wink; A Dash to the Pole; The New Senior at Andover; The White Crown, and

Other Stories; The Burglar who Moved Paradise. *Hou. Ll. Lo. Lov. Rob.*

Ward, Mrs. H. O. *See Bloomfield-Moore, Mrs. Clara.*

Ward, James Harman. *Ct.*, 1806–1861. A United States naval officer. Elementary Course of Instruction in Naval Gunnery; Manual of Naval Tactics; Steam for the Million.

Ward, James Warner. *N. J.*, 1818——. A verse-writer; librarian, 1874–1895, of the Grosvenor library at Buffalo. Home-made Verses and Stories in Rhyme; Yorick, and Other Poems; Higher Water, a parody upon Hiawatha.

Ward, John. *N. Y.*, 1838——. Cousin of S. Ward, *infra*. A soldier and physician of New York city. The Overland Route to California, and Other Poems.

Ward, Julius Hammond. *Ms.*, 1837–1897. An Episcopal clergyman and journalist of Boston on the staff of The Boston Herald. Life of J. G. Percival, *supra*; The Bible in Modern Thought; Life of Bishop White, *infra*; Phillips Brooks in Massachusetts; The Church in Modern Society; The White Mountains, a Guide to their Interpretation. *Ap. Do. Hou.*

Ward, Lester Frank. *Il.*, 1841—— A botanist and geologist employed in the United States Geological Survey. Guide to the Flora of Washington and Vicinity; Sketch of Paleontological Botany; Synopsis of the Flora of the Laramie Group; Types of the Laramie Flora; Geographical Distribution of Fossil Plants; Dynamic Sociology; The Psychic Factors of Civilization; The Principles of Sociology. *Ap. Gi.*

Ward, Matthew Flournoy. *Ky.*, 1826–1863. A writer of Louisville. Letters From Three Continents; English Items.

Ward, Mrs. May [Alden]. *O.*, 1853——. The wife of a clergyman in Franklin, Massachusetts. Petrarch; Dante: Sketch of his Life and Works; Old Colony Days. *Rob.*

Ward, Nathaniel. *E.*, *c.* 1580–1652. A Puritan clergyman, minister at Ipswich, 1634–36, and a resident of the colony of Massachusetts until 1646, when he returned to England, and was rector of Shenfield in Essex, 1647–52. He is famous as the author of The Simple Cobler of Aggavvam in America, a piece of satire as able as it is vindictive and intolerant. The first code of laws made in New England was drafted by Ward in 1639, and formally adopted in 1644. It is styled The Body of Liberties. Mercurius Anti-mechanicus, or the Simple Cobbler's Boy with his Lap-full of Caveats, is usually attributed to Ward, and probably with truth. Other writings ascribed to him are, A Religious Retreat Sounded to a Religious Army; A Sermon before Parliament (1647). *See Tyler's American Literature; Memoir by John Ward Dean, 1868.*

Ward, Samuel. *N. Y.*, 1814–1884. A once prominent banker of New York city who published Lyrical Recreations.

Ward, Thomas. *N. J.*, 1807–1873. A littérateur of New York city. A Month of Freedom; Passaic: a Group of Poems; Flora, or the Gypsy's Frolic, a pastoral opera; War Lyrics.

Ward, William Hayes. *Ms.*, 1835——. A Presbyterian clergyman of New York city, editor of The Independent, and eminent as an Assyriologist. Notes on Oriental Antiquities.

Warden, David Baillie. *I.*, 1788–1845. A consul and secretary of the United States legation at Paris from 1804 until his death. Origin and Nature of Consular Establishments; Inquiry Concerning the Intellectual and Moral Faculties and Literature of the Negroes (1810); Description of the District of Columbia; Bibliotheca Americana Septentrionalis; L'art de vérifier les dates: chronologie historique de l'Amérique; A Statistical History of the United States.

Warden, Robert Bruce. *Ky.*, 1824——. A lawyer formerly of Cincinnati, but since 1873 of Washington. A Familiar Forensic View of Man and Law; A Voter's Version of the Life and Character of Stephen Douglas; Private Life of Salmon Chase.

Warder, John Aston. *Pa.*, 1812–1883. A Cincinnati physician very active in promoting a general interest in forestry and landscape gardening. Hedge Manual; American Pomology.

Ware, Henry. *Ms.*, 1764–1845. A Unitarian clergyman of Massachusetts, pastor of Hingham, 1787–1805. His election in the latter year to the Hollis professorship of divinity at Harvard University precipitated the dissensions which ultimately resulted in dividing the Congregational body into Unitarian and Trinitarian portions. Letters to Trinitarians and Calvinists; Inquiry into Foundation, Evidences, and Truth of Religion. *See Sprague's Annals of the American Pulpit.*

Ware, Henry. *Ms.*, 1794–1843. Son of H. Ware, *supra.* A Unitarian clergyman of Massachusetts, pastor of the Second Church in Boston, 1817–30, and Parkman professor at Harvard University, 1830–42. The Vision of Liberty, an ode; Hints on Extemporaneous Speaking; Discourses on the Offices and Character of Christ; Sermons on Small Sins; On the Formation of Christian Character, which has been very widely read; Life of the Saviour; Lives of Priestley and Noah Worcester, *infra. See Memoir by John Ware, infra; Sprague's Annals of the American Pulpit. A. U. A.*

Ware, John. *Ms.*, 1795–1864. Son of H. Ware, 1st, *supra.* A Boston physician, professor of medicine at Harvard University, 1832–58. History and Treatment of Delirium Tremens; Hints to Young Men on the Relation of the Sexes; Success in the Medical Profession; Life of Henry Ware, *supra. A. U. A.*

Ware, John Fothergill Waterhouse. *Ms.*, 1818–1881. Son of Henry Ware, 2d, *supra.* A Unitarian clergyman of Baltimore, and subsequently of Boston. Wrestling and Waiting; Sermons; War Tracts; The Silent Pastor; Home Life. *El. Le.*

Ware, Mrs. Katherine Augusta [Rhodes]. *Ms.*, 1797–1843. The wife of a United States naval officer. She published The Power of the Passions, and Other Poems.

Ware, Mrs. Mary Greene [Chandler]. *Ms.*, 1818——. Wife of J. Ware, *supra.* Elements of Character; Thoughts in My Garden; Death and Life.

Ware, Nathaniel A——. *Ms.*, *c.* 1780–1854. A Southern writer whose later years were spent in Philadelphia and Cincinnati. Views of the Federal Constitution; Notes on Political Economy.

Ware, William. *Ms.*, 1797–1852. Son of H. Ware, 1st, *supra.* A Unitarian clergyman of New York city, 1821–36, whose historical novels are still popular. Letters from Palmyra, republished as Zenobia; Probus, afterwards called Aurelian; Julian; American Unitarian Biography (edited); Lectures on the Works of Washington Allston; Sketches of European Capitals; Life of Nathaniel Bacon in Sparks's American Biography; Sermons Illustrative of Unitarian Christianity; Unitarianism the Doctrine of Matthew's Gospel. *See Allibone's Dictionary; Sprague's Annals of the American Pulpit. Est.*

Ware, William Robert. *Ms.*, 1832–——. Son of H. Ware, 2d, *supra.* A professor of architecture in Columbia College School of Mines from 1881. He has published Modern Perspective. *Mac.*

Warfield, Benjamin Breckenridge. *Ky.*, 1851——. A Presbyterian clergyman and educator, professor of didactic and polemical theology at Princeton Theological Seminary from 1887. The Divine Origin of the Bible; Introduction to the Textual Criticism of the New Testament; The Canon of the New Testament; The Gospel of the Incarnation, include his more important works.

Warfield, Mrs. Catherine Anne [Ware]. *Mi.*, 1816–1877. Daughter of N. Ware, *supra.* A Kentucky novelist who with her sister Eleanor wrote The Wife of Leon, and Other Poems; The Indian Chamber, and Other Poems. Her own separate writings include, The Household of Bouverie; The Romance of the Green Seal; Miriam Monfort; Hester Howard's Temptation; A Double Wedding; Lady Ernestine; Miriam's Memoirs; Sea and Shore; The Cardinal's Daughter; Ferne Fleming; The Romance of Beauseincourt.

Warfield, Ethelbert Dudley. *Ky.*, 1861——. A lawyer and educator, president of Lafayette College, Easton, Pennsylvania, from 1891. The Kentucky Resolutions of 1798, an Historical Study.

Waring [wā'ring], **George Edwin.** *N. Y.*, 1833——. An eminent sanitary engineer, since 1895 superintendent of the street-cleaning department of New York city. The Sanitary Drainage of Houses and Towns; A Farmer's Vacation; The Bride of the Rhine; Tyrol and the Skirt of the Alps; Village Improvements; Farm Villages; Elements of Agriculture; Draining for Profit and Draining for Health; Book of the Farm; How to Drain a House; Sewage and Land Drainage; Sanitary Condition of City and Country Dwellings; Modern Methods of Sewage Disposal. *Co. Hou. Vn.*

Warman, Cy. *Il.*, 1852——. A Colorado journalist who was for a time a railway engineer. Tales of an Engineer, with Rhymes of the Rail. *Scr.*

Warner, Adoniram Judson. *N. Y.*, 1834——. A Federal officer during the Civil War, since 1866 a resident of Ohio. Appreciation of Money; Source of Value in Money.

Warner, Amos Griswold. *Ia.*, 1861——. A professor of applied economics in Leland Stanford Junior University, who, beside reports as superintendent of charities for the District of Columbia, has published, American Charities: a Study in Philanthropy and Economics; Three Phases of Coöperation in the West. *Cr.*

Warner, Anna Bartlett. "Amy Lothrop." *N. Y.*, 1820——. Sister of S. Warner, *infra*, and co-author with her of Say and Seal; Wych Hazel; Books of Blessing; Ellen Montgomery's Bookshelf. Among her separate novels and religious and other works are, Dollars and Cents; My Brother's Keeper; Stories of Vinegar Hill; The Fourth Watch; The Other Shore; Three Little Spades, a Child's Book of Gardening; Gardening by Myself; Up and Down the House. *Har. Lip. Ran.*

Warner, Beverley E——. *N. J.*, 1855——. An Episcopal clergyman of New Orleans. English History in Shakespeare's Plays. *Lgs.*

Warner, Charles Dudley. *Ms.*, 1829——. A popular novelist and essayist of Hartford, editor of The Hartford Courant from 1867, and one of the editors of Harper's Magazine from 1884. As a humourous writer he presents the literary and not the newspaper aspect of American humour. My Summer in a Garden; Backlog Studies; Saunterings; Being a Boy; Baddeck and that Sort of Thing; Mummies and Moslems; In the Wilderness: Adirondack Essays; Life of Washington Irving; Life of Captain John Smith; In the Levant; My Winter on the Nile; A Roundabout Journey; On Horseback, a Tour in Virginia, North Carolina, and Tennessee, with Notes of Travel in Mexico and California; The Work of Washington Irving; Studies in the South and West; Southern California; A Little Journey in the World; Their Pilgrimage; The Golden House; As We Go; As We Were Saying; The Relation of Life to Literature; Our Italy. *See Vedder's American Writers; Foley's American Authors. Har. Ho. Hou.*

Warner, Eliza A——. 18——. A writer of Northampton, Massachusetts, among whose works are, Tom Tracy; The Red House; Our Two Lives.

Warner, Susan. "Elizabeth Wetherell." *N. Y.*, 1818–1885. A once famous novelist of Highland Falls, New York, whose Wide, Wide World, a priggish religious tale appearing in 1849, attained an extraordinary popularity in America and England. Among her other works are, Queechy; The Old Helmet; Stephen, M. D.; The Hills of the Shatemuc; Melbourne House; Daisy; Diana; The Law and the Testimony, a theological work. *Lip. Put.*

Warner, Zebedee. *Va.*, 1833——. A minister of the sect of United Brethren. Christian Baptism; Rise and Progress of the United Brethren Church; Life of Jacob Buchtel; The Roman Catholic not a True Christian Church.

Warren, Cornelia. *Ms.*, 1857——. Miss Wilton, a novel. *Hou.*

Warren, Gouverneur Kemble. *N. Y.*, 1830–1882. A lieutenant-colonel in the engineer corps, major-general of United States volunteers, and brevet major-general in the United States army. Explorations in the Dacota Country in 1855; Exploration of the Country Between the Missouri and the Platte Rivers; The Battle of Five Forks, Virginia.

Warren, Henry White. *Ms.*, 1831——. A Methodist bishop living in Denver. The Bible in the World's Education; Lectures on the Bible in English; Sights and Insights, or Knowledge by Travel; Studies of the Stars; Recreations in Astronomy. *Har. Meth.*

Warren, Ira. *Ont.*, 1806–1864. A journalist and physician of Boston. Causes and Cure of Puseyism; The Household Physician.

Warren, Israel Perkins. *Ct.*, 1814–1892. A Congregational clergyman, editor of The Christian Mirror at Portland, Maine, from 1875. Three Judges; Chauncey Judd; The Seaman's Cause; Sadduceeism; The Parousia; The Book of Revelation: an Exposition, include his principal works. *Cr. Fu.*

Warren, John. *Ms.*, 1753–1815. A Boston physician, professor of anatomy at Harvard University from 1783. He was a brother of General Joseph Warren who fell at Bunker Hill. Mercurial Practice in Febrile Diseases.

Warren, John Collins. *Ms.*, 1778–1856. Son of J. Warren, *supra*. A Boston physician who succeeded his father as professor of anatomy at Harvard University in 1815. He was one of the founders in 1820 of the Massachusetts General Hospital, and its chief surgeon till his death. He published, Cases of Organic Diseases of the Heart; Surgical Observations on Tumors, and lesser works. *See Life of, by E. Warren, 1860.*

Warren, John Collins. *Ms.*, 1842——. Son of J. M. Warren, *infra*. A professor of surgery at Harvard University from 1887. The Anatomy and Development of Rodent Ulcer; Pathology of Carbuncle and Columnal Adipose; The Healing of Arteries after Ligature in Men and Animals; Surgical Pathology and Therapeutics.

Warren, Jonathan Mason. *Ms.*, 1811–1867. Son of J. C. Warren, *supra*. A Boston physician. Surgical Observations, with Cures and Operations. *See Allibone's Dictionary.*

Warren, Mrs. Mercy [Otis]. *Ms.*, 1728–1814. Sister of James Otis, *supra*, very prominent as a literary figure in her day, and especially esteemed as a political satirist. The Gronp, a political satire; History of the American Revolution; three tragedies, including The Adulator, the Sack of Rome, The Ladies of Castille; Poems: Dramatic and Miscellaneous. *See Griswold's Female Poets of America; Mrs. Ellet's Women of the Revolution; Life of, by Alice Brown, supra, 1896.*

Warren, Nathan Boughton. *N. Y.*, 1805——. An author of Troy, New York. The Ancient Plain Song of the Church; The Order of Daily Service, with the English Musical Notation; The Holidays; Hidden Treasure, a Goblin Story.

Warren, Samuel Edward. *Ms.*, 1831——. An educator of Newton, Massachusetts. Elementary Projection Drawing; General Problems of Shades and Shadows; Problems in Stone Cutting; Descriptive Geometry; Machine Drawing; The Sunday Question, are among his published works.

Warren, Thomas Robinson. *N.Y.*, 1828——. A traveller and merchant. Dust and Foam Tracks; The Yachtsman Primer; Shooting, Boating, and Fishing; On Deck; Juliette Irving and the Jesuit.

Warren, William. *Me.*, 1806–1879. A Congregational clergyman at Gorham, Maine. School Geography; Household Consecration; The Spirit's Sword; Twelve Years Among Children; These for Those.

Warren, William Fairfield. *Ms.*, 1833——. A Methodist clergyman, president of Boston University from 1873. Paradise Found: the Cradle of the Human Race at the North Pole; The True Key to Ancient Chronology; In the Footsteps of Arminius; Constitutional Law Questions in the Methodist Church; The Quest of the Perfect Religion; The Story of Gottlieb. *Fl. Hou. Meth.*

Warriner, Edward Augustus. *Ms.*, 1829——. An Episcopal clergyman of Montrose, Pennsylvania. Victor La Tourette; Kear, a Poem; I Am That I Am, a Metrical Essay.

Warriner, Francis. *Ms.*, 1805–1866. A Congregational clergyman who was a United States naval chaplain, 1831–1834. The Cruise of the Potomac.

Warrington. *See Robinson, W. S.*

Washburn, Charles Ames. *Me.*, 1822–1889. A diplomatist who was minister to Paraguay, 1863–68. The History of Paraguay; From Poverty to Competence: Graduated Taxation; Political Evolution; Philip Thaxter; Gomery of Montgomery. *Le.*

Washburn, Edward Abiel. *Ms.*, 1819–1881. An Episcopal clergyman of Broad Church views, rector of Calvary Church, New York city. The Social Law of God; Voices from a Busy Life, a volume of verse; The Relation of the Episcopal Church to Other Bodies; Epochs of Church History; Beatitudes, and Other Sermons. *Dut. Wh.*

Washburn, Emory. *Ms.*, 1800–1877. A lawyer of Worcester, 1828–56; was governor of Massachusetts, 1854–56; and professor of law in Harvard University, 1856–76. Sketches of the Judicial History of Massachusetts; History of Leicester, Massachusetts; Treatise on American Law of Real Property; American Law of Easements and Servitudes; Testimony of Experts; Lectures on the Study and Practice of the Law. *Hou. Lit.*

Washburn, Francis. *N. Y.*, 1843——. An Episcopal clergyman of Newburg, New York. Meditations on Charity; The Soul Athirst, and Other Sermons; Thoughts on the Lord's Prayer. *Wh.*

Washburn, Israel. *Me.*, 1813–1883. Brother of C. A. Washburn, *supra;* governor of Maine, 1861. Notes, Historical, Descriptive, and Personal, of Livermore, Maine. *See Bibliography of Maine.*

Washburn, Peter Thacher. *Ms.*, 1814–1870. A lawyer of Woodstock, Vermont, and governor of his State in 1869. Reports of the Supreme Court of Vermont; Digest of All Cases in the Vermont Supreme Court.

Washburn, William Tucker. *Ms.*, 1841——. A lawyer and novelist of New York city. Fair Harvard; The Unknown City, a story of New York; Spring and Summer, a collection of verse.

Washburne, Elihu Benjamin. *Me.*, 1816–1887. Brother of C. A. Washburn, *supra*, but adding an "e" to the family name. A statesman who was secretary of state in 1869, and minister to France, 1869–77. Sketch of Edward Coles and the Slavery Struggle of 1823–24; Recollections of a Minister to France. *Scr.*

Washington, Booker Taliaferro. *Va.*, 1856——. A distinguished educator of African descent, president of Tuskegee Institute in Alabama from 1881. A writer on educational subjects.

Washington, Bushrod. *Va.*, 1762–1829. Nephew of G. Washington, *infra.* A jurist of Richmond, Virginia. Reports of Cases in the Virginia Court of Appeals; Reports of Cases in the United States Circuit Court, Third District, 1803–27. *See Life by H. Binney, 1858.*

Washington, George. *Va.*, 1732–1799. The first president of the United States, and known to general literature by his Farewell Address. His writings, including his Diary and Correspondence, have been edited in fourteen volumes by W. C. Ford, *supra. See United States histories; Lives by Marshall, Bancroft, Irving, Paulding, Sparks, Weems, Ramsay, E. E. Hale, Lodge, and many others; Allibone's Dictionary. Put.*

Washington, Mrs. Lucy Hall [Walker]. *Vt.*, 1835——. A temperance reformer and verse-writer, the wife of a Baptist clergyman at Port Jervis, New York. Echoes of Song; Memory's Casket.

Wasson, David Atwood. *Me.*, 1823–1887. A Unitarian clergyman of Massachusetts, prominent as a radical thinker, who lived at West Medford after his retirement from the ministry. Poems; Essays: Religious, Social, Political. *See Memoir of, by O. B. Frothingham, supra. Le.*

Waterbury, Jared Bell. *N. Y.*, 1799–1876. A Presbyterian clergyman who was city missionary of Brooklyn. Advice to a Young Christian; Voyage of Life; Sketches of Eloquent Preachers; Southern Planters and Freedmen, are among his works.

Waterhouse, Benjamin. *R. I.*, 1754–1846. A physician who was professor of medicine at Harvard University, 1783–1812, and of natural history at Brown University, 1784–91. Lectures on the Theory and Practice of Medicine; The

Principles of Vitality; The Botanist; The Journal of a Young Man of Massachusetts, a novel.

Waterman, Thomas Glasby. *N.Y.*, 1788–1862. A lawyer of Binghamton, New York, who published The Justice's Manual.

Waterman, Thomas Whitney. *N. Y.*, 1821——. Son of T. G. Waterman, *supra.* A lawyer of Binghamton who, besides editing many legal works, has written, The Civil Jurisdiction of Justices of the Peace in New York; Civil and Criminal Jurisdiction of Justices in Wisconsin and Iowa; Principles of Law and Equity; The Law of Set-Off; The Law of Trespass; The Law Relating to Specific Performance of Contracts; The Law of Corporations other than Municipal.

Waters, Mrs. Clara [Erskine] [Clement]. *Mo.*, 1834——. An art-writer of Boston. Handbook of Legendary and Mythological Art; Painters, Sculptors, Architects, Engravers, and their Works, a Handbook; Christian Symbols (with K. Conway, *supra*); Artists of the Nineteenth Century and their Works (with L. Hutton, *supra*); Life of Charlotte Cushman; Eleanor Maitland, a novel; Stories of Art and Artists; Naples, the City of Parthenope; Venice, Mediæval and Modern; Constantinople, the City of the Sultans; History of Painting for Beginners and Students; Rome the Eternal City. *Est. Hou. Sto.*

Waters, Robert. *S.*, 1835——. An educator of Hoboken, New Jersey. Life of William Cobbett; Shakespeare Portrayed by Himself; How Genius Works its Wonders.

Waterston, Mrs. Anne Cabot Lowell [Quincy]. *Ms.*, 1812——. Wife of R. C. Waterston, *infra*, and daughter of J. Quincy (1772–1864), *supra.* Verses by A. C. Q. W.; Adelaide Phillipps, a Record.

Waterston, Robert Cassie. *Me.*, 1812–1893. A Unitarian clergyman of Boston. Thoughts on Moral and Spiritual Culture; Arthur Lee and Tom Palmer.

Watson, Beriah Andre. *N.Y.*, 1836——. A physician of Jersey City. Amputations and their Complications; The Sportsman's Paradise, or the Lake Lands of Canada.

Watson, Elkanah. *Ms.*, 1758–1842. A noted traveller and agriculturist. Men and Times of the Revolution, his best-known work, is mainly autobiographic. Other works of his are, Tour in Holland in 1784; History of the Canals in the State of New York from 1788 to 1819; Rise of Modern Agricultural Societies; History of Agricultural Societies on the Berkshire System.

Watson, Henry Clay. *Md.*, 1831–1869. A journalist of Philadelphia, and subsequently of California. Camp-fires of the Revolution; Camp-fires of Napoleon; Romance of History; Lives of the Presidents; Nights in a Block-House; Old Bell of Independence; The Yankee Teapot; Heroic Women of History; Universal Naval History. *Le. La.*

Watson, James Craig. *Ont.*, 1838–1880. A professor of astronomy in the University of Wisconsin at the time of his death. He discovered several asteroids and comets. Popular Treatise on Comets; Theoretical Astronomy; Simple and Compound Interest Tables.

Watson, James Madison. *N. Y.*, 1827——. An educator of Elizabeth, New Jersey. Handbook of Gymnastics; Manual of Calisthenics, and a series of Independent Readers.

Watson, John Fanning. *N. J.*, 1780–1860. A bookseller, and subsequently a banker, of Philadelphia. Historic Tales; Annals of Philadelphia.

Watson, John Whittaker. *N. Y.*, 1824–1890. A journalist of New York city. Beautiful Snow and Other Poems; The Outcast and Other Poems.

Watson, Paul Barron. *N. J.*, 1861——. Grandson of J. F. Watson, *supra.* A lawyer of Boston. Marcus Aurelius Antoninus; Bibliography of Pre-Columbian Discoveries of America; The Swedish Revolution under Gustavus Vasa, a very effective study of an important epoch in Swedish history. *Har. Lit.*

Watson, Sereno. *Ct.*, 1826–1892. A noted botanist of Cambridge, curator of the Herbarium of Harvard University, 1888–92. Bibliographical Index of North American Botany; Botany of California (with Gray and Brewer).

Watson, William. *Ms.*, 1834——. A professor of mechanical engineering.

Technical Education; Course in Descriptive Geometry; Course in Shades and Shadows.

Watson, Winslow Cossoul. *N. Y.*, 1803——. Son of E. Watson, *supra*. Treatise on Practical Husbandry; Pioneer History of the Champlain Valley; History of Essex County, New York.

Watterson, George. *N. Y.*, 1783–1854. A Washington lawyer who was the first librarian of Congress. Letters from Washington; The Wanderer in Washington; Course of Study Preparatory to the Bar or Senate; The Lawyer, or Man as He Ought Not to Be.

Watterson, Henry. *D. C.*, 1840——. A journalist of Louisville, long prominent as editor of The Courier-Journal. Oddities of Southern Life and Character.

Wayland, Francis. *N. Y.*, 1796–1865. A Baptist clergyman eminent as a metaphysician, who was president of Brown University, 1827–55. Elements of Moral Science; Intellectual Philosophy; Human Responsibility; Elements of Political Economy; Occasional Discourses; Moral Law of Accumulation; Domestic Slavery Considered as a Scriptural Institution; Sermons to the Churches; Principles and Practice of Baptist Churches; Letters on the Ministry of the Gospel. *See Allibone's Dictionary; Lives by his sons, 1867, Murray, 1890.*

Wayland, Heman Lincoln. *R. I.*, 1830——. Son of F. Wayland, *supra*. A Baptist clergyman, editor of The National Baptist at Philadelphia, 1872–1894, and editor of The Examiner from 1894. Life and Labors of F. Wayland (with his brother); Faith and Works of Charles Spurgeon.

Wayman, Alexander Washington. *Md.*, 1821–1895. An African Methodist bishop. My Recollections; Cyclopedia of African Methodism; Wayman on Discipline.

Wead, Charles Kasson. *N. Y.*, 1848——. An electrician of Hartford. Aims and Methods of the Teaching of Physics; Lecture Notes on Sound and Light.

Weaver, George Sumner. *Vt.*, 1818——. A Universalist clergyman. Lectures on Mental Science; Hopes and Helps for the Young; Aims and Aids for Girls; The Ways of Life; The Christian Household; The Open Way; Moses and Modern Science; The Heart of the Word; Lives and Graves of Our Presidents.

Weaver, Jonathan. *O.*, 1824——. A clergyman of Ohio, bishop of the Church of the United Brethren. Discourses on the Resurrection; Ministerial Salary; Divine Providence; Universal Restoration not Sustained by the Word of God.

Webb, Alexander Stewart. *N. Y.*, 1835——. Son of J. W. Webb, *infra*. The president of the College of the City of New York from 1869, and during the Civil War a general in the Federal army. The Peninsula; McClellan's Campaign of 1862. *Scr.*

Webb, Charles Henry. "John Paul." *N. Y.*, 1834——. A journalist now living at Nantucket very popular as a humourist in the earlier part of his career. Liffith Lank; St. Twel'mo'; John Paul's Book; Parodies in Prose and Verse; Vagrom Verse. *See Hart's American Literature. Hou.*

Webb, Mrs. Frances Isabel [Carrie]. *N. J.*, 1857–1895. A magazinist of New York city. A Tiff with the Tiffins; Gala Day Books; A Breath of Suspicion.

Webb, James Watson. *N. Y.*, 1802–1884. A journalist of New York city, minister to Brazil, 1861–69. Altowan, or Life in the Rocky Mountains; Slavery and its Tendencies.

Webber, Charles Wilkins. *Ky.*, 1819–1856. A journalist and traveller who was killed in Walker's expedition in Nicaragua. Hunter-Naturalist; Tales of the Southern Border; Old Hicks the Guide; Gold Mines of the Gila; Shot in the Eye; Adventures with Texas Rifle Rangers; Wild Scenes and Song Birds; History of Mystery; Spiritual Vampirism; Texan Virago; Wild Girl of Nebraska; Romance of Natural History. *See Bibliography of Texas. Lip.*

Webber, Samuel. *Ms.*, 1759–1810. An educator of Cambridge, professor of mathematics in Harvard University, 1789–1806, and president of the same, 1806–10. He published a System of Mathematics that was for a long time the only text-book on that subject in use in New England colleges.

Webber, Samuel. *Ms.*, 1797–1880. Son of S. Webber, *supra*. A physician of Charlestown, New Hampshire. Zogan, an Indian Tale, in Verse; War, a Poem.

Webster, Albert Falvey. *Ms.*, 1848–1876. A magazinist of New York city the best of whose short stories are, Little Majesty; An Operation in Money; Miss Eunice's Glove.

Webster, Daniel. *N. H.*, 1782–1852. A distinguished statesman who was a graduate of Dartmouth College in 1801. He represented New Hampshire in Congress, 1813–17, and, removing to Massachusetts in 1816, was a representative from that State, 1823–27. He was a member of the Senate, 1827–41 and 1845–50, and secretary of state, 1841–1843 and 1850–52. He died at Marshfield, Massachusetts, October 24, 1852. He was a master of English style, the best of his orations on especial occasions being those delivered at the second Pilgrim centennial in 1820, on the laying of the corner-stone of Bunker Hill Monument in 1825, and the eulogy of Adams and Jefferson in 1826. *See Parton's Famous Americans; Private Life of, by C. Lanman, supra; Whipple's Great Speeches of Webster, 1879; Atlantic Monthly, February, 1882; Lives by Curtis, Lyman, Smucker, Everett, Fletcher Webster, Tefft, Lodge; Appletons' American Biography; Johnson's Universal Cyclopedia; Allibone's Dictionary; Reminiscences of, by Harvey; Biographical Encyclopædia of Massachusetts. Co. Lit.*

Webster, John White. *Ms.*, 1793–1850. A chemist who was professor at Harvard University, 1824–50, and was tried and executed in 1850 for the murder of Dr. Parkman, *supra*. Description of the Island of St. Michael; Manual of Chemistry. *See Reports of Trial by Bemis and Stone.*

Webster, Nathan Burnham. *N. H.*, 1821——. An educator of Norfolk, Va. Outlines of Chemistry.

Webster, Noah. *Ct.*, 1758–1843. A famous lexicographer, best known by his Spelling Book and his American Dictionary of the English Language (1828). His great dictionary is still published, being revised and enlarged from time to time, and edited according to the principles laid down by its originator. The unabridged edition is now called the International Dictionary. Among his other works are included, A Philosophical and Practical Grammar of the English Language; The Prompter, or Common Sayings and Subjects; Rights of Neutrals; Dissertations on the English Language; A Compendious Dictionary of the English Language (1806). *See North American Review, April, 1829; Life by H. E. Scudder, 1882; Allibone's Dictionary.*

Webster, Pelatiah. *Ct.*, 1725–1797. A once famous political economist of Philadelphia. Essays on Free Trade and Finance; Essay on Credit; Political Essay on the Nature and Operation of Money, are among his writings.

Webster, Richard. *N. Y.*, 1811–1856. A Presbyterian clergyman, pastor at Mauch Chunk, 1835–56. History of the Presbyterian Church in America till 1760.

Webster, Warren. *N. H.*, 1835——. An army surgeon during the Civil War. The Army Medical Staff; Sympathetic Diseases of the Eye, from the German of Mauthner.

Weed, Clarence Moores. *O.*, 1864——. A professor of zoölogy and entomology at the New Hampshire College of Agriculture and the Mechanic Arts, Durham, New Hampshire. Ten New England Blossoms and their Insect Visitors; Insects and Insecticides; Fungi and Fungicides; Spraying Crops. *Hou. Ju.*

Weed, Thurlow. *N. Y.*, 1797–1882. A journalist of note who founded The Albany Evening Journal in 1830. Letters from Europe; Autobiography. *See Memoir by Thurlow Weed Barnes. Hou.*

Weeden, William Babcock. *R. I.*, 1834——. A woollen manufacturer of Providence. The Morality of Prohibitory Liquor Laws; Social Law of Labor; The Economic and Social History of New England, 1620–1789. *Hou. Rob.*

Weeks, Edwin Lord. *Ms.*, 1849——. An artist of note. From the Black Sea through Persia and India. *Har.*

Weeks, John M——. *Ct.*, 1788–1858. An inventor of Salisbury, Vermont. Manual on Bees; History of Salisbury.

Weeks, Robert Kelley. *N. Y.*, 1840–1876. A lawyer and verse-writer of New York city whose poems are not without individuality and a very measurable degree of charm. Twenty Poems; Episodes and Lyric Pieces. *Ho.*

Weeks, Stephen Beauregard. *N. C.*, 1865——. An historical writer. Bibliography of the Historical Literature of North Carolina; Church and State in North Carolina; The Press of North Carolina in the Eighteenth Century; Southern Quakers and Slavery. *J. H. U.*

Weeks, William Raymond. *Ct.*, 1783–1848. A Presbyterian clergyman of Newark, New Jersey. Nine Sermons; Pilgrim's Progress in the Nineteenth Century; Scripture Catechism.

Weems, Mason Locke. *Va.*, 1759–1825. An Episcopal clergyman, famous as a book agent in his day, but at one time rector of Pohick Church, Mount Vernon, where Washington attended. He was an erratic personage whose regard for truth is far from being the strongest feature of his biographies. His Life of Washington, which as early as 1811 had reached an eleventh edition, is still the most popular life of its subject, as from some points of view it is the most entertaining. He wrote, also, Lives of Marion, Penn, and Franklin, which are as untrustworthy as his more noted performance. *Lip.*

Weidenmeyer, John William. 1819–1896. A writer of New York city. Catalogue of North American Butterflies; Real and Ideal, a volume of verse; Themes and Translations; American Fish and How to Catch Them; From Alpha to Omega.

Weidner, Revere Franklin. *Pa.*, 1851——. A Lutheran clergyman, professor of systematic theology at Augustana Seminary, Rock Island, 1885–1891, and subsequently at the Lutheran Seminary, Chicago. Commentary on Mark; Exegetical Theology; Historical Theology; System of Dogmatic Theology; Grammar of New Testament Greek; Commentary on the Hebrew Text of Obadiah; Method for Study of New Testament Greek. *Scr.*

Weir, James. *Ky.*, 1821——. A Kentucky romancer. Lonz Powers, or the Regulators; Simon Kenton; Winter Lodge.

Weir, John Ferguson. *N. Y.*, 1841——. The director of the School of Fine Arts at Yale University from 1869, and professor of painting and design there. The Way: the Nature and Means of Revelation. *Hou.*

Weiss [wīss], John. *Ms.*, 1818–1879. A Unitarian clergyman of very radical views who was pastor at Watertown, Massachusetts, and was prominent as an abolitionist. Wit, Humor, and Shakespeare; American Religion; The Immortal Life; Life of Theodore Parker. *Rob.*

Weiss, Mrs. Susan Archer [Talley]. *Va.*, 1835——. A verse-writer of New York city whose poems were first collected in 1859.

Weisse, John Adam. *F.*, 1810–1888. A philologist, born in Lorraine, who came to America in 1840, and ten years later settled in New York city, where he was president of the New York Philological Society. Key to the French Language; Origin, Progress, and Destiny of the English Language and Literature; The Obelisk and Freemasonry.

Welby, Mrs. Amelia [Coppuck]. *Md.*, 1819–1852. A versifier of Louisville whose sentimental lyrics attained an extraordinary popularity in their author's lifetime. Poems by Amelia. *See Griswold's Female Poets of America; Coggeshall's Poets of the West.*

Welch, Adonijah Strong. *Ct.*, 1821–1889. A lawyer and educator of Michigan and Iowa, president of Iowa Agricultural College, 1869–83. Analysis of the English Sentence; Object Lessons; Talks on Psychology; The Teacher's Psychology.

Welch, John. *O.*, 1805——. A jurist of Ohio. Mathematical Curiosities; Index Digest of Ohio Decisions.

Welch, Philip Henry. *N. Y.*, 1849–1889. A journalist and humourist of New York city. The Tailor-made Girl; Said In Fun. *Scr.*

Welch, Ransom Bethune. *N. Y.*, *c.* 1825–1890. A Presbyterian clergyman, professor of Christian theology at Auburn Seminary. Faith and Modern

Thought; Outlines of Christian Theology.

Welch, William Henry. *Ct.*, 1850——. A Baltimore physician, professor of pathology in Johns Hopkins University from 1884. General Pathology of Fever.

Weld, Mrs. Angelina Emily [Grimke]. *S. C.*, 1805–1879. Wife of T. D. Weld, *infra*, and daughter of J. F. Grimke, *supra*. Letters to Catharine Beecher, a review of the slavery question; Appeal to the Christian Women of the South; Sacred Palmlands.

Weld, Horatio Hastings. *Ms.*, 1811–1888. An Episcopal clergyman of Riverton, New Jersey. Corrected Proofs; Life of Christ; Women of the Scriptures.

Weld, Theodore Dwight. *Ct.*, 1803–1895. A reformer of Boston, long prominent as an abolitionist. The Bible Against Slavery; American Slavery As It Is; Slavery and the Internal Slave Trade in the United States.

Weller, George. *Ms.*, 1790–1841. An Episcopal clergyman once prominent in Tennessee and Mississippi. Vindication of the Church; The Weller Tracts.

Welles, Charles Stuart. 186——. A physician who has published Boheme (verse); Lilian; The New Marriage and Other Uniform Laws.

Welles, Gideon. *Ct.*, 1808–1878. A journalist and politician, secretary of the navy, 1861–69. Lincoln and Seward.

Wellington, Arthur Mellen. *Ms.*, 1847–1895. A civil engineer of distinction. The Computation of Earthwork from Diagrams; The Economic Theory of the Location of Railways; Car-Builders' Dictionary; Field Work of Railway Location. *See Annual Cyclopædia, 1895. Wil.*

Wells, Mrs. Catherine Boott [Gannett]. *E.*, 1838——. Daughter of E. S. Gannett, *supra*. A Boston essayist and novelist who has contributed largely to periodicals. In the Clearings; Miss Curtis; Two Modern Women; About People, a collection of essays; several Sunday-school manuals of ethics and normal methods. *Hou. Lip.*

Wells, David Ames. *Ms.*, 1828——. A distinguished writer on economics. Familiar Science; Science of Common Things; Our Merchant Marine; Primer of Tariff Reform; Practical Economics; Local Taxation; Robinson Crusoe's Money; Study of Mexico; Recent Economic Changes; Relation of the Tariff to Wages; Principles of Taxation; Production and Distribution of Wealth. *Ap. Har. Put.*

Wells, Henry Parkhurst. *R. I.*, 1842——. A lawyer of New York city. City Boys in the Woods; Fly Rods and Fly Tackle; The American Salmon Fisherman. *Har.*

Wells, J—— C——. 18——. A legal writer of Ohio. Delineation of the Law of Limitation in Illinois; My Uncle Toby: his Table Talks and Reflections; Questions of Law and Fact; Treatise on the Doctrines of Res Adjudicata and Stare Decisis; On the Separate Property of Married Women under the Separate Enabling Acts; E Pluribus Unum; Magna Charta, or the Rise and Progress of Constitutional Civil Liberty in England and America; The Jurisdiction of Courts; Powers and Duties of Ohio County Commissioners.

Wells, Mrs. Kate Gannett. *See Wells, Mrs. Catherine.*

Wells, Samuel Roberts. *Ct.*, 1820–1875. A phrenologist of New York city, long a member of the publishing house of Fowler & Wells. The New Physiognomy; Wedlock, or the Right Relations of the Sexes.

Wells, William Harvey. *Ct.*, 1812–1885. An educator of Chicago, superintendent of the city public schools, 1856–64. Historical Authorship of English Grammar; several popular text-books on English Grammar.

Wells, William Vincent. *Ms.*, 1826——. Great-grandson of S. Adams, *supra*. Explorations in Honduras; Walker's Expedition to Nicaragua; Life of Samuel Adams.

Welsh, Alfred Hix. *O.*, 1850–1889. A professor of English in Ohio State University from 1885. Development of English Literature and Language; English Literature in the Eighteenth Century; The Conflict of Ages; Man and His Relations; Plane Trigonometry. *Sil. Sc.*

Welsh, Herbert. *Pa.*, 1851——. A philanthropist of Philadelphia, prominent as a champion of the rights of the Indians. Civilization among the Sioux Indians; Four Weeks among some of the Sioux Tribes; A Visit to the Navajo, Pueblo, and Hualpais Indians.

Wendell, Barrett. *Ms.*, 1855——. An assistant professor of English at Harvard University. The Duchess Emilia, a romance; Rankell's Remains, a novel; Life of Cotton Mather, *supra;* English Composition; Stelligeri, and Other Essays; William Shakspere, a Study in Elizabethan Literature; Ralegh in Guiana, a play. *Do. Scr.*

Wesselhoeft, Conrad. *G.*, 1834——. A well-known homœopathic physician of Boston, professor of pathology and therapeutics in the Boston University School of Medicine, who has translated Hahnemann's Organon and contributed extensively to homœopathic journals.

Wesselhoeft, Mrs. Elizabeth Foster [Pope]. *Ms.*, 1840——. Wife of C. Wesselhoeft, *supra.* A Boston writer of popular juvenile tales. Jerry the Blunderer; Sparrow the Tramp; Flipwing the Spy; Old Rough the Miser; The Winds, the Woods, and the Wanderer; Frowzle, the Runaway. *Rob.*

West, Andrew Fleming. *Pa.*, 1853——. A professor of Latin in Princeton College from 1883. The Philobiblion of Richard de Bury; Alcuin and the Rise of the Christian Schools. *Scr.*

West, Mary Allen. *Il.*, 1837–1892. An Illinois educator who was Knox County superintendent of schools, 1873–1892. Childhood: its Care and Culture.

West, Nathaniel. *I.*, 1794–1864. A Presbyterian clergyman of Philadelphia. The Ark of God the Safety of the Nation; Popery the Prop of European Despotism; Babylon the Great; Right and Left Hand Blessings of God; Complete Analysis of the Whole Bible.

West, Stephen. *Ct.*, 1735–1819. A Congregational clergyman, pastor at Stockbridge, Massachusetts, 1759–1819. Essay on Moral Agency; Life of Reverend Samuel Hopkins, *supra ;* Evidence of the Divinity of Christ; Duty and Obligation of Christians to Marry Only in the Lord. *See Sprague's Annals of the American Pulpit.*

Westcott, Thompson. *Pa.*, 1820–1888. A Philadelphia journalist, editor of The Sunday Dispatch, 1848–84. Life of John Fitch, the Inventor of the Steamboat; The Tax-payer's Guide; Official Guide to Philadelphia; Historic Mansions of Philadelphia. *Co.*

Weston, Mrs. Mary Catherine [North]. *N. Y.*, 1822–1882. Calvary Catechism; Synopsis of the Bible; Jewish Antiquities; Biography of Old and New Testament Characters. *Dut.*

Weston, Roxana. 1800–1891. A verse-writer of Skowhegan, Maine, whose poems were published in 1889.

Wetherell, Elizabeth. *See Warner, Susan.*

Wetherill, Charles Mayer. *Pa.*, 1825–1871. A professor of chemistry at Lehigh University, 1866–71; The Manufacture of Vinegar.

Wetherill, Julie K. *See Baker, Mrs. J.*

Wetmore, Mrs. Elizabeth [Bisland]. *Ts.*, 1863——. A journalist of New York city. A Flying Trip Around the World. *Har.*

Wetmore, Prosper Montgomery. *Ct.*, 1798–1876. A once prominent citizen of New York city. Lexington, and Other Fugitive Poems; Observations on the War with Mexico.

Wharey, James. *N. C.*, 1789–1842. A Presbyterian clergyman of Goochland County, Virginia. Baptism; Sketches of Church History. *See Sprague's Annals of the American Pulpit.*

Wharton, Anne Hollingsworth. *Pa.*, *c.* 1845——. A Philadelphia writer. The Wharton Family; Virgilia; St. Bartholomew's Eve; Colonial Days and Dames; Through Colonial Doorways; A Last Century Maid, and Other Stories for Children; Martha Washington, a biography. *Lip. Scr.*

Wharton, Charles Henry. *Md*, 1748–1833. An Episcopal clergyman of Burlington, New Jersey, rector of St. Mary's Church, 1798–1833. Reply to Bishop Carroll's Address to the Roman Catholics of America; Proofs of the Divinity of Christ; Concise View of the Principal Points of Controversy between Protestant and Roman Catholic churches.

Wharton, Francis. *Pa.*, 1820–1889. Son of T. I. Wharton, *infra.* An Episcopal clergyman of Boston, professor of ecclesiastical and international law in the Episcopal Theological School at Cambridge. Criminal Law of the United States; Medical Jurisprudence; State Trials of the United States; The Silence of Scripture; Treatise on Theism; Precedents of Indictments; The Law of Homicide in the United States; The Conflict of Laws; Law of Agency and Agents; Digest of International Law (with M. Stillé, *supra*); The Law of Negligence; Commentary on the Law of Evidence in Civil Issues; The Law of Contracts. *Lip.*

Wharton, Henry. *Pa.*, 1827–1880. Son of T. I. Wharton, *infra.* A lawyer of Philadelphia. Practical and Elementary Treatise on the Law of Vicinage.

Wharton, Thomas Isaac. *Pa.*, 1791–1856. A lawyer of Philadelphia. Digest of Cases in United States Court, Third District; Reports of Cases in Pennsylvania Supreme Court; Memoir of William Rawle, *supra.*

Wharton, Thomas Isaac. *Pa.*, 1859——. Son of H. Wharton, *supra.* A journalist. A Latter Day Saint; Hannibal of New York.

Wheat, John Thomas. *D. C.*, 1800–1888. An Episcopal clergyman in Tennessee who published a very popular Preparation for Holy Communion.

Wheatley, Charles Moore. *E.*, 1822–1882. A mineralogist of Phœnixville, Pennsylvania, who published a Catalogue of the Shells of the United States.

Wheatley, Phillis. *See Peters, Mrs.*

Wheatley, Richard. *E.*, 1831——. A Methodist clergyman of New Jersey. Cathedrals and Abbeys in Great Britain and Ireland. *Har.*

Wheaton, Henry. *R. I.*, 1785–1848. A diplomatist and an eminent authority upon international law, chargé d'affaires to Denmark, 1827–35, minister to Prussia, 1835–45. History of the Progress of the Law of Nations; Elements of International Law (completed by Lawrence); History of the Northmen; Reports of Cases in United States Supreme Court; Digest of Supreme Court Decisions from 1789 to 1820; Life of William Pinkney in Sparks's American Biography. *See Westminster Review, July, 1847; Allibone's Dictionary.*

Whedon, Daniel Denison. *N. Y.*, 1808–1885. A Methodist clergyman, editor of The Methodist Quarterly Review, 1856–84. The Freedom of the Will; Commentary on the New Testament; Commentary on the Old Testament; Essays, Reviews, and Discourses; Statements: Theological and Critical. *Meth.*

Wheeler, Andrew Carpenter. "Nym Crynkle." *N. Y.*, 1835——. A dramatic and musical critic of New York city. The Chronicles of Milwaukee; The Twins, a comedy; The Primrose Path of Dalliance, a theatrical tale.

Wheeler, Benjamin Ide. *Ms.*, 1854——. A professor of comparative philology at Cornell University from 1886, and of Greek also from 1888. Life of Alexander the Great; The Greek Noun Accents; Introduction to Study of History and Language. *Put.*

Wheeler, Charles Gardiner. *Ms.*, 1855——. Nephew of W. A. Wheeler, *infra.* A writer formerly of Winchendon, Massachusetts, and later of Topsham, Maine. Who Wrote It? a literary index, and Familiar Allusions, both begun by his uncle, were completed by him. The Course of Empire: Outlines of the Chief Political Changes in the History of the World. *Hou.*

Wheeler, Charles Stearns. *Me.*, 1816–1843. A classical scholar who published an edition of Herodotus from the text of Schweighäuser.

Wheeler, Crosby Howard. *Me.*, 1823——. A missionary to Turkey. Little Children in Eden; Letters from Eden; Ten Years on the Euphrates; Odds and Ends; Grace Illustrated.

Wheeler, Daniel Hilton. *N. Y.*, 1829——. A Methodist clergyman, president of Allegheny College, Meadville, Pennsylvania, 1883–87. Brigandage in South Italy; By-Ways of Literature; Our Industrial Utopia and its Unhappy Citizens. *Mg.*

Wheeler, Henry Nathan. *Ms.*, 1850——. Formerly an instructor in mathematics at Harvard University and now engaged in educational publishing work in Boston. Plane and Spherical Trigonometry; The Elements of Logarithms; Second Lessons in Arithmetic. *Gi. Hou.*

Wheeler, John Hill. *N. C.*, 1806–1882. A diplomatist who was minister to Nicaragua, 1854–57. History of North Carolina; Legislative Manual of North Carolina; Reminiscences and Memoirs of North Carolina.

Wheeler, Junius Brutus. *N. C.*, 1830–1886. Brother of J. H. Wheeler, *supra*. A military engineer, professor at West Point, 1866–85. Civil Engineering; Art and Science of War; Elements of Field Fortifications; Military Engineering.

Wheeler, Mrs. Mary Sparks. *E.*, 1835——. A Philadelphia writer. Poems for the Fireside; Modern Cosmogony and the Bible. *Meth.*

Wheeler, William Adolphus. *Ms.*, 1833–1874. A librarian of Boston who, besides editing an edition of Webster's Dictionary, was author of Noted Names of Fiction; Familiar Allusions; Who Wrote It? a literary index. *Hou. Le.*

Wheelwright, John Tyler. *Ms.*, 1856——. A Boston lawyer. Rollo's Journey to Cambridge (with F. Stimson, *supra*); A Child of the Century, a novel; A Bad Penny. *Lam. Scr.*

Wheildon, William Willder. *Ms.*, 1805–1892. A journalist of Charlestown, Massachusetts, 1827–70, and long a resident of Concord, in the same State. Letters from Nahant; Contributions to Thought; New History of the Battle of Bunker Hill; The Arctic Regions; Curiosities of History.

Whelan, James. *I.*, 1823–1878. A Roman Catholic bishop of Nashville. Catena Aurena, or Papal Infallibility no Novelty.

Whelpley, Samuel. *Ms.*, 1766–1817. A Baptist clergyman (from 1806 Presbyterian) and educator of New Jersey. Letters on Capital Punishment; a once popular Compend of History; The Triangle, a theological discussion.

Whipple, Edwin Percy. *Ms.*, 1819–1886. A Boston essayist and critic, whose writing was as discriminating as it was vigourous and epigrammatic in style. Character and Characteristic Men; Literature and Life; Essays and Reviews; Success and its Conditions; Literature of the Age of Elizabeth; Recollections of Eminent Men, with Other Papers; American Literature, and Other Papers; Outlooks on Society, Literature, and Politics; Rufus Choate, a volume of personal recollections. *Har. Hou.*

Whipple, Squire. *Ms.*, 1804–1888. A civil engineer of note. The Way to Happiness; Treatise on Bridge Building; The Doctrine of Central Forces.

Whistler, James Abbott McNeill. *Ms.*, 1834——. An artist who from 1863 to 1892 lived in London, and in Paris from the latter date. Ten O'Clock; The Gentle Art of Making Enemies. *Hou.*

Whitaker, Alexander. *E.*, 1588–after 1613. An Episcopal clergyman who came to Virginia in 1611. He baptized Pocahontas, and officiated at her wedding. Good Newes from Virginia, one of the very first books written in the colony. See Tyler's American Literature.

Whitaker, Epher. *N. J.*, 1820——. A Presbyterian clergyman, pastor at Southold, Long Island, from 1851. The War of Death; New Fruits from an Old Field; Ready for Duty; Collection of Original Hymns; History of Southold, 1640–1740; Old Town Records.

Whitaker, Mrs. Mary Scrimgeour [Furman] [Miller]. *S. C.*, 1820——. A New Orleans writer. Poems; Albert Hasting, a novel.

Whitaker, Nathaniel. *L. I.*, 1732–1795. A Presbyterian clergyman in New England and Virginia, popular in the colonial period. Discourses on Reconciliation; Discourses on Toryism, which were widely read.

Whitcher, Mrs. Frances Miriam [Berry]. *N. Y.*, 1812–1852. A still popular humourist who was the wife of an Episcopal clergyman in Elmira, New York. The Widow Bedott Papers; Widow Spriggins, and Other Sketches.

White, Andrew Dickson. *N. Y.*, 1832——. A distinguished diplomatist and educator, minister to Germany, 1879–81, and to Russia, 1892, president of Cornell University, 1867–85, appointed ambassador to Germany in 1897. Lectures on Mediæval and Modern History; The New Germany; History of the Doctrine of Comets; European Schools of History and Politics; Studies in General History; Paper Money Inflation in France; The Warfare of Science with Theology. *Ap.*

White, Carlos. *Vt.*, 1842——. Ecce Femina, an Attempt to Solve the Woman Question.

White, Catherine Ann. *N. Y.*, 1825–1878. A former Superior of the Convent of the Sacred Heart, New York city. The Students' Mythology; Classical Literature; Bible Literature.

White, Charles. *Ind.*, 1795–1861. A Congregational clergyman and educator, president of Wabash College, Crawfordsville, Indiana, 1841–1861. Essays in Literature and Ethics.

White, Charles Abiathar. *Ms.*, 1826——. The State geologist of Iowa, 1865–70, and on the United States Geological Survey from 1882. Report of Iowa Geological Survey; Physical Geography of Iowa.

White, Charles Ignatius. *Md.*, 1807–1877. A Roman Catholic clergyman of Washington, long pastor of St. Matthew's Church. Life of Mrs. Eliza Seton, *supra*. He translated, from the French, Chateaubriand's Genius of Christianity, and other works.

White, Daniel Appleton. *Ms.*, 1776–1861. A jurist of Salem, Massachusetts. The Jurisdiction of the Massachusetts Court of Probate; New England Congregationalism in its Origin and Purity; Eulogy on Nathaniel Bowditch.

White, Eliza Orne. *N. H.*, 1856——. A writer of Brookline, Massachusetts. Miss Brooks; When Molly was Six, a juvenile tale; Winterborough; A Little Girl of Long Ago; The Coming of Theodora. *Hou. Rob.*

White, Mrs. Ellen G—— [Harmon]. 18——. Wife of James White, *infra*. The Spirit of Prophecy.

White, Emerson Eldridge. *O.*, 1829——. An Ohio educator, superintendent of the Cincinnati public schools from 1883. The Elements of Pedagogy; School Management.

White, Greenough. *Ms.*, 1863——. An Episcopal clergyman and educator, professor of English at the University of the South, Sewanee, Tennessee, 1885–1887, and professor of ecclesiastical history and polity there from 1894. Sketch of the Philosophy of American Literature; The Rise of Papal Supremacy; Outline of the Philosophy of English Literature. *Gi.*

White, Henry. *Ms.*, 1790–1858. A Congregational clergyman of Maine and New Hampshire, who published, The Early History of New England.

White, Henry Clay. *Md.*, 1850——. The State chemist of Georgia from 1880. Complete History of the Cotton Plant; Elementary Geology of Tennessee (with MacAdoo).

White, Horace. *N. H.*, 1834——. A journalist, editor of The Chicago Tribune, 1864–74, and since 1883 one of the editors of The New York Evening Post. The Silver Question; The Tariff Question; Coin's Financial Fool; Money and Banking Illustrated by American History; The Gold Standard. *Gi.*

White, James. 1821——. A Seventh Day Adventist elder who published, Life Incidents of the Great Advent Movement.

White, James Terry. *Ms.*, 1845——. A publisher of New York city, but formerly a resident of San Francisco. His volumes of original verse comprise, Christmas Greeting; Bouquet of California Flowers; Flowers from Arcady; Captive Memories.

White, John. *Ms.*, 1677–1760. A Congregational clergyman, pastor at Gloucester, Massachusetts, 1703–60. The Gospel Treasure in Earthen Vessels; New England's Lamentations for the Decay of Godliness (1735).

White, John Blake. *S. C.*, 1781–1859. An artist, lawyer, and dramatist of Charleston. Foscari; Mysteries of the Castle; Intemperance; Modern Honor; Triumph of Liberty.

White, John Silas. *Ms.*, 1847——. An educator of New York city, master of the Berkeley School from 1880.

Boys' and Girls' Plutarch; Herodotus and Pliny. *Gi.*

White, John Williams. *O.*, 1849——. A professor of Greek at Harvard University from 1877. Greek and Latin at Sight; First Lessons in Greek; The Beginner's Greek Book; An Illustrated Dictionary to Xenophon's Anabasis (with M. H. Morgan). *Gi.*

White, Matthew. 18———. Harry Ascott Abroad; One of the Profession; My Mysterious Fortune.

White, Pliny Holton. *Ct.*, 1822–1869. A Unitarian clergyman of Coventry, Vermont, but prior to 1859 a lawyer there. History of Coventry.

White, Mrs. Rhoda Elizabeth [Waterman]. 18———. Portraits of My Married Friends; From Infancy to Womanhood, a Book for Young Mothers; What Will the World Say? a novel.

White, Richard Grant. *N.Y.*, 1822–1885. An eminent Shakespearean scholar and littérateur of New York city. His critical twelve-volume edition of Shakespeare appeared in 1865, and the Riverside edition in 1883. His original works comprise, Words and Their Uses; Every-Day English; England Without and Within; Biographical and Critical Handbook of Christian Art; Shakespeare's Scholar; Memoirs of Shakespeare; Studies in Shakespeare; The New Gospel of Peace, a political satire; Revelations: a Companion to The New Gospel of Peace; The Fate of Mansfield Humphreys, a novel; The Fall of Man, or the Loves of the Gorillas; The American View of the Copyright Question; The Chronicles of Gotham. *See Atlantic Monthly, February, 1882; Foley's American Authors. Hou.*

White, Sallie Joy. *See White, Mrs. Sarah.*

White, Mrs. Sarah Elizabeth [Joy]. *Me.*, 18———. A Boston journalist. Housekeepers and Homemakers; Business Openings for Girls. *Lo.*

White, William. *Pa.*, 1748–1836. The first Protestant Episcopal bishop of Pennsylvania. Memoir of the Episcopal Church; Lectures on the Catechism; Comparative View of the Controversy Between Calvinists and Arminians, are among his writings. *See Life by Bird Wilson, 1839; Sprague's Annals of the American Pulpit. Dut.*

White, William Allen. *Ks.*, 1868——. The Real Issue, and Other Stories. *Wy.*

White, William Charles. *Ms.*, 1777–1818. A lawyer and dramatist of Worcester, Massachusetts. The Country Cousin; The Poor Lodger; Compendium of the Laws of Massachusetts.

White, William N——. *N.Y.*, 1819–1861. A bookseller of Athens, Georgia, who edited The Southern Cultivator. Gardening for the South; Scientific Gardening.

Whitehead, Charles Edward. *N. Y.*, 1829——. The Campfires of the Everglades, or Wild Sports in the South.

Whitehead, William Adee. *N. J.*, 1810–1884. A prominent citizen of Newark, New Jersey. Biographical Sketch of William Franklin; Contributions to the Early History of Perth Amboy; East Jersey Under the Proprietary Governments.

Whiteley, Mrs. Isabel [Nixon]. *N. Y.*, 1859——. A Philadelphia writer. The Falcon of Langéac, a romance. *Cop.*

Whitfield, Henry. *E.*, 1597–1658. A Puritan clergyman who came to New England in 1637, and was one of the founders of the New Haven colony. He returned to England in 1650. Helps to stir up to Christian Duties; The Light Appearing; Strength out of Weakness.

Whiting, Charles Goodrich. *Vt.*, 1842——. A journalist of Springfield, Massachusetts, on the editorial staff of The Republican. The Saunterer: Essays on Nature. *Hou.*

Whiting, Henry. *Ms.*, c. 1790–1851. A United States army officer. Otway, the Son of the Forest, a Poem; Sanilæ, a Poem; The Age of Steam; Life of Zebulon Pike, in Sparks's American Biography.

Whiting, Lilian. *N. Y.*, 185——. A Boston journalist. From Dreamland Sent, a volume of verse; The World Beautiful, two collections of essays; After her Death: The Story of a Summer. *Rob.*

Whiting, Samuel. *E.*, 1597–1679. A Puritan clergyman, pastor at Lynn, Massachusetts, 1636–79. Oratio quam Comitijs Cantab. Americanis, etc.; The Last Judgment; Abraham Interceding for Sodom.

Whiting, William. *Ms.*, 1813–1873. Descendant of S. Whiting, *supra*. A Boston jurist whose chief work, The War Powers of the President and the Legislative Powers of Congress, has been widely read. *See Duyckinck's American Literature. Le.*

Whitlock, George Clinton. *Vt.*, 1808——. A Methodist clergyman and educator of Iowa. Elements of Geometry; New System of Surveying.

Whitman, Bernard. *Ms.*, 1796–1834. A Unitarian clergyman, pastor at Waltham, Massachusetts, 1826–34, and prominent as a controversialist. On Denying the Lord Jesus; Letters on Religious Liberty; Village Sermons; Friendly Letters to a Universalist. *See Sprague's Annals of the American Pulpit; Memoir by J. Whitman, infra.*

Whitman, Charles Otis. *Me.*, 1842——. A naturalist of note, head professor of zoölogy in the University of Chicago from 1892. He established The Journal of Morphology in 1887. Methods of Research in Microscopical Anatomy and Embryology.

Whitman, Jason. *Ms.*, 1798–1848. Brother of B. Whitman, *supra*. A Unitarian clergyman of Portland, Maine. Memoir of B. Whitman, *supra;* Young Man's Assistant; Young Lady's Aid to Usefulness; Week Day Religion; Discussions on the Lord's Prayer.

Whitman, Mrs. Sarah Helen [Power]. *R. I.*, 1813–1878. A poet of Providence whose Still Day in Autumn, her finest effort, still finds an honoured place in anthologies. Hours of Life, and Other Poems; Edgar Poe and his Critics. A complete edition of her poems appeared in 1879. *See Easy Chair of Harper's Magazine, September, 1878.*

Whitman, Walter [commonly **Walt**]. *N. Y.*, 1819–1892. A poet regarding whose claims to the title much controversy has raged. During the Civil War he served as a volunteer nurse in the Washington hospitals, and, after holding a government clerkship till 1873, removed to Camden, New Jersey, where the rest of his life was passed. Leaves of Grass, his first book, appeared in 1855, a vigourous protest against established rules of versification in its utter formlessness. Drum Taps, which included the now famous Lincoln elegies, When Lilacs Last in the Dooryard Bloomed, and O Captain, My Captain, followed in 1865. The republication of his poems in England in 1868 aroused instant attention there, and excited extravagant praise in some quarters. His rejection of rhyme and metre will probably always repel the mass of readers. His later works include, After All Not to Create Only; A Passage to India; As a Strong Bird on Pinions Free; Two Rivulets; November Boughs; Good Bye My Fancy; Sands at Seventy; Specimen Days and Collect; in prose, Franklin Evans, or the Inebriate; Democratic Vistas; Memoranda During the War. *See O'Connor's Good Gray Poet; Burroughs's Notes on Whitman, and Study of Whitman; Walt Whitman, by R. M. Bucke; Whitman, by W. Clarke; Whitman: a Study of Democracy, by Triggs; Whitman: a Study, by J. H. Symonds; Annual Cyclopedia, 1892; Life of, by W. S. Kennedy, supra; Cheney's That Dome in Air; In Re Walt Whitman; Foley's American Authors; T. Donaldson's Walt Whitman the man.*

Whitmarsh, Caroline. *See Guild, Mrs.*

Whitmore, William Henry. *Ms.*, 1836——. A genealogist of Boston. American Genealogy; Elements of Heraldry; History of the Old State House, Boston; and many genealogies.

Whitney, Mrs. Adeline Dutton [Train]. *Ms.*, 1824——. A very popular writer for girls. She has lived at Milton, Massachusetts, for many years. Friendly Letters to Girl Friends; Faith Gartney's Girlhood; The Gayworthys; A Summer in Leslie Goldthwaite's Life; Hitherto; We Girls; The Other Girls; Real Folks; Sights and Insights; Odd or Even?; Bonnyborough; Boys at Chequasset; Homespun Yarns; Ascutney Street; A Golden Gossip; Patience Strong's Outings; Mother Goose for Grown Folks. She has also written, The Open Mystery: A Reading of the Mosaic Story; Just How, a Key to the Cook Books; and in verse, Pansies; Daffodils; Holy Tides; Bird Talk; White Memories. *See Vedder's American Writers. Hou.*

Whitney, Anne. 1821——. A sculptor and poet of Boston. Her only volume of Poems appeared in 1859. Bertha is her best known poem.

Whitney, Caspar. *Ms.*, 1861——. A journalist of New York city, a prominent advocate of amateur sports. A Sporting Pilgrimage; On Snow Shoes to the Barren Grounds. *Har.*

Whitney, James Amaziah. *N. Y.*, 1839——. An agricultural chemist. Relation of the Patent Laws to Development of Agriculture; The Chinese and the Chinese Question; Shobab, a Tale of Bethesda in verse; Sonnets and Lyrics; The Children of Lamech (verse).

Whitney, [Joseph] Ernest. *Ct.*, 1858–1893. An instructor in English for some years at Yale University. Poems of the Pike's Peak Region (1890).

Whitney, Josiah Dwight. *Ms.*, 1819–1896. A professor of geology at Harvard University from 1865, and State geologist of California, 1860–74. The United States; The Metallic Wealth of the United States; Barometric Hypsometry; Polypetalæ and Gamopetalæ; Contributions to American Geology; Names and Places, Studies in Geography and Topographical Nomenclature; Geological Survey of California; Yosemite Guide Book; Geological Survey of Iowa. *Lip. Lit.*

Whitney, Mrs. Louisa [Goddard]. *E.*, 1819–1882. Wife of J. D. Whitney, *supra.* The Burning of the Convent; Peasy's Childhood: an Autobiography.

Whitney, Peter. *Ms.*, 1744–1815. A Congregational clergyman, pastor at Northborough, Massachusetts, 1767–1815. History of Worcester County (1793).

Whitney, Thomas Richard. *N.Y.*, 1804–1858. A journalist of New York city, member of Congress, 1855–57. The Ambuscade, a Poem; Defence of the American Policy.

Whitney, William Dwight. *Ms.*, 1827–1894. Brother of J. D. Whitney, *supra.* A philologist of eminence, professor of Sanskrit at Yale University from 1854, and of comparative philology, also, from 1870. He edited The Century Dictionary. Language and the Study of Language; Compendious German Grammar; Oriental and Linguistic Studies; Life and Growth of Language; Essentials of English Grammar; Sanskrit Grammar; Practical French Grammar; Roots, Verb Forms, and Primary Derivatives of the Sanskrit Language; Max Müller's Science of Language. *See Atlantic Monthly, March, 1895. Ap. Gi. Ho. Scr.*

Whiton, James Morris. *Ms.*, 1833——. Grandson of J. M. Whiton, *infra.* A Congregational clergyman of New York city. New Points to Old Texts; Is Eternal Punishment Endless?; The Gospel of the Resurrection; Beyond the Shadow; The Divine Satisfaction; Early Pupils of the Spirit; The Evolution of Revelation; The Law of Liberty; Turning Points of Thought and Conduct; Gloria Patri. *Wh.*

Whiton, John Milton. *Ms.*, 1788–1856. A Presbyterian clergyman of Antrim, New Hampshire. Sketches of the Early History of New Hampshire, 1623–1833.

Whitsitt, William Heth. *Tn.*, 1841——. A Baptist clergyman of Louisville, professor of ecclesiastical history at the Southern Baptist Theological Seminary from 1872. History of the Rise of Infant Baptism; History of Communion Among Baptists; Life and Times of Jude Caleb Wallace; A Question in Baptist History. *Mor.*

Whittaker, Frederick. *E.*, 1838——. Son of H. Whittaker, *infra.* A Federal cavalry officer during the Civil War, and subsequently a journalist of New York city. A Defence of Dime Novels by a Writer of Them; Life of General Custer; Cadet Button, a Tale of American Army Life; Bel Rubio, a novel.

Whittaker, Henry. *W.*, 1808–1881. A law-office clerk in New York city. Practice and Pleading Under the Codes; Analysis of Decisions in Practice and Pleading.

Whittaker, James Thomas. *O.*, 1843——. A prominent surgeon of Cincinnati. Lectures on Physiology;

History of Tuberculosis; Theory and Practice of Medicine. *Clke.*

Whittemore, Thomas. *Ms.*, 1800–1861. A Universalist clergyman of Boston. History of Modern Universalism; Notes and Illustrations of the Parables; Commentaries on Daniel and Revelations; Life of Hosea Ballou; Autobiography.

Whittier, John Greenleaf. *Ms.*, 1807–1892. A famous New England poet, born at Haverhill, Massachusetts, December 17, 1807, and all his life a member of the Society of Friends. He was one of the early abolitionists, and edited The Pennsylvania Freeman, 1838–39. After 1840 he lived at Amesbury, Massachusetts. Among the most characteristic of his shorter poems are, My Soul and I; The Eternal Goodness; In School Days; The Last Walk in Autumn; The Playmates; My Psalm. His prose writings include, The Stranger in Lowell (1845); The Supernaturalism of New England (1847); Leaves from Margaret Smith's Journal (1849); Old Portraits and Modern Sketches (1850); Literary Recreations and Miscellanies (1854). His work in verse comprises, Legends of New England (1831); Moll Pitcher (1832); Mogg Megone (1836); Poems (1838); Lays of My Home (1843); Voices of Freedom (1849); Songs of Labor (1850); The Chapel of the Hermits (1853); A Sabbath Scene (1853); The Panorama (1856); Home Ballads and Poems (1860); In War Time (1862); National Lyrics (1865); Snow-Bound (1866); The Tent on the Beach (1867); Among the Hills (1868); Ballads of New England (1870); Miriam (1870); The Pennsylvania Pilgrim (1872); Hazel Blossoms (1875); Mabel Martin (1876); Centennial Hymn (1876); The Vision of Echard, and Other Poems (1878); The King's Missive, and Other Poems (1881); The Bay of Seven Islands, and Other Poems (1883); St. Gregory's Guest, and Other Poems (1886); At Sundown (1890–92). He was also the compiler of Songs of Three Centuries; Child-Life; and Child-Life in Prose; and the editor of John Woolman's Journal. *See Scribner's Magazine, August, 1879; Harper's Magazine, February, 1883; Century Magazine, December, 1883; Hazeltine's Chats About Books; Steuart's Letters to Living Authors; Lives by Underwood, Brown, Pickard, W. J. Linton; Personal Recollections of, by Mrs. Claflin; Whittier: Notes of his Life and of his Friendships, in Authors and Friends, by Mrs. Fields; Memorial of, from his Native City, 1893; Allibone's Dictionary; Annual Cyclopedia, 1892; Whittier, by B. O. Flower; Cheney's That Dome in Air; American Song, by A. B. Simonds; Foley's American Authors. Hou.*

Whittingham, William Rollinson. *N. Y.*, 1805–1879. The fourth Protestant Episcopal bishop of Maryland. Fifteen Sermons. *See Life, by W. F. Brand. Ap.*

Whittlesey, Mrs. Sarah Johnson [Cogswell]. *N. C.*, 1825——. Heart Drops from Memory's Urn; The Stranger's Stratagem, and Other Stories; Herbert Hamilton; Bertha the Beauty; Spring Buds and Summer Blossoms.

Wiard, Norman. *Ont.*, 1826–1896. An inventor and military engineer of distinction whose specialty was the manufacture of ordnance. The Solution of the Ordnance Problem.

Wickersham, James Pyle. *Pa.*, 1825–1891. An educator of Lancaster, Pennsylvania, State superintendent of public instruction, 1866–81, minister to Denmark, 1882. School Economy; Methods of Instruction. *Lip.*

Wickes, Stephen. *L. I.*, 1813–1889. A physician of Orange, New Jersey. Living and Dying: their Psychics and Physics; History of Medicine in New Jersey; Sepulture: its History, Methods, and Requisites; History of the Newark Mountains.

Wickes, Thomas. *N. Y.*, 1814–1870. Brother of S. Wickes, *supra*. A Presbyterian clergyman of Marietta, Ohio. Exposition of the Apocalypse; The Son of Man; The Household; Economy of the Ages.

Wiggin, Kate Douglas. *See Riggs, Mrs.*

Wigglesworth, Edward. *Ms.*, 1693–1765. Son of M. Wigglesworth, *infra*. A Congregational clergyman, Hollis professor of theology at Harvard University, 1722–65. An Answer to Mr. Whitefield's Reply to the College Testimony; Doctrine of Reprobation

Briefly Considered, are among his writings.

Wigglesworth, Edward. *Ms.*, 1732–1794. Son of E. Wigglesworth, *supra.* A Congregational clergyman who succeeded his father in the Hollis professorship at Harvard University in 1765. Calculations on American Population; Authority of Tradition Considered.

Wigglesworth, Edward. *Ms.*, 1804–1876. Grandson of E. Wigglesworth, 2d. A lawyer and merchant of Boston who published Reflections, a collection of apothegms. *El.*

Wigglesworth, Michael. *E.*, 1631–1705. A Congregational clergyman, pastor at Malden, Massachusetts, 1656–1705. The Day of Doom, his chief work, appearing in 1662, was for more than a century the most popular poem in New England. It is an epic of the Last Judgment, not without gleams of poetic merit, but full of what must be styled savage theology. Meat Out of the Eater is a much inferior poem, but was very popular for a long period. God's Controversy with New England, also in verse, and A Short Discourse on Eternity, comprise his remaining works. *Tyler's American Literature; Life by John Ward Dean.*

Wight, Orlando Williams. *N. Y.*, 1824–1888. A Universalist clergyman and physician, appointed State geologist of Wisconsin in 1874. The Philosophy of Sir William Hamilton; Lives and Letters of Abelard and Héloise; Lectures on the True, the Beautiful, and the Good; Maxims of Public Health; People and Countries Visited in a Winding Journey round the World. *Ap. Hou.*

Wight, Peter Bonnett. *N. Y.*, 1838——. An architect of New York city. One Phase in the Revival of Fine Arts in America.

Wikoff, Henry. *Pa.*, 1813–1884. A writer whose life after 1834 was passed mainly in Europe. He was commonly known as Chevalier Wikoff. Reminiscences of an Idler; Louis Napoleon Bonaparte; Life of Count d'Orsay; My Courtship and its Consequences; Adventures of a Roving Diplomatist; A New Yorker in the Foreign Office; The Four Civilizations.

Wilbour, Charles Edwin. *R. I.*, 1833–1896. An Egyptologist who has published a Life of Victor Hugo and a number of translations from the French.

Wilbur, Hervey. *Ms.*, 1787–1852. A Congregational clergyman and educator of Massachusetts among whose writings are, Elements of Astronomy; Lexicon of Useful Knowledge.

Wilcox, Cadmus Marcellus. *N. C.*, 1826–1890. A United States army officer. Rifles and Rifle Practice; History of the Mexican War.

Wilcox, Carlos. *N. H.*, 1794–1827. A Congregational clergyman of Hartford, popular as a verse-writer in his day. The Age of Benevolence. *See Duyckinck's American Literature; Griswold's Poets and Poetry of America.*

Wilcox, Mrs. Ella [Wheeler]. *Wis.*, 1855——. A very popular verse-writer and novelist of New York city. Maurine, and Other Poems; Drops of Water, temperance poems; Shells; Poems of Passion; Poems of Pleasure; The Song of the Sandwich; The Beautiful Land of Nod, poems and prose for children; Custer, and Other Poems. Her prose work includes, Men, Women, and Emotions; Mal Moulée; Was It Suicide?; A Double Life; Sweet Danger; Perdita and Other Stories; An Erring Woman's Love; Men, Women, and Emotions; Adventures of Miss Volney. *See Bibliography of Wisconsin.*

Wilcox, Marrion. *Ga.*, 1858——. A New Haven writer. Real People; Señora Villena.

Wilcox, Phineas Bacon. *Ct.*, 1798–1863. A lawyer of Columbus, Ohio. Condensed Reports of Ohio Supreme Court; Ohio Forms and Practice; A Few Thoughts by a Member of the Bar; Practical Forms in Action, etc.; Practical Forms Under Code of Civil Procedure.

Wilde, Richard Henry. *I.*, 1789–1847. A New Orleans lawyer who wrote Conjectures and Researches Concerning Tasso, but is known chiefly as the author of the graceful lyric, My Life is Like the Summer Rose. *See Griswold's Poets and Poetry of America; Mrs. Johnson's Our Familiar Songs.*

Wilder, Alexander. *N. Y.*, 1823——. A physician and journalist of

New York city. Lectures on Scientific and Literary Subjects; Intermarriage of Kindred; Life Eternal; The Ganglionic Nervous System, are his principal writings.

Wilder, Burt Green. *Ms.*, 1841——. A physician, professor of physiology at Cornell University from 1867. What Young People Should Know; Emergencies; Health Notes for Students. *Est. Put.*

Wilder, Daniel Webster. *Ms.*, 1832——. A Kansas lawyer and journalist who has published The Annals of Kansas.

Wildwood, Will. *See Pond, F. E.*

Wiley, Calvin Henderson. *N. C.*, 1819–1887. A Presbyterian clergyman and educator in the Carolinas. Adventures of Old Dan Tucker; Utopia, a Picture of Early Life at the South; Scriptural Views of National Trials; Alamance, a novel; Roanoke, or Where is Utopia? *See Hart's American Literature.*

Wiley, Harvey Washington. *Ind.*, 1844——. A chemist of note, chief of the chemical division of the United States Department of Agriculture from 1883. Principles and Practice of Agricultural Analysis: Part I., Soils; Part II., Fertilizers; Part III., Agricultural Products.

Wiley, Isaac William. *Pa.*, 1825–1884. A bishop of the Methodist Church from 1872. The Fallen Missionaries of Fuh Chan; The Religion of the Family; China and Japan: a Record of Observations. *Meth.*

Wilkes, Charles. *N. Y.*, 1798–1877. A naval officer of distinction. Narrative of United States Exploring Expedition During the Years 1838–42; Western America; Theory of the Winds.

Wilkes, George. *N. Y.*, 1820–1885. A journalist of New York city, editor of The Spirit of the Times from 1850. History of California (1845); Europe in a Hurry; Shakespeare from an American Point of View.

Wilkeson, Frank. *N.Y.*, 1845——. A journalist. Recollections of a Private Soldier in the Army of the Potomac. *Put.*

Wilkie, Franc[is] Bangs. *N. Y.*, 1832–92. A Chicago journalist. Petrolia, or the Oil Regions of the United States (1865); Davenport, Past and Present; Walks About Chicago; The Chicago Bar; Great Inventions and Their Influence on Civilization; The Gambler, a Story of Chicago Life; Pen and Powder; Personal Reminiscences. *Hou.*

Wilkins, John Hubbard. *N. H.*, 1794–1861. A Boston writer whose Elements of Astronomy (1822) was long popular as a text-book.

Wilkins, Mary Eleanor. *Ms.*, 1862——. A novelist of Randolph, Massachusetts, whose rank as a short-story writer is among the very first, her work displaying the greatest skill in constructive details as well as accurate perception in characterization. Her fictions deal almost entirely with phases of New England rural life. A Humble Romance, and Other Stories; A New England Nun, and Other Stories; Young Lucretia, and Other Stories; The Pot of Gold, a collection of juvenile tales; Jane Field; Pembroke; Madelon; Giles Corey, Yeoman, a Play; Jerome, a Poor Man; The Adventures of Ann; Comfort Pease and her Gold Ring; The Long Arm (with J. E. Chamberlin, *supra*). *Har. Lo. Rev.*

Wilkinson, James. *Md.*, 1757–1825. A soldier who served in the American Revolution and in the War of 1812. Memories of My Own Times. *See Gayarré's Spanish Domination in Louisiana, 1854; Gilmore's Advance Guard of Western Civilization, 1887.*

Wilkinson, John. *Va.*, 1821——. A Confederate naval officer who has published, The Narrative of a Blockade Runner.

Wilkinson, William Cleaver. *Vt.*, 1833——. A Baptist clergyman and educator. Poems; A Free Lance in the Field of Life and Letters; Webster, an Ode; The Baptist Principle; The Epic of Saul; The Dance of Modern Society; College Greek Course in English, and other text-books. *Fl. Fu. Meth.*

Willard, Ashton Rollins. *Vt.*, 1858——. A lawyer of Boston. A Sketch of the Life and Work of the Painter Domenico Morelli; Legislative Handbook Relating to the Preparation of Statutes. *Hou.*

Willard, Mrs. Emma [Hart]. *Ct.*, 1787–1870. A noted educator of Troy, New York. Journal and Letters from France and Great Britain; History of the United States; Universal History in Perspective; Treatise on the Circulation of the Blood; Last Leaves of American History; Poems. She wrote the well-known poem, Rocked in the Cradle of the Deep. *See Life, by John Lord, supra; Hart's American Literature.*

Willard, Frances Elizabeth. *N.Y.*, 1839——. A temperance reformer of prominence. Woman and Temperance; How to Win; Woman in the Pulpit; Nineteen Beautiful Years; Glimpses of Fifty Years; A Great Mother. *See A Woman of the Century. Fu.*

Willard, John. *Ct.*, 1792–1862. An eminent jurist of New York city. Equity Jurisprudence; Treatise on Executors, Administrators, and Guardians; Real Estate and Conveyancing.

Willard, Joseph Augustus. *Ms.*, 1816——. Son of Sydney Willard, *infra.* Clerk of the Superior Court of Massachusetts for Suffolk County, from 1865. His connection with courts of justice began in 1846. Half a Century with Judges and Lawyers. *Hou.*

Willard, Samuel. *Ms.*, 1640–1707. A Congregational clergyman of Boston, president of Harvard University, 1701–07. Of his many works, A Complete Body of Divinity is the best known. Others are, Peril of the Times Displayed; Covenant-Keeping the Way to Blessedness; Ne Sutor Ultra Crepidam. *See Sprague's Annals of the American Pulpit.*

Willard, Sydney. *Ms.*, 1780–1856. A descendant of S. Willard, *supra.* A professor of Hebrew at Harvard University, 1801–31. Hebrew Grammar; Memories of Youth and Manhood.

Willard, Sylvester David. *Ct.*, 1825–1865. An Albany physician, surgeon-general of New York at the time of his death. The Willard Asylum for the Insane was named for him. Biographical Memoirs of Physicians of Albany County; Annals of the Albany County Medical Society.

Willcox, Orlando Bolivar. *Mch.*, 1823——. A United States army officer. Shoepack Recollections; Faca, an Army Memoir.

Willett, Joseph Edgerton. *Ga.* 1826——. A professor of natural science in Mercer University, Macon, Georgia, from 1849. The Wonders of Insect Life.

Willett, William Marinus. *N. Y.*, 1803–1895. A Methodist clergyman and educator. Scenes in the Wilderness; A New Life of Summerfield; Life and Times of Herod the Great; Herod Antipas; The Messiah; The Restitution of All Things.

Willey, Austin. *N. H.*, 1806–1896. A Congregational clergyman of Maine, long prominent as an abolitionist, and the editor of The Advocate of Freedom, 1839–58. After the latter date he lived at Northfield, Minnesota. Family Memorial; History of the Anti-Slavery Cause in State and Nation.

Willey, Benjamin Glazier. *N. H.*, 1796–1867. A Congregational clergyman of New Hampshire who wrote a History of the White Mountains.

Willey, Henry. *N. Y.*, 1824——. A botanist, lawyer, and journalist of New Bedford. List of North American Lichens; Introduction to the Study of Lichens; Synopsis of the Genus Athona.

Williams, Alfred Mason. *Ms.*, 1840–1896. A Providence journalist, editor of The Journal. The Poets and Poetry of Ireland; Studies in Folk-Song and Popular Poetry; Sam Houston and the War of Independence in Texas. *Hou.*

Williams, Mrs. Anna [Bolles]. "Jak." *Ct.*, 1840——. A writer of Springfield, Massachusetts, who has written a number of popular juvenile tales. Birchwood; Professor Johnny; The Fitch Club; Who Saved the Ship? ; Rolf and His Friends; Scotch Caps; Giant Dwarf; Riverside Museum. *Cr.*

Williams, Mrs. Catherine R—— [Arnold]. *R. I.*, c. 1790–1872. A Providence writer. Original Poems; Religion at Home; Tales: National and Revolutionary; Fall River, an Authentic Narrative; Neutral French; Annals of the Aristocracy of Rhode Island; Aristocracy: a novel.

Williams, Charles Frederic. *Ms.*, 1842–1895. The Tariff Laws of the United States, with Explanatory Notes; Index of Cases Overruled by the Courts of America, England, and Ireland from 1873 to 1887. He edited the last eight volumes of The American and English Cyclopædia of Law.

Williams, Edwin. *Ct.*, 1797–1854. A writer of New York city. The Politician's Manual; New Universal Gazetteer; Book of the Constitution; New York as It Is; Arctic Voyages; The Fortunate Puzzler; The Statesman's Manual; The Twelve Stars of the Republic, comprise his chief works.

Williams, Eleazer. 1787?–1858. An Episcopal clergyman at Green Bay, Wisconsin, supposed by some persons to have been Louis XVII. of France. He published A Spelling-Book in the Language of the Seven Iroquois Nations, and other works in Iroquois. *See The Lost Prince, by Hanson.*

Williams, Francis Howard. *Pa.*, 1844——. A littérateur of Philadelphia. His plays include, The Princess Elizabeth, a Lyric Drama; The Higher Education; A Reformer in Ruffles; Master and Man; Theodora, a Christmas Pastoral. Other works are, Atman, a Story· The Flute Player, and Other Poems; Pennsylvania Poets of the Provincial Period. *Cas.*

Williams, George Huntington. *N. Y.*, 1856–1894. A professor of inorganic geology at Johns Hopkins University from 1892. Elements of Crystallography.

Williams, George Washington. *Pa.*, 1849–189–. A writer of African descent who served in the Federal army during the Civil War, and as lieutenant-colonel of artillery in the Republican army of Mexico, 1865–67, and who was minister to Hayti, 1885–86. History of the Negro Race in America; The Negro Troops in the War of the Rebellion; History of the Reconstruction of the Insurgent States. *Har.*

Williams, Henry Shaler. *N. Y.*, 1847——. A professor of palæontology at Cornell University from 1871. The Bones, Ligaments, and Muscles of the Domestic Cat; Geological Biology. *Ho.*

Williams, Henry Willard. *Ms.*, 1821–1895. A Boston physician, professor of ophthalmology at Harvard University, 1871–91. Our Eyes and How to Take Care of Them; Diagnosis and Treatment of Diseases of the Eye; Practical Guide to Study of Diseases of the Eye.

Williams, Jesse Lynch. *Il.*, 1871——. A littérateur of New York city. Princeton Stories; The Freshman, a book for boys. *Scr.*

Williams, John. *Ms.*, 1664–1729. A Congregational clergyman of Deerfield, Massachusetts, carried captive to Canada, with many of his parishioners, by the French and Indians in 1704. The Redeemed Captive is a graphic account of heroism and suffering during the period of captivity.

Williams, John. "Anthony Pasquin." *E.*,· *c.* 1765–1818. An English journalist who came to the United States after being very unpopular in England. Poems; Legislative Biography; The Hamiltoniad; The Dramatic Censor; Life of Alexander Hamilton.

Williams, John. *Ms.*, 1817——. The fourth Protestant Episcopal bishop of Connecticut, and presiding bishop from 1887. Sermons; Studies on the English Reformation; Ancient Hymns of Holy Church; Thoughts on the Gospel Miracles; The World's Witness to Christ; Studies in the Book of Acts. *Wh.*

Williams, Roger. *W.*, 1607 - 1683. A famous clergyman, minister at Salem, Massachusetts, but banished from the Massachusetts Bay colony in 1635 on account of his views upon religious liberty. In 1636 he founded the city of Providence, and was the chief citizen of the Rhode Island colony until his death. He was the first upholder of the doctrine of liberty of conscience in its entirety, and actively sustained his theories in many controversial works. Key Into the Languages of America; The Bloudy Tenent of Persecution for Cause of Conscience; The Bloudy Tenent Yet More Bloudy by Mr. Cotton's Endeavour to wash it white in the Bloud of the Lambe; Mr. Cotton's Letter Lately Printed, Examined and Answered; George Fox Digg'd Out of his Burrowes, include his principal works. *See Tyler's American Litera-*

ture; Mudge's Footprints of Roger Williams; Allibone's Dictionary; Johnson's Universal Cyclopedia; Appletons' American Biography; Dexter's As to Roger Williams; Lives by Knowles, 1834, Gammell, 1846, Elton, 1852, Straus, 1894; Bibliography of Rhode Island.

Williams, Samuel. *Ms.*, 1743–1817. Grandson of J. Williams, 1st. A Congregational clergyman, Hollis professor of mathematics at Harvard University, 1780–88. A Natural and Civil History of Vermont (1809); History of the American Revolution.

Williams, Samuel Wells. *N. Y.*, 1812–1884. A secretary and interpreter of the American Legation in China for many years; after 1877 professor of Chinese at Yale University. China, the Middle Kingdom; Easy Lessons in Chinese; Chinese Commercial Guide; Tonic Dictionary of the Chinese Language in the Canton Dialect; Syllabic Dictionary of Chinese; Chinese Topography. *See Allibone's Dictionary; Life by F. Williams, 1888. Scr.*

Williams, Stephen West. *Ms.*, 1790–1855. Great-grandson of J. Williams, 1st. A physician who was medical professor in Willoughby University, Ohio, 1838–53. Catechism of Medical Jurisprudence; American Medical Biography; The Williams Family in America (1847).

Williams, Thomas. *Ct.*, 1779–1876. A Congregational clergyman of Providence. Ten Sermons on Important Subjects; The Domestic Chaplain; Rhode Island Sermons.

Williams, William R——. *N. Y.*, 1804–1885. A Baptist clergyman of New York city, pastor of Amity Street Church, 1832–85. Religious Progress; God's Rescues, or The Lost Sheep, the Lost Coin, and the Lost Son: Discourses on Luke; Miscellanies; Lectures on the Lord's Prayer; Lectures on Baptist History; Eras and Characters of History. *Bap. Har. Ran.*

Williamson, Hugh. *Pa.*, 1735–1819. A statesman and physician who was a member of the Continental Congress. History of North Carolina; Observations on the Climate of America.

Williamson, Isaac David. *Vt.*, 1807–1876. A Universalist clergyman of Cincinnati and other cities. Argument for the Truth of Christianity; The Crown of Life; Philosophy of Odd Fellowship; Philosophy of Universalism; Rudiments of Theological and Moral Science.

Williamson, Joseph. *Me.*, 1828——. A lawyer of Belfast, Maine. The Maine Register and State Reference Book; Bibliography of Maine; History of Belfast. *See Bibliography of Maine.*

Williamson, Julia May. "Lura Bell." *Me.*, 1859——. A verse-writer of Augusta, Maine. Echoes of Time and Tide; The Choir of the Year.

Williamson, Robert Stockton. *N. Y.*, 1824–1882. A soldier and military engineer. Report of a Reconnoissance in California for Pacific Railroad Route; Use of the Barometer on Surveys; Practical Tables in Meteorology.

Williamson, Walter. *Pa.*, 1811–1870. A homœopathic physician of Philadelphia. Diseases of Females; Instructions Concerning Diseases of Females.

Williamson, William Durkee. *Ct.*, 1779–1840. A Bangor lawyer, governor of Maine in 1820. History of Maine from its First Discovery to the Separation from Massachusetts.

Willis, Nathaniel Parker. *Me.*, 1806–1867. A once popular New York littérateur, much overrated in the earlier part of his career, and now neglected. His prose, though pleasing, is almost all of ephemeral merit, and his verse is sentimental rather than thoughtful. The latter includes the once widely read Sacred Poems; Melanie; Lady Jane and Humorous Poems; Poems of Passion: while his prose comprises Hurry Graphs; People I have Met; Pencillings by the Way; Inklings of Adventures; Letters From Under a Bridge; Famous Persons and Places; A Summer Cruise in the Mediterranean; The Convalescent; Out-Doors at Idlewild; Paul Fane, a novel; Al Abri, and other works of lesser importance. A complete edition of his poems appeared in 1868. *See Life by Beers; Allibone's Dictionary; Lowell's Fable for Critics; Foley's American Authors. Cr. Scr.*

Willis, William. *Ms.*, 1794–1870. A Portland lawyer. History of Portland; History of the Law, Courts, and Lawyers of Maine.

Williston, Seth. *Ct.*, 1770–1851. A Presbyterian clergyman in New York State. Discourses on the Sabbath; Moral Imperfections of Christians; Harmony of Divine Truth; Millennial Discourses, are among his writings.

Williston, Timothy. *N. Y.*, 1805–1893. A Presbyterian clergyman. Orthodox Paths Restored; Talks to My Bible Class; Christ's Millennial Reign; Premium Essays.

Willson, [Byron] Forceythe. *N.Y.*, 1837–1867. A verse-writer at one time on the staff of The Louisville Journal. The Old Sergeant, and Other Poems. *See Atlantic Monthly, March, 1875. Hou.*

Willson, James McLeod. *Pa.*, 1809–1866. Son of J. R. Willson, *infra.* A Reformed Presbyterian clergyman of Philadelphia. The Deacon; Bible Magistracy; Civil Government; Social Religious Covenanting; Witnessing.

Willson, James Renwick. *Pa.*, 1780–1853. A Reformed Presbyterian clergyman in New York and Pennsylvania. History of the Church of Scotland; The Written Law; Historical Sketch of Opinions on the Atonement.

Willson, Marcius. *Ms.*, 1813——. An educator of Vineland, New Jersey. Civil Polity and Political Economy; Mosaics of Bible History; and many school text-books. *Har.*

Wilmer, Lambert A——. *Circa* 1805–1863. A Philadelphia journalist. New System of Grammar; The Quacks of Helicon; Life of De Soto; Our Press Gang, an Exposition of the Corruptions of American Newspapers (1859); Recantation: a Poem; Somnia; Liberty Triumphant.

Wilmer, Richard. *Va.*, 1816——. The second Protestant Episcopal bishop of Alabama. The Recent Past from a Southern Standpoint. *Wh.*

Wilmshurst, Zavarr. *E.*, 1824–1887. A journalist of New York city. The Viking, an epic; The Winter of the Heart, and Other Poems; The Siren; Ralph and Rose, a Poem.

Wilson, Alexander. *S.*, 1766–1813. A Scottish ornithologist and verse-writer who came to America in 1794. He is often called the father of American ornithology. Watty and Meg, a narrative poem; American Ornithology, or the Natural History of the Birds of the United States (continued by Charles Lucien Bonaparte). *See Life by G. F. Ord; Life by Brightwell, 1860; Allibone's Dictionary. Co.*

Wilson, Mrs. Augusta Jane [Evans]. *Ga.*, 1835——. A once popular novelist living at Mobile. Her writings had at one time an extraordinary vogue, but are now much less read. Beulah; Macaria; Vashti; St. Elmo; Inez, a Tale of the Alamo; Infelice; At the Mercy of Tiberius. *See Manly's Southern Literature. Dil.*

Wilson, Henry. *N. H.*, 1812–1875. A Massachusetts statesman who was vice-president of the United States at the time of his death. History of Anti-Slavery Measures; Rise and Fall of the Slave Power in America. *See Life and Public Services of, by G. E. Nason. Hou.*

Wilson, James Grant. *S.*, 1832——. Son of W. Wilson, *infra.* A littérateur of New York city who, besides editing Appletons' Cyclopædia of American Biography, has published Poets and Poetry of Scotland; Mr. Secretary Pepys and his Diary; Love in Letters; Bryant and His Friends; Centennial History of the Diocese of New York; Life of General Grant; Life of Fitz Greene Halleck; Sketches of Illustrious Soldiers. *Dil. Har.*

Wilson, James Harrison. *Il.*, 1837——. A United States army officer. China: Travels and Investigations in the Middle Kingdom; Life of Andrew Alexander; Life of General Grant (with C. A. Dana, *supra*). *Ap.*

Wilson, James Patriot. *Del.*, 1769–1830. A Presbyterian clergyman of Philadelphia. Lectures on the Parables; Essay on Grammar; Common Objections to Christianity; Easy Introduction to Hebrew, are among his works.

Wilson, John. *E.*, 1588–1667. A Puritan clergyman, the first pastor in Boston, and long prominent in the ecclesiastical and civil affairs of the colony. Some Helps to Faith; Famous Deliverances of the English Nation, a poem; The Day Breaking if not the Sun Rising of the Gospel with the Indians in New England.

Wilson, John. *S.*, 1802-1868. A Scottish printer who came to America in 1846, and established himself in the printing business in Cambridge. A Treatise on English Punctuation is his best-known work, but he wrote others on Scripture Proofs of Unitarianism; The Concessions of Trinitarians; Unitarian Principles Confirmed. *A. U. A.*

Wilson, John Grover. *Del.*, 1810-1885. A Philadelphia clergyman, originally of the Methodist Protestant denomination, but after 1855 the church of which he was pastor was known as the Ebenezer Independent Church. Among his various works are, Discourses on Prophecy; Writings in Prose and Verse; The Sabbath and Its Law; Atheism and Theism.

Wilson, John Laird. *S.*, 1832-18—. A journalist of New York city, but prior to 1866 a United Presbyterian minister in Scotland. The Battles of the Civil War; Life of John Wycliffe. *Su.*

Wilson, John Leighton. 1809-1880. A Presbyterian missionary to Africa. Western Africa: its History, Condition, and Prospects (1857). *See Life by Du Bose, 1895. Har.*

Wilson, Peter. *S.*, 1746-1825. An educator of New York city, classical professor at Columbia College, 1780-1792 and 1797-1820. Rules of Latin Prosody; Introduction to Greek Prosody; Compendium of Greek Prosody.

Wilson, Robert Anderson. *N. Y.*, 1812——. A lawyer of California. Mexico and its Religion, reissued as Mexico, California, and Central America; New History of the Conquest of Mexico.

Wilson, Robert Burns. *Pa.*, 1850——. An artist and verse-writer of Louisville. Life and Love, a volume of verse.

Wilson, Samuel Farmer. *Ct.*, 1805-1870. A New Orleans journalist. History of the American Revolution, long a popular work.

Wilson, Samuel Graham. 18——. A Presbyterian missionary in Persia. Persian Life and Customs. *Rev.*

Wilson, Theodore Delevan. *L. I.*, 1840-1896. A naval architect of note in the government service. Ship Building, Theoretical and Practical.

Wilson, Thomas. *Pa.*, *c.* 1768-*c.* 1828. A Philadelphia printer. Principal American Military and Naval Heroes (1821); The Picture of Philadelphia for 1824.

Wilson, [Thomas] Woodrow. *Va.*, 1856——. A professor of jurisprudence at Princeton College. Congressional Government: A Study in American Politics; The State Elements of Historical and Practical Politics; An Old Master, and Other Political Essays; Division and Reunion, 1829-1889; George Washington; Mere Literature, and Other Essays. *Har. He. Hou. Lgs. Scr.*

Wilson, William. *S.*, 1801-1860. A Scottish verse-writer who became a bookseller and publisher in Poughkeepsie, New York, in 1854. Poems, edited by B. J. Lossing (1870).

Wilson, William Dexter. *N. H.*, 1816——. An Episcopal clergyman of Syracuse, professor of philosophy at Cornell University, 1868-86. History of the Reformation in England; The Church Identified; Psychology; The Foundations of Religious Belief; Elementary Treatise on Logic; Live Questions in Psychology and Metaphysics; Introduction to the Study of the History of Philosophy. *Ap.*

Wilstach, John Augustine. *D. C.*, 1824-1897. A lawyer of Lafayette, Indiana, who has published a translation into English verse, with variorum notes, of the complete works of Virgil; also a translation of Dante's Divina Commedia into English verse. *Hou.*

Wilstach, Joseph Walter. *Ind.*, 1857——. Son of J. A. Wilstach, *supra.* A lawyer of Lafayette, Indiana. Horatian Odes; Montalembert: a Character Study.

Wiman, Erastus. *Ont.*, 1834——. Formerly a prominent capitalist of New York city. Chances of Success.

Winans, Ross. *N. J.*, 1796–1877. An eminent inventor. One Religion: Many Creeds.

Winchell, Alexander. *N. Y.*, 1824–1891. A professor of geology at the University of Michigan, 1854–73 and 1879–91. Sketches of Creation; Pre-Adamites; Doctrine of Evolution; World Life; Science and Religion; The Geology of the Stars; Thoughts on Causality; Sparks from a Geologist's Hammer; Geological Excursions; Geological Studies; Walks and Talks in the Geological Field. *Har. Sc.*

Winchell, Newton Horace. *N. Y.*, 1839——. Brother of A. Winchell, *supra.* State geologist of Minnesota. Geology of Minnesota; Annual Reports on the Geological Natural History Survey of Minnesota from 1872.

Winchester, Carroll. *See Curtis, Mrs.*

Winchester, Elhanan. *Ms.*, 1751–1797. A Universalist clergyman of Philadelphia, but in earlier life a Baptist minister. New Book of Poems on Several Occasions; Universal Restoration; Prophecies to be Fulfilled; Progress and Empire of Christ, a Poem. *See Life of, by E. M. Stone, 1836.*

Winchester, Samuel Gover. *Md.*, 1805–1841. A Presbyterian clergyman of Philadelphia, and subsequently of Natchez. Companion for the Sick; Family Religion; The Theatre.

Winebrenner, John. *Md.*, 1797–1860. A German Reformed clergyman of Harrisburg, Pennsylvania, founder in 1830 of the Church of God, a sect commonly known as Winebrennerians. Regeneration; Practical and Doctrinal Sermons; Brief Views of the Church of God.

Wines, Enoch Cobb. *N. J.*, 1806–1879. A Congregational clergyman, widely known as a philanthropist, who laboured extensively in behalf of prison reform. Two and a Half Years in the Navy; A Trip to China; Hints on Popular Education; How Shall I Govern My School; Commentaries on Laws of the Ancient Hebrews; Adam and Christ; Prisons and Reformatories of the United States and Canada; State of Prisons and Child-Saving Institutions Throughout the World.

Wines, Frederic Howard. *Pa.*, 1838——. Son of E. C. Wines, *supra.* Formerly a Presbyterian clergyman, but now devoted in official and private capacities to various reforms connected with the defective, dependent, and criminal classes. Punishment and Reformation, an Historical Sketch of the Rise of the Penitentiary System; The Liquor Problem in its Legislative Aspects (with John Koren). *Cr. Hou.*

Wing, Conway Phelps. *O.*, 1809–1889. A Presbyterian clergyman of Carlisle, Pennsylvania, long active as an abolitionist. Among his writings are, History of Cumberland County, Pennsylvania; History of the Presbyteries of York and Carlisle.

Wingate, Charles Edward Lewis. *N. H.*, 1861——. A Boston journalist. Shakespeare's Heroines on the Stage. *Cr.*

Wingate, Charles Frederick. *N. Y.*, 1847——. A sanitary engineer of New York city. Views and Interviews on Journalism; Plumbing and House Drainage; Twilight Tracts.

Wingate, George Wood. *N. Y.*, 1840——. Brother of C. F. Wingate, *supra.* A lawyer and soldier. Last Campaign of the Twenty-Second Regiment; Manual of Rifle Practice; On Horseback Through the Yellowstone.

Winser, Henry Jacob. *Ba.*, 1833–1896. A journalist of New York city, and subsequently of Newark, New Jersey, United States consul at Sonneburg, Germany, 1869–81. The Great Northwest; The Yellowstone National Park; The Seat of a Thousand Industries, a description of Newark.

Winship, Albert Edward. *Ms.*, 1845——. An educator of Boston, editor of The Journal of Education. Methods and Principles in Bible Study; Life of Horace Mann, *supra.*

Winslow, Mrs. Catherine Mary [Reignolds]. *E.*, 183——. Best known as Mrs. Erving Winslow. A once popular actress of Boston, and since her retirement from the stage well known as a public reader. Yesterdays with Actors; Readings (with notes) from the Old English Dramatists. *Le.*

Winslow, Charles Frederick. *Ms.*, 1811–1877. A physician. Cosmography; The Cooling Globe; Force and Nature.

Winslow, Edward. *E.*, 1595–1655. A notable member of the Plymouth colony who succeeded Bradford as governor of that colony in 1633. Good Newes from New England; Hypocrisy Unmasked; New England's Salamander; The Glorious Progress of the Gospel Among the Indians of New England. *See Tyler's American Literature; Bibliography of Rhode Island.*

Winslow, Mrs. Erving. *See Winslow, Mrs. Catharine.*

Winslow, Helen Maria. *Vt.*, 1851——. A Boston journalist. The Shawsheen Mills; A Bohemian Chapter.

Winslow, Hubbard. *Vt.*, 1799–1864. A Presbyterian clergyman who held charges in Boston and other localities, and among whose writings are, Hidden Life; Moral Philosophy; Doctrine of the Trinity; Controversial Theology; Christian Doctrines; Young Man's Aid to Knowledge, a very popular work; Intellectual Philosophy.

Winslow, Miron. *Vt.*, 1789–1864. Brother of H. Winslow, *supra.* A Presbyterian missionary in Ceylon and Madras. Hints on Missions to India; Sketch of the Missions; Comprehensive Tamil and English Dictionary.

Winslow, Stephen Noyes. *Vt.*, 1826——. A Philadelphia journalist. Biographies of Successful Philadelphia Merchants.

Winslow, William Copley. *Ms.*, 1840——. Son of H. Winslow, *supra.* An Episcopal clergyman of Boston widely known as an Egyptologist. Israel in Egypt; The Store City of Pithom; A Greek City in Egypt; The Pilgrim Fathers in Holland.

Winsor, Justin. *Ms.*, 1831–1897. The librarian of Harvard University. He was editor of The Memorial History of Boston; Narrative and Critical History of America. His original works include, Reader's Handbook of the American Revolution; Cartier to Frontenac: Geographical Discovery in the Interior of North America in its Historical Relations, 1534–1700; Christopher Columbus; The Mississippi Basin: the Struggle in America between England and France, 1697–1763; Was Shakespeare Shapleigh?; History of Duxbury; The Westward Movement. *See Bibliography of Maine. Hou.*

Winter, William. *Ms.*, 1836——. A prominent littérateur and dramatic critic of New York city. Poems; The Trip to England; The Jeffersons; English Rambles; Shakespeare's England; Gray Days and Gold; Old Shrines and Ivy; Shadows of the Stage; My Witness, a Book of Verse; The Wanderers, a collection of poems; Thistle Down, a Book of Lyrics; The Queen's Domain, and Other Poems; The Convert, and Other Poems; Brown Heath and Blue Bells; George William Curtis: a Eulogy. *See Foley's American Authors. Hou. Kt. Mac.*

Winthrop, John. *E.*, 1588–1649. The first governor of Massachusetts. Arbitrary Government Described; History of New England from 1630 to 1649. *See Tyler's American Literature; Letters of, to Margaret Winthrop; Lives by R. C. Winthrop, infra, 1867, J. H. Twichell, supra, 1891; Atlantic Monthly, January, 1864.*

Winthrop, John. *Ms.*, 1714–1779. Great-grandson of J. Winthrop, *supra.* A professor of mathematics and natural philosophy at Harvard University, 1738–79, and the foremost teacher of science in America in his century. Lectures on Earthquakes; Account of Some Fiery Meteors; Lectures on the Parallax.

Winthrop, Laura. Sister of T. Winthrop, *infra. See Johnson, Mrs. L.*

Winthrop, Robert Charles. *Ms.*, 1809–1894. Descendant of Governor Winthrop, *supra.* A Massachusetts statesman, a lifelong resident of Boston, noted for the polish and refinement of his oratory. Addresses and Speeches; a Life of Governor John Winthrop; Memoirs of Henry Clay, Washington, Bowdoin, and Franklin. *See Smalley's Studies of Men. Lit.*

Winthrop, Theodore. *Ct.*, 1828–1861. Descendant of Governor Winthrop, *supra.* A brilliant young novelist who entered the Federal army at the outbreak of the Civil War and was killed at the battle of Big Bethel. John Brent; Cecil Dreeme; Edwin Brothertoft; The Canoe and the Saddle; Love and Skates; Life in the Open Air. *See Atlantic Monthly, August, 1861, and August, 1863; Life and Poems of, edited by his sister; Nichol's American Literature. Ho. Int.*

Winthrop, William Woolsey. *Ct.*, 1831——. Brother of T. Winthrop, *supra.* A United States army officer, professor of law at West Point. Treatise on Military Law; Digest of Opinions of the Judge-Advocates-General of the Army. *Lit. Wil.*

Wirt, Mrs. Elizabeth Washington [Gamble]. *Va.*, 1784–1857. Wife of W. Wirt, *infra.* Flora's Dictionary.

Wirt, William. *Md.*, 1772–1834. A famous Virginia statesman and orator, attorney-general of the United States, 1817–28. Life of Patrick Henry; Letters of the British Spy. *See Memoir by J. P. Kennedy, supra. Co. Har.*

Wise, Daniel. "Francis Forrester." *E.*, 1813——. A Methodist clergyman and religious editor of Boston. Personal Effort; Heroic Methodists; Boy Travellers in Arabia; Some Remarkable Women; My Uncle Toby's Library; Uncrowned Kings; Summer Days on the Hudson; Men of Renown, are among his numerous works. *Meth.*

Wise, Henry Alexander. *Va.*, 1806–1876. A Virginia politician, minister to Brazil, 1844–47, governor of Virginia, 1856–60, in whose administration occurred the celebrated John Brown raid. Seven Decades of the Union; Memoir of John Tyler.

Wise, Henry Augustus. *N. Y.*, 1819–1869. Cousin of H. A. Wise, *supra.* A United States naval officer. Story of the Gray African Parrot; Captain Brand; Los Gringos; Tales for the Marines; Scampavias, from Gibel Tarak to Stamboul.

Wise, Isaac Mayer. *Bo.*, 1819——. A Jewish rabbi of Cincinnati from 1854, president of Hebrew Union College. History of the Israelitish Nation; Essence of Judaism; Judaism: its Doctrines and Duties; The Martyrdom of Jesus of Nazareth; The Cosmic God; History of the Hebrew Second Commonwealth; Pronaos to Holy Writ. *Clke.*

Wise, John. *Ms.*, 1652–1725. A Congregational clergyman of Ipswich from 1780 until his death. A strong, vigourous writer, almost the first of the American colonists to declare his belief in a government founded on human equality. The Church's Quarrel Espoused; Vindication of the Government of New England Churches. *See Tyler's American Literature. C. P. S.*

Wise, John. *Pa.*, 1808–1879. A once noted aëronaut. System of Aëronautics; Through the Air, or Forty Years' Experience as an Aëronaut.

Wise, John Sergeant. *B.*, 1846. A lawyer of New York city. Diomed: The Life, Travels, and Observations of a Dog. *Lam.*

Wisner, William. *N. Y.*, 1782–1871. A Presbyterian clergyman of Rochester, New York. Incidents in the Life of a Pastor; Civil Liberty.

Wisner, William Carpenter. *N.Y.*, 1808–1880. Son of W. Wisner, *supra.* A Presbyterian clergyman at Lockport, New York, 1837–76. Prelacy and Parity.

Wisser, John Philip. *Mo.*, 1852——. An instructor at West Point from 1878. Chemical Manipulations; Modern Gun Cotton; Practical Instruction in Minor Tactics and Strategy; Report on Military Schools of Europe. *Ap.*

Wistar, Caspar. *Pa.*, 1761–1818. A Philadelphia physician, professor of anatomy in the University of Pennsylvania, 1792–1818. System of Anatomy for Use of Students in Medicine.

Wister, Mrs. Annis Lee [Furness]. *Pa.*, 1830——. Daughter of W. H. Furness, *supra.* A noted and popular translator of many German novels. With F. H. Hedge, *supra*, Metrical Translations and Poems. *Hou. Lip.*

Wister, Owen. *Pa.*, 1860——. Son of Mrs. S. B. Wister, *infra.* A lawyer and littérateur of Philadelphia. The New Swiss Family Robinson; The Dragon of Wantley, a romance; Red Men and White, a collection of frontier stories. *Har. Lip.*

Wister, Mrs. Owen. *See Wister, Mrs. Sarah.*

Wister, Mrs. Sarah [Butler]. *Pa.*, 1835——. Daughter of Frances Kemble. A Philadelphia writer who has published, A Boat of Glass, a poem; translations from Alfred de Musset.

Withers, Frederic Clarke. *E.*, 1826——. An architect of New York city, the designer of the reredos in Trinity Church in that city. Church Architecture.

Witherspoon, John. *S.*, 1722–1794. A Presbyterian clergyman, president of Princeton College, 1768–94, eminent in his day as a leader of opinion, both political and religious, and one of the signers of the Declaration of Independence. Ecclesiastical Characteristics; Thoughts on American Liberty; Sermons on Practical Subjects; Leading Truths of the Gospel; Letters on Marriage; Sermons on Various Subjects. *See Sprague's Annals of the American Pulpit; American Historical Review, July, 1896.*

Witherspoon, Theodore Dwight. *Al.*, 1836——. A Presbyterian clergyman in Louisville from 1882. Children of the Covenant; Letters on Romanism.

Withington, Leonard. *Ms.*, 1789–1885. A Congregational clergyman, pastor at Newbury, Massachusetts, 1816–1885. The Puritan, a series of Essays; Penitential Tears; Solomon's Song Translated and Explained.

Wolcott, Roger. *Ct.*, 1679–1767. A colonial governor of Connecticut, 1750–1754. Poetical Meditations. *See Everest's Poets of Connecticut.*

Wolf, Edmund Jacob. *Pa.*, 1840——. A Lutheran clergyman, professor in the Theological Seminary at Gettysburg from 1874. History of the Lutherans in America.

Wolfe, Theodore Frelinghuysen. *N. J.*, 1843——. A physician and littérateur of Ledgewood, New Jersey. A Literary Pilgrimage Among the Haunts of Famous British Authors; Literary Shrines: the Haunts of Some Famous American Authors, — two widely popular books. Among his professional works are volumes on Tetanus; Anæsthesia, and other medical subjects. *Lip.*

Wolle, Francis. *Pa.*, 1817–1893. A Moravian clergyman and educator of Bethlehem, Pennsylvania, eminent as a botanist. Desmids of the United States; Fresh-Water Algæ; Diatomaceæ of North America. *Wn.*

Wollenweber, Louis August. *G.*, 1807–1888. A German printer who came to America, and, after editing several German papers in Philadelphia, removed to Reading, Pennsylvania. Sketches of Domestic Life in Pennsylvania; Treu bis in den Tod; Zwei treue Kameraden.

Wood, Alphonso. *N. H.*, 1810–1881. An educator of Brooklyn whose text-books were very popular. Class-Book of Botany; First Lessons in Botany; Leaves and Flowers; The American Botanist.

Wood, Benjamin. *Ky.*, 1820——. A journalist of New York city, member of Congress, 1861–65. Fort Lafayette, or Love and Secession.

Wood, Charles. *N. Y.*, 1851——. A Presbyterian clergyman of Germantown, Philadelphia. Saunterings in Europe.

Wood, De Volson. *N. Y.*, 1832–1897. A professor of mathematics and engineering at the Stevens Institute, Hoboken, New Jersey, from 1872. Treatise on Resistance of Materials; Construction of Bridges and Roofs; Elements of Analytical Mechanics; Elements of Coördinate Geometry; The Mechanics of Fluids; Trigonometry; Thermodynamics; Theory of Turbines. *Wil.*

Wood, George. *Ms.*, 1799–1870. A treasury clerk at Washington. Peter Schmeil in America; The Modern Pilgrim; Marrying Too Late; Future Life (1858), reissued in 1869 as The Gates Wide Open. *Le.*

Wood, George Bacon. *N. J.*, 1797–1879. A Philadelphia physician, medical professor in the University of Pennsylvania, 1835–60. The Dispensatory of the United States (with F. Bache, *supra*). The Practice of Medicine; Therapeutics and Pharmacology; Introductory Lectures and Addresses on Medical Subjects; History of the University of Pennsylvania; Lives of S. G. Morton, F. Bache. *See Gross's Sketches of Contemporaries. Lip.*

Wood, Henry. *Vt.*, 1834——. A philosophical essayist and novelist of Boston. Natural Law in the Business World; Political Economy of Natural Law; God's Image in Man; Ideal Suggestions Through Mental Photography; Edward Burton, a novel; Studies in the Thought World. *Le.*

Wood, Horace Gay. *Vt.*, 1831–1893. A New Hampshire lawyer, who practised in New York city in his latest years. The Relation of Landlord and Tenant; Treatise on the Law of Nuisances; Master and Servant; The Law of Fire Insurance; Limitation of Actions at Law and in Equity; On the Statute of Frauds; The Law of Railroads; Legal Remedies of Mandamus and Prohibition.

Wood, Horatio Curtis. *Pa.*, 1841——. Nephew of G. B. Wood, *supra*, a medical professor in the University of Pennsylvania from 1866. The Phalangidæ of the United States; Researches upon American Hemp; Brain Work and Overwork; On Fever; Nervous Diseases and their Diagnosis; Thermic Fever, or Sunstroke; Therapeutics. *Lip.*

Wood, James. *N.Y.*, 1799–1867. A Presbyterian clergyman and educator in Indiana. Old and New Theology; Treatise on Baptism; Call to the Sacred Office; The Best Lesson and the Best Time; The Gospel Fountain; Grace and Glory.

Wood, Mrs. Jean [Moncure]. *Va.*, 1754–1823. The wife of James Wood, who was governor of Virginia, 1796–99. She was socially prominent in her day. Flowers and Weeds of the Old Dominion, a book of verse.

Wood, John. *S.*, c. 1755–1822. A Scottish writer who came to America in 1800 and settled in Richmond, Virginia. Among his writings are General View of the History of Switzerland; History of the Administration of John Adams.

Wood, John Seymour. *N.Y.*, 1853——. A lawyer and littérateur of New York city, editor of The Bachelor of Arts. Gramercy Park, a story of New York; College Days, or Harry's Career at Yale; Yale Yarns; A Coign of Vantage; An Old Beau, and Other Stories; A Daughter of Venice. *Ap. Cas. Do. Put.*

Wood, Mrs. Julia Amanda [Sargent]. *N. H.*, 1826——. A Roman Catholic writer of Sauk Rapids, Minnesota. Myrrha Lake; Hubert's Wife; Annette; Strayed From the Fold; From Error to Truth; The Brown House at Duffield.

Wood, Mrs. Sarah Sayward [Barrell] [Keating]. *Ms.*, 1759–1855. A novelist whose sentimental fictions include, Duval; Ferdinand and Almira; Amelia, or the Influence of Virtue; Tales of the Night; The Illuminated Baron.

Wood, William. *E.*, 1580–1639. A Puritan colonist who came to New England in 1629. He founded the town of Sandwich, Massachusetts. New England's Prospect, a descriptive work partly in verse. *See Tyler's American Literature.*

Wood, William Maxwell. *Md.*, 1809–1880. A United States naval surgeon. Wandering Sketches; A Shoulder to the Wheel of Progress; Hints to the People on the Profession of Medicine; Fankwei, or the San Jacinto in the Seas of India, China, and Japan.

Woodberry, George Edward. *Ms.*, 1855——. A prominent literary critic of New York city, professor of literature in Columbia University, editor, with E. C. Stedman, of the complete works of Poe. He has also edited a complete edition of Shelley, with Memoir and Notes. A History of Wood Engraving; The North Shore Watch, and Other Poems; Life of Edgar Allan Poe; Life of James Russell Lowell; Studies in Letters and Life. *Har. Hou.*

Woodbridge, Samuel Merrill. *Ms.*, 1819——. Kinsman of W. C. Woodbridge, *infra*. A Dutch Reformed clergyman, professor at Rutgers Theological Seminary, New Brunswick, New Jersey, from 1857. Analysis of Theology; Faith: its True Position in the Life of Man.

Woodbridge, William Channing. *Ms.*, 1794–1845. An educator of Hartford. Universal Geography (with E. Willard, *supra*). Modern School Geography; Letters from Hofwyl.

Woodbury, Augustus. *Ms.*, 1825–1895. A Unitarian clergyman of Providence from 1851. Plain Words to Young Men; The Second Rhode Island Regiment; Historical Sketch of Rhode Island Prisons and Jails, include his principal works.

Woodbury, Daniel Phineas. *N. H.*, 1812–1864. A general in the Federal army during the Civil War. Sustaining Walls; Theory of the Arch.

Woodhull, Alfred Alexander. *N. J.*, 1837——. A United States army surgeon. Notes on Military Hygiene; Studies in the non-emetic use of Ipecacuanha. *Lip. Wil.*

Woodruff, Hiram. *N. J.*, 1817–1887. A noted horse-trainer who wrote The Trotting Horse of America. *Co.*

Woodruff, Mrs. Julia Louisa Matilda [Curtiss]. "W. M. L. Jay." *Ct.*, 1832——. An author and compiler of New York city. My Winter in Cuba; Shiloh; Holden With the Cords; Bellevue; Daisy Seekers, and various compilations. *Dut.*

Woods, Mrs. Kate [Tannatt]. *N. Y.*, 1838——. A writer of Salem, Massachusetts. Six Little Rebels; Dr. Dick; Out and About; The Wooing of Grandmother Grey; Grandfather Grey; Children's Stories; Toots and His Friends; The Duncans on Land and Sea. *Cas. Le. Lo.*

Woods, Katherine Pearson. *W. Va.*, 1853——. The Crowning of Candace; John: a Tale of King Messiah; From Dusk to Dawn; A Web of Gold; Metzerott, Shoemaker, a protest against social injustice; Mine and Thine. *Ap. Cr. Do.*

Woods, Leonard. *Ms.*, 1774–1854. A Congregational clergyman of Massachusetts, professor at Andover Seminary, 1808–54. Letters to Unitarians; Inspiration of the Scriptures; Memoirs of American Missionaries; Church Government; Lectures on Swedenborgianism; Examination of the Doctrine of Perfection. *See Park's Life and Character of.*

Woods, Virna. *O.*, 1864——. An educator of Sacramento, California. A Modern Magdalene, a novel; The Amazons, a lyrical drama. *Fl. Le.*

Woodward, Ashbel. *Ct.*, 1804–1885. A physician of Franklin, Connecticut. Vindication of General Israel Putnam; Vindication of Army Surgeons; Life of General Nathaniel Lyon; Medical Ethics, include his principal writings.

Woodward, Annie Aubertine. Sister of J. J. Woodward, *infra. See Moore, Mrs. A.*

Woodward, Calvin Milton. *Ms.*, 1837——. A St. Louis educator, professor in Washington University from 1868. History of the St. Louis Bridge; The Manual Training School: its Aims, Methods, and Results.

Woodward, Joseph Janvier. *Pa.*, 1833–1884. A United States army surgeon. Outlines of the Chief Camp Diseases of the United States Armies, as observed during the present war (1864); Medical and Surgical History of the Rebellion (with G. Otis). *Lip.*

Woodward, Francis Channing. *Ct.*, 1812–1859. Nephew of S. Woodworth, *infra.* A once popular writer of juvenile tales, among which are, Uncle Frank's Home Stories; Stories for Little Folks.

Woodward, Robert Simpson. *Mch.*, 1849——. A mathematician, professor of mechanics at Columbia University from 1893. Latitudes and Longitudes of Certain Points in Missouri, Kansas, and New Mexico, and many scientific papers of value.

Woodworth, Samuel. *Ms.*, 1785–1842. A journalist and verse-writer of New York city who wrote, The Champions of Freedom, an historical romance; Melodies, Duets, Trios, Songs, and Ballads, but who will be longest remembered as the author of the famous lyric, The Old Oaken Bucket. *See Foley's American Authors.*

Woolf, Benjamin Edward. *E.*, 1836——. A popular playwright, among whose plays are, The Mighty Dollar; The Professor; The Doctor of Alcantara.

Woolley, Mrs. Celia [Parker]. *O.*, 1848——. A novelist, formerly of Chicago, now (1897) in the Unitarian ministry at Geneva, Illinois. Roger Hunt; A Girl Graduate; Rachel Armstrong, or Love and Theology. *Hou.*

Woolman, John. *N. J.*, 1720–1772. A Quaker itinerant preacher of New Jersey, in whose writings occurs the earliest protest in America against the slave trade. His ethical teachings have won the highest praise from many quarters. Essays and Epistles; Serious Considerations; On the Keeping of Negroes. His famous Journal, by which he is most widely known, has been edited by the poet Whittier. *Hou.*

Woolsey, Abby Howland. 18—1893. A New York philanthropist. A Century of Nursing; Lunacy Legislation in England; Handbook for Hospital Visitors; Hospital Laundries.

Woolsey, Sarah Channing. "Susan Coolidge." *O.*, 183——. Niece of T. D. Woolsey, *infra.* A poet and popular writer for young people. A resident of Newport, Rhode Island. Old Convent School in Paris; The New Year's Bargain; What Katy Did; A Guernsey Lily; For Summer Afternoons; In the High Valley; A Short History of Philadelphia; The Barberry Bush, and Other Stories About Girls; Verses; A Few More Verses, include the more important of her writings. *Rob.*

Woolsey, Theodore Dwight. *N. Y.*, 1801–1889. A Congregational clergyman, president of Yale University, 1846–71, long eminent as a scholar and thinker. Political Science; Communism and Socialism; Introduction to the Study of International Law; Essay on Divorce and Divorce Legislation; Helpful Thoughts for Young Men; The Religion of the Present and the Future; Eros, and Other Poems. *Lo. Scr.*

Woolson, Mrs. Abba Louisa [Goold]. *Me.*, 1838——. A Boston lecturer on English literature. Woman in American Society; Dress Reform; Browsings Among Books; George Eliot and Her Heroines. *Har. Rob.*

Woolson, Constance Fenimore. *N. H.*, 1838–1894. A novelist whose work was much above the average level of fiction, Horace Chase being her best novel. Her other works include, Castle Nowhere; Lake Country Sketches; Two Women, a poem; Rodman the Keeper: Southern Sketches; Anne; For the Major; East Angels; Jupiter Lights; The Front Yard, and Other Italian Stories; Dorothy, and Other Italian Stories; Mentone, Cairo, and Corfu; The Old Stone House. *See Appletons' Annual Cyclopædia, 1894. Ap. Har.*

Worcester, Alfred. *Ms.*, 1855——. A physician of Waltham, Massachusetts. Monthly Nursing; A New Way of Training Nurses; Training Schools for Nurses in Small Cities; Small Hospitals.

Worcester, Joseph Emerson. *N. H.*, 1784–1865. A distinguished lexicographer and philologist of Cambridge. Geographical Dictionary; Gazetteer of the United States; Sketches of the Earth and Its Inhabitants; Elements of History; Outlines of Scriptural Geography; Comprehensive Primary Dictionary. His greatest work is his well-known quarto Dictionary of the English Language, first published in 1860. *Lip.*

Worcester, Noah. *N. H.*, 1758–1837. A Unitarian clergyman, pastor at Brighton, Massachusetts, 1813–37, who was prominent in the Unitarian controversy. He edited The Friend of Peace. A Respectful Address to the Trinitarian Clergy; The Atoning Sacrifice a Display of Love, not Wrath; Last Thoughts on Important Subjects; Causes and Evils of Contentions Among Christians. *See Sprague's Annals of the American Pulpit.*

Worcester, Noah. *N. H.*, 1812–1847. A physician who was professor of pathology in Western Reserve College, Hudson, Ohio. Symptoms, Diagnosis, and Treatment of Skin Diseases.

Worcester, Samuel. *N. H.*, 1770–1821. Brother of N. Worcester, 1st, *supra.* A Congregational clergyman, pastor at Salem, Massachusetts, from 1803. Letters to Dr. Channing on the Unitarian Controversy; Discourses on the Covenant with Abraham. *See Life of, by S. M. Worcester, infra.*

Worcester, Samuel Melanchthon. *Ms.*, 1801–1866. Son of S. Worcester, *supra.* A Congregational clergyman, professor of rhetoric at Amherst College, 1825–34; pastor at Salem, Massachusetts, 1834–60. Essays on Slavery; Life of Samuel Worcester, *supra.*

Worcester, Thomas. *N. H.*, 1768–1831. Brother of N. Worcester, 1st. A Unitarian clergyman. Call for Scripture Evidence that Christ is God; The True God but One Person; New Chain of Plain Argument.

Work, Henry Clay. *Ct.*, 1832–1884. A popular song-writer of Chicago. Marching Through Georgia; Grandfather's Clock, are perhaps the best known of his songs.

Workman, Mrs. Fanny [Bullock]. *Ms.*, 1859——. Daughter of A. H.

Bullock, *supra*, and wife of W. H. Workman, *infra*. A littérateur who has lived much abroad. With her husband she has written, Algerian Memories: a Bicycle Tour over the Atlas to the Sahara; Sketches Awheel in Modern Iberia. *Ran.*

Workman, William Hunter. *Ms.*, 1847——. A physician who is co-author with Mrs. Workman, *supra*, of Algerian Memories, and Sketches Awheel. *Ran.*

Worman, James Henry. *P.*, 183——. An educator who has filled professorships in various colleges North and South. Complete Grammar of the German Language; Elementary German Grammar; L'Echo de Paris.

Wormeley, Katharine Prescott. *E.*, 1832——. A translator of prominence who has translated the novels of Balzac and the plays of Molière, and is the author of The Other Side of War; Life of Balzac; The United States Sanitary Commission; Hospital Transports. *Rob.*

Wormly, Theodore George. *Pa.*, 1826——. A Philadelphia physician, professor of chemistry in the University of Pennsylvania from 1877. Methods of Analysis of Coals, etc.; The Micro-Chemistry of Poisons. *Lip.*

Worthen, William Ezra. *Ms.*, 1819–1897. A civil engineer of prominence. Cyclopædia of Drawing; First Lessons in Mechanics; Rudimentary Drawing for Schools.

Wright, Carroll Davidson. *N. H.*, 1840——. A statistician of distinction, United States Commissioner of Labor from 1885, and professor of political science in the Catholic University at Washington from 1895. Census of Massachusetts, 1875; The Factory System of the United States; The Relation of Political Economy to the Labor Question; Annual Reports of Massachusetts Bureau of Statistics, 1873–88; Convict Labor; Strikes and Lockouts; Working Women in Large Cities; Railroad Labor; Marriage and Divorce; Cost of Production of Iron, Steel, etc.; Cost of Production of Textiles and Glass; Industrial Evolution of the United States. *Fl.*

Wright, Chauncey. *Ms.*, 1830–1875. An instructor in mathematical physics at Harvard University. Philosophical Discussions; Darwinism. *See Biographical Sketch, by C. E. Norton, supra; Memoir, by J. B. Thayer.*

Wright, Elizur. *Ct.*, 1804–1885. A journalist of Boston long prominent as a reformer. A Curiosity of Law; The Politics and Mysteries of Life Insurance; Savings Bank Life Insurance; Myron Holley and What He Did for Liberty and True Religion; a translation of La Fontaine's Fables.

Wright, Fanny. *See D'Arusmont.*

Wright, George Frederick. *N. Y.*, 1838——. A Congregational clergyman and geologist, since 1884 attached to the United States Geological Survey in the Department of Glacial Geology. The Glacial Boundary in Ohio; Studies in Science and Religion; Logic of Christian Evidences; The Relation of Death to Probation; Divine Authority of the Bible; The Ice Age in North America; Man and the Glacial Period; Life of Charles Grandison Finney, *supra*. *Ap. Hou.*

Wright, Hendrick Bradley. *Pa.*, 1808–1881. A lawyer of Wilkes-Barre, Pennsylvania, Member of Congress, 1853–55, 1861–63, and 1877–80. A Practical Treatise on Labor; Historical Sketches of the Wyoming Valley.

Wright, Henrietta Christian. 18——. The Golden Fairy Series; Children's Stories of American Progress; Stories of the Great Inventors; Stories in American Literature; Stories in English Literature; Stories of American History; The Princess Liliwinkins. *Har. Scr.*

Wright, Henry Clarke. *Ct.*, 1797–1870. An anti-slavery reformer and lecturer of prominence in his day. Man-Killing by Individuals and Nations a Wrong; A Kiss for a Blow; Defensive War a Denial of Christianity; Human Life Illustrated; Marriage and Parentage; The Living Present and the Dead Past. *Le.*

Wright, John Stephen. *Ms.*, 1815–1874. A Chicago manufacturer who established The Prairie Farmer in 1840. Chicago: Past, Present, and Future.

Wright, Mrs. Julia [McNair]. *N. Y.*, 1840——. Wife of W. J. Wright, *infra*. A prolific writer of temperance and religious tales, the latter being strongly anti-Roman Catholic in character. Among them are, Almost a Nun; Priest and Nun; Scenes of the Convent; The Gospel in the Riviera; A Wife Hard Won; A Million Too Much. *Co. Lip.*

Wright, Mrs. Mabel [Osgood]. *N. Y.*, 1859——. Daughter of S. Osgood, *supra*, and great-niece, on the maternal side, of Susanna Rowson, *supra.* A nature writer of Fairfield, Connecticut. The Friendship of Nature, a series of out-door studies; Birdcraft, a field-book of New England Birds; Tommy-Anne and the Three Hearts: a Natural History Story; Citizen Bird, a bird book for beginners. *Mac.*

Wright, Mrs. Mary [Tappan]. *O.*, 1851——. A writer of Cambridge, the wife of Professor J. H. Wright, of Harvard University. A Truce, and Other Stories. *Scr.*

Wright, Marcus Joseph. *Tn.*, 1831——. A brigadier-general in the Confederate army during the Civil War, and subsequently a lawyer of Memphis. Life of General Winfield Scott; Life of Governor William Blount; Reminiscence of the Early Settlement of McNairy County, Tennessee. *Ap.*

Wright, Robert Emmet. *Pa.*, 1810——. A lawyer of Allentown, Pennsylvania. Aldermen and Justices of the Peace; The Office and Duties of Constable; Pennsylvania State Reports, 1861–65.

Wright, Robert William. *Vt.*, 1816–1885. A Connecticut lawyer and journalist. The Church Knaviad; Vision of Judgment; The Pious Chi-Neh; Life: its True Genesis, a refutation of evolution; Practical Legal Forms.

Wright, Thomas Lee. *O.*, 1825——. A physician and journalist of Bellefontaine, Ohio. Notes on the Theory of Human Existence; Disquisition on the Ancient History of Medicine; Inebriism: a Pathological and Psychological Study.

Wright, William. *I.*, 1824–1866. A journalist of Paterson, New Jersey. The Oil Regions of Pennsylvania (1865). *Har.*

Wright, William Bull. *N. Y.*, 1840–1880. A physician and educator of Buffalo. Highland Rambles, a Poem; The Brook, and Other Poems.

Wright, William Burnet. *O.*, 1836——. A Congregational clergyman of Boston, and more recently of Buffalo. Ancient Cities from the Dawn to the Daylight; The World to Come; Master and Men: the Sermon on the Mountain practiced on the Plain. *Hou.*

Wright, William Henry. *N. C.*, 1814–1845. A military engineer in government service. Brief Practical Treatise on Mortars.

Wright, William James. *Vt.*, 1831——. A Presbyterian clergyman and educator, professor of metaphysics at Westminster College, Missouri, from 1887. Tracts on Higher Mathematics.

Wyatt, William Edward. *N. S.*, 1789–1864. An Episcopal clergyman of Baltimore, rector of St. Paul's Church, 1814–64. Christian Offices; The Parting Spirit's Address to His Mother.

Wyckoff, William Cornelius. *N. Y.*, 1832–1882. Son of W. H. Wyckoff, *infra.* The scientific editor of The New York Tribune, 1869–78. Silk Goods in America; American Silk Manufacture.

Wyckoff, William Henry. *N. Y.*, 1807–1877. A Baptist clergyman and educator of New York city. American Bible Society and the Baptists; Documentary History of the American Bible Union.

Wyeth, John Allan. *Al.*, 1845——. A surgeon of New York city, founder, in 1880, of the New York Polyclinic and Hospital, the first graduate medical school in America. Essays on Surgical Anatomy and Surgery; Text-Book on Surgery. *Ap.*

Wylie, Theodore William John. *Pa.*, 1818——. A Reformed Presbyterian clergyman of Philadelphia. English, Latin, and Greek Vocabulary; The God of Our Fathers; Washington as a Christian.

Wylie, Theophilus Adam. *Pa.*, 1810–1895. A Reformed Presbyterian clergyman and educator, professor of ancient languages in the University of Indiana from 1864. History of the University of Indiana.

Wyman, Edwin Allen. *Me.*, 1834——. A clergyman of Malden, Massachusetts. Acquaintance with God, or Salvation and Character.

Wyman, Jeffries. *Ms.*, 1814-1874. A physician and scientist of distinction, Hersey professor of anatomy in Harvard University, 1847-74. He was the author of Fresh-Water Shell-Mounds of the St. John's River, Florida, and many scientific monographs of much value. *See Atlantic Monthly, November, 1874; Biographical Memoirs of National Academy of Science, vol. 3.*

Wyman, Mrs. Lillie Buffum [Chace]. *R. I.*, 1837——. Poverty Grass, a collection of short stories.

Wyman, Morrill. *Ms.*, 1812——. Brother of J. Wyman, *supra*. A physician of Cambridge. Practical Treatise on Ventilation; Progress in School Discipline; Autumnal Catarrh. *Hou.*

Wynne, James. *N. Y.*, 1814-1871. A physician of New York city. Lives of Eminent Literary and Scientific Men of America; Importance of the Study of Legal Medicine; The Private Libraries of New York.

Wynne, Mrs. Madelene [Yale]. *N. Y.*, 1847——. Daughter of Mrs. Yale, *infra*. A Chicago artist and worker in silver. The Little Room and Other Stories. *Wy.*

Wythe, George. *Va.*, 1726-1806. A Virginia lawyer, professor of law at William and Mary College, 1779-89, and a Signer of the Declaration of Independence. Decisions of Cases in Virginia by the High Court of Chancery (1795).

Wythe, Joseph Henry. *E.*, 1822——. A Methodist clergyman and physician of San Francisco. The Microscopist; Curiosities of the Microscope; Agreement of Science and Revelation; The Science of Life; Biblical Biology; Easy Lessons in Vegetable Biology; Physiology of the Soul. *Meth.*

X

Xariffa. *See Townsend, Mrs.*

Y

Yale, Mrs. Catharine [Brooks]. *Vt.*, 1818——. A writer of Deerfield, Massachusetts, wife of the inventor of the Yale lock. Story of the Old Willard House of Deerfield, Mass.; Nim and Cum, and the Wonderhead Stories. *Hou. Wy.*

Yarrow, Henry Crecy. *Pa.*, 1840——. A physician in Washington, curator of the reptile department in the National Museum. Introduction to the Study of Mortuary Customs Among North American Indians.

Yates, John Van Ness. *N. Y.*, 1779-1839. A lawyer of Albany. Collection of Pleadings and Practical Precedents, with Notes; History of the State of New York (with J. Moulton); Principles and Practice, etc., in Cases of Writs of Error (with T. Tillinghast).

Yeaman, George Helm. *Ky.*, 1829——. A lawyer of New York city, minister to Denmark, 1865-70. The Study of Government.

Yoakum, Henderson K——. *Tn.*, 1810-1856. A lawyer of Huntsville, Texas. History of Texas from its First Settlement to its Annexation to the United States.

Youmans [yoo'manz], **Edward Livingston.** *N. Y.*, 1821-1887. An eminent scientist who, though partially blind for many years, wrote and lectured extensively, beside editing The Popular Science Monthly, 1872-87. Handbook of Household Science; The Culture Demanded by Modern Life; Alcohol and the Constitution of Man; Chemical Atlas; Correlation and Conservation of Forces (edited). *See Life of, by J. Fiske, supra. Ap.*

Youmans, Eliza Ann. *N. Y.*, 1826——. Sister of E. L. Youmans, *supra*, and his assistant in his studies and researches. First and Second Books of Botany; Descriptive Botany; Lessons in Cookery. *Ap.*

Youmans, William Jay. *N. Y.*, 1838——. Brother of E. L. Youmans, *supra*. A physician and scientist of New York city, and editor of The Popular Science Monthly from 1887. Pioneers of Science in America (edited); co-author with Huxley of Elements of Physiology and Hygiene.

Young, Alexander. *Ms.*, 1800-1854. A Unitarian clergyman of Boston, pastor of the New South Church. Chronicles of the Pilgrim Fathers; Chronicles of the First Planters of the Colony of Massachusetts Bay, 1623–36. He edited The Library of Old English Prose Writers.

Young, Alexander. *Ms.*, 1836–1891. Son of A. Young, *supra*. A Boston journalist on the editorial staff of The Post. History of the Netherlands; Young Folks' History of the Netherlands. *Est.*

Young, Andrew White. *N. Y.*, 1862–1877. A journalist of Warsaw, New York. First Lessons in Civil Government; Citizens' Manual of Government and Law; The American Statesman; National Economy: a History of the Protective System; History of Warsaw; History of Wayne County, Indiana. *Clke.*

Young, Augustus. *Vt.*, 1785–1857. A jurist of St. Albans, Vermont. On the Quadrature of the Circle; Unity of Purpose.

Young, Charles Augustus. *N. H.*, 1834——. An astronomer of note, professor of astronomy at Princeton College from 1877. The Sun; A General Astronomy; Elements of Astronomy; Lessons in Astronomy; Uranography. *Ap. Gi.*

Young, Jesse Bowman. *Pa.*, 1844——. A Methodist clergyman, editor of The Central Christian Advocate from 1892. What a Boy Saw in the Army; Days and Nights on the Sea. *Meth.*

Young, John Russell. *Pa.*, 1841——. A journalist formerly of New York city and now of Philadelphia, minister to China, 1882–85. Around the World with General Grant. He has edited The Memorial History of Philadelphia.

Young, Mrs. Julia Evelyn [Ditto]. *N. Y.*, 1857——. A novelist and verse-writer of Buffalo. Adrift, a Story of Niagara; Glynne's Wife, a Story in Verse; Thistle Down. *Lip.*

Young, Loyal. *Ms.*, 1806——. A Presbyterian clergyman in Pennsylvania and West Virginia. From Dawn to Dusk; Ecce Diluvium; Interviews with Inspired Men; Commentary on Ecclesiastes.

Young, William. *Il.*, 1847——. A dramatist of note whose plays include, Pendragon; The Rajah; Jonquil; The Rogue's March; Ganelon; Joan of Arc; If I Were You; Young America; The House of Mauprat (with J. G. Wilson). He has also written Wishmakers' Town, a volume of verse.

Z

Zabriskie, Francis Nicoll. *N. Y.*, 1832–1891. A Dutch Reformed clergyman. Golden Fruit from Bible Trees; The Story of a Soul; Behold a Ladder; Life of Horace Greeley. *Fu. Ran.*

Zachos [zăk'os], **John Celivergos.** *Ty.*, 1820–18—. A Unitarian clergyman and educator. New American Speaker; Analytical Educator; Phonic Primer.

Zahm, John Augustine. *O.*, 1851——. A Roman Catholic clergyman, procurator-general of the Congregation of the Holy Cross, now (1897) living at Rome. Evolution and Dogma; Bible, Science and Faith; Sound and Music; Catholic Science and Scientists. *Mg.*

Zeisberger, David. *Ma.*, 1721–1808. A noted missionary of the Moravians in Pennsylvania and Ohio. Delaware and English Spelling-Book; Sermons for Children; Dictionary in German and Delaware; Essay Toward an Onondaga Grammar. In 1888 his Diary from 1781 to 1798, including the narrative of his eventful life among the Indians of Ohio, was translated from the original manuscript in German by Eugene Bliss, and for the first time published. *See Life of, by E. de Schweinitz, supra, 1870; Bibliography of Ohio.*

Zenos, Andrew Constantinides. *Ty.*, 1855——. A Presbyterian clergyman, professor of biblical theology in McCormick Theological Seminary, Chicago, from 1891. The Elements of the Higher Criticism; Compendium of Church History. *Fu.*

Ziegler, Henry. *Pa.*, 1816——. A Lutheran clergyman in Selinsgrove, Pennsylvania. Natural Theology; Apologetic Theology; Catechetics; The Pastor; The Preacher; Dogmatic Theology; The Value to the Lutheran Church of Her Confessions.

Zogbaum, Rufus Fairchild. *S. C.*, 1849——. An artist of New York city. Horse, Foot, and Dragoons, or Sketches of Army Life; All Hands. *Har.*

Zubly, John Joachim. *Sd.*, 1725–1781. A Presbyterian clergyman of Savannah, prominent during the period of the American Revolution, as an opponent of the Declaration of Independence. The Real Christian's Hope in Death; Sermon on the Repeal of the Stamp Act; An Humble Inquiry into the Nature of the Dependency of the American Colonies upon the Parliament of Great Britain; The Law of Liberty: a Sermon on American Affairs.

Zundel, John. *G.*, 1815–1882. A musician, organist of Plymouth Church, Brooklyn, 1850–78. Modern Organ School; The Amateur Organist; Treatise on Harmony and Modulation.

ADDENDA

A

Aaron, Samuel. *Pa.*, 1800–1865. A Baptist clergyman and educator of Mount Holly, New Jersey, prominent as an anti-slavery advocate. He published a number of popular text-books. Faithful Translation.

Addison, Daniel Dulany. *W. Va.*, 1863——. An Episcopal clergyman of Brookline, Massachusetts. Life of Lucy Larcom, *supra*; Life of Edward Bass, First Bishop of Massachusetts. *Hou.*

Addums, Mozis. *See Bagby, G. W.*

Alemany, Joseph Sadoc. *Sp.*, 1814–1888. A Roman Catholic missionary of Spanish birth, who came to the United States in 1841, and was made archbishop of San Francisco in 1853. He resigned his office in 1883 and returned to Spain. Life of Saint Dominic.

Allen, David Oliver. *Ms.*, 1800–1883. A Congregational missionary in Bombay for many years. India, Ancient and Modern.

Andrews, Charles McLean. *Ct.*, 1863——. A professor at Bryn Mawr College, Bryn Mawr, Pennsylvania. The Historical Development of Modern Europe from the Congress of Vienna to the Present Time; River Towns of Connecticut; The Old English Manor. *J. H. U. Put.*

Appel, Theodore. *Pa.*, 1823——. A German Reformed clergyman and educator in Lancaster, Pennsylvania. College Recollections; Beginnings of the Theological Seminary; Letters to Boys and Girls about the First Christmas at Bethlehem; Life of John Williamson Nevin, *supra*.

Ashmore, Ruth. *See Mallon, Mrs.*

Aspinwall, Mrs. Alicia [Towne]. 18——. A writer of juvenile tales, living in Brookline, Massachusetts. Short Stories for Short People; The Echo Maid and Other Stories. *Dut.*

Astor, John Jacob. *N.Y.*, 1864——. Cousin of W. W. Astor (page 12). A Journey in Other Worlds, a scientific romance. *Ap.*

Atlee, Washington Lemuel. *Pa.*, 1808–1878. A noted surgeon of Philadelphia. Ovarian Tumors and Ovariotomy.

Audsley, George Ashdown. *S.*, 1838——. A Scottish architect and art writer of note, now (1898) living in Plainfield, New Jersey. With his brother, William James Audsley, he has published Colour in Dress: a Manual for Ladies; Floral Decoration of Churches; Cottage, Lodge, and Village Architecture; Outlines of Ornament in the Leading Styles; Popular Dictionary of Architecture and the Allied Arts, in ten volumes; Polychromatic Decoration as applied to Buildings in the Mediæval Styles; and (with James Lord Bowes) The Keramic Art of Japan. His separate works include Guide to the Art of Illuminating and Missal Painting; Handbook of Christian Symbolism; The Art of Chromo-Lithography; Notes on Japanese Art; The Ornamental Arts of Japan.

Avery, Elroy McKendree. *Mch.*, 1844——. A prominent educator in Cleveland. Among his many school text-books are The Complete Chemist;

School Physics; Modern Principles of Natural Philosophy; Modern Electricity and Magnetism.

Avery, Isaac Wheeler. *Fl.*, 1837–——. A lawyer and journalist of Atlanta. Digest of the Georgia Supreme Court Reports; History of Georgia.

Aylesworth, Barton Orville. *Il.*, 1860——. A clergyman of the Christian denomination, now (1898) pastor in Denver. Song and Fable.

B

Bacon, Alice Mabel. *Ct.*, 1858——. A teacher in the Hampton Institute, Virginia. Japanese Girls and Women; A Japanese Interior. *Hou.*

Bagby, Albert Morris. 18——. A writer of New York city. Miss Träumerei: a Weimar Idyl, a popular musical novel. *Lam.*

Bagby, George William. "Mozis Addums." *Va.*, 1828–1883. A Virginia journalist and lecturer, of some note as a humourist. John M. Daniel's Latin Key; What I Did With My Fifty Millions; Meekins's Twinses. *See Hart's American Literature.*

Bailey, Mrs. Urania Locke [Stoughton]. "Una Locke." *Ms.*, 1820–1882. A Providence writer. The School at Elm Oak and the School of Life; The Crooked Tree; Dr. Plassid's Patients; Star Flowers; Holiday Tales (with F. L. Pratt).

Bailey, William H——. *N. C.*, 1831–——. A prominent North Carolina lawyer whose later life has been passed in Houston, Texas. The Conflict of Judicial Decisions; Onus Probandi; Self-taught Law; The Detective Faculty; The Fifth North Carolina Digest (edited). *Clke.*

Balch, Elizabeth. *N. Y.*, 1845–1890. A writer whose life was spent mainly in Europe. Mustard Leaves, or a Glimpse of London Society; Zorah, a Love Tale of Modern Egypt; An Author's Love, the answers to Prosper Mérimée's "Letters to an Inconnue."

Baldwin, George Colfax. *N. J.*, 1817——. A Baptist clergyman of Troy, New York. Representative Men of the New Testament; Representative Women from Eve to Mary; Model Prayer; Notes of a Forty-one Years' Pastorate. *Bap.*

Ballantine, William Gay. *D. C.*, 1848——. A Congregational clergyman and educator, president of Oberlin College, 1891–96. Inductive Logic. *Gi.*

Ballard, Harlan Hogue. *O.*, 1853——. An educator in Berkshire County, Massachusetts. Three Kingdoms; Handbook of Blunders in Writing and Speaking; The World of Matter; The American Plant Book (with S. P. Thayer).

Ballard, Mrs. Julia [Perkins]. *O.*, 1828–1894. A writer of children's books of notable excellence. Gathered Lilies; Lift a Little; Little Gold Keys; The Hole in the Bag and Other Stories; Insect Lives, revised and republished as Among the Moths and Butterflies. *Put.*

Barton, William Eleazar. *Il.*, 1861——. A Congregational clergyman, pastor in Boston from 1893. An associate editor of the Bibliotheca Sacra, and a writer of history, theology, and fiction. The Wind-Up of the Big Meetin' on No Bus'ness; Life in the Hills of Kentucky; Early Ecclesiastical History of the Western Reserve; Sim Galloway's Daughter-in-Law; The Truth about the Trouble at Roundstone; A Hero in Homespun: a Tale of the Loyal South; The Story of the Psalms. *Lam.*

Bates, Herbert. 186–. A Cincinnati journalist, but earlier a member of the faculty of the University of Nebraska. Songs of Exile. *Cop.*

Beale, Charles Willing. *D. C.*, 1845–——. A romance writer of Arden, North Carolina. (His wife, Mrs. M. Beale, is mentioned on page 22.) The Ghost of Guir House.

Beard, Daniel Carter. *O.*, 1850——. An artist and illustrator of New York city. What to Do and How to Do It; The American Boys' Handy Book; Six Feet of Romance; Moonlight; The American Boys' Book of Sport. *Scr.*

Beauregard, Pierre Gustave Toutant. *La.*, 1818–1893. A noted brigadier-general in the Confederate army during the Civil War. Principles and Maxims of the History of War; Report of the Defence of Charleston; A Commentary on the Campaign and Battle of Manassas (1891).

Behrends, Adolphus Julius Frederick. *H.*, 1839——. A Congregational clergyman, pastor of the Central Church in Brooklyn from 1883. Socialism and Christianity; The Philosophy of Preaching; The World for Christ. *Scr.*

Bellows, Albert Jones. *Ms.*, 1804–1869. A Boston physician. How not to be Sick; The Philosophy of Eating. *Hou.*

Beman, Nathan Sidney Smith. *N. Y.*, 1785–1871. A Presbyterian clergyman long settled in Troy, New York. The Old Ministry; The Influence of Freedom on Popular and National Education; Letters to John Hughes; Episcopacy Exclusive; Four Sermons on the Atonement.

Bendire, Charles Emil. *G.*, 1836–1897. An ornithologist of note, honorary curator of the department of oölogy in the United States National Museum, a captain and brevet major in the United States army. Life Histories of North American Birds. *See Science, February 12, 1897.*

Berenson, Bernhard. *Lithuania*, 1865——. An art writer now (1898) living in Florence, Italy. The Venetian Painters of the Renaissance; Lorenzo Lotto: an Essay in Art Criticism; The Florentine Painters of the Renaissance; The Central Italian Painters of the Renaissance; The Drawings of the Florentine Painters. *Put.*

Bernadou, John Baptiste. *Pa.*, 1858——. A United States naval officer in the employ of the naval department at Washington from 1888. A Trip through Northern Corea in 1883–84.

Bicknell, Anna Louisa. *F.*, 183—. ——. The Story of Marie Antoinette; Life in the Tuileries under the Second Empire. *Cent.*

Bicknell, Thomas Williams. *R. I.*, 1834——. A prominent educator of Rhode Island and Massachusetts. Memoir of William Lord Noyes; A History of Barrington, Rhode Island; John Myles and Religious Toleration in Massachusetts.

Bigelow, Andrew. *Ms.*, 1795–1877. A Unitarian clergyman of Boston. Leaves from a Journal; Travels in Malta and Sicily.

Bigelow, Lafayette Jotham. *N.Y.*, 1835–1870. A lawyer and journalist of Watertown, New York. Bench and Bar: a Digest of the Wit, Humor, and Asperities of the Law.

Bill, Ledyard. *Ct.*, 1836——. A former publisher of New York city, but from 1874 resident in Paxton, Massachusetts. Ten Pictures of the War: Lyrics; History of the Bill Family; A Winter in Florida; Minnesota: its Character and Climate; History of Paxton.

Bliss, George. *Ms.*, 1830–1897. A prominent lawyer of New York city. Treatise on the Law of Life Insurance; Annotated Edition of the New York Code of Civil Procedure, usually styled "Bliss's Code."

Blodgett, Mrs. Mabel [Fuller]. *Me.*, 1869——. A writer of Brookline, Massachusetts. The Aspen Shade, a novel; Fairy Tales; In Poppy Land, a book of fairy tales; At the Queen's Mercy, a tale of adventure. *Lam.*

Blunt, Stanhope English. *Ms.*, 1850——. A colonel in the ordnance department of the United States army. Firing Regulations for Small Arms; Instructions in Rifle and Carbine Firing in the United States army. *Scr.*

Bolles, John Augustus. *Ct.*, 1809–1878. A Boston lawyer. Treatise on Usury and Usury Laws; Essay on a Congress of Nations.

Bonsal, Stephen. *Md.*, 1863——. A journalist of New York city, special correspondent of the New York Herald in Cuba and elsewhere, and secretary of the United States Legations in Peking, Madrid, and Tokio, 1890–95. Morocco as It Is; The Condition of Cuba. *Har.*

Bourne, Edward Gaylord. *N. Y.*, 1860——. A professor of history at Yale University from 1895. The History of the Surplus Revenue of 1837.

Bowser, Edward Albert. *N. B.*, 1845——. A professor of mathematics and engineering in Rutgers College, New Brunswick, New Jersey, from 1870, and a mathematician of promiinence. Analytic Geometry; Differential and Integral Calculus; Analytic Mechanics; Hydro-mechanics; Academic Algebra; College Algebra; Plane and Solid Geometry; Elements of Trigonometry; Treatise on Trigonometry; Logarithmic Tables. *He. Vn.*

Boynton, Charles Brandon. *Ms.*, 1806–1883. A Presbyterian clergyman of Cincinnati. Journey Through Kansas (1855); The Russian Empire; The Four Great Powers; History of the American Navy During the Rebellion; Doctrines and Duties. *Ap.*

Boynton, Henry Van Ness. *Ms.*, 1835——. Son of C. B. Boynton, *supra.* A journalist of Washington city, brevetted brigadier-general for service in the Federal army during the Civil War. Sherman's Historical Raid; Was General Thomas slow at Nashville?; The National Military Park: Chickamauga–Chattanooga. *Clke.*

Brewster, Anne M—— Hampton. *Pa.*, 1818–1892. A writer whose later life was passed in Rome. Compensation, or Always a Future; Saint Martin's Summer.

Brewster, Charles Warren. *N. H.*, 1812–1868. A journalist of Portsmouth, New Hampshire. Fifty Years in a Printing Office; Rambles about Portsmouth.

Bridgman, Frederic Arthur. *Al.*, 1847——. A noted painter of oriental subjects. Winters in Algeria.

Briggs, Le Baron Russell. *Ms.*, 1855——. A professor of English at Harvard University from 1885 and dean of the University from 1891. Original Charades. *Scr.*

Brimmer, Martin. *Ms.*, 1829–1896. A prominent citizen of Boston. Egypt: Three Essays on the History, Religion, and Art of Ancient Egypt. *Hou.*

Brown, Charles Rufus. *N. H.*, 1849——. A Baptist clergyman, professor of Hebrew at the Theological Seminary, Newton, Massachusetts. The Aramaic Method, Part I., Text, Notes, and Vocabulary; The Aramaic Method, Part II., Grammar. *Scr.*

Brown, Solyman. *Ct.*, 1790–1876. A Swedenborgian minister of New York city. Essay on American Poetry (1814); Dentologia; Dental Hygeia.

Browne, Causten. *D. C.*, 1828——. A lawyer of Boston. Treatise on the Construction of the Statute of Frauds. *Lit.*

Bruce, Henry. 18——. A littérateur who has written James Edward Oglethorp and the Founding of the Georgia Colony; Samuel Houston and the Annexation of Texas. *Do.*

Bryan, William Jennings. *Il.*, 1860——. A noted politician of Lincoln, Nebraska, prominent in 1896 as the Democratic candidate for the Presidency. The First Battle: a Story of the Campaign of 1896.

Buckalew, Charles R——. *Pa.*, 1821——. A prominent United States Senator from Pennsylvania. Proportional Representation; An Examination of the Constitution of Pennsylvania.

Buel, Clarence Clough. *N. Y.*, 1850——. An assistant editor of the Century Magazine. Battles and Leaders of the Civil War.

Bullock, Charles Jesse. *Ms.*, 1869——. An instructor in economics at Cornell University. Introduction to the Study of Economics; Finances of the United States from 1775 to 1789.

Burroughs, Stephen. *N. H.*, 1765–1840. A once famous adventurer whose Memoirs of My Own Life (1811) were long popular. In his later years he was a successful and beloved educator in Canada.

Buntline, Ned. *See Judson, Edward* (page 214).

Byrne, William. *I.*, 1836——. A Roman Catholic clergyman, vicar-general of the archdiocese of Boston. Catholic Doctrine.

C

Callender, Guy Stevens. *O.*, 1865——. An historical writer who has published English Capital and American Resources in 1815–1860.

Canfield, James Hulme. *O.*, 1847——. An educator of Ohio, president of Ohio State University from 1895. Taxation; Short History of Kansas; Local Government in Kansas.

Carpenter, William. *E.*, 1830–1896. An eccentric English printer and stenographer who removed from England to Baltimore in 1879. He strenuously advocated the theory that the earth is flat, revolving on a central axis with the sun stationary over the centre. Among his various writings are, The Earth Not a Globe, by Common Sense; Sir Isaac Newton's Theoretical Astronomy Examined and Refuted by Common Sense; Water not Convex; Proctor's Planet Earth; Something About Spiritualism.

Cavazza, Mrs. *See Pullen.*

Chancellor, Eustathius. *Va.*, 1854——. A physician who has published Researches upon Treatment of Delirium Tremens; Gonorrhœal Articular Rheumatism; Woman in the Social Sphere; Marriage Philosophy; Correlation of Physical and Vital Forces; The Pacific Slope and its Scenery.

Chanler, William Astor. 1867——. Through Jungle and Deserts: Travels in Eastern Africa. *Mac.*

Chapman, Frank Michler. *N. J.*, 1864——. A well-known ornithologist, assistant curator of the department of ornithology and mammalogy in the American Museum of Natural History, New York city. Hand-book of Birds of Eastern North America; Bird-Life: A Guide to the Study of our Common Birds. *Ap.*

Cheney, Charles Edward. *N. Y.*, 1836——. A bishop of the Reformed Episcopal church, consecrated in 1873, and rector of Christ Church, Chicago, from 1860. The Evangelical Ideal of a Visible Church; A Word to Old-Fashioned Episcopalians; The Prayer which God Denied, and Other Sermons; Enlistment of the Christian Soldier.

Child, Frank Samuel. *N. Y.*, 1854——. A Congregational clergyman of Fairfield, Connecticut, known as a lecturer on historical subjects. The Boyhood of Beecher; Be Strong to Hope; The Friendship of Jesus; An Old New England Town; The Colonial Parson of New England; A Colonial Witch. *Ba. Scr.*

Childs, Thomas Spencer. *Ms.*, 1825——. An Episcopal clergyman of Washington city, but for many years prior to 1890 in the Presbyterian ministry. The Heritage of Peace; The Lost Faith; Difficulties of the Scriptures Tested by the Laws of Evidence.

Clark, Frederick Thickstun. "Frederick Thickstun." *Pa.*, 1858——. A novelist of Denver, Colorado, whose stories deal with phases of Western life. A Mexican Girl; In the Valley of Havilah; On Cloud Mountain; The Mistress of the Ranch. *Har. Hou.*

Cleveland, [Stephen] Grover. *N. J.*, 1837——. The twenty-second President of the United States. The Self-Made Man in American Life. *See Lives by Chamberlain, 1884; Hensel, 1884; King, 1884; Welch, 1884; Dieck, 1888; Grover Cleveland, by J. L. Whittle, 1896; The Hawaiian Incident, by J. A. Gillis, 1897; Atlantic Monthly, March, 1897. Cr.*

Cole, William Morse. "Christopher Craigie." *Ms.*, 1866——. An educator resident in Concord, Massachusetts, now (1898) a university extension lecturer on economics. An Old Man's Romance. *Cop.*

Collins, Louis. *Ky.*, 1797–1870. A journalist and jurist of Maysville, Kentucky. Historical Sketches of Kentucky; History of Kentucky.

Colvocoresses, George Musalas. *Gr.*, 1816–1872. A United States naval officer. Four Years in a Government Exploring Expedition.

Commons, John Rogers. *O.*, 1862——. A professor of sociology at Syracuse University from 1895. The Distribution of Wealth; Social Reform and the Church; Proportional Representation; State Supervision for Cities. *Cr. Mac.*

Converse, Florence. *La.*, 1871——. A novelist of New Orleans. Diana Victrix. *Hou.*

Cook, William Henry. *N. Y.*, 1832——. A physician of Cincinnati. Physio-Medical Surgery; Woman's Book of Health; Physio-Medical Dispensatory; Spermatorrhœa; Science and Practice of Medicine.

Cook, William Wilson. *Mch.*, 1857——. A lawyer of New York city. Stock and Stockholders, Bonds, Mortgages, and General Corporation Law, a work which has passed into several editions; The Corporation Problem. *Put.*

Coonley, Mrs. Lydia [Avery]. *Va.*, 1845——. A Chicago writer of pleasing verse. Under the Pines, and Other Verses; Singing Verses for Children. *Mac. Wy.*

Cooper, Samuel. *Ms.*, 1724–1783. An influential clergyman of Boston, eminent as a preacher and pastor of Brattle Street Church, 1744–83. Beside a number of published sermons he was the author of The Crisis, an argument for a colonial excise. *See Sprague's Annals of the American Pulpit; Tyler's Literary History of the American Revolution.*

Cory, Charles Barney. "Owen Nox." *Ms.*, 1857——. An ornithologist of Boston. A Naturalist in the Magdalen Islands; Birds of the Bahama Islands; Southern Rambles; The Beautiful and Curious Birds of the World; Birds of Haiti and San Domingo; Catalogue of West Indian Birds; Hunting and Fishing in Florida; The Birds of Eastern North America; How to Know the Shore Birds of North America; How to Know the Ducks, Geese, and Swans of North America; The Birds of the West Indies; Key to the Water Birds of Florida. *Est. Lit.*

Craigie, Christopher. *See Cole, W. M.*

Crevecœur, Jean Hector Saint-John de. *F.*, 1731–1813. A writer of French birth who settled in Pennsylvania at the age of twenty-three, long famous for his Letters from an American Farmer, which was translated into French, German, and Dutch; a work which had much influence in stimulating emigration to America, and a distinct literary value. His other works include La Culture des Pommes de Terre; Voyage dans la Haute Pennsylvanie et dans l'État de New York. *See Tyler's Literary History of the American Revolution.*

Crosby, Fanny J. *See Van Alstyne, Mrs.*

Cuckson, John. *E.*, 1846——. A Unitarian clergyman of Boston, pastor of the Arlington Street Church from 1892. Faith and Fellowship. *Hou.*

D

Dallinger, Frederick William. *Ms.*, 1871——. A politician of Cambridge. Nominations for Elective Office in the United States. *Lgs.*

Davis, David D——. *Pa.*, 1854——. A Presbyterian clergyman, professor of Semitic philology and Old Testament theology at Princeton Theological Seminary from 1888. Genesis and Semitic Tradition; The Sunday-school Teacher's Bible Manual. *Scr.*

Davis, William Thomas. *Ms.*, 1822——. A lawyer and historical writer of Plymouth, Massachusetts. Ancient Landmarks of Plymouth; History of Plymouth; The Bench and Bar of the Commonwealth of Massachusetts.

De Fontaine, Felix. *Ms.*, 1832–1896. A journalist of Charleston during the Civil War, but subsequently, and for the greater part of his career, on the staff of The New York Herald. Gleanings from a Confederate Army Notebook; Army Letters of Personne, 1861–1865; News from the Front.

Dixon, Frank H——. *Min.*, 1869——. An assistant professor of political economy at the University of Michigan. State Railroad Control, with a History of its Development in Iowa. *Cr.*

Dodge, Walter Phelps. *Sa.*, 1869——. Nephew of William Walter Phelps, American Minister to Germany, 1889–93. A littérateur now (1898) living in London, and practising at the English bar. Three Greek Tales; As the Crow Flies from Corsica to Charing Cross; A Strong Man Armed.

Dresser, Horatio Willis. *Me.*, 1866——. A Boston writer, editor of the Journal of Practical Metaphysics (1898). The Power of Silence; The Perfect Whole; In Search of a Soul.

Dunning, Edwin James. *N. Y.*, 1821——. A Cambridge writer, but in earlier life a dentist in New York city for many years. The Genesis of Shakespeare's Art: a Study of his Sonnets and Poems. *Le.*

Du Pont, Henry Algernon. *Del.*, 1838——. A brevet lieutenant-colonel in the United States army. Cavalry Tactics; Artillery Tactics.

E

Eastman, Charles Rochester. *Ia.*, 1868——. A scientist of Cambridge, an assistant in the Museum of Comparative Zoölogy. Beiträge zur Kenntniss der Gettung Oxyrhyna. He edited and translated from the German of Karl von Zittel a Text-Book of Palæontology. *Mac.*

Elliot, Daniel Giraud. 18——. An ornithologist of Chicago, at one time president of the American Ornithologists' Union. Monograph of the Pittidæ or Family of the Ant Thrushes; The New and Heretofore Unfigured Species of the Birds of North America (1869); The Life and Habits of Wild Animals; Classification and Synopsis of the Trochilidæ; North American Shore Birds; The Gallinaceous Game Birds of North America; and many ornithological monographs.

Ernst, Oswald Hubert. *O.*, 1842——. A military engineer with the rank of major. A Manual of Practical Military Engineering. *Vn.*

F

Fisher, Sidney George. 1808–1871. A lawyer of Philadelphia. The Trial of the Constitution; Kansas and its Constitution.

Fiske, Amos Kidder. *N. H.*, 1842——. A journalist of New York city. Midnight Talks at the Club, a series of social essays; Beyond the Bourn; The Jewish Scriptures; The Myths of Israel. *Scr.*

Flandrau, Charles Macomb. *Min.*, 187——. A former instructor in English at Harvard University. Harvard Episodes. *Cop.*

Fletcher, Horace. *Ms.*, 1869——. A writer whose life has been largely spent abroad, and who is now (1898) living in Berlin. Menticulture; Happiness. *S.*

Foster, David Skaats. 18——. Rebecca the Witch, and Other Tales in Metre, first issued as The Romance of the Unexpected; Spanish Castles by the Rhine, a Triptychal Yarn. *Ho.*

Frazar, Douglas. *Ms.*, 1836–1896. A colonel in the Federal army during the Civil War, brevetted brigadier-general of volunteers at the close of the war, and subsequently a citizen of Somerville, Massachusetts. The Log of the Maryland; Perseverance Island; Practical Boat-Sailing. *Le.*

G

Gilbert, Howard Worcester. *Pa.*, 1819–1894. An educator in Pennsylvania, once prominent as an abolitionist. Aldornere, a Pennsylvanian Idyl, and Other Poems.

Gilder, Jeannette Leonard. *Pa.*, 185——. Sister of R. W. Gilder (page 146). A journalist of New York city, editor of The Critic. Taken by Siege, a novel. *Scr.*

Glasgow, Ellen. *Va.*, 1875——. A novelist of Richmond, Virginia. The Descendant: a Novel. *Har.*

Goodell, William. *Ms.*, 1792–1867. A Congregationalist missionary in Syria and Turkey, 1822–55. (His son of the same name is mentioned on page 150.) Come-Outerism; American Constitutional Law and its Bearing upon American Slavery; The Democracy of Christianity; Slavery and Anti-Slavery; The Old and the New, or the Changes of Thirty Years in the East; The American Slave Code in Theory and Practice; American Slavery a Formidable Obstacle to the Conversion of the World.

Goodwin, Hermon Camp. *N. Y.*, 1813–1891. A journalist of Central New York. The Pioneer History of Cortland County and the Border Wars of New York; Life of John Jacob Astor; Legends of Poland; History of Ithaca, New York; Edgar Wentworth.

Goss, Elbridge Henry. *Ms.*, 1830——. A writer of Melrose, Massachusetts. Life of Colonel Paul Revere; Melrose Memorial.

Gray, Morris. *Ms.*, 1856——. A Boston lawyer. Treatise on the Law of Communication by Telegraph. *Lit.*

Grier, James Alexander. *Pa.*, 1846——. A United Presbyterian clergyman of Pennsylvania, professor in Alleghany Theological Seminary. Secret Societies; Biography of Jeremiah Rankine Johnston.

H

Hale, William Bayard. *Ind.*, 1869——. An Episcopal clergyman of Middleborough, Massachusetts, who has contributed noteworthy articles on religion and sociology to The Forum. Phillips Brooks: a Memorial; The Eternal Teacher; The Making of the American Constitution: a Genesis of Nationality; The New Obedience: a Plea for Social Submission to Christ. *Lgs.*

Hallowell, Mrs. Anna Coffin [Davis]. *Pa.*, 1838——. Wife of R. P. Hallowell (page 167). James and Lucretia Mott: their Life and Letters. *Hou.*

Hallowell, Mrs. Sarah Catharine [Fraley]. *Pa.*, 1833——. A Philadelphia journalist, an associate editor of the Public Ledger from 1877. On the Church Steps; Nan, the New-Fashioned Girl.

Hamblen, Herbert Elliott. "Frederick Benton Williams." *N. H.*, 1849——. A New York writer who has had a varied experience as sailor and railroad man. On Many Seas; The General Manager's Story; The Mystery of the Dead Man on the Davit; A Tough Experience; Will Kimball's Adventures, are among his works. *Mac.*

Hapgood, Norman. *Il.*, 1868——. A journalist of New York city, now (1898) on the editorial staff of the Commercial Advertiser. Literary Statesmen and Others, a collection of essays of notable excellence. *S.*

Harben, Will[iam] N[athaniel]. *Ga.*, 1858——. A novelist of New York city. White Marie; Almost Persuaded; A Mute Confessor; The Land of the Changing Sun; From Clue to Climax. *Cas. Lip. Mer.*

Harding, Chester. *N. Y.*, 1843——. A former secretary of the United States legation at Pekin. The Real Chinaman. *Do.*

Harrison, Benjamin. *O.*, 1832——. The twenty-third President of the United States. This Country of Ours. *See Life of, by L. Wallace. Cent.*

Hazen, Charles Downer. *Vt.*, 1868——. A professor of history at Smith College, Northampton, Massachusetts, from 1894. Contemporary American Opinion of the French Revolution; a translation of Borgeaud's Adoption and Amendment of Constitutions in Europe and America. *J. H. U. Mac.*

Henderson, Marc Antony. *See Strong, G. A.*

Herrick, Robert [Welch]. *Ms.*, 1868——. An assistant professor of rhetoric at the University of Chicago. The Man who Wins, a novel; Literary Love-Letters, and Other Stories. *Scr.*

Hicks, Lewis Ezra. 18——. A professor of geology in Denison University, Granville, Ohio. A Critique of Design Arguments: an Examination of the Methods of Reasoning in Natural Theology. *Scr.*

Hill, Henry. *N. Y.*, 1795–188–. Southern Africa; Recollections of an Octogenarian.

Hoffman, Charles Frederick. *N. Y.*, 1830–1897. Brother of E. A. Hoffman (page 188). An Episcopal clergyman, rector of All-Angels Church, New York city, 1873–97. All the Week Through; Days and Nights with Jesus.

Horton, Edward Augustus. *Ms.*, 1843——. A prominent Unitarian clergyman of Boston. Noble Lives and Noble Deeds.

Horton, George. 18——. An American consul at Athens. Songs of the Lowly; In Unknown Seas; Constantine: a Tale of Greece under King Otho; Aphroessa. *Wy.*

Houghton, Mrs. Louise Seymour. *N. Y.*, 1838——. A writer of New York city, on the editorial staff of The Evangelist. Beside publishing a number of translations of foreign juvenile works and of Sabatier's Saint Francis of Assisi, she has written Fifine; The Sabbath Month; Faithful to the End; The Log of the Lady Grey; Antipas, son of Chuza, and Others whom Jesus Loved. *Ran. Scr.*

Howe, Mark Antony De Wolfe. *R. I.*, 1864——. Son of M. A. De W. Howe (page 198). A littérateur of Bristol, Rhode Island. Shadows, a book of verse; American Bookmen. *Cop. Do.*

Hughes, Thomas Aloysius. *E.*, 1849——. A Roman Catholic clergyman of the Society of Jesus, now (1898) attached to the Saint Louis University at Saint Louis. The Acolyte, a Story for Catholic Youth; Four Lectures on Anthropology and Biology; Loyola and the Educational System of the Jesuits. *Scr.*

Hughes, Thomas Patrick. *E.*, 1838 ——. An Episcopal clergyman of New York city from 1885, and for twenty years previously an English missionary in Northern India. Notes on Muhammadanism; Dictionary of Islam; Ruhainah, a Story of Afghan Life; American Ancestry. He has also published several text-books in Pushto, the Afghan language, and several editions of Afghan poets. *Scr. Wh.*

Humphreys, Frank Landon. *N.Y.*, 1858——. An Episcopal clergyman resident (1898) in Morristown, New Jersey, who has written and lectured on musical and historical themes, and is an authority upon church music. The Evolution of Church Music; The Mystery of the Passion; English Church Music; Men of Understanding; Carols and Carolling; Chaplains of the Revolution. *Scr.*

Hunt, Edward Bissell. *Ms.*, 1822-1863. A military engineer. Union Foundations: a Study of American Nationality.

Hunt, Sanford. *N. Y.*, 1825-1896. A Methodist clergyman of prominence, long associated with the Methodist Book Concern. Handbook for Trustees of Religious Corporations in the State of New York; Laws Relating to Religious Corporations in the United States. *Meth.*

I

Ide, Mrs. Frances Otis [Ogden]. "Ruth Ogden." *L. I.*, 1853——. A popular Brooklyn writer of juvenile tales. A Little Queen of Hearts; His Little Royal Highness; A Loyal Little Red Coat; Courage; Little Homespun. *St.*

Ingle, Edward. *Md.*, 1861——. An historical writer. Local Institutions of Maryland; Local Institutions of Virginia; Southern Sidelights. *Cr. J. H. U.*

Inman, Henry. *N. Y.*, 183——. A United States army officer. The Old Santa Fé Trail: the Story of a Great Highway. *Mac.*

Ireland, John. *I.*, 1838——. The Roman Catholic archbishop of Saint Paul, well known as a writer and speaker upon educational themes. The Church and Modern Society.

J

Jak. *See Williams, Mrs. Anna* (page 425).

K

Keasbey, Lindley Miller. *N. J.*, 1867——. A professor of history and economics at the University of Colorado, 1892-94, and at Bryn Mawr College, Bryn Mawr, Pennsylvania, from 1894. The Nicaragua Canal and the Monroe Doctrine. *Put.*

Keely, Robert Neff. *Pa.*, 1860——. A Philadelphia physician. In Arctic Seas.

Keith, Charles Penrose. *Pa.*, 1854——. A lawyer of Philadelphia. The Provincial Councillors of Pennsylvania between 1733 and 1776, and those Earlier Councillors who were sometime Chief Magistrates of the Province, and their Descendants.

Keith, Sir William. *E.*, 1680-1749. A royal surveyor-general of customs in America and subsequantly lieutenant-governor of Pennsylvania and Delaware. The History of the British Plantations in America, Part I.: The History of Virginia, 1738; Public Spirit; Papers and Tracts; On the Subject of Taxing the Colonies.

Kellogg, John Harvey. *Mch.*, 1852——. A physician of Battle Creek, Michigan, for many years editor of Good Health. Ladies' Guide in Health and Disease; Home Handbook of Hygiene and Rational Medicine; Man the Masterpiece; Plain Facts for Old and Young.

Kent, Charles Foster. *N. Y.*, 1867——. A professor of biblical literature and history at Brown University from 1895. A History of the Hebrew People; Outline Study of Hebrew History; Wise Men of Ancient Israel; Students' Chronological Chart of Biblical History; History of the Jewish People. *Bap. Scr. Sil.*

Kimball, Hannah Parker. *Ms.*, 1861 ——. A Boston poet, whose work in-includes Soul and Sense, and Other Verses; The Cup of Life, and Other Poems; Victory, and Other Verses. *Cop.*

Kinley, David. *S.*, 1861——. An educator in Illinois, professor of economics and dean of the college of literature and arts at the University of Illinois. The Independent Treasury System of the United States. *Cr.*

Kipling, Rudyard. *E. I.*, 1865——. A distinguished English writer, born in Bombay. He was educated in England, but was for some years in the Indian civil service, leaving India, however, in 1889. Later he married the sister of C. W. Balestier, *supra*, and made his home in Brattleboro', Vermont. The greater part of his work in prose and verse has an East Indian *locale*, but some of his latest stories have an American local colouring. As a writer of fiction his rank is deservedly high, and in The Seven Seas, as well as in the Recessional, published after the Queen's Jubilee of 1897, he has abundantly vindicated his claim to the name of poet. His prose comprises Plain Tales from the Hills; Wee Willie Winkie, and Other Stories; The Light that Failed; Soldiers Three; The Naulahka (with C. W. Balestier, *supra*); The Jungle Book; The Second Jungle Book; Captains Courageous; The Walking Delegate; Life's Handicap. His verse includes Barrack Room Ballads, and Other Verses; Departmental Ditties, and Other Verses; The Seven Seas. *See The Critic, January 21, 1893; The Fortnightly Review, November, 1893; The Forum, June, 1895, and December, 1896; Atlantic Monthly, January, 1897; Review of Reviews, February, 1897. Mac.*

Knowles, Frederic Lawrence. *Ms.*, 1869——. A littérateur and educator in Tilton, New Hampshire. He has published, Practical Hints for Young Readers, Writers, and Book-Buyers, and edited Cap and Gown, a collection of college verse; The Golden Treasury of American Songs, and other verse compilations. *Kt.*

Knowles, James Davis. *R. I.*, 1798–1838. A Baptist minister of Boston. Memoir of Mrs. Ann Judson; Memoir of Roger Williams.

L

Lanman, James Henry. *Ct.*, 1812–1887. Uncle of C. Lanman (page 223). A lawyer and littérateur of New York city. History of Michigan (1842).

Laurie, Thomas. *S.*, 1821–1897. A Congregational clergyman of Providence. Dr. Grant and the Mountain Nestorians; Woman and her Saviour in Persia, reprinted as Morning on the Mountains; Glimpses of Christ; The Ely Volume, or The Contributions of Foreign Missions to Science; Assyrian Echoes of the Word.

Learned, William Law. *Ct.*, 1821–——. A jurist of Albany who edited The Journal of Madam Knight (page 220), and published The Learned Family, a genealogy.

Lewis, Alfred Henry. "Dan Quin." 18——. A journalist of New York City. Wolfville, episodes of cowboy life.

Lloyd, John Uri. *N. Y.*, 1849——. A botanist and pharmacist of Cincinnati. The Chemistry of Medicine; Elixirs: their History, Formulæ, and Method of Preparation; Etidorhpa, or the End of Earth, the title of which is Aphrodite reversed; The Right Side of the Car; The American Dispensatory (with John King); Drugs and Medicines of North America (with C. G. Lloyd), and many contributions to professional journals. *Clke.*

Lord, Augustus Mendon. *Cal.*, 1861 ——. A Unitarian clergyman of Providence. A Book of Verses.

Loud, Mrs. Marguerite St. Leon [Barstow]. *Pa.*, *c.* 1800–18—. A verse-writer of Philadelphia. Wayside Flowers.

Loveman, Robert. *O.*, 1864——. A writer of Dalton, Georgia, whose verse displays much quiet beauty of thought and expression. Poems. *Lip.*

Lush, Charles Keeler. *Wis.*, 1861–——. A Milwaukee journalist. The Federal Judge, a political novel. *Hou.*

M

McCulloch, Hunter. *S.*, 1847-——. A verse writer of Philadelphia. From Dawn to Dusk, and Other Poems. *Lip.*

McHenry, James. *I.*, 1785-1845. A physician of Philadelphia, whose poems and sensational novels once attracted attention. His fictions include: O'Halloran, or The Insurgent; The Wilderness; A Spectre of the Forest; The Hearts of Steel; The Betrothed of Wyoming; Meredith. His other works are, The Pleasures of Friendship; Waltham; The Antediluvians, a Narrative Poem in Ten Books; The Usurper, a tragedy.

Mackie, Pauline Bradford. *Ct.*, 1873——. A novelist of Washington city. Mademoiselle de Bernay: a Story of Valley Forge. *Lam.*

Mackubin, Ellen. *Il.*, 18———. A novelist of Baltimore. The King of the Town, a novel. *Hou.*

Main, Thomas. *S.*, 1828-1896. A mechanical engineer, professor of shipbuilding in the Webb Academy of Shipbuilding, New York city. History of the Steam Engine.

Mallon, Mrs. Isabel [Sloan]. "Ruth Ashmore." 18—. A popular writer on deportment. Side Talks with Girls. *Scr.*

Martin, Mrs. Jane [Percy]. *E.*, 1847-——. A story-writer of Pendleton, Oregon. Lost and Saved.

Mason, Lowell. *Ms.*, 1792-1872. A famous Boston musician who, beside publishing many collections of sacred and secular music which included many pieces of his own composition, was the author of Musical Letters from Abroad, and several musical text-books.

Mason, Mary Augusta. *N. Y.*, 18———. An adopted daughter of C. M. Dickinson (page 98). With the Seasons, a collection of verse of more than average merit. *Ran.*

Mason, William. *Ms.*, 1829——. Son of L. Mason, *supra*. A musician of New York city. Easy System for Beginners (with Hoadley); Piano Forte Technics (with Mathews); Touch and Technic.

Mead, Theodore Hoe. *N. Y.*, 1837-——. A manufacturer in New York city. Our Mother Tongue; Health Without Medicine; Horsemanship for Women. *Do.*

Meigs, William Montgomery. *Pa.*, 1852——. Son of J. F. Meigs, *supra*, grandson of C. J. Ingersoll, *supra*. A lawyer of Philadelphia. Life of Josiah Meigs; Life of Charles Jared Ingersoll.

Mifflin, John Houston. *Pa.*, 1807-1883. An artist and author of Columbia, Pennsylvania. Rhymes of an Artist. He was a portrait and miniature painter of much delicacy.

Mifflin, Lloyd. *Pa.*, 1846——. Son of J. H. Mifflin, *supra*. A poet and artist of Columbia, Pennsylvania. At the Gates of Song, a volume of one hundred and fifty sonnets; On the Slopes of Helicon and Other Poems; Memorial Day Ode; The Hills: a Poem; Conversation as a Fine Art. *Est.*

Mifflin, Samuel Wright. *Pa.*, 1805-1885. Cousin of J. H. Mifflin, *supra*. A civil engineer of Pennsylvania. Location, for Railway Engineers.

Moffat, William David. *N. J.*, 1865——. Son of J. C. Moffat (page 258). A New York writer of stories for boys, business manager of The Book-Buyer and Scribner's Magazine. The County Pennant; The Crimson Banner; Brad Mattoon; Not Without Honor, a novel.

Moody, William Godwin. 18———. Land and Labor in the United States; Our Labor Difficulties. *Scr.*

Morison, John Hopkins. *N. H.*, 1808-1896. A Unitarian clergyman, pastor at Milton, Massachusetts, 1846-1885. Life of Honorable Jeremiah Smith; Disquisitions and Notes on the Gospel of Saint Matthew; The Great Poets as Religious Teachers. *See John Hopkins Morison, Memoir, 1897.*

Murfree, William Law. *N. C.*, 1817-1892. A lawyer of Murfreesboro, Tennessee, and, in later life, of St. Louis. His daughters, F. N. and M. N. Murfree, are mentioned on page 266. A Treatise on the Law of Sheriffs; Official Bonds; Practice before Justices of the Peace.

N

Nash, Henry Sylvester. *O.*, 1854——. An Episcopal clergyman of Cambridge, Massachusetts, professor of New Testament interpretation in the Episcopal Theological School from 1884. The Genesis of the Social Conscience: the Relation between the Establishment of Christianity in Europe and the Social Question. *Mac.*

Nox, Owen. *See Cory, C. B.*

Nutting, Mary Olivia. 18——. Our Summer at Hillside Farm; Steps in the Upward Way; The Story of William the Silent and the Netherland War.

O

Ogden, Ruth. *See Ide, Mrs.*

O'Reilly, Bernard. *I.*, 1823——. A Roman Catholic clergyman and educator, formerly of New York city, but from 1887 domestic prelate of the papal household. Mirror of True Womanhood; Life of Pius IX.; True Men; Key of Heaven; The Two Brides, a novel; Life of Leo XIII.

P

Paine, Albert Bigelow. *Ms.*, 1861——. A littérateur of New York city. Rhymes by Two Friends (with W. A. White); The Mystery of Evelyn de Lorme; Gobolinks (with Mrs. Ruth Stewart); The Dumpies (with F. Van der Beck).

Paterson, Stephen Van Rensselaer. *N. J.*, 1817-1872. A verse writer of New Jersey, whose version of The Moss Rose, from the German of Krummacher, is his best-known poem. Poems of Twin Graduates of the College of New Jersey (with W. Paterson, *infra*).

Paterson, William. *N. J.*, 1817——. Brother of S. V. R. Paterson, *supra*. A jurist of Perth Amboy, New Jersey. Co-author, with his brother Stephen, of Poems of Twin Graduates of the College of New Jersey.

Peabody, Selim Hobart. *Vt.*, 1829——. An educator, president of the University of Illinois, 1880-91. Natural History for Children; Elements of Astronomy.

Pepper, George Wharton. *Pa.*, 1867——. A lawyer of Philadelphia. The Borderland of Federal and State Decisions; Pleading at Common Law and Under the Codes.

Percival, Henry Robert. *Pa.*, 1854——. An Episcopal clergyman of Philadelphia. A Digest of Theology; The Doctrine of the Episcopal Church; Invocation of Saints treated Theologically and Historically. *Lgs. Put.*

Peters, John Punnett. *N. Y.*, 1852——. An Episcopal clergyman and archæologist of New York city. Nippur, or Explorations and Adventures on the Euphrates. *Put.*

Pollard, Percival. *P.*, 1869——. A New York littérateur, born in Pomerania of English and German parentage, and resident in the United States from 1885. Figaro Pictures, a collection of short stories; Cape of Storms, a novel; Posters in Miniature; Dreams of To-day. *Wy.*

Powderly, Terence Vincent. *Pa.*, 1849——. A noted labor leader of Scranton, Pennsylvania, admitted to the bar in 1894. Thirty Years of Labor.

Powell, William H——. *D. C.*, 1838——. A lieutenant-colonel in the United States army. The History of the Fifth Army Corps, 1861-1865; History of the Fourth United States Infantry; Tactical Queries; Records of Living Officers of the United States Army (1890). *Put.*

Prall, William. *N. Y.*, 1853——. An Episcopal clergyman of prominence in Detroit from 1891. Civic Christianity. *Wh.*

Pratt, Cornelia Atwood. 18——. A novelist who has published A Book of Martyrs; The Daughter of a Stoic. *Scr.*

Priestley, Joseph. *E.*, 1733-1804. A celebrated English scientist and Unitarian theologian, who came to the United States in 1794 and settled in Northumberland, Pennsylvania. From 1780 to 1791 he was pastor of a Unitarian chapel in Birmingham, but in the latter year his house and chapel were burned by a mob. He was one of the foremost scientists of his time, the discovery of oxygen being his most important contribution to scientific knowledge. Among his many works are: Rudiments of English Grammar; Theory of Language and Universal Grammar; History and Present State of Electricity (1767); Vision, Light, and Colours; Experiments and Observations relating to Natural Philosophy; Familiar Letters to the People of Birmingham; General History of the Christian Church; Notes on all the Books of Scripture; The Doctrines of Heathen Philosophy compared with those of Revelation. A collection of his Theological and Miscellaneous Works (excluding those upon science) appeared in twenty-six volumes in 1817–32. *See Brougham's Lives of Philosophers; Dictionary of National Biography, volume 46.*

Pullen, Mrs. Elisabeth [Jones] [Cavazza]. *Me.*, 18——. A littérateur of Portland, Maine. Don Finimondone: Calabrian Sketches.

Putnam, Eben Frederic. *Ms.*, 1868——. Son of F. W. Putnam, *infra.* A genealogist of Salem, Massachusetts. His principal work is a valuable History of the Putnam Family in England and America.

Putnam, Frederic Ward. *Ms.*, 1839——. A noted archæologist of Cambridge, professor of American archæology and ethnology at Harvard University from 1886, and curator of the Peabody Museum there from 1874. His professional papers, reports, and other contributions to science are exceedingly numerous and valuable.

Putnam, John Pickering. *Ms.*, 1847——. An architect of Boston. The Metric System of Weights and Measures; The Open Fireplace in All Ages; The Principles of House Drainage; Improved Plumbing Appliances.

Putnam, Samuel Porter. *N. H.*, 1838–1896. A writer who, after holding successive pastorates in Congregational and Unitarian churches became known as an extremely radical thinker. Prometheus: a poem; The Golden Throne: a Radical Romance; Four Hundred Years of Free Thought.

Q

Quin, Dan. *See Lewis, Alfred Henry.*

R

Rantoul, Robert. *Ms.*, 1805–1852. A prominent anti-slavery congressman from Massachusetts. The Republic in the United States; Memoirs, Letters, and Speeches, edited by Luther Hamilton (1854).

Reddall, Henry Frederic. *E.*, 1852——. From the Golden Gate to the Golden Horn; Who Was He?; Schoolboy Life in Merrie England; Courtship, Love, and Wedlock; Fancy, Fact, and Fable; Life of Henry M. Stanley.

Reeder, Charles. *Md.*, 1817——. A merchant and manufacturer in Baltimore. Caloric: a Review of the Dynamic Theory of Heat.

Reid, Mayne. *I.*, 1818–1883. An Irish writer who came to the United States in 1838, and for a number of years lived and wrote in Philadelphia, but subsequently made his home in London. He was a prolific writer of tales of adventure for boys. Among them are, The Rifle Ranger; The Quadroon; Osceola; The White Chief; The Yellow Chief; The Lost Mountain, a tale of Sonora; The Lone Ranch; The Land of Fire; The Boy Tar; Afloat in the Forest; Boy Hunters; Forest Exiles; Plant Hunters; Desert Home.

Roberts, William Charles. *W.*, 1832——. A Presbyterian clergyman, president of Lake Forest University, Illinois, 1886–92. Letters on the Great Preachers of Wales.

Rollins, Mrs. Clara [Sherwood]. *Mo., c.* 1868——. A Boston writer of short stories. A Burne Jones Head; Threads of Life. *Lam.*

S

Sanford, Ezekiel. *Ct.*, 1796–1819. A writer who published in 1819 A History of the United States before the Revolution.

Schofield, John McAllister. *N. Y.*, 1831——. A distinguished soldier, commander of the United States army from 1888. Forty-six Years in the Army. *Cent.*

Scidmore, Eliza Ruhamah. *Ia.*, 1856——. A writer of Washington city. Alaska; Jinrikisha Days in Japan; Guide to Alaska and the Northwest Coast; Westward to the Far East; Java: the Garden of the East. *Ap. Cent. Lo.*

Scott, William Amasa. *N. Y.*, 1862——. A professor of economic history and theory in the University of Wisconsin. Repudiation of State Debts. *Cr.*

Sealsfield, Charles. *A.*, 1793–1864. An Austrian author resident for some years in the United States, whose original name was Karl Postel. Tokeah or the White Rose, published in German as Der Legitime und die Republikaner; Transatlantische Reiseskizzen; Der Virey und die Aristokraten, a Mexican novel; Lebensbilden aus beiden Hemisphären, reissued as Morten oder die grosse Tour; Deutschamerikanische Wahlverwandtschaften; Süden und Norden.

Sellers, Edwin Jaquett. *Pa.*, 1865——. A lawyer of Philadelphia. Genealogy of the Jaquett Family and other genealogical works.

Shackford, Charles Chauncy. *N. H.*, 1815–1891. A Unitarian clergyman, pastor in Lynn, Massachusetts, 1846–65, and from 1871 professor of rhetoric at Cornell University. A Citizen's Appeal in Regard to the War with Mexico; Social and Literary Papers. *Rob.*

Shuey, Mrs. Lillian Hinman. *Il.*, 18———. A novelist of California. Hilda; Don Luis' Wife: a Romance of the West Indies. *Lam.*

Sidney, Edward William. *See Tucker, Nathaniel Beverly* (page 390).

Sizer, Nelson. *Ms.*, 1812–1897. A phrenologist of Brooklyn. How to Teach; Forty Years in Phrenology; Heads and Faces; Right Selection in Wedlock; Resemblance to Parents.

Smiley, Francis Edward. *Pa.*, 1858——. A Presbyterian evangelist of Philadelphia. The Evangelization of a Great City.

Smith, Nora Archibald. *Pa.*, 186——. Sister of Mrs. Riggs (page 315). A writer upon kindergarten themes. The Children of the Future. With Mrs. Riggs she has written The Republic of Childhood; The Story Hour. *Hou.*

Sommerville, Maxwell. *Va.*, 1829——. A professor of glyptology in the University of Pennsylvania from 1894. Engraved Gems; On the Meinam, with Three Romances of Siamese Life and Customs. *Lip.*

Stevens, Augusta De Grasse. *N. Y.*, 1865–1894. A novelist and art critic whose home was in London for many years. Distance, a novelette; Old Boston, an American Historical Romance; The Lost Dauphin; Miss Hildreth; The Sensation of the Season; A Romantic Inheritance. *See Black's Notable Women of To-Day. Ap. Scr.*

Stevens, Charles Wistar. 18———. Fly Fishing on the Maine Lakes; Revelations of a Boston Physician.

Stevens, Isaac Ingalls. *Ms.*, 1818–1862. A major-general of the United States army, killed at the Battle of Chantilly. Campaigns of the Rio Grande and Mexico; Report of Explorations for a Route for the Pacific Railroad from St. Paul to Puget Sound (1855–60).

Stone, Witmer. *Pa.*, 1866——. An ornithologist of Philadelphia, among whose writings are, Bird Waves; The Birds of Eastern Pennsylvania and New Jersey; Report on Birds collected in Yucatan and Southern Mexico.

Strong, George Augustus. "Marc Antony Henderson." 182———. An Episcopal clergyman now (1898) living in Cambridge, but formerly a professor in Kenyon College, Gambier, Ohio. The Song of Milkanwatha, and Other Poems, the title poem a witty parody of Hiawatha.

T

Thickstun, Frederick. *See Clark, F. T.*

Tufts, Henry. *N. H.*, 1748–1831. A notable vagabond, whose autobiography furnishes a valuable picture of certain phases of New England life a century ago. It was published in 1807, with the title, A Narrative of the Life, Adventures, Travels, and Sufferings of Henry Tufts. *See T. W. Higginson's Travellers and Outlaws.*

Tyler, Charles Mellen. *Me.*, 1832——. Kinsman of M. C. Tyler (page 392). A professor of the history and philosophy of religion at Cornell University from 1891. Bases of Religious Belief, Historic and Ideal.

U

Updike, Wilkins. *R. I.*, 1784–1864. A Rhode Island lawyer. Memoirs of the Rhode Island Bar (1842).

V

Van Alstyne, Mrs. Frances Jane [Crosby]. "Fanny J. Crosby." *N. Y.*, 1820——. A well known blind hymn and song writer of New York city. Her hymns and songs are over five thousand in number. A Blind Girl, and Other Poems; Monterey, and Other Poems; A Wreath of Columbia's Flowers.

Vaughan, Benjamin. W. I., 1751–1835. A once prominent scientist and political economist who lived at Hallowell, Maine, from 1795. His writings nearly all appeared anonymously. The Calm Observer; Ten Hints to Wise Men; The Rural Socrates, a translation from the German of Hirzel, include a portion of his writings.

W

Watson, Augusta Campbell. 18——. An historical novelist. Dorothy the Puritan; The Old Harbor Town; Lynnport; Beyond the City Gates, a story of Dutch New York. *Dil. Dut.*

Watson, Edward Willard. *R. I.*, 1843——. A physician and verse writer of Philadelphia. Songs of Flying Hours; To-day and Yesterday. *Co.*

Watson, William Frederick. *Ont.*, 1862——. A professor of chemistry in Furman University, Greenville, South Carolina. The Children of the Sun, and Miscellaneous Poems.

Webster, Arthur Gordon. *Ms.*, 1863——. A professor of physics at Clark University, Worcester, Massachusetts. The Theory of Electricity and Magnetism.

Wenley, Robert Mark. *S.*, 1861——. A Scottish thinker and a leading exponent of the spiritual reaction in philosophy, professor of philosophy in the University of Michigan from 1896. Socrates and Christ; Aspects of Pessimism; Contemporary Theology and Theism; Introduction to Kant; Preparation for Christianity in the Ancient World. *Scr.*

Wemyss [weems], **Francis Courtney.** *E.*, 1797–1859. A theatrical manager in New York city. Chronology of the American Stage, 1752–1852.

Wharton, Henry Redwood. *Pa.*, 1853——. A physician of Philadelphia. Text-Book on Minor Surgery and Bandaging.

Whitman, William Edward Seaver. *Me.*, 1832——. A journalist of Augusta, Maine. The Ship Carpenter's Family, a story; The Wealth and Industry of Maine.

Wilcox, Delos F[ranklin]. *Mch.*, 1873——. A lecturer and writer of New York city. The Study of City Government; Municipal Government in Michigan and Ohio. *Mac.*

Williams, Frederick Benton. *See Hamblen, Herbert.*

Wilson, Bird. *Pa.*, 1777–1859. An Episcopal clergyman from 1829, but previously a noted lawyer of Philadelphia. Abridgement of the Law by Matthew Bacon; Memoir of Bishop White. *See Memorial of, by Bronson, 1864.*

Wyckoff, Walter A[ugustus]. *E. I.*, 1865——. A lecturer on sociology at Princeton University, born of American parentage at Mainpuri, in the northwest provinces of Hindustan. In order to ascertain the actual conditions surrounding the American workingman, he spent two years in toil as an unskilled labourer, an experience described in The Workers: an Experiment in Reality. *Scr.*

Y

Young, Claiborne Addison. 18——. A Unitarian clergyman in Canton, Massachusetts. Way Songs and Wanderings. *Est.*

www.ingramcontent.com/pod-product-compliance
Lightning Source LLC
Chambersburg PA
CBHW022010110726
47901CB00006B/1469

* 9 7 8 3 3 3 7 2 8 0 1 9 2 *